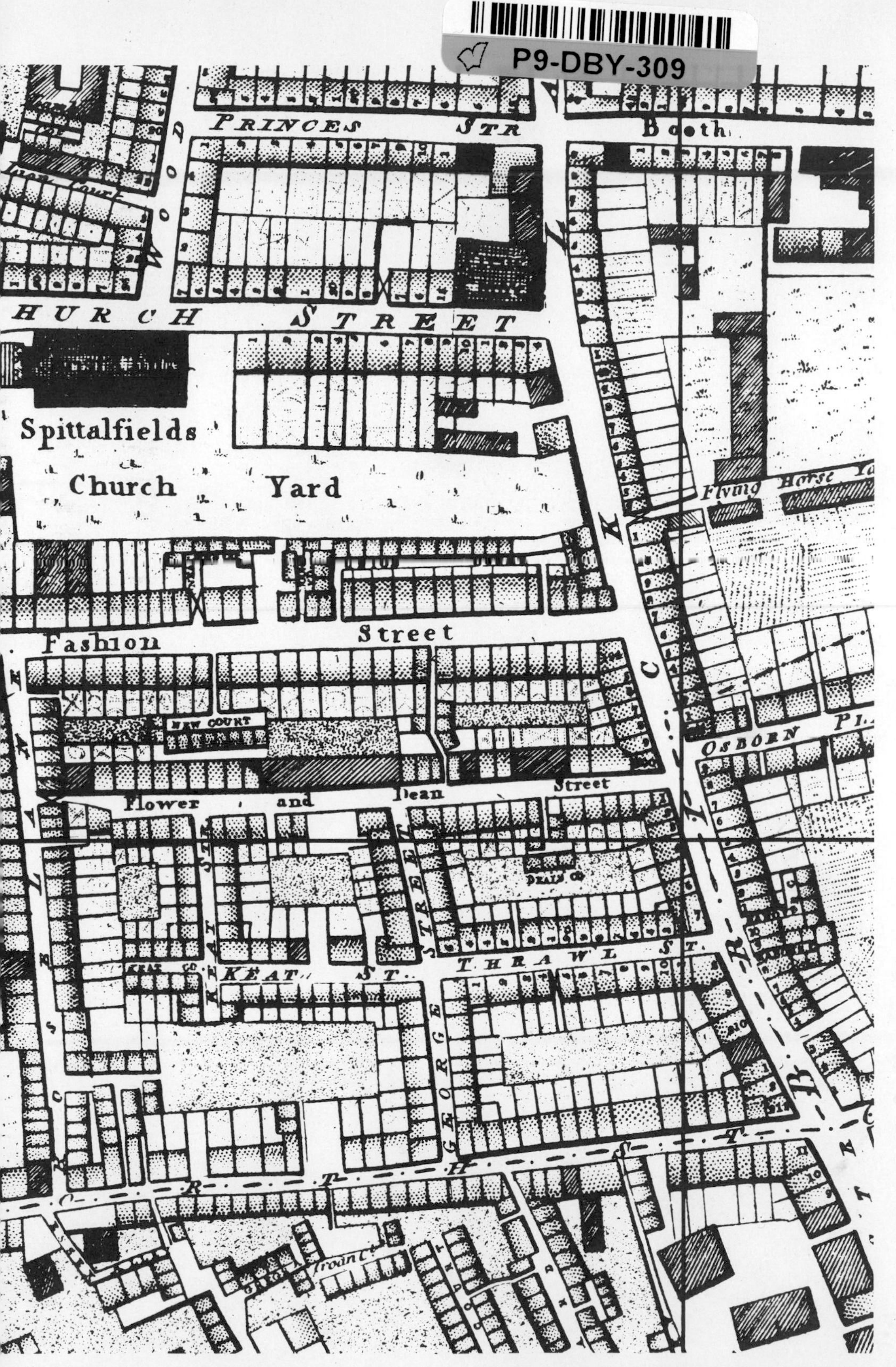

SPITALFIELDS (Scale: 1″=50 yards)

THE QUINCUNX

THE QUINCUNX

CHARLES PALLISER

BALLANTINE BOOKS · NEW YORK

For My Mother

(4th May 1919—22nd February 1989)

NOTE ON COINAGE

Twelve pence make one shilling (1s.). Twenty shillings make one pound (1£).

There are also these coins: A farthing, four of which are worth a penny (1d.). A ha'penny, two of which are worth a penny. A crown which is worth five shillings and a half-crown (2s. 6d.). A sovereign which is worth one pound. A guinea which is worth twenty-one shillings (1£ 1s.).

 Published in the United States by Ballantine Books, a division of Random House, Inc., New York, and distributed in Canada by Random House of Canada Limited, Toronto. First published in Great Britain in 1989 by Canongate Publishing Limited.

Map details from the Horwood Map (1813 edition) are reproduced here with permission, and from film supplied, by Harry Margary, Lympne Castle, Kent in association with The Guildhall Library, London.

Library of Congress Cataloging-in-Publication Data

Palliser, Charles.
The Quincunx / Charles Palliser.
—1st American ed.
p. cm.
ISBN 0-345-36463-5
I. Title.
PR6066. A43Q85 1990 89-91787
823'.914—dc20 CIP

Design by James Hutcheson
Illustrations by Jenny Phillips

Manufactured in the United States of America

First American Edition: February 1990

10 9 8 7 6 5 4 3

CONTENTS

Paddington
Hyde
Park
Map 1
Map 4
Map 2
Green Park
St. James's Park
Queens Palace
Knights Bridge
Pimlico
Chelsea
Tothil Fields
Ranelagh
Hospital
Vaux Hall
Lambeth
Piccadilly
Oxford
Street
Holborn

LIST OF MAPS

METROPOLIS OF LONDON *c* 1800

Quid Quincunce speciosius, qui, in quamcunque partem spectaveris, rectus est? (Quintilian)

PART ONE
THE HUFFAMS

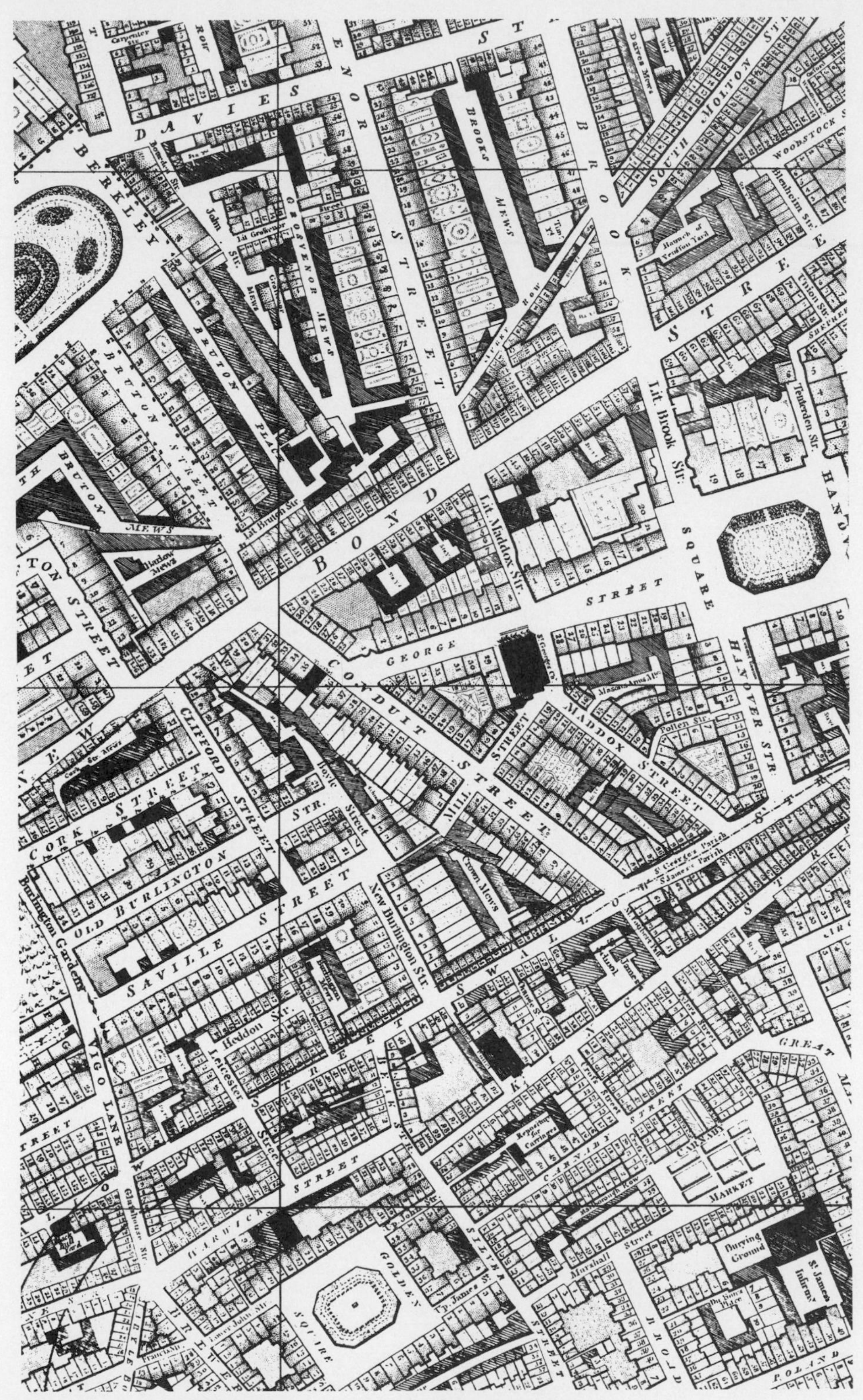

MAYFAIR AND SOHO (Scale: 1″=115 yards)

The top of the page is West

BOOK I

A Wise Child

CHAPTER I

It must have been late autumn of that year, and probably it was towards dusk for the sake of being less conspicuous. And yet a meeting between two professional gentlemen representing the chief branches of the law should surely not need to be concealed.

Let us imagine, then, how Law might have waited upon Equity.

Approaching a particular house in a street near Lincoln's-inn-fields, Law, embodied in the person of a small, pale-faced gentleman of about forty years of age with a large head, mounts the steps and rings the bell. The door is immediately opened by a young clerk. The visiter steps inside, is relieved of hat, great-coat, and gloves, and is then ushered into a small dark room at the rear of the house. There he sees a figure seated at a little table at the other end of the chamber. The clerk noiselessly withdraws. The gentleman who is already there rises with the briefest of bows and indicates a chair opposite him before the fire. The newcomer seats himself while the elder man takes his chair again and brings his gaze to bear upon his guest. Equity is some fifteen years the elder, with a high-coloured complexion, a lofty nose and a face most remarkable for a pair of black bushy eyebrows.

There is a long pause and at last the newcomer clears his throat: "It has been an honour, sir, to receive and obey your summons."

There is a note of polite interrogation in this observation but Equity appears not to hear it for he continues to gaze at his guest.

After another minute Law asks nervously: "May I know how I can be of assistance?"

"Did you take the precautions I requested?" the host asks.

"Indeed I did. I am certain that no-one followed me here."

"Good. Then our meeting has probably been kept from the knowledge of a third party."

"A third party? My dear sir, you intrigue me. To whom do you refer?"

"I shall ask the questions," the other gentleman replies with only the slightest emphasis on the pronoun.

His guest flushes.

The elder gentleman takes something from his pocket and says: "Now, you have a client whose name I have written on this piece of paper which I ask you to be good enough to read." He holds it out for a few moments and when Law has looked at it and nodded in confirmation, he replaces it: "Very well. Then I will lose no time in coming to the point: the document which your client possesses has the capacity to damage very materially the interests of the party for whom I have the honour to act, and in view of this … "

He breaks off for on Law's face is an expression of manifest bewilderment: "My good sir, I assure you I know nothing of such a document."

"Come, come. Not two weeks past your client sent a copy of it to us demanding money and giving your name for correspondence."

"That may be so … that is to say, I am certain that it is so if you state it to be. But I beg you to believe that I am no more than a receiving-office in this transaction."

"What do you mean?"

"That I merely forward letters addressed to me in my client's name. I know no more of that individual's affairs than a letter-carrier does of the correspondence he collects and delivers."

The other gazes at him and says: "I am prepared to accept that that may be so." The younger gentleman smiles but his expression alters at the next words: "Then tell me the whereabouts of your client."

"My dear sir, I cannot."

"Beg your pardon, I'm forgetting to put up my stake," the elder says and brings out from his pocket something that crackles as he lays it on the table.

Law leans forward slightly to look at it. There is surely an expression of yearning on his face. Then he says: "I assure you, my dear sir, I am quite unable to oblige you."

"Oh-ho!" the elder gentleman exclaims. "You think to bargain with me, do you? I warn you not to try it or you will find that I am able to apply quite other inducements."

"No indeed, sir," the other stammers. "You entirely mistake my meaning. Your generosity quite overwhelms me and I only wish I could deserve it. However, it is wholly impossible for me to assist you."

"I advise you not to attempt any of your games with me, my good fellow," the other says in a brutally contemptuous tone. "I have made enquiries enough to know how ill these high-principled scruples become you. I've 'smoked your lay' — isn't that how they call it in the jargon of your clients?"

The other gentleman becomes quite pale. He begins to rise from his chair but his eyes fall on the thing on the table and he stays in his seat.

Equity goes on: "Do you wish me to give you the catalogue — or perhaps I should say, calendar — of activities in which I know you to be involved?"

When Law makes no answer Equity continues: "A little brokerage of doubtful bills, rather more squeezing of debtors, and a great deal of tutoring witnesses? Is that not so?"

The other gentleman answers with dignity: "You have misunderstood me, my dear sir. I merely meant that I do not possess the information you seek. If I had it I would most willingly give it to you."

"Do you take me for a fool? How do you communicate with your client, then?"

"Through a third-party to whom I forward my client's letters."

"That's better," the other growls. "Who?"

"A gentleman of the highest respectability who has been some years retired from my branch of our profession."

"Most intriguing. Now be good enough to write down that gentleman's name and address for I cannot identify him, even though your branch of the profession is hardly replete with gentlemen to whom that description applies."

The other laughs shortly and joylessly. Then he takes out a pocket-book, writes "Martin Fortisquince, Esqr., No. 27 Golden-square", tears out the leaf and hands it to the other gentleman.

Equity takes the paper from him and without looking at it says abruptly: "In the event of my needing to speak to you again we will communicate as before." He reaches into a dark corner of the room beside his chair and tugs gently at a bell-rope.

Law rises with his eye on the thing on the table. Seeing this Equity carelessly pushes it towards him and he slips it into his pocket. Just as the door opens and the clerk appears again, Law hesitantly reaches out his hand towards his host. He, however, appears not to notice the gesture and Law hastily returns his hand to his pocket. The clerk ushers him to the door, restores to him his hat, great-coat, and gloves, and in a moment he finds himself out in Cursitor-street again. He sets off at a rapid pace occasionally looking anxiously behind him. When he has rounded several corners he draws into a quiet door-way and removes the package from his pocket. He cautiously counts it, counts it again, puts it back, and then sets off again more slowly.

CHAPTER 2

Our house, the garden, the village, and the country for a mile or two thereabouts — this was my world, for it was all I had known, until that last summer when a new one opened before me at Hougham. And now that I seek an image for the undertaking I am embarked upon, I recall a glorious afternoon during that summer when — still unaware that I was to leave so soon — I escaped from the confinement under which I had long chafed and lay, exulting not so much in my freedom as in my having stolen it, on the bank of the stream that ran through Mortsey-wood and on to the forbidden land towards the north.

Forgetful alike of my reasons for escaping and the precious minutes that were slipping by, I gazed, entranced, into the limpid depths. For there I glimpsed strange creatures that flitted away so quickly when I looked at them that I wondered if they were merely shadows — effects of the sunlight through the water upon the weeds and the dappled, pebble-strewn bed that vanished when I moved my head. And then in the attempt to see more, I poked the weed and pebbles with a stick, and only raised a dark cloud that obscured everything. And though it seems to me that the recollection is like that clear runlet, yet I have set myself to search back into my memory. And now that I clutch at my first reminiscences I recall only the sun, the warm breeze, and the garden. I remember no darkness or sunlessness or shade from that earliest time when the outlying cottages of the village marked the furthest limits of my world.

It may be that we are aware only of the warmth and the daylight and the sun at that most fortunate age, and that if there are moments of darkness and cold they pass over us like a dreamless slumber, leaving no memory behind them. Or it may be that it is only the first touch of the cold and the dark that wakes us from our earliest sleep.

The first moment that separates itself from what had come before is late on an afternoon of cloudless sunshine when the shadows were beginning to lengthen. Tired after my play, I was swinging on the gate into the lane that ran along the side of the garden. From the topmost lawn at the back of the house where we were now, a series of terraced lawns descended, linked by a gravelled path and steps and surrounded by a high red-brick wall with espaliered apricot-trees against it. On each terrace the walnut and mulberry-trees extended their long thin arms protectively over the encircling flower-beds, in one of which Mr Pimlott was now at work some distance below us. And almost out of sight at the bottom of the garden, was the tangle of stunted trees and thick bushes we called the "Wilderness"

I recall the rough feel of the gate as I clasped its top in my hands to hold myself steady for each swing. The metal spikes were hot in the sunlight and the rust and black paint came flaking off in my fingers. With my feet thrust between the uprights of the gate and my frocks pressed against the frame, I pushed off from the jamb-post bending my body one way and then the other so that the gate swung out to its fullest reach and then fell back under its own weight, gathering speed as the ground sped past until it crashed home with a loud clang. I knew I wasn't supposed to do this, of course, and my mother had already reproved me as she sat on a garden seat at her work a few paces away.

Backwards and forwards I swung, lulled by the rhythm of the squeaking hinge, with the sun warm on my face, and the soft breeze carrying to me the scent of flowers and the smell of freshly-cut grass. I would close my eyes to listen to the loud buzzing of bees, then open them to gaze upwards at the blue sky and fleecy clouds that circled dizzily over my head as the gate hurtled downwards.

Suddenly a harsh voice that seemed to be right at my ear said: "Stop it at once, you wicked creatur'. You know that ain't allowed."

Distracted, I let the gate crash against the jamb harder than I intended and was stunned by the blow. For a moment I wasn't sure if I was really hurt, but whether I was or not, I knew how to appeal for reassurance.

I was taking a deep breath for that purpose when the voice came again: "Don't you set to a-bawlin', now. You're too old for that."

"But I'm hurt," I cried out.

"Then you've been justly sarved," Bissett jeered as she seated herself beside my mother.

"It's not just," I cried. "It was your fault for calling out like that."

"Don't answer again, dearest," my mother said.

"I hate you, Bissett, you always spoil things."

"You wicked child! I can see I s'all have to take my hand to you again."

"No you shan't for Mamma has forbidden you," I jeered.

"Why no such thing, you story-teller!"

Yet I knew it was true for my mother had promised me it was, but before I could say so she laid her hand to her mouth unseen by Bissett and I consented to hold my peace. Bissett, still grumbling about my wickedness, picked up her work: "I'll have no more of your malpertness. Now stand there in my eye and don't make no more mischief."

Though I was indignant at being ordered to stay, at least Bissett didn't know that there was nowhere else I wanted to be just then, for the great treat of the day was about to take place.

"It's too bad, ma'am, it really is," Bissett began. "She's let her work go for nought these last few days hangin' around Limbrick's workmen."

"Oh, but they've just about finished now."

"And glad I'll be to see the back of 'em. For I hate to have men in the house. Nasty noisy creatur's! And a fearful nuisance they've been with their buckets and their hods and their ladders. And that young mawkin and Mrs Belflower — who ought to know better — invitin' 'em into the kitchen five times a day."

"I understand," put in my mother timidly, "one of them is a cousin of hers."

"Cousin," repeated Bissett darkly. "If you mean that young good-for-nought, Job Greenslade, well, kissing-cousins is what they are, if cousins at all. Out companying at all hours! It may not be my place to say it, but I'm sure there are many well-conducted, natty girls in the village," Bissett went on, speaking with difficulty through a mouthful of pins, "would sarve a lot better than her, ma'am."

"But she's a good-natured, honest girl for all her faults. And Master Johnnie's fond of her. And then we should help her in her mother's recent sorrow."

Bissett sniffed expressively. "Sorrer," she repeated. "It's a rotted pea as you'll get of a rotted pod. You're too soft on the gal, ma'am."

At this moment I heard the cattle approaching from the direction of the High-street and an instant later they came crowding past the gate accompanied by a boy who was something of a hero to me for the nonchalant way in which he wielded his stick as he followed the herd. The dismal lowing and the way they competed for passage through the narrow lane were delightfully frightening, and I knew I was safe because of the sturdy gate that stood between us. But today something unprecedented happened. Suddenly one of them seemed to catch my eye — I can describe it in no other way — and began to make its way across the flow towards the gate, butting its way through the herd with an awful purposefulness. I knew in an instant that it had some terrible and irresistible mission to accomplish that involved me, and yet I could not stir to save myself. As the animal's huge head came thrusting towards the gate I saw its bulging blood-stained eyes rolling in their black leathery sockets, its huge teeth parting as if to close again upon my cheeks, and its thick, twisting, pointed horns like strange tree-trunks rising from the matted grass-like brown hair. I knew the gate would splinter and give way in an instant if that mighty head should be borne against it, and yet I continued to stand and stare, unable to move.

Then at last I turned and ran, my heart pounding in my ears while my legs rose and fell without seeming to carry me over the ground. Through my tears two blurred figures were visible a few yards away, rising to their feet and looking towards me in alarm — the one slender and flower-like in a bright gingham dress, the other standing out as a stark white shape against the greenness of the grass.

"That nasty cow!" I wailed. "Don't let him hurt me!"

In a moment I had buried my face in the starched white apron of my nurse and her arms were about my shoulders as she pressed me tightly to her and soothed me with the chiding, almost jeering, tone that she used on such occasions.

I best remember Bissett at this period as a crisp, slightly astringent aroma of starched apron and gown, a faintly apple-like smell, fresh and a little forbidding.

When I close my eyes I can remember looking up at a reddish face fringed by the few strands of grey hair that were visible beneath her lace cap. Her eyes were a pale shade of grey and her mouth was thin — and grew thinner on the rare occasions when she pressed her lips together in such a way that they gave the impression, without compromising themselves, of going up a little at the ends.

Now surely a few tears were permitted, but Bissett shook me and said: "Come, you ain't a baby no more. Why, in no time at all, you'll be a growed man and have to take care on your mother."

I looked at her in surprise but at that moment my mother called out: "You're safe now, my dearest. The cows have gone. Come and kiss me."

I tried to, but Bissett held my arm tightly: "Don't mar him, ma'am," she said. "And see, you've your work that he'll disarrange."

I broke free of her grip and made for my mother's lap, sending her needles, thread, and embroidery-frame crashing to the ground. I heard Bissett scolding us both but I didn't care.

I don't need to close my eyes to summon up the remembrance of my mother: the cascade of fair curls that flowed over her shoulders and down to her bosom so that when I snuggled up against her now my hands and face were plunged in among the soft scentedness; the sweet face with its gentle mouth; and the wide blue eyes that were bright now with tears for my own grief.

"Don't you let him bother you, ma'am," Bissett objected. "Look at your work, now, fallen all in a tumble on the grass."

"It's of no account, nurse," my mother said.

"Why so it is, indeed! Good cloth and thread! Let him go and plague Mr Pimlott."

"Yes, Johnnie. Why not find Mr Pimlott and ask him what he is doing. He seems to be making a hole. Do you think he can be burying something?"

"Why, I know what it is," my nurse interrupted. "I meant to mind and tell you, ma'am: he's aiming to make hisself a nice new weskit out of what rightly belongs to you. But it ain't his property but yourn since it's on your land and it's your time as he's doing it in."

My mother sighed but I heard no more for in an instant I was flying away across the terrace and then down the steps and over the grass-plat whose smooth surface was marred by a small mound of earth.

"Mr Pimlott! Mr Pimlott!" I cried as I raced towards the edge of the lawn where he was at work. "What are you doing? Can I help you?"

He was kneeling down and at my approach he raised his sun-darkened face and looked at me with an expression I could not read. I was rather in awe of him, partly because he was that strange creature, a man, and the only one I knew at all well. I wasn't sure what being a man meant, except that he was large, the skin on his face looked rough, and he smelt of earth and tobacco.

"Now, little mester," he said, "don't ye come a-pestering me with questions. I aren't paid to abide 'em, like some."

"But Bissett told me to come and find you so that you can give me something to do."

"That ain't no consarn of mine. Mrs Bissett don't give me orders, the Lord be praised. Though she sometimes thinks she do."

I watched him for a few moments as he worked in silence. He was reaching into a hole that was more like a burrow than a pit and manipulating a long-handled tool with awkward jabbing strokes.

"What are you doing?" I asked.

He made no reply but looked up at the sun shielding his eyes from its still bright glare. Then he withdrew the tool so that I saw how very long it was, and began banging it up and down on the grass to dislodge the earth trapped by the head. For its shape was very strange indeed with the blade curved almost into hooks on either side. He laid it down and began to gather up his other tools and place them on the grass beside the great wooden box in which he kept them.

"What have you been doing today, Mr Pimlott?" I asked in desperation.

Still without replying he began smearing thick grease like clear honey across the metal parts of the tools before wrapping each one up in a piece of soft-leather and carefully placing it in the box. They had always been objects of fascination to me: the fearsome spikes of the forks, the dibble with its two prongs for extracting thistles, and the spades with their heavy wooden handles polished smooth by use, the iron clamps that held metal and wood together, and above all, the blades that glittered so brightly and so surprisingly where the bare metal was kept shiny by being rammed hard and often into the earth.

"What's this one called?" I asked him, indicating the long-handled one with the curiously hooked blade. "Is it a spade or a trowel?"

"Don't you touch it," he said. "It's very sharp."

"And this one?" I asked, and pointed to another that I had never seen him use.

He glanced at me. "That? Why, that's my grubbin'-hoe."

"What do you use it for?"

He looked at me for a long moment: "Why, I grubs."

Encouraged by this reply, I looked round at the signs of his work: "Why have you dug up that tree?" I demanded, indicating a pear-tree lying on its side with its roots brutally exposed.

"On account of it has the canker."

"The canker," I repeated. Now here was an interesting new word and I repeated it several times to extract its full flavour. "What is the canker?"

"It's a distemper as trees gets. And people, too. It rots 'em both away from inside."

At this he opened his mouth suddenly, exposing a few blackened stumps, and made a harsh noise that I took for a laugh.

"But it looks all right. It seems a shame to kill it."

"Why, anythin' old or ill is to be throwed away or killed. And who has the right to pull up that tree if not I?"

"Why do you, Mr Pimlott? Surely it's my mother's tree?"

He turned away from me and delivered over his shoulder the longest response I had ever heard from him: "You want to know why? Because I planted it, that's why. A dozen year or more a-fore your mither even come here, let alone you. What did you think? That it just growed of its own self? Everythin' in this world has to be planted. And needs tending. Like yourself, with Mrs Bissett a-tendin' of you. That is, if she done her work instead of leavin' it to gossip and make trouble and let you come and bother folks as has work to do if she don't."

When he had finished I allowed a minute or two to pass before my curiosity overcame me again: "Are you burying the tree in that hole?" He shook his head. "Are you going to plant another?"

"No. If you has to be told, I'm setting a trap for Old Mouldiwarp."

"You mean 'mole', Mr Pimlott. That's the proper word."

"I means what I says."

"But why are you trapping him, Mr Pimlott?"

"On account of he comes in and digs up your mither's grass-plat as she pays me to keep nice. He don't reckernise no rights of property, don't Old Mouldiwarp. And so he must be killed."

"But that isn't right."

"Right, Master John?" He turned to me and looked at me keenly: "When he comes straight in and takes however many muck-worms he wants without so much as a by-your-leave?"

I could see the error in this argument immediately: "But we don't want the worms."

"You don't want the worms? No, in course you don't want the worms. But no more don't you want for no-one else to come boldly in and ketch them worms, being as they're yourn."

I thought about this because I was sure there was a reply, but without waiting for me to find it, the gardener went on: "Well, howsomever, he's ketched enough worms and now I'll ketch him, for he has something I want, and if I'm clever enough I'll get it of him. And that's the way the world goes: if you don't eat him, he'll eat you."

"So are you digging a hole for him to fall into and be caught?"

Mr Pimlott grimaced: "Not him. He's a deal too 'cute for that. He lives underground, don't he? So holes is what he knows about just the way I knows about plants and Mrs Bissett knows about other folks' business. Oh no, you have to be clever to ketch Old Mouldiwarp asleep."

"Then how will you do it, Mr Pimlott?"

"The only way is, you have to make him ketch himself." He indicated the excavation. "This is one of his own burrers, see, so he won't be a-feared of no trap. So I digs out a deep hole inside of it — which is what that there molin'-spade is for — and at the bottom I s'all place a gin with a spring and then cover it over with all leaves and earth. And if I've been canny enough, then Old Mouldiwarp'll come looking for muck-worms and he'll spring it and get ketched by his leg or mebbe his snout. And then I'll make him turn tailor and fashion me a new coat."

For a moment I imagined a captured mole holding a needle and thread in its delicate little paws and stitching away, and I laughed in disbelief. Seeing that I didn't understand Mr Pimlott touched his waistcoat which I had often noticed because it was so shiny and darkly glossy.

"But that's horrid!" I whispered in delight. I looked at the moleskin and it seemed strange to me that something so beautiful should come from the damp earth.

"That's why I aren't using a trap. I want his coat unsp'iled."

"How cruel!" I cried and thought of the mole struggling and dying in the darkness. Mr Pimlott laughed shortly. Now I remembered something and exclaimed: "But Bissett said the mouldiwarp isn't yours to make use of."

"Oh did she?" Mr Pimlott said, turning away.

"How many do you need for a waistcoat?"

Now, however, he appeared not to be listening as he fastened his box, picked it up, shouldered the long-handled tools, and began to make his way to the top of the garden. I watched him touch his forehead to my mother and nod briefly at Bissett before he went out through the gate into the lane and turned towards the High-street and his neat little cottage nearby.

Now that I suddenly found myself alone at the bottom of the garden, a daring and wicked thought came to me. I looked to see that Bissett and my mother were not observing me, and made my way through the apple-orchard, where I was truly out of sight, and into the Wilderness that lay beyond it. I passed quite easily through the tall grass, overgrown shrubs, and tangled bushes at the edge, but beyond that were ancient, stocky trees that spread their twisted branches into phantastic shapes as if pleading for more light, and here the darkness began to close about me and the sinister branches seemed to be reaching out to me like the long fingers of huge hands. Although I was only a few yards from the garden with its murmur of bees and rustling of trees in the gentle wind, it was as if I had passed through a door into another world for here there was no sound at all.

Something fluttered against my face, and as I brushed it away, suddenly there was a shape in front of me: a face with sightless eyes like the marble sculls I knew from the monuments on the walls of the village church. The features were worn away — cankered, it occurred to me — and the surface of the stone was like a skin that was deeply pitted. Terrified, I stepped back but to my horror found myself held in a firm grip. I pulled again but to no avail. My heart pounded, and I felt a panic beginning to rise inside me. Desperately I wriggled again and at last came free. As I began to back away I heard a cry that seemed to come from a very long way away. It came again and I recognised the voice of my nurse.

Almost grateful for the summons, I fought my way back through the tangled undergrowth into the bright sunlight of the garden.

"Master Johnnie!" Bissett was calling from out of sight at the top of the garden. "Where are you?"

Was it my imagination or was there a note of fear in her tone? I hastened up the steps and when I gained the upper terrace I found her turned to her right and I followed her gaze.

My mother was standing at the gate with an individual whom I had never seen before. He stood in the lane talking to her with passionate intensity, his eyes fixed on her face and his hands (one holding a stick) gesticulating, while she listened with her eyes cast down, nodding her head occasionally. My first thought was that he might be a pedlar, for they were the only strangers who came to the house and he seemed to be trying to sell my mother something. But then I saw that he was not dressed like one and carried no pack.

In age the stranger was between my mother and Bissett, and although not tall, he had the head of a much larger man. A mass of curly, reddish hair tumbled about his ears from his high-domed head. His animated face on which every passing emotion seemed to register, was dominated by a large beak-like nose. His mouth was wide and thin and his eyes, deep beneath the jutting eye-ridges, were large and very blue. He was wearing trowsers which had once had a pattern of checks and squares but were faded so that the design was barely discernible; a coarse round frock-coat whose green cloth was worn bare in places; and a white stock that, although of fine wool, was now of a yellowish hue. I might not have taken all this in if Bissett had not been watching them so closely, but seeing my mother like that it suddenly came to me that she had a life of which I knew nothing, and in that moment she seemed herself a stranger to me.

The man broke off when he saw Bissett and me looking at him, and touched his hat ceremoniously to each of us.

"And a very good evenin' to you, too, mistress, and to the little genel'man. I was jist explainin' to this young lady," he addressed himself to Bissett but with a friendly eye included me in his speech, "how it is that I find meself, a stranger passin' through this country to seek work, havin' to seek charity of strangers, which is a thing I haven't never done a-fore."

He spoke rapidly, and in a manner that was unfamiliar to me, so that I had to strain to catch his meaning. As he talked he glanced backwards and forwards between my mother and my nurse as if trying to judge which of the two it was the more important to win over.

"So will you help a poor honest workin'-man down on his luck," he said to my mother, "to find a night's lodgin' and wittles arter a hard day's tramp?"

"Be off with you," Bissett suddenly cried.

In an instant the man's face darkened and his brows drew together as he turned towards Bissett.

"Get off now," Bissett called out again, perhaps alarmed by his expression. "Or I'll go for Mr Pimlott."

The stranger's features lightened instantly and he said: "Why, I'd be happy to speak to the genel'man of the house."

At this Bissett glanced towards my mother who blushed and looked down. Puzzled, the man turned to me: "Where is your father, young genel'man?"

"I don't have one."

"Come, young master," he said, smiling at my mother, "everyone has one."

"Oh no, I never have had one."

"Take yourself away, and your impertinence," Bissett cried.

As if she had not spoken the stranger addressed my mother: "What do you say, Mrs Pimlott? Will you not spare a few pennies?"

"Mr Pimlott's the gardener, you silly man," I cried. "Our name's Mellamphy."

"Why then, Mrs Mellamphy," he said. "Will you sarve me?"

"I ... I don't believe I have any money with me."

As my mother spoke she nervously touched the cylindrical silver box which always hung from the chain around her waist on which she kept the household keys, and I noticed the man's large eyes rest inquisitively on it.

"What," he said, pointing to it, "not even in there?"

She looked up at him for the first time with an expression of alarm and shook her head vehemently.

"No siller in the house?" he said. "Not even a few coppers?"

Still looking into his face my mother said: "Will you bring me a six-pence from my writing-desk, Bissett?"

"I will not, ma'am," said my nurse stoutly. "I'll not leave you and Master Johnnie out of my sight while that rag-a-bond is here."

"I believe we should help him, nurse. I believe it would be better."

"Show a little charity, miss'is," the man said boldly to Bissett.

"Charity's for them as desarves it, but you've a gallows face and I'll warrant the Law knows summat of you. The only place I'll go is to fetch the constable and then we s'all see."

"Why, damn you, you old meddler," the stranger shouted, his features hardening suddenly. With an oath he stepped forward, raising his stick and putting his other hand upon the gate as if to open it. My mother screamed and stepped back, while I ran forward to defend my territory.

"Don't you dare come in here!" I cried. "If you do I'll kick you so hard you'll fall over and then I'll sit on you until Mr Pimlott comes."

He scowled down at me as my mother and nurse hurried forward to pull me back from the gate, but then as he looked towards them there appeared a smile that frightened me more than his previous grimace: "Why you didn't think I meant to come in, did you? I amn't sich a flatt as to bring the Law down upon me like that."

"I'll run for the constable now, ma'am, while you take the boy inside," said Bissett breathlessly.

"Don't give yourself the trouble," said the stranger laconically. "I'll bid you good day, Mrs Mellamphy," he added and, shrugging his shoulders, turned and walked quickly up the lane.

My mother knelt with her arms around my neck, and hugged me: "You were so brave, Johnnie," she said, kissing me and laughing and almost sobbing at the same time. "But you mustn't, you mustn't."

"If he'd come in I'd have frightened him away," I boasted.

Looking over her shoulder and through the mass of golden curls, I watched the stranger walking away with an odd, lolloping stride, his shoulders strangely hunched. Just as he reached the corner of the High-street he turned to look back at us. Even from where I was standing, I could see an expression of such concentrated, black-browed malevolence that it burned itself indelibly into my memory. My mother didn't see this, but I noticed that Bissett had intercepted that look, and I saw her spit surreptitiously on her right index finger and swiftly draw a cross between her eyes.

"Come, Johnnie," said my mother. And the three of us, my mother still keeping her arm on my shoulder, made our way through the back-door into the kitchen.

The cool, spacious kitchen which seemed so dark as we passed into it from the sun-lit garden, had originally been the "house-place" of the ancient farm-house which formed the original core of our cottage, as its huge chimney-place and white, scoured and sanded stone-flagged floor testified. This was Mrs Belflower's domain, and we now found that good-natured body standing over the fire preparing our tea. I broke from my mother's hold and danced across the floor towards her:

"Mrs Belflower, Mrs Belflower," I sang out, "a rag-a-bond just tried to get into the garden but I drove him away. I wasn't frightened at all."

"Well, just fancy! Isn't that nice, dear. I only hope it's given you a good appetite for your tea," said the imperturbable cook, turning towards us and wiping her large red hands upon her apron. She had a kindly face as plump and pale as one of her own puddings wrapped in muslin, and rather vague blue eyes that didn't quite meet your gaze.

Disappointed, I tried again: "He was very fierce, and he said he'd roast me alive if he caught me."

"Lor' save us," said Mrs Belflower rather distantly, her eyes straying to the sideboard where the tea-things were waiting.

"Why, shame on you, Master Johnnie!" Bissett exclaimed. "He said no such thing. You know you mustn't tell stories."

"But Mrs Belflower tells stories!" I cried.

"I'm sure I hope she does not," Bissett said gravely.

"But everybody does: Mamma reads me stories and Mrs Belflower tells me them and even Sukey. Everyone does but you," I added bitterly.

My mother said quickly: "But we don't say they're true when they're not, Johnnie."

Bissett commented darkly: "The child has a deal too much fancy, that's what it is."

"'Tis a terrible thing," Mrs Belflower put in diplomatically, "when dacent folks is harassed and parsecuted in their own houses by such ruffians."

"It usen't to happen. I nivver heard on it when I wor a gal," Bissett agreed. "'Tis all them Irishers workin' on the new 'pike — besides all them that come over for the harvest now. I don't know why they can't stay in their own country for they do us no good here but take the bread from the mouths of honest Englishmen."

"Why mayn't I see the turnpike?" I cried, reminded by her words of an ancient grievance.

"I don't believe he was Irish," said my mother quietly, while Mrs Belflower sympathetically slipped into my hand a small piece of ginger-bread.

"No?" said Bissett. "Well, for sartin he wasn't a this-country-man by his speech. It weren't the speech of a Christen man, hardly."

"He was from London," my mother said.

"London," I repeated. I had not heard the word before and the flat, slightly metallic syllables were oddly mysterious.

"Aye," said Bissett. "That seems like enough for that's a place where folks aren't safe in their own houses, by all accounts."

My mother started and turned pale: "What do you mean?"

Bissett looked at her shrewdly: "Do you not rec'lleck that terrible business a few year back, Mrs Mellamphy? It must have been around about the year Master Johnnie was born or a little a-fore that."

My mother stared at her in dismay.

"Aye," said Mrs Belflower. "Along the Ratcliffe-highway, you mean, when two famblies was murdered as they slept in their beds."

"Aye, you've hit it. And there was another, too, about that time — or was it earlier? — when a rich old man was murdered by his own son, or somethin' o' that natur'," Bissett put in and my mother turned away. "It was at Charing-cross. Is that near the Ratcliffe-highway?" My mother said nothing and Bissett went on: "So what I say is, ma'am, to be on the safe side, send that gal for the constable and he'll see that tramper out o' the parish."

My mother spoke with her back still turned to us: "I don't believe that's necessary, nurse. He's best left alone."

"Anyways, she ain't here," Mrs Belflower objected. "She's gone down to 'Ougham to visit her uncle." (I might add here that the villagers always referred to "going down" to Hougham even though that village was on higher ground — for the stream that passed through Mortsey-wood behind our house ran down from there — as if to visit the village involved a moral lapse.) "The poor old man was took of a fever last night. They heard about it at home just now and sent young Harry round to fetch her down there."

"What, upped and gone without no by-your-leave?" Bissett exclaimed. "That gal takes a deal too many liberties. When will she be back?"

"She only left a minute ago," said Mrs Belflower, rather resentfully.

Between her and Bissett there existed a state of permanent though rarely overt hostility. As England and Russia have long struggled for mastery along the border from Constantinople to the North-west Frontier, so these two faced each other from their domains of kitchen and nursery and struggled for the upper hand throughout a range of less clearly defined spheres of influence. Sukey was their Ottoman Empire.

"Why, who give her leave to go, Mrs Belflower?"

"I done, Mrs Bissett."

"Then I don't believe it were your place."

"Nor no more it ain't yourn to tell me mine."

My mother turned suddenly and stamped her foot, exclaiming: "Hold your tongues! Both of you!"

"Well I nivver," said Bissett and we all three looked at her in surprise.

"Bring the tea-things, Mrs Belflower, and come with me, Johnnie," she said and walked quickly out of the room. I obeyed, leaving Bissett and the cook in a sudden, outraged alliance.

We went from the older half into the spacious hall, in the newer part of the house, from which led the sitting-room and breakfast-room where we took our meals (except, oddly, breakfast which we had in the little parlour). As we entered the breakfast-room I asked: "Tell me about London."

"Is everyone conspiring to drive me mad?" she cried. Then she turned and hugged me and said: "I'm sorry, Johnnie. It's not your fault."

We seated ourselves at the table and she went on: "I used to live there. That's all there is to know."

"When? I thought we had always lived here?"

"Oh, it was before you were born."

"Tell me about before I was born."

At this moment Mrs Belflower came in and began to set out the tea-things.

"We won't talk about it now," my mother said.

"And what did the man mean about my father? I never had a father, did I?"

I noticed Mrs Belflower's back stiffen over the side-table where she had put the urn. My mother looked at me reproachfully and I felt a stab of pain mingled with a strange pleasure at the realization that my questions were causing her grief.

"I heard someone say once that I was a 'poor fatherless boy'," I went on. "So that must be right, mustn't it?"

"Thank you, Mrs Belflower," my mother said. "I can do the rest myself." When she had left the room my mother said to me: "Who said that to you, Johnnie?"

"Oh, someone in the chandler's shop said it to Bissett. So tell me!"

My mother clasped and unclasped her hands: "When you're older," she said at last.

"When? At Christmas?"

"Not this Christmas."

"Then the one after next?"

"No, darling. Perhaps the one after that."

Thirty months! It might have been as many years.

Although I tried to persuade her, she would neither bring the date nearer nor answer any more of my questions.

When Mrs Belflower had returned and finished clearing the table, my mother asked her to bring her writing-stand and letter-case from the parlour and we went into the sitting-room — a beautifully light room with a good view of the High-street. Then she unlocked her escritoire and took out the large pocket-book in which she wrote her letters, as was customary in that time before the Penny Post. While she was writing I got out my soldiers and marshalled them on the carpet, but since my mother wouldn't look at what was going on when I asked her to, it wasn't as much fun as usual. Usually I dreaded the moment when Bissett would knock on the door and I would be condemned to bed and sleep, but tonight I was, if not looking forward to it, at least resigned. And there was still the prospect of teazing Bissett.

However, this evening at about the time that my arrest was due, there was a sudden hammering at the street-door. We both started and my mother looked up from the letter she was writing and exclaimed:

"Who can that be at this time?"

We heard Bissett answer the door and a moment later she came into the room, the flow of her indignation in full spate: " 'Tis really shameful, ma'am. Those men have left that ladder out there in the airey right under the winder of the parlour as if this was their own yard."

"Oh yes. They told Mrs Belflower that they had had such difficulty getting it over the railings that they hadn't time to do it tonight and they would come back for it tomorrow. But who was it at the door?"

"The letter-carrier's gal," Bissett answered indignantly. "That Sally, a saucy-faced little baggage. Coming to the front door bold as brass. Said she was a-feared to go up the lane in the dark, but I told her off for that, you can be sure. Nivver too young to larn your place."

"And did she bring anything?" my mother enquired.

"Aye, she brung you this, with ten-pence to pay which I give her myself."

She reached into the pocket that hung by her hussif while my mother took the letter and handed her the money from her escritoire.

"Well," said my inexorable gaoler, "this young gentleman's for bed, as soon as he has cleared up his play-things."

Now of course I was determined that I didn't want to go: "Oh, Mamma, can't I have just a little longer?" I begged.

"Well, just a few minutes," she said absently as she broke the seal.

I smiled triumphantly at my nurse and her face darkened as she strode quickly from the room. At that moment a smaller, sealed missive fell from my mother's letter and landed on the floor near me. I picked it up and as I handed it to her my eyes fell on the superscription, which, as I held it, was upside down. I had only just begun to learn my letters but I knew that our name began with an "M", and since this was easy to recognise even inverted, I was surprised to see that the name on this smaller epistle began with a different letter — a "C". I could not think of any explanation for this.

Pretending to be still playing, I watched my mother put down the letter she had read first and quickly tear open the smaller missive. It must have been short for she read it quickly, and frowned and bit her lip. She then placed the two letters inside the silver case and locked it with one of the keys at her waist. She looked up and saw that I was watching her.

"This was my father's," she said, showing me the case. "He gave it to me on the day ... " She broke off.

"Tell me!" I exclaimed. "When did my father give it to you?"

She looked at me in sudden surprise and I saw that her face was flushed. Then she laughed: "I was talking not of your father but of mine. You see, my father was your grandfather."

"I think I understand," I said slowly. "Tell me about him."

"Now, Johnnie, we've just agreed not to talk about any of that until you're older. But I have some good news to tell you. How would you ... "

At that moment Bissett's entry interrupted us. Just as she was about to take me into custody, my mother held out the letter-case and said: "Bissett, will you put this in the parlour so that I'll be sure to see it in the morning, for I must remember to answer it first thing."

I stood up quickly and snatched it from her: "I'll do it!" I cried.

"No, Johnnie!" my mother exclaimed but I ran from the room.

Bissett had left a burning candle on the hall-table to see us upstairs and I seized it and went into the parlour. Because the old part of the house was built so low, the parlour looked into an area — a dark little yard between the house and the road — so that although it was cozy enough in the winter when a fire was lighted and the curtains drawn, on summer days it had a mournful air. By the light of the candle I now examined the leather-bound case with its heavy silver clasps which I had never been able to look at before. Engraved upon a silver plate was a design that I recognised because I had often seen it on our cups and plates and on the silver cutlery: a rose with four petals. But here five of these roses were incorporated into a design in which four of them stood at each corner of a square with the fifth in the centre. There was also a line of writing beneath it and I vowed that very soon I would be able to read it. Not daring to delay too long, I laid the case on the sideboard among the breakfast things. When I came back into the sitting-room I found my mother and Bissett waiting for me sternly.

"That was very naughty, Johnnie," said my mother. "I don't know what has got into you today. I was going to tell you something nice but now it will have to wait until you deserve to hear it."

And so, truly like a disgraced prisoner with nothing to say on his own behalf, I was handed over to my guard and led away.

I had always dreaded the journey up the ancient staircase with the treads creaking behind us to my room in the older part of the house, and so even on this occasion, as soon as Bissett and I left the sitting-room I reached out for her hand.

"Get along with you," she said irritably, pushing my hand away. "If you're old enough to worrit and fret your poor mamma so, you're too old to need your nurse in the dark."

It wasn't the darkness that terrified me but the mysterious shapes and shadows created by the flickerings of the candle as if it were summoning creatures of the night that scuttled out of sight as you moved towards them, like the huge spiders I saw only too often and which seemed to me to have more legs than could ever be required for any innocent purpose. I had particularly loathed them ever since Bissett had described to me how they fed on living creatures.

"Why," Bissett scolded, "for all your bold sauciness, I believe you're affrighted of your own shadder."

Indignant at this charge, I hurried ahead and in a moment we gained my room which was at the end of a short dark passage that led from the landing. It was small and narrow with a floor that sloped steeply downwards towards the windows, while the low ceiling was sharply angled, because of the steeply-pitched roof, so that it, too, converged towards the end of the room where the window was. There was little space in the room for furniture, and apart from an ancient black press and a chair, there was only an old chest in which I kept my play-things. A threadbare Turkey-carpet covered the floor beside my bed, and on the walls were two framed prints that my mother had given me: a large coloured engraving of the Battle of Trafalgar — a mass of tattered sails and puffs of smoke — and above it a small mezzotint of my hero, Admiral Nelson.

"Now no more of your nonsense. Hurry and get into bed," Bissett scolded.

"Where do you think that man is now?" I asked thoughtfully.

Indignantly she replied: "I'm sure I don't know, but I dare say miles from here, asleep in some ditch."

"How I should like to sleep in a ditch!"

"Mebbe one day you will," she said grimly. "And for sartin if you carry on as you have today. But I'll wager he ain't the only one abroad now. That gal won't be home tonight, mark my words. Nor most probably in the morning nayther. Why your mither lets her get away with scamping her work ... ! Well, 'tis not my place to say. But this is what comes of dealing with the ungodly. 'Tis no better than heathen, this parish, and as the Good Book says, evil communications corrupt."

Now, at last washed, and clad in my night-shirt, I prepared to clamber into bed. This was not easy for it was in a sort of ancient oaken box fitted into a recess by the door and was several feet above the level of the floor.

"I'll warrant your mamma 'ull not come up tonight when you've been so bad," Bissett said as she tucked my bedclothes in.

I didn't believe this but naughtily I said: "Then will you tell me a story instead?"

"You know very well I shall not. Stories are lies."

"But the Bible is full of stories," I said.

"That's quite different, and well you know it."

"How is it different?"

"You ask too many questions. Ask no questions and you'll be told no lies."

"Why should anyone lie?" I demanded. "And if you can tell me a lie then you can tell me a story as well since you've just said they're the same thing."

"You're a wise child, Master Johnnie," Bissett said very gravely. "The devil makes use of such wit as yourn. There's some things as can't be argyed about. You know they're true on account of God speaks 'em straight to your heart."

At that moment I heard my mother's tread along the passage. I smiled triumphantly at my nurse and as my mother came in Bissett said: "You're a deal too kind to him, ma'am. If you ask me, he wants a father's hand."

My mother started and then said somewhat haughtily: "That will be all, Bissett."

My nurse moved to the door holding the candle: "Good night, Master Johnnie."

"Good night, Bissett," I replied.

With a glance at my mother she added: "Be sure and mind you say your prayers now."

I nodded and she left the room.

When I was sure she was out of hearing I said: "May I hear a story, Mamma?"

She read me a story every night and I loved the ritual of choosing as much as the story itself. My favourites were the ones that frightened me most — "The History of Jack the Giant-killer", "The Children in the Wood", "The Tale of Death and the Lady", and "Chevy Chase". Above all I loved *The Arabian Nights* as much for the strange words — Sooltans and Ufreets and Djinns — as for the fabulous world of the stories. There was one tale that had frightened me so much on the only occasion that my mother had read it that although I longed to hear it again, I had never dared to ask her for it.

"No, Johnnie. You've been too naughty this evening."

"Oh please! I'm sorry about the letter-case."

"It wasn't just that. Bissett's right, I'm too indulgent with you. I'll read you a story but to show you that I really am hurt, *I*'ll choose it and it shall be that one about a man who spies upon his wife and has a horrible surprise as a punishment for his curiosity, for curiosity is always punished, you know."

I nodded, not daring to speak, for this was the very story that had frightened me so much.

My mother took down the book from the shelf over my bed and began to read the tale of Syed Naomaun who married a new wife who was very beautiful. But after a time he was struck by the fact that she ate only a grain of rice a day. He saw that she went out of the house almost every evening, and so one night he followed her. She walked out of the town and seemed to be passing the graveyard when he lost sight of her in the shadows of the trees. "So he crept forward and as he came closer," my mother read on, "he saw that she was seated upon the wall beside a female goul and ... "

I could bear it no longer and, with a scream, I thrust my head under the bedclothes.

"There, there, Johnnie," said my mother, patting my head through the blankets. "It's only a story. It didn't really happen."

"Didn't really happen?" I repeated as I emerged from beneath the blankets. "But it says so in the book!"

"You'll understand when you're a little older."

"You always say that," I protested. "It's not fair."

She looked at me intently: "I'm sorry I was a little upset today, Johnnie, but I've had some rather bad news. That letter was to say that Uncle Martin is unwell."

"Is that all?" I asked.

She looked down: "Yes, there's nothing else to worry about. Now, you will go straight to sleep, won't you?"

I nodded. She quickly kissed me, picked up the candle and stole from the chamber squeezing the door shut behind her. I strained to follow her light step making its way along the uncarpeted passage and down the stairs until it was out of hearing.

Since it was a still, almost windless night and nothing was passing in the road, the only sound was the gentle rustling of the trees. After some time, from the borders of slumber, my ears caught the faint jingling of bells in the far distance, and then the hollow, echoing rumble of huge iron-hooped wheels labouring over the uneven metal of the road. That, I knew would be the carter whose waggon travelled overnight to Sutton Valancy. It clattered and rumbled past the house and I traced it into the distance along the road out of the village.

Sleep was reclaiming me when suddenly I became aware of the low murmur of voices very near to the house. My first thought was that Sukey might have returned, but then I realized that they were men's voices. I wondered if I dared to leave my warm safe bed and brave with my bare feet the spiders that might be lurking on the floor. I managed to place my feet on the ground and begin to cross the chamber. I started once at something that moved behind me, but it was only my own shadow crossing the light that came round the edges of the shutters. Because of the thickness of the wall, the window was set in a recess several feet deep and had a window-seat onto which I now clambered. Noiselessly I lifted the bar that secured the shutters and drew them back. The moonlight flooded in and by its aid I opened one of the casements and knelt to look out. I could see nothing that moved except, on the wide High-street before me, the shadow of clouds passing the face of the moon. The railings that separated the house from the carriageway caught my eye as they glinted in the bright moonlight, and then for a moment, as my gaze moved on, I was puzzled by something lying at the bottom of the area on my side of the building, before I recognised it as the ladder left by the men working on the roof.

Raising my head I could just make out the chimneys of the houses opposite above the tops of the trees that lined the other side of the road. Our house stood on the outskirts of the village and the few houses here were set far apart from each other. I could see no lights in any of the other dwellings and it seemed to me that I might be the only person awake in the world. Suddenly a dog barked and the sound was so clear, though it obviously came from far away, that I realized that whoever had been out there must have gone or I would have heard their footsteps.

At that moment I heard noises from within the house and recognised the sound of Bissett coming up to rest. Quickly I hurried back to bed, crept between the sheets and was soon asleep.

CHAPTER 3

I ran through a door and found myself climbing stairs. Round and round and up and up I went and all the time I could hear the sounds of my pursuer behind me. The staircase seemed to go on forever and as I ran my heart pounded and my legs laboured without seeming to be conveying me at all. I looked back and saw something advancing up the stairs just behind me with a strange smoothness of motion. It was a large, pale face that was hideously pitted as if by the smallpox and whose deep eye-sockets seemed to be staring sightlessly at me. There seemed to be no body supporting it but only a trailing black garment. As it grew closer the figure grew taller and taller so that now it was no longer beneath me but towering above me, its great arms spread out like the wings of a bird or the webs of a huge bat, and I knew that it was about to pounce.

In my sleep I screamed, and then I found myself awake, my heart thumping, my forehead bathed in sweat, and the bedclothes scuffed up around me. Had I really screamed and called out? I seemed to have started no echoes for the room was still and peaceful in the moonlight which streamed through the open shutters. And then, as I looked at the window I saw a head framed within it.

This must still be the dream and I must have only dreamed that I awoke, I thought, for no-one could reach up to this window. I couldn't see the features, for the moonlight was coming from behind so that the face itself was in shadow, but the head was large and had a lot of hair which stuck out. But how could I be dreaming, for my eyes were open? Was I only dreaming that my eyes were open? Or was it that ...

"Keep quiet or I'll tear off your arm and beat you to death with it!"

I wanted to shout with relief for the voice was that of the tramper. So it was no dream that I was trapped in! I watched as he clambered through the window and came and stood over me: "Not a word to nobody that you knowed me or I'll come back and cut your throat. I promise. And your precious mam's too."

At that moment we both heard footsteps in the passage. With an oath the man went back to the window and swiftly climbed out. A moment later my mother was in the room, holding a candle and gazing at me in dismay. It all happened so quickly that I almost wondered if the stranger had been in my chamber at all.

"What is it," she asked. "What's the matter, Johnnie?"

I was about to speak when suddenly a face came round the edge of the door: gaunt, the features glaring, the hair rising strangely in silhouette. I screamed and my mother looked behind her in alarm.

Bissett came in. I had never before seen her in her night-gown and with her hair in a net.

"There was a man!" I cried.

"What do you mean?" my mother asked in alarm.

"He was here. I saw him at the w-window," I managed to sob.

"Oh Johnnie, that was a nightmare."

"I told you what it would lead to, ma'am," said Bissett.

"N-no," I persisted. "He was really there."

"How could he be there?" said my mother mildly. "No-one could get up to the window without a ladder."

As she said this she faltered and I saw Bissett glance at her. While my mother stayed by my bed with the candle, my nurse quickly went across to the window and looked out.

Without turning round she said gravely: "Aye, there's that ladder up against the wall here sure enough."

My mother gave a cry and I noticed that one hand reached to grasp the slender box that hung from the key-chain that she must have snatched up when she left her bed. I wriggled aside to watch as Bissett clambered onto the window-seat and peered out. As she did so there was a loud crash which seemed to come from directly underneath us.

"They're coming at last!" my mother exclaimed in terror.

She clung to me so tightly that she hurt me. As that moment there was a second blow louder than the first and accompanied by the sound of splintering wood.

Bissett came back from the window and stood over us, a tall gaunt figure in her long night-gown. Her voice was oddly calm as she reported: "They've broke into the parlour, ma'am. I jist seen one of 'em getting through from the airey as I put my head out."

"Mercy!" cried my mother. "They've come to murder us."

"Fiddlesticks!" Bissett snapped.

Still clinging to me, my mother began to weep, and to my amazement Bissett seized her by the shoulders and shook her fiercely: "Be silent," she demanded. "We're in no danger. Not less'n you cry out and draw their notice to us."

"You don't understand," moaned my mother. "They've come to kill us, me and Johnnie."

"They're only thieves, ma'am. They seen the ladder and thought to break in easy."

"No, no! You're wrong," my mother cried. "You don't understand. Go to the window and call for help."

"No, indeed," said Bissett. "That would be dangerous."

"You must believe me," exclaimed my mother. "They'll have firearms and they'll be on the way up here now."

Bissett crossed to the door, closed it, and then leant with her back against it.

"Well, they won't be able to get in if they try. But most like they're more frighted nor us and only want to get out."

"Then let me go and look," I said, trying to pull myself free from my mother's grip.

"No, Johnnie," exclaimed my mother anxiously, pressing me back into the bed.

"Bide there," said Bissett. "We'll give 'em time to be gone. 'Tis safest that way."

We waited for what seemed an age, staring at each other in silence as we strained our ears for the slightest sound. With her arms still about me, I could feel that my mother was shivering, though it was a warm night. At last my keener hearing detected something: "Do you hear that?" I asked.

Bissett cautiously made her way to the window and looked out: "There they go," she exclaimed. "I've just seen one of 'em go up the road."

"Oh, thank heavens," sighed my mother.

Then we all started and stared at each other in dismay as footsteps approached down the passage. The door opened slowly and Mrs Belflower appeared, magnificent in a night-gown and night-cap and carrying a candle. She was pale with terror.

She collapsed onto the bed and it was some minutes before she was able to tell us her story. Sleeping at the back of the house (and very heavily) she had not been woken by my cries, but she had heard sounds from downstairs and so had gone down.

"When I got to the foot of the stairs," she went on, "I could see someone at the door trying to pull back them bolts as sticks so bad. I hadn't brung no candle but there was light enough for me to see: 'twas a man! A stranger."

"Oh you must have been terrified," exclaimed my mother.

"No, ma'am, for I didn't think. I jist said: 'Who are you and what are you a-doin'?' And he said ... " She glanced at me and said: "Well, nivver mind what he said. Then he just kind of girned and went on, cool as you like, pulling at them bolts. In a minute he had 'em free, and then he jist opened the door and made off."

"What did he look like?" asked my mother.

However, she was unable to describe the man at all and even when my mother prompted her with a description of the tramper she could neither confirm nor deny that it might have been he. She was the only one of us, of course, who had not seen him that afternoon. Remembering the threat the man had made, I said nothing.

Bissett suddenly said: "Did you open them shutters, Master Johnnie?"

"No," I said and then felt myself blushing at my words. But it wasn't a lie for I had not meant to leave them unfastened and besides, it occurred to me, if I were to explain that I had heard voices I would have to tell the whole story and expose my mother and myself to the threat the man had made.

There were many questions that could be left to the morning, but the one that had to be decided now was that of the dispositions for the remainder of the night. There was some discussion of whether Mr Pimlott should be summoned to keep guard, but since even the redoubtable Bissett was reluctant to venture the few yards to his house, the scheme was abandoned in favour of other precautions. Mrs Belflower announced that she would go back to her bed but leave her door open.

"Let me stay with you," I said to my mother.

"There's no call for that," Bissett put in. "I'll watch the rest of the night, but I'll warrant they'll not come back. And if you take him, we shall have all that to-do over again of getting him to sleep on his own."

"No we shan't," I protested.

"I think nurse is right, dearest. You'll be quite safe here now."

"Why do you always do what she says?" I demanded.

"I don't," she said, blushing slightly. "Very well, I suppose one night won't hurt." And so, despite Bissett's forebodings, she took me back to her bed for the remainder of the night.

When I awoke the next morning it seemed perfectly natural that I should be in my mother's bed. As usual she had already risen and as I pulled back the curtains and looked round the chamber I saw that everything was as always, and yet seemed unfamiliar: the clothes-press and wash-stand stood where they always did and on the dressing-table was the beautiful japanned box with its picture of a tiger-hunt and the silver clasps at the corners like claws. Then suddenly the events of the night came flooding back and I remembered that the room seemed unfamiliar because I no longer slept there.

As I came down the stairs some minutes later I started at the sound of a man's voice, but when I reached the hall I saw that it was Mr Emeris. He was bent with considerable dignity over the lock and the bolts on the street-door. Even in this position he cut a magnificent figure in his brown great-coat with its gold braiding, his dark plush knee-breeches, and tri-corn hat, and with his truncheon dangling from his belt. As village-constable, beadle (in which capacity and carrying a different staff of office, he ushered the other gentle-folks into their pews on Sundays) and sexton, he was a complete parish administration in himself. While I sat at breakfast with my mother in the parlour, I could hear his deep slow tones in the hall murmuring on in a steady, reassuring growl against the voices of Bissett and Mrs Belflower.

"The burglar seems not to have taken anything," my mother told me. "Last night Bissett found two silver candlesticks near the front door that he must have dropped while he was trying to get out, but nothing else seems to be missing."

"Oh good. We frightened him away before he had time."

"Yes," she replied. "That might be so."

At that moment there was a knock at the door and Mr Emeris entered backwards, opening the door as little as was necessary to admit his large frame and drawing it to immediately behind him, saying to someone in the hall: "I'll have you say that again later, mistress, thank you kindly."

He shook his head and sighed as he removed his hat and seated himself, at my mother's invitation, on the sopha.

"Have you come to any conclusions, Mr Emeris?"

"I reckon I've about puzzled it out, ma'am," he answered with composure.

"Don't you want to know what I saw?" I cried. For I wanted my moment of importance even though I was determined to conceal the most interesting part of my experience.

"Why I've heerd that already from your mither and Mrs Bissett," he answered. "Now the way I see it, ma'am, is this: he knowed that ladder had been left there. Now Mrs Bissett has told me about one of the slaters, Job Greenslade, as has been workin' on the roof. It seems he keeps company with your help-maiden, Sukey Podger."

"I can't believe Sukey could have been involved!"

"You can't argue with hard evidence, ma'am. I found summat outside the winder in the airey."

With a theatrical gesture indicating that we would have to rein back our curiosity, he stood up and went out as my mother and I looked at each other in surprise. When he returned a moment later Bissett, who had been lurking in the hall and obviously ambushed him, came in with him. He was carrying something and my heart missed a beat as I looked at it for it was a mole-spade and the twin brother of the one Mr Pimlott had been using the day before.

"See this, ma'am," cried Bissett, snatching it from him and brandishing it like an angry Roundhead with a pike-staff; "this is a slater's tool!"

"Now, now, Mrs Bissett," the constable said reproachfully, retrieving his piece of evidence. "This is my business, if you please. Now it seems, ma'am, as Job Greenslade and your gal Sukey has been seed often and often at night in the village."

Bissett added: "Almost every night."

"In view of that and the ladder being left there and this tool and all, I reckon I've got enough to lay an information against him before a Justice and have him took up."

I had been listening with growing dismay for I knew and liked the young slater: "But it wasn't Job!" I exclaimed.

"Why, Master Johnnie, you said you didn't see the man proper so how could you know?" Bissett said quickly.

I dared not admit the truth, but another objection occurred to me: "But Mrs Belflower saw the man and she would have recognised him if it had been Job."

Bissett and the constable exchanged looks at this and he said: "When you're as old as I am, young genel'man, you'll know as things ain't always so simple as they appear."

"That's right," Bissett said. "Mrs Belflower's too partial to that gal by half. And to young Greenslade, too."

"I cannot believe it was Job," my mother declared. "You really don't think, Mr Emeris, that it was the tramper who came begging yesterday?"

"I do not. It were jist chance that he happened to come by that same arternoon. And only consider, ma'am, the fambly what that gal come from."

"Aye," Bissett put in, "and as you've jist said, Mr Emeris, she was seed last night with Job. And she was out all night."

At that moment we heard a banging at the back-door. Mr Emeris and Bissett exchanged glances and as she made for the door he said: "Don't let her speak to Mrs Belflower."

She returned with Sukey who was red-eyed and exhausted and now looked stunned at finding herself brought before the majestic embodiment of the Law.

"I'm sorry I stayed out so long, ma'am," she said timidly. "You see, uncle was took bad (and aunt is poorly, as you know) so I was up all night with him till my sister come up."

"Oh Sukey, it's nothing to do with that," my mother began.

Mr Emeris held up his hand warningly: "If you'll be good enough to let me examine her, ma'am."

At this word Sukey visibly blenched. However, frightened as she was and the more so as she gradually realized what was being charged against her and Job, she remained unshaken in her assertion that she had gone directly to Hougham and had stayed there until just now. Even Bissett's attempts to break this story down were unavailing, though she reduced the girl to tears. And so Mr Emeris had to concede that the evidence against her and Job was inadequate to justify seeking a warrant yet — though he remained convinced of the guilt of at least the latter and sure that he would succeed in proving it once he had shewn the tool to Mr Limbrick and examined Job himself.

The sun was shining from a clear sky when, early that afternoon, we left the house, my mother in a white walking-gown and straw bonnet against the sun and I in my white beaver hat and pale blue frock-coat. We set out towards the centre of the village and after a few minutes passed the little old church with its big, untended graveyard. The smoke ascended straight up into the blue sky from the low-browed cottages with their dark little windows.

As we walked we discussed the great event and my mother repeated her belief that the burglar had been the tramper.

"If I see him again," I vowed, "I'll hold onto him and shout for Mr Emeris."

She suddenly stopped and said anxiously: "Promise me, Johnnie, that you'll never speak to anyone you don't know?"

"But there never are any strangers in the village." I added bitterly, glancing to our right: "That's why the inn has shut down its livery-stables."

Almost opposite the church stood the village's only inn, an old, half-timbered building which seemed to lean into the road as if peering sideways for possible customers. And so it might well have done, for now that the turnpike was finished that took the high road half a mile away from the village, no travellers ever stopped there and it had sunk to the status of a mere public-house. The carriages that had rattled through the village on their way to change horses there until a year ago were no more than a dim but glorious memory for me now.

"Can you read the sign?" my mother asked.

"Yes," I said. "The Rose and Crab." Then I had to admit: "But I'm not really reading it because I know what it says, though I would recognise the 'R' and, of course, the 'C' even if I didn't know that that was what they were. If you see what I mean."

When, long ago, I had asked my mother why the inn had such a strange name, she had suggested that the crab referred to was the type of apple. However, the painting on the sign was so weather-worn (and its limner so maladroit) that although the rose was clearly recognisable, the object beside it might have been anything, and I liked to believe that it represented the sinister and spider-like sea-creature rather than the familiar fruit.

"You'll soon be able to read properly," my mother said and we discussed this as we passed through the centre of the village. From this point the houses began to thin out again, and a stream ran along the right-hand side of the road as it descended towards the Green which now lay before us, a wide meadow with houses all round it and a muddy pond in the middle. Our quickest way would have been to keep on towards our right along its edge by way of Silver-street where I knew Sukey's family lived. However, my mother never went that way because the stream flooded the road and it was altogether not a very nice part of the village. So we now skirted the Green and bore to our left.

As we were passing the little house on the edge of the Green where two elderly sisters kept a school and where I had often seen the scholars going in and out carrying their books and slates, I asked: "When I can read really well, shall I go to school there?"

"No, I shall continue to teach you. And we'll have such fun in our own little school. I asked Uncle Marty to buy a lot of books for us, and he said in his letter yesterday that he had despatched them so they should arrive any day now. This was the news I said last night I was going to tell you." She raised her hand to her forehead: "Oh, I didn't answer his letter this morning, what with all the excitement. Will you remind me later, Johnnie?"

"What sort of books will he have chosen, do you think?"

"Well," she answered, "because he has been a little unwell, he had to ask another gentleman we both know, Mr Sancious, to choose them."

We passed the pond into which the stream drained, and at the end of the Green reached the bridge where the road forked. The left-hand road ran round the village in a large circle and was the way we always went, but the other went up Gallow-tree-hill towards the turnpike and we had never taken that road.

"Please let's go up the hill."

"You've been told over and over again that there is no gallows there now."

That was true, but I could not believe that there could be nothing at all to see: "I don't care about that. But you know what I want to see."

"Oh very well, we'll go a little way up it but not as far as the turnpike."

To begin with the road was a deep, narrow lane between a high wall on our left and overgrown hedges on the other side so that it was impossible to see anything as we walked. Once we had to flatten ourselves against the wall as a great cart came rumbling down the hill towards us bouncing over the stones embedded in the surface of the road. Further on, the wall on our left was broken down so low in places that we could see through it the rich, rolling green slopes of the valley decorated with occasional trees.

"I believe I can see something shining," I exclaimed. "Do you think it can be a lake?"

"Those are the park-woods of a great estate," my mother said softly.

"I can see deer!" I cried.

"Yes, they preserve game." As we walked on she added: "And that reminds me, Johnnie, you must never ask Sukey about her father. It would cause her great pain. I will explain it to you when you're older."

I was hardly listening for the turnpike must soon be in sight. At intervals I jumped up to try to see over the high hedgerows, and once as I did so I caught a glimpse of the top of a big waggon up ahead of us at a right-angle to the way we were coming. A little further on I could see, without having to jump, the high bales of straw it was carrying and a man perched on top, but I could not see the driver or the horses so that the man seemed to be sailing magically over the tops of the hedges like the boy in the *Arabian Tales*, and moving surprisingly rapidly for so large a vehicle — certainly faster than I could walk. Excitedly I turned back and shouted: "It must be on the turnpike!"

"We must turn back now," she said.

"Just a little further," I begged.

"No. It's turning bad and I believe it's going to rain."

It was true that the blue sky was darkening a little in the east, but in the west the sun was still shining.

She reached towards me but I ran off and up the hill. As the slope flattened towards the summit, the lane grew wider and then turned into a muddy delta-mouth with the ruts of cart-tracks radiating out from it to the left and right. Then suddenly I was upon the road itself: a wide, perfectly flat, stony strip extending in both directions, sometimes vanishing for a few yards in a hollow of the ridge's summit but appearing again inexorably, until it disappeared from view at a distance of two or three miles in either direction. I scuffed at it with my foot, and only managed to dislodge a few small stones, for the surface was of a hard, tarred kind I had never seen before which was covered all over with gravel. Beside the turning there was a milestone bearing the legend: "L: CLIX", and I knew now what city the "L" stood for.

It was late afternoon and the sky was beginning to change to a darker blue as a cool wind began to blow. I looked down towards the village which seemed very far away and very small and tried to make out which roof-top was ours. I turned in the other direction towards the park and I now saw that there was an entrance a few yards away that gave directly onto the turnpike. It had high pillars on either side, each surmounted by a stone globe, and its great gate was standing open.

At that moment my mother came up with me, panting hard, and seized my shoulder: "You *are* wicked. Bissett is right."

"Oh now that we're here, do let's wait and see if a stage-coach comes!" I cried.

Before my mother could answer, a carriage and pair emerged from the entrance. The equipage was of a magnificence that I had never seen equalled even in the days when the Rose and Crab had still put up travellers. It was a brightly-varnished canary-yellow landau with a splendidly-attired coachman on the box and drawn by two superb matching greys. But what particularly caught my attention were the arms emblazoned in the pannels.

The carriage turned towards us and I noticed my mother suddenly grow pale. As it came rumbling past us it seemed to me that it slowed down for I had time to take notice of the two figures inside who, as it appeared, leaned forward to the window and stared out at us.

The occupants were an old gentleman and a boy some years older than I. The gentleman was on our side of the carriage and I saw him clearly. He had scanty grey hair receding from a high-domed forehead that was disfigured, as was his face, by large blotchy patches that made me think of the brownish bodies of spiders. He had a long jaw that jutted out and over which his lower lip hung down. But most striking of all were his eyes which were red and deep-sunken with dark folds of wrinkled skin beneath them. As the carriage passed, his head seemed to turn as if riveted on my mother's face, and she, equally, turned as if unable to resist returning that sinister gaze.

"I knew we shouldn't have come here," she muttered when the carriage had passed us. "Oh Johnnie, what have you done? Come, we must go back immediately."

She set off the way we had come and now I had to run to catch her up.

"Who was that old gentleman," I asked her. "Did you know him?"

"Don't ask me any questions, please, Johnnie," she suddenly exclaimed. "You've already been very bad indeed."

As we walked swiftly home almost in silence, I was thinking about something I dared not ask her: I had noticed that the shield emblazoned on the carriage-door was divided diagonally into two halves. One of them contained a crab, vividly portrayed with its numerous legs emerging from the shell and its ugly pincers at its head — so I was surely right about the Rose and Crab! But what had particularly struck me was the other half of the shield which contained exactly the arrangement of five four-petalled roses that I had seen only the day before on the silver letter-case.

When we got home I was surprised to discover that in our absence the carpenter and blacksmith, summoned by Bissett on my mother's instructions, had been hard at work. Both the front and back doors now had stronger bolts, and all the windows that could be reached from the ground had bars across them. Even the back-gate from the garden was now spiked and had a padlock. There was more to come for the next day the men would return and top the garden-wall and the gate with metal spikes. Moreover, my mother insisted that from now on the servants should ensure that the back-door was bolted at dusk and the garden-gate padlocked.

My attention was deflected from this, however, by the discovery that a large parcel had been delivered by the carrier. Although my mother tried to insist that I should not open it until I had finished tea, I made such a fuss that she at last agreed to let me unwrap it immediately. To my delight, it contained a box of about twenty horn-books which were illustrated by beautiful wood-cuts, many of them coloured.

"Oh do let's start straight away," I cried as I opened one after another in delight.

"Very well, but first I must answer Uncle Marty's letter and thank him for advising Mr Sancious so well," my mother said, and went out of the room.

A moment later I heard a cry of alarm, and she came hurrying back into the sitting-room.

"My father's letter-case is gone!" she cried.

We started to search every conceivable place, summoning Bissett, Mrs Belflower and Sukey to help us. Eventually we had to concede that it was not to be found.

"He must have took it, ma'am," said Bissett, not needing to be more specific.

"I suppose so," said my mother. And then, as if to herself, she murmured: "I would rather he had taken almost anything but that."

I looked at her in surprise and said: "Was it worth so much?"

"Why, Master Johnnie," Bissett exclaimed, "it was silver!"

My mother, however, merely shook her head sorrowfully.

"And Mr Emeris," Bissett confided when the other two had left the room, "come round while you was out to say as how Mr Limbrick swore on his solemn oath as that tool ain't nothin' to do with Job nor with slatin' neither." She shook her head: "The sinfulness o' folks sometimes beggars believing."

"I never believed Job did it," my mother said. "Nor that Mrs Belflower recognised him."

Bissett, however, remained convinced that Job had been involved, and would not be satisfied until she had carried her point.

CHAPTER 4

The arrival of the parcel of books from London initiated a new era of my life. Every morning, after breakfast, my mother and I would sit on opposite sides of the table in the sitting-room, she with some work on her lap and a primer propped open before her from which she would read me my lessons, and I listening to her or else crouched over my slate or cyphering-book with my tongue between my teeth as I frowned in concentration over the letters I was forming or the sum I was trying to work out.

Although my mathematical studies made slow progress under my mother's tuition, I greatly enjoyed being read to and persevered in learning to read for myself.

Even before I could make out the meaning of the letters, I was fascinated by the appearance of books — their illustrations and design. Above all, I was intrigued by heraldry and maps, especially the latter of which there were many examples in the house — and in particular one huge vellum example portraying the land around Hougham and dated to nearly a hundred years ago which I used to study for hours. (Mysteriously, it bore in one corner in an ancient hand Uncle Martin's name — "Fortisquince".) Because of this interest of mine, my mother arranged for Uncle Martin to send me a map of London and so one day a huge parcel arrived: a vast and fascinatingly detailed map which had been published in twenty-two enormous sheets just the year after I was born. I pored over it for hours, marvelling at the vastness of London. It became a city of the imagination to me rather than a real place, and my desire to read the hundreds of street-names spurred me on to learn my letters. Soon I devoured DeFoe's *Journal of the Plague Year* and Strype's edition of Stow's *Survey of London* and followed them on the map, fascinated by the changes I could discern taking place between the different periods. By this means I came to "know" the metropolis and believed I could find my way around at least its central districts.

I suppose I became what is called a queer child. I remember looking out of window at night and thinking how strange it all was, that the trees were just there and the houses, and the stars and the moon above them, and strangest of all that I was there and studying them. I knew God was looking down at me for Bissett and my mother had told me so. My nurse had told me how if I was good I would go to Heaven for ever and ever and if I was bad I would go to Hell. Once as I lay in bed I tried to imagine "for ever and ever". I perceived a vast gulph into which I was falling and falling and falling for it had no bottom to it, and the imagination of it made my hair prickle and my heart began to pound for everything I knew — my mother, my nurse, the village — became tiny and meaningless and far-away as I plunged on and on into this endless crevice — until at last I was able to force myself to think of something else.

I was terrified — as I suppose all children are — of things being random and arbitrary. I wanted everything to have a purpose, to be part of a pattern. It seemed to me that if I behaved unjustly I denied the pattern and by creating something ugly and meaningless, forfeited the right to judge that something unjust had been perpetrated against myself and, even more important, the right to expect that there was any justice or design in the world. I wanted my life to involve the gradual unfolding of a design, and whether I have been successful in this remains to be discovered.

Once I had learned to read, books became a great source of pleasure to me. In the histories and romances that I devoured — lying for hour after hour on the floor of the sitting-room with the light of the window falling over my shoulder — I found a kind of freedom and a richness of experience that I missed in the confined circumstances of my life. And if at times I grew tired of this, then for a diversion I would look out of the great window and watch the villagers pass the house. There went James Fettiplace, the surgeon's assistant, and then Mr Passant, the post-master, with his little girl. And there in the rain balancing on her pattens was Miss Meadowcroft. And now that it was a sunny day here came the Yallop boys — the sons of the village's general chandler — with the young curate who tutored them. The adults rarely looked at the house, but the children occasionally did so and it seemed to me that they often smiled and laughed as they glanced towards us. I had spoken to none of these people but their lives intrigued me and I made up stories about them — that Mr Yallop had run away to sea when he was a boy and made a fortune and married Mrs Yallop by elopement. And the curate was a wealthy duke in disguise who had come to the village in order to woo Miss Laetitia Meadowcroft, the Rector's daughter. I asked Mrs Belflower and Sukey about them and what they told me seemed duller and yet in a way stranger than my inventions.

As the months passed and a year went by and then another, and I became bored with spinning my top and trundling my hoop around the terraced grass-plats, I chafed increasingly at my confinement to the house and garden. I might remark, incidentally, that I never saw the mole-spade in Mr Pimlott's possession again. (And this confirmed my suspicion that he had lent it to the tramper to effect his entry.) Neither did I ever venture back into the Wilderness, at first through fear but then it was something else that restrained me — a superstitious desire, I think, to leave something unexplored, to have something that I feared as dangerous and yet knew I could face up to and find to be safe after all.

I particularly resented my afternoon walks because the village-children used to jeer at me when they saw me walking with my mother or Sukey as if I were under guard, and so I used to run on as far ahead of my escort as I could in order to look as if I were alone. I envied the children for running barefoot in the summer when I used to see them on the Green playing their elaborate games of chuck-farthing and kiss-in-the-ring and drop-the-handkerchief. And on the long summer evenings I watched them playing at shuttlecock in the wide street from the front windows of the house.

Above all, and later, as I grew bigger and my walks extended further, I envied the boys of my age whom I sometimes heard shouting above our heads where they were bird-nesting in the high branches or whom I glimpsed in the distance swimming in the river — the white flash of their bodies visible as they dived from the bank. Once or twice while I was walking with Sukey we met one of her brothers, especially Harry who was only a few years my senior, and he always seemed to be doing exciting things: helping to drive cattle, or tenting crows, or harvesting. And quite often it came about that we fell in with Job and that he happened to be walking our way.

I liked Job, particularly because, when he and Sukey were not giggling and whispering to each other, he told me about the things he had done as a boy. He had been very keen on swimming and I conceived the idea that he might be permitted to teach me. I asked my mother about this and at last she agreed.

And so one fine Sunday afternoon that summer, Job and I went to the mill-pond on the river at Twycott. He was a good teacher and on that first day I learned a great deal. I was impressed by the way he dived from the bank and swam underwater and I envied this ability and yet was terrified of the thought of emulating him, especially when he would swim beneath the water-gate of the abandoned mill. He tried to teach me but seeing how frightened I was, he desisted and contented himself with improving my skill in merely swimming.

Our lessons became a regular occurrence on Sundays, and afterwards Job would walk home with me to have tea in the kitchen with Sukey and Mrs Belflower. One day only a few weeks later, however, Sukey told me with tears in her eyes that I would not be seeing him again for a very long time. He had gone to "'list" as a soldier. (She told me that this was because of the way Mr Emeris — prompted by Bissett — was pursuing him with his suspicions of involvement in the burgling of our house.) I was so disappointed at this interruption of my swimming-lessons that my mother had the idea of asking Sukey if the eldest of her young brothers, Harry, could continue the lessons. She looked a little doubtful at this but said she thought it could be arranged.

So next Sunday it was Harry who accompanied me to the river, largely in silence for he spoke rarely and seemed uninterested in my conversation. He was a well-built, straw-haired lad with a big jaw and pale blue eyes. His approach was much more pragmatic than Job's for he insisted that I should first of all learn to stay under the water in order to overcome my natural fear of it, and his conviction that this was desirable seemed to increase when he found how frightened I was at the prospect. To this end he seized me with relish and held me under the surface while I struggled and fought. I really believed I was drowning and I recollect that when he at last released me and I pulled myself onto the bank and lay there gasping and spluttering, I was sure that I was going to die. I looked at a nearby gate — just an ordinary gate into a field — and I recall to this day how it looked exactly like a picture in a frame. And for several days I found that everything I looked at seemed to be framed in this way, as if I were seeing it for the first time.

Strangely enough, Harry's method seemed to work, for my fear of being underwater vanished and I became so skilful that he and I would compete to see who could swim fastest beneath the sluice of the water-gate. But the following summer he was too busy with his work to continue to teach me and my mother refused to let me swim alone — though I was privately convinced that I was safer without than with my professor.

I turned more and more towards books. Parcels of them arrived regularly from Uncle Marty and there were, besides, many in the house. I read whatever was in the library (by which I should be understood to mean, scattered throughout the house for there was no room set aside for that purpose) and soon discerned that there were several distinct categories. There were new books sent to my mother and myself from London and these were romances, novels, tales for children, and so on. Then there were much older volumes — none of them less than fifty or sixty years old — most of which were on dry and dreary subjects connected with estate management and farming, but there were also books of history and travel among these as well as a Latin primer. I knew they formed a distinct group for, apart from their age, they had very plain book-plates with only a heraldic design of an eagle, above which were the initials "D. F." These were to be distinguished from another group of books that were for the most part twenty or thirty years old and from which the book-plates seemed to have been removed. These volumes were entirely devoted to the subject of law and I put them aside in disgust. And finally there were a number which I supposed to have belonged to my mother when she was my age, though I was not sure of this because there was no name inscribed inside them. To speak more accurately, in all but a few instances the edge of the fly-leaf had been cut off.

Now that I could read for myself I perused all of *The Arabian Nights* — those exotic but often brutal and even indecent stories from whose full force my mother had tried to shield me. I particularly enjoyed the long tale in which the resourceful — but, as it seemed to me, surely often unscrupulous! — youth Alla ad Deen plunged into a series of extraordinary adventures as a result of which he was able to enrich his impoverished mother. And now I read to the very end the tale of Syed Naomaun who followed his wife to the graveyard one night and found her with a female goul.

I contracted the habit — or acquired the ability, for I do not know which to call it — of losing myself (or perhaps finding myself?) in a book and cutting myself off from the world. (And, to anticipate for a moment, this was often to prove very useful.) I read works of philosophy, travel, history and literature before I even knew what these words meant or how to distinguish between them. The strange bye-ways I wandered down, the vistas I glimpsed, the dark windings I passed through — all these I cannot hope to enumerate. Though often confused and befogged I was constantly excited by a glimpse of something vast and profound and mysterious. I lost myself amid the spacious "orotund lucubrations" of the last century (the great Cham), or the helter-skelter rushing of the drama and prose of the century before. I read — and above all in Shakespeare — of passions whose nature I often could not understand but whose expression thrilled me. I read about the lepers who roamed England hundreds of years ago ringing a bell and crying out "Unclean! Unclean!" with hoods over their faces to hide their ravaged features until they became too infirm, when the Burial service was read over them and they were locked away in leper-houses. Curious to know how the truth about the East matched the *Arabian Tales* I had loved so much, I devoured travellers' tales and read of hereditary and secret castes of worshippers of many-headed goddesses who strangled their arbitrarily-chosen victims by night as sacrifices to their deities, or of other votaries who hurled themselves to their death beneath the wheels of the great waggons carrying an image of their god. And I read of the hated and reviled Indian caste that only crept out at night to remove the night-soil.

My mother had long read Sir Walter Scott's works to me and now that I grew older I began to read his romances for myself — those works in which narrative and history are so adroitly blended and made to change places. Perhaps because of my reading of history-books, I became fascinated by the past, and always wanted to know how things had come into being. My elders could not satisfy my curiosity except that Mrs Belflower told me stories of the great families of the locality, but her tales seemed to me not to be historical for they were never precisely placed in time.

I became more and more curious to know about the past. Where had I come from? Where had my mother lived? She hated to be asked and would tell me nothing beyond the bare fact that she had grown up in London. Now that it was borne in upon me that we were not of the village, I was filled with a desire to belong, to have roots, to know of a past before I was born.

The only clew I had to follow lay in the books. I looked more closely at those which I assumed had belonged to my mother. And now in a few cases I found the letters "M. H." written in a corner of the fly-leaf and since I knew that my mother's name was Mary, I assumed that the initials were hers. Now I examined the law-books which I had earlier cast aside and noticed that although they had once had a book-plate pasted in, all of these had been torn out. However, since this had not always been done very well, by comparing a number of them I was able to reconstruct the original. This took the form of a shield with the familiar design of the five quatre-foil roses. Above it were the words "Ex libris J. H." and beneath it another line of writing which, as I gradually re-assembled it, I found to be the mysterious words: *Tuta rosa coram spinis*. This was very puzzling, but by now the time was approaching when my mother had promised to satisfy my curiosity on this subject and others, and so I was prepared to wait as patiently as I could until Christmas.

I suspected that the words were in Latin. This language was not one of the subjects my mother had undertaken to instruct me in, but I recognised it from church on Sundays when we attended divine service. And it was on one of these occasions that something happened that I must now describe.

It was autumn and as we walked to church that morning — my mother in her yellow silk gown with her merino cloak and best bonnet and I in my top boots, blue coat, canary waistcoat, white cravat, and creamy breeches — the season's combination of fullness and foreboding was in the air. The chestnuts were bursting from their sheaths and we passed several young men carrying baskets of hazel-nuts, filberts and beech-nuts that they had been into the woods early to gather, following the tradition of the village, in order to give to the girl they admired. And the martins were clustered on the chimneys and thatch of the cottages ready for their departure.

As usual we slipped into our little boxed pew (we had our sitting far away at the back and behind a pillar) before almost anyone else had arrived. And so while the church orchestra of clarionets, trumpets, trombones, bassoons, French horns, fiddles, and bass-viols buzzed and twittered as they tuned their instruments, I watched Mr Emeris — holding his mace before him with stately dignity — usher the great ones of the parish through the throng of villagers who were already standing in the body of the church and now parted respectfully, and into their boxed pews at the front. These were entailed upon the freehold of their houses and it had been a source of irritation to me ever since the beginning of my heraldic interests that we did not have one of those pews that commanded such a fine view of the chancel.

Finally the Rector, Dr Meadowcroft, ascended into the three-decker pulpit.

Then Clerk Advowson at his reading-desk below called the number of the first hymn and the service began. As the orchestra wheezed and squeaked its way through the Morning Hymn I gazed as usual at the multi-coloured shadows cutting across the dust-beams that were cast by the stained glass windows.

The hymns bored me for their language was dull. But I relished many of the words and phrases of the *Book of Common Prayer* and the psalms, especially the names of the sins, which sounded too dramatic to be anything I could ever be guilty of: vengefulness, uncharitableness, idolatry, covetousness, uncleanliness and wantonness. I had no idea what many of these words meant and when I later found out I was usually disappointed that they were names for things that I already knew. The sermon, however, was the part I most looked forward to, though this was not because of anything the Rector ever said. (I had gradually realized that he had a two year cycle of sermons, modestly trusting that that would be long enough to consign them to oblivion in their hearers' memory.) But the sermon gave me the leisure to study the pale marble memorials with which the walls near us were adorned, to try to make sense of the Latin inscriptions, and to wonder what had become of these families who were so boastful of the ancientness of their lineage and the virtues of their members. I recognised none of them except as parts of nearby village-names: le Despenser, Delamater, Mompesson, Torkard, Satchville, and Lacy which were repeated in Hampton Torkard, Stoke Mompesson, St. John's Lacy, and so on.

From where our pew was, however, I could not properly see the most magnificent monument in the church which was up against the wall of the chancel. I knew that as soon as the service ended my mother would follow her invariable practice of leaving before anyone else and I formed the resolution on this day to try to get a closer look at it. So when she rose during the final hymn I slipped out of the pew and advanced. When I smiled back at her I saw that she was staring at me in dismay. Undeterred, I waited up at the front and saw for the first time what happened after we had left the church: the pew-holders waited until Dr Meadowcroft had had time to take up his position at the door and then filed out, shaking hands with him and exchanging a few words.

While this was happening I went forward to look at the monument. It was like a huge high table of stone with another beneath it, and it was the lower one that struck me first for it was a skeleton lying in grinning mockery of the figure above it in exactly the same position. The effigy on top was the figure of a knight in splendid armour and with his arms folded piously across his chest. He was sculpted in cold black marble that was in places pitted and in others polished to a shine by people brushing by. The face was badly cankered by time and its expression unreadable, but the inscription on a brass inlay below his feet, though worn almost smooth, was still legible: *Geoffroi de Hougham: Eques*. Peering more closely I saw that there was a further line beneath: *Tuta rosa coram spinis*.

At that moment my mother seized my arm and hissed: "You're a wicked, wicked boy."

She led me towards the door and we found ourselves in the queue that was processing past the Rector.

As we came up with him he held out his hand to my mother with a look of surprise: "I wish you well, Mrs Mellamphy. I often see you there at the back while I'm preaching, and reflect that there is more rejoicing in Heaven ... you know?"

My mother coloured and nodded briefly.

As we walked away I commented: "What a silly thing to say. There's never any rejoicing in that church."

She was taciturn and still angry with me, though this occasioned me little concern for I had much to think about as we walked home and ate the dinner that Mrs Belflower had ready for us. I was so curious to know the explanation for these discoveries that I resolved to appeal immediately to my mother for an answer, even though we were still several months from Christmas.

Therefore, as we were having tea later that afternoon — safe and snug inside the house while outside the wind began to rise, I asked: "Mamma, what does 'J. H.' mean? I found it in some of the books."

"Oh, Johnnie," she said, "finish up your bread and butter and stop asking questions."

"I want some of that lemon cake," I said, pointing to one of Mrs Belflower's masterpieces that stood on the table, though the rule was that I had to eat all of my bread-and-butter first. "And I want to know about 'J. H.' And what that sentence in Latin means."

"My father told me it meant 'the rose is safe within its thorns'. It was the family-motto. That means, it was what they tried to live by."

It seemed to me a fine idea to have a motto to live by, but the sentiment — with its suggestion of defensive concealment — struck me as a shameful one.

"And he was 'J. H.', wasn't he?" I asked. She hesitated and I went on: "Mamma, you do remember, don't you, that you promised to tell me what I wanted to know next Christmas? You might just as well tell me now."

"Well, what do you want to know?"

"First, what was your papa's name?"

"That's something I can't tell you, Johnnie."

At that moment there was a knock at the door and Sukey came in: "Shall I take away the tea-things now, ma'am?"

"Yes, Sukey," my mother said, and then catching my eye she added: "But leave the cake and a plate for Master Johnnie."

Remembering an earlier occasion when a question in the presence of Mrs Belflower on the same topic had embarrassed my mother, I added: "And I want to know about my own papa." My mother stared at me in surprise and I saw Sukey turn her head suddenly from where she was working. My mother left the table and went over to sit on the sopha in the window as Sukey, carrying the tray, left the room.

Then she spoke again: "Do you know the box with the picture of a tiger-hunt which stands on my dressing-table?"

I nodded.

"Will you run up and fetch it now?"

I hurried from the room, but out in the hall I had to slow down abruptly for Sukey was standing at the foot of the stairs with the tray precariously balanced in one hand while the other was in the pocket of her apron.

She turned suddenly when she heard me: "Oh, Master Johnnie, you did startle me."

"You silly creature," I said. "Whatever are you doing? Stand out of my way."

I ran up the stairs, fetched down the japanned box and handed it to my mother.

She laid it on the sopha between us and then turned to me: "I'm going to say something to you now that is very serious. I had not intended to say it for some time and it may be that you are not old enough to understand it yet, but I fear I may not delay it for very much longer. I have to decide whether or not to do something. If I am to do it, I must do it soon, and once I've done it, I cannot undo it ever again. And it concerns you very deeply. Do you understand?"

"Yes," I said. I noticed that as she spoke she touched with her fingers the slender box that she wore at her waist.

"Now, my dearest," she went on, "you must help me to choose. If I decide to do this thing, then you and I will go on being poor but the important thing is that nobody will try to harm us or to take you away from me."

"But why should anyone want to do that?" I asked.

My mother lowered her eyes for a moment before she looked up at me and said: "You remember that I began by saying we had a choice? Well, if I decide not to do this thing that I spoke of, then we may just possibly one day cease being poor."

"Will we be rich? Rich enough to buy a carriage and horses?"

"No, not as rich as that, but rich enough to start you in a good profession. But in that case we might be in danger."

"What kind of danger?"

"We have a wicked enemy," she answered gravely, "who might try to harm us. Do you recall that man who broke into the house?"

"Yes, of course!" I exclaimed, blushing slightly for I remembered how I had allowed Job to fall under suspicion when I might have cleared him.

"Well, I believe he was sent by our enemy. So do you understand how difficult it is for me to decide? You must help me to choose what is best."

"Is the danger to myself or to you?" I asked.

"A little to me, but mainly to you."

"Then I'm not afraid of anything happening to me," I declared. "And I'll stop anyone hurting you."

She gazed at me thoughtfully: "Well, I won't do anything just yet anyway."

"What about the box?" I asked.

"I believe you ought to know a little more," she said, and choosing one of the keys from the chain, she undid the lock. Then she lifted the lid and, removing a piece of dark blue velvet that rested on the contents, took out a package tied up in crepe-paper. She unwrapped it to reveal a little heart-shaped locket attached to a golden chain. "See, this is how it opens," she said and pressed a tiny knob on the side so that the lid opened to reveal a painting in miniature.

"May I look at it?" I asked and she handed it to me.

The painting depicted the head of a young lady and of a young gentleman in each of the halves of the heart. I easily recognised the lady as my mother, looking very young and, I thought, very beautiful. The young gentleman was very handsome, too, with large, soft, brown eyes in a delicate and rather melancholy face.

"Is that my papa?" I asked.

My mother lowered her eyes and said softly: "The likenesses were taken a few days before we were married."

"And where is he now?"

She shook her head.

"Tell me. You said you would. It's not fair. Why won't you?"

"I didn't say I would tell you everything," she said tearfully. "I can't, Johnnie."

"Yes you can. You said you would. You've broken your promise to tell me."

Sadly she wrapped the locket up again and replaced it in the box. Just at that moment we heard the sound of running feet and immediately the door was flung open. To our surprise Mrs Belflower burst in, panting and flushed. She stopped when she saw my mother's face and glanced at me. Then she exclaimed: "Oh ma'am, please come at once. She's going at her something wicked."

"Why, what's the matter?" cried my mother, starting up.

"She had it in her pocket, but then she has the right, though I will say she has always ate her share and more. But she says she hasn't no right without she's gave leave."

My mother quickly went out followed by Mrs Belflower.

Resenting my mother's failure to keep her promise, I took out the locket and opened it again. Idly I turned it over and found that engraved on the reverse were two pairs of intertwined initials so elaborately rendered that it was difficult to make them out. One set was the familiar "M. H." while the other looked like "P. C." I remembered the puzzling letter "C" that I had seen the day of the burglary and wished that I could recall the rest of the word which would now be meaningful to me. As I was replacing the locket I noticed something peeping out from beneath the velvet and, moving it a little, saw the corner of a piece of paper. My curiosity overcoming my scruples, I lifted the cloth and found beneath it a sheet of paper folded in two and sealed with a great piece of red wax which bore the impression of the four-petalled rose that was so familiar to me. There was an inscription which, though faded and slightly smudged where dark stains appeared to have been smeared randomly across the paper, was easily legible: "My beloved son — and my heir: John Huffam".

Hastily I covered the letter again with the piece of velvet. Huffam! How strange that the name that was signified by that ubiquitous letter "H" was one that I had always known, although under a different spelling! A train of possibilities began to appear before me, but my reverie was interrupted by the return of my mother.

"Is anything amiss?" I asked.

"No. There has been a little misunderstanding, but it has all been straightened out now," she said with a tired smile.

She locked up the box and handed it to me: "Now put this back and then it will be time for Mrs Belflower to see you into bed. Sukey has gone home for tonight."

"Isn't she well? And what's wrong with Bissett?"

"She's not exactly unwell, but nurse is a little under the weather tonight."

I knew what that meant, and I was delighted at the exchange.

So it was Mrs Belflower instead of Bissett who came panting up the stairs after me uttering the most bloodcurdling threats as I ran ahead of her screaming and laughing, all fears of the lurking shadows forgotten in the excitement of the chase.

"Now hurry up," she scolded a few minutes later. "'Tis a cold night to be out o' your bed. And just listen to that wind getting up."

She held my night-shirt over my head and I struggled into it. As the clean, starch-smelling linen enveloped my head dimming the lights of the candles, I swam in a kind of white mist until eventually I thrust my head through the top and re-emerged into the light to find Mrs Belflower securing the shutters.

"Terrible what it's done to the corn," she remarked. "They say 'tis the worst harvest for many a year. I don't like to think what the price of a quartern loaf will be come Christmas-tide. There'll be people in the village nigh on ... " She broke off. "I hope that gal ain't abroad still in this."

"She'll be home by now," I said, sitting up in bed, as I watched her bustle about putting my clothes away.

"Unless she's gone down to see her aunt and uncle. He's bad again, seemingly." She shook her head: "Poor gal. Her family is a worrisome burden to her. But they're from 'Ougham and it's a bad village, so it's no more nor you'd expeck."

At that moment there was a flash of lightning.

"Why is it a bad village?" I asked.

"That I can't say but bad it is from high to low. For even the Mumpseys, who are estated folk and own nigh everything there — and up here, for the matter of that — are a bad lot. There's plenty of tales are told of them and their doings."

"The Mumpseys," I repeated. I did not recognise the name. The sound of distant thunder rolled across the fields towards us and I felt a shiver of excitement for I loved storms. "What sort of stories?" I asked.

"Mostly stories about how they fust come by that great house and the land. You see, they got it of a fambly that had lived here since, oh, since the very start of time when the Romans built the barrers up on the Downs."

"And what was their name?" I asked.

"'Ougham, like the village, though which come fust I couldn't take it upon myself to say."

Huffam! So there had been a family here of that name! The descendants of Geoffroi! Surely I must be connected with it!

"Will you tell me the story?" I begged.

"'Tis too long for now."

"But I won't sleep with that storm!"

Another flash of lightning was followed almost immediately by a loud clap of thunder.

"Very well," she said, and lowered her ample person onto the end of my bed. "This is the story of how a terrible curse fell upon the house and land and anyone who ever owned 'em."

"Oh good!" I exclaimed, for I loved Mrs Belflower's curses. They nearly always ended in duels or madness.

"Well, the 'Ougham fambly lived in that big house on the edge of the village down there. They dwelt there peaceful enough for hundreds and hundreds of years until they started dying out, as old famblies will. So at last it happened that there wasn't nought left on 'em but an old man and his three children — two daughters and a boy. And the son was a young rascal called Jemmy. I call him a rascal for he was very spendy and lost all his fortin' on high play and drink and all manner of wicked mischief in Lunnon Town."

"What manner of mischief, Mrs Belflower?"

"All manner," she said firmly. "Well, he married a rich heiress who brung him fifteen thousand pound and he had a son and a daughter by her. The boy was called John."

John Huffam!

"Like me!" I cried.

"Aye, 'tis a common enough name. And they christened the gal Sophy.

Well, he spent all of his wife's fortin' in a few years and treated her so bad that he broke her heart and she died. And so he carried on until at last no-one wouldn't lend him no more money. And then he heard tell of a money-lender as lived in the City of Lunnon as everybody said was the devil — or nearest kin to him for they said he weren't come of no Christen-folk — and he was called Old Nick. So one day Jemmy went to ask Old Nick to lend him thirty thousand pound. And Old Nick said to him: 'What have you got to pledge?' And Jemmy said: 'I shan't have nought until my father dies.' And Old Nick said: 'Here's the bargain I'll offer you: take it or leave it. I'll lend you thirty thousand pound if you'll fust make away with your father. Then when you've come into the estate you must give me your daughter, Sophy, as my wife. You can keep the land for as long as you live, but if you fail to redeem the money then when you die Sophy's children will have it.' So Jemmy agreed to this for it was no hardship to him, and Old Nick told him how he was to make his father quiet and he give him the means."

"And how was he to kill him?" I asked.

She looked at me thoughtfully: "How do you reckon?"

"The best way would be with poison."

"Aye, you guessed aright. So Jemmy come back to the big house and the very next night, as he and his father sat up drinking, he put the p'ison into the old man's wine and he drunk it and died in terrible agony. So Jemmy inherited the estate and Old Nick loaned him the thirty thousand pound and in return Jemmy give him his daughter, Sophy. And she was only seventeen and mighty handsome, and Old Nick was an ugly old man, so she was mortal sad."

Just as Mrs Belflower reached this point I was irritated to hear my mother approaching. I didn't want her to know I was asking anything about the Huffam family in case she guessed that I had seen the letter.

"You both look very comfortable," she said as she came in.

"I was just starting to tell Master Johnnie a story," Mrs Belflower explained.

"I believe he enjoys your stories better than the fairy-tales I read him," my mother said smiling at me.

"No, I don't," I said. "I like them both. But the stories Mrs Belflower tells are true stories because they happened to real people."

"Do go on, cook," my mother said.

"No, please tell it to me another time, Mrs Belflower," I said quickly.

"That's very rude of you, Johnnie."

Mrs Belflower heaved herself to her feet: "I'll not stay now you've come, ma'am. I'll say goodnight, and goodnight to you, Master Johnnie."

She bent over the bed and kissed my forehead.

"Goodnight, Mrs Belflower. And thank you for telling me that story."

"Sleep well, my dear. I hope that storm don't come no closer."

When she had gone out my mother said: "Johnnie, you were very rude to Mrs Belflower just now. And you were unkind to me earlier."

"No I wasn't."

"But you were. Please try to be better."

"I don't need to try," I insisted. "I am better already."

She sighed then bade me good-night, kissed me, extinguished the candle, and left the room.

As I snuggled under the bed-clothes I heard the wind moaning softly as it prowled around the house, rattling the doors and windows as if seeking some way to get in. Now with a flash of lightning that lit up my room in an eerie white light and left my eyes dazzled as the darkness returned, the storm at last broke. As the rumble of thunder rolled overhead there was the first sudden downpour of rain that was hurled against the rattling windows like showers of pebbles thrown in handfuls. I thought of the fields of beaten-down grain that lay around the house, under whose wet straw the mice and birds must now be huddling in terror.

Surely I was connected with the Huffam family! There was the similarity of the motto and also the evidence of the letter I had seen. Then another thought came to me: the seal had not been broken. My mother had never opened the letter! Then did that mean that it was not addressed to her? If so, then to whom was it directed?

I tried to keep my mind on this, but other thoughts came to me. How strange to have bricks and slates around me, keeping the cold and the water out. And yet now that the wind buffeted the house in wave after wave with a shock that made the shutters and window-frames bounce and rattle, I wondered how long it could withstand such blows, for I recalled Sukey's stories of cottages in the village whose rooves had had their slates stripped off by high winds, and I thought of the roof above my head being scattered like a handful of dead leaves flung up in the air. Of course, animals had hides and birds had feathers that kept the rain from soaking them, like the tarred canvas I had seen stretched over the backs of waggons. And so with thoughts like these, even before the storm had spent itself, I must have fallen asleep.

CHAPTER 5

The weather next day was cold and louring as if ill-tempered after the debauch of the night before. Since the storm had kept my mother awake and given her a headache and because Bissett, who was anyway still "under the weather", declined to escort me on my afternoon walks now that their range had increased with the length of my legs, that task fell to Sukey. In consequence, I achieved the ambition I had nursed for so long.

"Let's go up Gallow-tree-hill," I suggested innocently as we left the house and made towards the village.

"Now you know that ain't allowed," she said. "Anyway, fust of all we must stop by mither's for a moment."

"But that's not fair," I protested. "That's not allowed either."

Sukey turned a worried face towards me: "Uncle has been took bad agin and I want to larn how he is. You won't get me into no trouble at home will you, Master Johnnie?"

Now my mother had not issued an explicit prohibition against my going to that part of the village, but this was only because she did not know that Sukey ever went to her own house when I was with her.

"Not if you promise to take me to the turnpike today."

"To the turnpike?" she said cheerfully. "Why, very well. We'll go round by Lower Hempford."

I was surprised and even a little disappointed to have secured so easy a victory and thought the less of Sukey for compromising so easily.

It occurred to me that she was secretly going against my mother's wishes just as I had done yesterday in looking at the locket and the letter. If Sukey could do it perhaps it was not wrong then, and yet I felt it was so because I had not wanted my mother to catch me in the act. Perhaps it was that while to do something that was forbidden was naughty it was not nearly as wicked as, for example, lying or stealing are. If my mother had asked me when she came back into the room, then I would have had to admit the truth rather than lie.

We soon reached Silver-street, which straggled along the southern edge of the Green and consisted of two rows of low cottages on either side of the stream which ran down its centre, supposedly kept within its wide and indeterminate channel, but frequently overflowing onto the footways on either side — as it was today after the storm. The cottages, with their bulging walls of lath and earth and their mouldering thatched rooves, seemed to be trying to hide themselves in shame by slipping back into the muddy ground from which they were scarcely to be distinguished. We came opposite Sukey's cottage and since we were on the wrong side of the stream, had to walk across on a series of large flat stones in the water.

"Now be good and wait here," said Sukey and went inside.

Sukey's cottage leant up against an exactly identical one, as if each were trying to support itself by leaning against the other. It had only one window and this was a small hole stuffed with rags and kindling-wood. Stamping my feet and blowing on my fingers, I stood at the door and watched some ragged children carrying a bucket of water to another of the cottages. Two boys came past carrying bundles of wood along the opposite side of the stream. One of them was a little older than me and the younger one about my age. They were poorly dressed, wearing ragged clothes that were too large for them and with their bare feet wrapped in sacking as was usual amongst the village-children when the cold weather came.

"Where are you from?" the elder cried, and he and his companion ominously laid down their bundles.

"You're from the Rector's, aren't you?" the other one shouted.

I shook my head.

"Yes you are," the older boy insisted. "Your father is his brother that's visiting there."

"No, you're mistaken," I said mildly.

"Then who is your father?" he sneered.

I hesitated and he cried out: "He won't tell us!" I saw the younger boy pick something up. Before I knew what he was about a stone hurtled towards me and thudded into the grass a few feet away. The other boy bent and picked up another.

"I'll fight one of you fairly," I called out. "But this isn't fair."

"Yaagh!" came the reply and two stones hurtled toward me. Both of them missed me, and the older boy shouted: "Come, Dick! We'll go across and catch him between us."

Carrying several stones a-piece they began to cross over the ford, pausing a little way across to fire another broadside at me.

Fortunately one of the stones struck the door of the cottage behind me and a moment later Sukey rushed out with a basket over her arm which she raised threateningly though she could hardly have intended to hurl it across the stream: "Be off with you, Tom o' Joe," she cried, "or I'll get your dad to tan the hide off your back for ye! And you, too, Dick o' Bob!"

With muttered threats the boys picked up the bundles of wood and made off.

"Are you all right, Master Johnnie?" Sukey asked anxiously.

"Yes, Sukey," I replied. "They didn't hit me. And if they'd come across I would have given them more than they'd bargained for."

"Well, no harm done then, thank goodness," Sukey said and began to move off.

"But why are we going this way?" I asked for we were going towards Gallow-tree-hill.

"I must take some vittles to my poor aunt," she replied, indicating the basket. "There's nobody else can go. We can get to 'Ougham and back before your tea if we hurry. But you must promise not to tell nobody as to how I took you that way."

"Oh yes, I promise!" I exclaimed with delight for I had been told that the lane to Hougham ran for some distance alongside the turnpike-road.

Well, Sukey was being very naughty! And yet I had done even worse things than I had done yesterday, for I had never told anyone that the burglar spoke to me and therefore that I knew who he was. And I had never mentioned to anyone the business of the mole-spade. Just when I believed I had found the courage to ask the old gardener himself about it, he had stopped coming.

"Sukey, what has become of Mr Pimlott?" I asked.

"He won't be doing no more work for your mother. He has gone to the poorhouse now."

"Why?"

"On account of he's too old and ill to look arter hisself. Like poor Uncle. He'll lose his place soon, so the steward has told him and aunty, for he's too poorly to keep the lodge. And if he has to leave the cottage he don't have no settlement in that parish and so they'll have to go back to where he were born."

Could Mr Pimlott have had a hand in the burglary? I asked myself once again while Sukey was chattering on. I had not believed so at the time, partly because I recalled how fiercely he had seemed that afternoon to be defending my mother's property against the poaching mole. Yet I wondered now if, young as I was then, I had misunderstood him. Or had the tramper simply acted alone?

"I never believed that Job took part in the burglary," I remarked.

"Lor', Master Johnnie, I don't know why you should say his name so sudden like that when he's been in my thoughts all day. He's j'ined up for a sodger and gone away, you know, and all on account of Mr Emeris kept on trying to have him took up on one charge arter another."

Perhaps I had been wrong not to speak out, even at the risk of making trouble for Mr Pimlott. "Sukey," I asked, "how can it be right for you to take me this way when you know my mother does not wish it?"

"But uncle's ill! I've got to go!"

"So sometimes you can decide to do what's wrong if it would be more wrong not to do it?"

"Aye, that's it, Master Johnnie," she said gratefully.

"Then," I pounced gleefully, "that's like saying you can choose to break the law when it suits you. Why, Sukey, that man who broke into our house might have said the same, you know."

I was fascinated to see how powerfully this thrust appeared to affect her for she stopped suddenly and stared at me apparently unable to speak.

"But if he was hungry, Master Johnnie," she began in a rush, "or say if he had to watch his children crying for hunger and he knowed that there was something he could get for food as the persons as owned it didn't want for theirselves and didn't even know as they owned it, and that it would be hard for him and dangerous, too, to ketch it, then mightn't it be right for him to try to take it?"

Once again, I wished my mother had not forbidden me to ask Sukey about her father. Anyway, the answer to her question was very simple: "No, Sukey, for if you have no law then everybody would take everything from everybody else. And then where should we all be?"

That silenced her. But it was an interesting thought that you could do something wrong if you had a good enough reason for it.

"So what will you say if my mother asks where we have been?" I asked. "Will you tell a lie by saying that we didn't go near the turnpike?"

"But it ain't the 'pike you're forbidden!" she cried and then broke off.

Not the 'pike! Then why had my mother always been so reluctant to come this way? We walked on in silence for some minutes as I thought about this. After a time I gave this up and returned to another puzzle: "Sukey, can you tell me about fathers? Oh, I don't mean your father," I added hastily, and she flushed. "I mean my own."

"I don't know nothin' about that, Master Johnnie."

"But all I want to know is, could he have died many years before I was born?"

"Why, I don't believe so. No, I'm sartin sure not."

We walked on in a thoughtful silence. Some minutes later, just as we reached the turnpike Sukey suddenly said: "My dad broke the law. There now, I didn't ought to have told you that and I shan't say no more."

I stored this away to think about later for by now my mind was on the 'pike and my disappointment in finding that there was no vehicle upon it in sight in either direction. We continued along it for about half a mile with the wall of the park on the left, and in that time only a couple of waggons and a light chaise passed us.

"Time to turn off, Master Johnnie," Sukey said sorrowfully as we reached the turning to Hougham.

"Mayn't we wait a little?" I asked.

At that instant I thought I heard a metallic wailing note in the distance.

"Oh listen, Sukey," I exclaimed. "Here comes something."

"We must hurry, Master Johnnie," she protested.

The road ran up a long slope to a bend about a mile away, and I fixed my eyes upon that point. Suddenly something appeared there. Even before I could construe what I was looking at I heard the clattering of horses' hooves — more of them and faster than I had ever heard before. Now I could make out the coach and team as they came thundering towards us at full gallop. I saw the blinkered heads of the horses, raised and rearing backwards and pulled to one side as if they were reluctant to advance, and yet at the same time their great fore-legs were always thrusting forward as if to pull the road towards them. I saw the cloaked figure of the driver on the box holding his long whip before him, and then the body of the vehicle itself, gleaming and painted bright red. At that moment Sukey clutched me and pulled me back with sudden violence onto the wide grass verge.

Now it was almost upon us and the thunder of the hooves and the great metal-clad wheels on the hard surface of the road grew and grew until it seemed to be pounding and clattering inside my head. Then the horses were passing us, their huge heads and rolling eyes seeming only inches from us, their coats gleaming wet with sweat, and after them the great lurching monster of the coach itself, with the face of the inside passengers briefly glimpsed through the windows, and the driver and the outsides huddling together against the wind on the top.

In an instant it was gone, and from beneath Sukey's arm I looked at its swaying back as it bounced across the uneven surface of the road.

We were both silent for a moment, and then I said: "Did you see, Sukey? That was the York to London coach. The Arrow."

"Was it, boy?" Sukey said, her face still flushed with excitement. "How do you know?"

"It had it written on the side in big golden writing," I told her proudly, for Sukey, of course, did not know her letters. "Though of course," I added regretfully, "it wasn't the Royal Mail."

"What am I thinking of!" she exclaimed suddenly. "We must be gettin' on."

So we hurried down the lane with the high wall of the demesne still on our left. It was badly delapidated so that in places we could easily look down into the park as it sloped towards the bottom of the valley where we saw a line of thick bushes and trees marking the course of a hidden stream until it broadened out into an expanse of grey water which was the lake.

We skirted Stoke Mompesson with its broad high street with rows of handsome cottages on either side, and then another half a mile further, a straggling group of rough-cast hovels on our right marked the beginning of the village that was our goal. And a very squalid hamlet it was in comparison to Melthorpe, looking to me like an extended version of Silver-street, made up of mean one-story houses built of furze-branches, mud and mortar, and in many cases with turves for rooves. I expected the big house to be nearby but there was no sign of it.

"The village was moved, see," Sukey explained. "So now it's out o' the paritch as the estate is in."

And so we had to walk for another ten minutes before Sukey said: "That's where my aunt lives." She indicated a small cottage that stood beside a pair of tall stone columns topped with globes. They framed a set of lofty black double gates with elegant filigree iron-work fancifully wrought into flourishes and flowers, which were secured by a large padlock and chain, and whose railings rose to sharp points.

"Now you'll be all right to wait here for a little and won't get up to no mischief, will you, Master Johnnie?"

I nodded agreement and she went into the cottage. Overcome by curiosity I approached the gate and peered through the bars, whose black paint was peeling off, revealing the rust underneath. Beyond was a courtyard with a paved surface whose stones were not merely overgrown with moss and grass but had become loosened and dislodged by the passage of long years of neglect.

Some distance away I could see the shape of a house looming up. Although it was sideways on to me, its huge size was apparent, and so, too, was its state of delapidation. Its windows were either shuttered or the paint was flaking off the bars and frames; no smoke rose from its chimneys, many of which were missing pots; slates had slipped from the part of the roof that was visible to me; and altogether the house appeared to be a deserted and uninhabited ruin.

As I watched, however, a figure, dressed in the clothes of a working man and pushing a hand-barrow, came round the corner of the house. He began to gather up the pieces of fallen masonry and shattered slate that lay about on the ground, presumably blown down in the storm the night before.

After a moment two more figures approached from round the corner of the house. I watched them, knowing that I should move away from the gate, but something prevented me. The great empty house of Hougham (or was it Huffam?) seemed to have touched some chord inside me, and awakened, it seemed to me, an echo in my innermost being whose summons I was powerless to resist.

As the newcomers came close enough for me to be able to make them out, I saw that they were a little girl of about my age and a tall, elderly lady, and that both of them were dressed in black. The lady stopped to talk to the workman, but the little girl must have seen me for she continued to walk slowly up to the gate opposite me. Her face was very pale — so pale that I wondered if she had been ill — so that her dark eyes looked all the darker. She held her hands inside a muff she carried in front of her, and a strange, solemn little figure she made altogether.

"You're not one of the village boys, are you?" she said.

Under the terms of the promise I had given my mother, I wasn't allowed to speak to strangers, but, I reasoned to myself, surely this only referred to adults and so a little girl did not count.

"No," I replied.

"I'm strictly forbidden to have anything to do with the children from the village," she explained.

"But don't you live in the village?"

"No. I live here."

"Do you mean in that big house?" I wondered.

"Yes."

She spoke as if it were the least interesting fact in the world.

"Is that lady your mother?"

"No," she replied. "My mother is dead. And so is my father. You see, I'm an orphan."

An orphan? Here was an interesting word and I felt envious of her right to it. Then I supposed I was at least halfway towards being an orphan too.

"That lady is the housekeeper here," she explained. "Of course, I should have a governess. I've had several, but my guardians said that none of them suited. Mrs Peppercorn is very strict about not allowing me to speak to strangers."

Behind the little girl I could see the tall figure of the housekeeper still engaged with the workman. They appeared to be having a difference of opinion, for the man tried several times to turn away but she continued to address him until he had to turn back.

"She is very short-sighted and must not be able to see you," the little girl continued. "But when she does, she will tell you to go away and I will be punished."

"Punished?" I asked. "In what way?"

"I will certainly be sent to bed without my tea," she said in a very matter-of-fact tone. And then added: "And perhaps whipped."

"Whipped?"

She withdrew one hand from the muff and I saw that the back of it had a series of painful red welts across it.

"Then perhaps," I said, "I should go away before she sees me."

"No," the child replied very definitely; "I should like to talk to you for a little longer. There is no-one else here to talk to."

"Have you no brothers or sisters?" I enquired.

"No. There is only Mrs Peppercorn and Betsy, and two other servants whom I am not permitted to speak to."

"And is there no-one else in that big house?" I asked.

"No-one at all," she said. "But, you see, most of it is shut up. We only use a few of the rooms. I wish there were other children here. Do you have brothers and sisters?"

"No," I said; "I don't know any other children either."

"What's your name?" she asked.

"John Mellamphy," I replied.

"Is that all?" she asked in surprise.

"Yes. What's yours?" I answered.

"It's very long. Do you want to hear all of it?"

"Yes, please," I said.

She took a breath, closed her eyes, and recited: "Henrietta Louisa Amelia Lydia Hougham Palphramond." She opened her eyes and (still in a single breath) explained: "My mother was called Louisa, and Henrietta and Lydia are for my great-aunts. I don't know about the others, though."

"But Hougham?" I exclaimed. "Is that spelt like the name of this village?"

"Yes," she said. "H-o-u-g-h-a-m."

Prompted by the desire to show that I, too, possessed a claim greater than might be implied by the bare two names I had admitted, I exclaimed: "I've got that name too! At least, I believe my grandfather's name was the same as that, only spelt 'H-u-f-f-a-m'. That's the name of the family that used to own this house and this village and all the land around here, you know."

"Oh I don't think that can be right," she said.

"Oh yes it is." (What an unpleasantly contradictory little girl it was!) "You see the Mumpseys ... " I hesitated. "They got it from the Huffams."

"The Mumpseys! You mean the Mompessons. Only the village-people pronounce it that way."

I flushed with shame. Of course I knew that name from the memorials in the church. Why had I not made the connexion when Mrs Belflower mentioned it?

"You must be mistaken, you see," Henrietta went on, "because I know that my guardian's grandfather built this house."

"But perhaps his name was Huffam?"

"I don't think so, for my guardian is Sir Perceval Mompesson."

I burned with humiliation. Then the wretched Mrs Belflower had got it completely wrong and so probably my idea that I was connected with this place was mistaken. It was this girl who belonged here if Sir Perceval Mompesson was her guardian!

Absorbed as we were in our conversation, we had not noticed that the housekeeper had left the workman and approached the gate until she spoke from a few yards away:

"I shall write to Mr Assinder to complain of the insolence of that fellow. He has the effrontery to tell me that that window cannot be repaired without ... " She broke off, raised the lorgnette which hung by a chain round her neck, and then exclaimed: "Miss Henrietta! Is that a *boy*?"

"Yes, Mrs Peppercorn," said Henrietta calmly.

"Can you possibly be talking to a village child in defiance of your guardian's strictest injunctions?"

"He's not from the village, Mrs Peppercorn," said Henrietta coldly.

"Indeed?" The housekeeper stared at me through her lorgnette. "I see he appears to be a gentleman's son." Then she said: "What is your father's name?"

The question threw me into confusion. For one thing, I was deeply conscious of my undertaking to my mother not to speak to strangers, and yet surely I could not be so impolite as to refuse to answer a direct question?

"He is called John Mellamphy," Henrietta said.

"Mellamphy," she repeated. "I know of no good family of that name in the vicinity. However that may be, Miss Henrietta, you have disobeyed Sir Perceval's instructions. We will return to the house immediately while I consider your punishment."

"Although he is a stranger, Mrs Peppercorn," Henrietta said, "yet he says his grandfather was called Huffam which is one of my names, so perhaps he is not quite a complete stranger."

"Indeed?" said the housekeeper, turning back towards me quickly. "Where does your father live, Master Mellamphy?"

"I cannot tell you."

The housekeeper's mouth tightened into a thin line at what she must have taken for a piece of impertinence, and she was about to speak when Sukey came running up: "Oh Master Johnnie!" she exclaimed. "You bad boy! You know you mustn't talk to strangers. What would your mother say?"

She seized my hand and began to pull me away: "Come," she said. "We're going to be late. Melthorpe's a good hour's walk from here."

As I turned away, I caught a last glimpse of Henrietta still standing with her pale face pressed against the black iron-work of the gate like a prisoner, while the housekeeper placed a black-gloved hand upon her shoulder.

"Oh, Master Johnnie," said Sukey as we hurried out of the village; "I hope you haven't got me into trouble. Please don't say nought about coming here this arternoon. Not to your mother, and not to nobody besides."

"But Sukey, if my mother asks where we've been, I can't tell her a direct lie, can I?"

She halted suddenly and since she was still holding my hand, brought me to a stop too. She turned to face me and said solemnly: "I beg you, Master Johnnie, don't say nought that might make me lose my place. I know you're a good-hearted boy at bottom and wouldn't want to do no harm to my fambly."

"Will you promise to let me go up to the 'pike when we go our walks together, and stay there as long as I want?" She nodded. "Very well, then. I promise."

We walked on again, and after a few yards Sukey broke out: "Oh, I wish we hadn't come to 'Ougham today. I don't know what ill mayn't come of it. And my uncle is going fast. And then my poor aunt'll be turned out."

I was hardly listening for I was wondering how it could be that Henrietta and I were connected and whether that meant that I was also linked in some way with the Mompesson family.

When we got home my mother, hearing us at the back door, came into the kitchen as we were removing our outer garments: "You're back very late," she said. "I was worried about you. Where have you been?"

The question was addressed to both of us. I blushed and looked away, but instantly Sukey, also bright red, replied: "We went by Over-Leigh way, ma'am. And the lanes was very bad."

"But you must have gone further than that," said my mother. "You're more than an hour later than usual."

Sukey stood in red-faced confusion and cast a desperate look at me. Almost before I knew what I was going to say I heard the following glib speech issue from my mouth: "When we got back to Over-Leigh, the ford had flooded so much that we couldn't cross it there, and we had to go round by the path through Mortsey-wood."

I tried not to look at Sukey who was staring at me.

"Then you must be hungry," said my mother, and it was with a mixture of relief and dismay that I saw that my lie had been believed. I had spoken in order to protect Sukey for she was right: one could lie if it were justified. But if that were so then one could do other things and there was no longer any clear pattern to be followed through the world. And beyond even that, I felt a sense of power and excitement at having created something which had been made real by my mother's crediting it — an afternoon spent innocently and busily between Over-Leigh and Mortsey-wood.

BOOK II

Friends Lost

CHAPTER 6

Let us imagine that we are standing, on a wintry afternoon some years ago, in the west-end of Town. The dusk thickens, rendering even gloomier that great prison-house of fashionable society, so that all those grim and lofty streets and squares seem in the gathering mist to be riding at anchor like so many aristocratic Hulks designated for the detention of Society and its transportation to the waste shores of fashionable boredom. The grimmest and gloomiest of all of them is Brook-street. The grimmest and gloomiest of all the houses in Brook-street (which is, in point of fact, where we are) is one whose brightly-painted scutcheon over the street-door proclaims its aristocratic pretensions, as do the lofty and blank windows which gaze upon the opposite side of the street with a kind of grimace of fashionable hauteur. Of all these windows the loftiest and the blankest is the centre window of the huge state-room on the first floor.

Standing beside us on the pavement is an individual in a shabby great-coat who has the brim of his hat pulled down over his eyes. He is looking up at one of the houses. We, likewise, raise our heads, averting our eyes from the sight of Poverty and gazing instead towards the haunts of Wealth, Arrogance, and Power.

Only just visible, since no lights have yet been lit inside the room, against the centre window on the first floor is a tall figure. With the means at our disposal, however, we are not condemned to remain on this cold pavement but are able to enter the chamber. From inside which, the figure can be seen to be that of a gentleman in black standing with his back against the window and addressing a lady and another gentleman. The lady sits on a chaise-longue, while the second gentleman reclines on a chair with a rug over his legs which are resting on a foot-stool in front of him.

Taking them in the order of courtesy, Arrogance — the lady on the chaise-longue — is the epitome of aristocratic British beauty, tall, stately, and handsome but with a suggestion of cruelty in her thin mouth. Wealth, reclining opposite her, bears in his visage the record alike of an ancient lineage and of centuries of spoliation — the cold blue eye of the brutal thane, the high nose of the acquisitive Norman, and the sallow jowls of the avaricious Tudor courtier jostling for the spoils of Dissolution. And as for Power, standing at the window, his character speaks only too clearly through the bushy black eyebrows, the jutting ridges above the eyes, and the reddish face of one who brooks no opposition from an inferior.

As we enter the room Power is saying: "But if this is the case, at least we now know that she has a child which, whatever the circumstances, was born in wedlock. And that is wholly to our advantage."

"Assuming, of course," the lady says languidly, "that her father's legitimacy is not disproved."

"Well, since the other side has not been able to achieve that in fifty years, I doubt if they will succeed now," Power answers firmly but respectfully. "Though I would feel much reassured on that point if only the record of that marriage could be brought to light. And incidentally, this latest piece of intelligence has given me an idea of where to look for it."

"How intriguing," says Arrogance though she speaks without the vulgarity of manifest enthusiasm. "Do, pray, explain what you mean."

"If you will permit me, I will make myself clear in a moment. But if this is indeed the woman we have been seeking, then the audacity of her choosing that village for her place of residence is breath-taking."

"I examined my employee minutely," the lady says in a cool and very dispassionate tone; "and she is absolutely certain that the servant accompanying the child mentioned the name."

"It's preposterous!" Wealth exclaims impatiently. "It's a damn-fool notion. A fox don't run to earth in the very kennels of the hounds that are chasing it!"

"At first hearing such a view was precisely my own," comes the calm voice from the window. "But the fact is confirmed to my satisfaction by the connexion that exists with the place through her ... protector, Fortisquince."

"What course of action do you recommend?" the lady asks.

"I suggest that we make a direct approach and meanwhile continue with the more oblique initiatives we have already undertaken. For the first ... "

He breaks off as two footmen enter carrying lighted candles.

"Shall we do the curtains now, my lady?" one of them asks.

"Yes, carry on, Edward."

The gentleman in black moves away from the window and advances into the room while the footmen place the tapers on side-tables around the chamber and then draw the curtains. There is silence until the door has closed softly behind them. Then — for why should Power even notice Servitude? — he continues to speak as if there had been no interruption: "For the direct approach, I mean — with your approval — to take a journey into the country and speak to her myself."

"Is that wise," says Arrogance in surprise, "in view of the scrutiny that attends you? If the other side should find her ... "

She breaks off.

"I am confident I can elude my observers," returns Power. "One of them is in the street at this moment which is why I was standing in the window. They are so spoiled by my generosity in making myself conspicuous that they become careless, and that is when I slip away."

The lady smiles briefly and then says: "And do you believe she will part with it?"

Before he can reply the gentleman in the chair suddenly interjects: "Take a couple of stout fellows and force it from her."

"With great respect, there is no reason, as I have so often had the honour to state, for turning the law into your enemy when you can use it as your ally."

"I think we need not disinter that discussion again," says the lady sharply.

"I believe, however, that she will see reason," Power continues.

"Aye," cries Wealth. "She must know that we hold all the aces."

Power smiles at the lady: "I prefer to say that we have her in check. And while I am there I intend to make a further search for the missing record we spoke of a moment ago, for I am reminded of the connexion between that village and the history of your family and hers. The vestry or the graveyard may hold the record that we seek." He pauses, glances cautiously towards Wealth, and then says: "I will also take the opportunity to discuss certain matters with the steward."

The lady shakes her head at him warningly but it is too late for Wealth exclaims: "Don't bring that up again. Fellow's worked for me for years. And his uncle before him. I won't hear a word against him."

Smoothly Power goes on: "I was merely going to say that I would discuss with him the private bill for the enclosure of the common-land."

"Indeed," says the lady. "That wretched bill. Tell me, what progress has been made?"

The gentleman draws a sheaf of papers tied up in red cord from his portmanteau and at the lady's invitation seats himself on the sopha beside her. He begins to untie the knots he has made. Ah, how many miseries lie enfolded by that cord! How many lives strangled by the knots he has made. We shall leave them at their work.

CHAPTER 7

Although I often thought about Henrietta, Sukey and I never went to Hougham again together. Apart from any other consideration, her uncle did indeed die a few days later and so after that she had no reason to go.

In the months that passed — and winter began early that year — I noticed that my mother seemed particularly cast down after receiving letters from London, but she would not tell me if anything was wrong.

Christmas-tide approached and as I was returning from one of my walks with my mother or Sukey in the late afternoon we would meet bands of waits made up of local boys together with members of the church-orchestra carrying their instruments, all with Christmas green hung round them as they went from house to house (though never to ours) to solicit for candied fruit or small coins in return for their singing.

Late one morning a few days before Christmas I went into the kitchen, lured by the sweetly-pungent fragrance of cinnamon and ginger and cloves, and found Mrs Belflower grating spices and beating eggs as she made the Christmas pudding — not, of course, for that festival but for the following year. (In fact, we were destined for the first time in my life to eat that pudding without her.)

"Will you help me by stirring in the charms?" she asked, indicating the little pile of coins and tokens on the table.

"Very well," I said rather unenthusiastically, for although in past years I had enjoyed this task, I now felt I that it was a little beneath me.

"Remember, you has to make a wish. But only one. And you mustn't nivver tell it or it won't come true."

"Oh I remember all that. But I say, Mrs Belflower, will you finish telling me that story now?"

"Which one, my dear?"

"How the Mompessons stole the land from the Huffam family by deceit," I said. When she looked a blank I added: "You remember, Jemmy Huffam cheated his own son, John, out of his inheritance."

"Now I rec'lleck, my dear. But jist put me in mind, where had I got to?"

"Jemmy having to kill his father because he's borrowed money from Old Nick."

"Aye, now I mind. Well, when Jemmy arst for the money Old Nick said to him: 'What have you got to pledge?' And Jemmy answered: 'Nought but my soul.' And Nick said: 'I'll take that, but you're still a young man and you might make me wait fifty year so you'll have to promise more nor that a-fore I'll lend you no money.' Well, the long and the short of it was Old Nick told him 'you must make a legal deed givin' the estate to me and my heirs if so happen you don't pay the money back.'"

"For his children would be Jemmy's grandchildren anyway, wouldn't they?"

"I daresay, my dear," she replied rather absently. "(I'll jist thicken it a little and then you might drop the fust coin in.) So Jemmy said: 'I agree'. But then Old Nick said: 'But you have a son, John, and if you try to keep him out of the estate he'll have the law on his side. So we must draw up a contract between us that nothing can break.' Well, he drew it up and Jemmy signed it with his own blood."

"And then he murdered his father," I cried, "by putting poison in his wine" (here I dropped in a worn six-pence) "and he died in agony."

"Right enough. And his cries was heard all through that great house and even as far as 'Ougham."

"Is that the house that is there now?" I asked quickly.

"The very one," she said stirring steadily.

"Then it can't have been!" I exclaimed in triumph. "For it wasn't built then."

"Why, I believe you're right, my dear. There were an older house nearby which I don't know what happened to it, and that's where it were." Undismayed, she went on comfortably: "Well, time passed and Jemmy kept up his evil ways, drinking and gambling and I don't like to say what not. And one night he was playing dice with Sir Parceval Mumpsey. Now Sir Parceval ... "

"But this can't have been Sir Perceval!"

"And why not, my duck? (Put another o' them charms in now.)"

"Because you said this was a long time ago and I know he's still alive," I said as I added to the mixture a badly bent George II guinea which was the finest of all the charms and was always found in my helping of the pudding.

"Then this must have been his father," said Mrs Belflower imperturbably, "who was also called Sir Parceval. And he was very rich and owned thousands upon thousands of black slaves, and at his wedding in London the King and Queen come to see him married to one of the greatest ladies in the land, and hundreds of black slaves marched through the streets behind the bridal carriage which was all of gold. (I'm about ready for another charm. That old furrin coin with the lady's head.) And so the night I was a-telling you on, he was playing Hazard with Jemmy 'Ougham and ... "

"Hazard? What is that?"

" 'Tis a game at dice, as I understand."

"But what does it mean?" dropping the charm into the bowl and closing my eyes briefly to make a wish — a wish that is only now close to coming true.

"Mean? Why, should it mean anything? 'Tis only a name and names don't mean nought. So like I say, he gambled with Sir Parceval that night but fortin and the bones ran cross and he lost all he owned. At last he had nothing left to wager except the estate. And although he knowed it wasn't rightly his to risk since he hadn't paid back all that money, he staked it on a single throw. And Sir Parceval throwed a five and that meant Jemmy had to throw a five too. But he throwed crabs instead and so he lost."

"Crabs?"

"That's what they call it when you throw a bad cast. And so Jemmy gived up the estate to him. And that's why the Mumpseys took the crab for their device, and them five flowers, too, which were the 'Oughams' badge. And now Sir Parceval started to build hisself that fine new house at 'Ougham with I don't know how many great ball-rooms and staircases and state rooms. And he had it laid out so that the main block and the wings were like the five dots on the face of a die: one at each corner and one in the middle."

"But it isn't that shape at all!" Remembering that no one was to know that Sukey had taken me there, I added lamely: "I mean, so I've been told."

"Why, he only built the middle and the front two wings on account of he ran out of money hisself, for all his great wealth. Though not before he had pulled down most of the old village to lay out the park for miles all around it. Now, Old Nick was very angry with Jemmy and they say he frighted him to death. And because Jemmy could not pay him back the fifty thousand pound ... "

"You said thirty before."

"Well, it had mounted and mounted till it was fifty now. However that may be, he took the promise that Jemmy had signed and went to the Lord High Chancellor with it, and tried to make him force the Mumpseys to give up the estate."

"In favour of his wife, Sophy, and her children, since she was Jemmy's daughter?"

"In course. (You have minded well, Master Johnnie.) But them Mumpseys wouldn't give way for they said they had won it fairly, and the argyfying went on and on and they say it has gone on to this very day."

"But didn't John have a better claim than the Mompessons?"

"Why, I'd nigh on forgotten about him. You're quite right, Master Johnnie. And what happened was this. Sir Parceval had a beautiful daughter called Lady Liddy and John met her and they fell in love."

I sighed, for the story had just been reaching its most crucial point. "I know," I said quickly. "After a lot of silly misunderstandings they eloped and were married. Now tell me about John's claim and why he didn't get the estate back."

"Aren't you the 'cute one," Mrs Belflower answered cheerfully and carried on stirring the pudding for a few moments before saying: "They 'loped right enough but whether they were married you must wait and hear. But before they 'loped, Lady Liddy come to John and told him how her father boasted that he had cheated Jemmy."

"I know!" I cried. "He had played with cogged dice!"

"That's right. And what's more, she gived him a signed confession she had got from her father saying as it was true. And then they 'loped up to 'Ougham."

"But why did they do that?" I asked in surprise.

"Why? On account of lovers allus 'loped in them days. But Sir Parceval follered 'em up and he and John fought a duel in a square of four trees before the Old Hall where there was a statue in the middle. And Lady Liddy looked out from the window and she hoped and prayed that no harm might befall either one of them, but that John might win. And so it happened, for John disarmed Sir Parceval and had him at his mercy. But just at that minute Lady Liddy saw the statue come to life and it was no statue at all but a stranger all in black. And before she could cry out to warn her lover, the stranger come up behind John and stabbed him in the back."

"What? He was killed?"

"Indeed he was," she said, stirring vigorously and smiling with maddening complacency.

"But are you sure he didn't marry Lady Liddy and have children?"

"Quite sure, and she nivver married nobody for she went mad of grief, poor soul."

"And who was it who killed him?"

"Why, nobody knows. But sartin it is that an old man is seed around 'Ougham to this very day. Clad all in black he is and with a face like death. And folks say that 'tis Old Nick hisself. Though others say 'tis the old father who was murdered. And others again say 'tis Jemmy himself who forfeited his soul and cannot leave this world. However that may be, ever since then the curse of Chancery has laid upon the Mumpseys for they have never prospered and that's why the great house lies empty and the lands are undrained and the walls broke down and the farms untenanted."

As she spoke I shivered and recalled the old man who had so alarmed my mother.

"There, I reckon that's about done. Will you pass me that dish?"

And yet, I recalled as I handed it to her, his carriage had borne the crab and five roses so he must be a Mompesson. But this was a silly thought for he was not a ghost, and, anyway, I had doubts about the truth of large parts of this story — particularly the bit about John having been killed without leaving any descendants. For I was certain I was a descendant of the Huffam family.

CHAPTER 8

Apart from the wind, it was good walking weather that afternoon when Sukey and I set out, for the ground was frozen hard under a light sprinkling of snow and the muddy ruts of the High-street rang beneath our feet. We had decided to take the lane towards Over-Leigh, but Sukey wanted to call on her mother beforehand and that meant going through the village and then retracing our steps.

She shivered under her thin red cloak: "This easterly is a lazy wind: it goes through ye instead of round ye."

"You are silly not to have worn something warmer," I said.

In my good thick merino top-coat I didn't mind the cold and I knew that when I got home Mrs Belflower would have a spicy plum-cake and a dozen Christmas-pies smoking from the oven. The high-day was very close now and many of the cottage-doors were dressed with holly and hulver branches and in the windows were the tall waxen candles standing ready to be lighted.

As we approached the church Sukey said: "We'll cross over just here, Master Johnnie, for I don't like to go too near the burying-ground at this time of the year."

"Whyever not?" I asked.

"Don't you know what day it is today?" she exclaimed, turning to me round-eyed with alarm. "'Tis the Eve of St. Thomas!"

"What does that mean, Sukey?"

"It's when the fetches walks."

"What is a fetch?"

"Why, don't you know nought?" she said. "That's the day when the ghosts of the dead rise up and come to seek the living as will die during the coming twelvemonth." I shivered and clasped her hand. "If you see one of 'em," she went on, "it means you or someone near you is going to die."

We quickened our pace and hurried past the graveyard without daring to look. A few yards further on we came to the Rose and Crab, outside which I was surprised to see a smart chaise and horses standing.

"Why Amos," said Sukey suddenly, addressing a boy of about my age. I had not noticed him for he was standing almost hidden between the two horses and holding their bridles. "Whatever are you doing?"

"Genel'man axed me to hold the horses a piece while he went to find the clerk," the boy answered.

"Who was it?" she enquired.

"I dunno. An outcomeling. Said he'd give me a penny."

"Well mind you bring it home," said Sukey. "And you might find something nice if you make haste."

"I've to fetch the kindling from the Common fust," rejoined the boy. "Tell mither I shall be late with it on account of this."

"I will," said his sister and we resumed our progress. When we reached the cottage Sukey looked at me doubtfully and said: "It's too cold for you to stand there today. You'd best come in."

"If you're worried about those boys, I'm not afraid of them. If they bother me again I'll clod stones back at them."

"No, Master Johnnie," Sukey insisted; "you'll have to come in. I should never be forgived if you ketcht a cold standing there."

She lifted aside the door which was unhinged and I followed her in through the low entry. For some moments I could see nothing because of the gloom, and when I drew breath I was nearly stifled by a mixture of acrid smoke and a fetid animal-like stench. I felt sticky hands clasping my own and warm bodies pressing against me, and just as fear began to well up inside me, my eyes adjusted to the darkness enough to discern that my assailants were no more than a crowd of small, half-naked children. They were pressing round me and Sukey and reaching into her pockets as she smilingly pushed them away. The near-darkness was because the cottage's two tiny windows — mere holes in the cracked and ancient stud-work — were blocked with rags, and because the smoke from the hearth where cakes of dried dung were smouldering was billowing back into the living-space.

"Away with you," protested Sukey, seizing a small child and pulling its fingers from my coat. "Leave the young genel'man alone."

"Where is it, Sukey?" the children were crying. "What have you brung us? Is it in here?"

"In a minute," she said, glancing towards me. "Now give us room to move."

She took my arm and guided me towards the hearth. At that moment an old woman, whom I had not noticed before, came hobbling forward.

"This is Master Johnnie," said Sukey. "Sit with him while I 'tend to the little 'uns."

The old woman gave a smile which revealed that she had only three teeth in her head, and, seizing my hand, steered me towards the single piece of furniture I could see which was a battered old chair before the hearth: "Bless you, young master," she said; "and your sweet mother, who has been the saving of me and mine many and many a time. Sit ye down by the fire for 'tis a mortal cold day."

I did so and was now able to look around me. The cottage consisted of a single chamber about the size of our sitting-room and had a floor of beaten mud with a gutter running down it. There was no ceiling so that above our heads stood the naked beams — on which there were fowls roosting — and above them the hanging, cobwebbed thatch.

The old woman stood beside me still smiling and nodding as she spoke: "I'm sorry the fire's no better. Amos has gone for wood on the Common."

"We met him and he said he'd be late back," Sukey said. "He was holding a genel'man's horses outside the inn."

As she spoke I saw her pull something from her pocket, divide it up and then hand it out to her younger brothers and sisters who seized it greedily. Seeing my gaze upon her she coloured slightly and looked away.

"Will you take a cup o' milk, young master?" the old woman asked. "'Tis our own cow's as we grazes on the Common."

I shook my head, trying to keep my mouth closed as much as possible.

"Keep a piece for Harry, mither," Sukey said, pressing something into her hand.

So this was her mother! I had taken her for the great-aunt.

"Will you not stay for your aunt's coming?" the old woman asked.

"No, for Master Johnnie and I should be on our way now," Sukey said, to my relief.

I got up and, having taken my leave of Sukey's mother with unceremonious speed, made for the door. As I passed one particularly grubby child I noticed that she was holding in her hand something that looked exactly like a piece of the almond-cake my mother and I had had for our tea the day before and had left half-eaten.

Once outside, I turned my face to the cold wind and breathed in, letting the air rasp in my throat and lungs.

CHAPTER 9

We walked between hedges that were bright with hawthorn berries and saw periwinkles and the starry blue flowers of the myrtle peeping out from the light dusting of snow, although we sought in vain for early snow-drops. As we went along I thought about what I had just seen. It was very wrong to steal. I looked at Sukey who was more silent than usual. But then there were so many mouths to feed.

"How many brothers and sisters have you, Sukey?"

"Seven," she answered.

That seemed a very large number.

"And shall there be any more, do you think?"

She turned her large eyes towards me: "My dad's been gone five years, Master Johnnie."

Silence fell again as I pondered this.

We walked as far as Offland, a little hamlet beyond Over-Leigh, and on the way back we were so cold that we had to blow into our clasped hands to keep our fingers from going numb. And so, as we approached the village, I suggested daringly: "Why don't we take the short way?"

"The short way?" Sukey's eyes grew round as she guessed my meaning.

There was an overgrown path through the graveyard which we quite often used in the summer. To take that way on a warm sunny afternoon was one thing, but to do so late on a cold winter's evening — and St. Thomas's Eve moreover! — was quite another.

However, Sukey hesitated for only a moment: "Why, we shall!" she exclaimed. "I ain't a-feared."

By now it was deep dusk as we entered the big overgrown church-yard through the back-gate. The wall here was broken-down for the ground behind the church had long ago been abandoned and no attempt was made to keep it neat. And so, since the path was obscured by overgrown grass and weeds, we soon wandered from it and had to pick our way through the undergrowth, sometimes bumping against a hidden gravestone.

"Oh Master Johnnie," whispered Sukey from a few yards ahead of me, "it ain't right to cross the dead this way. I wish we hadn't come."

"Don't be such a milk-sop," I jeered, a little comforted by her dismay.

Suddenly she stopped, and in a voice that chilled me cried: "There's a corpse-light!"

I followed her gaze in horror, for she had often told me about the flickering fires that hover above a grave, foretelling disaster. It was true! Some way over on our left towards the High-street a muted light was glowing and flickering above one of the larger vault-graves that was surrounded by high railings and lay under the shadow of a great yew-tree.

We both quickened our pace as far as was possible and the church was looming up ahead of us in the near-darkness when I dared to look round again. The light was no longer where it had been, but then to my horror I saw it — and it was much closer to us than a moment ago.

"It's following us," I cried.

"Oh mercy upon us!" Sukey sobbed and somehow we fought our way through the remaining yards of rough ground until we reached the rude path which encircled the church, where we broke into a run.

Then suddenly, as we rounded the corner of the church, a dark shape separated itself from the greyer shadows ahead and loomed up a few feet in front of us, blocking our way. We froze, and Sukey clutched my arm so fiercely that her grip hurt me: "My poor dad's fetch!" she moaned. "I knowed it!"

A bright light suddenly dazzled us and I heard a sob from Sukey. Then the light was shut down and I saw that it came from a dark-lanthorn that was being held aloft.

Just as my fear was diminishing, the apparition hailed me with horrible familiarity: "Master Mellamphy?"

The voice was that of an elderly gentleman, and now I could see a pair of piercing dark eyes beneath jutting brows.

"Yes," I answered, my voice quavering a little, and I heard Sukey muttering in terror.

"I've come all the way from London to see your mother," the gentleman said. He wore a black broad-brimmed hat that shielded his face from the light, and a black great-coat and carried a black cane. "Now I don't suppose you know anyone who lives as far away as London, do you?"

"Oh yes I do," I said, my courage returning.

"Oh indeed?" said the gentleman. "Now whom do you know there?"

"Don't you speak to him, Master Johnnie," said Sukey suddenly.

"Don't be so rude and silly, Sukey," I said.

The stranger turned towards her and said very softly: "I advise you, young woman, to hold your peace until asked to speak."

"You can't be Uncle Marty," I said, "because he's ill."

"No, you're quite right," he said. "I'm not Uncle Marty. Try again."

"Please don't speak any more, Master Johnnie," Sukey pleaded, pulling my arm towards her; "or you shall make me lose my place for disobeying your mother's orders."

"So perhaps you're Mr Sancious," I suggested, shaking Sukey off.

"No," he said briskly as if pleased by my wrong answer, and he reached into the pocket of his great-coat. "You see," he went on; "you do not know me even though I know you. But there's a half-sovereign for your guesses."

I took it and I gazed in delight at the shiny little coin which felt satisfyingly heavy on my palm. Gold! This was the first such coin I had ever seen, for sovereigns and half-sovereigns had only been introduced a couple of years before.

"Now in recompense," the gentleman said, "take me to your mother's house."

"I don't know as we should," said Sukey.

"Now look at this, young woman," the stranger said, again drawing something from his pocket; "I have a half-sovereign here for you if you are going to be sensible."

He held it out to her on the palm of his flat hand, and it gleamed in the light from his lanthorn.

"No, I shall not take it," said Sukey shaking her head. "I'll not take money from no fetch."

"Don't be silly, Sukey. He's not your father's fetch. He's a living gentleman."

"But mebbe that's what a fetch is, when you thinks you've seed one, even if it ain't."

There was no reasoning with her and I felt ashamed to be associated with such stupidity before so imposing a gentleman. "Take no notice of her," I said to him. "I'll show you the way."

He thanked me and we set off. Yet as we left the church-yard and made our way back along the High-street in silence, it was oddly as if the stranger were leading us, although it was we who knew the way.

In honour of our visiter I marched up to the front-door while Sukey went round to the back. I hammered at the knocker and Bissett opened the door with an expression of indignation that turned to amazement when she noticed the stranger.

"Good day, my good woman," the stranger said. "I am pleased to make your acquaintance."

To my surprise Bissett made an awkward curtsey holding her pin-before in front of her, accompanying it by a kind of smirk, while she muttered: "I'm very honoured, sir."

As she stood aside he entered, removed his hat and handed it and his cane to her and then did the same with his great-coat, revealing that he was wearing a black frock-coat, knee-breeches, and a long waistcoat with a fine cambric kerchief at his neck. Also visible was a gold half-hunter with a guard from whose watch-chain hung a veritable treasury of fobs and seals. He was the first gentleman other than the rector whom I had seen at such close quarters, and his dress and bearing put the clergyman in the shade — though his expression was even less benign for his prominent brows seemed to be permanently bristling and his reddish face looked as if an explosion of anger was always imminent.

"I have business with your mistress," the gentleman continued, and then with a wave of his hand he indicated Sukey, who by now had come through the house and was helping me to remove my boots: "Your fellow servant apparently entertains the deepest suspicions of me and was most reluctant to direct me here."

"Be about your work," Bissett snapped. "How dare you be so impertinent to a gentleman who has to do with your mistress? Go on, get along with you." Sukey retreated to the back-apartments and Bissett turned back to the stranger: "I'm sorry your honour was troubled by her," she said. "A foolish village mawkin that don't know how to conduck herself in dacent company."

"Well, I see I'm dealing now," said the stranger, "with someone who has seen something of the world."

Bissett reddened with pleasure at this and made another curtsey.

"Now will you be good enough to tell your mistress that a gentleman from London wishes to see her. I will announce myself for my name will mean nothing to her."

"Yes, sir," Bissett said.

"I'll go," I cried and ran towards the sitting-room door. I burst into the chamber crying: "A gentleman from London to see you! He knows Uncle Martin!"

My mother looked up in alarm. I rapidly told her of our encounter but before she had time to speak Bissett knocked quickly and flung open the door with the words: "A gentleman to see you, ma'am."

As the stranger strode unceremoniously in I saw my mother rise from the sopha in dismay: "Who are you, sir?"

"I am a solicitor and my name is Barbellion. How do you do, Mrs ... " He paused and then said very deliberately: "Mrs Mellamphy."

My mother flushed and said: "What do you want with me?"

He said softly: "I want the codicil."

She turned pale and her hand went instantly to the long narrow box she wore at her waist. I watched Mr Barbellion's eyes follow this movement and then saw my mother register his look with a deepened expression of alarm. Then, with a pitiful attempt to recover her composure, she said: "I don't know what you're talking about. You must have the wrong person."

"Come, let us not waste time. Your son and I have made friends already, and he has told me about Mr Sancious and his Uncle Marty — that is, Mr Martin Fortisquince."

These successive revelations came as hammer-blows beneath which she sank back onto the sopha with her hands across her face. When after a few moments she took them away, it was to direct towards myself a haggard look of deep reproach: "Johnnie! You shouldn't have spoken to him. You know you weren't to speak to strangers."

"But he made believe he knew you. I only told him ... "

"Hush, Johnnie, don't say any more. Mr Barbellion, I have been expecting something like this for a long time. I guessed that my enemy had found me, but will you tell me how?"

To my horror he directed towards myself what I took to be an expression of secret complicity: the housekeeper at Hougham! I hoped he would say nothing.

"That is of no account. But in speaking of my client as your enemy, you melodramatize. Far from meaning you harm, I have instructions to offer you fifteen hundred pounds for the document."

"I will never sell it. I know why your client wants it and what ill that would bring to my son and me."

"You are quite mistaken. My employer has your interests and those of your child at heart. Indeed, I am further instructed to make you this offer: my client is willing to take your son off your hands and undertake his education at his expense."

"No," my mother cried, and gripped my arm tightly. "This is what I have always feared. Leave this house immediately."

His cheeks darkened: "Madam, I am not accustomed to this kind of treatment."

It seemed to me very wrong to treat such an array of fine linen and such a display of watch-chains and seals with so little respect: "Mamma, you shouldn't be so impolite."

"Be silent, Johnnie. You don't understand."

Mr Barbellion stood up and strode to the door. He opened it and turned: "I believe you will come to regret your present conduct very bitterly."

"You see, Johnnie? He is threatening me!"

Mr Barbellion shrugged his shoulders and made a snort of contempt. Bissett, who must have been hovering outside, appeared in the door-way carrying his hat, cane, and great-coat.

With a curt bow he said: "I wish you good day. Your admirable servant will show me out."

The door closed behind him and my mother and I stared at each other in dismay.

After a moment's silence she exclaimed: "So now he knows where I am!"

"Who?"

As if she only now remembered my presence she said: "Hasn't Mr Barbellion gone yet?" He had obviously not, for we heard voices in the hall. "I won't feel safe until he has left the house. Safe! We'll never be safe here again now. If only I'd thought to tell him I'd destroyed it as I once meant to!"

"Mamma," I said in desperation, "please tell me what all this means."

"What can he have to say to Bissett? Listen!"

At that moment we heard the street-door bang shut. I crossed the room and looked out of window.

"He's going down the steps," I reported.

"Thank goodness!"

"Tell me. What danger are we in?"

"We're not in danger, Johnnie," she insisted, looking at me wildly.

"You told him we were!" She turned away as if in agony, and I felt as if I was pushing a blade into her side, but one that cut me as much as her. "And there's something funny about our name, isn't there? What is it?"

She shook her head.

"You must tell me," I cried.

"I won't tell you anything. You can't be trusted."

"That's not true!"

"Yes it is. You told him that we knew Uncle Marty. If you hadn't, I could have denied it."

The thought that she did not know the full extent of what I had done made me the angrier at this accusation: "That's not fair!" I cried. "I hate you!"

"You must not speak to me like that!"

"I hate you and I wish you weren't my mother!" I cried and ran out. I hurried to my own room almost blinded by tears and flung myself on the bed sobbing. My mother's face was before me as I pounded the pillow with my fist. It was true what I had said, that I hated her. Hated her for being so frightened of Mr Barbellion and for being so unhappy. To show her that I had meant what I said, I wouldn't go down for my tea!

Feeling better after taking this resolution, I thought over what had happened and tried to fit together everything that I knew into a single design. My mother seemed to think that the burglar all those years ago was sent by our enemy, just as Mr Barbellion was. But could it instead be that Mr Barbellion had found out our hiding-place from my incautious words to Henrietta and her companion a few months ago? And what had he meant to imply about our name? Could it be that "Mellamphy" was not our real name? But how could it not be? I was John Mellamphy just as much as the house was a house. How could I have a "real" name that I didn't know? In that case, was there a real me that went along with it and that I also didn't know? The very idea was absurd.

It was late by now and she had not come up. I listened to the sounds in the house, waiting for the soft footfall along the passage. I waited for a long time but it did not come. Then I heard it at last. Some demon of perversity, however, made me close my eyes and pretend to be asleep. I heard my mother come into the room, wait for a few moments, and then softly withdraw again. When she had gone I wished that I had spoken to her, but it was too late now.

CHAPTER 10

When I came down to breakfast the next morning I wanted us to make up our quarrel but I was determined not to be the first to yield. However, my mother's manner as she greeted me was cold and reserved, as if hurt that I had not stayed awake for her coming last night:

"I really am very angry at your behaviour yesterday, Johnnie," she said. "You must apologise to me for the cruel things you said."

I was about to answer indignantly when Sukey came into the room looking very frightened: "The letter-carrier has just brung this, ma'am."

She held out a letter which I saw was surrounded by a black border.

"Martin!" my mother exclaimed, seizing it from her. She quickly read it while I studied her face. She bit her lower lip and, after a moment, looked up at me sadly and said: "Yes, he is dead. He died two days ago."

"The fetch!" Sukey exclaimed. "Then mebbe it weren't my dad's!"

"Be about your work, Sukey," my mother said and the girl went out. My mother reached across the table and took my hand. "We have nobody now, Johnnie, but each other."

"Are you very sorry?"

She shook her head gently: "It was a release for him. But it makes things worse for us. You see, this is his house."

"His house!" I exclaimed. I had never doubted that the house belonged to my mother.

"Yes, it has been in his family for many years. His father was land-agent to an estate nearby and so Uncle Martin spent part of his childhood here with his mother. He allowed us to have it at what they call a peppercorn rent but his widow says here she will have to charge us a real rent: forty pounds a year!"

"How unkind! She must be a horrible old lady."

"No, you're quite wrong. She is only a few years older than I."

"And will she still receive your letters from Mr Sancious and forward them?"

"Why, how sharp you are, Johnnie," my mother said in dismay. "However did you learn that?"

"I know 'Mellamphy' isn't our real name, is it?"

She put her hand to her head: "Please don't start that again, Johnnie. No, if you must have it. It isn't."

"Then what is our real name?"

"No, I won't tell you that. Not yet. One day you'll know everything."

"Then tell me at least how you chose the name 'Mellamphy'?"

"I chose it at hazard. I saw the name on a board."

The thought made me feel dizzy. Then if something as important as one's own name which seemed so rich in meaning could be so meaninglessly random, then perhaps all names — and even words, for weren't they merely names? — were equally accidental and lacking any essential connexion with what they designated? I turned shuddering from this possibility. "Please tell me why," I begged.

"Not now, my dearest. But I promise you that whatever happens, one day you will know everything. I have already started to make sure of that."

This was a further mystery and I wondered if it were connected with the letter I had seen in the japanned box that held the locket, but she would say no more on the subject.

"I will miss Uncle Marty's advice about money," she went on. "From now on I will have to consult Mr Sancious, for I just don't know what to do. We can't afford to pay another forty pounds. The poor-rate is so high now and is going up all the time."

"Don't you think, Mamma, that we really have more servants than we need?"

We gazed at each other with guilty excitement, feeling, I think, a little as if we were secretly plotting the death of one of them.

"What are you thinking, Johnnie?" she almost whispered.

"Well, Sukey's wages are only fifteen shillings a quarter, so we would not save very much by losing her. But Bissett's are twenty pounds a year, and Mrs Belflower's twenty-five. And you know, we can't do without a cook, but I don't need a nurse now, do I?"

"No," my mother said, watching me intently.

"Then give her notice," I said, and she nodded, her eyes sparkling with excitement.

BOOK III

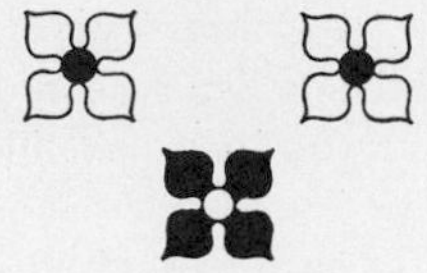

Fathers

CHAPTER 11

A little more than two months later, Lady Day came round which was the time appointed for Mrs Belflower to take her leave of us. My mother had explained to me immediately after the interview with Bissett which was supposed to result in her dismissal, that as soon as she had raised the need to dispense with one of the servants, Bissett had leapt with such alacrity to the conclusion that it was to be the cook and had sympathised so much with her distaste for breaking the news to Mrs Belflower, and at the same time so cheerfully assured her that a cook — unlike a children's nurse who was getting on in years — would experience no difficulty in finding other employment, that my mother had not had the heart to tell her that it was she herself who was the chosen sacrifice, and so what Bissett had assumed — or had pretended to — had actually become the case.

So early that morning Mrs Belflower stood in the front hall with her boxes packed, waiting for the carrier to arrive. His road-waggon would convey her to the nearest post-town, Sutton Valancy, where she would take the coach to her new employer, who lived far away in a village in the extreme west in a county I had never even heard of. When the crunch was heard of the waggon's wheels on the road outside, Sukey could restrain her tears no longer.

"Now you be a good gal," said Mrs Belflower to Sukey in a would-be stern tone whose effect was somewhat marred by the steady stream of tears running down her cheeks. "Mind what I larned you and don't overcook your greens." She enfolded the weeping girl in her arms, and then, gently disengaging herself, turned to my mother. They held each other's hand and both tried to smile: "I've been so happy here, ma'am. I don't expect I'll ever be so happy anywhere again. You've been a good, kind mistress that I couldn't wish for better."

"Oh Mrs Belflower," my mother exclaimed, "I only wish ... " She broke off.

"I do understand the need for it, Mrs Mellamphy, and I pray all will come out for the best with you and the little master."

They embraced each other and gave way to tears. And so a very dismal sight must have been presented to the carter and his boy when they came into the hall to carry the boxes out to the waggon. At this moment Bissett came from the kitchen and stood beside me at the door, and as we looked at each other I was sure that she knew how much I wished it were she who was going. Then Mrs Belflower quickly released my mother and tottered slightly as she made towards us and I suddenly realized that she was really quite old to be starting over again in a new place. Bissett held out a hand as if to protect herself against any more compromising gesture.

"Goodbye, Mrs Bissett, and God bless you," said Mrs Belflower grasping the proffered hand. "We've had noises, you and me, as 'twould be foolish to deny. But I've always respected you as a person that lives by the lights of her religion."

"Goodbye, cook," said Bissett; "and I hope you will come among godly people and find the light of grace yourself. I will pray for that."

She released the hand and Mrs Belflower stood with a troubled expression as if wondering whether to speak.

"Ready now," said the carrier loudly at that moment, putting his head round the door.

Mrs Belflower started at the summons, and then turned quickly to me: "I shall always think about you, Master Johnnie, and wonder what a fine young man you are growing up to be who will take care on your mother." As she stooped to kiss me she said in a low voice: "Be sure not to make things no harder for her."

"I don't know what you mean!" I said, pulling myself away from her.

Mrs Belflower shook her head gently and then after a last embrace from my mother and Sukey, she made her way down the steps and was helped up onto the cart. Until it had rumbled out of sight we stood on the steps waving.

The house seemed very empty without Mrs Belflower and we conducted ourselves as if in mourning.

A week or so later my mother sent Sukey to summon me to her. When I entered the sitting-room I found that she was at the escritoire and had on her most business-like expression. "Johnnie, I have just heard from Mr Sancious that Uncle Martin left us nothing, as I had expected."

"But he should have!" I exclaimed.

She blushed.

"Why do you say that?" she asked.

"Why, he was your uncle, wasn't he?"

"I called him 'Uncle' but he was no blood-relation to me," she said, still looking rather conscious.

"No blood relation to us?" I exclaimed. I thought about this. Then a question I had pondered ever since I had seen the locket rose to my lips: "Mamma, is my father still alive?"

She blushed: "Johnnie, I ... I don't know how to answer you. One day you will know everything. I promise. But the good news I wanted to tell you is that Mr Sancious has agreed to advise me on my financial affairs."

At that moment there was a tap on the door and Bissett came in: "I didn't realize as Master Johnnie was here. I should like a private word with you, ma'am, if convenient."

"We had just finished," my mother answered. And so, taking the hint, I went into the kitchen where I found Sukey sitting, sobbing into her apron, at the table.

"Has she been teazing you?" I asked. "You should stand up to her."

"It ain't jist that, Master Johnnie," she said. "I've heerd some bad news. Do you mind that fetch as we seen in the buryin'-ground the Christmas a-fore last? Well, I feared it was my dad's. But when I hadn't heerd nought by this Christmas jist gone by, I thought he was all right. But on'y yesterday my poor mither got a letter and when we taken it to the clerk he told us as it said my father was dead. He'd died a-fore Christmas so it *was* his fetch we seed." She hid her face in her apron again.

"But this is March, Sukey. Why did it take so long to hear?"

"The letter had a long ways to go, Master Johnnie," she replied and would say no more than this.

When, after some time, Bissett came into the kitchen I went to ask my mother what she had wanted, but she refused to tell me.

CHAPTER 12

Equity summons Law once again, and so a second time you may follow in imagination your quarry — who is, of course, Mr Sancious — to the house in Cursitor-street. Equity — who, as you likewise know, is none other than Mr Barbellion — is again waiting in the shadows of the same dark little room, but this time Mr Sancious enters with an air of self-confidence. Only the curtest of greetings is exchanged between them and they seat themselves at opposite ends of the table.

"To what do I owe the honour of this ... invitation?" asks Mr Sancious.

"I require your further assistance."

"On the same terms as before?"

"To the penny," answers Mr Barbellion with a sneer.

Mr Sancious smiles: "I am not sure that I can oblige."

"Indeed? And what has changed your mind?"

"Just this: Mrs Clothier has recently taken me more largely into her confidence."

"I understand. You mean that your price for betraying her confidence has gone up. Continue."

Mr Sancious scowls and says: "I wish to know who your client is and why he is so anxious to obtain the document."

"But I, you see, am not at liberty to disclose my client's affairs."

Mr Sancious flinches at this but goes on: "But my dear sir, your name is so widely-known and respected within our profession that the identity of the great families who form your clientship is certainly no secret. Consequently, it has not been difficult for me to learn that the party in whose interests you are acting must be one of the following: the Earl of Chester, the Viscount Portsmouth, the families of Verney, Waldegrave, De Temperay, Mompesson, and de Coverley. It can only be a matter of time before I establish which of these it is."

"And what then?"

"Simply that I would be able to set a fair price on my services."

"I see. But are you saying that the fact that Mrs Clothier has confided in you is the strongest card you hold?"

"Do not speak of cards, my good sir," Mr Sancious replies with a well-bred shudder. "I deplore games of chance and never take risks on principle. Say rather, that I have you in check."

"If we are talking in those terms, let us say that you are trying to fool's mate me." Mr Sancious flinches. "If you know so much, do you know where she is?" There is a silence and the attorney flushes and looks down. "You see I know," Mr Barbellion goes on, "that you still have to write to her through Fortisquince's widow. And since she has not trusted you enough to tell you even her whereabouts, I doubt if she has told you anything else."

"How do you know all that?" Mr Sancious says in indignant surprise.

"That is my affair. But I am not wrong in thinking you do not know her whereabouts?"

Biting his lip, Mr Sancious shakes his head.

"I warn you to learn from this," Mr Barbellion goes on, "that I too despise games of chance. If I play with dice I ensure — to borrow terms from your professional acquaintance — that they are cogged. Now, will you assist me?"

Mr Sancious nods and the other gentleman takes from his pocket-book another sheaf of bank-notes and places it upon the table: "Very soon Mrs Clothier will write to ask you if she can afford to raise the wages of a servant. You will reply advising her in the strongest terms that she cannot."

"Is that all?" the attorney asks in surprise.

"That is all for the present," Mr Barbellion replies and while he pulls the bell-cord, his guest rises, picks up the sheaf, and hurries to the door.

CHAPTER 13

At the end of the street Mr Sancious crosses Chancery-lane and plunges into a maze of dirty back-streets. As he walks he mutters angrily to himself and bites his lip. But now he slows his pace and glances back several times as if he has heard something. Then he begins to walk faster, his hand clutching his pocket. He turns into a long and curving alley. By the end of it he is almost running. Just as he turns to look back someone shoots out of the mouth of a lane beside him. Mr Sancious presses himself against the wall, his heart pounding, and holding his arms in front of his face as if to ward off a blow: "Prig from me and I take my oath you'll be twisted for it!"

The other man, however, says in surprise: "I ain't on that lay. It's Mr Sancious, ain't it? I've been follering you for a wery long time, guv'nor."

Mr Sancious looks out through the shield formed by his arms. Before him is a tall, poorly-dressed individual with a large head with close-cropped reddish hair, a big nose, and bright, eager blue eyes.

"Following me! What do you mean? Who paid you?"

"Nobody never paid me. I've been watching you for days waitin' for a chance to speak to you in private, like this. You are Mr Sancious, ain't you?"

The lawyer nods.

"And a 'torney?" Mr Sancious nods again. "You're the only cove o' that name I could hear on. It was you what saved Conkey George from being marinated, wasn't it?"

Mr Sancious nods again: "What do you want of me?"

"He was a pall o' mine. But it's the other way around, guv'nor. I got something what I reckons you wants." At this he reaches into a pocket and brings out a crumpled piece of paper which seems to have been torn from a larger sheet. He holds it out for Mr Sancious to see.

"It's upside-down," the attorney gasps.

"Be damned to it," mutters the other man. "'Tis all one to me." He turns the paper round and Mr Sancious peers at it.

"I cannot read it," he says. "It's not close enough."

He reaches towards it but the other man steps quickly back: "Don't lay a finger on it. Can you foller it if I say it?"

"I believe so."

The other man recites: "'To kerkude, you should soon receive the play-things and books what I have arst Mr Sancious to purchase. Speaking of which cove, you will see as I ingclose another letter under cover from that genel'man. I must warn you as he has been a-tryin' agin, in wery indireck ways, to find out from me your whereabouts and I believe he would give a great deal to know.'" As the stranger repeats these last words he stares intently at Mr Sancious's face, as that gentleman peers at the letters in the dim light of the alley-way. "Well, are you in for the game?" the stranger demands folding the letter up and putting it back in his pocket.

"Possibly," mutters Mr Sancious. "But is the direction given?"

"Oh-ho," says the other man. "So you still want to know it, do you? Jist like it says here."

"I'll tell you what, my good man. I'll give you a guinea for that letter."

"A guinea!" the other man repeats in such a tone that Mr Sancious quickly says:

"Very well, we will discuss it. But somewhere else, for heaven's sake."

"The Swan-with-Two-Necks in Lad-lane?"

The attorney nods and they set off, the stranger leading the way along dark passage-ways whose walls drip water, through sunless back-courts which have no front, and along dingy side-streets, until they reach a run-down old drinking-house, with paint peeling from its front and its windows obscured by dirt. In a few minutes they are seated in a boxed-off section against the bar separated by wooden partitions from the rest of the tap-room with a glass before Mr Sancious and a tankard before his companion.

"That letter was written nearly two years ago. How came you by it and why have you taken so long to find me?" Mr Sancious asks as he drinks the brandy and water before him.

"Now that's a story," the stranger says, pouring half of his quart of porter down his throat. "It was the summer before last. I had reasons for getting off the stones jist then what I'm sure you won't expeck me to go into. Now I'm a j'iner by trade, and there was a great fambly what I'd worked for in Town off and on for years and I heerd as how they was doing some work on their country-house down in ——shire and got took on by the steward what I knowed. (Though in a general way I don't have no fancy for the country.)"

"What is the name of the family?" asks Mr Sancious.

"In my own time and my own way, if you please, Mr Sancious. When I gived that over I set out to go on the tramp back up to Town again. Well, I didn't have no blunt so I stopped at a crib to arst for wittles. I went up a lane off the high road. There was a young lady with a little boy in the garding."

Mr Sancious leans forward at this.

"Well, the young lady was all right, but there was an old witch of a sarvint with her, a nuss-maid or some such. And she purwented the young lady from giving me nothin'. And she said things to me that weren't called for, neither." At the memory his face darkens and he mutters an oath under his breath. "And then the young 'un starts on at me, too. Shouting and bawling. So I goes back up the lane to the road and just at the corner an old file calls out: 'What did they say to you?' So I tells him, and it seems he's the gardener there and has a grudge agin 'em, or agin everybody as far as I can tell. And he says: 'Mebbe you'd like to get square with 'em and do yourself some good?' And I says: 'What have you got in mind?' And he says: 'Look where they've gorn and left that ladder down in that airey. That's an invitation if ever I seen one.' Well, I sees what he meant and lets him know it. And then he offers me a bite of supper and so I goes into his cottage. And he gives me a long spade for hooking the ladder up when I get over the railing, and tells me which of the upper winders is a room that nobody don't sleep in. So that night I climbs on top of the railings and gets the ladder while he plays bo-peep. Well, it goes all right at fust. I gets down into the airey, and then I puts the ladder agin the wall and climbs up to the winder. Well, I've got my kifers with me, so I gets to work on the shutters. But arter a bit I finds I can't get them open no-how. Not without making a lot of noise, anyhow. Then I notices that the shutters of the next winder are unbarred, so I thinks: 'Well, if I'm very quiet I can mebbe get in that way even if there is someone sleeping. Leastways, I can take a look.' So I gets up there and I'm just openin' the shutters to look in when I'll be blessed if that same boy don't wake up and start screaming fit to bring the roof down. Well, next thing, I find I can't move the ladder 'cause it's got jammed into the angle of the wall and the ground on account of my weight. Well, the only thing now is to get through one of the winders down there. So I breaks the shutter-clasps and then smashes through the glazing-bars. So I climbs in and jist for the sake of me own self-respeck I ketches a hold onto some candle-sticks, but they was too big to carry easy, so I drops 'em. All I takes for my pains is a letter-case. A silver 'un. So then I gets the street-door open and I jist bolts. And the old file is waiting for me up the road and he says, 'What did you get?' Well, I knows he could make trouble and anyways he sees the case in me pocket. So I shows it to him, then I rips the lid off of it and throws it into the ditch and runs off. And when I looks back there he is, a-grubbin' in the weeds for it. So arter that I keeps on running the rest of the night, ready to jump off the road into the hedge if I sees or hears anything coming behind me, 'cause I knows if I'm ketched with that letter-case, it's Botany Bay or the tree with only one leaf for me. Well, towards dawn I makes it to a big old barn where I'd kipped on the way down on account of it being about two days' tramp from Mumpsey-park."

"From where?" asks Mr Sancious quickly.

"Mumpsey-park. That's the big house what I told you of. Mumpsey's the name of the people what owns it."

"Mumpsey," Mr Sancious says and shakes his head.

"Well," the man continues, "I wraps the letter-case up in a piece of soft-leather to keep it dry, and don't even think to open it up. Then I hides it in a hole in the wall and keeps on a-runnin'. Well, then it were more than a year a-fore I goes down there agin, but a six-month back, I goes to the barn and finds the letter-case jist as I'd left it. That's when I opens it and finds the screeve inside. Well I was going to throw it away but then I thinks to meself 'Well, I've heerd on screeves and dockyments as is worth a deal of money,' so I decides not to.

Now as it happens, Mr Sancious, my eddication was sorely neglected, first on account of my father being a lushington and secondly 'cause even though when I was a younker I 'tended the Floating 'Cademy at Chatham, the truth is I larned more about picking oakum and gettin' beat than about conning my books. So the long and the short of it was, I showed the screeve to my brother's gal. She's a sharp 'un and can read you off any amount of words faster nor a dog can trot — both writin' and print. So that's how I heard on a Mr Sancious as was a split-cause and was so eager to find the direction on the front of this cover. It's taken me a deal of time and trouble since then to run you down. So, Mr Sancious, don't you talk to me about no guinea."

"Well my good man, what figure would you consider appropriate?"

"Fifteen."

"Good heavens!" exclaims the attorney. "You have a grossly inflated idea of the value of that piece of information. You don't imagine that anyone else will offer you anything at all for it, do you?"

The other man drains his tankard and rises from his seat: "Mebbe not, but if it ain't worth fifteen to you then no more shan't you have it neither."

"Stay!" As he sits down again Mr Sancious takes out his pocket-book and removes some of the bank-notes he received from Mr Barbellion. He hands them across the table while the letter is passed to him.

The man holds each of them up to the light of the oil-lamp hanging on a nail nearby and then, apparently satisfied, puts them in his pocket: "Well, it's been a pleasure doing business with you."

Mr Sancious glances up from the letter: "Stay a while. I may have further need of you."

The man seats himself agreeably and watches Mr Sancious's features while he reads. The letter bears the heading "No. 27 Golden-square, 23rd. July", and is signed "Martin Fortisquince". The final paragraph reads:

"To conclude, you should soon receive the play-things and books which I have asked Mr Sancious to purchase. Speaking of whom, you will see that I enclose another letter under cover from that gentleman. I must warn you that he has been endeavouring once again, in very indirect ways, to find out from me your whereabouts and I believe he would give a great deal to know. I regret to tell you that my condition is no better and once again my beloved wife is having to write this letter at my dictation. I fear that the house is being watched and that your enemy has somehow discovered that I know your whereabouts."

Mr Sancious turns the paper over and sees on the cover: "Mrs Mellamphy The Cottage, Mortsey-manor-farm, Melthorpe, ——shire".

"Mellamphy!" he repeats softly: "So that is her real name." He glances at the other man who is watching him curiously: "I may have need of you. Will you help me?"

"For more of this," he replies, patting his pocket and smiling, "I'll do anything you arst me, guv'nor."

"Then how may I find you when I want you?"

"Leave word here."

"What is your name?"

"'Barney' will find me."

"Very well," says Mr Sancious, rising to his feet and pulling his great-coat about him. "But never come to my house or my office. Do you understand?"

"Oh, I understand," says Barney and briefly rises to bow as, with a curt nod, Mr Sancious goes out. He looks after him and repeats: "I understand, all right."

CHAPTER 14

Though I shall, of course, not speculate on his motives, it seems that Mr Sancious now believed that his mysterious client's real name was Mrs Mellamphy and was intrigued by the fact that there was such interest in her and in her whereabouts. He now had the advantage that he knew her address and so, armed with this piece of knowledge, he went to the one person who (he believed) could tell him what he wished to know.

And so a few days after the incident recounted above, Mr Sancious knocks on the door of a house in Golden-square and it is opened to him by a timid servant-girl who, when he utters his name, answers: "My mistress got your letter and is a-waitin' for you, sir." She takes his hat and great-coat and leads him to the morning-room where a lady is seated upon an elegant ottoman.

He enters with a gracious smile upon his lips but when he sees her he stops in apparent surprise. Then he smiles again and says: "I am Mr Sancious. I believe it must be your mother that I have business with."

"I think that unlikely, Mr Sancious," the lady says with a faint smile. "My poor mother has been dead for twenty years. I am Mrs Fortisquince."

"Forgive my blunder. May I say in my defence that it was entirely natural?"

Mrs Fortisquince smiles and indicates a chair near the ottoman.

"Please accept my sincerest condolences, dear lady, on the decease of your husband who was highly respected by his humbler confrères amongst whom I number myself." The attorney sighs as he seats himself.

"You are very kind, Mr Sancious. Very kind. But may I ask to what I owe the honour of this visit?"

"I have come on the subject we have in common."

"I had assumed so. You mean Mrs Clothier?"

As Mr Sancious speaks he watches her face closely: "Yes, or Mrs Mary Mellamphy." The widow inclines her head in recognition of the name and slightly raises one eyebrow. "I see you are surprised that I know that name," the attorney continues, "but Mrs Mellamphy has very recently done me the honour to take me into her confidence."

"Indeed?"

"And so," Mr Sancious continues, "I now know that she lives in retirement with her son in a village called Melthorpe. I also now know about her difficulties with ... " He hesitates and looks at her knowingly as if waiting for her to speak. She does not, so he goes on: "Well, shall we call them 'a certain distinguished family'?"

He may call them what he likes for all the widow appears to care: "Mr Sancious, I confess to being a little surprised since I had believed that Mrs Clothier was resolved to confide her whereabouts to nobody apart from my late husband and myself. But I still cannot perceive the purpose of your visit to me."

"It is a delicate matter, ma'am. I am seeking certain information about Mrs Mellamphy."

"You surprise me again, Mr Sancious. Since she has, as you say, taken you fully into her confidence, I wonder what I can help you with that she cannot tell you herself?"

The attorney wriggles rather uncomfortably on his chair: "Well now, Mrs Fortisquince, it is sometimes the case that an attorney might wish to keep his client in ignorance of enquiries he is making on that client's behalf."

"You intrigue me, Mr Sancious. My late husband having been an attorney, I have acquired more than a merely superficial knowledge of legal practice, and yet I have never heard of such a thing. Under what circumstances might this be so?"

Mr Sancious looks very knowing: "Well, ma'am, where for example the attorney becomes aware that there are remote possibilities of eventualities occurring to affect his client's interests either for good or for ill, and does not wish either to alarm his client or to raise hopes that may be unfulfilled."

"And of course you have Mrs Clothier's interests at heart," the widow remarks.

"Indeed I do, ma'am," he answers earnestly.

"You promise me that absolutely?"

"I do unreservedly. I should be grossly betraying my honourable profession if I confessed to any other motive."

Mrs Fortisquince appears to reflect for some moments before saying: "If I were to agree to help you, what would you like me to tell you?"

"I need to know her unmarried name and something of her family connexions."

"Mr Sancious, I am again at a loss to understand you. You know the name of the family into which she married, and since it is one that is known — not to say, notorious — in the commercial world, you should, with very little trouble, be able to learn what you wish by that means."

"Mellamphy? Notorious?" he begins in surprise, then breaks off. "I beg your pardon. Her real name. Of course. Clothier. I was becoming confused."

"I was saying that I greatly regret that I am unable to tell you anything more. My late husband involved himself in Mrs Clothier's affairs as an act of simple kindness, and I therefore feel that her interests are really no business of mine."

"Thank you, Mrs Fortisquince," the attorney says, accepting his dismissal and rising with a smile. "I am most grateful to you."

As Mrs Fortisquince speaks she rises and pulls the bell-rope beside her: "But I have told you nothing that you did not already know."

"And in doing so have been most helpful."

As the door opens Mr Sancious bows and withdraws, while his hostess sits frowning slightly on the ottoman.

CHAPTER 15

Let us imagine that it is near shutting-up time on a cold wet winter's evening and that we are following Mr Sancious once again a day or two after we last encountered him. He descends Ludgate-hill, making for the river through a labyrinth of back ways until, a little to the west of Upper-Thames-street, he finds himself at the top of a dark narrow alley which declines by a cobbled lane towards one of the old Thameside stairs. He cautiously descends and, reaching the river's edge, peers about him. The only light is coming from a window in the ground-floor of one of the tall houses whose backs line the alley. It appears that the premises are being employed as a counting-house, and when Mr Sancious peeps through the filthy window-panes he sees that the gas is burning low and that, although it is very cold, the coal-fire is banked up.

As Mr Sancious walks into the outer office a figure rises from a high desk and comes towards him. He is about fifty, of middling height but stoutly-built, with a balding head and a rather round puffy countenance that is very red about the eyes and nose. He is clad in a snuff-coloured coat with large brass buttons, a canary-yellow waistcoat, and velveteen breeches. "Good evening, sir. Have I the honour of addressing Mr Sancious?" he asks, dabbing at his watering eyes with a large handkerchief.

"That is my name," the attorney replies with a smile.

"Then my Guv'nor is expecting you, sir. Will you be so good as to come this way?"

The clerk is about to turn away when the lawyer arrests him with a movement of his hand: "One moment, if you please. It is now six o'clock. When my business here is finished I will be close upon my usual hour for dining. I have another engagement hereabouts and since I am unfamiliar with this neighbourhood, I wonder if you could be so good as to direct me to a nearby eating-house?"

"Nothing easier, sir. There's Millichamp's just at the corner of the alley. You may have remarked it as you came in."

"And can you give it a personal recommendation?"

"Oh yes, sir. I usually take my dinner there. In fact, I'll be going there very soon myself."

"Then I may have the pleasure of seeing you there," says Mr Sancious with a little bow.

"It would be an honour, sir," replies the clerk with a corresponding bow.

"What the devil is keeping you, Vulliamy!" a voice suddenly shouts from the inner office. "I don't pay you to gossip, you infernal rattle!"

"No indeed, sir, just coming," says the clerk pushing open the door and showing Mr Sancious the way.

The private closet is small and pervaded by a bitter smell that puts Mr Sancious strangely in mind of dead flies. It is so dark that it is with difficulty that the lawyer makes out a figure lurking in a dusty corner at the opposite end. He hears a rustling of papers and then a high thin voice: "What do you want of me, Mr Sancious?"

Mr Vulliamy turns up the gas-jet projecting from the wall by the door and then withdraws. There is just enough light for Mr Sancious to make out that the old gentleman who is Mr Vulliamy's Guv'nor — now blinking at the light and shielding his eyes — is small and thin with a pale face. His features are sharp, his pale grey eyes flickering restlessly and his thin mouth frequently opening slightly as he runs his tongue suspiciously along his upper lip. He is wearing a small wig that sits on his scull like a rotted cauliflower, a yellowed stock, a long green coat of old-fashioned style which is patched and dirty, a waistcoat whose faded stripes are still visible, and tight nankeen breeches.

"I have come to enquire about the placing of a sum of money on behalf of a client of mine," the attorney answers.

At these words the old man's face is lit up by an almost innocent expression of delight.

"Have you indeed?" he exclaims and scuttles out of his corner towards his visiter, his skinny legs seeming to carry him along almost independently of his body and his will. Now Mr Sancious sees that although he is so thin he has an incongruously bulging belly. As the old gentleman reaches out one of his long arms the attorney takes his hand and flinches slightly at its clamminess. "Then I'm very pleased to see you, Mr Sancious. I thought you were here on quite another matter. Please sit down and make yourself comfortable." Mr Sancious does so as the old man smiles and rubs his hands together: "Will you take something?"

"You're very kind, sir."

"Brandy and water?"

"Thank you."

"Very good," says the old gentleman as if his guest had said something very witty. But suddenly he screeches, "Brandy and water, Vulliamy, and double-quick."

The door opens and Mr Vulliamy hurries in carrying a bottle, glasses, and a flask of water in a small tray. He bangs the tray down on a table and quickly retires.

"Now, sir," says the old gentleman when he and his guest have each a glass in their hand. "Did you mention a figure? I believe not."

"Shall we say, about one thousand pounds?"

"Why not? Why not?" says the elderly gentleman, his hands beginning to tremble.

"And perhaps a further sum later," adds the attorney.

"A further sum," the old man repeats. "Very good. Now, sir, I have a number of interests at the moment, but an excellent spec that I can particularly recommend is the Consolidated Metropolitan Building Company. I will tell you frankly, sir, that I am a promoter of the company for I believe in being absolutely truthful."

"I expected no less a declaration from your reputation," the attorney replies.

The old gentleman stares at him for a moment before going on: "Quite, quite. Now your client is in luck for it happens that not all the share-issue has yet been subscribed. Yes, I think I can find you a thousand pounds' worth, though I might not be able to promise as much in a week or two." He begins to rummage through the piles of papers on the desk and shelves, smiling at intervals at the lawyer. After a moment he glances towards the door and scowls: "Vulliamy!" he suddenly screams.

The door opens and the senior clerk shambles in, wiping his mouth on his handkerchief.

"The Consolidated Metropolitan Building Company," the old gentleman snaps. "Find me a prospectus."

"The Consolidated Metropolitan Building Company," Mr Vulliamy repeats, glancing at the attorney who sits with an appearance of utter calm watching the other two. "Are you sure, sir? Are you absolutely sure?"

"Of course I am sure, you fool! Get out of here and find them!"

Mr Vulliamy turns and shuffles out. The old man smiles at the lawyer: "A sad case, sir." He glances meaningfully at the glass before him: "A lushington. I only retain him in my service from reasons of sentiment. He has an invalid wife and a crippled child. Perhaps it's reprehensible of me, but it is, I hope, pardonable. You see, he has been with me from a boy."

The old gentleman sighs heavily, while the attorney replies: "Your feelings do you credit, sir."

"Oh do you say that, sir? Most reassuring. Of course, he is only entrusted with the most menial tasks. Nothing of a confidential nature, I do assure you. He knows very little of my business."

At this moment the door opens and Mr Vulliamy returns with a printed document which he lays on the desk before his employer and then goes out.

The old gentleman seats himself behind the desk, dips a pen into the inkstand, and looks up: "Now, sir, I need some information, if you will be so good. The gentleman's name is ... "

"It is a lady."

"A lady?" he says in surprise.

Mr Sancious nods slowly, watching his interlocutor's face very closely: "Living in the country." Another pause. "With a small child." Another pause, but the old gentleman's face registers no change of expression. "A boy," Mr Sancious concludes.

"Very good. And the name?"

The attorney hesitates for a moment before pronouncing "Mellamphy".

The old gentleman's face undergoes no change as he bends over his paper and begins to write.

"Mrs Mellamphy," Mr Sancious says. And he spells it out.

"Yes, yes, so I assumed, Mr Sancious," he says impatiently and then looks up and smiles. "And the direction?"

"To be reached under cover to myself."

"Very well." He puts the paper on one side and picks up the prospectus. "Now, my dear sir, as I say, I am one of the agents for the Company which is undertaking the speculation. It has been so fortunate as to acquire the head-lease of a plot of land extending to four and a quarter acres and sited in a most desirable part of the metropolis as yet unbuilt upon, between Pimlico and Westminster. May I refer you to the second page?" He opens out the document and points to a portion of a map which is engraved thereupon.

"Not perhaps the most fashionable part of the city?" suggests the attorney. "Or the most salubrious?"

"Not at present, sir, the most fashionable, perhaps, but a very salubrious district (once the Bason and the marshes are drained) and adjacent to the Grosvenor estate which is being built upon and which families of the highest respectability are increasingly favouring." He clears his throat and continues: "The price the Company has agreed to pay is forty-five thousand pounds which is a remarkably advantageous one. And as is customary, it has mortgaged the lease, though, of course, this will be redeemed as soon as enough shares have been sold."

"Of course."

"The mortgagee is the highly respectable banking house of Quintard and Mimpriss."

"I know the house," Mr Sancious says, "and its unimpeachable reputation."

"Excellent," the old gentleman says with a little simper. "Plans have already been drawn up by the most distinguished architects and surveyors for the construction of one hundred and seventy-eight dwelling-houses." He opens out the prospectus and lays it on his desk, inviting Mr Sancious to look. Both gentlemen study a plan on which the proposed lay-out of streets and squares is plotted. "You will see that the designs, for the most part, involve gentlemen's — indeed, noblemen's — houses of the most distinguished elevation and soundest construction. The Company has so far raised about ten thousand pounds and under the terms of the mortgage, undertakes to pay the Bank three thousand five hundred pounds per annum for twelve years until the balance has been paid together with the interest. But this will only start in two years, as is usual. And so this makes the investment very safe."

"So it would seem."

"Now the Company intends, as is customary, not to undertake the work itself but to sell building-leases to a main contractor for six thousand pounds per annum, and it will be down to the contractor either to sub-contract or undertake the entire project. Once the dwellings are erected the main-contractor will be paying six thousand pounds per annum to the Company. So as you will see, the Company's profit can hardly be less than two and a half thousand pounds a year and at virtually no risk."

"I have just one question," says Mr Sancious and leans back as he enunciates it: "Will there be a clause about time and completion in the terms offered to the main contractor?"

From his smile it appears that nothing could have given the old gentleman greater pleasure than to have the opportunity to answer such a question.

"Yes, Mr Sancious, and I perceive you are well up to the game. The contract will have a standard clause making no rent payable for the building-lease until half of the houses are completed."

Mr Sancious merely raises one eyebrow and the old gentleman continues: "That is customary, as you doubtless know, in order to provide an inducement to commit the required amount of capital in the building-work."

"And yet," Mr Sancious suggests, "it means that so long as that condition is not fulfilled, the contractor may sell any houses that are finished and take the profit without the Company receiving a brass farthing!"

"In theory," the old gentleman concedes, as if the thought has just struck him. "Yet since you are so knowledgeable, you will clearly perceive that such a clause is, despite appearances, greatly to the advantage of the Company."

"Indeed?" says Mr Sancious.

"Oh yes, for given his capital outlay, the contractor cannot possibly clear a profit until far more than half of the houses are finished and sold."

Mr Sancious seems to reflect and then remarks off-handedly: "And then there is the freeholder, who retains the ground-rents."

The old gentleman looks at him in surprise and the lawyer explains: "You see, a freeholder continues to hold the reversionary interest in the land and therefore the right to re-enter for breach of covenants or to distrain for debt."

"*You* are the lawyer," the old gentleman graciously concedes, "and I am certain you are correct. But I assure you, there is no question of such an eventuality arising."

"Can you be so sure? Who is the freeholder?"

In obedience to this question, the old gentleman looks through his papers, pursing his lips as if in deep perplexity. After a minute he looks up and says frankly: "I can't tell you for the transaction was in the name of a nominee, the Pimlico and Westminster Land Company, behind which the real freeholder is concealing himself. But I assure you there is no question of the Company defaulting on what it owes the freeholder. Bear in mind, my dear sir, that Quintard and Mimpriss are behind us."

"Indeed, Quintard and Mimpriss. A name to inspire confidence."

The old gentleman smiles and Mr Sancious says: "Well, sir, the manner in which you have answered my questions has settled any doubts in my mind as to the soundness of this project."

The old gentleman's smile grows wider.

"I have no doubts at all," the lawyer says, smiling back. "None."

"You're very kind, sir," the old gentleman says.

"It's a bubble, ain't it?" the lawyer says, still smiling.

The old gentleman's expression of affability is transformed into a scowl: "What do you mean, sir?"

"It's a flatt-trap."

"Why, how dare you!" the old gentleman exclaims in outrage, rising from his chair. Then he clutches his chest and falls back wheezing and coughing. "Mustn't alarm myself. Very bad for me," he gasps.

"You have misunderstood me, sir," says Mr Sancious blandly as he remains comfortably seated in his chair, playing with his gloves. "I am very interested indeed in your project. I believe that you and I can do business together very profitably."

The old gentleman stares at him: "Then you intend to advise your client to make the investment?"

"Assuredly. I shall urge her most forcefully to purchase a thousand pounds' worth of stock."

"In the Consolidated Metropolitan Building Company?"

"Precisely. And moreover, I have a little capital of my own which I would like to place at a profitable rate of return."

The old gentleman looks puzzled: "But surely ... "

Mr Sancious laughs: "Oh, not with the Consolidated Metropolitan Building Company. I would very much like to purchase a share in the freehold."

He and the old gentleman stare at each other. Then the latter says: "I dare say it might be possible to establish the identity of the freeholder. And it's not impossible that that party might be amenable to an offer."

"I do hope so," Mr Sancious comments.

"And if we were able to agree terms, Mr Sancious," the old gentleman continues, "would you be interested in acting as the main-contractor?"

"What would it involve?"

"Very little: the creation of a company which would exist only on paper as the chief-lessee. All the work would be sub-contracted to little masters. Even that would not fall to you if you know of a tradesman — a mason or a joiner or something like that — who is reliable?"

"Reliable?" Mr Sancious repeats. "You mean, my good sir, one who could be trusted to inspire confidence in others?" The old gentleman nods. "Why, I believe I might." He leans back comfortably and raises his glass. "I like the suggestion. Then let this moment mark the birth of, shall we say, the West London Building Company."

The two gentlemen toast each other.

"I see we have much to talk about," the attorney says. "I hope we will both lay our cards frankly upon the table, Mr Clothier."

BOOK IV

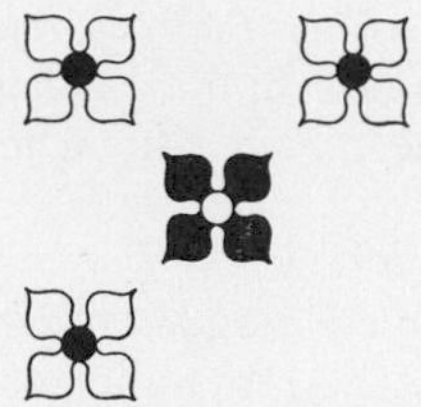

Speculations

CHAPTER 16

The eating-house called by the name of Millichamp's still stands (at least, it did so a few months ago) at the corner of Upper-Thames-street and Addle-hill. Here a little later the same evening Mr Sancious might have been observed, having been directed by the potboy to the Snuggery where, in one of the little wooden boxes along the bar, he finds Mr Vulliamy comfortably discussing a mutton chop and caper sauce with a glass at his elbow.

"My dear sir, you look excessively comfortable," he exclaims.

Mr Vulliamy raises his large, melancholy head and half-rises from his seat to bow a greeting. "I should be honoured if you would join me," he mutters with a weak smile.

Mr Sancious seats himself opposite the head-clerk with a cheerful smile: "That is a remarkably fine-looking chop," he remarks pleasantly. "I think I will order one for myself. And a glass of something to go with it. Mr Vulliamy, will you do me the honour of taking wine with me?"

Yes, Mr Vulliamy will, and so the orders are given to the boy.

"Upon my soul," Mr Sancious muses, "it is a pleasure to do business with your governor. Such an affable gentleman of the old school."

"Does he strike you that way, sir?"

"Indeed he does," Mr Sancious says just as the boy brings the bottle. "I can easily picture him surrounded by laughing grandchildren, Mr Vulliamy. I imagine he enjoys the most cheerful domestic circumstances?"

"Wife dead," Mr Vulliamy mutters. He brightens as Mr Sancious pours him a glass.

"Is that so? Ah well." Mr Sancious shakes his head sadly and then takes a drink. "Daughters?"

"None."

"Indeed? Not even a daughter-in-law?" Mr Vulliamy makes no response, so Mr Sancious remarks idly: "I don't seem to know of another Mr Clothier in the City." When there is still no answer he asks: "I say, I don't seem to have heard of another gentleman of that name."

At this Mr Vulliamy's left hand seizes an invisible pump-handle and rises and falls energetically while he looks at Mr Sancious.

That gentleman laughs pleasantly at this implication that he is "pumping" his companion, and pours him a second glass.

Mr Vulliamy drinks from it and then says: "As you say, Mr Sancious, there is no young Mr Clothier engaged in any trade, commerce or profession in London."

At this juncture Mr Sancious's dinner is laid before him and he appears not to notice what has just been said. But a few moments later he asks: "A grandson, perhaps?"

Mr Vulliamy shrugs his shoulders.

Mr Sancious turns the conversation to other subjects, and while he eats, the clerk addresses himself to the remainder of the wine. When the bottle is empty the attorney orders another and some time later, when half of it has vanished down Mr Vulliamy's throat, Mr Sancious remarks: "This is a fine scheme your employer is helping to promote, the Consolidated Metropolitan Building Company."

Mr Vulliamy nods and smiles.

"It was most injudicious of the freeholder — whoever he is hiding behind the Pimlico and Westminster Land Company — to have sold so valuable a lease for so little," the attorney muses.

"Does it strike you like that?" Mr Vulliamy asks, meaningfully.

"You mean that the freeholder knew what he was doing?" Mr Sancious exclaims. Mr Vulliamy looks a little surprised at so perspicacious an inference, but the attorney goes on: "My dear sir, how can you say such a thing?"

Mr Vulliamy first lays a rather unsteady hand to the side of his nose and then points to himself.

"I understand! You are the nominee in whose name the Pimlico and Westminster Land Company is held! On behalf of whom, I wonder?"

At this Mr Vulliamy leans forward on one elbow and winks knowingly, though the effect is somewhat spoiled by the elbow missing the edge of the table.

"Mr Clothier!" the lawyer cries, and his companion nods again looking rather taken aback at his interlocutor's quick understanding. "Then I believe I understand it all! But how he must trust you!"

"Oh, he's very sure of me," Mr Vulliamy remarks, shaking his head.

"And likewise, you must trust him," Mr Sancious remarks amiably. "For public knowledge of this could harm both of you."

"How could I not trust him? I assure you, Mr Sancious, I am deeply indebted to him. How could anyone fail to trust him when he talks so much about Justice? And has sacrificed so much to that accursed suit?"

"What suit?"

Perhaps Mr Vulliamy has had a particularly arduous day, for now his head begins to nod forward as he speaks: "Come, Mr Sancious, you must know of it. It's common gossip in the City. He has been pursuing a suit in Chancery for many years."

"Indeed? I seem not to have heard of it. Against whom?"

"Against a family called Mompesson."

"Mompesson?" Mr Sancious echoes. "Mumpsey, by heavens!" he exclaims, then quaffs from his glass to hide his surprise. A moment later he says: "Are you certain there is no daughter-in-law? There is no young Mr Clothier, you say. But was there once one?"

But Mr Vulliamy leans forward and, as if his head has suddenly become very heavy, rests it on his arms which are laid on the table.

Mr Sancious stands, takes him by the shoulder and shakes him: "Was there a son who died?"

There is no response from the other gentleman. The attorney shakes him more and more roughly. At last, seeing that he is asleep, he pulls the bell-rope and when the pot-boy appears says to him: "Find me a ticker-porter. I believe I saw one lounging at the next court-entrance as I came in."

The boy hurries away and while he is gone Mr Sancious gazes with no friendly expression at his fellow-diner, now snoring loudly as he lies with his face on the table and his elbows brushing against the remnants of his dinner. After a moment the boy returns with an unkempt individual in a greasy great-coat. The attorney dismisses the boy and says to the porter: "Do you know the Swan-with-Two-Necks in Cheapside?"

The man smiles: "Aye, as the worst flash-house in Town."

"Stow that and cock your lugs," the attorney says and then lowers his voice so that the man has to bring his head forward to obey him.

CHAPTER 17

One morning a few weeks after Mrs Belflower had gone, I went to the drawing-room after breakfast for my usual lesson and found that my mother had on her reading-glasses which she always wore for "business". She looked up with a smile and said: "I've had such a kind letter from Mr Sancious. He must have thought a great deal about my affairs for he advises me very strongly not to grant Bissett's request. For you see, she asked me for higher wages now that some of Mrs Belflower's work falls to her as well."

So that was what she wanted to say to my mother that time while Sukey was telling me of her father's death!

"Mr Sancious says he is very concerned that our income is too low to meet our present expenses, and certainly no new ones. You see, the government has reduced the amount of interest it pays on the consolidated funds I have. In other words, we are really quite poor now, Johnnie."

"Is there any way we can stop being poor?"

"Yes, Johnnie, for he advises me to change my present investments to a better one."

"That sounds like a wonderful idea!" I exclaimed. "I wonder Uncle Martin didn't think of it."

"Well, he was rather old-fashioned, my dear."

"Then what does Mr Sancious say you should do?"

"It's very complicated and I don't understand it entirely, so I don't think you will. But I'll read it out and see if it makes it easier." She adjusted her reading-glasses and began, stumbling over some of the hard words: "'We consequently beg to suggest that the monies, to the value of one thousand pounds, at present with the Consolidated Funds be removed therefrom and laid out in the purchase of shares in the stock of the Consolidated Metropolitan Building Company which we have referred to above. The Company's purpose is to undertake the speculative improvement of a piece of land in the westernmost portion of the metropolis, the leasehold to which it has acquired on highly favourable terms. We would be failing in our duty if we omitted to warn you that there is always a risk attendant upon any such venture, but in this case we have every confidence in the Company, whose Directors are personally known to us. Moreover, title to land — even leasehold — is the surest form of security. By reasonable probabilities, we estimate that within two years the capital value of the lease — and therefore of equity shares in the Company — will have at least doubled.'" My mother looked up at me: "You see, Johnnie, Mr Sancious seems very sure that it is a good idea doesn't he? And nothing can be safer than land and houses, can it?"

"No, nothing!" I cried, though I had made very little of this.

"If we invest a thousand pounds as Mr Sancious suggests, then for the next two years we will be very poor because we will have to live on the money that is left in the Funds."

"A thousand pounds! Do you think, Mamma, that we should? After all, Mr Sancious says there is a risk?"

"But he will be very hurt if I don't, since he has gone to so much trouble on our behalf."

"That's so. But I know! Let him have three hundred pounds."

"Yes, perhaps that's best. That's still a great deal of money so he can't be too offended."

"And twice that is six hundred!"

"Very well. I will write him to say that. I am glad that I asked you. You are clever." She flung her arms round me: "And soon we will have nothing more to worry about. Six hundred pounds! And it may be even more than that! This is a great day. We must celebrate. I know: I will make negus!"

The prospect of this wonderful undertaking, which was carried out only on the most special occasions, excited me because of what it signified and not because I liked the final result — though since my mother always assured me that one day I would, I always expected that this momentous event would happen very suddenly. When she had run into the kitchen and returned with the hot water and other ingredients, she stirred in the sugar, lemon, cinnamon, sherry and one or two other things as we talked about how Mr Sancious' foresight meant that I would be able to go to a good school and enter a proper profession. Then we toasted each other (I with a quarter of a tumbler) in the hot liquid that was so sweet yet bitter.

"I still don't like it," I said. "What's that nasty taste?"

My mother laughed. Then she said gravely: "Now I must face Bissett." She poured herself another tumbler and said: "Will you ask her to come, Johnnie?"

"Are you going to give her notice? That would save a great deal of money."

"Well," my mother said rather anxiously, "she might choose to leave."

I ran into the kitchen where I found Bissett standing, red-faced and arms akimbo, in the middle of an exchange of words with Sukey who sat on a chair before the hearth sobbing into her apron.

I gave Bissett my mother's message, and when she had left the room I said cautiously: "Can I do anything to help, Sukey?"

She looked at me, sniffed, and said: "Will you play at the cards with me?"

"I'm forbidden to game," I said sadly.

"It ain't them sort," she said, pulling from her pocket a pack of greasy cards whose designs, as I saw when she spread them on the table, were quite strange. "They're for tellin' of fortins."

"I'm sure that wasn't forbidden me," I said.

So she plied the cards in the hope of comforting herself with brighter visions of the future, but however often she tried to get a better fortune, the cards persisted in foreseeing only the direst calamities. She was deeply down-cast by what she called her ill luck, and though I tried to raise her spirits by telling her that she could avert the worst now that she had been forewarned, she insisted that it was not like that for coming events were fixed. We were so preoccupied that although we were listening out for her step, we didn't hear Bissett before she had opened the door. She looked at the cards strewn on the table with repugnance but to my surprise she merely muttered "More heathenish tricks" and turned away.

I returned to the sitting-room where I found my mother sitting on the sopha and looking rather pale.

"Well, is she going to leave?" I asked.

"Don't speak like that, Johnnie," she said slowly. "I believe she must be much fonder of us than we think."

"Why do you say that?" I demanded.

"And she is certainly very loyal," she said reflectively.

She would say no more than this.

Bissett's demeanour during the next few days was strangely forebearing, as if she were suddenly resigned to the moral deficiences in those around her.

CHAPTER 18

The duties assigned to the various members of our household re-arranged themselves in the weeks and months that followed the cook's departure. Bissett now acquired unchallengeable authority over Sukey (and became so tireless in her pursuit of an ideal of cleanliness that I have seen her many a time make Sukey black-lead the kitchen grate all over again before she would let her go home). Meanwhile my mother, with Sukey's assistance, took on the cooking, and I have to admit that I found that I missed Mrs Belflower more and more as time passed. Now bereft of the astute house-keeping experience of the cook, we tried to save money by economizing on clothes, provisions, candles, and coal, especially as prices were increasing because of the badness of the times. Meanwhile scenes between Bissett and Sukey of the kind that I have just mentioned having interrupted, grew more and more frequent. We had a bleak first Christmas without Mrs Belflower's cheerful good-nature and excellent fare, the memories of both being fresh in our minds. Other memories, too, remained fresh and I had been in the habit of asking Sukey about Hougham in the hope — never satisfied — of hearing news of my little friend. Since her aunt had now come to live with her, however, she was scant of intelligence from that village and at last I gave up even soliciting it. My studies continued, and now I found the old Latin primer I had come across long ago and began to study that language. One result of my efforts was that I was able to see that the motto which had seemed so dishonourably circumspect, could on the contrary be translated to mean: "The rose of safety must be sought in the midst of danger".

In the late Spring of the new year Mr Sancious wrote to explain something about the progress of our investment, and my mother showed me the letter which she said was very good news. The Company, he wrote, had entered into a friendly arrangement whereby it assigned certain of the sub-leases on the improved ground-rents to the respected banking-house of Quintard and Mimpriss. He pointed out that the only disadvantage to share-holders was that there would be a slight delay in the completion of the contract.

"You see, Johnnie," my mother commented. "I knew it would be all right. You were quite wrong to say that we should not have invested more. Fortunately your mother understands these things better than you do."

The delay, however, turned out to be more than slight for although the following Spring was the end of the two years and therefore the moment that our investment was originally to have matured, the months passed without Mr Sancious finding himself able to give my mother a firm date by which a return could be expected.

That summer I became increasingly bored and irritated at being left to amuse myself on my own, for I was strictly forbidden even to talk to other children. One glorious day in July, however, I took advantage of a misunderstanding between my mother, Bissett, and Sukey about which of them was keeping an eye on me, and slipped out of the house. As I made my way towards the village I encountered three boys of my own age whom I had often watched and envied. I hailed them and they answered me, though in a slightly surly, suspicious manner. They let me tag along behind them and we made our way towards an abandoned barn on the outskirts of the village. I understood that some secret and even illicit project was in hand, and, knowing from hints dropped by Harry that ratting and even cock-fighting were practised by the boys of the village, I felt a stirring of excitement.

As we entered the dimly-lit barn I made out something on the floor before us, something that hissed and moved convulsively as we approached. There were whoops of delight from my companions and cries of "Got her at last!". The thing before us was a black cat — very obviously a female — which was caught by one leg in a gin-trap. It was a hideous animal — its legs as thin as sticks but its belly hugely distended. It was trying to run away but, held securely by a length of cord, was only able to flatten itself on the ground, arching its back, and spit at us. Although I had never cared for cats — finding them sly, two-faced creatures — I was horrified by this. And I became the more so when my companions began to pick up the big stones which I now noticed were lying all around, as if they had been thrown there on previous occasions.

It seemed to me that ratting was fair because the rats had the chance to escape from or even to resist the dogs, and cock-fighting matched two creatures on equal terms. But this was ugly and cruel! I began to protest and tried to explain these principles to the other boys, but they ignored me and began to clod stones at the terrified animal. When I tried to stop them physically, they turned their attention to me.

I was seized and punched in the ribs several times and then thrown to the muddy ground and rolled in the dirt. Although I managed to escape without further injury, since I had to return home in this condition, I could not conceal what had happened and was punished (on Bissett's insistence) by being sent to bed without my supper.

As summer gave way to autumn I saw my mother becoming more and more tired and preoccupied. Winter arrived and by the time Christmas approached we had heard nothing from Mr Sancious. On the afternoon of Christmas-eve there was a hard frost and snow was threatening, but the three of us — my mother, Sukey, and I — seized the chance offered by the sunny, windless day to gather armfuls of evergreens in Mortsey-wood and to find a Yule clog which I dragged home behind me. And so that evening when — to Bissett's disgust who was outraged by these "pagan ways" — we had arranged the evergreens around the house and set the clog to burning in the fireplace in the sitting-room, my mother and I exchanged gifts and tried to recapture the Christmases of the past.

Afterwards the post-master's daughter came with a letter and so, leaving my mother to read it, I went and sat in the kitchen and listened to Sukey telling ghost-stories, as she plucked the goose for the morrow and pounded spices for the stuffing and the mulled wine. The room was full of the bitter-sweet scent of cinnamon and cloves, but I missed the presence of Mrs Belflower and knew that somehow the dinner, despite the trouble we had all gone to, would not be as good as in the old days. Bissett was darning stockings and pretending not to listen to Sukey's tales, but occasionally she could not resist a disapproving or sceptical remark.

"And from that day to this, nobody in the village ain't nivver seen him again," said Sukey as she concluded a particularly horrible story about the disappearance of an impious sexton.

"Stuff and nonsense," muttered Bissett. "You've no business to be filling the child's head with such things."

At that moment my mother came into the room. "Johnnie," she said, "will you come? I wish to discuss something with you."

I followed her into the sitting-room and we made ourselves comfortable on the window-seat. By the faint light from the sky we could see the snow falling as if with a quiet and secret purpose.

"My dear," my mother began, "I don't quite know what to make of this letter from Mr Sancious."

"Are we to receive some money soon?"

"I don't really know. Let me read you part of his letter: 'The foreclosure of the mortgage, following upon the defalcation of the contractor, is an eventuality not to be contemplated on the estimable principle that' — good heavens, Johnnie! — '*Crastinus enim dies solicitus erit sibi ipsi. Sufficit diei malitia sua*.' (I believe that must be Latin.) 'However, the subscription of more capital by the present share-holders would entirely forestall this prospect, and we therefore advise you in the strongest terms to make a further investment of five hundred pounds. We enclose the necessary documents for your signature.' What do you think, Johnnie?"

"Mamma, it sounds to me as if something has gone wrong."

"Surely that cannot be so or why would he advise us to put in more money?"

"In order to save what we have invested already. But I think we should not throw good money after bad."

I had often heard Bissett use this phrase.

"But then if you're right we might lose all the money we have put in!"

"That is so, but you said we could afford to lose three hundred pounds."

"Well, yes, I know I did," she said, looking down and colouring. "But you see, Johnnie, it's really more than that."

She hesitated.

"You mean we would also lose the money that we would make if everything turned out well?"

"Yes, that's just what I meant. So don't you think that it is worth risking some more?"

"I suppose so."

"Very well, then. Let us do as Mr Sancious advises and invest another five hundred pounds."

She sat at her escritoire to write the letter immediately and told me to ask Sukey to take it to the post office on her way home that evening, for she was being allowed to spend the night with her family on account of the approaching holiday.

Just as my mother had wafered and sealed the letter, we heard running feet and Sukey burst into the room: "Come quick! Oh, please ma'am!"

"Why, whatever is the matter?" exclaimed my mother, starting up in alarm.

"There's two fetches at the back-door, and they're a-trying to come in!"

"Now don't be so foolish, Sukey. You know what it is: you have frightened yourself with your own stories, haven't you?"

"No, ma'am, they're real. We was sitting there not two minutes back when we suddenly heard a scratching and a scraping at the door. I looked out of window and ... " She broke off and her voice trembled: "I seen two pale faces a-staring back as sure as I'm standing here now."

My mother looked at me in alarm and although I felt a tremor of dismay run through me, I saw clearly where my duty as the man of the house lay and marched resolutely (in appearance anyway) towards the kitchen with Sukey straggling at the rear.

As we entered we found Bissett standing at the open back-door and shouting "Be off with you!" into the darkness.

"Who is there?" asked my mother.

"Two no-goods come a-begging, Mrs Mellamphy," said Bissett, turning her head briefly towards us. Then she turned back and shouted: "You heard me. Be off now!"

"Let them come in," said my mother. "We cannot turn anyone away tonight of all nights, and in this weather."

"I don't think you're doing the right thing, ma'am," protested Bissett, but seeing that my mother was resolved, she opened the door and stood back.

In came a woman dressed in a long ragged gown with a woollen shawl over her shoulders which was covered in snow. As she entered, blinking in the sudden light, she staggered slightly. Her drawn face was pale as ashes and I could see why a sudden glimpse of it had so alarmed Sukey. Though she was far from slender, the flesh seemed to hang loosely upon her face. After her came a boy who seemed by his size to be a year or two younger than I and was wearing a long, torn great-coat that hung loosely upon his slight frame.

"Oh, the poor things," said my mother, and she led them both to chairs onto which they collapsed.

They leaned back and closed their eyes, and I saw that they were both shivering. The woman's face was lined and careworn, and her hair had streaks of grey, so that she seemed very much older than my mother.

"The little feller seems nigh past it," said Sukey who had timidly come forward.

My mother began to chafe the woman's hands between her own and Sukey did the same for the boy.

"Warm up some broth, please," my mother said to Bissett.

Disapprovingly, Bissett set about doing so, first stirring the fire which had been banked up for the evening.

"What's wrong with the boy?" I asked Sukey in a whisper, for he seemed to have fainted away.

"Near starved wi' cold, Master Johnnie. And his mither, too. Look at them thin clothes. Nobbut rags."

The woman opened her eyes and looked around her in a dazed manner. When she saw the boy she seized his hands from Sukey and began to rub them vigorously. At last he opened his eyes. The woman began to sob and catching hold of my mother's hand she carried it to her lips and kissed it: "Oh thank you, thank you, ma'am. You've saved us, so you have."

My mother gently removed her hand and said kindly: "Can you eat now? I think you should."

Sukey brought over a bowl of the broth that Bissett had heated up, and the woman began to spoon it into the mouth of the boy. Only when he had swallowed enough did she begin to help herself. "I'm beholden to you, ma'am," she began. "I don't know what mightn't have happened to me and Joey if you hadn't sarved us."

The food and the warmth revived them. I now saw that the boy was a handsome lad with large brown eyes and a nose that turned up a little at the end. Yet his face had a somewhat watchful, suspicious expression as if he could not quite believe that we meant him no harm.

My mother said: "I know by your speech you're from London. What are you doing so far from home? And out in such weather clad like this?" The woman closed her eyes and my mother said: "Leave it till tomorrow. You're too tired now."

"No, ma'am, I'll try to make it clear, only my head's in such a whirl. We've been working in Stoniton." (This is what I shall call the manufacturing town some twenty miles to the north which she named.) "When we come down here, my goodman was took on at the big house in the next village, but there wasn't no work for Joey and me so we had gone on there to look for a place. Well, we found work of a sort. Then two days back we had word by the carrier that my George had heard some bad tidings and gone back to Town sudden. So we left as soon as we could and come down yesterday morning from Stoniton."

"Good heavens!" my mother exclaimed. "Did you come so far in this weather in one day! How did you travel?"

"Mostly on foot, ma'am, but we got a ride of about five mile of a good man driving a waggon. The worst of it was what we found waiting for us when we got back to the great house. The reason my man returned so sudden to Town ... " Here her voice trembled and I thought she was going to begin weeping. But she mastered herself and went on: "He'd had word that the other children ... are sick of the Irish fever. We've three others, you see. So I've got to get back as quick as I can."

"Of course, of course," my mother murmured. "But even so, was it wise to continue your journey in the snow?"

"The old lady at the big house wouldn't let us stay, on account of my husband had throwed up his work so sudden, though the young lady there — governess I believe they call her — tried to persuade her to. We were so cold and hungry that we tried more than a few houses in the village, but they all said they couldn't do nothin' for us. So we had no choice but to keep on walking. When we come to the turnpike-road up yonder, I was for walking along it to the next big town, but Joey said we should come into Melthorpe and we'd be sure to find kind people here. Joey pulled me along when I wanted to lay down and die. Like I said, ma'am, we walked all through the village without stopping anywheres, for Joey said he would know which house would be best to stop at as soon as he seen it. So we come to this one. I call it providence, ma'am. There ain't no other word for it."

"No, indeed," cried my mother, clapping her hands together. She smiled at the boy who, I thought, scowled slightly. "And what made you try this house?" she asked him.

"Dunno," he said, looking away.

"Well, I'm very glad you did," she said.

"It's getting late," said Bissett. "You'll want to be on your way."

"Of course not," my mother exclaimed. "They cannot think of going out again tonight."

"We can stay?" the woman asked.

"Why, of course. But Sukey, it is late. You must go or Mr Passant will have gone to meet the mail and this letter will miss the last post before Christmas."

"If they must stay, then let them sleep in one of the outhouses," Bissett whispered to my mother quite audibly.

"Certainly not. They need warmth and comfort. We must make up a proper bed for them. This is the warmest room in the house, so it shall be in here."

"They'll dirty the linen," Bissett hissed.

"No matter," said my mother.

"You're too soft, ma'am," said Bissett indignantly. "I would not suffer them to lie in my beds. Who knows what varmin and nastiness they have broughten with them? To be sure, if they must stay here they may lay upon the floor. You're too careless of your good things. Those sheets cost good money that will be thrown away."

Yet although Bissett grumbled she set about her duties once she saw that my mother was determined, and with Sukey's assistance a mattress and bedclothes were conveyed into the kitchen and arranged in front of the fire. Then Sukey was given the money for the postage and set off home muffled up against the snow and carrying the letter.

Something woke me in the middle of the night. Unsure whether it was my dream or a noise from outside, I lay awake straining to catch any sounds but hearing nothing. Then I remembered our visiters and, wondering if they were all right, I got up and, cold as it was in my night-shirt, went along the passage groping my way in the dark since I had no light. When I reached the door to my mother's room, which was ajar, I heard her breathing in her sleep. I smelt burning as if a taper had been recently extinguished there, and at that moment I thought I heard a faint noise from below. I crept down the stairs, still in complete darkness, and looked round the kitchen door. In the dim reddish glow of the fire I saw the large form of the woman stretched out on a palliasse before the hearth. But the mattress beside her was empty! I felt my way towards the front of the house and as I entered the hall I saw a faint glow from the open door of the parlour. Very cautiously I advanced towards it and looked round the edge of the door.

The light came from a rush that the boy was holding. He was standing by my mother's escritoire and appeared to be running his free hand over the lid and around its sides.

"What are you doing?"

He jumped and as I entered the room presented to me a face of horror: "I wasn't doin' nothin'! I was jist lookin'."

"I could see that. But why?"

"'Cause I ain't nivver seen sich prime stuff. Look at this wood. It's rare."

I felt proud to own such things and think nothing of it. "But why did you go into my mother's room?"

"I nivver done. I haven't been upstairs."

"That's strange, for I smelled a rush on the landing."

"Well, now that I rec'lleck, I did go jist a little way up them stairs. But I didn't go into no room."

"You are silly to come in here in the dark, you know. I could have shewn you everything in the morning."

He looked at me oddly for a moment and then said: "I nivver thought of that. See, I meant no harm. Don't tell nobody, will you?"

"Of course not. What is there to tell?"

So, rather puzzled, I returned to my bed while Joey went back to the kitchen.

CHAPTER 19

The next morning I was awoken by Bissett's brisk: "Good morning, Master Johnnie."

"Good morning, Bissett," I said sleepily. "How are they?"

"They're in the kitchen and eating as big a breakfast as if there'd nivver been nothin' amiss with them," she replied dourly as she drew back the curtains. There was thick hoar-ice on the windows that had made frost-flowers, and the light that streamed in had a peculiarly pale brilliance. "Ah," she said, "just look at that."

I jumped out of bed and ran over to the window. The light was reflected from the surface of the silent, snow-encumbered landscape. In the distance I heard the sounds of horns that boys always blew on Christmas morning.

"Oh isn't that lovely!" I exclaimed.

"Well," said Bissett with a kind of grim pleasure, "there'll not be much visiting this Christmas for them as likes to go gadding about upon the Lord's holy day."

After breakfast my mother and I went into the kitchen where we found the woman and the boy seated in front of the fire and drinking from big mugs of tea. By the efforts of my mother and with the assistance (unwilling, I believe) of Bissett, a complete new wardrobe had been found for both of them. Several of my clothes had been given to the boy, including a pair of stout walking-shoes. Now rested and in their new clothes they presented a much rosier picture than on the day before. A little colour had returned to their faces though they were still pale and hollow-cheeked. Since the boy was so much slighter than I, my clothes hung somewhat loosely on him, though as they were mainly garments I had outgrown, the fit was not too bad. He looked as gloomy as before although his pallor was better.

"Will you tell me your story?" my mother asked.

"Are you sartin you wants to hear it, ma'am?" she said and glanced towards myself.

"I am very curious to do so."

"Very well," she said thoughtfully. And so when my mother and I had made ourselves comfortable in two of the other chairs, and the strangers' mugs of tea had been replenished, she began: "Well, it's long tale, ma'am, but one that's little like to interest you to hear minced too fine, for it is a common enough one, pity only knows. Our name is Digweed and we live in Cox's-square, Spitalfields. My George, the father of that boy, is a time-sarved mason by trade. And a skilled j'iner, too. And don't hardly take a drop when he's working. Seen the damage of it in his own dad, he says. And then there's the young 'uns: Joey here and then his sister, Polly, who is a wonderful child for all she's only going on ten. Many's the time she's saved us from starvation, or the work'us, or nussed us through sickness. Then there's the other boy, Billy, who's only seven and a fine lad. And there's Sally, too, the eldest." I noticed that her right hand clasped and unclasped as she spoke these words. Then she went on quickly: "Well, until three or four years back we'd been making a dacent living for my George was a paid-up member of his S'iety and respected by his fellows and trusted by the little masters who gived him a deal o' work. Then the slack time started and George didn't get no more work. We were all right at fust, though we saw trouble coming to others. At fust, he worked in the dishonourable part of the trade — though he nivver gived short measure. But he was working under the book-price and somehow the S'iety larned this and struck him off. Arter that the only work he could get was for that new gas-company in Horseferry-road. He was doing the brick-lining and it was very hot and none too safe, and the wages was mortal low. Why, bless you, we was poor as rats. Well, we was just about making do when our fortins took a turn for the worse. There was some trouble at work and my George was hurt. His arms and leg and his face. He was in the 'Spital for four months and then couldn't work for another year. Things wasn't good for the gas wouldn't do nothin' for us at fust but then at last they gived us some money as a set-off. But then on account of his arm, George couldn't get work of no kind at all. It was about this time — Christmas three year ago — that ... a sartin indiwiddle come to us." Her face darkened. "Well, he was wery friendly. I reckon he'd heard that George had that money. Mind, I don't say he meant to do us harm. Mebbe the worst thing he done was he took that boy to live with him to save us another mouth to feed. Joey ain't nivver been the same boy since, though he wouldn't nivver tell his dad nor me nothin' about that time."

I glanced curiously at Joey who hung down his head guiltily.

"Anyways, what this person done was, he purwailed upon George to set up as a small master himself since the S'iety wouldn't let him work no more for the honourable masters and to come in with him on a contract to take a lease and build a house in the marsh-lands out beyond Westminster. (That's the reg'lar way of doing things.) For with the set-off from the gas, we had just enough to do it. Some of the other small masters took on two or three houses but George and his partner only took on one between the two on 'em, though it was a big 'un for they were meant to be fine houses for the gentry. So they had to pay the plaisterers and other j'iners themselves. And all the money went into that. And more, for this indiwiddle didn't have no blunt at all. We had to feed ourselves and, worst of all, to buy all the building-stuff. And George wouldn't use nothin' but the best stock brick, and he had noises with his partner over that. And also on account of how this indiwiddle didn't do none of the work as he'd promised, but spent all his time drinking with other tradesmen and trying to purwail upon 'em to take up contracts, too. Well, next thing is, arter about six months he says he wants to pull out. And so George bought out his share — oh, it was a fair price but it was more money than we'd bargained for at the start. And so as time went on we pawned almost everything we owned — our few sticks, clothes, bedding, cups and plates — everything save a few clothes and the tools he needed. But we had to raise more money somehow. Well, the pawnbrokers what we'd pledged everything to was willing to lend us money, but at a terrible rate of interest. You wouldn't know nothin' about it, ma'am, but there are wicked men in Town what feeds on poor people like us."

My mother shook her head slowly at this as if, to my surprise, she understood the allusion.

"Well, so we borrowed forty pound, and that meant we had to pay back eighty at the end of six months. At the beginning of last year George had about finished work on the house and then we larned some bad news: a man come round from the main-contractor and told all the small masters that on account of some kind of difficulties that I nivver understood, the people what owned the land had the right to seize it back on account of they hadn't been paid no rent or something. It was nothin' to do with us, but it seemed we could lose everything without no set-off: all the money we'd paid for the lease and all the work and the bricks and the wood and all what we'd put into the house and paid others to do. It didn't seem right."

Here my mother looked at me in dismay.

"This man said to all the small masters as how they should sell out to the main-contractor who, in course, couldn't offer them nothin' like a fair price for the work they'd put in on account of the difficulties he was in himself. He would offer them a hundred pound for each house, take it or leave it. And if they left it, they might lose everything. Well they'd done about three hundred pound worth of work on each house. Some of 'em said they wouldn't sell at that price and sure enough the freeholder went to law and seized their houses without paying nothin' at all. And then the contractor dropped his price even lower on account of that. So then the rest on 'em sold and George did too and got no more nor forty pound for the house. But the strange thing is, ma'am, that the main-contractor what now owned nearly all the half-built houses was able to finish and sell 'em, for the freeholder nivver did seize any more on 'em. I nivver understood that and thought there was something wrong there."

"What was the company called?" I asked.

"It was the West London Building Company."

My mother and I glanced at each other in relief.

"Since then things have been worse than before on account of the badness of the times. They say the harvest failed in Ireland this summer and sartin it is there's been many more poor Irishers in Town than ever before to bring down the price of work and raise the rents."

"So how have you lived since then?" my mother asked.

Mrs Digweed glanced nervously in my direction before replying: "My George has had to take to the shores, ma'am. And with that and my washing we've jist about managed to keep body and soul together. But then last winter he took sick with the damp on his chest — and worse than that! — off the work he was doing. We nigh on starved then, for the pawnbroker what I told you about was taking four shillin' a week off of us for what we owed. And because we couldn't pay it back fast enough, we was getting deeper and deeper into debt all the time. Well then in the Spring, this same indiwiddle as I told you of come to see us again. It was a long time since we'd seen him, and to tell the truth, I was none too glad when I set eyes on him. But he seemed to be bringing us some good news this time. He said he'd heard that there was some work to do at the great house up at Hougham."

"The great house?" my mother repeated. "You must mean Mompesson-park?"

"I believe the name was something like that, ma'am."

"But the house has been empty for years!" my mother exclaimed.

"Seemingly the fambly's coming back there, ma'am, if it's the same house. Well, my George went to see the steward in Town and got took on. So we talked it over and agreed to leave the young 'uns in Town. George was from here as a boy but it was the fust time that I'd ever gone beyond the lamps. Then, like I told you last night, Joey and me had to go on to Stoniton. And that's where we were until we heerd the tidings from Town. Well, that's all there is to say. And now we have to get on home."

She rose from her chair as she spoke.

"Gracious Heavens!" cried my mother. "You surely cannot propose to continue your journey today!"

"We have rested and we have ate, and thanks to your goodness we have got warm clothes and good stout shoes that will take us up to Town easy."

"But not on foot," my mother persevered, seeing that she was determined. "At the very least, I insist upon giving you the money to pay for your fare by stage-coach. You can pick it up at noon on the turnpike where it passes the turning to the village."

A troubled expression appeared on the woman's face: "I don't like to take money, thank you kindly, ma'am. We're so deep in debt already, we dare not take on no more."

"But if you take the coach you can be with your family by early tomorrow instead of three or four days from now. And Joey looks much too tired to go on today by foot. And I don't mean it as a loan but as a gift."

The woman's weary face as she looked at her little boy was a battle-ground of conflicting emotions. At last she spoke: "We'd pay you back, ma'am, Joey's dad and me. He would say that as sartin as me if he were here now. We'd not like to be beholden." Then she added timidly: "How much would the fare be for the two of us?"

My mother glanced at me: "Two outsides would be about twenty-four shillings," I said.

Mrs Digweed's eyes widened in horror. "I don't know how long it would be a-fore we could pay back that much," she murmured. "We couldn't put aside more than that in a quarter even when my husband was working in the honourable trade."

"Please don't worry about that," said my mother.

"Since it's Christmas-day," Sukey put in, "the coach that passes the village at noon will be nigh on empty."

"Sukey will go with you to show you the way to the cross-roads."

"Then I will take your money, and thank you ma'am, thank you," the woman said. "Bless you, you have a workin' heart for the poor."

My mother smiled and said to me: "Johnnie, will you come into the parlour for a moment?" When we were alone she asked: "Do you think this can be the same enterprise? The name of the company was different."

"It seems to be the same scheme. And there are several companies involved."

"If so, it seems a strange coincidence. And what that woman said has made me uneasy. I wish I hadn't sent that letter last night. Do you think I should write to Mr Sancious to say that I have changed my mind about putting more money into it?"

"Very well, if it will make you easier, though I don't really see why you should be worried."

"Then Sukey can take the letter to the post-office on the way to the cross-roads."

"It's Christmas-day, Mamma, the office will be closed."

"Well if it is then Mrs Digweed can take it to London."

"Do you think we should entrust so important a letter to her?"

"Whyever not?" my mother cried as she sat down and began to compose it.

I begged her to allow me to accompany Sukey and the Digweeds to the turnpike and, seeing how disappointed I would be to miss this chance of seeing the coach stop to take up passengers, she agreed. While she wrote the letter I went up to my room to make ready, and also to act surreptitiously on a resolution I had formed as I listened to Mrs Digweed's story.

The leave-taking and the formalities which accompanied the handing-over of the money and the letter were taking place when I returned to the hall. Mrs Digweed insisted on my mother's writing down her name and the direction of our house.

Eventually the four of us set off through the quiet village, peaceful under its blanket of snow and the only signs of life the chimneys from which the smoke was ascending straight up into the cloudless sky. The two women walked on ahead, leaving Joey and me to follow.

"Do you think the guard will blow his horn when he stops the coach?" I asked Joey.

"I don't care," he said. "I've travelled on a coach many and many a time."

"Have you? Where?"

"With my uncle. In Town and thereabouts."

"How old are you?" I asked.

His answer surprised me: despite his slighter stature (and I myself was small) he was only about six months younger than myself. I was relieved to know that he was not very much younger, as I had believed, since that would have made the fact that he had done and seen so much all the more galling.

The little general shop that served as a post-office was indeed barred and shuttered and so Sukey handed the letter to Mrs Digweed with another tuppence for the postage in London.

"Of course everything's locked up today, just as I said it would be," I pointed out.

"Everythin' save the buryin'-ground," Joey remarked for we were just passing it as I made this remark.

"Don't be silly, graveyards are never locked up."

He looked at me with a very irritating air of superiority: "They are in Lunnun. 'Less there's a mort-safe."

"Oh be quiet about London," I cried and pushed him, determined not to ask what that word meant.

He pushed me back much harder so I seized him by the arm, but he managed to wriggle free and hit me on the chest. At this moment Sukey and Mrs Digweed pulled us apart and we walked the rest of the way separated by them.

We reached the cross-roads in good time and had some minutes to wait before the coach came in sight along the snow-covered road. I began waving my arms as soon as I saw it, and to my delight the guard did indeed blow a long blast on his horn as it slowed down and drew to a steaming, jangling, stamping halt abreast of us. The guard confirmed that there were places outside, the money was handed over, and the two new passengers helped up as I watched enviously.

Just as they were getting settled and a moment before the guard gave the signal to the driver to set forward again, I broke from Sukey's hand-hold and ran to the side of the coach calling out to Joey: "Here, catch this!" I threw up the little purse I had fetched from my own room and which contained all the money I had saved, a sum amounting to one pound, four shillings and three-pence, and which included the half-sovereign that I had received from Mr Barbellion in the church-yard. (I had kept it from some superstitious feeling, and was now relieved to see it go.)

The coach pulled away before Joey and his mother had time to open the purse, but when it was about fifty yards from us I saw him half-standing to wave back at me, while his mother clutched his legs to prevent him falling over.

For several weeks my mother and I talked frequently of Mrs Digweed and her son, wondering what they had found when they got to London. (I took great pleasure in finding on my map the place where they lived.) And for some time afterwards she seemed thoughtful and melancholy, and it occurred to me that the mention of London had brought back into her mind memories and associations that she hadn't thought about for a long time. It was strange to reflect that she had had experiences of which I knew nothing at all. She spent more time writing and it didn't seem to be letters that she was composing in her pocket-book. Bissett had a low opinion of our visiters, insisting that the creature's story was a string of lies and berating my mother for her innocence in having believed any of it. Eventually Mamma came to accept that the woman might have been exaggerating the wrongs and hardships that her family had endured after her husband's injury in the explosion at the gas-works. (Once I happened to overhear Bissett say to her, shaking her head as she spoke: "I'm sure I smelt gin on that woman's breath.")

Their visit had had its effect on me too and had made me restless. I did not believe that we had been lied to, and neither was I surprised by the apparent connexions between their lives and ours — for at that age we expect everything to concentre upon ourselves and do not see such patterns as coincidences. I was disturbed, however, when I reflected that Joey, at about the same age as myself or a little younger, had already and for several years worked to earn his living. He knew London and had had experiences which I could hardly begin to imagine. I became impatient to grow up and leave the village, and I believe that my mother saw this and that it distressed her.

CHAPTER 20

The letter entrusted to Mrs Digweed reached its destination but it must have arrived too late to undo the effect of the earlier one, for about a week after Christmas my mother received a reply from Mr Sancious saying that he had already undertaken the transaction on her behalf and that it could not be undone.

The winter passed away and on a wonderful morning in April I came down to breakfast and found my mother studying another letter from her man of business.

"What is the news?" I asked.

"Very good," she answered, smiling. "It seems that the Company is to raise a great deal more money because its prospects are so excellent."

"And does that mean we will get our money at last?"

"I'm sure we will."

"Let me see the letter," I said and she let me take it. "We beg to advise you," Mr Sancious wrote, "that at the extraordinary board-meeting of directors of the Consolidated Metropolitan Building Company duly held on the Monday of last week, the Chairman reassured those present as to the continuing soundness of the Company's prospects."

"But Mamma," I said, "this doesn't look very good at all. Why did they need to be reassured?"

She looked at me in surprise: "But Mr Sancious says I should buy more shares, so he must think things are going well."

I read on: "The Chairman announced that a further subscription of shares was being offered to those already holding stock in the Company's equity, the monies to be used to meet its current mortgage liabilities. We therefore, Madam, urge you to purchase another five hundred pounds' worth of shares in order to protect the investment you have already made."

I looked up: "But that doesn't sound good at all. I think he means that if you do not put in more, you will lose everything."

She gasped: "Don't say such things, Johnnie."

I turned back to the letter which ended: "And since you have no money left in ready cash we enclose a promissory note at six months by which date the situation will have resolved itself. You should accept the bill by signing it in the presence of a witness."

"Why does he say you have no money left?"

She started weeping: "Johnnie, I have something terrible to tell you. After we discussed it all that time ago and agreed to invest just three hundred pounds, I decided to buy more shares than that."

"What! Why did you do that?"

"I was afraid Mr Sancious would be offended if I didn't, and besides, it seemed such a good investment."

"How much?"

"A thousand pounds," she sobbed.

"How could you be so foolish!"

"Don't speak to me like that. I did it for your sake. And anyway, if it comes to that, it's your fault, too, Johnnie."

"What do you mean?"

"Why, don't you recall, just before Christmas when that woman and her little boy came, I wanted to sacrifice the investment I had made but you agreed that it was right to put in more money."

I exclaimed: "But I didn't know that you had invested so much already! That meant you were putting in the last money we had!"

"But the more I stood to lose the more reason there was for trying to save it!"

"No, the more reason for not risking any more! You're so silly!" I cried. "And how could you do it without asking me? I hate you."

She hid her face in her hands and wept and I rushed out of the room. I ran up to my own bed-chamber and hurled myself onto the bed sobbing. Why did she do such things? Why was she so rash? And to have hidden her actions from me was so underhand. I vowed that I really would stop loving her from now on. She was weak and foolish and from now on I would be strong and cold towards her.

After several hours I felt better and prepared myself to receive her when she came up to bid me goodnight. I don't believe I had quite determined to make an apology but I'm sure I had resolved that I was not going to upbraid her again. But I waited and waited and at last realized that for the first time ever she was not going to come. I wondered what she was doing and it occurred to me that she might be feeling very much as I felt now. Perhaps she was finding it just as difficult to forgive me for what I had said as I was to pardon her for what she had done. But what I had said had been true and she had been silly and deceitful.

I slept badly and next morning at breakfast I was cold and silent and didn't look at her. But then our gaze met accidentally and I could see that she had been crying. I don't know which of us was first, but we both burst into tears and threw our arms around each other and laughed and cried. But even as I hugged her I felt something cold and hard inside me that didn't quite melt then.

When we had gone into the sitting-room and seated ourselves my mother said: "What should we do about this business, Johnnie?"

"I suppose we will have to do as Mr Sancious suggests, otherwise we might lose even more."

"I suppose you're right," she said and we turned back to the letter:

"In order to raise this sum we have secured an arrangement with a broking-house of the utmost respectability under which you may accept a bill of hand dated at six months. What this means is that, in return for five hundred pounds now you undertake to repay that amount, with interest, on a date six months from now once the Company has consolidated its position. We have pleasure in enclosing the appropriate document, stamp-duty paid, for you to sign in the presence of a witness."

"I have so little left," my mother said, "I don't know how we will manage for the next six months."

"We cannot afford to keep Bissett, can we?" I said softly and she shook her head. "Then let me ask her to come and witness the bill and then you can explain everything."

"I suppose I must."

So I summoned Bissett from the kitchen where bread-making was in progress. She went out dusting her floury hands on her apron and I stayed behind to talk to Sukey.

"Have you heard, Master John, the common is to be 'closed?" she said as she kneaded.

"By whom?"

"Why, the Mumpseys, in course. Mr Assinder has spoke to us all and says we s'all be the better of it, for we're all to have a piece of land of our own."

"Well, I hope he may be right."

Sukey put the dough on top of the oven and covered it with a cloth.

Just then the door opened and my mother entered. "Will you both come to the sitting-room immediately?" she said gravely.

Looking at each other in surprise we followed her out. In the sitting-room we found Bissett sitting with an expression of great solemnity on the sopha. My mother seated herself beside her while Sukey and I stood together facing them.

"Now Johnnie," my mother began; "I know you always speak the truth. Has Sukey ever taken you to places you ought not to have gone?"

The thought of Hougham flashed into my mind. In the hope of deflecting attention from that episode I said boldly: "Yes, she has taken me to her mother's cottage several times."

"Jist as I said, ma'am," Bissett muttered.

"And did you ever see her give food from here to her family?"

"Well," I hesitated; "just once, but I'm sure it was only left-overs."

"That's still stealing," put in Bissett. "She's only allowed what she eats here as part of her wages. But I'll wager more than left-overs has gone from that larder."

"What is the truth of this, Susan?" asked my mother.

Sukey began to sob: "I did take things home, ma'am, but I never took nought save what was due to me. I'm 'lowed to keep the old tea-leaves and grouts and coffee-grounds and the ashes."

"'Cordin' to who?" Bissett asked.

"Mrs Belflower always let me."

"She ain't in the question no more."

"And I ate less myself often and often so as I could take more home."

"Well, but you should have asked me, you know, Susan. It's very wrong to take what doesn't belong to you, under any circumstances."

"'Ougham, ma'am," Bissett suddenly muttered, to my dismay.

I saw Sukey colour up suddenly.

My mother turned to me: "Now, darling, did Sukey ever take you to any other places you were not supposed to go?"

I hesitated but looking at Bissett's triumphant and watchful expression I said: "Yes, we went to Hougham once."

"I told you so, ma'am!" exclaimed Bissett.

"Now Johnnie," said my mother; "I know it was a long time ago and you were very little, but please try to remember if you spoke to anyone there."

I saw Sukey watching me fearfully and thought of the fate of her family if she lost her place. After all, it wasn't her fault that I had spoken to Henrietta. "No, I don't remember," I answered. As I spoke I caught Bissett's eye and the strangest look passed between us: surprise, suspicion, suppressed indignation and I don't know what. It was as if she was certain that I was lying. But how could she be?

"You don't remember?" my mother prompted.

"I'm sure I did not," I answered.

My mother was obviously relieved. "Well, Sukey ... " she began.

"Be firm, ma'am," Bissett said in an undertone.

"You know, Susan, you have broken my trust and with the bad news about money that I've just heard, I'm afraid I'll have to give you your wages."

"But they've nothing to keep them but what she brings them," I protested.

"You see, ma'am?" said Bissett. "You've been supporting the whole fambly out of that kitchen. No wonder we've found it so hard to manage and arst each other many a time where the money was going!"

"You've been very good to me, ma'am," Sukey sobbed. "I wish I hadn't of done it, and I knowed it was wrong."

"Go and colleck your things," said Bissett. "And before you leave this house I'll look through everythin' you take."

"I don't think you need to do that," my mother murmured, but Bissett glanced at her sharply and she fell silent.

Sukey flung her pin-before over her face and ran from the room.

"But Bissett," said my mother, who was clearly upset by this scene, "even without Sukey's wages, I can't afford to keep you on now, either."

"Never you mind about my wages," she replied. "I'll stay with you anyway, ma'am. Even if you can only pay me no more than you paid Sukey."

I was astonished by Bissett's response, and in particular by her equation of herself in this way with the despised servant-girl.

My mother seized her round the neck and hugged her: "Oh, Bissett, you're a true friend!" she exclaimed.

"I know where my duty lies," Bissett said harshly, standing stiffly and not returning my mother's hug.

Her eyes met mine over my mother's shoulder.

"How did you come to know all that about Sukey?" I demanded. "It was years ago that we went to Hougham."

Her face darkened slightly and after a moment's hesitation she replied: "I heard it in the village."

I stared at her angrily and at that moment a number of suspicions fell into place.

When she had left the room to superintend Sukey's departure, my mother said to me: "How loyal Bissett is. I do feel guilty now for sometimes thinking that she cared too much for money. It's clear that she loves us. You know she agreed to accept a cut in her wages that other time when I told her I could not go on paying her so much and we expected her to leave?"

Sukey went home that same evening, and what kind of reception she must have had when she brought the news home, I hated to think. Before she left I might record, since I have to record so many thoughts and actions to my own discredit, that I persuaded her to accept the two shillings and a few pence that I had accumulated from my allowance. My mother was also crying when she took leave of her under the watchful eye of Bissett, but I saw her manage to slip some coins into the girl's hand.

BOOK V

Relations

CHAPTER 21

It is the late evening of a dark wet day and the shutters of the counting house down by the river are drawn and bolted. Inside the inner closet Mr Clothier is sitting with Mr Sancious, both bent over papers which are spread out on his desk. The fire is burning low and before it stand a pair of chairs and a table with two tumblers upon it. These, like the bottle of wine propped against one of the fire-dogs and gently mulling, are waiting for the two gentlemen to conclude their business.

"Well, Mr Clothier," says the attorney with a smile, "now that the West London Building Company has gone into liquidation without ever paying anything for its lease, the Consolidated Metropolitan Building Company is unable to pay its ground-rents to the freeholder. I therefore see no alternative to a declaration of insolvency and the institution of proceedings of bankruptcy."

"Exactly so, my dear sir," the old gentleman responds brightly. "I am lost. Utterly lost. Every last blessed penny."

"You take it remarkably well, sir."

"I believe I do," the old gentleman says with a droll expression and shaking his head.

"With true Christian fortitude," the lawyer adds and the old gentleman looks at him sharply and then smiles.

"I wonder how Quintard and Mimpriss will take it," the attorney speculates, "when your company defaults on the mortgage and they find the leasehold worth so much less than their advance."

The old gentleman smiles uneasily.

"They were very rash to accept the mortgage," Mr Sancious muses. Then he says suddenly: "You must have a friend at court there."

Mr Clothier looks at him suspiciously and then mutters: "Nonsense, nonsense. It's still a fair price. But I congratulate you, Mr Sancious. That man of yours was very sharp. The joiner. He brought plenty of gulls into the game."

"He has been well paid for it. But you remind me that I have a request to tender on his behalf: would you allow him the use of one the properties?"

"Why, they're the freeholder's now!" the old gentleman says with a laugh.

"Then shall I ask Vulliamy?" Mr Sancious says sweetly.

"Eh, how do you know about that?" Mr Clothier gasps in amazement.

"How else should I know but from himself?"

"I almost begin to be afraid of you, Mr Sancious," the old gentleman confesses. "You're so wide-awake. Yes, Vulliamy is the nominal freeholder, if you must know." He stands and moves towards the hearth: "Now, my dear sir, will you do me the honour of taking a glass of wine with me?"

"The honour would be entirely mine, Mr Clothier."

The two gentlemen seat themselves in front of the fire and the host pours the wine. Then Mr Sancious leans back comfortably. "You say you are surprised by how much I know, Mr Clothier. Will you bear with me while I tell you a story?"

"Go ahead, my dear sir," the old gentleman responds, slightly nervously.

"I think you will find an interest in it. Let me emphasize that it is only a story." The other gentleman nods and he goes on: "Very well, then. Let us suppose that in the course of my professional duties I discovered that a client of mine was very anxious to remain hidden. Let us suppose that I found out from whom it was that my client wished to remain concealed, and that it was revealed to be two parties who were as anxious to find that person as she — for it is a lady — was to remain concealed. And each eager to do so before the other party."

By now Mr Clothier is sitting up straight in his chair and staring intently at the other gentleman. He is about to speak, but Mr Sancious holds up a hand: "Patience, please, my dear sir. Let us suppose that I encouraged this client to invest all her little capital."

At this Mr Clothier sharply draws in his breath.

The attorney continues: "In, let us say, a promising project which, due to unforeseen circumstances, unfortunately failed. And that I got her, in an attempt to extricate herself from her difficulties, to sign a bill for five hundred pounds. And then suppose further that I learned that a very respectable and well-to-do gentleman — much like your good self — was one of those who wanted to find that person. Suppose further that I knew that she had in her possession a document and guessed that this gentleman wanted to obtain it. And then let us suppose that I learned that this gentleman was involved in a suit in which a large amount of property was at stake, and that the document was relevant to that. Now, supposing all that to be the case, would you have anything to say to me, Mr Clothier?"

"Does she have a child?" the old gentleman stammers.

"I am struck by the fact that that should be your first question. Your feelings do you credit, my dear sir. Indeed she does."

At this the old gentleman gives a cry and rises to his feet as the glass falls from his hand.

CHAPTER 22

After Sukey's departure it necessarily followed that I was occasionally allowed to go out alone in the afternoon on those days when my mother was unable to accompany me. On one such occasion early in July, as I began to walk towards the village I noticed a stranger lounging against a tree by the Rose and Crab. An "outcomeling" being a fairly unusual sight in Melthorpe, I took special note of him. He was of middling years and wore a wide-awake hat, a fine green great-coat, and hessian boots of a kind that I had rarely seen before. By his dress I would have taken him for a gentleman, but his lounging, idling manner suggested otherwise. He took no notice of me and I walked on.

Since it had been raining hard all morning, though the sun had come out as I left the house, the ways were muddy underfoot. As I passed Farmer Lubbenham's Sixteen-acre between the Moat-piece and the Green, I heard the noise of a set of clappers and saw a boy tenting the crows. He wore a patched round frock and a blue cap — both drenched from the morning's rain — and was shaking at intervals the three heavy wooden slabs which were attached by cords and the central one of which had a handle. It seemed to me to be very fine to be out alone in the fields all day. Enviously, I waved to him but he appeared not to notice me.

I walked on, looking at the green swathes of newly-growing corn and the hay-fields either already tedded or standing in their luxuriously-scented quiles. I walked to the top of Gallow-tree-hill and then back, making a full circuit of the Green. As I approached the Sixteen-acre again, the boy was standing near the hedge so that I now saw that it was Harry, Sukey's brother.

I greeted him and he stared at me in a somewhat surly way through his clear blue eyes.

"Who's that cove as follered you when you went past?" he asked.

"I don't know what you mean."

"Here he comes agin," Harry answered and then began to shake the clappers furiously as he moved away.

I turned in surprise and saw that the stranger I had seen earlier was coming into sight behind me, a considerable way back and walking with a careless, slouching sort of gait. I walked on and he stayed behind me all the way up the High-street.

Now it came to me that if I were to call at the post-office-cum-general-store to see if the post had brought anything I would be marking a new stage in my shouldering of the responsibilities of the household. At first Mr Passant, the post-master, made some difficulties but at last he consented and to my surprise he handed me, in addition to a letter for my mother, one addressed to Bissett. My mother's letter was in the hand of Mrs Fortisquince and I supposed that it contained an enclosure from Mr Sancious. Bissett's letter had a seal — for this, of course, was before the time of envelopes — whose impression I could not make out. I walked homewards studying it and as I rounded the corner opposite the church, saw ahead of me two figures standing close together before the Rose and Crab. I recognised one of them as the stranger and the other was Bissett. Immediately they separated, the stranger crossing the road and entering the church-yard, while Bissett came towards me.

"Who was that man, Mrs Bissett?" I asked.

"How should I know?" she replied curtly. "He only arst me to set him on the way to the Green."

"I should think he would know that since I saw him there," I said. Bissett seemed about to say something but I went on quickly: "Here's a letter for you."

She snatched it from me and stuffed it into her basket. "You've no business collecting the post," she said. "Don't never do it again, do you understand?"

"I think that's for my mother to say," I said.

"We s'll see what your mother says," she answered and began to walk on saying: "I've my marketing to do now. Go straight home."

After that injunction, of course, I made a circuit past our house and over the fields towards Mortsey-wood, getting my boots (whose cleaning now fell upon myself) thoroughly muddy so that Bissett would know what I had done. When honour was satisfied, I went home and found my mother in the sitting-room. I gave the letter to her and when she opened it there was, indeed, a letter inside from Mr Sancious with only the customary brief covering note from Mrs Fortisquince. As my mother read I saw a growing horror on her face.

"What has happened?" I exclaimed.

She stared at me in terror: "We are ruined."

"What? How can that be?"

For answer she repeated phrases from the letter: "'The Company has defaulted on its mortgage and the bank has foreclosed. The Company has therefore gone into liquidation and the lease has been redeemed by the freeholder.'"

"But Mr Sancious said it was so safe. He said we could not lose our money!" I protested.

She began to weep and the letter fluttered from her hand to lie on the carpet. I picked it up and the characters swam before my eyes for a moment or two but one sentence stood out: "The house having broke for a sum far in excess of its assets, you are consequently liable, as a shareholder, for that amount of the outstanding debts to which your shareholding is proportionate, namely up to thirty shillings in the pound." A cold chill seemed to clutch at my heart as I read these words. I continued: "There is also, of course, the bill whose term falls due within a few weeks. There can be no question of renewing it under the present circumstances and its redemption is therefore a matter of the utmost priority. To effect this your only course of action is to sell all that you own. If you have anything of value that could be sold you should do so in order to realize this sum wholly or in part. We can take it upon ourselves to sell at a very reasonable commission anything of this nature that you may possess."

I folded the letter away in my pocket, for my mother, lying sobbing on the sopha, was in no state to hear the rest of it.

"How unlucky I have been!" she was sobbing.

I would have chosen another term, I reflected coldly as I looked down at her.

At that moment Bissett entered without knocking. She glanced at my mother and with a shake of her head directed at me went to her.

"What's amiss, Mrs Mellamphy? Has the boy been unkind again?"

"There's no need for you here, Bissett," I said. "She's had some bad news."

"It's 'Mrs Bissett' and I'll judge whether or no I'm needed."

And so I could do nothing as Bissett led my mother out of the room and up to her own chamber. When they had gone I took out the letter and read it again. Why had Mr Sancious asked if we had anything that could be sold when surely he knew that there was nothing? Nothing, that was, apart from that mysterious document of which the lawyer was surely unaware. Who was this man and how much did he know about us? And what was his part in the disaster that had befallen us?

When I came down to breakfast the next morning I found my mother already at the table. She was dark-eyed and pale of face.

"Did you sleep well?" I asked.

"Oh yes," she said wistfully. "Mrs Bissett made me such a wonderful sleeping-draught that I went off immediately. And I had such marvellous dreams."

When we had helped Bissett to clear away the breakfast things, we went into the drawing-room and sat together on the sopha. Without saying anything of my suspicions, I told her that I thought that Bissett should be kept from involvement in our problems as far as possible, and she said she agreed. Now we estimated what our property would be worth and reckoned it to be not less than three hundred and not more than five hundred pounds.

"Then with the hundred pounds left in the Consols," I said, "we have more than enough to pay back the five hundred pounds."

"But then we should have no money left at all!" my mother cried. "And how should we live now that we have nothing coming in?"

"I don't know, Mamma, but from what Mr Sancious says, I believe we should pay off that bill or else our debts will increase."

She was silent for a few moments and then said: "There is one last hope."

"Do you mean, to sell that document?"

She shook her head in surprise but when I pressed her to tell me what in that case she did mean, she would say nothing more. However, she opened her escritoire and spent the rest of the morning composing a letter. In the afternoon we walked into the village and put it in the post-office.

It was about six o'clock the next evening and my mother and I were in the drawing-room when we heard the sound of a carriage pulling up outside. I looked out of window and saw just at the foot of the steps a gleaming phaeton drawn by two splendid beasts. With a sense of added excitement I noticed that emblazoned on the side-pannel was the crest I remembered so well: the crab and the five roses. As I watched, a footman in magnificent livery who was standing on the back, swung himself to the ground and came up the steps. There followed the most tremendous hammering that I had ever heard. My mother and I gazed at each other in terror. After a moment we heard Bissett hurrying from the back of the house past our door, and then the muffled sounds of an exchange in which we could not catch the words. Then I saw the magnificent being reappear as he descended the steps and then climbed back onto the carriage. The driver shook the reins and the vehicle moved quickly off.

I turned and saw that Bissett had come into the room and was holding out a letter: "What do them Mumpseys want of you, Mrs Mellamphy?" she asked. " 'Twas them for sure, for they're the only folks in this country as has Lunnun servants and carriages, as I knows on."

"Thank you, Mrs Bissett," my mother said, taking the letter and, catching my eye, she said no more.

Bissett waited for a moment and then:

"Well, I've plenty of work to do if nobody else has," she said, and left the room shutting the door behind her rather fiercely.

Glancing nervously at me my mother opened the letter. "The hand is very difficult to read," she said, peering at it closely. "Why, he will see me!" Then she bent forward again to decypher it: "Tomorrow," she added and then looked up at me and said in surprise: "And, Johnnie, he wishes you to accompany me."

I felt a surge of pride at being summoned in this way, but it was mingled with apprehension, too.

"Why?" I asked.

She looked away and at last said: "It is a good sign. It means that Sir Perceval is interested in your welfare."

Why should he be? I demanded. What was the connexion between him and us? She would say no more, however, and I gave up asking. She allowed me to look at the letter (written in what — had it not been Sir Perceval's hand — I would have called an illiterate scrawl) but its burden was as plain as her account of it.

That night I lay in bed thinking about my mother's unhappiness. I had always believed that I had power over reality, that by exercising my will I could change things in the great outer world. It was a secret gift that I would never — indeed, could never — use unless I was in desperate circumstances, but which was always latent within me. At some time I might find myself imprisoned, perhaps, in a dungeon, and then, late at night when my gaolers had gone to bed, I would call upon this mysterious power and by its agency bore a hole in the wall or pull apart the bars of my cell and so escape.

Now I lay in the darkness listening to the rustling of the trees and wondering whether to summon up this power and test its efficacy in this unforeseen situation in which what was wanted was not physical strength but money. After lengthy reflection, I decided that its time had not yet come and I would not risk offending and so perhaps losing it by calling upon it prematurely. Comforted by this decision, I drifted at last into sleep.

The next morning my mother and I, wearing our best clothes, set off through the village and up Gallow-tree-hill. It was a beautiful day with only a gentle breeze blowing, sending the fleecy clouds scudding across the blue sky. The distant hills melted into shapelessness like a faintly blue mist, and in the sloping park-land to our left, the trees swayed gently like thick green feathers. At the top of the hill, to my surprise, instead of following the turnpike-road towards Hougham village, we went up to the gates of the demesne from which the carriage had come those many years before that had so alarmed my mother. They now stood shut, but my mother boldly knocked on the window of the porter's lodge in the shadow of the great gate-posts, and the man came out with an ill grace, wiping the back of his hand against his mouth, and opened one of the gates to admit us.

"This is more direct, Johnnie," my mother explained; "and anyway it is the right way to come when you are making a call."

So we began to walk along the carriage-drive which led gently downwards through the park in a succession of curves. It was lined with tall elm trees like those that stood in groups, elegantly interspersed down the sides of the valley into which the drive descended. As we looked down, we saw how the course of the stream along the bottom of the valley was marked by a line of willows as crooked as the vein along an ancient arm.

As we walked I urged my mother to answer my questions of the day before, but she was still reluctant. Then as we rounded the last curve and the landscape opened before us, she stopped. Ahead of us the wooded slopes of the valley undulated into the distance, and more than a mile away as the ground rose I could just make out a grey rectangle which I took to be the great house.

My mother said softly: "All of this was once my grandfather's."

I had been right! All that I had guessed from Mrs Belflower's story was true! I remembered stirring the Christmas pudding all that time ago and the wish I had made then.

"You see, my father was called John Huffam, for you are named for him," she went on. "Now, Johnnie, you must never tell anyone of our connexion with that name because it could be very dangerous."

I blushed at the memory of my indiscretion to the little girl and the lady who had been with her.

My mother did not notice: "The family dwindled and my father was the last to bear the name. So you and I are the sole descendants."

"They were a very old family, weren't they?"

"I suppose so."

"And did they build the great house we're going to?"

"I'm not sure. I believe it's not terribly old and there was another house, the Old Hall which is near here. I believe we might be able to see it in the distance."

"How did all this come to belong to the Mompessons?"

"Ah, that is the whole point. A long time ago my grandfather, James, got into difficulties over money."

"James? Did he lose heavily because of high play and drink?"

She looked at me in surprise: "Why, I believe all the gentlemen did in those days."

"And did he murder his father?"

My mother stopped suddenly and stared at me in horror: "Whoever told you that?"

"It was one of Mrs Belflower's stories," I said defensively.

"Well, it's nonsense, utter nonsense." She walked on: "You must never speak like that again." After a few moments she continued: "I was telling you how he sold the estate to his brother-in-law, the grandfather of Sir Perceval."

"So now the Mompessons own it?" I asked in disappointment.

"Well, I'm afraid it's not quite so simple. I only wish it had been. Now everything hangs upon that sale, Johnnie, and it is because of it that we are here today, for part of the contract was that Sir Perceval's grandfather made an agreement to pay in perpetuity to James and his heirs a certain income from the estate, that is to say, an annuity. That is quite a regular way of paying for something if you don't have enough money. It's a kind of mortgage. I inherited it from my father and you will inherit it from me."

"Is it very much?"

"Yes, a very great deal: nearly fifteen hundred pounds a year."

"Goodness! Then we're rich?"

"No, of course not, because they stopped paying it when my father died."

"Why? How could they?"

"Oh, Johnnie, please don't ask so many questions. There are reasons that I ... There are many reasons. It's partly because there has been a suit in Chancery about the ownership of the estate for many years because of that sale."

"Who claims ownership of it?"

"That is no concern of ours."

I surveyed the park and reflected that it would be a fine thing to look on all this as my own.

As we progressed, the sunken stream that I knew ran through our own

Mortsey-woods came in sight emerging from a spinney that coursed along the valley's floor. Further along and on our left we glimpsed the silvery glint of water, and after some minutes saw that there was a long, narrow lake beneath the steep wooded hill opposite us. Eventually the drive curved down to run along one side of it, winding in and out of the folds of the valley so that the great house vanished and re-appeared at intervals.

"Look," my mother said. "Beyond the lake there are chimneys above the far slope. I believe that must be the Old Hall."

I could just make out the tall twisting chimneys in the distance. As I stared I asked: "Who lives there now?"

"It's a ruin. Nobody has lived there for many years."

"But tell me, who was bringing the suit?"

My mother's face darkened: "Our enemy."

"Who is that?"

"I've told you that I won't tell you."

"You must."

She refused and we walked on in silence.

We reached the end of the lake where it narrowed to form a long stretch of water curving around the front of the mansion for here, on the other side of an elegant bridge and on top of a slight rise, stood the house itself.

Suddenly my mother said: "One day you'll know everything. I'm writing a relation of my life so that you will understand ... understand everything, but only when you are old enough."

"When can I read it?" I demanded.

"When you come of age. And there is also a letter from my father that you may read then."

The letter I had seen in the japanned box with the tiger-hunt which held the locket that my mother had shewn me! The letter was for me!

"Must I wait so long?" I protested.

"Yes," she said quietly. "Unless something happens to me."

Puzzled by her meaning, I walked on in silence.

We were near the house now and, viewed straight on rather than from the side as I had seen it on my visit to Hougham with Sukey, it was an imposing building. Its central block was lofty and surmounted by a pediment with Corinthian columns forming a high portico whose entrance one reached by means of a pair of semi-circular steps thrusting forward like the claws of a crab. This portion was flanked by two wings, linked to it by a curving section.

In a few minutes we had begun to ascend those steps and my heart began to pound with excitement. When we arrived at the tall, glazed doors at the top a servant in the livery of scarlet and chocolate that I had seen the day before, strode forward with a slight bow. As he straightened it seemed to me that on his otherwise impassive features was a hostile stare of enquiry, as if demanding to know who dared to ascend these steps after making so undistinguished an arrival on foot.

To this august being and his powdered wig my mother replied: "Will you please tell Sir Perceval and Lady Mompesson that Mrs Mellamphy and her son are here. I believe they are expecting us."

The footman eyed us coldly. "Very good, ma'am," he answered. "Will you please to enter and wait here?"

Although he deferentially indicated the open door behind him and stepped back to allow us to pass, the tone in which he spoke made this less an invitation than an instruction. Obediently, we stepped across the threshold and found ourselves in a large entrance-hall, high-ceilinged and marble-floored, with magnificent doors in every wall. Great fires of hewn logs were burning in the two fireplaces, and a number of high-backed chairs were set against the walls, but it was quite deserted. Standing in the very centre was a huge urn decorated with stone garlands and rams' sculls. High up at intervals on the tops of the friezes were busts of bony white heads which were quite bald and bore little circlets of flowers like crazy wigs.

The footman had followed us in and now disappeared through one of the doors. We stood hesitating in the centre of the vast room.

I indicated two unoccupied chairs and said in an undertone: "Shall we sit down?"

"Do you think we ought?" she whispered back.

I was annoyed that she was so cowed and seeing this, she chose a seat and sat down. I stood beside her.

We waited for what seemed a very long time. At last the footman reappeared and advanced upon us. Towering over us, he bellowed:

"Sir Perceval and Lady Mompesson will receive you in the justice-room. Kindly be good enough to follow me, madam."

The justice-room, I repeated silently. This venue seemed to augur well.

"Should he come?" my mother asked, glancing anxiously at me.

"Sir Perceval and Lady Mompesson was most particular, madam, that the young genel'man should be brung to the ante-chamber adj'ining of the room what they will receive you in."

And so we set off, following that broad back as the footman strode ahead at such a pace that we had almost to run to keep up with him. How many passages we walked along, how many stairs we climbed, how many huge rooms we traversed, I have no idea. Yet, dazed as I was at being inside that house at last, I could not help noticing that the livery on the back turned to us was patched and worn, the epaulettes tarnished and the stocks in which the magnificent calves were encased were yellowed and much-repaired. Similarly, the carpets were threadbare and everywhere there was an air of delapidation and neglect.

At last, from the landing of a magnificent staircase we passed into a small room where it was made clear to me that I was to wait. The footman advanced to the other end of the room and, flinging open the lofty double doors that led into the next chamber, bellowed: "Mrs Mellamphy!"

With a timid glance back at me, my mother went through the doors. The servant drew them shut behind her and, with a stern look at myself as if defying me to misbehave, went out through the door to the landing. I was left in absolute silence. I pressed my ear against the door through which my mother had vanished, but could hear nothing. I looked around me. The room had no windows, and the walls, except where pictures hung, were lined with book-shelves containing severely uniform leather-bound volumes which seemed never to have been touched.

Suddenly I heard the sound of footsteps running lightly past the door by which we had entered. The runner was panting heavily and seemed to be in distress. After a moment I heard the sound of another, equally quick but much heavier person running as if in pursuit. Just outside the door the pursuer seemed to overtake the pursued, and I heard the sounds of a scuffle. A girl's voice cried out: "No, don't, don't!" Then there was a sharp cry of pain, and the sound of the pursuit resumed as the two ran out of hearing.

I seized the heavy handle of one of the great doors and turned it, then cautiously pushed. The door moved. Bringing my eye to the crack I had thus opened up, I looked along the passage that led from the landing. It was empty, but after a moment I heard the sound of running feet and a figure appeared coming towards me. It was a girl of about my own age, but there was something strange about the way she was running. Then I recognised her as the pale-faced child I had met at the gate of this house all that time ago.

She was almost upon me now, and I pushed open the door and called out: "Henrietta!"

She looked at me in amazement but slowed her run.

"Come in here!" I whispered and I think at that moment she remembered me. She ran in, squeezing herself through the gap with surprising difficulty, and I quickly pushed the door shut. A moment later the heavier footsteps came running down the passage, passed the door, and faded out of hearing.

Henrietta stood panting and gazing at me. She was wearing a plain dark dress with a blue sash and her long black hair fell in ringlets around her face that seemed, for her black eyes, so pale.

"Do you remember who I am?" I asked in an undertone.

She nodded as if too out of breath to speak and as she did so I noticed that her arms and head appeared to be oddly constrained, so that as her head moved so the rest of her upper body seemed to follow. She leaned back against the door and there was a clattering sound of two hard objects colliding and I was disconcerted by this for it made her seem something strange — like a creature made of wood.

"You're the boy I met whose name is the same as one of mine," she gasped.

"Who was chasing you?" I asked.

"Tom."

"Does he hurt you?"

She pulled up one sleeve a little way and showed me her forearm: it was covered in bruises and had several long scars.

I shuddered: "I'll fight him for you!"

"If it wasn't for this thing I could scratch his eyes out!" she said, indicating the wooden contraption strapped to her shoulders.

"What is it for?"

"It's a back-board. It is to rectify my posture."

Suddenly she broke off and listened intently. In a moment I heard the footsteps that had just run past the door. They were coming back, but this time at a walking pace. We froze until they had gone past, then Henrietta said: "Even he will soon guess that I am here." She moved back towards the door.

"Are you ever allowed out alone?"

She looked at me in surprise: "Why do you ask?"

"Because I should like to meet you. Should you like to have me as your friend?"

She seemed to reflect before she replied: "Yes, I think I should like to have a friend. I'm never allowed out alone or permitted to go outside the park. But on Sunday afternoons, if it's fine, my governess and I walk to the Pantheon. I must go now."

"Then I'll try to meet you one day. Where is it?" (I was determined not to ask what it was.) "And won't your governess stop you from speaking to me?"

"It's in the little wood above the lake. You can find it easily because of the cascade that runs down from it. And as for ... "

At that moment the door opened softly and a young lady, whose footsteps we had not heard, came in. She wore a plain dark dress and was tall and, I thought, very beautiful: her clear grey eyes and well-shaped mouth conveyed an impression of gravity nicely balanced with playfulness and wit.

"Are you hiding from your cousin again?" she asked with concern. Then she noticed me and smiled.

I recalled Mrs Digweed saying that the young governess here had pleaded her cause with the housekeeper and smiled back at her.

"This is the boy I told you about, Miss Quilliam," Henrietta said.

"How do you do, Master Mellamphy," she said, holding out her hand. "I have heard a great deal about you."

I looked at Henrietta in surprise. What could she have said? Before I could speak she began to talk about our hopes of meeting again. Miss Quilliam listened gravely and asked me some courteous but searching questions which I believed I could answer without betraying any of my mother's confidences.

"Then we may, mayn't we?" Henrietta asked.

At that moment the door was flung violently open hitting the young lady's back and hiding her behind the door. A burly youth sprang into the room with an exultant shout at Henrietta: "You sly creature! I guessed you had tried to hide in here! But I'm too clever for you, ain't I?"

The youth was about seventeen, quite tall and sturdily grown. He had a coarsely-featured red face and short, carrotty hair. He was wearing dark-blue mixture pantaloons, Wellington boots and a black waistcoat. He did not look anything like the boy I had seen in the carriage all those years ago. (In fact it was not he but his brother whom I had seen, as I later understood.) He had just seized Henrietta by one arm and raised his hand as if to strike her, when he caught sight of me: "Hello! What have we here?"

He lowered his hand but tightened his grip on the little girl.

At that moment the young lady, pushing the door out of the way, stepped forward and said: "Mr Tom! That is not the way to enter a room."

"What, are you here too, missy?" he exclaimed.

"Release Miss Henrietta. I have told you before: a young gentleman does not play with boys and girls still in the school-room."

"Ride your own mare, missy," Tom said. "I ain't your scholar."

"Please, Tom!" Henrietta protested.

"Who are you, boy?" the youth said, with an insolent emphasis on the last word.

"Let go of her," I demanded.

"How dare you speak to me in that way," he retorted. "What is your business here? Why did they let you in?"

"I have as much right to be here as you," I said angrily. "More right, if justice were done."

At this the youth sketched a coarse laugh rather than laughed, as if indicating that amusement was called for rather than that I had said anything funny. In the face of such stupidity combined with such arrogance I felt a hatred I had never experienced before.

"Mr Thomas, if you do not release Miss Henrietta I shall have to report your conduct to your tutor," the young lady said.

"I don't care a fig for him!" the young gentleman replied.

I stepped up to him and said: "Let go of her or I will hit you."

Suddenly he released Henrietta and swung his fist at me striking me in the chest so that I stumbled backwards, lost my balance, and fell to the floor. Henrietta cried out and, lying on the floor, I saw the youth hit her in the face quite hard with the flat of his hand. The young lady ran forward and laid a hand on his arm but he shook her off and advanced towards me, drawing back one booted foot as if to drive it into my face.

I rolled aside and seized one of his shins but he gripped me by the head and began to bang it — though not as hard as he might have — against the wall. Henrietta began to hit him on the shoulder and he elbowed her aside.

At that moment a commanding voice said: "What in the name of goodness is going on here?"

Tom coloured and moved sheepishly away from me. As I scrambled to my feet I saw a tall lady standing in the door-way into the adjoining room. Although she was some years older than my mother, I could see that she was far from old but was in that puzzling region between the two states. There was something in her face that made me think it handsome rather than beautiful — and certainly not pretty — and as she looked at us now, anger and disdain were manifest upon it.

"Will nobody answer me? Miss Quilliam, what is the explanation for this extraordinary scene?"

"I hardly know, Lady Mompesson, for my own scarcely preceded your arrival."

"Indeed?" she said with a horribly deliberate kind of icy surprise. Her gaze swung round: "You screamed I think, Henrietta. Why?"

Henrietta glanced at the youth and he made a growling gesture with his mouth: "I only cried out when John fell over, Aunt Isabella."

The lady's lips pursed slightly: "And what have you to say, Tom?"

"I was only kicking up a bit of a lark, Mamma."

She shuddered: "Must we be subjected to the language of the stables?"

"Henrietta's right," I said. "It was nothing. I only tripped."

Lady Mompesson's gaze was turned upon me but so expressionlessly that I almost wondered if I had spoken. Then she addressed herself to Henrietta: "You have no business to be in here. Go to the school-room immediately with Miss Quilliam where you will be punished for your disobedience."

Henrietta, accompanied by the young governess, quickly left the room without looking at me.

"As for you, Tom." She paused and looked at him reflectively. "Go to your governor and tell him to give you something to do. And ask him to wait upon me after dinner. It is time we had another of our little talks."

"It wasn't my fault, Mamma," Tom whined. "She came in here and I came to find her because I knew she had no business in this room. Then this boy attacked me."

"You're a liar and a bully," I exclaimed. "She only hid in here because you were chasing her."

"Mamma, how dare this boy insult me?" cried the carrot-haired youth. "Why, he is not even a gentleman's son."

"Then," I said angrily, "neither are you, for I don't believe a gentleman would treat his cousin as you have just done." (Of course, I meant Henrietta.)

"Master Mellamphy is, as he reminds us, doubly entitled to our courtesy, for he is also a guest in this house," Lady Mompesson said to her son. "Be on your way now, Tom. This young man and I have business to attend to."

With a glare at me the youth slouched out of the room while Lady Mompesson with a muttered "Follow me" passed through the door-way into the next room, and I obeyed her, my heart pounding in excitement at the implications of what she had just said.

The room was vast and seemed even vaster by virtue of its being in half-darkness with the curtains pulled across the tall windows at the opposite end. A few lighted candles stood on side-tables around the walls. In the centre was a high-backed chair on which my mother sat with her back to the door by which I had just entered. Facing her was an old man reclining on a chaise-longue under a richly-embroidered covering, with his feet resting upon a gout-stool.

As we approached my mother looked round and gave me a timid smile. Looking at the old man's face I remembered the long sunken cheeks, the bleary eyes with their folds of skin beneath them, the protruding jaw and the stained skin, for he had changed not at all: it was the old gentleman in the carriage who had alarmed my mother the day after the burglary so long ago.

"This is the boy," said Lady Mompesson pushing me into the centre of the room so that I stood between the chaise-longue and my mother's chair.

"Bring him closer," said the old man.

Lady Mompesson pushed a bony fist into the small of my back and I was shoved forward.

Sir Perceval raised a spy-glass to one blood-shot eye and stared at me for a minute.

"He seems rather small," he pronounced eventually, speaking in a slurring drawl. "Is he not very robust?"

"He is well and strong, Sir Perceval, thank Heavens," said my mother.

"Excellent," he said without enthusiasm. "I am glad to have been reassured on that point."

Lady Mompesson seated herself on an elegant sopha beside her husband and uttered a request in the tone of a command: "Now will you show Sir Perceval and myself the item we have spoken of."

"Go back to the other room and wait for me, Johnnie," my mother said.

Surprised and disappointed, I protested: "Mayn't I stay?"

"Why not let him?" the old gentleman asked. "It consarns him, don't it?"

"If you wish it, Sir Perceval," my mother said timidly and looked at me reproachfully. "But you must promise to be silent."

I felt a little guilty at this victory and yet triumphant too. I nodded and moved towards her so that I stood beside her in her chair and we faced the other two.

My mother took one of the keys that hung from the chain around her waist and undid the lock that secured the slender document case which she always carried. Sir Perceval leaned forward eagerly as she found another key and unlocked the case itself. From it she took out a small paper that was rolled up into a cylinder secured by two brass rings at either end. None of us seemed even to breathe as she slid the rings free and carefully unrolled the paper. Standing behind her chair I could see that it was a single sheet of thick parchment covered with writing. Partly because I was too far away, but also because of the nature of the character which was beautifully regular but very strangely formed, I was unable to make out any of the words. A large red seal was affixed to the bottom of the paper, and there appeared to be three signatures just above it, for their irregularity contrasted with the rest of the writing.

"Let me look at it," said Sir Perceval, reaching out a bony, be-ringed claw towards it although he was much too far away to reach it.

My mother drew back and pressed the paper close to herself: "No, Sir Perceval," she exclaimed. "Please forgive me, but I must not allow you to touch it." He muttered something and sat back. She held it up so that they could see it and said: "I hope you will accept this as proof that my claim to the annuity is valid."

"Without prejudice to that question, Mrs Mellamphy," said Lady Mompesson, "we will go so far as this: assuming that that is the codicil of which you sent us a copy some seven years ago, we are prepared to purchase it from you."

My mother gasped: "Purchase it!" she exclaimed.

"In consideration," Lady Mompesson went on, "of the sum of fifteen hundred pounds."

"But it is not for sale!"

"That is our final offer," said Lady Mompesson, "and I assure you that you are wasting your time if you believe it will be increased."

"No," my mother insisted. "I cannot sell it."

"But, Mamma," I broke in, "only think: fifteen hundred pounds would save us from having to sell all our things."

I saw Lady Mompesson glance at Sir Perceval with a look of triumph at my words.

"Oh Johnnie, you shouldn't have said that." She addressed the Mompessons: "It is true that because of some ill fortune I have suffered, my son and I are penniless and I have no means of supporting us. And certainly no prospect of educating him to take his place in the world in the way that his birth ... "

"Madam," drawled Sir Perceval, "be so good as to come to the point."

My mother flushed and began to speak more hurriedly: "That is all I have come to ask for today: the annuity that I am entitled to."

"But you see, Mrs Mellamphy," Lady Mompesson replied languidly, "my husband and I do not admit that you are entitled to it, and that for reasons that our legal representatives have in the past seven or eight years on frequent occasions communicated to yours, and that we ourselves rehearsed at length not five minutes ago." She paused and then turned her gaze briefly on myself before saying dispassionately: "Do you wish me to repeat them now?"

"No," said my mother quickly, "please do not."

"But what we are prepared to offer you is a single payment for the codicil."

"But it is not mine to sell, Lady Mompesson." As she spoke my mother restored the document to its case and locked it up.

"I beg your pardon," Lady Mompesson said icily, "I do not understand you, Mrs Mellamphy."

"I tell you frankly I believe this to be a device," Sir Perceval said.

"No!" my mother cried. Then she went on in a lower tone but as if struggling to master her feelings: "I promised my father I would keep it. This document cost him ... cost him ... " Here she faltered and broke off.

"I said it was a question of price," the baronet exclaimed.

"I don't mean that!" my mother exclaimed. Then she reflected for a moment, glanced at me and said: "I promised my father that I would pass it on to my heir. And, moreover, I know you would destroy it if I sold it to you."

"And why the deuce should we not do so? Once we'd paid for it ... "

"A moment, Sir Perceval," his wife interrupted him. "*If* we did so," Lady Mompesson began frigidly; "and mark that I say 'if' since to do so would be to put ourselves in peril of an action for contempt of court since the document might be material evidence in a suit still before the courts; *if* we did so, it would be because we believed it to be a forgery."

"If it is a forgery then why are you so eager to have it?" I cried.

"Your son is very insolent, Mrs Mellamphy," said Lady Mompesson in a matter-of-fact tone. "Nevertheless, I will answer that highly impertinent question. Even a forgery could damage our interests by prolonging that infernal suit."

"It is not a forgery," my mother exclaimed. "My father was convinced of that."

Lady Mompesson smiled coldly: "But you see, my dear Mrs Mellamphy, your father might well not have been the most reliable authority in this matter. Consider how much he believed he stood to gain by it."

My mother looked at her and bit her lip. "I hardly know how to take your meaning, Lady Mompesson. I can't believe that you can be so cruel as to ... " She paused and then said impulsively: "But I can assure you that the other party to the suit believes it is genuine."

They both glanced quickly at each other.

"What the deuce do you mean?" Sir Perceval demanded.

"Somehow that party has learned that I have it and now knows where I am."

"What evidence do you have for this?" Lady Mompesson asked.

"My house was broken into one night some time ago in an attempt to steal this document."

This revelation had an extraordinary effect. Sir Perceval uttered an oath and his wife rose to her feet staring at her husband in amazement.

My mother now appeared dismayed by the response her words had provoked: "I didn't mean to tell you."

"The deuce you didn't!" exclaimed Sir Perceval. "That determines it!" As if forgetting his bed-ridden state, he lifted the covering that lay over his legs and went to stand up. Then he realized what he was doing and said impatiently: "Isabella, ring the bell."

"No," my mother cried, standing up quickly and looking fearfully towards the door.

"Let me deal with this, Sir Perceval," Lady Mompesson said calmly as she seated herself again.

At her request, my mother cautiously resumed her seat.

"And what makes you believe, Mrs Mellamphy, that this burglary was perpetrated by that party?" Lady Mompesson demanded.

"The burglar took nothing except a letter-case of mine," my mother explained. "I'm sure he hoped to find the codicil in it."

"That hardly constitutes conclusive proof," Lady Mompesson remarked drily. "And is it likely that that party could have discovered your whereabouts when our own efforts to do so failed completely? Until the merest accident," she added, glancing at me in a way that chilled me to the bone.

"I don't know," said my mother uncertainly.

"In brief, Mrs Mellamphy, you only mentioned the burglary in an attempt to intimidate my husband and myself into offering you a higher price by implying that you might allow the codicil to pass into the hands of our opposites, either by sale or by negligence."

"Oh well done, Isabella!" the baronet called out.

"No!" my mother cried in anguish. "How can you think I would be so dishonest?"

"To be frank," Lady Mompesson said, "I can't decide, Mrs Mellamphy, whether you are the most ingenuous or the most duplicitous individual I have ever had dealings with."

"You can't believe that I would ... Surely you must realize how dangerous ... " She broke off. "Perhaps you will believe me when I tell you that I have recently turned down an offer from that party to sell it."

Again this piece of news fell on the Mompessons like a thunderbolt.

"Just as I said!" Sir Perceval exclaimed: "The woman is attempting to force up the price by involving us in a squalid auction."

"That's not true, Sir Perceval!" said my mother, rising to her feet and taking me by the hand. "And I don't believe it's right of you to speak of me like that!"

Lady Mompesson was looking at her strangely and ignored her husband's remark: "Tell me, Mrs Mellamphy, how much were you offered and when?"

"Fifteen hundred pounds. The same as your offer. A lawyer came to me three or four years ago."

Lady Mompesson smiled very faintly, and a thin-lipped, cruel smile it seemed to me.

As my mother began to move towards the door, Sir Perceval called out in a commanding tone: "Wait!" My mother turned. "Our final offer is seventeen hundred pounds."

"You still don't believe me! Don't you see how you are insulting me?"

"I understand," the baronet said savagely. "You believe that you will obtain a larger sum from our antagonist. Well, it may be so but I warn you, you'll need a very long spoon if you intend to sup with that gentleman."

"I don't, I won't," cried my mother, now near to tears. With difficulty, she pulled open the great doors and ran from the room.

With a last glance back at Sir Perceval, his face suffused with rage as he propped himself on one elbow, and at Lady Mompesson who was still smiling, I followed her.

The footman who was standing outside the door moved suddenly to cut us off on the landing and then, with a disapproving glance back at us, led us to the entrance-hall where (I felt) he almost shoved us out down the steps, slamming the high portals behind us.

I was too angry and she too upset for there to be much speech between us. I felt that we had been disgraced and humiliated and I brooded long at the shamefulness of my mother's demeanour. Though I longed to ask her how these grand folks were related to us and what their business was with her, I knew she would answer none of my questions.

CHAPTER 23

After this I was determined to meet Henrietta, even though it meant defying my mother's wishes. The following Sunday I was unable to carry out this project because she accompanied me on my afternoon walk. But the Sunday after that the intensity of the heat and the ferocity of the sun shining from a clear sky, gave her such a head-ache that there was no question of her coming with me. With secret exultation I left the house and took the quickest way towards Hougham — along the course of the stream through Mortsey-wood.

When I reached the road to Over-Leigh where the park began, I lost the stream which ran underground into a culvert from this point. I easily entered the park, however, over the broken-down wall and made my way through a spinney where the hanging vines clung to the moss-covered trees as if the copse had turned in upon itself and was weaving a cloth for protection against the sun. As I hastened through it, the twisted branches of the dead trees clutched at my shoulders and arms, and the woodbine and brambles impeded my legs.

After some time I caught a glimpse of the lake ahead of me and knew that what I was looking for should be on my left. I heard the sound of falling water and cautiously left the cover of the wood and crossed part of the park that afforded little concealment. Ahead of me I saw a cascade falling some thirty feet into the lake and as I approached, a building came in sight further up the slope. The cascade came from a stone bason at the foot of this erection which, when I got nearer, I saw was a circular edifice with a colonnade of pillars above each of which was a stone figure. So that was a Pantheon!

I waited but nobody came. I walked about and looked at this strange construction, feeling that the statues reminded me of something that I could not recall. After an hour I cautiously crept through the woods and peered down at the great house. It had a very deserted air: few of the chimneys were smoking and I saw no-one come or go.

Now I had to hurry home because I was going to be late. To save time, I turned along the road when I reached the park-boundary, instead of tracing the stream back through Mortsey-wood. The way was dusty and I became hot and tired. Just as I was approaching the Green, a carriage came up behind and halted beside me.

"Which is the road to Nether-Chorlton, young master?" the driver called down to me in what I was now able to recognise as a London accent.

"You take the right-hand fork at the cross-roads up yonder," I replied; "and follow the road through the village. At the other end you look out for the first lane on your left."

At that moment the window on my side was lowered and a lady wearing a veil against the dust appeared: "Little boy," she said very sweetly; "would you be kind enough to ride with us and show my coachman the way for fear that we may miss it?"

I knew that I would be disobeying my mother's injunction to have nothing to do with strangers if I accepted. On the other hand, I reasoned, the carriage would pass my house and so it would get me home all the quicker and so make her less worried. From her voice and figure, I made out that the lady was barely grown up and I could detect no harm in it. While I stood hesitating, she opened the door and the driver climbed down and lowered the steps.

I was very tempted by the idea of riding in such a fine carriage beside such a charming young lady, and since I could perceive that there was nobody else with her, I could see no reason against it: "I should be very happy to set you on your road," I replied.

I climbed up, and then the driver raised the steps and closed the door behind me.

"How kind you are," the lady smiled at me as I seated myself beside her. "We have become fearfully lost among these horrid dusty back-lanes and my friends will be worried about me."

The carriage moved and I felt a surge of pride at my first ride in such a vehicle. We seemed to be going very fast and as I looked out of window the ground seemed far below me.

We reached the cross-roads and to my surprise the driver brought the vehicle to a halt.

"Why, did he not understand me when I told him to take the right-hand way?" I asked the young lady. "I will tell him again."

I went to put my head out of window but at that moment a man emerged swiftly from the bushes beside the road and leapt up, pulling open the door. It was not difficult for him to effect this for he was quite the tallest man I had ever seen.

While he got in he smiled triumphantly and then seized my arm as he seated himself opposite me, thus pulling me forward to within a few inches of his face. This was very white with deep black eyes, a lock of black hair with streaks of grey falling over one part of it, and a thin mouth which was twisted into a crooked smile: "Now I have you, young man," he said, his hand gripping my arm so hard that I nearly cried out with the pain.

The carriage began to move off again and I realized that it was taking the opposite lane from the one into the village: "Why, this is not the way to Nether-Chorlton!" I cried.

"You had no trouble, then?" the man asked the young lady.

"None," she answered. Then, in a tone that was not at all kindly, she said: "Master Mellamphy was very anxious to help."

How did she know my name? My mind raced. I could not see her features through the veil but her voice sounded so unpleasant now that I wondered how I had ever thought it sweet.

The carriage was taking the road up Gallow-tree-hill towards the turnpike-road, and I knew that once on it our pace would be too fast to allow me any chance of escape. If I was to make the attempt it had to be soon, while we were still labouring at not much more than walking pace up the hill. I remembered that only a few yards further ahead the road wound steeply to the left at the point where a small stream splashed across it. Here it would have to turn so sharply that it must almost come to a stop.

"You are hurting me," I protested, hoping to induce a change of position which could only be to my advantage.

The man took no notice and I began to struggle.

The young lady leaned forward and slapped my face: "Sit still, you odious little monster!"

"Let him sit between us," said the man. "That way we may both secure him."

This was better than I had hoped. He rose from his seat opposite us and at that instant the vehicle tilted abruptly as it began to take the turn. Not expecting this, the man lost his balance and loosened his grip on my arm.

I had braced myself in anticipation of the movement of the carriage so that

I was able to kick him on the shin with all the strength I could muster. With an oath he let go of my hand and I flung myself across the young lady towards the handle of the door on her side. Now I was out of reach of the man, and I managed to open it before the girl realized what I was doing. But then, recovering herself, she seized the tails of my jacket. I was looking down into the swollen stream now and it seemed to be a long way below me, but I jumped and felt my jacket tear before I splashed into the water and fell on my hands and knees. I was stunned for a moment, but the water was only a few inches deep and although I was bruised I had done myself no serious injury.

I scrambled quickly to my feet and made off down the road as fast as I could. When I glanced back I could see that the man had jumped down and was in pursuit of me. I could not hope to match him for speed for on the road he would be bound to overtake me with his long stride, but I knew the surrounding countryside intimately and amongst the undergrowth my small size would be an advantage, so I plunged into the wood at my left. Here I was able to slip beneath branches that obstructed him, but even so I could hear that he was gaining upon me.

My only chance was to take the risk of stopping and hiding. I dived into a thick clump of bushes and froze. Seconds later he came crashing past me and went on some yards ahead. Then he stopped as if to listen for me. He paused for some time and then, fortunately concluding (as I supposed) that I had got out of his hearing, went on ahead.

I cut back towards the road and rejoined it at a lower point. Then I ran as fast as I could until I reached the safety of the village. I realized from the way people looked at me how strange an appearance I presented, but probably those who saw me imagined that I had merely been the victim of some boyish accident. I wondered what to tell my mother for, soaking wet as I was, covered in mud, my clothes torn by briers and my jacket ripped almost in two, there could be no question of keeping from her that something had happened. It seemed to me to be permissible to tell her a lie to keep her from worrying. But what could be the meaning of my adventure? Could Bissett have had anything to do with it? Yet I was sure that the man was not the one whom I had believed to be following me and to whom I had seen her talking some weeks before.

I was trying to make haste but I saw that the parish-clerk, Mr Advowson, who was crossing from the church to his house just over the road, was hailing me as if he had something important to say. He looked at me round-eyed in amazement and before I had time to think, I found myself telling him — a parish-clerk to whom I was telling a lie! — that I had fallen from a tree and torn my clothes in the course of my descent.

"Well, well. Very glad I am that there's no harm done, Master Mellamphy. Now tell me, did they find you?" Seeing the expression of surprise on my face he went on: "A young lady and a gentleman — at least I believe he was a gentleman, but he was remarkably tall, that's sure as death or quarter-day, remarkably so. Anyway, they were looking for you not half an hour since. Old friends of your mother, yes, that's what they said. Very old friends. And that they'd called at her house and learned that you had gone a walk in this direction and so they had come looking for you, not having much time to stay."

"No, Mr Advowson," I called as I ran off. "No friends of mine or my mother found me."

How could my mother have sent them after me? I kept asking myself as I ran the few hundred yards to our house. When I burst into the front parlour I found her sitting with Bissett over their work.

My mother gasped when she saw me and I cried out: "Why did you send them after me? They nearly succeeded!"

"Who?" my mother exclaimed. "What do you mean? What has happened to you?"

Now I saw it all. They had lied to Mr Advowson, and it was too late for me to disguise the truth from my mother. I noticed that Bissett was — or at least, appeared to be — as surprised and upset as my mother. I told them the bare facts and then answered their questions.

I could not describe the young lady because of her veil but when I mentioned that the man was extremely tall my mother gasped: "How tall? Can you describe him?"

"The tallest man I ever saw!" I cried.

In horror she asked: "Did he have a long pale face and a thin mouth?"

I nodded, still gasping for breath.

"And black hair," she went on in horror; "falling over one side of his forehead?"

"Yes," I said in amazement. "That's him precisely, except that his hair was streaked with grey."

At this she staggered and nearly swooned but Bissett and I held her and helped her back to the sopha. "It's he, it's he!" she moaned, rocking herself backwards and forwards.

"Who, mother? Who do you mean? How do you know him?"

"This is what I have always feared," she stammered. Then she said to Bissett: "I knew I was wrong to let you persuade me to let him go out alone." She turned to me, gripping my arm: "Never again will you go out by yourself while we live in this village. Either Mrs Bissett or I must always be with you. And we will never go beyond the village."

My mother kept her word and from that moment onwards I became a kind of prisoner. I was restricted to the garden — except for my walks which were always under escort — and the locks and spikes that had been installed on the gate and the walls after the burglary now became the means of keeping me in.

CHAPTER 24

Three weeks passed and it was now late August. During this time I had been chafing at having to keep the house. After dinner that Sunday I was in the garden for it was another beautiful afternoon, although this time much cooler and damper for there had been a shower in the morning and there were rain-clouds still about. I was alone for my mother and Bissett were indoors.

Suddenly I thought of exploring the one part of my domain that was still mysterious to me: the Wilderness at the bottom of the garden. A moment later I had pushed my way through the undergrowth of hazel and briers, penetrated the spinney, and found myself beside an abandoned pool — a dark-green expanse on which the dappled shadows of the trees played and which was surrounded by its broken circle of stone. I gazed into it in the hope of glimpsing some ancient survivor from the distant era when the pond must have been tenanted by goldfish similar to those which still inhabited the two smaller ponds on the upper terrace; but nothing seemed to move beneath the surface. As I stared I became aware of the silence. I looked behind me and started at finding at my shoulder the face that had frightened me all those years ago.

It disturbed me even now but in a different way. Though it was only an image, yet the features, worn away and made grotesque by time and weather, were still human and horribly suggested the idea of deformed, agonised suffering. And yet even as I felt this, I was able to see that the face belonged merely to a water-nymph or goddess who had lost both her arms at the shoulders. But now I saw that there was an arm about her waist and realized that she was being held by another figure which was behind her so that the strange angle of her head was explained by the fact that it was directed towards that other figure, most of which was missing, with whom she was struggling. It reminded me of something that I could not recall.

Then I noticed that there was an inscription incised in the stone base. It was so worn and over-grown with moss that it was difficult to decypher, but I was almost certain that it read *Et Nemo in Arcadia*, which even my little Latin was able to make sense of though I could not understand its bearing.

I went on and after that the thicket grew darker and denser so that it was not without a struggle that I finally won my way to the very wall. To my surprise I saw that it had an old entrance whose door was secured by a massive padlock and chain covered in rust. My hopes rose but were dashed when I ascertained that although the door was broken in places, it was still stout enough to resist my attempts to force it. And then I looked more closely at the chain and realized that, formidable though it looked, it was severely rusted. I found a large stone nearby and tried smashing it down on one of the links where it crossed the jamb. After a few blows the chain parted in a shower of rust. The next problem was to move the door which had become almost a part of the ground. However, after some minutes I was able to push it far enough to allow me to squeeze round it. I did not hesitate, and a moment later found myself in the abandoned orchard which belonged to the farm that lay at the end of the lane. The farm-house was out of sight some distance away and so it was no wonder that the door had been so completely forgotten.

Now I felt truly free, but I did not know what to do with my unexpected liberty. I thought of going to Hougham again, for it might be that my absence would not be noticed for a couple of hours and that would be long enough to get there and back. On the other hand, the house was probably still empty. Anyway, I resolved that I would first make for that direction by way of the stream at the bottom of the valley. And so I set off, carefully skirting the farm on my right, and reached the runlet without seeing anybody.

After a few hundred yards the stream broadened out and was shaded by high trees so that where their shadows fell across it the depths were visible. And now it was that I lay on my stomach on the bank and gazed into the limpid waters. The shadowy shapes of what might be lampern, stickle-back, trout, and bull's-head moved mysteriously about. I imagined what it would be like to be a creature of that silent, beautiful world. I watched for some time scarcely daring to draw breath, and then I became aware that there was a dim shape that might have been a fish or a shadow of the weed. And so I took a stick and poked at it and only stirred up clouds of mud. The surface of the water seemed to lose its gleam and I looked up at the sky. It was beginning to cloud over and it must be getting late. At that moment the resolution came to me: Yes, I would go to Hougham.

I swiftly made my way along the banks, under cover of the thick wood which grew along the stream's length. When the path faltered and progress became difficult, I removed my boots and stockings, and, carrying them tied round my shoulders, waded along the shallow bed.

I made rapid progress by this means, and soon reached the road to Over-Leigh a mile or two further on. Now I was on Mompesson land. The dark clouds were gathering towards the southern horizon although the sun was still shining from an expanse of blue in the other direction.

As before, I made my way cautiously towards the strange building that must be what Henrietta had called the Pantheon. Suddenly I saw a servant-girl sprawled on a stone beside the pool, dozing in the sun. I was surprised since I had not expected to find anyone. Perhaps she was a servant left in the house who was taking a rest from her work. I looked carefully around from behind the cover of the trees and caught sight of a small figure not far away. I made a signal with my arm and when Henrietta — for she it was — saw me she nodded her head. Then she put her finger to her lips and looked towards the servant-girl. I nodded and she pointed further up the slope to where the ground was thickly timbered again. Moving from tree to tree, I crept past the sleeping servant, then followed Henrietta into the wood keeping track of her only by the sound she was making and an occasional glimpse of her head. We were tracing the streamlet, which came trickling down to supply the bason below us, as we climbed towards the little building.

When I caught up with her she was waiting for me on the steps out of which the stream was gushing.

"I believed you would keep our tryst," she said. "I was looking out for you."

Not daring to ask what a "tryst" was, I said: "Are we safe here?"

"Yes. Nobody ever comes to the Pantheon, and I believe everybody has forgotten that it exists."

"What is a Pantheon?" I asked, swallowing my pride.

"It's a summer-house, of course."

As I looked at it I suddenly remembered that what I had been reminded of earlier that afternoon when I saw the sculpture of the two figures fighting in our garden was this: the statues standing here on top of the circular colonnade. The style seemed to be the same and the stone was worn in just the same way.

Now as I looked down I saw what looked like tall brick chimneys rising above the woods that covered the valley: "What are those?"

"That's the Old Hall."

Of course. My mother had mentioned it. I went a little way down the slope and peered at it through the thick trees. I saw spiralling chimney-stacks of decorated bricks rising from ancient gables and bare beams where slates had fallen away. The place was filled with the wood-pigeons' liquid bubblings and the wood had the sense of a murmurous green echo. Now I saw a group of four elm trees below me on a level with the old building which was still just out of sight. The trees were in a square and suddenly Mrs Belflower's story of the duel came back to me. Was it true? Yet I could see that there was no statue in the middle of the square, though there was one beneath each of the trees.

I went back to my companion and we sat down, making ourselves comfortable on a low balustrade beside where the water gushed out.

"I cannot stay more than a few minutes," I said. "I must get back before my absence is discovered. I wish I had found you when I came three weeks ago. Where were you?"

"My guardians decided suddenly that we should all go back to London immediately after I met you."

"Immediately after?"

"Yes. That very afternoon. We set off the next day."

"Then why have they returned after so short a time?"

"You are mistaken. They are still there." She paused and I saw that she was upset. "Something happened in London. Miss Quilliam was dismissed. I have been sent back here under the care of the housekeeper again."

"Why was she dismissed?"

She shook her head: "I don't know. Nobody would tell me anything and she wasn't allowed to say goodbye. But I can't believe any ill of her. She was the first governess I ever cared for. I am sure that is why they have sent her away."

I told her how sorry I was and how much I had liked Miss Quilliam and then I explained how I had managed to escape and that I might never be allowed another such opportunity. I ended: "But if I can, I will come again."

"You will not find me," Henrietta replied gravely. "On Tuesday I am to go away from here, probably for many years."

"Where are you going?" I asked.

"I am being sent to school. In Brussels," she added. "My guardians say they have given up hope of finding a reliable governess."

"Are you sorry to go?" I asked.

"No," she said after a moment's reflection. "I will be free of Tom. And apart from you and my great-aunt, I have no friends."

"Then we may not meet again for many years," I said.

"Or perhaps never," she said gravely. "And you will forget me."

A little surprised by her solemnity, I began to protest that I would not, but she interrupted me: "Let me give you a keepsake to remember me by. The ladies always do in the stories."

Quickly she slipped a ring off one of her fingers and passed it to me. It was a band of pewter set with a piece of red glass which had the letters "L. R." engraved on the face.

"I cannot ... " I began.

However, she said firmly: "Oh it is not worth anything or I would not have been allowed to keep it. But it belonged to my mother."

"Then if it was your mother's, it must be very precious to you," I protested.

"Yes, it is very precious. But that is why I wish you to have it."

I made to put it in my pocket but Henrietta said: "You must promise to wear it always."

"I promise to keep it," I said, slipping it on. "But I have nothing to give you," I cried in vexation. I hastily reached through my pockets but could find nothing amidst all my boy's treasure of string, strange-shaped stones, chestnuts and mysterious pieces of iron, except a small implement for removing stones from horses' shoes which was very precious to me. I contemplated giving this to her but I felt it would be wasted.

"I have another ring," Henrietta said, bringing out one which was similar to the first but had no initials on it. "You give it to me," she said handing it to me.

Rather puzzled, I did so.

"Now we have to kiss each other farewell," she announced. "And then you walk away quickly only glancing backwards once."

"Are you sure about the kiss?"

She moved a pace nearer to me and, glad that there was nobody to witness the shameful deed, I quickly kissed her cool cheek and then obeyed the rest of her injunction.

Just before the trees engulphed me I turned back and saw the small figure still standing motionless holding her hands crossed in front of her. I wasn't sure if I was supposed to wave but I raised one hand in a stately greeting and then passed under the shadows of the trees.

I retraced my steps through the park quickly but still cautiously, the more hurriedly because I was aware that the sky to the north had darkened suddenly. A few minutes later, as I hurried along the course of the stream beyond the road, I saw a great purplish thunderhead mustering, and then a cool wind sprang up and a bank of driving rain became visible approaching from my right. I knew that if I followed the same course home and so took the longer way round to gain the orchard and thence the gate into the garden, I would be caught by the rain. I therefore decided to make for home by the quickest way, so I left the stream and ran up the fields towards the village. The sheet of rain, sparkling in the sun as it approached, came nearer and seemed to be drawing a curtain of shadow in its wake. As I reached the first houses it overtook me and I was drenched in a fine spray. Still hoping to get home unseen, I ran down the High-street intending to get up the lane, into the orchard, and so back into the garden before my mother and Bissett had had time to wonder why the sudden shower had not brought me in.

However, when I reached our house I saw a carriage standing outside it and this was so unusual that, instead of turning up the lane, I went directly to the front.

My mother and Bissett were standing on the steps with a strange gentleman, and they seemed to be in the middle of an argument while the rain fell heavily on them. My mother was holding something out to him and waving it at him. Bissett seemed to be trying to pull it away from her and the gentleman was making disclaiming gestures with his hands.

"I'll give it to you if you'll only bring him back," my mother was crying.

Bissett was saying: "Give it to him, just give it to him!" And she was trying to snatch from her the silver document-case which was attached to her key-chain.

Meanwhile the gentleman was saying: "I know nothing of this. I only wish to purchase it."

I approached and when my mother caught sight of me her face was transformed: "Johnnie!" she cried.

She embraced me laughing and sobbing hysterically as the rain ran down our faces, and I tried to push her away.

"Oh thank heavens! Thank heavens!" she cried.

"I hope you will see now, madam, the absurdity of your allegations," the gentleman said ill-temperedly, and I recognised him now as Mr Barbellion.

"What happened? What happened?" my mother cried, pressing me against her.

"Let go of me," I protested. "Nobody tried to harm me. I got out of the garden by myself."

"Why you wicked boy!" Bissett cried. "You've affrighted your poor mother nigh to death!"

"There, madam, and I think you owe me an apology," said Mr Barbellion.

"Go away, go!" my mother cried.

I burned with shame at her conduct and the more so at the haughty courtesy with which he responded: "Madam, I will bid you good-day."

With slightly absurd dignity in view of the rain that was running down his cheeks, Mr Barbellion raised his hat and set off down the steps towards his carriage.

"Come inside, Mamma," I said.

I led her in and shut the door. Bissett brought out the *sal volatile* and eventually my mother was calm. Anxious as I was to know what had happened, I was determined to say nothing until Bissett was out of the room. When at last she had withdrawn I asked my mother for her story. And so I learned that Mr Barbellion had presented himself not long before my return. My mother had instantly sent Bissett to find me and while she was doing so had reluctantly consented to an interview with the lawyer. He had talked again of taking custody of me, and my mother had understood him to be threatening to have me declared a ward of Chancery, though she refused to explain to me how this could be done. And then he had offered eighteen hundred pounds for the codicil. At that juncture Bissett had returned to say that I could not be found. My mother had instantly leapt to the conclusion that he had abducted me and was demanding the codicil in exchange for my return, and this is what had brought on the scene that I had interrupted.

"Even if I was wrong to accuse him this time," she said, "I'm sure it was he who was responsible for the attempt last month. He is working for our enemy."

"We don't know who he is working for, Mamma," I insisted.

"But Johnnie, eighteen hundred pounds! It was as if he knew that Sir Perceval offered us seventeen hundred! He has intelligencers everywhere!"

"Who does?"

"Our enemy!"

"Who is that? Please tell me."

She would not, and I saw that it would be dangerous to press her any further. She kept repeating that he would do anything to get hold of the document.

"But Mr Barbellion didn't take it even when you offered it to him and Bissett tried to make him," I pointed out.

However, she was convinced that she was right. "And it's all your fault, Johnnie," she went on. "It was very wrong of you to disobey my orders and leave the garden like that."

"It wasn't my fault that Mr Barbellion chose to come just then," I protested. "If he hadn't, you would probably not have known I had gone and no harm would have been done."

Bissett made up one of her strong sleeping-draughts and my mother retired early. For the rest of that long summer evening I thought over the events of the last few weeks. It seemed to me that my mother's account of Mr Barbellion's motives — or rather, his actions, for that was all we knew for sure — did not really make sense. Was she confused or was she hiding something from me?

A week or two after this I asked my mother about the sculpture in the garden. She explained to me that Uncle Martin's father — who had originally bought the house — used to be the land-agent at Hougham and had inhabited part of the old hall. (So that accounted for the old map I had found with the name "Fortisquince" on it.) When Uncle Martin's mother came to live here in retirement she had brought the sculpture with her from the old hall as a keep-sake. So it had come from there! Perhaps even from the vacant place in the centre of the four trees!

A few days later came the following letter so strangely addressed that it was testimony to the intelligence of the Post-office that they had sent it even to the right county:

"Wrote from numbr 6 Cocks sqare spittlefeelds in londun on The 8 of Oggust

"dear Miss melermfy wich J am writen this for miss Digwid on acount of not been nor mistr D pertikler scullards for to say. thank yu very much for yowre goodnes to myself and joiy wich we had a bad truble com upon her when she com back to lundon for she fond our too yungers chilren poly and bily was took. and also the eldest gorn now mstr d heven gorn bac to the shoors in opes to beable to sen th rest of the munny toords crismuss an with bess opps and rspeks miss maggy diggwid her mark X"

Folded inside was a bank-note for two pounds. We discussed this for some time in the attempt to decypher its meaning, but remained unclear on several points. The next day my mother told me she had sent the money back and had told Mrs Digweed to regard the loan as a gift. She had also expressed her condolences if she had understood the letter correctly. She remarked rather mysteriously that she had told Mrs Digweed something that would make it impossible for her to repay the balance of the loan.

CHAPTER 25

I understood the meaning of my mother's words when, a little under three weeks later, I awoke from a deep slumber in what seemed the depths of the night to find her standing over my bed with a candle. She was looking down at me with an expression of suppressed excitement.

"What is the matter, Mamma?" I asked sleepily.

"You must get up and dress quickly, my dearest," she said. "We must be ready to leave in half-an-hour."

"To leave!" I exclaimed, sleep falling away from me. "Why, where are we going?"

"Come down now. Mrs Bissett is warming some milk for you."

"But where are we going?"

"Do hurry, Johnnie," she said, pulling back the bedclothes. I jumped out of bed and began to dress.

"Put on some warm clothes. It will be chilly when it gets late."

"Is it not late already?" I asked.

"It is only a little after midnight. Make haste."

"Are we going somewhere?"

"Yes."

I was by now almost dressed.

"Where?" I demanded.

"I will not answer any questions."

"Why not?"

"Well, you haven't always been very good at keeping secrets."

I flushed at this reminder of my indiscretions to Mr Barbellion in the church-yard and before Sir Perceval and Lady Mompesson, and I reflected that there were others that she did not know of. Strangely, that made me even angrier: "It's not fair. You must tell me."

"I dare not take the risk, Johnnie. You might say something quite accidentally."

"But who is there to tell? I won't tell Bissett." Then a suspicion occurred to me: "Or have you told her?"

"No. Mrs Bissett knew nothing until two hours ago when I asked her to stay up and help me pack. And she is very hurt that I haven't told her any more."

I was slightly mollified by this. When we went down and I found in the hall two trunks which I had only ever seen before in the attic I began to get very excited. One of them was already locked and secured by heavy leather straps; the other was open and almost full. We went to the kitchen where we found Bissett preparing a kind of cross between a late supper and an early breakfast. She was in a very sour mood indeed.

"Besides anythin' else, if you had told me a-fore now I could have got things ready."

"I'm sorry," my mother cried. "Oh, Mrs Bissett, I hate to part with you like this, after all you've done. I do so hope you will find another place."

"Too late to mind that now, Mrs Mellamphy," Bissett replied, vigorously scraping the butter as thinly as possible on a slice of bread.

My mother sighed. "Hurry up, Johnnie. The chaise will be here soon."

"A chaise! Where is it from?"

"I wrote to the Lion and the Unicorn in Sutton Valancy. It should arrive at half-past midnight."

"And where will it take us?"

"Wait and see."

"It don't seem like regular Christen conduck, gallivanting off in the middle of the night like folk that haven't paid their score."

"But I've explained all of that, Mrs Bissett," my mother protested mildly; "and you agreed to it. And you know, six pounds in lieu of notice is three months' wages."

I gasped at my mother's generosity.

"Aye, but how much work is there going to be to sell the furniture and settle with the chandler's and them others in the village, that's what I been arstin' meself?"

"It shouldn't take more than two weeks."

Bissett sniffed. "And where am I to send the money left over from the sale when I've paid off the tradespeople?"

"I do not know yet. I have no lodgings arranged in ... where we are going."

Bissett slowly shook her head: "You don't trust me, do you, Mrs Mellamphy?"

My mother looked at her for a moment and then turned to me as I was finishing my bowl of hot milk and fingers of bread and butter: "We can take very little with us now, Johnnie, so if there are any of your books or play-things that you really can't bear to leave behind, go and find them now."

I jumped up.

"Not so quick, young man," Bissett said. "That boy's so journey-proud he'll do hisself or us some mischief."

Seizing a candle, I hurried out. And now the significance of what was about to happen overtook me. I would be leaving, in a very few minutes, the house in which I had, as far as I was aware, spent all my life, and going I knew not whither. Suddenly I thought of my map of London, and though I had no idea what our destination was, I decided I could not bear to set off without the reassurance that it offered. Quickly I found it, rolled it up, and placed it in one of the boxes waiting in the hall.

Now I wanted to bid farewell to the house and I went from room to room in a peculiar state of sorrowful excitement, lingering the most time in my own little chamber. My reverie was interrupted by the sound of a carriage drawing up outside and then by a knocking at the door which seemed — especially at that unhallowed hour — to thunder through the house. I went down to watch and in a few minutes our two trunks and our boxes had been loaded by the driver and post-boy.

When I went back to the kitchen I found (somewhat to my surprise and, I admit, my chagrin) that my mother and Bissett were now on much more amicable terms.

My mother was carefully wrapping something up: "I will take my embroidery and work-basket in the coach. I dare not lose it for if the worst happens, this is what will be keeping us, Johnnie."

And so now my mother and I, warmly clad in top-coats and comforters, assembled in the hall for the final leave-taking. My mother put out her hand to our old servant and it was rather stiffly held and shaken.

"I hope we may meet again, Mrs Bissett," my mother said, and I could see that she was about to weep.

"If not here below in this Vale of Tears, then in a better place, I trust, Mrs Mellamphy," Bissett replied.

Suddenly my mother flung her arms around Bissett and embraced her. Bissett neither resisted nor returned her gesture but when my mother disengaged herself and stumbled through the door and down the steps I could see that the old servant was moved almost in spite of herself.

As she turned to me her expression was troubled: "You take care on her, Master Johnnie. She don't always know what's best to do. You'll soon be old enough for it to be you as looks arter her." She seemed to hesitate for a moment, before she said: "That Mr Barbellion, now. Your mother is mistook to be so a-feared on him. Trust him, for your own sake."

"I'll remember you said that, Bissett," I answered.

We exchanged a long look.

She glanced away first and I held out my hand: "Goodbye," I said.

She looked at my hand with surprise: "You seem so growed-up, Master Johnnie, I hardly know how to take leave of you."

"Then let it be like this," I replied and she took my outstretched hand.

"And yet," she said wonderingly; "this is the same child as I've nussed on my knee when you was in petticoats."

We shook hands and a moment later I clambered into the chaise. The driver closed the door and raised the steps and the vehicle moved off. As it pulled away we looked back and waved to the figure standing in the open door lit only by the candle she carried, and who held her arm up in a gesture of farewell.

It was the first time I had been out so late at night and my first proper ride (apart from the brief moment in July) in a carriage. As we rumbled through the sleeping village where hardly a light was showing — except where we passed labourers working their own plots by the light of lanthorns — I wondered whether the eyes of any secret watcher were upon us. In the blackness that surrounded us, it seemed unlikely.

There were occasional little flashes of light from glow-worms but only the faint moonlight shed any illumination when it peeked from behind a cloud. In its light my mother smiled at me reassuringly from her seat opposite, and I wondered if she were also thinking back over the years we had passed in Melthorpe and speculating on whether we would ever see the village again, or was she too much preoccupied with the difficulties that lay ahead of us? What, I wondered, was presaged by this disruption of the pattern of my life — the pattern, rather, that I had assumed?

Once the carriage was on the turnpike-road it gathered speed, and its regular, swaying motion was in danger of lulling me back to the sleep from which I had been snatched little more than an hour before. Although I was determined to savour every moment of the great adventure, in fact I slumbered and only awoke as we rumbled into the courtyard of the inn at Sutton Valancy.

"What hour is it?" I muttered sleepily.

"It is half after two," my mother answered. "The night-coach departs from here at three-quarters past the hour."

The heavy-coach called the Farmer, which rumbled along the high road from here to the far North, was waiting in the yard and almost ready to go forward. Since we were the last to board I was able to fancy that it was being kept back for us. There were people travelling overnight on top of the coach huddled under travelling-capes, and all manner of portmanteaus and bandboxes and carpet-bags and traps and boxes were strapped onto the roof and bulging from the hind-boot. There were even hampers of game and hares hanging their long ears about the coachman's box which detracted considerably, it seemed to me, from his coachmanly dignity. We climbed into the cavernous, ill-smelling interior where the other dozen "insides" were already ensconced and had staked out their territorial claims. The guard blew a blast on his horn and the great vehicle lumbered out of the yard and turned into the silent High-street. We maintained a sedate rather than an exciting pace and I had to admit to myself that when we went up a steep hill we were travelling only at foot-pace.

After a little I asked: "Why are we going to the North? Whom do you know there?"

"Be silent, please, Johnnie," she whispered. "I will explain later."

However, I kept on insisting until she agreed to say more once the other passengers had fallen asleep.

Then she began to whisper: "We are not really going to the North. If anybody attempts to follow us I hope they will pursue us almost to the Borders. But in fact when we reach Gainsborough we will board the Regulator from York which leaves there at twenty minutes past five, on which I have reserved places for us."

"The Regulator! A mail-coach!" I breathed. "Then we are going to London?"

She nodded. "We are no longer safe now that our hiding-place is known. But in London we can hide easily."

For some minutes I considered what she had told me. Then I said: "But it's a very silly design, Mamma, to have come this way. For the Regulator goes through Sutton Valancy on the way to London."

"You must not speak to me like that," she hissed.

"Don't you see? If someone tries to follow us but doesn't know we have gone north, he will most likely search for us at Sutton Valancy and probably catch up with us there."

She was hurt by my words and we sulked until I fell asleep for the rest of the stage. However, when we arrived at Gainsborough I was so excited that I forgot I was annoyed with her. We waited in the travellers'-room but I soon found my way out to the yard.

"When is the Regulator due?" I asked a man in the royal livery of scarlet and gold.

He drew from its pocket an enormous watch: "Four and twenty minutes and forty-five seconds after five o'clock," he announced, as if the dial had so informed him.

"I'm travelling by her," I said, modestly.

"Are you, so? Well, she's a tip-top goer and no mistake. Two leagues an hour she'll keep up all the way to Lunnon. And the stoppage here for the change will only take forty-five seconds or Tom Sweetapple, her guard, will want to know why."

At a few minutes before the time he had mentioned we heard distant blasts on the horn. Immediately the man flung open the door of the travellers'-room and bellowed: "All out for the Regulator!"

Precisely to the second the coach, painted bright scarlet and with the royal arms blazoned on its sides, swung in through the entrance to the court-yard and like the chorus of a well-rehearsed opera the men who appeared to have been standing idly round went into action.

The coach halted in the centre of the yard and I saw the guard, holding his timepiece in his hand, stand up to shout instructions to the ostlers. Led by one of them we quickly boarded the coach, finding that the other seats were empty. I lowered the window to watch as the two "outsides" were almost thrown onto the box by the ostlers. With extraordinary speed the horses were changed, buckets of water were thrown against each of the wheels, and the letter-bags were tossed up to the guard and stowed by him in the hind-boot. Meanwhile a waiter hurried out carrying a glass which he handed up to the coachman who was buried in coats like a human cauliflower and wore a brightly-striped waistcoat and jockey boots. A hand reached out and seized it, his head was thrown back, and the glass thrust back at the waiter who stretched up on tip-toe to take it.

The coachman signalled to the guard that he was ready to go forward and the latter blew a blast on his horn. At this the ostlers threw the horse-cloths off and then scattered. The coachman shook the reins and touched up the horses, and the vehicle seemed to surge forward like a coiled spring.

It seemed only a moment before we were out on the high road. Now we hurtled past everything that we met and nothing delayed us, for even before the turnpike lamps came in sight, the guard blew his horn to warn the 'pikemen and the gates were opened as we reached them. More and more vehicles appeared now as the dawn lightened. We overtook heavy stages that towered over us, neat little gigs that were galloping along as fast as they could go, smart broughams and elegant phaetons and chariots. Only the lightest post-chaises could keep up with us for any distance but even they were forced to halt at the 'pikes.

My mother urged me to try to sleep but there was far too much to see. It was the dawning of a beautiful day — the last of that summer — and as the coach rattled south, the rich flat farmland unrolled past us displaying its bridges, rivers, woods, and neat little villages. There were so many things I had never seen: a lofty aqueduct arching over a steep valley, canals with barges being towed along them by patient horses, a great cathedral squatting amongst the little rooves of a town like a huge beast, and so much more.

At last I must have succumbed to sleep, for I remember coming to partial wakefulness as I was being carried from the carriage into a lighted, bustling room, and I recall moments of sleep and near-wakefulness succeeding each other until once again I was being lulled by the swaying of a carriage and the rhythmic clattering of hooves — though this time the movement was gentler and the clattering was louder.

When I awoke properly, I found myself wedged between my mother and a strange gentleman whose head lay lolled against the back of his seat and who was snoring loudly. Opposite us sat three other travellers in a similar condition.

At intervals we rumbled into the yards of inns in little towns where we made brief stops while the guard stood beside the coach with his timepiece in his hand watching the ostlers change the horses, or longer stoppages for a hasty luncheon or a gobbled dinner. Once as we passed through a city, I poked my head out of window and looked up to see a great castle towering over the street. And once at a cross-roads I saw something hanging that seemed to be a collection of iron and bone and tarred cloth.

"What was that?" I asked.

My mother shuddered and her neighbour said: "They haven't done that much for ten years, thank heavens."

In the afternoon I remember looking out, as we made our way along the bottom of a gentle valley, at the water-meadows beside the little river. The countryside was of that richly golden green that it acquires late on a fine day towards the end of a wet summer. As the sun began to sink behind the horizon a pale mist appeared over the low-lying water-meadows — so common in that country of dikes that we were passing through. The mist was swirling around the legs of the cattle unconcernedly grazing at the edge of the water so that they looked almost as if they were wading through deep water and bending their necks in order to crop at the powdery gold that swirled about their feet.

I dozed off again, resting my head against my mother's shoulder, and half awoke a little later to feel the weight of her own head resting against mine as she slept.

THE HUFFAMS

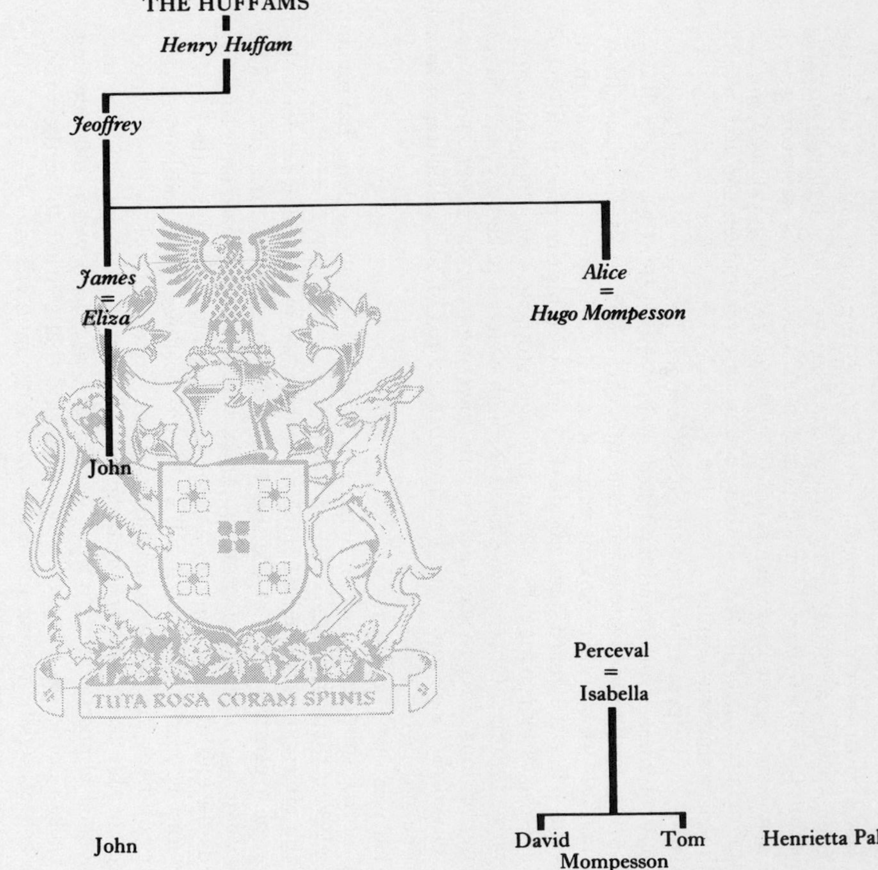

Characters who never appear directly in the narrative are in *italics*.

PART TWO
THE MOMPESSONS

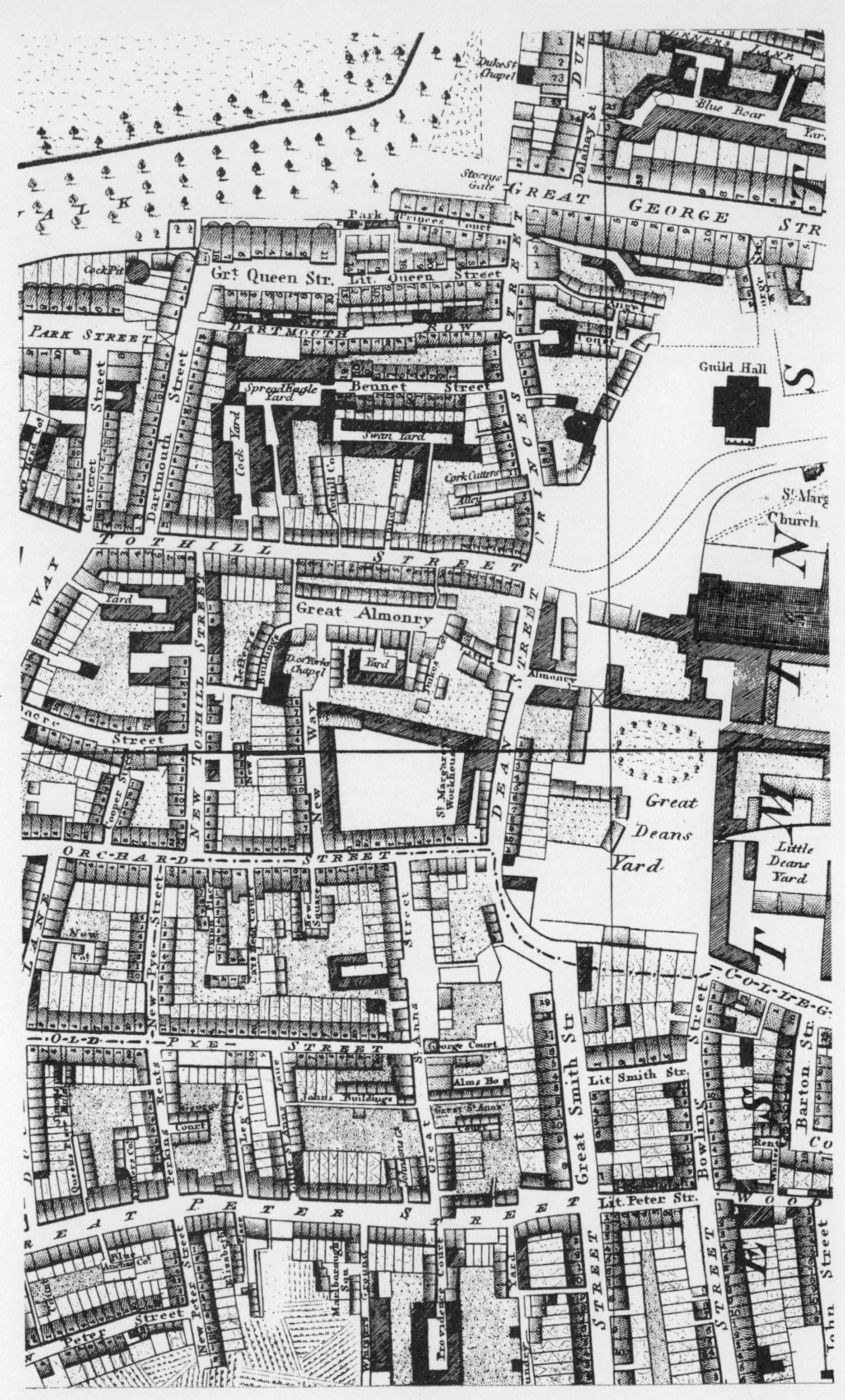

WESTMINSTER (Scale: 1″=90 yards)

The top of the page is North

BOOK I

Spoiled Designs

CHAPTER 26

A lamp-lighter, working his way along the street of tall, dull houses upon a corner of which we are standing, blows on his cold fingers, picks up his ladder, and goes on to the next lamp. And so all down the length of the street small points of light appear, briefly flaring up before settling down to a steady glow. And now along the pavement trails a little fatherless family in rags, poor unhappy exiles of Erin, our sad sister-island. Wretched, cold, hungry fellow-creatures! So close to the haunts of Idleness and Dissipation. We shall let noble Poverty pass by, for our business is again with Wealth, Arrogance, and Power.

For once more we are outside Mompesson-house. This time it is ablaze with lights for it is one of Lady Mompesson's "Friday nights". You know the kind of thing: Weipert's band is playing quadrilles, the livery-servants are in evening dress, additional servants who have been hired from an agency are pretending to belong to the house and to know where everything is and yet keep bumping into each other and blundering into the wrong chamber. The state-rooms are dazzling and filled with the slightly honeyed fragrance of the best wax-candles. In short, all that the insolence of Opulence can offer when Old Corruption gathers is on show, and ....

But enough, for it appears that elegant writing is not what is required. Very well. Sober truth then, without digression.

It must have been towards ten o'clock that Mr Barbellion (Power) dismounted from nothing grander than a hackney-coach and, to the contempt of the link-boys and footmen guarding the steps, was recognised by the butler and allowed to enter the house. He ascends the stairs and in the grand salon full of gentlemen in court dress and their ladies in silk and jewels, makes his way towards Lady Mompesson (Arrogance) as she looks at him with an expression as close to surprise as good breeding permits.

"This is an unlooked-for pleasure, Mr Barbellion," she says coldly.

He appears to flush at this and perhaps it would not be too fanciful to suppose that he resents it. But no motives! That is the rule.

However that may be, he says something like: "My lady, I would not have presumed to intrude if it had not been upon a matter of the utmost urgency.

My agent has just ridden up post from Melthorpe. Mrs Mellamphy — as she calls herself — has fled."

"Fled! And gone where?"

"To London, but beyond that I do not know."

"You do not know, Mr Barbellion?" she repeats frigidly. At that moment a courteous smile appears on her face and she bows towards a gentleman wearing the uniform of an Imperial ambassador on the far side of the room.

Mr Barbellion flinches: "I am afraid my agent lost her, Lady Mompesson."

"He should not have done. He was being well paid for his pains."

"Lady Mompesson is doubtless correct," Mr Barbellion replies with a slight bow.

"How came he to be so remiss?"

"In the very early hours of this morning he was roused at the Rose and Crab inn by a message from his informant to the effect that Mrs Mellamphy had just left for London. He naturally set off in pursuit of the night-coach, but when he overtook it he found that she and her son were not on it. So, assuming that they had travelled post, he himself proceeded to Town, making enquiries at each of the inns that post along that road. He found no trace of them."

"I see," Lady Mompesson says, and drums with her fingers on her fan. "Then why do you say she has come here?"

"She confided as much to my informant."

"Has it not occurred to you that she might have been lying? I take her for a cunning dissembler."

"I think that unlikely, Lady Mompesson. It is more probable that because my agent was apprised of her departure so soon, he somehow overtook his quarry on the road."

"Overtook her! How extraordinary. But if she is here, she must be found. As long as she has that codicil ... " She breaks off and Mr Barbellion nods. "You did right to report this to me, Mr Barbellion. Sir Perceval has not my appreciation of the delicacy of the affair."

"Sir Perceval's directness," says Mr Barbellion, "is in the fine old tradition of the English gentleman, but in this case something more circumspect is called for."

"Precisely my view. Tell me, why do you think she decided to flee, Mr Barbellion? Did she realize that your agent was observing her, for he seems to have made a bad business of it."

"I believe she fled on account of the attempt to abduct the boy that took place on the very day that I visited her. She actually accused me of responsibility for that. How absurd! As if I would ever involve myself in anything that exposed me so dangerously."

"I believe I can account for her fear of yourself, Mr Barbellion. From something she said when she came to Mompesson-park two months ago, she is under the misapprehension that you are acting for the other party."

"I see!" Mr Barbellion exclaims. "Then that explains much."

"However, I am very alarmed to hear that the other party found out her whereabouts and attempted to seize the child."

"Indeed. In fact, I believe that it was through her own attorney that our opposite discovered where she was hiding."

"Yet you assured Sir Perceval and myself that that man — (What is his name, Sumptious?"

"Sancious," Mr Barbellion murmurs.

"Quite so.) — That that man could be, if not precisely trusted, then at least relied upon."

Mr Barbellion flushes. Surely he must have felt ... But no, let us speculate no further.

He murmurs: "I fear I was mistaken, Lady Mompesson. He had the audacity by some means to discover Mrs Mellamphy's hiding-place and, doubtless realizing the value of this intelligence, to sell it to the adverse party."

At that moment the baronet, who is reclining upon a sopha near the door into the next room, catches sight of his solicitor and beckons to him.

"I am alarmed to learn it," Lady Mompesson says. "But I see Sir Perceval has noticed you. Just before you go to him, I want to say something. We seem to be singularly unlucky in tutors and governesses."

"So I have heard from Assinder. Mr David Mompesson is recovered, I trust?"

Lady Mompesson draws her lips together: "Indeed, but I was not referring to that regrettable incident. My allusion was to Tom's governor who has also left, though under much less reprehensible circumstances. There was some unpleasantness over what Sir Perceval sees as a boyish prank. Be that as it may, we are in need of another governor. Will you look out for one — and this time find a young man with a somewhat robuster disposition?"

"I shall take charge of that, Lady Mompesson. And before I go, I have some grave news from Hougham. Now that the autumn rents are in, Assinder informs me that the rent-roll is down again and I fear the figure is alarmingly low. Much of this is due to the old difficulty: tenants cannot be found who are willing to take on a farm whose poor-rate is at least equal to the rent."

"I thought Mr Assinder was dealing with the problem of the settled poor?"

"He informs me that he is proceeding as fast as is practicable, Lady Mompesson. But at the same time, I must caution you again that ... "

He breaks off and looks at her speculatively.

"I am prepared to acknowledge that you are correct about Mr Assinder," she says. "But I warn you, Sir Perceval still refuses to hear a word against him."

Sir Perceval beckons again, this time with an impatient shake of his head, and receiving a cold smile of dismissal, the solicitor leaves Lady Mompesson with a bow and crosses to the baronet.

CHAPTER 27

We changed horses twice during the night, though I have only a very confused memory of being carried half-awake from the darkness of the carriage into the bright lights of the coffee-room. When I awoke I found myself leaning against the shoulder of my mother who was still slumbering. On my other side was an elderly gentleman, also fast asleep, at whose slowly opening and shutting mouth I gazed in fascination. It was a dark and gloomy morning for the good weather of yesterday had departed — or perhaps had stayed behind as we journeyed South. The sky was low and grey and a drizzling rain fell at intervals, so that we seemed to have passed suddenly from the golden end of summer to the grey beginning of autumn. We travelled on all through that long day and the next night, and although it had all seemed so exciting at first, my spirits quickly sank with the boredom and confinement of the swaying carriage.

In the early dawn the coach rumbled beneath the arch of an inn-yard. My mother half woke up, looked out of window and sleepily asked: "What is this town?"

"Hertford," the elderly gentleman answered, waking with a snort. "The Blue Dragon."

My mother started and came suddenly awake.

At that moment the guard bellowed at us that we had five minutes, and in great haste we left the coach and hurried to the travellers'-room. (Here, to my amazement, there was a gentleman being shaved in a corner of the room as we ate.)

"We are nearly arrived," my mother said as we drank our coffee.

"Mamma, whom do you know in London?" I asked.

"I know no-one except Mr Sancious. I will go to him as soon as possible in order to ask his advice about how we can manage with so little money."

Now I broached a subject I had for some time brooded over in secrecy: "Mamma," I began, "has it ever struck you that Mr Sancious may not have behaved well by us?"

She admitted that this had occurred to her and now that the question was before us, we frankly discussed whether it was in good faith that he had given us such disastrous advice. When my mother made much of the fact that he could have no motive for having deceived us, I told her that Mrs Digweed's story about how her husband had lost money in a building speculation suggested that the scheme we had been encouraged to put money into might have been a fraud from the very beginning. And then I pointed out how suspicious was Mr Sancious' interest in whether we had anything to sell, and asked her if she thought he might have had any way of knowing that we had the codicil and that it was valuable to other people.

At this she fell silent for a long time and then said: "Yes you may be right. Perhaps it was he who betrayed us to our enemy, although I don't understand how he could have found the way to him. But it's true that he has always known my real name and that might have aided him."

Despite my attempts, I could not persuade her to tell me what she called "our real name", though I guessed it was the one beginning with "C" that I had seen all those years ago before I could properly read.

Finally I asked: "Mamma, what name shall we go under now?"

She looked at me in surprise: "What do you mean?"

"I think we should use another in case anyone is searching for us."

"Another name! How strange that it should be here ... " she began softly and then broke off.

She would not tell me what she meant (and it was long before I found out), but she agreed that we should choose a new name. We thought of the little hamlet near Melthorpe called Offland to which we had often walked, and settled on that. How strange names are, I reflected, repeating to myself "John Offland".

"So now we have no-one to go to," I said. "Except for Uncle Martin's widow?"

"Oh, Johnnie, we can't do that. I hardly knew her. She was a young woman when I was only a little girl."

"But wasn't she your cousin?"

"I suppose so. Our families were connected in some way, but not very closely for my father did not know hers. And about the time she married Uncle Martin my father and he quarrelled and I had very little to do with her afterwards."

"What was the quarrel about?"

"Oh never mind now. It's a very long story. You'll know all about it one day."

I was about to ask what she meant by these hints that she had dropped before, but at this moment the guard interrupted us with a warning that the coach was about to go forward. The gentleman who had been seated opposite us did not get back in but two new passengers — a genteely-dressed lady with a youth a few years older than I — boarded the coach and we set off again.

The lady — who introduced herself as Mrs Popplestone (travelling with her son, David) and to whom my mother, rather shame-facedly, returned that we were Mrs and Master Offland — struck up a conversation with my mother and they were soon fast friends.

Long before I saw London I smelt it in the bitter smoke of sea-coal that began to prickle my nostrils and the back of my throat, and then I saw the dark cloud on the horizon that grew and grew and that was made up of the smoke of hundreds of thousands of chimneys. After some miles the villages became more frequent, straggling along the road as if reluctant to leave its protection, and the gaps between them grew shorter. At last they came to be so many and the gaps so few that I exclaimed, "Surely this is London!" But my mother and the nice lady and her son laughed and assured me that we still had some way to go. I went through this exchange several times more, for I could not believe that the streets of shops and fine houses which were now almost continuous were only overgrown villages lying outside the capital.

I could see that my mother was almost as excited as I was. "It seems bigger than ever," she said softly, her eyes glittering.

At last, however, we passed through the turnpike that was at that date on the New Road, and my fellow travellers admitted that indeed we were in London. And now I was amazed that we travelled on and on through street after street without coming out at the other side of the town. Moreover, I had never seen or imagined streets like them: I was overwhelmed by their width, by the height of the buildings, the volume and the variousness of the traffic — magnificent private carriages that swept past us with a disdainful flourish of their horses' tails, shabby hackney-coaches, black coal-waggons, huge lumbering drays — and the press of foot-passengers along the pavements like two vast crowds hurrying in opposite directions.

After nearly an hour we entered a particularly wide street which Mrs Popplestone informed me was Regent-street but which I did not recall from my beloved map — and, indeed, it had been constructed since that was printed. Now the coach slowed almost to walking pace for here the carriageway and pavements ran together in one dangerous crowd of men and youths and horses and carriages like a wild, moving market-place. There were sallow-skinned boys in black coats with flat round hats and with ringlets hanging down on their cheeks — "Jews", my mother whispered — who were running in amongst the carriages offering articles for sale at the windows: oranges, gingerbread, nuts, pen-knives, pocket-books, and pencil-cases. And other men and boys were thrusting papers through the windows of carriages, and when one hurtled through ours I picked it up and saw that it was a play-bill. (At last I would go to a real theatre!) And there were yet others running into the middle of the streets at peril of their lives with shovels and buckets. It was like a waking dream: the noise of the vehicles rumbling and clattering over the paved streets, the cries of street-vendors, and the ringing of the newspaper-sellers' bells. All of this filled me with a mixture of excitement and fear.

Now we encountered a lock of carriages and came to a halt, surrounded by handsome vehicles of a number and variety I had never dreamed of. On our right was a fine landau painted scarlet and beautifully varnished, with a coat-of-arms emblazoned on the side-pannel which was repeated on hanging folds of the gold-fringed hammer-cloth on which the coachman and the whip sat. There were two footmen standing abreast up behind wearing tri-corns and coats with huge gold shoulder-knots, each carrying a gold-headed cane sloped across the roof, and both of them were staring as if sightlessly ahead. There was an even more elegant equipage on the other side, for in addition to the two footmen it had a boy in a striped waistcoat and small wig who stood on the platform and who caught my eye and smiled in a manner that made him my mortal enemy.

Above all I was astonished by the flaring gas-jets lighting the streets and shop-windows, for they had been lit quite early on that dark and rainy September day. I had never heard of such a thing, for gas lighting had not at that date reached our village. I looked at my mother and saw that her cheeks were flushed as if the same emotions had taken hold of her.

"So many gas-lamps!" she exclaimed. "And only look at the plate-glass and the gas in the shops. When I was last here only three or four streets in St. James had gas lighting and few of the shops had such windows."

"My dear!" Mrs Popplestone exclaimed, while her son smiled disdainfully; "You can't have been in Town for simply ages and ages!"

My mother coloured and looked down.

The coach which had flown like a bird along the highway seemed to have become a clumsy monster in these streets, constantly coming up against other vehicles, being shouted at by drivers and narrowly missing foot-passengers who dived in front of it at the crossings. It reminded me of the ducks on the village-pond which swam so gracefully over the water but waddled awkwardly when they came ashore.

Now that the vehicle was going so slowly I had a chance to examine my new fellow-citizens. On this broad street (which my mother whispered to me was called Haymarket) the fashionably-dressed and the poorly-clad mingled promiscuously. Brushing past the ladies and gentlemen, often with a footman walking behind them carrying an ivory-topped cane, were many who looked like beggars: men in fustian and corduroy with their sleeves tied with string, women in ragged gowns, and little girls selling flowers whom I took for beggars. On every side the eye and ear and nose were assaulted: by posters and placards pasted on every wall and paling, by bellmen crying the events of the day — a lost child or ship or motion in the House — by the stalls selling roast chestnuts or baked potatoes or cooked shell-fish.

We now approached a district which was being extensively demolished, for the Royal-mews were being taken down and a great public square opened up. My mother looked around in amazement as if half-recognising the place. With a sudden blast on the guard's horn the coach came almost to a halt and then lumberingly turned and passed under a high arch and along a narrow alley-way into the yard of an inn whose sign proclaimed it to be the Golden-cross.

"We are not to stay here, are we?" I asked my mother as we gathered up our possessions and prepared to get down.

"No," she whispered. "This is too expensive."

"And besides," I replied, "it would be easy for anyone to find us here. Then where shall we go?"

"I don't know," she replied.

Mrs Popplestone, who was standing beside us with her son, must have overheard this last exchange, for she now said: "My dear, we are going now to a very respectable private-hotel, Bartlett's, in Wimpole-street. I can recommend it. Will you and your son not share a coach with us since we have no luggage to speak of?"

My mother thanked her and accepted her offer. But then a problem arose for when the coach-driver saw how many we were and how much luggage my mother and I had, he demurred.

"You know I can't take that much," he said to Mrs Popplestone reproachfully.

"Then," she said to my mother, "it is very simple. You and I will go on ahead with the luggage and the two young gentlemen will follow on foot. My son knows where the hotel is."

This seemed a very sensible arrangement and so our luggage was loaded and the two ladies boarded the coach. (But not before I had insisted on unpacking my map and removing the sheets that portrayed the central districts, putting the rest of it back in the box.) Master Popplestone and I followed the coach out of the yard by another alley-way and found ourselves in the Strand directly opposite to the gloomy old front of a great mansion whose façade was surmounted by a stone lion. (When I learned much later that this was Northumberland-house, I understood why my mother was so upset at finding herself so suddenly here of all places.) Soon losing sight of our quarry, my companion and I took to the bye-streets.

As we twisted and turned I quickly lost my bearings, so preoccupied was I in drinking in the sights: the laundresses in clogs carrying bundles on their heads, the pie-men ringing their bells and crying "Rare hot pies!", the stalls selling oysters and apples and pies and cockles, and at each crossing the sweepers with their long brooms. There was much that daunted me: in the high narrow airless streets, looking at the sky was like peering up from the bottom of a well; and the iron grilles on the houses on all sides reminded me of tombs. London must be a very dangerous place, I thought, for in the main streets all the shops had guard-irons. But those shops! I gazed through the plate-glass windows of the print-shops longing to dawdle there, but Master Popplestone hurried me on.

Suddenly he halted and cried: "Wait here! I must run an errand for my mother!" and disappeared into a nearby milliner's-shop. I waited outside so distracted by the sights that it was with a sudden shock that I realized that a long time had passed. I went into the place and not seeing my companion, I asked a shop-boy.

When I had described him he said: "You must mean that young genel'man what come in here a bit back. Why, he runned straight out agin through the back-door."

I could not think what to make of this but I had no leisure to reflect, for I now realized that I was lost and had no idea where the hotel was to which my mother had gone. In mounting alarm I wandered about, and now it seemed to me the street-sellers were directing their cries at me — the orange-sellers crying "Chase some oranges! Chase my nonpareils!" as I hurried past and the long-song sellers barring my way with shouts of "Three yards a penny!" And once I passed a stall where a big bold woman held out a half-skinned live eel on a long fork that squirmed at me hideously as she grinned and said something.

I tried to consult the map but since I had no idea where I was it was of no use. I showed it to a man chosen from among the passers-by at random, but he had never seen one before and had no idea what to make of it.

Luckily, however, I remembered the name of the coaching-inn and at last I managed to find my way back to Charing-cross. I waited at the entrance to the yard for a good hour until a hackney-coach stopped and my mother dismounted.

She was distraught and as soon as she saw me ran to hug me, crying: "Is she not here?"

When she was able to speak coherently this was the story she told me: When the coach had halted outside the hotel, Mrs Popplestone had insisted upon settling the fare and had asked my mother meanwhile to enter the hotel to say that she, Mrs Popplestone, was returned and required assistance with her luggage. My mother had done so leaving everything in the coach, and had found to her surprise that nobody at the hotel knew her companion's name. When she had gone back into the street she had found, of course, that the coach had driven off. So all our luggage was gone!

"I waited and waited but she did not return," she kept saying. "And you didn't come either, Johnnie. But it must be a misunderstanding. Surely she will come back here when she finds I am no longer at the hotel?"

It took me some time to convince her that we had been robbed and then she broke down and wept: "How could she do it? I cannot believe it! She was so kind and so respectable. Oh, Johnnie, we have nothing but the clothes we stand up in! Nothing!"

She kept repeating that we had been unlucky, and this irritated me for I thought we had been foolishly trusting. All the time aware that people were staring at us, I led her into the coffee-room. The waiter asked me what the matter was, and when I told him our story, he said it would be a waste of our time to lay an information before a magistrate, and when he took no more notice of us I saw that what I had taken for sympathy was merely curiosity.

At last, when my mother was more composed, we engaged another coach, instructing the driver to take us to a respectable private hotel of his acquaintance. So a few minutes later Mrs and Master Offland alighted before a house in Clifford-street with a modest sign announcing — or, rather, intimating in a genteel under-tone — that it was "Nevot's Private Hotel". There — having explained to an uninterested clerk why we had no luggage — we engaged rooms and ordered a small luncheon to be brought to us.

We assessed the implications of our loss — all the silver, the good china, and the fine clothes whose sale we had been counting upon to support us. How would we keep ourselves now? Cautiously I raised the prospect of selling the codicil to Sir Perceval, but my mother became so upset at the idea and talked so incoherently of her father and how such a betrayal would break her heart, that I vowed never to mention it again. After a time I asked her if she did not think that in view of our situation, we should go to Mrs Fortisquince after all.

She sighed and said: "Yes, I suppose so."

Later that afternoon, therefore, we made our way towards Golden-square where Uncle Martin's widow lived.

CHAPTER 28

As we approached Regent-street, the number of poor people on the streets increased. Noticing that many of them were heavily laden with possessions, I asked my mother the reason for this, but she merely shook her head. Here there were many little girls (some much younger than I) selling flowers, and I noticed that they did not stop us but addressed themselves only to gentlemen — perhaps finding them softer-hearted, it occurred to me.

Mrs Fortisquince's house was on the western side of the shady square which, though so close to the great thoroughfare which had been recently constructed, was quite retired. We found her name etched on a new brass plate and when we rang, the door was opened by a pleasant young maid who, when my mother explained that she was a connexion of Mrs Fortisquince's who had come to London unexpectedly and gave her name as "Mrs Mellamphy", showed us into an upstairs parlour and left us. The room, its walls hung with rich flock papers, was most elegantly furnished with tables and chairs of walnut, a marquetry side-table with a matching glass above it, and a satin-covered ottoman. There was a magnificent Turkey-carpet on the floor, and in a corner were a large harp and a pretty pianoforte, on top of which lay some fine needlework and several books. Although the day was quite warm, there was a fire burning in the grate. We waited without sitting down and listened to distant voices and the sound of doors opening and closing in other parts of the house.

At last we heard a step upon the landing, the door opened and a lady came into the room. She was tall, distinctly handsome, and although only a few years older than my mother had the manner of one much her senior. She had a high straight nose between two clear blue eyes, a strong jaw and a thin mouth. She was wearing a half-mourning dress and a cap trimmed with black lace and mourning-ribbons. Her air of gravity was increased by the stately manner in which she entered the room and closed the door behind her. Then she and my mother looked at each other for a moment, neither of them smiling. At last Mrs Fortisquince smiled and my mother timidly did the same.

"Mary, after so many years! Is it truly you?"

She stepped forward and they embraced quickly.

"Dear Mrs Fortisquince," my mother said.

"'Mrs Fortisquince!'" that lady repeated. "You must not be so cold, Mary. Have you forgotten that you used to call me Jemima?"

"No, of course not. Of course not, Jemima."

"That's better, my dear Mary. Pray seat yourself."

My mother did so and Mrs Fortisquince, having made herself comfortable on the ottoman, now turned and gazed at me with a mysterious half-smile for some moments before saying softly:

"And with such a grown-up young man!"

"This is Johnnie," said my mother.

"Of course it's Johnnie!" she said. "Why, the resemblance is so obvious. Do you not think so?" She turned to my mother who lowered her eyes. "Well, don't you?"

"I ... I'm not sure."

"Indeed? You do surprise me. Surely he features your father quite remarkably?"

"My father? Yes, he does," my mother said readily, now looking up.

To my surprise, Mrs Fortisquince looked directly at her rather than at me and said: "But I can see nothing of his own father."

My mother reddened and looked down again: "No, indeed?"

"Positively not a trace. Can you?"

My mother looked at her timidly and with a quick glance at myself, briefly put her hand to her lips.

Mrs Fortisquince turned to me raising her eyebrows: "Sit down, young man."

I perched on the edge of the only remaining chair which was before the fire, where the heat was intense for there was no screen.

"How long must it be since we last met?" Mrs Fortisquince mused.

"Many years," my mother murmured.

"Let me consider, when was the last occasion?"

I saw my mother bite her lip.

"Ah, of course," Mrs Fortisquince suddenly. "How could I have forgotten? It was that night, was it not?"

My mother nodded dumbly.

"My dear, I should not have spoken so thoughtlessly. But such a long time," Mrs Fortisquince said reflectively. "And so much has happened. I am intrigued to know what brings you to Town. Has there been a change at last in the melancholy circumstances of your poor ... ?"

"I know nothing of that," my mother interrupted and glanced sharply towards me: "Johnnie, will you go outside and wait on the landing until I come for you?"

"There is no necessity," said Mrs Fortisquince. "You need tell me nothing."

My mother flushed.

"But then I wonder what brings you here now. And how mysterious that you did not write to me first!"

"There was no time. I will explain. But, Jemima, I have said nothing to you of ... I am so sorry about ... "

She paused.

Mrs Fortisquince sighed: "I am, of course, profoundly bereft. But it could at least be no surprise. With a husband so much more advanced in years than oneself it is an event that one must always have foreseen. But enough of my own sorrows. Tell me what brings you to Town."

"That is very simply told. I have lost everything. Johnnie and I are penniless."

"I am horrified to learn it," Mrs Fortisquince said equably. "Pray tell me how such a thing came about."

So my mother had to rehearse the whole sad story. Mrs Fortisquince, who appeared to accept the news with considerable philosophy, became more and more interested as her tale progressed. She asked a number of questions about the nature of the speculation, the assignment of leases, and the redemption of the mortgages, which were of such a technical nature that we did not know how to answer them; and she appeared to be particularly interested in the precise terms of the advice that Mr Sancious had given my mother and in the nature of the financial obligations that she had incurred and of which she now went in fear.

Clearly struck by her curiosity, my mother asked: "Do you think Mr Sancious cheated me? You see, Johnnie thinks I should have nothing more to do with him because his advice turned out so badly."

"How absurd," she said, turning and smiling at me. "What an imaginative child it must be. My dear Mary, I am sure Mr Sancious played an entirely honourable part. There is always an element of risk in such a speculation and you admit yourself that he did not disguise this from you."

"There you see, Johnnie," my mother said, smiling at me triumphantly.

"Building speculations," Mrs Fortisquince explained, "have been extremely profitable, but at the same time they have ruined many people in the last few years. I think you should certainly go and see this Mr Sancious again. He will advise you on how to make the best of your present circumstances."

"Thank you, Jemima. I believe I shall." Then my mother went on: "But as if that were not bad enough, we were robbed of all our luggage when we arrived here."

"How terrible," Mrs Fortisquince said calmly.

There was a pause and seeing that nothing further was to come, my mother, her eyes cast down, went on falteringly while I burned with shame: "Until some money arrives from the sale of our furniture, we have literally only a few pounds to live on."

"I am profoundly relieved to know that you are expecting some money," Mrs Fortisquince said. "I know only too well what it is to be pressed by creditors. It may surprise you to learn that I am myself somewhat embarrassed for money since my late husband — because of injudicious dispositions in his latter years — left me considerably less well provided for than I had anticipated. Were it not for that, I would gladly assist you."

At these words my mother looked at me with a lack of reserve which laid bare how these words had disappointed and hurt her. I felt a sense of shame on her behalf that was mingled with resentment against Mrs Fortisquince.

"What will you do?" that lady asked. "I suppose you will have to accept a situation as a governess?"

"If I must," my mother answered.

"Well, just fancy!" Mrs Fortisquince exclaimed with a bright smile. "Isn't it strange how things turn out? To think that I was once a governess when you were the adored child of a wealthy gentleman." When my mother did not return her smile, she moved slightly as if preparing to stand and said: "But how kind of you to think of coming to see me so soon after your arrival. Especially when you have had so many other things to think about."

Presumably hearing the note of dismissal in her voice, my mother said: "I think we should go now, Johnnie."

"My dears, must you?" said Mrs Fortisquince as she rose and rang the bell. As we stood she asked with languid curiosity: "Where are you staying?"

Before my mother could answer I replied: "The Golden-cross, Piccadilly."

My mother looked at me in astonishment and horror. I frowned slightly to indicate that she should not contradict me.

Since the young servant came in at that moment, Mrs Fortisquince did not notice this exchange. She kissed my mother farewell at the door of the room. "Mind you come and see me again, soon," she said, and the way she paused before that final word strangely conveyed the exactly contrary effect.

We descended the stairs and the maid accompanied us to the street-door. As soon as it slammed shut behind us my mother exclaimed: "Johnnie, whyever did you tell such an untruth?"

"I didn't like her," I said.

"What can you mean?"

"Why did she want us to trust Mr Sancious so much?"

"Oh do stop that, Johnnie. You're quite unreasonable about Mr Sancious. Why did you lie to her?"

"Mamma, don't you think she could be connected with whoever it is who is looking for us, and that is why she wanted to know how to find us?"

"No, Johnnie, of course not." Then she hesitated: "Well, I suppose it is just possible."

"Anyway, there's nothing to be gained by having anything more to do with her, is there?"

"I suppose you are right."

"Then, Mamma, tell me what Mrs Fortisquince meant by 'that night'? And who were you talking about?"

She clutched my arm: "Not now, Johnnie. Please. I promise you that one day you will learn everything. Only don't force me to tell you anything now. I should not have taken you there, only I thought she ... "

"Thought she what, Mamma?"

"I thought she would help you if not me. For the sake of others."

CHAPTER 29

Though this whetted my curiosity further, she would say no more and we were both silent as we walked back. I went over the conversation I had heard, trying to find an explanation that would fit what I knew, almost as if I were trying out different keys to turn a lock. What could have happened on that night so long ago when my mother and Mrs Fortisquince had last met? And who was the mysterious person whose "melancholy circumstances" she had referred to? Above all, what was the mystery about my father? And what were Mrs Fortisquince's feelings towards my mother — and even myself?

When we got back to the hotel it was time for a light supper and then we retired. (When I commented on how dirty our clothes were, my mother explained that it was caused by the London blacks from the coal burning in the many chimneys.) Lying on the sopha in our sitting-room, I slept badly on my first night in Town for the noises were so different from those I was used to: the rattle and rumble of carriages, the clatter of hooves on the cobbles, the shouts of the watchmen calling the hours and then at first light the cries of hawkers and the crash of church bells. Waking before dawn, I lay listening for sounds within the hotel and wondering what was happening back at Melthorpe. Was Bissett rising as early as usual in the empty house? Were the cattle going down the lane on their way to their grazing? And Mr Passant opening up the shop? It was strange to think of life continuing in the village just as always when I was there no longer.

After breakfast my mother made enquiries of the hotel-proprietor and learned of a person called "Marrables" in a nearby street who kept lodgings and was believed to have rooms free. We went there immediately and found No. 37 Conduit-street to be clean and respectable-looking and the landlady the same. The only accommodations available, however, comprised the two bed-chambers and a sitting-room on the first pair back; and the rent, including the services of the maid, was four pounds a month.

I tugged at my mother's arm and whispered: "That is far too much."

"We have to live somewhere," she whispered back. And so she insisted on engaging the rooms and, despite my protests, handed over the first month's rent.

On the way back to the hotel I remonstrated with her for her extravagance.

"You can't expect me to do without a servant-girl," she protested. "And anyway, Bissett will soon be sending us some money."

"We don't know how much, Mamma. We should work everything out and see how much we can afford."

"Sometimes you talk as if you didn't trust me," she said bitterly, and we quarrelled fiercely.

However, when we had returned to the hotel, ordered the reckoning to be made up, and begun to pack our belongings, she consented to sit down at the table and help me to work things out. We found that at that moment we had 24£ — less the 8s. or so that we anticipated for the reckoning. We expected that Bissett would send us about 40£, and I argued that even taking that into account, we could not afford to live at so high a rate.

"But you have left out of consideration the money that I will make from the sale of my *petit point*. I am a fine needlewoman, you know, and people will pay a great deal of money for good work."

"Are you sure of that, Mamma?"

"You are unkind, Johnnie," she said. "You don't want to think well of your mamma. But I know about clothes and I remember how much I used to pay when I was a girl, and I'm sure prices have gone up since then. And besides, if it came to it, I could always accept a situation as a governess."

I recognised the phrase with its implications of gracious acquiescence.

"You'd hate it," I protested. "You don't know what a hard life it is."

"Why, what do you know about it?" my mother exclaimed with an angry smile.

"I *do* know about it. That time we went to Mompesson-park, I saw how Lady Mompesson treated the governess. And the day I escaped from the garden — you remember? — I went to see the little girl I met there, and ... "

"Oh Johnnie," she interrupted. "That was very naughty of you."

"Nobody knew I was there except Henrietta," I said indignantly. "Anyway, I was going to say that she told me how much her governess, Miss Quilliam, had had to endure and that finally she was dismissed very suddenly and unfairly."

My mother remained unconvinced, however, and I raised another objection: "But even supposing you could endure it, where would *I* live?"

"You should have to board at a school. We should find one nearby."

"I should hate that. And if you are going to work, then so am I."

"Don't be silly. You're much too young."

"Many boys and girls as young as I work — and younger too. Sukey's little brothers and sisters do."

"That's different, that's the country. That's just minding the cattle and that kind of thing. That's not real work. It's not the same in London."

"Yes it is. Joey works."

"Who is Joey?"

"Joey Digweed, the boy who came to our house with his mother at Christmas!" I said indignantly.

"Oh yes, but that's quite different. And anyway, you would earn too little. It's much better that you go to school now so that you may enter a profession and can earn your living as a gentleman. But anyway I'm sure it won't be necessary."

"But if you were to accept a post as a governess, how much do you suppose your salary would be?"

"I should think at least 30£ for I paid Mrs Belflower 25£ and I am sure that a lady — who, you know, lives on terms of equality with the family — must be paid more than a cook."

"Very well. Then how much would be needed for my school?"

"Well, since you will be boarding during the vacations, your fees and expenses must be about 15£. Then there will be additional expenses — clothes for both of us, physicians' bills and medicines, holidays and occasional treats — and for this we should allow 10£. That means we could save 5£ a year and so in five years — by the time you're of age to be articled or apprenticed — we will have, adding the money due from the furniture, a total of about 60£ which should be more than enough for the premium."

"I wonder if a governess would receive so much," I said. "I have an idea: why don't you register for such a post and find out what the salary would be, and then we may ask to be sent details of offers and may accept one that is really desirable?"

My mother reluctantly agreed. We went downstairs and while she was settling the reckoning, I went into the coffee-room where, out of idle curiosity, I picked up a newspaper. My eye was taken by advertisements for schools on the front page, most of which said something like: "Boarding establishment for the education of the sons of gentlemen. Excellent tuition. Fees 60 guineas p.a. and extras." The lowest figure I could find for any school in London — or, indeed, within a hundred miles of it — was 25 guineas. However, the advertisements for some of them, all of which were far away in the North, said things like: "Children disposed of on the most reasonable terms. Twelve guineas a year or thirty guineas for final disposition." I also noticed advertisements for governesses and their wages were all between 15 and 30 pounds.

When my mother came to find me I hastily put the newspaper down. She looked grave and I soon found out why:

"The reckoning was fourteen shillings, Johnnie. London seems to be much more expensive than I'd expected. You know, I think we should try to live in a provincial town instead."

"But we came here to escape being found, Mamma!" I protested, loath to surrender the prospect of becoming a Londoner so soon.

"But we have done that now, Johnnie. Nobody will be able to pursue us beyond the Golden-cross-inn. So perhaps we could find a way to settle in a nice town. I'm sure we'd love Salisbury. I passed through it once many years ago and it was so pretty with its cathedral and the old Close around it, I thought I should love to live there one day."

"Or Hertford," I suggested watching her face closely. "That looked nice, I thought."

She flinched and turned away: "No, not there."

We now left the hotel and were soon at Mrs Marrables' house. When we were installed in our rooms we arranged our few possessions and then, as parlour-boarders, took our dinner downstairs.

Afterwards, when we had returned to our rooms and my mother had made herself a hot toddy, she said: "I feel a lot more cheerful now. I should write to Bissett now that we have an address to tell her."

I had reasons for thinking this was not a good idea but I was loath to make them explicit: "Mamma," I said; "I think you should delay writing because we may decide we will have to move soon. And you shouldn't want her to send a bank-note here if we had left, should you?"

"Oh Johnnie, you are tiresome. Of course we won't move from here for a while. But very well. I won't write yet. Anyway, she won't have had time to sell everything."

I suggested we should go to a registry-office tomorrow and also start to look for a school for myself: "And when we are at the office, shall we ask if we can learn Miss Quilliam's address?"

My mother laughed: "Really, Johnnie, you can't claim acquaintance after meeting her just once."

"But we know no-one else in London, do we?" She said nothing so I repeated: "Well, we don't, do we?"

"Very well, we will ask for her."

She fell silent but a few minutes later she spoke gravely: "After we have been there, there is somewhere I must go."

"Where?" I asked in surprise. "Is it far? Must we take a coach?"

"I must go alone. And you must not ask me about it now and must promise that you will not ask me any questions when I return."

I was much perplexed: "But you told me you know no-one in London apart from Mrs Fortisquince and Mr Sancious!"

"I said I had no friends. But I asked you not to question me!" she exclaimed and seeing that she was upset I turned the subject: "But we do have friends in London, for you are forgetting Mrs Digweed and Joey."

"Oh yes," she began to laugh. "But I don't imagine we will claim acquaintance of them."

We were tired after our busy and successful day and once I was in bed I soon drifted into sleep.

So early the next morning we set out for the largest of the registry-offices which was not very far away in Wigmore-street.

On the way my mother stopped at a shop-window and pointed out some embroidery-work: "Look at that. It's the kind of work I could do. Let's just go in and ask how much it is."

We did so and, discovering that it was enormously expensive, emerged feeling much encouraged.

With the aid of my map we made our way into a very grand district where many of the streets and squares were closed off by posts and chains at one end and had gates at the other with liveried porters and watch-keeper's boxes. After we had been walking for some time we realized that we had lost our way and, seeing our obvious perplexity, a well-dressed gentleman of middle years came up to us and asked where we were looking for.

"Wigmore-street?" he repeated. "It is the first on the left. Is it the London General Office that you seek?"

When my mother confirmed that this was so, he glanced at her kindly and said: "Then I compassionate you from the depths of my heart."

"Is it so very terrible a life?" my mother faltered.

He looked at her keenly: "I have known governesses who were among the most miserable of creatures, despised by their charges and humiliated by their employers. Yet it need not be so. Perhaps I could be of service in finding you a position with a good family."

My mother seemed taken aback at this. She murmured: "You are very kind, sir."

"Come," he said, "permit me to accompany you in the direction of Wigmore-street, and perhaps I can persuade you not to throw yourself upon its mercies."

Obviously surprised, my mother allowed him to walk along with us.

After a few steps he said: "I am Mr Parminter of Cavendish-square. Allow me to give you my card. And please come to me if I can be of any assistance."

He reached into his pocket but my mother suddenly halted and said: "Pray do not give yourself the trouble."

"But I should be very glad to help you," he said pleasantly.

At this my mother drew back and said as if trying to speak very haughtily: "Thank you for your assistance, sir, but we can find our way from here and I wish to trouble you no further."

Without giving him time to reply she bowed very slightly and walked on. As I hurried after her I glanced back and saw the gentleman watching us with an expression which I took to be one of mild amusement.

"But Mamma," I said when I caught her up, "why did you not accept his offer when the gentleman seemed so kind?"

She merely shook her head and hurried on.

We reached Wigmore-street a moment later, found the Office on the second floor and entered. A notice indicated that there were two rooms, one for the employers and one for the governesses. In the appropriate one we found a long wooden counter running the length of the great chamber, behind which a clerk stood talking to a seated lady and consulting at intervals the large books stacked around him and on shelves behind him. A number of ladies were seated in our half of the room waiting their turn. We gave our name to a boy who sat behind a desk near the door and told him what we wanted. He wrote our name down, indicated seats and passed the slip of paper to the man behind the counter who merely glanced at it and put it on one side.

We sat down and had to wait a long time, but when at last the name of "Offland" was called the clerk cried out: "Hurry along there. I ain't got all day."

He was a slight man with a lugubrious but sharp-featured countenance and thinning hair visible beneath a small wig. When we were before him he asked, without raising his eyes from the ledger he was writing in: "Where 'ave you been in sarvice, Mrs Offland?"

"In service?"

"Yes, that's what I said."

"I have never been."

At this he looked up for the first time: "That's bad." Then he noticed me: "This your young 'un?"

"Yes," my mother admitted.

"Widder?"

My mother reddened and nodded.

The man gazed at her searchingly.

"He would board at a school," she said.

"In course," he said. "But even so, famblies don't like a governess to have a child. Governesses is single, as a rule. In course, you couldn't see him 'cept by arrangement?"

"I did not know that."

"Well, now you know," he said. "Or, though I never ought to say this, you could leave him out of question."

"What do you mean?"

"Oh my, ain't you green. Well, I ain't going to say no more. Anyways, let's see what you have got to offer. Can you speak French?"

"Yes," said my mother.

"Straight-up Parigian like you was born to it?"

She shook her head: "Not so well as that."

"What about Italian?" he asked severely.

"No," she almost whispered.

He closed his mouth as if in resignation: "Well, can you sing and play the pianny-forty?"

"Yes, fairly well."

"Famblies don't want fairly well, they want bang-up." He sighed heavily and fiddled with his shirt-cuffs: "Drorin'?" he suddenly demanded.

My mother looked at me in dismay. I nodded to encourage her.

"Pretty well," she stammered.

"I don't think you'll sarve," he said grimly. "I don't know if it's worth my time to write you down. Anyways, have you anyone to speak for you?" Seeing that we did not understand he said irritably: "What character can you furnish?"

My mother gazed at me in dismay. Why had we not thought of this?

"Mrs Fortisquince," I said.

My mother looked at me in surprise and the sharp-eyed clerk noticed this and looked at both of us sceptically.

"Who is Mrs Fortisquince and where does she live?"

"The lady is the very respectable widow of a legal gentleman," I said. "She lives in Golden-square."

The man rudely snapped his fingers: "Faugh to your Mrs Fortisquince and Golden-square. We wants a title or a bang-up West-End address at the very least."

"But wouldn't she suffice for a family in ordinary circumstances?" my mother asked.

"Perhaps you know more about it than I do," he said rudely. "Such famblies is more pertickler about tip-top connexions than the aristoxy theirselves." To our horror he tore out and crumpled up the page of the ledger on which he had begun to write my mother's answers. "We won't take you on. There ain't no p'int."

"No point?" my mother repeated.

"You could try for a position as a children's nurse," the man added. "Your

Mrs Fortisquince would sarve for that. But we don't touch that sort of work. You want a sarvints' hirin'-office for that. Now move along, please."

As she turned away I tugged her sleeve: "Miss Quilliam," I reminded her.

"We can't," she whispered.

"You promised," I urged and reluctantly she turned back.

"Can you give me some information?" she asked. "I wish to find a friend of mine — that is, of my son — who may have been registered with you. A Miss Quilliam."

"I seem to rec'lleck the name. But what's it to me?"

"I beg your pardon?"

"What's it worth to me to bother with it?"

"He wants money," I whispered.

"How much?" she whispered back.

"Two shillings," I suggested, wondering if it was worth such an investment.

My mother drew the coins from her reticule and placed them on the counter. The clerk took them up as if absent-mindedly, his attention preoccupied with opening a large volume lying nearby. He ran a finger down the page and at last said: "Yes, I thought I rec'llected the name. Was registered with us while in the employment of the family of Sir Parceval Mompesson of Brook-street and Mompesson-park, Hougham." Here he looked into space reflectively and an almost wistful expression appeared on his features: "A most elegant establishment. We've sent them many a governess while their two young genel'men was in the school-room. And more recent, too, for the young lady. Oh yes, very many."

"Can you tell me by whom she is presently employed?" asked my mother, breaking in upon his reverie.

"No, I can't," he said abruptly and frowned.

"But won't you look," I protested.

"I don't need to," he said. "She ain't registered with us no more. She come in here about a month or two back and wanted to register again, but I couldn't do nothing for her."

My mother and I looked at each other in dismay.

"I don't understand," she said.

He gave us a very mysterious, knowing look accompanied by a piece of pantomime which involved laying one thick finger alongside his nose and shaking his head significantly: "She left without a character."

This confirmed what Henrietta had said, but here was an unforeseen obstacle to our finding her.

"Well then, will you at least be so kind as to tell me her address," my mother asked.

"She didn't leave one, there being no call."

"But have you no address for her?" I demanded.

Reluctantly he looked at the greasy page of his great tome: "According to this, previous to her engagement with Sir Parceval's fambly, she lodged at No. 26 Coleman-street. (Now that's still a wery good address, for all it's in the City.) But there ain't no reason to suppose she's there now." He shut the book with a bang: "That's all I can do for you."

"You remembered all the time that you couldn't help us," I protested. "You shouldn't have taken the two shillings!"

"Move along," he said threateningly. "There's others waiting."

My mother took me by the arm and we went out and began to walk disconsolately towards our lodgings.

"Why was he so unkind?" my mother asked.

"Because he's a beast," I cried.

"Johnnie," she said a few minutes later, "if ever I did need to accept a situation, do you think we dare give Mrs Fortisquince's name?"

Now that I had time to consider it I answered: "I don't think it would be safe to let her know where you were, Mamma."

She agreed and we continued on our way. When we got back and had had dinner, my mother put on her bonnet and set off on her mysterious errand.

While I waited for her I tried to amuse myself by looking at one of my favourite books which had survived the theft because I had been carrying it, but the pictures that had interested me when I gazed at them in Melthorpe seemed strangely flat now. Perhaps it was because I was at last in London and therefore adventure and excitement lay all around me; though if this were so, then this house and this street seemed disappointingly mundane. I closed the book and, seating myself at the window, looked at the evening sky as the sun sank over the horizon, and watched the cowls slowly turning on the chimney-tops and the sparrows hopping about in the gutters of the houses opposite.

At last I heard the door-bell and Jennie going to answer it. Then I detected a light step outside and when my mother came in I knew immediately that something had occurred that had moved her deeply. As she removed her bonnet she looked at me without seeming to see me and I could not tell whether what had happened was good or bad. She seemed excited as if inspired by some unanticipated hope, and yet at the same time saddened as if some dark shadow of the past had fallen upon her. When I spoke to her she looked away suddenly and took a long time to answer me. It was only with considerable difficulty that I was able to observe my undertaking and refrain from asking her any questions while we made our supper of the bread and cheese she had brought back.

Afterwards she sat at the table and began writing in her pocket-book. When I went to my bed a couple of hours later she was still writing, and, happening to awaken some hours later, I crept into the sitting-room and saw her still bent over the table scratching away with her quill.

CHAPTER 30

I was worried by the realization that it might be less easy than we had assumed for my mother to find work as a governess, but she was less concerned since she was anyway determined to earn her living by her needle. So the next morning we strolled up and down Regent-street before at last choosing one of the grand shops selling gowns. As we entered a shop-woman came forward smiling and made a little bobbing curtsey.

"Good morning," my mother began nervously. "I wish to offer to do fine embroidery work for you."

The woman did not understand at first, and my mother had to repeat her words. Then her face darkened and she came up close to us and hissed: "You never ought to have come in the front. Don't you know no better than that?"

"Where should I go?" my mother asked in dismay.

"Out of here and round the back."

We turned and left with as much dignity as we could muster, then went round the mews and with difficulty identified the rear of the premises. Then, directed by a youth loading boxes onto a hand-cart, we climbed a pair of back-stairs to a big bare room beneath the roof where about twenty women — predominantly young — were sitting round a huge table heaped with materials, and stitching so intently that they hardly glanced up as we came in — except for one, who was older than most of the others, and who was putting on her bonnet as if to leave.

"What do you want?" said another older woman, rising and coming forward to speak with a mouthful of pins.

My mother repeated her words and the woman answered brusquely as she turned away: "You're wasting my time. Be off with you."

"How dare you speak to a lady like that!" I cried.

She turned and said scathingly: "Oh, a lady is it? I nivver heard of no lady peddling her work."

My mother pulled me from the room but as we slowly descended the stair she said: "Why must they be so impolite?"

By the door we were overtaken by the woman who had been making ready to leave.

"You see, my dear," she said kindly, "there ain't no call for fancy work. The ladies do it themselves, you know, and bring down the price to nigh on nothing."

"But I must find work to keep myself and my son!"

"Your only hope is to find plain-sewing. But there's no call for it just now since the Season hasn't begun, and I don't know if you could do the hours if you aren't bred to it."

We thanked her and she hurried away.

"I don't believe it," my mother exclaimed. "There must be people who want fine work. If only that wicked woman hadn't stolen my things I could show them a piece and I'm sure they would buy it."

However, what this woman had told us was confirmed — at least as far as I was concerned — during the next week or so as we traipsed from one mantua-maker's shop to another, often received with considerable discourtesy, though occasionally with kindness.

To my relief, my mother seemed strangely cheerful in spite of these discouragements. In the evenings she divided her time between working at a piece of embroidery that I assumed must have survived the theft, and writing in her pocket-book.

One evening when I was particularly cast down at having failed once again to persuade her that it would be wiser to attempt to find a situation as a governess at one of the registry-offices that remained to be approached, she said: "It will be all right, you know, Johnnie. I have a design."

"What do you mean by a design?"

"Wait and see," she said, shaking her head with a mysterious smile.

It was about this time that I suggested to her that we should find a cheaper lodging without waiting for the expiry of our month's tenancy. For on our journeyings through the poorer streets we had observed cards in the windows advertising rooms to let at much lower prices. She reluctantly agreed and we picked out one nearby in Maddox-street that seemed clean and respectable. The landlady, Mrs Philliber, appeared to be a pleasant and decent woman and we negotiated with her for a single room at 7s. a week.

Mrs Marrables was not pleased that we wished to end the tenancy so soon and refused to return any of the first month's rent unless she could find another tenant for that period. This was undeniably fair, but fortunately she found another person who was anxious to take the rooms immediately and at a higher rent than we were paying her. She declined, however, to return the whole of the unexpired portion of our rent and now revealed an aspect of her character that we had not seen before:

"Why, Mrs Offland, there's all the fuss and bother I've had and that has to be considered. Time is money, you know, and I'd be robbing myself and my family not to take it into account."

I prevailed upon her, at last, and we compounded with her to receive a rebate of a week's rent and took possession of our new room that afternoon. Now, on closer acquaintance, it became clear that although our new lodgings were only a few streets away from our old, the district was much less respectable, and I saw that my mother's spirits sank.

"I know!" I cried. "Let us have a feast to celebrate our new home!"

She clapped her hands together: "Yes! And then I will make negus! And it will be just like the old days. You're right, Johnnie. This will be our home from now on, so I will write to Bissett to send the money here."

So we enlisted the help of the young maid-servant, whom we sent out for two chops and four-pence-worth of muffins and a little brandy for the negus. Meanwhile we put the plates to warm behind the fender and made the room ready. When the girl brought her purchases back — together with some baked potatoes from the cook-shop and a jug of milk, a handful of spices, and two eggs purchased from Mrs Philliber — my mother broiled the chops over the fire on a grid-iron suspended on a couple of trivets. As we ate them we felt very jolly and pleased with ourselves, and except for a certain burnt quality on the outside and an undeniable rawness inside, the chops were excellently cooked.

Then, while I speared the muffins on a toasting-fork and grilled them, my mother set about making the negus. As I watched her she seemed suddenly very innocent and vulnerable, filled now with delight at the prospect of the negus and, I guessed, at the thought of writing to one whom she loved and trusted. I feared that she had not yet realized how difficult things were going to be for us and I felt oddly as if I were older than she. I had seen strangers look at her with so cold and calculating an expression that I felt that I could take nothing for granted — and certainly not Bissett's loyalty.

When the negus was ready she poured me a third of a tumbler and we toasted each other in the hot, fragrant liquid.

I gasped: "It tastes even nastier than usual!"

She laughed and sat down to begin her letter.

"Are you telling her our address?" I asked.

"Of course, my dearest. How else should she know where to send the money! You are funny."

I hesitated, but I could not bring myself to say anything.

She glanced at me, the point of the quill pressed thoughtfully against her cheek as she pondered: "I am telling her to deduct from what she sends us all her expenses — arranging the sale, paying for this letter, and so on — and, in addition, a quarter's wages in lieu of notice." She removed the point of the pen leaving an inky trace on her face: "Do you think that is fair?"

"Indeed. And perhaps more generous than we can afford to be!"

She frowned: "Do you think I should ask her to take less?"

"No, I think we must treat Bissett well."

"Yes, Johnnie," she said delightedly. "That's just what I think. You know, she is really our only true friend."

We confided the letter to the post-office the next day. Assuming that Bissett had had time to sell the furniture and settle with the creditors, we expected to hear from her by the end of the following week.

When by that date no letter had arrived, my mother assumed that it was taking her longer to settle up than we had calculated. We had other, more pressing worries by that time, anyway, for it had been a week of further disillusionment. For one thing, we had become concerned about our new lodgings, for the house was dirty and often rather noisy late in the evenings, while the servants, though friendly, were careless and slovenly. And Mrs Philliber frequently smelt unmistakably of spirits and on those occasions tended to be robustly informal.

Additionally, still convinced that she would be able to earn our keep by doing fine embroidery, my mother had insisted that we start looking for a school for me. I had protested and told her the size of the fees that I had seen in the newspaper, but she had remained obdurate.

The first academic establishment we visited was in Goodge-street and was kept by a gentleman with a very red nose, an unsteady gait, and an equally uncertain grasp of English grammar. The second was up a dirty bye-street off Fitzroy-square where, after a long silence, our knock was greeted by a grubby curtain moving cautiously at a window. Then the door was opened by a thin man in patched clothes who, declaring himself to be the "High-master", instantly remarked conversationally that he had never had to answer the door before but as it happened the maid-servant, the cook and the kitchen-boy had all been given a holiday that day and the parlour-maid had been sent out on an errand that very minute. We went in and, noticing that we were struck by the absence of furniture in the hall, the High-master mentioned that it had all been sent away for French-polishing. He led us into the school-room and we found that the establishment appeared to consist of two small frightened boys covered in ink and chilblains and wearing collars that were too large for them.

That evening I put it to my mother that since there was clearly no point in her continuing to look for orders for fine work, we would have to consider other ways of earning our living and therefore abandon the quest for a school.

She smiled and said: "But you're quite wrong, Johnnie. I have a surprise for you. I have finished my design."

She held up a piece of *broderie anglaise* and I saw that it was a length of silk with beautifully worked designs in silver and gold of the kind I had often seen her undertake at Melthorpe.

"I thought all your good stuffs had been stolen. Where did the material and the thread come from?" I demanded.

She blushed: "I bought it, Johnnie."

"How much did it cost?"

"Three pounds," she said, looking away.

"Was it?"

She reddened: "Well, the thread was another two pounds. But don't you see, when I show this, I will be certain to get work."

"It was very wrong of you not to ask me before spending so much!" I cried, feeling a surge of rage at her simplicity and deceptiveness.

"I knew you'd stop me if I told you," she exclaimed, near to tears.

We quarrelled and, unreconciled, both sobbed ourselves to sleep. Next morning a sort of peace was restored between us and, making the best of our appearance, we set off for New-Bond-street. There we entered a grand shop (by the rear entrance, of course) and found the forewoman.

Before my mother had finished her introduction, she seized the material, briskly unrolled it and, with a grimace, held it stretched out: "Why, this was a dacent piece of silk what I might have done something with, only you've gorn and sp'iled it."

My mother flushed and I cried: "Why, whatever can you mean?"

Ignoring me the woman said to my mother: "This is journey-man work. Look at the size of them stitches and the unevenness of the lines. I'd send any girl out of my shop what did work like that. And it's a provincial style as well. Take it away and begone with you."

I cannot bring myself to describe how we dragged ourselves out of there nor how, after finding explanations of the woman's attitude that served to rally each other's spirits (for our previous night's quarrel was quite forgotten), we tried other shops, only to hear the same verdict — though usually less offensively worded.

So now at last accepting the impossibility of what she had been hoping for, my mother consented to visit the other registry-offices. Here, however, my worst fears were confirmed for we met with the same reception as at the first one: there were far too many educated women competing for places for there to be any likelihood of employment for one without excellent references, experience and a greater degree of proficiency than my mother could claim. At each office we remembered to enquire for Miss Quilliam, and it was strange that although none of the clerks could tell us anything of her, they always seemed to recognise the name as soon as we mentioned it.

The realization that even the dreaded recourse of governess was not open to her was a heavy blow for my mother. And so now we began the dreary round again, this time visiting those much more squalid registry-offices which undertook to find positions as lady's companions or children's nurses. But even here the lack of a reference from a previous employer or even of a "good name" — a character reference from a respectable individual — proved to be an insurmountable obstacle since we had decided that we dared not ask Mrs Fortisquince.

"Is there no-one who knew you before you lived in Melthorpe?" I asked her again after a day of renewed disappointments.

She shook her head. "My father and I lived very quietly. We knew almost no-one."

"What about whoever it was you went to see that day soon after we arrived?" I demanded irritably.

She shuddered and shook her head: "Oh no, that wouldn't serve at all."

Yet even if she could have found such work and we were enriched by our little capital due from Bissett, I could see that, since the usual terms were "all found" and 10£ a year, living would be very hard and there would certainly be nothing to spare for my education.

At last, deciding that her only marketable skill lay in her ability as a plain needlewoman, my mother went back to the first mantua-maker's shop in Regent-street from which we had been turned away.

By chance we encountered in the mews the woman who had spoken to us kindly before, and when my mother explained what she had come for this time, she said: "Let me see your hands." She took them in her own: "So white and fine. Look at mine."

They were as hard as horn and yet were covered in little sores where she had been pricked by the needles.

"Nobody will take you on, my dear. You could not work fast enough. Nor could you stand the long hours. Fourteen, at least, and often sixteen or seventeen, and sometimes we have to work all night at no notice. And all for ten shilling a week." She glanced at me and added in a low voice: "But a young woman with a pretty face need never go hungry in London."

My mother blushed as if at the compliment and I felt reassured by this. There were kind people here after all and we would be all right.

She was at least correct in her assumption that my mother would fail to find employment, though it was only after we had spent many hours walking the long grey streets without success that we acknowledged this.

By the end of the following week — that is the third after we had sent the letter — there was still no reply from Melthorpe. Now worried by this at last, my mother wrote again. Our little reserve of capital was disappearing quickly and the rent which had seemed so self-denyingly parsimonious when we had moved from our original lodgings, now began to seem an extravagance that was no longer justifiable. Yet we were reluctant to move again because of the waste of time and money involved, and when a smaller chamber at the top of the house came available at 5s. a week we negotiated with Mrs Philliber and moved into it.

The room — which was a section of the garret that had been boarded off — had no fireplace so we now ate our food cold or occasionally treated ourselves to something hot from a nearby pastry-cook. The weather was still mild but it would be getting colder, and I wondered how we could face the winter there. It was a dreary little chamber with hardly any view except of the neighbouring rooves and no sunshine, and perhaps because of this our spirits gradually wore down. Often in the late afternoon while my mother was out searching for work, I would sit with a book in my hand and look out between the chimney-pots to watch the sparrows in the eaves hopping around like tiny cripples on crutches, and then suddenly whirring their wings and taking flight out of my sight — and how I envied them!

After spending the day traipsing around the streets — for a coach was now out of the question even for the longest journeys and there were no omnibuses at that period — my mother was exhausted and often wet through if it had been raining. As the weather grew colder, the thin summer clothes that were all we had became increasingly inadequate, and we had seriously to deplete our little capital in order to buy ourselves great-coats.

It became my mother's custom to make herself a bowl of negus every evening, though as we grew poorer she dispensed first with the eggs and then the milk and finally the spices. It was as if — or so it seemed to me — she was trying to convince herself by this ritual that all was well. And certainly she grew more cheerful afterwards, though she was frequently out of sorts in the morning.

By the time a month had passed since the first letter to Bissett, we had only four pounds left and I privately calculated that, with rent and food, we were living at the rate of 12s. a week. It was clear to me that without the money we were expecting, we could not continue long at this rate. And when the winter was upon us we would need to spend money to keep warm, perhaps necessitating a move to another room for I could not see how we could live without a fire.

BOOK II

Understandings

CHAPTER 31

Once again Mr Sancious finds himself outside the door of No. 27 Golden-square. When he is led into the presence of the widow she smiles coldly and says: "Why, Mr Sancious, what can you want of me?"

"It concerns Mrs Mellamphy again. Or, rather, Mrs Clothier. Ma'am, I am desperate. I throw myself at your feet. I must find her."

"Gracious heavens, Mr Sancious! Such passion! Has she absconded without settling your account?"

She indicates that he should sit, and as he does so Mr Sancious forces his lips to part and draw back from his teeth: "Oh very droll, ma'am. Ha-ha. But this is deeply embarrassing to me. Indeed, more than embarrassing. She has disappeared and I believe she may have come to Town. I must find her."

"Your concern for her welfare does you credit. But am I to assume that you are no longer in her confidence, as you once boasted of being?"

The attorney flushes: "The truth is, ma'am, she lost some money in a speculation over which I advised her."

"And she has taken into her head the notion that you did not deal with her honestly?"

The attorney fails to conceal his astonishment: "You are very acute, madam. That is exactly the case. Her suspicions are quite absurd, of course."

"Of course."

"Have you any idea where she might be?"

"Set your mind at rest on that score. She is in Town."

"Oh thank heavens."

"I have seen and spoken to her in this very room not three weeks ago."

"Then pray tell me where she is."

"Wait, Mr Sancious. We must understand each other perfectly. I think you were not frank with me on the last occasion we met."

"Madam!"

"Do you remember that I asked you whether you had Mrs Clothier's interests at heart? If I were to ask you that question now, what would you answer?"

The two watch each other very closely.

Then the attorney says: "My answer would be that I have them at heart precisely to the extent that you have yourself."

The young widow smiles.

"That is very satisfactory," she says. "But before I tell you anything, I must know why you desire to find her and who you are working for."

He hesitates and she says: "Come, frankness, Mr Sancious. You can't be disbarred for it, you know." When he still fails to reply she says: "I suspect that your principal is Mr Silas Clothier."

"You are right," he answers in surprise. "And since you know that, then you must understand how vital it is to his interests to obtain the document which Mrs Clothier has in her possession."

"The document," she repeats vaguely.

"That the Mompessons are trying to obtain," he says, "because it destroys their right to the Hougham property."

He breaks off for Mrs Fortisquince turns away suddenly.

"Are you all right, madam? Shall I ring for your maid?"

"No, I am quite well, I thank you." After a moment, she turns back to him: "Mr Sancious, I will help you. But I must tell you frankly that I too have no idea where Mrs Clothier is now, beyond the mere fact that she is in London."

"Then I have told you this for nothing!" the attorney says angrily, rising to his feet.

"No, Mr Sancious. For I believe I may be able to assist you. I take it that Mr Clothier will reward you for finding her?"

He nods.

"In that case, I am sure you and I will be able to reach an understanding."

He seats himself again.

"However," she continues, "it is absolutely crucial that my involvement be kept from Mr Clothier."

He looks at her curiously and she says: "Oh, the reason for that has to do with long-past events. You could have no interest in them. But there are matters on which you and I have a common interest."

"My dear madam," the little lawyer says, "from this moment on, your interests are mine."

CHAPTER 32

When, even by the end of November, no reply had come from Melthorpe, we had found ourselves facing a crisis: we had no money to pay the following week's rent. As this moment had approached I had begged my mother to tell Mrs Philliber the frank truth as soon as possible, but she would not. Having given up the search for work, she had begun to spend the day listlessly in that increasingly cold little room until it was time to go to the post-office. On the way home she would purchase our supper and something for the negus, and it was on the latter item that much of our money had gone.

My mother had delayed the crisis by promising Mrs Philliber that the money was coming, but one morning at the beginning of December — by which time we owed a week in arrears — the landlady came boldly into our little chamber and said bluntly: "It ain't coming, is it?"

"Why, how can you say such a thing!" my mother cried. "I expect it tomorrow."

"No," I said. "I'm afraid it seems that it isn't."

"Johnnie!" my mother cried.

"I ain't a cruel woman," Mrs Philliber said. "But I've my own to think on and I must be paid." She looked round the room curiously: "Surely you must have something you could sell?"

My mother followed her gaze in alarm as it swept the naked room, and I saw her seize and hide the fatal piece of material.

Her gaze swung back to rest upon us: "Them clothes you're wearing would fetch a few pound," she said. "And they're for summer so what will you do now that winter's upon us? Why don't you sell 'em? Then you can pay me what you owe and still buy some slops for winter?"

My mother resisted the idea of exchanging our own clothes for inferior and second-hand garments, but eventually we managed to bring her round.

"Let me trade 'em for you," Mrs Philliber said. "I'll wager I could git more for 'em than what you could. And I promise I won't cheat you."

I believed her and so we came to an agreement under which she would take a small commission and, of course, deduct her rent. She estimated that they would fetch some five or six pounds clear of the exchange, and this was encouraging news for we could live on such a sum for some time.

We gave them to her, reducing ourselves to our great-coats. As she was about to leave the room with them over her arm, she suddenly looked at my mother closely: "Is that case silver?" she asked, indicating the slender container that hung at my mother's waist.

"No, only silver-gilt."

"I'll wager I could get a pound or two for it," she said. "And something for your ring." She raised her eyes to my mother's neck. "But I'd take my oath that locket is silver."

My mother gripped it in alarm: "I would not think of parting with this."

"Don't be silly, Mamma," I cried.

"Oh? It has tender associations for you, does it?" Mrs Philliber enquired with sympathetic inquisitiveness.

"I ... yes," my mother stammered.

The landlady shook her head: "Well, my dear, the time may come when it's all that stands between you and starvation. And if it does, I think that you could get four or five pound for it. You shouldn't take less than three. Remember what I said."

She left the room.

"Now, Mamma," I said, "you must not be silly about that locket."

"Johnnie, don't speak to me like that."

"But you don't understand," I cried. "We have nothing. And the money from Melthorpe is not going to come."

Now that I was being so frank I brought up something that I had often thought about: "And we must think of selling the codicil to Sir Perceval."

"No!" she cried. "Anything but that."

We quarrelled about it and by the time Mrs Philliber returned we were both sullen and resentful. However, we were cheered by her news for she had been as good as her word and once she had taken her back-rent we were left with enough to keep us for a few more months. Moreover, I was delighted with what

Mrs Philliber had purchased: a pair of white cord trowsers with a blue waistcoat and matching cut-away jacket with brass buttons and a white beaver-hat.

We still hoped for the money to arrive from Melthorpe, and even discussed the daring possibility of my mother's going down there by the public coach as an outside passenger to find out what had happened. However, this would have cost at least five pounds and we decided that this was too great a risk to undertake.

No news came in the next weeks and by the time Christmas was upon us, my mother had given up hope of finding work without a character. A few days before the festival she suggested to me that it would be a good idea to pay our respects to Mrs Fortisquince and find out how she was disposed towards us in our present plight in the hope that she might offer some help.

I could not argue against the wisdom of the proposal but I stood out for one condition: "By all means, but let us not reveal to her where we are living."

My mother agreed to this and suggested that we should take her a gift.

"How could we?" I demanded.

She picked up that ill-fated piece of embroidery and said sadly: "I am sure she will value this. She always loved good things."

We observed the day itself very frugally with a small fowl which Mrs Philliber permitted my mother to broil at her kitchen-fire, and with mince-pies from the pastry-cook. In the afternoon we set off through the silent streets.

When we knocked on the door the young maid-servant answered it with a smile of welcome: "Oh, Mrs Mellamphy, it is good to see you again. The miss'is is from home, but I know she'll be sorry for missing you, for she has often said she hoped as you'd come back."

My mother beamed at me in triumph and said: "Then may we wait?"

"Oh ma'am, I'm a-feared she's gone down into the country. She won't be back till the day arter tomorrer. But please to leave me your direction for I know she was anxious to find you."

"She has gone away at Christmas?" my mother exclaimed. "I hope there is nothing amiss?"

"Oh no," she replied, adding with the perfect appearance of logic: "She's only gone to Canterbury."

My mother handed over our gift and asked her to wish her mistress the season's greetings from us.

"Very well, Mrs Mellamphy," she said. "But will you tell me your address, please?"

I touched her arm warningly.

"We are about to move to a new one," she said, remembering the excuse we had prepared. "I will let Mrs Fortisquince know it when I know where it is myself."

"But please tell me where you live now, ma'am. The miss'is expressly told me that if you ever come while she was from home, I should find it out. I will get into trouble if you don't tell me."

My mother blushed and looked at me in dismay.

"We will send word of it in a few days," I said rather magnificently, as if we had ranks of servants at our bidding. Then I took my mother's arm to lead her away.

"Well said, Johnnie," she whispered.

"I wonder why Mrs Fortisquince is so anxious to find us."

"Perhaps she wishes to help us."

She said it without conviction and it seemed to me that she accepted this as evidence that Mrs Fortisquince was not to be trusted.

As the months passed and our money ran out again, we drifted towards another crisis and one to which I could see no favourable outcome if my mother persisted in refusing to sell either the case or the ring.

I thought often about the codicil for which Sir Perceval and then Mr Barbellion had offered us so much money. Seventeen hundred pounds would end all our worries, and it was reassuring to know that in the last resort we could presumably raise money by that means. But at the same time I began to feel a vague sense that without knowing why they were so anxious to obtain it, it would be a mistake to part with it. Perhaps my mother had very sound reasons for her unwillingness to surrender it. I recalled the day she had shewn me the locket and spoken of a decision she was trying to make. It involved a choice between the possibility of wealth but the certainty of danger if she chose not to do something. Now I believed I understood: alarmed by the burglary, she had been thinking of destroying the codicil. Then surely I was right to suspect that it might be the means to our entering upon great riches!

My mother now began to spend time in the kitchen with Mrs Philliber and increasingly often she came up late and woke me up by taking a long time making ready for sleep. Then she often lay in bed all morning complaining of a headache.

Towards the end of February the money from the sale of our clothes ran out, and one morning the landlady came up for one of her little talks. Reluctantly, my mother consented to sell the document-case, and handed it to her, carefully placing the codicil in the pocket she wore beneath her petticoats and in which she carried her pocket-book.

I had wondered whether to offer to sell the ring which Henrietta had given me, and I now showed it to Mrs Philliber.

She looked at it with contempt: "Only a bit of pewter and glass," she sniffed. "Ain't worth even a penny."

Flushed with irritation at her words, I nevertheless felt relief that I had no obligation to part with my keep-sake for although the world of innocent childhood in which we had pledged our love to each other seemed so distant, I still remembered the passionate and black-eyed little girl with affection.

The sale of the case brought a couple of pounds which kept us going for a few more weeks, but one morning in the middle of March our circumstances changed dramatically. I had gone out to buy us some rolls for breakfast and as I came in I noticed a man standing on the opposite side of the road. I thought I had seen him there a few days before and reflected for a moment on the oddity of this. However, I had reason to forget about this as soon as I got upstairs, for I found an unpleasant scene going on. Mrs Philliber was standing at the door of our little room and speaking very loudly on the subject of the rent.

"I have no money, I tell you," my mother cried.

"Then sell that blessed locket," the landlady cried and I saw that her face was flushed in the way I had come to recognise meant that she could be quite dangerous.

"I can't! I won't!" my mother protested.

"Well pawn it then, and you can redeem it when that blessed money comes — if it ever does."

"I dare not. I might lose it."

"Well, my dear, you'll have to do something or out you'll have to go. And that blessed boy."

She threw in this last remark apparently in honour of myself, for I gained the top landing at that moment. When I entered the room I found that my mother had buried her head in her arms.

"Then will you at least part with the ring?" Mrs Philliber asked, still from the door.

"My wedding-band?" my mother said, raising her head in surprise.

"Yes," she said and added sarcastically: "Or does that have sentimental associations?"

"Yes, it does," said my mother softly. "But I'd rather lose it than the locket. How much is it worth?"

Mrs Philliber advanced into the chamber, took my mother's small pale hand in her big red one and studied the ring: "Mebbe two pounds."

"But it cost far more than that, I'm sure. Only look at the workmanship!"

"They sell and buy them simply by the weight of gold, my dear." She studied the engraving: "What are the letters?"

"'P' and 'M' intertwined in a circlet of roses."

"And the roses makes a big 'C', ain't that right? Very pretty, but of no value to nobody else. First thing the silversmith will do, he'll burnish 'em off."

I had never noticed these letters. What could that mysterious "C" stand for?

"But I need a wedding-band."

"Indeed you do," said the landlady. "But they're not difficult to obtain." She cackled in anticipation of her joke: "Easier to come by than husbands. And a deal less bother to keep."

"Very well, I will sell it," said my mother.

"Come, I have a proposal. You and I will go now to a goldsmith I know of hard by here who will give us a fair price. And for a few pence he will give you a brass ring with the same initials worked upon it. What do you say?"

She nodded her consent.

"Then put your bonnet on and we'll go now."

"I need not come, need I, Mamma?" I asked.

"No, Johnnie. Stay here. I won't be very long. On the way back I'll buy something nice for our dinner."

I kissed her and she went out with Mrs Philliber. As I watched them from the window I remembered the stranger I had seen earlier, and noticed that he was no longer there.

After about an hour I heard a loud ringing at the bell of the street-door. I assumed it was my mother returning before Mrs Philliber who had her own key, but when the little servant answered the door, I heard men's voices. Then there was a rush upon the stairs, the door of our room was unceremoniously opened, and a crowd of strangers burst in.

Foremost among them was a red-faced man with a nose like a wen, who was wearing a three-cornered hat and carrying a silver rod. He looked round the room and, with a sweep of the arm that embraced the few possessions scattered about, shouted at me: "Are these the effects of Mrs Mellamphy, formerly of Manor-farm-cottage, Mortsey by Melthorpe, in the County of etc. etc.?"

I stood bewildered.

"Yes, yes, they are," said another man impatiently.

He was tall with a long, drooping pale face and I thought I recognised him from somewhere but in the excitement of the moment, could not place him.

"Now, now, Mr Espenshade, not so fast," said the man in the three-cornered hat. "There is a proper form to be gone through."

"Damn your forms," Mr Espenshade said. "I recognise the boy. But the woman isn't here. I said you should have let *me* watch the house." As he spoke he crossed the room and seized me by the arm, gripping me tightly. "We've got the boy at the least."

"Let me go," I said.

His grip tightened until it hurt. Now that I had had time to collect my wits I realized that there were only three men.

"I watched from eight sharp and never seen her leave the house this morning," said the one who had not yet spoken, a burly individual in a green coat with a face like a London brick — flat and reddish. He turned to the man in the three-cornered hat: "Then I come and told you so, Mr Fewster."

"That's when she must have gone out, you confounded simpleton," cried Mr Espenshade.

The burly one was the man whom I had seen across the street!

Mr Fewster now said with considerable dignity: "There ain't no call for language like that, Mr Espenshade. You can't guard against an accident of that natur'."

Mr Espenshade muttered something I couldn't catch, and then, giving me a shake, he said: "Where is she?"

I shook my head.

"Where has your mother gone?"

The maid, Susan, had followed the men up and was standing, pale with fright, at the door.

"Send up your mistress," Mr Fewster ordered her.

"Please sir, she ain't here. She's from home, too."

He turned to me: "Tell us where your mother is."

"Who are you?" I cried. "What right have you to come in here in this manner?"

"Every right in the world, young man," said Mr Fewster drawing himself up and pushing out his chest so that I feared his polished brass buttons would pop. "I am the sheriff's officer for the jurisdiction of the Marlborough Street Commission of the Peace. And this gentleman," he said, indicating the individual in the green coat who bowed ceremoniously in my direction, "is Mr Beaglehole who has the honour to be my deputy."

"The bailiffs," Mr Espenshade said grimly.

"What do you want with us?" I cried.

"We're putting in an execution."

I gasped. The bailiff drew from his pocket a piece of paper and laboriously unfolded it. "I have here a warrant for the securing of the body of Mrs Mellamphy formerly of etc. etc. to be brought before the Commission of the Peace in the County of Middlesex; and likewise for the distraint of all the effects of the said person. The warrant has been issued by the local magistrate and backed by the one here and the capias transferred to me."

Seeing my bewilderment Mr Espenshade said: "In plain English they're taking up your mother and seizing all her goods."

"But why?" I demanded.

"I am acting under a warrant issued for the recovery of debt," the bailiff said.

"But I don't understand. We owe nothing!"

"Oh indeed?" he said satirically. "That's not the view of the following plaintiffs at whose suit I am acting." He unfolded the paper and began to read out a list of names: "Henry Yallop, Anne Peege, Elizabeth Passant, Michael Treadgold ... "

"We're losing our time," exclaimed the man holding me. "We must find where the woman is."

Mr Fewster stared at him in reproachful silence and then continued to read: "James Passant, Bartholomew Kittermaster, and Jane Parchment."

"Those are all tradespeople in Melthorpe!" I exclaimed. "But they have all been paid."

"Apparently not, young gentleman," said the bailiff.

"But Bissett was to pay them with the money from selling the furniture!"

"Bissett? I seem to know that name."

He turned over the paper and searched it until he found what he wanted: "Ah yes. 'This warrant is issued on information received from Mrs Bissett of etc. etc. to the effect that the present whereabouts of the person named are at No. 31 Maddox-street in the Parish of St. James.'"

"Bissett gave that away!" I gasped.

"Don't forget your main business," said Mr Espenshade.

As he spoke, and perhaps because I was thinking of Bissett, I suddenly remembered with a shudder of horror when it was that I had seen him: he was the man who had followed me the day I had met Harry and whom I had then seen speaking to Bissett outside the Rose and Crab!

"I don't need you to remind me," said Mr Fewster indignantly. Then he turned to me: "Now tell me where your mother is."

"I don't know."

Mr Espenshade gripped even harder and shook me. At that moment I heard a step upon the landing. The three men heard it too and in silence we all turned towards the door. It opened as far as it could, since it was obstructed by the bailiff and his assistant, and a woman's voice said: "What's going on in there?"

I recognised the newcomer as our landlady, but Mr Espenshade let go of me and swiftly crossed the room. He pulled open the door and Mrs Philliber, who had obviously been pushing at it, almost fell into the room. He seized her by the arms from behind.

"How dare you?" she protested and tried to pull herself free.

He followed her still holding her arms.

"Let me see your face, damn it!" he said.

"Who in heaven's name are you?" she demanded.

"She's *my* prisoner!" cried Mr Fewster. "Let her go!"

Seizing my opportunity I moved across the room until only the bailiff's deputy was between me and the door.

"Take a hold on her, Beaglehole!" Fewster cried.

"That's my miss'is," cried Susan, adding to the uproar.

The deputy moved forward to obey his master's orders and Mr Espenshade, catching sight of Mrs Philliber's face and realizing that she was not the person whom he wanted, let go of her and looked round for me. At that moment I reached the door.

"Hold the boy!" Mr Espenshade cried.

"I don't have no warrant to hold him," I heard Fewster say.

"Damn your warrants. He's going to warn his mother!"

Mr Espenshade made a rush towards me but I managed to get out of the room and down the stairs. I heard him come crashing after me as I shot out of the street-door, and once I was out in the street I sped round the first corner and then the next. I ran the full length of the street and on reaching the next corner looked back just before turning it, and saw that my pursuer was still behind me. Knowing that I could not hope to keep ahead of him in a fair match, I dived into a dark alley-way and flattened myself against the wall, my heart thumping. To my relief he ran past without even glancing into the entrance. I emerged cautiously a few moments later, tormented by the thought of how urgently I needed to warn my mother not to return to the house.

Very circumspectly and by a roundabout route, I made my way back until I was in a bye-street opposite the lodging-house. From here I could see anyone entering or leaving, but I was far enough away to make it unlikely that my pursuers would notice me. Mr Espenshade was standing on top of the steps scanning the street in both directions, while the two bailiffs were in conversation with the driver of a gig that was waiting outside the house.

From here I would be able to see my mother before Mr Espenshade if she came up Pollen-street behind me, but only at the same time as he if she came along Maddox-street. Knowing that there was no possibility of her being able to evade her pursuers in the way that I had, I could not wait passively for her to spring the trap prepared for her.

Mr Beaglehole now clambered into the gig and it drove off, leaving the bailiff and Mr Espenshade standing talking together. But then, to my delight, they went up the steps and shut the door. Just for the few moments while they were ascending to our room, I had my chance and I knew what I had to do, though it was contrary to all my instincts for safety. I thought suddenly of the Huffams' motto: "Safety is to be sought in the midst of danger". There was only one place from which I could see almost as well as they, but without any chance of their seeing me. And so I ran across the street and up the steps until I stood at the street-door. From here I could command almost as good a view as they could from the upper windows.

I had been peering anxiously along the street in either direction in the hope of spotting my mother for a few minutes when a fellow lodger came up the steps. When he nodded at me and seemed surprised to find me standing sentinel there, I signalled to him to say nothing. He knocked and the door was opened. Luckily Susan did not look round it for she might have cried out in surprise at seeing me.

At last I saw my mother, recognising her bonnet bobbing above the crowd of heads. My heart rapidly beating, I forced myself to walk at an ordinary pace towards her. There were many foot-passengers on the pavement and I had to hope that my pursuers would not recognise me from above and behind. Fortunately, for she might have made some sign of recognition which could have been observed, my mother did not see me until I was within a few paces of her. As I reached her I kept walking and cried: "Turn around and follow me."

I had time to see an expression of surprise appear, then I was past her. I dared not turn to see if she were following. My ears straining for sounds of pursuit, I continued to the next corner and turned into Regent-street. I waited for what seemed long minutes — but could only have been seconds — until, to my inexpressible relief, my mother appeared round the corner.

"What is this game, Johnnie?" she asked, smiling anxiously.

"It's not a game!" I cried. "It's the bailiffs. We must get away."

A hackney-coach was passing and I ran into the street to wave to the driver. He stopped his horses and got down with what seemed to me to be deliberate slowness to lower the steps, and I urged my bewildered mother to get in. "Keep driving!" I shouted, pulling down the blinds, as the coachman raised the steps and mounted again to his box.

As we lumbered along I explained to my mother what had happened, leaving Bissett's name unmentioned. As I saw her horror, the full enormity of our predicament now dawned upon me.

"But how can they have a warrant?" she asked.

I did not speak.

"Something must have happened to Bissett," she said. "That is why she has not written. But what can it be?"

This was not the occasion to embark upon such a discussion. Our plight was desperate for we now possessed in the world only what we had with us.

"How much money have you?" I asked.

She took her bulky pocket-book from her reticule.

"We sold the wedding-band for two pounds and two shillings," she said. "And the brass ring cost three-pence." She held out her hand with a forced smile and showed me. "I had my initials worked on it."

I saw that the letters "MC" were crudely engraved. (What could that "C" stand for?)

"Then Mrs Philliber took her back-rent and ten shillings for the next two weeks, so that leaves only about a guinea."

"What a pity you paid for two weeks," I sighed.

"She insisted, Johnnie," she said timidly.

Apart from this, we had the clothes we were wearing and the locket which Mrs Philliber had told us was worth several pounds.

"I wonder, can Bissett have betrayed us?" my mother said. "I believe she must have, for no-one but she knows our address." She turned to me in panic: "She must be in league with Mr Barbellion and our enemy!"

"Later, Mamma," I said. "We cannot think of that now."

She started muttering to herself, her face white and fearful. I caught a few words: "Enemy ... Silas ... destroy us."

I saw that she was shivering. When I raised one of the blinds and looked out of window, I did not recognise the street.

"We must stop the coach," I said, "or the fare will take all our money."

I put my head out of window and cried out to the driver. We got out and paid the fare which was 1s. 6d. As the driver was folding up the steps I said: "Please, can you tell us where we are?"

He made no answer but got back on the box. I asked him again. He muttered something I did not catch as he shook the reins and moved off.

We were in a long gloomy street of shabby houses, very poorly-lit by a single oil-lamp halfway along it. We stood at the side of the carriageway and looked at each other in dismay: we had never been out so late in a strange neighbourhood.

"Where are we?" my mother asked me.

"I don't know," I said.

She began to tremble: "Oh Johnnie, what will become of us?"

"Come," I said. "We have not done so badly. We have escaped pursuit. No one knows where we are."

"Not even we ourselves," she said and to my alarm she began to laugh, but I became even more alarmed when the laughter turned into sobs.

I put my arm round her shoulders. "It will be better in the morning," I said. "But now we must find shelter for the night."

Dusk was approaching and it was getting cold. Although my mother was wearing her out-door clothes, I had run out of the house without my great-coat or hat.

"We have enough money to find a lodging for tonight," I said. "But we must learn where we are."

I put this question to a decent looking working-man who was passing.

"This is Smiffle," he said.

Recognising the name that I had not caught on the hackney-coachman's lips, I remembered something from my study of my map: "Is that near Coleman-street?"

"It ain't so far," he said and gave me directions.

"Did you hear that, Mamma?" I said.

She replied dully: "No."

"We're in Smithfield, so the street where Miss Quilliam lives, or at least used to live, is quite near. Let us go there."

She made no response and realizing that it fell to me to take the initiative, I took her arm in mine and led her in the direction the man had pointed out.

It was late by the time we found the street and rang the bell of No. 26 which was a tall, gloomy-looking building in a street whose houses seemed to be eyeing each other askance in genteel distaste.

On learning from the maid who answered that she did not know Miss Quilliam's name, my mother gasped and staggered. The girl looked at her sympathetically and asked us to come in while she enquired of her mistress. The lofty hall — filled with the scent of flowers that stood in bowls upon elegant side-tables — was only dimly-lit by bees-wax candles, but I could see how fine the furniture was: the rosewood cabinets, the ancient oak-cased clock, and the shield-backed chairs against the walls. My mother slumped onto one of these and I chafed her hands.

After a few minutes another servant-girl returned with a sharp-featured woman of about fifty who, as she approached, eyed us narrowly. She was very clearly in a superior class to Mrs Philliber or even Mrs Marrables, and I could imagine how unfavourable an impression my lack of a hat and coat and my mother's exhausted state were making upon her.

"I am Mrs Malatratt," she said. "My servant tells me you are enquiring for Miss Quilliam?"

"Yes, we are friends of hers," I took it upon myself to explain.

Mrs Malatratt indicated her surprise at my answering: "Is this lady ... unwell?"

"She is very tired," I said. "That is all."

She looked at me closely and then turned to examine my mother who glanced up and tried to smile at her but, failing to do so, bit her lip and lowered her head.

"Miss Quilliam is no longer here," Mrs Malatratt said. "She left this house to take up a position in the household of Sir Perceval and Lady Mompesson almost a year ago." She rolled the names and titles out with obvious relish.

"Thank you," I answered. "But we know that and also that she left that position quite recently."

"That is so," Mrs Malatratt said reluctantly, as if unwilling to let go of these illustrious names. "Whom, might I ask, have I the pleasure of addressing?"

"Our name is Mellamphy."

"If you are friends of Miss Quilliam I confess I am surprised that you do not know where she is."

"Miss Quilliam did not expect us to come to London so soon," I said, trying not to exceed the limits of truth. But seeing an expression of polite surprise on the landlady's face, I added: "It is possible that she has written to the place we have just come from to tell us her new address."

"I see," Mrs Malatratt said, looking in the most genteel way as if she believed not a word of my explanation.

If she was not going to trust us, then I felt a sense of freedom from the need to constrain myself to the literal truth: "We have arrived from the country only today after a long journey." I named the county and said: "From near Hougham where Sir Perceval is a ... " I hesitated and then contented myself with "a neighbour of ours."

"Indeed?" she said.

"Because of a misunderstanding our boxes have been sent to the wrong address on the other side of the metropolis. We were taking a coach to go there and as it passed along this street I remembered that Miss Quilliam had said she once lived here. Seeing that my mother was so tired, I stopped the coach with the idea of finding shelter here for tonight."

"Very well," said Mrs Malatratt and, with a sense of triumph mingled with guilt at the fluency of my lies, I realized that I had not deceived her but rather had provided the kind of explanation that was required. "But I am sorry that I cannot help you to find Miss Quilliam. As you say, she left Mompesson-park last summer — towards the close of July, as I recall — and stayed here for a night or two. When she left she undertook to leave a forwarding-address, but she has not done so."

"Then you know nothing more of her?"

"Merely that she called in only a fortnight ago to ask me to keep for a little longer one or two trunks she had left here. I was happy to oblige her. She left no direction but I believe I understood her to intimate that she had taken lodgings at the other end of Town."

The West-end! I glanced at my mother in dismay. She did not look back, but I caught the eye of the maid-servant who was looking at me with an expression I could not make out. She now glanced at her mistress with what I took to be timidity and dislike.

Mrs Malatratt looked at us appraisingly: "If you desire to be accommodated I can let you have a room for tonight only. It will be 3s."

I knew that we could find somewhere else for a shilling or eighteen-pence, but at that hour we might find difficulty. Looking at my mother who was still holding her face in her arms, I decided to accept.

"Payable in advance," Mrs Malatratt added.

I reached into my mother's reticule and beneath the pocket-book with its mysterious bundle of documents, I found our few remaining coins.

"Take them to the Blue Room, Nancy," Mrs Malatratt said and with a slight nod she retired magnificently.

I helped my mother to her feet and we followed the maid upstairs to the chamber specified which was beautifully furnished with a large bed and fine damasked hangings.

Nancy drew me to one side and in an undertone asked if we would care for something to eat. Then she whispered: "It ain't right, what she said."

"What do you mean?"

"And this ain't no place for you and your mam. I dursen't say more." Then she slipped out of the room. A few minutes later she brought us a little bread and milk, but as if she regretted her earlier indiscretion she avoided my eye and hurried out.

I had difficulty persuading my mother to eat even a little and I could not prevent her from returning to the subject of Bissett's betrayal: "There was enough value in the furniture to settle all our debts. What could she have done with the money?"

"Tomorrow, Mamma," I pleaded. "We should sleep now."

"Why did she do it, Johnnie?" she said suddenly. "I shall never forgive her. Never. After all I have done for her."

Eventually she stretched out on the bed and fell into a fitful slumber. For some time I lay in the pale moonlight that entered between the curtains and watched her sleeping with feelings of dark foreboding. What was the connexion between Bissett and Mr Espenshade? And if it was she who betrayed our address — as it surely must have been — then who paid her to do so? And why? These questions kept me from sleep, but later I was awakened several times when a carriage drew up outside the house and the street-door was slammed.

My mother seemed more cheerful the next morning but I could see that she was making a deliberate attempt to be brave and optimistic and I was irritated by this. I wondered how she would take the revelation of the full extent of Bissett's treachery.

Nancy brought us our meagre breakfast and as we ate it I explained to my mother exactly what had happened at Mrs Philliber's, confirming that it was at Bissett's instigation that the bailiff had been able to find us.

"So I was right about her," she said calmly.

"Yes, but not only that. The man who was with the bailiffs — Mr Espenshade, they called him — was somebody I have seen before."

I described how he had followed me one day at Melthorpe, and how I had seen him talking to Bissett.

My mother was horrified and the more so when I recounted my suspicions of our former servant going back over a long period. I now told her of the understanding that I suspected Bissett had entered into with Mr Barbellion on the occasion of his first visit, and of the mysterious errand to the post-office which I had interrupted and which I guessed was for the purposes of communicating with him.

"That is bad news, indeed, Johnnie," she said, reaching to take my hand. "But now I have something to tell you. I told her we were coming to London."

"Oh, Mamma!"

"It was the night we left the village. She was so hurt that I wouldn't tell her where we were going. It was while you were collecting your things."

"And yet you wouldn't tell me!" I exclaimed. "And I recall that I wondered why she was so much less irritable when I came back. Oh, Mamma! Then perhaps she went and told that man — Mr Espenshade — and he followed us to London."

"Surely not!" my mother cried.

"Well, perhaps not," I conceded. "For after all, if our enemy and his people knew where we were, I wonder why they chose to wait until you had sent Bissett Mrs Philliber's address?"

This was a mystery that we could not resolve.

"We can expect no money from Melthorpe now," I pointed out a few minutes later.

"What shall we do, Johnnie?"

"We must sell the locket," I said.

"No, I couldn't bear to part with it!" she cried.

"Don't be silly!" I said. "It's only an old piece of metal."

"You don't understand," she said tremulously. "It's all I have left of ... "

She broke off.

"Of what?" I demanded. She would not answer and I said angrily: "Then I don't know what will become of us."

"Johnnie, there is one other thing? Do you remember the document that Sir Perceval and then Mr Barbellion wanted to buy?"

"Yes, of course," I said. "You mean the codicil?"

"Yes. Well, we could offer that to Sir Perceval again."

"I thought you were not willing to part with it?" I said reproachfully. For I had thought about it often and come to the conclusion that if so many people were so anxious to obtain it, then it would be prudent not to part with it too easily.

"It would be painful because I made a promise about it," she said hesitantly. "A solemn promise. To my father. Just before he died. But I think he would want me to part with it now that we have nothing."

I begged her to explain more but she would not. I argued that it would be better to sell the locket but since she adamantly refused, we at last agreed not to part with either of these things.

"Mamma," I said. "I have an idea. Do you remember Mrs Digweed and her little boy who came to our house the Christmas before last?"

"Yes, of course."

"Well, don't you think it would be a good idea to find them?"

"Why, whatever for?"

"We are now as badly off as they. And they at least know how to be poor, which you and I must quickly learn."

"But how could we find them?"

"I remember that they lodged in Cox's-square, Spitalfields, and I believe that is not very far from here. So why don't we go there and look for them?"

"Well, why not? After all, what does anything matter any more? What does it matter what becomes of us? We are lost now."

"Don't be like that," I said angrily.

At this her pretence of equanimity collapsed and she started sobbing. It was some time before I had undone the damage and she had recovered her composure. While she was making ready to leave, I acted on an idea I had had and wrote a brief letter to Miss Quilliam reminding her of the occasion we had met, indicating that my mother and I were now in London without friends or means of subsistence, and asking her to leave an address at which we might reach her. I gave the letter to Nancy who undertook to put it into her hands when she returned and to retain for us any reply.

We left the house and enquired the way to Cox's-square. As we approached it the streets grew poorer and poorer and our spirits fell. The heavy sweet stench of a nearby brewery hung over the area, there was a public-house at every corner, and half-naked children swarming in the gutters called out to us for money when they saw how we were dressed — for in that district even our dowdy garments stood out. It wasn't merely the shabbiness of the clothes of the people we passed in the street that struck me, but their faces — pale, sallow, the skin often hideously pitted — and the eyes of many seemed empty as if they were in a stupor. I saw numerous swollen noses and black eyes, and many of those we passed were pigeon-breasted and had drooping shoulders and bandied legs.

The houses grew increasingly delapidated: the doors peeling and cracked, the stonework discoloured by a rotten green slime where the guttering had given way, and many of the windows broken and stuffed with rags. We passed many narrow slits in the walls through which people were disappearing or from which they emerged.

When at last we reached "Petticut-lane", to which we had been directed, we found that we ourselves had to pass into such a narrow alley-way in order to reach our goal. Finding ourselves in a dark court with a heap of refuse in the centre, we looked at each other in amazement.

"It was No. 6 wasn't it?" my mother asked.

I nodded for the stench was so terrible I did not want to open my mouth. The doors had no numbers.

"Which is No. 6?" I asked a little girl.

She pointed towards one of the entrances whose steps were broken and whose battered door was half-open. We climbed the steps and knocked.

A boy called out: "Keep on knockin', the footman can't 'ave 'eard you."

"Bless you," said a woman passing by. "You just go straight in and find the room you want."

We passed into the dark hall, unsure of what to expect. There was a door on our left which was ajar and we went up to it and my mother called out: "Mrs Digweed?"

A woman's voice responded: "Come in."

This was most encouraging and we pushed open the door and advanced into the room. However, the face that greeted us as we passed round the door, though cheerful and friendly, was not that of Mrs Digweed. The woman was about forty-five, neatly dressed, and with an open, pleasant countenance. Over her shoulder I could see that the chamber, which seemed bright and clean though it was not large, was full of people. A man lay sleeping in a makeshift bed in the corner, a young woman and two little girls were preparing food at the fire, and two younger children were playing with some pieces of coal on the cracked stone floor before the hearth. They looked up curiously at our entrance but then went on with what they were doing.

"You're not the family called Digweed?" I asked since my mother seemed overwhelmed by what she saw.

"Never heerd on 'em," she said. "Our name's Sackbutt."

I was aware of my mother turning sharply to me and not wanting to see her disappointment I ignored her and asked: "So they're not in this house?"

"I can't say so much," she said, looking at us with interest. "But come in and sit down. You look fair done up. Meg, clear them things off of that settle."

As she turned away my mother looked at me with her nose wrinkled to indicate her distaste but I nodded at her that we should accept the invitation. So we seated ourselves, I on a very precarious chair and my mother on the single decent piece of furniture, a battered and patched settle.

"Let me see," said Mrs Sackbutt, counting off on her fingers; "there's the Sneezums and the Glatts and the M'Tongues down here. But I don't know about all the rest of the house. There's ... "

My mother interrupted: "Do you mean that each family has one room?"

"Yes," said Mrs Sackbutt with unmistakable pride. "There ain't no sharin' down here, though as I says, I can't answer for the rest of the house."

My mother turned a ghastly face towards me.

Oblivious of this, Mrs Sackbutt continued: "There's the Clinkenbeards in the first-pair front, and the Meatyards in the back, so they've got two rooms apiece, though in course they pays more than what we do."

"Do you mean that you pay for this?" my mother cried.

"In course," said Mrs Sackbutt in surprise. "Why, you are simple. Are you Irish?"

"No, we've just come from the country," I explained.

"Four shillin' a week. Why, you pays everywhere except p'r'aps a few places like the Holy Land or the Devil's Acre or the Rookery at Mitre-court in Hatton-garding and such, and I wouldn't go there, not if I was able to crawl nowheres else."

The man muttered in his sleep and turned over.

Mrs Sackbutt went on: "But as for here, why, the landlord's deputy, Mr Ashburner, comes round regular every week and if you can't pay, why, out you go."

I saw my mother shudder. Did she know the name? That was an absurd thought. How could she?

"He takes most of the rents for here and Bell-lane," Mrs Sackbutt went on.

"Bell-lane!" my mother exclaimed. "Is that near?"

"Why the next street to this," the good woman answered.

My mother blenched. What *did* she know of this place?

"Are you all right?" Mrs Sackbutt said. "You look poorly. Will you take something? A little gin?"

Rather to my regret, she accepted.

"We should be going, Mamma," I said. "Thank you for your help, Mrs Sackbutt. We'll enquire of the rest of the house."

"Why don't your mother wait here while you go?" she asked. "She looks fair done in."

"Yes, Johnnie, I am very tired," my mother said.

I agreed and Mrs Sackbutt placed two glasses on a sideboard and pulled open one of its drawers. There was a cry and there — to our amazement — was a small baby lying in an old egg-chest in the drawer that was lined with straw. It was sucking a teat made of a bag of plums.

"Why," my mother exclaimed. "That can't be good for the child!"

Mrs Sackbutt smiled cheerfully: "Bless you, that's only a nuss-child. And it does her no harm."

While my mother took the baby out and began to nurse her upon her lap and

Mrs Sackbutt poured out two tumblers from a stone jug, I left the chamber and climbed the battered staircase to knock at each door. My search was without profit for nobody had heard the name of Digweed, and as I went from one room to the next I realized that this was because the occupiers came and went too quickly for the house to have a common memory. I wondered where they came from and went to, for this, I reflected, must be the very bottom of the pit of degradation, and I could not conceive that there could be anywhere more debased than this.

The signs of poverty increased as I ascended, for above the floor on which the Sackbutts lived I commonly found two families inhabiting a single chamber. (They were large for the houses in the square had long ago been built as fine merchants' dwellings.) In the first I was assailed by a strong stench which came from the paste the whole family were using for making cigar-boxes. A broken flower-pot propped open the window-frame but smoke from the chimneys outside was billowing in and adding to the foetid atmosphere. In the next room there was nobody but a small boy holding a baby that looked like a limp bundle of rags. There was a bucket full of soaking rags on a rickety deal table, the grate was oozing cinders, and a cracked tea-cup stood on the floor.

Most of the rooms had little furniture — perhaps a single turn-up bedstead with a bag of straw and a dirty and scanty coverlet — and the windows had in many cases lost their glass whose place was supplied by sheets of cloth covered in tallow to let a little light through. Yet in many of them an attempt had been made at decoration and there were flower-pots containing flowers or in some cases mere dried sticks where the plants had long ago died.

When I had tried every door, I decided to try all the other houses in the square in case we had mistaken the number, or in the hope that even if the Digweeds had gone, someone might remember them and know where they were now. The first chamber I tried on the ground-floor of the next house was the dwelling of a sweep and although the front room was fairly clean, I saw over his wife's shoulder a back chamber containing nothing but a huge pile of soot and beside it an empty bird-cage. I opened another door when there was no response and found an old woman holding a plucked chicken that was visibly putrid, who screamed abuse at me so that I hastily closed it again. The next room was deserted and bare except for a pile of rags, a broken table, and a small girl of about five and a baby — both sitting on the floor.

I need not go on. Many of the occupants of these houses were stunned by hunger or incapacitated by drink or spoke no language that I recognised, but of those who could reply in English, none of them — at least of those who would answer me — could help me, and in despair I almost decided to abandon the search.

Then I knocked at the door of a garret-room at the top of No. 10 and although the woman who opened it (holding it only a little ajar) said: "I nivver heerd tell on 'em, young master," an old man's feeble voice from the room behind her called out: "Digweed? Aye, I rec'lleck a fambly of that name."

"No you don't," the woman said without turning round and beginning to close the door.

"Why, I do," the querulous voice insisted. "They lived four houses along, I b'lieve."

The woman still held the door, looking at me discouragingly.

"No. 6?" I said. "Yes, that is so."

With a warning shake of her head, the woman opened the door, allowing me to see that she was holding a baby to her breast, and I entered.

The chamber was small but clean and tidy and the walls, though they came down from the low ceiling at a sharp angle, were freshly whitewashed. A clean old man with a grizzled white chin sat before the fire looking at us.

"Here, sit down, young 'un," he said, and with a smile showed me his complete range of teeth: two shiny yellow stumps.

I sat in the ancient chair opposite him that he indicated.

"Digweed, you say?" he began. "For sure, I mind 'em well for the master gived me baccy and the mistress brung me poultices for the rheumatiz and the little lad runned messages for me. They moved away, though. Now when was that? Let me think. They had the fever that time it was so bad here."

"Yes," I said with mounting excitement. "That's them."

"Why, I rec'lleck now. 'Twas the winter I broke my leg. That was four or five year agone."

I was disappointed for it had sounded like them and yet if this was so it could not be. But the woman broke in impatiently: "Why, father, that was only a year or two back."

"Aye," he agreed. "Mebbe it was. Two on the children died. Is that right?"

"Yes," I said, remembering the letter we had received and the news that we had been unable to interpret. "But where did they go to when they left here?"

He frowned: "I can't call it to mind. In fact, I don't believe I ever knowed it."

I slumped down, and after all I had endured I found myself fighting back tears. "Do you know of anyone who might know?"

"Hold hard," he said, "I believe I might. How I knowed 'em at all was on account of Barney. I believe he was the master's brother, or mayhap the wife's. Anyways, this Barney (I never heerd no other name), he worked mates with some coves what I done some work with. This is going back more nor ten year now. Jerry Isbister and Pulvertaft, they was." Here he paused as if remembering something, and then he suddenly looked at me strangely: "Would you know anything about the lay they was on?"

I shook my head.

"Well, howsomever, they worked mates together for many a year. And with others, too, in course. (There was Blueskin for one. Nobody couldn't forget him.) I helped 'em once or twice but I hadn't the stomach for it, but that's how I come to know Barney."

Though I wanted to ask questions for I was intrigued by these words, I was afraid to interrupt him because he might lose the tenuous thread.

"Well, arter I gived up I heerd they had a turn-up. Barney and Pulvertaft agin Isbister. Then him and Pulvertaft went over the water."

I glanced at the daughter in surprise and she mouthed: "Down the Borough."

"But I believe Jerry knows of Barney still," the old man went on. "I rec'lleck he said summut about him not three month back when I met him one day coming down Field-lane with his hoss and cart."

"Longer back than that, dad," the woman put in, with a meaningful glance at me. "You've been laid up of that leg of yourn for more than a year."

"'Why, Sam'el,' he said to me," the old man continued, ignoring her words, "'it does a man good jist to lay eyes on you. I declare, your phiz'd ripen cowcumbers.' That's what he said," old Samuel said chuckling. "'Your face'd ripen cowcumbers.'"

"Do you know how I can find any of these men?"

"That I don't for I nivver heerd tell what become of Barney beyond that he 'tended the Floatin' 'Cademy at Gravesend."

He began to cackle and I glanced at the daughter who shook her head at me in bewilderment.

"And the others? Where do Isbister and Pulvertaft live?"

"Isbister lives in Parliament-street hard by Bethnal-green. Now is it No. 8 or No. 9?"

"And Pulvertaft?"

"I've heerd tell he lives in a nethersken in what they call the Old Manor-house down the Old Mint."

"Father, you're going back nigh on ten year now," his daughter protested.

Seeing there was no more to be got from him, I expressed my gratitude and rose to leave.

"Come again, young feller," he called out. "Maybe I'll mind some more."

As his daughter let me out she held the door between me and her father and said: "Now he's stuck up here all day, and nobody don't bother with him, he don't care what he says to be took notice of."

I thanked her and went back to my mother. I found that she had recovered her cheerfulness for there was colour in her cheeks again and when I said I had had some success, she greeted the news with a cry of joy and clapped her hands. I tried to emphasize how indirect was the connexion with Mrs Digweed that I had found, but she hardly listened. She had forgotten her lack of interest in finding her and was all for setting off immediately. Mrs Sackbutt confirmed to me what I had suspected about the relative distances of the two addresses I had learned: Bethnal-green was fairly near, but the Mint was on the other side of the metropolis.

"Bethnal-green!" my mother exclaimed. "Why I remember it. Uncle Martin had a summer-house there. It's so pretty! Do let's go there!"

Fate seemed to have determined that it should be so, and therefore we took leave of our kind hostess and set off. There was a light rain falling, but oblivious to this my mother was laughing and smiling as we walked along Wentworth-street and turned up Brick-lane.

"I don't like to see you like this," I said.

Her smile faded as if she had been struck: "You only want me to be miserable."

"Of course I don't. But you must keep a hold on yourself."

"Why? What does anything matter any more!" she said.

"That's silly."

"We mustn't quarrel!" she cried and stopped then flung her arms around me. "It'll be all right, Johnnie. I know it will. We will find the Digweeds and stay with them. And then perhaps find work. Or if we have to, we will go to Sir Perceval and sell the codicil to him. You'll see. It will all come right at last."

"Of course it will," I said, detaching myself from her embrace.

Though it was late afternoon and the dusk was gathering, carts and waggons were rumbling busily past us and the pavements, cracked and broken in many places, were crowded with ragged foot-passengers.

Once we were in Bethnal-green-road, I tried to use the map (which fortunately I had in my jacket pocket when I left Mrs Philliber's) but it bore little resemblance to this district, for whole streets of houses stood where according to the design there should have been gardens. The metropolis was growing so fast that the map was already out of date, although it had been published only a few months after my birth.

"I remember this road so well," my mother said, looking around. "We used to come here on Sundays in the summer when I was about your age. It was so peaceful. You'll see, the countryside begins just here. We would hire a coach and Uncle Marty's servant would come on ahead and lay out the food in the summer-house so that it would be waiting for us."

After a few minutes, however, I could see that she was puzzled by the absence of countryside or gardens. And when she saw a church on our right she said: "I'm sure I remember this. And yet it seems so different."

For some time we had been passing row upon row of little two-roomed or four-roomed dwellings in straggling streets or stifling courts, and now she glanced at me several times in growing perplexity.

"Are we lost?" I asked.

"I don't understand: we should be there by now. I don't remember any of this."

"I believe this might be the place, Mamma. Look, that court is called Mulberry-gardens. These houses look new although they're so broken down."

She spoke in a faint and distant voice: "I believe you may be right."

"And look," I cried, "there are summer-houses."

In an overgrown piece of waste-ground just off the high-road were a number of single-storied wooden buildings with verandahs and projecting supports for canvas awnings that must have once fluttered in the summer breeze. Now, however, they were rotting, green slime covered the walls, and they were near collapse, for they were forty or fifty years old. Yet to our surprise there were dim lights in them and we saw people entering and leaving.

As we advanced my mother became more and more upset and when she clutched my arm I could feel that she was trembling.

"Where was Uncle Marty's summer-house?" I asked. "Can you remember? Perhaps it is still there?"

"I don't want to see it!" she cried. "Oh Johnnie, everything's so horrible now, I can't bear it!"

We quickened our pace and hurried through the darkening streets until we reached the Green. There we enquired out the way, and had great difficulty in finding Parliament-street which turned out to be a dark little conspiracy of tiny houses crouched around a gloomy and diminutive square. Like most of those that had been thrown up in the last few years, it had a built-up parapet with a roof rising above it like a high hat, and windows that were too large for the front and looked like bulging eyes. We had no difficulty finding the house we sought, for a cart stood outside No. 8 bearing on its side the painted legend "Jeremy Isbister: General Carrier".

A burly unshaven man of about forty opened the door to our knock. He had small bloodshot eyes on either side of a prominent but broken nose, and wore a neckcloth which was none too clean. He stared at us with hostility from orbs that were like the "eyes" of a potato that remain when it has been peeled, deep and black in the white flesh. His close-shaven scull, too, was like a fuzzy potato with its knobs and dents all visible. His big head was held low as if, like a cautious turtle's, it was ready to disappear back between the shoulder-blades.

"Who are you?" he demanded.

"We are friends of the Digweeds," I said.

"Digweed!" he exclaimed in dismay. "Did he send you here?"

"No," I answered. "And it is Mrs Digweed that we know."

He scrutinised us: "I nivver heerd o' no Mrs Digweed. What's your business with her? Who sent you here?"

"If you are Mr Isbister, we were told you know a man called Barney, who is some kind of kin to Mrs Digweed."

The small eyes appeared to me to widen, but he began to close the door saying "I don't know no Barney. Is that good enough for you?"

At this my mother gave a cry and staggered against me so that I had to hold her up.

The man looked at her curiously: "She looks about done up. Don't you have nowhere to go?"

I shook my head.

"Nor much blunt, I s'pose?"

I shook my head again: "We hoped to find shelter with Mrs Digweed."

He looked at me with an appraising expression: "You're a bright lad," he said. "I'll wager you can read?"

"Yes," I said.

"Anything at all, print or writing?"

"Yes."

"And write a fine genel'manlike hand, too?"

"That too," I agreed.

He stared at me intently with his mouth slightly open but he said no more and I turned away, supporting my mother as best I could. When we had taken only a few steps he called out: "Wait! Do you want a shake-down for tonight?"

I turned back but hesitated.

"I have a chamber free," he went on, "what I lets in the usual run o' things. I had to turn the last fambly out a couple of nights back. You can have it tonight for ten-pence."

"I think we should go on, Mamma," I whispered.

"Oh let us take it for tonight, Johnnie," my mother said. "I am so tired."

Mr Isbister was listening to our conversation anxiously.

"May we see it?" I asked.

He turned and advanced into the passage, and as he did so bellowed: "Molly!"

He looked back and impatiently beckoned us with his head to come inside. As we stepped across the threshold into the dark passage, a strange smell that I could not identify struck me: it wasn't just the cabbagey, potatoey, smell of the poor that I had become familiar with, but something darker and earthier. As we jostled each other in the narrow passage a big slatternly woman appeared from the back room.

She had been baking and was wiping her floury hands on her pin-before, but it seemed to me that there was something indefinably unclean about her. In the midst of her mealy-white fat face that was floury and doughy (like the ill-baked bread and cakes that I was to learn she was constantly making), lurked two deep black eyes. It was a habit of hers constantly to wipe her hands on her dirty apron as if — it seemed to me — preparing to use her fists.

"What do you want?" she said irritably.

The man jerked his head at us: "They want the chamber for tonight."

She looked at us contemptuously: "Can you pay?"

"We'd like to see it first," I said.

"First pair back," she said.

"You can take it for the week for two shillings and six-pence," the man said suddenly.

"Oh can they!" exclaimed the woman angrily.

As her husband took her arm and said something in an undertone, my mother and I went upstairs. The room was small and dark with one soot-begrimed little window which looked into a dirty back-yard. There was an ancient truckle-bed which was stripped bare and a thin straw palliasse on the floor. We looked at each other in dismay.

"It's very dear for one night," I objected, wrinkling up my nose at the smell of damp and that something else that seemed to pervade the house. "I don't like those people. I don't think we should stay."

"But it's getting late and I can't go any further. I can't, Johnnie. I don't want to go onto those streets again. And where would we go?"

"Well," I said. "Just for one night."

When we got downstairs Mr Isbister was standing in the dim passage and smiling.

"Will you do me and me wife the honour to take a glass o' best nine-penny with us, ma'am?"

My mother nodded and made to enter the parlour but Mr Isbister put his arm out and held the door: "Why, the parlour ain't fit for company jist now." He turned and led the way into the kitchen where he poured a large tumbler of gin for each of us, and healths were drunk. I left mine untasted.

"Well, my dears," Mrs Isbister said with a simper that was more disquieting than her previous hostility, "is the room to your liking?"

"We wish to take it for one night," I said.

"I see who makes the decisions!" cried Mrs Isbister. "Bless him, he's quite the little master isn't he?"

"Yes," said my mother. "He bullies me terribly sometimes." She looked at me reproachfully.

"No, I don't."

"I love children," said Mrs Isbister and to my horror reached out a large, doughy fist to stroke the top of my head. "We buried three. Mr Isbister and me," she said mournfully.

He sighed heavily and asked: "Another, ma'am?"

My mother held out her glass and he filled it and they toasted each other again.

"Would you like the money now?" my mother asked, opening her reticule.

"There's plenty of time for that," Mr Isbister said. "We'll trust you."

"You've got to trust someone in this world, haven't you?" Mrs Isbister said. "That's what Mr Isbister and me allus says."

My mother nodded and smiled at me as if to invite me to share her good opinion of our new landlords.

"It's a nice room," Mr Isbister said. "You'll sleep sound as a bat in winter."

The Isbisters lent us some ragged sheets and blankets and the straw palliasse was made up for me. My mother went to sleep quickly but I stayed awake for an hour or so and my fears were not allayed when I heard the Isbisters very late that night come up to the other chamber quarrelling drunkenly.

CHAPTER 33

Rather to my surprise, since I believed that carriers started work very early, I was the first of the household to wake up the next morning. By half past seven there was still no sound from the Isbisters, though I thought I heard a noise below. I got out of bed and dressed, leaving my mother still asleep though tossing and turning restlessly. As I descended the stairs, I could hear snores coming from the Isbisters' room. From below there was the sound of the fire-grate being riddled and when I went into the kitchen I found a girl of about fourteen kneeling before the hearth and furiously clearing the fire.

"Hello," I said. "I'm John. Who are you?"

To my surprise she did not even look at me. This didn't seem very friendly or even polite, and altogether she looked a most unprepossessing young woman, covered from head to foot in powdered black, and with a pallid, bony face and blistered red hands. I looked round the room. There were a number of large baskets along one wall which, though they were covered by a piece of cloth, appeared to be full of clothes.

I went to find a baker and a dairy in order to buy a penn'orth of rolls and a little milk for our breakfast, and when I had done this I returned upstairs and consumed my share while I waited. When my mother awoke a little after eight I urged her to make ready as quickly as she could so that we could leave the house immediately.

"I don't believe I can," she said.

I was disturbed to see that she was feverish and pale.

"Can't you make an effort?" I asked.

"No, and anyway, where should we go?"

It was clear that she was ill and so I said I would tell our hosts when they got up, and let her sleep again.

However, I had a long wait. At last, late on towards midday, I heard them rise and descend. A few minutes later I went downstairs, and hearing me on the stair, Mr Isbister bellowed from the kitchen:

"In here!"

I went in and found them making their breakfast of bread and cheese and washing it down with porter which the girl was serving.

"You clumsy creatur'," Mrs Isbister was saying to the girl as I entered, but when she saw me she forced her features into a smile.

When I told them of my mother's state they said they were sorry and insisted that we should stay until she was recovered.

Mr Isbister scratched his head: "Why, I suppose I could use a sharp lad for a few days to carry messages and hold the horse. In course, I'd jist be doing you a favour. So let's say you don't pay us no rent and that'll keep us square. All right?"

I nodded.

"That man's so kind," his wife said to me. "Why, I've knowed him give up a day's work to help his brother when it weren't nothing to his own good. Do you know, I believe I could find something for you to do as well. You could fetch and carry the out-work for me, for this idle gal's too slow." She turned quickly and cried, "Why, Polly, haven't you set that fire on yet?" aiming a slap at the girl who moved smartly out of the way.

When I had told my mother what had been agreed, I came down again in order to be ready to go out on the cart. The girl was black-leading the fireplace while her employers rounded off their breakfast with a few glasses of gin, and I stood at the door waiting for my orders.

"What would you like me to do, Mr Isbister?" I enquired at last.

"Nothin' for now," he said, leaning back and loosening his belt a few notches. "I'll want you by and by, though, for I have to take a half-anker of Hollands from Lime'us to Hackney. But arst her."

He pointed a finger over his shoulder at his wife who nodded towards one of the baskets and said: "Take that to Mrs O'Herlihy in Smart's-gardings. Tell her to bring home what she's done."

Carrying the heavy and awkward basket with difficulty even though it was empty, I set off. At last I was working! Just beyond the little square was a nightman's-yard where a number of old women, each carrying a leather bag, appeared to be raking through the ash-heaps with sticks, and from one of them I enquired out my way to Smart's-gardens. I had to cross places where pools of black liquid lay blocking the narrower streets and often flooding right across the courts so that it was impossible not to wade through them. Great mounds of waste lay in the courts and I hated to think what this place must be like in the hot weather.

Around here most of the streets were new, but they had been thrown up carelessly in the former pleasure-gardens and straggled haphazardly across wild wastes of mud and stones. There were no street-lamps or pavements, and in many places the carriageway was not made up at all but was merely an expanse of mud. The yards and the little gardens that seemed to grow nothing but broken railings and old china were often not distinguished from the public thoroughfares, or were marked off only by rotting palings; and all about there were piles of rubble, old herring-casks lying on their sides, broken glass, weeds, and always and everywhere there were dirty children rolling among the dirt or tossing ha'pennies.

I found the dirty little street — really no more than a few short rows of houses built in higgledy-piggledy fashion — and asked for the O'Herlihys. The house they inhabited was the same size as the Isbisters' but a different family had each of the rooms. The people I sought possessed the kitchen, and when I entered I found almost the whole family — two women, three girls and even two little boys — hard at work stitching. The room was hot and close for it was illuminated by stinking tallow-dips, and there was paper stuffed in the broken panes of several of the windows which rose and fell as I opened and closed the door. With a shudder I saw that the walls were alive with wood-lice and moved a step away.

Mrs O'Herlihy, who rose and came forward, had a lined, anxious face and yet — I realized with surprise — was only a few years older than my mother.

She seemed frightened at the sight of me and the basket: "I hope she won't make no bates for poor work." She sighed and said: "She ain't the worst of the sweaters, but she's bad enough."

Mrs O'Herlihy loaded the basket with finished garments and I helped her to carry it back, and hard work it was to chart a course that would keep it clear of the filth.

"What took you so long?" Mrs Isbister demanded when we staggered into the over-heated kitchen. Her face was flushed and there was a stone jug and a tumbler on the table before her. Her husband sat frowning judicially at the other end of the table with his large hand clasping another tumbler.

She began to lift the garments out — I now saw that they were all waistcoats — and examined the linings, the buttons and the button-holes of each one carefully. Triumphantly she held one up and cried: "Look at this! I ain't a-goin' to pay you for work like this! You've sp'iled that lining. It'll come out of what I owe you and you won't git no more work of me."

"Oh please, mim," Mrs O'Herlihy pleaded, "it's only a little sp'iled. One of the chillun must've done it. Let me take it back and do it again."

"Wery well. But I'm still bating you for it on account of you've sp'iled the material."

"Oh please, mim, my good man's been out of collar for four months."

"Here's the blunt," Mrs Isbister responded, flinging the coins down on the table so that one of them rolled onto the floor. "Take it or leave it. There's plenty to do the work if you don't want it."

Mrs O'Herlihy picked up the money and with a little bob towards Mrs Isbister and a nervous glance at her husband, hurried from the room clutching the waistcoat.

"What are you a-starin' at?" Mrs Isbister cried to me. "Look alive now! Git on to the Parracks in Coopers-gardings and tell them to bring their work home if they want any more."

As I turned to leave she grabbed me by the shoulder and thrust the big basket at me: "Where are you goin'? You're to take this with you, in course. And mind and don't be so long this time."

It was a relief to get out of the house and as I hurried away I noticed that there was a bladder-drier's a few doors along, and wondered if the smell might come from there for it gave off a terrible stench.

Now I had to plunge into one of the former gardens which was a wilderness of broken-down palings, criss-crossed by treacherous ditches and dotted with summer-houses — either abandoned and overgrown with vegetation or still inhabited. Wide lakes of putrid water and huge mounds of debris and filth lay everywhere, but in amongst the mud and the undergrowth, makeshift cabins had been thrown together with rooves of tarred canvas. My goal turned out to be a rickety wooden structure, built perhaps sixty years earlier as a summer garden-house, in whose single tiny room a whole family yet again was at work.

When I explained my errand Mrs Parrack, almost in tears, said: "I haven't got none ready. We've all been sick of the low fever. I'll do it by Monday, on my solemn word."

So I left and now, as I hurried back, I realized what I was reminded of by the rotten thatch, the leaning chimneys, the holes in the rough-cast walls that had been stopped with hurdles and straw, and by the livestock — the numerous chickens scratching around in the dirt, the pigs snorting in little outhouses, even ducks waddling through the black ponds that drained from the heaped middens, and donkeys grazing dolefully in tiny back-yards. The district was like one of the tumbledown hamlets around Melthorpe — except that it went on and on and on, and the smells were not those of the farm-yard for the leaking ash-heaps were foul, the dark and noisome stalls that sprouted like blighted mushrooms amongst the undergrowth of the waste-lands sheltered human beings, and, as I was to realize later, the cries and moans and sudden outbreaks of bark-like yelpings that occurred throughout the night, were made by men and not beasts.

When I got back and told Mrs Isbister the outcome of my errand, she shouted: "You little flatt. You should have took what she'd done. Most like, she's pawned it. And then you should have gone on to the M'Quhaes."

"But please, you didn't tell me," I protested.

"Don't answer me agin," she shouted. "Go to the M'Quhaes in Crabtree-row. And if they don't have nothing, go to the Lamprills up Whiskers-gardings."

In this manner I hurried backwards and forwards a number of times, all the while worrying about my mother and hoping that we would soon be able to leave. Then in the late afternoon when I was slumped exhausted and unregarded in a corner of the kitchen while Mrs Isbister was haranguing Polly, Mr Isbister rose a trifle unsteadily to his feet, wiped his sleeve across his mouth, and told me to make ready to come with him. I just had time to hurry upstairs where I found my mother sleeping restlessly, her face flushed, before my new master and I strolled to the livery-stables nearby. Here we fetched his horse which we led back and put to the cart.

The horse seemed as lazy as its master — though much thinner — and was stubborn to move off at the command. "Why, drat you, Gunpowder!" Mr Isbister cried, shaking the reins: "Burn my body if I don't sell you for glew!"

We were in motion at last, however, and this was a welcome respite for me. We drove to Limehouse to fetch a great barrel of Hollands which we delivered to a public-house in Hackney, and all I had to do was to hold Gunpowder's head while Mr Isbister directed the warehousemen and then the pot-boys. After that we came home and when he had shewn me how to unharness the horse, I took the beast back to the stable. Although my master did nothing for the rest of the day, his wife kept me busy until night-fall.

My mother was no better in the evening and when I had fetched and consumed a ha'penny pease-pudding from the pastry-cook — my mother could eat nothing — I fell exhausted into bed. She was in the same state the next morning and the day passed in much the same way, for Mr Isbister lay even later in bed, then rose and immediately began drinking, while I spent the morning running errands for his wife. I was sent to fetch and harness the horse in the afternoon and we made one journey to Aldgate to pick up some boxes to deliver to Poplar. But then I was instructed to take the horse back and for the rest of the afternoon Mr Isbister sat in the kitchen drinking.

In the evening my mother was a little better and she and I were eating some cold pies from the pastry-cook when we heard a number of men arriving one after the other. The sound of drinking and laughter was heard all evening and had not abated by the time we went to bed. Towards midnight I was woken by sudden noises and as I listened it became clear not only that the men were leaving the house, but also that they were trying to do so quietly. Then, to my surprise, I heard the cart setting off and reflected that Gunpowder must have been fetched from the livery-stable so late by special arrangement. I wished our room gave onto the street so that I could look out, for I wondered what Mr Isbister and his companions could be doing at this late hour. I fell asleep before I heard the cart return, and the next morning my master did not rise until noon, and did not go out at all that day.

When we had been there three days my mother was better and that evening, the 26th. of March, I asked her if she felt well enough to leave the next day.

"I believe I do," she said. "But, Johnnie, we've been getting on so well here, why don't we stay a little longer?"

"No," I insisted. "They're not nice people."

Yet what did I have against them — apart from the way they treated Polly and the out-workers, and even the poor old horse?

"Don't be silly. They've been very kind in letting us stay for nothing. And where else can we go? We're not going to be able to find Mrs Digweed and that was a foolish idea anyway. And your Miss Quilliam won't help us either. And we need somewhere to live while I look for work and try to find you a school."

"School!" I exclaimed. "How can we afford that? Don't you understand how little we have now?"

"Don't speak to me like that, Johnnie," she said indignantly.

I persisted, however, in my attempts to persuade her to leave.

"Oh very well," she cried at last. "If you're so set on it, we'll go and starve on the streets."

We went downstairs and, finding the Isbisters as usual drinking in the kitchen, told them of our decision. They looked taken aback and Mrs Isbister said:

"We're wery sorry to larn it. Will you stay for a moment and say farewell with a nice glass of best Cream o' the Valley, my dear?"

Avoiding my warning gaze, my mother accepted and seated herself.

"In course a place like this ain't good enough for you," Mrs Isbister began. "For you're a real lady and I respecks that. Oh, I know you think I'm low, and so I am, powerful low," and she glared round fiercely as if defying anyone to deny it. "But I know I'm low and that makes me not as low as them as don't."

"Draw it mild, old gal," Mr Isbister murmured.

"But I will say on me own behalf as how I knows a real lady. And for how? On account of I lived sarvint to one for nigh on ten year. Oh wery ladylike she was with her fine chaney and her fambly silver and all that. Everythin' had to be jist so. I left her at the last for I could not abide her prims and prissums."

"Oh that does sound awful," my mother said. "I know I always try to be good to my servants."

Mrs Isbister scowled briefly at this: "So does I. For that's the best way to git work of 'em. Though that gal!" She shook her head. "It's a kindness to keep her up to the mark for she'll slip if I don't. But as for my mistress what I was a-tellin' you on, oh, she was a Tartar and no mistake. That fust day I come, she says, 'Do this, Meg,' and I says, 'With respeck, that ain't my name, ma'am,' and she says, 'Why, Meg, we allus calls our maid that on account of it's easier to bring to mind.'" Mrs Isbister glared round as she reached this conclusion and angrily drained her glass.

"She don't want to hear all that," Mr Isbister interrupted. He turned back to us: "Mrs Isbister and me is wery sorry you're going, you and the younker."

"He's as fond of that boy as if he was his own," Mrs Isbister commented with a doughy simper, and her hand came snaking somewhat erratically towards the top of my head. I moved slightly sideways and it clawed the back of my chair instead.

"And he's so sharp he's been wery useful to us," Mr Isbister went on.

"Yes, he is clever," my mother agreed, smiling at me nervously. "I wish we could stay, but Johnnie believes we should go."

I glared at her.

"But whyever should you go?" exclaimed Mr Isbister. "And jist for the boy says so!"

"I need to find work."

"What kind?" Mrs Isbister asked.

"Needle-work."

"Are you good with your needle?" Mrs Isbister asked.

"Yes," my mother said proudly. "I am."

"Why, I could put some plain-work your way. You wouldn't have to do nothin' low," Mrs Isbister went on. "You and me would work here wery snug and cozy. It'll be to the credit of the connexion to have a real lady."

My mother turned to me and her smile faded as she saw my expression. "What harm can it do for just a few weeks?" she asked in an undertone.

But the Isbisters were so close that I could not tell her all I suspected, so I merely glared.

"Then here's what I'll offer," Mr Isbister said. "You don't pay no rent for the room and you work for the old ooman here, and we'll give you six shillin' a week for yourself. In course," he added as an afterthought, "that's with the boy's work throwed in."

His wife nodded and smiled.

It seemed to me strange that they were prepared to pay so much more than the going rate when there were many women nearby who would work for much less. Was I wrong to suspect and dislike them?

"Only six shillings! I had hoped for more," my mother said.

Though I was irritated by this, I hoped that her ignorance would prevent the bargain from being struck.

"More?" Mrs Isbister cried, then broke off suddenly and drained her glass.

Mr Isbister leaned forward quickly: "I reckon you can see your way to a little more than that, can't you, Molly?"

She looked back at him steadily for a moment and then said stiffly to my mother: "For a real lady like you, it's worth seven shillin'."

Though still disappointed, my mother agreed to these terms. The contract had to be celebrated, and several times while he drank, my new master smiled at me and said: "Why, you'll live like a fighting-cock from now on."

When we at last went up to our room my mother was more cheerful than I had seen her since we had fled from our former lodgings. She remarked upon our good luck in having run across such people, and, almost gaily, she said: "I didn't like Mrs Isbister at first, I must confess, for her appearance is not in her favour. But I believe she is a good creature at heart."

"You promised we would leave," I said reproachfully.

"Oh don't start that!" she cried.

I pursued it no further, but when she extinguished the candle and bade me good-night I made no reply.

The next morning my mother slept late and when I went downstairs I found that, as usual, Polly and I were the only creatures awake in the house. I tried again to make her answer me but she appeared to be entirely deaf, and even when I stood in her way she stepped round me without looking at me. It was nearly nine o' clock before the Isbisters emerged from their room and they were both in a very bad mood. My mother came downstairs at the same time as they, and Mrs Isbister, having scolded her for her lateness, put her to work stitching shirt collars despite her protest that she had not breakfasted. And she gave me errands to run that kept me busy all morning.

Mr Isbister and I went out on the cart in the afternoon and when I got back I found my mother and Mrs Isbister still in the kitchen. My mother was stitching away and looked up at me with an exhausted smile when I entered. Our benefactress, who was sitting with a jug of gin and a tumbler on the table before her, now grudgingly admitted that it was time to end work and handed over a shilling. When we were safely upstairs my mother began to tell me how hard Mrs Isbister had forced her to work. Choking back the words that rose to my lips, I contented myself with extracting a promise that we would leave there as soon as we had saved a few shillings. We were both almost too tired to eat and were soon fast asleep.

About two weeks passed in much the same way. At times Mrs Isbister was extremely rude and unkind to my mother who then tearfully complained to me, but at other times our mistress would make up for it by being fulsomely friendly. I would go into the kitchen with the baskets and overhear her in her most oily and ingratiating mood as she sat by the gin bottle talking to my mother as she worked:

"That gal," she would often begin. "I don't know what to do with her. (Yes, you help yourself. That's right.) But sarvints is allus an infernal nuisance, as you know yourself, Mrs Offland."

To illustrate her point she would often seize Polly by the hair and pinch her, but the girl neither complained nor resisted. On Mondays a horrible snivelling old woman with red eyes, Mrs Peppiatt, came to help with the wash, and not only was the wretched slavey unmercifully harried on two fronts, but my mother also became the object of their spiteful interest. It was clear to me that Mrs Isbister delighted in having a "lady" to patronize and humiliate, and it infuriated me to see my mother accepting worse and worse abuse from her each day. I do not know whether my mother's acquiescence towards her mistress or her complaints afterwards to me angered me more, but, annoyed by the latter, I refrained at first from telling her the things I had seen in the district. When at last I began to describe them, she either refused to listen or else accused me of making them up.

My master's work involved going to public-houses a great deal while I waited outside with the horse and cart. (When it rained, Gunpowder and I grew soggy, and it was not surprising that the horse did not take fire when the whip was applied.) It seemed reasonable that Mr Isbister should patronize taverns in order to hear of work, but I began to realize that the carting he mainly did was between the bar and his lips, and at this he drove a brisk trade.

Increasingly I puzzled over the Isbisters' behaviour for I could make no pattern out of what I witnessed. By this time, I had established that it was Mr Isbister's wont, regularly every two or three nights, to go out with his cart at about midnight in the company of a number of other men, returning four or five hours later. Then he would sleep most of the next day and begin drinking when he arose. Then another part of the pattern became apparent and began to teaze me.

Late one Sunday afternoon, about a week after the scene I have just described, Mr and Mrs Isbister came downstairs with an air of self-consciousness. She was wearing a fine silk gown with a velvet cloak, and a magnificent bonnet. Mr Isbister was dressed in a bottle-green top-coat with a pale blue undercoat, canary waistcoat and salt-and-pepper trowsers. Polly was despatched to Bethnal-green-road and when she returned a few minutes later in a hackney-coach, her master and mistress got in and I heard him give the order "Bagnigge-wells tea-gardings, my good man." They came back very late, sullen and unsteady as they climbed the stairs. The following Sunday they appeared once again resplendently dressed — on this occasion for the country — and this time (as I overheard) hired a coach for the day to take them to Richmond.

Where, I asked myself, did the money come from that paid for these parties of pleasure? It did not seem to me that Mrs Isbister was "sweating" on a large enough scale to account for their comparative opulence.

As April wore on, however, this pattern changed. Mr Isbister went out at night on the cart only once in the first week and after that not at all, and there were no more fine clothes on display or trips in coaches. They quarrelled more often and more noisily than before and spent a great deal of time drinking. At least, however, the weather was beautiful now: fine, very dry and still pleasantly cool even in the sun.

It was at about this time that there occurred an incident which should have encouraged me to believe in the good intentions of our patrons. Since the winter clothes that Mrs Philliber had purchased on our behalf were both heavier and of finer quality than we required, my mother and I decided to sell them for lighter garments and raise some money to enable us (I hoped) to get away.

It seemed prudent to ask advice of Mrs Isbister and so one evening, just before finishing work, my mother said to her: "Do you know how much this coat of Johnnie's and his linen shirt and my spencer are worth?"

"No," Mr Isbister suddenly objected. "Don't sell 'em. Leastways not the boy's good things: that cut-away and the silk neck-kerchief."

We all — including his wife — looked at him in surprise: "It's good for the business," he said, "to have a smartly-dressed boy on the cart." And then, to my amazement, he brought out of his greasy coat-pocket a half-sovereign and handed it to my mother with ceremony: "Buy what you need with that," he said. "I want him to look like a young swell."

"Why, you're too generous," Mrs Isbister cried. She turned to my mother: "I'll take that from your wages, Mary."

I saw my mother flinch at this use of her name.

"No you won't," Mr Isbister said. "That's from me."

My mother and I hastened upstairs as they began to quarrel.

"Mother," I said, "we must leave this place."

She looked at me in alarm: "Whyever do you say that?"

"Because of them."

"How can you say that? Of course, she makes me work very hard but at least she pays me something. And without that, where would we go and what would we do?"

"We must try to find something else," I insisted. "We can't stay here for ever, and now is the best time to look for other work. The summer is approaching and the start of the Season."

"No," she said. "I dare not leave here."

"But you promised we would go when we had money."

"But a half-sovereign isn't enough, Johnnie. And there are so many things that we need. I must have some decent clothes and I can't bear not to have proper bed-linen. I can't."

We quarrelled about this and she was reduced to tears. Now feeling guilty for what I had said, I tried to comfort her.

"Then if you really want to please me," she said, "let us go out now and buy what we need!"

I agreed reluctantly, for the half-sovereign represented our best chance of escape. As we left the house we heard Mrs Isbister's voice raised: "When are you ever a-going to get some more pickled pork?"

"Don't start on that agin!" the man of the house shouted just before we closed the street-door.

We hurried through the muddy streets of the neighbourhood towards the high-road, for it was Saturday-night and the street-market was drawing towards its climax. In the flaring gas-lights the faces — the features often squashed together or misshapen — loomed at us from the shadows like a theatrical show: the drawn faces of the very poor, the laughing faces of those in funds or already drunk, but always, in one form or another, misery and fear and shame and desperation, whether clothed in rags or in tawdry finery, and everywhere a profligacy of children — children of all ages, children in tatters, dirty, with unkempt hair, their chests pinched inwards and their legs bowed, and with running sores on their faces or on their limbs that were visible through their rags; children running, fighting, stealing, swarming in the kennels.

This was the first time we had ventured into the market so late, and we drew together in dismay.

We bought (second-hand, of course) some more clothes for my mother and some bed-linen and a pair of boots for each of us, and the half-sovereign soon disappeared. However, once she was wearing her new bonnet and cloak, my mother's spirits rose.

When we got back we heard the Isbisters in the middle of a fierce quarrel.

"I'm having to work myself half to death," the lady of the house was shouting as we opened the door.

"It's the blessed weather," her husband responded. "Is it my fault that it's so bad?"

We were stealing up the stairs at this moment and I don't think my mother heard this remark which puzzled me, because the weather had remained fine and dry for a couple of weeks.

"You know there ain't no things to be had when it's like this," Mr Isbister shouted.

We had not been quiet enough, for just as we reached the door of our room, Mrs Isbister came into the hall. She looked up at my mother and said thickly: "Why, Mary, you do look nice."

My mother drew back to take my arm: "Thank you, Mrs Isbister."

That lady glowered and, reaching for support from the door-handle behind her, said: "From now on you call me 'ma'am'. Is that understood?"

"Yes," my mother said softly.

"Yes what?"

"Yes, ma'am."

When we had shut the door behind us, she said: "Oh Johnnie, I think she's horrible. If only we could go! I wish we hadn't spent that money."

"Then let's go now anyway!" I urged.

A look of terror appeared on her face: "No, I dare not."

She seemed so frightened at the thought that I pursued it no further.

The weather continued sunny and dry. It was a few days after this, on the 13th. of April, that Mr Isbister told me late one morning to put on my new clothes and get Gunpowder from the livery stable and harness him to the cart. I noticed when I got back with the beast that a piece of tarred sacking was hanging over the driver's side of the cart in such a way as to obscure the name painted on it.

We set off and after some time were driving along Old-street and then up the City-road, a district which was quite strange to me. Then, just after we passed a large building on the side of which I saw the sign "St. Luke's", we turned the corner and Mr Isbister reined in Gunpowder.

He glanced behind him up the street and then said to me in a low voice: "Now listen, young 'un. I've been good to you and yer mother, haven't I?" I nodded. "Now it's your chance to show your gratitude. All right?"

"Yes."

"I want you to go to the infirmary ward and arst for Mr Pulsifer who is the superintendent. When you find him, tell him you've come for Mr Leatherbarrow. He's the uncle of a friend of mine, Bob Stringfellow. Bob hasn't time to fetch the old feller himself, so he's arst me to do it."

"But Mr Leatherbarrow doesn't know me. Will he come with me?"

"Don't consarn yourself about that," Mr Isbister answered, with a smile.

"Very well," I agreed.

"That's prime," he said. "I knowed you was up to the game."

"Where will he go?" I asked, for there was room for only two people on the seat.

"On that straw back there," Mr Isbister said, jerking his head.

I supposed he would be more comfortable if he could lie down since he had been ill.

"That puts me in mind o' something," Mr Isbister went on. He reached into his pocket and brought out a coin. "Now you see this here shilling? You're to show it to Mr Pulsifer and say it's for helping you to get the old feller onto the cart out here. Is that clear?"

"Yes," I said.

"If he arsts, say there's a friend o' yourn with the cart what can't help on account of I've got a gammy arm. See?" I nodded, reflecting that this did not seem to have prevented him from heaving bales of cloth a few days before. I reached out for the coin and he handed it to me saying earnestly: "There'll be one for yourself if this goes off all right."

I got off the cart.

"Go to the gate round the front," he said, pointing back the way we had come. "And remember, he's in the infirmary ward."

I went through the gate and up to the porter's lodge where I was given directions. When I passed into the building the sounds from the street were suddenly muffled, and as I began to walk along a long dark stone-flagged passage I heard nothing but the echoes of my own footsteps and the distant sounds of raised voices.

I passed a yard with a high wall through the gate of which I saw men, women and children — all wearing their distinctive garb and the parish badge — picking at thick knots of tarred ropes. And in another yard there was a loud and mysterious rumbling, though I was unable to see what was making it.

When I had made my way to the infirmary I was directed by one of the attendants to Mr Pulsifer, a tall and sallow-faced individual with a thin, fastidious mouth.

When I gave him my message he looked at me curiously: "Do you have a coach?"

"No, but a person is waiting outside with a cart. I have a shilling for your attendants to help me get Mr Leatherbarrow onto it."

"Follow me," he said, looking at me sceptically.

As we left the room he picked up a candle and lit it from a gas-jet while he called to two other men: "Hey Jack! Jem! This way!"

Two burly individuals who had been lounging against the wall smoking a pipe and chatting together, now followed us out of the long room and along a gloomy passage.

"Nobody visited him when he was ill," Mr Pulsifer said, turning to look at me intently. "It's strange his nephew should want him now."

As we descended some steps and entered a cold dark room in the cellars, I wondered at the inappropriateness of such a chamber for a convalescent old man. Mr Pulsifer led us over to a corner of the room where there was a wide wooden ledge like a sideboard on which I now saw, by the light of his candle, a large shape covered by a piece of cloth. While Mr Pulsifer raised the candle Jack pulled back the cloth.

"There he is," Mr Pulsifer said.

I went closer, my eyes straining in the dim light. Then I felt a surge of horror and all my perplexities were instantly resolved: an old man was lying there who, by his marble-like flesh and staring eyes, was no longer in a state to be injured by a ride in a jolting cart. Because of the near-darkness, the men did not notice my expression. The two assistants picked the awful object up, and, one holding the feet and the other the shoulders while Mr Pulsifer led the way with the candle, carried it back the way we had come. The superintendent took leave of me — with a final suspicious look — as we passed through the infirmary, and the other two followed me with their burden out into the street.

I led them to the cart, where Mr Isbister was standing by the horse's head, and they laid the body down. I covered it with some of the straw and handed the shilling to one of the men, who both touched their hats politely towards my master — the more politely since he had his face turned away from them — and went back into the building. When they had gone Mr Isbister got back onto the box and as the cart rolled off, he smiled at me and began to whistle tunelessly.

"Mr Isbister," I said, "Why did you not warn me that Mr Leatherbarrow ... " I broke off.

He laughed: "I was a-feared you might be skeered. But now you know there ain't nothing to be a-feared on."

After a few minutes he pulled the cart up at the corner of the City-road and Old-street.

"Make your way home from here," he said and handed over a coin. "There's that shilling for being a good lad."

I took it but felt a certain disquiet as I climbed down and walked away. After a few yards I glanced back and saw to my surprise that Mr Isbister had not moved off but was watching me. Just before I turned the corner I looked round again and saw him still keeping his eyes on me.

I walked about the streets lost in thought. Had Mr Isbister really been simply helping his friend? If it was something more than this, I could not understand how he could be profiting by it. And what should I tell my mother? I resolved merely to say that my master had given me a half-holiday and a shilling to enjoy it.

When I came out of my reverie I realized that I was near Coleman-street and on an impulse turned aside to call in. The little servant, Nancy, answered the area-bell (I dared not ring at the street-door now) and told me that Miss Quilliam had not been back since our visit.

As I reached the door of the Isbisters' house half an hour later, it opened and my mother and Mrs Isbister appeared. They were both laughing and clutching each other as if for support, but when my mother caught sight of me standing a few yards away and watching her, she flushed and said: "Why, Johnnie, whatever are you doing here?"

I told her of the half-holiday and the shilling, at which she exclaimed: "How lucky! We were just going to the shop. Now you can run round and buy another quart of … "

She broke off and looked at Mrs Isbister, giggling and covering her mouth with her hand.

"The Reg'lar Flare-up," Mrs Isbister, who was having difficulty standing, put in.

"I shan't," I declared. "We need the money for other things."

"Why, that ungrateful ill-mannered young rascal," Mrs Isbister said.

"Johnnie, you must respect … respect and obey your mother. Now do as I tell you."

"It's my money," I cried. "I earned it."

Mrs Isbister sucked in her breath through her teeth at this: "I've told Jerry agin and agin as how that boy ain't worth the bother."

Furious and ashamed, I turned and ran down the street. I walked about for a couple of hours and bought a meat pie which I ate sitting on a broken wall near the church. Where could we go and how could we earn our bread? And yet we had to get away from these people, for I had begun to form an explanation for their interest in us. Our only hope lay in selling the document that the Mompessons and Mr Barbellion (on behalf of our mysterious enemy) were so anxious to obtain. And until I knew why it was so important to them, I was reluctant to try to persuade my mother to do so.

When I got back I could hear Mrs Isbister and my mother still in the kitchen, so I went upstairs and got into bed.

I could not sleep and was still awake when my mother came upstairs several hours later.

"You must not speak to me like that before other people," she said carefully.

"I hate to see you with her," I answered. "She's horrible."

"She's not," she cried. "Of course she's vulgar and uneducated, but she means well."

"She doesn't," I said. "Can't you see? Mamma, we must go away from here. I'm sure I can earn more than Mr Isbister gives me."

"You?" she said in surprise. "How much could a little boy like you hope to earn? You know, Johnnie, you live on the money I get from Mrs Isbister. It is I, not you, who keeps us."

"That's not true," I cried. "You're kept on charity. I know how little Mrs Isbister pays other women for the work you do."

"You're only saying that to hurt me," she said. "Why do you do it?"

We argued ourselves into silence, and though my mother fell asleep quickly, I lay awake. After an hour or so she began coughing and woke up, and then we both lay in the darkness for some time listening to the other's breathing and pretending to be asleep.

Nearly three weeks had passed and my mother had been spending more and more time with Mrs Isbister and yet was increasingly at odds with her and resentful of her treatment. Then on the morning of the 3rd. of May, as we were about to go out on the cart, Mr Isbister told me to put on my best clothes and make myself look smart. When I saw the cart I was not surprised to see the sacking in place once again.

We drove in silence for some time but as we began to go down Cheapside, Mr Isbister suddenly cleared his throat and began to speak. He told me a rambling and incoherent story concerning a friend of his, Ben ("You've most likely seen him coming and going at the crib."). It appeared that Ben's mother had recently died, and the old woman had always wished to be laid to rest beside her husband in the burying-ground at St. Giles-without-Cripplegate. Ben's sister, however, with whom he was not on the best of terms, had prevailed upon the family of her mother's employers — for malign but unspecified motives of her own — to bury their late servant in a different ground. And since they had obtained her ticket to the hospital and paid for her medicines, "the coves at Bart's will do as they say." If, however, I were to compose a letter purporting to come from the old woman's employer, Mr Poindexter, and instructing the authorities to surrender the body to his son and servant — "That's me and you, see?" — then the old woman's dying wish could be gratified and Ben's peace of mind restored.

At this point he appeared to notice the expression of dismay on my face for he licked his lips and said: "There's two shillin' in it for you."

"I don't think I can oblige you, Mr Isbister," I said.

The effect of these words was dramatic. His face darkened suddenly and his little black eyes appeared to protrude. He leant towards me and, lowering his voice, spoke rapidly:

"Then you're both out tonight, you and your blessed mother. Why do you think I took you in? I can get a good price for that room. And boys to help on the cart is ten a penny. And the old ooman says your mother is so slow and stupid she costs her more than her work's worth in ... "

As he talked I thought of what sudden eviction might do to my mother. And yet the alternative was hateful.

I realized that Mr Isbister was watching me hungrily: "Say three shillin', then?" he said.

He had mistaken the nature of my scruples, but it might be better to dissimulate them.

"Five," I said.

"You're a hard 'un, but all right," he said in ill-disguised relief.

He produced the materials, I wrote the letter, and we drove to the hospital and drew up outside the back-gate in Well-yard. I went in and played my part successfully, once again noticing, as two of the porters helped me to carry out my prize, that Mr Isbister kept his face averted.

He drove off and halted at the same place as before, gave me my money and told me to get down and walk home. I looked back and although he was sitting on the cart watching me, I now acted upon an intention I had formed after the last incident. I passed around the corner but after a few moments crept back just as the cart was moving off. It turned and went back up Old-street and, staying well back, I tried to keep up with it.

The difficulty was not, as I had anticipated, that the cart went too fast for me, for I found that I could just manage to keep up with it because it was slowed down by the other traffic. The problem was that, in the press of other vehicles, I could not distinguish it unless I kept so close that Mr Isbister would see me if he looked round. And so at the intersection with Goswell-street, where I had difficulty in crossing, I lost sight of it.

As I made my way home I debated my best course of action. Given that I had no conclusive evidence of what Mr Isbister was doing, was I prepared to force my mother into complete poverty and homelessness on the grounds of my suspicions alone?

As I entered I heard low voices coming from the kitchen and looked in. The room was lit only by the dull glow from the grate and my mother and Mrs Isbister were sunk in their chairs at the table and did not notice me.

"Please don't call me that," my mother was protesting.

"I'll call you what I please. Givin' yourself them airs as if you was a fine lady."

"You've no right to say that."

"Oh, haven't I? How dare you speak to me so disrespeckful. Why, Meg, you would 'ave starved, you and that blessed boy, if we hadn't've took pity on you. We on'y keep you out of charity."

"How can you say that when I work so hard!"

"Work! Why, you're so slow and you sp'il more than you make. And that's to take no account of what you cost me in ... " She broke off and looked up: "Who's that?"

I crossed the room and almost pulled my mother from the chair.

"Come," I said.

Protesting feebly she allowed me to lead her upstairs where she staggered into our chamber and sat heavily on the bed. When I reproached her for letting Mrs Isbister abuse her, she started weeping and begging my pardon. I gave it rather grudgingly, and she dozed off. I tried to sleep as well, but she began coughing in her sleep and that and the events of the day running through my mind prevented me. The dampness of the house was bad for her lungs and I feared that the long hours she had to work, and other things, were sapping her strength. Yet could I force her to leave the comparative safety of that house? If only I could be sure of what Mr Isbister was involved in! And now it was that the resolution came to me: I would follow the cart the next night that Mr Isbister and the other men went out on it!

CHAPTER 34

My opportunity seemed to come only a few days later, for one afternoon two of Mr Isbister's companions arrived at the house earlier than usual. They stayed in the parlour drinking and I could hear their laughter and shouts as I sat upstairs with my mother.

Suddenly Mr Isbister came out into the hall and roared up the stairs: "Jack! Come down here!"

I obeyed and when I found him standing at the door he pushed a couple of shillings into my hand: "Look sharp and bring us three quarts of nine-penny, there's a good lad. Arst for Jerry's reg'lar and they'll sarve you the Real Knock-Me-Down."

When I got back from the gin-shop round the corner and knocked on the door, Mr Isbister pulled it open but instead of simply taking the bottles from me as he had done on previous occasions, he said: "Come in and meet the lads."

Reluctantly I entered the hot little room for the first time for it had always been forbidden to me before, and now the smell made my nose work though I wanted it not to. My master and his two companions had already consumed several jugs and if not actually "knocked down" they had certainly taken considerable punishment. I recognised them as the men I had seen on previous occasions, though I did not know their names. One was very fat and the other extremely thin. Mr Isbister beckoned me forward and then seated himself so that I was standing as if on a stage before the three men.

"You haven't seen my new boy, have you?" he said.

"He don't look worth much," said one of the men.

He was so enormously fat that his chest and stomach seemed almost perfectly spherical and his chin appeared to rest on the top of his chest for I saw no sign of a neck. He had small black eyes which, set in an oddly small head with thick black curls, seemed to be restlessly staring about them as if in surprise at finding themselves stuck at the top of such a monstrous form. I saw something move and realized that he was carrying a couple of bull-dog pups in his capacious pockets.

"He may not look like much, Ben, but wait until you hear him speak. Now say something to show the genel'men," Mr Isbister urged me.

"Mr Ben," I said, "I am very sorry about your mother."

He stared at me in obvious amazement: "*I*'m wery sorry about the infernal old nuisance, meself, but I'm damned if I see that she's any consarn of yourn."

I looked towards Mr Isbister in surprise.

He leaned forward: "Your mother, Ben," he prompted. "Your blessed mother as passed away t'other day. It was Jack here what fetched her from the dead-house at Bart's so as you could bury her beside her old feller, according to her dearest wish."

"Be damned if I hadn't forgotten," said Ben. He turned to me: "Well, thank you, my young cully." He looked at Mr Isbister: "How did you manage that? They're too wide-awake there, I thought. Finesilver's a sharp 'un."

Mr Isbister smiled: "See this boy dressed up like a little genel'man and carrying a letter from his dad wrote out proper and sealed and everything." He suddenly screwed up his face and, speaking several tones higher than usual, said: "Excuse me, Mr Finesilver, I ham most confounded sorry to trouble you, but my dad arst me to give you this here letter and for you to give me the thing mentioned in it what he wants collected."

Ben and Mr Isbister roared and slapped their knees at this sally. The thin man smiled and drank from his tumbler.

"So how much do you owe us, Jerry?" Ben asked.

"Not a brass fardin!" Mr Isbister exclaimed, the smile disappearing very quickly. "That was on my own account."

"Your own account be damned! I won't take gammon. You know what we agreed," Ben said. "Share and share alike: everything what we hears, the time what we puts in, every blessed thing. Eq'al money for eq'al risk. Ain't that right, Jem?"

"That's right," the other man agreed, and wiped his nose emphatically with the back of his sleeve.

"I'll tell you what, Ben: you can whistle for it," Mr Isbister replied cheerfully.

"Why, honour among genel'men," said Ben raising his massive body from the chair with difficulty. "That's the company's blunt not yourn."

Mr Isbister looked up at him as he loomed before him blocking his light, then calmly drank from his tumbler before speaking: "Sit down, Ben." He added conversationally: "Or I'll beat your phiz to a pulp."

Ben sank back into his seat like a pierced pig's bladder.

Mr Isbister turned to me and said genially: "Take a seat, Jack. Here Jem, pour the lad a wet. And will you take a second glass yourself?"

Jem, who had a long melancholy face and weak eyes, replied: "Why, I will. Always wet both eyes, says I." He poured me a large tumbler. "Here, lad, take it slow and it'll do you no harm."

I sat on a chair near the door and pretended to drink the raw spirit whose very smell I had come to loathe.

"We had a boy when I was fust on this lay a good few year back," Mr Isbister said expansively. "And wery useful he was, too. But he weren't no gentry-boy like this 'un. And the Jew has got a boy now, but Ikey's boy don't speak as nice as what this 'un do. And Jack here'll read you off print or hand-wrote letters faster nor a dog kin trot. And write 'em, in the bargain."

Jem looked at me curiously and even Ben, who had appeared not to be listening, turned a speculative eye upon me.

"So you reckon," said Jem, "to put him to work, what with the reg'lar line of business being so bad the last few weeks ... "

Mr Isbister interrupted quickly: "Exackerly."

There was a pleasant silence while the three men — even Ben, who was still sulking — looked at me and drank contemplatively.

"I reckon it's the weather," Jem said. "It's too dry. We wants a nice damp spell."

Mr Isbister agreed: "Warm and wet. This dry weather ain't no good to no-one. It's jist the same in the winter. Cold and dry ain't no use to us."

"There jist ain't enough things," said Jem. "Pertickerly with the competition. There's a deal too much. The trade can only support so many."

"Too many on us and what happens?" Mr Isbister replied. "Why, the price comes a-tumbling down. It's the Cat's-meat-man what's sp'iling the trade for all on us, the honourable men."

"What's he getting?"

"Lampard and Morphew pays twelve for a long, five for a small long, and two for a small."

The others drew their breath sharply through their teeth.

"It's a scandal!" said Ben, speaking for the first time since his altercation with my master.

"Why, it don't show no respeck, do it?" Jem agreed. "Twelve pound!"

They shook their heads.

Jem turned to Mr Isbister: "Things don't fetch what they used to. What was it you used to get when you started this lay, Jerry?"

Mr Isbister sighed: "Nigh on twenty for a long. Them was the days. Jist a-fore the War come to an end. There weren't nobody in the trade but us and the Jew."

"Aye, you and Blueskin was working mates with the Cat's-meat-man and Barney then, wasn't you?" said Jem.

I pricked up my ears at this.

"Aye," Mr Isbister said, adding quickly: "But then we fell out with 'em and started on our own. So that left him and Barney down the Borough and arter that there was a deal o' competition between us."

"But then not long arter that him and Barney come off at hooks, didn't they?" Jem said.

"Aye, the Cat's-meat-man 'peached on him about seven year back. He had to leave Town and go down into the country but when he come back the Cat's-meat-man got him took up. He done a couple o' year at Gravesend at the Floating 'Cademy a-fore he managed to buy his ticket."

"He's a rum nut, the Cat's-meat-man," put in Ben.

"When he was young," said my master, "there wasn't nobody in Town to match him — barring gin."

"Why did you and Blueskin fall out with him?" Ben enquired sharply. When Mr Isbister didn't answer he said: "Ain't it true that Blueskin sarved his brother out?"

"You've got the wrong pig by the ear," Mr Isbister said dismissively. "That were never down to Blueskin."

"I heerd the same," Jem agreed. "They say he stuck him with a knife on account of a noise over the blunt."

"Tell us the story, Jerry," said Ben. "Or are you a-feared o' Blueskin?"

"I ain't a-feared of Blueskin or no man," Mr Isbister insisted.

At that moment the door opened and a man came in very quietly, and this was all the more striking since he walked with a limp and I saw that he had a wooden leg. He was completely bald, had a thin mouth and an almost fleshless face with blue-grey eyes so pale that they seemed to vanish as you looked into them. He said softly: "Nobody heerd me knockin', you was a-having sich a good time."

He appeared to address these words to the whole company, but he smiled at Mr Isbister, if that was the right word for such a scull-recalling grimace.

Mr Isbister stammered: "Why, Blueskin, my good fellow. Come in and set yourself down."

"What was you all a-talkin' about so cozy?"

There was an uneasy silence.

Then Mr Isbister said: "We was saying that business being as bad as it is, the lad here can help us."

Blueskin smiled at each of them and said softly: "Oh, was you?" Then he turned his cold gaze upon me and I felt a chill as he scrutinized me with those disconcerting eyes.

"I don't think we should use him," said Jem.

"Whyever not?" Mr Isbister exclaimed.

"It ain't right, that's all."

"Well, perhaps we won't need to," Ben said. "Is there anything in from the searchers?"

"No," said Mr Isbister. "Old Nellie out in St. Botolph's work'us sent word to say she had something, but then it weren't no good. Relatives come for it."

They sighed and shook their heads.

"Relatives!" said Ben scornfully, and the others muttered in agreement.

"Has any on you had any luck today with the blacks?" Mr Isbister asked.

Ben and Jem shook their heads.

"Nothing," said the latter. "I walked around till my feet was sore."

"I followed one," said Blueskin. "From Great-Tower-street. It looked a good 'un." At this the others smiled, but then Blueskin added softly: "Only then it went down the Borough."

Their smiles disappeared.

"Then that ain't no good to us," Jem said. "The Boys o' the Borough will have that one."

"I don't see why they should," Blueskin said. "The Cat's-meat-man comes up this way. Why shouldn't we go down there?"

None of the others met his eye and he went on: "That's the way I reckoned it, so I paid Sleeth fifteen to forget to lock the gate same as last time."

"We'll settle next time," Mr Isbister said, "when we'll have done some business."

"We'll settle now," Blueskin said very gently, and with a scowl my master reached into his pocket and handed over fifteen shillings.

"While you got your blunt handy, Jerry," Ben began as Mr Isbister shot him a hideous look, "you can settle up for what we talked about earlier." He turned to Blueskin: "Jerry got the boy to colleck a thing from Bart's."

"Is that so?" Blueskin said. "Well done, Jerry. Cop us the blunt."

With an ill grace Mr Isbister gave each of the three men two sovereigns.

"What, only ten?" said Blueskin ironically. "You was done brown. Especially with things so hard to come by just now!"

"It weren't a good 'un," said Mr Isbister.

"What about Harry's share?" Jem asked.

The other three looked at each other.

"Harry won't know," Blueskin said. "Leastways, not if none on us don't tell him."

"So that's another ten each," Ben said.

As Mr Isbister counted out the money and gave it to them, Jem protested mildly: "I don't think we should. It ain't honourable."

"Don't you want your share?" Mr Isbister snarled.

Jem pocketed it ruefully.

"Well," asked Blueskin, looking round the room, "who's game for the go tonight?"

"Have you forgot the drubbing the Boys o' the Borough give us last time?"

Mr Isbister asked indignantly. "Look at this." He rolled up a sleeve and held up an arm: "Be damned if I haven't still got the scars where the Cat's-meat-man pinked me."

Blueskin said softly: "I ain't forgot at all, not at all, Jerry. That's why I says we can't let 'em have it all their own way, or where will it end?"

"I'm cap'n," said Mr Isbister. "I decide."

"It's our living that's getting took away from us. We all decide," said Blueskin gently.

"That's the ticket," said Ben, and even Jem grunted in support.

"So what do you say?" asked Blueskin, turning to them.

"We ain't had no luck for weeks," said Ben uncertainly.

"You want a broken head, do you?" my master sneered.

"See, last time we wasn't ready for 'em," said Blueskin to the other two as if Mr Isbister had not spoken. "But if they come tonight we'll make 'em welcome."

"Aye, that's right," cried Ben, glaring at Mr Isbister. "We'll win the horse or lose the saddle, says I!"

"What do you say, Jem?" Blueskin asked.

"I ain't happy, but if you go I'll make one with you."

"There's a plucky Briton!" Ben exclaimed, turning his massive body so that he could glare at Isbister. "So we'll go! And if anyone says contrairy, then damn him for a yellerbelly!"

"Well, Jerry?" Blueskin asked quietly.

"Why, I'll come. In course I will. Did I ever say different?"

Blueskin thumped the table beside him and looking round at the others, cried: "So we'll go a-wooing, then?"

Ben and Jem laughed and Blueskin shouted: "Go on, Ben, give it to us."

Ben began to sing to the tune of "Wapping Old Stairs", and the others passed the jug round as they joined in the chorus, the comical point of which was to come in early cutting off the last line. As they did so they banged their tankards down on any nearby surface. All this time, to my dismay, Mr Isbister, singing in a tuneless bass, kept his gaze fixed upon me with a smile that I found more disturbing than any grimace. It was as if he were inviting me to admit that I was enjoying the joke:

"Jack wooed a cold, cold lady
To leave her mother's side.
Jack was a bashful wooer;
She would not be his …

Chorus:
"Kneel upon the lady's shift
To arst her for her hand;
And don't mind if she's stiff,
And don't mind if she's stiff.

"Jack told his dad his troubles:
'The lady is too proud
And stiff to let me take her,
A-wearin' of her … '

Chorus:
"Kneel upon ... etc.

"The old 'un answered Jacko
In these most helpful terms:
'You'll have to straddle her boldly
Or leave her to the ... '

Chorus:
"Kneel upon ... etc."

As the song finished with a climactic clattering of tankards, Mr Isbister said to me: "Well, young 'un, how do you fancy j'inin' us tonight?"

"No, Jerry," Ben suddenly put in. "How do we know we can trust him not to nose?"

"Oh I think we can trust him," Mr Isbister said placing his arm over my shoulders and pulling me close to him. "He knows what's good for him and his mam."

"I don't want to, Mr Isbister," I said.

He got to his feet looking down at me with deep malevolence in his little black eyes. "You don't want to," he repeated, advancing upon me.

I stood up as he approached and began to move away.

"I've trusted you," he said. "You know enough to queer our pitch."

He seized me with one massive fist bunching up my coat-front and pushed me back suddenly against the wall.

"I say Jerry, lay off him," Jem objected mildly.

"What's a half-long worth just now?" Blueskin asked quietly.

Ben laughed but Mr Isbister, holding his face an inch or two from mine, said: "You don't think I took you and your mam in out of pure kindness do you? You ain't that simple, are you?" To emphasize his point he banged my head hard against the wall. "It ain't just a matter of throwing you and your mam out. Oh no, it's gone too far for that. If I can't trust you ... " He broke off. "Boys like you is fetched out of the river or found in the Fleet-ditch, oh, three or four times a week. So do you still say you ain't a-coming tonight?"

"No, not tonight," said Jem. "Not if we're going down the Borough and there's a fair chance of trouble."

"All the better," said Mr Isbister. "He can hold the hoss and keep an eye on the cart." For added emphasis he gave me a blow to my head which sent it back against the wall. "Well, what do you say?"

I was saved by a remark from Blueskin: "Jem's right. He'd jist be in the way. Wait till we find a gate that wants squeezing through."

Mr Isbister looked at me resentfully: "All right, not tonight," he said. "But next time we go out you'll come with us. Now be off."

He stood aside so that I could pass, and I left the room. Outside in the dark little hall I paused and breathed deeply. I heard the voices of my mother and Mrs Isbister arguing together in the kitchen, and suddenly I felt that I could not bear the house any longer. I ran out and then hurried through the streets at random, bent simply on getting as far away from there as I could and resolved that I would never go back.

I walked for a couple of hours, going over and over in my thoughts the choices that were available. If only something had come of my attempt to find Miss Quilliam. That reflection made me suddenly realize that I was not far from Mrs Malatratt's house and I hurried thither.

When I knocked on the kitchen door Nancy opened it and smiled at seeing me: "I've got something for you at last. The genel'man come and settled the account so she's been 'lowed to take the boxes. She left this."

With these puzzling words, she reached behind a tray propped against the wall on a sideboard and handed me a letter. I turned it the right way up and saw that the superscription was simply one word: "John".

"I can't speak now for the mistress has jist rung the bell," Nancy said and closed the door.

As I mounted the area-steps I opened the letter — my first proper letter! — and read the elegant hand with my heart thumping:

"No. 47, Orchard-street,
"Westminster,
"The 4th. of June, 18--.

"My Dear John,

"Certainly I remember you, though that time at Hougham now seems to belong to another world.

"I grieve to hear of the misfortunes that have befallen you and your mother, and I dearly wish it were in my power to help you. But only conceive what I must mean when I tell you that I am now in much less fortunate circumstances even than when you saw me last. However, though I fear I have very few means to help you, whatever may lie within my power I will perform — and more than gladly. If you and your mother wish to come to me, you will find me at the above address.

"In the meantime I remain,
"your very obedient servant
"no less than your friend,
"*Helen Quilliam*."

I was a little disappointed, and as I made my way quickly home, I speculated on whether I should persuade my mother to accept Miss Quilliam's offer, and on how we would maintain ourselves if we did. Before I could urge her to leave the protection of the Isbisters, I decided, I had to be absolutely sure that my master was involved in something as nefarious as what I suspected. And then it came to me: I would follow him and find out tonight!

It was nearly nine o'clock by the time I got back. I crept up to our room and, listening to the sounds of drunken laughter from the parlour and the quarrelling voices of the two women from the kitchen, consumed the saveloy and bread-roll I had bought on the way home.

When, after a couple of hours, my mother at last came up to bed I could tell that it was not the occasion for a rational discussion of the future. Shortly afterwards, Mrs Isbister ascended the stairs, muttering drunkenly to herself. My mother quickly fell into a deep sleep and, except for her coughing, her breathing was soon deep and regular.

Time passed slowly and all the while I could hear shouts and laughter punctuated by bursts of song issuing from the parlour. It was not until a little after midnight that I heard the men leave the house and instantly I slipped out of bed, pulled on my clothes in the dark, and left the room, squeezing the door shut behind me. Reassured by the sound of Mrs Isbister still breathing heavily in her sleep, I stole downstairs and, once in the kitchen, released the catch on the window, opened it, and climbed out, gently lowering it behind me.

I now found myself in the little yard at the back of the house which was empty except for a water-butt, a heap of broken bricks and slates, and a dead rat, and which was surrounded by a high wall with a gate. I had scanned it from our window during the day and now scrambled over the gate without much difficulty, and then cautiously made my way along the dark little lane between the surrounding back-yards until I gained the street. Mr Isbister's three companions were standing by the cart, and as I watched from round the angle of the house, my master himself approached leading the horse, which he had obviously just brought from the livery-stable. He harnessed it as quietly as possible in the light of the lanthorn that Jem held for him, and a few minutes later they boarded the cart and it rolled away. I kept well back when it set off and only emerged from concealment as it reached the end of the street. Now I would find out if I was going to be able to keep pace with it.

Fortunately it was a fine night with many stars and a large bright moon, so that I could follow the cart's progress from a considerable distance without losing sight of it. Though by the same token, I had to be more careful not to be observed. Mr Isbister kept the horse to a walk until he reached the high-road, probably to avoid attracting notice. I had never been out so late and though I was surprised by the volume of traffic and the number of foot-passengers on the road, I felt some alarm at the prospect of venturing into the dark bye-ways. Now Mr Isbister set the horse going at a trot — though fortunately for me a slow one, on account of the number of passengers.

At first I was able to keep up with little difficulty by maintaining a steady and gentle run, but after fifteen minutes I was beginning to tire. The cart made its way steadily westward along Bethnal-green-road and then turned south into Shoreditch. By the time it was going at a good trot along Bishopsgate I began to flag and it drew steadily away from me. With my heart and lungs on the point of bursting and my feet in considerable pain because of the poor condition of my boots, I nearly cried aloud with frustration and anger at the thought that I would lose the vehicle after all. Since I had no more reserves of strength or wind, however, there was nothing to be done and a few minutes later it was out of my sight. I assumed that it was going to cross the river by London-bridge but beyond that, I knew I had no chance of regaining my quarry. Yet still I ran on for it was easier to do that than to admit defeat.

Just as I reached the bridge, I suddenly realized that a vehicle that was pulled in to the side of the road a few yards ahead of me was the cart! I had nearly run upon it! I hastily ran up Lower-Thames-street and then crept back to watch. This was a stroke of luck and it gave me the chance to get my breath back. After some minutes a figure approached from Upper-Thames-street to the west and, after a few words were exchanged, climbed aboard as the cart moved off. I assumed that this was the man, Harry, whom they had referred to.

It went through the toll-gate on the bridge and a moment later I followed, slipping through the horse-gate so that the toll-taker, busy with his leather apron and money-pocket, did not even notice me. Once the cart had entered the Borough it went only a short distance down some side-streets and then drew up in an unlit lane. I stayed some distance away and watched the five men get down and take from the back of the cart certain objects which I could not make out because they were wrapped in sacking. And they were taking other precautions against noise for I heard not a sound. Then four of them made their way down an alley-way that led off the lane, and now I could see that they were carrying dark-lanthorns and long-handled tools. Above the tops of the houses on that side I saw the spire of a church. The fifth man stayed with the cart and as I crept past it in the darkness on the other side of the lane I thought that I could make out that it was Jem, and I could see that the piece of tarred sacking was in place.

I dared not go down the alley-way after the men in case they looked back, so I cut through other streets until, by a kind of tacking, I came up against a wall topped by railings and peered through. I could just discern dark figures moving among the pale stones and then was able to make out what it was that they were unwrapping. I needed to see no more. Exhausted, horrified, and in need of respite before setting off on the long walk home, I leant against the wall trying not to hear the faint sounds of metal striking earth.

Suddenly I heard a noise from behind me: footsteps were approaching down the alley-way! I left the wall and pressed myself into a door-way opposite it just as a group of six or seven men approached. I felt the back of my neck tingle as I realized that they were treading as soundlessly as they could and then saw that they were carrying long staves.

The man in front, who appeared to be directing the others, was of very striking appearance, as I saw in the pale moonlight that fell directly upon him. Though he was small he had a strangely large head for so diminutive a figure, and it jutted out like a tortoise's. As I watched he lifted a hand to halt his followers, and raised his head to listen. His face was sallow and his mouth was a mere slit, but he had a huge beaked nose and very deep eye-cavities, and as I watched him seeming to sniff the air, I sensed an animal-like eagerness that frightened me.

Immediately behind him was a tall, good-looking young man with frank, manly features that contrasted strangely with those of his dwarfish leader. At another signal from the latter, the men pulled kerchiefs from their pockets and wrapped them about the lower part of their faces so that they resembled a party of sufferers in search of a dentist. Then after a few muttered words they passed through the gate by which the others must have entered.

From the faint sounds I heard a minute afterwards, I realized that the newcomers had attacked Mr Isbister's gang and that a fight was taking place. But it was a very strange kind of conflict, for those involved were taking pains to make as little noise as possible, and though I heard the muffled thud of club and spade against person several times, I heard no voices except once when there came a cry of pain which was quickly bitten off.

I knew I should get away while I was still undetected, and so at last I tore myself from the railings and retraced my steps. When I reached the lane where the horse and cart were I began to creep cautiously past, though nobody seemed to be in attendance. As I did so I saw something lying in the ditch at the side of the carriageway and when I went closer I found to my horror that it was a man. He was motionless and when I went right up to him I saw that it was Jem and that he was bleeding from a wound to the head. Of all of Mr Isbister's gang he was the one whom I least disliked.

I hurried on my way and in the next street came across a couple of horse-drawn carts guarded by two men carrying dark-lanthorns and cudgels. I worked my way round them by back-lanes and then ran as fast as I could and did not stop until I reached the toll-gate on the bridge. From there I alternately walked and ran, exhausted as I was, for I had formed a resolution which I needed to act on very quickly.

I met nobody now except the occasional milkman and a few market-carts and then some children on their way to the early morning market at Bethnal-green where they presented themselves to be hired out for the day. When I reached home I found the street was quiet, though the dawn was already beginning. I hastily climbed back over the wall and in through the window, reassured to find that the house was perfectly silent. Now the smell from the parlour made me gasp for breath — for I understood why I had so often been forbidden to enter it — and I longed to be out of there. As I passed Mrs Isbister's door I heard her still snoring as before and when I gained our room I saw a shape in the bed and assumed that my mother was sleeping as I had left her.

When I had lit a tallow-candle, I called softly: "Mamma, wake up."

I leant over her and now saw with horror that she was doubled up as if in pain. Her face was turned away from me and she was moaning, and fearing that she was ill I touched her shoulder. She muttered something and moved restlessly, her eyes flickering open and shut until I shook her gently and, with a start, she woke up. She turned her face to me still in the grip of sleep and I felt a shock of dismay for she looked strangely old. With her lips drawn down her mouth seemed toothless like an old woman's and her eyes stared blankly at me without recognition.

Then she seemed to know me, and yet she looked at me strangely as if afraid of me.

"Is it you?" she asked timidly.

"Yes, it is I: Johnnie."

"Who is Johnnie?" she said and frowned. Then her face cleared and she smiled and was herself again, and yet not entirely for now I saw how much the last few months had aged her, and I felt an obscure sense of foreboding for the future.

"Oh Johnnie," she said. "I was having such a horrible dream!" She bit her lower lip and seemed about to speak. "But no matter," she went on, after a pause. "Is it time to get up already?"

"It's about four o'clock."

"So early!" She looked at me in surprise. "But why are you dressed?"

"Hush!" I said. "We must not wake Mrs Isbister."

She looked bewildered and I knelt beside the bed and took her hand in mine: "Mother," I said, "will you believe me if I tell you that we must go from this house immediately?"

"Why, what can you mean?"

"I have been out tonight. I have learned something about Mr Isbister. I don't want to tell you what it is. Just believe me."

She looked at me strangely: "How like my father you are. I was dreaming of him just now. You don't trust me, either, do you?"

"Will you believe me, Mamma?"

"But where would we go?"

I pulled out Miss Quilliam's letter and explained my visit to Coleman-street.

She read the letter, then looked at me uncertainly: "But Johnnie, it seems as if she is no better circumstanced than we."

"But at least she offers us somewhere to go."

"But I have work here, and we have food and drink and shelter. And I have all my possessions," she said, looking round the room. "I cannot leave them."

"What possessions?" I said angrily. "Nothing at all compared to what you left in Melthorpe. And we can take them with us if you wish."

"But things are going so well here."

"How can you say that? You know how unkind Mrs Isbister is to you! You know you hate her."

"She is often kind. When we have finished the day's work."

"Kind!" I exclaimed. "That is not kindness. She wants to have you in her power."

She flushed then looked down and her hands played restlessly on the edge of the sheet: "I won't go. I'm frightened."

"If you won't come I will go alone." Saying it gave me a strange sense of exultation, but as I looked at her horror I felt a stab of pain.

"No, Johnnie!"

"I mean it!"

"How could you manage? What would become of you? You would starve." She shuddered. "Don't say such a thing."

I stood up and began to put my things together, as best I could through my incipient tears: "I am going. Come with me or stay here."

"Then I must go with you. But this is very wicked of you."

"Then we leave now."

"Do you mean today?"

"I mean within the hour or less. Mrs Isbister is fast asleep but may wake soon, and *he* may return at any moment."

It did not take us long to prepare for we had very little: a bare change of clothes each, some sheets and blankets, and a few plates, cups, knives and forks. While my mother dressed I made these up into two bundles, the crockery carefully padded with the clothes to prevent them from making a noise as we left the house. When all was ready, and the little chamber as empty as when we had first come there, my mother looked wistfully at some of the clothes she had been working upon.

"Johnnie, do you think it would be awfully wrong to take some of this work?"

"What do you mean?"

"She has not yet paid me for them. If I took some of the garments it would cover what I am owed for the last few days. And perhaps a little over for I believe she hasn't been paying me a fair price."

"Mamma," I exclaimed. "That would be theft!"

She looked as if I had struck her.

"Yes," she said. "You are right." Then she began to sob: "What has happened to me? How can I be thinking of such a thing?"

"Hush," I whispered.

She looked at me wildly and, no longer keeping her voice down, said: "You know, sometimes I think of such terrible things. I dare not tell you."

"You will wake Mrs Isbister," I said desperately.

This seemed to recall her to herself and she grew calmer.

"Quickly," I said. "It is getting late."

The light was coming in through the barred shutters (we had to draw them at night for the window had no curtains) and there were the sounds of foot-passengers in the street. We picked up our bundles and began to creep down the stairs.

Mrs Isbister was still snoring like a hedgehog (as Sukey used to say) and we retraced without difficulty the course I had taken a few hours earlier through the malodorous house. I opened the kitchen-window and helped my mother to climb through, then passed the bundles to her.

We found ourselves out in the raw morning air of the street without mishap and had begun to make our way towards Bethnal-green-road when, in the next street but one, I heard a cart approaching. I drew my mother into a door-way in case it should be Mr Isbister and my precaution was justified for as the vehicle passed I saw him hunched malevolently over the reins. His coat was covered in mud and so was his face. One eye was swollen and half-shut, and there was a great purple bruise on his left temple. As the cart clattered past I felt a profound sense of relief that we were no longer at his mercy.

I glanced at my mother to parry her questions about his appearance but she said nothing, and once the vehicle had turned the corner we hurried on our way.

We now had to cross the metropolis almost from its eastern to its western extremity, and we had only eight-pence to sustain us. It was a laborious walk carrying our bundles, but at least it was a warm summer's night and we did not need to hurry.

As we slowly covered the weary miles the dawn began to suffuse the sky behind us with a gleaming pinky-orange light that presaged a fine day. We stopped to rest often and once to buy a small loaf for our breakfast, keeping half of it for our midday meal. That left us with four-pence which I calculated to be enough to reach Miss Quilliam's lodging, but I hated to think that we would arrive as abject beggars.

"I know this place," my mother said as we approached the Temple Bar at midday. "My father used to bring me here when I was a child when he came to visit his lawyer." After a moment she added bitterly: "How strange it is to walk down this street as a beggar when I last saw it from inside a fine carriage. I knew nothing of these back-streets then." She turned to me: "Oh Johnnie, I was having such a nightmare when you woke me. My father was holding out his arms to me and I thought he was welcoming me for he seemed to be smiling, but when I got closer I saw that he was covered in blood and his mouth was twisted as if he were in fearful pain."

She shivered and I said: "Are you cold, Mamma? It's going to be a beautiful day."

"How my father would grieve to see us like this," she sighed. "He had such great hopes for his heirs."

"What hopes?" I demanded. "Why?"

She refused to say any more, but I was convinced that it was something to do with the codicil.

Then as we passed Northumberland-house at the western extremity of the Strand, she began to talk of her father again, mentioning that his house was near here and that was why she knew the district. Despite my entreaties, however, she would not show me which street the house was in.

"Did my grandfather know me?" I asked.

"No, you were not born when he ... when he died."

"When did he die?"

"Nine or ten months before that," she replied.

"And what did he die of?"

She gripped my arm and said passionately: "Don't ask me that. You'll know one day, I promise."

To distract her, I stopped a respectably-dressed young clerk who was passing and enquired the way.

He looked at us with manifest curiosity: "Orchard-street?" he said. "Yes I know of it. It's in the Devil's Acre."

My mother looked at me with dismay at these words but I avoided her gaze.

"Will you tell us how to reach it?" I asked.

"Keep straight along here, then turn right and follow your noses. You could smell your way to it blindfolded."

I thanked him and we walked on with heavy hearts.

"I wonder why he called it that," my mother said bleakly.

I made no reply for I felt that I knew and that the answer would become all too clear. And I was right, for the streets grew poorer and shabbier and a profound and insidious stench became increasingly unignorable.

CHAPTER 35

The Devil's Acre stood on what was then the western extremity of the metropolis, for beyond it stretched the empty, marshy, clayey district which was known as the Neat-houses and beyond that the wilderness of the Four-fields. To its east lay the Palace of Westminster and the ancient Abbey, by whose Dean and Chapter the Devil's Acre had been owned from the beginning of historical records and by whose right of sanctuary it had been created.

Orchard-street, in which we soon found ourselves, was one of the principal thoroughfares of that unhappy district, and although its houses had been very fine when they were built, for many years they had been the dwellings of the most poverty-stricken. Windows were broken and covered by paper or stuffed with straw, street-doors had disappeared, gutters and waste-pipes hung crazily down the sides of the buildings, tufts of grass and weeds sprouted under the eaves, and on the rooves whole areas of slates were missing. Although it was now afternoon the street had a sullen, ill-tempered air as if it had been up too late the night before and had drunk more than was good for it.

No. 47 was a little less delapidated than its neighbours. Its street-door stood open and now, wiser than before in the customs of the poor, we went into the dark hall and knocked at the first door on the left.

After some delay a poorly-dressed man appeared and held the door open only enough to look out: "What do you want?"

"We are looking for a young lady called Miss Quilliam," I said.

The door slammed and we heard the man speaking to someone in the room. Then it opened again just enough for him to say hastily: "Back two-pair."

Ascending the ancient staircase, many of whose treads were wanting and whose banister rocked as we held it, we knocked on the door indicated to us, and to my delight a voice that I knew called out: "Pray enter."

I pushed open the door and we found ourselves inside a large high-ceilinged room. Although the weather was sunny and there were two lofty windows, it was dimly-lit and I saw that this was because one of the windows had several missing panes covered by rags and the other had its shutters drawn. The great chamber bore many traces of its former state: the walls were pannelled in dark wood and there were elaborate mouldings around the windows and the door-frames and on the corners of the ceiling. But its present condition revealed the poverty of its occupant — the floor had only bare boards and there was very little furniture — though everything was clean and neat.

A woman wearing a plain grey gown sat at the unshuttered window and had clearly been sewing when we had knocked for she laid down her work now as she looked towards us. When I came closer and saw her face I would hardly have recognised her as the fine-looking young woman I had encountered only a little less than a twelvemonth previously. Her features were drawn and pale, and her eyes seemed larger. We looked at each other for a moment and it was as if she knew my face as little as I knew hers. She stayed where she was and we advanced into the room.

"John!" she cried, "and John's mother!"

Her voice was the same and at its sound that summer day at Hougham came flooding back into my memory.

"Come closer," she said. I went up to her and she put her work aside and took both my hands between hers, then leant forward and kissed me.

"You're not too old to be kissed, I hope," she said. "And yet you look so much older that I did not know you at first. But tell me quickly, have you any news of poor Henrietta?"

I told her of our last meeting and that she had said she was being sent to Brussels.

Miss Quilliam sighed: "A convent-school! But at least she will be getting away." Then she exclaimed: "What am I thinking of! I must be forgetting my manners."

She turned to my mother and held out her hand. My mother took it, hesitated for a moment while she looked into her face, then flung her arms around her and started sobbing.

"My dear, you are safe now, you are quite safe," Miss Quilliam said, quite as if she were the elder, looking at me with concern over my mother's shoulder. I was divided between pride in having such an acquaintance and shame on my mother's behalf.

"At last we have found a friend," my mother cried.

"Yes you have," Miss Quilliam declared, making my mother comfortable beside her. "And how clever of Johnnie to have found me! I can't tell you how surprised I was to receive your letter." She looked at me: "However *did* you find me?"

I said proudly: "Through the clerk at the London General registry-office."

She looked at me oddly as if about to say more. Then she exclaimed: "But you have come a long way and must be hungry! Let me give you something."

"Miss Quilliam," I said, looking round and unsure how to express myself on this delicate point, "I see you are not in prosperous circumstances and as for us, why, we are beggars. We have but four-pence in the world."

"Then I am much richer than you." She smiled and added: "By nearly two hundred and forty times, for I have three sovereigns and some shillings. So I have wealth enough for all of us."

I looked at my mother, weary and hungry after the day's exertions but now animated by an impulse of hope in our newly-rediscovered friend, and I ceased to protest.

Leaving my mother on the window-seat Miss Quilliam rose and began to cross the room, and I now saw how thin, how very thin, she was. Then to my alarm, after she had taken just a few steps, she staggered slightly and only just managed to return to her seat.

She winced, but seeing our expressions of dismay, forced a smile and said: "I have been ill, but I am so much stronger now that I forget my weakness."

"I will make the tea," I said. "Tell me where everything is."

She consented and so, under her direction, I boiled a kettle in a corner of the vast fireplace where a few coals were gathered, and while the tea was mashing, toasted some slices of bread. This was all there was to eat or drink except for a small jug of milk and another stone jug.

Later, while we ate, my mother and I, at Miss Quilliam's prompting, began a condensed version of our history, omitting nothing of importance — except that neither of us seemed to think it necessary to mention that we had a document which others were anxious to obtain. I felt a little guilty at not confiding fully in our friend but it seemed prudent to mention the codicil to nobody.

I noticed that Miss Quilliam consumed very little, but while my mother and I were still eating, she said to me: "Will you be kind enough to bring me that jug by the chimney-piece and the glass beside it?"

I did so and she poured herself a measure saying: "I find it restores my strength a little."

She offered some to my mother who glanced at me timidly and declined.

When we had finished, Miss Quilliam asked some questions which were pertinent without being in the least prying.

Then she said: "You say you are penniless, but I know that you have at least something of value." My mother looked at me in alarm which vanished when Miss Quilliam went on: "I refer to the clothes you are wearing, which would bring several pounds."

"If it comes to that we have something much more valuable ... " my mother began.

Fearing that she was after all about to mention the codicil I quickly said: "Yes, indeed we have. Mother, show Miss Quilliam the locket."

"Not that, please, Johnnie," my mother said.

Her face showed that she was struggling, while Miss Quilliam looked from one to the other of us in surprise.

At last, however, my mother reached for the locket round her neck and showed it to our hostess: "If necessary," she said, "I could raise money by this."

"Yes," said Miss Quilliam examining it with interest. "That would assuredly fetch several pounds."

My mother restored the locket to its place with a reproachful glance towards me.

"Now as to the future," Miss Quilliam said, "I will help you as best I may. But as I wrote in my letter, I fear that I am almost destitute myself. Of course you may stay here as long as you wish, for anyway this room is far too large for me."

"That is very kind of you," my mother said.

Miss Quilliam looked up at her: "Not at all. I have been seeking to underlet it, so I am happy to have you as tenants. There is a bed" (and she indicated a straw mattress in one corner) "and Johnnie may sleep in the little closet."

"How much should we pay you as our share of your rent?" I asked.

"Oh, Johnnie," my mother said. "Miss Quilliam did not mean that."

"Of course she did," I insisted.

"I only wish," Miss Quilliam said, "that I could let you have it for nothing. But let us say, two shillings?"

"That is very little," I said. "But it may still be too much for us for I don't know how we will earn any money."

"You said you did plain-work for that woman," Miss Quilliam said to my mother. "There are some good souls in the room across the landing who give me such work, and it may be that they can find some for you as well. Mr Peachment is a slop-tailor and he and his wife have been very good to me. For some months I have been keeping myself with my needle by helping them to do out-work for a slop-shop. I owe them a great deal, for they saved my life. You see, shortly after arriving here, I was taken ill and Mrs Peachment nursed me. I will take you to meet them tomorrow in the hope that they will be able to offer you some work — at least while the Season lasts."

"You are very kind. But have you given up hope of finding employment again as a governess?" my mother asked in surprise.

Miss Quilliam appeared not to hear and my mother did not repeat the question, for there were many others to be asked and answered on both sides.

After a short time, however, since my mother and I were tired, it was settled that we should retire to bed. The unpacking and disposition of our two bundles of possessions took but little time and the vast room looked hardly any the less bare for the new additions.

I made myself comfortable in the closet, which was, in effect, a small chamber off the larger one as is often found in houses of that period. Miss Quilliam gave me a mattress of quilted straw on which I spread a sheet and then crawled under one of our two blankets.

I heard the voices of the two women murmuring together until I fell asleep. Once when I awoke — or half-awoke — I thought I heard someone sobbing and the sound of a gentle voice rising and falling. I slept badly for there were noises from the street and on the stairs and in the other parts of the building all through the night: loud arguments and drunken singing and once someone hammered at the barred door and tried to get in.

BOOK III

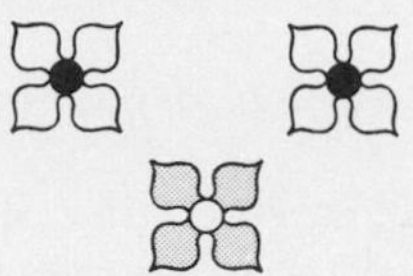

Secret Benefactors

CHAPTER 36

The next morning Miss Quilliam took us to meet the Peachments. As we entered their chamber I had the impression of crowdedness in contrast to the emptiness of Miss Quilliam's and realized that this was because, although it was no larger, it had to serve as kitchen, bed-chamber, living-room and workshop for the parents and no less than seven children ranging in age from near full-grown to an infant in arms — all of whom were now present. Yet it was clean and neat for all that. Moreover, it was made even smaller by an arrangement of faded and threadbare Turkey-carpets hung from ropes hooked to the walls (putting me in mind of a dingy tent from the Arabian Tales) which served to separate one corner.

Although it was not yet seven everyone was busily at work: a number of little girls and boys were cutting out pieces of felt and sewing them into the shapes of dolls, while their elders were stitching pieces of cloth and button-holes under the direction of their parents.

Mr and Mrs Peachment were friendly and their soft West-country speech fell gently on my ear after the insistent rise and fall of London speech.

"I can spare ye some work from the slop-master," Mr Peachment said to my mother when the situation had been put to him; "like I've been doin' for the other young lady, for this is the busiest time o' the year." My mother thanked him and he added: "But 'tis unpossible to say how long 'twill endure. When Parlyment rises and the Season ends then there shan't be a mite o' work no more."

"We'll not deceive ye," said his wife with a kindly smile. "If there's but little work it must go first to our own."

"It's hard to scratch a living here," her husband said reflectively. "Lunnon folks is so mortal 'cute."

As he spoke he laid one finger along the side of his nose, and he repeated this phrase a number of times in his conversation and always with the same gesture as if it indicated that, sharp though they might be, he had the measure of them.

The question of what I should do was also resolved for it emerged that the Peachments' eldest boy, Dick, who was a year or two my senior, and who earned a few shillings a week by selling in the streets the dolls made by the younger children, had been offered an opening in the "costermongering line" as his father proudly expressed it. And so it was suggested that my mother and I should buy the tray and the current stock and that I should assume his function.

The negotiations were protracted and made difficult by the commercial attitudes of the two parties:

"Why," Mr Peachment kept saying, "we don't want to take more than a fair price of you."

"What would that be, do you reckon, Mr Peachment?" speculated his wife.

Here Dick, scowling at us, said something to his father in an undertone who shook his head, upon which the boy walked away angrily to the other end of the room.

However, with the mediation of Miss Quilliam it was at last settled that I would pay five-pence a week for the use of the tray, purchasing the dolls at four-pence and letting them go to the public for a shilling. And, moreover, it was agreed that Dick would take me out that very morning in order to initiate me into his mysterious art.

When Miss Quilliam had paid over the money on our behalf, I strapped on the heavy tray and Dick and I left the house.

"Me mam and dad is green," he said sullenly, breaking his silence only as we reached the end of the street. "They could have got more of you than they done."

I noticed that his speech was already more London than Dorsetshire.

"Fair price!" he snorted. "I told 'em a fair price was what you'd pay. I told 'em, but they wouldn't take no heed." He kicked a loose paving-stone.

Encouraged by his volubility, I asked him several questions about my new profession, but he said nothing. And so we walked on in silence — I having to struggle to keep pace with him since he was unencumbered — until we reached the corner of Fleet-street and Chancery-lane, where even though it was long after eight, crowds of people were still hastening to work.

"This here's your walk," he said. "But you have to be here earlier than this or you'll lose it."

"And what do I do?" I asked.

To my astonishment he suddenly seized one of the articles of sale and, brandishing it ferociously above his head, shouted: "Dolls! Buy my dolls!"

Then he banged it back in the tray: "That's what you do. And be ready when the traps' deputies pull you up for their blunt."

"What do you mean?" I asked.

"Lor'! Ain't he green!" he exclaimed to an imaginary auditor. "I ain't got all day. You're up to the game or you ain't."

With these words he walked away without looking back.

Now that I had to make my entry onto the stage of commerce, I found it extremely difficult to raise my voice and shout, convinced that I would be ridiculed if I tried. At last I managed it and to my surprise the foot-passengers — far from pausing to jeer at my feeble screech — continued to hurry past without looking at me. I shouted louder and directed my attentions towards particular individuals, but during the course of the morning I succeeded in selling only one doll.

There was a puzzling incident when, after about an hour, two men came up to me, one lean and sharp-featured, the other with a bland, shiny face.

"Cut away, young 'un," the thin one said. "This here's our pitch."

"What do you mean?" I demanded.

"We keeps the streets hereabouts," the one with the fleshy features said confidentially; "and anyone what wants to work 'em has to square us."

"But that's not right!" I cried. "These streets are free to anyone."

He lowered his face to within a couple of inches of mine and said: "Hook it or it'll go the worse for you."

They walked away and, indignant at this threat to the native liberties of an Englishman, I continued to sell. I soon forgot about the incident for I had discovered a serious problem in the form of street-boys who ran up, grabbed my wares, and hurried off until I learned to watch out for them and turn my tray to the wall until they had gone.

Early in the afternoon, a policeman came up to me and said: "Move along, young shaver."

When I protested that I had acquired the right to this walk from its previous occupant, he smiled perfectly affably and said: "Why, you surely don't believe he didn't pay for the privilege, do you?"

"Then I will, too," I said.

He nodded judicially and walked away.

A little later his deputies re-appeared and, when I assured them that I had sold only one doll, agreed to accept a mere tuppence on the grounds that I was only a beginner.

I sold no more that day and returned home exhausted and dispirited to find my mother and Miss Quilliam stitching furiously.

"Isn't it time to stop now?" my mother asked Miss Quilliam when she had greeted me.

"Heavens, my dear, not yet."

"Mrs Isbister let me stop at seven or eight," she protested.

They worked on while I fetched and prepared a meagre supper of herring and cold potatoes, and then at last Miss Quilliam declared that it was time.

My mother and I drank porter with our meal, but Miss Quilliam poured herself a tumbler from the stone jug, and then added a few drops of dark liquid from a small bottle.

They resumed work while I explored her library (three battered volumes) and read a few pages of one of Sir Walter Scott's historical romances.

Seeing this Miss Quilliam, whose spirits had lifted, cried: "I shall teach you, Johnnie. It will be quite like the old days with Henrietta. I love to teach."

We thanked her and my mother exclaimed: "How can you bear to live like this when you could be a governess again?"

Miss Quilliam looked up and coloured. After a moment she said: "I think you said yesterday that you learned of my former lodging at Mrs Malatratt's house from the registry-office in Wigmore-street?" We nodded and she glanced from one to the other of us uncertainly. "I don't know what lies about me you may have been told ... " she began, and then broke off.

My mother and I looked at each other in surprise and shook our heads.

"We heard nothing," my mother said.

"I am relieved to find it so," Miss Quilliam said and then she continued somewhat excitedly: "The truth is that upon my first coming to London I lodged at Mrs Malatratt's house. And when, upon entering the employment of Sir Perceval and Lady Mompesson, I departed from there, I left some boxes behind me for safe keeping. Last summer I went back there after leaving my position, and Mrs Malatratt refused to restore my property to me."

"How could she do that?" my mother asked.

"Oh, she said that ... she demanded that I should pay her an extortionate rent for the space they had occupied. But when I went back just a week ago and found your note, Johnnie, she at last let me have them. Their contents were of little value and I have sold them to pay debts incurred during my illness."

She had not needed to say so much and the subject was allowed to drop when Miss Quilliam offered my mother a drink from her jug.

She looked at it wistfully and blushed when she caught my eye. Then she poured herself a tumbler, saying defiantly: "It restores my strength and helps me to sleep."

The next day I did a little better on the streets, and during the next days and weeks I learned how to manage some of the hazards that threatened. However, I sold very few dolls and earned at most two or three shillings a week clear profit.

At first Miss Quilliam was true to her word and when I came home and we had eaten, she would take out her books and I discovered what a good teacher she was. However, it was difficult for me to summon the strength to devote myself to this after a day on the streets, and she was exhausted, too, after working from first light until late at night. Although usually after supper (of which she ate very little) she would revive for a while, she would often become too restless to concentrate and would walk up and down the room talking wildly. Then after an hour or two a reaction would set in and she would become listless and dispirited. So after a few weeks my lessons were allowed to lapse.

Though we had much to be grateful for, our situation remained extremely precarious. Often my mother and I had no money at all to pay our share of the rent at the end of the week when the landlord's deputy came round on collecting-day, and in effect we lived on Miss Quilliam's little stock of capital. We also subsisted on "tick" at the dirty little general chandler (generally called the "tally-shop") at the street corner, paying something weekly towards the total, but never clearing it entirely. This meant that we had to purchase their inferior and over-priced goods, for Miss Quilliam warned us that they would demand repayment of the whole sum if we withdrew our patronage.

During this time I became increasingly annoyed by my mother's frequent reproaches for having forced her to leave the Isbisters where (she said) we had been so much better off. Moreover, from being wasteful and extravagant, she became increasingly obsessed with obtaining money and unwilling to part with it. Most irritatingly she became convinced that the Peachments — manifestly honest and generous as they were — were cheating her by not paying her adequately for her work, and she even complained to me on occasions that Miss Quilliam worked her too hard. Her mood ranged between deep depression and strange light-heartedness, for I often got back from the streets at night and found her oddly animated and then (though her mood never lasted long) I was cheered. And yet I knew that this way of life was damaging to her health, although it was not until one evening several months later that I understood how very dangerous it was.

As I became increasingly familiar with the neighbourhood I realized how much more desperate was the plight of many of our neighbours, for my mother and I were at least able-bodied and capable of scraping a living. Those ancient streets — largely unlit, unpatroled, and unvisited by the dust-collector — harboured nests of the most abject poverty. The stench that hung over the district was augmented by the presence of breweries and above all by the gas-container at the premises of the Gas, Light and Coke Company which were then in Great-Peter-street (and with which my own destiny was much later to be indirectly connected). There were haunts of criminality, too, among the warrens of the poor, and (since the poor find it safer to prey upon each other) the streets were infested by pick-pockets and sturdy beggars who would demand money even in the open street by day. Miss Quilliam warned us of the gangs of armed men who sometimes blocked off a whole street at both ends and attacked the shops "by escalade" like a Crusader army, while others robbed the foot-passengers.

And so the summer wore on. We awoke shortly after five o' clock and while my mother and Miss Quilliam began their work, I drew water from the pump in the yard at the back, washed in a leaden trough beneath the cistern, then carried up the water, lighted the fire, and boiled a kettle. We made our breakfast as quickly as possible and then by seven o'clock I was on my way to my pitch in one or other of the streets leading from the suburbs into the City. My best customers at the beginning and end of the day were clerks and people of that kind, but in the morning and early afternoon my "walk" was amongst the fashionable shopping streets of the West-end.

One morning, finding that the City was almost deserted, I abandoned trade for the day and set off for home. Approaching Westminster, I encountered crowds of people in holiday dress making in the same direction, and asked someone what was going on.

"Why, it's the risin' of Parlyment," he answered with a sneer as if only a simpleton could fail to know it.

So that was the explanation for the emptiness of the City! Along the route from St. James to Westminster there were crowds gathered to watch the royal procession return, and mounted soldiers to protect His Majesty from the popular displays of feeling to which he had occasionally been exposed. Quite near our street I came across a gaily-painted wooden box with streamers of coloured ribbons, before which was gathered a crowd of children with their nurses and governesses — and further back some urchins of the street.

Mr and Mrs Punch had reached that stage in their domestic relations when they were furiously throwing the baby backwards and forwards in anticipation of its final ejection through the window by its male parent.

"You improvident creature," Mr Punch cried in a nasal squeak, "you didn't never ought to have had it. What was you a-thinkin' of?" With these words he flung his off-spring at his wife who neatly caught it round the neck.

"Why, you monster, don't you love your own little child?" asked his wife in a much deeper voice than her spouse.

"How should I love it if it conflicts with my interests?" her husband demanded. "I can't afford another mouth to feed!"

"What's the cost matter to you?" his spouse retorted. "We shall get our reg'lars of the paritch."

"Why, woman, that's just what will beggar the country and bring us all to our ruin!" Punch riposted in deeper and much better modulated accents.

"Humbug!" Joan cried. "There's wealth enough and it's only equitable that the rich should help the poor. Why, I know Lady Decies has ten thousand a year and she ... "

The young audience was becoming increasingly restless at the turn the performance was taking, and some were beginning to drift away.

"Don't speak to me of Equity!" interrupted Mr Punch in an even deeper voice than before. "You're a Jacobin! An incendiarist!"

This exordium was interrupted by a man's voice from behind the little stage that sounded oddly like Joan's: "Hit me, you ideot!"

Mr Punch instantly obliged by raising his truncheon and bringing it down hard upon his wife's head, and the children who remained roared with delight. To their even greater joy, Mrs Punch turned her infant into a weapon and banged it a number of times over her husband's head. While Punch and Joan continued to trade blows they did not speak but the sound of a fierce argument could be heard coming from behind the box. The voices were too muffled to be heard distinctly, though occasional phrases were comprehensible: "property rights ... irresponsibility ... population".

Suddenly Mr Punch turned away from cudgelling his wife and demanded of the remaining members of the audience in a squeaking voice: "Children, have you ever considered the relation of the means of production to the growth of population?"

I saw some of the governesses and nurses exchange looks of outrage, and in a moment there were only a few jeering street-urchins left. Though his wife continued to smash their child down upon his head Mr Punch took no notice of her.

"Only grasp that principle and its terrible implications and you will perceive that while we flatter ourselves as a polity that we are in control of our destiny, the truth is that we are powerless," he declared passionately, his voice now unequivocally that of an ordinary man.

While he was speaking, Joan ducked down with the baby leaving her husband on the stage alone.

"How then may we become free? Only by harmonising ourselves with the randomness of life through the untrammelled operation of the market."

While Punch was making this speech his wife reappeared carrying a saucepan which she had substituted for the baby, and crept up behind him.

The few children who were still watching cried: "Look out behind you, Mr Punch! Look sharp, you silly puppet!"

"Puppets, that's all any of us are," Punch remarked, catching only this word.

"Hold your noise, you fool," shrieked Joan, thumping him on the head. Then in a lower and gruffer voice she added: "They don't want to hear that."

It occurred to me now that when the puppeteers emerged at the end to pass the hat round they would find nobody but myself and a few ragged laughing boys, and, embarrassed at the thought, I walked quickly away.

In the next street the crowd was gathering along the pavement and, finding a good site on a street-corner, I could not resist the temptation to take up my pitch.

During the next hour or two I sold more dolls than I had ever done in a whole day, though the press of the crowd made it difficult to keep a hold on my tray and several times boys snatched objects or even money from me. Then the procession at last returned and there passed the most magnificent carriages I had ever seen or imagined — each with a squadron of mounted and plumed out-riders on matching bays. At that moment a crowd of boys and youths approached and one of them — a tall, ungainly youth with a jutting jaw and deep-set eyes — appeared to notice me and to draw the attention of some of the others. They ran up and, while the eyes of the rest of the crowd were on the procession, knocked over my tray. They seemed to be impelled by mere high spirits, but the one who had incited them stayed behind when they passed on and pushed me to the ground so hard that for a moment I was stunned. He stood over me, reached into my pockets, and extracted all the money I had taken. Then he was, I think, about to kick me for he had got so far as raising one foot when he was suddenly pulled backwards so unexpectedly that he lost his balance and fell.

The gentleman — or was it a gentleman? — who had done this looked down at him and remarked benignly: "My most excellent young man, you will learn in due course, I hope, the virtue of moderation. A kick would have been a wholly unnecessary expenditure of energy."

The youth, as he stood up and dusted his trowsers, replied venomously: "Oh won't Squeezem Jack jist be pleased with you! I should say so. You'd better look for another pitch, that's all." Then he slunk off and was lost in the crowd.

As my saviour helped me to my feet I had the chance to look at him. He was tall and stooping with rounded shoulders and a rotund figure and was about fifty years of age. His face, which wore an expression that I can only describe as one of indignant good humour, was red-cheeked and adorned by little half-lens eye-glasses above which bristled a pair of very bushy eyebrows that gave his physiognomy an expression of permanent surprise. His appearance did not efface but recorded the history of his dressing: a neckerchief carelessly tied, stockings ill-matched, and the act of shaving ill-completed. His stained and patched coat was covered in a fine powder and when I knew him better I understood that this was because of his habit, on becoming passionately eloquent on a subject as he often did, of throwing rapid pinches of snuff in the direction of his nose so that it flew about him like a golden mist. He wore an ancient wig which somehow always contrived to get turned round so that the queue hung over one ear, impairing the tenuous dignity of his appearance still further.

"Silverlight, restrain yourself!" this gentleman suddenly cried, and following his gaze I saw another individual standing anxiously some distance away with a number of what looked like wooden boards, a bundle of material, and a large box sitting beside him on the pavement.

He was much shorter and slighter than his companion, and about ten years younger. Though so small he had a large head and jaw and possessed quite the most distinguished nose I had ever seen on a human face — indeed, so distinguished was it that the rest of his features were cast into shadow both literally and figuratively by this magnificent organ. Unlike his companion this gentleman was dressed very carefully and I owe it to him to say that in times to come, however severely straitened his circumstances, I never but once saw him when his linen was not impeccable and his clothes equally neat.

"Beast! Animal!" this gentleman was crying as he shook his fist at the retreating youth. "I shall go after him!" he shouted, making as if to take up the pursuit.

"Noble fellow, be calm," the larger gentleman shouted and leaving me he rushed to hold onto the coat-tails of his friend who appeared to be making violent attempts to break loose, though fortunately the cloth held.

"Impulsive creature," my rescuer cried. "You'll endanger your life which — remember! — it is the first duty of the rational man to preserve."

"Humbug! The first duty of the Rational Man is to defend his principles!" the little man shouted. "And the principle of Retributive Justice is sacred. He must be punished!"

The little gentleman, however, gave up the attempt to pursue my attacker and I now had the chance to express my feelings.

"It was very kind of you," I began.

To my surprise, while the little man beamed at this, the elder gentleman started back as if I had struck him.

"Kind! Fiddlesticks!" he exclaimed almost irritably. He turned to his companion: "Do you think so, Silverlight? Was it kind?"

"Indeed it was," he said in what seemed to me an oddly malicious tone.

"It's cruel of you to say so!"

"Well," I said trying to make peace, but sadly puzzled, "It was at the least a fortunate chance for me."

This remark, however, fared no better: "A tautology," the elder gentleman exclaimed. "Chance rules all things."

"On the contrary," the other insisted, "there is a pattern in all that exists if only we have the wit to perceive it." He turned to me: "I believe some Principle of Design may have been at work on this very occasion, for I know you. You're the young gentleman who lodges with Miss Quilliam, are you not?"

As I nodded I remembered that I had seen them on the stair once or twice.

"We are neighbours of yours, for we lodge for the moment with a simple family of the name of Peachment," he continued. "An entirely temporary arrangement until our circumstances improve."

Now I recalled that I had once or twice seen the two gentlemen assisting each other up the stairs late in the evening.

"Of course!" I exclaimed. "You live in the portion of their room that is ... "

"Quite, quite," Mr Silverlight said quickly. "I have seen you in the company of the lady I take to be your mother?"

I nodded.

He held out his hand: "My name is Silverlight and my friend is Pentecost."

Mr Pentecost also shook my hand. "Come," he said, "there will be nothing to be gained by working the rest of the day. Let us accompany you home in case that misguided creature takes the dictates of self-interest to excess."

"It will be a pleasure," Mr Silverlight said, "to restore you to the loving arms of your charming mother."

They turned to pick up the objects lying beside them on the pavement and as they did so I realized who they were: "You're the Merry Andrews!" I cried.

"Indeed we are," the elder said somewhat bashfully. "Have you seen our work?"

"Only a little," I replied, in fear that they would ask me for my opinion.

"Don't you think there's too much political economy?" Mr Silverlight asked me as we began to make our way homewards.

"Well, perhaps just a little," I said tactfully.

"You see, Pentecost?" said Mr Silverlight. "I've told you a thousand times, Punch and Joan can only bear so much. The children don't like it."

"Fiddlesticks! It's your infernal ideas they don't like. Even a child can see through them. And if it comes to that, Silverlight, there's a deal too much good society in your patter."

"But for satirical purposes, my dear sir, surely it is justified! Or do you mean that I'm too harsh?"

"No, Silverlight," Mr Pentecost said quickly, "I'll do you the justice to say I think you show great restraint in your treatment of the *beau monde*."

When we got back I took them to meet my mother and Miss Quilliam, both of whom were alarmed to see my bruised and blood-stained appearance. While they fussed and worried over me, my two rescuers stood in the door-way.

"Here are the gentlemen who saved me," I kept saying but it was some time before it was established that I had received no serious injury and until then nothing else could be thought of. I made the introductions and my mother warmly expressed her gratitude.

"I am delighted, utterly enraptured," Mr Silverlight said, bowing first to my mother and then to Miss Quilliam, "to have been of service. But dear ladies, I did nothing, nothing at all. What was it to show five or six ruffians that I was not afraid of them? They soon ran away when they saw what mettle they had to deal with."

My mother and Miss Quilliam, insisting that they enter and be seated, moved their work out of the way and lighted another candle.

While they were doing this, Mr Silverlight squeezed himself into a corner of the window, moved a piece of paper covering a broken pane and then stretched on tip-toe to look over an intervening roof to where the sun was setting: "Why, how I envy you. You have a western aspect! I think a western aspect best. Pentecost's chambers and mine face east. So dreary in the evening, one finds."

"Yes," said my mother. "It is often very dreary."

"Gentlemen," Miss Quilliam said, "will you do us the honour of taking a glass of best nine-penny?" With a smile she added: "It is the finest we have to offer."

"It is we who should be honoured," Mr Silverlight answered with a bow. When he caught sight of the gin-bottle he exclaimed: "Ah, the Out-and-Outer! Pentecost favours the Regular Flare-Up which I confess I find a trifle rough. But this has a delightful smoothness." He turned towards Miss Quilliam and said with another little bow: "I perceive you are accustomed to the fine things of life."

"I certainly became so," she answered, "at one period of my life."

"Indeed?" said Mr Silverlight inquisitively.

"I refer," Miss Quilliam continued with a slight blush, "to the time when I resided in the house of Sir Perceval and Lady Mompesson." She added with a smile: "Though to the best of my recollection the Out-and-Outer was not served in their drawing-room." Seeing an expression of astonishment on Mr Silverlight's features she explained: "I was governess to their ward."

"A private governess!" Mr Silverlight breathed. "And with one of the most ... prominent families in the land."

"They are known to you?" Miss Quilliam asked.

"By name and reputation," Mr Silverlight said, and added haughtily: "Though I have not had the pleasure of being received by them. Many members of the aristocracy are, however, personally known to me. You see, I chummed — I should rather say, shared a lodging — with the nephew of Sir Wycherley Fiennes Wycherley, that is to say, Mr Fiennes Wycherley Fiennes. In fact, we were on terms of the utmost intimacy. His is a sad tale. Perhaps you know it? Wycherley Fiennes spent four thousand pounds in five years and ended badly. Squandered it all on cards and at Hazard."

"While you lived in chambers with him?" Miss Quilliam exclaimed. "You quite alarm me, sir. I hope you were not involved."

Mr Silverlight coloured and stammered: "It was afterwards that I knew him, as it happened. Pentecost knew him too."

Mr Pentecost nodded without looking at his friend.

"It gave me," Mr Silverlight went on, "innumerable opportunities to witness at first hand the corruption of the ruling classes."

Miss Quilliam and my mother stared at him in amazement.

"Ladies," Mr Pentecost said sternly, "I warn you, my friend Silverlight is a Radical of the most scarlet dye. Indeed, he is a very violent Democrat and positively all but an incendiarist."

Though I had little idea what these terms meant, from the way Mr Pentecost spoke them — his eyebrows standing up and his left hand extended accusatorily as if denouncing his companion, while his right hand plied his nose with snuff — I took them for terms of opprobrium. And this made it all the more puzzling that Mr Silverlight appeared to take them as compliments, for at these words he blushed and smiled in embarrassment as we all directed our gaze towards him.

"My friend does me no injustice," he said. "I am a mortal foe to Old Corruption which at times has trembled to hear my very name."

"Gracious Heavens!" my mother exclaimed.

"Do not be alarmed, ladies," Mr Pentecost said; "for if he roars it is, I assure you, as gently as any sucking dove."

"Are you an enemy of the superior classes, even though you know them so well?" asked Miss Quilliam, who appeared quite unperturbed.

"It is *because* I have lived amongst the aristocracy and know their profound corruption that I am their enemy," Mr Silverlight said. "Yet I have known men of altruism and generosity amongst them. And I believe that it is from them that the leaders of the poor must come."

"Humbugs and frauds every man-Jack of them!" Mr Pentecost snorted. "You're the only man I ever knew to possess true altruism, Silverlight." At these words his companion indulged himself in a smile which disappeared as his friend went on: "And that's only because you're such a confounded fool."

My mother turned away from Mr Pentecost in evident distaste and said to his companion: "Whom do you mean, Mr Silverlight? My father was a friend of Sir Francis Burdett, though he did not share all his opinions."

Why had my mother not told me this about my grandfather when she was ready to confide it to a first-met stranger? I wondered indignantly.

"Why," Mr Silverlight cried in delight, "I had the honour of knowing Sir Francis well. You know he stood for this seat?"

Here my mother nodded, to my surprise for I had never known her express any interest in politics.

"For we are in the constituency of Westminster and St. Giles," he went on. "The most radical of all seats."

"Aye," said Mr Pentecost, "for everyone has the franchise, however poor and rascally."

"How absurd," said Miss Quilliam.

Mr Silverlight turned his large head and melancholy eyes upon her: "I am distressed to find you an opponent of the universal suffrage!"

"I do not believe that government of the nation can be entrusted to a rabble who cannot govern even themselves," she answered.

Mr Silverlight shook his head sorrowfully at these sentiments, but Mr Pentecost said: "It matters not who has the suffrage since power will always lie with those who possess the wealth. And their interests must of necessity be opposed to those of the mass."

"Whether that is true now, which I deny most emphatically, it was not true ten or a dozen years ago," Mr Silverlight insisted. "When Burdett and I fought this seat the poets and aristocrats, Shelley and Byron, and many others fought beside us. Those were fine times! The best of the superior classes were united with the best of the poor in pursuit of Justice!" As he spoke he brushed back the thin hair on his high dome which glistened in the candle-light. Looking at his noble profile and hearing such elevated sentiments I felt moved and inspired. I could see that my mother was also impressed by our guest.

Suddenly he broke off and said: "But I must not make speeches or I will bring down one of Pentecost's around my ears."

"Oh how I wish I had known poor Shelley," my mother murmured.

"I regard the gentlemen Radicals you speak of as misguided," Miss Quilliam said to Mr Silverlight. "Indeed, as a dangerous symptom of disease in their otherwise honourable class."

"Honourable!" I exclaimed. "After the way the Mompessons treated you?"

Everyone directed their gaze at me and while my mother shook her head at me in silent reproof, our guests then turned in surprise towards Miss Quilliam who looked extremely conscious.

"As a class I respect them," she said; "though the Mompessons as individuals treated me badly. For as members of that class they have obligations that in my case they failed to observe." At this both gentlemen shook their heads and Miss Quilliam went on: "Those who possess great wealth at the same time incur weighty obligations to their dependants. The Mompessons do not live upon their estates in order to return the wealth to those who have helped to create it, but spend the rents of their tenants profligately in the capital."

As she spoke I thought of the delapidated farmlands and tumbledown cottages that lay around Melthorpe and its neighbouring villages. Surely Miss Quilliam was right. I looked at my mother who was nodding at these words, but the two gentlemen looked away as if embarrassed.

Seeing this Miss Quilliam raised her voice slightly: "A nation is surely a family and like any family has weaker and stronger members who must serve or rule over each other according to their weaknesses and strengths, and thereby procure the advantage of all."

"Oh yes!" I cried and she smiled at me.

And though my mother reached out to quiet me she murmured, "Oh surely that is so!"

Mr Pentecost, however, snorted while Mr Silverlight gently shook his head.

"My dear young lady," the former began, "your opinions reflect the largeness of your heart rather than the extent of your experience. The Mompessons are only too typical of their rank, for like every class and every individual they are animated solely by self-interest."

At this Mr Silverlight smiled at the rest of us and gently shook his head as if in comic warning.

"Self-interest is all that drives us," Mr Pentecost went on. "But we are infinitely resourceful in finding ways to disguise this bleak truth from ourselves and others, and hence arises the prevalence of hypocrisy and self-deception. For this reason you must ignore what men say and consider only what they do."

Mr Silverlight, who had been evincing signs of impatience, now cried passionately: "I can keep silent no longer! Motives are what matter. Give me a man breathing the fine full fire of altruistic nobility, and I will value him above all else."

"You're a child, Silverlight," Mr Pentecost said, shaking his head. "Only actions speak and they say but one thing: serve yourself. And it is right that it should be so, for it is the complex interplay of innumerable self-interested actions in a free market that constitutes what we call society and so gives us what freedom of choice we have."

"You are wrong," Miss Quilliam said. "For otherwise there would be no such thing as charity."

This was an unfortunate remark for Mr Pentecost snorted angrily at this word: "Charity is always self-interested and therefore hypocritical."

I saw my mother gasp at this and turn away.

Miss Quilliam, however, answered calmly: "Charity may arise from the desire to be seen to be charitable, but surely nobody would attempt to deny that hypocrisy is a force for the good in society?"

"I deny it!" cried Mr Silverlight. "I am sworn foe to hypocrisy and all forms of humbug. I care not what it costs to say it."

"Noble fellow," said Mr Pentecost, shaking his head. "But you're a child in these matters."

Miss Quilliam, however, smiled before going on: "You cannot explain the desire to be seen to be charitable simply from self-interest, Mr Pentecost. And therefore you must grant that some kind of mixture of conscience, divine prompting, instinct and tradition of which one is not fully aware is what determines one's actions. Each of us finds true happiness — if at all — only in harmony with our society, and the impulse to charity arises from this."

"My dear young lady," said Mr Pentecost, appearing to be much moved by these words. "I hardly know where to begin to attempt to set you right. All social and economic life is warfare between individuals and between classes and this is absolutely inevitable. It makes no sense to speak of what ought to be: this is the Law of Necessity."

Mr Silverlight said nothing but his high forehead gleamed at us from the near-darkness and he was smiling as if asking for understanding for his friend's absurdities as Mr Pentecost now went on to speak of how everyone hunts and preys upon everyone else or at best feeds on everyone else like parasites on a dog. And this, he insisted, is what we call society.

My mother put her hands over her face, but without noticing this he continued: "And it is right, or at least desirable, that this should be the case, for this parasitical system that makes use of waste operates in a self-regulating way. Nothing is wasted and so society extracts its full value from things and people."

Miss Quilliam argued against this that society was not parasitical but organic. Individuals and classes were not at war but dependent each upon the other.

The contentment of each in his proper place was the end of society and was attainable in the future as it had been once in England's happy past.

Mr Pentecost dismissed this, insisting that misery for the majority was inevitable because, since society was constituted by competition, there must be losers as well as gainers. For this reason the most that could be achieved was the happiness of the largest number and there was a felicific calculus by which this could be calculated. In order to arrive at this estimate of its best interests, society must always ask what use something was, and the best — indeed the only — way to establish the value of something was on the free market. So there must be competition in order that everything and everyone should be bought and sold at its true value which was always the lowest price at which its existence or manufacture could be justified. And the reason for England's present distress was that this delicate mechanism was being interfered with.

As the evening advanced the two gentlemen responded in opposite ways to the hospitality extended to them, Mr Pentecost flapping his arms in his excitement so that he looked like a duck trying to get into flight and all the while showering himself with snuff, while Mr Silverlight sat gazing dolefully at the two ladies or smiling mournfully at his friend's impassioned oratory. And when Mr Pentecost was amused by something — and the strangest things had this effect on him — he threw his head back and laughed in short barking cries, which stopped as suddenly as they started.

I could not smile and neither could my mother for I saw that his words had profoundly depressed her. What Mr Pentecost was saying seemed to me so repellent that I could not square it with his kindly demeanour. How could he believe and say such terrible things? And did he really behave in that immoral way himself? And yet what he was saying could not be dismissed for it did cast light on Bissett's motives and those of people like Mrs Marrables and the Isbisters.

"Must everything be bought and sold," I asked him, following an association of ideas of my own. "Is nothing sacred?"

"Nothing," he replied. Almost as if he had read my mind, he went on: "Even our laws against cannibalism are the product of mere superstition, and in circumstances where human life depended on their suspension then it would be inevitable — or, as you might say, right — that they should be suspended."

"Oh no!" my mother exclaimed, covering her ears with her hands. "I cannot listen to any more of this!"

Mr Pentecost looked at her in alarm but his companion rose and said sternly: "Come, Pentecost. It is late. And you have forgotten yourself, my good fellow." He turned to my mother: "Forgive us. We find ourselves so rarely now in good company."

He bowed and then almost tugged his friend out of the room.

When the door had closed behind them my mother sighed: "Thank Heavens he has gone! I don't ever want him here again, Johnnie."

"To which gentleman do you refer?" asked Miss Quilliam.

"That horrid Mr Pentecost, of course," she declared with a shudder.

"Why," Miss Quilliam said, "I believe his worst side is his outside."

"And that's quite bad enough," my mother said and the subject was dropped.

I was also upset by Mr Pentecost's vision of society as a spiderly, cannibalistic, irrational pursuit of self-interest. I didn't want to believe that he was right. On the other hand, what Miss Quilliam had said inspired me. Yes, that was the finest thing, to be a great landlord and act benevolently for the sake of one's dependants!

Miss Quilliam picked up the little green bottle that I saw so often in her hand and shook it. She looked puzzled and shook it again. Then rising she said: "I must go out for a few minutes."

"But it's so late!" I objected.

She left and, intrigued, I examined the bottle and saw that it was labelled "The Black Drop". As I lifted it to my nose my mother called out "Don't, Johnnie!" It had a sweet, slightly pungent smell that seemed familiar.

Miss Quilliam came back in ten minutes and poured herself a tumbler of gin to which she added a couple of drops from the fresh bottle she had brought.

Noticing that I was watching her, she coloured and then said: "They call it the poor man's friend for it brings sweet solace when either the body or the mind is in pain. It has saved me often. I take only three or four grains now."

It was almost with relief that I saw my mother pour herself a tumbler of "Cream o' the Valley".

A few days later I happened to be on the landing when Mr Pentecost and his friend came up the stairs. They courteously invited me into their Eastern potentate's tent in the corner of the Peachments' room and I found it quite a cozy little arrangement.

"Sit yeself down," Mr Pentecost said.

As I obeyed I asked: "How long have you and Mr Silverlight known each other?"

"Why, more years than I care to count," Mr Pentecost answered. "Ten or twelve, I should think, eh, Silverlight? We made our acquaintance in, shall we say, less happy circumstances than these."

"I was in Equity at that time," Mr Silverlight said with dignity. "That noblest of man's achievements in social justice."

Mr Pentecost snorted.

"In short, I was a lawyer," Mr Silverlight continued, ignoring his friend.

"And what about you, sir?" I asked the other gentleman.

"I have pursued many avocations," he replied.

These, I now discovered, included a wide range of things: at various times he had insured in the Lottery, worked as a bill-broker's agent, copied manuscripts for a theatre, and so on.

"But I have, like my companion, had some experience of that maze of confusion and depredation strangely named the Common Law," Mr Pentecost went on. "I say 'strangely' for in its stupidity and irrationality it exceeds even what is common."

"There I concur with you my friend," said Mr Silverlight.

"But, Mr Silverlight, I thought you just praised it!" I protested.

"My good young friend," Mr Silverlight said superbly, "pray do not make the vulgar error of confusing the Law and Equity."

The rebuke was so magnificent that I dared not ask for elucidation.

"On occasions," Mr Pentecost went on in order to help me out of my difficulty, "I have earned my bread as a humble handmaiden to both Law and Equity — that is to say, as a jobbing writer. A very high quality of penmanship is required for Chancery engrossing and law-copying. I can't do it any longer because I am getting too old and my eyes poor and my hands unsteady." Here he held out one hand and it was indeed quavering. "But I occasionally engross a common law deed or writ, even now."

"I too have done a number of things," Mr Silverlight said. "When I was young I was in commerce, but though I inherited a good connexion, I got into difficulties through no fault of my own. My downfall was that credit was only too easy to obtain."

"You trusted people too easily?" I asked.

"The reverse," he said. "Alas, too many trusted me." He shook his head: "Greed is a terrible thing."

"Indeed," his friend said. He turned to me: "You see, greedy tradesmen were only too ready to sell to poor Silverlight and take his notes at a discount in preference to taking bank-paper at face-value. Too much of that goes on."

Indeed, I reflected, I had better reasons for agreeing with him than he could know of.

"Because of it, we are heading for a smash," Mr Pentecost went on in words that turned out to be prophetic. "Mark my words, the whole paper kingdom will come tumbling down in a year or two like a house of cards. You see, giving credit implies trust and is therefore — on the present scale — an utter absurdity. For trade is universal cheating and so inherently inimical to the notion of trust. But the mania is being whipped along by the pettifogging attorneys for they make huge fortunes from bankruptcies, insolvencies, compositions, and debtors' gaols."

"Well, they made a deal of money out of me," Mr Silverlight sighed.

"That's true," Mr Pentecost said. Then somewhat timidly he added: "But also, Silverlight, you know you rather brought it upon yourself by gaming."

"Nonsense, I never game," said Mr Silverlight stiffly. "Though occasionally I have speculated at the game of Hazard."

Mr Pentecost turned to me: "You see, Silverlight lost a great deal of money by playing in accordance with a mathematical system that assumed a design in the way the numbers come up on the dice."

"I was not taking a risk for there is such a design," Mr Silverlight insisted, and I noticed a vein in his prominent forehead beginning to pulse.

"Fiddlesticks!" Mr Pentecost said with an affable laugh. "Yet you are right in a manner of speaking, for all of life is a risk. There is no order or rationality."

"Certainly not in your own conduct," Mr Silverlight said meaningfully.

Mr Pentecost looked at him gravely: "I have wounded you, my friend, and believe me, I had no intention of doing so." He reached into a pocket, took out a large watch and consulted it. "But you have reminded me that I must leave you for a while."

"Where are you going?" Mr Silverlight asked and, receiving no reply, watched his friend curiously as he pulled on his coat and left.

When we were alone Mr Silverlight said: "He disappears like that now and then. I cannot help speculating about his motives. An honourable man for all his queerness, but one never knows. The evening we met you it distressed me to see him offend your charming mother and the other delightful young lady. (Incidentally, how are they? ... Excellent, excellent. Please convey to them my kindest sentiments.) But as for my friend ... I call him Mount Vesuvius for brimstone and rubbish are continually being emitted from his mouth. I must put you right on one or two things he said that evening for I hate to see the bright hopes of Youth blighted by the cynicism of Age. You know, Pentecost is wrong about the notion that ideas are determined by economic circumstances. One must start with abstract principles — Justice, Equality — and condemn society if it falls short when it is measured against them."

I nodded my agreement and he went on: "Pentecost is quite wrong. There is a Design in every part of our lives if we can but perceive it. I am a Deist and accept the argument from Design as proof of the existence of a Supreme Spirit of Reason. Reason and not self-interest forms the ordering principle upon which society is founded. The whole economic order must be changed to bring it into conformity with rational Justice."

He was soon in full flight and I listened enraptured. Mr Pentecost was wrong. Society could be better, could be perfect! And yet as I returned to our room I felt deeply confused, for I liked Mr Pentecost and could not understood how he could really believe the views he expressed.

When I entered I found my mother very subdued and a little later she went to bed and slept soundly. This was a rarity, for she was often kept awake by coughing and would then light a tallow-dip and write for hours in her pocket-book.

During the weeks that followed I came to know the two gentlemen better and often stayed to talk to them when I went to the Peachments' room at the end of the day to buy more dolls for the following morning. My mother continued to refuse to have anything to do with Mr Pentecost and so I kept my visits to them secret from her. As I sat in their tent pretending to sip at a small glass of Cream o' the Valley, Mr Silverlight told me stories of Mr Wycherley Fiennes and his charming mother, My Lady Blennerhasset (who, I recall, had married again after being widowed), who had visited her son occasionally. Though he excepted her and several other members of the aristocracy from his strictures, he was eager to make clear his general detestation of Old Corruption and the system which permitted placemen to rob decent, talented young fellows of their rightful position. While clarifying for me the precise relation between different members of the nobility, he would consult his copy of Webster's Royal Red Book, and as the evening warmed, he would often read aloud from this, taking turn and turn about to recite from the scurrilously Radical Black Book long lists of the sinecures and pensions enjoyed by the Establishment. And often and often he would wax eloquent on the subject of Reason and Virtue and their interconnexion as he picked the lice from his linen. And usually by this stage Mr Pentecost would be throwing pinches of snuff in the direction of his nostrils and declaiming about the necessity of suffering while tears rolled down his cheeks.

Sometimes I was present when they rehearsed a new piece of business for Punch and Joan, and it was rather terrifying to me to see how, while Mr Pentecost (as Punch) lurked in waiting for his victims, his kindly features became quite savage. And then, like nothing so much as a sinister spider, he made the puppet shoot out to pounce upon them and afterwards jump around the stage hugging himself with glee. And similarly Mr Silverlight, who played with such convincing innocence each successive victim — the Turncock, the Foreigner, the Beadle — then became quite malevolent when, in the character of Ketch, it fell to him to hang his friend. (Mr Pentecost once admitted to me that the character of Punch seemed quite to take him over while he was manipulating him.) I might add that, of course, the two gentlemen's disputatiousness was not suspended during these occasions, and the rehearsals were punctuated by cries of "Not like that, you fool!" and "Quicker, dolt, quicker!"

One evening I met them as I was returning home, and as we walked along Mr Silverlight declaimed loquaciously against the civil list and the whole apparatus of jobbery that kept honest merit unrewarded.

"I agree," said Mr Pentecost. "It is only if the system is left to operate freely that the political economy is self-regulating. But I fear that it is being interfered with by Privilege. But even more so by state-charity."

Mr Silverlight disagreed with this, of course, and launched into a eulogy of social Justice. Then suddenly he broke off in mid-flight as if in alarm. When I turned my gaze towards what he was looking at, I could understand why he had been so disconcerted. Before us was an old man whose face was horribly scarred and pitted and whose red eyes seemed to stare ahead so that the countenance seemed hardly human. He was in rags and had a grizzly white beard, and beside him and attached to him by a length of rope tied to its collar was a large mangy brute of a dog.

"Who is there?" he said, turning his head towards us and holding it at a slight angle.

"Why, my old friend," Mr Pentecost exclaimed. Then he coloured slightly.

I looked at the three of them: Mr Silverlight silent with dismay, Mr Pentecost embarrassed, and the old beggar turning his head from one to the other in bewilderment.

"Why, is it you, Mr Pentecost?" he said. "I thought it was, it was ... Well, never mind what I thought. I wouldn't have spoken to you if I had known it was you, sir."

"I ... I ... Well, I am very glad that you did," Mr Pentecost stammered. "Let me present you. This is a very old friend of mine, Mr Tertius Silverlight."

The beggar put out a hand and that gentleman reached out his own with manifest reluctance and shook it slightly.

"I'm pleased to make your acquaintance," the old man said.

He raised his face towards Mr Silverlight with eager inquisitiveness, but that gentleman merely nodded without speaking, and after a moment the old man lowered his head as if disappointed.

Mr Pentecost pushed me forward: "And this is a very young friend, Master John Mellamphy."

I held out my hand and the beggar stretched forth his towards me but missed my own by a considerable distance. Mr Pentecost nudged me to take it and now I realized that the man was blind. I shook it.

"Master Mellamphy, this is Justice," said Mr Pentecost.

"And Wolf," said the old beggar and the dog bared its teeth and growled.

There was an uneasy silence which was broken by Mr Pentecost: "My good fellow, Silverlight and I were just agreeing on the iniquity of the system of sinecures and pensions."

"Aye," said the beggar warmly. "You know that I'm a sworn enemy to that, too. But unlike you, Mr Pentecost, I oppose it as contrary to social justice."

"There, Silverlight, you have an ally," Mr Pentecost said. But his friend merely coloured and avoided his eye. Could it be that he was embarrassed to be supported by so humble an ally? I wondered.

The conversation came to an uneasy halt.

"I'm sorry to have bothered you, Mr Pentecost," said the old man.

"Not at all, not at all, my dear friend," Mr Pentecost said. "But we should be on our way."

The beggar saluted us and we walked on for the length of the street in silence.

"Now there," said Mr Pentecost, "is a man who has given his sight for his principles — misguided though they are."

I was about to ask him what he meant when at that minute Miss Quilliam came up behind us: "I saw that poor old man accost you," she said. "Did you give anything to him?"

"Certainly not," Mr Pentecost cried indignantly. "I will have no truck with charity!"

"Indeed, and why not?"

"Nothing, young lady, is so precisely calculated to bring about the collapse of society."

"How can that be?" Miss Quilliam asked with a tired smile just as we reached the street-door to our house.

"Why, Miss Quilliam, pauperism is necessary to our society. You shake your head, but you see, it is needed in order to preserve the self-regulating mechanism of the free-market in labour."

At this moment Mr Peachment came down the stairs towards us and Mr Pentecost appealed to him: "Why, Mr Peachment, if you could get twelve shillings a week for doing nothing, would you work for thirteen?"

It took some time to convey this notion to him. Then a smile appeared on his tired face: "Why, I reckon not, Mr Pentecost."

"Of course not!" he cried triumphantly. "The price of labour must be settled by the lowest price that a man will accept. If this is unnaturally raised by charitable subventions to twelve shillings, then everything will collapse."

"Why," said Mr Peachment, "I only wish the paritch would behave thus by us, for I fear that unless things pick up, me and mine will have to return to Dorset and go into the 'House, for we cannot scratch a living here."

"I am distressed to learn it, Mr Peachment, but you must have seen for yourself how the parish provision is demoralizing the English peasantry. Can you deny that they marry without being independent, they save nothing when they could, and they spend money on drink when they have it? Alas, they need the fear of starvation to make them work."

"Aye, but the paritch harries 'em cruel, Mr Pentecost."

"My very point!" he cried. "The persecution by the parish of those likely to become chargeable is making Old England into a tyranny. Only by abolishing charity and therefore the right of the parish to evict people, will this be ameliorated."

"If the parish is such a tyrant, Mr Peachment, why are you going back?" Miss Quilliam asked.

"Why, I have no settlement in Lunnon and therefore cannot claim relief."

"You see?" cried Mr Pentecost. "A free market in labour is the only solution."

"That may be so," Mr Peachment said. "But if you'll excuse me, I must be on my way."

He passed on and we walked on up to our landing as we talked.

"I have to tell you frankly, Mr Pentecost, the abolition of relief is a repugnant idea," said Miss Quilliam smiling as if at a clever but misguided pupil. "We need more charity, not less. And if you are correct — as I concede that you are — to say that society is breaking down, the reason is the failure of the propertied classes to fulfil their obligations and take those measures which would forestall pauperism." She hesitated and then went on: "In the case of my own family, for example, a certain patron failed to keep his promise of a living to my father and thus precipitated him into acute poverty."

"You are both in error," cried Mr Silverlight, who seemed now to have recovered his composure. "Only in a society founded upon the Law of Reason can Justice for all be won."

"Faugh!" exclaimed his friend. "The Law of Reason is a Chimaera. The Law of Necessity is what governs men and that is why only the prospect of starvation will teach them what their real interests are."

"But if men act from rational self-interest as you have often said, Mr Pentecost," I asked, "why do they need to be starved into knowing what is good for them?"

"A hit! A palpable hit!" cried Mr Silverlight.

"Deluded imp!" exclaimed Mr Pentecost but he softened it with a smile. "Men do not know what their true interest is, for their narrow view needs to be modified by the objective reality of society."

"The boy is clever," said my patron. "That you cannot deny, Pentecost."

"You are right, Mr Silverlight, and it grieves me that his education is being neglected," said Miss Quilliam. "I wish I could teach him as I did at first, but I fear I have not the strength."

"Why, of course not," Mr Silverlight said. "But I have an idea: I could do it!"

"Certainly not!" his companion cried. "I would not permit you to fill his head full of nonsense. I will take it upon myself to teach him."

"Then you have three tutors now, Master John," said Miss Quilliam, smiling at me. "What do you want to learn?"

"I want to learn the Law," I said.

"You do not mean the Law but Equity," said Mr Silverlight.

"What is the difference?" I asked. "Is there any?"

Mr Silverlight shuddered: "There is indeed."

Mr Pentecost vigorously shook his head at me behind his friend's back.

At that moment the door to our room opened and my mother appeared, looking drawn and pale. "Whatever kept you?" she said dully to Miss Quilliam, seeming not to notice the rest of us. "Have you got it?"

Miss Quilliam glanced at me.

Mr Pentecost said: "John, come and share our dinner."

"Yes," said Mr Silverlight. "And I will try to put you right."

So while Miss Quilliam went into our chamber, I followed the two gentlemen into theirs. Once we were snugly ensconced and the water for their brandy was heating in a chafing-dish hung on a trivet over the Peachments' fire, they began to explain the point to me — interrupting one another at each sentence and quarrelling over the meaning of almost every term.

The Common Law, Mr Silverlight asserted, was a low, mechanick, ungentlemanly business which was concerned only with the strict application of precedent and statute regardless of the merits of the case concerned. And to go to Law was to play at Hazard, for procedure was all-important and was bedevilled by complex and arbitrary rules, for example, governing entry upon process. This meant that a case might be thrown out on a technicality which had nothing to do with the justice or injustice of the cause.

"But Equity, my young friend," Mr Silverlight said, "is very different. It is practised in the High Court of Chancery which is a court of conscience. That means that it is concerned with Principle, with what ought to be, regardless of what actually is. The Law surrenders before the randomness of life and the power of mere accident, while Equity attempts to achieve something perfectly just and based upon Reason."

There was a derisive snort from his friend.

"That is poppycock," he said. "Why, you're just making patterns! These ideas don't depict reality any more than the set of perfect squares that Wren conceived for rebuilding London after the Great Fire, could ever have represented the reality of a great metropolis. My dear young friend," he said turning to me, "pray don't let Silverlight's enthusiasm mislead you. Chancery is the most notoriously unjust court in the kingdom!"

"But only think," his companion cried, "of the noble principles embodied in it! Whereas in the Common Law there are writs not rights, in Chancery rights are of supreme importance. And whereas legal rights in realty can be lost over time if not defended, equitable rights are imperishable!"

"Realty?" I asked in bewilderment.

"Land and houses and so on," Mr Pentecost whispered to me since his friend was in full flight, "rather than personalty — money, investments, and that sort of thing."

"Equitable rights are immortal," Mr Silverlight exclaimed, "showing us an image of the Justice of the Supreme Being!"

"What does that mean?" I asked in excitement.

"It means," Mr Pentecost explained for his friend had fallen into a rapt day-dream, "that if a will comes to light no matter how late, then the property will be restored to the rightful owner, and if he is dead, then to his heirs however remote. You see, Equity abides by the principle *ubi remedium, ibi jus*. That is to say, rights arise from remedies. In other words, if you can prove title to land then you own it. If someone else can prove a better title, then he owns it. There is no absolute title to realty."

"And does the same hold true for a codicil?" I asked, remembering how my mother's father had hoped that the codicil might lead him to wealth.

He assured me that it did, and this gave me much to think about.

This was the first of what I came to think of as my law tutorials, for during the next few weeks my two friends generously instructed me in the fundamentals of both Law and Equity. And a very strange education it was for almost whenever Mr Silverlight taught me something in impassioned terms, Mr Pentecost contradicted him, but was at least as knowledgeable and could cite precedents from memory with remarkable ease. And so I came to understand those almost theological distinctions on which Equity is founded: between tenure and estate, between seisin and possession, between seisin in law and seisin in deed, between barring and breaking an entail, between vested and contingent interests, between interests which are vested in interest and those vested in possession, between conveyance by fine and by common recovery, and many others.

Although Miss Quilliam knew and approved, I had to keep my visits secret from my mother who was, anyway, increasingly distant and silent in the evenings.

One evening late in the summer I was with my two legal tutors in their tent when we heard a knock and then Mrs Peachment's voice raised in welcome. A moment later, Miss Quilliam appeared at the flap.

"Your mother," she said to me, "is writing mysteriously in that pocket-book of hers, so I thought I would come and find you."

"Pray come in, dear young lady," said Mr Silverlight, rising and placing the bottle out of the way beneath a coat.

"You are very civil, sir, but I would not venture into the private apartments of two gentlemen."

"Then pray be seated here at the fire," said Mrs Peachment, who had over-heard this. "And let the gentlemen come forth."

"That is very hospitable of you!" Mr Pentecost cried advancing ceremoniously into the Peachments' portion of the room as if into a strange house, bowing courteously at his hosts.

When we were all comfortable Miss Quilliam asked me: "What progress have you made in your studies?"

"I have been learning about Justice," I answered cautiously.

"Humbug!" cried Pentecost.

"Noblest of Man's creations," Mr Silverlight sighed.

"And about the law of real property," I finished.

"And how the rights of property must be reduced," Mr Silverlight said.

"On the contrary. How it is the primary function of the Law to protect property!"

"Quite correct," said Miss Quilliam. "For that is the basis of our freedom."

"How sad to see young Loveliness holding hands with aged Cynicism!" Mr Silverlight cried. "Property is a crime against society!"

Miss Quilliam and Mr Pentecost glanced at each other in mutual disbelief at this.

Before either could answer Dick Peachment said: "Then for s'iety to take it back ain't no crime. And I'm a member of s'iety, ain't I?"

"Well said," cried Mr Pentecost while his companion looked dismayed at this practical application of his dictum.

"Oh, sir, please don't encourage the boy," his father said.

"You see where your doctrines lead, gentlemen?" Miss Quilliam said reproachfully. "The corruption of this misguided youth will lie upon your consciences."

"And why shouldn't I sarve meself?" Dick asked. "I've often heerd you two genel'men tell as how all the nobs do."

"There is no reason at all why not, so long as you recognise the risk of being caught."

"Mr Pentecost!" Miss Quilliam exclaimed.

"Dear young lady, the Law is no more than an arbitrary construct designed to protect the wealthy."

"This is pernicious, Mr Pentecost. The Law has real moral force for each individual: to dwell in society is not to have the freedom to choose which laws to obey as one might choose which bonnet to put on."

"On the contrary, dear young lady. One chooses to obey or disregard the Law simply on the calculus of self-interest. Whether one is a duke with an income of fifteen thousand a year or a pick-pocket, one asks oneself the same question: is it easier to obey this particular law or can I profit from breaking it? In almost every case the duke answers yes, the pick-pocket answers no for the Law was designed by the former against the interests of the latter. The rest of us have to answer differently according to each case."

As I looked at the shocked faces around me — except for Dick's which wore a reflective expression — I felt a profound sense of excitement mingled with feelings of dismay, for if this was right, then everything was arbitrary and uncertain.

"I cannot stay any longer to hear such abominable ideas," Miss Quilliam said, rising to her feet.

"Dear lady, I will accompany you," Mr Silverlight said with a reproachful glance at his friend. "I have something I wish to say to you and Mrs Mellamphy."

When they had gone, and Mr Pentecost and I had retired to his tent, I said: "But if you believe that self-interest is the ruling principle of human affairs ... "

Then I paused, not knowing how to express my point delicately.

"How have I done so badly for myself?" Mr Pentecost said. "Well, people don't always manage to live by their principles, I'm afraid. I was a sad disappointment to my family in this respect. They were in trade and when they realized how unfit I was to inherit my father's connexion, he took a very high-minded step and disinherited me — as he was quite right to do, for I would only have lost the money. I have always lost any money I ever had."

"Do you mean you have been unlucky like Mr Silverlight?"

"Gracious me, have I taught you nothing? There is no such thing as luck. I brought my woes upon myself by once foolishly acting against my principles. As a consequence, I am being sought by creditors, though I have nothing to give them. Fortunately they do not know where I am."

He had acted against his principles. I was afraid to think what he might mean, but, needing to get away, I left him a few minutes later. I returned to our own room feeling, as always when I entered it from the Peachments, that it was much gloomier than the other which was always full of people and life.

Now I found Mr Silverlight saying to my mother and Miss Quilliam: "Dear ladies, some friends of mine and of Pentecost — excellent people though simple, very simple — are holding a ... well, an assembly or rout or what you will, a week tomorrow night. It would be a privilege to be permitted to escort you there."

I saw my mother blush with pleasure.

"Thank you," Miss Quilliam replied gravely. "We would be honoured, would we not, Mary?"

"Yes," my mother cried. "I haven't been to anything like that for simply ages." Then she frowned: "Oh, but Helen, only think: we have nothing to wear!"

Miss Quilliam glanced at Mr Silverlight who smiled very charmingly and said: "Set your minds at rest. The elegant and unaffected apparel in which I see you now will be perfectly in order."

This remark did not achieve its aim, for when he had gone my mother was full of the great question of what to wear and how to appear at her best.

"Do you think, Helen," she said after a reflective pause, "we might meet someone there ... I mean, some gentlefolks who will appreciate us for what we are and take pity on us and help us to take up our rightful position in society?"

Seeing that Miss Quilliam was at a loss for a reply, I asked: "Am I to come, Mamma? What shall I wear?"

"Why, Johnnie, I think you're too young to go to a ball. And besides, you haven't been invited, you know."

The great day announced by Mr Silverlight came at last and my mother and Miss Quilliam finished work early and spent a couple of hours dressing each other's hair and helping each other with their clothes. By nine o'clock, when there was a knock at the door, they really did look very handsome and lady-like. When Mr Silverlight and his friend entered, the two ladies — both of whom were now offended with Mr Pentecost — managed to greet him with a display of goodwill. The two gentlemen, too, looked quite elegant — particularly Mr Silverlight who had clearly taken even more trouble than usual with his toilette.

"It's such a fine night," that gentleman said with a smile, "that I thought we might walk, if you were agreeable."

"Indeed," said Mr Pentecost, smiling at Miss Quilliam and my mother; "it's really no distance at all."

"Yes," said my mother. "Let us by all means leave the carriage at home."

Mr Silverlight laughed as if she had said something rather clever.

And so, the ladies holding their dresses above the mud of the unpaved way, we set off — for I had prevailed upon my mother to permit me to come. With the aid of Mr Pentecost's lanthorn, we went a little way along Orchard-street and turned up a dark alley into New-square. This mis-named place was no more than a court of low dwellings, work-shops and store-houses thrown up a few decades before in the back-gardens of the former fine mansions of Orchard-street. From somewhere in a corner of the dark yard in which we found ourselves, we heard the scrape of fiddles, the lilting of cornets and fifes, and the drone of pipes, all punctuated by the crash of dancing feet. We went up to one of the low door-ways and as we stood at the threshold, my mother turned to Miss Quilliam in dismay. Before us we could see a large chamber — really a kind of rotting outhouse — which was blazing with the glare of rushlights secured to the bare walls which were splashed with lime where the plaister still clung to the decaying bricks. There was a swirling mass of bodies and shadows, for people were dancing in couples or in groups on the earthen floor, while others were drinking from great pewter cans and singing.

"But this isn't ... " said my mother and faltered.

I could see how disappointed she was and it made me angry with her.

"Come, dear ladies," said Mr Silverlight, advancing into the building.

We walked a little way in and were assailed by a strong smell of mould and rotting wood mingling with the acrid stench of the burning rushes and the odour of heated human beings crowding together, and tobacco and drink.

"I can't stay here!" my mother gasped. "Not with these people."

"My dear lady, I don't know quite what you anticipated," said Mr Silverlight. "Our good hosts are poor unhappy exiles of Erin — our sad sister-island — and therefore somewhat rough and ready in their ways, but perfectly respectable in their own manner, I promise you."

"Let us leave, Helen," my mother whispered.

At that moment a man came forward: "Why, bless your Worships' honour. We're glad to see you at the jig. And so would Thady be for he loved a ranty."

"Thady?" Miss Quilliam repeated. "Is this your friend who is our host, Mr Silverlight?"

"Sure and Thady isn't the host," the Irishman went on. "This is for him. We are waking poor Thady."

"Waking him!" cried Miss Quilliam. "Why, can he be asleep in all this noise?"

The man laughed: "Asleep, do you say? *Acushla machree!* But will you see him?"

Without waiting for our response he turned and we all followed him to a corner of the shed where there was a straw palliasse with a candle in a silver-gilt candle-stick at the head and the foot. An old woman wrapped in a dark and ragged cloak was squatting on the floor at the head. As I looked at the body, I recognised Thady as a neighbour of ours.

Saying something to the crone in their own language, the man poured some liquid from a jug into a tumbler which he then held out to her, and then did the same for my mother and Miss Quilliam.

"It comes to this in the end," he said. "So we might as well enjoy ourselves."

My mother seized the tumbler and drank it down. Then she flung it aside and plunged forward into the mass of dancers and Mr Silverlight hurried after her. I watched as they began to waltz, whirling in and out amongst the others.

As I listened to the wild lilting of the fiddles playing reels and the moaning of the bagpipes and screeching of the fifes, all counterpointed against the stamping feet, it occurred to me that we might have been in a cabin in the far west of Ireland.

My mother was still dancing with Mr Silverlight and as they passed me I saw her smiling at him and reflected that this was the first time for a long period that I had seen her happy — though I could not have known that it would also be the last. Seeing her partner smile back at her as he held her I wasn't sure that I really liked Mr Silverlight after all.

Now Mr Pentecost held Miss Quilliam rather stiffly and they sedately picked their way through the couples and the lines of men linking arms and dancing in rings in the Hibernian fashion. As I sipped my beer by the wall I wondered if I was alone in feeling that the gaiety on display bore a desperate air, as if for everyone there the pleasure in the moment was overshadowed by fear of what lay ahead now that the winter was approaching.

The rushlights casting long shadows on the filthy walls as the dancers swirled were beginning to assume strange forms when I heard a voice saying: "Come, it's time you were in bed, young fellow."

Mr Pentecost took my arm and hurried me back to our house, almost carrying me upstairs and into our room. He gently laid me on my bed and I quickly fell asleep so that I never knew when my mother and Miss Quilliam returned. I did not ask them the next morning for they were both pale and tired and my mother complained of a head-ache.

My fears were vindicated, for this turned out to have been the last happy moment before the long slide into disaster brought about by the imminence of winter and the consequent slackening in trade. This meant that Mr Peachment was able to give my mother and Miss Quilliam less and less work. They tried various other expedients to keep themselves profitably employed — pin-making, button-manufacture, lappel-sewing — but with little success. There were so many people prepared and able to work even longer hours than they could and for even less remuneration, that they could not compete. And so by the beginning of October our plight was desperate.

By now the three of us were making about five shillings a week in total and even this was decreasing. The rent was three shillings and the landlord's deputy allowed no arrears, so that the first Saturday we were unable to pay we would find ourselves homeless from the following Monday. We were only able to survive on Miss Quilliam's slender savings which she insisted on sharing with us, and it was clear that unless trade picked up substantially, we would soon be destitute. Moreover, as the winter approached our expenses would increase considerably for we would need to burn both coal and tallow-candles in order to be able to work for longer hours. Moreover, neither my mother nor I had any winter clothes. In the light of this, it seemed to me that the time had come to sell the locket.

So one evening in the middle of October when Miss Quilliam was next door with the Peachments and my mother was still sewing by the little light that remained, I raised the question.

"Mamma, we cannot continue to live on Miss Quilliam's money."

She looked at me in alarm: "What can we do?"

"We must sell the locket."

She gasped and reached for it where it hung: "I knew you were going to say that. I don't think I could bear to lose it."

"But we have no choice."

"It is the only thing I have left to remind me of that brief time when I was happy."

Tired, cold and hungry as I was after a day on the streets, I felt a surge of irritation: "But only be reasonable. How else are we going to eat and stay warm?"

She seemed to be finding the courage to say something: "Johnnie, I've been thinking. Now please don't be angry with me, but why don't we offer to sell the codicil to Sir Perceval after all?"

I thought of what I had learned about the law from the two gentlemen and the understanding I had begun to acquire of how my family's claim might be valid.

"No," I said. "That would be very silly. I'm sure it's worth a great deal more than they would ever give us for it."

"We should never have left Bethnal-green," she sighed.

I was suddenly angry and wanted to blurt out the horrible truth about the Isbisters.

"Those people may not have been very charming," she went on. "But they were good to us."

"Then go back there!" I cried.

Now, in exasperation, I told her what I had seen that night I had followed the cart to the graveyard. To my annoyance she refused to believe me, telling me I was merely remembering the story of Syed Naomaun and his wife that had frightened me all those years ago. I was furious at this and we quarrelled fiercely.

Afterwards I reproached myself and asked her pardon, and at last she forgave me and kissed me and said she was sorry for being such a goose but that the idea of losing the locket was almost more than she could bear.

Then I said: "Well, would you agree to pawn it? We would have to keep up the interest payments or we would lose it, but if we got some money we could redeem it."

She reflected.

"Yes, I believe I could resign myself to that," she said at last. "We will ask Helen's advice when she comes in."

Miss Quilliam agreed that my idea was a reasonable one. We would raise less by pawning than by selling but on the other hand, if we could redeem it in the spring when our earnings should rise, it would be a useful form of security for the future.

So the next morning my mother and I went out into the surrounding streets to look for the sign of the three golden balls. At the first we came to, on the corner of Orchard-street and Dean-street, we followed a pointing hand that led up an alley-way to a back-door. Inside we found ourselves in a dark passage at the end of which were a number of wooden boxes. We entered one of them, bolted it on the inside, and waited at the counter while the taker dealt with someone in a neighbouring box. On the racking behind the counter were shelved the pledges: jewellery, watches, pelisses, bed-ticks, wrappers, duffles, Waterloo medals, and so on.

After a few minutes the man attended to us.

"What will you give me on this?" my mother asked, taking the locket from around her neck.

The taker took it and looked at it very closely: "One pound ten shillings," he answered.

She hesitated but I remembered that Mrs Philliber had said we should not take less than three pounds for it, so I led her out of the office and impressed upon her that this was the very least she should accept. We walked on and the next, in Princes-street, offered us two pounds, then the next only one pound and six shillings.

In the fourth, which was a little further up on the corner with Bennet-street, the man behind the counter looked at the locket without much interest. He had a squint and carried one shoulder higher than the other so that his chin was forced into his collar-bone at an angle.

"One pound and five shillings," he said.

My mother shook her head. Then he opened the locket and it seemed to me that he was suddenly interested. He examined the initials with particular attention, then studied the two miniatures, glancing at my mother to compare her with her painted likeness.

"I'll give you two pound on it," he said.

My mother declined and turned to go.

"Wait," he called out. "What do you want?"

"Three pounds."

"I can't go so far, but I'll give you two pounds fifteen shillings."

My mother hesitated.

"Two pounds seventeen shillings," he said.

"Very well," my mother said.

"Don't do it," I whispered.

"What a silly boy you are," she said. "Whyever not?"

I could say nothing, except that I had vague suspicions. So I stayed silent.

"What name shall I write on the duplicate?" the man asked.

My mother hesitated.

"Halfmoon," she said. "Mrs Halfmoon."

I looked at her in surprise. Why had she chosen such a strange name? We had once walked down a street whose sign bore that legend, but what had made it lodge in her memory?

"Interest payable monthly," the man said as he handed the duplicate over.

She took it and the money and put them in her outside pocket, and we left the shop. When we got home we paid Miss Quilliam back some of what we had borrowed over the last few months.

Later we exchanged our fine clothes for cheaper but warmer garments. This was a crucial step for, as Miss Quilliam pointed out, it would henceforth be impossible for my mother to appear as a lady in the cheap and ill-fitting garments she now wore.

That terrible winter of bitter memory was now approaching, and as the days grew darker and colder we found it more and more difficult to work. When I went down to the yard in the morning, there were often people slumbering on the stair who had taken shelter there from the cold. I had to break the ice in the leaden cistern before I could bring up the water for our tea, and by this time my mother and Miss Quilliam would be working by the light of dips so that the stench of tallow already filled the room. Although we encouraged each other with the thought of Christmas, it was not that we anticipated being able to mark it with any kind of celebration, but simply that we hoped that the Season would begin not long after that and therefore that the demand for all manner of clothes-making would increase.

My mother's cough grew worse and I would often lie in the cold and darkness resenting the way she was keeping me awake and yet feeling a terrible anguish for her. We all suffered from the low-fever and my mother, in particular, from night-sweats and bad dreams that brought her suddenly awake and crying out in terror.

Yet there were times even then that I remember with some tenderness. I recall one misty afternoon late in November when I had met the two gentlemen — who had also abandoned work early because of the weather — and we had walked home together. As we had passed the Abbey it had loomed up vast and black, the mist making it seem that there was nothing behind it. In the distance the houses — save for the occasional yellow flickering of a lighted window — were indistinguishable blocks of darkness whose chimneys and gables alone were visible against the lighter shades of the sky. And higher up the blue vault became a liverish purple where the sun still shone feebly on the top of the mist.

Mr Pentecost and Mr Silverlight had invited me to share their supper and as we were finishing it Miss Quilliam had come in saying, "There you are, Johnnie. I thought you might be here."

The four of us — for after the party my mother had returned to her refusal to speak to Mr Pentecost, and, indeed, now included Mr Silverlight in her anathema as well — often gathered in the tent in the Peachments' room. And so Miss Quilliam (who had overcome her reservations about entering it) joined us where we were snugly toasting muffins before the fire.

"Your mother," she said to me, "is writing furiously in her pocket-book. Do you know what it is?"

"I believe it is an account of her life. There are things she will not tell me, but she wants me one day to know the whole truth."

I nearly bit my tongue, for I had uttered one of the controversial terms I tried to avoid.

"The truth!" cried Mr Pentecost indignantly.

"Indeed, the Truth. A noble ideal."

"Nonsense! The truth is a lie, a fiction. Why, there is more truth in the silliest romance than in the most elevated history."

"That may be so," said Mr Silverlight. "I myself have written several plays and epic romances in verse which have been ignored because of the petty envy of the managers and the book-sellers. And I must own, there was a great deal of Truth in 'em. Perhaps I could turn my hand to a novel, for there would be more money in that. I know how well I could write the sections on High Society — from a satirical angle, of course — but I couldn't stoop to the low-life and the intrigue. I know I should be no use at all at plotting."

"Oh, leave that to me!" Mr Pentecost said.

"Are you such a designing creature?" Miss Quilliam said with a smile. "I begin to be quite afraid of you."

"I believe I should be good at tracing out intrigues," Mr Pentecost admitted as if rather ashamed of it. "But I readily acknowledge that what we call the motives of other people are entirely mysterious to me."

"That is surely a serious handicap in an aspiring novel-writer," suggested Miss Quilliam, smiling at me.

"On the contrary, for motives do not matter. All that matters is what people do."

"That is nonsense," said Mr Silverlight. "Motives are all that is important. Apart from elevated language and the design of the whole."

"Design of the whole!" Mr Pentecost cried, and I believe his indignation cost him a six-penn'orth of snuff. "How can there be a design, my ridiculous fellow? Life is too random and arbitrary for that."

"You're wrong. Reason provides Man with his clew to the design that underlies the Universe."

"The argument from Design!" Mr Pentecost exclaimed, his eyebrows shooting up. "Discredited decades ago!"

"The purpose of a work of Art," Mr Silverlight continued as if he had not spoken, "is that Man may trace this out and find the pattern for himself. In any novel I collaborated upon everything would be a part of the whole design — down even to the disposition and numbering of the chapters."

"Fiddlesticks! Novelist-writers are liars. There is no pattern. No meaning save what we choose to impose."

"Your views, it seems to me, are complementary rather than in conflict," Miss Quilliam suggested pacifically. Then, glancing with amusement at me, she went on: "So perhaps you should collaborate. Mr Silverlight could take responsibility for describing the motives of the characters (particularly, of course, in the upper ranks) while you, Mr Pentecost, could concentre your talents upon the elements of plotting and intrigue."

I smiled at the notion, for I thought it would be like their Punch and Joan show.

"A capital idea!" Mr Silverlight cried. "But I think I should have to take charge of the design of the whole."

"Not for a minute!" exclaimed his friend.

Miss Quilliam and I left the prospective collaborators arguing about this and returned to our chamber which we found in darkness. From the gloom my mother said slowly and indistinctly: "Why were you so long? I was all alone here and I was so frightened. Why did you stay with those horrid men?"

Miss Quilliam lit a candle and I saw my mother slumped in her chair with her pocket-book and her pen fallen to the floor before her. Our friend gestured to me to withdraw, so I entered the little closet where I slept. Why was my mother confused and childish like this so often now? And why was she suddenly so hostile to Mr Silverlight? I fell asleep listening to the murmur of their voices.

The fog was even thicker the next day. And in the days that followed, the misery of the poor increased. As a consequence of a disastrous harvest, the price of a four pound loaf rose from the eight-pence farthing it had cost when we had arrived in London to eleven-pence only this short time later.

As Yule-tide approached, the weather, which until now had been wet but not unusually cold, deteriorated. A hard frost gripped the land and stopped all employment in the brick-fields and the market-gardens which were at that time so numerous around the metropolis. To make matters worse, an East wind blew so steadily that ships could not come up the river to unload. Then a week before Christmas the Thames froze over as it had not done for forty years and all those involved in the river trade — coaling, wherrying, ballasting, ship-wrighting, and many others — were cast out of work.

We observed rather than celebrated Christmas, not daring even to halt work for the day. On Boxing-day deep snow fell in the capital and brought to a halt what little outdoor-work was still in train. Gangs of men patroled the metropolis and suburbs carrying the implements of their trades — hods for brick-layers, rakes for market-gardeners, and so on — and raised the traditional cry: "Froze out! All froze out!" as they proffered their hats for alms. The number of people begging in the streets visibly increased, as did that of street vendors, while against this the quantity of foot-passengers declined. Faced with this competition my earnings dropped even lower.

Worst of all, however, was the effect of the weather on the fashionable Season. Because of the state of the roads His Majesty and his family remained at Windsor and many of their most elevated subjects chose to emulate them by staying in the country after Christmas. And so the start of the Season, that usually occurred in the middle of January, was delayed; Parliament did not reassemble and race-meetings were cancelled. All of this meant that the hoped-for demand for clothes on which we were relying failed to appear and we, like many other trades — tailors, shoe-makers, dress-makers, cabinet-makers, harness-makers, saddlers, servants, cabmen, farriers — suffered in consequence.

The streets around all the workhouses were thronged with people seeking relief, nearly all of whom were refused outdoor assistance. I myself saw some of those who had been turned away from St. Anne's workhouse by Drury-lane, then accost well-dressed foot-passengers for alms in a threatening manner, and meanwhile reports circulated that mobs had attacked bread-shops and eating-houses in Whitechapel.

One morning at the end of January Mr Peachment told us that Dick had failed to return the night before. At first they were very alarmed for his safety but after a few days they realized, after going over and over the things he had been saying for the past few months, that he had deserted them. This was a heavy blow to the family for they relied on his earnings, and Mr Pentecost expressed to the parents his deep contrition for having put ideas into the boy's head.

Our large, lofty-ceilinged room with its partly-unglazed windows dissipated all the heat that was so dearly bought. We tried to make a chauldron of coal last two weeks by keeping only a handful of cinders burning during the day and huddling together as we slept at night. All of us suffered from chilblains and cold sores, as well as the colds and coughs that particularly affect those new to London.

The winter, instead of ending in February, actually worsened for now there came a frozen fog — heavy, foul-smelling, and yellow — which for days at a time granted scarcely a glimpse of the sun. On such occasions there was little point in my going out with my tray for I could sell nothing on the streets. Food-prices rose and the value of made things dropped, for there were no buyers.

Needless to say, the two gentlemen (whose means of livelihood were as badly affected as mine) frequently argued about the implications of what was happening. Mr Pentecost believed that the bad times would regulate themselves, and that when wages fell low enough employment would start again. Mr Silverlight, on the other hand, insisted that things would spiral into disaster and said cheerfully that he lived in daily hopes of a popular rising. He rejoiced, he said, to hear of a bread-shop being attacked.

Despite his display of cheerfulness, however, I could see that Mr Silverlight was finding it hard to endure the privations that were now forced upon him. Gradually the furniture disappeared from the Caliph's tent, then Mr Pentecost's watch, then articles of clothing. Mr Silverlight remained as well-dressed as always, until one day at the very end of that terrible February, when I came home and met him hurrying down the stairs muttering to himself, clad in a shabby coat I had not seen before and wearing no neckcloth. I had never seen such disarray in his dress, and indeed never saw such a thing again.

The next day Mrs Peachment, two of her children, and Mr Pentecost fell ill of a high fever. When I went into the other room that evening I found the latter lying on the bed with a flushed face and wandering in his thoughts: "Where is Silverlight?" he kept saying. Surprised not to find him present, I asked Mr Peachment. That honest fellow drew me to one side and explained in an undertone that he must have stolen away during the hours of darkness for they had found him and his belongings gone that morning and they had not seen him since.

I was puzzled by this but was to become even more confused the next day.

Miss Quilliam and I did what we could for our neighbours that evening. Then late the following afternoon, as I was returning from an almost profitless trawl of the streets, I heard my mother shouting at someone as I reached our landing: "Begone! I want nothing to do with you!"

There was a man standing at our door accompanied by a large dog which was baring its teeth and growling at my mother, while Justice — for I now recognised the old beggar — was trying to quieten it and to reassure her.

"I'm only seeking Mr Pentecost," he said, turning towards me when he heard my voice.

I calmed my mother and coaxed her into our room. Then I explained to the old man that our friend was ill.

"I'm powerful sorry to larn that," he said. "Mr Pentecost has sarved Wolf here and kept the poor beast alive. Many and many a time he's brung a piece of polony or a pork-pie when I had nought to give him."

Since old Justice wanted to see Mr Pentecost I knocked on the door of the opposite room and led him into it. I was relieved to see that my old friend had fully recovered his senses, and to my surprise, when he saw who my companion was, he caught my eye and blushed.

"It's most extraordinary that you have not received anything," he said when Justice explained why he had come. "For I was so concerned when I knew I was falling ill that I told Silverlight about you — or, rather, that is to say, about Wolf — and asked him to take a shilling to you so that you could purchase something for the dog. I cannot imagine what can have happened."

I broke it to him gently that his friend had left him but this merely plunged him further into bewilderment.

"Gone?" he kept repeating. "Why, the poor fellow can't manage without me. Hopelessly trusting, you know. Quite a child."

Old Justice had been brooding thoughtfully and now said: "Mr Silverlight? Was that the genel'man that you was with that day I met you and the younker here?"

"That is so."

The old man shook his head thoughtfully and I believed he was about to speak, but he seemed to think better of it.

"Wolf looks hungry. I still have a shilling left," Mr Pentecost said, looking in fact at his master.

Justice resisted but at last he was persuaded to take the money for the sake of the wretched beast. However, a few minutes later he returned with some meat-pies which he insisted on sharing with Mr Pentecost and the hound, and I left them making a feast on the straw mattress in the corner of the tent. I was rather puzzled as to what to make of all of this and although on the face of it there seemed grounds for suspecting my old friend of a breach of his strict principles on the subject of charity, I was reluctant to think the less of Mr Pentecost.

I soon had other matters to occupy me, however. For when I got into our room my mother came forward and greeted me anxiously:

"How much have you brought?"

I showed her the few pence I had earned and she seized the coins and began to put on her bonnet.

"Have we no food?" I asked.

She nodded and hurried out.

When she came back only a few minutes later she was much calmer and sank into her chair without removing her bonnet. When she made no move to produce anything to eat I reproached her. She did not answer and I went over to her. To my surprise, I saw no purchases.

"What have you done with the money?" I demanded.

She smiled at me.

Suspicions that I had long nursed came crowding upon me. I lifted her hands that were lying on her lap and found what I had expected. The cork had already been removed.

"How long have you been taking this?" I demanded.

"It does me no harm," she said, smiling dreamily. "Helen takes it."

Miss Quilliam came in just at this minute.

"Is this your doing, Miss Quilliam?" I asked, holding up the little dark-green vial.

"I have never encouraged your mother," she said, colouring slightly. "For I once became enslaved to it. I only saved myself from its clutches by recording the number of grains I was taking and forcing myself to reduce the amount day by day." She shuddered. "I would not want any friend of mine to have to endure that."

"It lets me sleep even when I cough and it gives me such beautiful dreams, Johnnie."

"Then let me take it," I cried angrily, removing the cork. "I want some beautiful dreams, too!"

"No," Miss Quilliam cried, crossing to me and snatching it from me. "In small quantities it brings sleep, in larger amounts strange visions, but in excess it is a deadly poison if you are not habituated to it, Johnnie. That is why they call it the best friend of the poor. It robs you of life but leaves no sign of the means of death to shame your friends."

I looked at my mother who had fallen into a slumber.

With much to brood upon, I went to bed and slept badly. Before dawn I was awakened by a loud noise from across the landing. When I went out to look I found Mr Pentecost — still pale and thin from his illness — standing between two men whose cocked hats and silver staves of office I knew so well.

He smiled when he saw me: "Well, my young friend, I'm for the Fleet again."

So he had been a Fleet prisoner before that!

"On what account?" I asked.

He looked discomfited and said: "I believe I told you that I was being sought by my creditors. The truth is a little more complicated. The fact is that some years ago I backed a bill for a friend."

Here was a frank confession of his hypocrisy in acting contrary to his principle of self-interest, and I blushed to hear it from him.

"I dare say you're wondering how we managed to find you arter all these years, Mr Pentecost," one of the bailiffs began in a friendly tone.

"My good fellow," Mr Pentecost interrupted quickly, catching my eye, "not for a minute, I assure you."

There was nothing that could be done and to the dismay of the Peachment family — and, indeed, of the whole stair — he was given a few minutes to gather his scant possessions before being led away and put in a waiting hackney-coach.

In the weeks that followed I thought often of Mr Pentecost when I had leisure from my own concerns. A few days after the arrest of his patron, the old beggar had come again and was deeply upset to learn of his fate.

"Why," he said, shaking his head, "Blind Justice knowed it when he heerd his voice. A leper don't change his spots, ain't that what they say, sir?"

When I pressed him to explain his meaning — which I feared I partly understood — he merely shook his head with a sad smile and shuffled down the stairs.

The winter eventually came to an end in the middle of March and trade picked up a little. I was aware that the first monthly payment of interest on the locket was now due, and I knew my mother would be determined to raise the money. And so it happened, for she starved herself to put a little aside and although we had an argument about it, when the time came she went back to the pawn-broker and had her duplicate endorsed for a further month. She managed to do the same in April and May but after that our plight deteriorated so much that it became clear that the locket would have to be forfeited.

I came to this conclusion because at the end of May Mr Peachment warned us that the Season appeared likely to terminate sooner than usual because of its unpropitious start. He added that he suspected that the garret-master from whom he sub-contracted work, was on the point of going out of business because of this. Moreover, I knew that he and his wife no longer had Dick's earnings to help them and that after the departure of Mr Pentecost and Mr Silverlight they had failed to find a tenant to whom to let the other half of their room because trade was so depressed.

During these months I had continued to think about my old friend and several times I went past the begging-grate (which was an iron grille let into the wall in Fleet-market) where one of the prisoners always stood to beg, with the words "Pray, remember the poor debtors," hoping that one day it would be Mr Pentecost's turn. It never was he, however, and at last I summoned the courage to ask the prisoner I found there if he knew anything about him. He knew his name and told me he was seriously ill and his life despaired of.

Now it began to get hot and an oppressiveness settled on those miserable streets that was as onerous as the fogs of January. By the end of June my mother had not managed to save enough to pay the next month's interest and although she was very upset about this, I was not sympathetic.

On the evening of the 22nd., we were sitting in the near-darkness (for when we had no work we did not light even a tallow-dip) when there was a knock at the door and Mr Peachment came in with a very long face.

"It's the end," he announced. "The slop-master don't have no more work to give me. And he says he never will, neither."

The blow was not the less bitter for having been long expected. My mother gave a cry and Miss Quilliam reached out to take her arm.

"What will become of you and your family?" she asked him.

"We'll sell everything, and go back to where we come from."

Miss Quilliam poured something for my mother and herself from the stone jug. "Will you take something with us?" she asked him.

He shuddered slightly: "I will not, I thank you. No disrespeck 'tended, but I seen what it done to my own dad."

"Why must you go back?" asked my mother.

"Don't you know that? Why, no Relieving Officer in none o' the Lunnon paritches will grant an order into the 'House if you don't have no settlement. They pass you back to your own paritch. So we'll return to Dunsford where we come from three years back on account of there weren't no work."

When he went out a few minutes later we sat for some time in silence in the gloom. Then my mother's voice came from the darkness: "What will become of us?"

"I don't know," Miss Quilliam replied, pouring out for herself and my mother a generous portion of gin.

"My dear Helen, have you no friends you can turn to?" asked my mother.

"None that I could bring myself to beg help of. But as for you and Johnnie, I recollect you once told me you have a legal settlement in London through your husband."

I was astonished to hear this and looked at my mother.

"I dare not go there," she said. "It would be far too dangerous."

"Why?" I demanded, but she only shook her head.

"My dear, I believe you have no choice," Miss Quilliam said gently.

"What would it be like?" she whispered.

"You would be fed and clothed. The food would be that thin gruel they call stir-about, but there would most likely be a little meat on Sundays. And you would wear pauper dress and the parish badge. You would be put to picking oakum which is unpleasant and painful though not crushing work."

"Would we be separated?" my mother asked.

"You would be in the same house and allowed to speak through a grating for a few minutes a week. But after a time they would probably try to find a master in another parish to bind Johnnie to as apprentice, since then the burden of keeping him if anything happened to him would fall on the rates of that parish."

As she spoke I recalled the workhouse I had visited on Isbister's errand, and the rumbling noise I had heard which I had more recently come to understand was the sound of a treadmill.

After a few moments my mother took her hands away from her face and said: "Then I suppose it must be so." Then she asked: "But what of you, Helen? Do you mean to go upon the parish too?"

"Anything but that!" she exclaimed extravagantly. Then she said more collectedly: "My circumstances are different. I am responsible only for myself." She hesitated, and then said: "Besides, I was there once."

She raised her glass to her lips and drank as if to wash away the memory.

"You were a pauper!" my mother gasped. Her friend nodded. "Tell me about it."

Miss Quilliam glanced towards me, then drank off her glass, poured another and said: "No, Mary, I think not."

We spent the next hour or two in sorting out our few possessions. Miss Quilliam was to take almost everything my mother and I possessed — though that was little enough, Heaven knows! — to recompense her for our unpaid debts and because all our goods would be taken from us when we entered the 'House.

I went to my bed and fell quickly into a light slumber, from which I was suddenly awakened by Miss Quilliam saying: "Is he asleep?"

I lay still and kept my eyes closed.

"Yes," my mother answered.

"Mary," she said rather recklessly, "now that the time is approaching for us to part, tell me frankly whether you heard any slander against me from Mrs Malatratt or that odious man at the registry-office?"

"No, certainly I did not."

There was a silence and then Miss Quilliam said: "I would like you to know more of my story."

She began and, unable to sleep, I lay and listened to the clear, musical voice that came out of the darkness. Outside our room I heard the sounds of Orchard-Street preparing itself for the night: in the building the rushing of feet upon the stairs and hammering upon doors with raucous oaths, and in the street sudden bursts of shouting and wild laughter. But the story that I was not supposed to know held me so that I heard nothing of these distractions.

CHAPTER 37

My misfortunes began before I was born for my parents' marriage was a love-match which was struck in defiance of both their families and without the blessing of either. Neither possessing an independence, every ill consequence followed from this imprudence. My mother's father died when she was a little child, and left to the support of his widow no greater fortune than could be looked for from a naval lieutenant who had passed much of his life on half-pay and had earned no prize-money, since this was long before the late wars. At his death, therefore, my grandmother was left almost destitute to bring up two young children in a mean dwelling near the dock-yard in Portsmouth. Every sacrifice was made — including my mother's education — to prepare her elder brother for entry to the Navy in the hope of his restoring the little family's fortunes. Alas, he died of the yellow-fever in his sixteenth year while serving as a midshipman in the West-indies. My grandmother now had no recourse but to take in lodgers. One of them was a young curate just down from the University and, of course, he and my mother fell in love — poor innocents! He had but fifty pounds a year for his curacy. He did, however, have the prospect of preferment to a comfortable living in due course, as I shall explain.

Because his own father had opposed his wish to take orders, he had been able to do so only with the aid of a benefactor, Sir William Delamater. It was this wealthy baronet who not merely paid for my father's studies at Cambridge, but subsequently procured for him the curacy at Portsmouth.

Virtually disowned by his parent, my father could not think of marrying. But now Sir William once again revealed his generosity — though with disastrous consequences in the event — by promising my father the reversion of a benefice to which he had the advowson. This was nothing less than the rectorship of the parish in which lay his principal seat, Delamater-hall, and which, in tithes, emoluments, and compositions, was worth not less than 1200£ a year besides having attached to it a fine house. The present incumbent being a gentleman much advanced in years, though in good health, my father's entry into the living could not be long delayed.

Although my parents postponed their marriage for two years, by the expiry of this period neither of the two old gentlemen concerned had done what was hoped of them: my grandfather had not changed in his opposition and the elderly rector had made no move towards claiming his heavenly reward. Then it was that my father made a fateful decision. Unwilling either to delay his marriage any longer or to make further claims on Sir William's generosity, he sought out a money-lender in the City from whom he borrowed 300£ against an annuity of 100£ to start at five years from that date and run for twelve. By the time the annuity was to fall due, he expected — reasonably enough — to have entered upon the benefice and therefore to be able to pay it without difficulty. And with the 300£, little as it was, my parents married and set up home in a cottage in Portsmouth. I was born within a year and mercifully remained the only child to survive infancy.

The rest is simply told and I think I see that you have anticipated the outcome. The elderly incumbent did not die but instead defeated expectations by outliving his patron, for when I was four, Sir William, a hale and hearty man still in the prime of life, died on the hunting-field. This melancholy event occurred only a few months before the repayment of the loan was due to commence. The heir to his estate and property — as to his title — was Sir Thomas Delamater, his nephew, and a gentleman of whom my father knew little — and that little boded ill. He wrote to him immediately, condoling with him on his loss and explaining his uncle's promise and the hopes he had built upon it. The new baronet answered in the coldest and most formal tones: Sir Thomas had no knowledge of any promise made by his uncle since it had never been expressed to him while he lived and no record was found of it after his death either in his testament or any other papers. My father would, as an ordained member of the church, understand that under the circumstances Sir Thomas, while not doubting that such an undertaking had been made, could not be bound by it on a matter upon which he had a duty to exercise his conscience. (This from a man who had given proof upon proof in the infamous irregularities of his private life of how little he held in respect the tenets of the Christian religion!) Moreover, Sir Thomas had himself already promised the reversion of the benefice to a collegiate companion of whose worthiness for the position he had direct knowledge. Finally, Sir Thomas deeply regretted that my father had been so precipitate as to enter upon a commitment involving others which was founded upon so insecure a prospect, but my father would understand that Sir Thomas could not allow his feelings to deflect him from his duty.

My father's situation was now desperate. The money-lender who had advanced him the loan soon learned of his misfortune — you appear surprised, but it seems that these people have a web of agents and intelligencers in all the legal, financial and ecclesiastical offices — and began to threaten an action for debt which would assuredly lead to my father's incarceration.

My father made a last appeal to his father which went unanswered. Knowing that he faced arrest and indefinite confinement if he stayed in England and consumed with anxiety for the prospects of my mother and myself, my father determined upon a desperate step. It was possible at that date — and for all I know this may still be the case, for the period I speak of is barely fifteen years ago — for a young clergyman to obtain without undue difficulty the post of Junior Chaplain to one of the East India Company's stations. The comparative ease with which such posts could be secured was not due merely to their poor remuneration — 70£ was the best one could expect — but principally to the extreme insalubriousness of the area and the high rate of mortality among Europeans who went out there. Obtaining such a post in the cantonment of Cawnpoor in the province of Allahabad, my father employed the larger part of his first quarter's salary, which was paid in advance, in insuring his life for 500£. He assigned the policy in trust to myself, with my mother and grandmother as trustees, and it is my belief that as far as was reconcilable with the ethical teachings of his church, he intended that his imminent death should at once cancel his debt and secure the prospects of his widow and his child. His intention had been to sail for India alone, but my mother insisted on accompanying him and when he saw that to continue to refuse was to offer a surer threat to her health than to allow her to have her way, he consented.

So they sailed for Calcutta, leaving me in the charge of my grandmother. Of course the climate did all that was hoped and within a few months of landing my father's design was fulfilled with respect to himself. The same, alas! was true for my mother. The remainder of his purpose, however, was not achieved for he had been badly advised. Indeed, will you believe me if I say that I suspect that the attorney he consulted might have been in colleague with the money-lender and that he deliberately misled my father? For far from his death freeing his estate from all obligation to the money-lender, that individual was able to go to court and secure the 500£ before the insurance company even paid it to my grandmother. And he could surely only have known of its existence from the attorney.

I was therefore left, now in my seventh year, completely dependent upon my grandmother whose only income was derived from the lodgers to whom she rented two upper floors of the small house that she leased and who, besides being old, her temper frayed by her own worries, and in poor health, was ill-fitted to the sole care of a young child. She discharged her obligations and sent me to a day-school where I benefited as far as was possible from the education available, and did so well that I was at last entrusted with some teaching as a pupil-monitor.

My grandmother died when I was fourteen and since her lease on the little house expired with her, I was at a stroke deprived of protector, income and home. When her estate was settled and her debts paid I, as heir-at-law, was left with only a few shillings.

Now it was that I had no alternative but to take the course I have already hinted at and to seek the aid of the parish authorities. I will not describe the humiliations and insults I was forced to endure. Let it suffice to say merely that the Master and Matron of the 'House were brutal and ignorant people who took delight in the opportunity to lord it over one of genteel birth.

Desperate by some means to get away, I now wrote to my only relation. My letter to my grandfather was answered by an attorney representing his estate who informed me that he had died and left everything to found an alms-house in his memory. He sent me 10£ and made it clear that that was all I could expect.

Far from ending my trials, this initiative on my part made them worse. For now the Board of Guardians of the Poor, as the most efficacious way of ensuring that I would not be a burden upon the parish, was disposed to add ten pounds to my ten in order to make up the premium required to apprentice me to a dress-maker in Southampton to whom they had sent girls in the past. I, however, had aspirations above this: I wished to be apprenticed to the school where I had done well and whose proprietors were anxious to take me as an apprentice-teacher at a reduced premium. Their intentions were not in the least charitable: they knew how much work they would be able to extract from me, in return for board and lodging that they would have hesitated to offer to a scullery-maid. But even the reduced premium was 40£ and the Board refused to make up the short-fall. I was heart-broken at the prospect that lay before me. However, I wrote to ... that is to say, aid came from an unexpected quarter. And so I was able to be apprenticed as I had wished.

During the two years that followed I worked diligently in order to profit from every advantage that the school could offer me. These were not unhappy times even though, except among the girls, I had no friends, for I discovered in myself an aptitude for teaching and a pleasure in it which, since my highest ambition could only be to secure a good place as a school-teacher or governess, confirmed my belief that I had taken the right course.

CHAPTER 38

When my apprenticeship was out, the proprietors offered me a permanent post but refused me the remuneration that I knew my talents and industry entitled me to. And so we agreed to part — I with no great reluctance for the two sisters who owned and directed the establishment were hard and narrow women with whom I had little sympathy.

Now it was that I came to London and shortly afterwards was so fortunate — as I then believed — as to procure an appointment in the Mompessons' household. I was at first, briefly, in Town and then my charge and I removed alone to their place down in the country. I soon came to love that strange, unhappy child, Henrietta, and to love her all the more as I came to see how she was treated by the rest of the family, including even the servants. It would not be right for me to express myself with complete frankness on the subject of my employers — especially since you have told me they are connexions of yours — so I will content myself with saying that the less I had to do with Sir Perceval and Lady Mompesson the happier I was. No such constraint deters me from saying that in their sons, David and Tom, comparable examples of devious selfishness and cruel stupidity, respectively, would be very hard of discovery. But I over-run myself, for while Henrietta and I were at Hougham for the first months that summer — only two years ago, but how remote it seems! — I was very happy. She and I were alone except for the housekeeper, Mrs Peppercorn, and some other servants. She was a melancholy child but would not be drawn on the source of her unhappiness — which I attributed to her having been orphaned at an early age — and she never once uttered a complaint about her treatment by her relatives. Dismayed by the fact that she was forced to wear a back-board, I remonstrated with her guardians by letter, though to no avail. I was also disturbed to discover the deep welts she bore on her hands, about whose origin she would say nothing. At that happy time I did not suspect the truth.

Gradually I won Henrietta's trust and became that timid creature's first — or almost her first — friend. The idyll, however, could not last and the family, apart from Mr Mompesson who would not be drawn from the pleasures of the capital, came down later in the year, as you know, for it was shortly after that when I first met Johnnie. Now I saw how my employers neglected and disparaged my little charge, and permitted Tom to bully and torment her. This was bad enough but when, after Christmas, the whole household removed back to the house in Brook-street, an unexpected difficulty presented itself. Although I tried as far as possible to exclude myself from the family — and that was not difficult for my chamber and Henrietta's were on an upper floor and we usually consumed our meals together in the school-room — it was impossible to be altogether withdrawn. I therefore encountered Mr Mompesson on several occasions and before long found that I could not conceal from myself an attention on his part towards me. This was something I had not had to endure even from his boorish brother — in whose company I had sometimes found myself down at Hougham — whose intellectual resources were fully engaged by his dogs and his horses. Naturally I attempted to avoid Mr Mompesson as far as possible, but he began to force his presence upon me, and worse, find occasions to speak to me alone. When I made it a rule never to address him save in the presence of a third person, he grew increasingly importunate and offensive on the few occasions when I was unable to avoid his company.

Finally, he found me one day alone in the library, barred my egress, attempted unacceptable freedoms, and, at last, growing angry at my resistance, delivered himself of a remark that was unpardonable. In deep distress I forced my way past him and went immediately to Sir Perceval and Lady Mompesson. I burst upon them in their sitting-room distraught and almost in tears, complaining of their son's conduct in a manner that should have compelled belief and respect. The effect of the way they received me was like a blow on the cheek. They treated me with haughty disdain, implying that I was making too much of what was no more than a display of youthful high spirits. I withdrew with as much dignity as I could and once back in my room concluded that this refusal to take my charge seriously put me in an impossible position. A young woman in my situation could not risk exposure to conduct of the kind Mr Mompesson was inflicting upon me, and I saw clearly that my wisest course was to seek other employment. Yet I also knew that the situation I faced was the perennial lot of young governesses — particularly those unfortunate enough to be possessed of personal attractions which exposed them to danger. And so I felt that I had to triumph over the situation instead of fleeing from it, with the near certainty of encountering it again. An even more powerful motive for remaining than this was my desire not to abandon Henrietta. Since we had come to the London mansion I had learned from her great-aunt, who had rooms in the house, something of the motives that had led Henrietta's guardians to take her under their protection.

I therefore resolved to stay but to keep myself apprised of other situations in case my position at Brook-street became unendurable. It was for this reason that I registered myself with the London General Office, and very fortunate that decision turned out to be since it was by that means that you and John discovered me.

CHAPTER 39

One evening Mr Mompesson found me alone in the library — an eventuality I tried to avoid, but I could not completely deny myself the pleasure of reading. In marked contrast to earlier occasions, however, he represented himself as extremely apologetic for his previous behaviour. Glad to conciliate him, I accepted his apologies. Then in the most charming manner — for he can be very charming — he told me he wished me to do him the honour of accompanying him, with a party of friends, to Vauxhall-pleasure-gardens the following evening in order to make amends to me for his past conduct. He assured me that one of the party would be a widowed lady of the utmost respectability, a Mrs Purviance, who was an old acquaintance of his mother.

I felt that it would be unwise to reject his invitation if it were truly tendered in a spirit of reconciliation, because to do so might be to encourage him to return to his former demeanour towards me. Also, if I am completely frank, the idea of a party of pleasure did not repel me, stultified as I was by the narrow penury of my way of life. Yet I could not but be suspicious of his motives and so I told him that I insisted on hearing from his parents not merely their consent to his proposal, but their express desire that I should accompany him and his companions; for otherwise, I argued, there would be an impropriety in a mere governess being included in such a party. Though I expected and half hoped that he would reject this stipulation out of hand, he seized eagerly upon it, said that it was as much as he had expected, and insisted on ringing the bell to summon a servant to ask his parents to admit him to their presence. The footman, Edward, took the message, but returned to say that Sir Perceval and Lady Mompesson had withdrawn for the night — although it was only a little after ten.

Mr Mompesson appeared cast down by this, but then he suggested that I write them a note instead. I consented, and dashed off a few lines, in which I did not request their permission to accompany their son but rather indicated that he had invited me and that I was unwilling to accept unless they particularly wished it. At Mr Mompesson's suggestion, I mentioned the name of Mrs Purviance as one of the proposed party. A few minutes later Edward brought back a three-cornered note of the kind that I had received before, the contents of which — in Sir Perceval's distinctive hand, which would be called illegible from anyone of lesser rank — were to the effect that he and his wife not merely approved of the proposed party, but positively desired that I should accept the invitation. You may imagine the conflict of emotions I experienced: there are occasions when we wish to be impelled into an action by which we are tempted but against which our judgement protests. Though apprehensive — and yet excited, too — I felt that I was bound by my undertaking to Mr Mompesson to accept his parents' decision, and I therefore consented to make one of the party. As you may conceive, I passed a restless night. I will forgive you if you smile when I tell you that my want of an appropriate costume was a cause of considerable concern, and the next day I had great difficulty in adapting what clothes I had to fit the occasion in the little time free from my responsibilities. Henrietta, though much less interested in dress than most girls of her age, aided me in my preparations and lent me her cachemire shawl. And the maid who waited upon herself and her great-aunt, kindly offered to dress my hair.

The following evening found me, then, modestly, though adequately, attired and waiting anxiously in my room. Because Sir Perceval and Lady Mompesson were dining out, Mr Mompesson had arranged that after taking them to their engagement, the carriage should return for us. So at nine o'clock I came down to find Mr Mompesson in the Great Parlour in the company of Mrs Purviance, in appearance a very respectable lady of about fifty years of age who, from her conversation, was on terms of intimacy with numerous members of the aristocracy and who expressed her regret at not having the opportunity of seeing Lady Mompesson that evening.

It was, therefore, with a sense of reassurance that I entered the carriage and was driven to the gardens — in itself an adventure for me. At the gate we met by previous arrangement the fourth member of our party, a young man whose surname I did not hear but whom Mr Mompesson addressed as Harry. He was handsome, though rather poorly dressed, and as I was soon to discover, very clever and extremely charming.

This gentleman escorted us into the gardens while Mr Mompesson paid at the door. As we walked about in the drawn-out summer dusk, I, naturally, conversed mainly with Mrs Purviance, who impressed me as a woman of fashion and taste. The conversation of the gentlemen seemed, from the snatches I heard, to be confined to the green baize and the turf, for it was all of how "Such-and-Such had dropped a monkey at the Fishmonger's" and "whether the filly would take the bit".

When the conversation became more general, it seemed to me that Mr Mompesson was taking pains to speak to me with respect and courtesy as if to one of his own rank, and for the first time I began to feel that he had qualities which had not previously been apparent.

It was a beautiful evening and for an hour or two we strolled about looking at the coloured lanthorns hidden in the branches of the trees, admiring the fountains and the new cosmorama and the Moorish-tower, and listening to the orchestra which performed in a painted and arched stand in the centre. Around us were the most fashionable and elegant members of Society and I was very excited to be mingling with them on terms of equality. As the evening wore on, however, the better families grew fewer and an altogether different clientèle appeared: servants aping their masters, apprentices on stolen leave, and servant-girls with their sweet-hearts. I believe it was upon seeing this and observing my dismay at it, that Mr Mompesson proposed that we should dine.

Mrs Purviance assented readily but Harry said: "Why, I don't believe I'm hungry. In fact, I'm sure I'm not."

"Set your mind at rest, Harry. I shall pay for everything," Mr Mompesson said, leading us towards the supper-room. "No, I beg of you, Harry, don't protest."

"I shouldn't dream of it," Harry said, also smiling. "For here you are, industriously increasing your credit."

"How's that? You mean decreasing it?"

"On the contrary. Why, going into debt is like digging the foundations of a house: the deeper you go, the higher the house may rise. You can always know who is deepest in debt by the opulence of their establishment."

"There is some truth in that," Mrs Purviance said, as we seated ourselves at one of the tables protected by a painted awning. The table had an elegant epergne heaped with rare fruits and sweetmeats, and a little way away a band of French horns and clarinets were playing French waltzes.

Mrs Purviance went on: "I recall that shortly before he was forced to flee his creditors, Lord Quantock added a ball-room to Quantock Castle."

"By that chop-logic, my dear fellow," Mr Mompesson said to the other young man, "I should have taken you for a millionaire."

"So here you are, Mompesson," Harry continued, parrying Mr Mompesson's remark with a smile, "digging away as industriously as any Irish navigator. Have you ever considered, Miss Quilliam, how very hard a fashionable debtor has to work? And all from mere selflessness! Only from pity for his creditors, for if he goes for smash then he'll bring down whole families of honest money-lenders. Why, do you know, Miss Quilliam, Mompesson here has a family of Jews whose happiness depends entirely upon him?"

"There is some truth in your nonsense, Harry."

"There is always truth in it," he interrupted. "As someone said of Virgil, I fling about my nonsense with an air of majesty."

"Indeed," Mr Mompesson resumed. "If the truth be known, my creditors begged me to borrow of them."

"Precisely! You hooked them and not the other way round, as is usually supposed. And it weighs on you, I know — the security of all those little Abrahams and Rebeccas. No wonder you envy me, for true peace of mind comes only when one has nothing."

"If that is so," said Mr Mompesson, "then my family will soon attain the state of highest bliss."

"Fie, Mr Mompesson!" Mrs Purviance exclaimed. "You should not jest upon such matters!"

"Fear not, Mompesson, for there will always be greedy fools enough to lend you more. Did not Horace (or one of those old Romans) refer to this when he said: credit is long, life is short?"

"I'm confounded if I know. I had a little Latin beaten into me at school but it was painlessly taken out again at the 'Varsity. I leave book-learning and all that sort of collar-work to you."

"It's true that I have to work hard," Harry said, looking a little put out at this; "but you've studied for your profession, too: the life of a leisured gentleman is not easy. Why, my friend Pamplin sometimes takes an hour choosing his neckcloth."

"A most elegant young gentleman," Mrs Purviance murmured, smiling at me.

"You're fortunate to be spared such labour," Mr Mompesson said with a satirical smile. "For you have but two of that article: one for use and one for superfluity."

"And am therefore all the more of a gentleman," Harry said lightly. "For according to one definition I have read, a man is a gentleman if he has no visible means of gaining his livelihood. And that is certainly my case."

"I believe an invisible means is implied, Harry," Mr Mompesson said. "For otherwise your definition would mean that hundreds of gentlemen are confined in Newgate and several dozen hanged there every year."

"In equity that should be so," Harry said with a droll smile. "But most of the 'gentlemen' you refer to have an invisible means of gaining their livelihood, so your reservation can hardly apply. A better definition I have heard is that a man will not be black-balled by White's if he ties a good knot to his handkerchief, keeps his hands out of his breeches-pockets, and says nothing."

"But that test would permit even my brother Tom to pass muster!" Mr Mompesson cried.

"For shame, Mr Mompesson," Mrs Purviance protested mildly, trying not to smile with the two young gentlemen.

Feeling that I should say something or be convicted by my silence of stupidity or pride, I said: "A gentleman is surely one whose birth and breeding are matched by his manners and conduct, whatever his personal fortune may be."

"How well you express it, my dear," Mrs Purviance said.

"Excellent sentiments," Harry said. Then he went on with a smile that did not conceal his anger: "And yet a man whose manners are those of a boor and whose conduct is infamously irregular, is received as a gentleman in a family where he would not be given a place as the meanest servant. You know whom I refer to, Mompesson."

"No man," Mr Mompesson said, "can be an absolute boor who has four thousand pounds clear per annum."

"By that reckoning," said Harry, "you're a couple of thousand short of acceptance in good society."

"I positively don't know how you would know anything about good society that you did not hear from me," Mr Mompesson said coldly.

Harry flushed but continued to smile as he turned to me: "Pray don't think, Miss Quilliam, that Mompesson patronizes me. The truth is, I patronize him. By insulting him in company I encourage the idea of his humility and magnanimity. I am like the Old Cumberland Beggar, in that poem of the atrocious Wordsworth, who goes about providing opportunities for the exercise of charity and thereby benefits his fellow men."

"Then you are a greater benefactor than anyone I know," Mr Mompesson said quickly. He turned to me: "He even tried to benefit my father in the manner he has just described."

I thought Harry winced at this, but he said gaily: "Indeed I did. But unfortunately the old gentleman declined to avail himself of the opportunity."

"And yet Sir Perceval has such a strong sense of family," Mrs Purviance commented. "Only look at his kindness to that poor child Henrietta."

"It is precisely because my father has that sense that he declined to profit from Harry's benevolence," Mr Mompesson remarked, and if I was puzzled by Mrs Purviance's words, I was the more so by his. Was Harry or was he not a relative of Sir Perceval?

"How is ... " Harry quickly began, as if to turn the subject.

Mr Mompesson, however, rode over him: "I heard such a good thing the other day. I was talking to Berkeley Tessymond at White's."

"Is he not," put in Mrs Purviance, "the recorded son of the late Earl of Huntingdonshire and therefore the elder half-brother of the present earl?"

"Exactly so, and therefore jocularly called the Early of Huntingdonshire," Mr Mompesson said with a sidelong glance at myself. "He was talking of his paternity and quoted something that had been said to him by a young Frenchwoman he met at Mrs Mauleverer's in Hill-street. Possibly you know the house, Mrs Purviance?"

That lady merely nodded somewhat curtly and he went on: "They were discussing her origins and she said that although one did not always know one's father, which was a pity, one was certain to have had one, which was a consolation."

Nobody laughed and I turned away to conceal my blushes. At this moment the waiter began to lay the dishes before us.

"What is this?" Harry demanded of the man, staring at his plate in comical surprise.

"Veal, sir."

Harry stabbed it with his knife: "Then it is veal tottering on the edge of beef."

We laughed and the moment of embarrassment passed. The others were drinking freely of a white wine which they told me was called Tokay, and which they assured me — urging me to partake of it — was hardly stronger than table-beer. Certainly this seemed so from the quantities they were quaffing without visible effect, and so, at last, unwilling to seem stiff and unconvivial, I consented to drink a very little. I later realized that it must have been stronger than I knew at the time, but it was perhaps through its effect that I found my tongue and began to talk, hoping that I was not making too manifest my gratification at finding myself, quite for the first occasion in my life, in the company of witty and educated people.

Afterwards we strolled to the firework-ground where I saw the finest display I had ever witnessed: Bengal lights that blazed above our heads and seemed to drop glittering fires upon us, serpents that appeared to spit flames as they revolved, and magnificent rockets that burst in the air sending out whirling galaxies of many-coloured stars.

The time passed so very pleasantly that when Mr Mompesson suddenly said — "Be a good fellow, Harry, and go and see if Phumphred has brought the carriage back." — I was quite alarmed to discover that it was almost midnight.

Harry flushed at Mr Mompesson's tone but he did as he was bid. When he returned to say that the vehicle was waiting at the gate, I thought the evening was at an end, but Mr Mompesson said: "Come, the fresh air has made me hungry and I am sure the rest of you must be, too. I propose we take supper before we return."

The other two exclaimed in delight at this proposal and I therefore felt some dismay at the speech I believed I had to make: "Indeed not, Mr Mompesson. I could not think of such a thing. Sir Perceval and Lady Mompesson gave permission for no such extension of the evening."

Mr Mompesson tried to persuade me that it was implicit in their reply, but I was obdurate. When the others expressed their disappointment at the curtailment of the evening's pleasure, I said: "If you would be so good, Mr Mompesson, as to direct the coachman to take me home, there is no reason why you and this lady and gentleman should not go elsewhere without me."

"By no means," Mrs Purviance exclaimed. "To break up a party of pleasure in such a way would be monstrous and unthinkable."

I blushed for I felt that I was at a grave disadvantage in not knowing how to conduct myself in fashionable society, and feared I had suggested something that was not *comme il faut*.

As we began to walk towards the gate Mr Mompesson said: "I understand and respect your scruples, but you need have no fear. Mrs Purviance will be present, and I am certain you cannot think that she would lend herself to any action that savoured in the least of impropriety?"

This made it difficult for me to continue to resist, and I found myself in a state of confusion from which Mrs Purviance herself rescued me by saying: "It is unkind of us to seek to persuade Miss Quilliam to act in disregard of her scruples."

The kindness with which she spoke had the effect of allaying my suspicions, and without reflecting any further I exclaimed: "I will not abridge the evening's pleasure for merely selfish reasons. Mr Mompesson, I accept your invitation with gratitude."

I was wrong and readily acknowledge it now. But consider my situation: I had never had an evening of such excitement in all my life; I had drunk a glass or two of wine to which I was wholly unaccustomed; and, foolishly, I was afraid to seem provincial and ignorant of good society. How often do we make decisions — or let them be made by default — because we weigh insignificant factors like these in the scale against much weightier ones!

The carriage took us to a street near Leicester-square where, at past midnight, I was amazed to find the pavements thronged with people of both sexes who appeared to be among the most fashionable members of Society. Everything dizzied and overwhelmed me: the flaring gas-jets, the plate-glass windows, the magnificent carriages and liveries, and the profusion of lights, rich perfumes, and the odours of exotic foods. Yet even as I admired, I was not so dazzled that I failed to see the expressions of cunning, selfishness, despair, and other emotions on the countenances of the glittering denizens of those streets.

On alighting from the carriage we entered a fashionable supper-house in Panton-street where Mr Mompesson was obviously known for he was greeted respectfully by name. We were led upstairs and shewn to a private dining-room in a manner which seemed to imply — though how could I be judge of such things? — that it had been reserved for us. There a repast of richness and delicacy beyond my experience was quickly laid before us. I was very careful to drink nothing but soda-water, for I was on my guard; not a word, however, was uttered during the meal that gave me the slightest cause for suspicion.

Suddenly, as we were sitting over our ices and hot-house fruits, the door opened and to my dismay Tom Mompesson entered. He was in regimentals for he had very recently been gazetted to a cornetcy. It was equally apparent that he had passed the evening in soldierly conviviality.

As we stared at him he cried: "I am't too late for grubbing, am I?"

"There are ladies present, Tom," his brother said warningly.

"Why, what a surprise!" Harry said, looking at the newcomer with ill-concealed distaste.

"Ladies?" the younger Mr Mompesson said, blinking and squinting at myself and Mrs Purviance. "Why, dammit, so they are! I declare, well done, old fellow." Then he turned to Harry: "What the deuce do you mean by saying it's a surprise?"

"Tom," his brother commanded. "Don't stand there by yourself like a noun substantive for want of a chair." He smiled at me as if to reassure me in the face of this new situation: "Have I remembered my grammar, Miss Quilliam?"

As Tom Mompesson advanced, blundering into the table as he seated himself, Harry said: "More grace, Tom. Try to follow the advice of Chesterfield and do everything in minuet time."

"Minuets be damned. The only time we military fellows know is double-time."

"My congratulations on your commission, Mr Thomas," Mrs Purviance said.

"My dear fellow," said Harry with a glance around the table; "is there any hope of your being sent out to clear up this trouble with Constantinople?"

"Cons ... Consent ... Be deuced! Is that in Burma?" the new arrival asked, downing a glass of champagne.

The other gentlemen laughed and Mr Mompesson said to me: "I think you could teach my brother the use of the globe, Miss Quilliam, with profit to himself and, perhaps, to our nation's foreign policy. Though rectifying the deficiences of his education would be a large task. His last tutor, though an excellent shot, was, I believe, wholly illiterate."

"Pay no attention to them, Mr Thomas," Mrs Purviance said. "They are envious of the magnificent costume."

"It is certainly very fine," Harry said, and added wickedly: "Could we not send that out to frighten the Ottoman?"

"A capital idea!" Mr Mompesson exclaimed. "A whole army of 'em. Stuffed with straw and with a headpiece of wood under the helmets. I'll be sworn no Turk of them could tell the difference."

"When I think of England defended by an army of Toms," Harry began with mock-solemnity, "I say to myself: thank God for the Royal Navy."

"What are you saying?" Mr Thomas Mompesson said angrily, pouring himself another beaker. "Deuce take your cleverness! I'm glad I am't as clever as you."

"I assure you, I whole-heartedly reciprocate that sentiment."

"And yet," said the hapless cornet's brother, "deuce take me if I don't feel myself growing dull from mere good-natured sympathy with you, Tom."

"Why, if it's jokes you want," Mr Thomas Mompesson said, smiling in my direction, "I'll tell you a good story I heard in the mess last night from Masterson." He began to laugh: "It's about a private soldier of Ours. That's the 25th. Hussars," he explained to me.

"I hope this is fitted to the present company," Harry said.

"Aye, for it's a story about a lady, don't you see? Well he was a good-looking fellow, it seems. In Saunderson's battalion. (Did I say that already?) They saw service at Barakpoor in that mutiny, don't you know? What was I saying? Oh yes, your friend Pamplin would care to meet him, I dare say, Harry. Anyway, it seems ... Hah, hah, hah."

He became speechless with laughter and his brother said: "Well, what of it, you poltroon?"

"It seems he caught the fancy of a lady, a rich widow in the town."

"I warned you, Tom," his brother said angrily. "Now hold your tongue."

"And she invited him to an assignation," the cornet continued.

I looked at Mrs Purviance and saw to my distress that she was smiling good-naturedly. Mr Mompesson, however, attempted to shout his brother down but the cornet persevered:

"And Masterson asked him what he'd brought back and be damned if the fellow didn't show him a bank-note of twenty pounds!"

At this he laughed immoderately until he suddenly broke off. I was looking down but I heard him say angrily: "Dammit if I ain't forgot something. It was deuced funny when Masterson told it."

"Bring your man next time, Tom, to stand behind your chair and laugh at your jokes," said Harry, standing up and opening the door. "It's too hard for you to have to cut them and laugh at them in the bargain."

"Out you go, Tom," said his brother, lifting him to his feet. "You're not fit for decent society."

Protesting and cursing, he was bundled into the passage and the door shut behind him.

All I could think of now was getting away from there, and I hardly noticed when, just at this moment, a waiter brought in a note for Mr Mompesson. He read it and told us that a party of friends of his, who were also known to Harry and to Mrs Purviance, were dining elsewhere in the establishment and had recognised the Mompesson crest on the carriage at the door. Before I understood what was happening, the two gentlemen were leaving the room in order, they explained, to speak to their friends. A moment later, Mrs Purviance also made her excuses and left me.

I was relieved to find myself alone. An instant later, however, the door opened and Mr Thomas Mompesson came blundering back into the room saying: "Deuce take it if I ain't remembered the point of Masterson's story. You see, he told the fellow the honour of the regiment was at stake and he should bring back proof of ... "

At this point he broke off and stared round the room. "I say, missy, have they all gone and left you? Why, then we shall be cozy together, shan't we? Come, give me a buss."

As he advanced towards me I rose to my feet to try to escape, but since he stood between me and the door I was unable to flee.

"Come a step nearer, Mr Mompesson, and I will scream," I declared.

He stood blinking at me and swaying slightly: "Why, you minx. This ain't what Davy told me you'd say."

"How dare you!" I cried.

"Why, dammit," he cried and stepped forward.

At that moment the door opened and you may imagine my relief when Mr Mompesson entered. He appeared to take in the situation at a glance for he seized his brother by the scruff of his collar and swiftly ejected him, turning the lock behind him.

Nearly swooning with relief, I found myself, without resistance, enfolded in Mr Mompesson's arms. Now, however, I discovered a new peril for my rescuer began to shower kisses upon me, and I realized that I had substituted one danger for another, and a much worse one. He told me he had fallen passionately in love with me and said that he could not know a moment's rest until I was his, and much more in that vein. When I protested, he accused me of coquetry, saying that I had set out to drive him mad with passion and had now succeeded and must bear the consequences. In brief, he made a proposal of a nature which I was wholly unprepared to listen to, imploring me to appoint a rendez-vous. When I refused to countenance such a suggestion, he accused me of mere prevarication and eventually grossly insulted me with a proposition which put a monetary value upon my chastity.

The more I opposed his desires the more inflamed he became, and when I reflected that I was alone in a locked room with a rich and unscrupulous voluptuary in a house in which a woman's cries for help would not be answered, I realized that I had to act decisively to defend myself.

I hardly know whether to be proud or ashamed of what followed. Reaching behind my persecutor I snatched up a fruit-knife from the table and threatened him with it. He laughed at me and reached out to take it. I am not sure how it happened or what my intention was, but as he seized my hand the point of the knife bore down against his face and cut a wound from above his eye to the cheek-bone. Instantly he was blinded by the flow of blood and forced to release me. In a moment I had unlocked the door and was fleeing along the passage, down the stairs and out into the street.

The insults I endured as I made my way through that infamous quarter I will not recount. A scene that had appeared so magnificent from the window of a carriage now presented itself in a very different light to a young woman unescorted and immodestly dressed for the streets. For, having had to abandon dear Henrietta's shawl in my precipitate flight, I was bare-shouldered. Under these circumstances it was impossible to ask my way without exposing myself to insult, and for more than an hour I wandered in circles, constantly finding myself drawn back into that whirlpool of vice that swirls about Leicester-square. How could I have seen that place as anything but the resort of wickedness and misery! Now it flashed before my eyes like a hideous dream: the desperate or reckless faces of the women in their tawdry dresses, the coaches crawling along the kerb, the cigar-divans and coffee-houses open all night with flambeaux burning outside them to draw in the vicious or the lost.

At last, however, I reached the house in Brook-street, conscious of the irony that I had had to seek refuge in the abode of my enemy, and terrified that if I had wounded him seriously I might find the authorities waiting to take me up. But now I became aware of an unanticipated difficulty for the house was in darkness and my timid knocks — I dared not hammer harder for fear of waking the whole household — failed to summon the nightwatchman. By now the carriage must have returned, whether or not it had brought Mr Mompesson home, and Jakeman, having locked up, would be in a drunken slumber — according to his unvarying practice — at the back of the house. After fifteen minutes I gave up the attempt and walked round to the mews where I found all dark in the coachman's house and no light showing in the grooms' quarters above the coach-house. Though I felt a deep repugnance at the idea of raising these servants and exposing myself to the gossip of the whole establishment, I reflected that the head-coachman, Mr Phumphred, was a kindly man whose discretion might be relied upon.

I therefore knocked at his door until he came down in his night-shirt and admitted me. He was amazed to see me and explained that Mr Mompesson had told him, when the rest of the party had left the supper-house, that I had made my own way home in a hackney-coach. And yet, he told me, his suspicions had been aroused, especially by the fact that Mr Mompesson's face was cut — though, he assured me, only very superficially. He had taken Mrs Purviance to her house and then left the two young gentlemen in the neighbourhood of Covent-garden where he believed Mr Mompesson intended to find lodging at the Hummums Hotel, and had then brought the carriage home, assuring the nightwatchman, before going to bed, that all of the party who intended to return that night were safely back.

Without telling him what had happened I gave him to understand that I had been ill-used and begged him to say nothing of my arrival under these circumstances. He implied that he knew enough of his young master to understand what I meant, and gave me the undertaking I sought. (I might add that so far as I know he was as good as his word.) He let me out through the back-door of his quarters into the yard by the laundry, from which I was able to enter the house by the kitchen-door — which, fortunately and quite improperly, is left unlocked at night to enable the laundry-maids to start their work in the morning without rousing Jakeman.

As you may conceive, I spent a second sleepless night — for now that I reviewed the evening it came to me that I had been the victim of what I can only call a charade. Of Mr Mompesson's wicked design there could be no doubt; his brother, vicious and brutal though he was, might be as much a dupe as I; but about the role that the other two members of the party had played I could only speculate.

CHAPTER 40

Although I felt that my position in the house was now unendurable, yet I dreaded to be forced to desert Henrietta whom I had come to love like a sister. I took my decision, and very early in the morning I wrote a note to my employers begging the favour of being permitted to wait upon them as soon as possible.

By the time my breakfast-tray had been removed, I had received no reply. All during morning-school with Henrietta I found myself constantly on the verge of weeping, and though I longed to tell her the whole story and hated having to dissemble, I knew that it would not be right to obtrude such a tale upon her innocence and thereby implicate a man who was, after all, her cousin — though I knew how little affection or respect she had for him.

At last, at about noon, a footman summoned me to the breakfast-room where I was received by my employers who were sitting at the table. Sir Perceval rose as briefly as possible and indicated that I should take a chair some distance from where they were sitting.

I began impulsively: "Your sons have grossly insulted me. Without an apology, I can stay no longer under this roof."

"Bigad, young woman," Sir Perceval exclaimed. "What in the name of damnation are you talking about?"

"Mr Mompesson has organised a base conspiracy against my person and my honour in which Mr Thomas Mompesson has played a shameful part. Both gentlemen must apologise in your presence and undertake never to speak to me again."

"Hoity toity, missy!" Sir Perceval began. "You take a deuced high tone ... "

His wife, however, interrupted him: "I cannot accept that my elder son would dishonour himself in the way you say."

"Nor Tom neither," the baronet exclaimed. "He's a rough and ready sort of boy but a true-hearted Briton."

As if her husband had not spoken, Lady Mompesson continued coldly: "Will you therefore describe, Miss Quilliam, precisely what you allege has occurred?"

Her manner of uttering these words stung me as much as their matter, but I collected my thoughts and described how Mr Mompesson had asked me to accompany him to the Gardens. I laid stress on the scrupulousness of my demand that Sir Perceval and herself should explicitly approve my joining the party, and my self-possession returned as I became conscious of the blamelessness of my own conduct. But when I came to a description of the exchange of letters, Lady Mompesson curtly bade me stop and explain myself.

"I know," she said, "of no such communication."

At this I felt a first intimation of alarm, but I remembered that I still had Sir Perceval's reply to my note and handed it to him.

He glanced at it briefly: "A counterfeit," he pronounced. "Clever, I grant you, but nevertheless a fraud."

He crumpled it up and threw it in the fire.

Now my self-possession began to dissipate.

"What can this mean!" I exclaimed. "This is the reply that the man-servant carried back from you."

Clearly fraud had been practised upon me, but I was uncertain who had collaborated in it. The fact that Sir Perceval had so swiftly destroyed my one piece of evidence was, to say no more, unfortunate.

"Even if this story were true," Lady Mompesson said, "I am amazed that you could be so ... naif, let us say, as to imagine that we could countenance your visiting a pleasure-gardens at night in the company of our son. At the very best your discretion is at fault; at worst ... " She broke off.

I saw that if I did not keep calm I was lost. "I am not so naif, Lady Mompesson," I replied. I turned to her husband. "That letter referred to a Mrs Purviance, did it not?"

"It did," he confirmed.

"Your son assured me that this lady, who was to be a member of the party, was an old friend of yours, Lady Mompesson."

"Stuff!" she cried. "I never heard the name until this moment."

At this I cried: "Send for your son! Let me, in common justice, challenge him to deny that I am telling the truth."

"What!" she exclaimed. "Our son to be arraigned by a governess! You are impertinent, Miss Quilliam."

"Then at least send for the man-servant, Edward," I begged.

They looked at each other and Lady Mompesson nodded. Sir Perceval pulled the bell-rope that hung behind his chair.

"Leaving aside this question of the note," Lady Mompesson went on, "what is the rest of your allegation?"

Mastering my anger with difficulty, I described the incident at the supper-house while they listened in silence, occasionally glancing at each other with what seemed to me to be expressions of disbelief and contempt. Just as I had finished describing my escape, the footman entered.

"Edward," said Sir Perceval, "did you, the day before yesterday, carry a letter from Miss Quilliam to myself and Lady Mompesson, and convey my reply back to her?"

He looked at all of us as if in surprise: "No, sir," he said. "I ain't never carried no message from Miss Quilliam. I don't attend upon the governess and nivver have. That's the third footman's charge."

"That will be all," Sir Perceval said.

As the man went out he glanced at me and I knew from his look that Mr Mompesson had bribed him. I had had occasion once or twice to rebuke him for his slackness in attending upon me and I guessed that he resented me. Now I understood that my employers were as much victims of the deception practised by their son as I. For a moment I reflected on its ingenuity and realized that I had proof of nothing. Even if I were given the chance to challenge Mr Mompesson I would gain nothing, for he would assert that I had readily accepted his invitation and that the story of the exchange of notes was a fabrication designed to protect myself in retrospect. He would also deny having assured me that Mrs Purviance was a friend of his mother. In short, I had proof of nothing — the very note had been destroyed — and all the evidence was against me. The significance of my position was quickly spelt out to me.

"I am prepared to credit," said Lady Mompesson, "at least this much of your story: that my son invited you to the Gardens and that you accepted his invitation; and that you afterwards accompanied him to what was clearly a night-house in an infamous district of the metropolis of whose character I cannot believe even the greenest girl from the country could really be in ignorance. Your conduct displayed extreme indiscretion — to say the least — for one in your position and that, I take it, is why you have concocted that story of the letter from Sir Perceval and the forgery in support of it. In making you that invitation my son cannot be blamed for anything more than the predisposition towards gallantry natural in a young man. Whether or not he offered you the insult you allege seems to me to be entirely by the way, for once you had consented to go with him and two utter strangers to such a place as that at such an hour, you had clearly forfeited the claim upon a gentleman's respect to which every honourable woman of superior rank has a right."

I listened with the strangest feeling of detachment. There was nothing I could say in my defence for I had been completely outwitted and I only wondered whether Lady Mompesson really believed me guilty of what she charged, or whether she knew very well what her son was capable of.

At that moment she said: "All that puzzles me about the incident is the question of what your motive is in making this allegation. Do you want money for refraining from making a scandal? If so, I assure you, we are not to be so easily intimidated."

"Aye," put in Sir Perceval, "try the worst that you can do, young woman. I should like to see you."

My eyes were clouded with tears and I was afraid to trust my voice: "Lady Mompesson, Sir Perceval, I beg you not to disbelieve me. If you do, you are collaborating with your son in the ruin of a defenceless creature whose good name is her only fortune."

"Sir Perceval," Lady Mompesson said, "will you be good enough to ring the bell again?" He did so and then his wife said to me: "If you think you can prevent me from circulating to all the registry-offices at this end of Town a statement that I am unwilling to provide you with a character, then you are mistaken. That should show you how little I am afraid of your threats."

At that moment the footman entered in response to the summons.

"Robert, ask Mr Assinder to attend immediately," Lady Mompesson said.

When the servant had gone I said: "I have made no demands for money and no threats, Lady Mompesson. And your action would make it impossible for me ever again to earn my living in the only way open to me that is compatible with my upbringing and station."

To this she merely answered: "An individual in my position has a responsibility to Society to protect others against the entry into their family of a brazen adventuress."

My eyes burned at these monstrous words. Before I could answer there was a knock and the steward entered.

"Mr Assinder," Lady Mompesson asked, "have this person's wages been paid to the quarter?"

"They have, Lady Mompesson," he replied, looking at me with insolent surprise.

"She leaves the house this very day — in fact, by the end of the forenoon."

"Very good, my lady," Mr Assinder answered.

"I owe it to myself," I exclaimed, "not to accept passively such ill-usage before a third party, but to state unequivocally that I repudiate the allegations made against me."

From this moment Lady Mompesson neither looked at nor addressed me. She said to the steward: "See that she has no communication with Miss Henrietta before she goes."

"Oh cruel!" I cried. "May I not explain why I am to part from her so suddenly?"

Still Lady Mompesson ignored me:

"Do not leave her until she is out of the house. Then come to me and tell me she is gone."

I stood unable to move, so great was my astonishment at being treated in this way, until at last Mr Assinder took me by the arm and led me from the room. As we passed through the hall he sent a footman for the housekeeper, and when she joined us they accompanied me to my rooms and watched as I packed my boxes. The grief that was uppermost in my mind was the idea of leaving Henrietta without saying farewell and explaining something of what had happened, for I dreaded to think that she would hear a version of events that would cast discredit upon me. Though I hoped to be able to send a message through Fanny, the lady's maid who attended upon Henrietta and her great-aunt, I was given no opportunity to do so.

A hackney-coach was summoned and I was put into it with my boxes by Mr Assinder and the housekeeper like a chamber-maid caught stealing the linen. All the servants must have assumed I had been convicted of some grave offence, and I hated to imagine how the scene which the steward had witnessed between myself and my erstwhile employers would be embroidered in the telling. Though I had been fighting back tears in the determination that I should not weep before my enemies, now that I was alone in the coach I gave way to my grief. When the driver had put up the steps he peered through the window to ask me where he should go, and now for the first time the full extent of my plight was borne in upon me with the realization that I had nowhere to go and no friend to help me. I directed him to drive to my former lodgings in Coleman-street, even though I knew I could not afford to stay there longer than a night or two. Since the end of the quarter was only three weeks away, I had little of my last wages left, and when I had paid the fare I possessed in all the world but three pounds and a few shillings.

I stayed at Mrs Malatratt's house that night and the next while I began my search for cheaper lodgings and some means of earning my living. When I gave my name at two of the three registry-offices for the employment of governesses, the clerk would not even put me on the books. At the third he pretended to, but I saw that this was a courteous fraud. It became clear that Lady Mompesson had kept her word, but even if she had not, I would have found it almost impossible to find suitable employment as I discovered when I resorted to inserting and answering private advertisements in the newspapers. For the difficulty was that, having no character from a previous employer, I could not account for my time since leaving the school in Portsmouth, and therefore found that no respectable family was prepared to consider me.

I took cheaper lodgings and it was now that I had the altercation — about which you know — with Mrs Malatratt over the boxes that I had left with her the previous year, and whose quite valuable contents I now wanted to sell, for she suddenly demanded that I should pay an extortionate rent for the space they had occupied.

My history since that time is quickly told. I had to keep moving to ever more inexpensive lodgings and as my savings dwindled was forced to take up plain-work to earn my bread. I found too little of that to keep me, and shortly after I came here I fell ill from the low-fever and want of nourishment, and believe I would certainly have died had not Mrs Peachment nursed me.

A few weeks before you found me, I received a visit from one who appeared to regard herself as an old friend, and who must have devoted a considerable effort to tracing me through Mrs Malatratt. This was none other than Mrs Purviance, who came to offer me money and assistance. I declined both of them for I have had leisure to reflect on the events of that fateful night, and I believe that Mrs Purviance played no honourable role in the charade that was practised at my expense.

BOOK IV

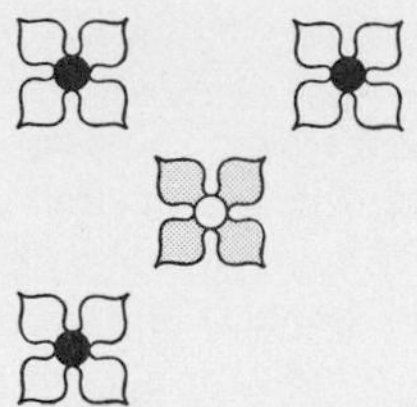

Faces from the Past

CHAPTER 41

Once again I invite you to accompany me into the private closet of the old counting-house by the derelict wharf, where Mr Clothier, red-faced, is shouting at Mr Sancious: "Then where the deuce is she?"

"I don't precisely know, but … "

"Find her! You cheated me. You haven't been just with me, Sancious. You undertook to deliver her up. You've taken my money under false pretences and that's a thing I shan't stand for. Everyone thinks they can cheat me. There's no justice left in England now! I was cheated in the cradle!"

"But pray consider what I have risked for your sake, Mr Clothier. Barbellion knows that I betrayed him because of the abduction attempt. He is a man to be feared amongst us lawyers. He may destroy me. But I will find her, my dear sir, do not fear. And when I do, remember that I have her promissory note."

"What if Barbellion gets to her first? Do you know how long I have laboured to outwit those accursed Mompessons?"

"*I*'ll get to her first, I promise you. I have an ally who is trusted by her."

The old gentleman stares at him: "Whom do you mean?" He comes close and peers into the attorney's face: "Who is he?"

"You must not ask me."

"Why the devil not?"

"Because I have undertaken to conceal that individual's identity."

At that moment there is the sound of the street-door banging and then rapid steps in the outer office.

Mr Vulliamy, without ceremony, bursts into the closet flushed and excited: "I have found her! I have found her!"

He turns and beckons to someone behind him, and there shuffles in after him a short man with a hunched back wearing a greasy benjamin and carrying a fur cap in his hand. He gazes at the old gentleman in a somewhat sideways manner as if too awed to look at him directly, and pulls at his forelock.

"Come, Acehand," Mr Vulliamy prompts him. "Tell your story to Mr Clothier."

The stranger shuffles his feet and says: "Why, it's like this. Mr Vulliamy comes round to see the books jist now and I shows him this and tells him about the young ooman as pledged it. A young ooman with a boy."

As he speaks he brings something from the depths of his pocket and lays it on his palm. Mr Sancious leans forward to look at it but the old gentleman keeps his glittering eyes on the face of the pledge-taker.

"Well, I looks at it and I thinks, Hello, I reckon I knows that there face. But I couldn't call it to mind. Anyways, this was, oh, seven or eight months agone and she come in every month since then to pay the interest. Name of Halfmoon. And each time I thinks and I thinks but it ain't no good. And then suddenly it comes into me head. For I only seen him jist the once, Mr Clothier, sir, when I met you with him many years back. (You wouldn't call it to mind, sir, but I was walking one Sunday on Bow-common with me old ooman.) He was hardly more nor a lad for that was nigh on twenty year agone. And I knowed that ... That's to say ... Well, I said to meself, Mr Clothier will want to know about this. So I told Mr Vulliamy here about it and he brung me straight to you." With timid resentment he adds: "Runnin' all the way."

The old gentleman takes the locket and holds it up to the window. After a moment he turns, suddenly pale now, and says: "Why, you're quite right. I am most confoundedly glad to see this. When is the interest next due?"

"Why, in about a week."

"Thank you, Acehand. You will be rewarded for your astuteness. See to it, Vulliamy." He adds in an undertone: "Give him a guinea."

"It's a honour, sir, to be of help to your fambly," the pledge-taker says and shuffles out.

The old gentleman stares at the attorney in triumph: "A fiddlestick for your help! And your blessed ally!" he cries (though he doesn't say "blessed"). Then in an undertone he says to himself: "I think I see my way clear now."

"My assistance is available whenever you need it," Mr Sancious says.

"Yes, yes," the old gentleman mutters rudely.

The attorney bows curtly and takes his leave. As he goes out he passes Mr Vulliamy in the door-way, who comes in and says to his employer: "I gave him his reward and he was very grateful."

"Good, good," the old gentleman says.

"And what about *my* reward, sir?"

"Oh very well. What did I say? Twenty guineas?"

"You undertook to cancel one of the bonds. Do you not recall?"

"Did I, by heavens?" He glares at his managing-clerk: "Well, if I said so then I will. Never let it be said that I do not keep my word." Then he takes a key from around his neck and unlocks a strong-box in a dark corner of the chamber. He removes a document and hands it to Mr Vulliamy who opens it, nods, and then passes it back. His face twisted with pain, the old gentleman rolls it up again and thrusts it into the flame of the candle and when it has blazed up, throws it into the fireplace.

Watching the delight apparent on Mr Vulliamy's face as the paper turns to shiny ash, the old gentleman locks the strong-box again, amiably remarking: "Don't forget, I still have the other." Then he beckons his clerk nearer and says softly: "Follow Sancious day and night. I want to know everything he does and everybody he sees."

"Why, Mr Clothier!" the clerk exclaims. "Do you trust nobody?"

"Nobody," the old gentleman answers calmly. "Nobody but you," he adds, glancing towards the strong-box.

CHAPTER 42

By the time Miss Quilliam had finished her relation, dawn had largely chased away the brief summer night and the candle-flame glowed yellow in the pale light.

"What a terrible story," my mother sighed. "How you have suffered, Helen."

I heard the murmur of their voices as they made preparations to retire, and before I drifted into sleep myself, the narrative I had just overheard ran through my mind and I wished I could have asked Miss Quilliam some questions. She had not, for one thing, explained how, arriving in obscurity from a provincial town with no friends in London, she had come to be employed by the Mompessons. And I fell asleep thinking about other things in her account that had puzzled me.

When I awoke an hour or two later the dawn light was coming in through the grimy windows and it was clear that it was going to be another hot sunny day. I found my mother asleep and no sign of Miss Quilliam.

When my mother wakened a few minutes later she explained that our friend had gone out to make some purchases.

"What has she gone for?" I asked rather irritably. "I'll wager it's ... "

"Don't be harsh on her, Johnnie. She has had such a hard life, you know. When I was no more than the age she is now I had experienced nothing but kindness and comfort."

"Perhaps that made it easier for her," I suggested.

"I don't believe anything has been easy for her. While you were sleeping she told me her story."

"Did she tell you everything, Mamma?"

"No," my mother answered. "I am sure she left some things out and changed others." I was intrigued by this and wondered if she had noticed what had alerted me, but then, as she went on, I realized that she had interpreted Miss Quilliam's motives very differently: "I imagine that she left things out because she wanted to spare my feelings." She considered for a moment and then said: "And yet I can hardly imagine how her story could be any harsher than what she recounted."

At that moment there was a knock at the door. At my mother's cry of "Come in!" a well-dressed lady of about fifty entered.

She was tall and handsome, and, resplendently dressed in a grey beaver hat with an ostrich plume, a blue silk dress, and a velvet shawl trimmed with ermine, and carrying a magnificent reticule of linked steel rings, she seemed not in the least discomposed at finding herself in so incongruous a situation. Indeed, self-possession was the distinctive feature of her frank, even bold, countenance, for although she seemed surprised at seeing us, she smiled very graciously:

"Do not let me disturb you, good people. I expected to find a young lady of the name of Miss Quilliam, but I presume that she is no longer living here?"

"Indeed she is!" my mother cried. "She has only gone out for a few minutes."

The strange lady repressed a start of well-bred astonishment at my mother's manner of speech. She looked at her closely as she smiled: "I am delighted to know it," she said, "for I have come to this district especially to visit her."

As she spoke she glanced round the bare room and surveyed our sparse possessions with an air which, though it clearly read the story of poverty and distress that they told, was oddly inoffensive.

"Pray be seated," said my mother who had risen and now indicated a chair.

The lady settled herself in the best, though battered chair, not quite managing to conceal her distaste at its appearance.

"I wish I could offer you something," my mother said, standing by her; "but we have nothing at all. I could send my son to borrow some tea of a neighbour."

"Do not think of it," the stranger said. Then, laying her hand on my mother's arm, she continued: "My dear, I perceive that you were bred to something very different from this, and that you have not borne poverty for very long."

"That is so," she answered in a trembling voice. "I have been very unlucky."

"Won't you tell me how you came to this?"

My mother hesitated and the lady glanced towards me: "Is it a story of betrayal?" she asked in a tone of deep compassion.

"Yes," my mother answered and I guessed that she was thinking of Bissett.

"We poor women," the unknown lady said, shaking her head. "It is our lot to suffer, to trust and to be betrayed. Is this of recent date?"

"Yes," my mother said. "Only a year ago the three of us were so happy together, and now ... "

She broke off and the lady looked at her compassionately.

"My dear, if it would not distress you, I would very much like to hear your story. But what am I thinking of to forget my manners so completely! For you must have no idea of whom you are speaking to. I am an old acquaintance of Miss Quilliam. My name is Mrs Purviance."

"Oh yes," said my mother. "Helen has spoken of you."

"Indeed?"

"She told me only last night how very badly she was treated by her former employers," said my mother.

"She was indeed," Mrs Purviance agreed rather vaguely. "She is not strong enough to earn her bread by the kind of work she has taken upon herself. I have told her that with her gifts she could do something better fitting her station, and I have been trying to persuade her to take shelter under my roof."

"That is kind. Very kind. I have been very concerned about her health."

"You see, my dear, I am fortunate enough to be a widow of independent means. I have a house in Gough-square — No. 5 — a most respectable address. (The Great Cham himself resided in the square!) And there I receive a great deal of good company. Indeed, only the very best company. You do understand me?"

"Oh yes."

"I am always on the *qui-vive* for well-brought-up young women who have fallen upon misfortune. And they must be possessed of a certain savoir-faire. Now you, my dear, are very charming." She reached up to touch my mother's tresses: "You are like a marigold with your fair hair and forget-me-not eyes."

My mother smiled with pleasure: "You are kind."

"Nothing pleases me more than to find a sister in distress. But Miss Quilliam — Helen — is too proud. I hope you wouldn't be too proud." At this my mother shook her head. "For I would be very glad," Mrs Purviance continued, "to offer hospitality to you at any time."

"Would you indeed?"

"Most assuredly." She glanced in my direction: "Only I am afraid I could not accept a child."

My mother's disappointment was so manifest that it cut me like a knife.

She exclaimed: "Oh, we could not be parted."

"But surely some arrangement could be arrived at? He could board at a school perhaps?"

"We should both hate that! But anyway I could not afford it."

"My dear," exclaimed Mrs Purviance with a patronizing smile, "I haven't made myself clear. I see we have much to talk about." She glanced at me. "But I wonder if this young gentleman might find something at a pastry-cook's to spend a six-pence on?"

She opened her reticule and was bringing out her pocket-book when the door opened and Miss Quilliam came in.

When she caught sight of our visiter her face took on an expression I had never seen on it before. Her colour drained away and her eyes seemed to narrow and grow hard: "I am surprised to find you here again, Mrs Purviance."

"My dear, how very glad I am to see you looking so much better than on the occasion of my last visit."

"What do you want?" Miss Quilliam said coldly.

"Well, my dear Helen — may I call you that? — I came to learn how you were and to renew my offer, but finding you out I have introduced myself to this delightful young lady." She hesitated as she turned towards my mother: "Miss ... ?"

"Mrs Mellamphy," said my mother. Then she gently added: "Johnnie is my son."

"Ah, of course. How stupid of me," Mrs Purviance said, recovering quickly: "You said so, did you not?"

She now conveyed to us that she was charmed to make our acquaintance and shook hands with both of us.

"I give you the answer now that I gave you before," Miss Quilliam said to her. "I do not desire your assistance."

"Well, my dear, the time may come," Mrs Purviance said, rising to her feet and brushing down her gorgeous silk dress as if afraid that it had taken some infection from the chair; "when you will think more kindly of me." She smiled very sweetly at my mother: "I fear I must go without hearing your story. But if you will come to my house one morning, I will be very glad to listen to it then. Be sure to come before noon."

"Thank you Mrs Purviance," said my mother, "I will do so."

"Now will you remember the direction?" she began. "It is ... "

"I assure you, Mrs Purviance," said Miss Quilliam, "that Mrs Mellamphy has as little use for your kind of assistance as I."

My mother looked from one to the other in perplexity.

"My dear Miss Quilliam," said Mrs Purviance, "I think you must let this lady decide for herself." As she walked towards the door she turned and took something from her reticule: "Now I am going to offend you both, I know. But I cannot leave this scene of poverty with a clear conscience when I have so much money in my purse."

She took out a coin but made no attempt to give it to Miss Quilliam. Instead she laid it down on the little table at which we worked and ate.

"I will not have it back," she said, "so you must do with it what you will. Please use it, if only for the child's sake." As she reached the door she said: "I will not trouble you another time, Miss Quilliam. Goodbye."

My mother and I returned her greeting but Miss Quilliam inclined her head very slightly and continued to stare at her with a cold and hostile expression which relaxed only when the door closed behind her.

My mother said timidly: "How much did she leave? Go and see, Johnnie."

I went and looked at the bright gold coin without picking it up: "A sovereign."

The three of us could live well on such a sum for three weeks, and we now had only a shilling or two and no prospect of earning any more.

"To take that woman's money would bring nothing but evil," Miss Quilliam said.

"How can that be?" asked my mother.

"The part she played in the events I told you of was at best equivocal," Miss Quilliam said. "But since then I have learned things about her which I would tell you if I were not satisfied that she will not show her face here again, and if I had not prevented her from giving you her address."

My mother glanced at me guiltily, but refrained from telling her friend that our visiter had earlier given the direction to her house. "Then if we are safe from her," she said, "surely there can be no harm in using the money?"

"I will not touch it," said Miss Quilliam. "Do with it what you will. Only do not ask me to share anything that comes from it."

She raised the stone jug and poured a glass of what little remained.

My mother picked up the coin and whispered to me: "Johnnie, we will buy bread and something from the pastry-cook."

"And candles," I suggested.

Miss Quilliam must have caught the last word: "Not candles," she objected, "for I would derive benefit from them and I have a superstitious fear even of that."

"Then Johnnie," said my mother in the tone she used when she said something she knew I would disagree with; "we will use some of the money to pay this month's interest on the locket. It must be paid by today or I will forfeit it, and I need only one shilling and six-pence."

"What nonsense," I cried. "We can't waste money like that."

"But Johnnie, it would be an investment for it is worth far more than what we pledged it for."

"But you know we will never be able to redeem it!"

"Don't say that!" she cried. "We will one day. All will be well again just as it was before. You will see."

I looked at her in surprise and she said: "The codicil. We will sell it for a great deal of money."

I glanced towards Miss Quilliam who gave no sign of having heard.

"We must do nothing rash," I whispered, for what I had learned of the law from the two gentlemen had convinced me that the codicil could be worth much more to us than anyone would give us for it.

Seeing how upset she was at the prospect of losing the locket, however, I reluctantly consented to her wishes. By the time we had made our purchases at the pastry-cook's and eaten them (rather guiltily while Miss Quilliam sat at the other end of the room), it was early evening. The pawn-broker stayed open until ten o'clock, so we set off in good time through the warm streets and arrived there about an hour before the office was due to close.

The taker glanced up as we entered and it seemed to me that he took particular notice of us for he smiled and when my mother presented the duplicate and the money, he said: "I must ask you to wait a minute," and disappeared into a back-room. He was gone some time and I thought I heard voices talking softly. Then he came back and completed the formalities, endorsing our ticket for a further month.

When we returned to the street I glanced back and noticed two men — one of them strikingly tall — come out of the shop behind us. This surprised me for I had thought there were no other customers there. My suspicions having been aroused by this, I glanced round occasionally as we made our way home, and each time I thought I saw two figures stop and shrink back into the shadows. Darkness had fallen by now and although I felt safe enough on the crowded, lamp-lit streets, as we turned up Bennet-street I reflected that we were approaching Spread-Eagle-yard and the long, dark and empty alley that led from it into Tothill-street, and I wondered whether to advise my mother that we should take the longer way round. I was reluctant, however, to alarm her with what might be groundless suspicions.

Halfway along the alley I heard running feet. I turned but before I could even see our assailants I felt myself being seized from behind by strong arms. I began to scream but a hand was clasped over my mouth. I heard a cry from my mother that was choked off, and now I could see that she was being gripped by a second man who was at least six and a half feet tall.

"You know what we want," the tall man said. "I'm not going to ask you for it a second time. This is what I mean."

I heard the sound of his hand striking her hard against the face.

Then he said: "Now I'm going to take my hand away so you can tell me where it is. If you scream my friend will twist the boy's arm off."

My mother gasped: "Don't harm him! I'll find it."

I tried to shout out that she should not, but I was unable even to open my mouth. There was just light enough still for me to be able dimly to make out the figure of my mother's assailant. As well as being so tall he was cadaverously thin and I had the strangest feeling that I knew him. Suddenly I remembered: *he was the man who had jumped into the carriage on the occasion when the young lady had tried to abduct me from Melthorpe!* Yet how could that be? How could this man have found us so long after?

"Hurry up," the man holding me urged.

"It will take time," my mother cried, "for it is in an inner pocket beneath my petticoats."

"Just give her a sign that we don't have all day," said the tall man, and in obedience to this the one holding me drove my head against the wall. I felt a wave of nausea and seemed to be falling into a deep shaft.

Then as if from a great distance I heard my mother cry: "Oh please don't hurt him. I am finding it."

"Then hurry," shouted the tall man.

At that moment I heard the sounds of voices and laughter and thought at first that it was the effect of the blow on my head. But they were real! For a group of people was making its way towards us along the lane from the direction from which we had come.

"Damn it, Jack, do you hear that!" the man holding me exclaimed. "I told you we should have put them in a coach and done the job at our leisure."

"Never mind that now. Just keep a hold of the boy," Jack shouted. "And keep your mouth shut as I told you."

The men and women, about six or seven of them, were almost upon us. Their arrival had distracted the attention of the man holding me enough for me to manage to get my teeth apart and then close them with all my strength on a fleshy part of the hand that was fastened over my mouth.

The man swore and his grip weakened enough for me to shout: "For God's sake help us! We're being robbed!"

"She's my wife!" my mother's assailant cried.

"That's not true!" my mother exclaimed. "They are robbers!"

"You can't be flatts enough to believe such fustian, can you?" Jack shouted.

"Who are you crying a flatt?" said an Irish voice, speaking indistinctly.

"Mind your own business, Murphy," Jack shouted.

At this, the intoxicated Irishman struck him so that he let go of my mother who ran towards my attacker. Jack tried to follow her but several of the Irishmen grabbed him and seeing this, my assailant let go of me and tried to release his friend. As I moved away I glimpsed my tormentor's face: flat, reddish, topped with bristling eyebrows.

"Run, Mamma," I shouted, and we hastened down the alley as fast as we could. Within a minute or two we had gained Tothill-street, crossed it and dived down the lane opposite into the ancient and now infamous Almonry and then made our way through the back-courts into Orchard-street. Now that we were clear of any possibility of pursuit we slowed to a walk.

"Did they hurt you?" my mother sobbed, panting hard.

"No," I replied.

"Who were they and how did they know I have the codicil?" my mother cried.

"They followed us from the pawn-shop," I gasped.

"You are bleeding!" she cried catching sight of my face as we approached a street-lamp.

"I am not badly hurt," I said. "Come we must get home."

My mother stopped suddenly: "Is it safe to go home?"

"Yes," I said. "They do not know where we live. That is why they had to wait for us at the pawn-broker."

And yet, I asked myself, how could they have known to find us there? I hesitated to ask my mother any questions about this.

When we burst in upon Miss Quilliam a few minutes later I could see in her expression of alarm as if in a looking-glass, how ghastly we looked. One side of my mother's face was bruised so that it rose in a livid welt, and her lip was cut and swollen, while blood from the top of my head was running down my cheeks and neck, making it appear that my injuries were much worse than they were. We looked at each other in the light of the candle that Miss Quilliam lit and then my mother flung her arms round me weeping.

It was some time before poor Miss Quilliam could get any sense from us, but at last, while she bathed our injuries, we told her the bare facts of what had happened. To our disappointment we discovered that all but a few shillings of the money left from Mrs Purviance's sovereign had gone, presumably dropped in the course of my mother's attempt to produce the codicil, but the document itself was still safely in her possession. Miss Quilliam, who of course knew nothing of the codicil, listened curiously as we spoke of it and must have wondered as she gathered that it had been the cause of the attack.

"I'll never be able to get the locket back now," my mother kept sobbing.

Seeing how over-wrought and exhausted she was, Miss Quilliam put her to bed after giving her (somewhat to my dismay) a powerful draught to make her sleep.

When my mother was asleep Miss Quilliam held a whispered conference with me at the window. As we spoke we glanced occasionally at the bed across the room where, lying with the faint moonlight upon her face, my mother looked very young, so that it was almost as if she were a sleeping child under discussion by her anxious parents.

"This was no mere robbery was it?" Miss Quilliam began.

I shook my head.

"And it was a document in your mother's possession that they sought?"

I nodded for I believed no harm could come of confirming this.

"May I ask what it is?"

I hesitated, remembering Bissett's betrayal. Yet surely I could trust her?

"I know very little about it," I said, "except that it is a codicil to a will."

She said gravely: "You're very young to shoulder such a burden, but I must tell you that I don't believe your mother has the strength to bear up very much longer — I mean the strength of both body and mind."

I nodded.

"Can you think of any means of obtaining money?" Seeing me hesitate she prompted: "Is the codicil of any value, that someone is so anxious to obtain it?"

I remembered how suspicious I had become when Mr Sancious had made the same suggestion, but surely there could be no possibility of Miss Quilliam knowing any more than she was able to guess?

"Some people once offered to buy it," I said. "But my mother refused to sell it, although they offered a very large sum."

"I see that you don't mention their names. But tell me if you believe it was they who were responsible for this attack?"

I felt a particular delicacy in suppressing the names of the Mompessons since they were known to Miss Quilliam, but this was not my secret to divulge.

I said: "I don't believe they would go so far. However, from things that my mother has let drop it seems that there is another party who is determined to get hold of it and who would gain so much by it and is so ruthless that he would use any means."

I told her about the attempt to abduct me from the village and that I believed the same monstrously tall man was involved in both attempts. Then I went on: "My mother says that if this enemy of ours obtained it, our lives would be in danger, for he could only profit by it if she and I were both dead."

"How very strange. I don't understand enough about the law to know how that can be. What a pity that our legal acquaintances are no longer to hand."

I blushed at these words for I felt embarrassed at withholding from her what I had learned from the two gentlemen.

"But then what would be the consequences," she went on, "if the party who tried fairly to buy it, were to succeed in doing so?"

"My mother has told me that they would destroy it," I answered, "for in some way that I do not understand, its existence endangers their interests."

"Stranger and stranger," she said. "Then why has your mother refused their offer since it would at once end your financial hardship and put you out of danger?"

"I don't know," I said, rather shame-facedly. I was unable to admit that it was I who had dissuaded her from taking this course of action because of what I had learned about the law of inheritance of real property.

"Then don't you think we must persuade her to sell it?"

How much did she know, I wondered as I gazed into her grey eyes — so clear that it seemed unthinkable that she could be acting on hidden motives. For more reasons than I could calculate, I believed I could not tell her what Mr Pentecost and Mr Silverlight had shewn me to be a possibility. And she was surely right that our only reasonable course of action, now that we were in want and danger, was to sell the codicil to the Mompessons.

"I suppose so," I said.

It was now very late and we retired to rest. Sleep failed to come, however, as I lay wondering whether to trust Miss Quilliam and remembering some of the puzzles in her story. How had she obtained her post with the Mompessons? How was it that she could afford such expensive lodgings as Mrs Malatratt's on first coming to London? And then there was the business of the trunks: she had told us when we first came to her that they contained nothing of value, but in her account had appeared to contradict this.

The next morning, which dawned fine and dry though with intimations of later rain, we rose and breakfasted late. Then Miss Quilliam and I raised with my mother the question of selling the codicil.

I asked her if she thought that the party who had once offered for it would still be interested: "Oh yes," she replied. "More anxious than before, I imagine."

At the suggestion, however, that we should therefore offer to sell it to them, she said in alarm: "No, Johnnie, I can't do that."

"But why not?" I cried.

"I made a promise to my father. He spent so much time trying to obtain it. And it cost him ... it cost him his life."

"Whatever do you mean, Mamma?"

"Don't ask me about that!" she cried. "I shouldn't have said anything."

"Tell me at least, what did you promise him?"

"That I would hold it in trust and pass it on to my heir."

"Then you mean, it's really mine?"

"Yes, but only when you reach twenty-one."

"But why was it so important to your father to pass it on to me?"

She looked at me reproachfully and at last said: "Oh, Johnnie, you are wrong to make me tell you. But since you're determined to know, it's because it could be the means of bringing us a great fortune of which our family was cheated long ago."

"I guessed it!" I cried. So Mr Pentecost and Mr Silverlight had been right! "Tell me how!" I begged.

She shook her head: "I won't. And anyway, I don't understand it. It's too complicated. There's a letter that explains it all."

I knew that, for I well remembered the letter I had seen in the casket all those years ago which had first brought to my attention the name "Huffam".

Seeing that I was wavering, Miss Quilliam said: "Johnnie and I believe you should sell it."

Reluctantly I stood by my earlier undertaking, and so, supported by Miss Quilliam, I argued that my grandfather had had the best interests of his daughter and her heirs at heart in requiring that promise, and that in the present circumstances those interests were best served by parting with rather than retaining the codicil. Moreover, if she were holding it in trust for me then it was in a sense mine to dispose of as I chose.

She began to weaken and I followed up my attack: "Possession of it endangers us. We may be attacked again."

This frightened her and now at last she agreed to sell it. Miss Quilliam and I exchanged a surreptitious look of triumph.

"Mamma," I said, "will you now tell Miss Quilliam who the people are who wish to purchase it?"

"They are known to you, Helen," she said. "They are Sir Perceval and Lady Mompesson."

"I wondered if that were the case," she said, to my surprise, and my suspicions came flooding back. Then she laid my fears somewhat to rest by explaining: "For I know that they are cousins of yours, and you have never told me what errand took you to Mompesson-park that day I met Johnnie."

The problem now arose of how we should communicate with the Mompessons. My mother was terrified at the thought of either of us venturing onto the streets again because she was convinced that the whole district was being watched by agents of our enemy. This made difficulty enough, but she also feared that it would be unsafe for us to approach the Mompessons' house in case an observer had been posted outside to watch out for us. Although this seemed to me an irrational and excessive fear, I saw that there was no reasoning with her.

"Why can you not simply send a letter?" Miss Quilliam asked.

"Oh no!" she exclaimed. "That would not serve. It might be intercepted. I am sure he has an agent in the Mompessons' household. So any communication from myself must be taken by someone whom I can trust absolutely."

There was a short silence which was ended by Miss Quilliam saying reflectively: "I suppose *I* could take a message."

My mother clasped her hand and said: "Oh Helen, would you? But it would have to be placed directly in the hands of Sir Perceval or Lady Mompesson."

Miss Quilliam nodded.

My suspicions of her smouldered into life again.

"But Mamma," I cried, "it's too much to ask Miss Quilliam to do that. You forget how she was humiliated and persecuted by them."

They looked at me in surprise and I blushed to think how close I had come to revealing that I had overheard her story.

"Hush, Johnnie," Miss Quilliam said. "It will be hard to appear before them, but I will do it since I see it is the only way."

While my mother expressed her thanks, Miss Quilliam and I looked at each other and the thought tormented me: what were her motives?

In order to secure her admission to the house, my mother, with advice from Miss Quilliam and myself, wrote the following letter to the baronet:

"The 16th. of July 18--.

"Sir Perceval Mompesson:

"I am now prepared to sell the Codicil for the figure previously discussed between us. The Bearer of this will tell you where I am to be found. I urge you not to delay, for the other interested Party is close upon my Track.

"M. C."

I was intrigued to notice the initials with which my mother had signed the note. What *was* our real name?

Miss Quilliam looked out of window and seeing that the sky was clouding over, picked up the single ancient umbrella that our little household possessed and, in a hail of thanks and good wishes, left the room. It was now the middle of the morning and since we could not expect her to return for several hours, an anxious, restless period began.

"Mamma," I asked, "will the Mompessons really destroy the codicil?"

"Yes."

"Why?"

"I don't know if I should tell you," she answered, twisting her hands in her anxiety. "But then, what harm can it do now? Well, I will tell you. As far as I understand it — and, as you know, I have no head for legal matters — it casts doubt on the legality of their ownership of the estate at Hougham."

"And does it," I asked in excitement, "give you and me any right to the estate instead?"

The question caused her obvious pain: "Not in itself, but under certain circumstances it could. But they are so remote! Oh Johnnie, don't force me to tell you any more. I am betraying the trust my father laid upon me for your sake by selling it. Don't remind me of my guilt."

"But I have encouraged you to sell it," I said. "I am not reproaching you. I am only curious. May I not at least be permitted to read it before it is lost for ever?"

She wrung her hands in anguish. "Oh I don't know what to do."

Though I felt that I was being cruel, something beyond mere curiosity made me go on: "I think you should allow me to make a copy of it, Mamma."

"Very well," she said at last and drew out the package of soft-leather from which she removed the much-folded piece of parchment.

She handed it to me and when I tried to read it I saw that it was engrossed in a style of legal hand which I had never seen before and which, with the strange terminology, made it very difficult to understand.

Although it was much too soon for any result, my mother now took up her station at the window to watch for the return of Miss Quilliam and, perhaps, a representative of the Mompessons. Meanwhile I sat at the table and began to copy the codicil. Although the date it bore was so remote, it was in such good condition — apart from the fold-marks — that it might have been written that morning. Copying it was a laborious business since at first I could not interpret the letters but simply transcribed them slavishly without understanding. Gradually, however, the hand became familiar to me and I was able to make sense of it — of the words at least if not their meaning:

"I, Jeoffrey Huffam, do this day annex to this my last Will and Testament these Presents in witness whereto I set my hand and seal. Namely that I hereby create an Entail upon all the lands and hereditaments, tenements, messuages, and holdings: which Entail is vested in my Son, James, and the Heirs of his Body. In default of such Heirs the Entail shall pass to my only Grandson, Silas Clothier, on condition that he be alive at the determination of the aforementioned line. In the event of this Condition not being fulfilled, then the Entail shall pass to my Nephew, George Maliphant, and the Heirs of his Body.

"Witnessed in the presence of:

"Name. [*Illegible*.]

"Name. [*Illegible*.]

"Signed and sealed this Third day of September in the Year of Our Lord 1768 under the hand of Jeoffrey Huffam."

"Jeoffrey Huffam was your grandfather, wasn't he?" I asked.

"No, my great-grandfather," she said unwillingly. "So James was your great-grandfather, and John, my father, was your grandfather."

"Can you explain why Jeoffrey added this to his will?"

"He wanted to secure his property to his descendants for he feared that his son would sell it after his death. And so he tried to create an entail upon his heirs."

"And you and I are his heirs, aren't we?" She said nothing. "Aren't we, Mamma?"

She nodded.

"Then what happened to the codicil?"

"Somehow it was stolen when Jeoffrey died and that was why James was able to sell the estate."

Remembering what the two legal gentlemen had taught me I cried: "But that means that James did not break the entail but merely barred it."

My mother shuddered: "That is what my papa used to say, though I never understood what it meant."

"It means that the Mompessons have only the base fee to the estate which gives them nothing but the right to possession — seizance. That was all that James sold them when they bought the estate. You and I have inherited the fee-simple, though it is of no advantage to us. You see, the Mompessons retain the estate only while there is an entailed heir. If the line fails, then the fee-simple passes to the heir who has the right of remainder and he possesses the estate." I looked at the codicil and said: "That is someone called Silas Clothier. Who is he?"

She looked away.

"It's he who would inherit if you and I were to die," I prompted her. "Is he still alive? He must be very old." Still she said nothing. I remembered that she had once uttered this name in fear, and so I said: "He is our enemy, isn't he? It was he who sent Mr Barbellion to try to buy the codicil and who tried to abduct me when that failed and then bribed Bissett to betray us, and it was he who had us followed and attacked yesterday, wasn't it?"

She would say nothing and, seeing that my questions were frightening her, I gave them up.

Towards the middle of the afternoon while I was still sitting at the table studying the original and my copy, I was startled by a gasp. I looked up and saw that my mother had gone pale and was staring into the street. When I hurried to the window and looked out, I saw Miss Quilliam coming along the street in the company of a strange gentleman. And yet he was not strange for I seemed to know him: the burly figure, the heavy jowls and staring eyes beneath bushy brows. Just before they approached so near to our house that they passed from my view, I recognised him: it was Mr Barbellion!

"Betrayed!" my mother exclaimed. "We have been betrayed to our enemy!"

"Come!" I said, taking her arm and drawing her towards the door. As I passed the table I seized both the original document and my copy of it.

At the door, however, my mother refused to move any further.

"It is too late," she cried. "We cannot escape. We will meet them upon the stair."

"No, we'll go up," I cried.

She made no move, so I dragged her through the door and up the stairs to the next landing. As we climbed we heard footsteps on the flight below us, but we just managed to stay out of sight. (Often and often have I reflected on how differently our lives would have turned out if we had been a moment slower!) As we gained the top-most landing we heard a quick knock on our own door and then the sound of Miss Quilliam and Mr Barbellion going in.

"Quickly!" I whispered, "and quietly!"

I pulled her down the stairs, past our own door which the new arrivals had closed behind them, and out into the street. We ran to the end of it and up the next one, and then chose another at hazard and kept on running in this fashion until we were exhausted and knew not where we were.

We had come into a district of the metropolis that was quite strange to us, and, having entered through a wicket-gate, found ourselves in the quiet little yard of a large old church that stood between us and the bustle and clatter of a great thoroughfare. The fine weather of the morning had gone and it was now drizzling desultorily. Gasping for breath, we sat on a low wall.

My mother put her hands over her face: "I cannot understand it," she sobbed. "I cannot understand how she could do such a thing to us."

Indeed, I could not understand it either, but in the additional sense that I could not comprehend how Miss Quilliam had known where to find our enemy. For if even *I* had not been able to learn from my mother who these people were, how could *she* have known? Could it be that there were ramifications far beyond what I had imagined, and that her connexion with the Mompesson family had — in all innocence on her part — somehow led associates of our enemy to her? Or was it simply by chance that she was involved with them? I could not believe, however, that coincidence could stretch so far. The remaining and most horrible possibility was that she had been involved in the conspiracy from the very beginning. And yet I found it difficult to believe that she had betrayed us, though I could imagine no other explanation for her arrival with Mr Barbellion. I was about to raise this with my mother and try to untangle this web of apparent coincidences, accidents, and significant events, but I saw that she was past all reasoning.

"First Bissett and now Helen!" she cried. "Whom can I trust? To have known us for so long and have shared so many hardships, and then to deliver us into the power of our enemy!"

"We can't be sure that she did," I tried to object. "There may be some other explanation."

She wasn't listening for suddenly she said: "Where is the codicil?"

"I have it," I said. "Shall I keep it?"

"No," she cried. "Give it to me!"

She spoke with fierce, suspicious intensity as if she did not trust even me. I pulled it from my pocket and she snatched it from me with a wild look, folded it up in its package, and stuffed it into her own pocket.

Now I had to think of our situation. We were without lodging, hungry, and literally without a penny since we had given what little money we had to Miss Quilliam for any expenses incurred on her errand. It now began to rain more heavily and dusk was not far off. We were poorly dressed to withstand the rain, and, seeing my mother's fevered condition I feared for the consequences if we did not soon find shelter, food and warmth. I remembered what Mrs Sackbutt had said about places where one could find bare refuge for a penny or two, but I could see that my mother needed more than that.

"Listen," I said impatiently, for it seemed to me that only one course of action presented itself: "We must go to Mrs Fortisquince."

My mother shook her head. Her lips moved and, unable to catch the words, I leaned forward: "Mrs Purviance will help us," she muttered.

"No," I said. "She has no reason to help us. Mrs Fortisquince has." She was the widow of my grandfather's oldest friend and, moreover, was herself a cousin of ours. "She must do something for us."

Her lips moved again: "I don't trust her."

"We need not trust her," I said. "But the only alternative is the workhouse."

She shuddered: "I would be passed back," she muttered.

"Back where?" I asked quickly.

"To Christchurch," she said. "It would be too dangerous."

Christchurch, I thought. So that was the parish where my mother's settlement lay. The very parish in which Cox's-square and Bell-lane were which my mother had seemed to have some knowledge of that time we had gone to Mrs Sackbutt's house! I would have leisure to reflect on this later.

"Then it must be Mrs Fortisquince, must it not?" I said.

She said nothing.

Suddenly the bell in the tower beside us began to strike the hour. It seemed to me an innocent enough sound, but my mother looked up with an expression of horror and then glanced wildly around.

"St. Sepulchre!" she cried, and started to her feet.

She hurried through the gate at the other end of the narrow yard and in bewilderment I followed her into Giltspur-street. Almost opposite us stood the grim edifice of Newgate but, as if not noticing it, my mother hastened towards Holborn past the church in whose shadow we had rested.

After a few yards she stopped suddenly and I caught up with her. She was staring at an inn-sign hanging above us and depicting the face of a ferocious Moor carrying a cruelly curved scimitar. (It was the famous Saracen's-head which denoted the inn of that name.)

She turned away muttering to herself and appearing not to see me: "The sword and the crescent moon. And the blood."

She seemed to me to be remembering one of my stories from the *Arabian Tales*. But before I could remonstrate with her she set off at a run into the maze of stinking lanes and back-ways around Smithfield. I hurried after her and it was long before she slowed and halted.

She looked at me as if in a stupor.

I took her hand and said: "Come. We must go to Mrs Fortisquince."

Wearily she nodded and we set off.

We walked and walked as the sky grew darker and darker, and after a few minutes the rain began pouring down and soaked through our clothes. My mother's steps grew slower and feebler, and I had to keep urging her on. Neither of us knew this part of the metropolis — we were in Clerkenwell — and yet as it grew dark we became increasingly reluctant to ask the way of strangers, and therefore it happened many times that we missed our way and found that we had laboured the length of a long street only to have to turn back and retrace our steps. Now for the first time I was tempted to beg, but I knew the danger of being taken up by a constable for this offence, especially in the better streets that we were at last approaching. However, I looked in the face the few well-dressed foot-passengers whom we encountered with what I hoped was an expression of proud importunity — forced to this expedient not for myself but on behalf of my mother, — and once I was rewarded when a poorly-dressed woman gave me a penny. I used it to buy a small piece of bread and we shared it between us on one of the frequent stops to rest that my mother's state of exhaustion necessitated.

CHAPTER 43

The nearer we drew to Mrs Fortisquince's house the more worried I became about the way she would receive us. If she had been so unfriendly when we were far from absolute penury, how would she behave now that we were penniless and almost in rags? Yet surely she could not refuse to help us?

It was past midnight when we reached the house in Golden-square and no lights were visible. I wondered if it would be better to walk the streets for the night and apply at the house early the following morning, but the sight of my mother, her hair and clothes drenched and her teeth chattering, emboldened me. I rang the bell and as it clanged on the other side of the street-door it seemed a fearful violation of the night's silence.

In a few moments lights appeared at the upper windows, we heard sounds upon the stair, and then Mrs Fortisquince's anxious voice came through the door: "Who is it?"

I hesitated and then answered: "John Mellamphy and his mother."

There was a pause before we heard bolts being slid back, and then the door opened the few inches permitted by its chain. A candle was held towards us and then the chain was released and the door swung back to reveal Mrs Fortisquince and her maid-servant, both in night-attire, staring at us in obvious surprise.

"It really is you," Mrs Fortisquince exclaimed, and to my relief she smiled in the most welcoming manner. "Come in, come in," she urged.

We entered and, while the servant secured the door again, Mrs Fortisquince led us into the parlour and bustled about lighting candles.

"My dears, I'm so glad to see you. I've thought about both of you so much and wondered why you did not ever return here."

At these words my mother threw herself into her arms and embraced her.

"My poor Mary," Mrs Fortisquince said, stroking her shoulder, "I can't begin to tell you how often I have asked myself where you were and what you were doing. I sent to the Golden-cross to find you but they had no record of your ever having stayed there. So mysterious!"

My mother blushed and glanced at me reproachfully.

"It was so kind of you to bring me a gift at Christmas," Mrs Fortisquince went on; "but that foolish girl I had then, Dorcas, did not remember to ask you for your address. You must tell me everything. Why did you not come back to me?"

"Johnnie would not let me!" my mother cried.

"Indeed? Whyever not?"

"He didn't trust you," she said. "He's so suspicious and mean-minded now that he quite frightens me."

Mrs Fortisquince stared at me with the strangest expression. "Only fancy," she said. Then suddenly it was as if only now she realized how exhausted and how ill-clad we both were. "Why, you're both soaked to the skin! What am I thinking of! Checkland will make up beds for you and light fires upstairs, while I warm up some broth. Your story will keep till the morning."

My mother was almost asleep on her feet but recovered enough to take a small amount of nourishment before we were led upstairs to a room in which a blazing fire had been lighted and the two beds warmed for us. Mrs Fortisquince helped my mother off with her wet dress and noticed that she clutched the package she wore in a pocket under her top petticoat.

"Come, let me take that from you," she said, holding out her hand for it.

"No," said my mother abruptly.

"Come, my dear, don't be silly."

But my mother moved away with a look of fear on her face.

"Please leave it, Mrs Fortisquince," I said. "She always sleeps with it."

"Of course, of course," she said, and left us a few minutes later.

What a pleasure it was to sleep between sweet-smelling linen sheets again in a bed that was free of vermin! My mother was quickly asleep but I lay awake for some time reproaching myself for my earlier mistrust of Mrs Fortisquince and wondering how many of our sufferings over the previous two years might have been avoided if my mother had not followed my advice.

When, very late the next morning, we went downstairs to breakfast, our hostess showed herself again so solicitous and concerned that I would have decided for certain that I had misjudged her before, had it not been that I still felt a shadow of unease in her presence. I could see that my mother now trusted her completely, however, for when Mrs Fortisquince insisted on hearing what had happened since we last saw her, she told her everything: How she tried to find a post as governess. How we became poorer and poorer because, instead of receiving some money from the sale of our furniture, we had been cheated and betrayed by our old servant. And how, as a consequence, we had been pursued by bailiffs.

At this point Mrs Fortisquince cried: "Bailiffs! So you are in danger of being arrested?"

My mother confirmed this and I watched Mrs Fortisquince anxiously, fearing that we were putting a perilous weapon into her hands if she were not well-disposed towards us.

"How much is the sum involved?" she asked.

"A hundred and fifteen pounds."

"But my dear, you must not worry about so small a sum as that! I will stand surety for you and pay that debt so that the warrant is quashed."

While my mother thanked her I told myself that if she kept her word, I had certainly misjudged her. And clearly her financial circumstances had improved since our last meeting.

"But I have no means of paying you back," my mother said. "And only a very uncertain prospect of gaining money."

"Indeed?" Mrs Fortisquince said. "And what is that?"

And so my mother told her about Miss Quilliam and how she had appeared for so long to be well-disposed towards us. "Then she betrayed us," my mother said.

"Mamma, we cannot be certain of that," I pointed out.

"My dears, how odious!" Mrs Fortisquince exclaimed. "Whatever happened?"

"Well," said my mother, glancing at me nervously while I frowned at her, "I have a document which ... which could be worth a great deal of money."

"Indeed? That must be the object that you were so very unwilling to part with last night. You were most odd about it, my dear."

"I have a fear of losing it, for it could be very dangerous to Johnnie and me if I did. What happened was that I resolved to sell it ... "

"To sell it?" Mrs Fortisquince interrupted. "To whom?"

Before I could intervene, my mother said: "To Sir Perceval Mompesson."

"Really?" Mrs Fortisquince said abruptly. After a moment, she went on: "And what part did this Miss Quilliam play?"

"I asked her to go to Sir Perceval with a letter from me. But instead she went to ... to the agents of that party who wishes nothing but harm to myself and Johnnie. So we were forced to flee our lodgings and had nowhere to go but here."

"I see," Mrs Fortisquince said slowly, her eyes cast down. Then she looked up, smiled at both of us and said briskly: "And thank heavens you did come here! Now the first thing is to pay off the horrid bailiffs. Where can we find them?"

I gave her the address of the magistrate's office at which the warrant had been backed, and she sent her maid there immediately in a hackney-coach. She was back within the hour and we learned that the full amount due now came to one hundred and thirty pounds with costs included. Mrs Fortisquince sent Checkland back with a bank-draft for that figure, and by the time we had eaten a late luncheon my mother had in her possession a quittance for the full amount. She embraced Mrs Fortisquince and the two women clung to each other weeping.

When tears had been dried and dresses tidied, they got down to business.

"Now I must sell the codicil," said my mother. "But how shall I approach Sir Perceval?"

Although she paused as if for Mrs Fortisquince to make an offer, that lady said nothing and at that I felt that my suspicions about her interest in the codicil must be ill-founded.

My mother went on: "It seems unjust to trespass further on your kindness, but I wonder if you would undertake this?"

Mrs Fortisquince hesitated and then said: "I see no reason why not."

"Thank you," said my mother. "And since I want to be able to repay you, could it be as soon as possible?"

"I can go this very afternoon if you wish it."

This was wonderful news! So my mother wrote another letter to Sir Perceval to the same effect as the first, a coach was summoned and Mrs Fortisquince set off. While we waited we began to make plans. When we had paid back Mrs

Fortisquince, I calculated that we would have enough, even if we invested in something as safe as the three per-cent Consols, to live comfortably.

"We will go to Salisbury," my mother declared. "It's so pretty, Johnnie. We'll take a little house in the Close and you shall go to day-school and we shall be able to keep a servant."

When Mrs Fortisquince arrived back a couple of hours later she was in high spirits. "Success!" she cried as she entered the house.

"How did Sir Perceval receive you?" my mother anxiously enquired. "Was Lady Mompesson present?"

"I will tell you everything, only let me get my breath back. You have met Sir Perceval, of course?"

"Yes, once," said my mother.

"But you do not know the house?"

"No, I was there once as a child, but I hardly remember it."

"Let me tell you then. Sir Perceval received me very warmly."

"Lady Mompesson was not there?" I asked in surprise.

Mrs Fortisquince turned to me smiling brightly: "No, indeed she was not. As I say, Sir Perceval received me very warmly — the effect of your little note, my dear. He was delighted that you now wished to sell the codicil and expressed himself perfectly satisfied with the terms proposed. I assure you, nothing so indelicate as a precise figure was mentioned. May I know what *is* the sum that you previously turned down?"

"Seventeen hundred pounds," my mother replied.

Mrs Fortisquince's eyes widened with astonishment. "Only imagine," she murmured, "how much he must want it." Then she went on: "Sir Perceval undertook that his man of business, a gentleman called Mr Steplight, would call upon you tomorrow to effect the transaction."

Though I was slightly worried as to whether Sir Perceval had the authority to transact business of this importance in the absence of his wife, it really seemed that at last the tide of our misfortunes had turned. After passing the happiest evening that my mother and I had known for a long time, we went to bed looking forward — for once — to the following day.

We seated ourselves at the window after breakfast the next day to wait for Sir Perceval's representative. At last, late in the morning, a magnificent carriage drew up outside the house, and to our delight we recognised the gleaming coat-of-arms painted on the door: for there were the crab and the roses which I recalled from the occasion when I had seen Sir Perceval coming out of the park at the top of Gallow-tree-hill. Two footmen in the chocolate and red livery that I remembered so well jumped down, released the steps, and opened the door.

Mrs Fortisquince came to the window just as a figure emerged from within the carriage.

"What a strange little man," my mother remarked. "That must be Mr Steplight."

"Oh, do you find him so?" said Mrs Fortisquince. "I think him rather distinguished. I suppose it must be he."

Mr Steplight had a very large head for his small body, with a high-domed forehead, sharp features and slightly protuberant eyes. He was aged between forty and forty-five, and his toilet and dress were extremely elegant without being ostentatious.

As the door-bell rang Mrs Fortisquince started smoothing down her dress, preparing herself just as nervously, it seemed, as we to greet her guest. When the servant announced him he came in and looked round with a promiscuous smile as if, not knowing who was who, he intended to leave no-one unsmiled at. When Mrs Fortisquince introduced herself and then presented my mother and myself to him, he bowed courteously to each of us, professed himself charmed to make our acquaintance, and then shook hands. I noticed that when he stopped speaking he dropped his gaze and lowered his eye-lids, revealing his rather sparse eyelashes, then slowly raised them. Mrs Fortisquince asked him to sit and signed to the servant to pass round biscuits and wine.

While Checkland was present Mr Steplight maintained, with a little assistance from Mrs Fortisquince, a smooth flow of courteous trifles — the weather (its delightful unreliability), that part of Town (so convenient!), the lock of vehicles coming from May-fair (so provoking), etc. etc. As soon as the servant withdrew, he modulated charmingly into the matter at hand: "I have come directly from Sir Perceval from whom I have received instructions, and I have a letter for you, Mrs Mellamphy, from that gentleman."

He handed it to her, she broke the seal, and I read it over her shoulder:

"No. 48, Brook-street,
"The 19th. of July.

"Madam:

"The bearer of this letter, Mr Steplight, is my trusted agent and confidential man of business. He is empowered by me to give you 200£ in return for the codicil. When its authenticity has been verified the balance of 1,500£ will be paid to you.

"*Perceval Mompesson*, Bart."

The baronet must have dictated it for the hand was very different from the illegible scrawl that I remembered we had received at Melthorpe. My mother and I looked at each other and read on each other's faces our bitter disappointment that only a part of the purchase-money was to be paid immediately. Yet it was understandable, for I well remembered how Sir Perceval and his wife had insisted, on the occasion of our interview with them at Mompesson-park, on the possibility of the codicil's being a forgery.

"What does this mean?" my mother asked.

"A mere formality, I assure you, Mrs Mellamphy," Mr Steplight said. "The balance will be paid within a day or two."

"We must have all of it before we part with the codicil," I said.

Mr Steplight smiled at me: "What a very precocious young gentleman. Most charming."

"Hush, Johnnie," said my mother. "But I am dismayed, Mr Steplight, not to receive all of it now."

"Notice that the precise sum outstanding is specified," Mr Steplight said. "In consequence, that letter itself is as good as a promissory-note. I am sure you cannot believe that a gentleman of Sir Perceval's standing would default on an undertaking to which he had engaged himself?"

My mother hesitated.

"The idea is preposterous," said Mrs Fortisquince.

My mother looked from one to another of us in perplexity.

"Don't give it up, Mamma," I cried.

Mr Steplight and Mrs Fortisquince both smiled at me — the former with manifest benevolence, the latter with a slightly forced demeanour.

"Most engaging," the man of business murmured. "What delightful errors little people fall into."

"Don't be silly, Johnnie," said my mother, and took the codicil from her pocket and unwrapped it.

Mr Steplight produced from his pocket-book a bundle of purple and white Bank of England notes for twenty pounds which he carefully counted. Then he held them out for my mother to take and she handed him the document. Mr Steplight glanced at it briefly as if it were of little interest and then secured it in his pocket-book.

He now rose to his feet and took elaborate leave of us, assuring us that we would see him again in a day or two. I watched from the window as he got back into the carriage and was driven away.

My mother paid Mrs Fortisquince back and put the rest of the money into a reticule that our kind hostess had given her. Later that afternoon Mrs Fortisquince treated us to a celebratory meal of roasted fowl, saddle of lamb, and quince-tart, to mark the beginning of our new lives; but though I was permitted to drink a whole glass of burnt champagne, I could not expel from my mind my reservations about the transaction that had just taken place.

We were not surprised to hear nothing from Mr Steplight the next day, but the day after that we stayed in the front parlour to watch for his return and when he had not come by the late afternoon, we began to grow concerned. When, no message having arrived, I finally went to bed, I could not get to sleep for worrying about the vulnerability of our position now that we had surrendered the codicil. Yet surely it could not be a forgery, for that could be the only reason why the agreement could be repudiated? When I reflected that we had the letter from Sir Perceval, I felt reassured and eventually, though somewhat disturbed by my mother's coughing, I drifted into sleep.

Suddenly I was wrenched from my slumbers by a loud hammering at the street-door.

"What can that be?" cried my mother.

We went out onto the landing and there we all — my mother, Mrs Fortisquince, the servant, and I — stared at each other in alarm. We descended to the street-door where Mrs Fortisquince called out to ask who was there.

"Sheriff's officers," came the reply.

My mother and I looked at each other in dismay at this while Mrs Fortisquince cautiously opened the door on its chain, looked round it and, apparently reassured as to the identity of the visiters, opened it wide. Three strange men in the familiar tri-corn hats and carrying silver staves came crowding into the hall, like a nightmarish repetition of the occasion when bailiffs had raided the house at Mrs Philliber's.

"Which is Mrs Mellamphy?" one of them asked. He had a flat face like a well-worn penny.

"What do you want?" Mrs Fortisquince demanded.

"We are acting on a writ for non-payment of debt," the man replied.

"The money has been paid!" my mother cried.

"You're the party, are you?" he said, turning to her, and to my horror he laid his hand upon her arm.

"I have a quittance!" she cried.

"That is so," said Mrs Fortisquince. "I paid the debt myself."

The officer looked taken aback.

"Find my reticule, Johnnie," my mother said.

I went into the dark parlour with a candle and found it lying on a table near the window. I took out the discharge and then something prompted me to remove the bundle of notes left in there and hide it inside my night-shirt. I went back into the crowded hall and handed the reticule to my mother who took out the paper and passed it to the bailiff.

He looked at it and laughed: "You've put the saddle on the wrong mare! This is a different one!" He consulted his documents: "I am acting in execution of a warrant for recovery of debt arising from the bankruptcy of the Consolidated Metropolitan Building Company."

I turned to my mother and saw that her face had taken on a ghastly pallor.

"Mr Sancious," she muttered.

She was right, for this was the name of the company involved in the building speculation which that gentleman had urged upon us and which had encompassed our ruin. I recalled his warning that as a shareholder my mother would be liable to a proportion of its debts once it had been established how far its liabilities exceeded its assets.

Something occurred to me: "How did you find us?" I asked the bailiff.

He turned to me with a look of amusement: "Never you mind that, young master. The question is: have you got the blunt?"

"How much is it?" my mother asked in a faint voice.

"Eight hundred pounds," he answered after glancing at his papers.

"Oh my dear, I cannot help you!" exclaimed Mrs Fortisquince.

My mother staggered and would have fallen if the bailiff and I had not supported her.

"Come into the parlour," said Mrs Fortisquince and while his deputies remained in the hall, my mother was assisted into that room by Mrs Fortisquince and the bailiff and helped to a sopha. The man then took up his position by the fire while the servant lighted candles.

He glanced round the room: "I am required to seize all personal possessions up to the approximate value of the debt if the monies are not paid in full."

"I have nothing," my mother muttered.

"I can confirm that," Mrs Fortisquince said. "This lady is a guest in my house with her son. They came to me a few days ago and brought nothing with them."

"I am afraid I must search your reticule," the bailiff said and my mother meekly gave it to him. He opened it and counted the money it contained. "Three pounds and some shillings," he announced. My mother looked up in surprise but I managed to catch her eye and nod slightly. "However," the bailiff went on, "I have reason to believe that you have in your possession a sum amounting to upwards of seventy pounds. Where is it?"

How could he have known this? I wondered.

"I do not know," said my mother.

The bailiff shook his head: "It will go hard for you, Mrs Mellamphy, if you try to conceal these monies."

Mrs Fortisquince turned to me: "Johnnie, did you take it?"

I shook my head.

"You are making things worse for your mother," she said.

Reluctantly, I brought out the notes.

"Very wise of you, young sir," the bailiff commented. He carefully counted the money, wrote out a receipt for my mother, and put the notes away. "Now, ma'am, you must make ready to come with us."

"Where?" my mother cried.

"To my house."

"To your house! I don't understand! What is it?"

"The spunging-house," he said brutally.

"What will happen to me?"

"You will be held until the writ is returnable. That is, until you are brought before the court."

My mother was crushed under this blow.

"I will come too," I said.

"No, Johnnie," she protested.

"I may come, may I not?" I asked the bailiff.

"Yes," he said. "But then there'll be two on you to pay for, that's all."

So it was settled. We were allowed a few minutes to dress and make ready, and were then put into a hackney-coach which had been waiting outside.

"Please help us," my mother begged Mrs Fortisquince through the coach-window.

"My dear," she replied from her door. "I promise to continue what I have begun. You will see."

The coach moved off and we were driven through the dark and silent streets into a part of the metropolis that was wholly unfamiliar. In the occasional flashes of illumination as we passed a street-lamp, I could see that this sudden shock to my mother after the brief period of relief was a serious blow. She looked haggard, her eyes were dulled, and when we at last reached the bailiff's house in Great-Earle-street, Soho, and were led inside, she seemed to be taking little notice of what was happening to her. When the bailiff's wife had led us to a small, bare chamber which had bars on the windows, and had locked the door upon us, my mother gave way to a fit of weeping. She clung to me but as her tears ran down my cheeks and I muttered mechanical words of reassurance, I was trying to understand what was happening to us. How did the bailiff suddenly know where to find us after so long? And how did he know that we had a large sum of money? My suspicions of Mrs Fortisquince returned in force.

We passed what remained of the night in broken slumbers and awoke weary and oppressed. My mother learned from the bailiff that since that day was a Sunday, she was not to appear before the magistrate until the following morning. The man's wife explained to us that our accommodation and board would be added to the debt already outstanding, and it may be imagined whether or not this sharpened our appetite for the wretched breakfast her servant laid before us. When, an hour later, we were told that we had a visiter and were escorted to the dreary little parlour, we expected Mrs Fortisquince, but to our surprise it was Mr Steplight who entered the chamber.

His self-possession was undimmed by the venue and he greeted us with the elaborate courtesy of the earlier occasion: "Dear lady, I am deeply grieved to find you under these melancholy circumstances. I have come from our mutual acquaintance, the inestimable Mrs Fortisquince, who told me of last night's sad event."

"Have you brought the rest of the money?" my mother asked anxiously.

"To my profound regret, there remain certain formalities."

"But the codicil has been accepted as genuine?" I asked.

"Certainly," he said.

Reassured by this, we smiled bravely at each other.

"There are a number of preliminaries to be settled," Mr Steplight went on. "First, Sir Perceval is very concerned about the safety of your son."

I heard this with amazement, but after a moment's thought I believed I understood why this should be so.

"He does not believe he is safe in London," Mr Steplight continued. "He therefore desires that he be sent to school in the country."

"Yes, that is exactly what I have already decided. We were going to take a house outside London, but because of this new warrant I may not have enough money."

Mr Steplight smiled: "Set your mind at rest on that score, Mrs Mellamphy. Sir Perceval is prepared to pay for your son's schooling over and above the money he owes you."

"He is very kind!" my mother cried. "You see, Johnnie, I knew it would be all right in the end. Only imagine, you and I will be together and safe."

"Not precisely, my dear lady," Mr Steplight said smoothly. "Sir Perceval feels strongly that your son should board, and at a school in a secluded part of the country. Only thus can his safety be perfectly assured."

"Board?" exclaimed my mother in dismay. "Where?"

"In consultation with myself he has already chosen a school which is in a suitable position to provide that necessary assurance of safety."

He named a county far in the North.

"So distant!" my mother exclaimed.

"Far from those who wish him harm," Mr Steplight parried.

"No," my mother said decisively. "I won't be separated from him. He may go to school near me."

Mr Steplight shook his head sadly: "I am very sorry, but in that case I am not empowered to pay to you the balance of monies."

"But it's my money," my mother protested. "He promised to pay me."

"And he is perfectly willing to do so once these trifling conditions are met."

My mother looked from one to the other of us in perplexity.

"Mamma," I said, "why should I not go to this school? You could take a little house nearby and I could come to you for the week-ends and the holidays. Think of the alternative: you will go to prison."

Seeing that she was in an anguish of uncertainty, the confidential agent pressed home the attack: "Your son is right. And if you were in prison, what would become of him, exposed as he would be to your enemies?"

"Yes," she muttered.

"You know you may trust Sir Perceval to act in the best interests of your son, do you not?"

My mother shook her head as if in a daze: "I suppose so. I have been told so."

"My dear lady, you hardly seem convinced. Do you not understand that the effect of the codicil is that Sir Perceval and his family only possess the estate as long as there is an heir to the original Huffam line?"

"That's right, Mamma," I cried. "Mr Pentecost and Mr Silverlight explained the law to me. The codicil means that you and I are the last of the entailed line to the fee simple, so that the Mompessons now only hold a base-fee to the property. If we were to die without leaving an heir, then title to the property would pass to the person named as heir in remainder — Silas Clothier."

My mother shuddered but the lawyer looked at me in amazement. Then he smiled: "How remarkable. You are absolutely correct, young man." He turned to my mother: "So you see, don't you, that it is essential for Sir Perceval's peace of mind that your son remain alive and in due course grow up to marry and provide future heirs to the entail?"

"Yes," she said. "I suppose so."

I turned to Mr Steplight: "But you must pay my mother the money still due to her."

"How very astutely you do business, young sir," he said, smiling benevolently at me. He turned to my mother and said: "I shall by all means give you eight hundred pounds immediately to clear this debt, and the balance when your son boards the coach. If you accept these terms, I have the monies with me."

Though we were disappointed by this further prevarication, his conditions seemed reasonable and so we consented. He pulled out a bundle of bank-notes, counted them, and passed them to my mother.

"Now I suggest you send for the bailiff," he said.

We did so, and I enjoyed his surprise and disappointment when my mother showed him that she had enough to pay off the debt.

"How long," Mr Steplight asked him, "do you need before you can obtain a formal discharge and have the warrant respited?"

"If it weren't Sunday," he said, "I could do it by this afternoon. But it will be noon tomorrow at the earliest."

"Very well," Mr Steplight said. "Take the money now and give this lady a receipt. Add on your costs and fees due up to midday tomorrow. And don't try any of your bailiff's tricks with me, my friend. I'm too sharp a bird for that."

"Why, I can see that, sir," the man answered glibly; "and I'd be a fool to try it."

The business was quickly done and when the man had gone Mr Steplight said: "Tomorrow noon will suit me very well. I will be back then with places booked for Master Mellamphy and myself on the three o'clock coach."

"So soon!" my mother exclaimed.

"The sooner he is out of London the safer he will be," Mr Steplight replied.

"But he has nothing, no linen or change of clothes or books or even a box."

"Then he is taking all that he will need there," Mr Steplight replied. "Of that I can assure you, Mrs Mellamphy."

"You are going with me?" I asked him.

"Yes. Sir Perceval did me the honour to say that he would not confide this responsibility to anyone whom he trusted less than myself. Those were his exact words. You may see from this how very seriously he takes your son's welfare, Mrs Mellamphy."

"I will come too!" she cried.

I thought I saw a brief flicker of something like anger in the eyes of the baronet's confidential agent.

"Though it would be charming to have the advantage of your company, dear lady," he said smoothly; "it is a long and tiring journey. And an expensive one. Sir Perceval will pay your son's fare but he has made no offer to pay yours."

"Don't come, Mamma," I said. "You are still unwell and you need every penny of what you have left."

"I am resolved on coming," she said.

"Very well," said Mr Steplight, smiling suddenly. "That is agreed and I will reserve three seats at the coach-office."

He took leave of us a few minutes later and we were led back to our own room and locked in again. How much lighter our hearts were than when we had left there only an hour or so ago! Yet these sudden changes in our fortunes were bad for my mother's health, it seemed to me, and for the rest of that evening I watched her with concern. As we discussed the future I noticed a kind of recklessness and excitement that I had not seen in her before.

We were up early the next morning and each hour dragged slowly by as we waited for the bailiff to bring the discharge. His wife agreed to send out one of the servants to purchase some articles that we would need for the journey and a few that my mother was convinced I would require at the school and which she packed into a bundle. By the time our meagre luncheon was brought to us in the parlour and Mr Steplight was due within the hour, the bailiff had still not come. We were finishing the meal, which neither of us had much appetite for, when the bailiff knocked and came in. It was immediately apparent that he brought bad news.

"Do you have it?" my mother asked.

"I do not, ma'am," he replied. "For when an investigation was made to see if you could be whitewashed — that is to say, a bill of indemnity be drawn in your name — it was found that there is another warrant out against you."

"Another?" she gasped, staggering backwards.

He glanced down at a piece of paper in his hand: "A matter of a bill of five hundred pounds drawn by yourself some years ago and never paid."

It was the one that Mr Sancious had persuaded her to sign in order to increase her investment in the company!

"That bill!" my mother cried. "But how has it come to light now? Who has it?"

The bailiff screwed up his features and squinted at the paper. "Someone has bought it up, but I can't read the name," he said, and held it out to my mother.

She looked at it, uttered a faint cry and would have fallen if I had not caught her and helped her to a chair.

Seizing the paper, the bailiff withdrew from the room.

I chafed her hand to revive her.

"What was the name?" I asked, but she merely shook her head.

"I'm lost, I'm lost," was all she would say, though I begged her to tell me what the name was.

Though she was now resolved that my departure for the North should be postponed, I guessed that Mr Steplight would insist on adherence to the original design. And I was right for when he arrived a few minutes later and heard the news and my mother's request, he was obdurate:

"Out of the question, Mrs Mellamphy. I must be back in Town by Thursday morning which would be impossible if we leave any later than early this afternoon. I am only empowered to pay you the balance when your son boards the coach in my custody."

After some argument my mother, seeing that he was immovable, at last agreed.

"Please give my mother the direction of the school so that she may write to me," I asked.

He wrote it on a piece of paper and my mother carefully put it away.

Then Mr Steplight pulled out his repeater. "We must leave here in ten minutes to be sure of the coach," he said.

Considerately, he withdrew to wait in the hackney-cab.

I took up the bundle in which my few possessions were secured and it only remained for us to kiss and part.

"I will come up to see you as soon as I can," my mother said.

"No, Mamma, don't be silly. When you've paid off this bill you won't have any money left at all."

"No, dearest," she said, stroking my cheek.

"Are you paying attention, Mamma? I shall be taken care of now, but what shall you do?"

"I don't know." She seemed stunned by the sudden changes in our fortunes and simply gazed at me with her eyes shining with an unnatural glitter. "All that matters is that you will be safe now."

"No, you must listen to me," I insisted. "Find cheap lodgings, or live with Mrs Fortisquince if she offers to have you. I believe we must have misjudged her before. And yet, I'm not entirely sure. Be very careful, won't you? Are you listening, Mamma?"

"Yes, darling," she said.

"Try to find work while you live on what will be left of Sir Perceval's money. There should be a little."

I gave her the map which she carefully placed in her pocket-book.

"Look after it," I told her. "For I shall want it back."

I felt that it would help her in that great city and be a kind of talisman.

We embraced, I picked up my bundle and we went into the hall to tell the bailiff we were ready for my departure. He allowed my mother to stand at the street-door to wave me off, though he insisted on keeping his hand on her arm. When I had climbed into the coach and seated myself beside Mr Steplight, he handed the balance owing to my mother through the window. As the vehicle moved off I looked out of window and saw such an expression of longing on her face that I turned away but then I looked back and could see how hurt she was that I had averted my head. What would become of her, I wondered. And when would I see her again?

CHAPTER 44

As the vehicle drew away Mr Steplight's smile faded and he fell silent, staring out of window. When we reached the Golden-Cross-inn he seized me by the arm and held onto me until we boarded the coach for the North. I was surprised to see that the inside was full up, but I assumed that someone had only just that minute secured the place he had presumably booked but which my mother was, in the event, not occupying, and so I made no comment on it.

As the coach clattered through the streets I sank back in my seat, taking no interest in the sights as I brooded on what this latest delay to my mother's release could mean. Could it have some significance that I had not grasped? Mr Steplight and I made a fine pair of travelling-companions, for he addressed no word to me nor even looked in my direction during all the first stage so that I might have been a parcel he had shoved onto the seat beside him.

North of London we ran into a cold clammy mist which lay in the hollows like a fine veil of gauze through which the sun appeared as pallid as a huge moon, bringing a chill against which — for all that it was July — my coat gave no protection. We travelled through the afternoon and the evening, and then halted briefly to take a late supper before going on in the night-coach.

We travelled through the next day and then late that evening I saw in the darkness occasional flashes of fire and heard strange noises. When I asked my companion what this meant he merely shrugged his shoulders, and so for three or four hours I stared out in bewilderment at the ghastly lights that flickered around us on both sides. I became aware of a foul stench of a kind that was familiar to me from the gas-works in Westminster but much more pungent, and when we stopped to change horses in the dirty, cavernous hold of an inn-yard I leaned out of window and called to one of the ostlers: "Please, what is that smell?"

He seemed puzzled by my question but at last responded, in an outlandish accent, with something that sounded like: "That'll be t' mains, yoong mester."

This left me none the wiser but as we journeyed on and I dozed and awoke and dozed again, the dawn slowly crept upon us from our right hand and the oppressive smell and the fires were left behind and a landscape of rolling hills and villages was revealed by the pale cloud-obscured sun.

At the next large town we breakfasted at about five in the morning and then took the branch-coach. And now, as we continued yet further northward, the countryside grew bleaker as we entered a land of high moors broken only by steep ridges and stony outcrops. More and more dismayed by Mr Steplight's manner towards me, and puzzled that a school should be located in such a desolate landscape, I tried to make him tell me something about the academy to which he was taking me. Now it was that he smiled for the first and last time on that journey when he turned to me briefly and said: "*Crastinus enim dies solicitus erit sibi ipsi. Sufficit diei malitia sua*. That is to say, 'Sufficient unto the day is the evil thereof'." The words jogged my memory but it was long before I remembered where I had last heard them.

At a gaunt inn that stood at an empty cross-roads in the middle of a vast landscape, we parted from the coach and Mr Steplight hired a chaise. The road we took ran to the west straight across the undulating moorland and here there were very few farmhouses and they all turned windowless walls to the east; and when I looked back I saw their small low windows on the other side like eyes that were narrowed to follow us.

Though I had revolved the business of the codicil again and again in my mind with the feeling that there was something strange that I had not been able to put my finger upon, I had got nowhere. But now, when I tried to see the whole affair from the point of view of the self-interest of each of the other parties involved, the anomaly came to me suddenly: "Mr Steplight," I said, "if Sir Perceval intended to destroy the codicil when he sent you to buy it, then how was it also necessary to his interests to keep me alive?"

He turned and looked at me very strangely — almost with a kind of pleasure

— compressing his thin lips. Then he looked away again as if reading his fortune in the barren landscape.

At last the driver turned off the high-road and trundled carefully down a rough track. To my surprise we appeared to be approaching a farm. We passed some fields, marked by stone walls but otherwise barely distinguishable from the uncultivated terrain all around, and in one of them I saw three thin, poorly-dressed boys at work. We drove into the farm-yard where two large mastiffs chained up by the gate barked angrily at us. Ahead of us was a long low stone farmhouse in the midst of a dirty yard in which lay heaps of mouldering straw and refuse. Enclosing the yard were two tumbledown ricks, a midden, several delapidated outbuildings, and a drying-ground, in which some more boys were threshing corn with flails. Like those I had already noticed, they had pinched faces and deep-sunken eyes underscored by dark smudges, and were wearing ragged trowsers and shirts. A well-dressed burly youth stood by, holding a whip and apparently over-looking them.

The chaise stopped at the door of the farm-house and we got down. Mr Steplight knocked and a little maid-servant peered anxiously round the edge of the door as it opened.

"I am Mr Steplight," my companion said. "I believe Mr Quigg is expecting me."

"Oh yes, sir, come in," she said, curtseying and pulling back the door.

We entered and found that the door opened straight into the "house-place", a large stone-flagged kitchen-cum-hall.

"Mr Quigg is in the library. Will you come this way, please, sir."

She knocked on the door and showed us into a small room which, in view of its designation, was chiefly remarkable for the complete absence of books. A fat red-faced man, with what I would now call a brandy-painted nose, half-rose from the table at which he was sitting as we entered, pushing something into a drawer and wiping his sleeve across his mouth. He was about fifty and, wearing a high neck-cloth, a bottle-green coat, and mud-spattered boots and gaiters, looked exactly like the farmers I knew from my Melthorpe years. The two gentlemen saluted each other as if they had never met and yet knew each other.

"My letter has preceded me, then, Mr Quigg?" said my companion.

"I ken nowt aboot yon," he replied in the broad speech of the country. "But it cwome yester forenoon. 'Troost yow had a good journey. Pray be seated, and tak' a glass of wine, my good sir."

When this ceremony had been carried out and the two gentlemen had toasted each other, Mr Quigg looked at me: "Yon's t' lad, I tak' it?"

"It is."

He turned and pulled me roughly towards him:

"Give me tha pook."

I stared at him in bewilderment and he laughed unpleasantly and cuffed me on the side of the head. "Why, art deaf? Tha hast cloth ears? Then Cloth-Ear is rightly tha name. I want tha boondle."

He seized my "poke" from me, untied it and then shook its contents onto the floor: a few shirts, and some articles carefully packed by my mother.

"Turn out tha pockets, Cloth-Ear."

I handed over the few coins I had and he put them in his pocket without counting them. "Put on yon," he said, handing me a bundle of what looked like rags. While I was exchanging my trowsers and shirt for these, Mr Quigg said pleasantly to his visiter: "Would yow care to see t'other lad?"

"I would indeed."

Mr Quigg went to the door, put his head round it and bellowed: "Send Mealy-Plant in here." He came back rubbing his hands ingratiatingly: "I reckon yow'll be reet glad to see what we've made on him, Mr Steplight, and will report t' same to t' party consarned."

Mr Steplight glanced warningly towards me and said: "I'm sure I can rely upon you."

"Very good," replied Mr Quigg, looking at me as I stood in my newly-acquired rags. "And now to business, Mr Steplight," he said briskly, and he gripped me painfully by the arm and propelled me towards the door and out of the room, slamming it behind me with the words: "Stop there."

I waited in the house-place, grateful for the few moments of respite to try to understand what was happening. This was like no school I had ever heard of!

After a few minutes a pale ragged boy a year or two younger than I came in.

He glanced at me timidly and said in the soft accents of the South: "Should I knock or wait, do you think?"

"I don't know."

"I'll be beaten whichever I do," he said and knocked softly. The door opened suddenly, Mr Quigg seized him roughly by the arm, hitting him about the head to encourage speed, and dragged him into the room slamming the door behind him.

I reflected that no-one could be pleased with what had been made of that boy. A few minutes later he was thrust out of the room as the door was slammed behind him.

"Are you to come here?" he said to me shyly.

"Yes."

"Then I am very sorry for you."

The door opened and Mr Quigg stood glaring at us: "What dost tha think th'art doing?" he shouted. "Get back to work."

As the boy moved away Mr Quigg struck out at his head and shoulders, slewing him sideways with the force of the blow as he ran.

"Mischievous young devils, Mr Steplight," he said, as that gentleman followed him out. "They need a firm hand."

He seized my shoulder, gripping so hard that I nearly cried out, and pushed me before him out to the chaise. Mr Steplight climbed in and shook hands with the headmaster.

I said: "Goodbye, Mr Steplight."

He glanced at me briefly without acknowledging me, and then the chaise pulled away.

Mr Quigg tightened his grip and shook me to emphasize what he was saying: "Now th'art to start afternoon school."

"Please sir," I protested, "I've not eaten since early this morning and I'm very hungry."

Mr Quigg removed his hand in order to hit me across the face: "Tha dostna speak until th'art bidden."

Again gripping my shoulder, he led me — to my surprise — not back into the house but across the yard towards the outbuildings I had seen from the chaise where a group of boys were threshing corn.

"Here's a new 'un, Hal," he said to the youth with the whip who had a nose like a parrot's bill. "Cloth-Ear."

"All right, Cloth-Ear, get to work," said the burly youth.

I picked up the flail but since I had no idea how to use it, I had to be shewn — which involved much cuffing and swearing.

Mr Quigg watched benignly for a few minutes this commencement of my studies, and then strolled back towards the house.

Now, hungry and thirsty as I was, I was forced to work for the next three hours at the exhausting task of threshing, with only a single break of a few minutes. The hand-staff of blackthorn blistered my hand as I swung the swupple. Then once we had threshed the corn from the ear, we had to winnow it to separate the corn from the husks and chaff, and the dust that was raised by the winnowing-fan made us gasp and choke.

We laboured under the sharp gaze of Hal who seated himself on a bale of hay and smoked a pipe. But if any boy slacked Hal cried out in the manner of a coachman and "touched him up" with his whip. At last our over-looker allowed us to stop and then led us to a delapidated barn outside which there was another group of boys of various ages who were being supervised by yet another youth with a whip — this one thin and cadaverous, and his face badly pitted like a frost-bitten leaf in autumn.

These two counted us: "Eleven with the new 'un makes twelve," Hal called out. "It's one of tha's that's wanting, Roger."

"Mealy-Plant," the thin youth replied. "He's on his way."

And a few minutes later the boy I had spoken to outside Mr Quigg's library came into the yard from one of the fields, staggering with exhaustion.

"Get in!" shouted Roger and cracked the whip above our heads alarmingly.

All the boys hurried into the barn and I followed them. It was empty except for bales of decaying straw and there was more straw underfoot above a layer of mud. There was a strong musty smell of rot which grew intenser when the door was secured behind us. The only light came through the gaps between the boards, and in the near-darkness no-one spoke. We laid ourselves down on the straw, too tired for speech. After several minutes we heard the wooden cross-bars being raised and the door was opened by Mr Quigg who entered followed by the two young men each carrying a bucket. The boys rose wearily and stood back while Roger and Hal poured the contents of the buckets into a large wooden trough and I saw that they were nothing but potatoes. None of the boys moved and all kept their eyes on Mr Quigg. When the youths had finished he stepped forward holding up his hand as if to quell an uproar:

"Now young genel'men, I ken how hoongry yow mun be after yowr labours in t' fields of larning. How do I ken? Why, on account of I ken what boys are. How do I ken what boys are? On account of I wor one myself. But don't go thinking I had the advantages of a superior eddication like what yow're getting. Oh no, indeed. I wor turned out by my fond pappy to yarn my living at no more nor seven year old, so yow boys are lucky and yow should be grateful."

He made this speech regularly. Later I was told that he had been a porter at a school in Wakefield and that this was his closest experience of education.

He looked around at us with a cruel smile, waiting as if enjoying the suspense. At last he shouted: "Now get it!"

All the boys ran forward to reach into the trough and to my horror began fighting amongst themselves. Three of them were bigger and heavier than the others and these — two of whom were almost plump by comparison with their fellows — pushed the smaller ones aside and seized as many of the potatoes as they could, tucked them into their shirts which they held out before them, and carried them away to a corner of the barn. Mr Quigg and his sons (for that is who I learned the two youths were) urged the other boys on with shouts and occasional blows of the whips. When the bigger boys had eaten their potatoes they came back for more. Hungry as I was I could not bring myself to join in the fight.

"Good lads," Mr Quigg cried out giving the three bigger boys a hunk of barley-bread each. Then he addressed me, jeeringly: "Art tha not hungry now, Cloth-Ear?"

I shook my head and he struck me with the whip. I crept away and watched from the shadows. A boy who had a humped back and short, misshapen legs was fighting off some of the smaller fellows to seize a few of the potatoes that were left. I noticed that the boy I had spoken to, the one addressed by Mr Quigg as Mealy-Plant, was, like me, making no attempt to obtain any of the potatoes although he was one of the comparatively larger boys.

When the trough was empty Mr Quigg and his sons went out and I heard the cross-bar slam into place. A minute or two later the monotonous howl of the yard-dogs turned into a series of frenzied barks as the sound of their chains being unlocked became audible. I heard them approach and then saw their muzzles shoved through the wide gap under the door of the barn as they scratched at the wood, whining savagely. No notice was taken by my new companions, and then the thinnest of the three bigger boys began working at a flint and tinder until at last he lit a tallow-dip and somewhat dispelled the darkness.

Now I saw the young cripple hold out a potato to a large but vacant-faced boy who took it without looking at him and put it straight into his mouth. Then the crippled boy went over to the one I had spoken to outside Mr Quigg's library who was lying as if exhausted on the straw, and held out a potato to him.

"Here you are, Stephen," he said.

"Thank you, Richard." He took it and looked across at me: "But he had nothing either."

Stephen broke the potato in two and held out one half.

"It's yours," I said, shaking my head, though I was in pain from hunger.

"I'm not hungry," he said.

"I wish I had another," said the crippled boy.

At that moment the boy who had lighted the dip said: "Here's one I was keeping for later."

He brought over a potato and I accepted it. It was half-raw inside and burnt outside, but I ate it with as much pleasure as if it had been the most exquisite delicacy.

The boys now gathered round me and in the faint light of the guttering dip I saw a circle of drawn, pale faces with sunken eyes and gaunt cheeks. The three largest boys were in rather better sort than the others, all of whom were emaciated, clad in rags, filthy, and infested with vermin, especially their shaggy heads which they constantly scratched.

"Who sent you here, Cloth-Ear?" demanded the largest and oldest. He had a somewhat brutal face with a broken nose. He was stuffing a pipe as he spoke and now leaned forward to light it at the candle.

"Don't call me that. My name is John."

He and the burlier of the two other biggest boys looked at each other quickly as if secretly amused, then he gripped me by the throat and forced my head back: "I'll call you what I please. I'm captain here. Now answer my question. Who sent you here?"

"M-My mother." I gasped.

"Who is your father?" he asked.

"I don't know," I said.

He said something brutally coarse and his companion laughed noisily, revealing that he had only a few blackened stumps for teeth. Then he banged my head against the wall and let go of me so that I fell to the ground. He and the other boy walked away.

Richard helped me to my feet.

"Why does your mother want you out of the way?" he asked matter-of-factly.

"Out of the way?" I repeated.

For answer he drew one hand across his neck and smiled grimly.

"I don't understand," I said. "I've been sent here because my mother's friends want me to be safe."

The boys laughed joylessly.

"Oh you'll be made safe all right," said the one who had given me his potato.

"My mother does not mean me harm," I protested.

"Are you sure?" he asked. "We were all sent here by our friends. Most of us are love-children as I am. My name's Paul." He indicated the crippled boy: "That's Richard. He's not a love-child. His parents wanted to get rid of him because of his back. But *he* is," he said, pointing to the boy with the vacant, staring face. "We call him Big Thom because that's Little Thom." He indicated a smaller boy with a sharp-featured countenance and pale eyes.

"I don't know what I am," said Big Thom. "I don't remember nothing before this. 'Cept beatings."

"He was sent here for being disobedient," Paul went on. "He was wild when he came."

Paul pointed out the other, smaller boys and told me their names quickly as if they were of little significance. They were lying down on the straw and pulling it over themselves — indeed, several of them were already slumbering. One was weeping in his sleep and from the darkness the self-proclaimed captain cried out: "Shut thy noise before I shut it for thee, thou mammy-sick babe! And bring that dip over, Paul."

Paul quickly lighted another and gave it to Richard.

"Who are those two?" I asked Richard softly as Paul obediently went over to his captain.

"That's Ned," he answered. "And the other is Bart. His lieutenant. They're Quigg's favourites." In an undertone he added: "Paul's one of them, too, because he's older."

Ned pulled a pack of cards from under the straw and they began a noisy game of vingt-et-un.

"What is for early school tomorrow?" Little Thom asked sleepily, lying back on the straw.

"Threshing and ploughing again," Richard answered.

"When will we start proper lessons?" I asked.

They laughed mirthlessly.

"What could they teach us?" Richard said. "None of them can even read or write. They have to get their maid-servant or one of us, to deal with their letters."

"Is it just in the summer that we work on the farm?" I asked.

"Bless you, no. The autumn's the hardest," said Stephen.

"When do we start pulling potatoes?" Little Thom asked.

"Another month at least," Richard said. "But that's no good. You can't eat murphies raw."

"Yes," Stephen agreed, "carrot and turnip-pulling are best for that."

"I found some mushrooms this afternoon," said Little Thom.

"Did you eat them?"

"No, I didn't dare. They weren't like any mushrooms I've ever seen."

Cautiously he pulled something out of his pocket and opened his palm. Richard held the dip over them and we all leaned forward.

"Where did you find them?" Richard asked.

"By the gate from the yard into the Fifteen-Acre. Just by where Davy is. Does anyone know, dare I eat them?"

I recognised them from my mushrooming expeditions with Sukey. "No," I said. "You certainly can't. They're called Death-caps and they're very dangerous."

"Are you sure?" Little Thom said disappointedly.

"Yes. Give them to me and I'll throw them away."

"Oh," he said, "I know a trick worth two of that."

I didn't understand for a moment what he meant. "No, I'm not going to eat them," I said. "Put them on the ground."

Suspiciously he did so and I put my foot on them and crushed them into the mud and straw of the floor.

"Hush!" Richard whispered suddenly, and we all fell silent, our ears straining.

We heard what sounded like footsteps at one side of the barn, but then came a low growl and the boys relaxed.

"It's only one of the dogs," Richard said.

"We were afraid it was Roger," Stephen explained to me. "He often spies on us like that."

He lay back and pulled some straw over himself. In a few minutes he was fast asleep.

Richard glanced at him: "He is being worked harder than any of us."

"Yes," said Little Thom, "he is being treated the way they did poor Davy. Today he was ploughing for longer than ever."

He turned away and began to make preparations for sleep.

"Ploughing!" I exclaimed to Richard. "Surely he is not strong enough to handle a team!"

"A team?" He smiled grimly. "You'll see."

"And they're punishing him more often than any of us," Little Thom muttered.

"Yes," agreed Richard. He added softly: "Just like poor Davy again."

"Can you do nothing?" I asked.

"What?" Richard demanded.

"Can you not tell your friends when you write?"

"Write?" Richard cried. "You are green! We cannot send letters."

"But do you never go home?"

"Never," Richard said. "The fees cover the holidays as well."

"But do your friends never visit you?"

"Our friends!" Richard exclaimed. "Do you think we would be here if they cared for us?"

"Then can you not escape?"

"Where to?" asked Richard. "If we had anywhere to go or anyone who wanted us we would not be here."

"But wouldn't anywhere be better than this?"

"It's impossible to escape from here," Richard said. "Nobody ever has."

As if to mark his words, the dip guttered and went out. The others now lay down and prepared to sleep and I did the same, pulling the straw about myself. It stuck into me most painfully and the dust made me gasp and splutter. Since I had eaten nothing since breakfast at the inn, apart from the potato Paul had given me, I was so hungry that I was in pain.

Why should Mr Steplight have brought me to this place when he had stressed that it was so clearly in Sir Perceval's interest that I should be well looked after? Could it be that Mr Steplight did not understand what kind of establishment it was? Surely not, for he had met Quigg and seen Stephen and the other boys. In that case, was he deceiving Sir Perceval? Or, a more frightening thought, could it be that the baronet was acting dishonourably towards my mother and myself? Was it, as I had asked the attorney during the journey, because he no longer needed me now that he had the codicil and was going to destroy it?

I wondered if there were any way to smuggle a letter to my mother, but then I reflected that it would merely torment her for she would be powerless to do anything. To come and fetch me away — even if it were in her power to release me from Quigg — would be far beyond her pocket.

One thing was clear to me: I had to escape. And it had to be sooner rather than later because I could see how much stronger I was than all but the three biggest boys. It was plain to me that, worked and fed as the others were, I would be getting weaker and weaker from that moment. Eventually, worn down by the exertions of the day I fell asleep.

The next morning we were awoken early by Hal and Roger entering the barn and laying about them with their whips. They had a stack of wooden platters which they threw to the ground as we scrambled for them, and then they ladled from a bucket a helping of cold oat-porage which, I realized later, was always cooked — or, rather, over-cooked — the evening before with the potatoes and left to cool overnight. Immediately after this we were driven out into the yard and divided into two work-gangs. I was allocated to Hal's and, with three or four others, was led by him out of the yard. As we went through the gate into a big field I noticed a number of Death-caps in the weeds near some grassy mounds and a newly-dug heap of earth. Hal marched us to a distant field where we were put to clearing stones and then building a boundary-wall with them. Stephen had gone off with Roger's gang.

The labour was not as arduous as threshing had been the day before, and we were not so closely under the over-looker's observation. And so as I worked I was able to think about the way of dividing up dinner that I had seen the previous evening and that the boys had told me was practised every night. It meant that the biggest boys obtained far more than their fair share while the smallest obtained too little — and Stephen almost nothing — and merely wasted their strength in hurting each other. It occurred to me that Mr Silverlight would have insisted — and Mr Pentecost have denied — that there was a better way. And surely Mr Silverlight was correct.

Hal allowed us half-an-hour to rest after our "piece", and then we worked on until late afternoon, when we returned for dinner. Just as on the previous day, the brothers tipped the buckets of potatoes into the trough and we had to wait while Quigg delivered his usual oration, then clapped his hands as the signal to rush forward and begin struggling for the potatoes.

Again, I hung back and noticed that Stephen did the same. As before, the bigger boys made off with an armful and both Richard and Big Thom managed to wrest several potatoes from the younger boys by using their comparative size and strength, while Little Thom also did fairly well by picking up any that were dropped in the *mêlée*. Once again the losers were the smallest boys who were reduced to fighting over the few potatoes remaining.

While I was watching this, Quigg suddenly came up behind me and seized me by the hair, raising me to tip-toe.

"Art tha trying to cheat me?" he asked.

"What do you mean, sir?" I gasped.

"Dost reckon that if tha dostna eat tha munna be made to work?" he snarled. "But tha sall see: I sall get my share of work from tha."

He slapped me hard on the face and the force of the blow, as he simultaneously released his grip on my hair, felled me. As I picked myself up it occurred to me that he paid no attention to the fact that Stephen was similarly making no attempt to fight for food.

When the Quiggs had gone, securing the door behind them and then releasing the dogs, I said to my friends: "Why do you let them make you do that?"

"What other way is there?" Richard asked as he handed a potato to Stephen and then offered one to me.

"No," I said. "I won't take it because you fought for it."

I saw Stephen redden at the implied reproach.

"What should we do?" Richard asked.

"We should divide them up fairly. Everyone should get two, three, or four, according to his size, and after that the remainder should be divided equally. That is the principle of Equity."

I had spoken loudly enough to be heard by the others:

"Stuff!" jeered Ned. "This is the fairest way. The ones who need it most are the strongest and so they get what they need."

"Aye," said Bart. "What's fairer than that?"

"*You* get more than you need," I said. "While others get too little or nothing."

"So what?" Ned sneered and turned back to his game of cards.

"Don't you see," I said to the others in an undertone. "It doesn't have to be this way. We out-number the other three and we could seize all the food and divide it up fairly."

The very thought frightened them, and yet I could see that it excited them, too. They resisted, but their argument amounted to no more than that because it had always been done that way, there was no other way of doing it, and by the time I settled down to sleep I believed I had won my case.

The next day I was assigned to Hal's work-gang again and spent the day collecting stones as before. I took the opportunity, during our baiting-time, to tell the other boys what had been agreed the previous night and, though fearfully, most of them consented to support me. Richard had done the same in Roger's gang and so that evening, when Quigg gave the signal for us to start fighting, nobody moved. Somewhat surprised, Ned and Bart swaggered forward and collected an armful each but Paul, whom I had forewarned, hung back. As the captain and his lieutenant began to move away, I moved forward and seized some of the potatoes. This was the agreed signal, and to my relief enough of the other boys now supported me to enable us to over-power Ned and Bart. I threw them four potatoes each and shared out the others.

The Quiggs were amazed at this turn of events and accused me of being a trouble-maker and of having arranged the whole thing to get more food for myself. Obviously at a loss as to their course of action, they contented themselves with driving us with brutal blows of their whips into the barn. When they had left us I told Ned and Bart that from henceforth this was the way that the food was to be shared out. They were sullen and said very little, but Paul agreed to abide by the new rules.

The next day Quigg himself took a gang to which I was assigned and I spent an exhausting day threshing corn. When the signal was given at dinner-time no-one moved except me, and I shared out the food as before. The Quiggs, who were furious again, urged Ned and Bart to fight us but, seeing how united we were, they declined.

The rest of the boys were euphoric at their victory and I was particularly gratified to think that Stephen would at last be receiving his fair share, for he seemed to me to be visibly weaker even than when I had arrived.

The next day I was assigned to Roger's gang and so was with Stephen for the first time. To my bewilderment, as we set off Roger threw at him a kind of leather harness attached to wide pieces of leather and made him, helped by Little Thom and myself, carry a heavy two-handled wooden implement consisting of a beam about six feet long with a triangular metal blade at the end.

When we reached the field we were to work in, the mystery was solved. To my amazement Stephen secured the harness round his waist, thereby attaching the pieces of leather to his thighs. He then held the implement before him and I now realized it was a breast-plough. The field had been harvested and our task was to burn-brake it which is to say, to pare the stubble so that it could be burnt. This meant that Stephen had to push the heavy share before him with his thighs which were protected by the leather clappers. My task was to walk ahead of him pushing the picket, the blade, from side to side at the correct level. I found this extremely hard work — and somewhat dangerous — but the effort required by Stephen to supply the driving force must have been far more arduous.

"Can't you let it rise?" he gasped once while Roger was watching the others who were removing stones, digging drainage-ditches, and repairing walls.

I realized that it was easier to cut the stubble the higher the blade was, and so I let the picket rise. But when Roger came back he quickly noticed and cut me with the whip. And so after this I only dared ease Stephen's labour very briefly when Roger was not near, even though he begged me to do it more often.

Roger stayed near us sauntering about smoking his pipe but occasionally running with his whip raised to strike at any of the others whom he suspected of slacking. He gave us all fewer and shorter rests than his brother did, but it was clear to me that he was determined to work Stephen and myself particularly hard.

After a couple of hours Stephen was so exhausted that he could hardly stand.

Seeing this, Roger walked behind him constantly striking him on the shoulders with the whip.

At last I cried out: "Let me do it! You're killing him!"

Roger looked at me with a strange smile: "Tha'rt in a hurry," he said. "Wait tha turn."

At least, I reflected as Little Thom and I helped Stephen to stagger home at the end of the day, he would get his handful of potatoes. However, I noticed that the Quiggs seemed unusually pleased with themselves and when the time came for the distribution of the food, I found out why.

When the potatoes had been emptied into the trough Roger and Hal placed themselves between it and us and then Quigg beckoned Ned, Bart, and Paul forward and told them to help themselves to as many as they could carry.

"Don't, Paul!" I called out, earning myself a lash from Roger's whip.

"Hold hard, lad," Quigg said to his son, to my astonishment. He grinned at me: "Let him see he's beat fair."

The triumvirate began to eat the potatoes and when they had almost all gone, Quigg picked out about half of the rest of us — including the two Thoms but not Richard or Stephen or me — and ordered them forward. Then he told them to eat as many of the remaining potatoes as they could. After glancing anxiously at us, they began to do so.

"Stop!" I cried. "Share them with us or we'll all be the worse of it."

The appeals from the rest of us made no impression, however.

Then Quigg cried to us: "Come and fight for 'em if you want any."

Despite my attempts to urge them to hold back, the boys who had been left with Richard and Stephen and me ran forward and began fighting their former comrades while the Quiggs roared with laughter. Richard and I continued to exhort them not to, but at last Richard himself — with a shame-faced grimace towards Stephen and me — joined in the *mêlée*.

I knew that the cause of Equity was lost. And so it turned out for the next evening the boys fought for the food exactly as they had before my initiative, and now, to the immense satisfaction of the Quiggs, I was forced to do so myself. So Richard and I fought in alliance against the smaller boys and managed to gather just enough for ourselves and Stephen.

Although it was the end of July, during the next days the sky was low and grey and at intervals a drizzling rain fell. I foresaw with dread a procession of days like this following one another until I was numbed and starved into submission. I had to escape. And yet I could not imagine how Richard and Stephen, the one crippled and the other weakened by illness and hunger, could make the attempt.

The next week or two dragged past during which I was either burn-braking or stone-picking — which was exhausting because we had to use a rake to get the stones up and load them into the box to carry to where a wall was to be built. Because of the long daylight hours we carried our dew-bit to the fields for our breakfast to save time. I could not grow accustomed to the diet of hog-peas, oatmeal, buttermilk, "turmot-tops", oaten cakes that were often thick with mould, and occasionally pieces of bacon. And always the black rye-bread. I knew I would get weaker on this regimen and I learned from the others how much worse things would be later in the year when winter came and we would be put to flailing corn and making hurdles in the freezing barn.

The composition of the gangs was different each day but I noticed that

Stephen was always put into Roger's. I soon discovered that Hal was the least brutal of the three Quiggs and always rejoiced when he was my tasker. When, for example, we were working far from the farm-house, and our midday "piece" was brought by the little maid-servant — bent over as she bore a bucket of potatoes or a basket of bread — Hal always allocated the food reasonably fairly himself, whereas his father and brother always made us fight for it.

Now it was that I had a nightmare which has often come back to me since then. I dreamed that a dark hunched shape was approaching me and though I tried to flee, it bore down on me relentlessly and loomed over me. Just as I realized with horror that it was a huge spider, it spoke to me in a soft, frightened voice that I recognised: "Help me. Help me, Johnnie." I started back and tried to run but my limbs would not move. Shuddering, I stared at those waving legs and tentacles not wanting to recognise the face I feared to find in the midst of them. Then in heart-breaking tones she said: "I don't want to be like this."

I started out of my sleep in a sweat to find my companions sleeping peacefully around me. All my doubts and fears were renewed, and so the following evening I brought up the subject of escaping again.

"It's impossible," Richard said. "You must have seen as you came that the farm is surrounded by wild moorland for miles and miles in every direction. There are no villages and only a few scattered sheep-farms."

"So even if you managed to get off the farm," Little Thom went on, "you could not seek shelter from anyone in the neighbourhood for they all know of the rewards the Quiggs offer for returning one of us. And if you could not seek shelter you would need to get off the moors very quickly or the Quiggs would catch you. You see, there is only one road and they would use the dogs to scent the way you had taken, and then they would overtake you on horseback."

"Then," I said, "could I not simply strike out across the moors ignoring the road, so that the Quiggs would lose the advantage of their horses?"

"Yes," said Richard, "but it would be slow going and difficult to keep a straight course, and the dogs would catch you quickly."

"Unless it were raining," I said, "so that the scent could not be followed."

"It would be too dangerous to attempt if the weather were not fine," Stephen objected.

"But all this is foolish," Richard protested, "it is impossible to get out of the farm itself. We are guarded during the day by the Quiggs, and at night we are locked in here and the dogs are let loose."

"Then," I asked, "has no-one ever escaped?"

Nobody seemed to want to answer.

At last Little Thom said in an undertone: "Only two fellows have ever tried. One of them died on the moors and he's buried near Davy. But Thom nearly got away." Seeing my surprise he added: "He wasn't simple then. They beat him, you see, and after that he was stupid."

"Why was he caught?" I asked.

There was a silence and it seemed that the three were avoiding each other's eye.

"Someone 'peached on him," Little Thom said eventually. "We never found out who."

"So whoever it was might do it again if I tried?" I asked.

None of the three looked at me.

"Then if I were to try, would any of you come with me?"

Little Thom shook his head: "See what happened to Thom."

"How could I?" asked Richard, touching his leg.

"What about you, Stephen?"

He looked at me sadly: "I have no-one to go to."

He said it so flatly that, though we had learned a little of each other's story, later that night as we lay down to sleep I asked him to tell me the rest.

"I am an orphan," he said. "For my Papa died when I was a baby and my Mamma a few years later. I have only two relatives in the world. One is my half-brother, Henry. You see, my Mamma was married before she became my Papa's wife, only Henry's Papa died. He's quite a lot older than I and I don't know him well. He is studying law in London. I know he has very little money, for his Papa and my Mamma were very poor. My own Papa left a little money in trust for me."

"Money?" I repeated. "Then there's your chance."

He shook his head: "It is administered by my aunt, who is my only other relative. She is my guardian, but she took no interest in me after my Mamma died, and so I stayed on at the school in Canterbury that I was boarding at. I wish she had left me there for I was quite happy, but at Christmas last year she suddenly came to visit me. She asked if I would like to go to a different school. I did not want to and told her so. But she was very kind and brought me a soldier. (A Prussian with a real sword. You should have seen it, Johnnie!) She said I should do nothing I did not choose to do, and that she would leave me to think it over. A week or two later Henry came to see me. He was very kind, too, and advised me to do as my aunt wished. So because of that I agreed to be sent here."

"Why should your aunt wish you ill?"

"I don't know. Except that if I died she would inherit the money held in trust for me. But it is very little — only a few hundred pounds — and she has lots of money for her husband was rich."

"That is strange," I said. "But perhaps she does not know how you are treated."

"No, perhaps not. But she has not written to me or visited me and I have not been allowed to write to her."

"Has Mr Steplight not visited you on her behalf?"

"No. That time when he brought you was the first occasion I have met him or heard his name."

"What of your half-brother?"

"Henry would be very distressed to know what is being done to me. But he could do nothing."

We lay without speaking in the darkness and after a time I heard his breathing become slow and rhythmical. Perhaps it would not be possible to help him to get away, it occurred to me, and in that case I should think only of myself.

The next day was the last of July, but it was pouring with rain so heavily that even with our pieces of sack over our shoulders, we could not work in the fields. I was put into Roger's gang with Stephen and three of the other boys, and we were led to one of the "laithes" — or barns — and put to work topping turnips while Roger walked round us carrying his whip under his arm and losing no opportunity to bring it into play. It was exhausting labour for I had to bend over to hold the turnip steady, then swing the cleaver hard to separate the top from the rest at peril of severing a finger if I made a small mistake. I spurred myself on by imagining that each turnip was the head of one of the Quigg family and I executed Roger many times more frequently than either his parent or his brother.

Stephen was working in front of me and I watched him anxiously, aware of how much weaker even than me he would be after what he had endured. Roger was behind me at one moment when I noticed Stephen glance round, then put something in his mouth.

At that instant Roger shouted from behind us: "I seen tha, Mealy-Plant!"

As he spoke he strode towards him and Stephen tried to swallow what he had in his mouth but it was too large, and he choked. When Roger reached him he forced his mouth open and made him spit it out.

He held up the piece of turnip and said gleefully: "Aren't tha going to ketch it now! I should say so!"

He did not raise his whip to Stephen, but ordered us back to work and strutted up and down grinning broadly.

"What will happen?" I asked one of the boys.

"A roasting," he answered.

When, an hour or two later, we were marched to the barn for dinner, I saw Roger standing in conference with his father and noticed that he glanced towards us as he spoke.

Before the food was given out Quigg bellowed: "Nothing for you, Mealy-Plant! You've had your dinner." Then he clapped his hands for our attention and called out: "Listen, young genel'men. You're to assemble in the school-room after dinner."

A shudder ran through the boys and they glanced at Stephen.

While I was eating I whispered to Paul: "What's a roasting?"

"Quigg will flog him until he passes out," he answered.

"Can we not stop him?"

"How can we?"

"But for something so trivial?"

"They've taken every occasion to beat him," he replied. "They don't need a good reason."

After dinner Roger and Hal rounded us up and led us into the house-place — for that was the "school-room" referred to by Quigg, though this was its sole scholastic function, as far as I ever learned. We assembled at one end and the three Quiggs faced us at the other. Mrs Quigg temporarily abandoned her persecution of the little maid and emerged from her kitchen, and she looked a worthy mate for her husband — big with a broad, staring face and angry eyes. Now it was evident to me how absurd any idea of resistance was: we were eleven near-starving, sick boys against three grown men with whips and sticks, as well as a large and muscular woman.

Stephen was gripped by Hal and made to double over across the table while Roger pulled up his shirt. I saw that his back, pitifully thin, was already ridged with welts. Meanwhile Quigg who was carrying a thick leather strap, strode forward and began a speech:

"A boy from Quigg 'Cademy may not be as book-larned as other scholards. He may not be able to speak Ancient Greek well enow to pass t' time o' day with a Ancient Greek. Similarly with Latin and a Ancient Latin. We ain't ashamed o' that. But one thing a Quigg boy will be is honest. I know a boy is always hungry however much he gets fed. I know he'll tak' what he can if he ain't watched. But if there is one thing I will not abide in this 'cademy it is thieving. When we ketches a thief we makes an example of him."

As he pronounced these last words he removed his coat and unfastened the top and bottom buttons of his waistcoat. Then he took a couple of paces back and raised his arm. I saw the belt flying through the air but I winced just before I heard the sharp crack followed by a cry from Stephen.

The boys murmured and Roger shouted: "Quiet! T' same for any boy as cries out another time."

As if in a nightmare I saw the arm go back again, and again saw the strap arching downwards, and heard Stephen cry out again. A third time the arm was raised and the strap descended. There was a crack but this time no sound came from Stephen. When I opened my eyes I saw Quigg panting heavily and undoing another button. I forced myself to look: there was a spreading mass of blood on the white skin of Stephen's back. He lay quite still.

Quigg began to raise his arm again. All I remember of the next few seconds is a reddish haze before my eyes for I have no recollection of crossing the intervening space. Then I recall Quigg's face staring down at me.

"Hit him again and I swear I'll kill you!" I cried.

I remember the expression of surprise — almost of wounded indignation — that appeared on the brutal red face. I remember being seized from behind by Roger and Hal and I recall Quigg's words: "Tha munna be in such a hurry, Cloth-Ear. Tha turn will cwome."

I remember seeing Quigg aim his fist at me. I recall the first blow on my chest, and I have a memory of the second to my head. But after that I remember nothing except misty blotches swimming around me and far-away voices calling me.

When I came round my head was aching and I opened my eyes with difficulty. I found I was lying on a layer of straw and there was a guttering light nearby. I had no recollection of who or where I was. Then I recognised Richard's face looking down at me and I remembered everything.

"How is he?" I asked.

For answer Richard glanced to one side of me and when I turned my throbbing head I saw that Stephen was only a foot or two from me, lying on his stomach as if asleep. His back was heaped with rags which were soaked with blood. The act of raising my head had brought on a thudding ache and I laid it on the straw again. There was no sound inside the barn. I closed my eyes.

I don't know how long I slept. When I opened my eyes again both Stephen and Richard were exactly as they had been.

"Will he be all right?" I asked.

Richard said nothing.

"Is it the same day?" I asked.

He nodded.

"Is it late?"

"About midnight."

I drifted back to sleep and dozed and awoke a number of times. Each time I did so I found Richard watching Stephen and me, and once I saw him raising the injured boy's head to help him to swallow a little water. Stephen was muttering to himself but I could not make out the words. Somewhat reassured by this, I slipped back into unconsciousness.

When I woke again I heard birds singing and realized that it was near dawn though it was still dark in here and the other boys were sleeping. I turned my head and to my delight found Stephen's gaze upon me. He was now lying on his back with his shoulders slightly raised on an old bale of straw. Though his face was very white he appeared well for he smiled at me. I smiled back at him with relief and looked at Richard, who averted his eyes.

"Hoping you ... wake soon," Stephen whispered.

"How are you?" I asked, leaning forward to catch his words.

"Don't try to speak, Stephen," said Richard, looking at me indignantly.

"Pain much less," he replied.

"I had to turn him over," Richard explained to me. "But he said his back was no longer hurting."

I could see that the straw beneath him was red.

"Are you sure, Stephen?" I asked.

"Yes. Pain less. But no time," Stephen whispered. He broke off and began to gasp for breath but all the while his eyes stayed fixed on my face and glittered at me.

"Don't speak," Richard cried.

Stephen began to breathe more regularly but his whisper was even lower now: "John. Must escape. Soon. You next ... after me. Quigg."

I shook my head: "How can I escape? How could I get off the moors?"

"Money. ... My shoe. Hid. Before arrived."

Looking at me in surprise, Richard moved a little distance away and picked up Stephen's shoes.

Stephen's eyes were half-closed and I had to lean forward to catch his words: "Half-brother. Go. Tell him 'bout me."

"But I could not escape without the other fellows knowing. And one of them would 'peach on me! The one who 'peached on Big Thom."

"No," he gasped. "Not be 'peached. Sure."

I looked at him wonderingly, for how could he be so certain? Surely only by one means! He was struggling to speak again and although I dreaded to hear more I could not stop him.

Richard had been pulling up the inside of one of the shoes and now he said: "I've found something. It's wrapped in a piece of paper."

"Give ... John," Stephen managed to whisper, then he shut his eyes.

Richard passed it to me and when I unwrapped it I found a shining half-sovereign. I smoothed out the paper and glanced at what was written on it: "Henry Bellringer, Esq., second bell-handle on the right-hand door-post, No. 6, Fig-tree-court, Barnards-inn. Half-brother of Stephen Maliphant."

I knew that latter name. I had read it recently. Indeed, I had written it myself. Then it came to me: one of the beneficiaries mentioned in the codicil I had copied out only a few weeks before at our lodgings in Orchard-street had that name!

"Is that your name?" I asked. "Maliphant? Is that why Quigg calls you that ugly word?"

"Don't speak to him!" Richard cried. He studied his face and then placed his hand upon his chest.

Stephen's eyes remained closed and he didn't answer.

"Stephen!" I whispered.

I reached out my hand to touch his shoulder, but Richard gently took it and held it between his, and we remained like that until the light of day crept into the barn through the gaps in the wooden walls, and the other boys awoke to learn of the awful visiter who had come among us while they slept.

CHAPTER 45

From that moment onwards I dedicated myself to escaping. It seemed the only way to avenge Stephen and I felt it my bounden duty to tell his half-brother his story in the hope that he would be able to do something against the Quiggs. I concealed the half-sovereign, still wrapped in its mysterious piece of paper, in my own shoe. What little energy left to me after the day's work I could spare from thinking about my escape, I devoted to puzzling over the question of why I had been sent to this place and the related enigma of why Stephen had the same surname — and a very uncommon one — as one of the beneficiaries of my great-great-grandfather's codicil made forty years before either of us was born. Confirmation that there was some kind of connexion between him and myself lay in the fact that Mr Steplight had an interest in both of us. Beyond this point I could not advance, but I found it difficult to accept that these links between us were merely coincidental.

The next morning, the Quiggs had shouldered Stephen's body and borne it out of the barn as if it were a sack of malt. (Later I noticed that there was a freshly-dug mound among those I had remarked by the gate into the Fifteen-Acre where the Death-caps grew.) I was assigned to Roger's gang and had the leather harness thrown at me. So I found myself drawing the plough day after day and in all weathers. It proved to be a severe strain on the heart and lungs, for the strap passed over the ribs so that breathing in was extremely arduous. Moreover, the skin of my shoulders and chest quickly became a raw mass of skin and blood. The toll on my strength soon became apparent and I knew I had to get away before I became too debilitated to be capable of the attempt.

Richard and I discussed my escape long and late, and with his help, I broke the problem down into its constituent parts.

First there was the difficulty posed by the existence of a spy for the Quiggs which meant that I could not risk trusting any of the other boys. (I tried to forget what Stephen had said and hoped I had misunderstood him.)

Secondly, there was the problem of getting out of the farm-enclosure. This seemed impossible during the day since we were watched all the time by one or other of the Quiggs, and anyway I needed to flee at night in order to gain a head-start over my pursuers. Yet at the very moment we were locked into the barn for the night after dinner, the dogs were released by Quigg and were so fierce in their unfed state that even Roger and Hal had to be safely inside the house before their father released their chain, and by dawn even he could not approach them with impunity if he were not carrying great pieces of meat to throw to them while he chained them up.

Thirdly, even if I managed to escape from the farm, I had to get off the moors — and very quickly. As Little Thom had pointed out, I could not risk asking for help at one of the few farmhouses in the vicinity because I might be betrayed. Once they discovered I had gone the Quiggs would use the dogs to track me and, on horseback, would certainly overtake me unless I had the greater part of the night to put distance between myself and them. I would have to decide whether I was going to go across the moors where the dogs could follow me, but the horses would be less of an advantage; or whether I would stay on the road. If I chose the latter course, then the dogs and horses could follow me very rapidly, but I might succeed in getting taken up by a passing vehicle. On the other hand, there would be few of these, particularly at night. Beyond that, and the question of how I was to travel the several hundred miles to London with only half a sovereign, and what I would do when I got there, I did not even begin to speculate. The crux of the problem remained how to get out of the locked barn and away from the dogs. I could think of no feasible solution, and I knew I would have only one chance.

The weeks dragged past and as the summer slipped away I felt I was losing my best opportunity for escape. Once autumn arrived the dangers of being out on the moors at night would become considerable, and in the winter it would be impossible. In compensation, however, the Quiggs' guard would be more relaxed and the longer nights would give me more time before my disappearance was discovered in the morning.

During this period my sleep was disturbed by terrible dreams that left me more tired the next morning than when I had lain down to rest: I wandered among great cities that were engulphed in vast holocausts with swirling flames obscuring the sky or I hung over the edge of ravines so deep that I was looking down at wisps of cloud floating far below me and concealing the bottom. But the one that left me feeling most alarmed was one that I had again and again: I was walking down a long dark passage and suddenly met my mother, but instead of greeting me she backed away as if in dismay and then turned and walked swiftly into the darkness ahead of me so that I lost sight of her.

One evening, towards the middle of October, the Quiggs gave us our great-coats for the winter — foul old garments made for men and heavy with grease. Under these we were to sleep and we would wear them at work in the fields instead of the sacking.

When the Quiggs had gone, Big Thom held his great-coat out in disgust: "I don't want this 'un. This was Harry's."

Richard held out the one he had been given and said: "Then take this instead."

"Who was Harry," I asked him as Thom snatched it and tried it on.

"He took ill with the fever last winter."

"What happened to him?" I asked as we lay down on the straw and pulled our coats over us.

"Nothing," he answered. "He was put in the little outhouse beyond the hay-rick. The Quiggs made some of us carry him there because they were so afraid of catching it. They thought it was the Irish fever. They threw food and water in to him every day. After a few days they had Ned and Paul put him where they bury us, beyond the wall by the house, so that the dogs can't dig us up — you know, where Stephen is."

An idea began to take form in my mind. "I wish I knew for certain that it was Stephen who 'peached on Thom," I said. "Because while I don't know I dare not trust anyone."

Then I realized what I had said and looked at Richard. He had reddened and avoided my eye so that I was afraid I had hurt him by my accusation against his friend.

I lay awake for some time thinking about the idea his words had given me.

I thought he had fallen asleep but once I saw the glitter of his eyes in the faint light from the moon that came through the gaps in the walls.

The next day I managed, on my way to the fields with Roger and the rest of his work-gang, to look at the outhouse — hardly more than a shed — that Richard had mentioned. To my delight I saw that it was built of wood and that the weather-boarding was very delapidated.

After dinner that evening Richard and I held a whispered conference: "I am going to take ill," I told him. "I want them to believe it is something infectious."

"They will be suspicious," he objected, "and suspect that you are feigning."

"I know. But I will not be feigning. Just you see."

He looked puzzled and then said: "Be careful."

"I want you to help me frighten them," I said.

"They don't trust me," he objected. "And they know you and I are friends. Ask Paul to do it. They will believe him."

"I dare not. He might be the one who 'peached on Thom. If it wasn't Stephen, then it might have been any one of them."

Richard looked at me strangely. "Why do you say it was Stephen?"

I told him of his words just before he died.

He was silent. "It wasn't Stephen that 'peached on Big Thom," he said at last.

"How can you know?" I objected, but even as I spoke I saw the answer in his face and felt a cold chill run through me.

"I couldn't bear to let you go on thinking it was Stephen," he said, without looking at me.

"Then ... But why?" I demanded. Richard was silent. "They forced you to?" He shook his head. "You did it to protect someone? To protect Stephen? Or Davy?"

Richard shook his head again. "For the promise of being let send a letter home," he said. "And it served no good. If it was even sent." I turned from him in disgust. For a letter! He went on: "So now you can ask Paul. The Quiggs don't trust me any more." Then he added: "Stephen guessed." I got up and moved away and he said more loudly: "Stephen didn't blame me."

I moved my bed to another part of the barn and lay down beside Paul. I waited until the others were asleep, then I quietly woke him up and told him in a whisper what I wanted of him. He agreed and smiled at me enviously.

I now had one more operation to perform and it took several days of patient waiting. During this time I avoided Richard and was afraid to meet his eye for the sense of shame that welled up in me. To have betrayed a fellow-sufferer seemed to me to go against all my notions of what one should live by. No, it was unforgivable. Wholly unforgivable. Richard seemed to understand my feelings for he kept away from me.

The weather remained auspicious for my purposes: dry and not too cold. At last, one day in the middle of October, the chance I had been waiting for came. Roger led his work-gang to a field to the north of the farm and we returned in the evening through the Fifteen-Acre. I fell to the rear and just as I was passing into the yard I stumbled as if suddenly faint, and collapsed into the long grass beside the gate. I earned a lash of the whip from Roger as I picked myself up, but by that time I had achieved my purpose.

"I felt dizzy," I said.

He pushed me towards the barn and I staggered towards it as if unwell. As I ate my dinner I slipped into my mouth a couple of pieces of the two Death-caps

I had managed to gather. I wasn't sure what quantity I should eat but I had to trust to luck to get it right.

The effects came quickly. A few minutes later I broke into a sweat, my stomach was gripped by sharp cramps, and my head seemed to become a vast, echoing cavern. Suddenly I lost consciousness. I came round very quickly to find Roger holding me up and shaking me. He seemed to be speaking but I could hear nothing for the sound like rushing water that was in my ears. My tongue felt like a huge stone as I moved it in my mouth and I could not speak. Roger summoned his father for the sake of his superior medical understanding, and Quigg seized me from his son and hit me twice on the face. I saw a look of rage appear when this treatment failed to effect a cure. As if through a red mist I saw Paul's face. The rushing waters seemed to abate a little and I heard a strangely distorted voice saying:

"Please, sir, I think it's the Irish fever. A girl in our house died of it and she started the same way."

Quigg instantly let go of me and I fell to the ground. "Tak' him to t' 'firmary," I heard him gasp. "Tha and tha."

I felt myself being picked up and carried and then there was darkness and recollection ends. After this there are only vague memories of terrible fears and fierce pains, and even a strange joy at moments. How long I lay in a delirious fever I cannot say, but I believe I was in this condition that night, all the following day, and all the next night. But I may have lost a day or even two from my reckoning.

Certain it is that I awoke one morning at the first approach of dawn feeling perfectly recovered though very weak and exceedingly hungry. I was lying on a bed of straw and in the dim light I found a large pitcher of water standing beside me and five or six potatoes. A torn and filthy blanket was lying across me and I was still wearing the great-coat, but even when I drew them tight around myself and snuggled under the straw I was cold. About an hour later I heard the dogs being chained up, and when, some time after that, I heard footsteps coming towards my shed, I began to roll and moan. Through half-closed eyes I saw a figure peering in over the top of the door and then two potatoes landed beside me before, his duty to the sick discharged, my visiter retreated. I drank deeply but, hungry as I was, I dared not eat more than a few of the potatoes in case their disappearance was noted. When all was quiet I set about searching for one of the planks to loosen on the blind side of the shed — that is, the side away from the barn and the farmhouse. Finding a likely one I set to work but I made slow progress without tools and having to stop frequently to listen for the sounds of someone approaching. And it was as well that I did.

By midday I had managed to work the plank almost free when suddenly I heard soft footsteps coming across the yard. Instantly I lay down and feigned ill. Through my half-closed eyes I saw Roger looking down at me over the top of the door. He watched me for some time, then walked away without making any attempt to deaden his footsteps.

By the late afternoon I had made the board loose enough to be sure that I could pull it out quickly. Knowing that when the opportunity came, I would have only a few seconds to act, I tried to foresee as many eventualities as possible. The Quiggs would probably check on me at dusk either before or after distributing dinner and securing the barn, for their final action would be to release the dogs. My only chance to escape would lie between the moment they examined me and the release of the dogs — after which I would be torn to pieces if I was in the yard.

As soon as my chance came I must gather the potatoes and remove the board. I would have to replace it behind me in order to prevent the dogs from discovering that they could get into the shed for otherwise they might start to bark, and if the Quiggs were alerted to my flight so soon I would be overtaken before I had gone half a mile. Once I had secured it, I would then, keeping the shed between myself and the Quiggs, have to get over the wall before the dogs were released.

Then I could either head for the road or make my way across country. After chasing these alternatives round and round in my head for hours, I eventually settled for the latter course, calculating that in the eight or ten hours I could hope to remain unpursued until my flight was discovered, I could be off the moors and amongst the lowland villages and farm-steadings where I would be comparatively safe. What decided me was my realization that my pursuers would not be able to go very much faster than I across that rough terrain, despite being mounted, whereas along the road they would have an enormous advantage. Although it would be good scenting weather for the dogs since it was a cold dry day and the night seemed likely to be the same, it would benefit me, too, for although there would be no moon, the sky would be clear and the stars would shed enough light to enable me to see my way. I was fairly confident that I could find my direction by the heavenly bodies for I believed I could identify the Pole Star. My design was to head due South even though this was the way the Quiggs would assume I had gone, for the dogs would easily find my track and so there was no advantage in trying to baffle pursuit by describing a circle. Above all, the land to the north was inhospitable, but there were villages and towns not far to the South.

For the rest of that day I rehearsed this sequence of events and choices so that I could act without needing to think, made ready my shirt and jacket to hold the potatoes, and practised gathering them up quickly. At last, as the dusk thickened, I heard the boys returning from work. Watching through the gaps in the boards I saw them go into the barn and then the Quiggs carrying their dinner in. At last the Quiggs came out, carrying lanthorns for it was now nearly dark, and locked the barn-door. Were they going to ignore me and immediately release the dogs? It appeared that they were talking together and despite all that I had earlier decided, I was tempted to make my escape now in the hope that they would not check. But just at that moment one of the lanthorns separated itself from the other two and came towards me. Quickly I lay on the floor and peered through a crack between my eye-lids. The lanthorn was held up above the door and a couple of potatoes hit the straw beside me. As soon as the light was removed I gathered up the potatoes and stuffed them into my shirt, went to the loosened board and removed it as quietly as I could, then stepped out into the yard. I heard the barking of the dogs quicken in the way that indicated that they were about to be released. My heart thumping and my instincts urging me to run, I forced myself to replace the plank, wedging it firmly back in place. Then I hurried to the wall and began to clamber up it. Although characteristic of that country, being made of large stones which offered many holds for the hands and feet, it was more difficult than I had anticipated because of my weakened condition and the awkwardness of the potatoes inside my shirt. Indeed, as I reached the top, three or four of them fell and I dared not climb down for them since I would now be easily visible against the star-scattered sky from the farmhouse, were it not for the intervening barn.

Just as I began lowering myself down the other side I felt suddenly dizzy, and, rather than resist and risk injuring myself against the stones, I surrendered to the sensation of falling. To my horror, however, I fell much further than I had anticipated for there was a ditch on this side whose presence I had not suspected, and consequently I landed heavily and awkwardly.

Although I had bruised my knee and grazed my shins, as well as twisted my ancle, I did not think my injuries were any more serious. But I quickly had something else to occupy me, for I heard the dogs running over to this side of the yard, probably having heard the sounds of my fall which — I hoped — had eluded the duller senses of their master. From the noises the animals began making just on the other side of the wall, I realized that they had found the potatoes and were devouring them. Thank goodness they were consuming the evidence instead of carrying it back to Quigg! I breathed as quietly as I could and after a few desultory barks, they dashed away to another part of the yard.

I got up and felt a stab of pain when I put my weight on my right leg. It was obvious that I must abandon my intention of crossing the moors for I would be unable to scramble up ridges and jump across gulleys. I began to limp as fast as I was able towards the track that led up to the road and when I struck it I stayed parallel to it. I kept glancing round and just before I reached the crest of the ridge, I looked back at the farm for what I hoped would be the last time. I could see lights at two of the upper windows, but even as I watched one of them was extinguished. An occasional bark reached me but the farmstead looked completely at peace in the star-light and I hurried on. In a minute the road lay before me gleaming in the faint light. I took a moment to cram into my mouth one of the potatoes and then, turning left towards the South, I began to walk as fast as my injured leg would permit me.

I walked on through countryside which might have seemed beautiful if it had not been so inhospitable. My leg slowed me down considerably and, to my increasing disquiet, grew more painful with each step. I needed something I could use as a walking-stick, but in this treeless country that was not to be hoped for.

I limped on for more than an hour — my pace slackening as my leg grew more painful with each step — before I encountered anything except the tracks to three farms whose buildings I could see some distance off the road. Apart from these, there was no house, no cross-road, and no change in the featureless landscape. At the end of that time I saw a light approaching about two miles ahead and since I had decided that I would hide from any vehicle coming towards me in case its driver were stopped by my pursuers, I wasted precious minutes by lying down, when it was about a mile away, at the side of the road in the long grass and bracken — there being no wall or even ditch to provide concealment — until the vehicle, a light waggon, had rumbled past.

After another hour or so my frequent glances behind me brought to my attention a vehicle approaching from that direction. It was travelling fast and in case it could be a pursuer — though I knew the Quiggs kept no carriage — I hid once again and looked out at it. As it drew nearer, however, I saw that it was a stage-coach and since in Stephen's half-sovereign I had the fare to carry me two or three stages, I came forth and stood in the middle of the road waving my arms above my head. For answer the guard blew a long blast and I had to leap aside as the vehicle thundered past, the driver cutting at me with his whip. I was furious but I could understand their unwillingness to stop at night in that desolate place. Then I reflected that I had obeyed a foolish impulse, for one of the Quiggs might have boarded the vehicle behind me as the quickest way of gaining ground.

So I stumbled on for two or three hours, firmly resolved to conceal myself from any vehicle that approached from either direction, though none appeared to test me. Still I came to no cross-road and passed only a few farmhouses lying a mile or two off the road. I figured that it must be an hour or two past midnight and my mind kept turning to possible events at the farm: the discovery of my flight, the leashing of the dogs, the saddling of the horses, the departure of the Quiggs in pursuit. If these things had not occurred already they could not be long delayed, and with the dogs to tell them which way I had gone, two of the Quiggs would be able to gallop down this road at three or four times my pace, leaving the third to follow on foot with the dogs. I began a grim calculation: even assuming my absence was not discovered until dawn which was still four or five hours off, the Quiggs would need only an hour and a half to reach the point I was at, and perhaps a little over another half-hour to come up with where I would be by then. My injury had reduced my chances of getting off the moors to where there would be more roads to choose from.

Then, peering into the distance far ahead, I thought I saw a dark shape on the silvery road. Yes, surely there was a vehicle ahead for now I saw a couple of faint lights. I increased my pace as well as I could for my leg was hurting more than ever, and at the end of another mile or two I made out that it was an eight-wheeled road-waggon. It took me nearly an hour to come up with it and see that it was carrying huge bales of wool loosely covered by tarred sacking. When I saw that the out-rider was up beside the driver and deep in conversation with him, an idea came into my mind that plunged me into an anguish of indecision. Either I could keep walking as far and as fast as possible, taking the risk that if the road ran on like this and I was not taken up by a vehicle it could only be a matter of time before the Quiggs overtook me, especially since I was tiring rapidly. Or I could try to board this waggon — which was going at least as fast as I and probably, henceforth, faster — in the hope of throwing the dogs off my scent and of soon coming to a cross-roads or a forking of the way, for then my pursuers would be forced to choose and might take the wrong road. Against this, the danger was that they would overtake the waggon and search it and then I would be trapped.

I would play the long shot. I approached cautiously, hoping that neither the driver nor the out-rider would look back and catch sight of me in the dim gleam of the lamps projecting on brackets from the sides. The huge wheels rose above my head, concave and seeming to bend sinuously as they turned, crashing over the uneven stone surface of the carriageway. I eyed the tail-gate a few feet ahead of me on which was painted "Thomas Cavander and Sons: Carriers" and marked a foot-hold. I made a run and a jump and by means of this I managed to get one knee onto the top of the tail-board and then pulled myself over it and landed amongst the woollen bales. I crawled under a piece of the tarred sacking and arranged it so that I could look back at the road but not be seen by the out-rider if he turned round or dropped back. I longed to sleep but the jolting of the waggon, even through the bales I was lying on, and the smell of the oil from the lamps and the tar and above all the gamey sheep-smell of raw wool, made that impossible. I felt, anyway, that I should keep watch for a fork or cross-roads.

We travelled on for an hour or more and still none appeared. A couple of hours passed, and when I glanced out pale streaks began to appear in the eastern sky and I could see that there was snow on the crests of the hills. As the pale sun rose behind the thick layer of cloud, I saw that I was in a bleak country of furze and whinstone.

Then at last the waggon rumbled across some deep ruts and I saw first a finger-post and then over to my right another road alongside us receding at a widening angle. If my absence had not already been noticed, it was now being discovered, I knew, and I estimated that it would take my pursuers only two hours on horseback to reach the fork. Here they might divide, assuming the third had stayed behind with the dogs, and this suggested that until we came to at least another fork I was still very far from being safe.

BOOK V

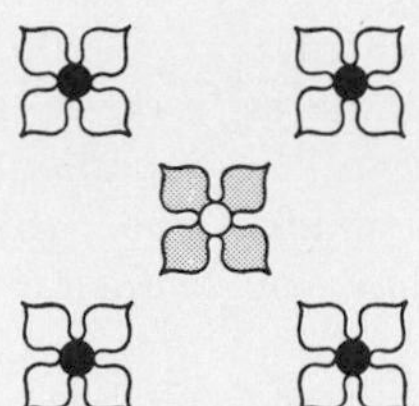

The Coming of Age

CHAPTER 46

We are again in the old-counting house down among the wharves of Blackfriars. Mr Sancious, carrying a portmanteau, enters the private closet smirking, and the old gentleman looks up at him from his chair across his table in keen anticipation.

"I have something for you," the attorney says.

He takes from the portmanteau a folded paper and opens it out so that the old gentleman, sitting on the other side of the table, can see it. Mr Clothier scans it for half a minute and then, rising with a fierce cry, reaches towards it. The attorney, however, steps backwards holding the document behind him.

"Fifty-five years I've waited for this," the old gentleman moans. "For heaven's sake tell me, how did you come by it?"

Mr Sancious smiles: "That is not my secret to reveal. But I can tell you that I used subtler methods than those that you employed. But come, do you want it?"

"Want it!" the old man repeats.

"Then what will you give me for it?"

"I'll give you what we agreed."

"Very generous of you," the attorney says.

He watches while the old gentleman unlocks his strong-box in the dark corner where it is hidden and reaches into it. Mr Clothier brings out a bundle of papers and gazes at them lingeringly.

Then he says: "What of the woman and the boy?"

"Have no fear for them."

"What do you mean?" the old gentleman almost whispers. "Are they ... ?"

The attorney merely smiles.

"You know it's worthless to me while they live," Mr Clothier says, staring at the paper in the lawyer's hand. "Is she alive?"

"Yes, but be assured that it will soon be worth many times more than you're giving me for it."

The old gentleman sighs. Then suddenly he says: "And the boy?"

"In due time. The people who have him are waiting for the word from me."

"As soon as may be!" the old gentleman cries.

"But don't you want this?" Mr Sancious asks, waving the document and then putting it back in his portmanteau while the old gentleman stares at it in anguish.

"Yes, yes, here's your money, curse you," Mr Clothier says, laying one of the papers on the table.

"The price has gone up," the attorney says. "For all my hard work and that of my helper, I want as much again."

The old gentleman is a pitiable sight as he stands, holding the bundle of bills from his chest and looking at the document in the attorney's hand. Then he says: "You're trying to cheat me! That isn't right! I'll pay you what we agreed and the same again when you bring me proof that you've made them both quiet."

"The same again for each of them," Mr Sancious says.

Mr Clothier is silent for a moment and then he nods: "Very well."

He draws out two pieces of paper from the bundle he is holding and says: "These are at three months drawn by the house of Pomeroy and due in six weeks. They are both backed by Shelmerdine and Tiptoft."

The attorney nods and while the old gentleman places them on the table (all the while holding onto one end of them), Mr Sancious lays the codicil beside them, in his turn keeping his hand firmly upon it. While the old gentleman scrutinises the document the attorney examines the bills. They nod at each other and then each relinquishes his grasp so that the exchange can be made.

When Mr Clothier has placed the codicil in his strong-box and locked it, he offers his guest a glass of wine "to mark the successful conclusion of our business".

When they have drunk each other's health, the old gentleman says: "Well, Sancious, what do you think the Pimlico and Westminster Land Company should do now?"

"Sell the freehold and put out all the capital."

"Sell it? With the way that the value of land in the metropolis is rising, we should hold onto it."

"Very well, Mr Clothier. Speculation in land is certainly very profitable at present."

"Then what should we do with the capital?"

"I had thought of putting it into government stocks," the attorney suggests.

The old gentleman snorts: "At two or three per cent?"

"Or mortgages," Mr Sancious suggests.

"Pshaw! One or two per cent more. I have a better suggestion. Why should we not use it to buy up discounted bills? That way we could double our capital in six months if the present speculative mania continues. For with prices of stocks rising so swiftly now, where will things be by Christmas?"

"Perhaps they will have crashed. I've never known such wild speculation. They say more than six hundred new companies have been promoted in the past twelvemonth."

"Nonsense! But even if the market falls and some of the acceptors break, the banks will have to pay up. We'll only buy paper endorsed by them."

"But if there's a general fall, will they be able to?"

"Upon my soul," the old gentleman exclaims, "don't you want to make your fortune? Of course, any commercial transaction involves risk because it's based on credit. You yourself have just gambled by accepting that paper of Pomeroy's from me. Even if the very worst happens and one or two of the banks close their doors, don't forget that all bills accepted by them are backed by the Bank of England."

"But that is only a *de facto* and not a *de jure* arrangement. Has it ever struck you that the money-market is like a gaming-hell where the players all agree to accept the ivory fishes as if they were worth a hundred pounds? What would happen if enough of the players declined to do so? They would become just pieces of ivory again."

"Nothing like that will happen. Why, I'm almost twice as old as you and I remember that the Bank suspended payments in gold only once. And that was in '97 at the height of the War and the blockade, when they issued paper instead. But bear in mind that if anything were to go amiss, neither you nor I are in jeopardy. Remember who the nominal owner of the Pimlico and Westminster Land Company is."

He jerks his head towards the outer office and at this Mr Sancious smiles and the two gentlemen raise their glasses.

CHAPTER 47

Before the dawn was fully accomplished the waggon had, to my relief, rumbled up to another cross-roads and borne left. Though even now I dared not assume I was safe, I laid my head against a bale and managed to slumber fitfully, tossed between waking and sleeping as the great vehicle jolted its way across the bleak uplands through the chilly dawn. Perhaps two or three hours later the waggon halted and I awoke to hear the driver and the out-rider applying the drag to each of its wheels. As it moved slowly off again and began to descend a steep hill, I peeked out from the sacking and saw a whitewashed public-house and then a row of low stone cottages. The surface of the road became cobbled and, realizing we were approaching a town, I waited for my opportunity. As the waggon slowed to less than walking-pace to take a bend, I jumped off (taking the weight on my uninjured leg) without being seen.

I found myself in the main street that ran steeply downhill towards a bridge. There were few people about at that hour, but following the smell of fresh bread I found a bakery and purchased a roll and a ha'penn'orth of milk with the half-sovereign. Seeing that there was a big inn down by the bridge and feeling that I needed to put as much ground as possible between myself and the Quiggs, I now conceived a daring design. I waited in the yard until an ostler came out of the stable and asked him if there were a public coach to the next town to the South.

He stared at me for a moment and then said: "Aye, for them as has t' bloont."

I said: "I have to get to York today. I've heard that my father is very ill."

"Seven shillin' outside," he replied.

I showed him the change from the half-sovereign, and he stared at me curiously: "T' coach leaves in an hour. Book ticket over yonder."

I purchased it from a sleepy clerk and the ostler allowed me to wash at the pump in the yard. Not wanting to make myself any more conspicuous than I had done already, I did not go into the travellers'-room but lingered in the yard and watched the coach being made ready. One of the maids saw me walking up and down swinging my arms against my sides, and smuggled out a cup of hot coffee.

When the time came to board the coach the other travellers emerged from the inn grumbling at the earlyness of the hour — which seemed dangerously late to me. To my dismay, for it would make me more prominent, I found that I was the only outside passenger, but when we pulled out of the yard, rumbled across the bridge and began to ascend the opposite hill my spirits lifted. Once we were up on the moors again, I found myself shivering with cold. Noticing this the guard invited me under the shelter of his own great-coat and I was the more grateful since this would conceal me from anyone we might meet on the road. In fact we met nothing except a few carts, then a string of pack-horses in a long line laden with fleeces for the wool-stapling towns, and finally the up-coach to whose driver our own coachman signalled with a laconic lift of his elbow.

The road remained deserted even as we began, after an hour or more, to descend from the lip of the high moors, and this caused me concern for I felt that my best hope of evading detection lay in the safety of crowds. However, leaning against the guard, I fell asleep and remember no more until a little after midday I was awakened by his fumbling for his horn upon which he then blew a prolonged blast.

Under any other circumstances I would have derived great enjoyment from our rattling entry into York, but as it was, I would have preferred to have got down on the outskirts. However, I had to allow myself to be borne into the yard of the city's principal coaching-inn and here my worst fears were realized for just as an ostler was seizing the lead-horse by the bridle, I noticed two men standing a few yards away by the door to the coffee-room: to my horror one of them was Quigg.

He was deep in conversation with a stranger — dressed in the gaiters, velveteen breeches, felt hat and heavy coat of a waggoner — and only glanced idly at the coach as it drew up beside them. Not knowing that I had any money, it would not have occurred to him that I could be travelling by that means.

The guard jumped down and began to speak to the ostler, thereby exposing me to Quigg's sight had it not been for the ample figure of the driver which was still between me and my enemy.

I had to freeze where I was — so close that I could hear the conversation:

"I'm chasing a yoong thief," he said. "He made off last night and me and my twa lads tracked him down t' high road this forenoon till he must have gotten hisself a cast, for t' dogs lost t' scent. So I sent my elder boy back with t' hounds and rode on with t' younger lad. He went round by Holmby and I cwome through Spentbridge for we didna ken which gate t' boy'd have tak'd. I'm meeting my lad here and if he doesna have t' young rascal wi' him then we'll most likely look for him here this forenoon and go on to Selby cwome t' afternoon." He had named the next town on the great road to the South. "For he'll mun pass through there if he's heading Sooth, as I believe he is."

The waggoner spoke but so marked was his speech that I could not understand a syllable.

In answer, however, Quigg described my appearance and concluded: "So keep yowr eyes open for t' rascal, will yow, and tell t'other lads and t' gate-keepers to do t' same? And if yow find him, ketch a hold on him and send word to me."

The waggoner appeared to consent to this and then asked another question.

"Why, a great-coat," Quigg answered. "But more nor yon, he's a runaway 'prentice so above all, hisself. It's robbing his friends as has paid t' premium, but worse nor that it's robbing me that's spent months larnin' t' lad his trade."

I admired the cunning of Quigg's pretending I was an absconded apprentice, for this denied me the protection of the law and enabled him to call on the help of the authorities.

To my dismay Quigg now hailed the guard of my coach and I realized that I was only seconds away from discovery. At that moment, however, the coachman, who had finished gathering up his belongings, stood up to descend. Concealed behind his broad figure I dropped down on the other side of the vehicle from Quigg as quietly as I could and, resisting the temptation either to look back or to run, walked out through the arched entrance of the yard.

Once out on the street I quickened my pace and then, breaking into a run, dived down a bye-street and then another and then another. In view of what I had overheard I realized that I could attempt to leave the town only after dark and that I would have to travel by night, and find a means of avoiding the turnpike-gates. Meanwhile, it would be dangerous to wander about the streets. Hunger, however, could not be resisted and so once I had bought a small loaf — leaving me two shillings and nine-pence of Stephen's half-sovereign — I found my way into the poorest part of the town down by the river.

Eventually I discovered what I was looking for: a deserted yard off a quiet bye-street where there was a range of abandoned outhouses which belonged to a former livery-stable. Although they were padlocked, the old door of one of them was so worm-eaten that I was able to remove it and then replace it behind me. In the dim light I could see that I was in a three-stall stable with a loft above, reached by a ladder which looked strong enough to bear my weight. I sat on an ancient manger and ate half of my bread, rejoicing that I was dry, relatively warm and for the first time fairly safe. The very smell of the stable — compounded of hemp because of the old sacks strewn about, of malt, of rotted wood and ancient straw — was oddly reassuring for it suggested that the place had been long abandoned. I cautiously climbed the ladder — to which surely no grown man would entrust himself — crawled into the musty straw in the darkness further back, pulled it around me and slept.

When I awoke it was nearly dark. I descended, ate some more of the bread, waited until night had fallen, and then ventured into the unlit back-lanes. By means of them I picked my way out of the town towards the North in case the roads to the South were being watched. After a mile or two I left the highway and, keeping the lights of the town always at a distance, made a wide sweep to the South, being careful to rejoin the road beyond the toll-house in case the keeper had been alerted. This manoeuvre cost me several hours, but at least my injured leg had so much benefited from the rest that I was able to keep up a brisk pace. This time I did not leave the carriageway to hide from other travellers except when I saw riders coming towards me, in case Quigg and Roger should be returning from Selby already. I reached the outskirts of that town before dawn and found a lonely barn to sleep in and there, with nothing more to eat than the last of my bread, I spent the day.

When darkness fell I skirted the town and pressed on South. As I walked, the harvest moon sailed above the horizon and the latticed windows of the darkened cottages I passed glinted in its light. When dawn was approaching I bought bread from a baker, who was overcome by floury surprise to have a customer so early. I found an isolated barn and slept for a few hours but then, feeling that I had eluded capture and could henceforward travel by day and sleep by night, I walked on in the bright mid-morning.

In this manner I made my way South. Occasionally a passing carter gave me a cast, but most of the time I walked, sleeping in barns by night. Often as I was sleeping under some straw in a musty byre or on a rattling cart, I started up from my sleep in the belief that my mother had called me, and it seemed to me that her voice sounded not frightened or anxious but strangely calm. As my money ran out I learned to beg — always on the watch for the constable — and when that failed, lived on raw turnips stolen from the fields, pea-shucks, and the dwindling produce of the autumnal hedgerows — sorrel leaves, berries, sloes, and crabs.

I have not leisure now to record the many adventures and the many strange meetings I had with the folk I met on the high-road: the packmen and wandering beggars, each with a wallet over his shoulder, and honest workmen upon the tramp and disembodied soldiers and crippled sea-men and cheap-jacks on their way to one or other of the statute-fairs and the man leading a dancing-bear with whom I walked for half a day. I met tinkers crying: "Any razors or scissars to grind? / Or anything else in the tinker's line? / Any old pots or kettles to mend?" When I went by the drove-roads and green-lanes I fell in with drovers leading cattle South from Scotland to be fed in Norfolk; and I often saw from a distance the dark-eyed, silent gypsies passing in their brightly-painted waggons. Ill-use I received from some, but charity from more. Yet even so, once my money had run out I had difficulty in obtaining food. At least once I walked a whole day on nothing more than a piece of bread and it was then — on the sixth day after leaving the Quiggs' farm — that I had an experience whose memory has haunted me all my life.

I had come to a district where the hamlets and farms gave way to a landscape of manufactories and canals and high hillocks of slag among which little lines of mean brick cottages started and broke off seemingly at hazard. Most of them were of recent construction but even so many were already in ruins, and often the carriageway sank several feet as if the land beneath it had caved in. The road and the buildings, the hedgerows and trees, and even the faces of the people I met, were covered with a fine layer of black ash and there was an oppressive smell like camphor. From behind high walls that ran alongside the road on one side there came the monotonous thump of a steam-engine and other sounds like the distant roar of malevolent seas. I drew my ragged coat about me to keep out the chill wind, but could do nothing against the dust and ashes that were blown into my mouth and eyes with every gust.

The faces of the country-people I had passed had been for the most part suspicious and closed and I had been better treated by my fellow way-farers, but the features of the people I met here were wild in either their misery or their exultation. And it seemed to be at these two extremes that the denizens of this place lived, for I saw many in the deepest poverty while others swaggered along in fine clothes. From either group my attempts to beg were unavailing, and since there were no hedgerows or fields to batten on, I became hungrier and hungrier. As evening approached I found myself surrounded by wide pits that belched flames and smoke from underground fires, lighting the ground up all around with a lurid flickering glow that made the shadows of the tall chimneys bend and waver alarmingly on either side of me. Now I remembered the fires that I had seen and the noises I had heard as I travelled north with Mr Steplight.

Further on I passed great hillsides of ashes which were the refuse of nearby lime-kilns. I was stopped by a small boy scantily clad in rags even on an October night who held out a grubby palm.

"I have nothing," I said.

"Sister's sick," he said, still holding out his hand.

"Where is your mam?" I asked.

"Gorn away," he said.

"Where do you live?"

He jerked his head.

"Where do you mean?"

He repeated the gesture and I looked at the great mound that rose up beside us. Some flimsy pieces of wood with tarred sacking over them had been placed across a space that had been hollowed out in the hillside. Now that I peered into the gloom I could see several of these makeshift shelters. I hurried on.

Even as night fell I walked forward for I wanted to get clear of that place of desolation, but it went on and on limitlessly. Hunger was making me light-headed and it became difficult to know if the noises I heard and the lights that flashed were inside my head or outside. It grew darker and darker and the sulphurous smell grew worse. I thought I had been walking for hours and could not tell why the dawn had not come. Now I began to have the strangest fancies: that perhaps the dawn would never come for the place I had entered was not on the face of the earth.

At last, I lay down a few paces from the side of the road and slept. It seemed to me that when I awoke it was still night for the same thick pall of smoke hung over the land and I walked on, and either a grudging daylight came at last or the smoke grew clearer. Then I was walking along a road on the edge of a town — or perhaps it was between two towns, for I could not tell where one ended and another began — and I came to a canal over which the road passed on an iron bridge. I looked down and there was a high, blank and windowless manufactory in pink brick like a boiled lobster with a row of dreary red-bricked cottages beside it and heaps of waste all around. There was a laden barge passing on the canal being drawn by no horse but with a little metal chimney puffing smoke, and there was a man at the tiller who was puffing on a pipe like a smaller imitation of the funnel. The building before me was immense with two high chimneys belching out smoke and long rows of arched windows and a hollow pediment in the centre through whose vast arch-way I could glimpse hundreds of men — black and almost naked — furiously pushing waggons heaped with coal on metal rails up to the very maw of a giant furnace where others fed it into the flames.

Then I was overcome by a sudden terror. What was I doing here in this nameless waste where I knew nothing and nobody and might lie down and die and not even my name be known to record my death? I must hasten on. Yet where was I going to? Whom, apart from my mother, did I know even in London? My hand was resting on the cold metal surface of the bridge's parapet and as I looked at the rusted surface it seemed to me that its pattern of stains and scratches was both meaninglessly accidental and yet the only thing that mattered in the world.

I walked on and the next thing I recall is that there was a high wall on one side of the way and that it seemed that I had been walking along that road all my life and would walk along it for ever. Despairing of its ever ending,

I lay down and slept, and then it seemed that I rose and went on and that I watched the most beautiful dawn I had ever seen unfold in the eastern sky, and that the land changed again and I came down into a delightful valley and found myself following a willow-bordered stream that flowed gently through a landscape of neat houses and well-kept fields dotted with clumps of trees like so many pleasure-demesnes. Still following the stream I entered a village by a foot-path that led along the backs of tall old houses, each with a walled sally-garden running down to the water into whose edges tall willows were weeping. Children were splashing about in the stream and their elders watching them from the ancient bridge accosted me with smiles and shook me courteously by the hand and pressed me to stay there. But I walked on. And later I must have lain down to sleep for I awoke and did not know where I was.

I went on again through the sullied landscape thinking about the sweetness of that village and remembering Melthorpe.

Gradually the waste-tips and canals and chimneys ebbed and the countryside came back. There was a smell of winter in the air and the sense of nature closing up and withdrawing made me anxious to quicken my pace. Then suddenly one morning a day or two later I saw on a finger-post a name I knew: *Sutton Valancy 12 mi.* Then Melthorpe could only be a few miles away! The thought gave me new strength for suddenly it came to me that I would go there. Sukey would help me!

On the ninth or tenth day after my escape I reached the well-remembered lane that led from the turnpike-road down Gallow-tree-hill to Melthorpe. It was late afternoon on a fine day and the familiar houses and fields lay in the autumnal sunshine of late October. How brief a time had passed since I last saw the village, but how much had happened! I made my way down the hill and past the Green, and there were the tumbledown cottages rising from the mud of Silver-street. The door of Sukey's was open and I went up to it, knocked and went a little way inside. All seemed at peace: a fire burned merrily in the hearth; a knitting-frame stood idle in a corner; some children — two girls and a boy — were sitting on the dirt-floor plaiting straw, and a woman was busied over a cooking-pot that hung over the fire. She turned on hearing my entrance and I saw that it was Sukey.

She stared at me for a moment, then a look of astonishment appeared on her face.

"Yes, Sukey. It's I."

With a cry she rushed towards me: "Master Johnnie!"

I felt myself pressed against her and so much of the past flooded back! After all that I had been through her welcome broke something inside me that had been holding firm, and I began to sob.

"For a minute I didn't know you!" Sukey cried, holding me at arm's length. "You're so much taller. And so thin." At this she hugged me again. "What has happened to you?" she cried. "And to your sweet mither? Is she in good cue?"

But when I tried to answer she hushed me and insisted that explanations should come later. I was seated before the fire and a bowl of the thick soup in the pot was ladled out and laid before me with a piece of the coarse barley-bread of the northern districts. Meanwhile Sukey put a skillet over the fire and fried some potatoes and a little bacon-fat which I consumed with relish after the broth.

When I had eaten this — the first hot food I had had for months — I was permitted to answer one question: "How is your mither?"

"When I left her she was well," I answered.

She read my meaning in my face.

"Wait while I get the children abed," she said.

When she had over-seen the washing and preparations for bed of the children — two little girls of about ten and six and a boy of eight — she came back to the fireplace and wearily seated herself beside me.

"How are all of you?" I asked.

Sukey looked down: "My mam died last winter. And Sally was carried off by the fever this Pack-rag Day."

"I'm sorry. And how are the others?"

"The girls help me with the work. Amos gets what work he can by the day. Jem starves the crows now for Farmer Lubbenham like Harry done."

"And Harry?"

She glanced down and then said: "He had a place as a farm-servant over towards Mere Bassett but he lost it for his bad ways, and now he's a roundsman on the paritch, like most of the men in the village. He's working on the 'Ougham estate right over beyond Stoke Mompesson. Most likely, he'll not be back till gone late."

She explained that a roundsman was a parish pauper who was hired out by the Overseer of the Poor each day to whichever farmer bid most for his labour.

Interested though I was, I could not stifle a yawn and Sukey insisted that I should sleep immediately and tell her my story when I awoke. Despite my protests, she laid an old straw palliasse in a corner of the cottage and the sight of it brought an immense yearning for rest upon me. I laid myself down and once I was lying there with a couple of ragged old blankets over me no-one would even have known I was there in the dark corner among the spiders.

I woke up late in the evening at the sound of a man shouting. For a moment, when I had recalled where I was, I wondered sleepily if it could be Sukey's father until I remembered that he was dead. I looked out from among the straw and blankets and recognised in the tall, brawny-shouldered figure with straw-coloured hair the boy I had known as Harry and who, though only three or four years older than I, was already a man. He flung some coins down on the floor and shouted: "That's all, so don't you complain none."

"Why it's good of you, Harry," Sukey said timidly as she stooped for the money. "Many a young man wouldn't bring back none at all. But I wish you wouldn't ... "

"If it wasn't for her I wouldn't need to. She'll have to go. I can't feed her and the young 'uns on my reg'lars."

"I know, I know," Sukey said propitiatingly.

What was it Harry was doing? I believed I could guess. I kept hidden while Sukey calmed him down, pulled off his boots, and heated up some food for him. At last he climbed the ladder, threw himself down on the straw near his sleeping siblings, and was soon deeply and stertorously asleep.

I crept out and in a whisper Sukey invited me to sit with her before the dying fire which gave all the light we needed. And now at her request I told her the burden of all that had happened since my mother and I had left the village.

Sukey said nothing until I had finished my account, and then, when she had expressed her indignation against all things Quiggish, she remarked: "But I can set you straight about what happened here arter you'd gone. It was all down to Mrs Bissett. What she done was, she sold off your mither's things to a higgler in Sutton Valancy. He come over and boughten everything. Sent two carts for it the next day. And many folks hereabouts said they would have paid a deal more if they'd been gave the chance, for your mither had some fine things. Folks saw them sold in Sutton Valancy for a mort o' money. Some said Mrs Bissett took a share herself, but I would not go so far."

"I see," I said. "So then there was not enough money to pay the creditors?"

"That is so. Mrs Bissett went round to each on 'em and offered 'em a few shillin' in the pound."

"But then why did they go to law?"

"Why, do you mind that Mr Barbellion?"

I nodded.

"Well, I believe him and her had an understanding. Mrs Bissett was a three-cunning creatur' and she got letters and met strangers that you and your mam never knowed nothin' about. And this Mr Barbellion come down a few days arter the sale and persuaded all the shop-keepers to club together and go to the magistrate agin her. Whyever should he do that, Master Johnnie?"

"Because he works for some people who are enemies of my mother and myself, Sukey."

"They must be indeed," she replied. "Though why they should choose to make trouble for you when they are so rich themselves and they're blood-relatives, too, by all accounts — why 'tis past my understanding."

I was astonished by her words. She seemed so well-informed when I was myself only dimly aware of the identity of these people.

"How do you know all this?" I asked.

"Why, it's common knowledge hereabouts that Mr Barbellion works for the Mumpseys."

I smiled for I saw that there was a misunderstanding: "No, Sukey. You're mistaken. There is no connexion between them."

"I'm not wrong, Master Johnnie. For Auntie Twelvetrees saw him often at Mumpsey-park. You remember her, don't you? Her goodman was lodge-keeper there."

"Then it is she who is in error. She may have seen the Mompessons' lawyer at Hougham," I conceded, "but I don't see how she could know he was the gentleman who came to see my mother on those two occasions."

"Why, you can ask her when she gets back for her bed-bit."

"Is she living here now?"

"She is. Just now she's sitting up with a neighbour who is thought like to go tonight or you'd have seen her. She had to leave the cottage in 'Ougham and could not go upon the paritch."

"But surely she must have had a settlement there?"

"Why, that won't sarve her none in 'Ougham, and she lost her settlement here when she married, so she is not boarded by this paritch, more's the pity. But at least she has a roof over her head."

Though not a very sound one, I reflected, looking up.

"She'll be gived a shillin' or two for tonight's watching." Lowering her voice even more she went on: "But on account of her rheumatiz and her hands being crippled you can't expeck her to yarn her bread, can you?"

"I remember the lace-making," I said.

"That's finished for the bobbin net-lace has taken away our trade, so now I make up knitted work and take it to the general shop. Auntie helps as she can."

"Then how do you all live?"

"Why, not badly now at all. Harry gets his reg'lars of the paritch — four shillin' a week, near enough, whether he's found work or no. I yarn a few pence for helping the women with their cleaning and washing. And there's my spinning." She indicated the wheel. "Though that's little enough for the hours I work. Me and Auntie go out washing, too. The children work at pea-picking and straw-plaiting and we all go leasing at the end of harvest, and then arterwards we collect the stubble to burn for fuel. But against that, we may no longer gather firing and furze and cut turves on the common, now that's 'closed. And in course we can't stint a cow no more."

"So the enclosure has done you harm?"

"Why, I'd not say that. Not at all. We got gave a piece of land as we sold for three pound. Though Harry was choked off the paritch till we'd spent it."

"Why are things so much worse?" I cried.

"Why, Master Johnnie, they're not worse!" she exclaimed in surprise, gesticulating to indicate that I should keep my voice down. "I reckon the vestry-men do the best they can but times are bad for everyone and there's a fearsome number of famblies on the paritch. It's the weather, and the Irish coming over and working under rates. The winters have been hard, and there's been times when there's been nought else to eat but nettles. But at least we don't have the freehold. Them's the ones I pity."

I was about to ask what she meant but at this moment — some time past midnight — Sukey's aunt came in saying in a loud whisper: "Heaven be praised! The Lord seed fit to roll away her mountain and she died under the Blood as peaceful as any saint in the county."

"Why, Auntie, Neighbour Treadgold weren't never no Methody!" said Sukey.

"Indeed, child. But the Lord is infinite in His mercy and she ketched a-hold of the foot of the Lamb as she was a-dying."

Then she saw a stranger sitting by the fire and it was some time before she could be made to recognise in me the neatly-dressed little boy she had last seen several years ago.

When she had taken off her bonnet, seated herself beside us, and eaten some of the broth that had been kept waiting for her, Sukey said: "Auntie, tell Master Johnnie the name of Sir Parceval's lawyer as you used to see come and visit him at 'Ougham."

She looked at us both in surprise and said: "Oh, you mean Mr Barbellion?"

Sukey looked at me in triumph.

I was taken aback, but I believed the old woman must have heard the name from Sukey and transferred it by mistake to Sir Perceval's lawyer.

"I think you must be mistaken, Mrs Twelvetrees," I said gently.

"No, I am not, saving your honour," she protested. "And I'll tell you what. Do you remember that day — oh, I don't know how many year agone now, for you were only a very little chap, saving your reverence — when that fierce genel'man all in black met you and Susan in the buryin'-ground hard by, and give you both such a fright as she told me about arterwards?"

I nodded.

"Well," she said, "that was Mr Barbellion, wasn't it?"

A chill ran through me at this for the old woman sounded very sure of her facts.

"Yes," I said. "But did you see him?"

"Well, just you listen to me a minute, saving your honour," she said tartly. "Now a little earlier that day I had been walking past the Rose and Crab with young Harry on my way here when that same genel'man, Mr Barbellion that I knowed from 'Ougham, pulled up in a chaise and arst Harry to hold the horses and promised him a penny. And when he got down he arst me to direct him to the vestry-clerk, so I showed him Clerk Advowson's house and left him there. And it was soon arter that as he scared you both, as Susan told me arterwards. And I can tell you what he wanted of Mr Advowson — and he can tell you himself that what I say is the Bible truth. And what he wanted ... "

I had stopped listening as I tried to work out the implications of this revelation, and, seeing the effect it had had on me, Sukey put her hand on her aunt's arm to quiet her. My world was turned upside-down by this news. First it occurred to me to wonder why the Mompessons wished my mother and me harm: why they had bribed Bissett to cheat us and then incited my mother's creditors to take action against her. They must have wanted to apply financial pressures against her in order to force her to sell the codicil to them. Well, they had achieved their purpose. But then I wondered if this revelation cast any light on the puzzling question of why they had sent me to Quigg's school since it was essential for their interests that I remained alive. I cast my mind back over the sequence of events that led me to the school: Mr Steplight had come to us at Mrs Fortisquince's and we had gone there because Miss Quilliam had brought Mr Barbellion to our lodgings in Orchard-street. Mr Barbellion! Suddenly it burst upon me that we had been mistaken in assuming that Miss Quilliam had betrayed us to our enemy that day. On the contrary, she had indeed gone to Sir Perceval and he had sent his attorney, Barbellion!

Now the room swam about my head as the question thrust itself at me: who, in that case, was it that Mrs Fortisquince had approached when, at my mother's request, she had ostensibly gone to Sir Perceval? If she had indeed gone back to the Mompessons then surely the confusion about Mr Barbellion would have been cleared up!

Therefore, perhaps she had not gone to them and so Mr Steplight was not their agent, even though he had come in the Mompessons' carriage and with their livery-servants in attendance. And there was that strange remark he had made in the carriage on the way to the school.

Now suddenly I began to see the solution. Mrs Fortisquince had not taken my mother's message to the Mompessons but had contacted our enemy! My original suspicions of her were justified. Her coldness when we first went to her and her warm reception of us the second time were in some way explicable in the light of this. And in that case Mr Steplight was an agent of our enemy. As I was staggering under this shock I suddenly realized that this meant that our enemy had the codicil for my mother had given it to Mr Steplight! And this meant that he — whoever he was — wanted both of us dead!

Now at last I knew why Mr Steplight had taken me to Quigg's school: the intention was to kill me. Well, I had escaped, but with a sickening sense of dread I realized that I had left my mother trusting Mrs Fortisquince and Mr Steplight and wholly in their power. But who was Mr Steplight? At that moment the Latin phrase he had quoted as we had travelled north swam into my mind and this time I recalled where it had come from: Mr Sancious' letter to my mother had employed the same tag in order to allay her worries about the investment! *Surely Mr Sancious and Mr Steplight were one and the same individual.* He and Mrs Fortisquince were in alliance! I had to rescue my mother from them. I would set off for London tomorrow.

I looked up and saw Sukey and her aunt watching me curiously. "I'm sorry, Mrs Twelvetrees," I said. "I didn't hear what you said."

"I was just saying that he wanted Clerk Advowson to show him some of the old paritch-books, seemingly."

She could be no more precise, but here was another puzzle to brood over. Why was the Mompessons' lawyer so interested in this parish? There were many mysteries now and the more I thought about what I had learned, the stranger it began to seem. Presumably it had been Mr Sancious who had been responsible for the attempt to abduct me from the village. But if that were so, how had he discovered where my mother and I had been living?

Shortly after this Sukey's aunt went to bed at the other end of the cottage and, seeing me silent and inattentive, my old friend suggested I should turn in as well.

When I was settled comfortably I whispered to Sukey who was banking up the fire with turves: "Do you recall that day Mr Barbellion so frightened us in the graveyard?"

"I shall remember it to my dying day!" she said with a shudder. "He were just like a great black fetch."

"What was he doing? Wasn't he looking at one of the old tombs?"

"I believe he were. Aye, 'twas that big one by the great yew."

"That's what I thought."

We wished each other good night and I tried to sleep. It came on raining heavily and water dripped through the thatch, but even without this, the things I had just learned would have kept me awake for a couple of hours. How had Mr Steplight come to Mrs Fortisquince's house in the Mompessons' carriage? Was he in some way connected with them, though their interests and those of our enemy were surely starkly opposed? And what was Mr Barbellion examining that day in the church-yard?

CHAPTER 48

The next morning I woke up long before first light at about four. I heard Sukey giving Harry his breakfast and shortly afterwards he went out. Mrs Twelvetrees now emerged and I also arose and found the floor an inch deep in muddy water which was running into the brick gutter down the middle.

"Why, bless you," Sukey said seeing my astonishment. "This happens 'most every time it rains."

While I was breakfasting on oatmeal and buttermilk Sukey's aunt went out to help a neighbour with her wash for the sake, as Sukey explained, of getting her dinner.

"Sukey," I said, "I mean to go on to London today."

"That's nonsense!" she cried. "I beg your pardon, Master Johnnie. But you need to rest and gather your strength."

"No," I said. "I've told you about my mother, haven't I?"

Seeing that I was determined she said: "Very well. But I can be just as stubborn."

She went to a dark corner and reached up into the thatch among the cobwebbed beams and then returned with a piece of soft-leather: "Hold out your hands."

I did so and she poured into them the contents of the little package. The money was mainly made up of pennies, ha'pennies, and farthings, but there were some six-pences and even an old shilling, bent so that the porcine features of the second George looked even more like a sucking-pig astonished to find itself wearing a wreath.

"Seventeen shilling and four-pence three-farthings," she said.

"I can't take this," I protested. "This is all the money you have, isn't it?"

"I know you'll pay me back one day."

"I can't leave you with nothing."

"But how will you get to Lunnon with only a few pence?" she asked, for I had not been able to conceal from her my penurious situation. "Take it for your dear mam's sake. It's to help her as much as you."

I saw the force of this, but I continued to resist, and only eventually was agreement reached. I took three shillings which I believed was just enough to get me to the capital.

I had one task to perform before I left and so, telling Sukey I would be back soon, I made my way to the church. I found the graveyard deserted except for a tall figure at work cutting the grass at the other end. I pushed through the unmown grass that grew waist-high and found the corner by the yew-tree where I believed Mr Barbellion had been standing with his lanthorn that winter evening I had first seen him. The tomb he must have been examining was an old vault-grave of nearly three hundred years of age with a high railing around it. The stone-work was overgrown with ivy and beneath that, moss clung to the surface. When I pulled some of the foliage away I found that the lettering was badly worn. I could, however, easily make out the name "Huffam" which occurred several times: there were a James Huffam, a Christopher Huffam, several John Huffams, (though I saw no Jeoffrey Huffam), as well as any number of Laetitias, Marias, Elizabeths, and so on, included as "Wife" or "Daughter of the Above". There were other names: Ledgerwood, Feverfew, Limbrick, and Cantalupe. Many of the dates were in Roman numerals and most were between about 1500 and 1600, the latest being 1614.

Passing into the church, which was deserted and gloomy, I made my way towards the door into the vestry. I knocked, and when there was no response, entered.

The only light came from a candle on a desk at the other end where a balding figure was bent over a great volume. He looked up and said indignantly: "What are you doing here, boy?"

"Don't you know me, Mr Advowson?"

He looked at me in amazement: "Master Mellamphy!" he exclaimed and reached for his wig that lay beside him and placed it on his head saying: "Scratches terribly, yes, scratches a man's scull beyond endurance." Then he said gravely: "I'm sorry about your mother's affairs. That was a bad business, a bad business." He glanced almost apologetically at my ragged clothes: "It grieves me to see you looking ... well, not as you were before."

When I had fended off without too much damage to the truth some preliminary enquiries about myself and my mother, I asked: "Mr Advowson, I know this is a strange question but it may be very important. Do you recall a gentleman coming here just before Christmas nearly six years ago?"

It seemed to me that he blushed.

"I believe I do," he said.

"It was a Mr Barbellion, wasn't it?"

He nodded solemnly.

"I have a particular reason for asking this. Will you tell me what he wanted to know?"

He sighed: "I always knew that ill would come of it. Yet it was not wrong of me to help him, surely?"

"May I ask what he wanted?"

"The first thing was to see all the entries relating to marriages going back many years. Oh, more than fifty years. We had to go through all the old parochial-registers in the vestry-chest. Every blessed one."

He turned and pointed towards a huge oaken chest with rusting metal clasps that was lying in the corner. There were two others nearby, even older and dirtier and rustier. "Why, we got back to the time almost before the old King and that's a great many years ago."

"What was he looking for?"

"That I cannot tell you, for whatever it was, he failed to find it. And very disappointed he seemed, yes, very disappointed."

I was disappointed, too. And yet it seemed to me that Mr Advowson, who carefully avoided my gaze, was holding something back. I examined the chests and noticed on the oldest of the three that there was a faded design emblazoned in red letters on the wooden top. When I looked more closely I recognised it as the quatre-foil rose that was so familiar to me.

"Did you search through that one?"

"No, of course not, young fellow," he said impatiently. "For that has nothing to do with this parish." He adjusted his wig and said: "Why you see, Master Mellamphy, it comes from old Hougham Hall and concerns nought but a family of that name."

Then that explained the rose design.

"Mr Barbellion did not wish to know about them?" I asked.

"Well if he did, he didn't mention the name to me. You wouldn't know anything of them, Master Mellamphy, for it was many years ago they lived around here. They used to own the property that the Mompessons have now. I recall my grandfather worked for them as a coachman. They lost everything many years back through foolish speculation and sold up to Sir Perceval's father."

"As it happens, I do know the name," I said. "And I noticed a tomb of theirs out there. If they only sold their land a generation or two ago, why did they stop being buried here in about 1614?"

"Why, they had their own chapel at the Hall from about that date. Extra-parochial, of course. Those records must be very old for the chapel was abandoned long ago — after a murder, so they say."

"A murder?" I exclaimed, for I recalled Mrs Belflower's story of the parricide and the elopement and the duel and was amazed that there should have been any truth in it. "Who was murdered?"

"That I don't recall," he said so off-handedly that I did not suspect that he was prevaricating. "They say round here that the chapel was de-consecrated on account of it, but that's so much fustian. But however that may be, certainly the muniments were moved here for safe-keeping about that time. And the chapel is in ruins now for the Mompessons don't use it."

"That's because they don't live on the estate, do they?"

He rubbed the wig so that it slid backwards and forwards across his bald head: "No, and more's the pity for the rent-money goes straight to London and there's little enough of it round here anyway. I respect Sir Perceval Mompesson as a landlord, though many don't, I know. For Stoke Mompesson — the home village on the estate — is an excellent place, very prosperous. It's a close village, of course, and that makes all the difference. They may achieve that here in Melthorpe one day and I hope they do for otherwise I see no hope. You see, the high poor-rates here are driving out trade."

There was no interrupting him and it seemed to me that he was talking on in this way in order to avoid some other topic: "I blame the greed of the farmers. For in the old days when I was a young man, farm-servants were hired for the year and lived with the family. But now since the price of food rose in the Wars, the farmers have started hiring labourers by the day so they don't have to feed them. Of course that means the men can't keep their families — especially now that the common is enclosed. And so the parishes have brought in the system of outdoor relief and the consequence is that the farmers get their labour cheap, for nigh on all the labourers are on the parish now as roundsmen. And that means that the shop-keepers pay for the farmers' labour through the poor-rate. And on that account, and also because there's so little money circulating around here now, many of them have gone for broke. (For example Mr Kittermaster was sold up and has gone.) That is why they were so ready to take action against your mother. But as I say, things may improve for the poorest of the freeholders are anxious to sell their cotts, though the trouble is that then they would go upon the parish and push the poor-rate up still higher. But now the Mompessons' steward has found a way of buying up the freeholds and making sure that this doesn't throw more of the poor upon the parish."

"That sounds very fair and generous of them," I said, rather grudgingly.

"Well, let's hope it succeeds or I despair of this village. But there was no call for the tradespeople to act like that against your mother. Yes, that was a bad business."

"So that is all you can tell me?"

He looked at me oddly and said nothing. I was about to take my leave when he suddenly spoke in a rush:

"There is one other thing. Mr Barbellion also wanted to see the register of baptisms."

"For the past fifty or sixty years?"

"No indeed. Much more recent. Just going back a very few years."

He was bright red now and the wig was being slid backwards and forwards so rapidly that I almost expected it to catch fire: "In fact, not to be roundabout with you, Master Mellamphy, it was your baptism that he was looking for. There, now it's out."

I was astounded by this but I immediately thought of the codicil and the significance of the fact that my mother and myself were the entailed heirs.

"I often wished to tell your mother in the past," Mr Advowson continued; "but Mr Barbellion asked me to say nothing of it. And he was most gentlemanlike in thanking me for my help. Yes indeed, most gentlemanlike. But I feel I can tell you now on account of what has happened to you and your poor mother, for I know he played a part in forwarding the action for debt against her."

"Might I see the entry now?"

To my surprise, since I had assumed that he had now made his confession and had nothing more to hide, he looked embarrassed again: "Certainly, if you wish. Now where is that blessed register? Put me in mind of the year."

I told him and he said: "And the month and day of your birth?"

"The Seventh of February," I said.

"Why then, that was the first year we had to keep separate registers for baptisms, marriages and deaths under Sir George Rose's Act. So I'll wager yours will be one of the first entries."

He opened the least ancient of the chests and brought out a folio volume bound in mottled calf, banged it down in a cloud of dust, and opened it up. I looked over his shoulder and, indeed, the entry that referred to me was the very first. There were three different hands: Mr Advowson's careful copper-plate, a neat hand that I did not recognise which had written "and father", and finally my mother's less tidy writing. The whole entry read thus: "*10th. February*: A fine frosty day. Excellent news of the capture of Cuidad Roderique by Sir A. Wellesley. Baptised John Mellamphy son of Mary Mellamphy of this parish, privately, being like to die. Mr Martin Fortisquince godfather and father: Peter Clothier of London."

As I stared at it Mr Advowson began nervously to speak: "How it happened was, I wrote it down to 'godfather' and when I pointed out to your mother that I should record the name of the child's father and his parish of settlement, Mr Fortisquince it was who added the words 'and father' and then they looked at each other. I was quite struck by their manner. And then she took the quill from him and added 'Peter Clothier of London'. But she would not give his parish."

Clothier! So that was the name represented by the initials "P. C." on my mother's locket! And the "M. C." with which she had signed her note to Sir Perceval. Then the Silas Clothier mentioned in the codicil was some kind of connexion of mine! But there was another shock: my mother's name was different from my father's. (Perhaps here lay the explanation of the rector's remark the day I had discovered the tomb of Geoffroi de Hougham and of our seclusion from the society of the village.) And yet I could not accept the most obvious implications of this. For one thing, I could have no legal claim of any kind if this were correct. I looked at Mr Advowson who, as if to confirm the conclusion I had drawn, glanced away with an embarrassed little cough. Something else occurred to me: this was the name that Quigg had been alluding to when he had named me "Cloth-Ear". Then how did Mr Steplight (alias Sancious) know that that was my real name? But *was* it my real name? Why had my mother apparently tried to conceal it? And why was she so unwilling to give my father's parish of settlement, which she had reluctantly admitted to me was Christchurch in Spitalfields? And what was the role of Uncle Martin in all of this?

Whatever the truth of the matter, it seemed to me that if Mr Barbellion was so interested in this entry, then I should have a copy made. (I should explain that there was no registration of births at this date, except by the parish.) If my life was in danger, it would be a wise precaution.

"Mr Advowson, if I could get enough money to pay you, could you make an official copy of it?"

"Indeed I could. But as to the fee, well, now it would need to be vellum or at least parchment, and be sealed and witnessed. Five shillings is the usual charge. But I dare say I could find an old piece of parchment. And seeing it's for you, Master Mellamphy, and ... well, seeing it's for you, as I say, I could do it for three. I wish I could say less but I can't rob my own children."

I thanked him and, telling him I hoped to return soon, I made my way back to Sukey's cottage where I found her at work on the knitting-frame while her aunt, who had returned, bustled about. I was sorry to find the old woman there for I wanted to ask Sukey something in confidence.

"She told me as how Neighbour Feverfew has been offered twenty pound for her freehold," the old woman remarked, in the course of a recital of the gossip gleaned during the morning's work.

"It's a pity you don't own the freehold, Sukey," I said.

"Oh no," she exclaimed. "For the freeholders get nought from the paritch no matter how sick and old they may be. That's why they choose to sell and go on the parish — that is, if anyone will buy."

"I see," I answered. "In that event, why would anyone buy?"

"Nobody will, leastways until just these last years," Mrs Twelvetrees put in. "But now the Mumpseys' steward is buying them up and then demolishing the cottages."

"Why?"

"They say he wants the village to be closed like Stoke Mompesson," Sukey said.

"Why," Sukey's aunt declared, standing up and making ready to go out again; "I remember when they pulled down the old village there. 'Twas when I weren't hardly more nor a gal. And they made the park where the village had stood and built the new one where 'tis now. And they barred the day-labourers from it and to this day they aren't allowed to rent cotts there. And so Sir Parceval pays no poor-rates and gets his pauper labour paid for by other paritches."

"And that's what they're doing here," Sukey explained.

"I see," I said.

So that was what Mr Advowson had meant by saying that the steward had found a way of buying out the freeholders without increasing the burden upon the parish's poor-rate!

"But where do the labourers live?" I asked.

"Many on 'em live a couple of hours' walk away as our Harry does now," the old woman said, fastening her bonnet. "Or if they can find a cott, they live in open villages like 'Ougham where there are none but freeholders. But it's a hard living for there are no rates collected and so there's no poor-relief. That's why I couldn't stay there when my goodman died."

"The Mompessons should have let you," I said.

She turned to me gravely: "Don't speak agin 'em, Master John. My good man sarved them all his life and had nought but respect for 'em all his days."

When the old woman had gone out I exclaimed to Sukey: "Why, they're not fit to own the estate! To own land is a great trust, you know, Sukey. Why, if I owned it, the tenants would be happy and contented and the stewards just and honest and the cottages would be rebuilt and the land drained and the stock improved and so on."

"Oh, that is beautiful, Master Johnnie. I wish it could come true."

"Why, Sukey, what would you say if I told you I might own it one day?"

At first she thought I was joking, but when I had explained to her a little about the codicil and my connexion with the Mompesson family, she saw that I meant it.

"But you see," I concluded, "if I am to have a chance of owning it one day, I believe I should have a copy made of my baptismal entry."

She instantly gave me the money I needed from her little leather packet, assuring me that it was hers and not Harry's. Promising to repay her many times over, I hurried back to the vestry.

Mr Advowson looked up in surprise at seeing me and reached for his wig: "Why, young fellow, to be frank, I didn't think to see you back. Let me see if I can find a piece of parchment."

He hunted through the nearer of the two oldest chests, but finding nothing suitable, then pulled out the oldest of them and brought out from it piles of documents and register-books. At last he found a parchment with a large piece that was blank at the bottom which he cut off.

As he began to sharpen a quill he said: "We need a witness. While I'm doing this, might I trouble you, Master Mellamphy, to step out and find the under-sexton? He'll be at work in the yard. His name is about all he can write but that will suffice. The sexton is ill or I'd send for him."

I left him laboriously copying the document with his head at the same angle as his quill, his accursed wig discarded beside him on the table, and his tongue half out of his mouth as if guiding the pen from a distance. When I regained the graveyard I saw the tall but stooped figure of a labouring man some way away and went towards him. When he turned I found to my surprise that he was known to me: he was bent now and his face was more lined, but it was Mr Pimlott. All my feelings of suspicion came flooding back and, giving no sign that I knew him, I explained my errand as to a stranger. Though he looked at me long and closely I could not tell if he recognised me. When he understood what I wanted, he stuck his spade in the ground with a sudden thrust. I looked at it and it seemed to me to be identical to the famous mole-spade.

As I turned and he followed me he suddenly said: "I noticed you a-fore. About an hour agone. You was looking at that grave."

I turned and he gave a sort of smile: "Why, I knowed you straightaways, Master Mellamphy."

I made no answer and he said no more to me until, having entered the vestry and signed the document where the clerk showed him, he suddenly noticed the old chest that had been pulled out from its usual place.

"Why, now there's a strange thing, Mr Advowson. That there rose on that chest. I ain't never seen but two others like that a-fore now." He turned to me: "And one on 'em was on that tomb."

"What tomb are you speaking of, Pimlott?" Mr Advowson asked impatiently.

"The big 'un under the yew."

Mr Advowson was fussily shaking a sand-box over the piece of parchment and paying little attention.

"And what was the other time?" I asked.

"Why, now there's the strangest thing. 'Twas on a silver box of your own mam's, Master Mellamphy."

He spoke with a strange kind of triumph and it seemed to me that he was making it clear that he had played a part in the burglary and its theft, for there was no other way that he could have seen that letter-case since he had never had reason to enter the room in which it was kept.

He walked out and I took the copy from Mr Advowson who was looking at me thoughtfully. I paid him and then I asked him if he would undertake to pass on to Sukey some money which I would try to send soon, and he consented.

"Mr Advowson," I said. "I believe I can do you a favour in return. I think I should tell you that when Mr Pimlott worked for my mother some years ago there was a burglary and there is good reason to believe that he was involved in it."

"Indeed, indeed?" the clerk said in dismay. "Thank you very much, Master Mellamphy. I will remember you said that."

I took my leave of him and made my way into the burying-ground where Mr Pimlott was now not to be seen. Of course I went straight to the ancient vault-grave and pulled off much more of the ivy and then cleared some of the moss with a piece of flint I found in the grass. Sure enough, incised on the surface of the central flat stone was the familiar design, though it must have been hidden by the vegetation for some years. But there was not just one quatre-foil rose but five of them in the design found on the face of a die.

When I got back to the cottage I gave the copy of the entry to Sukey, and she carefully wrapped it up in the piece of soft leather that had held her savings and concealed it in the thatch. I almost told her about my encounter with Mr Pimlott and what he had implied about the burglary, but remembering that the episode involved Job I hesitated to awaken painful memories.

In the evening as Sukey and I — her aunt was out watching with a sick neighbour — were sitting before the fire with the children and quietly eating our bed-bit, Harry came in.

"You mind Master Johnnie, don't you Harry?" Sukey said nervously.

He gave me a surly look: "Oh, aye. I mind him all right."

He seated himself before the fire and began to eat angrily, spooning the hasty-pudding into his mouth.

Nobody spoke until Harry announced defiantly: "I shall be out tonight."

"Oh Harry I wish you wouldn't."

"When can I come with you, Harry?" asked Jem, licking the back of his wooden spoon.

Sukey shuddered.

"When you're bigger and 'll be some use," Harry said shortly. Then he stood up: "I'm going out now, for I'm meeting the others at the Bull and Mouth. I'll take a six-pence or two, Sukey."

At this she looked so guilty that he sprang up and rushed to the place in the thatch where the money was hidden. When he found the piece of parchment in place of the coins, he demanded an explanation and when she told him that she had lent the money to me and why, he exclaimed: "You had no right. It's mine as much as yourn."

"That ain't so," she said mildly.

"All that blunt just for a bit of paper!" he said, scowling at me.

"But Harry, 'twas no more nor a bit of paper as took the common land from us, as I've often and often heerd you say yourself."

"Aye, that's true enough," he cried, seeming angrier with her than ever. "All the more reason not to meddle with such things." He glared at me as if I were the culprit: "Did she tell you how the Mumpseys paid for a private bill that let 'em 'p'int their own Commissioners to settle it all fairly. Fairly! All we got in exchange for our rights was a little piece of scrag land a good mile off that weren't no use to us and that we had to sell back to the Mumpseys for nigh on nought."

He jumped up and began to dance a jig, keeping his face directed upon mine while he chanted:

"The law locks up the man or woman
Who steals the geese from off the common,
But leaves the greater villain loose
Who steals the common from the goose."

The children sprang up and began to dance round him shouting out phrases from the rhyme and varying them with the rhythm of their clapping hands, while Sukey tried vainly to hush them.

Panting heavily, Harry stood over me: "But the worst of it is that they aren't working the land they've stole but grazing it, and that's throwed most of the men hereabouts upon the paritch and brung down the price o' labour all round. I lost my place as a farm-servant over towards Mere Bassett, for Farmer Treadgold could buy a roundsman of the paritch for a mort less nor he paid me. And now I'm a roundsman myself. I'm auctioned off by the day for what the overseer can get as if I were no more nor a black Negro slave. And all for my 'lowance of four or five shillin' a week."

"That's terrible," I said. "The farmers shouldn't be so greedy."

He laughed angrily: "Why shouldn't they get the other rate-payers to make up their wages if they can? *I* should if I was them. Take what you can for yourself and devil take the hindmost, say I!" He paused and then smiled recklessly as he went on: "And do it, too. Only that's more hazardous now, for snaring a rabbit on the old common can yarn you transportation for life."

"Surely not!" I exclaimed.

Harry's smile vanished and he demanded angrily: "Don't you know about our dad?"

"No," I said.

"He was caught by a man-trap on the Mumpseys' land. He lay there a night and most of the next day with his leg half-chawed through. Like a fox or a mole. He lost the leg and to top that, he was lagged and transported to Norfolk-island where he died of the gaol-fever."

A number of mysteries were resolved and I turned in dismay to Sukey: "Of course! So that's why that letter took so long to reach you."

She nodded.

"This is all wrong!" I cried.

"Master John was saying earlier," Sukey explained, "how everything could be ordered for the good of all."

Harry snorted: "Gammon! Why, the rich take what they can and so do the poor. The Mumpseys steal what they can of me and I steal what I can of them. They can buy the law to help 'em, but that's the only difference."

"Master John says everyone can help everyone else and then all would be the better of it."

"He wouldn't say that if he was rich."

"Why," Sukey exclaimed before I could prevent her, "for the matter of that, Master John might own the Mumpseys' land one day. That's why he wanted that dockyment copied."

"What?" said Harry, swinging round to scrutinise my face. "How can that be?"

I hesitated and then said at last: "I believe my mother's father had a claim on the estate which he was defrauded of."

Harry stared at me and whistled softly: "Well, well. Then if this here dockyment," and he picked it up, "should turn out to be worth the whole estate, I reckon you owe Sukey and me a share of it."

"And I promise to repay you a hundredfold the money you have lent me for it," I said.

"A hundredfold!" he exclaimed. "You should give us a share of the estate. Say a quarter."

"But that ain't fair, Harry," Sukey protested.

"Yes it is. For we've gived him more nor a quarter of all the money we have in the world, so it's only fair that he should give us a quarter back." He turned to me with a shrewd smile: "It's a speculation and speculators get their money back in proportion, don't they?"

"But you are imposing conditions after the event!" I objected.

"But you would have took it even if I'd been here and said the same then," he insisted and would not yield this point.

At last, therefore, and reflecting that, if nothing else, it would give Harry a reason for preserving the parchment which he might otherwise be tempted to destroy, I consented to his terms.

"Write it on the back of the dockyment," Harry insisted.

When I objected that I had neither pen nor ink, he mixed up some lamp-black, which he had scraped from the wall, with a little water and found me a pointed twig. With this I wrote below Mr Advowson's careful calligraphy: "I John Mellamphy promise to give Harry Podger and Sukey Podger one quarter of the Huffam estate if ever I come into it, as God is my witness." And then I signed it. Sukey replaced the package and shortly after this Harry went out.

The next morning Harry had not come back by the time I took my leave of Sukey. I travelled as before, but faster now that I was refreshed after my rest and impelled by a new sense of urgency.

I learned something — or believed I did — as I walked through Hertford a few days later, for late one evening, just as I passed the Blue Dragon inn where the coach had baited on the journey from Melthorpe that my mother and I made two years before, I noticed the name on a shop-board opposite: "Henry Mellamphy, Provisioner". I recalled my mother telling me how she had chosen the name at random from such a source and while I walked on in search of a quiet outhouse to spend the night, there came back to me the memory of how upset she seemed to be on that occasion at the knowledge that we had reached Hertford. Could this be the origin of the name?

When I arose at dawn the next day I could see a darkness over the sky to the South. The weather was fine and as I slowly advanced all that day I kept my eyes on the far horizon where the smoke rose like a great dusty-coloured mountain, dark below and at the centre, but growing greyer and bluer as it melted at the periphery into the infinite clear sky. And then as the dusk came on, the edge of the distant hills was lit by an unearthly glow as the gas-lit shimmer of the great Babylon stretched from side to side of the vast horizon. I slept that night in another outhouse and as I wearily advanced the next day, the weather grew worse and worse. Late that afternoon I reached the top of Highgate-hill and looked down towards the dark ocean of mist through which glimmering lights shone. Somewhere in that vastness was my mother. But how would I find her in the midst of that huge and crowded waste?

I passed under the Archway and an hour later went through the turnpike-gate on the New Road with eleven-pence ha'penny in my pocket at a little before noon on the 11th. of November.

In the hope that my mother was still there, I had decided to go first to Mrs Fortisquince but without making myself known to her, for that would risk losing the advantage that she and Mr Steplight (Sancious, as I guessed) did not know my whereabouts, nor even that I was in London. I went into a stationer's and parted with a penny in exchange for a sheet of paper, a quill and ink. I had had time to compose my letter in my mind so I now quickly wrote:

"To Mrs Mellamphy:

"I am in London. If you can, come as soon as possible or send someone to the church-yard where we rested after leaving Orchard-street. Sukey sends her best regards."

I left it unsigned, folded it, then made my way to Mrs Fortisquince's house in Golden-square and pushed it under the street-door. Then I went to the little church-yard to wait in the cold rain. I stayed there all that evening and all night and all the next day, when I was sure that my mother could not have received my letter. Then — very cautiously for fear that someone would be waiting for me there — I revisited the lodgings that we had lived in when we first arrived in London. Mrs Marrables and the rest of the household had heard nothing of her, and the same was true of Mrs Philliber at our old lodgings in Maddox-street. Now, feeling a growing sense of dread, I went back to Westminster and found a strange family who knew nothing of us living in the room we had shared with Miss Quilliam in Orchard-street. In desperation, I crossed the centre of the metropolis almost at a run, and when I had tapped at the kitchen-door of Mrs Malatratt's house, the little maid opened it and started back as she recognised me. But when I asked for Miss Quilliam she told me she had not been back since the occasion when she had given her the letter for me.

"No," she added, "I haven't seed nothin' on her since she got her dresses back."

"Is that what was in the trunks?" I asked.

"Yes," she sighed. "Such lovely silk ones as you nivver seed."

How did she come by such things? I asked myself as I walked away.

By now I had exhausted all the possibilities I could think of except one, and that one I was very loath to pursue. However, I made my way to No. 5 Gough-square — for fortunately I had remembered the address.

When I knocked on the area-door it was opened by a young maid-servant.

"I am looking for a lady," I began.

"What do you want of her?" she asked.

"She's my mother," I said. "I've come back to London from the country unexpectedly and she doesn't know that I'm here."

The girl looked at me curiously: "And is she one of the dress-lodgers?"

I didn't know what she meant so I answered: "I believe she may be lodging in this house. Her name is Mrs Mellamphy."

"Names don't mean much," she said. "And they're all 'Miss' here. But there's no-one of that name in the house. You'd best describe her."

I did so and the girl shook her head: "That don't fit none of the ladies that's old enough to be your mam. It sounds a little like Miss Quilliam, but she's much too young."

"Miss Quilliam!" I exclaimed. "Is she here."

The girl looked at me doubtfully: "Do you really know her? For I would be in terrible trouble if you was lying."

"Yes," I said. "And she may know where my mother is. Please let me see her."

"How do I know you really know her?"

"Her name is Helen, isn't it?"

The girl nodded: "I don't know. But I believe you anyway. I can't let you go up, though."

"Then please ask her to come down. I'm sure she will if you tell her that John Mellamphy desperately needs to speak to her."

"Mrs Purviance don't like 'em to come down here," the girl said. "I should lose my place if she ever knew. But I'll risk it. Promise you won't take nothin' while I'm gone?"

I gave my word and with a last glance over her shoulder the girl went up the stairs. She was braver and more generous than many a soldier.

After a long wait she came down, followed by Miss Quilliam who paused at the foot of the stairs when she saw me and spoke to the girl without taking her eyes off me: "Betsy, you've been very good. Would you be kind enough to leave us?"

Betsy went into the scullery and was heard for the next few minutes moving pots and pans about.

Even in the gloom of the kitchen I could see that Miss Quilliam's circumstances were very different from the occasion of our last encounter. She was dressed in a beautiful silk gown trimmed with lace, and as soon as I saw this I was shaken by a terrible understanding as everything fell into place. In fact, I already knew the truth, but now I could not hide from myself that I knew it.

In the near-darkness I could not establish whether her cheeks were lightly rouged or if they were red with consciousness.

We both found it difficult to speak.

At last she said with dignity: "I hope you will not reproach me for having betrayed you and your mother when I was commissioned to go to Sir Perceval. I am quite innocent of that at least."

"I know you are."

She looked at me with surprise.

I answered: "I have recently learned something which puts that incident in a quite different light. I will explain in a moment, but please tell me first what news you have of my mother. I have lost her."

She gazed at me for a moment: "I am afraid the news is not good."

"You don't mean ... ?"

"Oh no. She is alive and well. Or reasonably so. Let me tell you what happened. I went to Sir Perceval and spoke to him and Lady Mompesson. They responded as your mother had anticipated. Their man of affairs, Mr

Barbellion, was summoned to accompany me back to our lodgings with a large sum of money in bank-notes for the purchase of the document. When I found you had both fled — and remember that I had no notion why — Mr Barbellion was very angry at the futility of the visit I had led him upon. I owe it to myself to state that he gave me nothing. Now I was left destitute. I sold the few articles left in the room. Some of them were your mother's and I owe you money for your share, but I cannot pay you for despite these gorgeous clothes I have nothing. Finally I decided to come to this house and accept Mrs Purviance's hospitality."

I thought she shuddered slightly.

"It is better than the alternative. I am at least protected."

"And what of my mother?"

"Two weeks ago I saw her briefly."

"Where?"

She looked at me gravely: "In this house."

I turned away in pain.

"Do not blame her," Miss Quilliam went on. "She came to Mrs Purviance to ask her for help. She met me in the hall and reproached me for having betrayed her. I was astonished by her words, but I saw that it was best to leave her without attempting to defend myself. I think she came in all innocence believing that Mrs Purviance would give her food and shelter out of charity. Mrs Purviance told me she had been left with nothing after being cheated and lied to by people she believed were her friends."

"Where is she now?"

"Mrs Purviance has another house nearby. So far as I know, she is still there."

"Please tell me the address."

"No. 12 East-Harding-street."

She saw my anxiety to be gone and said, as a kind of farewell: "I am glad your mother will know that I did not betray her. I only wish I had money to give you. But I have none. I am only not starving. If I had more I would leave, and Mrs Purviance knows that very well."

"May I find you here again?" I asked.

"I will help you and your mother as far as I am able to," she replied. "But I fear it may be out of my power soon. Mrs Purviance wishes me to go to Paris. I am entirely in her hands now."

We shook hands and I left. As swiftly as I could I found my way to East-Harding-street and took up my station opposite No. 12. After some time I saw a well-dressed and lady-like young woman leave the house, accompanied by a maid-servant. As they walked up the street the servant fell further and further behind her until as they turned the corner they seemed to have no connexion. Another half-hour passed and then a second young woman came to the house accompanied by a gentleman. They rang the bell and were quickly admitted. The door was held open after them and a man who looked like a servant out of livery and who appeared to have been following them, slipped in before it closed.

It was getting dark and as I watched and waited, the lamp-lighter began to make his way slowly along the street carrying his ladder laboriously from post to post. Now a third young woman arrived accompanied like the last by a gentleman and again followed at a distance — this time by an old woman. The gentleman who had accompanied the second woman left the house. Some time later the woman herself left followed by the man-servant. By this time I had seen enough.

Then another couple came down the street and turned up the steps. It was difficult in this light and at this distance to see clearly, but I thought I recognised the figure despite the unfamiliar clothes. I quickly crossed the street and went to the foot of the steps as the gentleman rang the bell. The woman wore beneath her coat a silk dress, she had a fine bonnet and carried an elegant umbrella and steel-chain reticule. They both had their backs to me as they waited for the door to be opened. The gentleman leaned close to the lady and whispered something. I heard in response a kind of coquettish laugh — ghastly in its bright falseness, but particularly ghastly to me.

"Mamma," I said.

A face of horror was turned to me: the eyes unnaturally bright, the eyebrows painted and the cheeks inexpertly rouged. Beneath the paint and powder I could see that her cheeks were thin and her eyes feverish.

She backed away from me a few steps holding one arm up half-shielding her face: "Johnnie!" she cried.

As I looked at her in the light of a nearby street-lamp, I seemed to see her both as a stranger — so garishly dressed and made-up — and yet more penetratingly than ever before.

"What are you doing in London?" she exclaimed.

I believe she registered only the fact that it was I, and that I was not several hundred miles away. She did not notice how poorly I was clad.

"Leave me," she said. "Go back to where you are safe."

I shook my head, unable to speak.

"Leave me," she moaned. "I am not your mother now."

"What is going on?" said the gentleman. "Who is this boy?"

At that moment the door was opened by a severe-looking maid-servant of middle years.

"Will you come in," she said, more as a command than an invitation.

The gentleman hesitated and made as if to enter.

"Go back to the school," my mother said and began to turn away to go in.

I stepped forward and seized her arm.

"Come with me," I said. "You do not need to go in there."

"What is this charade?" the gentleman asked angrily.

"Come in, Miss Marigold," the maid said sharply.

My mother hesitated, looking at me with an expression of timidity and shame.

"You know what I have become?"

She struggled for breath.

"Dearest," I said. "Dearest mother, we will go away from here."

"Will you come in," said the servant angrily.

"No," said my mother.

"I don't understand this," said the gentleman, raising his voice angrily, "but I believe it is some trick to … "

"What is going on here, Annie?" said Mrs Purviance, appearing suddenly behind the maid. "I will not have a scene in the street."

"She won't come in," said the maid.

"I see," said Mrs Purviance. Her eyes fell on me and I believe she took in the meaning of the tableau instantly. To my surprise, she looked beyond us out into the gloom of the street and called softly: "Edward!"

Instantly a tall man who must have been lurking a few yards off, came up the steps behind us.

Seeing him the gentleman turned and began to descend the steps. "It's high time I was out of this," he said.

"Wait, I beg you, my dear sir!" Mrs Purviance called, but he hurried down the steps and up the street. "Edward, bring her in and send the boy away," she said softly.

"No, I'm never going back in there," my mother cried. "Come, Johnnie."

"Run, Mamma," I cried.

She turned but Edward held out his arms to prevent her from descending the steps.

"Not with those clothes," Mrs Purviance said.

She and the maid-servant seized my mother and as I moved forward to defend her Edward gripped me from behind so hard that my arms hurt.

"Bring the boy in!" Mrs Purviance ordered. "He'll make too much noise out here. We've already lost one guest."

"Help!" my mother shouted.

"Quiet her," hissed Mrs Purviance and the maid tried to cover her mouth with her hand.

"Don't struggle, Mamma," I said. "They only want your clothes."

In truth, I was not sure that that was all they did want, but I was afraid of what they would do to quieten her if she continued to struggle. We were dragged into the hall and the door was slammed behind us. My mother, still gripped by the two women, was sobbing and crying out and, to my horror, Mrs Purviance now struck her sharply across the face. I struggled but could not break free of Edward's grasp, one of whose hands was now clamped round my jaw to prevent me crying out.

"In there, quickly," Mrs Purviance said, and we were hustled into a room that led off the hall.

She lit one low gas-light and then closed the door.

"Release them both," she ordered, and my mother and I were let free. "Now, Miss Marigold," she said, "I cannot believe you intend to leave the security of this house. You know what awaits you. You remember in what circumstances I found you?"

My mother sobbed.

"Well, do you?"

She nodded.

"You know that that will happen to you again if you leave the Rules and my protection," Mrs Purviance went on. "Moreover, I gave security against your absconding and paid the necessary per centage of your debt. Have you forgotten that? Seventy pounds in total for the warrant of attorney and the payment to the Warden. How do you propose to repay me? You don't think what you've earned for me nearly repays the expenses you've incurred, do you? Your board and lodging alone amount to a further twenty pounds. However, I am a generous woman. You may go if that is how you wish to repay my generosity to you at a time when you were destitute and in despair. But if you go, you leave here as you came: with nothing. Is that understood?"

"Yes," my mother whispered. "I wish to have nothing from this house. I wish I had never entered it. You deceived me, Mrs Purviance."

"You would have died," she said contemptuously. "Edward, stay here with the boy. And Annie, go with her and make sure she leaves everything. Take what money you can find. All of it was given her by me. I must go and reassure the other guests in case they have heard anything."

The three women went out leaving me with Edward who watched me carefully. Seating himself by the door he pulled a newspaper from his pocket and held it towards the light.

After a few minutes he looked up, smiled and said: "Don't you believe she was gulled into it. She knowed the trade."

I stared at him with my heart pounding.

He ran his tongue around his lips and added with a smile: "I kin allus tell."

I threw myself at him and tried to hit him, but he caught my fist and viciously wrenched my arm behind my back twisting it so that it was agony. Then he released me and I retreated a few steps screaming at him until I threw myself to the floor and thumped the carpet with rage and misery.

After a few minutes my mother came in again with Annie. Now she was dressed as the poorest servant-girl, but, grotesquely, she was still rouged and powdered.

Mrs Purviance came in a moment later:

"Did she leave everything?" she asked Annie.

"Yes, ma'am."

"And has nothing now?"

"Only a pocket-book of her own. But there ain't no money in it."

Mrs Purviance turned to my mother: "Let me see it."

"No, it's mine," she protested.

Mrs Purviance glanced warningly towards Edward: "Show it to me," she said.

My mother took the pocket-book I knew so well from inside her dress, unclasped it and held it up so that the pages fell open revealing that there was nothing inside. She was holding something in place with her thumb.

"What's that?" Mrs Purviance asked.

"Just a letter and a map."

Mrs Purviance looked at them closely.

"Very well," she said.

"May we go now?" I asked, for Edward and Annie were still guarding the door.

"In a moment," Mrs Purviance said impatiently. Then she addressed my mother: "I thought I had little to learn of the baseness of the human heart, but you have taught me another lesson in ingratitude, Miss Marigold. When you came to me with nothing I gave you food and clothing. More than that, I gave you my time and attention. I introduced you to company and gave you the means to better yourself. Yet this is how you repay me."

My mother stood pale and wide-eyed before this onslaught.

"Come," I said, taking her by the hand.

"Leave this district and you become an absconded prisoner," Mrs Purviance said.

At a nod from their mistress the two servants opened the door, led us through the hall, and let us out of the street-door.

CHAPTER 49

It was quite dark now and although a steady drizzle was falling, the wind appeared to be rising. At the bottom of the steps my mother turned to me a timid, fearful face. I seized her and hugged her, kissing her cheek and covering my mouth with rouge. Then we looked at each other. She was pale and thin but her cheeks beneath the rouge seemed flushed with health.

I felt a strange kind of power at having her under my protection.

"I knew that at least you were safe," she said. "I wasn't brave enough to starve. I must tell you everything ... "

"Later," I said. "For now, we must find shelter."

"I have no money," she said.

"I have a little," I said, but in fact it was only five-pence ha'penny.

We set off at hazard up the street.

After a few yards she stopped and looked at me curiously: "But why are you dressed like that? Why, you're in rags!" Then in increasing anxiety she demanded: "What has happened to you? Why are you here in London?"

There would be time enough, I thought, to enter upon explanations that I knew would distress her.

"We must find shelter," I insisted. "Night is coming on."

"No, Johnnie," she cried. "I must know your story. Look at you! You're so thin!"

"Later," I replied. "I have an idea. We will go to Sir Perceval," I said, for I had considered this in advance. "Remember that it is in his interest that we remain well."

This was true since our enemy had obtained the codicil, but I must not let her find that out. I broke off because she was staring at me with a ghastly expression. Now I saw the hectic colour in her cheeks that I had taken for paint.

"Sir Perceval?" she repeated.

"What's the matter, Mamma?" I asked.

"Sir Perceval? No, we won't go there," she said vehemently. "I went there and was turned away."

"Very well," I said, surprised at this piece of news. All my doubts about the Mompessons and the fact that Mr Steplight (or Sancious) had arrived at Mrs Fortisquince's in their carriage, returned in force. Yet I could make no sense of this for the Mompessons must want us to remain alive. What she had said could not be correct. "But we must go somewhere."

"Where?" she asked.

"Where can we go," I said, "but the workhouse? If they will admit us."

"No," she cried, coming to a stop. "Not that. They would separate us."

"But," I said, "we have no choice."

"There is the river," she said softly.

I had heard of the Arches beneath the Adelphi as a desperate place of last resort. "Why, Mamma, the workhouse would be better than that. Christchurch is in Spitalfields and so not far from here."

I remembered that she had admitted that that was her parish of settlement.

She looked at me in terror.

"No!" she cried. "It would not be safe to go there!"

"Why not?" I demanded, remembering how frightened she had been at the prospect of going to the workhouse when Miss Quilliam had suggested it.

"Don't ask me that!" she cried and ran ahead of me. Suddenly she stumbled and almost fell.

"Why, you're ill!" I exclaimed. "All the more reason why we must go for help now."

"Only," she said, "if you will tell me your story. For we will be parted once we are there."

I dared not contradict her. And so, as we walked along, I told her about the school and how I had escaped. Then, to my eternal regret — but I was too exhausted to consider the consequences and was thinking only to remove her belief that Miss Quilliam had gone to our enemy — I began to tell her that I had learned at Melthorpe that Mr Barbellion was Sir Perceval's lawyer.

"So you see," I concluded, "she went to Sir Perceval as she promised, and Mr Barbellion was sent to buy the codicil from us."

My mother's mind, fired by a feverish excitement, had raced ahead. To my dismay she cried: "That means that Mr Steplight is working for our enemy! That explains why they treated me as they did! Mr Pentecost was right!"

"What do you mean? Who treated you in what way? What did Mr Pentecost tell you? I thought you never spoke to him?"

But she paid no attention for another horror had come to her and she looked round at me wildly, her eyes glittering unnaturally: "Silas has the codicil! That is what Mr Assinder meant!"

"Tell me about Silas! Who is he? And who is Mr Assinder?" I demanded, though I was sure I had heard that name not long before.

She was not listening: "We are in terrible danger! He will kill us! What my father feared has come to pass! And it was I who put it into his hands!"

"Do you mean Silas Clothier?" I demanded, recalling that this individual was a beneficiary under the codicil.

She paid no heed, however. I was burning to ask her about the name of my father — Peter Clothier — that I believed I had found on the baptism entry.

"What a fool I've been!" she exclaimed. Then she looked up the street we had walked along: "We are being followed!" she cried.

She began to walk faster and, weak though she was, I had difficulty in keeping up with her.

"No-one is following us," I said.

"Yes, yes. They know I was there, Silas and his agents. Mrs Purviance is one of them."

"Mamma," I said, "Mrs Purviance is not an agent of anyone — certainly not of our enemy. Do you not recall how we met her through Miss Quilliam?"

But at this my mother shuddered: "It was she who betrayed us!"

"No, it was not," I protested. "I have explained that."

"Yes, yes," she cried. "I met her again at Mrs Purviance's house. She was beautifully dressed. The money came from our enemy!"

I saw that it was useless to reason with her in this state of mind. And at the same time I began to wonder if she or I were right: were Miss Quilliam and Mrs Purviance members of what seemed to be a vast conspiracy against us? After all, Bissett, Mr Sancious or Steplight, Mrs Fortisquince and, though entirely innocently, even Stephen Maliphant, had all turned out to be implicated in one way or another in some kind of design whose origin and purpose were so far hidden from me.

"We must elude them," my mother cried and began to run.

Unable to do anything else, I ran beside her and she seized my hand.

As if she knew where she was going, she turned up a dark bye-street. It was unpaved and I found difficulty in running across the wet cobbles.

"We should be careful," I said. "There are other dangers in these streets."

She was gripping my hand so hard that it was painful. "Nothing is as dangerous to us as our enemy," she cried.

We had almost reached the end of the unlit street when, because of her exhaustion or her distraction, she stumbled and fell on the wet cobbles, letting go of my hand.

I helped her to stand and held her close to me. I noticed that now I was almost as tall as she.

"Mamma, we are in no danger except from hunger and tiredness. We must find food and rest for tonight, and shelter from the cold and rain. We must ask the way to the Spitalfields workhouse."

She stared at me wildly: "You don't understand. Silas has spies everywhere. If we went there he would find us out."

Now I believed I understood why she was so frightened of going to the workhouse or even, as Mr Advowson had told me, revealing her legal parish of settlement: this would enable her enemy to find her.

"But we have to go somewhere," I protested.

"Johnnie, all I care about is making you safe. My life doesn't matter. I loathe myself now."

"No, no," I said. "Don't speak like that."

"Quickly," she cried, "or they will be upon us."

She set off at a run again and I hurried after her.

I don't know how long we ran up one street and down another, my mother constantly looking back and hardly even seeming to be aware of whether I was with her or not. I lost all idea of where we were as we ran along unpaved and unlit lanes, into dark courts with their stinking ash-heaps, or through streets blazing with gas-lights where, late as it was, people crowded around market-stalls. Once we found ourselves in a blind alley from which my mother retraced her steps in terror as if expecting to find herself trapped.

At last she fell, this time from sheer exhaustion. Almost with a kind of relief, I pulled her to her feet and found that I had to hold her up. Now I saw that a profound change had taken place in her, and I felt my stomach go cold. How could I have thought she looked well? She only looked younger because she was so much thinner even than when I had last seen her.

The feverish brightness of the last couple of hours had given place to a dull stupor and her eyes no longer seemed to focus properly. In the light of a street-lamp nearby she looked at me strangely, as if unsure who I was.

Then her face cleared and became animated by joy: "Peter?" she said. "Is it you?"

"No, Mamma, it's Johnnie," I answered, but she did not seem to hear.

"Oh Peter, you've been away so long. You shouldn't have left me there alone, it was cruel of you. I've been so frightened and worried."

She wiped her sleeve against her mouth and I saw something dark appear on it.

"You've coughed up blood," I said.

"Blood!" she cried and drew away from me staring at me in horror: "Whose is it?"

"Have you done this before?" I asked angrily.

"Is it," she began in a horrified whisper, "is it *his* blood?"

The wind and rain had died down and yet I knew that it was as if the weather had stopped merely to draw in its breath for a worse onslaught. I had to find rest and shelter for her soon. I looked up the street and saw that a working-man was coming towards us.

I stopped him and said: "Please tell me where we are?"

"Field-lane."

I dimly recalled my knowledge of that part of London.

"Are we near Hatton-garden?"

He nodded.

"And Mitre-court?" I asked, for I remembered that Mrs Sackbutt — the friendly woman we had met when we were searching for the Digweeds — had mentioned this place as somewhere that one could find shelter very cheaply.

He looked at me curiously. "Yes, if you wish to go there."

"I wish we did not have to," I answered.

"Peter," my mother suddenly said. "I've lost your locket. I couldn't help it."

"Never mind about that now," I said.

"Oh but I do mind. I mind very much. But you see I dared not go back there."

The strange man said: "She looks done in. Is she your mother?"

I nodded.

He pointed the way he had come: "Go to the end of this street and turn right into Holborn. Walk a short piece and turn into Ely-place and then there's an alley-way between two of the houses on your left. But what do you want there?"

"A dry place where my mother may lie and rest tonight for just a penny or two. Will we find those?"

"You may do," he said. "Nobody knows who owns them houses, but someone will take a toll of you, you can be sure of that."

"I was afraid of your father," my mother persisted.

The man frowned sympathetically: "Your guv'nor's a hard 'un, is he? But have you no friends? No tin?"

"No friends, and only a few pence," I told him.

"I believe a storm is brewing. Your mother looks ill enough to have a chance of being admitted to the sick-ward of a workhouse for a few days if you have a settlement. Won't you take her there?"

"No, she is afraid."

"Then Mitre-court is your last hope. But it is an evil place. Trust nobody." He reached into his pocket: "I am out of collar and have a family, but I can see your case is worse than mine."

He brought out a penny and looked at it for a moment. Then quickly he found another and, pressing them into my hand, strode quickly off.

My mother had taken in none of this. One hand was restlessly stroking my ragged collar and she was looking at me with disconcerting intensity:

"Why is your coat torn, Peter? And where is this blood from?"

There was no blood upon my coat, though it was certainly torn. I gently detached her hand.

"Come," I said. "We must go this way."

As we set off she said cajolingly: "You won't leave me ever again, will you, Peter?"

"No," I said. "Never again."

"Will you take me home now? Won't Father be worried? Your argument with him was only a jest, wasn't it?"

Thinking it best to humour her I said: "Yes. We're going home now."

Following the directions I had been given, we walked on as the wind began to rise again and from Ely-place turned into a narrow and noisome alley-way which was partially obstructed by rotten-looking wooden props leaning against the houses as if for support.

My mother asked timidly: "Are you certain this is the way, Peter? I don't remember it."

"Yes, come on," I said.

The Rookery consisted of three or four delapidated buildings which had once been part of the palace of the Bishop of Ely, the rest of which — save the ancient chapel abutting on the north — had been demolished to build Ely-place, and the faded blazon of the bishop's key and mitre was still visible above the arch that led into it at the end of the alley.

Looking up at this my mother smiled and exclaimed: "Oh, this is the court at the side of Northumberland-house, isn't it?"

I nodded, remembering how she had recognised the streets around Charing-cross where that great mansion stood. Her father's house must have been near there.

Water poured down the sides of the buildings from the over-flowing gutters, and at the lowest point of the court a lake had formed through which we had to wade. Skirting the mound of filth that almost blocked the way, we entered one of the houses. Passing through an entrance whose door was broken from its hinges, we found ourselves in a dark hall. I tried the first door, and after some moments it was opened by a surly man who glared down at us. Over his shoulder I glimpsed other men sitting around a fire, looking anxiously towards us.

"We are seeking shelter," I said.

He merely jerked his head to indicate that we should ascend, and slammed the door shut.

I took my mother's hand and we began to climb. The stairs were so rotten and broken away as to be very dangerous in the darkness. On the next floor I asked at each of the doors and was turned away with curses. At last, on the floor above, a man who was unshaven and stank of raw gin stood behind the half-opened door and said: "There's a corner you can have. Over by Lushing Lizzie. A penny a night each."

I gave him the coins and he stood aside for us. My first impression as we passed in was of the stench which was appalling. It was a large chamber but with a low ceiling crossed by heavy beams which were encrusted with elaborate plaister-work, broken off in many places. The plaister was everywhere stained yellow or visibly damp, and in one corner the ceiling had collapsed entirely. The room was lit only by a rushlight burning by the fireplace and by its feeble light I saw that it contained more than a dozen people disposed in three or four groups about the floor, so that there was little space left.

Near the fireplace — where only a small blaze was smouldering — was a group of three women and a man and a number of sleeping children. There were a man and a woman lying on some straw in the middle of the room and an old woman in one corner by the windows, one of which was secured by battered shutters and the other stuffed with rags and paper where many of the panes were missing. The deputy who had admitted us joined three other men who were drinking in the opposite corner.

I led my mother over to the part of the chamber pointed out by the man, which was almost beneath the shattered ceiling.

She looked round and said: "How good it is to be back in my own dear room."

Of course, we had nothing: neither mattress nor pillow nor bed-covering, and no dry clothes to change into, but I tried to persuade her to lie down on the bare floor. Filthy as it was, it was at least dry. She took no notice of my attempts, however, and was taking part in an animated conversation with people whom she imagined to be present.

The old woman, noticing our arrival, came hobbling over, bringing a rushlight. A smell compounded of cheap spirits and dirt issued from her. It was impossible to guess her age: her nose seemed almost to meet her sharp chin, white wisps grew from hideous lumps upon her face, and she was dressed like a pile of dirty laundry.

She looked at my mother who was now smiling and laughing as she stroked my jacket:

"Dearest Peter, I had such a foolish dream. You'll laugh when I tell you. And yet it was too horrible to laugh at."

"How do, my pretty pair?" the old woman said. My mother smiled at her and the old woman said: "Old Lizzie will make you welcome. Who are you fleeing from, that you come to this place? Is it a father or a husband?"

"Father and husband!" my mother repeated, catching at the stray words. "Dearest Father, I see you have arranged everything just as it was before."

"Are you on your marriage journey?" persisted the old woman. "Is this your wedding day?"

"Why yes, I was married today," my mother exclaimed.

Grinning, the old creature held the light closer to me saying: "And is this the fine young groom?" Then she started back with a cackle: "Why," she said, "this is only a boy! Are you quizzing Old Lizzie? Fie," she exclaimed with ancient coquetry, "you naughty creatur'! To vex Old Lizzie so." Then, smiling toothlessly, she put her face down to my mother's and said: "Why, I know what it is. Am't I a downey not to have guessed?" She sniffed ostentatiously. "You're enjoying yourself, aren't you, pretty dearie?"

My mother looked at her in bewilderment.

"I'll wager you've had a treat of a kind gentleman, eh? Have you any to spare for Old Lizzie?"

I put out my hand to draw the old woman away.

"Leave her be," I said. "She's not well."

The old woman stopped smiling and looked at me: "Is she your mother?"

I nodded.

"Poor creatur'. She has a church-yard skin. But Lizzie will tend her."

She hobbled away and shortly afterwards returned with two ragged blankets and a heap of rags. I put one of the blankets on the floor to keep my mother's head off the bare boards and laid the other over her shoulders, and though I managed to persuade her to sit, she would not lie down but continued to conduct an animated conversation with her imagined interlocutors.

"She should eat something," I whispered.

The old woman shrugged: "Lizzie don't have nothing." Then she glanced towards the group of people near the fireplace: "But Lizzie can beg."

She went over to them and I saw her gesticulating vigorously before she beckoned me across. They were Irish and could not speak English. Indeed one of them was a very old woman who sat gravely amongst the others with an unlit cob in the corner of her mouth, and seemed to think she was still in her peat-cottage. The two other women muttered together in Erse and then the elder of them offered me a piece of bread in a small bowl of milk and would not take the penny I proffered for it.

I could persuade my mother to eat only a mouthful or two for all the time she was talking to herself, though directing her attention to me as if I were someone else.

She gazed at me intently: "Dear father, is it truly you? I've been so frightened. Let me stay here tonight."

The wind had been rising for some while and now a first shower of rain was suddenly flung against the windows like a handful of pebbles. I remembered how I had lain in my little bed-chamber in Melthorpe on many a winter night and heard a storm blowing, and how sometimes my mother had come to comfort me.

"Must I?" she cried in despair, more like a child than a grown woman. "But I don't want to. What do I want with a husband? I want to stay as we are now." Suddenly she seemed to listen closely and then turned and looked at me as if with dawning recognition: "Peter!"

At this moment the first flash of lightning lit up the room briefly and seconds later there was a roll of thunder.

"Try to sleep," I said.

"Yes, sleep. It's been such a long journey there and back again. But where is dear Mr Escreet? I want to tell him what a fright you all gave me. But now that I know it was only a game I believe I shall sleep at last."

"Yes, my pretty," said old Lizzie. "Sleep now and you'll be grand as five-pence come the morrow."

At this, my mother suddenly seemed to notice the old woman for the first time: "Who are you?" she exclaimed in alarm. Then more calmly she said with a pout: "Are you my watcher?"

"So you've been on that lay, have you?" the old woman cackled. "No, my dearie, I ain't. Though I was a dress-lodger in my time, too. And I've been a watcher. We all comes to it in the end."

"I can't sleep for the storm," my mother said childishly, for now it had broken upon us in its full force.

The wind rattled the windows and the thunder crashed and rumbled like cannon as if we were in the midst of a battle-field.

"Give me something to make me sleep, Helen," she said to the old woman. "I promise I won't tell Johnnie."

"Lizzie sees you're of gentle birth," the old crone answered. "Why, my Guyneys, when Lizzie was a gel she was in high keeping. She kept company at Mother Kelly's in Arlington-street. She was on the Town then. Why she was kept by a baronet's son," she said with a mincing flick of the head whose effect was grotesquely coquettish. "She lodged in Bond-street and rode down 'Dilly in her carriage dressed in a silk-gownd, and didn't all the folks stare at handsome Lizzie then!" Then she added sombrely: "But he died shoreditch for he was foul of the strawberries — the only marks of a baronet that he lived to show, poor devil! — or I might have been a Lady."

The old woman talked on in this vein and yet despite this and the vehemence of the storm, to my relief my mother lay back with her head against the heap of rags and closed her eyes. Once she opened them briefly and whispered something to the old woman who said:

"I don't have none, dearie. Nor no blunt to buy it."

At last, however, she fell into a fevered sleep, muttering occasionally and even opening her eyes several times and addressing people she believed to be present.

Suddenly Lizzie interrupted herself and looked at me sharply: "Have you any blunt?"

I shook my head.

"But you have rich friends?"

I wasn't sure how to answer for the best: "My mother has. And when she is better we will go to them."

She stared at me and then suddenly turned and hobbled away without a word. A few moments later I saw her go out of the room. I lay beside my mother on the naked boards, resolved to stay awake and watch over her.

The storm would not let me sleep anyway, for the wind was battering the house as relentlessly as waves crashing against cliffs. I heard tiles being stripped from the roof a few feet above my head and flung about like handfuls of playing-cards until they reached the ground. To my dismay water began to drip through the broken ceiling almost directly above us; then it became a trickle and within a short space of time the floor was damp.

Some time later the old woman returned. From somewhere she must have obtained money for she carried a stone jug from which she drank and now began to bawl out old songs. Then she tried to get the others in the room to dance. As the lightning flashed and the thunder roared, she began to pace around the sleepers huddled on the floor, loudly humming a minuet as her accompaniment and grotesquely curtseying to an invisible partner with all the flirtatiousness of fifty or sixty years earlier.

"Stow that! You infernal damned witch!" one of the men drinking with the deputy shouted. But his companions clapped their hands and called out obscene encouragements.

She danced on, tripping and stumbling over the sleepers by the fire. The young Irishman cried out something and pointed towards the younger of the two women who was in an interesting — indeed, an extremely interesting — condition. The old crone merely laughed at him and danced the more furiously, swinging the jug around her as she pranced round the room.

When she stumbled into one of the children the Irishman came up to her and struck her in the face. She threw herself at him, trying to hit him with the jug, but he seized it from her and flung her into a corner. She picked herself up all the while screaming abuse at him like nothing so much as an alley-cat hissing and snarling at a dog. My mother muttered and opened her eyes but did not awake.

At last the old woman, still spitting curses, lay down on the heap of rags in a corner and quickly fell into a deep snoring slumber.

Despite the noise of the storm and my intention to stay awake, the exhaustion I had undergone was too much for me and some time after this I must have slept myself.

CHAPTER 50

When I awoke I could not remember where I was. I raised my head and looked about me. It was still early and only a very little light was coming in through the unshuttered but dirty windows. In the hearth the embers of the fire were glowing, and in the dim light I saw sleeping figures huddled together and memory returned. The wind and the rain were still blowing, but the worst of the storm had spent itself. I turned the other way and to my joy found my mother's eyes upon me looking calm and as if restored to her right senses. She was half-propped up against the wall with the bundle of rags against her head.

Her expression was strange. During the night a change had come over her — and I did not know whether it boded well or ill. Her mental equilibrium was restored, but her eyes seemed to lie deeper, her cheek-bones were more apparent, and her lips thinner and disquietingly pale. She said something I could not hear and now that I looked more closely, I saw how weak she was, and that speech was a considerable effort.

"Don't speak," I said, getting up and moving nearer to her. "Save your strength."

She tried to raise her hand to draw me down beside her but was too weak. I sat down and took her hand.

"There is something I must do," she managed to mutter.

"Later," I said. "Tomorrow will do."

With an effort she shook her head and then went on so softly that I had to lean forward to catch her words: "Promise me," she whispered, "that you will never go to the house."

"Which house?" I demanded but she would not answer. "You mean your father's old house, don't you? But you forget, I don't know where it is. Where is it?"

She said nothing.

"Why should I not go there?" I persevered.

She merely shook her head.

"Tell me," I insisted.

"He might harm you."

"Who? Whom do you mean?" I asked.

She made a great effort to utter the one word: "Promise!"

"How can I promise when I don't know what I'm promising?" I said. "And why do you want me to promise now?"

As I spoke those words a sudden realization came to me: "No, Mamma! Everything will be all right."

She let her head fall back but a few moments later she tried to speak again: "My pocket-book," she whispered at last.

One hand clawed feebly at her pocket, hideously like the paw of a trapped animal. I reached in and removed the small leather-bound book I had seen so often. The piece of my map that I had given her fell out, but I saw that it still had something — a piece of folded paper or a letter — inside it. I was in a tumult of conflicting emotions. Was I at last going to learn about the mystery that had been withheld from me for so long? I showed the book to her and she nodded to me very slightly and then turned her head towards the fireplace.

"Burn it," she said.

My chest constricted and I had to struggle to draw breath.

"No," I cried.

"Please, Johnnie."

I shook my head, staring at her in horror. Was I destined never to know the truth about my origins?

"Then give it to me."

I handed it to her and she feebly leafed through it until, apparently finding what she sought, she seized a bunch of pages and tried to tear them out. It took all her strength before she succeeded, and then she lay back exhausted.

She passed the torn pages to me and said: "Burn these at least."

I crossed to the slumbering fire flickering in the grate and shoved the papers a little way into its red heart. I looked back and saw that my mother was watching me. I pushed the papers all the way in and they took fire and flared up. When I had watched the handwriting turn silvery against the blackening paper, I went back and knelt again beside her.

"My darling boy," she whispered, the words scarcely audible. "I don't want to leave you like this."

"You don't have to," I cried angrily. "What are you talking about?" Then more calmly I said: "Try to sleep now. It is still early. When it is day I will go out and buy us food. I have a little money still."

In truth I had but five-pence ha'penny. When that was spent, I thought, we would have to beg in the streets unless we took the course which seemed to me the safest and surest: "Mamma, I know you dismissed the idea of going to Sir Perceval for help. But that was when you were so confused and frightened. You do see, don't you, that it is crucial to his interest that we remain alive and well? And so he will want to help us to escape from our enemy and live securely and secretly. You do see that, don't you, Mamma?" I repeated.

She muttered something and I leaned forward to catch it: "No," she said softly.

"Yes," I insisted. "I understand these things better than you. Mr Steplight wasn't lying about that at least for I'm sure it's true that Sir Perceval needs us to remain alive and well, especially now that the codicil is in the hands of our enemy. Listen to what I am saying. We will go to him soon and ask him for help. We will not ask him for very much money. Only a hundred pounds a year. That is nothing to a gentleman as rich as he."

It was almost full day now and people were stirring in the room. I noticed old Lizzie watching us from her corner.

Suddenly my mother raised herself and looked at me with terrible intensity: "That's nonsense! Why are you saying such things? Mr Assinder told me: Sir Perceval and his wife don't care about us now. They don't need us alive." There was a terrible coughing deep in her chest. "Do you think I'm so foolish, you too?" she managed to gasp. "Must everyone lie to me?"

"Mamma, I don't understand you. It's me. Johnnie. I haven't lied to you."

"I know who you are," she said with that same look. "You've always despised me for a fool."

"No!" I cried. Then she began to cough as violently as if she were vomiting, and to my horror I saw flecks of blood spattering over her hands as she put them to her mouth.

I seized her arm and my hand almost closed round it, for it was so thin.

"Leave me alone!" she cried, shaking my hand away.

She stared round wildly and the pupils of her blue eyes seemed suddenly vacant now that I looked into them. And in that image of terror there came to me the time I had watched boys in Melthorpe stoning a cat they had trapped. Blood was dribbling down her chin now and her lips had turned blueish.

"I'm so frightened!" she gasped. "Help me!" Then, to my horror, she cried out: "Mamma!"

As if in response, the old woman came across and looked at the blood with a kind of eagerness: "Aye," she said. "As I feared. 'Tis the white plague." Seeing my expression she added: "Consumption."

"Get a surgeon!" I cried.

"Why," she chuckled grimly, "there ain't no sawbones as will come here. And besides, she's too far gone now."

My mother was gasping for breath and suddenly the old woman bent over her, pulled her head forward, and began thumping her on the back.

"Stop that!" I cried. She persisted until I seized her and pulled her violently away, and she retreated, muttering imprecations.

My mother fell back and lay quiet.

"I'm right, Mamma," I went on after a minute, hoping to reassure her. "You'll see. We will get some money from Sir Perceval and then we can rent a little house in Salisbury, like you said."

Her head was turned slightly away from me now and I wasn't sure if she heard me. I went on softly in case she was sleeping: "I will go to school and in a few years it will be time for me to be apprenticed and after that I will be able to keep us both." As I spoke my voice broke. "You'll see. It will be as it was before."

I bent over my mother whose face was still turned away from me. Her eyes appeared to be open and I wondered if she were not sleeping after all.

"Mamma," I whispered.

I felt a shadow fall across me and glanced up. The Irishwoman who had given me bread was beside me and was gazing at me with an expression I could not read. She reached past me and began to pull up the edge of the ragged blanket. She drew it further and further and when I saw her intention I put out my hand and cried "No!" She looked at me for a moment, and when I let my hand fall she went on pulling the blanket up until it obscured my mother's face.

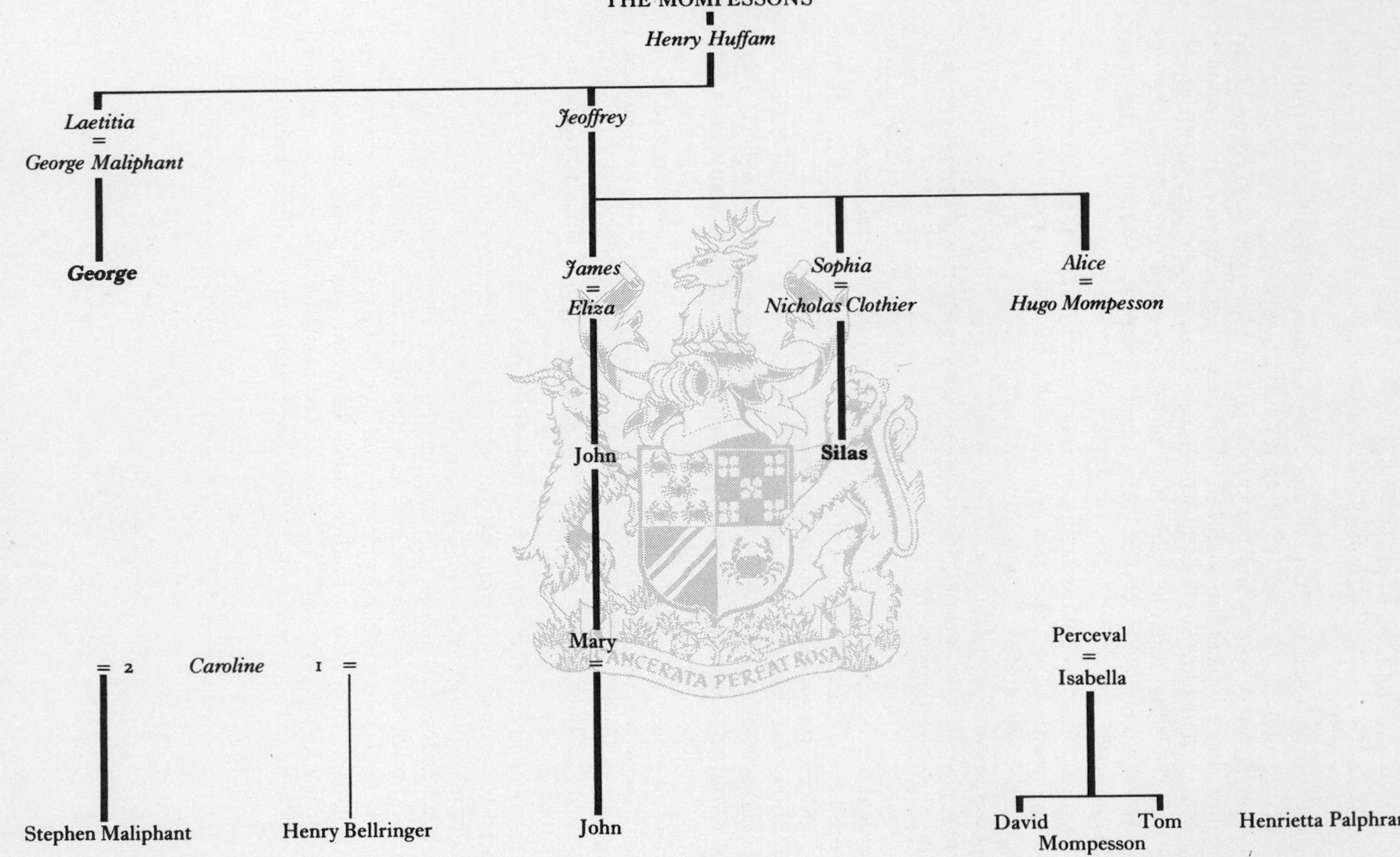

Characters who never appear directly in the narrative are in *italics*. Those who might possess the estate if Jeoffrey Huffam's suppressed codicil were in force appear in **bold** typeface.

PART THREE
THE CLOTHIERS

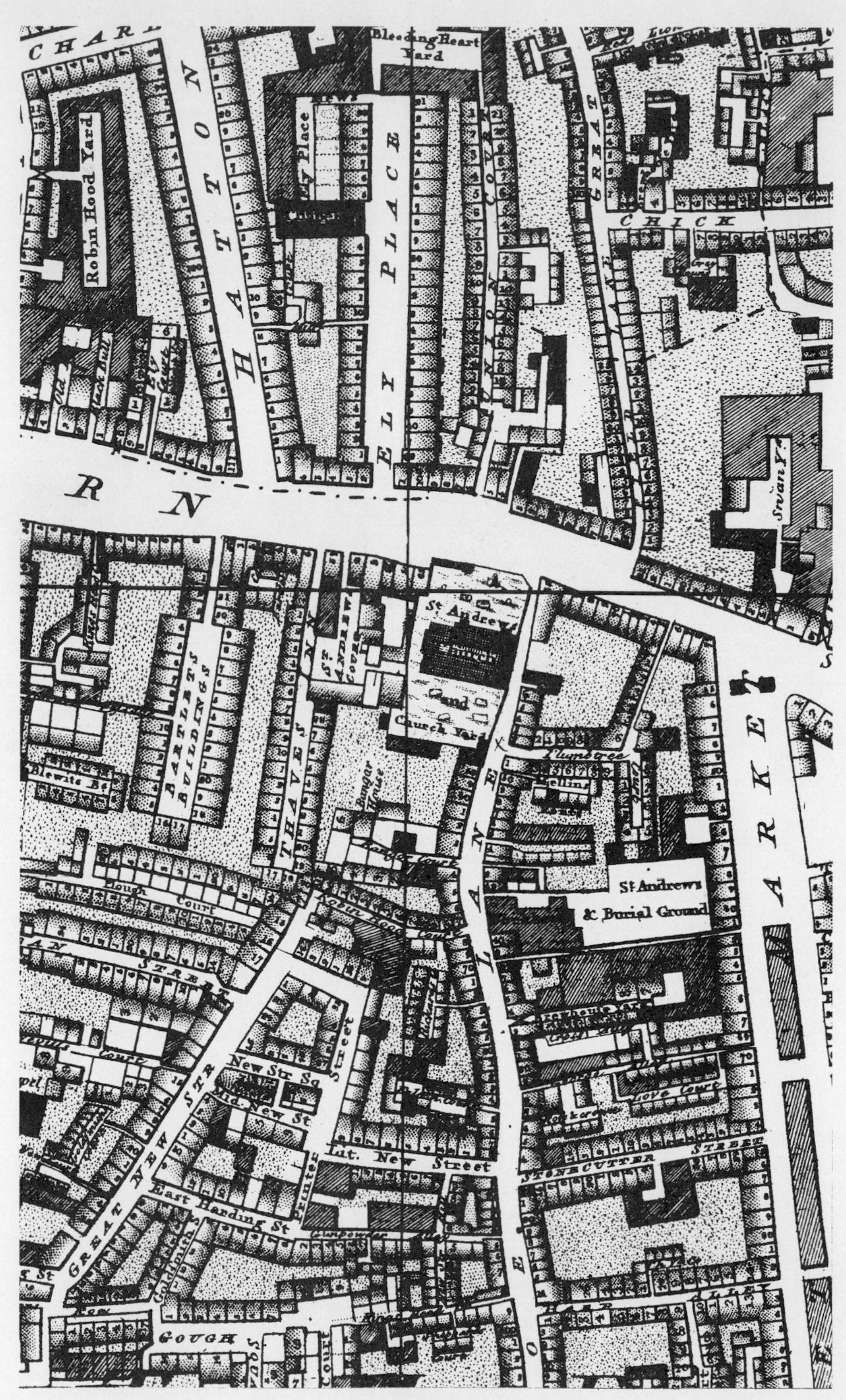

HOLBORN (Scale: 1″=70 yards)

The top of the page is North

BOOK I

Inheritances

CHAPTER 51

I invite you to return with me now to No. 27 Golden-square where, in that elegant morning-room with which you are familiar, we find Mrs Fortisquince in the middle of a rancorous argument with a guest.

"I don't understand how she did it," she is saying.

"Never mind how it happened. All that matters is that now we'll get nothing for her from the old man."

"It's hardly my fault that she got away."

"Oh no?"

"Certainly not. I believed I was the only friend she had in London. So she told me many times."

"She lied," Mr Sancious says bitterly. "You allowed yourself to be taken in by her plausible manner."

"It is ungracious of you to reproach me. You owe everything to my generosity. When Mrs Clothier and her son came to me for help, did I not frankly come and confide in you?"

"You confided in me, certainly, ma'am, but you have been rewarded for that. And as for frankness, well I'm sure I don't know how frank you've been. Why are you so anxious that old Clothier should not know of your involvement?"

"That is not your concern."

"Well, he'll have to know now for I'll not take all the blame upon myself."

Mrs Fortisquince fixes him with her gaze and says softly: "If you tell him, I promise you that you will regret it."

The attorney bites his lip and then says: "Well, I suppose he doesn't need to know. I'll take the brunt of his anger myself, then. But at least he'll be pleased that we've made the boy safe for him." She nods and he adds: "And soon he'll be even safer."

Mrs Fortisquince, however, says sharply: "I hope you don't mean ... "

She leaves the rest unsaid.

He stares at her in amazement: "But that's what we agreed!"

"Indeed we did not. We talked merely of making him safe."

"But I believed you meant what is usually meant by that term."

"I don't know what *you* meant by the term. *I* meant what is commonly meant: that we could lay our hands upon him when we wanted to. He must not be harmed. Not yet."

"Your concern for the boy does you honour," Mr Sancious says with a sneer.

"I promise you, if anything befalls him, I will go to the authorities."

"I think not, Mrs Fortisquince, for in that case the good Quigg might say more than either of us would wish."

They stare at each other and then the widow slowly smiles: "Come, it is foolish for us to quarrel when all we can achieve is to harm ourselves."

"Well said, madam. We can gain so much more by being friends."

Mrs Fortisquince rings for Checkland and instructs her to bring tea, and so ten minutes later the two are sitting comfortably together on the ottoman.

The widow looks thoughtfully at her guest and begins: "There is something I have been meaning to ask you for some time, Mr Sancious. As you perhaps know, I inherited from my husband some interests in landed property and securities."

The attorney nods gravely.

"While he lived, of course," Mrs Fortisquince goes on, "he handled them himself, and since his death my affairs have been in the hands of an attorney appointed by him as his executor. Though it seems disloyal to say it, I have not been altogether happy with his conduct of my affairs. In particular, now that the rate of interest on government stock has been reduced, I believe I could do better than my agent has been able to procure for me."

"Most certainly you could, ma'am!" the attorney exclaims. "Have you considered the bill-market?"

"I have not. Is it not rather uncertain?"

"No indeed. It's as safe as the Bank of England — quite literally so, for it is the Bank itself that ultimately backs up bills drawn upon the banking-houses. And the Bank has not even suspended payment in gold within your lifetime, for the last time that happened was in '97." (The lady smiles at the compliment.) "I have plunged heavily myself. And though at first I was hesitant, now I am glad that I allowed myself to be persuaded, for the market has soared so much that I only wish I had gone in earlier. The truth is, I have staked everything I have. The market has never done so well. Go in now, and I'll wager that by Christmas you'll bless me for it."

Mrs Fortisquince raises her cup to her lips, watching him thoughtfully.

CHAPTER 52

Of what happened then I have no clear recollection. I only recall shouting and screaming at the old woman and perhaps even trying to hit her, for I know that I had to be dragged away from her by the young Irishman. Then I remember feeling a sudden nausea and clutching my stomach in the belief that I was going to be sick, for I recall the expression on the man's face as he released me and stepped back. And after that I recollect throwing myself on the floor beside her, possessed by a terrible rage and hitting the rotten boards with my fist and digging my nails into my palms until they bled. And one thing more I recall — that I did not weep.

I had refused to recognise what was plainly visible in her face when I had seen her on the steps of Mrs Purviance's house just a few hours before, as if by denying it I could forestall it. I had prepared no defences against what had now happened and as the remorseless truth of it beat against me like an incoming tide, I felt myself collapsing inside like a fortress of sand built by a child. For I had never considered that she would die. And now as I thought of all the times I had answered her insolently or shewn my irritation at her or jeered at her understanding or pressed her too hard to reveal things she wished not to, I burned with remorse and rage.

Hours passed. I may have slept but I cannot say for there was no difference between my waking and dreaming nightmares: the hideous, unblinking, monstrous fact that she was dead. Then slowly I became aware that dim light was entering the chamber through the rag-stuffed and begrimed windows and that other people were stirring near me. I looked at the silent form beside me, the blanket still pulled over the face, and could not believe that she would not tug it away and smile at me and tell me it had all been a game. I heard rough voices, children crying, drunken shouts and curses from which one cry emerged: "Stow yer racket, for the last time." I did not look round to see if the speaker was addressing me but when I turned my head some minutes later I found that Lizzie was sitting near-by cross-legged, combing her straggling grey locks with one claw and watching me.

"Don't take on so," she said. "You'll get over it."

The thought horrified me: I did not want to be the person I would have to become if I ever got over it.

"You've no money to bury her, have you?" the crone continued.

I shook my head.

"You must go to the paritch," she said. "They will take care on her."

When I paid her no attention she seized my arm: "You've got to bury her dacent."

"Where do I go?" I asked in order to quiet her, for I thought it did not matter what became of her body.

She gave me directions to the house in Leather-lane from which the parish-clerk conducted his business and as she spoke it suddenly came to me that it did matter. It mattered very much. And as I rose to go a thought, a memory rather, occurred to me.

"Will you watch over her?" I asked.

"I will. Set your mind at ease."

I groped my way down the treacherous stair — still in near-darkness — and found myself in the flooded court. The storm had burnt itself out and the wind had fallen, but the louring sky shed little light and the rain still descended with a relentless malevolence.

The directions I had been given soon brought me to the house I sought where a young skivvy at the kitchen-door rather doubtfully admitted me to the scullery. There I was kept waiting nearly an hour while Mr Limpenny — for the girl had told me his name — finished his breakfast, for I had not realized how early it still was. At last the servant-girl led me into his presence in the "breakfast-parlour" where he sat over his teapot and the remains of his meal, reading *The Morning Post*.

"What do you want?" he asked abruptly, only half-lowering his paper.

I stood before him and tried to speak but no words came.

"Come, speak out, boy. Don't waste my time," he said testily.

"It's about my mother."

"I'll thank you to address me with respect," he interrupted.

"I beg your pardon, sir," I said. Then I attempted to go on: "My mother ... my mother has just died and I have no money to bury her."

"That's very fortunate," he answered.

As I stared at him in amazement he wiped his hands fastidiously on a napkin and went on: "We bury paupers once a week and by good chance tomorrow is our burying day."

Without looking at me, he stood up and walked out of the room.

Unsure what was expected of me, I followed him across the passage and found myself in a tiny room that, from the bundles of papers secured with pink ribbon, the old chests, and the tin deed-boxes that were piled in corners or stacked on shelves, obviously served as an office. "There are certain formalities to be discharged," he said, sitting at a little desk. He pulled out a drawer and removed a printed paper, mended a quill and glanced up at me: "Name of deceased pauper?"

"Mrs Mary Mellamphy, sir," I said, suddenly not wanting to reveal our true name.

"Mellamphy, female. Irish, I suppose," he said wearily. "What is the parish of settlement of your mother's husband?" Then with a sneer he corrected himself: "I should say, your father?"

"I don't know, Mr Limpenny."

He sighed. "You people. What makes you think you're entitled to come here and die at the rate-payers' expense without so much as a by-your-leave? I suppose it's nothing to you that you've deprived this parish of its right to reclaim the cost of burying your mother from her own parish of settlement? Why, do you realize it would cost two pounds to bury a pauper decently? The coffin alone would come to twelve shillings!"

No answer seemed to be required and I ventured none.

"I suppose you'll want someone to lay her out?"

"Yes, please."

"I should think so," he said indignantly as if I had denied the need for this. Then he added: "And the parish pays for that, too." He took another piece of paper and began to fill it in. "Address of deceased?"

"Mitre-court, sir."

"I might have guessed it," he said. He passed the second piece of paper to me. "Now take this order to No. 2 Ely-court and ask for Mrs Lillystone."

"And is that all?"

"What more do you want?" he demanded angrily, ringing a bell that stood on the desk. "Now get off with you."

The girl appeared at the door.

"Show this boy straight out," Mr Limpenny said. "Mind, I say straight."

Back in the street I looked at the piece of paper I had been given and saw that it instructed Mrs Lillystone to wash, lay out, and put into a shroud the body of a "female pauper" at the address given. When I had found my way to the house and knocked at the door, there was a long silence before an upstairs window was raised and the head of a woman appeared.

"What is it?" she said.

"It's my mother," I had to call up to her.

"Where are you from?"

"Mitre-court."

"I know. Is she near her time?"

"She has passed it," I said.

She stared at me hard then withdrew her head and banged the window shut. A minute or two later she opened the street-door and I saw that she was a large, slovenly woman in a gown that was none too clean. She was pulling on her bonnet and tying the strings.

"Come," she said. "There ain't no time to be lost in sich a case."

"I don't think you understand me," I said and handed her the order.

Without doing more than glance at it she gave it back: "That don't mean nothing to me. I can't read."

"It's for a laying out."

She laughed: "I thought it was the other thing," she said. "I heerd there was a woman there near her time. But then, it's all one to me, a laying out or a lying in. I sees 'em into the world and I sees 'em out. And more often nor otherwise, the one follows hard upon the other."

Suddenly she said "Wait!" and shut the door.

I huddled myself into the door-way to try to escape the rain which was still falling steadily. About ten minutes later Mrs Lillystone opened the door again and came out carrying a number of articles: a small copper, a tin bason, and over her arm a shroud of the cheapest material.

As we walked along she asked: "Did you leave her with a relative to watch?"

"Not a relative," I said. "An old woman."

She hissed slightly through her teeth but said nothing more until we reached Mitre-court when she exclaimed in distaste at the floods of foul water over which she had to venture on her pattens. She objected strongly to the condition of the stairs as if I were to blame, and made a great business of getting up them with the articles she was carrying, at the same time refusing to entrust any of them to myself.

When we entered the room it seemed to me that a silence fell among the people who were there and I saw to my surprise that while Lizzie was not to be seen, there was a family of strangers seated near our corner of the room. Mrs Lillystone and the middle-aged Irishwoman greeted each other and when I indicated to the layer-out the blanketed form in the corner of the room, she crossed to it and drew back the ragged covering.

"As I thought," she said. "Everything has gone."

I covered my face and turned away.

"The old woman stripped her," said a woman belonging to the strange family. "She said she was her daughter and she was going to lay her out, but she went away with her clothes and hasn't come back."

"She's left nothing but this ring," Mrs Lillystone commented and raised the hand.

I did not look.

"Aye, she could not get it off," said another of the interested neighbours.

I did not need to look for I remembered that it was the plain brass ring which my mother had exchanged on the day of the bailiff's raid for the gold wedding band that she had sold. It had her initials rudely etched upon it and was worth only a penny or two.

"Well, she's done some of my work for me," said Mrs Lillystone, rolling up the sleeves of her gown.

"You're not going to do it here, are you?" I protested.

"Where else?" she demanded.

"But it's not decent," I said, and indicated the other people in the room.

Those nearest murmured in agreement and made a point of ostentatiously turning their backs towards that corner of the chamber, but I saw that I had to submit to this arrangement.

The kind Irishwoman indicated that I should sit with them but as I made to move away, Mrs Lillystone said: "Not before you've filled this copper for me."

So I went down to the pump and when I returned and helped Mrs Lillystone to place the filled copper over the fire, I could not help noticing that she had bound my mother's face with a rag to keep the jaw closed. Shuddering, I joined the family of poor Irish as I had been invited, and they insisted that I share their pitiful breakfast of bread and herring, and, though barely able to speak more than a few words of English, tried to talk to me in an effort to distract my attention from the other end of the room.

At last Mrs Lillystone announced that she had done and I saw the long shape roughly stitched into the cheap winding-sheet.

"I found this under her," she said and held out the pocket-book with the letter inscribed with her father's name still in it.

I took it from her and pushed it into my jacket. Wryly I recalled my legal tutorials: I was her heir-at-law and everything she owned now belonged to me.

"The dead-cart will call early tomorrow," Mrs Lillystone said.

I expected her to depart but she stayed at the door looking at me strangely: "You won't want to stay here till then, will you?" She screwed her face into an expression which I realized was intended to express motherly sympathy. "Not with that in the room. Why not come and sleep in my house tonight?"

I don't know and I never will know how justified I was in suspecting her display of kindliness, but I had the darkest suspicions of her motives, for I had not forgotten Mr Isbister's allusions to the services of parish searchers. I merely shook my head, and, gathering up the implements of her trade, she left.

I watched beside the body all through the rest of that day and the long night that followed. The Irishwoman had given me a piece of dry bread at midday and a little of their porage in the evening, and I was not hungry. When dusk began to gather, the deputy who kept the room had returned and demanded his tuppence, pointing out that my mother occupied the same floor space and should therefore pay for it, or he would "catch it hot" from Mr Ashburner if he should happen to look in. However, when the other occupants of the room protested he had backed down and agreed to take only a penny.

Though I was determined to observe my vigil and not to sleep, I could not keep my resolution. My dreams, however, brought me no relief. I found myself in a great empty house, walking from one vast room to another or along passages so lengthy that though I carried a lanthorn their ends were lost in darkness. Then the floor began to creak and to sway and as I ran across it to find safety it crumbled beneath my feet and I crashed into the room beneath. Now there was a huge window before me through which I could see nothing but a great white moon in the black sky. Then the head and shoulders of a veiled figure appeared from below, and to my dismay the veil slipped away and revealed a face — and yet it was not a face, for the skin was deeply pitted, the eyes were blank, and the nose no more than a chewed stump. Now it grew larger and to my horror came thrusting at me through the window and I awoke in terror.

The morning dragged itself out and it was several hours before one of the Irish children called out something to me in his language from the window where he was watching.

I looked out and saw two men climb down from a cart that had halted at the entrance to the court. I went down and met them on the stair and when I had led them into the right chamber, they picked up their burden and carried it downstairs while I followed.

"That's the last of the outdoors," the driver called out as they came up to him.

I saw that the cart was laden with six similar burdens and now the seventh was placed — not very gently — beside the others. The two men jumped aboard, their feet nudging the shapes on the floor, and the driver flicked the horse into movement with his whip.

"Where are you going?" I asked.

"The work'us," one of them answered without turning to look at me.

I followed the cart in the desultory rain through the narrow streets. Nobody attended to us, except that once, as we passed a gaggle of urchins playing shove-ha'penny in the street, they broke off their game and followed us for a while chanting:

"Rattle his bones
Over the stones.
He's only a pauper
What nobody owns."

At last the cart went across Holborn and down Shoe-lane and then turned into a lane beside the workhouse and pulled up in a narrow yard. The driver took the horse from the shafts and led it away, and while one of the men went into the building the other sheltered from the rain under the arch of the gateway to light his pipe.

"How long will it be?" I asked.

He merely shrugged and so I stood waiting by the cart.

After half an hour a parish-beadle appeared: "Cut away, young 'un," he said on seeing me.

The man who was smoking caught his eye and merely glanced towards the cart.

"Very well," said the beadle grudgingly and went back inside.

I waited for several hours, and by the end of that time was thoroughly soaked. At last the driver re-appeared with the horse and while he harnessed it to the shafts again, the two men — for the other came back now — carried out four more shrouded objects from inside the building, two of them very small.

The cart moved off again and I found that I was the only mourner to follow it. It went only a few yards along the lane at a walking-pace and entered a small, dark square at the rear of the workhouse. As I looked round at the soot-blackened backs of the buildings, I became aware of a dank odour. Although in the gloom of a stormy winter afternoon before the lighting of the lamps, it was difficult to see clearly, I made out that there was a graveyard in the middle and that it was raised several feet above the level of the square and surmounted by a broken-down wall topped by an ancient and rusted iron railing. There was no church.

The cart drew up at the gate to this yard and one of the men dismounted and went through a door at the back of the workhouse. After a few minutes, during which I became increasingly aware of the smell, he re-emerged with a young curate who stood in the porch sheltering from the drizzle while the man came back to the cart and began to help the other two to lift down the shrouded forms and lay them on the muddy grass beyond the gate. Meanwhile the clergyman was reading aloud from a prayer-book and when I went closer to hear him I realized that he was rattling through a very abbreviated version of the Service for the Burial of the Dead.

A sexton carrying a shovel now appeared and, leaving the clergyman at his devotions in the porch, made his way along a muddy track through the burial-ground followed by the three men who each picked up one or two of the smaller objects from the cart. The sexton halted beside an area of naked freshly-turned earth and began to clear away the soil with his spade, while the other men dropped their burdens to the ground nearby and went back to bring the rest of them from the cart. As the earth was removed from the pit the stench became overpowering, and I quickly understood why when, a few inches down, the sexton's shovel began to uncover shrouded forms. As the last of the bodies was brought from the cart, the curate abandoned the shelter of the porch and accompanied the men, now holding a handkerchief before his face. He stopped some ten yards from the pit as the three men, with the help of the sexton, began to lift their burdens and drop them the few inches into what was now a trench a couple of feet deep.

Now that I understood, I ran forward and laid my hand on the arm of the sexton.

"No," I said. "Not in there."

"What else?" he asked turning to me a face that was cold and uninterested.

"Not like that," I cried.

"Do not demean this sacred rite," the curate called out in a startlingly deep voice, removing the handkerchief from his face for a moment in order to do so.

I was powerless to prevent what was happening. Still standing at a distance, the clergyman rapidly intoned the concluding words of the Burial Service, throwing a few pebbles towards the pit at the appropriate moment, and then walked quickly away, followed by the men from the parish. I watched as the sexton sprinkled lime from a bucket and then shovelled a few inches of earth over the fresh contents of the pit which now rose from the surrounding grass like a pustulent sore swelling to bursting — just as the graveyard itself bulged several feet above the level of the street.

The sexton finished his work and departed, I heard the cart move off, and I was left alone. Was that all there was to my mother's life? It seemed less than meaningless. I tried to pray but all I could remember were Dr Meadowcroft's bland phrases, and I found that I could not believe in a God who had done this. I thought of the peaceful church-yard at Melthorpe which was the resting-place of our forefathers and spoke aloud my promise: "If ever I am able, I will have you moved from this place."

The promise failed to comfort me and an insane thought of digging up that precious object and carrying it off occurred to me. Overcome by grief and rage and possessed suddenly by a dark fear, I found that I could not breathe in the foul air. My stomach went into spasms and I would have vomited if there had been enough food inside me. Hardly trusting my legs to bear me, I withdrew from the burying-ground to the edge of the square where the air was less intolerable. For after the betrayal by Lizzie, I suspected everyone and all that Mr Pentecost had said seemed to me to be justified now. To believe in altruism or generosity or any of the other things that Mr Silverlight had defended was absurd. I recalled the feigned solicitude — as it seemed to me — of Mrs Lillystone, and passed in review the faces of the three men from the workhouse and the sexton. I had only too much reason to know what further indignity might await the body of my mother.

And so for the rest of that day I walked round and round the square — so silent though the bustle of Fleet-market lay just beyond that row of houses! — as the gloomy afternoon turned to dusk and the shadows lengthened. When night came I huddled into a door-way opposite to the long pit. Still no tears came for they would have been in pity for myself and I felt none: I felt only anger. Anger against everyone: against Mrs Purviance, against Mrs Fortisquince, against the Mompessons, against old Lizzie. Above all, against myself.

Now it was that I vowed that never again would I place myself at the mercy of outward circumstances by allowing myself to love another individual.

With the cold and the rain and the cries of the watch, I slept badly. About three hours after midnight the watch discovered me and shone their lanthorns in my face. They questioned me harshly and ordered me to move on, so I roused myself and began a weary patrole of the square and the surrounding streets for an hour or so. After that I settled down in my old place and was left in peace for what remained of the night. I slept fitfully and awoke to the desire of death — the longing to prolong sleep. Who now cared if I lived or died? Nobody. So why should I care?

When the sluggish dawn came up I laid out a penny on a small loaf and then took up my post again. The next day and the following night passed in the same way, except that having now only four-pence-ha'penny left, I bought no food. But this did not worry me for I could see no reason to live once my present task was fulfilled.

By dawn on the second day I believed that my vigil had been long enough to defeat the purposes of Isbister and his like. The weather was getting colder and it came to me that I should remain out in the streets that day, and then the following night find somewhere to conceal myself — a hidden kennel or over-grown yard — and simply fall asleep there in the expectation that I would never wake again.

How guilty the Mompessons would feel when they heard how my mother had died — and then of my death, too. They would be alarmed, too, for our deaths would dispossess them. But then it came to me that our mysterious enemy would be delighted, for this would give him the Hougham estate. In that case, I would not give him the satisfaction of having achieved his desire. I must remain alive.

With that thought animating me, I set off for Mitre-court, knowing nowhere else to go. I had just enough strength to find my way back to that room which I hated having to enter again, and when I gave up my penny at the door I now had only three pence and a ha'penny left. The Irish family had gone, but Lizzie lay before the fire in a drunken stupor, an empty stone jug beside her. I lay down beside her, with no feeling of anger towards her for I only remembered that she had shewn a sort of rough kindness to my mother — whatever her motives had been. I slept all that day, then in the evening went out and spent a ha'penny on a loaf of bread, then returned to the room at the expense of another penny — except for the remaining tuppence, the last money I had in the world — and slept again.

CHAPTER 53

When I awoke the next morning the desire to live was strong in me, though I felt in some way that it was a betrayal of my mother to want to survive her. But then I told myself that on the contrary, I owed it to her to stay alive, that it would have grieved her to know that I was to follow her. Something was taking place inside me which I did not understand, for the rage I had felt since her death had been transformed by finding its vehicle. I wanted justice. I wanted to bring it home to those people who had brought about my mother's death. Much as I hated them, I did not mean those whose actions had merely contributed to it, like Bissett and Mrs Purviance, or who had apparently refused her aid at the end like Sir Perceval and Lady Mompesson and their creature Mr Barbellion. (And yet I could not understand why my mother had said they had turned her away, for I knew that it was crucial to their interests that a Huffam heir remained alive. Surely she must have been delirious when she had spoken of it?) No, the individuals I wanted to bring to justice were those who had cold-bloodedly contrived my mother's destruction for purposes of their own: the mysterious "Silas" who must be the "Silas Clothier" mentioned in the codicil as the heir in remainder, and the creatures who, I suspected, had been part of his conspiracy — Mr Sancious (or, as he had called himself, Mr Steplight) and Mrs Fortisquince.

Now I was hungry and the fact that I had no money forced me to think about my future. I thought of the vastness of London with its teeming millions close-packed in streets and squares, or tiny courts and alleys. In all that huge crowd — each member of it preoccupied with his selfish concerns — I knew nobody to whom I could apply for aid, nobody who cared whether I lived or died, nobody at all — except perhaps Miss Quilliam, and she could do little enough for me. My head spun at the thought of the huge, meaningless, uncaring city around me and at the realization that I had no idea what to do next. Justice! That was the idea to hold onto. Only justice gave the world back a pattern and therefore a meaning, for without it there was nothing but incoherence and confusion. I would go to Miss Quilliam and perhaps she would help me to secure justice against the Mompessons, for they had done her harm; and with this thought I set out for Coleman-street.

As I was hurrying through Soho I noticed on a high narrow house in a dark street a brass door-plate bearing the legend "James Lampard: School of Anatomy". I remembered that name on Isbister's lips and now I understood what the point of his dreadful trade must be. I could not shake the thought of it off, and as I walked along I saw all those I encountered as pigs, brutal animals, self-interested, creatures of mere appetite. I did not wish to belong to such a race. Everywhere I saw jowls heavy with self-satisfaction, starched linen framing faces of utter bestiality, bare arms displaying jewelled bracelets.

Perfumed beasts, animals strutting in stolen finery — that was all my fellow beings seemed to me.

When I had descended the area stairs of the house in Coleman-street I found I was in luck for, having knocked at the kitchen door I discovered that the little maid was alone. She stood at the door, however, without letting me in.

"I dursen't," she said. "The mistress has forbid it. She was very angry with me for letting you speak to Miss Quilliam."

"But I must see her," I protested.

"You can't," she said with a kind of triumph. "She's gone away."

"Where to?" I asked with a stab of foreboding.

"To Paris."

I remembered that she had mentioned this possibility when I last spoke to her. The girl must have seen my disappointment — indeed, my dismay — for, indicating that I should wait, she closed the door for a moment and re-appeared with a piece of bread and half a saveloy.

"Go quickly," she said, pushing the food into my hand and shutting the door.

CHAPTER 54

As I walked slowly down the street lingeringly consuming this gift, I reflected that my situation was now truly desperate. I knew that no workhouse — and Heaven knew what kind of fate would await me there! — would admit an able-bodied boy of my years, especially one without any claim to a settlement in any parish in London. I would be reduced to scavenging for scraps around the markets or "mud-larking" on the shores of the river, and wondered how long I could survive that way. And yet I had no alternative, for I knew no-one in the metropolis to whom I could turn unless I made another attempt to locate Mrs Digweed. But that would mean going all the way to the Borough in search of Pulvertaft and after my experiences with Isbister — and all the more in the light of what had just happened — I shrank from the thought of seeking out anyone who had been connected with him. Moreover, I felt that my link with the Digweeds was very tenuous — and growing more so with each passing month.

At that moment I remembered that there was one other individual to whom I could go: Stephen Maliphant's half-brother, Henry Bellringer. Indeed, since I had promised Stephen that I would carry to him the news of his death, I had not so much a right as a positive duty to go to him. The consideration that I could not hope for much assistance from him since Stephen had told me how very poor he was, made me feel the less reserve about seeking him out in so impoverished a state.

I recalled the address of his chambers — No. 6, Fig-tree-court, Barnards-inn — and, reflecting that it was strange to live in a tavern if one were very poor, made my way there. The inn revealed itself to be a building of very shabby appearance and nothing like any other hostelry I had ever seen for there was no stable-yard and I could see no sign of a dining-room or coffee-room. It seemed to be no more than an ordinary court, except that the entrance was through a porter's lodge.

I knew that I had no chance of being granted admittance dressed as I was, so I lurked out of sight outside the lodge and then hurried past when the gate-keeper's attention was engaged by a gentleman leaving the building. I ventured through several inter-connected courts and found that the one I wanted was the dingiest and darkest. To my surprise I saw that there were names painted on boards at the bottom of the stairs for it suggested a degree of permanency on the part of the guests that was unusual in an inn. However that might be, I was reassured to find that Mr Henry Bellringer did indeed occupy chambers on staircase No. 6.

I climbed up the stairs and reached what I believed was the top floor without finding his name on any of the doors. Then I noticed an additional short and rickety pair of stairs beyond the main one. I took this way up to the garret under the roof where, indeed, I found another door with the name I was seeking inscribed upon it. The outer door stood open but the inner was closed and I knocked upon it.

It opened. A young man stood in the door-way and stared at me, and indeed in my dirty and ragged clothes and with my grimy face, I must have seemed a surprising and somewhat alarming figure. The young man was about three- or four-and-twenty years of age and was dressed as a gentleman, though, I could see, a very poor one.

He addressed me with no more formality than the occasion seemed to warrant: "Who are you? What do you want?"

"Are you Mr Henry Bellringer?"

He was clearly surprised by my intonation, which must have been very different from what he expected.

"I am," he said with an expression in which curiosity now predominated over repugnance.

"I am a friend of Stephen Maliphant."

He gave a start of surprise and scrutinized me for several moments, then he smiled slightly and said: "Then you had better come in."

As soon as he smiled I saw the resemblance to Stephen and this, as much as the kindness that the smile and the invitation expressed, gratified and reassured me. If I was any judge of physiognomy — the art of reading the mind's construction in the face — then this young man was honest and good-hearted.

A moment later I found myself in a small chamber which seemed all the more confined because of its steeply sloping ceiling. A door led into another room, which was hardly larger than a cupboard as far as I could see. A very small fire consisting of a countable number of coals was flickering in the hearth and did little to combat the cold of a winter afternoon, for although it was only the middle of November, winter had arrived. A worn Turkey carpet made a pitiful attempt to cover part of the floor. Two easy-chairs stood before the fire, a sopha was between it and the door, and a desk with an upright chair stood near the single small and dirty window. In truth everything was near everything else, so small was the chamber.

"Sit down," my host said, and I sank into one of the chairs. "You look done up," he went on. "I wish I had something hot I could give you. The fact is that I'm rather short of tin just at present and I don't have anything here."

"Please don't worry," I said, though hunger was making me faint.

"Let me lend something to Uncle," he said and looked round. His expression expressed comical dismay and indeed there seemed to be nothing worth pawning in the room. There were no ornaments, no pictures, and no clock. The furniture was so shabby and broken down as to be almost useless for its intended purpose and certainly worthless. There were no books except for some large and ancient tomes on the desk, on which lay the implements of writing: a sander, a quire of paper, a pounce-box, wafers, a brass frame like a lectern, a tablet, and a pen which he had obviously been nibbing when I had interrupted him.

"I must have something left," he said, "though strictly between ourselves, Uncle's been rather greedy just lately. I've had a run of bad luck. (I shouldn't say luck, for that's a fool's notion.) So nearly everything has gone up the spout already." He laughed and then, seeing my gaze upon the books he explained ruefully: "They aren't mine. I only wish they were, but they're from our office."

My pride revolted at the idea of receiving charity from one who was so clearly himself in need, and who could joke so bravely about his poverty.

"No, no," I said, "I couldn't think of allowing it. My friends will look after me."

He looked relieved and seated himself in the other chair.

"Your parents?"

"I have no father." I hesitated. "And my mother is dead."

"But you have friends with money? That's a very fine thing."

"Yes," I agreed. I noticed his gaze upon my garments and feeling that this claim accorded strangely with the figure I presented, I said: "They have been trying to buy me new clothes and clean me up, but I haven't had time. I've only just got back to Town from Yorkshire."

"Ah yes," he said. "You were at school with my half-brother down there?"

I nodded, wondering if he had learned anything yet of Stephen's fate for the cheerfulness of his tone suggested that he had not. His next words resolved that doubt and made my heart sink at the realization that I was to be the bearer of bad news.

"How is the dear lad?" he asked, smiling pleasantly.

I could not answer and seeing my confusion his smile gradually faded.

"Is he ill, or ... "

He broke off and I was forced to say: "I am afraid he is dead, Mr Bellringer."

He turned away and covered his face with his sleeve.

"Poor Stevie," he said after a moment. "When did this happen?"

"The very end of July. I am surprised and grieved that you did not know."

"There is no-one who would have told me. His aunt and I are not on any sort of terms. But you have not told me what he died of?"

"They killed him," I answered without reflecting.

I had considered long beforehand what I would tell Stephen's half-brother about the circumstances of his death and had decided to play down the Quiggs' brutality. I spoke as I did now because, tired and hungry as I was, it was easier to tell the truth. As soon as I had spoken I realized that it would have seemed wrong to have disguised the truth, and I believe that without knowing it I was influenced in this conviction by the bereavement I had just suffered.

Henry started at my words: "Can this be true?"

So I described the circumstances leading up to the boy's death — murder, as I called it — sparing nothing but taking care to avoid exaggeration. He listened without interrupting me with an expression of sympathy that deepened when I came to the brutal beating his half-brother had received.

When I had finished he looked at me gravely and then said: "Now, look here, old fellow, I remember that my own schooldays were deuced awful. I went to a good birchen academy and was whipped often enough. I think every schoolboy in England believes at some time that he is at school to be starved and beaten to death. Now, ain't that so?"

"Yes," I agreed.

"But the Quiggs do sound a worse set of rascals than most. Thank heavens you're clear of there now and back with your friends."

"You didn't believe my story, did you?" I said, and realized to my dismay that I was close to tears. "You think I made it up about Stephen being beaten to death."

"Now, now, old fellow," Henry said in a kindly tone. "I think you've had a very bad time and so you're seeing things as worse than they really were. That's all. One gentleman doesn't accuse another of lying." He exclaimed with comical indignation: "Dammit sir, that's a duelling matter!"

I smiled uncertainly and he went on: "I only wish I had known what a fearful place that was. But what could I have done for Stevie when, as you can see only too plainly, I can scarcely keep myself? And I had no legal standing to interfere. His guardian was his aunt."

"Should I find her out and tell her what I have told you?"

"Oh no," he said hastily. "Those people — what are they called, the Quiggs? — will have informed her of his death."

"Do you think that Miss Maliphant ... ?"

He interrupted: "Of whom do you speak?"

"Stephen's aunt."

"Oh, that ain't her name now. She married. But what about her?"

"Well," I said, "I wondered if she knew what was happening." Seeing his expression of bewilderment I went on: "You see, I believe I was sent to the Quiggs to be put out of the way."

"To be kept there, do you mean, all during the year?"

"More than that. In the hope, the expectation even, that I would never leave."

He stared and then smiled oddly: "I say, steady on, old man. I see what you mean, but that's pitching it a bit strong. What makes you think that?"

I told him that Mr Steplight — the man who had escorted me there — appeared to have a responsibility from Stephen's aunt to report back on his condition, and that since Stephen was visibly malnourished this tended to inculpate her.

"'Steplight'", Henry repeated. "No, I've never heard the name, I'm certain." Then he laughed: "As for the idea that his aunt was behind this! Well, she might not have cared for him a great deal, but I think you're going rather too far. And anyway, what motive could she possibly have for such a thing?"

"You don't know of one?"

He looked suddenly serious: "Let me give you some advice, old man. Don't tell the story about the Quiggs beating Stephen to anyone else. And above all, don't talk about his aunt like that. I know something about the law, and I warn you that there is such a thing as slander and it's a very serious business."

I saw that he meant well so I nodded as if in acceptance of this. I had mentioned Stephen's family-name because I was curious about it, so now I said: "May I ask you if you are related to the Maliphant family?"

"No, unfortunately not," he answered with a smile. "You see, after my father died when I was a very young child, my mother married again. Her second husband was Timothy Maliphant, Stephen's father. (Both families lived in Canterbury and that is how my mother met Maliphant.) Our mother, alas, died very shortly after Stephen's birth and he and I were brought up by our respective fathers' families so we knew each other only very slightly."

Since Henry's connexion with the Maliphant family was so tenuous, I decided not to mention to him the coincidence — if it was no more than that — of the name appearing in the codicil drawn up by my great-great-grandfather.

"I said 'unfortunately' just now," Henry continued, "because my father, unlike Stephen's who had a modest independence, was a very poor man." He smiled mischievously: "Timothy Maliphant's annuity, incidentally, was inherited by Stephen and held in trust for him until his majority, but it died with him. I mention that in case you're wondering if it could have been a motive for someone to murder him."

I blushed for the thought had occurred to me, and indeed it did seem to me now that I had been excessively morbid in my suspicions.

"My own people, the Bellringers," he went on with considerable bitterness, "are connected with some of the most ancient families in the kingdom. The blood of the Plantagenets runs in my veins. And we once had wealth — far more than the Maliphants, if it comes to that. But it was all lost long ago in foolish speculations, lotteries, card-play and other sorts of gambling. And my great-grandfather was cheated of his birth-right." Suddenly he laughed: "And so I, the last of my family, have been left a great inheritance that no duke's son could hope for: the chance to make my own fortune without the aid of patron or money. As you have probably deduced from these great dusty volumes, it is the profession of the law that I am preparing myself for."

"Stephen told me you were a lawyer," I said.

"Not yet," he said smiling. "I have still to complete my articles."

"I have thought of the law," I said. "Is it very difficult without much money?"

"Yes," he replied. "You need to have been to one of the public schools and to be vouched for by a respectable lawyer in order to be accepted as a pupil. Then you need the premium of about a hundred pounds. And on top of that, you require enough money to keep yourself for the years of your pupillage and articles. My family was only able to furnish me with a part of the premium and so I've made my way by law-writing for luckily (though I hate that word) I seem to have the knack of all that kind of thing."

"Do you mean writing Acts of Parliament?" I asked in awe.

He laughed. "That's rich! No, indeed. I am the lowest quill-driver, chained to my desk like a galley-slave and merely copying documents. I was in the middle of engrossing a conveyance when you knocked."

He gestured towards the table and I saw that lying there was a large piece of parchment in red and black ink, and covered in lines ruled in pencil.

I took the hint. He had been very friendly but I really had no further reason to stay apart from reluctance to return to the cold streets.

"I must go," I said. "Or my friends will be growing concerned about me."

I didn't know if this pretence took him in, but it served as a useful fiction that got me to the door without further embarrassment.

We took each other's hands and he said: "Thank you for coming to tell me about Stevie." He paused. "Why, I don't believe you told me your name!"

In my weariness all the names I had used appeared before me. I could not remember why I should use one rather than another and therefore could not choose, so I replied: "John, just John."

"Very well, John," he said, smiling.

We shook hands, then he closed the inner door and I descended the steep staircase.

CHAPTER 55

I dragged myself back towards Mitre-court, using my second last penny to buy a piece of bread on the way. The very last coin I gave to the deputy, feeling a strange sense of release now that I had no money at all and no idea of how I would eat or where I would sleep the next day.

The chamber's occupants had changed again and I recognised none of them. As I lay down on the bare boards I felt the contents of my jacket-pocket digging into me and remembered that all this time I had been carrying about with me my mother's pocket-book with the letter enclosed in it. When I had thought of them I had been unable to bring myself to look at them, but I pulled them out now and examined them by the little light coming through the dirty windows. I was pleased to see the map though I noticed that it had not been unfolded since I had given it to my mother before I set off for the North with Mr Steplight. Then I leaned my back against the wall, opened the pocket-book and began to read my mother's rather untidy hand. The first entry was dated to that long-distant day when Sukey and I had met Mr Barbellion in the graveyard at Melthorpe and then in the evening I had lain awake waiting for my mother to come up to me after our quarrel:

"*First Relation:*
"*The 18th. of December, 1819.*
"My dearest Johnnie,

"You don't understand, of course you don't. How could you? You were unkind but you didn't know what you were saying. You don't understand what Mr Barbelion's coming here means. It means that our Enemy has found us. And you led him to us! But it's not your fault for you are not old enough to understand. I'm not really angry. I will go upstairs now and make it up with you.

"You were asleep. I watched you for fear that you might be pretending, but I believe you were really sleeping.

"I want you to understand everything and so I have decided to write an account of my life before you were born. You will not read it until you are grown up and can understand everything in it. Some of it will be very hard for you to bear and for me to tell you if I am to tell you all of it. I will give this to you on your twenty-first birthday and let you read it. Or perhaps I will let you find it when I am dead."

I heard my mother's voice so clearly that now for the first time I felt a sense of loss that was unmixed with anger, and at last tears began to cloud my vision. I tried to ignore them and persevere in my reading, but I could not go on and so, stretching myself out against the wall, I abandoned myself to my grief.

It might have been an hour later that, the force of my sorrow having spent itself, I found that I was still clutching the pocket-book and noticed the letter sticking out from it. I removed it and inspected the big red seal representing the quatre-foil rose with which it was fastened and the rusty patch of faded discoloration that I had long ago childishly taken for blood.

The superscription read "My beloved son — and my heir: John Huffam". That was my grandfather's name, but was the letter addressed to his son-in-law ("My beloved son") and my mother ("my heir"), or to the former alone? *Addressed, in fact, to my father!* Who was my grandfather's heir? But now as I looked at the seal, it came to me that my mother could never have broken it! Then why had she not opened the letter if it was addressed to her? Did that imply that she took it to mean that her husband rather than herself was the heir referred to? And did that suggest that she believed he was still alive? I hesitated. Had I the right to break the seal if he was still alive? Surely I had some right to open it now. So I broke it and began to read the folio sheet I found inside:

"Charing-cross,
"The 5th. of May, 1811.

"Claim to Title of Hougham Estate:

"Title in fee absolute held by Jeoffrey Huffam. Allegedly conveyed by James and possession now Sir P. Mompesson. Subject of suit in Chancery.

"Codicil to Jeoffrey's will of '68 criminally removed by unknown party after his death. Recently restored through honesty and perseverance of Mr Jeo. Escreet. Creates entail vested in my father and heirs male and female. Legality of sale of H. estate? P. M. not dispossessed but now only dependant right of base fee, while fee absolute to self and heirs?"

I broke off here in bewilderment. What kind of letter was this? It was a jumble of fragments! And as for what it was saying, it seemed that it merely confirmed what I already knew: namely, that the codicil to Jeoffrey Huffam's will did not confer upon my grandfather's heirs any right to the title to the Huffam property since that title had been alienated — however dubiously — by his father, James, in the process of selling the estate to the Mompessons. All of this I had learned by copying out the codicil itself, and Mr Sancious (alias Steplight) — if he could be trusted — had expounded: my mother, and now, as her heir, I myself, held nominal title to the Hougham estate, but this conferred neither title nor right to possession.

My head aching and my stomach in pain from hunger, lying on the bare and dirty floor and straining my eyes in the near-darkness, I felt little interest in these obscure words. There was more of it but the light was fading fast and since I could only read with difficulty my grandfather's hand, I could see no purpose in continuing. I saw the words "will" and "rights" and stopped reading. Bitterly disappointed, I folded the letter and put it back inside the pocket-book. I do not know what I had hoped for from the voice of my deceased grandfather, but what I seemed to have found was an obsessive mind brooding over hair-splitting legal niceties in the hope of vindicating imagined rights. It grieved me to think that my mother had cherished this letter for so many years, for it seemed just another example of how misguided and pointless so much of her life had been and how many misjudgements she had made.

I attempted to make myself comfortable on the floor but it was long before I fell asleep, and then my dreams were haunted by leering faces coming at me from the darkness muttering insanely about codicils and title.

BOOK II

Honour Among Gentlemen

CHAPTER 56

It seems that they had arranged to meet in the Piazza Coffee-house just around the corner (speaking topographically) from the Office of the Six-clerks, though in a different world in every other sense. So here are two of them — both dressed in the height of fashion — awaiting the third. Though one of them is even now barely familiar, the other two were well-known to you. Mr David Mompesson wore a rifle-green frock-coat, a white top-hat, a sky-blue coat with yellow buttons and trowsers and a gold watch-guard, and the gentleman who arrived with him was clad in a dress-coat and tight trowsers with white silk stockings and long-quartered pumps. When the third gentleman joined them a few minutes later, wearing a shabby great-coat and a somewhat worn beaver-hat, Mr Mompesson introduced him to his companion:

"Harry, you've heard me speak of Sir Thomas."

"I have," he says with a brief bow as he takes the proffered hand which is be-ringed and manicured.

The two smile formally at each other.

"I sent to meet you here, Harry," Mr Mompesson goes on, "because I want to avail myself of some of your legal advice."

"Well, you've come to the right shop."

"Shop? Why, I hope you ain't going to make me fee you for it?"

"Not yet, but one day I shall. But if we're going to talk law we'd best not do it here."

"Why should we not go on to the Finish?" suggests Mr Mompesson.

As you probably know, he was alluding to a *tonish* but extremely disreputable coffee-shop in another part of Covent-garden.

"I have a better notion than that!" cries the young baronet. "Let us go to a Hell!"

"Thomas is a notorious black-leg," Mr Mompesson explains to his legal companion. "I sometimes wonder if his ruling passions aren't really the turf and the baize."

"The injury is at least only to one's pocket," Sir Thomas answers with a laugh. "Whereas a moment with Venus may condemn you to a lifetime with Mercury."

The other gentlemen smile (the shabbily-dressed one rather uneasily) and Sir Thomas says to Mr Mompesson: "I see you still bear the scars of an encounter with the fair sex."

Mr Mompesson flushes then, raising a hand to his forehead, protests irritably: "It's healed now. It was more than two years ago, dammit. Can't you let it drop?"

You and I, of course, know what member of the gentle sex inflicted this wound upon the future baronet and under what circumstances. Little wonder that he had no taste to be reminded of it!

"Come," says Sir Thomas rising from his seat, "we're getting dull and we shall quarrel. Let us go to Wetherby's."

So they make their way to Henrietta-street, and ring at a dark little door which is secured with knobs of iron. After a moment a small wicket with iron bars across it opens and a voice demands: "Who is there?"

"Friends," Sir Thomas replies. "We are sent by Stanhope Mountgarret."

He winks at his companions.

"Come in one at a time," the unseen voice returns and, as the sound of a bolt being drawn and a heavy chain falling is heard, the door swings back. From behind it the Cerberus who guards the entrance to this Hell holds a lanthorn briefly in each gentleman's face as he passes and then secures the door behind them.

They find themselves in a dark hall but from there they enter a large and magnificent apartment ablaze with candles and high looking-glasses whose existence could hardly be guessed at from the decrepit appearance of the house.

From the cashier seated at a desk in one corner, Mr Mompesson and Sir Thomas each purchase thirty guineas' worth of ivory fishes.

"You won't play?" Sir Thomas asks their companion.

He flushes while Mr Mompesson smiles.

"Never," he answers. "On principle."

And so, while Harry looks on disdainfully, the other two proceed to lose their money at Hazard. When they are quite cleaned out they lounge with Harry on the chairs and sophas in one of the other apartments, drinking the iced champagne that the establishment generously makes available.

"Why the aversion to play?" Sir Thomas languidly asks.

"The question doesn't arise," Harry answers stiffly. "My circumstances do not permit it."

The baronet looks him up and down with a bored smile as if to imply that from his appearance that is only too obvious.

"But I have another reason," Harry goes on, as if stung by this insolent appraisal. "My own family lost a great deal of money through play. My great-grandfather once had considerable wealth but he dissipated it all in gaming."

"Your great-grandfather," the baronet drawls. "That's going confoundedly far back, ain't it?"

"Not so far," Harry retorts. "He is still alive."

"Must be deuced old," Sir Thomas comments.

"Of course," Harry replies impatiently. Then he hesitates and, looking at Mr Mompesson, adds: "And yet he has neither forgotten nor forgiven the wrongs done to him, for he has been the victim of terrible injustice."

"Yes, yes," Mr Mompesson says quickly. "But don't for heaven's sake start on that now."

"It's very well for you," Harry says angrily. "Your family has profited by it."

He breaks off and both he and Mr Mompesson glance at the baronet as if afraid they have said too much.

"You intrigue me," Sir Thomas says. "Won't you tell me the story?"

"Well, if you must," Mr Mompesson says off-handedly. "It goes back to the absurd tale that my great-grandfather won his property down at Hougham in a game of Hazard, but there is no foundation in it. The truth is more mundane: he bought it from James Huffam."

"Yet such things happen," Sir Thomas protests.

"To win or lose everything on the fall of the dice," Harry says with a shudder. "I play no games of chance but I will take you on at chess where luck plays no part and my fate hangs or falls by my own cunning."

"If it's a question of cunning, you should play at cards," Mr Mompesson says. "But why do you jib at games of chance when life itself is a dice-game? If I win, very well. If I lose, why then, I shall have to accept my fate."

"No, you can make your fate," Harry replies. "You don't have to accept it."

"Gammon!" exclaims the baronet. "Life is a game of Hazard."

"That is a facile view," Harry says venomously. "There are patterns and they can be understood and mastered. That is the appeal of Equity to me."

"If it comes to that," returns Sir Thomas, "Hazard can be mastered if you play with a pair of cogged dice."

"As your great-grandfather knew," Harry says to Mr Mompesson.

"I wish the old fellow had known about this damned codicil!" that gentleman exclaims, doubtless intending to divert his companion from this dangerous topic.

(And I might presume to add that Harry would undoubtedly have had the best of the argument had the three young men continued it, for Equity is indeed an imitation of divine Justice, and the nearest image we have of the hidden Design that rules all things.)

"What's this?" Sir Thomas asks.

"It's a codicil to the will of James Huffam's father that has been laid before Chancery," Mr Mompesson answers gratefully. "And its conditions may be set up in place of those in the original will that old Huffam made. The codicil entails the estate upon James instead of bequeathing it outright, and so if the Court accepts it, that would mean that he had no clear title to the estate to sell to my great-grandfather."

"So do you lose the property?"

"No, it ain't so simple as that. You'd better explain it, Harry."

So Harry begins: "The codicil would mean that Mompesson's family acquired only a base-fee in the title while the fee-simple passed to the entailed heirs of James. So long as there is a Huffam heir, there is no difficulty. But if that line dies out (or is disproved), then the fee-simple in the property passes to the next entailed heir and in *that* event, Mompesson's family are dispossessed."

Sir Thomas whistles softly then asks: "And is there still a Huffam heir?"

Mr Mompesson and Harry glance at each other.

"We don't know," Mr Mompesson says. "There were two but they've gone missing. You see, they have nothing to gain from holding the fee-simple. But now that the story of the codicil is abroad, nobody will take my paper or my father's except at the highest discount. Even now when the money-market has gone so crazy that it seems that any paper with a signature to it is tradable."

"You're in deep?" Sir Thomas asks.

"Frankly, we're all to pieces. The governor's steward down at Hougham is lining his pockets at our expense, but my old fellow refuses to see it even though my mother and Barbellion have shewn him clear evidence. As for myself, why, I've borrowed so much on post-obits that even if the governor died tomorrow, it might be too late to save me from a complete smash."

"How deep are you?" the baronet asks.

Mr Mompesson leans forward and says softly: "Fifteen thousand."

The baronet whistles slowly.

"If the governor finds out, there'll be the devil of a blow-up. The only thing that can rescue me," Mr Mompesson goes on, "is to find myself an heiress."

"Why," says Sir Thomas, "I know of a likely filly and I believe I could help you to her."

"What is she like?"

"Well, she ain't one of your whey-faced demure misses who are only too tediously biddable. She's a woman of spirit. And I can promise you, you will never suffer a moment's anxiety for her reputation."

"In short, she's an ugly old virago," Mr Mompesson says, laughing.

"Well, the truth is, she has somewhat overstood her market by keeping her price too high. But I promise you, she's a Smithfield bargain: she'll bring you property with a rent-charge of ten thousand. You'll be famously rich. And to show gratitude, you can buy me a place in the Patent-office."

"Well, at least she'd keep me out of the hands of the Jews."

Sir Thomas laughs and says: "I didn't promise you that. Wait until I've found out if she's really on the market and if you're interested I'll tell you more about her."

"You're making me anxious, Tommy. Perhaps she'd do for that cankered blossom of our house — as our motto has it — my brother Tom. They sound as if they'd make a fine couple."

"But that wouldn't do any good for you," Sir Thomas objects.

"Yes it might," Mr Mompesson replies. "For Harry has an idea and that's what I wanted to speak to him about." He turns to him: "Tell him what we were talking about the other day."

"Tom could be married," Harry begins, "and then a Chancery commission convened which could be relied upon to declare him a lunatic. (These things can be arranged in most cases.) Mompesson here would become his committee with complete discretion to handle his affairs."

"Most ingenious," says the baronet. "But it would take time so it won't help you in the short term."

"As far as that goes," Harry says, "I could put you onto a broker who would take your acceptances."

"Why," exclaims Mr Mompesson, "that's excessively generous of you, Harry. Positively altruistic, I declare."

"You're a lucky devil, Mompesson," Sir Thomas exclaims. "You've found a marriage-broker and a bill-broker on the same day!"

"Yes," the future baronet answers, smiling at his friends. "And I wonder which intends to take the larger commission?"

CHAPTER 57

When I awoke the next morning my first thought was that I had no money and no prospect of acquiring any. I knew how difficult — nay, impossible — it would be to find work without skills or physical strength, and my only other recourse, begging, was not only uncertain but also dangerous, for I knew that I could be taken up for this offence and sent to the treadmill.

Deciding that if I were now forced to seek charity I should at least do so from those on whom I had some claim — however slight it was — I resolved to make one last attempt to find the Digweed family. I still remembered Pulvertaft's address that old Sam'el had given me two years ago, and although it occurred to me to wonder if he would still be living there now, my faith in the Digweeds and what they could do for me was so irrationally strong — perhaps because of my state of hunger and exhaustion — that I was convinced that if I could only find Pulvertaft, all would be well. And so I set out to walk into the Borough, repeating the name "Digweed" to myself over and over again as if it were a magic talisman which had the power to lead me to safety like something from my beloved Arabian Tales, and quite forgetting not only the circumstances under which my mother and I had met Mrs Digweed and her son, but also our experiences with the Isbisters whom we had encountered in our pursuit of them.

I had a long and exhausting walk before I found myself in the notorious district called the Old Mint, and it was getting dark as I began to enquire for the Old Manor-house which Sam'el had told me was the nethersken (low lodging-house) where Pulvertaft dwelt. I found it at last in Blue-Ball-court. Though it was old, it was like no manor-house that I had ever seen or read about. It was a low, two-storied tumbledown house lying up a dark back-alley and surrounded by a heaving sea of broken cobbles rising and falling like frozen waves. Only a few faint gleams of light came from the barred shutters and a little smoke rose secretively from its crumbling chimney-stack. There was a wooden staircase at one end leading to the upper floor so that one could come and go without reference to the main room or "kitchen" on the ground floor, which was reached by a door at the bottom of the stairs. I now knocked on this. There was a long pause and then a dirty-faced woman wearing a woollen shawl over a tattered gown and with her unkempt hair straggling to her shoulders, opened the door a few inches and I made my enquiry.

"He might live here," she said. "Then agin, he might not. Leastways, he ain't within doors now."

"May I stay for him?"

"I can't stop you," she replied and the door was shut in my face.

So I settled down to wait a little way up the stairs. People slipped in and out of the door beneath me at frequent intervals, and others passed up and down beside me. As the night approached, ragged men and boys came and laid themselves down to sleep on the landing above me and on the stairs, getting kicked and trodden on by those who passed, some of whom were not in a condition to be very considerate towards others. Exhausted as I was I quickly fell asleep, though I was woken a number of times when someone blundered into me and then showered abuse on me by way of apology. Once, waking in the near-darkness to feel something gently tugging at me, I realized that someone was trying to steal my pocket-book. I seized it, there was movement amongst the sleeping forms beside me, and in the little light there was, I saw a small figure escaping down the stairs. I tried to stay awake after that.

At last a man came out of the door carrying a stub of candle and, regardless of the sleepers around him, shouted up the stairs: "Where's the younker what's waiting?"

"Here," I said, coming down to him.

"And who might you be, my fine cull?"

When he lowered the candle to look at me and I saw his face, I realized with a shudder of horror that I knew him: he had been the small man with the tortoise-like head and great beaked nose whom I had seen when I had watched the Borough gang attack Isbister's men in the graveyard.

I must have stared at him in amazement for he reached out and shook me: "I say, what d'you want of me?"

And yet it did not surprise me that it should be this man. To the contrary, it seemed inevitable that through all the vastness of London the stranger I had come to find should turn out to be someone I had encountered before. There was clearly a design lying behind the apparently meaningless events I was experiencing.

"The old man, Sam'el at Cox's-square, directed me here," I said. "Are you Mr Pulvertaft?"

"I might be. What do you want?"

"I am looking for a family called Digweed. Do you know them?"

It seemed to me that a look of interest quickened in his face at this: "I might. What business do you have with them?" But before I could answer he seized my arm: "Come in here."

He pulled me through the door and I found myself in a long, low room in near-darkness but filled with the noise of fifty or sixty people laughing, shouting, singing, crying and swearing. The only light came from a few guttering dips stuck in brackets in the walls, and from a blazing fire at the other end before which a number of people were sitting drinking from tankards, while one man was sprawled intoxicated on the floor. Another in a similar condition was sitting at a table nearby with his head and arms lying on its surface, completely oblivious to his surroundings. The walls were of naked stone and the floor was of bare boards sprinkled with foul saw-dust.

I did not take all this in at first, for my assailant, having slammed the door after us, blown out his candle and thrown it on the floor, then pushed me back against the wall holding my head up with one hand: "Now what's your business with Digweed? Tell me the truth or I'll make cat's-meat of you."

In all that noise and drunkenness, no-one paid us any notice or could have heard us if they had.

"I want to ask his wife for help. Once — some years ago — my mother and I gave some assistance to Mrs Digweed. Now I am in need of help myself."

He looked at me closely. "His wife?" he said. "There ain't no Mrs Digweed so far as I know, or rather, there's a deal on 'em." He laughed. "You say the old man sent you here?"

I nodded as far as I was able.

"How do I know you're telling the truth?"

He scrutinised me while he smiled mirthlessly. Then he reached into my coat pocket. "Is there anything in this?" he asked, pulling out the pocket-book.

"Only writing," I said. He shook it and my grandfather's letter and my map fell out. He picked them up, looked at the letter holding it upside-down, then at the map — clearly making as little sense of it, — and then shoved them back into the book and returned it to me.

There was a silence during which he frowned as if he was calculating.

At last he said: "The only Digweed what I know is Black Barney. The last I heard on him he was living in a carcase beyond Westminster."

"A carcase?" I repeated in horror.

Tired and hungry as I was, my mind was in a peculiar state of receptivity so that at that word a vision came unbidden into my fancy of the man I was seeking as a huge white maggot boring into a human cadaver.

"Aye," said Pulvertaft. "Betwixt the Neat-houses and the Old Bason."

These words meant nothing to me but I recorded them in my exhausted mind so that they became part of the litany I repeated to myself: "Digweed, Black Barney, Neat-houses, the Old Bason".

"Cross by the new bridge and arter the turnpike, follow the road along the shore until you come to the new way what they're a-building. That'll take you straight there."

I began to move towards the door but the man called out: "Hold hard!"

I turned and saw that he was staring at me with an expression of cunning and eagerness: "He'll want to know how you found him," he said.

"What should I tell him?" I asked meekly.

"Why, what should you tell him but the truth?" he answered cheerfully. "And here's your time of day: give him this message from me. Will you remember it?"

"Yes."

"Then tell him: 'Dan'el arsts if he can jine the fakement at Henrietta-street on Christmas-eve.' Now can you say that agin?"

I repeated this mysterious formula to his satisfaction.

"Don't forget for if you do, I'll hear of it and, my word! won't you come in for it! Now be on your way." And, as if to encourage me, he pushed me to the door and out into the darkness, securing the door behind me.

CHAPTER 58

Muttering to myself my precious talismanic formula, I made my way back towards the river. It was an hour or two before dawn and the press of vehicles converging on the metropolis was getting thick, though the road grew more deserted once I had crossed the river by the new Regent's-bridge at Vauxhall and turned westward along the shore of the river — at that time quite empty and uninhabited.

Behind me was the vast octagonal shape of the new Millbank-penitentiary, and before me the Distillery with the white-lead works a little beyond it, whose stinking smoke I could smell with increasing sharpness as I drew nearer. After a quarter of a mile I came to where a new carriageway was being constructed and struck north-westward across what was then an area of market-gardens merging into a wilderness of abandoned pleasure-gardens, rough ground, and marshland which was known as the Neat-houses. The road was unlit, unpaved and deep in mud, except where puddles the width of ponds and half a foot deep forced me to wade through them. Several times I tried to ask the way of one of the few foot-passengers I encountered, but each of them hurried on when I approached.

After some minutes I saw the angry glow of fires ahead of me, and when I got closer I found I was surrounded by brick-fields where heaps of ashy rubble were burning fiercely, for here the clay of the swamp was being turned into bricks for the extensive new building taking place. Around me were the mean huts of the brick-yard workers, and in the flickering, smokey light from the ash-heaps I saw huddled forms where shelterless people were sleeping for warmth as near to the kilns as they dared. As I ventured on I saw in the distance a forest of derricks and masts where the Grosvenor-canal had just been opened and barges from the East of the metropolis were bringing rubble for the Bason to be filled in, though of course I knew nothing of this at the time.

The dawn-light was beginning to appear in the eastern sky over the City and I had left the river nearly a mile behind me when I reached the first of the lots marked out by hoardings and broken-down palings. When, a little further on, I spied some houses, I was surprised to see that they were all in darkness, for I guessed it was by now between eight and nine. On drawing nearer, however, I found that they were only constructed to the height of their first stories. Yet they had been standing for some time for they were weathered, and I realized that they had been abandoned before completion.

As I advanced northward the houses acquired their upper stories, then their rooves, and then in some cases their internal appointments and windows — though the carriageway and pavements had not been made up — so that I found myself walking through a skeleton of a city with a network of ghostly streets and squares precisely laid out but in varying stages of completeness. At last I found a street in which several houses seemed to be complete — although they had no chimney-stacks or doors or glazing in their windows which, like the door-ways, had planks nailed across them. To my delight I saw that one of them showed signs of being inhabited: a faint light appeared between the timbers across one of the windows on the ground floor. I ascended the imposing steps and hammered on the makeshift door. It was pulled a little way back and a man stared at me suspiciously around its edge.

"I'm looking for Black Barney," I said.

The man blinked then pulled his head out of sight and began to secure the door. Then his head re-appeared and he looked me up and down: "Try the carcase two streets up and on the left. But don't say I told you."

He vanished before I could thank him.

The streets had no names, of course, but in the one that had been indicated I found only one house that showed signs of being occupied.

It was even larger than the first one and I mounted the handsome steps with a feeling of trepidation, as if I expected to be ignominiously repulsed by magnificent footmen. Yet it was clearly unfinished for the naked stone-work of the ground-floor awaited its covering of stucco, and the windows had boards nailed across them — though unlike the other houses they were secured from the inside and more carefully fitted so that no light escaped, and it was this that had suggested that the building was inhabited. The house had no area-railings or bell-pull, but it was the first I had seen that had a proper street-door.

I knocked on it and after a long delay it opened a little way and a young woman peered round it. From what I could see of her she was not dressed like a servant at all, but very finely and inappropriately for that early hour. She was small and had dark hair worn in ringlets and was rather pretty, though there was a look in her eye that suggested she might have a fierce temper.

"I'm looking for Mr Digweed," I said.

"There ain't no-one here of that name," she said and began to close the door.

"Mr Barney Digweed," I said, desperately.

She looked at me in surprise. "Is it Barney you want?" she said. "That is, I ain't saying there's no-one here called Barney. Jist you wait there."

She closed the door. Then I saw a piece of the board covering one of the windows being pulled back, and then a man's face observing me. After a moment the door opened again and the same man stood looking down at me, the girl visible behind him. He was tall and strongly-built with a large head rising steeply to a high forehead, a shock of reddish hair and a big broken nose between two strangely beautiful blue eyes. To my astonishment, he was dressed as a gentleman in a fine blue merino-jacket with a cream waistcoat and white duck trowsers. He was staring at me with hostility.

My first feeling was one of deep disappointment: if this was Mrs Digweed's husband his appearance suggested that little good would come to me of the connexion from which I had hoped for so much. I also felt an obscure sense that I knew this man from somewhere, yet I was sure I had not seen him since I had been in London.

"Are you Mr Barney Digweed?" I asked nervously.

He looked at me appraisingly and then said slowly: "I am Black Barney if it's any consarn of yourn. Who are you?"

"Mr Pulvertaft directed me to you," I said.

I was sure that the name startled him but he kept his countenance impassive as he replied: "I'm not saying as I've ever heerd on such an indiwiddle. What do you want?"

"I'm looking for Mrs Digweed."

"Why?"

"Please tell me if you know her. Is your name 'Digweed'?"

"Be very careful, boy. Don't arst questions like that. It's impartinent, ain't it, Nan?"

Over his shoulder I saw the girl laughing.

He went on: "But suppose my name was what you jist said, what then?"

"Then I would ask you for help. I am alone and have no money."

"Why should anyone help you?"

It was not a question so much as a dismissal, and he began to shut the door even as he spoke.

Despairingly I cried out: "Mr Pulvertaft gave me a message for you!"

He looked at me keenly: "Well?"

"'Daniel asks if he can join the fakement at Henrietta-street on Christmas-eve,'" I recited.

Instantly Barney seized my upper arm squeezing it so tightly that I cried out, and then, wrenching it mercilessly, pulled me through the door and banged it shut. In the darkness of the windowless hall I could see almost nothing and I felt rather than saw that Barney brought his great head down close to mine and hissed:

"Say that agin!"

I repeated it.

"Do you hear that, Nan?"

"Aye," she said.

"Get Sam and the others," he said without looking round and I heard the girl move away.

"How do you know Pulvertaft?" Barney demanded, increasing his grip on my arm as an encouragement to frankness and confidence.

"The old man, Sam'el, in Cox's-square, sent me to him when I asked him for Mrs Digweed."

"The devil he did," he commented.

At that moment a crowd of people — as it seemed to me — hurried up carrying candles and in the flickering light I saw to my surprise the flash of jewels, the glitter of gold watch-chains, and the sheen of rich velvets, and noticed that the faces of some of the women were painted.

"Listen to this," said Barney and I was made to repeat Pulvertaft's words yet again.

They were received with whistles and exclamations of surprise and dismay.

"Someone has nosed on us," said Barney.

"That's for sure," cried one of the men.

"And the Cat's-meat-man has sent this boy to tell us he wants to be cut in or he'll blow us up," Barney said.

The Cat's-meat-man! The man that Isbister and his companions had talked about as the one who was spoiling their trade! It was Pulvertaft! (I recalled how he had used that expression.) In my dazed state it seemed entirely right that everything should connect in this way.

"What'll we do, Barney?" said the young woman who had opened the door to me, her voice rising above the babble of noise provoked by my message.

"We'll tell him to go to the deuce, that's what," Barney said.

There were murmurs of approval at this sentiment, but one of the men said: "Not to speak out o' turn, that ain't for you to say, Barney. We'll have to decide it all together."

He was short, about the same age as Barney, and had a thick black beard, a large, high nose, deep brown eyes and a most lively and engaging countenance. He wore his hair in a pigtail like a sailor and was clad in a blue pea-jacket.

"Aye, Sam's right, Uncle," another young woman said, like the first very handsome — but much taller and fair-haired — and just as beautifully dressed. "And we'll have to wait till Jack gets back."

Barney glowered at the others.

"When will that be, Sal?" asked Sam.

"I don't know," the girl said. "He's out on that job over by Hackney and it all depends on ... "

"Never mind about that," Barney cut in, and glanced from her to me warningly. Then, smiling at me unpleasantly, he added: "As for this young shaver, we'll cut him up and send him back like a parcel o' butcher's meat to show our feelings."

For a moment I believed him, but by the way the others laughed I realized that this was a pleasantry.

"No, my fine cull," he said to me, seeing my alarm. "You ain't worth the trouble of carving you up."

He opened the street-door again, pushed me through it and then propelled me down the steps so hard that I stumbled and fell the last few steps. He laughed and began to shut the door. I was torn between relief at escaping and dismay that my last chance of finding Mrs Digweed was about to be lost.

The latter predominated and I said quickly, my voice rising to a shout: "At least tell me if you know Mrs Digweed!"

"Still harping on that?" he sneered. "Whyever should you think anyone would help you?"

"Because my mother and I helped Mrs Digweed once," I cried. "Three years ago this Christmas. If you know her, please help me for her sake."

The door was closing.

"She'll remember," I cried. "It was in Melthorpe."

The door was suddenly thrown open and Barney stared down at me for a long time with an expression which I found unfathomable.

Then he said in a rough voice which belied the sentiments he was expressing: "You look fair knocked up. Come in and take something to warm you. I'm sorry I spoke a mite rough."

I hesitated, wondering at this sudden turn-around. Had I touched his conscience or his heart after all? It seemed so by his eagerness now, but I thought there was a calculating look in his eye that I did not trust. However, faced with an offer of food and warmth I had no choice but to accept rather than resign myself again to the hunger and cold of the friendless streets, and so I ascended the steps. I would be on my guard, I told myself, and would trust no-one — least of all this man. As I reached the door I staggered and he reached out his hand and seized me by the shoulder, this time gently though firmly, and led me back into the house.

"Then you are Mr Digweed?" I said, as we re-entered the hall which was now deserted.

He brought his great head down close to mine and whispered hoarsely: "I don't want you never to say that name agin, not to me nor to nobody else. Obey me and I'll see you right. Cross me and I'll tear off your arm and beat you to death with it! Is that understood?"

"Yes," I said.

"Tell nobody here nothing about yourself. 'Cept me. All right?"

Again I gasped my acknowledgement of this condition.

Still holding me he escorted me the length of the great dark hall and then pushed me ahead of him through a door-way to the right — which had no door — into the strangest room I had ever seen.

CHAPTER 59

It was a large, lofty drawing-room which would, under altered circumstances, have been very handsome. A number of people were in it, most of them drinking and playing cards and smoking while others, although it was early in the forenoon and despite the noise and thick smoke, were fast asleep and sprawled, men and women together, on carpets and cushions that lay scattered about. As I had half-glimpsed in the hall, many of those present — both sexes — were gorgeously dressed in the height of fashion like the girl who had opened the door to me, while others were clad in clothes that were almost rags. So while many of the women were wearing silk gowns with rich lace trimmings, and some of the men had on velvet coats and satin waistcoats, others wore the usual fustians and drabs of the poorest class. This was perplexing enough, but perhaps the strangest incongruity was that between, on the one hand, the luxury of the clothes and furniture and, on the other, the incompleteness of the edifice.

The windows, as I had seen from the street, were boarded over so that even though it was day, the room had to be lit by numerous oil-lamps. The walls were of bare brick without plaister or pannelling, though one was only aware of this where they were visible, for most of their area was concealed by rich hangings of the most exquisite woven stuffs. And the floors were covered by expensive carpets and rugs which lay about in careless profusion, over-lapping each other or folded double to form makeshift beds.

Of course I did not by any means perceive the splendours and squalors of the chamber all at once. In fact, as I entered I staggered at the smell of the lamps and the heavy perfumes and when Barney pushed me towards a sopha, I sank onto it. A young woman — not the one who had answered the door, but the tall, fair-haired one who had spoken in the hall about Jack and who was equally finely dressed — was sitting at the other end and arguing fiercely with some of her companions. She was wearing evening dress that left her shoulders and upper arms bare except for her jewels — which looked real enough to me. She and her companions broke off their argument when they saw Barney and myself.

"Do something for him, Sally," said Barney, nodding to me.

She frowned and held to my lips the glass she had been drinking from: "This will do you no harm. It's wine."

I sipped and felt a warmth spreading inside me. Then she turned away and began to speak to one of the men. Her handsome features suggested to me a languid apathy and boredom that seemed to be waiting to be moulded and made use of. As I looked round some of the sleepers around us began to wake up, and they and a few of the others whom I had seen in the hall came over.

"Why 'ave you brung the boy, Barney?" asked one of the men.

"Send him to rightabouts," called out Sam, the bearded man with the pigtail. Disconcertingly he accompanied this suggestion with the friendliest smile at me in which he showed several gold teeth.

"Don't we have enough to worrit about already?" said a man with a mean, ugly face who was somewhat incongruously wearing a beautiful satin coat and carrying many rings and seals at his fob. "What with the Cat's-meat-man being onto us."

"You're right, Will," said Sam. "The boy will be no more use to us nor a horse with a wooden leg."

"He might make a snakesman," suggested a masculine-looking female wearing a man's hat and a sailor's jacket glazed with oil and pitch, whose face was deeply pitted with the smallpox and whose teeth were absolutely black. Beneath the hat I saw that her hair was a vivid red.

"No, he's too big, Poll," Will objected.

"Is he flash?" asked the girl who had answered the door.

"The boy stays, Sam," Barney announced. Turning to the girl who had opened the door to me he said: "And no, he ain't flash, Nan."

"What, have you turned soft, then?" she jeered.

"You're mad," said the man with the jewels. "He'll get in the way of trade." He glared at me with eyes that were like two swelling bruises, and then suddenly struck me a stinging blow in the face: "Don't look at me like that."

"Lay off him," Nan cried.

Barney glared at him: "If you don't like it, Will, you can sling your hook."

"Well, we'll see what Jack says about it, that's all," Will muttered rebelliously.

"What Jack says don't matter," Barney said angrily. "I'm cap'n, not him, though some on you seems ready to forget it. I say the boy stays."

This was received in silence, with only a few mutterings from Will and one or two of the others. But then Barney went on: "And I say we go ahead even if someone's split on us to the Cat's-meat-man."

At this there was an outburst of angry protests until Sam raised his voice above the hubbub and there was silence: "We can't settle nothin' till Jack's back."

Barney flushed with rage as this was greeted with cheers, and when Sally smiled triumphantly at him, he shouted: "I told you to look arter the boy!"

She pouted angrily: "I ain't no nussmaid."

"Nan, you see to him," Barney said.

"What's a fakement?" I asked Nan in an undertone. "The one on Christmas-eve," I added since she looked puzzled.

"It's a party," she said, smiling at Barney, and then poured me a glass of wine.

"That's right," he said to me. "And when we've fed you up, Sally will take you to buy some good togs up West so you can come to it with us. All right?"

I nodded. Despite my reservations, the prospect of food and warmth was irresistible.

"Well, if he's staying he'll have to tell us his story," Will said.

"So don't stand there sparrer-mouthed. Tell us who you are, young covey," said Sam.

I glanced nervously at Barney and saw him press his lips together warningly. So very cautiously, and avoiding all names, I told them no more than the bare outlines of my story: that my mother and I had lost everything in a rash speculation urged on us by a dishonest attorney, that we had come to London, that things had gone badly, and that she had died a few days ago. I said nothing of the Mompessons, nor Mrs Fortisquince, nor the Isbisters. Barney listened intently but asked no questions, while the others came and went and put to me several enquiries which I was able to answer without giving much away.

Nan seemed sympathetic, particularly at the narrative of my mother's death, but when I reached the conclusion she said: "It's about the greenest story what I ever heard. It sounds to me like you and your mam was properly done brown by that lawyer cove."

"What was his monicker?" Sam asked.

Barney frowned at me behind his back. I was saved from having to reveal Sancious' name for at that moment there was a noisy interruption.

A group of people burst into the room, the foremost and tallest of the men beginning to talk very loudly and excitedly as he entered: "We're safe. It ain't us they're arter at all. It's Peg they've lagged." At this there were cheers and everybody in the room — whether they had been sleeping or eating or drinking — got up and crowded round him, cheering him on, laughing, intoning mock-jeers, or asking questions. Sally had jumped from the sopha as soon as he entered and he seized her around the waist and kissed her. As she stared at him her previously petulant features were transformed into an image of interest and vivacity. Still gripping her he went on excitedly with his tale: "Listen if this ain't the rarest thing you ever heerd tell. Bob and me's down in 'Ackney jist now and we sees this old cove ... "

"Look at Meg!" Sally cried and everyone did so and saw that the girl, small and black-haired with greenish eyes, was weeping.

"She was Peg's best girl once," Sally cried and Meg looked at her venomously.

The young man laughed and, still holding Sally, went on with his story which was about how Peg (what a strange name for a man!) had been caught cracking a crib at Old Ford, but I took in almost nothing of it for I was looking at him intently. As well as being tall and young, he was extremely handsome with a frank, open face and clear blue eyes. He was dressed as a swell with a tall black hat, a fine blue waistcoat, and black top-boots, though his broad-skirted green coat gave him an elegantly ruffianly air. Everyone crowded around him, and I noticed that only two people remained at a distance. One of them was Barney who stayed on the sopha beside me watching him with an expression that I could not interpret. The other was Sam who had hung back but now went forward smiling as much as any of the others. But it was several moments before I had eyes for anyone except the newcomer for I was trying to recover from my surprise at having recognised him: he was the tall man who had been with Pulvertaft in the graveyard at Southwark.

As I was struggling to take in the implications of this, Barney suddenly got up, interrupting the celebratory scene to shout: "Hold your fool tongue, Jack! The boy don't want to hear all our fambly business."

Jack broke off and turned to stare at Barney with an expression for a moment of profound hostility which he quickly modified.

Barney smiled and gestured towards me: "Why, Jack, you haven't been introjuced to our guest yet. We mustn't forget our manners. He don't want to hear your most interesting and instructive story a-fore he's had the pleasure of making your acq'aintance, do he? Especially as he won't understand and appreciate it. Leastways, not as you would wish."

Some of the others laughed at this, and Jack smiled at me and held out his hand: "Pleased to meet you, young 'un."

It was done so naturally and he had such a frank, cheerful countenance that I would have liked him immediately, if it had not been for my previous knowledge of him. How was it that he had been with Pulvertaft only eighteen months previously when that individual appeared to be an enemy of the people I was now with? Had he changed allegiances? I recalled from what old Sam'el had told me that even Barney and Pulvertaft had once been together, and had worked with Isbister. Or was Jack still allied with Pulvertaft, but clandestinely? Did that explain what the Cat's-meat-man had meant by his warning that if I forgot the message he would learn of it — that Jack would tell him? Well, I would keep my mouth shut and pick up what I could, for it might be dangerous to reveal what I knew.

I took Jack's hand and he glanced enquiringly at Barney.

"This is John. He's brung a message from the Cat's-meat-man."

Jack's expression showed nothing but anger and surprise. I was quite certain of that.

"What?" he exclaimed.

"Tell him your message, John," Barney prompted and I repeated it yet again.

Jack's face darkened: "Be damned!" he exclaimed. "Someone's put the mark on us!" He looked round at the others who were all watching him and Barney now.

"That's what we reckoned," Sam said.

"If I ketch that summun they'll be very sorry. Sorry they was ever born."

"So you don't think we should agree to cut him in?" asked Sam.

"Cut him in!" cried Jack. "Cut him up, rather!"

This piece of wit was generously received by his audience.

"That's my Jack," someone called out.

"But if we don't, he can sp'il it for us," Sam protested.

"Let him dare," cried Jack.

"I agree with Jack," said Barney and there was a laugh. He added: "For once."

"But we all have a say," Sam protested.

"Yet there ain't much purpose if them two both wants it," said Nan.

"You seem very keen to give over," said Jack, turning to Sam angrily.

It seemed to me to be very strange that they should be so concerned at Pulvertaft knowing about a party they were making up. Why should they not invite him? It seemed unkind not to.

"What do you mean by that?" Sam demanded.

"Jist wondering who it was what blabbed."

"Well it wasn't me," Sam said, but he looked embarrassed and guilty: "I'm jist saying, now that he does know we have to cut him in or call it off."

I was very puzzled by this. Why should Pulvertaft's knowledge prevent the gathering taking place?

"That ain't so," insisted Jack. "We can go ahead with the fakement and be ready for him if he tries anything."

"That's a fool argument," said Sam. "He could rub us all to the white by leading us into a trap. And since there is a nose amongst us, he'll know exactly what we're a-doing."

There were murmurs of approval at this and I saw some of the gang clearly wavering. Even Jack was speechless and he, like the others, glanced towards Barney.

He was about to speak when his eye fell upon myself. "Why!" he cried. "Here's us forgetting all about young Johnnie here who can't be in the least bit interested in all this. Tell you what, Nan will take you to find something to eat and show you where you can shake down. All right?"

So I followed Nan out of the room and across the hall into one that was similarly furnished. The only difference was that in this chamber the carpets were covered in stains which were mainly, so far as I could see, from spilled wine, for bottles of Tokay and champagne and the finest glasses of cut-crystal were scattered about broken or half-full. And sweet-meats and delicacies and baskets of hot-house fruit were similarly strewn across the floor. This, I assumed, was the dining-room and later I found that it was called the Red Parlour in reference to its walls of naked brick.

"There's plenty of vittles," Nan said. "So take what you want. And then you can find anywhere you like to shake down. There's a mort of rooms empty at the top of the house and in the cock-loft."

Then she went out of the room.

I was hungry and the sight of the food was very tempting. But first I wanted to hide my papers, so I went along the hall to the stairs. To my surprise I found that the staircase had neither floorboards nor balustrades but was a naked assembly of stringers and dowels. So with difficulty I made my way to the upper story where I found that none of the floors were boarded so that the scantlings and trimmers were exposed, except where planks had been clumsily laid to make gang-ways and habitable areas. It was therefore extremely difficult to walk across these rooms and, I imagined, almost impossible in the dark since one had to step from joist to joist and was faced with a fall into the chamber below if one missed one's footing.

Intrigued, I explored the rest of the house and found that there were no window-frames or shutters but all the windows had been boarded over, and there were no doors — except for the street-door and the one between the hall and the drawing-room. This, together with the fact that there were no ceilings, meant that there was little privacy, and every conversation could be overheard. None of the internal walls had been lathed and plaistered let alone pannelled or wainscoted so that the naked brick was everywhere visible, except where it was obscured by hangings in the drawing-room. In short, the carpentry but not the joinery work had been done, and the mason's but not the plaisterer's.

I went to the back of the hall and found that in place of a door the rear entrance was secured by timbers nailed crossways. It occurred to me that if it was proof against entry it would also be impossible to get out through it.

The house was a large and imposing mansion — indeed I pass it quite frequently now and it is occupied by the Earl of N------ who, I imagine, has little idea of its previous history, — and it possessed so many rooms that every individual or couple was able to have one, though, as I came to realize, they mainly used the two large chambers on the ground floor for taking meals, conversation, and even sleeping. So I found evidence of occupation — clothes strewn about, cakes, sugar-plums, and orange-peel scattered over the rugs and floor-coverings — in all the chambers on the first and second floors, and it was not until I reached the top of the house that I found an unused set which was, perhaps, destined to form a nursery or governess's accommodation. I had two small chambers — an inner with no windows, leading into an outer which had a window in the roof with some boards nailed over it — and made myself comfortable, apart from the inconvenience of there being no floorboards.

I searched for a place of concealment for my mother's pocket-book. Since the room was unceiled, the naked rafters and slates of the roof were visible above me and it was not difficult to find an excellent hiding-place in a corner behind one of the beams where it was very dry and dark so that no-one could find an object there unless they knew precisely where to look.

Then I went back downstairs to the dining-room and carried a number of rugs and draperies up to my lodging and made a shake-down. I returned and addressed myself to both the food and the drink. All the time the discussion went on in the other room, and I heard loud angry shouts and occasionally could make out a few phrases. After the long period of privation I had endured it is not to be wondered at that I indulged somewhat too freely, and in fact, made myself quite ill and more than a little drunk. Feeling dizzy and sick, I passed out and must have slept for an hour or two, awakening to hear the sounds of argument continuing from the other room and then dozing again.

Then I was aware of being picked up and carried and, with an odd sense of reassurance, I felt that my pockets were being searched. After that I fell deeply asleep and dreamed of pale-faced men like maggots and gorgeously-clad women in silk dresses that rose behind them like glittering wings, living in a carcase and battening on its rich rotting meat. And in the middle Barney, with his big face and long arms, was like a great blotchy red spider spinning invisible nets from his entrails and hauling in more prey for the others to feed on.

I woke up feeling (in Mr Isbister's phrase) as if I had two heads. Finding that my pockets had indeed been thoroughly searched I resolved that, despite the plentiful supply of food, I would leave as soon as I felt stronger.

I didn't believe that Barney would give me something for nothing. My experience of the Isbisters had taught me that. In that case, why had he taken me in and imposed me on the gang despite opposition? And what was the significance of Jack's connexion with Pulvertaft? Now that I considered it, I realized that the coincidence of my recognising both Pulvertaft and Jack was extremely puzzling, even though I knew from what old Sam'el had told me and then what I had heard from Isbister, that all of these men had worked together many years before.

And above all, what was the explanation for the way these people lived? Where did their money come from and why were they living here like this? Perhaps listening to their conversation would provide me with the answer to at least this last question.

This strategy turned out to be difficult when I began to practise it later that day. At first, when I saw them looking as if they were engaged in serious conversation and approached as inconspicuously as I could, they fell silent or quickly turned the subject or ordered me to "Hook it!". However, as the day wore on they grew more used to my presence, and I was sometimes able to stay within ear-shot. I was very puzzled by what I could understand of their speech — they used so much cant that it was often incomprehensible — for they seemed to be discussing a straightforward commercial business. They talked a great deal of things being bought and sold in the way of business, of people being bent or straight, and of a share of the profits being sent to someone who had gone abroad.

There was a great deal of coming and going throughout the day with hackney-coaches arriving and vans bringing goods of the most luxurious quality from shops in Oxford-street and Bond-street.

Once I heard Nan recounting an adventure in one of these grand places: "Didn't the shop-man stare when he seen my purse full of gold!" she exclaimed. "I'll wager he thought the paper was screens."

And my bewilderment was as great as the shop-man's.

All this time I was studying my new companions. The man-like woman was Carrotty Poll who was good to me in a rough way, so long as she was sober. Two others — who were apparently sisters and were called "Smithfield" and "Billingsgate" — I learned to avoid, drunk or sober. Though I was at first repelled by the sinister appearance of a man who wore a pale brass nose in the middle of his face and was called "Silvernose", I later found him to be one of the kindest of the gang. (I was told that he had suffered his injury in the Wars, though this was said with so much private significance that I doubted it even then.) I never cared much for Bob, a youngish man with a weak, rather brutal face. Will always hit me when he noticed me, but Sam and Jack were usually friendly.

I was often puzzled by the fact that many of them had a variety of soubriquets or "by-names" in addition to or instead of their usual ones. So Jack was sometimes "Quicksilver Jack" or just "Quicksilver" or even "Quick". Barney was often called merely "Black".

I tried to obey Bissett's often-repeated injunction to keep my mouth closed and my eyes and ears open. Above all, I watched Barney. He smiled constantly except when angry (as he often was) or when his gaze lighted upon Jack. His expression suggested always that he was about to jeer, and he was continually inviting the others to laugh at the victim of the moment — whether absent or present.

As that first day advanced into evening more and more was drunk. Gambling broke out and soon led to quarrelling and, later on, there was dancing when someone brought out a fiddle. I was petted by the women when they remembered me and ignored by the men, and, in general, I was treated well — if encouraging me to eat far too many sweet-meats and getting me drunk on Marsala can be so called. These jollifications continued all night and into the dawn, though I fell asleep and woke up a number of times. Finally I awoke to find everyone else asleep and a grey morning peering through the boarded windows. I made my breakfast on the remains of a meat-pie and some fragments of seed-cake.

I believe that another day passed as before, though, to anticipate a little, I found that the distinction between night and day was so entirely disregarded in that house that it was often difficult to be sure of the day of the week or even the time of day. To the best of my belief, then, it was the third day after my arrival that I was talking to Sam in the dining-room when Barney came up to us.

He cuffed me under the chin and said: "All right, young feller?"

"Barney," I asked, "Sally calls you Uncle. Does that mean you are really of the same family?"

"That's right. In fact, we're all one big fambly. Sam here's my little brother and Nan's my cousing and Will's my nevy and so on."

Sam grinned at me and nodded.

Not sure whether to believe this I went on: "And why do you live here? In this lonely place?"

"Why this is our new house what we've bought and paid for and we're waiting for it to be decorated," Sam said. "It's wonderful not to have no neighbours nearby, for one doesn't want to bother 'em with one's noise."

That sounded more plausible. "And what do you all do?"

The two grinned at each other.

"Why, do I dare trust you?" Barney asked with a smile.

I nodded and he went on: "Well, you might say we perform a public benefaction. You see, there's a deal of paper credit circulating on the money-market. Now, do you know what that is?" I shook my head. "Well, say Sam here needs money, so he borrers it and signs a bill and gets cash for promising to repay the full amount at six months. Now that bill is a kind of money and it's bought and sold and its vally depends on whether the file what buys it thinks Sam will be able to pay it. There's many people as makes it their business to know these things and if Sam comes into a fortin of an old aunt, why then the vally of his bill goes up."

"But if he doesn't pay it when it falls due?" I asked, remembering my mother's experience.

"Why, then I get someone to take another bill of me," Sam said, "and use that money to pay the first. And if nobody won't, why then I try to get a friend to back it."

"But if you can't do that," I asked Sam, "what will become of you?"

"Then arst for me at the Fleet or the Marshalsea," he answered with a laugh.

I remembered my poor old friend, Mr Pentecost.

"But the p'int is," Barney said, "what happens to that bill when nobody don't believe no more that Sam can pay it so it's discounted and discounted until at last it's nigh on worthless. Now someone buys it for next to nothing and he passes it on to me."

"Who is he?" I asked.

"Nivver you mind," Barney said quickly. Then more affably he went on: "Well, what I does is I restore the bill's credit. This is how I does it. Now say you're a tradesman and own a big shop selling joolery or carpets or clothes. One day I turns up with my wife in a fine carriage with sarvints and orders jewels and pays for 'em in ready cash. Then a few weeks later I comes back and does the same. Now you're getting very glad to see me, aren't you? Then one day I finds myself a little short on cash so I pays with a discounted bill — not a big 'un — and you're a bit doubtful, but you don't want to lose my custom by offending me. So you takes it and it's all right for your banker finds it's a good 'un. Then a little arter that I offers you a discounted bill for a lot more and you take it. Now you find its credit ain't as good as you thought it was. And you don't nivver see me agin." He and Sam laughed and he went on: "But have I robbed or cheated you? No, for it's down to the person what drawed that bill to pay you. It's them what's robbed you."

Though I was relieved to know that Barney and his relatives were not involved in anything that was actually illegal, yet I was disturbed by the dishonourableness of what they were doing.

Still chuckling, Sam went out of the room. Barney stared at me and said: "Now that I've been so frank, tell us the rest of your story."

I managed to give him a great deal of circumstantial detail but to avoid mentioning any names. The part he was most interested in was the most recent, for he seemed anxious to know about my mother's death. It was hard for me to speak of this. To my surprise, he appeared to be particularly concerned to know where she was buried and under what name. Eventually I told him that the parish was St. Leonard's and that she had been buried under the name of "Offland".

After learning this he seemed satisfied and shortly afterwards he left me.

A day or two later — I have no idea whether it was the day or night — I was dozing on my shake-down when I was awoken by whispering voices in the room below. Whoever was there clearly did not know that my rooms were above that one. Then, to my surprise, I realized that the two speakers were Barney and, of all people, Jack.

"Are you sartin?" I heard Barney say.

"I am. In course I didn't hardly believe it meself, but, like I say, Sal told me without knowing what it meant. If you don't believe me, Barney, you arst her yourself."

"I will."

Then they moved away and I heard no more. What could it mean for the two rivals to be talking in secret? And what were they discussing? I thought

I learned the answer to this only a few hours later, when, with most of the others, I was in the drawing-room when Barney suddenly burst in with Sam behind him.

Barney was shouting: "Where's Nan?" She came forward and he cried: "You've been prigging, haven't you?"

"No I never!" she exclaimed.

Barney brought a piece of jewellery from his pocket: "We jist found this in your gear!"

"I ain't nivver seen it a-fore!" Nan screamed.

"I seen you prig it in Bond-street yesterday," Sally cried.

"You're lying! It's a plant!"

"You know the rule," Barney said. "No private business."

So my suspicions about the honesty of my new friends were unfounded: Nan had stolen something and was being expelled for it!

The others murmured their assent.

"She planted it!" Nan cried pointing at Sally.

"I never did!"

"Yes you did and I know why. On account of how Jack likes me." There were some cries of "That's right!" and, fortified by this, Nan went on: "You're jealous so you've made this up."

The majority, however, were not sympathetic and remained silent.

"You'll have to leave the partnership," Barney said, and glanced at Sam and then Jack. These two both nodded gravely.

"You'll have to go, Nan," said Jack gently. "We have to be able to trust each other."

Will, Nan's usual fancy-man, put up a stout defence of her innocence and threatened to leave with her, but when his bluff was called he withdrew. Nan protested, wept, then turned to shouting abuse and threats, but the opinion of almost all was against her and eventually she conceded defeat and, still protesting her innocence, left the house.

As Christmas came closer I heard many references to the party that was to come off at Henrietta-street on Christmas-eve. It seemed strange to me that they were so excited at the prospect for many of them went out nearly every night in a big group led by Barney, returning only towards dawn. They dressed very carefully for it, so that the women looked like ladies and the men almost like gentlemen. Meanwhile, those who stayed behind amused themselves with a kind of continuous party: drinking, dicing, eating and quarrelling.

By now I was familiar with their way of life and since they were guarding their tongues much less in my presence, I became clearer about how they earned their living, though several mysteries remained. Members of the company came and went at all hours, but very rarely brought others there — and these had to be vouched for and were watched carefully. When they weren't sleeping they were amusing themselves in the ways I have described. Nobody except Jack and Sally ever read, and they had only two interests: either the fashionable papers and the *Court Guide* (for the "family" took a keen interest in the comings and goings of fashionable Society) or the *Hue-and-Cry* (which is a publication of the police which lists crimes and names the individuals sought by the authorities).

One evening Meg and another of the women came back from making a visit to Peg at Newgate and as we all gathered around them in the drawing-room, they described how they had spoken to him through a hatch in the wall of his ward. They reported that his trial was on the calendar for that Sessions and that he was confident that Pulvertaft would buy off his prosecutor, who was the house-holder at Old Ford whose house he had been caught breaking into.

Barney, who was sitting a little apart from the rest of us in conference with a stranger, laughed ironically at this and said: "Aye, just as he done for me in '17."

The man with him, who had one of the most villainous faces I had ever seen and that reminded me of Mr Pentecost's Punch, laughed and said: "I rec'lleck that, Barney. You got knocked down for a seven, didn't you? It was Limping Jem what blowed on you, and he got a pony of the Cat's-meat-man for that."

The conversation turned to the question of which of the beaks were honourable and could be trusted to keep their word. The stranger, whom the others addressed as Mr Lavender, told a story about an "old feller" who had taken a bribe and then gone back on his undertaking by "marinating" the man concerned, and everyone vied to express their outrage at this conduct.

"How's the lay you're on now?" Mr Lavender asked the company conversationally.

Some of them glanced down as if embarrassed but Barney said: "Why, you can speak freely a-fore him."

There was a discussion of the business that Barney had described to me.

In the course of it I heard an allusion to "slang bills" and I asked indignantly: "But Barney, you told me that you were passing real bills and so you weren't doing anything dishonest."

There was general laughter in which Mr Lavender joined as heartily as the others.

Then Barney, who had by now drunk a lot, said: "Why, you are green. Slang bills is even cheaper to buy than real ones."

I was in confusion now. So, after all, they were criminals!

"But then why was Nan sent away for prigging?" I exclaimed.

"Why, don't be such a flatt!" Barney cried amid jeers from the others. "That was for prigging on her own account when she could have blowed us all up. We're a swell-mob, see, and that means we has to pass for swells."

As I was thinking about the implications of this, Barney's guest took his leave. At first I was horrified to realize the kind of people I was among. Or rather I believed I was horrified. Certainly I knew I should be. But I could not think of these people and what they were doing as evil. What did it mean to be evil? Certainly, there was something I did not at all like in Barney at times, and in one or two of the others at all times — Will above all. But I could not see that the others were anything worse than irresponsible and selfish. I remembered Mr Pentecost's idea that the law is an arbitrary construct designed to protect the wealthy, and now it seemed to me that he was right. How had I ever been so foolish as to accept Mr Silverlight's view that there is a higher morality which we must obey whether or not it coincides with the law? On the contrary, each of us chooses to obey or break the law simply on the calculus of self-interest. And if these people chose to take the risk of breaking it with all the dangers they knew so well, that seemed rather fine and brave.

"So that's all right for Henrietta-street at Christmas," said Mr Lavender at the door of the drawing-room. "Our fellows'll keep far away that night."

He and Barney shook hands and when he had seen him out of the street-door,

Barney came back into the room saying: "Now there's a real genel'man as you can do business with."

After all, I knew what respectable society was: it was Mrs Fortisquince and Mr Sancious and Sir Perceval. And when I thought of what they had done, I could not find it in me to condemn the stealing and fraud of the people I was among. For they had taken me in and given me shelter and food when those who had some obligation to do that had hounded my mother and myself to destitution. I now began to feel — in an inversion of my earlier view of them — that I was the parasite who was living off them without contributing anything.

Someone suddenly punched my arm, interrupting my reverie.

"Well, you'll make one with us one day, won't you, young 'un?" It was Sam who had spoken, and now he was looking at me with a golden smile.

I nodded eagerly: "Yes, I'd like to."

"Then you can come to the fakement with us at Christmas," Barney said.

"You'll see," Sam said. "There ain't nothing to match it. It's like gaming for high stakes but with the odds in your favour."

"But with all to lose if they go agin you," Barney added, pulling his neckerchief tight around his neck and jerking it.

"How did you get into it?" I asked Sam.

"Me? I nivver knowed no different, my cully. I was bore and raised to it. I was jugged when I was eight year old and had my fust whipping when I was a thirteener. But I was nothing but a low gonoph then. Until I come to know Barney."

His friend and captain laughed and said: "That was the time when my ears was quick to the toll of a passing bell." His blue eyes glittered at me. "You know the lay I mean?" I nodded, though I was determined to say nothing of my connexion with Isbister. "It weren't agin no law, for the law says there ain't no property in a corpse."

The others laughed at the technical term. "You'll be knocking us down at the Old Bailey at this rate, Barney," Sam jeered. "Has your 'torney friend offered to 'prentice you yet?"

Ignoring their teazing, Barney, who had been drinking heavily, went on: "Why, this is going back more nor ten year now. A-fore I knowed Sam and Jack, I was working mates with Jerry Isbister and the Cat's-meat-man and Peg. Well, we was doing good, on'y then we come off at hooks, me and the Cat's-meat-man agin Isbister and Peg. The Cat's-meat-man reckoned as Peg 'peached on his brother what was turned off for cracking a crib. Him."

At this last word he waved his pipe in the air. Seeing that I didn't understand, he showed me the stopper and explained that it was a memento carved from the shin-bone of the brother of the Cat's-meat-man. It had been procured at some personal inconvenience after the body had been sent to be publicly dissected. Here there was a discussion of whether this was more or less honourable than the former practice in which the corpse of an executed man was hung at a cross-roads gibbeted in chains with iron bands forged on it to hold together the bones which had been wrapped in tarred calico. I recalled the thing that my mother had shuddered at in the coach on the way from Melthorpe and that, despite my interest in Gallow-tree-hill, I had failed to recognise.

Barney returned to his story: "So me and the Cat's-meat-man started to work down the Borough and, on account of there was more work than we could handle, we looked out for other culls. And that's how Sam come in with us and a little arter that, Jack, and you was on'y a young boy at the time," he added, turning to him. "We cracked a few cribs, too, and that was what we was 'peached on for, a year or two later. We had to break up and run for it. Arterwards I found out as how it was the Cat's-meat-man that done it. God rot his bones for it! I reckon he believed I'd had a hand in nosing on his brother. Well, so then I has to leave London so I goes up north to where my kin comes from." He shuddered. "Rot the place. All trees and fields. Well I lays low up there. Though I won't pretend I didn't crack a crib or two. But when I thought it was safe agin I come back up to Town. That was a mistake for I was took up a couple of days later. Someone in Dan'el's pocket must have 'peached on me. I nivver knowed for a long time how Dan'el done it. So then I done my naval training at Gravesend for two year." The others laughed at this allusion to the prison-hulks. "And when I managed to buy myself out me and Sam and Jack took up the sack-'em-up lay agin, but the Cat's-meat-man had made himself cock o' the walk on the other side of the water by then so we decided to give it over and leave him to fight it out with Isbister. And that was a sharp move, for last year he finished old Jerry."

I knew that he was referring to the attack in the Southwark graveyard that I had witnessed.

"But about then," he went on, "I made the 'q'aintance of a fly 'torney. (And it's on account o' him that we're in this crib now, though that's a long story that'll keep for another day.) And it was he what got me into the bill-passing lay." Then he looked at me appraisingly and said with a sly smile: "But that ain't the best o' what I've done."

Carrotty Poll said jeeringly: "Why, you're always a-boasting of something you done, aren't you, Barney?"

"Did you make a man easy?" I asked.

He smiled and touched the side of his nose.

I felt a thrill of excitement run through me. I was sure I had guessed correctly. "When? Who was it?"

"A nob. A long time back," he said. "What years are you?"

I told him.

"Why, then it was the year a-fore you was even bore."

He would say no more but I had enough to think about. There was nothing in his story that explained why Jack was with Pulvertaft the night I had seen them at Southwark and I therefore assumed that he had no idea of this. Surely then Jack was Pulvertaft's intelligencer among the company? I realized now that by using me to send that message, Pulvertaft was warning Barney and the others that he knew what they were planning — for I now understood that the "fakement" was in fact a criminal undertaking. Presumably he was requiring them to share the spoils with him.

About a week later came the day of Peg's trial at the Old Bailey before the Court of King's Bench. Jack, Sally and Meg went and when they came back they described it:

"Didn't old Peg look took aback," Jack exclaimed to the laughter of the others (except Meg, who was in tears), "when he seen the persecutor a-standing there!"

And so, because Pulvertaft had indeed failed to buy off the prosecution, Peg was found guilty and taken back to Newgate.

Now he had to wait for a few days since sentencing was passed on prisoners in batches only at the end of the Sessions. Though some had had to wait six weeks, he was lucky since he was one of the last to be tried. I was told by the others that at the Old Bailey the "old fellow" customarily passed sentence of death on nearly all capital convicts, but I understood that this would not be the end of the matter. As expected, Peg was indeed cast for death and was moved to the "salt box" (the condemned cell) in the Press-yard to be near the New Drop. He now had to wait for the Recorder's report in the hope of being respited. But two weeks later his sentence was confirmed.

Now the convicted murderers were executed immediately but all those sentenced to die for offences short of murder were referred to the King in Council. This was the last chance for beyond this lay only an appeal to the Secretary of State and that required more money and influence than Peg's friends — even had they been trying — could be supposed to have.

On the night of the 15th. of December a number of the company went to Newgate to wait for the news of Peg's fate, for the Recorder came directly to the prison to report on the decisions of the King, arriving from Windsor late at night. The rest of us passed the time in eager anticipation while I imagined the scene that had been described to me: the anxious crowd of relatives and well-wishers gathered at the grim gatehouse, the approach of the carriage with its out-riders, the Governor going to meet Black Jack (the Recorder) accompanied by the Ordinary (the chaplain), and then the long wait while the latter went from cell to cell giving each of the condemned the decision for life or death. And then finally the Warden went to the gatehouse and read out the list of respited prisoners to the crowd of relatives and friends.

At about two in the morning Sally, Jack, Meg (weeping hysterically) and the rest burst in to say that Peg had not been among the fortunate ones. His execution was six days hence.

As soon as the hubbub that greeted this had died down, Barney, Jack, and Sam clapped their hands and Barney shouted: "Listen to this. Our little Christmas party in Henrietta-street. It's to be brung for'ard by a few days."

Amid the shouts of surprise and protest that arose at this, Barney and the other two smiled at each other.

"What day?" asked Billingsgate.

"Nivver you mind," Barney replied.

"Why the change?" cried out Will.

"On account of the Cat's-meat-man," Barney replied. "For he thinks it's going to be on Christmas-eve, so this way we can ketch him out."

"No we can't," Will objected. "Not if one of us is spying for him."

Barney, Sam and Jack were smirking at each other with self-satisfaction.

"But there ain't nobody nosing for him," Jack said.

A hail of questions flew at the three: "What do you mean? You said a-fore that there's a spy amongst us?"

"There was," Barney said. "But there ain't no more."

"Do you mean it was Nan?" asked Will indignantly.

"That's right," said Sam. "Me and Barney and Jack found out it was her. Arter that time all on us talked about it when the boy here brung the message from the Cat's-meat-man, the three on us talked it over and agreed that it wouldn't do jist to find out who Dan'el's nose was and make 'em quiet because then he'd know he had to try another way to steal a march on us. We settled that we'd have to do it so as he wouldn't smoke that we'd found out Nan was his nose. That way he'd stick to his design. So Nan will have told him she was drove out of the company on account of Sal put the mark on her."

Jack broke in: "See, we agreed that I would tell Sally we knowed Nan was the Cat's-meat-man's nose and get her to let on as how she was jealous of her and me."

There were good-natured roars and whistles at this. Jack glanced at Sally with a smile and she stared around with a bold grin in her pleasure at her own ingenuity.

"And Sally come up trumps," said Barney. "So Nan thinks that Sally planted that jewellery on her out of pure spite, and that it don't have nothing to do with her being Pulvertaft's nose."

As he was speaking Sally accepted gracefully the tributes that were offered to her play-acting abilities.

Only Will was not smiling. "I don't believe Nan was no spy," he said.

"Oh don't you, Will?" jeered Barney. "Well Jack and me dodged her one night and she went straight to Dan'el's crib down the Old Mint."

Will flushed with annoyance at being so conclusively defeated. I remembered the occasion when I had overheard Barney and Jack immediately before Nan's trial. Presumably this was at last the full explanation of their conversation, though I was still a little puzzled when I tried to make it fit.

"Now we haven't said what the new day for the fakement is to be," Barney went on. "And we ain't going to until the very last moment. And so that nobody won't tell the Cat's-meat-man even by mistake, nobody ain't 'lowed to go out alone from now until it's done."

"What?" jeered Will. "Not even you?"

"In course *I* can," said Barney. "But nobody else. Not even Jack nor Sam. When we go out to work together, everybody will watch everyone else to see that nobody don't meet nobody or pass on no message. And we'll be guarding the door here to make sure nobody don't try to sneak out."

This was not well received but the necessity for it was acknowledged, so it was accepted with an ill grace.

So from that moment someone guarded the street-door — the only way of getting out of the house — day and night.

The next day — or, rather, after the next period of sleep — Sally met me in the hall and suddenly said: "Come on and get ready. We're going up West."

"What for?" I asked, believing it was late at night.

" 'Cause Barney says so," she answered. "Now hurry up."

"I'm ready now," I said.

She looked at me in distaste: "Is them the best togs you've got?" (She was in a blue silk gown and a cachemire shawl.)

"They're the *only* ones I've got."

"Then no wonder you need some more," she said enigmatically. "Come on, Sam," she called and when he had appeared from the Red Room we were let out by Will who was keeping the door.

I was surprised to discover that it was daylight. But even so, I almost felt frightened to leave the house after spending all that time there. It seemed that Sam was to accompany us, but as we walked through the half-built city in the direction of Vauxhall-bridge-road, I could get no answer to the questions I put, for Sam and Sally were too busily engaged in a flirtatious conversation to notice me.

We picked up a coach at the first stand and although the driver stared at my ragged appearance, his doubts must have been laid to rest by the magnificence of my companions, for Sam was also finely-dressed. Sam ordered him to take us to Shepherds-market and then wait there to take us on to Bond-street where, as he rather impressively expressed it, we had further business.

"What are we doing at Shepherds-market?" I asked.

"You can't go into a respectable shop like that," Sally remarked as we boarded the vehicle, without bestowing any illumination upon me.

They sat together opposite me and as the coach moved off Sam started trying to put his arm round her. At first she giggled coquettishly and urged him in the most provoking way not to be so silly, but after a time she grew irritated.

"Do leave off, Sam," she said impatiently, and he grew sulky and stared out of window.

When we reached the entrance to the market we left the coach and went to a shop selling second-hand clothes. I felt a keen sense of disappointment that I was not to be clothed in the style of the rest, yet even so I entertained some reluctance to accept a gift from them. However, there was nothing for it and I helped Sally to choose me some decent clothes.

"Aren't these rather dear?" I asked when I saw what she had selected.

She laughed: "Barney's gave me more than enough."

"Why should Barney spend money on clothes for me?" I asked Sally.

She and Sam exchanged glances.

"You want to look nice for going to Tuck-up Fair, don't you?" she asked. "And, besides, you don't know but that you might be able to return the favour."

I was wondering what she meant by this when the shop-keeper showed me where to go in the back premises to try on the clothes we had chosen.

To my surprise, Sam left Sally and stationed himself by the back-door. Removing my rags, I attired myself in my new garments and reappeared before Sally who pronounced herself satisfied — though in rather grudging terms.

"What shall I do with these, miss?" asked the shop-keeper, indicating my old rags.

Sally shuddered: "Burn 'em."

We returned to the carriage and it moved off again.

Some way along Piccadilly Sam suddenly said: "I've got something to do. I'll find you again at the shop."

He stuck his head out and attracted the driver's attention and when the coach stopped, jumped down and disappeared amongst the crowd.

"Why are we going to Bond-street?" I asked.

"To order your new togs," Sally answered irritably. "Bless me, you are slow, Johnnie. How old are you?"

I told her and she answered: "You seem less, perhaps because you're not tall of your age. I've a brother about your years, or a little younger. But he seems older than you in some ways."

This was a very interesting piece of information, especially if Barney really were her uncle. If that were more than a figure of speech or a jest, then it occurred to me that Barney might be not the husband — as I had assumed — but the brother-in-law of Mrs Digweed. In that case, Sally's younger brother might well be none other than Joey. I tried to remember if he or his mother had mentioned an elder daughter and if so, whether they had referred to her name.

"Where is your brother? What's his name?" I asked.

"Oh, he's living with my mam and dad," she said. "I ain't seen 'em, though, since I've been with Barney."

"Is he really your uncle?"

I longed to ask her if his second name was Digweed but I remembered the undertaking I had given him not to mention that name.

She looked at me sharply: "We don't arst each other no questions in the company. It ain't businesslike, Barney says. So don't you ever do it again. Is that understood?"

I nodded.

"And don't answer none, either. Whoever arsts you," she said meaningfully.

We had reached Bond-street by now and when Sally had paid the fare we entered a magnificent tailor's establishment where I was measured for a complete costume. As this ritual was being concluded Sam returned, strolling into the shop as he lit a cheroot like any young buck about town.

"Don't let on to no-one that I made off, will you?" he asked off-handedly.

As we travelled back in another hackney-chariot, I felt pleased with myself as I anticipated my appearance in my fine new clothes. But why had Sam broken Barney's injunction?

All during the week that followed my companions speculated on Peg's circumstances and state of mind and took pleasure in enlightening my ignorance by telling me about the customs and rituals that attended upon judicial death. We were all going to the hanging and had to be there early to obtain good places, so on the eve of the execution there was to be a "rantipole" at the end of which we would set off for Newgate. My new clothes had arrived the day before and so this was my first opportunity to appear in them on a worthy occasion. While the others danced to Sam's fiddle, I sat beside Barney and he described to me how at this very moment Peg and the other condemned prisoners who were to hang with him would be attending chapel, and would be preached to on the subject of death, sitting in a pew painted black and with a row of coffins draped in black laid out before them in which their mortal remains would lie the following day.

"Poor old Peg," Bob sighed. "Do you reckon he'll die game or chicken?"

"Game," Barney replied. "I'll lay you a crown at six to four agin it."

"How did Peg come to be working with the Cat's-meat-man?" I asked Barney when Bob had accepted these odds. "I mean, if he suspected him of 'peaching on his brother?"

Jack and Sally, who had been whirling round the room, now threw themselves onto the sopha near us.

"Well, it's like this. Ever since Sam and Jack and me gived over the sack-'em-up lay, the Cat's-meat-man and Jerry Isbister has been fighting it out between 'em. Then about a year ago the Cat's-meat-man outwitted him just like he got the better of me. It seems he made it up to Peg and told him he didn't believe no more that he had a hand in 'peaching on his brother."

There was laughter at this and Jack cried: "Fancy Peg being such a flatt!"

"And he bribed him, too," Barney went on, "to lure old Jerry into a trap down the Borough. There was a fierce mill by all accounts and old Jerry was soundly thrashed. One of his men got pinked. And that was the end of Jerry's company. He's had to go back into the carting line, I hear. Peg started working with the Cat's-meat-man but now he's 'peached on him, in revenge for his brother, I b'lieve, for I'll wager that was his game all along."

"Did you say someone was stabbed?" I asked.

"That's right," Barney said off-handedly. "Who was it, do you know, Bob?"

"A cove called Jem, I heerd. Dead."

I felt my heart pounding. I remembered seeing him lying in the gutter but I had never thought of this.

Without stopping to think what I was saying, I turned to Jack and blurted out: "Did you see who pinked him?"

There was a silence and the others looked from me to Jack in amazement. It was not so much my words that surprised them as Jack's response: he turned quite white and stammered something. Barney watched us both closely and then said to me:

"Why, I don't believe you've understood the half of what I've told you. Jack wasn't working with Isbister then. That was years back."

"That's right," Jack said, smiling in a rather uneasy manner.

Sally was staring at Jack in dismay and though I tried not to look at him I caught his eye a few minutes later and found him watching me narrowly. My slip had dispelled the earlier conviviality. We fell silent and I watched Sam fiddling furiously, his golden teeth glinting from the depths of his black beard as he smiled and nodded his head at the dancers while he threaded his way through them. I saw Barney glance at me and then at Jack several times.

"Time to be off," Barney said after a few minutes.

While Bob hurried out to bring hackney-coaches from the nearest stand, I went to fetch my new great-coat for the weather was taking a frosty turn.

Jem dead. And murdered, in effect, by Peg who had been in league with Pulvertaft to lure his companions into the trap at Southwark. Perhaps oddly in view of what I had just learned, I felt a sudden revulsion at the thought of seeing him hanged.

Coming back down those dangerous stairs in the darkness I heard a sound on the upper landing and was suddenly seized from behind and my head banged against the wall. In the faint moonlight that came through the window I could just make out the face that was now thrust into mine — the features so unlike those of the habitually good-natured and handsome Jack.

"Why did you say that?" he demanded.

"It was a mistake! I didn't see you." Then, foolishly, I added: "They had masks on."

"So you know what I'm talking about," he said through gritted teeth and slammed my head against the wall for emphasis.

My answer had placed me in greater danger.

Now he whispered gently: "Say anythin' about that agin and you're dead."

In a moment he was gone.

I remained on the landing reflecting on my plight. What was my life worth now? Why should he hesitate to make me quiet? I had to get away. I would refuse to accompany them tonight and seize my chance while they were all out of the house.

As my confederates assembled in the hall in all their finery, laughing and joking as if on their way to another rantipole, I said to Barney: "I don't want to go."

He looked at me in a manner that recalled the occasion when I had first come to the house, then gripped my arm and led me out to where the coaches were waiting for us. He pushed me into one of them and slammed its door.

As it moved off he brought his great head towards me, increasing his grip on my arm until it was agonizing. I was terrified that he would ask me what I had meant about Jack, but to my surprise he said:

"That was a wrinkle you told me about your mam! Her name and the paritch."

How could he know that I had been lying? And why did he care?

With a smile that was more frightening than any grimace would have been, he said: "Tell us the truth."

I shook my head: "That was the truth."

He leaned back. "We shall see," he said.

We arrived at Newgate in the middle of the night and yet we found a large crowd already gathered before the Debtor's Door, stamping their feet and rubbing their hands against the bitter cold. As we approached we heard the sound of hammering. With considerable difficulty we pushed our way nearer and when Sam generously raised me to his shoulders I could see the New Drop — the ancient scaffold which usually stood in the Press Yard and which was now being erected in Newgate-street in front of the prison. While we waited, my companions joked about the price that various bits of the condemned man would fetch once his body had been dissected. Were they taking this tone in order to conceal the depth of their feelings? Were they really insensitive to the fact that only a few yards from us two men — for there was one other to be executed — were at that very moment waiting in their cells for the footsteps that meant the Sheriff and Under-sheriffs were approaching? That one of them had been the companion of several of them — even though he had betrayed them — and the lover of another of them?

Hawkers were already going through the crowd crying the "sorrowful lamentations" and the "execution-song" — both of them allegedly composed by the doomed man, though Sally assured me that Peg could not write his name. They were also selling a very fanciful life-story which, as further evidence of its lack of veracity, contained an account of the execution.

"He's sold his life to pay for his funeral," Sam explained.

"What'll be left of him to bury," Will remarked cheerfully.

Sharp on the hour of seven a bell nearby began to sound and the crowd responded with a muted cheer.

I recognised that bell and glanced round. Just behind me stood the church of St. Sepulchre where my mother and I had paused after fleeing from Mr Barbellion that day when Miss Quilliam had brought him to Orchard-street. I understood now that she had been frightened by the steady, unrelenting tolling that every Londoner knows, for it sounds the knell of those wretches who are unfortunate enough to hear their own death-bell rung. And a little further away was the sign of the Saracen's-head which had also alarmed her for some reason.

"They're taking 'em to the Press-room now," Barney said, his face intensely concentrated. "They're unironing 'em and pinioning 'em.

At a minute to eight there was movement at the Debtor's Door. We heard cheers in the crowd in front of us.

"What's happening, John?" Sally begged, for, perched on Sam's shoulders I had the best view.

"There they are!" I said. "There's a party of men, some of them are in dark green livery and carrying pikes."

"The Sheriff and Under-sheriffs," Jack said.

I described the others who were identified by my companions as the Governor and the City Marshal.

"One of them has just come out with a mask over his face!" I exclaimed. "Is that the other one to be hanged?"

"No, that's Calcraft," Barney jeered.

Of course. It was the hangman rather than the victim who needed the protection of anonymity.

"You'll know Peg when you see him!" Barney added, and there was laughter from the others.

He was right in a sense that he had not intended, for now I saw a man come through the door wearing ordinary dress, his wrists pinioned by cords before him, and walking awkwardly. For a moment I could not see why.

Then Bob called out: "Don't twist the blessed leg! It ain't done nothing!"

He had a wooden leg! Hence the cruel nick-name "Peg".

"Blueskin!" I exclaimed, for it was he.

The shouts of laughter at Bob's sally hid my exclamation from all but Jack who looked at me in a way I have never forgotten.

The laughter turned into cries of "Hats off!" from all over the crowd. Barney and Sam took up the cry, removing their own and holding them before them. There was a gentleman in front of us wearing a high hat which he did not remove.

Barney reached forward and knocked it off. "I can't see through your damn' tiler!" he shouted.

"Game or dunghill?" cried Bob.

I explained that I could not see Peg's face for he was holding his head down and slightly turned away.

"What *can* you see, Johnnie?" Sally urged.

"There's a gentleman wearing canonicals walking beside him and he seems to be reading aloud from a book."

"That's the Ordinary and he's a-reading of the Burial Sarvice," Sam said with a kind of awed relish.

All the while the bell was tolling the death-knell and now there was only a faint murmur from the vast crowd as if we were collectively holding our breath. The execution-party moved forward towards the awful construction. They mounted the steps and now the prisoner advanced to the front like an actor coming forward to deliver a soliloquy. He seemed to be looking straight at me now. He raised his bound wrists before him and shook them at the crowd which broke the silence by roaring back. He seemed to be grinning. The crowd drew in its breath again.

Barney struck Bob on the shoulder: "I've won! I knowed Peg'd come up trumps."

At the insistence of my companions, I described how the dead man was led by the officers until he stood over the drop. Then the hangman placed a cap on his forehead which hung down so that it covered his eyes, and then pushed into his hands a white handkerchief.

"When he drops it," Barney whispered, "Calcraft draws the bolt."

Someone — was it the Sheriff? — shouted: "Silence!"

The crowd held its breath for an eternity.

I saw the handkerchief flutter and closed my eyes for a moment as a hideous cry broke from a thousand mouths. When I looked again the body was hanging like a puppet with the knees below the level of the scaffold.

Barney released a long sigh.

"Thank Gawd," Meg said, "he went quick and clean."

Then she began to sob.

"They'll twist the other now and then cut 'em down at nine," Sam explained. "Calcraft will strip 'em and then they'll be took to be dissected. Who's for going to watch?"

Meg shook her head. My gorge rose at the thought. I climbed down from Sam's shoulders and made an attempt to slip into the crowd, but I was seized by Barney. He gripped me and held on during the second hanging, which I made no attempt to see. Then, still with his arms locked around me, he hailed a hackney-coach. Some of the others were staying to watch the dissections, but the rest of us returned to the house. As we rode back, most of the party now drunk and quarrelsome but Jack eyeing me intently all the while, I had only one thought in my mind: how to escape.

CHAPTER 60

Later that day in the afternoon Barney, Sam and Jack suddenly came into the Red Room where most of us were, and clapped their hands for attention.

"It's tonight!" Barney cried.

Everyone began to talk at once, laughing and smiling as if with unqualified delight — but it seemed to me that some of them looked frightened, too.

"You all know what to do," said Sam. "Get ready now."

And so they began to make their preparations — the women dressing up and painting and powdering themselves, and the men, apart from Will and Bob who were delegated to stay behind and guard the house, similarly arraying themselves. To my dismay I noticed Sam cleaning and loading a small pistol.

In the middle of this bustling scene Barney beckoned me into the hall: "Put on your new togs," he said. "You're coming with us."

"I shan't," I declared.

His face darkened and he repeated: "You shan't? What the devil do you mean by that?"

As he spoke he struck out at me and though I had time to dodge the main force of the blow, his fist glanced off the side of my head.

"Why do you think I took you in?" he shouted. "Why do you think I paid for them togs?"

How I wished I knew!

"Then I'll give them back," I said, near to tears with the pain of the blow, "and you can let me go."

"Stow that," he growled. "I've got other plans for you. Now do as I say."

"Lay off him, Barney," said Sally, coming down the stairs in a beautiful yellow silk dress I had not seen before.

"Shut your noise, gal," he answered. "We need a boy tonight. You know that."

"I can get one," she said calmly.

When Barney looked at her in surprise she beckoned him towards her and they whispered together for a minute or two. Then he nodded and came back to me.

"Next time you do as I bid," he said, wrenching one arm behind my back to make his point. "Understand?" I nodded, wincing in pain and he released me and bellowed: "Will!"

When that individual hurried up, Barney gestured towards me: "You and Bob make sure the boy don't get out while we're away. Otherwise you'll answer for it."

Will nodded, looking at me in a way that made clear that it would be a pleasure to catch me trying to.

When the two hackney-coaches that had been sent for arrived, the party boarded them exactly like an expedition of pleasure setting out from a fine house in Mayfair. Will and Bob secured the street-door behind them and then settled down to play cards and drink in the drawing-room.

After Barney's words I was more determined to escape than ever before, and yet I could see no way to do so. Stepping adroitly from joist to joist, I wandered about the dark and empty house, holding a lighted candle-end, and tried all the boards across the windows on the ground-floor and the back-door. This merely confirmed that without tools I had no chance of getting out.

I was bitterly disappointed for it seemed to me I could hardly hope for a better opportunity. Then it occurred to me that this was at least a good moment to read my mother's pocket-book in peace, for if either Will or Bob came up the stairs I would have warning and be able to conceal it again. I retrieved it from its hiding-place (leaving there the map and that tiresome letter of my grandfather's) and then with the candle beside me, made myself comfortable on my makeshift bed. Then I opened it, my heart pounding as I saw the familiar hand.

BOOK III

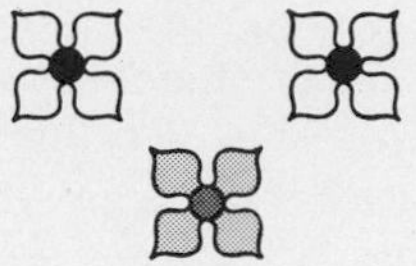

The Wedding Night

CHAPTER 61

FIRST RELATION:

The 18th. of December, 1819.

My dearest Johnnie,

You don't understand, of course you don't. How could you? You were unkind but you didn't know what you were saying. You don't understand what Mr Barbelion's coming here means. It means that our Enemy has found us. And you led him to us! But it's not your fault for you are not old enough to understand. I'm not really angry. I will go upstairs now and make it up with you.

You were asleep. I watched you for fear that you might be pretending, but I believe you were really sleeping.

I want you to understand everything and so I have decided to write an account of my life before you were born. You will not read it until you are grown up and can understand everything in it. Some of it will be very hard for you to bear and for me to tell you if I am to tell you all of it. I will give this to you on your twenty-first birthday and let you read it. Or perhaps I will let you find it when I am dead.

The 19th. of December.

How strange that just as I start to tell you about the past, I should learn of Uncle Martin's death! So much of what I have to tell you conserns him.

I was born in my Father's house at Charing-cross and until the day I married, I lived there with him, for my mother had died when I was very young. I won't tell you where exactly it was for I don't want you ever to go there. It was a big old house and our Family had lived there for many many years. I believe it had once been very grand and from the upper floor there was a view into the Royal Gardens of Northumberland-house, but by the time I remember it the district was no longer fashionable.

It was not a nice place. Soldiers were quartered in the public-houses all around and I was always frightened of them with their greased pig-tails and rough manners. There were often fights amongst them. And when the King held a Drawing-room the life-guards stood all around the Park and if we were going for a walk, my nurse and I weren't allowed past and had to go home for the Park was the only place I could go — and only in broad daylight, of course, though even that was not always safeguard enough. I was always made to look down while we passed the wall along the Privy-gardens. And the Rummer-tavern was nearby.

It was a queer, gloomy house — indeed, I suppose it still is unless it has been destroyed. My Father said it was built on the site of a medeaval priory — St. Mary Rouncivall — and used to show me the old carvings on the back of the houses in the next court which he said had been part of it. The house was in a quiet court set back from the street and had a small paved yard before it with a vestibble where the street-door was. When it was built the front was the back, but long ago other houses had been built between it and the street, so it was turned around and the vestibble was built on. You could reach the street by an alley-way directly from the back-door, and that is important as I will try to explain one day. It was a tall and rambling old place with many low dim rooms pannelled in dark wood and a great staircase where there was a big hall in the centre into which all the rooms led. There was a sword with a curving blade hanging crossed with a halbeard on the wall of the side-hall, and Mr Escreet used to frighten me by telling me the sword had been used to kill someone many years ago.

My Papa saw very little company for he had only one interest. We had almost no relatives for either my Papa or his Father before him had quarrelled with most of them. I had two little rooms on the second floor at the back, near my governess's rooms, where I spent most of my time either with her or most likely by myself, for the governesses never staid long, and so I fear I never learned very much. My Papa passed the better part of every day in his Library reading law-books and writing legal papers, or else consulting with his legal advisers at their Chambers. You see, the one thing he cared about was regaining the Rights to the Hougham Propperty that he believed he had been cheated of.

Mr Escreet was the only other person who lived with us. He was already an extreamely old gentleman when I was a little girl, and had been with my Family since my Great-grandfather's time for he had been a kind of confidencial Secretary to him when he was a very young man, and now he helped my Papa with his legal work for he had been bread to the law. He was a kindly old gentleman — though he would often become very mellancolic for no reason that anybody could dissern, [*These words were crossed out:* especially when he had been] — and he was my best playmate when I was very little.

Apart from Mr Escreet, there was only Mr Fortisquince — Uncle Martin as I called him then — and his connexion with our Family was also very antient, for his Father had been the land-agent at Hougham when my Great-grandfather owned the Estate there. He was of an age with my Papa and they had been brought up almost as Brothers. You see, my Grandfather had died when Papa was only a few months old and then his mother died when he was a small child of three or four years. And Uncle Martin's own mamma had died as well when he was very young. (You remember, the lady who lived once in this little cottage of ours?) And so Uncle Martin's father took Papa to live with him and his son at Hougham, where Sir Perceval Mompesson's Father, Sir Hugo, had retained Mr Fortisquince as his land-agent after he had purchased the Estate from my Grandfather. Mr Fortisquince lived in the Old Hall (or, at least, in part of it for there was another wing that was used for something else). And so you see my Papa grew up as a poor orphan on the very Propperty which had until recently belonged to his Family, and I believe it rankled with him that the new owners condessended to him when they noticed him at all. When I say that he was poor, I should explain that all that he had inherited was an annuaty charged upon the Estate that had been established as one of the terms of the sale by his Father. (The sad truth is that his poor Father had been a spend-thrift who had disappated most of his inheritance even before he had come into it, so that the Propperty was heavily encumbered by the time his own Father died, and that is why he had had to sell it on unfavourable terms.)

Papa and Uncle Martin attended the University at Cambridge together (for there was just enough money left for that) and when they came down, Mr Escreet invited them to lodge in the old house. I should explain that it had been bequeathed to him (to Mr Escreet, I mean) by my Great-grandfather in recognition of his services and he had been living alone there for many years by that time. (He had once been married but his wife had died long before. My Papa told me that he believed he had had a child who had survived to adulthood but had brought little joy to him, and to the best of my knowledge this subject was never mentioned by anyone in the house.) So the two young men lodged in the house while they studied the law. Mr Escreet became very fond of both of them and my Papa loved him in return, but it grieved Mr Escreet greatly that Uncle Martin never seemed to return his affection. This arrangement lasted until, a few years later, Uncle Martin married and set up his own establishment. (His wife died when I was still a very little child, and left him no children.)

Now I should explain why it was that my Papa was convinced that he had a claim to the Title of the Hougham Estate. The reason for this was that when he first came to London when he was no more than a boy of sixteen, he went to see Mr Escreet who confided to him a Secret: that he knew for a fact that my great-grandfather, Jeoffrey Huffam, had added a Codacil to his Will not long before he died and that this had been concieled at his death. But Mr Escreet was convinced that it was still in existance and could be found. The point was that it created an entail laid upon my Grandfather which meant that his sale of the Propperty to Sir Hugo was invalid since he had not broken or barred it. Mr Escreet encouraged Papa to save up the money he would recieve from the annuaty so that he might one day be able to buy the Codacil. Papa became very exsited by this, and plunged into the Chancery Suit. (I should have explained that his Grandfather's Will was already being disputed.) Uncle Martin, who, as I say, had never liked Mr Escreet, blamed him for encouraging Papa to believe that he had a chance of regaining the Hougham Propperty and wasting his life and his fortune in persuit of this. As it turned out, Mr Escreet was vindacated and Uncle Martin proved wrong, for one day when I was seventeen, something happened which changed everything.

SECOND RELATION:

The 12th. of April.

Wait until you find out how clever your Mamma has been. The profit on a thousand Pounds will make such a differance to us. Three hundred would not have been nearly enough to save us. And we were wrong to speak of her as we did. She is loyal. Johnnie, you will regret your words to me about her. Even though I told her that I could not pay her the wages she had asked for (for Mr Sancious advised most strongly against it), she told me that she would stay with us after all.

To go back to what I was telling you before: One afternoon my Papa summoned me the Library. Mr Escreet was there and they both seemed very exsited about something. Papa told me that Mr Escreet had just revealed to him that he had found the Codacil! Uncle Martin arrived at that moment and my Father asked Mr Escreet to recount the whole Story. To the best of my recollection this is what he told us: As I believe I have said, about forty years before, he had been the confidencial Agent of my Great-grandfather, Jeoffrey Huffam. The old gentleman had been so worried that at his death his son (my grandpapa) would sell the Propperty to pay his debts, that he had added a Codacil to his Will entailing it upon him in order to make it harder for him to do so. (And since my grandpapa, James, was not married then — and for other reasons as well — the old gentleman wrote the entail in such a way that if my grandpapa died without leaving an heir, then the Estate would be inherited by Silas Clothier, who was at that time his only grandson.) However, when the old gentleman died a year or two later, someone had secretly removed the Codacil. Mr Escreet had spent many years searching for it for he had had a shrewd suspicion (he said) of what had happened to it. At last he had found it and its owner was prepared to sell it for 4,000£.

When he had finished telling us this Uncle Martin asked him if he would withdraw for a few minutes. Papa objected to this, protesting that he had no secrets from the old gentleman, but Mr Escreet became very offended and insisted on leaving the chamber. When he had gone Uncle Martin asked Papa if he entirely believed his Story. My Father answered indignantly that he did. They discussed raising the money and Papa suggested mortgaging the annuaty on the estate. Uncle Martin opposed this because he said it endangered my future and he added that, besides, it might not be easy to raise money against it on the money-market for there were rumours that the Mompessons' affairs were in a parlous State. He had learned nothing of this from Sir Perceval and Lady Mompesson when he had recently paid them his annual courtesy-visit (for he still observed this on account of the connexion that once existed between his Family and theirs), but he said it was generally known that the rent-roll was falling year by year since they put nothing back into the land. And he said: *It grieves me to think of the improvements to which my Father devoted his life, being permitted to sink into ruin. But the point is that far from risking your income on a wild venture of this kind, you should be trying to reduce your expenses and put money aside in case it ceases altogether.*

Papa said: *That kind of Prudence is not in my nature and in urging it upon me I believe, Martin, that you forget the motto of my Family:* 'Tutor rosa corum spines', *that is, the flower of safety lies within the perilous thorns. And that is why I suggest this: My cousin, Silas Clothier, will also benefit from the discovery of this Codacil and he has plenty of ready money. I will offer to let him buy it jointly with me.* And he seated himself at his desk and began to write.

Now Johnnie, this is where I have to explain something. Mr Silas Clothier, although considerably older than Papa, was his first cousin by vertue of his, Mr Clothier's, mother being the daughter of Jeoffrey Huffam. (She was Sophia Huffam and that Alliance had been the cause of a great deal of trouble on account of the Clothiers not being considered gentile enough for the Huffams.) In this way he had inherited an interest in the Chancery Suit to which he was a Party, though he and Papa had quarrelled over it many years before and had not been on any sort of terms since then. He had two sons, Peter and Daniel. Uncle Martin had always feared and distrusted Mr Clothier, and so for this reason he was surprized and horrorfied by Papa's suggestion. But he had another reason, so now he said: *It is true that both Clothier and you have good reasons for wanting to lay the Codacil before the Court. But apart from the fact that he is a rogue, your interests and his are in direct conflict: for if Escreet is correct, Clothier or his heirs can inherit the Hougham Estate only if he is still alive at the death of yourself and Mary.* At this Papa laughed and kissed me and said: *Precisely. And there can be no likelyhood of that. Mary is forty years his junior.* But Uncle Martin was not reassured by this and begged him to change his mind and when Papa proved unyielding, he even offerred to lend him the money himself on certain conditions. And this is where I have to .... No, I need not go into that here though I will try to explain it all soon.

Mr Escreet was now summoned back into the room. He was close to tears and I was very affected. He said: *I have served your Family for fifty years since I was hardly more than a boy, Mr John. And now, to be banished from the chamber in order to have my voracity and my motives discussed! It's too much for mortal flesh to bear.* Papa rose and embraced him: *Dear old frend, pardon me. There was no question of your motives being impewned. My daughter and I trust you absolutely.* But when Papa told him that he was going to ask Mr Silas Clothier to lend him the money to purchase the Codacil, Mr Escreet was horrorfied and said that he and Mr Clothier were bitter Enemies and now he allied himself with Uncle Martin in exorting him to have nothing to do with the old gentleman. Papa, however, was not to be moved. The Die was cast and the invitation was sent asking Mr Clothier and his sons to pay us a morning visit.

They came a few days later. Mr Escreet disappeared to his own appartments as soon as he heard their knock. Old Mr Clothier was a small wisened man with bow legs. He was much older than I had expected and had a sharp, cunning face that I didn't care for at all. He was carefully and neatly dressed in an old-fashioned style. His elder son, Daniel was a large man of at least forty with a rounded figure and a round fleshy face. He was very soberly dressed and looked every inch the respectable attorney — which is what he was, an attorney, I mean. He looked much older than his Brother and could almost have been mistaken for his Father. Yet Peter looked as if he had no relation to the other two at all. He was of middle height and slender with a pale, mellancoly face and large brown eyes. When he smiled, which he did very rarely, his countenance was transformed and all trace of sadness vanished. He was elegantly dressed in the style of a fashionable young gentleman.

The servant handed round wine and cake and Papa and his cousin made peace. Old Mr Clothier was obviously intrigued to know why he had been invited. After a few minutes Papa rose saying: *Come, old frend. We will go to Busyness aand leave the young folks to make each others' aquaintance.* It was strange to hear him speak thus for in years he was not very much older than young Mr Clothier and in appearance and manner he seemed younger. He took old Mr Clothier by the arm and guided him out of the room. Now, Johnnie, I must explain everything. I must explain everything about your Father before I go on. But I will wait until I have the strength.

THIRD RELATION:

Christmas-day, 1822.

That poor woman! How much she has endured. And I fear for what she might find when she returns home. So much about the past and about London came back to me while I listened to her. There were things in her Story that touched very closely on my own life. Your questions about her have made me decide that I must tell you everything here, though I have put off writing about it for two years.

Now I have to make my Confession. I know that by the time you read this you will be old enough to understand. I have promised to tell you about your Father and now I will. I must first go back to what passed when Uncle Martin was trying to dissuade Papa from having anything to do with Mr Clothier. You must know that what ...

[*At this point several pages were missing where my mother had torn them out and forced me to burn them.*]

... that happened that night before we arrived at the Inn at Hertford, as you shall learn.

Now I've said it at last!

Now I must go back to the first time I met the Clothiers. While Papa was talking to the old gentleman in the Library I was attempting to converse with his sons. I found it extreamely difficult because young Mr Clothier was determined to dominate the conversation while his Brother became more and more reserved and tacitern, and yet what he had to say interested me much more than his Brother. For young Mr Clothier talked only of himself, his legal practice, and his household as if I could be interested only in him. When he mentioned his little daughter, I fell with relief upon this topic and asked him about her. I hadn't realized that he was even married and I caused myself, if not him, a great deal of embarassment by making it necessary for him to explain that his wife had died in giving birth to the child. Papa had neglected to tell me anything about our visiters.

At last my Father and old Mr Clothier rejoined us. The old gentleman looked extremely exsited and shortly after that they took their leave, though not before pressing Papa and myself to honour them by returning their call. When they had gone my Father embraced me and said: *He has agreed! He is as enthusiastic for the Codacil as I am.* He had no time to tell me more for we had to dress for dinner. But when Martin arrived Papa recounted to us how Mr Clothier had agreed to lend him the money. Martin asked about the terms and whether the old gentleman had made any conditions and at last Papa said: *He insisted on some security. So I consented to an annuaty on my life at twenty per cent, and to assign the policy to him.* Martin was annoyed at this for he said that it was contrairy to my interests for if Papa should die before the Loan was paid back then the principal would be a charge upon his Estate. Papa said: *Stuff and nonsense! By the time I die I will have regained the Estate and paid back the Loan.* Martin said: *You're too rash, John. What if you should die sooner than you expect?* (Oh how those words have haunted me!) I begged them not to continue the topic, but Martin persisted and said: *I made no such conditions in* my *proposal. Tell me frankly, John, are there any other conditions you have not told me of?* I saw how bitter he was. Papa said nothing. Then Martin said: *I am sure you will both be pleased to learn that I am after all getting married.* My Father cried: *Then you're a fool! As I said to you the other day, a man of your age who has done without a wife for so many years has no Busyness aquiring one now.* Martin was hurt at this, but when he said that his bride was to be Jemima, a cousin of ours, Papa, who had never liked her, made it worse by saying: *The hussy is only after your money. You know she has none of her own and will be condemned to a life of governessing unless she marries.* I feared that he would tell him that she had once tried to trap him into marriage (which I had never believed) but that he had seen through her tricks, but of course I could say nothing. Martin said: *You have already made it clear that you do not believe that a young woman could come to love an old man like me. I can forgive the asspersion upon my own commonsense, but you do an injustice to my intended wife that I cannot ignore. Withdraw those words or I can no longer remain under this roof.* Papa refused and so Martin left the house. I was quite relieved, though of course I was sorry that (as it seemed) Papa had lost his oldest frend.

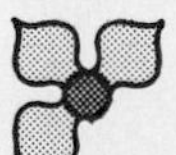

FOURTH RELATION:

The 6th. of April, 1823.

Perhaps it was wrong of me not to tell you, but I meant it for the best. You were unkind to say those things. After all, Mr Sancious assured us the Investment would do well, and you thought so too. I was unlucky, that is all.

The Clothiers came again a number of times during the weeks that followed. On the first three or four occasions Peter accompanied his Father and Brother and while the two Fathers were closeted together in the Library, the three of us talked in the Drawing-room. I liked Peter better and better the more I came to know him, while my feelings for Daniel remained the same. It gradually became apparent to me that something was troubling Peter and that he seemed to be a little timid of his Brother. Then one day Daniel joined his Father in the Library to discuss some legal matters connected with the Loan and Peter and I were left to converse alone. Now Peter was more forthcoming and talked of his childhood and his mother who had died when he was quite a boy. He had loved her very much and had been very lonely after her death and unhappy at the school his Father had sent him to. Then he began to talk about the Busyness that his Father and Brother were involved in and he said: *One may obey the laws of men and yet offend against those of God.* At that moment his Brother entered the room and looked at him angrily and said: *What are you saying? You must not bore the young lady.* I said that he had been interesting me very much which appeared to annoy his Brother. They took their leave shortly afterwards.

The next day Mr Clothier and his elder son came but this time without Peter. They offerred no explaination for his absence, and while old Mr Clothier withdrew to talk Busyness with Papa, young Mr Clothier staid with me. I asked him how his Brother was and he said: *I am afraid, Miss Huffam, that he is indisposed today, as he occasionally is.* I said that I was sorry to learn that his health was not good. He looked at me mysteriously and said: *Let us speak of happier subjects.* (I remember how, as he said this, he laid his hands together on his knees and slid the fingers of his two hands in and out of each other. His hands were podgy and red and the fingers reminded me of raw sausages.) He began to talk about his young daughter. His affection for his child was the only side to young Mr Clothier that I found any sympathy for. Very soon he began to speak of his desire to marry again and, though I attempted to steer him away from so personal a topic, he was determined to persist. To my horror he started to tell me that he believed he had found the right woman at last. I pretended to fail to percieve his meaning and by delaying in this way was at last rescued by the entry of our two Fathers.

The old gentleman came in rubbing his hands together and looking at me in the most knowing way and said: *I hope we are not interrupting.* Mr Daniel Clothier smirked at this and to my distress Papa smiled at me as if he too were in the joke. Young Mr Clothier said: *Well, Father, if it comes to that, you know, Miss Huffam and I were getting along very well without you.* The old gentleman said to my Father: *Young folks, eh, Huffam?* To my relief they left soon afterwards, but when they had gone my Papa said: *My dear child, I am glad to see how well you and Mr Daniel Clothier appear to understand each other.* I could not restrain myself from bursting out that I detested him. My Papa said: *I am very surprized to learn it. And disapointed, too, I may say. For, my dear child, have you considered the advantages of an Alliance with that Family?* I could not speak and he said: *Your and my interests in the Suit would then be identical to those of the Clothier Family: the Codacil would restore my Grandfather's Title to the Hougham Propperty to me, as my heir you would inherit it, and your marriage to old Clothier's son would mean that the children of that union would be his heirs as well as mine.*

Hardly knowing what I was saying, I asked him which son he refered to. He said: *For my part it makes no odds at all, but I understood Clothier to mean Daniel. I would be perfectly content to leave the choice to you, and if you have an objection to the elder son, then by all means take the younger.* My head was in a whirl at this. After a moment Papa asked: *Then shall I tell old Clothier you're agreeable?* I cried out in alarm and he said angrily: *Do you refuse then?* I protested that I did not mean that either and he asked what in heaven's name I *did* mean. I could not speak and he said: *Come, my dear, I must say something to Clothier for he's very anxious about this.* Then he suddenly cried: *I have it! Let me tell him you that do not object to having one of them?* I nodded and he kissed me and called me his own girl. He sent this message to Mr Clothier and a few days later informed me that the Deed governing the terms of the Loan had been signed.

A few days later all was ready for the purchase of the Codacil. Mr Clothier and his elder son came to the house in the morning and met Mr Escreet who was very nervous. It was strange to see him so frightened of so little a gentleman! Mr Clothier counted out the money — 4,000£ in bank-notes! — and paid it over to Papa who signed a Deed (which was then witnessed by Mr Escreet) and gave it to him. Papa then gave the money to Mr Escreet who left the room.

Nearly an hour ticked away very slowly by the Grandfather clock. My Father walked up and down the room rubbing his nose while the old gentleman sat chewing the end of his cane and his son stared out of window with his arms crossed. At last Mr Escreet returned and handed Papa a small package. He took it with trembling hands and carried it across to the lamp on the desk. He opened it and examined the piece of parchment he drew from it while Mr Clothier and his son watched eagerly. I saw that my Father's face was flushed and his eyes feverish and then noticed that old Mr Clothier was the same: his black eyes were glittering as he ground his teeth with impatience. His son was gripping his big hands together so hard that the pink flesh was white. At last Papa said: *This document is genuine. I am as certain of that as I can be of anything. You're a lawyer, see what you think, Clothier.* Young Mr Clothier crossed the room and almost seized it from him. After examining it for a long time, he confirmed my Father's judgement. Old Mr Clothier cried: *Read it, for heaven's sake!* So young Mr Clothier read it and when they had heard it out they discussed its implicactions. Mr Clothier said: *I have waited more than forty years to see this document laid before the Court. I am an old man and I cannot wait much longer. I hope you will set this in train tomorrow.* Papa carefully rolled up the document and placed it in the silver case which you have seen so often and which he had made ready to recieve it. He then secured this to his watch-chain and fob. Then he smiled and said: *Tomorrow is Saturday. I will do it on Monday. And until I hand it to the Court, I assure you that it will never leave my custardy. And now gentlemen, I beg you will do my daughter and myself the honour of accepting my invitation to dinner?* To my dismay, they did so. Because he had cause for cellarbration Papa partook freely of the wine though the two Clothiers remained sober and watchful. When the cloth was removed I retired to the drawing-room upstairs, but a few minutes later young Mr Clothier came in. As I made tea, he began to speak of the Codacil and the way it united the interests of our two families. Before I could say or do anything he had made me a flat proposal of marriage. I told him that I could not think of it. He said angrily that in that case our Fathers must have misunderstood each other, for his had very clearly recieved the impression from mine that I would look upon such a proposal favourably. At that moment the two gentlemen entered. I saw that Papa had taken more wine than was his usual custom. When Mr Clothier's son told him what had passed, the old gentleman said to my Father: *What is the meaning of this, Huffam?* I asked permission of Papa to withdraw, but he said to me: *This is d----d awkward for me, too. I told Clothier what you said to me. Now what's changed your mind?* I could not say anything. Old Mr Clothier said: *That's so, young woman. Your Father told me you had given your consent to marrying either of my sons.*

I managed to say that what I had said was that I had no objection to recieving a proposal from one of his sons. The old gentleman cried: *What is the differance?* I could not speak, but Mr Daniel Clothier said: *Ah, now I percieve. It is "one son" rather than "either" that the young lady is stippulating for, and evidently I have not the honour to be the favoured Brother.* Papa cried: *I believe that is right! I believe it is young Peter that she has in mind. Very well then, we shall have a wedding after all.* But old Mr Clothier cried: *No we shall not!* My Father said: *Why, what odds does it make whether she takes one or the other?* Mr Clothier shouted: *Daniel is my heir, not Peter. Why, Peter is ...* He broke off and exchanged a look with his son who said: *We've tried to keep it from you, Miss Huffam, but the truth is that my Brother has always been pecculier. In short, he is insane.* I cried out that this was a wicked lie and the old gentleman said: *Oh so you know all about it, do you? Then you'll know that for the last few weeks we've had to confine him to a safe room with a man-servant watching him night and day to make sure he don't injure himself. And as for you, Huffam, you undertook that your daughter should marry my heir, and now I find that isn't so.* Papa said: *I acted in good faith.* Mr Clothier said: *You've cheated me, Huffam. I would never have agreed to the Loan if I had not had your assurance on this point.* So Martin had been right to suspect that my Father had agreed that I must marry as a condition of the Loan! Papa cried: *Did you say "cheated"? How dare you, a Clothier, accuse a Huffam thus?* Then he seized my arm and gripped it so hard that it hurt. He said: *This is all your fault. Your girlish finicking has brought me into this embarassment. I won't be accused of acting dishonourably, do you hear me? You must stop mooning after Peter and make up your mind to have Daniel.* At this I burst into tears and Papa had to release me. Seizing my oportunity, I ran from the room. On the other side of the door I turned the lock then crossed in the darkness to the other door and turned that also. Now I was safe! I leant with my back against the door still sobbing, my heart near to breaking at the thought of what Peter was undergoing. Then, to my horror, I became aware of someone breathing in the darkness a few feet from me and my heart began to pound. Then a voice spoke: *Is that you, Miss Mary?* It was Mr Escreet. Now that my eyes were accustomed to the darkness I could see that he was sitting in his usual chair before the empty grate. He said: *I wasn't missed at the dinner-table, was I?* It was true. No-one had thought to send for him. He said: *Your Father needs me no longer, Miss Mary. He has the Codacil now and has forgotten all about me, though he wouldn't have it if it weren't for me.* He laughed and I wondered if he too had been drinking. Then he said: *And has he forgotten that the last thing the Clothiers desire is that you should have an heir, for any legitamate child of yours will stand between the entail and old Clothier?* I hurried out of the room and up to my own appartments.

FIFTH RELATION:

The 5th. of July.

I shall write to them and tell them what has happened. I am certain they will help us once they know the whole Story. After all, they are cousins of ours. And it is in their interests that you and I remain safe. But I'm not telling you about this because I don't want you to know. I shall go and see them without your knowledge.

The night after I was told about Peter I hardly slept a wink. It was true that I had seen him very dispirited and silent, but I could not believe what his cruel Brother had said. The next day and the next I kept to my appartments as much as possible and, on the only occasions on which we did meet which were at dinner, Papa kept up an angry silence towards me. Mr Escreet took his meals on a tray in his own chambers, and I would have done the same if my Father had permitted me. The next day at dinner he said: *After you left the room so uncerimoniously that night, Mr Clothier and his son told me some things about young Peter that I think you should know. His Family have long been aware of his severe predisposition to mellancoly. However, in recent years and particularly in the last months, he has developed a number of extrordinary delusions that suggested the onset of a more marked mental derangement, and this is why they have had to impose a degree of restraint upon him. They fear not only for his own safety, but for that of others as well. He has begun to make the most extrordinary accusations against his Father and Brother. And they warned me that we should be on our guard if he succeeds in comunnicating with either of us, which they assure me is most unlikely. And they tell me that his condition has worsened recently as a consequence ... as a consequence of what has happened in this house.* I asked him what he meant and he said: *I am afraid that he manyfests an obsession about you, my dear. He insists that he loves you and wishes to see you.* He cleared his throat and said with some embarassment: *The fact is, my dear, they tell me he speaks of you in terms of quite disrespectful familarity.* I was very affected by this, but not in the way that he intended. He went on to say that he and old Mr Clothier believed that the best course was for the marriage between myself and his elder son to go ahead as soon as possible, for only by seeing me as his Brother's wife would Peter accept that I was beyond his reach. But then something very extrordinary happened.

At that moment the maid-servant brought in a letter which, she said, had just been brought to the door by a porter. Papa looked at it in surprize and said: *Why, it bears the Mompesson seal.* I recognised the crest, four crabs in a square with another in the centre, and the motto *Chancerata Periat Rosa*. He broke open the seal and began to read. I saw the colour come into his face and asked if it were bad news. At first he did not understand me and then he said: *Bad news? To the contrairy. The best news I have ever recieved. The best news concievable.* He refused to answer any more of my questions but went to the Library and remained there until I withdrew for the night. When I went down to breakfast next morning I found him already there and in excellent spirits, except that he looked as if he had been awake all night. When he made no preparations for going to Court I asked him why. He told me he would not be going to his solicitor that morning after all to lay the Codacil before the Court for there need be no haste over it. I was astonished that he should speak in that way of the document which he had persued for so long, and which he had just plunged himself deeply into debt to pay for. Then he called me *Molly* — which he only said when he was being very affectionate. And he said: *You need not marry Mr Daniel Clothier if you don't wish it. You can do better than a Clothier.* I dared not say that I had no wish to do better than a Clothier, so long as I could choose him for myself. Old Mr Clothier came that evening to learn how he had fared in Court. Papa told me afterwards how furious he was to hear that he had done nothing about it. And to learn that Papa no longer supported the idea of my marriage to his elder son.

CHAPTER 62

Melthorpe. The 23rd. of July.

Oh Johnnie, I'm so alarmed! It was the same man! I'm sure it was he. Tall — horibly tall! — and with a lock of black hair. And a pale face. It must be. Then I was right that they have found us. Mr Barbelion must be working for them as I feared. We are undone. We must flee from here. I don't know what will become of us. Especially now that Sir Perceval has refused to help us as I believed he would. They were so unkind. To threaten to tell you about your Father like that! So cruel!

But you won't understand yet: For about three weeks old Mr Clothier grew more and more impatient with Papa. He came to the house almost daily and at last Papa gave instructions that he should not be admited and he went away in a fury. Then one morning while I was working in the front parlour, the maid-servant came in and announced that Mr Peter Clothier wished to see me. At first I thought she must have mistaken the name, but she insisted that she was right. It was indeed Peter who entered and I was terribly shocked by his appearance. He was very pale, his face thin and his cheeks unshaven, and his eyes seemed large and unnaturally bright. His cloathes were dirty and disordered. I asked him to be seated on a chair opposite mine. He made several attempts to speak and then said: *Miss Huffam, I must apologise for coming before you in this condition. I hardly have time to explain, for I must not stay here long if I am to make my escape.* I exclaimed at this word and he said: *I have been kept a prisoner in my Father's house. But I managed to bribe the man-servant to let me get away. My Father is trying to have me declared insane.* At this my mind was in a whirl. I had never doubted his sanity when his Father had tried to make me believe him mad, but now that I saw him like this. Then he said: *I have no time to speak of that. I have come to warn you and your Father of a plot against you. They tell me you are to marry my Brother. I warn you that if you do so, he and my Father intend to murder you.* I turned away so that he would not see the tears start in my eyes. Then what his Father had said was true! He was mad. He stood up and said: *I must go now if I am to get free. I believe I may have been recognised in the street by an Agent of my Father and followed here.* I asked him where he would go and who would help him and he said: *London is a big enough place to hide, even from my Family and their frends.* I longed to tell him to stay there, but what could I do? If Papa saw him now and heard what he was saying, he would surely have him returned to his Father. And perhaps that might be safest for him. And then on the way to the door he paused and said: *I had almost forgotten! One thing more. Do not reveal to any of my Family the name of the parish where your Father's parents were married.* I concieled my surprize and dismay at this remark and solemly assured him that I would do no such thing and we shook hands. I begged him to come back if ever he needed help and he thanked me and left the house. I watched him go. As he passed out of sight a very tall man emerged from an archway opposite and went quickly towards the street after him. Johnnie, *this was the man you described today!* The one who tried to abduct you! I am sure of it!

I didn't know what to hope for Peter. I thought it might be best if he were taken up by Agents of his Family, for I hated to think of him frendless and deranged adrift in the great city. I returned to the parlour. After long reflection, I decided to say nothing to Papa of this visit.

CHAPTER 63

London. The 22nd. of September.

So much has happened since I last wrote anything. I believe you are right about Jemima. She hates me. For I could see how spiteful she was being when she teazed me about your Father. I know I did her wrong. But it was unkind of her to talk about that night and Peter's *mellancoly circumstances* and so on. I should not have gone to her but I hoped she might know something for I could not come back to London without wanting to know, but it seems she does not. (I believe there is only one person I can go to. I hate to think of it but I must do it.) And writing about those times has made them live in my mind again. My Papa believed she was in league with old Mr Clothier, but I cannot think such a thing of her. I hated not being able to explain everything to you, but you were — I mean, are — too young to understand. You'll understand better by the time you read this. I hope you won't judge your poor Mamma too harshly. Now you understand why she doesn't like us. You were clever to see it! It was so painful to come back to London. In the coach I saw you looking so exsited and the past came flooding back with all its agonies. For you it was all so new and for me it was so painful. And to find ourselves in Piccadilly at the Golden-cross so near Papa's old house. And I knew that you knew so little. I decided we had to leave after that attempt to abduct you when I realized that it was the same man that Mr Clothier and his son had employed all those years ago. But when Mr Barbelion came again in August I made up my mind that we should go immediately. We have to escape from their knowledge again. I don't know how they found us, but I'm sure that man who broke in all that time ago was from them. But London will be very dangerous for us. And yet it's the safest place to hide.

Now I must go back to the evening after Peter came, and my Father and I were taking our tea in the front parlour after dinner when the servant-maid announced that old Mr Clothier was at the door. Papa told her he was at home and I decided to stay in the hope of hearing news of Peter. So he came in and sat down and drank tea with us and chatted aimiably about the weather and his walk through the metroppolis that day and the changes he had seen in London since he was a boy and the driving of the great new street through Soho and St. James and the construction of the Strand-bridge. And how he had come to that house when he was quite a young man, to visit my Grandfather (who was his uncle) in the company of his own Father. And then he began to reminnice about my Grandfather whom Papa had not known at all since he had died while he was still in the cradle. Then suddenly he said to Papa: *Your Father and mother caused a deal of bother, as you have most probably been told, by the manner of their wedding for they eloped and married in secret. Was it ever discovered where they went to?* The very question Peter had warned me against! Then I had been wrong about him! I was silently rejoicing over this when it suddenly came to me that he had said we would be in danger if his Father found out the answer to this question. Papa was saying: *Now that's a strange Story though one that, of course, I only know by hearsay. You must know that my Grandfather strongly disapproved of the match.* What could I do? I thought of feigning illness. I was in such distress of mind that I believe the old gentleman saw for I noticed him looking at me and I feared that I might betray that Peter had warned me. Papa went on: *My mother's Family, the Umphravilles, were small landowners whose fortunes had sadly declined, so that my Grandfather believed that they were not worthy of his son.* Papa went on with the Story while I listened in agony. At last, however, he concluded by saying that he did not know the answer to the question Mr Clothier had put. And the old gentleman looked extremely disapointed and suspicious at this.

When he had gone, I told Papa of Peter's visit and his warning about the marriage of my grandparents. He looked grave and said: *This means that the situation is worse than I feared. Old Clothier is plotting to destroy our claim to the Huffam entail so that as soon as the Codacil is accepted by the Court he will immediately inherit the Estate. You see, there has always been some mystery about my parents' marriage, and therefore those in whose interests it is to make such a claim have alledged that it never took place. It's not that he wants to find a record of it, but that he wants to destroy any such document if it exists. I imagine he has searched the London parish-registers and those around Hougham without finding it, and since the witnesses must be long dead, it cannot be proved that way.* Now that I was reassured that what Peter had said was not insane, I told Papa of his warning that the Clothiers planned to murder me. He took this seriously, too, and told me that Martin had warned him of rumours that old Mr Clothier poisoned his first wife in order to marry a rich widow who had also died. He said: *I don't say I believe this but if people say such things about him then it suggests what is thought of him. And your death would be in his interests, for remember that you and I must die without leaving an heir while old Clothier is still alive.* (Just what Mr Escreet had said to me!) *Therefore I believe that both you and I are in grave danger of our lives from the Clothiers once I have laid the Codacil before the Court. And that is why I have no intention of doing so. It is safe where it is.* As he spoke he touched it where it hung from his watch-chain. Then he said: *Besides, I may not need it now. Do you recal the letter I recieved a few weeks ago with the Mompesson seal? It was from someone in the Mompesson household who promised to obtain something in the light of which the Codacil is of no significance whatsoever.* Though I questioned him further, he would say no more.

Late one evening a week later I was reading in the front parlour. Suddenly I became aware of a faint tapping which seemed to be coming from the window, as if the twigs of a tree were being blown against the pane by the wind. But of course there was no tree outside the window. I took up a candle and went to draw the curtains back. I saw a pale face with wild eyes staring in at me. I stifled a cry and was about to ring for assistance when I recognised Peter. Although he looked so wild, I did not hesitate to let him in, remembering how I had earlier misjudged him. I went into the hall and as silently as possible unlocked the vestibble-door whose key (I might say) was always left on the inside, and then the street-door with its enormous key, and then drew back the heavy bolts which secured it. He came in and quickly explained that when he left the house the last time he had been followed by the very tall man whom I had seen — the one you saw in Melthorpe, Johnnie! This man captured him and took him to his Brother's house where he was locked up. He said: *To ensure that I would not escape again they put a servant to guard my door. Then they sent for the keeper of a private madhouse who is known to my Father, and instructed this man to sue out a Chancery Comision of* day inquiring lunattica*: a request for me to be examined and if found insane stripped of all my Rights and put in the power of my Family. The Comision examined me earlier this afternoon. I suspect that they have been bribed to return a verdict against me and so I decided to escape without waiting.* He had previously prepared a way out by means of a window and so succeeded in getting away. Then he said: *But perhaps I* am *insane. I have begun to wonder. What do you think, Miss Huffam?* It is true that he was speaking very fast and exsitedly, but I was quite certain that he was not mad and left him in no doubt of this. I told him that I was delighted that he had come to my Father's house for help and though he at first insisted that he had come merely to take his leave of me for he intended to flee England, I persuaded him to let me call Papa. For I told him that he was grateful for Peter's warning and that we had both realized that it had been because he had come to us with this warning on the last occasion that he had been caught. So I rang the bell and had my Father called. To my delight he smiled when he saw Peter and embraced him saying: *My dear boy, I am deeply grateful to you. It was honourable and generous of you to warn us about your own Father.* He insisted that he remain as our guest. Then he summoned Mr Escreet and took his advice on the legal situation. It was concluded that Peter was safe in the house even if the Comision found against him. Papa assembled the servants and swore them to secresy.

In the days that followed Peter never left the house and this was as well for we noticed strange men — one of them the tall man I had seen — loitering at all hours outside. Papa was very busy at this time with Mr Escreet on some mysterious Busyness that I guessed was connected with the letter he had recieved with the Mompesson crest. And so it happened that during the period that followed Peter and I were brought much together by circumstances, and we soon discovered that our feelings towards each other were the same. It was a bitter blow to learn that the writ of lunacy had indeed been issued. At times he became very mellancolic as he reflected on his position and the humillation of being indebted to the charity of those who were, despite our cousinhood, vertually strangers. He made it clear that he felt that in the circumstances in which he found himself — convicted of madness, pennyless and without any prospect of employment — he had no right to feel as he did about me. At last, however, he overcame his scruples and asked me to marry him and of course I accepted. The great question now was how Papa would recieve the news. Imagine our happiness when he declared himself delighted and said he had hoped that this would come about. I wept with joy and flung myself into his arms. I know he liked Peter and thought he had behaved well towards us. So you see, Johnnie, my Father and he liked each other very much and respected each other. I have never doubted that at least.

To our surprize Papa said: *The wedding must be as soon as possible. We need not wait for there can be no question of calling the banns or your Father,*

Peter, would learn your whereabouts. With that writ against you he can prevent the marriage from taking place, though if it can once be solemized, then it is completely unassailable. Apart from any other motive, he will try to prevent it because your heir would disinherit him. He summoned Mr Escreet who explained that all we had to do was to obtain a special licence from Doctors' Commons specifying a particular church. Papa said: *Then I suggest it be a week tomorrow and at the parish church of St. George's-in-the-Fields which is so far from here that it should be safe.* Peter and I were delighted at this. Then Papa said: *We will have a very private affair. I will give you away, of course, my dear. Mr Escreet will be groomsman, and we will find witnesses at the church. Even our own domestics must not know. I have it! We will simply tell them to prepare for a dinner-party that day and only when we get back will we announce the cause of the cellarbration.* Then Papa said something which astonished me: *I shall invite Martin and his bride to dine with us. And I will not tell even them of the joyous occasion we will be cellarbrating until they arrive.* His manner was very mysterious and I did not know what to think at the prospect of his healing the rift with his old frend. Martin to bring his new wife to my wedding! In the week that followed I interrupted him several times when he was with Mr Escreet and Peter, and they broke off with a guilty air. I worried, for I knew how far my Father allowed his better judgement to be overborne when the Suit was at issue. All went ahead as planned and the invitation was sent, and accepted by Martin. Under conditions of great secresy, a minature-painter came to take our likenesses for the locket that I have shewn you.

The day came that should have been the happiest of my life — the 5th. of May. The weather was beautiful and the cerimony went off very well. We returned to Papa's house for the wedding-breakfast at a little after midday. Papa announced the news to the servants and they became very exsited, the more so when he told them that they would be permitted to take the rest of the evening off once they had served dinner. Now Papa said he had something important to give to Peter to hold in trust for me. This was the Codacil which he now placed in the very same silver letter-case that was stolen from our cottage all those years ago. He made me promise that I would keep it safe and use it on behalf of my heir. He put in a letter as well which he told me was an explaination of legal matters. Then a little later that evening Martin and Mrs Fortisquince arrived and were told of the wedding. I didn't dare to look at him, but they both said the proper things, though afterwards I caught Jemima looking at me rather strangely. It was a difficult situation altogether and considering this, we sat down to dinner in tolerably good spirits. Yet even on that day, the conversation turned, as it always seemed to, to the Suit for Martin began to talk about the Mompessons. He said: *I was at Brook-street two days ago where I found the whole house upside down. I will tell you why so far as I understand it. But first, that reminds me, John, that I have brought ...* Papa interrupted him quite brusquely and I was surprized that he should leave a subject at all connected to the Suit once it had been started. He said: *Come, old frend. Let us not talk Busyness on this day.* Martin looked surprized but said nothing, though as the conversation moved on I noticed his wife staring at him and Papa. When the time came to bring in the dessert, my Father summoned the maids and the cook and presented them with four bottles of wine — two of champagne and two of madeira — and told them to be sure to drink the health of the bride and groom. He said he did not expect to see them above stairs until bed-time. They were delighted and went off to obey his orders. But now, as we drank our wine and ate the nuts and fruit, a quarrel sprang up between my Father and Peter. It was so sudden that I hardly knew where it came from. It was very striking that throughout it neither he nor Papa ever looked at me.

Mr Escreet was the innocent cause of the argument. The topic was started by Martin for he asked Peter: *Have you any idea of what you will do in the future, Mr Clothier?* He replied: *The only thing I know about is books. So I hope to set up on my own account as a book-seller.* Mr Escreet said that that would require capital and Peter said: *Yes, and Mr Huffam has generously promised to advance me a Loan.* Mr Escreet looked puzzled at this and said to Papa: *But surely the amount required will be beyond your present resources, Mr John?* Papa answered, addressing Peter: *I don't have much left on account of the extortionate terms of the Loan that your respected sire has favoured me with. However, I dare say I can spare a hundred or two.* I saw Peter frown but Mr Escreet said: *That is generous, Mr John, very generous.* I think if he had not spoken thus Peter might have let the subject pass, but unfortunately he said: *Generous it may be, but I'm afraid a couple of hundred — or even twice that sum — will not enable me, Mr Huffam, to establish the connexion that will permit me to keep your daughter as I believe you would wish.* Papa cried: *Indeed? And how much did you imagine I* could *spare? How much money do you think I have, now that your Family has robbed me blind? If you want money from me, get your rascally Father to moderate his userious terms for the Loan.* Peter said very quietly: *I must ask you, sir, not to refer to my father in that manner. He has wronged* me *but I do not believe he has done evil to you.* Papa struck the table and shouted: *What! Are you sitting there, a guest in my house, and defending the behaviour of that wicked rogue, Silas Clothier?* Martin and Mr Escreet both protested at my Father's words, but I noticed that Mrs Fortisquince was looking on with a faint smile as if secretly grattified by what was taking place. Peter said: *You did not have to borrow the money from him.* At this Papa got to his feet, looking very wild and angry, and shouted: *This is the morality of the tradesman! Take advantage of your customer's weakness to force extortionate terms upon him and then congratulate yourself for having done Busyness asstutely. And to think that the husband of my daughter sits at my table and defends that morality. And at the same time, asks me to give him money to persue his own roguish tricks to the detriment of other honest folks. Well, all I can say, young man, is that you must be as insane as your Father and Brother profess to believe if you really expect me to give you any capital at all.* When he said this he waited and looked at Peter. After a moment Peter stood up as well. Still he avoided looking at me and his demeanour was very extrordinary. He seemed almost ashamed of what he was saying. He said: *I beg you to consider your words or you will say something irredemeable.* Papa said: *Say something irredemeable? I have* done *something irredemeable! I have married my daughter to a tradesman, a sion of an antient Family of money-lending sharks, a ... a ... in short, a Clothier, for I do not believe I can find a noun in the English language as expressive of my contempt as that one.* At this I rose and cried: *Father, what are you saying?* He did not even glance at me. Now Peter said: *Sir, unless you withdraw your remarks you make it impossible — though this is our wedding-night — for my wife and me to stay under your roof any longer.* Papa said: *I won't withdraw a sylable.* Peter said: *Then we must depart. Come, Mary, rise and make ready.* Even now he did not look at me. I wept and pleaded with Papa to withdraw his words and begged Peter not to insist upon our leaving the house. Martin and Mr Escreet joined their voices to mine but my Father and Peter were unmovable. Peter asked me in an undertone if I had any money for he had none. I told him I had about thirty Pounds and he asked Mr Escreet to order a hackney-coach. I went upstairs to find the money and threw some cloathes into a box. I had never spent a night away from the house before and had little idea of what to take. I donned travelling-dress and came down. When the coach arrived, I took leave of Papa and the others in floods of tears and we boarded it. It drove off from my Father's door, and so began my marriage. Peter instructed the coachman to drive to the Sarricen's-head at Snow-hill. As I sat beside him I wondered if ever a wedding-night had begun more inauspisiously. Peter had shewn himself to be a complete stranger to me. When we reached the Inn he engaged a sitting-room where I waited while he and the hackney-driver took charge of our boxes. Peter returned a few minutes later to say that he would go to the book-keeper and secure our seats on the night-coach to Peterborough (on the way to Spalding), which was due to leave in a little more than an hour. I was amazed at this and asked him why we were going to Spalding. Did he have frends there? And why did we have to go so late? He said: *I beg you, do not question me.* And he opened his bag and unpacked a crimson great-coat which I had never seen before. He took off the one he was wearing which was green, and quickly left the room. I waited and waited and he did not come. Then at last he returned. He was away about forty minutes, I am sure it was no more. Forty-five at the very most. He came into the room smiling. (I am positive he was smiling.) When he approached me I saw that his hands were bloody. I started back in horror. He looked at his hands and said: *Yes, I have cut myself. But don't worry, it's only a scratch or two.* He washed the blood off at the wash-stand and when he turned again I noticed that the sleeve of his coat was torn. I drew his attention to it. He smiled and said: *I will tell you everything when we have time. But it will take quite a lot of telling.* So a few minutes later we boarded the coach and drove out into the dark streets. Peter remained silent until, as we left Islington behind us, he suddenly began to laugh. This was more frightening than anything, and I'm sure I need not tell you what I feared. Because of the presense of the other travellers I could not speak of what was uppermost in my mind and so we remained in silence.

However, when, at about three hours after midnight, we reached the first stage from London — the Blue Dragon at Hertford — he said, in his old, smiling manner: *We will stop here. You are too tired to go further, and there is no necessity for it.* He pressed my hand and said: *I will explain everything that has happened tonight as soon as we are alone.* So we alighted, and he engaged a room and ordered a sort of supper. When it was brought to us we sat down to it and he began: *My dear girl, how frightened you must have been. I hardly like to imagine what you must have thought: that you had married a madman at the very least. And that your Father had taken leave of his senses, too. But let me explain everything and set your mind at rest. What you saw tonight was a charade.* I asked him what he meant and he said: *It was a play, a representation, a piece of drollery. Your Father and I were not really quarrelling. It was all arranged between us beforehand.* Johnnie, I did not know what to think. He said: *Did you not notice how badly I performed my part? Whereas your Father entered into it so convincingly that I almost wondered if he were really angry. Kemble himself could not have acted better.*

But I dared not even look at you for fear that I would break down. I had been struck by this and now my doubts began to resede. He assured me that Papa's wounding taunts had been discussed beforehand. I asked him why he and Papa had arranged this charade and he said that they had not trusted my powers of deception. The purpose had been to decieve Mr and Mrs Fortisquince and to make them believe that a complete rupture had taken place between Papa and ourselves. This was the only way to secure our safety and that of our children. He said: *Far from our quarrelling over money, your Father gave me two hundred Pounds.* He brought out a thick roll of bank-notes and at the sight of this I believed him. It was now very late, or, rather, very early and we were both very tired. All seemed well now but later he returned to the topic. He took from the pocket of his crimson great-coat a package wrapped in brown paper and said: *This will explain everything. It was to fetch this that I went back to your Father's house when I left you at the Sarricen's-head.* He had gone back there? I was amazed to learn it and my mind was in a turmoil once again.

I asked him what was in it, but he said he would open it after breakfast and make all clear to me then. I begged him to open it immediately. I insisted, it was now nearly dawn. We argued about it but then at last he broke the seal, pulled open the wash-leather wrapping, and began to tug something from it. As it came free he said: *Here it is!* But then with a cry he dropped it on the floor. It was a thick bundle of bank-notes and it was covered in something dark and sticky! Peter's hands were now red and as he stood looking at me with an expression of horror he exclaimed: *What can this mean? How did this come to be here?* He picked up the package and, holding it gingerly, looked inside it. Then he said: *It's not here!* I begged him to tell me what he meant but he would say nothing. He insisted that he must go back to Papa's house immediately and that I must stay at the Inn. When I protested, he said: *You are safe here for no-one knows where you are. For you to return with me would defeat the whole purpose of our flight.* He rang for a waiter and ordered a post-chaise for London immediately. Then he opened the silver letter-case and showed me the letter and the Codacil beneath it (which is how he got blood on the letter) and then gave it to me saying: *Remember, if the Codacil were to fall into the hands of my Father you and your Father would be in danger.* He left me most of the 200£ that he said Papa had given him but took the bank-notes that were smeared with ... saying: *Wherever they come from, they do not belong to me and I must return them.* Then he washed his hands, embraced me and left the room. A few minutes later I heard the rattle of wheels and hooves and looked out of the sitting-room window. A post-chaise came out from the yard and passed through the arch into the street where, to my relief for I did not know what I feared, it turned back along the London road.

CHAPTER 64

37 Conduit-street, 24th. of September.

What she said upset me so much and made me think about those terrible things. I had to go and see him. It was horible to see that place again. I must not say more for I do not want you ever to find it. The house was still there and exactly as I remembered it, but even shabbyer and more delappidated. I rang the bell and waited and then rang it again several times before I realized that the bell-pull was not working. So I knocked and knocked. At last someone came to the door and opened it a few inches to peer out. I declared who I was and there was a long silence. Then the door opened and Johnnie it was he! Just as he looked when I last saw him! I asked him if he lived there alone. He said: *Who should live with me? An old woman comes in every day and cleans — unless she's drunk.* When I asked if I could come in he did not move for a moment, and then swung the door open. The hall was cold and dark and appeared not to have been cleaned for many years. He followed me saying: *Why have you come now when you never came nor wrote all these long years?* He seemed to be close to tears. I could not answer. I remembered how he had so often taken me upon his knee when I was a little child. But then I saw in the side-lobby that the sword and halbeard were hanging crossed on the wall in their old place. He saw me looking at them and said: *I like things to be where they've always belonged.*

He said: *Come to the plate-room. I have a fire there.* Johnnie the thought of going into that room. I said no. So he led me to the front-parlour. All the windows had their shutters closed and their moth-eaten and ragged curtains were drawn. We sat down and he offerred me wine, and I nodded to let him pour it but when he placed it on the table beside me I found I could not drink anything. He said: *All these years I have wondered where you were, not knowing if you were alive or dead. Fortisquince would tell me nothing. Nothing. He always hated me. I don't know why. Perhaps he believed something about me. Or he was jealous because your Father loved me. This was his revenge, to turn you against me and cut me out of your affections. What did he tell you? What evil thing did he make you believe about me?* I tried to tell him there was nothing but he said: *He must have poisoned your mind against me. Only consider, my whole working life has been passed in the service of your Family. Nearly seventy years. And then suddenly when your Father whom I loved like a son, when he ... then to find myself shunned by ... Oh Miss Mary, it was unkind.* Nobody has called me that for so long. I began to weep. He took my hand and now in such a kindly tone he asked me to tell him everything that had happened to me. I told him a little and he said: *Was there a child born? A Huffam heir? I must know that.* I remembered how Martin had insisted that your birth be kept a secret. I asked him why he wanted to know and he grew angry again and said that I distrusted him. He cried: *I've given the whole of my life to your Family. I've sacrificed everything — almost to my very soul.* That seemed such a strange thing to say. I told him I knew how much my Family was indebted to him and he said No, I did not. Nobody living knew that. He said: *You know I attended your Great-grandfather Jeoffrey on his deathbed? That I served your poor, wretched Grandfather as far as it lay within my power? And you ask why I should wish to know what the fate of the Family is now and whether it will endure?* I said I would tell him what he wished to know if he would tell me what happened that night, the last time I had seen him. He said: *So that is why you have come. Not to make amends for your neglect but because you want something from me.* I could not deny it. Then he said: *I gave evidence at the inquest and before the Grand Jury. Fortisquince must have told you. What more can I say now?* I told him what Peter had said to me, that the quarrel was a charade. Was it true? He was a long time before he said: *I will answer if you will tell me if a child was born?* I told him that I had a child. It was so strange. He looked away and bent over as if in pain or joy, I could not tell. When he turned back his eyes were full of tears. He said: *Then the Entail still holds. But you only said you bore a child. Tell me, is it still living? And is it a boy or a girl?* I said I would only answer if he would tell me what he had promised. And he said: *The quarrel was a charade.*

So then I begged him to tell me: What was the purpose of it? Why had he not revealed it at the inquest? Then was Peter innocent? He said he would say no more and he told me to tell him whether my child lived. I said I would not unless he answered my questions. Now he grew angry and rose from his chair and came towards me and I was so frightened Johnnie. He is so big and queer-looking. I smelt brandy. He said: *What did you really come for? You didn't think of me for all these years, did you? Now you come here making these accusations.* I started out of my chair and made for the door. I told him that I had wished to write to him but Mr Fortisquince prevented me. He said: *He poisoned your mind against me.* I got out of the room and back into the hall and opened the vestibble-door. He followed me, saying: *He thought I cheated your Father. I suppose you believe that, too. But if you think I have money you are wrong. I have nothing. Nothing but this worthless house. I have been unlucky. Damnably unlucky.* I got out into the street and away. I don't know if he truly meant to harm me, but one thing I am sure of: Johnnie, you must never go there. Never! I believe he is dangerous, that his wits have turned after all these years alone in that house. But at least now I know: Peter told me the truth about the quarrel. I don't know what that means but at least he didn't lie to me.

Now I must go back and tell you the rest. After Peter left me that day the long slow afternoon dragged past. I heard the sounds of arrivals and departures going on around me. Doors opened and shut and I heard steps along the passage outside, but nobody stopped at my door. I had no appetite to eat. Late in the evening the chamber-maid knocked to bring candles and a warming-pan, and was surprized to find me alone in the darkness. As you may imagine, I hardly closed my eyes that night. The next day came early for me, dark and overcast. Another weary day passed. I sat at the window watching everything that arrived, and whenever a post-chaise drove under the arch I waited for Peter's tread, but it never came. Then, just before midnight, as I was about to retire to rest there was a knock at the door and Martin came in. He looked at me for a moment with an expression which I could not read and then he told me what had happened.

I swooned and Martin summoned the servant who was waiting outside. She put me to bed and a surgeon was brought to prescribe a sleeping-draught. I awoke after a troubled sleep of a few hours and Martin told me the rest. When Peter had returned to the house yesterday, he had been searched and the bank-notes covered in blood had been found in his possesion. It had been confirmed that those very notes had been issued to Papa. Peter had been taken up and charged with the murder. Martin assured me that he was absolutely convinced that a terrible mistake had been made. (Oh Johnnie, what could I say? For I knew that he had gone back to the house and come back with blood on his hands.) When examined, Peter had refused to say anything at first. At last Martin had spoken to him alone and he had told him where I was and asked him to come to me. He had only waited to give evidence at the inquest and had then come straight to me. Now he summarized the evidence. He had advised Peter to say nothing as he was fully entitled to do. The witnesses — himself, his wife, and Mr Escreet had managed to avoid mentioning the quarrel that had driven Peter from the house. Fortunately, the servants, being below stairs all this time, had seen and heard nothing. After Peter and I left the house, Mrs Fortisquince had withdrawn upstairs to make ready the tea-things leaving the three gentlemen in the dining-room. Martin then gave Papa a package he had been entrusted with, and my Father left the room with Mr Escreet in order to place it in a safe place in the plate-room. Martin said: *They were only gone for a minute or two and I, having no heart for sitting over my wine alone after the distressing events earlier that evening, was about to join my wife upstairs, when Escreet returned to say that he and your Father would only be a little longer, and that your Father begged me to wait since he wished to discuss the evening's events in confidance. Escreet happened not to close the door as he went away and just a minute or two later I saw a strange man pass the door coming from the hall. I am certain it was not Peter for although he was about the same build, he was not wearing Peter's coat but a bright red one. I assumed that it was a man-servant whom I had not been told was in the house. A few moments later the same figure passed the door again. I began to wonder who it was, for it occured to me as strange that I should not know a new servant. And if it were a servant, I wondered why he did not seem to have come from the stairs down to the servants' quarters. Just a minute or two later I heard cries. I ran to the Library and found it empty. So I went into the plate-room and there I found a terrible sight. Your Father was lieing face downwards. He had been run through with the old sword that hangs on the wall of the back-lobby and which was still in his body. Escreet was lieing beside him and at first I thought he was dead, too, for his head was covered in blood. The strong-box was open and had been rifled. Now this is something I did not tell the inquest: Escreet regained his senses after a few minutes and told me that the person who had done this was Peter. I told him he must be confused because Peter had left the house some time ago, but the old gentleman insisted that he had come back. The servants were by now hysterical with fear that there was a murderer in the house. So I searched it from top to bottom and established that no-one was there. I found that the back-door was locked and that the only copies of the key were in the possesion of the cook and Mr Escreet. I went to the front of the house, where I found that the vestibble-door was broken and the street-door unlocked and open. I believe that the murderer entered the house by the street-door. Somehow he unlocked it and then smashed his way through the glass and wooden frames of the vestibble-door. I assumed that when I had seen him through the door of the dining-room he had been attempting to leave by the back-door but had found it locked and had had to return to the front and leave the way he had come. All this I worked out later. Now I called out to foot-passengers in the street to summon the watch and they arrived within a few minutes. But before they came, I went back to Escreet and told him that I had found nobody in the house and that he must have been confused when he said that he had seen Peter. He accepted this and said that he would not mention this to the authoraties. So when they arrived he told the constable that he had not seen his attacker. However, the servants repeated his words to the constable and so he was examined about them at the inquest. He said that he must have been wandering in his mind when he made this alligation against*

Peter. He now insisted that he had been struck from behind and therefore had not seen his attacker. But unfortunately, the coroner suggested to the Jury that he was lieing in order to avoid incrimmanating Peter. The waiter at the coaching-inn was found and testyfied that he saw you and Peter arrive and book seats for the night-coach. He then showed you to a private room and said he did not see Peter leave the Inn but could not testyfy that he had not done so. The result of the inquest was that, in accordance with the directions of the coroner, the Jury returned a verdict of wilful murder against Peter. He was charged and detained in custardy. He will now be indited before a Grand Jury. If they decide that there is enough evidence to return a True Bill against him he will be sent for trial. One other thing: When he was asked where you were, he refused to say. You may imagine the fears this provoked. But afterwards I saw him for a few minutes and he told me where you were and insisted that you be kept out of London. His great fear was that his Father and Brother would gain power over him again and perhaps thereby be the means of hurting you. Martin kept insisting that it was all a horible mistake and that Peter could not have been guilty. But he didn't know what I knew. He pointed out that there was no evidence against him except the bank-notes and Papa might well have given them to Peter unbeknownst to Mr Escreet. And there was no evidence of any motive once this alligation of robbery was set aside since the quarrel had not been mentioned. Neither was there any evidence to show that Peter went back to the house. The person Martin had seen was, he was almost sure, not Peter. The only other point against Peter was that the murderer had somehow opened the front-door without forcing it and this impliccated someone who had the oportunity to take a copy of the key. But this applied to other inhabitants of the house as much as to Peter. Against this, the fact that the murderer had had to break through the vestibble-door in order to get in suggested that it was not Peter for he could have made a copy of that key as well. Instead it suggested that the murderer was someone not connected with the household who had been acting on a sudden oportunity to pick the lock of the door or perhaps had even found it unlocked for some reason. Martin asked me if I could give any testermoney on Peter's behalf, for example by saying that he had staid with me all the time at the Inn. What could I do? I said nothing and he looked surprized and said that in that case I should stay out of it altogether and remain where I was until he returned to tell me the result of the Grand Jury hearing.

The time that dragged past, it must have been a week but I can't bear to recal it. At last Martin returned. He told me that Peter's Father and Brother had intervened and old Mr Clothier had used his power of attorney as Peter's committee in lunacy to appoint his attorney, and had appointed none other than Mr Daniel Clothier! This gentleman had instantly forbidden anyone — including Martin — to comunnicate with Peter. Martin said that the evidence to the Grand Jury given by himself and all the other witnesses was exactly as at the inquest, except that under examination by Mr Daniel Clothier, Mr Escreet had been forced into admitting that the reason why Peter and I had left the house was because a violent quarrel had sprung up between him and Papa. Mr Daniel Clothier had ellicited this ostensably because he was trying to use a defence of insanity and wanted to stress how strangely Peter had been behaving that night, but Martin was very angry about this because he said that until the quarrel was revealed, Peter had a reasonable chance. Now everything went against him. The prisoner had, of course, no right to give evidence, but the Judge had asked him some questions. And Peter had kept trying to insist that he did not wish to be represented by his Brother, that his Father had abused his power of attorney by appointing him, and that his Father and Brother wanted to have him hung because he knew things about them that could incrimmanate them. This had made a very unfavourable impression on the Jury. And when the Judge asked him to explain the quarrel he had had with his Father-in-law, Peter had come out with the most extrordinary Story: he said that it had not been a real argument but a kind of charade concocted between them with the collusion of Mr Escreet. He had insisted that far from their having really quarrelled about money, Papa had given him some of the bank-notes that had been found upon him and he had inexplicably found the others covered in blood in his pocket and had returned to London and gone to the house with the intention of finding out what had happened and returning them. Mr Escreet was examined again and testyfied that he knew nothing of the alledged gift of money to Peter, although as my Father's confidencial Agent he knew of all his financial transactions. As for the Story that the quarrel was a charade concocted beforehand, he only wished that that had been the case. At this juncture Mr Daniel Clothier had deposed that Peter had recently been found insane by a Comision of Lunacy and said that members of the Comision were present to confirm this, and that Mr Silas Clothier and servants from his household were also prepared to give evidence of the prisoner's insane conduct over the past several months. The Judge had then directed the Jury to find that Peter was unfit to stand trial by reason of insanity, and they had done so. Then the Judge had ordered that he be comited into the care of his Father who undertook to deliver him into the custardy of the keeper of a place called The Refuge. And the Judge had directed (Martin said) that the inditement be not withdrawn but ordered to be kept upon the record. Martin explained that this meant that Peter would remain in the madhouse for the rest of his life. If he ever seemed to have regained his sanity, he would have to stand trial for murder.

Though I was too distraught to be able to give any thought to my future, Martin insisted that I remain out of London and go into hiding for he feared that old Mr Clothier might try to gain power over me in order to obtain the Codacil. He reminded me that if it could be laid before the Court, then it was in the interests of the Clothiers that I should die, for now I was the sole Huffam heir whose continued existance was keeping old Mr Clothier from inheriting the Estate. He told me that he still owned his Father's old house in Melthorpe which was unoccupied and he said that I could live there without paying rent. When I suggested that it might be unwise to hide so close to Hougham, he argued that that was why it was so safe: nobody would think of looking for me there. (He said jokingly that to seek safety closest to danger was to live by my Family's motto.) It seemed so kind that I gratefully accepted and he escorted me there and made me mistress of the house. On the way there, I chose the name of *Mrs Mellamphy* and we gave out that I had been recently widowed and that Martin was my late husband's Father. Thank heavens I have already told you about all of this and need not go into it again. Afterwards, he engaged servants for me, Mrs Belflower and Bissett, arranged for the house to be made comfortable, and then returned to London to sort out my affairs. Of course, all of this compromised me and that is why I was treated as I was by the better sort of people in the village. Particularly when a few months later it became clear what my situation was.

Martin was my Father's executor — for Papa had neglected to change this after the breach between them. I was his heir, of course, but there was very little to inherit except the Hougham Annuaty — for even the house belonged to Mr Escreet. Martin had to sell the furniture and plate to clear Papa's debts — the largest of which was the four thousand Pounds owed to old Mr Clothier. (He managed to rescue a little of the plate and china and some books.) Once the Estate was settled, there was no more than a few hundred Pounds and the Annuaty. However, since I was a married woman all my personal Propperty belonged to my husband, and because he had been declared insane his legal personality was now vested in his committee who was, of course, old Mr Clothier. Martin feared that old Mr Clothier would therefore claim that the Annuaty should be paid to him on behalf of his son, and that is exactly what happened. Consequently, the Mompessons refused to pay it to either of us and old Mr Clothier took the issue to Chancery and made it a part of the Suit that he had been conducting for so many years (for Chancery spreads into everything thus when once you are involved in it), and Martin told me he feared that it would take many years to resolve. (Incidentally, he also mentioned that at about this time Mr Daniel Clothier quarrelled publicly with his Father and renounced him, saying that it was because of his shame and indignation over the way his Father had treated Peter. Martin said that he had repudiated his part in the old gentleman's Busyness, even going so far as adopting the name of his second wife when he remarried at about this time — for he had seen notice of this in the Gazette.)

For the first few months I lived on the money Peter had given me, with some assistance from Martin. But then I became aware that I was expecting a confinement. It was now that (as I have explained) Martin settled upon me the two thousand Pounds in the Consols that was what we lived on until I was cheated of it. But he insisted that (because of Jemima) this was the end of any assistance he could give me, beyond allowing me to occupy his house rent-free. He also warned me that there was a possibility that old Mr Clothier, in his capacity as the trustee of my husband, could gain custardy of you if he came to know of your existance, for he pointed out that any child of mine born in time would threaten his inheritance of the Hougham Estate. For this reason it was essential that the birth of my child and my whereabouts remain secret. Nobody outside Melthorpe — where I was known simply as Mrs Mellamphy — knew anything of your existance. Of course, Martin attempted to keep it from his wife though as you know, she found this out when he became unable to conduct his Busyness privately. After you were born he stopped visiting me because of her. I never gave up thinking about the mystery of Papa's murder and at the end of that first year — in the December before you were born — there was a terrible reminder of it when two families in the Ratcliffe-highway were slaughtered at night by a man who broke into their houses. I wanted to believe that the person who murdered Papa had not been Peter but someone from outside, and I wondered if it could be the same individual who had carried out those terrible crimes. But the authoraties caught the man they believed responsible and he hanged himself before he came to trial, so I could never find out. As time passed I thought of many things. I suspected everybody, everybody. Peter, Mr Escreet, and even ... Oh Johnnie, I could not bear to think that the Father of my child had killed my Papa! I imagined so many things. I even feared that it was I who was responsible — though all unwittingly — for the murder of my Father and the imprisonment of my husband. That it was not his fault for his passion for me had driven him to it.

As the years passed, I grew poorer and poorer and though Martin promised to make sure that you and I were never in absolute want, I feared what might happen if he should die soon, which was very probable in view of his poor health, for he had told me he dared leave me nothing. So then when you were about two years old, I did something very wrong and foolish from which all our ills have followed. I had the idea of making use of the Codacil to raise some money. I asked Martin whether there would be any profit in my laying it before the Court as Papa had originally intended, but he assured me that such an action would be of no advantage to me but would on the contrairy expose you and me to grave danger from the Clothiers. He urged that the wisest course was to sell it to the Mompessons in the certain knowledge that they would destroy it in order to remove the threat to their possesion of the Estate that it represented, thus making you and me safe from old Mr Clothier. I refused because of the promise I had made to Papa just a few hours before his ... I felt that that document had cost him his life and the passing of it on to me and my heir was the only thing he had atchieved during his life. It would be a terrible betrayal of him to surrender it to destruction. Then I began to wonder why Martin was so eager that the Mompessons should regain it and it even occured to me that he had their interests at heart more than he cared for mine. I thought of the fact that if Peter's Story of the charade was true, then it meant that Papa had not trusted Martin for some reason. (Now that I know for sure that Peter was telling the truth about this, I wonder more than ever if my suspicions were right.)

I therefore decided to act without his knowledge and to send to Sir Perceval a copy of the Codacil in order to support my claim to the Annuaty, for that way I could keep my promise to my Father and yet obtain the Annuaty. I did not realize that because the Codacil threatened his possesion of the Estate he would assume that I was trying to blackmail them and that was why he was so angry that time you and I went to see him. If only I had not mismanaged the whole affair, I believe he would have helped us for we are cousins. But everything bad came from that. For since I needed to conciel my whereabouts from Sir Perceval, I engaged an attorney, Mr Sancious, whom I chose at random from a reference in a newspaper reporting a trial. I wrote to him under cover to Martin whom I asked simply to forward the letter. I asked Mr Sancious to undertake to forward letters for me and he consented. Then I copied out the Codacil myself and had it sent by this means to Sir Perceval. So Martin knew nothing of this, and it should have been impossible for Mr Sancious and for the Mompessons to discover where I was living. However, as you know, both of them did discover this, though I never knew how. Sometimes I even wonder if Martin told Sir Perceval?

CHAPTER 65

Parlament-street, Bethnal-green. The 29th. of March.

How could she do it? When I had been so good to her? To betray me like that? To make us flee as if we were crimanals. Leaving everything: all my cloathes and possesions. I was always kind to her surely. I let her put most of the work on Sukey. I thought she meant well by us. Why do people ... And then that horible Mrs Mallatrat.

So much has happened since I last wrote! If I had only known how hard it would be I think I would not have brought us to London. But how unlucky I was to have been robbed by that wicked wicked woman just as we arrived. It all goes back to that, for I lost my embroidery then and that would have kept us.

We have been here a week now. It is horible. The chamber so small and dark. This district is so changed since I knew it. I tried not to let Johnnie see how upset I was. All gardens and green then and the dirty little cottages only further out then that are everywhere now. But the woman is kind, really, though she is so coarse and common. Johnnie is wrong. He is getting so stubborn now. She means well. I don't like her husband though.

The 10th. of April.

He was kind to buy Johnnie new cloathes. I believe he is fond of him. And yet he is not a nice man. She tells me he beats her. We are becoming quite frends now, though she makes me work so hard.

The 29th. of April.

Horible horible woman. How she humillated me. We must leave here.

Orchard-street. The 15th. of June.

I believe she will be good to us. She seems kind and honest. But I believe we should not have left those people we were safe there at least they fed us. Johnnie is becoming so bullying. How like Papa he is. I think of him so often now. I suppose because we are so near the old house. If he were to see me like this. I dared not tell him of my nightmare when he woke me last night. I dreamed of Papa covered in blood, his face his dear sweet face when he was ... did he recognise the He looked so surprized as if he knew the person who And saying that it was me who had done it to him. That I had brought.

The 24th. of July.

No time to write. I believe I work harder for Helen and the Peechments than for that woman. I told Johnnie we should not have left there. Only two grains.

The 30th. of August.

I wish I had some nice dresses to wear. I shall hate to look a fright in front of all those people.

The First of September.

It was horible. Horible. I am so ashamed. We should not have staid. And at the end, the gentleman — not a gentleman — whom I thought was so much nicer than Mr Pentecost ... But he accompanied me back while Helen staid and

The 16th. of October. Midnight.

It nearly broke my heart to part with it. Johnnie is cruel to make me give it up. But I shall redeme it one day. How it brought it all back to me. Those horible pawn-shops! The things that Peter told me. All that happened then. I cannot sleep for thinking of it.

2 o'clock.

I have told Helen everything. Papa's death. My marriage that was no marriage. Who Johnnie's Father is. Everything. She has given me a sleeping-draught.

The 18th. of October.

Such sweet dreams.

The 5th. of November.

She says I must start to keep a record.

2.

The 8th. of November.

3.

The 9th. of November.

3.

The 10th. of November.

5.
7.
6.
9.
10.

December.

11.
10.
12.
11.
14.
14.
13.
11.
15.
14.
14.

January.

17.
12.
14.
15.
18.
18.
19.
17.
19.
20.
24.

The 19th. of May.

It has been very bad. I did not believe I could live through so much, but with Helen's help I have done it. I shall never take that wicked stuff again.

The 22nd. of June.

What a sad Story! How unlucky she has been! Almost as unlucky as I. Lady Mompesson sounds a hard woman. To be so vindictave! Perhaps I was wrong ever to think they would mean well by me.

The 16th. of July.

They have found us! That man! That horible tall man! Who followed Peter that night and who tried to abduct Johnnie in Melthorpe. We cannot stay here. But how did they know where

No. 27 Golden-square. The 19th. of July.

She recieved us so kindly that I was overcome. I was wrong to let Johnnie persuade me not to trust her. She does not hate me at all. I once believed she had disliked me as a girl for I had so many things and she had nothing. But after all I was kind to her then. I gave her my old dresses to make up when she had nothing. And if she has disliked me and sought revenge, then after all … I believe I did her wrong. But how could Helen have betrayed. I cannot bear to think of it.

The 20th. of July.

Mr Steplight is such a funny little man but he is very courteous. Quite the gentleman. I don't believe Jemima likes him at all.

Great-Earle-street. The 22nd. of July.

Will it never come to an end. Just when I believed we were safe at last. How I wish I had … I cannot bear this place and these awful people. But how does he come to have the bill! Johnnie must not know that our Enemy has it, for now that we are in his power …

The 23rd. of July.

I have the most dreadful presentament about Johnnie, that I might never see him again. When he had gone with Mr Steplight I cried and cried. But at least he will be safe now.

The 26th. of July.

Mr Steplight's man has still not brought the money he promised. Mrs Fortisquince didn't come to visit me yesterday, but I expect her later today.

The 28th. of July.

Mr Steplight has not come, though he must have returned to Town by now. I want to know how Johnnie is. Mrs Fortisquince came today. She said that Charity to me was a waste of money because I would only spend it. Why is she so

The girl says she will get it for me. I have enough for just a little. No more for I cannot bear to go through all of that again.

1.

The 13th. of August.

Only a few shillings left and the horible man here has told me what will happen to me unless the balance is paid within two days: I will be brought before the magistrate and comited. I must go to them for help. He has agreed to escort me to their house for ten shillings. My last coins. We will go tomorrow.

1.

I am lost. Mr Assinder, the steward, recieved me and when I had explained everything he went to consult Sir Perceval. When he came back he said that Sir Perceval had told him to say that he had nothing to comunnicate to me and that he did not wish to be bothered on this subject any further. Now that Johnnie is safe they do not care what happens to me!

2.

The Common-side. The 18th. of August.

This is the first time I have been able to write since they brought me here. It was so humillating. There is nothing worse that they can do to me. At least Johnnie is safe.

2.

The 20th. of August.

He is still here! I never liked him. I thought him worse than his frend. I shall have nothing to do with him, though his letter seems frendly and kind.

The Master's-side. The 30th. of August.

The woman who nursed me while I was ill and who I believed was doing so from mere goodness of heart, was being paid by him! She told me so (though at his insistance she had undertaken not to) and I sent him a note. Her husband is the man he chums with — as they call it here. It was he who had me moved. He is coming when I am better recovered.

The 2nd. of September.

He has explained so much! I cannot write more until I have thought about it!

The 3rd. of September.

He has been very ill and is still in danger of his life. He is so kind. I was wrong about him. He has worked everything out from what I have told him. He says he fears that Mrs Fortisquince betrayed me though he says he cannot guess why for he never specculates. She has allowed me to be sent to this place. Perhaps it was even she who told my Enemy where I was. (Yet I cannot understand why Helen betrayed me. Or why Sir Perceval would not help me.) But he tells me not to specculate beyond what I know for sure. He never tries to guess the motives of other people beyond what he sees is manyfestly in their own interests. As for how old Mr Clothier came to have my bill — he says that Mr Sancious must have sold it to him. But how did those two come to join forces against me?

The 4th. of September.

He says he wishes he could get me out of here, but he cannot help me because he has nothing and is still deeply in debt himself. He is trying to raise enough to take the Rules. He got into debt by once acting against his most deeply held principals, when he backed a bill for a frend who had mismanaged his affairs so that he was in danger of losing his trading connexion. (And he lost it anyway and they were both sent here.)

The 6th. of September.

He has fallen very ill again and his life is despared of.

The 8th. of September.

Such sad news of Mr Pentecost. I am frendless again. I can now think of only one person to whom I can turn for help. But can I recal her address?

No. 12 East-Harding-street. The 10th. of September.

Thank heavens I thought of her! She has been kindness itself and I am now safe and have everything I could wish for. She came as soon as she recieved my letter and made all good with the authoraties by standing bail for me so that I can take the Rules and live as an out-prisoner. They know her well for she has helped other women in this way for her house is within the Rules. I don't know how I will ever repay her. When I told her that, she ordered me not to think of such matters until I was well and strong. She *is* good.

The 13th. of September.

I told her about Helen's betrayal of my trust and she was very horrorfied and vowed to cut her if she should ever encounter her again. She has introduced me to some of the other ladies who board with her. I only spoke to them very briefly, but they seem very pleasant. One of them told me they recieve a great deal of company. It has been so long since I have been in good company. She has promised to buy me a new gown so that I may recieve. She is really very generous, and as she says, in this world we have to help one another. I have everything of the best now: a maid to wait upon me and my own bed-chamber, and everything just as I like it.

The 14th. of September.

She has ordered me a beautiful new silk gown from the dress-maker. I do not know how I will ever pay her for it or when I will ever need to wear it, but she tells me not to worry about that.

The 15th. of September.

She tells me she wishes me to recieve visiters now. I hardly liked to decline since she has been so very kind, but I don't understand why her frends should wish to see me. However, I said I would do so. Mrs Purviance said I would be able to wear my new dress. So I am to go into company for the first time tomorrow.

The 16th. of September.

Thank heavens he is safe! That is all that conserns me now. It hardly matters what happens to me.

The 17th. of September.

Must leave here but I have no cloathes — save those she has given me — which she says belong to her — and no money and where could I go? I keep thinking of those creatures by the wall along the Privy-gardens!

The 18th. of September.

She tells me I am a fool and do not understand how the World wags, that no-one obliges anyone for nothing and I cannot have been so foolish as to believe that. I must be a disembling hussy and she will put up with my prevarracations no longer.

The 23rd. of September.

I am followed in the streets. If I tried to escape they would accuse me of stealing the dress.

The 24th. of September.

One of the women will help me to obtain it, she says.

The 25th. of September.

Thank heavens! There is one person here who is kind. Now I shall not care so much what happens to me.

1.

The 4th. of October.

I met Helen today! Here, in this very house! She went quite red with shame when I reproached her. So Mrs Purviance has been lieing to me. She has been sheltering her at another of her houses. To mislead me in that way! I must get away. I have done wrong. I have been so foollish.

3.

The 7th. of October.

I have been ill again. She was very unkind to me. I don't know why I am writing this any more for he will never see it. I will destroy it. He must never see me again. He must never know the Truth about me.

5.

The 9th. of October.

5.

The 13th. of October.

6.

The 28th. of October.

7.

9.

6.

9.

10.

BOOK IV

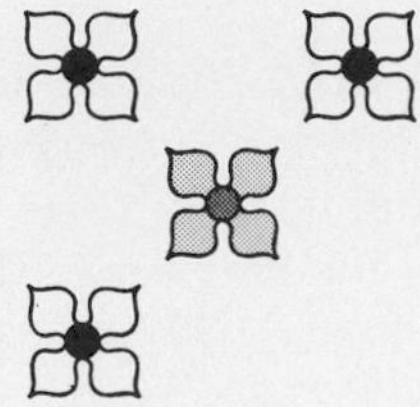

The Veil

CHAPTER 66

Speculation is surely foolish. Who can say what another individual's motives really are? They can never be known, and so it is surely wiser and juster not to speculate. All that can be said in this case is that Mr Vulliamy acted in a certain way. I cannot say if he was moved and angered by what he had heard, or whether he was motivated by self-interest and vengeance because of what Mr Sancious had just told him.

I must, however, begin with Mr Sancious. As he walks through the frozen streets blowing on his gloved hands he is surely unaware of the preparations for the festive season going on around him. Otherwise preoccupied, he makes his way towards the dingy counting-house by the old wharves.

When he arrives in the outer office he finds only Mr Vulliamy and the boy.

"Good afternoon, Mr Sancious," the former says. "Mr Clothier is on High 'Change. He is expecting you at this hour and will be back presently."

Mr Sancious takes the managing-clerk by the arm and leads him to the inner end of the office, leaving the boy sitting by the door. In a low tone he says: "This is a bad business, Mr Vulliamy."

The clerk shakes his head: "Never seen anything like it. Not even in '97 when I was no older than that younker. (That was a bad winter, too.) That was when the Bank of England suspended payments for the first and (as we hope) the last time."

Mr Sancious shudders and says: "The latest news in from the country is of three more provincial houses closing. I'll tell you frankly, I've been badly burned myself and am frightened for worse."

"I'm sincerely sorry to learn that, Mr Sancious. I pity all the poor widows and orphans who have lost everything. All those fatherless families, bless 'em." He wipes his hand across his eyes. "It's a sorry Yuletide they'll be keeping. Though for myself, why, the truth is that someone in my position is hardly any worse off."

Mr Sancious looks at him doubtfully and shakes his head. Then he says: "Are you sure of that?"

"Sure as I could be. Why, I have nothing to lose, I thank heavens." He laughs. "Mr Clothier has my paper to the tune of three hundred pounds. And so, far from having money, I'm deeply in debt and can be made no worse off by this."

"But the old man will be hit by it. And quite badly. They say Quintard and Mimpriss are close to breaking. So he'll surely want his pound of flesh from you."

For a moment the clerk looks alarmed. Then he smiles: "But my three hundred pounds won't make any difference, bless you, sir. And anyway, he knows I can't pay it. It suits him to keep it dangling over my head."

"But you haven't understood me, my good old friend. I am referring to the fact that you're, in effect, the Pimlico and Westminster Land Company. You must know there'll be no question of selling the freehold of any of those houses now."

Mr Vulliamy looks at him in surprise: "That's true enough, sir, but as I say, it makes my position no worse."

"But you're mistaken, my dear friend. By heavens, I'm glad to have caught you alone. There's been something on my conscience I've wanted to tell you for a long while. Your employer has been speculating in bills with the company's capital and, as you'll conceive in the present panic, he has lost heavily. There's no choice now but to declare the company bankrupt. And when that happens, the creditors will put you in the Marshalsea."

"I can't believe it! He wouldn't have done such a thing!" Then he pauses and after a moment exclaims: "Yes, I can. The old rascal. After all my years of loyalty!"

"Thank heavens I've got that off my conscience," the attorney says. "Now would you do something for me?"

"Yes, yes," the other mutters distractedly.

"Mr Vulliamy?" the lawyer says softly with a beatific smile.

The clerk comes out of his reverie: "At your service, sir. Yes, indeed. Anything you want. For the truth is, Mr Sancious, that I believe you may have saved me."

"Most gratifying," the attorney says. Then he asks: "What would you answer me if I were to say to you the name 'Fortisquince'?"

Mr Vulliamy looks at him in alarm.

"Ah-hah," says the attorney. "So you know it, do you?"

"No, that's to say, yes." He looks round nervously. "We cannot speak now, Mr Sancious. Pray let us meet."

At that moment the boy runs to the street-door and Mr Sancious says quickly in an under-tone: "Come to my office in the evening next Thursday."

As he speaks, the old gentleman enters wrapped in a muffler which the boy unwinds, circling around him like a shabby Maypole-dancer. All the while his employer's lean face glares at the attorney:

"I've just come from the money-market," he says. "Amphlett and Cleator have closed, and Bazalgette's, and also Hornbuckle and Ditmas."

Vulliamy shakes his head in dismay, looking at his employer intently.

Without even glancing at him, the old gentleman motions to the attorney to accompany him into the inner office.

"This is bad, very bad," Mr Sancious says, as the door closes behind them. "Some of the best houses have smashed. I have heard that even Quintard and Mimpriss may be in difficulties."

"Not in the least!" the old gentleman exclaims vehemently.

"Are you certain of that?"

"I am assured so by an unimpeachable informant."

"Indeed? Indeed?" the attorney mutters. "The truth is, I have been offered bills of theirs at a discount of fifty per cent."

"Take 'em!" the old gentleman cries. "Take as many as you can and buy the rest for me!"

"I am not buying on my own behalf but for another party," the lawyer says. "Alas, Mr Clothier, I have no cash. Our joint speculations have wiped me out completely. And, I fear, left the Pimlico and Westminster unable to meet its liabilities."

"The company will go into receivership," the old gentleman whispers, nodding his head towards the outer office.

"So he ... ?" Mr Sancious replies in an undertone, glancing towards the door.

The old gentleman draws one finger across his scraggy throat and smiles faintly.

"As a set-off to balance this," Mr Sancious says, "I have excellent news as far as our other business is concerned. What would you most hope to hear from me?"

Mr Clothier stares back and silently mouths one word.

The attorney smiles: "Exactly. My agent has informed me that that is the case."

"Excellent!" the old gentleman cries, clapping his hands and springing from his chair in excitement. Then he turns to the attorney and demands: "Can you furnish me with proof of this? Proof that will stand up in court?"

"Not yet, though I have been trying to. And I believe I will soon be in a position to satisfy you. However, you and I didn't bargain for that complication, Mr Clothier, and so it will cost you more. Meanwhile, I'll take what you owe me for this."

"Half now and half when you show me the proof," Mr Clothier insists.

The attorney nods reluctantly and once more the strong-box is unlocked and a bundle of notes handed over.

"Now as for the boy," the old gentleman begins.

"That is in hand, Mr Clothier. For my other piece of news is that he is secure again."

Mr Clothier hugs himself with glee. Then he stops and says: "But listen carefully. I want my instructions to be followed to the letter."

Since, of course, you know as well as I what they agreed to do, I will leave the two gentlemen there.

Meanwhile in the outer office Mr Vulliamy says to the boy: "Charley, run out for a bottle of best Hollands."

"But I can't get that no nearer than Paul's-church-yard, Mr Vulliamy."

"Never mind that. Do as you're bidden."

When the boy has gone Mr Vulliamy listens to the murmur of voices from the inner closet. Then he takes a piece of candle-wax, warms it over a flame and works it with his fingers. When it is soft he removes the great key from the street-door and quickly presses the wax onto it.

CHAPTER 67

When I came to the end of my mother's account I laid my head on my folded arms and rocked backwards and forwards in agony. A multitude of emotions that I could not have named were struggling within me. Now at last I knew the dark secret that my mother had kept from me: that my grandfather had been brutally murdered, and almost certainly by ... I could not let myself think of it. How my mother must have struggled during every waking minute to keep that imagination from her thoughts. How strange to think that I had believed I knew her so well and yet had no inkling of that. But then, how little I had understood! Only now did I know (as I then believed) who my father was. And that, as it seemed to me, my real name was indeed Clothier. And yet even then I wondered if this was so? Did that name have the right to claim me? Was it more mine than the name I had gone under for so long? Or than those my mother and I had chosen? It was the name I had been baptised under, certainly, and yet I did not want it to be mine. And, after all, the more I had learned, the more I understood how much was still hidden from me. What had been in the pages that my mother had destroyed? What had she wanted to keep from me? Was it something to do with my father? That he was still alive? And since Mr Escreet had confirmed the truth of his most incredible assertion, did that mean that my father was sane? But if he were sane did this not make him only the more guilty? My thoughts went round and round this terrible circle: if he was sane then he was hideously guilty. If he was anything less than guilty it could only have been by being insane. Mad or evil, evil or mad, there seemed no way out. How could I accept such a father as this? I repeated my mother's words: "I could not bear to think that the father of my child had killed my Papa!" I could not bear to think that either. Perhaps, then, another man had been responsible? Did not my mother's words, in several passages, point towards Martin Fortisquince? (Yet — God knows! — I had reasons for not wanting to believe that, either.)

And why would the old gentleman not reveal more? Were there yet more hideous revelations that he had spared my mother? Could I find my way to my grandfather's house and speak to him myself? Perhaps I could learn something from him that would vindicate my father? For though the evidence against him was convincing, yet there were others who had strong motives for wanting my grandfather dead. Old Mr Clothier and his elder son were so desperate that the codicil be laid before the court that they might not have shrunk from murder to ensure this. And the Mompessons, if it came to that, had the strongest reasons to prevent this happening, and I could not forget that Sancious (*alias* Steplight) had come to Mrs Fortisquince's house in their carriage. So were they involved with him in some way, improbable as it seemed?

It was now the middle of the night and there was silence in this uninhabited city of half-built houses, so different from the raucous noises of the crowded rookeries I had known. I had not noticed that it had got much colder while I was absorbed in the pocket-book, but now I pulled the bed-coverings over myself.

I thought of my mother's unhappy, wasted life. She had been too trusting but, more than that, she had had no purpose, no design, and had believed too much in luck. Her love for others had made her vulnerable. All this had made her a victim, merely drifting through a life that had no meaning towards a meaningless end. I would not make the same mistake. I would trust no-one but myself. There was no-one living now whom I loved and that made me free and invulnerable. I knew that there was no such thing as luck; there were only opportunities. From now on I would have a purpose, although at present I was too confused to know what it might be. For I became aware now of other emotions than pity and horror. I felt rage. Rage against Mrs Purviance, against Sancious, against Mrs Fortisquince. I wanted — I needed — to make them suffer. Especially the latter. I could not understand why she had behaved as she had. For what conceivable purpose could she have hounded my mother to her death? What grievance did she have against her? My mother seemed to refer to such a wrong but I could not make out for certain what it was. Then there were the Mompessons and their agent, Assinder, for now I understood what she had been talking about just before she died. So she had known, while I was trying to comfort her, that no help could be expected from that quarter. It would have cost Sir Perceval so little to have helped one whom his family had deeply wronged, and who had a claim of blood upon him as well as justice. At the same time I failed to understand why he had neglected to help her from motives of mere self-serving prudence, for I understood how crucial it was to his interest in the Hougham property to keep alive the entailed line.

Everything came back to the disputed title. So much in my mother's story that made no sense was connected with it. Why had my grandfather suddenly decided not to lay the codicil before the court when he had laboured to find it for so many years and had plunged deeply into debt to a man he distrusted in order to buy it? There were so many puzzles. If my father were sane and guilty then why should he have admitted to my mother that he had gone back to the house after leaving her at the coaching-inn? What happened there when he went back? Was he really surprised to find the bloody bank-notes when he opened the package at the inn in Hertford? At this thought I suddenly recalled my grandfather's letter and I shuddered, for now I knew what the stain was upon it that had so fascinated me as a small boy and that I had childishly interpreted as blood. And now that I thought of it, perhaps I had been too hasty in dismissing the letter that time when I had tried to read it a few days after my mother's death.

I remembered that the letter had gone on to refer to a "will" and that I had discounted this as the phantastic product of John Huffam's obsession with the Hougham estate. And yet perhaps such a document did exist. That assumption might account for some of the puzzling aspects of his behaviour. It might explain why he had so suddenly and surprisingly lost interest in the codicil. The document that had come into his possession, or that he had hoped to obtain, made the codicil redundant! In that case it must have been nothing less than a later will of Jeoffrey himself! If that were so, then presumably it superseded the original will! I remembered what Mr Pentecost and Mr Silverlight had told me: there was no statute of limitations applying to wills. And so the provisions of such a will would have the absolute force of Law! (Or, rather, Equity.) What were its provisions? Hastily I crossed in the near-darkness to where I had left the letter in its hiding-place, retrieved it and lifted it out. Something fell out with it. It was the map — or, rather, sections of it — that I had borne with me from Melthorpe and later entrusted to my mother. Suddenly I wondered if I could find on it my grandfather's house.

I moved the candle nearer and smoothed out the creased sheets. I knew the house was at Charing-cross, over-looked Northumberland-gardens, and was in a court with an alley-way to the street. I could see from the map that it must be either in Northumberland-court to the east of the mansion, or in one of the courts to the west: Trinity-place, one without a name, or Craigs-court. The nameless one seemed most likely.

Now I turned back to my grandfather's letter. I had just unfolded it and was about to start reading when I heard the gravelly sound of carriage-wheels in the unmade-up street. Hastily I put the letter and the map back in the journal and, getting out from under the blankets into the raw cold, stuffed it into the pocket of my jacket which was lying on the floor. Then I extinguished my candle and pulled aside a piece of the board that covered the window so that I could look out: Barney and the others were getting out of a couple of coaches whose drivers they had somehow persuaded to venture into this district at night.

As I heard the street-door opening I stole onto the upper landing just as the noisy throng, laughing and shouting with more exuberance than usual, entered the house and went into the drawing-room.

I crept down the stairs and entered the chamber above that room from which, because of the lack of a ceiling, I could hear everything as clearly as if I were down there with them, though my view was very restricted.

"You was wonderful, Barney," I heard Sally say. "I dunno how you done it so well. You was like a play."

Some of the others laughed appreciatively.

"We was lucky, wasn't we?" said Barney, the top of whose head I could just glimpse as he sat on the sopha. "We wiped their eyes for 'em!"

"How long will they be?" asked Meg.

"About two hours, Jack said," Barney answered.

"Sam told me he thought it would be longer," Sally said.

"Well, shan't we be glad to see 'em? That's all," Meg exclaimed.

There was a chorus of agreement at this.

"Well come on," said Will, "tell Bob and me what happened for Gawd's sake."

"Has the boy been quiet?" Barney demanded.

"Yes," said Bob. "He ain't so much as squeaked."

"We didn't need him arter all," Barney said. "Joey there come along and done what was wanted."

I leaned forward to try to see whom he was referring to but was unable to.

"But fust," said Barney, "there's somethin' I want to do a-fore I forget."

I leaned even further forward to try to see what he was doing, but could not do so without risking falling through the joists. Then as the others began to speak, I realized to my horror that he had left the room. I hurried as quietly as I could back onto the landing and heard him coming up the stairs from the ground-floor, mercifully slowly because of the difficulty of ascending those stairs in the near-darkness and because he was already a little drunk. I set off up the next flight and managed to keep out of his sight and get back into my room some way ahead of him. I hurriedly threw myself onto my makeshift bed, pulling the coverings over myself, and closed my eyes. Seconds later I heard heavy footsteps crashing along the joists of the landing, enter the room and then pause only a few feet from me.

A lanthorn gleamed on my closed eyes. I heard his steps advance and then I knew that he was leaning over me for I smelt gin and tobacco and heard his heavy breath. I was afraid that in my attempt to mimic sleep I was screwing up my eyes too much, and then wondered whether he would become suspicious if I did not pretend to be awoken by the light or whether he was so far intoxicated as not to realize how much noise he was making.

I was about to open my eyes when I heard him moving away and then crashing about the room. At first I dared not look in case he was watching me but at last I very slowly opened my eyes, fearing that he might catch their glitter in the light of his lanthorn. I saw that he was standing apparently facing me but in fact with his head lowered, intent upon my clothes which he had picked up from where I had left them on the floor.

I looked at him full square on and saw his heavy brow, his protruding eyes, his big nose and pointed jaw, and it was as if a veil was lifted from his face so that I saw it clearly for the first time. The years seemed to roll back and I was a small child again, pretending, just as I was now, to be asleep, but on that occasion lying in my own little bed in my mother's house and wakened suddenly from a nightmare to find that it was happening: the face I was now looking at was the face of the housebreaker I saw in the window at Melthorpe!

I closed my eyes and lay with my heart pounding so loud I was sure he must hear it. In my first shock of terror, I could not believe that this extraordinary connexion was a mere coincidence, and therefore I believed that the man standing a few feet away was the instrument of some inexorable and complex machinery of destruction that I was fated never to escape from, that was designed to wreak my ruin as it had that of my grandfather and my parents.

At last, however, Barney went out and when I was sure he had descended the stairs, I struck a flint and lit my candle for I needed the reassurance of the light as I tried to unravel the meaning of this extraordinary discovery. Suddenly it came to me that he had known of his connexion with me from the first. The reason why he had so mysteriously changed his mind about admitting me to the house was that I had mentioned Melthorpe and that had alerted him to my identity. But why should he be concerned with me? *Why, unless he was in touch with Sancious and the Clothiers?* That must be so! I thought of the attorney he had mentioned as the source of his fraudulent bills — surely that was Sancious! But how could this link between Barney and myself have come about? Since I knew nothing of the identity of the housebreaker and did not know if he had chosen my mother's house by chance or had come as the agent of one of our enemies, I could make no headway in following that line. But how had I come to encounter Barney again? I retraced my steps mentally: I had been directed here by Pulvertaft to whom I had been sent by old Sam'el whom in his turn I had found in searching for the Digweeds.

The Digweeds! That must be the answer for they linked Barney with my mother's house. At that realization it was as if the formless lump of links snapped straight and I saw the connexions that enchained me. Had Mrs Digweed and her son come to the house not by chance as they had claimed, but in connexion with the house-breaking that had taken place a few years before? I remembered how I had discovered Joey apparently searching my mother's escritoire that night they had stayed with us. Was he the same Joey that Barney had referred to just now? And yet it all seemed very fine-spun and wire-drawn. In strict logic, I could have no certainty that there was any connexion between Barney and Mrs Digweed. Yet if there was, then perhaps he was her husband? Though when I recalled her frankness and kindliness I could not believe that she was the consort of a criminal, and I did not want to. To accept that she had come to my mother's house fraudulently and abused my mother's generosity and trust was too horrible an idea to entertain. And yet I could see no alternative, except to assume that the re-appearance of the housebreaker in my life was the product of mere chance. Yet even this did not end the matter for if it were completely accidental, then in a paradoxical way that implied a kind of design. The thought made my head spin and at that moment there suddenly came into my mind the memory of Barney boasting that he had killed a gentleman. From what he had said, it appeared to have been about a year before my birth. If he were indeed so mysteriously connected with myself and my family and if he had acted as an agent of the Clothiers, could it not be that the murder he had hinted at was ... ? No, surely I was mad to speculate so far! Yet everything seemed to be connected and to fit together.

Now it came to me: my life had a design, but it was that of another! I wondered who held the threads of the conspiracy, who had spun them and why? But at least by seeing the pattern I had escaped being caught in the web. From now on I would no longer be a mere pawn of destiny. I would give my life a purpose and it would be to seek Justice. To seek Justice for my mother and my father and my grandfather and myself against those who had done us wrong. Against Mrs Fortisquince and her smiling duplicity. Against the cold-hearted and arrogant Mompessons. Above all, against Silas Clothier who surely held the threads in his mouth.

At any rate, I knew I had to get away, and this very night. Quickly and silently I got up and dressed myself, donning not the fine clothes that Sally had bought for me in the West-end, but the old slops she had purchased in Shepherd's-market when I had discarded my rags, for I wished to steal nothing from Barney and regretted having to take the great-coat and boots.

Once dressed and holding my boots in my hand, I glanced round the room before blowing out the candle: there was nothing else to take. Then as my arm brushed against the pocket of my jacket, I realized to my horror that it was empty. I searched the floor but eventually I had to concede that everything — my mother's pocket-book, the copy of the codicil which I had made, the map, and the letter from my grandfather — had been removed. That was what Barney had been doing when I had opened my eyes and recognised him! Feeling the loss of the pocket-book as a further assault upon my mother and my links with her, for a moment I gave way to my rage and pain. The loss of the other documents I felt as a dull ache which would grieve me later though I hardly had time to consider this now. I blew out the candle and left the room.

I crept down the upper flight wondering how I would manage to effect my escape since the street-door — assuming it were unguarded — was the only way out of the house and that required that I pass the door from the hall into the drawing-room. With the vague intention of waiting until everyone had gone to sleep, I went back to my station in the chamber above the drawing-room and began to listen.

I had obviously missed the recital of the evening's achievements.

"That's the right stuff!" Will was exclaiming in the midst of a chorus of hoots and laughter.

"Bli' me," cried Bob. "Wouldn't I love to have seen them swells' phizes when they laid their peepers on Jack!"

I heard the popping of corks and the sounds of celebration. Time passed. I had to remain alert to the sound of anyone coming up the stairs and to avoid falling asleep and toppling forward into the chamber below.

Card-games broke out, someone began to play the fiddle and I saw dancing figures whirling by below me. As the weary hours dragged by in drinking, gaming, quarrelling — and even fighting — I heard and glimpsed scenes of the most abandoned depravity to which my long exposure had still not inured me.

Suddenly I was awakened from near-sleep by Meg's voice: "Here, what o'clock is it?"

"A little arter four and a quarter," said Bob.

"Well, where's Sam and Jack, then?" she said.

"That's right!" cried Barney. "They should be here by now."

"Something's amiss!" cried Sally.

At that moment there was a knock at the door and, leaning forward, I saw Bob leave the room and a moment later heard him call out: "Who is it?"

I could not hear the reply but Bob shouted: "It's Jack!" He began to unlock the door as excitement mounted in the drawing-room.

Then I heard a sudden hubbub of voices, but amongst them cries of: "What's happened?" and "Where's Sam?"

Above the noise I heard Barney's voice: "Don't worry. It was only Jack what I expected. Not Sam."

"What do you mean?" Will called out.

"Me and Jack will explain," he answered. "And a wery interesting story it'll be, too." Then suddenly he broke off and cried: "By heavens, Jack, what's happened to you?"

There was a sudden silence and then I heard Sally scream and Jack's voice feebly saying: "I'm all right. I ain't a-dying, gal."

"You're all over blood!" she cried.

"I took a few knocks," he said.

"What happened, Jack?" Barney asked anxiously.

"Where's Sam?" Meg cried.

"Where's the blunt?" Bob demanded.

"Sam won't be comin' back and I ain't got the blunt. Pulvertaft nabbed it of me."

At this there was uproar for some minutes while Barney's voice, like an angry bull's, rose above the others and beat them into silence, until eventually it was quiet enough for Jack's feeble accents to be heard.

"Tell 'em what we knowed, Barney," Jack said in an exhausted tone, "while I ketch my breath."

He came into sight as he lowered himself onto the sopha, helped by Sally who seated herself beside him. She had something in one hand which she let fall to the floor as she began wiping the blood from her beau's face.

"You see," Barney began, "Jack and me knowed something we had to keep secret from the rest of you. Sam was Pulvertaft's nose all along."

There was uproar at this revelation. I remembered how Sam had gone off that time that he and Sally had driven to the West-end with me.

"How do you mean?" Bob cried. "So what about Nan?"

"She didn't do nothing," Barney said. "We only let on as how we b'lieved it was her."

"You mean you and Jack was lying?" Will said.

"Aye, and Sam, except that in course he knowed it weren't her because it were him, but he didn't know that we knowed that."

"I don't understand!" Sally cried and the others showed that they were equally puzzled.

"Well," said Barney, "you rec'lleck that time the boy brung the message from the Cat's-meat-man? So we knowed someone had sold us?"

As the others cried out at the memory, I peered down at what Sally had dropped, increasingly certain that it was my mother's pocket-book.

"Well, right arter that," Barney went on, "Jack smoked that it was Sam what was the nose. Tell 'em, Jack."

"Why it was Sal as put me onto him. One day she told me that she seen him talking to a bald cull with a wooden leg."

So here was the explanation of the conversation I had overheard between Barney and Jack when the latter had informed the former that Sally had told him something crucial without understanding its significance.

I looked at Sally, and was struck by the fact that at these words she started and stared at Jack.

"Peg!" several of the others exclaimed, referring, of course, to the man I had known as "Blueskin" whom we had seen hanged.

"That's right," Barney went on. "So I arst you, didn't I Sal, and you told me that was right."

Sally stared at him and then nodded slowly.

"So then I knowed as Jack was onto the nose," Barney went on.

"And jist to be sure," Jack said, "I dodged him and one day I seen him go down the Old Mint into the nethersken what Pulvertaft lives in. Well, I come back and told Barney and ... "

"Me and Jack," Barney interrupted, "settled as how we had to get rid of Sam, and do it so as Pulvertaft wouldn't get fly that we had rumbled him. That was the only way to stop him ruining our plans for the fakement. So we agreed to let on to Sam that we thought as how Nan was the nose."

So if I had overheard the rest of that conversation between Jack and Barney I would have heard them agree to pretend to Sam that they believed that Nan was the spy. And presumably Sally had helped them to incriminate her simply because of her spite against the other girl. But, of course, I knew that Jack, not Sam, was really Pulvertaft's secret collaborator.

"So Nan hadn't done nothing?" asked Will angrily.

"That's right," Barney went on. "So arter that me and Jack was letting on to Sam as how we thought we'd got rid of Pulvertaft's nose. And to ketch Pulvertaft on the wrong foot we agreed to bring the date forward by a week. But in fact we only done this to make Sam think we believed we'd wiped Pulvertaft's eyes, 'cause we knowed he'd find a way of telling him."

"But when did Sam have the chance?" asked Meg.

"Tell her, Sal," Barney commanded.

She remained silent.

"Sal told me," Jack said, "as how Sam sneaked off that day he went with her and the boy to buy togs. Ain't that right, Sal?"

Pale-faced, she nodded.

"So," Barney went on, "we knowed Pulvertaft would try to get the blunt of us once we'd got it. Now Sam was very keen that he and Jack should take it straight to the crib in Thrawl-street, so we guessed that Pulvertaft would either ambush them on the way or else be hiding there already."

"That's right," Bob agreed. "That's how I'd do it if I was Pulvertaft. Let Sam and Jack bring the blunt to me jist where I wanted it and then jump out on 'em with a couple of coves."

"That's the ticket, Bob," Barney agreed. Then he paused for a moment before saying: "So that's why me and Jack agreed that we would have to take the blunt of Sam a-fore that."

"So what happened, Jack?" Will asked.

"As soon as me and Sam left the hell, and got into that narrer lane from Bedford-court into Bedford-Bury, he pulled out a knife and tried to pink me. But I was ready for him, so I had my pocket-pistol and I made him quiet."

There was a stunned silence.

Suddenly Sally screamed and the horror of her cry made the hair on the back of my neck rise. Of course, she had had a fancy for Sam.

"Now listen, Sal," Barney said aggrievedly, "don't carry on like that. I've told you why we had to do it."

Sally buried her face in her hands and when Jack moved towards her she moved away on the sopha.

"Listen, Sal," he said, "I dared not wait no longer. He would have done it to me if I'd gave him the chance."

There were murmurs of agreement from the others. Sally was exhorted "not to carry on so" and several comments were passed implying that Jack's suspicions that her affections might be engaged by Sam were being given credibility by her attitude now. However, she remained distraught and tearful.

"So what happened to the blunt, Jack?" Barney asked.

"I left it too late," Jack said ruefully. "Right arter that Pulvertaft and another cove come round the corner. I didn't have time to re-charge the gun and they was on me in an instant. They beat me about the head and pulled the bag off me and I jist took to my heels."

This account was greeted with sympathy for Jack's appearance certainly suggested that he had been badly injured.

The mood of the gathering was now extremely grim, and though they continued to drink, as the realization dawned on them that they had, after all their efforts, been outwitted, they were now trying to numb themselves against their bitter disappointment. As the resentments that had been suppressed during the period of their common endeavour now surfaced, a number of fierce quarrels broke out and several of them deteriorated into brawls. Most of what was going on I had to deduce from the noises alone, but at one moment I was interested to see Sally, who had been sitting on the sopha, rise to her feet and move away in order to avoid Jack's attempts to embrace her.

I had wondered for some time how black were the crimes that these people were capable of, and now my worst fears had been far surpassed. Cold-blooded murder for reasons of mere profit and self-interest — murder of a friend and colleague, however disloyal he might have proved himself —

was a dark enough act to match my suspicions. And what Jack had done had been yet darker. I had to get away from there even at the risk of my life.

After a few hours the noises from below suggested that my former companions had fallen into a drunken slumber. This was the moment I had been waiting for: the street-door was not guarded and I should be able to pass through the hall unseen from the drawing-room under cover of darkness, for the late December dawn was not yet arrived.

I crept down the stairs — which was difficult without a light — and, holding my breath, passed the door of the drawing-room. The snores and drunken mutterings suggested that its inhabitants were now sprawled across the carpets and furniture in promiscuous disarray, as I had often seen them before.

As silently as I could, I began to undo the locks and chains with which the front-door was secured. I had released half of them when suddenly, because of the difficulty of doing it in the darkness, one of the great chains with a padlock attached fell to the floor with a noise that seemed to fill the house, echoing through the uncarpeted and empty hall and rooms. I could do nothing. There were still too many bolts and chains for me to be able to abandon caution and fling the door open and flee as I longed to do.

So I froze and waited for my fate. To my amazement, however, no-one came out of the drawing-room to challenge me. I had just concluded that the sound had seemed louder to me than in fact it was, when I seemed to hear a soft noise that might almost have been nothing more than a rat. I held my breath for as long as I could and when no further sound came, I decided it was safe to continue, and so I released the last of the locks and slid the door open.

A moment later I was out in the cold night air. I pulled the door to behind me in order that my escape should remain undiscovered for as long as possible, and made my way along the rough road, glancing back frequently. As I reached the corner of that ghostly street I took a last look behind me and it seemed to me that the door was open and a small figure was standing on the steps. But it was too dark to be sure that it was not merely a shadow, and I hurried on round the corner.

When I had gone a safe distance I paused to put on the boots. As I looked up I found before me a wooden board bearing the legend: "This ground to be let on Building Leases. Apply to Mr Haldimand, The West London Building Company". That was the company that had cheated the Digweeds and which I was sure had been involved in the speculation which had ruined my mother! Perhaps the house I had just left was one of those in which she had invested! Here were more coincidences! I had no time to ponder them, however, and hurried on.

CHAPTER 68

Walking north-eastward I soon left behind the empty streets of that half-built waste-land, crossed Vauxhall-bridge-road, hurried up Rochester-row and plunged with a kind of relief into the familiar warren around Pye-street and Orchard-street in Westminster. At first I looked back often and once or twice believed I saw a figure in the shadows that seemed to freeze as I turned, but now the streets grew too populous — even at that early hour — for me to be able to do this.

As I passed through St. James'-park, which was at that time a marshy field with a ruined Chinese bridge over the Dutch-canal, I turned often to look behind me — but all I believed I saw were the dark shadows of the park-women — those wretched creatures whose diseased features permitted them to ply their trade only by courtesy of the darkness of the unlit parks.

Except that I knew instinctively that safety lay in the crowded metropolis, I had not considered where I would go. So, passing the deserted bulk of Carlton-house Palace on my left, abandoned for five years and waiting now to be demolished, and then skirting the place where the great new square was being built on the site of the Old-Royal-mews opposite Northumberland-house, I kept steadily heading towards the pink and orange dawn that was rising over the City before me — beautiful but disturbing, too, for I knew it was a warning of even colder weather.

Although profoundly relieved to be free of that house and those people, I knew that my plight was desperate. I was hungry, I had not a penny, and the clothes I was wearing were hardly worth exchanging for any cheaper ones — apart from the great-coat and boots which I needed for protection against the December weather. The Asylum for the Homeless in Playhouse-yard, which only opened when the temperature fell below freezing, must be receiving inmates now, but I needed a ticket to get in.

I hardly knew how it came about but I found myself, as the pale sun rose, in the dank and noisome little square near the Fleet whither I had followed my mother a little over a month before. I remembered that date well — the ill-omened 13th. of November — but I was not sure what the date was today. Gazing at the ugly long mound beneath which my mother lay, I wondered how soon it would be before I would join her there. At length, however, I was recalled from these reflections by the memory that I had things to achieve. And so at midday I dragged myself away from there.

All that day I wandered aimlessly about the frozen streets, shivering with the cold and limping painfully for my feet were sore in the ill-fitting boots. I could not bring myself to beg but I went so far as to stare at people whose faces seemed kind. However, nobody stopped to offer money and I realized that, surrounded by importunate and experienced beggars as I was, I would have to make a direct appeal if I was to expect charity, and this I could not yet bring myself to do.

I reviewed the people I could go to for help: Mrs Fortisquince and the Mompessons were clearly out of the question now. They would not assist me, but anyway I would die rather than ask them. Miss Quilliam, who had little power to aid me anyway, was in Paris. After recognising Barney, I could no longer hope for anything good to come from finding Mrs Digweed. That left only Henry Bellringer and, knowing how impecunious he was himself, I could not bring myself to go to him. There was nobody besides, for surely I dared not go to Mr Escreet? Not after the way he had received my mother, and in view of her explicit injunction? And anyway, I did not know which street the house lay in.

That night I tried to sleep in the hall-way and on the stairs of houses in and around Drury-lane, but I was always driven out with oaths and blows. The next day, in desperation and keeping a careful watch for a police-officer or street-keeper, I began to beg, holding out my hand to passers-by with a few words of supplication. After only a few minutes, however, a cripple came towards me along the pavement, swinging his legs between two crutches and hopping like a sparrow. When he was a few feet away he rested on one crutch and, before I guessed his intention, swung the other towards my head. I moved and it caught me a painful blow on the shoulder.

"Why, I've bought this walk," he cried. "I pay my footing to work these streets. Cut away!"

I had similar experiences when I tried to beg in other places and learned by this means that all the decent streets were owned and sub-let by the police and street-keepers.

"Try down the Garding," a foot-passenger said, seeing me moved on by a sturdy woman in rags. "That's where boys like you goes." When he saw my incomprehension he added: "Common-garding."

I took his advice and arrived there at dusk. The market was over for the day and, apart from a few old women who were sitting on upturned baskets and shelling peas, the market-people were sweeping up and making ready to leave. Strewn around was the detritus of the day's trading — straw, shavings, broken boxes, and the like — and I now saw a number of ragged boys foraging for rotten fruit and vegetables amongst this rubbish. When I began to imitate them they told me to clear off, but then one of them, who was a year or two younger than I and had a crippled arm swinging uselessly at his side, said: "Let him be."

So the others ignored me and I managed to find a couple of apples and a tomato which were partially edible. Suddenly my new companions started and then all ran off.

The boy who had been friendly called out: "Hook it! The beadle!"

I saw the imposing figure of the market-beadle, with his golden epaulettes, his staff, and tri-corn hat, approaching round the corner of a row of stalls and took to my heels after the others.

When I ran up the next avenue I could not see them, but suddenly a head popped out from beneath an abandoned stall and a voice hissed: "In here."

I dived under it and buried myself among the straw. My rescuer was the boy with the crippled arm and as we lay hidden waiting for the market-beadle to go, he told me his name was Luke.

"How long have you had the key of the street?" he asked.

"Just a few days. What about you?"

"Longer nor I can tell. Ever since I rubbed away from me master. 'Cept when I was quodded for three months (and well-whipped twice in the bargain!) for prigging two buns and eight biscuits of a pastry-cook in Bishopsgate. That was when I was living in a brick-field by Hackney. A-fore that I had unfurnished lodgings under the arches of Waterloo-bridge, but it's rough there."

"What about your parents?" I asked as we cautiously emerged and renewed our search for food.

"Don't rec'lleck nothing about 'em. Fust thing I know, I was a sweep's boy down in Lambeth. That was all right, though some of the chimbleys was mortal narrer, but me master died and I was passed down to his son along with the connexion. He was a booser and hadn't no understanding of the trade. He sarved me wery ill. I had to eat the candles at night. He broke me arm once in a beating and it was never set and now it's useless. So at last I rubbed away."

I told him a little of my story in return, not concealing from him that I had not a penny to my name.

"I'll lay odds I could get something for that," he said indicating the ring that Henrietta had given me.

Doubting this and warning him that it was only worth a penny or two, I gave it to him in exchange for a piece of bread — resigning it with only a moment's regret. He left me and, not expecting to see him again, I continued to search for food with little success. Towards midnight, noticing that many of the costermongers and waggoners who had come in from the country were sleeping beneath their carts — most of them under a pile of blankets and great-coats — I was just beginning to wonder where to spend the night, when I felt my arm being nudged and discovered Luke grinning at me.

"Found you," he said, and held up two meat pies and a couple of polonies.

"So you sold it?" I said, taking the pie that he proffered me. "To whom?"

He nodded and bit into the pie as a hint that conversation was to be suspended. When we had eaten — leaving the polonies for breakfast — he suggested that we should find an unattended waggon and retire for the night.

"Won't it be too cold?" I asked.

"I ain't never cold," he said. "I wraps the 'Tiser over meself. Somehow no other paper won't do as well." As he spoke he looked through some abandoned newspapers lying on the ground and picked one up: "I knows the 'Tiser by the cat and horse on the front."

Puzzled by these words I looked to see what he meant and saw the lion and unicorn on the masthead. I followed his advice, but even the *Morning Advertiser* did not prevent me from passing a sleepless night. My thoughts were as bitter as the cold. If I had to live like this, then I did not want to live at all. Yet I must live in order to enforce justice against my enemies. Henry Bellringer, poor though he was himself, was my last hope. Surely, for his half-brother's sake, now that I was actually starving, I was justified in appealing to him for help?

By the time the pale misty dawn was breaking over the dark dome of St. Paul's, I had overcome my scruples and, saying farewell to Luke, I began to make my way towards Henry's chambers, eating my breakfast as I went.

Just at the corner of Chancery-lane and Cursitor-street, I saw a familiar figure: "Justice!" I called out, and the old man turned his blind face towards me like an animal sniffing its way.

He was unchanged except that he was carrying a leathern bag over his shoulder and was without his companion.

He smiled as I came up to him: "I remember you from your voice, Master John. That's the great blessing of blindness when you've been afflicted as long as I have."

Remembering something that I had heard from Barney's people, I asked: "Were you always blind, or were you blinded as a child to make a beggar of you?"

He chuckled: "Is that what they say? No, the truth is I lost my sight in gaol for I had the fever bad with the poor wittles and the darkness. The turn-keys gived me the by-name of 'Blind Justice' for they said I was as blind as Justice."

"Justice is not *blind*," I protested without thinking, for I was disconcerted by what he had told me; "but *blind-folded*, to show that she is impartial."

"Is that so?" he said with a gentle smile.

Suddenly I recalled that Mr Pentecost had told me that the old beggar had given his sight for his principles, and was puzzled to make these two explanations match.

"And how do you live now? Where is Wolf?"

"Why, I'm collecting for him." He touched the bag. "I does my rounds every day for people knows me and him now, and they gives me scraps for the old dog. He brings out the best in folks." He paused and I would write that he scrutinised me if it would not sound absurd. Then he went on: "I can tell that you're a-wondering what I was in quod for. Well, seeing as you're a friend of Mr Pentecost, I'll tell ye the tale. When I was a young man — oh, this is going back more than thirty year now to the time when the French wars was jist starting — me and a few other young fellows, 'prentices and young journeymen like myself for the most part, we was in a Radical s'iety. All we ever done was we met and talked about rising up like the French. But there was a government spy among us, a gentleman who pretended to be as Radical as us. More Radical, in fact. Mayhap he was, but was frightened into what he done. Who knows why a man does the things he does? Not even himself don't always. Be that as it may, he 'peached on us and we was all took up and stood a-fore the Privy Council. They sent us up for treason. What he said at the trial was all lies but it was b'lieved. Two on the others was hanged and the rest marinated — that is, transported. I was sent to the Hulks at Gravesend for seven years but respited arter three on account of I'd lost the use of my eyes. But the strangest thing, young master, is that I believed I heard his voice again not long back. In fact, it was that time I met you in the street with Mr Pentecost."

I was silent for a moment. I understood Mr Pentecost's words about the old man's principles now.

Then I said: "I have heard that Mr Pentecost is dead."

The old man sighed and shook his head: "The kindest individual I ever knowed."

"Where do you lodge now?"

"Why, to tell you the truth, I don't have no regular lodging. I sometimes pays my tuppence for a night's lodging but otherwise I sleeps under the stars. But are you well yourself and prosperous? You and your mam both?"

"Yes," I said. And as much to divert his enquiries as from any better motive, I said: "Let me give you this for Wolf. It's half a polony."

He hesitated and then said softly: "I cannot lie to you, Master John, for Mr Pentecost's sake. Old Wolf is dead."

I continued to hold it out to him. Then, recollecting myself, I said: "Take it anyway."

He accepted it, we took leave of each other and I continued on my way to Barnards-inn. This time when I tried to sneak past the lodge I was not quick enough, and the porter hurried out and seized me by the collar: "Where do you think you're going, boy?"

"I'm a friend of Mr Henry Bellringer. I'm going to call on him."

"Oh, you're a friend of Mr Henry Bellringer what you're a-going to call on him," he repeated, giving me a shake. "You'll have to conwince me as how he wants to see you fust, young feller. Perhaps you'll 'ave the goodness to send in your card?"

"Will you tell him that ... "

"What, do you think I'm going to carry messages for you? Are you simple?"

"But who will, then?"

"There ain't nobody here but me. But it's Thursday, ain't it? His laundress comes in later. She'll take it if she's a mind to."

So I took up my station in the cold street while the porter watched me at intervals through the lodge-window as he sat reading the newspaper in front of a cozy fire.

After a couple of hours a hideous old woman arrived carrying an enormous laundry-basket on her head. Wisps of reddish hair peeked out from under her dirty cap and she had a cob-pipe stuck in her mouth.

"That's who you want," said the porter, looking out of window.

"Will you take a message to Mr Bellringer?" I asked her.

She peered at me malevolently: "What's it worth to me?"

"I have nothing," I said. "But I'm sure Mr Bellringer will be grateful to you."

"Him?" she said sneeringly. "Grateful's about all I count on from him." Then she said: "Well, what is it?"

"Please tell him that Stephen's friend, John, wishes to see him."

She nodded curtly and passed in.

I waited and waited while several hours dragged by and it grew even colder. I walked up and down the street opposite the lodge swinging my arms around my body to try to keep warm.

Eventually the old woman came out. "What, are you still here?" she said.

"What did he say?"

She looked at me keenly and then said: "He wasn't there. He's gone away sudden."

"How long for?"

She and the porter, who was grinning through the window, exchanged glances.

"I dunno. Several weeks, I b'lieve."

She threw these words over her shoulder as she made off down the street with her basket on her head.

The porter slid open his window to say: "There you are, then. And I shouldn't think it would be worth your time to come back."

I set off dispiritedly down the street, having no idea where I was going. By this time it was late in the afternoon and snow was beginning to fall. I dared not contemplate another night in the open and without food, and one thought became clear to me, hazy though my mind now was. By barring all other paths, fate had forced upon me the outright defiance of my mother's explicit injunction: I had to go to my grandfather's old house and throw myself upon Mr Escreet's mercy. And after all, I had not in fact given her my word that I would not go there. But the question was, could I find it?

With the last reserves of my strength, I set off for Charing-cross. It was a fine evening for all it was so cold, and as I walked westward, the setting sun dyed the sky before me a bright blue that was faintly purple, as it shone through the thin racks of cloud which were like gauze — but dark at the centre and pale at the edges. And because of this, the buildings near me were reduced by the faint mist to a single shade of grey so that details were effaced.

I came first to Northumberland-court which I found to be a narrow street of small houses squeezed into the gardens of the houses in Northumberland-street on one side, and built up against the wall of the mansion on the other. These were not large enough to match my mother's description of my grandfather's house. Remembering from the map that there were courts on the other side, I passed the great Jacobean building and slipped into a narrow court-mouth between two of the high old houses. I went first into Trinity-place which I found consisted of squalid little dwellings made down into separate tenements. I came out and looked at the court before me. It was surrounded by the backs of the houses in Trinity-place and Charing-cross, except for a big old house that faced me and looked as if it had been there before any of the others were built. There was a paling before it and a skinner's yard behind that, and from the smells I guessed that the house was now being used as a tallow-boiler's. Though otherwise matching what I sought, it had no vestibule. The place was deserted, except that a man in a shiny cap was standing on the corner where the house protruded, and idly smoking a long-stemmed pipe.

Dispiritedly I walked towards him and then passed round the angle of the house. Suddenly I saw before me on the back of a big building in the next court two hideous faces carved in stone, now pitted and worn. I recalled how my mother had remarked on the stone-carvings at Mitre-court and confused them with those near her father's house. This was surely the place mentioned in her account! I turned to the right and there was a second big old house that had been hidden by the first. *It had a vestibule!*

Exhausted as I was, I felt close to tears when I beheld the building in which I believed so much had taken place. It was tall, gaunt and delapidated, and was set back from the court by a rusted railing; the windows were shuttered or had broken panes; the guttering hung down, and fallen slates lay along the foot of the wall.

I went up to the street-door which protruded from the house because of the vestibule, whose tiny windows were barred and obscured by grime. The paint had peeled so much from the ancient door that the naked boards were visible. There was a huge iron-rimmed key-hole into which I could have inserted all my fingers, and at about the level of my eyes was another metal-rimmed cavity which I took to be a judas-hole. On a brass plate, worn so smooth that it was almost unreadable, was the legend "No. 17" — which conveyed nothing to me. Then I saw that the heavy iron knocker was in the form of the familiar quatre-foil rose. So beyond doubt this was the house I sought!

I lifted this and let it fall. As it struck the hammer-plate the noise seemed to fill the court. I waited but nothing happened. I knocked again and with the same result. In growing despair now, I hammered several times, remembering how my mother had had to keep knocking.

At last I heard — or thought I heard — a faint noise. It seemed to me that the judas-hole was being slid aside, but when I tried to peer into it I could see nothing.

I stepped right up to the door and spoke. I did not choose the words but they came as if inevitably:

"My name is John Clothier. I am Mary's son. My mother is dead. I have nothing. Please help me."

There was silence, then it seemed to me that very slowly the cover of the judas-hole was being slid back into place. I waited for the door to open but it remained immobile.

I don't know how long I stood there and waited — I believe it was a long time — before I realized that the door was not going to be opened. I was almost delirious and cannot bring to mind exactly what happened after that.

I remember feeling passionate rage at this casual treatment — for this is what I conceived it to be. After defying the dying wish of my mother I was ready for insult, suspicion, further horrible revelations or danger, but I had not expected to be ignored. I felt that Mr Escreet — for I assumed it was he on the other side of the door — had no right to bar me from entering the house that had belonged to my family for so long.

I recall hammering on the great door until my fist was bruised. I believe I shouted — though I don't know what — and then I remember leaning my whole weight against the door and weeping, until exhaustion overcame me and I slid onto the top step and sat with my head against it.

It was now snowing heavily and the flakes were settling on my hair and jacket. The fancy came to me that it was strangely fitting that I should wait for Death at the door of the house where He had come so cruelly to claim my grandfather, and thereby had cast His shadow over the lives of my father and mother and therefore of myself. The Huffam line, I resolved, would end here. The pattern would be complete.

CHAPTER 69

I have no way of knowing whether I had been sitting in that position amidst the swirling whiteness for minutes or hours — beyond cold, beyond exhaustion, and waiting only for a sleep from which I would not awaken — when I became aware that I was being observed. A boy of about my own age was standing before me on the pavement, looking at me with an expression of curiosity and, I thought, sympathy.

"You look done up," he said.

I was unable even to nod.

"Are you hungry?"

He stepped closer and took out of a pocket a penny roll. I hesitated and he held it out still further so that I caught the sweet smell of freshly-baked bread. My hand reached out for it without my being aware of what I was doing and I crammed it greedily into my mouth, which was so dry and swollen that I could chew and swallow only with difficulty.

"My," he commented, "aren't you jist hungry? And you've been sleeping out these last few nights, haven't you?"

I nodded for speech required too much effort.

"Where are you going to shake down tonight?"

I shook my head.

"I ain't got no tin," he said, "but I know a place we can go. It's warm there and we can shake down on real beds and there's fair wittles, too."

His words evoked a kind of waking dream out of *The Arabian Nights*. In my confused, almost intoxicated, state of mind I believed I had only to stay there and wait and these things would come to me. They were not to be found by chasing after them in the manner that this boy described. That was a delusion. I felt more knowing and wiser than he. He should sit down and wait with me.

"He don't arst for no tin there, neither," my informant continued insistently. "He does it for charity."

I shook my head.

"Oh but he does," he insisted. "He's a friend of the poor. I'm going there now. Come with me and you'll see."

I had no strength to move.

"Come," he said again and shook me by the shoulder. I was comfortable where I was for I felt no pain from my hunger now and even the cold seemed less.

"Come on," he said relentlessly and began to tug my arm.

He seemed angry with my obstinacy as much as concerned for my welfare. He pulled me to my feet and it was easier to give in to him than to resist, easier to stand than to fall in the snow. Still holding me firmly by the arm, he led me back to the street. I walked beside him wondering why he had taken this interest in me, and resenting the fact that he had disturbed me when I was comfortable.

We walked out of time into a world grown suddenly quiet, for the snow muffled the foot-falls of the infrequent passers-by and dulled even the hooves and wheels of the few vehicles still abroad. As we walked there seemed to be nothing in the world but the motion of my legs and the gentle falling of the snow.

After some time the boy released his grip and I walked behind him, though he kept glancing back every few yards to make sure I was keeping up. I took no reckoning of the streets we were passing along, beyond noticing that we were heading directly away from the river into a district to the north of the metropolis that was strange to me.

The boy had got ahead and now waited for me to come up with him.

"It's a long way still." he said. "Can you make it?"

I tried to nod.

"You need something inside you. I wish I had some more wittles but that was the last what I gived you. Look, we'll stop at a house as we go along."

I shook my head for I knew of the danger of being given into the custody of the watch if we struck upon an unfriendly householder.

"Oh, don't worry," he said, seeing my expression, "we won't get into trouble. I can always tell a house where they're likely to sarve me. I ain't nivver been wrong."

I had no strength to argue and so we walked on, my companion now scrutinizing the houses we were passing and rejecting all of them. We were in the newly-built district of elegant streets and squares to the west and south of Islington. In many of the windows a tall white candle stood burning, wreathed in green-stuff. On the doors there were bunches of holly and laurel and several times we passed men unloading guinea-hampers from spring-vans.

As I found myself trailing after my new friend something about the situation — the snow, the cold, the hunger, the weariness, and an insistent boy urging someone on with the prospect of a welcome at a stranger's house — seemed to remind me of a distant incident that had happened to me or that I had read of or been told about. But I was in no state to tell reality from dream, or dream from memory. At last it came to me that I must be recalling Sukey's story of the "fetch": this boy was my other self and had come to lead me to my death. I felt no alarm or dismay at this reflection.

At last the boy paused before a house in a prosperous street that looked to me exactly like all the others. But when I came up to him I saw that he was looking across the area railings into the windows of a room on the ground-floor which were only slightly above us. The curtains were not drawn although it was by now late in the evening, and since the chamber was brightly lit the scene lay before me with the clarity — though the similarity did not occur to me at the time for I had never been to the theatre — of a stage-setting. This was the more so since in my state of consciousness everything was heightened and sharpened. What I saw was evidently a cheerful and loving family sitting at their dinner: the father and mother, well-dressed and genial, beaming from the opposite ends of the table at two young people between them who were obviously their children — a young woman and a boy two or three years younger than I who were smiling across the table at each other.

Good things to eat covered the table in careless profusion. I saw in the centre the remains of a roast goose, and waiting on the sideboard at the back of the room were fruit-tarts, custards, jellies, oranges, chestnuts and hot-house fruits. Even as I watched a door opened and a pleasant-faced middle-aged woman in a clean white gown carried in a blazing plum-pudding which she elevated in state as she approached the table. Behind her walked a young maid-servant bearing upon a silver tray a steaming bowl of punch. The family clapped in delight and smiled at each other. I was transfixed by the mysterious blue flame that flickered from the pudding. And now I noticed the holly and mistletoe hanging up around the frieze. Of course! It was Christmas! Memories of Christmases long ago came flooding into my mind and whether it was that or simply the effect of hunger, I began to feel dizzy and had to clutch the railings for support.

As the pudding was ceremoniously placed at the head of the table the father rose, went down to the opposite end and kissed his wife. And then each of the parents kissed each of the children, and the brother and sister paid each other the same compliment. Then the father returned to his place and began to serve the plum-pudding.

Outside in the cold and darkness my companion and I stared at each other. Then he went up the steps and, to my surprise, instead of ringing the area-bell, pulled the handle beside the street-door. My dizziness was increasing as, still standing on the pavement and staring at the window, I saw the family look at one another in surprise as if wondering who of their friends would call at such an hour at Christmas-tide. But it was getting difficult to see now for there seemed to be dark shadows at the edges of the lighted frame through which I was observing the room.

I turned and saw the older servant open the street-door. I heard her speaking to the boy, though their words were a meaningless buzzing. I saw them both glance towards me. But after that I knew no more for the blaze of light from the windows suddenly darkened and a great black wave seemed to rush over me.

Some minutes must have passed, but I can say nothing about them for the next time I was aware of anything I found myself lying on the snow surrounded by the anxious faces of strangers. And yet they were not all quite strangers, for amongst them there were the faces of the family I had been watching: the mother and father, and the two young people, as well as their servants. The mother and the daughter had thrown shawls over their shoulders, but apart from that all of them were dressed as they had been in the room, and the snow was falling heavily upon them. Behind them I saw the face of the boy who had accompanied me there.

"Poor boy, he seems half-famished," the kindly mother said.

"Yes," said the young lady. "And starved with cold, poor creature. Just look at those thin clothes."

"We must do something for him," the mother said. "Why, he's hardly any older than Nicholas. What can we do?"

"We'll bring him in," said the father. "We can't leave him to starve. Especially not on this day of all days."

It was too much of an effort to keep my eyes open and so I let them close. I felt myself being gently lifted and borne up the steps. I opened my eyes and saw that I was being carried by the father and the older servant. As we reached the street-door I looked back and saw that the boy who had accompanied me there was standing at the bottom of the steps looking up at me with a strange expression. Was it wistful, or envious at seeing me about to be borne into that region of warmth and plenty while he was left unnoticed outside? No, it did not seem to be expressing either of those feelings.

"Thank you," I said. "Thank you." Then I looked at the father: "But please give that boy something, too. He brought me here. He has nothing either."

"Oh never mind about that," the father said. "He'll have his reward."

"Thank you for bringing me here," I said to him.

He was still looking at me with a countenance that I could not fathom. Suddenly he said quickly: "I'll come back to see how you are. That is, if I may."

Before I could answer I was lifted across the threshold, then carried through the hall into the chamber I had seen through the window, and laid on a sopha. My strength failed again and I was conscious only of many hands helping me, of faces that wore expressions of concern and solicitude. A glass of hot wine was put to my lips and I sipped a little of it, rugs were laid over me, a cool hand was laid on my forehead, and a bowl of something hot and thick was held before me. But I could not take any of it for the rapid change, the sudden warmth and light, the noise of voices — all these were too much for me. Again I fell away, this time as if tumbling into a well that seemed to have no bottom.

CHAPTER 70

There followed a period of confusion and strangeness when I could not separate waking phantasy from dream or either of those from reality. I was in a carriage travelling late at night, or I was on the heaving deck of a ship in a storm, or I was labouring through the snow with someone who seemed at first to be my mother but then wasn't and yet was somebody's mother, or I was back in the foetid, over-crowded room in which my mother had died; but always I was oppressed by fear that something terrible was going to happen, or had happened, or was happening. At other times I seemed to be in bed in a small chamber with a fire, but then the fire came leaping out of the grate at me and turned into a vast conflagration and I found myself fleeing through the smoke-filled streets of a burning city pursued by long shoots of flame.

Whenever I awoke it seemed that faces peered down at me, and hands reached towards me to stroke my face or rearrange my bed-clothes. Many of the faces I knew. My mother's countenance smiled at me often, but then the smile turned into a grimace of pain. At other times the faces of Mrs Fortisquince, of Mr Barbellion, of Miss Quilliam, of Sir Perceval, and of many others, appeared before me out of the darkness — as in a theatre when the lime-light is ignited in fierce flashes — changed from one into another, and vanished again.

Frequently the faces were those of the family who had so kindly taken me in, and yet there was a strange and persistent feature: that when they looked at me their faces were transformed before my eyes into bestial shapes: the father's nose grew outwards and thickened, the nostrils flattened and became the naked level holes of a pig's snout. The young woman's eyes narrowed into thin slits that were overshadowed by huge black eyebrows, and the paleness of her face became the pallor of a piece of marble.

A surgeon came many times. I knew he was a surgeon by the way he looked at me while he held my wrist. He had a cold, cruel face that frightened me, and I was most frightened when I saw him smiling thinly in my direction while he spoke to the mother and father.

And often there seemed to be other people in the room. Lizzie from the rookery came in carrying a tray and then turned into the middle-aged servant. Mr Quigg stood over my bed until I saw that he had taken on the appearance of the father. And once I was convinced that Mr Steplight (whom I knew to be Mr Sancious) came in with the father and his daughter, and looked down at me and nodded and then that all three smiled at each other. On another occasion the chamber seemed to be full of people dancing round my bed: I saw Lady Mompesson waltzing with Mr Beaglehole, the bailiff, while Barney led Mrs Purviance through a square dance, and Mr Isbister scraped wildly at a fiddle. There were more people dancing round the room than I could distinguish and the noise was getting louder and louder until it seemed that my bed floated off the floor and up into the middle of the chamber and then I remembered no more.

The most real-seeming visiter of all those whom I afterwards decided I had imagined, was a hideous little old man who came in with the young lady and grinned down at me and hugged himself with delight. With his waving arms and skinny, bent legs encased in tight pantaloons beneath a bulging paunch, he horribly made me think of a great blotchy white spider as he strode round the room in a kind of ecstasy of malevolent triumph.

Then at last I woke up one day and knew I was recovered. I found myself lying amongst the lavender-sweetened sheets of a bed with a bag of camphor hanging near my head in a cozy little chamber with a fire crackling cheerfully in the grate, where vinegar was being burned on a shovel. It was the room I had seen in lurid glimpses during my delirium. And on a chair beside the fire sat the young lady reading a book.

After some minutes she looked round and seeing me gazing at her with eyes no longer clouded by fever she exclaimed: "Oh thank heavens, you are restored!"

She was very beautiful, I thought, with her pale face, blue eyes, and glossy black hair in ringlets hanging down over the collar of her muslin morning-gown.

"Yes," I said. "I believe I shall be all right now."

"We have been so concerned about you," she said, leaving the chair and coming to sit on the end of my bed.

"You are very kind. But why have you been so good to me, a stranger?"

She smiled and said: "Must one have a reason for acting charitably?" Seeing that I was about to speak she went on: "But hush now, do not over-tax your strength. There will be time for questions later. Only tell me now, what is your name?"

"John," I answered. Then I added: "Or Johnnie."

"Only that?" she asked with a smile.

I was not strong enough to face the question of what I was going to tell these kind people about myself and my history: to decide which name to reveal was to choose whether or not I was going to deceive them.

"May that do for now?" I asked. "I am so tired."

"Of course," she said.

"And what is your name?"

"Emma."

"That's a beautiful name," I murmured as my tongue grew suddenly too heavy to speak. "And what is your second name?" I managed to ask.

"My father is Mr Porteous."

"Miss Emma Porteous," I said.

"Please call me Emma," she said.

"Emma," I murmured.

"Sleep now, Johnnie," Emma said gently, but her injunction was unnecessary and I remembered no more.

During the next few days Emma was always at my bed-side when I awoke, and it was from her hands that I took the nourishment — at first, bread soaked in milk and honey — that slowly restored my strength. Occasionally she was replaced by her mother, but one or other of them was always in the room so that if I wakened in the night I was sure to see her sitting by the fire and reading or doing embroidery by its bright glow. I was very affected by the fact that they took it upon themselves to attend upon me rather than leaving it to their maids. The older servant-woman, Ellen, fetched and carried, but apart from her I did not even see any of the other domestics.

As I regained my strength and was able to stay awake longer and converse at greater length, the different members of the family came to sit with me. Emma's father was grave and reserved and sat staring through his rather small eyes and pressing his thick fingers together nervously as if in search of topics, but I felt that he was trying to convey his goodwill and kind intentions even through his rather stiff formalities. (Later Emma told me that he was very worried about something involving his work.) His wife was very solicitous and talkative, and, to confess the truth, rather tiring. The boy, whose name was Nicholas, was very friendly but he was several years too young for us to be companions, and he quickly grew tired of my company. It was Emma whom I liked best, and it was she who visited me most often and stayed longest.

A couple of days after our first conversation, she said, as she handed me a glass of hot lemonade and barley-water: "I still don't know your second name, Johnnie."

I had had time to consider how I would answer this question. I had tried to overcome my distaste at the idea of deceiving people who had been so kind to a complete stranger, by telling myself that it could not matter to them what they called me, since they knew nothing of me. For I had argued to myself that a name could not be a lie under those circumstances for it made no statement which was contrary to the truth. My name was what I chose to be called by, so why could I not choose a new name from now on? And yet reason it as I could, I could not avoid the feeling that it would be a poor return for their kindness.

Yet I also knew that it might be dangerous for me to admit that my name was Clothier, for I knew from my mother's account that it was well-known — not to say notorious — in London's commercial world. Therefore, if by confessing to it I revealed my connexion with the Clothiers, I would have to ask these good people to keep my identity secret, and in order to explain the necessity of that I would have to tell them a great deal of my story. Partly because I did not wish to think about it and partly because I was not sure what effect it would have on its hearers, I was reluctant to do this.

All this time Emma was looking at me curiously.

"I have had so many different names in my life," I said, "that I hardly know which is my real one."

"How very mysterious," she said. "What are they?"

I hesitated: "Will you accept one of them — Cavander?"

I had used this name once or twice, having remembered it from the time of my escape from Quigg's farm.

"Do you mean," she said gravely, "that that is not your father's name?"

Seeing me frown involuntarily, and, as I thought, misunderstanding why, she said quickly: "Or at least, not the name you were given at your baptism?"

I nodded.

"Do you not trust me?"

"Pray don't think that," I cried in dismay. "Not when you've been so kind to me — who have no claim upon your generosity. It is simply that if I told you my real name I would have to explain to you a great deal besides."

"Then why not do so? Are you afraid it would bore me? How foolish you are," she said, smiling. "I would like to hear your story, however long it takes."

"You are very kind," I said, feeling myself on the verge of tears. "But it's not only that."

"Ah, I see," she said sympathetically. "I have been very obtuse and selfish. It would distress you to narrate it." Then very gently she asked: "You have been betrayed by people you trusted, have you not?"

"Yes," I said. "But why do you say that?"

"Because I believe you like me, and yet I can see that you are unsure whether to trust me."

"I do like you," I cried. "And I trust you. I would trust you with my life. You and your parents have taken me in and tended me though I am a complete stranger to you."

She pressed my hand with a smile and said: "I am glad you like me. But let me reassure you since you are so mistrustful. A few days ago you asked me if there was a reason why my parents had taken you in. I will tell you now." She paused and her face grew grave: "Between my birth and Nicholas's, my parents had another child. A boy. They called him David. He was a sickly baby and ... " She broke off for a moment. "He would have been about your age and I know they think of him often. I believe it was partly for his sake that they acted as they did the other night."

I saw that tears were glistening in her beautiful eyes. But suddenly she glanced up and said with a smile: "Is that a selfish enough motive to satisfy your cynicism and misanthropism?"

I reached out to lay my hand on hers and said: "I have made a poor return for your generosity and trust. I will tell you my real name, though I hate it so much it pains me to speak it. It is Clothier."

It seemed to me that she registered a tremor of recognition.

"Do you know it?" I asked.

"I believe I have heard the name," she said. "But no more than that."

"Please mention it to no-one apart from your mother and father," I said. "I will tell you why I ask this when I feel strong enough."

"I promise. But will you tell me now, if even that will not cause you too much pain, where are your friends? Your father and mother, above all?"

"My father … I do not know. My mother is dead."

"Oh Johnnie," she said. "I am very sorry. Was this recently?"

"Yes," I said, "very recently."

"Do you mean, in the last few weeks?"

"Almost," I replied. "The 12th. of November last."

"I am sorry. I am afraid I have caused you pain. But tell me, if it would not distress you, where did this happen?"

"Here in London."

"I mean," she said, "in which parish? Where is she buried?"

The question was gently spoken but it brought back with overpowering vividness the dark room in the stifling court and the dank little square with its stinking graveyard.

"I cannot say," I said and began to weep.

"Never mind, never mind," Emma said, stroking my hand. "It was foolish and thoughtless of me to ask. There will be plenty of time for explanations when you are stronger."

I squeezed her hand. My tears had tired me and I was soon asleep, my hand still clasped in hers.

During the next fortnight or so I grew much stronger, until at the end of that period Dr Alabaster, the surgeon who had attended upon me every few days, declared that I would soon be ready to leave my bed. The family visited me as before, and Emma spent much of the day with me, either reading aloud, working while I dozed, or talking to me. A few days after our last conversation, I told her that I felt able to narrate the story of my life, and when I said that although I would find it easier to confide in her alone, I saw no reason to withhold my story from her parents, we agreed that she would recount it to them.

So during the week or so that followed I told her everything — except that I had decided to omit certain passages in my mother's life — and found her to be a good listener as well as a very acute one. I described my early years with my mother in Melthorpe and the onset of our money problems which arose, I explained, from my mother's trust in her attorney, Mr Sancious, who had conspired to cheat her.

I told her of the codicil which my mother had inherited from her father, and I explained its importance to the Mompesson family. I described my mother and Mr Fortisquince's attempts to get from them the money they owed her in the form of an annuity on their estate; and when I gave her an account of the way Sir Perceval and his wife had received my mother on the occasion when we had gone to their house, Emma was very indignant against them.

Though I described our flight to London, the rebuff we received from Mrs

Fortisquince, and the betrayal of our secret address to the bailiffs by Bissett, I did not go into much detail about our period with Mr and Mrs Isbister, obscuring entirely the nature of his nocturnal activities. Then I narrated our attempts to earn our living with Miss Quilliam, our descent into the bitterest poverty, our attempt to sell the codicil to the Mompessons, the misunderstanding about Miss Quilliam and Mr Barbellion, and the way we were then deceived by Mrs Fortisquince into conveying it into the hands of the false Mr Steplight and through him into the possession of our enemies. Emma seemed quite upset when I explained that these last were my father's family, the Clothiers, and particularly so when I elaborated upon their reasons for wanting me dead: that now that the codicil was, presumably, before the court, if I were to die while Mr Silas Clothier was alive, he would immediately become the owner of the Hougham estate. In order to make all this clear, I summarized what I had learned from my mother's account: my grandfather's obtaining of the codicil in collaboration with Mr Clothier, the events leading up to my parents' marriage and the murder of my grandfather, and my father's incarceration as a criminal lunatic.

Emma was very disturbed by this and now professed that she understood perfectly my reluctance to reveal my name. When I went on with my narrative she became very distressed as I described the school that Mr Steplight had taken me to, although I mitigated its horrors and omitted any reference to Stephen Maliphant and the treatment that had led to his death. Another omission I made was of all references to the situation in which I had found my mother on my return to London, merely saying that I had found her ill and in great poverty after being treated cruelly by Mrs Fortisquince and Mr Sancious and imprisoned in the Fleet. I was touched by how closely Emma followed my account for when I mentioned that my mother had been refused help by Sir Perceval, she expressed herself as much puzzled by this last circumstance as I was, since she had grasped the fact that it was — ostensibly, anyway — in the Mompessons' interest to maintain my mother's life as the Huffam heir. I found I was only able to give a very brief account of my mother's death, and my evident emotion affected my confidante very deeply.

"And where was this?" she asked.

I told her the name of the festering little court.

"And did you have to go to the parish for the burial?" she asked sympathetically.

"Yes, I did," I said, trying not to remember the circumstances.

"And under which name did you have her death registered?"

As I looked at her now she gazed steadily into my eyes and said: "I ask you that because of an idea that my father has had about how your safety might be assured which I will let him explain to you himself."

Feeling ashamed of myself, I said: "You are all very much better to me than I deserve. The answer to your question is that I gave the parish-clerk the name of 'Mellamphy'."

I went on with my story, describing how I had made my way to the "carcase" and lived with Barney and his gang until my gradual realization of what they were involved in led to my discovery that they did not stop even at murder. Emma was horrified by this, and also as baffled as I was by the discovery that Barney was the housebreaker from Melthorpe all those years ago.

Finally, I described how I had made my escape from the "carcase", gone to my grandfather's house and been refused entrance by old Mr Escreet, and had been found there by the boy who had brought me to Emma's house.

I should make it clear that I did not tell my story as coherently as I have summarized it here, for often one part of it required an explanation which carried me forward or backward out of chronological sequence. The part of it which interested her most — apart from my mother's death and burial — was my mother's account of the night of my grandfather's murder. We went over these events a number of times and she supported my suspicion that the will mentioned by my grandfather might have been the motive for his murder.

"What a pity you no longer have that letter of his," she said, and I was moved by the way she entered so passionately into my situation.

The day I finished narrating my story, she said to me: "My father would like to talk to you tomorrow about your future. Do you feel well enough?"

I said I did and when she had gone I reflected on how much lighter my burden of knowledge and responsibility felt now that I had shared it with a sympathetic listener.

When Emma came into my room the next day, she was accompanied by her father. While he pulled chairs up to my bed for himself and his daughter and solemnly seated himself, I reflected that he was the only member of the family I could not quite like. Throughout the interview that followed he spoke coldly and pompously, while Emma kept smiling at me on the other side of him, as if to represent the warmth and kindness that he felt but could not outwardly manifest.

"My daughter," he began, kneading his podgy fingers together, "has advised me of everything you have told her, and I have been considering by what means you may best be protected from those who might wish you harm. It is evident to me that much depends on the various suits being pursued in the Court of Chancery. Though," he said with a sneering smile, "as a humble attorney I am not qualified to penetrate the mysteries of Chancery. For that reason I have taken the liberty of consulting a solicitor, Mr Gildersleeve, who is a trusted friend of mine, and of laying before him the circumstances of your situation — of course, in the utmost confidence."

"You are very kind, Mr Porteous."

"Not at all, not at all," he said, seeming truly embarrassed by my gratitude. "Mr Gildersleeve's opinion is that now that you are — in the legal sense, at least — an orphan, the most effective way for you to be protected from the machinations of other parties is by going before the Court of Chancery itself and seeking its guardianship."

Go before Chancery! I felt a thrill of excitement at the prospect of penetrating to the very centre of the mysteries which had surrounded me all my life.

"What must I do?" I asked.

"The procedure, I understand, is very simple. You merely affirm your identity by an affidavit — in this case a verbal one — which must be supported by the evidence of witnesses. And they should be easy to find."

"But do you not think, Mr Porteous, that I am safest if my enemies believe me dead, as presumably they will if I simply disappear?"

"It does not matter what *I* think," he replied rather distantly. "Mr Gildersleeve believes that the situation is as I have had the honour to state it."

"But how could they find me now? No-one knows I am here."

"Are you sure of that?" he said. "My daughter tells me that the captain of the gang you found in that half-completed dwelling in the Neat-houses was the man who broke into your mother's house many years ago. Can you be sure that that was merely a coincidence? And if it was not, does it not suggest that the man may be an agent of your opposites? And in that case, you cannot be sure that he will not find you again."

I had to admit the force of this and concede that it might be safer to expose myself before the Court. But then I thought of an insurmountable obstacle:

"But will it not cost a great deal of money?"

"I will pay Mr Gildersleeve's fee," Mr Porteous said. "You have no need to concern yourself about that."

At this I felt my eyes begin to water. As if discomfited by this, Mr Porteous moved his chair a little further back and coughed into his handkerchief.

"You are kind to me," I stammered out. "You are like a family to me."

As if to relieve his feelings, he reached into his pocket and pulled out a sovereign which he handed to me with considerable solemnity.

"We *are* your family now, Johnnie," Emma said, pulling her chair forward and clasping my hand. She turned to her father: "May I tell him now, father?"

Mr Porteous nodded and she went on: "If you agree, Mr Gildersleeve will ask the judge to make you a ward of court, giving custody of you to my father and mother. They will adopt you, Johnnie, and then you will really be my brother. And you will be safe."

"*If* I agree!" I exclaimed.

Emma kissed me and Mr Porteous took my hand and awkwardly shook it with a rather uncomfortable expression as if embarrassed by the emotion he felt.

Mr Gildersleeve was to come the next day, they told me, in order to explain what would be required of me. When they had gone I lay unable to sleep for excitement, feeling how very strange it was suddenly to acquire a complete family. I was very fond of Emma already, I was sure that Nicholas and I would become friends, and Mrs Porteous seemed a thoroughly good-natured and motherly being. Yet I felt a vague disquiet all the same. I decided that it was because I found Mr Porteous cold, despite his generosity, and I could not readily accept the prospect of his having authority over me in that mysterious capacity of "father".

The next morning I was allowed to get out of bed and receive Mr Gildersleeve seated in a chair by the fire. He came at about ten, accompanied by Emma and Mr Porteous, and was revealed to be tall and thin with a sharp-featured face. He was near-sighted and had frequent recourse to an eye-glass which he wore upon a black riband that hung down over his pear-shaped form. He would raise it and peer through it at me and then mutter: "Most remarkable!" If he had not been a Chancery solicitor, I would have believed that he was distinctly slow-witted.

"So you are the Huffam heir," he said and held out his hand. "I have followed the suit, as have all those in my branch of the legal profession, with considerable interest for many years."

My visiters seated themselves around me and Mr Gildersleeve began: "The Master of the Rolls will be the presiding judge. First he will need to satisfy himself that you are indeed who you claim to be, and to this end we have subpoenaed a witness of unimpeachable respectability to support your affidavit."

"May I ask who is it, sir?"

He referred to his papers: "Mrs Fortisquince, the widow of a respected attorney."

"And you have already sub-poenaed her?" I asked in astonishment.

"Yes, several days ago," Mr Gildersleeve replied.

I glanced at Emma who said: "You see, Johnnie, my father was so anxious to set this in train that he went ahead as soon as he had heard enough of your story from me to know what needed to be done."

I said nothing, and Mr Gildersleeve continued: "Now, you must be very careful to utter not a word to the Master about being in danger from anyone."

"But surely that is the whole reason why I am to be made a ward of court, is it not?"

Mr Gildersleeve and the other two exchanged glances.

"Yes, so I understand," the solicitor said. "But the law does not recognise the same criteria of relevance that we do. We cannot make allegations against another party without positive proof. Otherwise we will simply confuse matters, and we don't wish to do that, do we?"

Somewhat puzzled, I nodded my head in agreement.

"Very well," said Mr Gildersleeve. "Now when we've established your mother's death — a mere matter of form, I assure you, once you've proved it upon oath and witnesses have testified to the same effect — then we will ask ... "

"Excuse me, please, Mr Gildersleeve," I interrupted. He paused and stared at me as if in amazement that I should dare to halt him in the middle of his disquisition. "I don't understand why this has to come up. I would really prefer it not to."

"You would prefer it not to," he repeated monotonously. "Master Clothier, I think you fail to understand that we are dealing here with the law. Your likes and dislikes have no place in a court. Your status as an orphan has to be proven. Do you understand that?"

"Yes," I said meekly while Emma made a sympathetic face at me.

"Now, with your permission," said Mr Gildersleeve, "I will continue. Once we have established this, then we will ask the court to make you a ward, granting custody to Mr Porteous. Now what is important is to make it clear to the Master how happy you are here. You are, are you not, happy here?"

"Yes, indeed. Happier than for a very long time."

"Excellent. Then I suggest you refer to Mr and Mrs Porteous as your uncle and aunt, in order to show the court how much you consider yourself to be one of the family. Do you understand?"

"Yes, I do and I will."

"Then that is really all I have to say to you now, young gentleman. I will see you in court soon."

We shook hands and, to my relief, Mr Gildersleeve left with Mr Porteous.

"Well, Johnnie," cried Emma clapping her hands, "in a few days you will be my brother!"

I smiled back at her but when I was left alone a little later I could not prevent a certain feeling of foreboding from overshadowing my mind. Events seemed to be moving very rapidly and with a logic that I felt was eluding my grasp.

And so not long afterwards the day came that had been appointed for my appearance. Since it had been decided — and I fully concurred — that Emma alone should accompany me, a man-servant was assigned to attend us in order to carry me, if I should need help. I was helped into warm outdoor clothes and, with the assistance of Frank, whom I had not seen before, boarded a hackney-coach with Emma.

We drove through streets which seemed alarmingly crowded and noisy after my period of seclusion, and passed districts that brought back painful memories: Holborn, Charing-cross, and then Westminster. We pulled up before a dingy little door in St. Margaret-street and by this undistinguished means entered an outlying building of the Palace of Westminster. Following Mr Gildersleeve's directions, Emma made herself known to an usher and we were led by him through a series of dark passages and gloomy little courtyards with dripping walls covered in green slime. All around us were the sounds of demolition and construction, for at that time Sir John Soane's handsome new edifice was building on the site of the warren of ancient galleries that had for so long accommodated the Court of Common Pleas and the Courts of the Exchequer.

Eventually we gained a draughty lobby where we were met by Mr Gildersleeve who was unblushingly clad in the most extraordinary costume that ever a sane man wore outside a masquerade. It was a billowing black gown with gold and purple stripes, the most inconvenient sleeves imaginable — for they hung almost to the ground — and a flowing white cravat. On his head was a grey powdered wig, and on his legs and feet knee-breeches and shoes with huge gold buckles.

We waited while Mr Gildersleeve held mysterious conversations with gentlemen similarly attired, which involved a great deal of head-shaking and narrowing of the eyes accompanied by the minutest possible of nods. After a few minutes an individual wearing an even more preposterous costume and carrying a kind of golden rolling-pin appeared and led us along a further and more bewildering sequence of ill-lit corridors, as if bent upon confusing us completely as to our whereabouts. At last, however, he ushered us into a small and must-smelling ante-room, and, while Emma and I waited here, Mr Gildersleeve went into what I took to be the further chamber.

Some half an hour later, we were summoned by another usher and led through the same door as the solicitor. To my astonishment, I found myself in a huge building, with a hammer-beam roof high above us, like an enormous barn, so large that I could not see its opposite end in the gloom of a wintry afternoon. Emma whispered that this was Westminster-hall and I felt a thrill of excitement at the realization that I was to find Justice in this revered building where Charles himself had stood trial.

In the corner nearest us were a number of benches and chairs facing a raised platform. Upon this a gentleman whom I understood to be the Master of the Rolls was seated on a high black wooden chair which looked most uncomfortable, and the individual with the golden rolling-pin now placed himself at a little desk before him and laid this object on its surface. The Master was wearing a costume in which it was so impossible to believe that he had knowingly attired himself, that it seemed that it was only by a polite conspiracy among his observers that no-one drew his attention to it. Its principal features were a capacious scarlet gown covered in embroidery executed in gold thread, and a huge wig enveloping his neck and shoulders that constantly threatened to obscure his features if he turned his head too quickly. His gravity clearly derived from the difficulty of keeping all of these garments in their proper place and it amazed me that he had any attention left to bestow upon the legal issues before him.

Emma and I were directed to the front row of the ranks of heavy old chairs facing the Master. There were a number of individuals clad in a variety of strange costumes seated around us who were whispering or rummaging through papers or reading enormous tomes or taking notes or arriving or going out, and among them I saw a figure that was familiar to me: Mr Barbellion. Noticing me looking at him, he directed towards me a tiny bow of his head and I responded in as close an imitation as I could manage.

As I gathered self-possession enough to look around me at the ancient pannelled walls and the high carved wooden chimney-piece in whose grate a vast coal-fire slumbered, I became aware that in the opposite corner at this end of the vast hall there was another and similar court-session taking place. (In fact, it was the Court of the King's-Bench.) I saw the candles and could hear the murmur of voices, while people came and went in the gloom. It all reminded me of nothing so much as a huge school-room with different forms being conducted simultaneously.

The Master and I were introduced to each other by Mr Gildersleeve and the old gentleman made much of seeing the Huffam heir at last.

"Do you know," he asked me, "that the suit began when my father was a very young man? In fact, he could not have been much older than you are now. What age are you?"

I told him and he wrote it down, remarking apologetically: "You must call me 'm'lud', you know." Then he went on: "I am very sorry not to see you in better health. Do you feel well enough to take part in these proceedings?"

"Yes, m'lud. I have been ill, but I am recovered."

The Master exchanged a grave look with Mr Gildersleeve who made a kind of courteous moue as if to qualify what I had said.

"Now," the Master said, "you are to be entered upon oath. Do you understand what that means?"

I assured him that I did and the formality was completed.

Then Mr Gildersleeve rose, sweeping his robes about him, and said to me precisely as if we were complete strangers: "Will you tell the court who you believe yourself to be: when and where you believe yourself to have been born and who you believe your parents to have been."

"I am John Clothier, sir," I began. I told him the date of my birth and that the place was Melthorpe. Then I went on: "I was brought up there by my mother and we lived under the name of Mellamphy which I thought was our real name, but much later my mother told me it was assumed. Her father, she told me, was Mr John Huffam of Charing-cross, London."

"And what name appears in the parish-register as that of your father?"

"Peter Clothier, sir."

"All this, m'lud," said Mr Gildersleeve, "can be confirmed both from documentary evidence and by a witness who is at hand now."

"Who is the witness?" the Master asked.

"Mrs Martin Fortisquince, m'lud. The lady is connected with the deponent and his late mother and was introduced to the deponent some three years ago by his mother."

The Master nodded and looked at Mr Barbellion who said: "M'lud, the party whom I have the honour to represent accepts without dispute that the deponent is Master John Clothier, formerly known as Master John Mellamphy. Indeed, we had ourselves assembled evidence to prove this, and I am grateful to my learned friend for doing something which appears to be in the interests of my clients rather than his."

At this he and Mr Gildersleeve bobbed at each other in what I can only call a kind of barbed bow. What Mr Barbellion had said confirmed my belief that the Mompessons needed me to remain alive, but I was puzzled by his suggestion that it was not in my interests that my identity be proved. Could this be an allusion to the danger I was in? It seemed to me strange that he should raise this issue.

"Then it appears, Mr Gildersleeve," said the Master, "that neither the documents nor the witness are required."

"M'lud, I am very pleased," said Mr Gildersleeve, expressionlessly. He shuffled his papers as if to mark a transition and then said: "I now ask the deponent to describe the circumstances of his mother's death."

This was a shock and I was only with difficulty able to stammer out the bare facts while Emma squeezed my hand in sympathy.

"You recorded your mother's death with the parish clerk?" Mr Gildersleeve asked. "Under what name?"

I told him, wondering that once again I had been asked this question.

Mr Gildersleeve turned to the Master: "M'lud, I ask the court to accept this evidence of the death of Mrs Peter Clothier, the daughter of Mr John Huffam."

The Master addressed Mr Barbellion: "Are you content?"

"In this case, no, m'lud, I am not since so much hangs upon it."

"Very well," said Mr Gildersleeve. "Let the first witness, Mr Limpenny, be called."

To my amazement the parish-clerk was brought in looking very much smarter than when I had seen him in *déshabille* at his breakfast-table. I turned to Emma in surprise but she did not look at me.

In answer to Mr Gildersleeve's questions the clerk confirmed what I had said, and once Mr Barbellion had cross-examined him without establishing anything more, he was released. Then the second witness was introduced, and this was Mrs Lillystone, the woman who had laid my mother out. The same ritual was gone through, and it was so extremely distressing to me to have to live through it again — this time under the gaze of strangers — that I covered my face with my hands.

When the woman had withdrawn, Mr Barbellion said: "M'lud, my party will accept this evidence of the death of the holder of the Huffam entail and its consequent devolution upon the deponent, Master John Clothier."

"Very well," said the Master, writing something down. "In that case, the story of the Huffam entail begins a new chapter. And let us hope that it will prove a happier one than any that has gone before."

Now Mr Gildersleeve gathered his robes behind him and said, raising his voice and dragging out his words like a parson intoning the service: "M'lud, I move that the court now order that the infant, weakened as he is by illness in mind and body, be made a ward and assigned to the tender solicitude of the lady and gentleman by whom he was lovingly tended when he came to them destitute and ill and whom he now knows and loves as his own family and has learned to call his uncle and aunt."

I deeply resented the reference to my illness having weakened my mind and wondered that legal gentlemen were allowed to insult those whom they were paid to defend.

As Mr Gildersleeve sat down the Master said: "This appears eminently suitable. Mr Porteous is a most respectable gentleman, and, I am given to understand, a trusted officer of the distinguished banking-house of Quintard and Mimpriss."

At this, however, Mr Barbellion rose: "M'lud, my party opposes this motion in the strongest possible terms."

Emma's hand tightened on my own.

"I cannot say I am surprised, Mr Barbellion," said the Master. "However, be good enough to tell me on what particular grounds you found your objection."

At that moment I noticed that Mr Gildersleeve turned and gave a signal to an usher who immediately left. Before Mr Barbellion, who had risen, could begin to speak, Mr Gildersleeve stood up and said: "M'lud, I ask your indulgence and that of m'learned friend for interrupting him, but I do so in order to ask leave of the court to permit Master Clothier to retire."

"I don't see any necessity for it, Mr Gildersleeve," replied the Master. "Pray continue, Mr Barbellion."

Mr Gildersleeve sat down and glanced angrily at Emma. Just as Mr Barbellion began to speak I noticed the usher return with Frank.

"M'lud," began Mr Barbellion, "under less extraordinary circumstances neither the party I represent nor I myself would seek to remove an infant from the custody of a family to whom it was attached by both affinity and sentiment."

At that moment Frank and the usher reached us but Emma waved them away. I was trying to follow what Mr Barbellion was saying for I was puzzled by his opening remarks. However, Mr Gildersleeve stood up again and Mr Barbellion stopped, stared at him in amazement, and then turned to the Master with his eyebrows raised as if dumbfoundered at the extraordinary effrontery of his colleague.

"Beg pardon, m'lud," Mr Gildersleeve boldly began, "but as I had the privilege of explaining to your honour before these further instructions began, the deponent has been grievously ill and his mental faculties are not fully restored. It is most desirable that he be permitted to leave the court now."

So that was what he had been saying to the Master! Altogether, I did not like the way things were going. And something that I had just heard was nagging at my memory. And how was I "attached by affinity" to the Porteouses?

"This seems an entirely reasonable request," said the Master. "Do you object, Mr Barbellion?"

"To the contrary, m'lud. For as far as my party is concerned, the continued good health of the residuary entailee is crucial to their interests, and that is why the issue of his guardianship is so important."

"Very well, Mr Gildersleeve. Master Clothier may leave the court. But before he departs I wish to establish the infant's own wishes."

He looked at me: "Tell me, Master Clothier, are you content to be legally entrusted to the guardianship of the family you are at present being looked after?"

I said nothing for I needed time to think about what I had learned.

"Well, young man," said the Master after a few moments, "are you happy to have your uncle take custody of you and be given the authority over you, until your majority, of a father?"

"He is not my uncle!" I cried. "And I do not wish it."

"Johnnie!" Emma hissed in my ear. "What can you be saying?"

"M'lud," said Mr Gildersleeve, merely raising one eyebrow with a smile of complicity for him and a frown in my direction.

The Master nodded: "What objection can you have?" he asked me.

"They mean me harm!" I cried. "I can't tell why, but I don't trust them."

Emma turned to me a face that I will never forget: cold and hard and burning with anger.

"You have carried your point, Mr Gildersleeve," the Master replied, nodding gravely. "This is most lamentable. The boy may withdraw."

Mr Gildersleeve nodded towards Frank and the usher and they immediately seized me by the arms, pinning them behind my back. Seeing what they were about I began to shout and struggle, but Frank laid his hand across my mouth as he picked me up, put me across his shoulder, and carried me swiftly towards the door while the usher followed, gripping my legs.

In the middle of all this I heard a few phrases of Mr Barbellion's address: "... highly unusual circumstances ... the closeness of the blood relationship ... a potential conflict with other interests ... "

Just as we got to the door the beadle who was standing there opened it. The two men carrying me started to go through it but Frank, who was in front, stopped when he found that someone was already coming in. The usher who was behind him could not see what was happening and, in the belief that the delay was caused by my resisting, pushed hard against me and Frank with the result that there was an undignified *mêlée* and we all came to a stop. The newcomer who had caused the confusion was a young man and from over Frank's shoulder I found myself face to face and on a level with him: it was Henry Bellringer!

He stared in amazement and, unable to speak, I struggled as much as I could in the hope that he would recognise me, even though half of my face was concealed.

"What the devil is going on?" he demanded.

I heard Emma say behind me: "Hurry. What is the delay?"

Henry looked at her and she quickly lowered her veil. "Why," he said, "fancy seeing you here, Miss ... "

"Be quick, Frank," she cut in.

Obedient to her command, the man-servant stepped rudely towards the door so that Henry was forced to stand aside, pressing himself against the jamb to let us by.

Just as we passed through the door I heard Mr Barbellion's voice for the last time: "... exposes that individual — and, indeed, the other members of his family — to invidious suspicions in the event of a melancholy occurrence that we must all hope will not take place, but of whose likelihood we have seen evidence today."

This was all I heard, for a moment later we were in the ante-chamber and the beadle had closed the door behind us.

The usher led us back the way we had come and I was bundled into the hackney-carriage which had been waiting for us, and held inside it by Frank on the journey home. When he removed his hand from my mouth I had nothing to say, and Emma, whose face had lost the expression I had seen so briefly in court, did not speak either except to sigh reproachfully: "John, John, after all we have done for you!"

I had much to occupy me as I tried to make sense of the day's occurrences.

Why had Mr Gildersleeve been at such pains to emphasize how ill I had been and to suggest that I was mentally deranged? Why had the judge taken up the usage that Mr Gildersleeve had suggested, and referred to Mr Porteous as my uncle? And what was the meaning of Mr Barbellion's strange words as I was being borne out? Had I made a terrible mistake to repudiate the generosity of Emma's family so openly, and thereby been guilty of the most culpable ingratitude?

When we got home Emma instructed Frank to take me to my room and put me to bed. He did so, removing my clothes — though not before I had managed to secrete in my hand the sovereign Mr Porteous had given me — and leaving me in my night-shirt. I heard him locking the door of the room as he left. Quickly, in case it was taken from me, I concealed the coin in the hem of my night-shirt.

All the remainder of the day I lay revolving in my head the words and actions I had witnessed that morning. I wished I understood the legal procedures of the Court of Chancery so that I might know what had really been going on. I thought of Henry. Had he recognised me? I wondered what he was doing there, and if it could be that he was a Chancery student. In that case he could have explained some things that puzzled me: why had the Porteouses been so anxious to take me before Chancery? And why were the circumstances of my mother's death so important?

Gradually a certain suspicion crept into my mind, one that accounted for so much that when I looked back over the scene before the Master and interpreted it in the light of this supposition, everything fell into place as part of the design. And yet it was so improbable, so conspiratorial, that the mere fact that I had entertained it alarmed me. How could I conceive such a thing! Perhaps I really was less well than I wanted to believe.

BOOK V

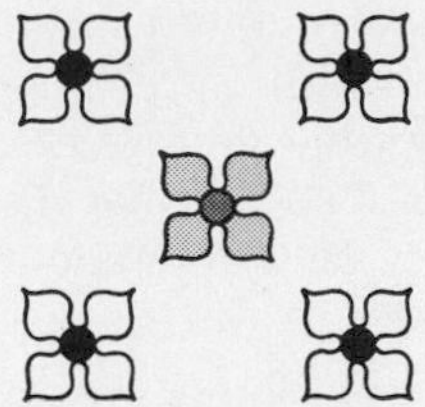

Friend of the Poor

CHAPTER 71

Once again the scene is the best parlour of No. 17, Golden-square. Mrs Fortisquince has a visiter, to whom she is saying angrily: "If only I had known before! This will have disastrous consequences."

"You should have trusted me. Tell me the whole story now."

"Trust you! Why should I trust you over this, Mr Sancious, when the advice you gave me on my own affairs has turned out so badly? I have lost every penny that I invested."

"And so have I! So has everybody. The very Bank of England came close to shutting its doors last Christmas!"

"That's all very well but it was I and not you who lost everything on those bills of Quintard and Mimpriss that you persuaded me to buy!"

"Only because I had no money left to purchase them on my own account, my dear madam, for I had already lost everything! Otherwise I would have plunged as heavily as you. I was assured of their worth by a source that I had every reason to believe. And to tell the truth, I now believe I was lied to, and I am sorry for it. I have been entirely frank with you, Mrs Fortisquince, but you have not been so with me. There is much that you have kept from me. I can't bear duplicity."

The widow flushes and stares at him haughtily: "Kindly explain your meaning."

"I have recently learned that the boy was followed to Barnards-inn," the attorney says. "Don't look so innocent, Mrs Fortisquince. I know that that is where Henry Bellringer has his lodgings!"

"Followed? Who followed him?"

"Ah-hah, you must allow me my little secrets if you are going to have yours. Now, what are you keeping from me?"

"Nothing," says Mrs Fortisquince. "It is a coincidence, that is all. A rather extraordinary one, but of no further significance."

"But you see, madam," Mr Sancious says, "I do not believe in mere coincidence. There are hidden webs connecting you to the boy and to old Clothier and to Bellringer that I don't entirely understand, though I comprehend more than you imagine." She stiffens at this and he goes on: "Oh yes. You see, when you warned me not to mention my acquaintance with you to that delightful old gentleman, you alerted me to a connexion between you. I fancied that that wretched creature, Vulliamy, might be able to illuminate it. I was able to do him a favour and in return he undertook to give me the information I sought. I have just met him and he was very communicative. Very communicative indeed."

The lady stares at him with cold fury.

"I'm sure you'd like to know what he told me." When she makes no answer he goes on: "Well, first he informed me that his employer has been requiring him to follow me. Consequently he knows about your connexion with me and has known about it for some time."

Mrs Fortisquince gives a cry and covers her mouth with her hand.

"I feared this intelligence would dismay you," the attorney continues. "For you see, Vulliamy explained the reason for that, too. I know the whole story, Mrs Fortisquince. Everything about your motives that puzzled me before is clear to me now."

She glares at him so remorselessly that at last he has to cast down his eyes. "You should have told me earlier," he says. "You should have trusted me. Even now, it's not too late for us to reach a new understanding."

The young widow stares at him speculatively.

CHAPTER 72

At the usual hour for my supper that evening the door was suddenly unlocked and Emma came in carrying my evening meal. I was surprised by this attention for since I had grown so much stronger, I had usually had my meals brought by Ellen. Emma smiled at me in quite the old way and sat on a chair beside me as I ate the thick mutton broth on a tray set before me.

"John," she began, "although my father and mother are very hurt, I have persuaded them that you spoke as you did because you have not yet recovered fully."

She paused but I said nothing.

"And while you were sleeping," she continued, "Mr Gildersleeve came to tell us that after we had left, the Master made the order assigning custody of you to my father. So you will really be my brother now. Isn't that wonderful?"

I nodded without looking at her and laid down the spoon, for I had little appetite.

Emma noticed this: "Come," she said, "do try to eat."

I shoved the bowl away.

"Why, you've left half of it!" She pushed the tray back. "You must eat in order to get well and strong again."

"I can't eat any more."

Emma seated herself on the bed and picked up the bowl and spoon. "Let me feed you as I did when you first came to us. Don't you recall how helpless you were?"

At this reminder of past kindness I felt an impulse of guilt, and as she smilingly held the loaded spoon towards me I forced myself to swallow. But my gorge rose and I shook my head.

"Very well," said Emma, standing and picking up the tray. Just for a moment I thought her face looked as it had at that terrible instant in the court-room. Then she smiled and was her old self again: "Let me prepare you a tumbler of camphor-julep to help you sleep."

"Thank you," I said. "That would be very kind."

When she brought it a few minutes later I had to disappoint her once again for I could not manage more than a few sips. However, when I promised to drink it later, she left it by my bed, kissed my forehead very sweetly, blew out the candle, and left the room. To my surprise, I heard her lock it behind her.

Sick at heart as I was, the thought of consuming anything revolted me, so when all was quiet I got out of bed with the intention of pouring the drink away, for I did not wish to wound Emma further. The window was locked so I went to a corner of the chamber where no carpet covered the boards, dipped my fingers in the tumbler and began to scatter the drops on the floor. As I did so the strangest thing happened: the liquid seemed to be red and slightly sticky. And yet in the queerest way I knew that it was not blood at all, for it was as if I was both dreaming and still wide awake. Now as I made my way back to the bed I became convinced that the room — though it looked as it had always done — was actually the one in which my mother died. And the bed-covers that I pulled over myself were the bundle of rags under which I had lain during those terrible nights at Mitre-court a few months before.

As I lowered my head and closed my eyes I found myself looking out through a window at a vast dark mass stretching towards the horizon and dotted with tiny yellow points of light. In the foreground the spires of buildings were etched against the pale magenta sky and I realized that I was almost on a level with them, hundreds of feet above the ground. Suddenly, impossibly, a shape appeared at the window and as I felt a swelling sense of terror, slowly defined itself as a pale face — remote, marble-like, watching me with empty, transparent eyes. Just as my terror became too great to bear, the scene changed and I found myself hurried through a series of visions of haunting beauty alternating with scenes of horror, so that I was swept from heights of terror to sweet agonies of reminiscence for something lost that I could not quite recall.

Once I found myself riding in a swaying carriage through the streets of a great city in a fiery dawn with the blazing red disc of the sun glaring above the horizon. When I put my head out of window and looked up, I saw dark billowing clouds blowing in great swirling eddies around the buildings which reared monstrously high beside me so that their tops were lost in the smoke, and I realized that the city was being engulphed in a vast conflagration. Opposite me in the carriage was a female figure who, though her veil was lowered so that her features were obscured, seemed to be strangely familiar. As I stared at her the veil grew darker and darker until her whole head was a black shadow. But now as the carriage lurched round a corner the sun caught it from a new angle and the outline of a scull began to appear. I did not want to know that face and I screamed and screamed and it seemed to me that I awoke and found myself in the bed-chamber in Mr Porteous' house, and yet it was not that familiar room for now the walls began to turn on their axes and the fire came leaping out of the grate and I was plunged back into a maelstrom of terrifying visions.

CHAPTER 73

For how long these phantastic scenes succeeded one another I do not know, but I believe they held possession of me all night. When I awoke the next morning — as exhausted as if I had not slept at all, my mouth dry and my head aching — I lay fearfully wondering if I were losing my mind, and trying to remember if I had ever heard that such dreams were a sign of the onset of madness, though at the same time I was haunted by a kind of nostalgia for some of what I had experienced.

Although it was still very early and the house was not yet stirring, I suddenly thought I heard a noise outside and without quite knowing why I did it, I half-closed my eyes to feign sleep. The door slowly opened and Emma's face appeared round it. To my horror, her expression was precisely as it had been at the moment in court yesterday when I had refused to accept her father as my guardian: the features cold and hard and her eyes narrowed. When she had crossed to my bed she picked up the empty tumbler, and in a voice cold enough to match her expression she said: "Are you awake?"

Taken unawares and afraid that she might have glimpsed my eyes between the half-closed lids, I answered: "Yes."

Was it my imagination, or did she seem to start at my voice?

"How are you?" she said tonelessly.

"Not very well."

Suddenly she exclaimed: "Well, what do you expect if you will not eat, you stupid little boy."

In that instant, as I looked at her and heard those words spoken in that tone, something I had long half-known rose to the surface of my mind and coalesced with my dreams of the night before: the young lady in the carriage, the veiled face, the angry words. *It was Emma who had tried to abduct me all those years before!*

Now I believed that I understood everything. All that had puzzled me about yesterday's transaction in court — Mr Barbellion's words about the "affinity of blood and sentiment" and the Master's reference to Mr Porteous as my uncle — now fell into place: *Mr and Mrs Porteous were my uncle and aunt! Daniel Clothier and his second wife!*

My horror was too profound to be dissimulated and I saw that Emma had perceived that some monstrous revelation had come upon me. For a moment she gazed at me and then she smiled or, rather, tried to for it looked to me to be a sickly imitation: "Have you guessed the real reason why we have been so kind to you, Johnnie?"

I nodded.

"Then say it."

"Your father is Daniel Clothier, my father's elder brother."

"Yes," she said. "We are your real family. My father took his present wife's name when he married a second time. So you see, I am something much better than your adopted sister: I am your real cousin!"

While she leant forward and kissed me, my mind was in turmoil. So she was Emma Clothier! That was how Henry Bellringer had been about to address her! (Though I couldn't imagine why he should know her.)

"You must be wondering why we kept it from you," she went on. "I will explain everything and then you will understand. But my father and mother should be here. I will summon them. How glad they will be to know that we may now tell you the truth."

Still smiling she went out. It was some time before she entered, with her parents behind her, crying: "Isn't it clever of Johnnie to have guessed!"

"Well done, old fellow," said my uncle, striding forward and holding out his big pink hand. I took it, remembering with an inward shudder what my mother had written about him. "You're a sharp one and no mistake," he added.

His wife hugged and kissed me and I wondered whether she knew as much as the other two. "Doesn't he look surprised!" she cried.

"You must be wondering why I changed my name," my uncle said, looking at Emma. "It's because I was so disturbed by my father's treatment of my brother."

"You mean my father?" I said.

He glanced at Emma.

"And so you see, Johnnie," she said, taking the old lady's arm, "my mamma is not my real mamma but my papa's second wife."

Her moving story of a brother who had died was an invention!

"But why did we keep this from you, you must be asking," my uncle exclaimed.

I nodded.

He turned to Emma again and she said: "We were going to tell you very soon, but we agreed to wait until you were stronger. Perhaps it was wrong of us but we were afraid of the consequences since you were so weak then."

"You were right, you were right," I murmured.

"You do understand what we were afraid of, don't you?" Emma said.

I nodded my head. I only wanted to be left alone to think about all this.

"We guessed that your poor mother had prejudiced you against us," Emma said. "And so it proved when you told me all the unkind, misguided things she had written about my dear papa."

Here was a new aspect of the affair: Emma had sat for hour after hour listening to my story and expressing horror at my relation of the behaviour of her father, and then gone into another room and conveyed the whole of my account to him!

"Your mother was sadly deceived," my uncle said. "We will explain all of this to you when you are fully recovered."

"But you must be wondering how it can have come about," Emma said, "that you have been reunited with us. How was it that of all the houses in London you chose to ask charity of, it should turn out to be your long-lost and unknown uncle's!"

I shook my head in bewilderment.

"It was Providence," my aunt cried. "The Lord be praised!"

"Yes, Johnnie," Emma said. "Extraordinary as it seems, it was mere coincidence that brought you to our door. It's the sort of thing that you expect to find only in a novel — and only when you know the author has been too idle to work it out any better."

Coincidence? No, I could not believe that. If there was an Author arranging my life, I could not think so ill of him.

"I guessed the truth very soon. Do you remember how I trembled when you told me your name was 'Clothier'?" Emma asked.

I nodded, recalling how I had described it as the name I hated above all others.

"I guessed then who you might be for my father speaks often of his poor brother's wife and her child. I dared not give voice to my suspicions for I feared the effect of the shock upon you of finding yourself among your 'enemies'." I blushed and she went on: "You had no reason to disbelieve what your mother told you. But we will explain it all to you and then you will understand the truth and no longer be frightened and mistrustful. Remember, Johnnie, we have all the time in the world."

"We should leave him now. He is looking tired," my aunt said.

"Yes, I should like to sleep," I said.

"Of course," said Emma. "It's still very early. In an hour or two I'll bring you your breakfast."

They withdrew, locking the door behind them, and left me in an anguish of doubt and fear. Could I believe that they had dissimulated their identity in order to protect me? Was everything that my mother had written about my uncle mistaken? I had to decide, for if she had been right then I was in grave danger for I assumed that the codicil had been laid before the Court of Chancery, and if it was now in force, then the only bar to the Clothiers' (or, rather, Porteouses') inheriting the Hougham estate was the continued existence of the Huffam line. And this, surely, was the explanation for what had happened during my appearance before the court: my mother's death had been proven in order that my status as the Huffam entailee might be established! And it was to make certain of my identity that it had been mentioned in court that "Peter Clothier" appeared in the Melthorpe register as my father.

So only my life stood in the way of Silas Clothier's immediate inheritance of the estate! Moreover, since he had to be alive at my death and must be a very old man by now, then his heirs — my uncle and Emma — must be impatient to see that condition fulfilled. No wonder that Mr Gildersleeve had laid so much emphasis upon my state of health! Nor that Mr Barbellion had raised objections to my uncle's being made my guardian!

How fortunate it was, I reflected, that my dreams had alerted me. Then suddenly I understood why I had had those visions: something had been put in my food! My heart began to thump as I remembered what Miss Quilliam had once said about laudanum: that in very small quantities it brought profound sleep, but in slightly larger doses it stimulated vivid and extraordinary phantasies, and that in still larger quantities it was a poison that was undetectable. Had Emma hocussed my supper and the sleeping-draught? And I had lived only because I had consumed so little of them? Or was I going mad that I should suspect such a thing?

Just as I reached this juncture, there was a gentle tap upon the door. I heard the lock turn almost noiselessly and Emma entered, smiling with her old composure, and bearing a platter of porage.

"Have you been sleeping?"

I nodded.

"Now you must eat," she said, making as if to hand me the platter.

I shook my head quite involuntarily for I was determined to eat nothing in that house. What the implications of this were I needed time to think about, for I could only see my way ahead clearly so far as that.

Emma looked at me sharply: "Well, I will leave it here for you," she said, placing it upon the table beside my bed. "Poor Johnnie," she went on. "What a shock to discover your wicked family so suddenly."

She spoke so naturally and so comically that I smiled. How much I wanted to believe that I could trust her and that all my imaginings were the consequences of my illness!

"Sleep again and try to eat when you awake," she said solicitously. "I will leave you now."

When I was alone again I directed my attention to another puzzling aspect of the business: how had I come here? I could not accept the explanation that had been offered, and now that I hunted back through the complex chain of events in which I was entangled, I remembered that it was the boy who had found me at the old house at Charing-cross who had led me here. At the time he had brought something to my remembrance, and as I tried to recall what it was a number of memories came flooding into my consciousness. Among them was the image of a weary walk through the snow from house to house. Where had I heard of this? Another picture swam into my mind: a fat, cheerful woman sitting in a warm kitchen. It was the kitchen of the house in Melthorpe! *The woman was Mrs Digweed! The boy who had led me here was her son Joey!*

In attempting to resolve one extraordinary coincidence, I had encountered another. And beyond this I could not advance for I could not understand why or how Joey Digweed could be connected with my uncle. It was like that other apparently inexplicable coincidence — that Barney was the housebreaker. Suddenly I wondered if there could be a connexion between that coincidence and this one, for I recalled how I had decided that Mrs Digweed's visit to my mother's house must have been connected with the earlier burglary. Although I could not disentangle them now, there must be secret connexions between all these events which proved that there was a conspiracy at work against me. Here was the consequence, not of blind chance, but of a hidden design. And so I knew that it was no mere accident that had brought me here, and therefore that Emma and her father were lying to me.

I was reassured by the logic with which I had arrived at this conclusion. I was not mad: there really was an extraordinary plot to entrap me. Whatever the truth of the matter, I knew I had to get away from these people as soon as possible.

I got out of bed and crossed to the window which I found to be secured by a bolt that I could not move. Moreover, since the chamber was on the first floor, I could see no way of getting down to the ground, and even if I could, I would be in a well-like little court from which there appeared to be no way out except through the house itself.

I had to get away soon for I was determined to eat nothing. And yet I could not let my relatives suspect that I feared I was being poisoned, and so I lifted the carpet by the bed and concealed the greater part of the food beneath it, treading it flat to make the lumps disappear. Then I got back into bed and although during the remainder of the evening the door opened and someone came in several times, I feigned sleep, not daring even to half-open my eyes.

All the time as I lay listening to the noises of the house settling down, I reviewed the practicalities. My clothes had been taken from me on my return from the court yesterday, I was still weak from my illness, and I had no money except for the sovereign. So how far could I hope to get barefoot and clad in only a night-shirt on a cold night in January? Indeed, where could I flee to, for I knew of no-one to whom I could go for help? Yet I had no choice, for to stay there was certain death.

I resolved to wait until about four o'clock when the house would be most deeply asleep and the dawn only a few hours away — for the cold of the streets would be perilous. And so as I struggled to stay awake, I listened to the clock on the landing counting out the hours: midnight, one o'clock, two o'clock.

CHAPTER 74

At last I heard the clock strike four. I collected and folded some of the blankets in order to drape them around myself, feeling no compunction at the theft. To my relief (and surprise), the door had been left unlocked for once. I stole onto the landing which was in complete darkness, and very slowly and cautiously I crept down the stairs. There was darkness here, too, except for the glow of the pilot-light of the gas-mantle in the hall, and knowing that the servants slept at the top of the house and the family on the first and second floors, I felt relatively safe down here. Since the back-door would lead me merely into the rear court, I had to make my escape through the street-door. I gently drew back first one bolt and then the other and the safety of the street seemed within my grasp.

Then out of the corner of my eye I suddenly became aware that a door had opened beside me and a figure was standing a few feet away.

"Is this how you express your gratitude?" said my uncle. "Has your mind been so poisoned against us?" He reached up and turned on the gas above us. As it flared up the shadows danced on his face. "How fortunate that I was working late and heard a noise."

"You weren't!" I cried, suddenly understanding how naif I had been. "You were waiting for me. Why, you had no light in that room or I would have seen it beneath the door. And that's why you left my door unlocked!"

Knowing that it was in vain, I pulled at the street-door which remained immovable.

"The key is in my pocket," my uncle said laconically.

Despairingly, I hammered with my fists at the door and shouted: "Help me! Let me out! Call the watch!"

My uncle moved forward with an oath and seized me. The noise I had made had awoken the house, or at least those in it who had been sleeping. As lights appeared upstairs and voices were heard, I kicked at my uncle's legs and screamed. My only hope now was to enlist the sympathy of one of the servants. Glancing upwards, I saw Emma and my aunt standing on the stairs in their night-attire. Behind them were Ellen — and I wondered that I had ever thought her face genial — and a young maid-servant whom I had only glimpsed before. The man-servant, Frank, came up from the basement fully dressed at this moment and, apparently taking in the situation at a glance, crossed to my uncle and helped him to restrain me.

"Into the back-room!" cried my uncle, and the two men started to drag me towards the rear of the house.

"You odious little monster!" Emma cried. "After all we've done for you!"

"Don't blame him, my dear," said her father. "Can't you see that he's not responsible for his actions?"

"No," I cried. "That's not true. I'm not mad." I addressed myself to the maid-servant who was staring at me in terror. "They're trying to kill me!

They tried to poison me! Please! Go to a justice and tell him what you have seen."

In a moment I was thrust into a chamber that led off the back-passage. In the light of the candle that someone was holding at the door, I had time only to see that it was bare of furniture or carpets, that it had no fireplace, and that there were iron bars on the inside across the single window which must look into the back-court. Then the door was slammed shut and I was left to the cold and darkness.

I realized that by trying to escape I had walked into a trap. The room was extremely cold and since I had dropped my blankets in the course of the scuffle at the door and there were no bed-clothes, I faced an uncomfortable and possibly even dangerous night in nothing but my night-shirt. I lay down on the bare boards, drew up my legs and folded myself into the smallest possible shape against the chafing cold, not daring to let myself sleep. They were trying to kill me. But I would not die.

Faint signs of dawn were manifesting themselves when the door opened and Emma appeared, accompanied by Frank and carrying food and drink. Fixing her eyes on me in the strangest way as if divided between fear, disgust, and pity, she set the dishes on the floor.

"I'll eat nothing unless you eat it, too," I said. "And drink nothing but water."

"I must hope you will get well," Emma said, "and see how absurd and unfair these suspicions are."

"And I'm very cold," I went on.

"Father says he dare not let you have either blankets or a fire."

She went out, leaving Frank to secure the door after her.

An hour or two later — but it became difficult to measure time — she returned with her father. They looked at the untouched food and drink and he said: "You are killing yourself. And all because you have been misled by that stupid and vicious creature, your mother."

"Don't speak of her like that!" I cried.

"I think you should know the truth," he said gravely. "It was your mother who was responsible for all the evil that came upon my wretched brother Peter. She set out to gain power over that innocent, weak-headed creature."

"Stop it!" I shouted. "I won't listen to your lies!"

I tried to put my hands over my ears but I could still hear his words: "She had already tried it with me, but I was too many for her. So she captivated Peter instead — heaven knows, he was such an innocent that it was not difficult — and gained complete power over him. What was her motive? I have often wondered, but I suppose she and that father of hers wanted a share of my father's wealth."

"Be silent!" I screamed.

"We're telling you this for your own benefit, John," Emma said. "The truth may be harsh, but you must learn it."

As I gazed into that pale face that I could still see was beautiful though now I saw nothing but hatred in it, I could not decide if she really believed what she was saying. It seemed horribly as if she did.

"Your mother and her father," my uncle continued remorselessly, "believed they could use my brother for their own purposes, but they were too clever. They drove him mad by trying to poison him against his own family. And it was because of that that he turned against your grandfather and murdered him."

"I don't believe he was mad!" I cried. "That was a wicked lie. Mr Escreet told my mother that what my father said about the quarrel being a charade was true."

"Told your mother," my uncle repeated with a sneer. "I warn you, you should not believe everything that woman said. For all I know it was she who persuaded Peter to the murder. Heaven alone knows for what motive. But no act of that woman's could surprise me." His eyes narrowed and he looked at me speculatively: "There's something I think you should know. I don't imagine you realize that Fortisquince ... " He broke off and, glancing towards his daughter, said: "But that can keep for later."

"No," Emma said with a kind of triumphant smile. "Tell him everything."

And so now it was that he told me something about my mother — or, rather, about my father — that I could not believe and yet could not dismiss from my mind.

Before he had finished, I threw myself at him and he pushed me away so that I fell on the floor. I lay there weeping with rage and despair while Emma and her father, smiling at me, went out.

Could any of these things be true? I felt the ground beneath me dropping away as I thought about them. My mother a deceiver? A liar? Something worse, even? Concealing beneath an appearance of trusting guilelessness a deeply duplicitous nature? It was true that she had kept from me the amount that she had invested in the fatal speculation. And she had bought that piece of embroidery without telling me. And later on she had become more and more suspicious and secretive, but that was surely the effect of her circumstances. As for what Mr Porteous had hinted at ... I could not bring myself to think about it.

At some time later that day — I have no means of telling when — Frank suddenly unlocked the door and threw a bundle of blankets into the room at me. I pulled them around myself as he secured the door again. By now my mind was beginning to wander and I was increasingly unsure where I was or what was happening to me. I only knew that I was trapped and it was now that the idea came to me that I should make enough noise to draw the attention of people outside the house. And so it was while I was holding onto the bars of the window and screaming at the dirty panes through which I could see nothing, that the door opened again and Emma's father entered. He was accompanied by Dr Alabaster and two strange gentlemen, and Frank walked behind them with a tray of dishes.

"Please help me," I said. "They mean to kill me."

As I spoke I was aware that my speech was slurred and I had difficulty keeping my gaze on their faces for they seemed to be great pale moons and I could hardly make out the features or distinguish one from the other.

"What makes you say that?" one of the strange gentlemen asked kindly.

"They are trying to starve me with hunger and cold."

"Are those not blankets you have around you, John?" asked the stranger. He indicated the tray that Frank was placing on the floor: "And food before you?"

I tried to explain that I had only just been given the blankets but I could not muster the words.

"The food is poisoned," I said. "I dare not eat it."

"Come, don't be foolish. Have something to eat, Johnnie," the man I had believed to be my uncle said in a tone he had never used to me before.

"I won't unless I see you eat it first," I said.

Mr Porteous looked at the others and they nodded gravely.

"Very well then, Johnnie," he said with a humouring smile; "if it will set your mind at rest, I will show you it is perfectly safe."

He spooned some of the food into his mouth and then poured himself a tumbler and drank it off.

"Oh, of course these are safe enough now!" I cried. And seizing the food and drink I consumed them with the ravenousness of a hungry dog while the gentlemen watched gravely.

"Now, Master Clothier," Dr Alabaster began.

"Don't call me that!" I cried.

"Why not? Is it not your name?"

"No, I hate that name!"

"Very well then, John," Dr Alabaster resumed calmly; "these gentlemen are going to put some questions to you. Will you try to answer them?"

I nodded.

"Will you tell us," the second stranger began, "who this gentleman is" (here he indicated Emma's father) "and how you came to be in his house?"

"They say he is my uncle," I said, "but I don't know what to believe. And I don't know how I came here. There has been a conspiracy against me. It goes back many years, you see, to the time when our house was broken into when I was a small child. The man who did it is living in a carcase by the Neat-houses. I believe he delivered me here somehow."

I trailed off and though I could see the two strange gentlemen turning to each other, I could not make out their expressions for their faces were mere blurred patches.

The first one now spoke: "My question is very simple. I want you to tell me how much it comes to if you add one shilling and eight-pence to six shillings and three-pence ha'penny and then take away four shillings and nine-pence three-farthings."

My head ached and I could hardly stand. I merely shook my head and said wonderingly: "I don't know, sir. But I'm not out of my wits. I know other things. I know that is a chair" (pointing to it) "and that is a man" (pointing to Frank).

"He can only just distinguish them," the gentleman said, shaking his head.

"I think we have seen enough," said the second gentlemen. "The order will be a formality."

"I expected no other conclusion," said Dr Alabaster.

"I hope, Mr Porteous," the second stranger said, "that you will not deal harshly with your maid-servant. She did what she believed was right."

"Rest assured," Mr Porteous replied. "I think I am known to be capable of magnanimity."

"It is fortunate," said the first gentleman, "that you have so safe a chamber as this: the bars on the window, the lack of a chimney-piece — all of these ensure that the poor lad cannot escape and can do himself no harm."

"That is due to a most melancholy circumstance," replied Emma's father. "This was the very place in which we had to confine my poor brother, this boy's father. The son has inherited his father's affliction."

"No," I cried. "That is not true! You're lying. Or else you were lying just now."

They shook their heads at each other and went out, and then the door was closed and locked. So this was the room from which Peter Clothier had made his escape to my grandfather's house!

I remember the rest of the day and the following night as a succession of spells during which I lost and regained consciousness — I cannot call it sleeping and waking. I ate no more and felt myself growing weaker and more fevered.

Then in the midst of the darkness of oblivion I recall lights flashing suddenly into my eyes, and someone seized me and when a foul-tasting strip of cloth had been tied around my mouth, my arms, almost jerked from their sockets, were thrust into something so that I could not move them.

I was picked up and carried through the house and flung into a carriage where I found myself pinned helplessly between two strong men. As the vehicle moved off, I struggled and tried to scream but the bandage over my mouth prevented me.

I was struck across the head and a voice that I recognised as Dr Alabaster's said: "Hold your noise, Clothier, and it will go the better for you."

I sat quietly after this. As the carriage turned into a broad, well-lighted street that must have been the New-road, I saw the face of Dr Alabaster gazing stonily through the window. I turned to look at the man on the other side of me and to my horror I recognised him: it was the tall man who had jumped into the carriage on that far-off occasion when Emma had attempted to abduct me, and who had later taken part in the attack on my mother and myself on the way back from the pawn-shop!

CHAPTER 75

It came to me then that I was indeed insane. To find coincidences and connexions everywhere was proof of it. At this realization, all power of resistance was gone and I reflected that it was as well that I was being taken where I was. Indeed, there seemed to me to be an irresistible inevitability in my being delivered over to this place: it was my destiny towards which my whole life had been moving and I felt a kind of relief that it had at last been attained.

After some time the man whom I had recognised broke the silence with an unpleasant chuckle: "This is in the way of being a regular branch of the family trade, ain't it, sir?"

"Aye," said Dr Alabaster. "And this one has inherited a kind of reversionary interest."

They both laughed and no more was said until after a long time the coach turned in through the gates that led to a gravelled carriage-drive. Already the night-sky was faintly suffused with light and against this I caught a glimpse of the outline of a large house. It had a strange appearance: like a wall-eyed dog I remembered seeing once, for the windows on the upper floors were whitewashed so that it was impossible to see in or out.

The vehicle stopped and I was bundled onto the gravel, picked up and dragged rather than led through the vestibule and into the entrance-hall, still with my arms secured behind my back.

Dr Alabaster went off without ceremony and his assistant was joined by a burly, ugly man who stared at me with a sneering smile as if I should know him. And now as I looked at his small squinting eyes, his eyebrows that seemed to be permanently raised as if in scorn of everything he saw, and his square flat face that was exactly like a red brick, it came to me that indeed I did know him: he had been the companion of the tall man in that attack! To judge from the keys that hung from a chain round his waist, he fulfilled the function of turn-key in this place.

I was now gripped by the shoulder and pushed before these two along a dark, stone-flagged passage at the end of which we entered a large room. It was the men's night-ward and at this early hour the patients were being awakened and dressed. I saw around me faces indicating all varieties of degeneracy, idiocy and mania: faces hardened by ill-usage and suffering, or broken by it, or borne up against it by a passionate sense of justification, or merely staring vacantly. Several were, like myself, wearing strait-waistcoats. I searched for a single face in which I could discern signs of intelligence and humanity and saw not one, until just at the end of the long room I caught the gaze of an old, white-haired man sitting on his low bed who seemed to be regarding me with an expression of interest and pity.

Then we were out of the room again and after walking down another corridor and descending some worn steps into a kind of cellar, we stopped before an iron door. The turn-key brought out a huge key from his chain. A moment later the great barred door swung creakingly open and I was pushed in.

I could make out nothing at first — except that there was deep straw on the floor for I felt it under my feet — since I was in absolute darkness, save that there was a tiny grating high up on one wall through which a little pale light crept. In a moment the door was swung to and locked behind me, but the two men remained for a moment watching me through the narrow grille on top of the door.

"Don't get too near," the turn-key said. "Mind how long the chain is."

"What an affecting scene," said Dr Alabaster's assistant. "Like the last act of a play."

They moved off still laughing and joking together. As silence succeeded their departure I realized that there was something in the darkness at the opposite end of the cell for I heard a faint rustling of the straw. I strained my ears and thought I detected the sound of regular breaths being drawn. I felt very afraid. I could not tell if it were an animal or if so, of what kind, and since my arms were still pinned behind my back I was helpless.

Now that my eyes were becoming adjusted to the gloom, I made out a shape against the far wall. Something was squatting on the floor. Now I saw that it resembled a human being. I heard the clinking of metal and saw that it was secured to the wall by a chain around its neck.

Slightly reassured, I took a step closer and the creature turned its face towards me and pressed itself back against the wall with its mouth hanging open and its tongue lolling out. I saw the thickly-matted hair and beard that ran together and almost covered the face, the wild staring eyes that seemed not to know which part of my visage to look at. And to my horror I recognised the face, recognised it despite the hair and the fierce grimace, recognised it from an image that had been engraved upon my inward eye from earliest childhood. Yes, the soft brown eyes and delicate features that I had stared at so long and so often as if searching in them for the meaning of my own life, were apparent in the face that now gibbered at me in the gloom of the cell: this wretched mad creature squatting in its filth amidst the straw, bore the countenance that I knew from the miniature on my mother's locket.

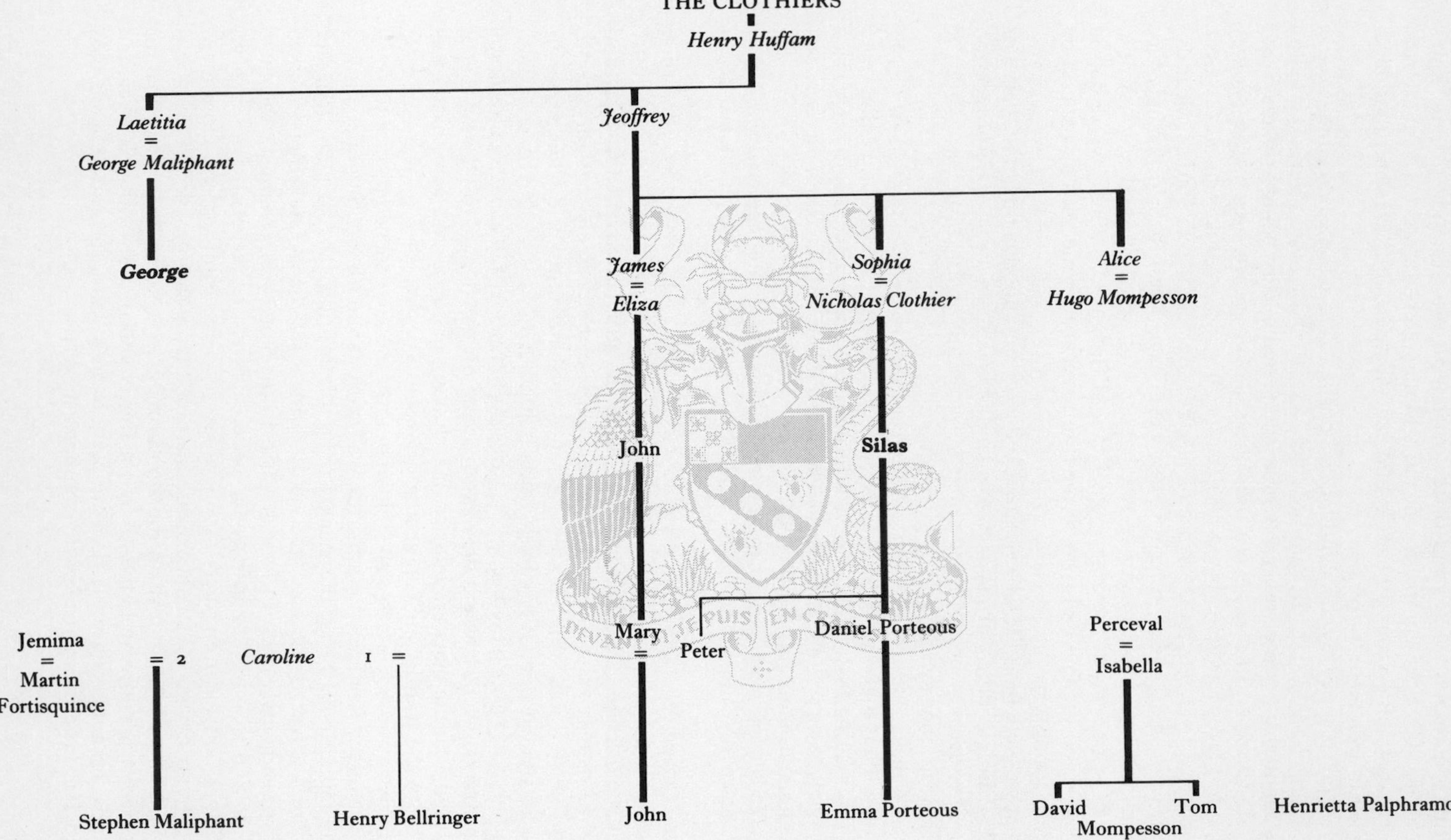

Characters who never appear directly in the narrative are in *italics*. Those who might possess the estate if Jeoffrey Huffam's suppressed codicil were in force appear in **bold** typeface.

PART FOUR
THE PALPHRAMONDS

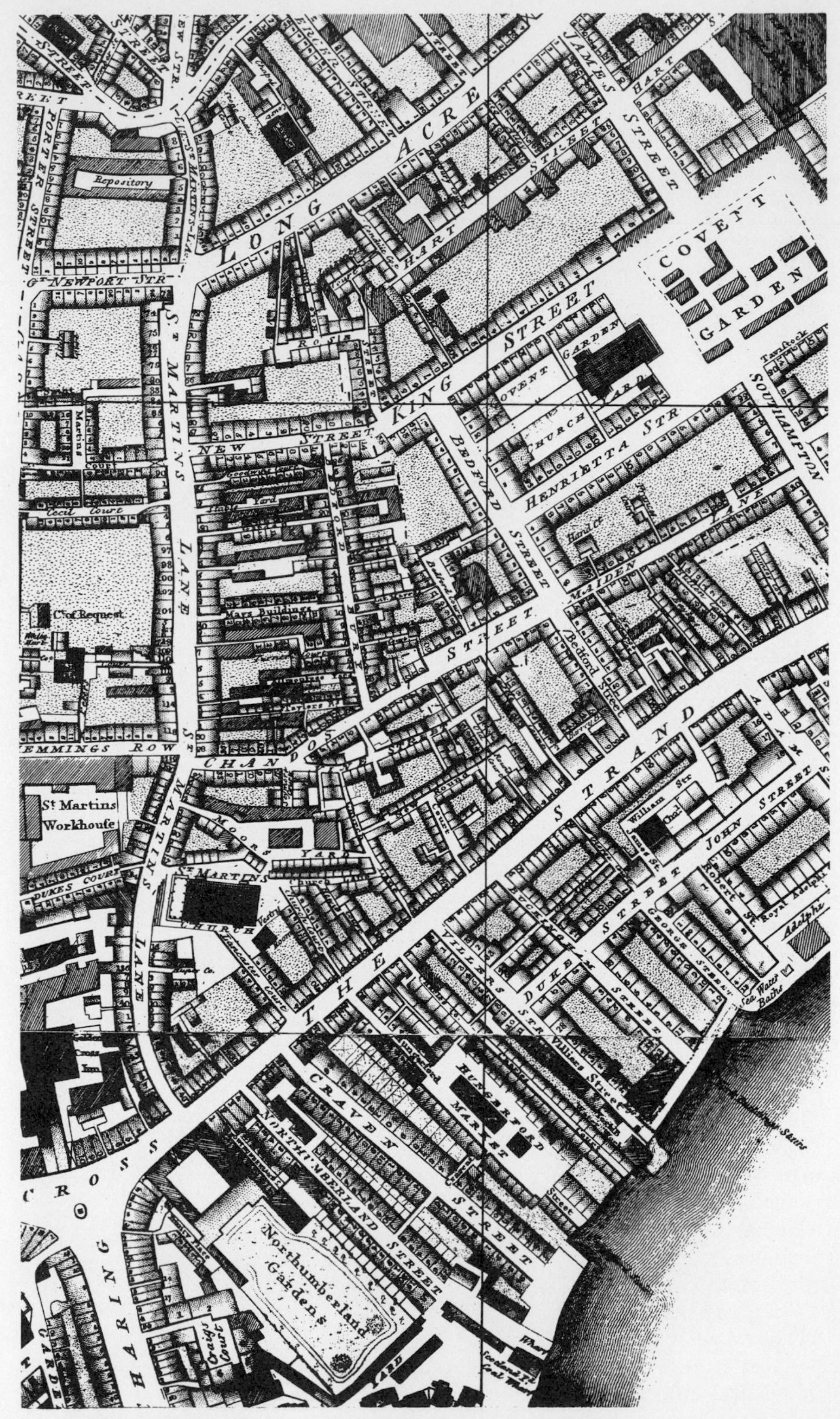

CHARING CROSS AND COVENT GARDEN (Scale: 1″=100 yards)

The top of the page is North

BOOK I

The Best of Intentions

CHAPTER 76

I invite you to enter in imagination the Great Parlour of the house in Brook-street and conceive how it must have been.

The elderly baronet is reclining upon an ottoman in the Drawing-room and addressing his heir, while his wife looks on from a sopha by the window:

"Outrageous! Absolutely outrageous! Almost as bad as that other rascal."

"Your father means that your conduct is only a little less deplorable than that of your brother," Lady Mompesson says calmly. "And less excusable, for your father and I hold him barely responsible for his actions."

"I give him up entirely," the baronet exclaims. "Entirely. He is being dismissed his regiment in disgrace. Never has a Mompesson ... "

He breaks off and after a moment his wife continues:

"Something will have to be done with him. And whatever it is will cost money. You appear to have no conception of the gravity of the situation. We are getting more and more deeply into debt."

"Going entirely to pieces! Damned Jews!"

"Nobody will take your father's acceptances," Lady Mompesson translates; "for our credit is destroyed now that the codicil has been laid before the court and we are threatened with the loss of the estate."

"Damnable bad news from Assinder, too."

"Ah, Assinder," David begins and his mother glances warningly at him.

But it is too late.

"I won't hear any more of that!" the elderly baronet cries. "He's the nevy of a man who served me and my father for forty years! And he's done damn' well by me, too!"

"He has succeeded admirably in bringing down the poor-rates," his wife says conciliatingly; "for he has largely excluded the settled poor. And the enclosure of the common land has been successful."

"That may be so, Father, but Barbellion ... "

"I know what Barbellion thinks," Sir Perceval shouts. "And your mother." He glares at her. "But it's nonsense. I'd trust him with my life."

He pauses and regains his breath.

After a moment, Lady Mompesson says equably: "Leaving that question aside, the fact is that he has estranged the chief tenants and in many cases their rents are gravely in arrears." Before her husband can protest, she turns to her son and goes on: "That is why your father's affairs are in so sad a state."

"And you're making 'em worse!" the baronet cries. "Spending your time and my money in the lowest gambling-hells. (Like that one that was robbed the other day. And serve its patrons right! Damn' fool pastime.) Hate to think how much you've squandered there. Now, tell me frankly, how much are your debts?"

Mr Mompesson looks at his mother and she purses her lips.

"A little over two thousand pounds," he answers.

The baronet looks somewhat mollified on hearing this figure: "Well, that's bad but it ain't impossible. There is only one thing for it: you must marry."

"The very course I have been thinking of myself, sir."

"Very well. But you know whom I am referring to."

"But Father, as I said the last time we spoke of it: I need a bride with ready cash. And I believe I have found one."

"I have told you before, the first priority must be to retain the estate."

"But not if we can't afford to keep it, Father. What would it matter if we lost the land as the price of remaining afloat?"

"Dammit, sir!" the baronet cries. "Have you no pride of family? Mompessons have owned land down there for hundreds of years."

"Oh come, Father. You speak of pride, but you know the truth. We acquired the estate by very dubious means. Your grandfather got that miserable creature, James Huffam, into his power and helped him to cheat his own son of his inheritance."

The baronet turns purple with rage and while his wife angrily signals to her son to leave the room, this is perhaps a good moment for us, too, to withdraw from this domestic scene.

CHAPTER 77

Through the long hours of darkness that followed I watched the wretched creature across the cell from me as I tried to make sense of what was happening. So this was the Refuge mentioned in my mother's narrative!

I thought of the procession of years — more than my lifetime — that he had passed here. It was a long time before it occurred to me that I was locked up with the murderer of my grandfather — since any hope I had nurtured that he might be innocent had been dispelled by the sight of that wild countenance — for this creature, now whimpering and huddling itself against the opposite wall, appeared to present no danger to anyone except perhaps itself.

For the first hour or so my cell-mate shook his chains as if trying to escape, but he was so firmly secured that he could hardly move. Then he set to moaning and rubbing his head against his upper arms which was all he could reach, constrained as he was by the links, and after some time the terrible idea came to me that he was weeping. It occurred to me to attempt to speak to him, but here a difficulty arose: I did not know how to address him.

Eventually I said simply: "Do you understand me?"

At my words he pressed himself back against the wall, staring at me in terror and trying to shield his face. And it was long before he was quiet again.

The long night dragged by. There were noises from elsewhere in the house for I heard a thin wailing sound that was so unrelenting that it might have been the wind — except that I believed it was a calm night.

So little light reached the cell that it was difficult to know when the dawn had arrived, but at what I took to be an early hour, Dr Alabaster came to the grille accompanied by the turn-key who had brought me there the night before.

My poor fellow-inmate cowered back at the sound of the mad-doctor's voice: "Good morning, Master Clothier."

I crossed to the grille and peered through it at the sallow features of Dr Alabaster.

"Don't call me that!"

"I trust you passed a pleasant night," he went on; "reunited, after so long a separation, with your esteemed parent." He held a lanthorn up to the grille so that it illuminated my face: "But I see that you appear tired. My fear is that he may have kept you awake with his eloquence. You must have had a great deal to talk over together. Has he told you of your distinguished grandfather — who I believe died before you could have the pleasure of making his acquaintance — and of his own affection for the gentleman and of its practical expression?"

He motioned to the turn-key to unlock the door and as it swung open he made a mock rush towards the chained creature who started back in terror. Without thinking I hurled myself at our tormentor, butting with my head since my arms were secured. The other man, however, pulled me away and hit me in the face so that I fell stunned onto the stone-flagged floor whose thin covering of straw gave little protection.

"Be careful not to mark the body, Rookyard!" exclaimed the doctor, brushing down his coat with a glance of deep resentment towards me. "I was warned that he was violent. We may have to use the Tranquillizer or the crib."

Rookyard smiled reflectively.

"Put him in one of the low grates," said Dr Alabaster. Then he said to me with a thin smile: "Now take leave of your father properly, as a dutiful and affectionate son."

When I did not move Rookyard propelled me violently forward so that the poor wretched creature cowered back against the wall.

"What an affecting scene," said Dr Alabaster.

He began to walk away up the passage but then turned and said: "Show yourself to be your father's son, Master Clothier, and don't disappoint your family's hopes in you."

There was a coarse guffaw of laughter from Rookyard and from the tall man, whom I now saw to be waiting in the passage. Then they pushed me before them in the other direction.

At the end of the passage we ascended some stone stairs — the turn-keys kicking and tripping me as I climbed — and then passed along another passage, then down some more steps into what seemed to be the cellar level of the building. Here we stopped and when the giant had unlocked another iron-grilled door, Rookyard pushed me through it so hard that I fell sprawling on the ground. As I picked myself up I found I was in a cell that seemed to me to be identical to the first, except that it was uninhabited: there was straw on the floor and a tiny barred window high up. There were no articles of furniture or, indeed, any contents except a narrow palliasse of straw, a jug and a wooden platter containing some cold porage.

Rookyard released me from the strait-waistcoat and then the door clanged shut behind me. Looking at the food and the water in the jug, it came to me that they were poisoned and so, despite my hunger and thirst, I determined neither to eat nor to drink, let the consequences be what they would.

My only hope lay in escaping, and with this in mind I examined my cell. The window was not only too high up to reach but also, with its iron bars, impossible to squeeze through. From the feeble quality of the light that came through it, I seemed to be below ground level and on a quiet side of the building. Peering through the small grille that surmounted the iron-bound door, I could see a little way along the passage in either direction by the faint lume of a distant gas-mantle. Holding the bars of the grille, I pulled myself up the door until I was just able to peer out of the bottom of the window on the opposite wall. I could make out a patch of waste ground with a scrubby grass-plat beyond it on which a broken wheel-barrow was lying on its side, and further off some untended shrubs and a large pond surrounded by a muddy swamp. There was no prospect of escaping that I could imagine.

The long hours dragged by and the cell was as cold as the other had been, and I was still in only my night-shirt. (I discovered that at least I still had the sovereign that I had hidden in its hem.) I was so hungry and thirsty that, towards noon, I nearly succumbed very suddenly to the temptation offered by the bason of congealed porage and the jug of cloudy water. But this would be to abandon the quest both to bring the Clothiers to justice for what they had done to me and my family, and to unravel the mysteries that surrounded me.

I was dozing on the palliasse when I suddenly heard something and looked up just in time to see an object being pushed through the grille and falling onto the straw on the floor. I rushed to the door but because of my limited angle of view was only in time to glimpse a figure passing swiftly and almost noiselessly along the passage away from me.

I picked up the object and found that it was half of a loaf of bread wrapped in a piece of muslin cloth that I found to be soaking wet. Here were the food and drink that I desperately needed! Then a suspicion came to me. This might be a ruse to lure me into consuming poisoned food when I would not eat what had been given to me. But then I wondered what I had to lose by taking this risk since otherwise I would die anyway?

So I made a lingering feast of the soggy bread and then tilted my head and wrung out the cloth into my mouth. No drink before or since ever tasted as sweet as that water, savouring though it did of the grubby cloth.

This must have been the early afternoon for it was only an hour or two later that it began to grow dark, or, rather, even darker, and so I found a dry corner of the cell and settled down to try to sleep.

CHAPTER 78

Dozing restlessly, I fancied I was dreaming that someone was calling me. But since I did not recognise the voice and since it was calling "John Clothier, John Clothier!" and I did not want to acknowledge that this name was mine,

I refused to answer the summons. Yet it came again and again and more and more insistently so that at last I woke up and lay with beating heart in the near-darkness and the bitter cold, having no recollection of where I was. Then I realized that someone was in reality calling to me by this hated name for I heard a loud insistent whisper repeating the syllables, and at that instant the memory of my situation came flooding back.

The unknown being who was addressing me was at the door of the cell. I rose and, advancing cautiously towards it, saw the outline of a face through the grille against the faint light that came from the passage. This individual was holding something through the bars and when I took it I found that it was another piece of bread wrapped as before.

"You are John Clothier, are you not?" said a gentle voice.

For a moment I was too stunned to answer and my visiter, who sounded like an elderly gentleman, asked again: "You are the son of Peter Clothier?"

"I am John Clothier," I answered hesitantly and reluctantly. "But who are you?"

"My name will mean nothing to you. I am Francis Nolloth."

He stepped back into the passage so that the little light there was from the gas-mantle some yards away fell on him. I saw that he was a small man of upwards of sixty with a mild, Quakerish face and a bald head, that he was looking at me with a kindly expression, and that he was the pitying figure I had seen in the night-ward — the owner of the single countenance on which I had so far seen signs of intelligence and compassion in that place.

"Thank you," I said as I began to devour the bread.

He stepped forward again to whisper through the grille: "They mean to poison you. Take nothing from them."

"How do you know these things?"

"I am a wardsman here and trusted by them." I must have revealed my dismay, for he went on: "Yes, I am an inmate of this place. But I am as sane as you."

"Don't say that," I protested. "I believe I am going mad."

"That's what they want," he said. "I know, for they don't notice me and so I hear many things, for my duties take me everywhere in the house and at all hours."

"Can you not escape?"

"Escape? To what? I have nothing in the world outside. I would be forced to beg my living on the streets."

"How can that be? Have you been here so long?"

"Longer than anyone. Longer even than Dr Alabaster himself, for he inherited me from his predecessor." Almost proudly he said: "I have been here more than five-and-twenty years."

"How is such a thing possible?"

"Oh it is a common enough story. I have not time to tell it now though we are safe for a little while because the night-porter is still in the kitchen. We will hear him when he comes this way and then I will go. As for how I came here, suffice it to say that I was so unfortunate as to be heir-at-law to a large estate."

"Can that be a misfortune?"

"Aye, for my brother and sister stood to inherit in default of myself and they had the means and the lack of scruple to have me put away. And so a medical gentleman was bribed to perjure himself. So you see, my case is similar to yours and your father's and to many others. But our time is too short to waste. Listen to me carefully. As I have said, I have overheard them talking about you and I know that you are in danger of your life. For as long as I may, I will pass food to you. But we must try to get you free of this place."

"Why are you endangering yourself for me?" I asked.

I wondered if this man had been ordered by Dr Alabaster to win his way into my trust like this, and although from his countenance I doubted it, I dared trust nobody.

"Should I need a reason? But if you must have one, ascribe it to my love for your father." He added gravely: "I have heard that you have seen him."

I tried to say "I have", but the words stuck in my throat.

"I am sorry for it," the old gentleman said. "But I promise you that he is not always as he is now."

"What do you mean?"

"When he first came here he was in complete possession of his faculties."

"He was sane?" I almost cried.

"Completely," Mr Nolloth replied.

At his words I felt a surge of relief. But an instant later I realized what this meant: if he was sane when he killed my grandfather then he committed murder. And yet if Mr Escreet had been telling the truth when he had told my mother that her husband was sane, was he also speaking the truth when he had said that the quarrel was only a charade? In that case, could Peter Clothier indeed be innocent?

"As I say, he was sane," Mr Nolloth said slowly, "but labouring under a great mental affliction."

He paused and I said: "Have no fear. I know — I have known for several months — that my grandfather was murdered by ... " I could not finish the sentence.

"By your father?" exclaimed Mr Nolloth. "Is that what you believe? Then allow me to lift that burden at least from your shoulders. Your father was completely innocent of that terrible crime."

I said nothing for another possibility had presented itself to me: that if the old gentleman were not an *agent provocateur* of Dr Alabaster's, then he might be a well-intentioned lunatic.

His next words, however, served somewhat to allay these suspicions: "I guess from your silence that you do not believe me. Why should you? I wish I had the time to explain it all to you. I have said that your father should never have been committed to this place. And he would not have been but for the plea of insanity that his father and brother entered in order to evade his indictment before the grand jury, for of course that was a ruse, a legal trick."

"Yes," I said, "but one intended to save him from ... from the consequences of being found guilty."

"No," Mr Nolloth said and laughed mirthlessly. "It was not intended to save him from the gallows but to give him into the custody of his father and then Dr Alabaster — perhaps a worse fate than execution. I promise you, he could never have been found guilty if the case had gone to trial. The evidence against him was wholly inadequate and the judge would have so directed the jury. Believe me, for I speak as a lawyer."

"You are a lawyer!"

"Yes, an attorney-at-law. I imagine you are surprised that my knowledge of the law has not enabled me to save myself from this place. The truth is that the laws and procedures relating to lunacy — particularly those of the court of Chancery — are wholly irrational and unjust and may easily be manipulated for unscrupulous ends. Like your father, I have the misfortune to be a Chancery lunatic — quite the most wretched, I assure you."

"But how do you know so much of his history?"

"He told me everything when he first came here — and he told it in such a manner that I did not doubt him for an instant."

"But if he was sane then ... " I began and could not go on.

"How does that square with the poor creature you saw last night?" the old gentleman gently supplied. "The answer is only too simple. Alabaster and his people set out to madden him — Hinxman (he is the enormously tall one) and Rookyard and the others, though I except Stillingfleet for I believe he has some vestiges of humanity left."

"How?" I said. "How can a sane man be turned into a lunatic?"

"How?" Mr Nolloth repeated. "Do not ask. But take my word for it that driving the sane mad is as profitable a part of the madhouse-keeper's trade as curing the afflicted. And they are so much more often successful in making than in unmaking lunatics that I have often wondered if we are not all insane, and what we name sanity is no more than a collective agreement to behave in the same mad ways. For the two are mingled strangely in that poor young man, your father."

Young? I thought in amazement. He must be five- or six-and-thirty!

"For even he," Mr Nolloth went on, "has periods of relative lucidity." His voice trembled slightly as he added: "I wish he did not."

"Why do you say that?"

He paused and then said: "At such times he thinks of his wife, your mother. Would it grieve you to tell me whether she lives and what has become of her?"

The request was gently expressed and I told him in a very few words.

He sighed and said: "I am sorry. Very sorry. I hope Peter never learns of this. Nor indeed of your existence — if you will forgive me for saying so — for I know that he rejoiced that no child was born of his brief marriage to grow up in danger and shame. But I fear that Dr Alabaster and Hinxman will tell him about both of you if he recovers enough to understand." Then he said sadly: "Your arrival here will accomplish several of their purposes together."

"What purposes?" I asked. "What do they intend for me?"

He hesitated before saying: "Do you understand how it is that your father's family would gain by your death?"

"Indeed I do!" I exclaimed. "It is on account of the codicil to my great-great-grandfather's will which Mr Escreet ... "

To my surprise he interrupted me: "I know all about how your grandfather purchased it through the agency of Mr Escreet. But tell me what has become of it since your father confided it to your mother's keeping at the inn in Hertford."

"I believe that it has very recently come into the possession of the Clothier family," I said and explained how my mother had been tricked into parting with it to Mr Sancious (disguised as Steplight), and my belief that he and Mrs Fortisquince were agents of the Clothiers.

"Then that explains what I have overheard. They must have laid it before the Court of Chancery, for the Master of the Rolls is about to sign an order making you a ward of court in less than a week."

"So I was right!" I exclaimed, remembering my assumptions about the significance of my appearance before the Court.

The old gentleman asked me what I meant by this and so I briefly outlined my mother's story and my own up to her death, then explained how I had been led into a trap at the house of Daniel Porteous and his wife; how I had been deceived into believing that I had encountered them by chance; how I had been taken before the court and perplexed by some of the things said and done there, then lied to (by Emma) in being told that I had been legally assigned to the guardianship of these people; how I had discovered the real identity of the family; and how I had tried to escape but had been detected and brought here.

"Then you understand," Mr Nolloth asked, "that at your death your grandfather, Silas Clothier, inherits the Hougham estate outright?"

I nodded and he said: "This is why Peter has always been so worried for the safety of your mother. The Clothiers' scheme is close to fruition, for from what I have overheard I believe they have instructed Dr Alabaster either to bring about your death or to ensure that you be truly mad before the Master's order can be signed, for otherwise the Mompessons will ask him to assign you to the custody of another doctor. So they must achieve their purpose within a week."

"But surely the Master would be suspicious if I ... " I protested.

I left the sentence unfinished.

"No," the old gentleman replied thoughtfully. "For only consider the matter from his point of view. He saw you before him in court ill and confused. Since then two justices of the peace have examined you (as required) and signed an order for your committal, and they can testify to your insanity. For what were you doing? Making absurd charges against your family and refusing to eat because you believed they were trying to poison you!"

"Then what do you think will happen to me?"

"A Commission of Lunacy convened by the Court of Chancery will most likely examine you and, assuming that it finds you to be insane, as I trust Dr Alabaster to ensure that it will, and the Mompessons' request fails, then you will stay here indefinitely. Though I don't think your life would be suffered to last very long in that event."

We were both silent for a few moments and then he said: "At all costs, you must escape from here, and as soon as possible. But how?"

I was about to speak when he whispered: "Listen!"

At first I could hear nothing, but then I detected a faint noise that might have been the clanging of a metal door.

"Yallop has begun his rounds," Mr Nolloth said. "I dare not stay longer. I will try to come again tomorrow night."

"Please wait for a moment," I said urgently.

"Yes, yes, I will think about how you might escape," he said hastily.

"It's not that," I replied. "Tell me why you believe Peter Clothier was innocent."

"Is that more important to you than escaping?" he asked.

"Yes," I said, "for I don't believe there is any way I can be got free of this place, and I must know the truth before ... "

I broke off but he said: "I understand. I will try to come again."

Without another word he left the grille and though I squeezed myself against it to see him go, he was so quick that he was already out of sight along the passage. He left me in a state of exhaustion, but too excited and moved to contemplate sleep.

The next day passed like the previous one: Rookyard brought food and water which I neglected in favour of bread that Mr Nolloth managed to deliver through the grille.

Late that night he appeared again at the door, to my delight, and brought with him more bread and water.

"I have been trying to think of how you might escape," he began; "but I have made no advance."

"Mr Nolloth, I beg you: please tell me what you know of my grandfather's death."

"If you wish it," he answered. "But first tell me, how much do you know of what happened the night he was killed?"

I explained what I had learned from reading my mother's account and said that although I had perused it only once, it was engraved on my memory.

"Then I will tell you without delay what will make all clear. Do you recall the gift which your grandfather received that night from Mr Fortisquince?"

I nodded.

"Have you any idea what it was, or, rather, what your grandfather expected it to be?"

"No," I said hesitatingly, but then in growing excitement I told him of my guess that the reason why my grandfather had lost interest in the codicil was because he hoped to obtain a document that was even more effective.

"You are perfectly correct," the old gentleman said. "What your grandfather expected to receive that night was a document of the utmost importance. This was nothing less than a will of Jeoffrey Huffam, your great-great-grandfather, dated later than the one which was probated."

My guess had been on target!

"And if, as I believe we may assume, it was not a forgery," the old gentleman continued, "then since a will remains effective no matter how long it has been lost sight of, once it had been probated it would have displaced both the original will and also the codicil about which there has been so much to-do."

"Then what would have been the consequences?" I demanded quickly.

"Very far-reaching for a great number of people. The will disinherited your great-grandfather, James, in favour of Jeoffrey Huffam's infant grandson."

"My grandfather!" I exclaimed.

"Precisely. John, then a child of a few months, became vested in the title to his grandfather's property. And therefore the sale of the Hougham estate by James would be retrospectively invalidated by the will beyond question, for James had no interest in the estate to convey. In short, if the will could have been probated it would have made your grandfather the outright owner of the estate immediately."

"His great ambition so close to being achieved!" I murmured. "The Mompessons ousted and the Clothiers thwarted." Many questions flooded into my mind but one of them thrust itself forward ahead of the others: "But where had the will been all those many years?"

"Apparently in the Mompesson family, for someone in that household wrote to your grandfather and undertook to obtain it for him."

"The letter with the Mompessons' crest," I cried, "that my mother mentioned!"

So that indeed explained why, immediately after receiving it, my grandfather had lost interest either in laying the codicil before the courts or in bringing about my mother's marriage with Daniel Clothier.

Then I asked: "But why should someone in the Mompessons' trust have wished to betray them? Who was this friend on the inside? And, indeed, why should the will have been kept by them for so long since it represented so grave a danger to their interests?"

"These are questions, young gentleman, on which your father and I have had a great deal of leisure to speculate, but without profit."

"I beg your pardon," I said. "Please continue. What happened, then, on that fateful night?"

"Not so fast. I must go back to the day about a week before that night when your mother and father informed your grandfather of their desire to marry. Did your mother tell you that he set the date of the wedding for a week hence and proposed to invite his old friend, Martin Fortisquince with whom he had quarrelled, and his new wife?"

"Yes, she was very puzzled by this."

"Here, then, is the explanation. Your grandfather had secret conference of your father and Mr Escreet and told them of the promise that had been made — though he did not identify the individual in the Mompessons' confidence. He explained that his unknown helper had proposed using Mr Fortisquince as the unwitting agent to convey the document from the Mompessons' house to himself. The intention was that the will would be removed from Sir Perceval's safe place on the morning of the wedding and would immediately be placed by the unknown party in the hands of Mr Fortisquince who would be told that it was a gift for your grandfather and should be given to him that very day. Mr Fortisquince, having no idea of the significance of what he bore, would bring it to the house that evening. So it was in order to provide Mr Fortisquince with a reason for coming to the house that your grandfather invited him and his wife to the wedding-feast."

"But why was this kept from my mother?"

"Let me tell my story exactly as I heard it from your father, and I hope all will come clear. Your grandfather, then, knew that as soon as Sir Perceval discovered the disappearance of the will he would fear that somehow it had come into the possession of the one person who benefited from it: your grandfather himself. And, moreover, Peter's father would learn for the first time of its existence — for it was a well-guarded secret."

"How would he learn of it? And why should it concern him?"

"He had at least one spy in the Mompessons' trust. And your grandfather also believed that Mr Fortisquince's new bride was paid by him to supply intelligence."

Mr Nolloth and I speculated about her motives and why my grandfather mistrusted her, but could come to no clear conclusion. Since reading my mother's pocket-book, I had often puzzled over Mrs Fortisquince's extreme malevolence against her.

"For obvious reasons, Peter's father took a keen interest in your grandfather's affairs," Mr Nolloth continued. "And of course this lost will would make the codicil worthless to him and destroy any chance of his inheriting the estate.

He would, like the Mompessons, realize that your grandfather was the party who stood to benefit from it, and would suspect that he had obtained it. He had already become angry and suspicious that your grandfather was delaying placing the codicil before the court. And he would have known, since your grandfather was so obsessed by the suit, that only a higher claim to the estate could prevent him from making use of the codicil."

"Then why did my grandfather not proceed with laying the codicil before the court in order to allay his suspicions?"

"Because once that was done your mother's life and his own were in grave danger. As yours is now."

"But would they not also be in danger once the Mompessons and the Clothiers knew that my grandfather had the will? For surely the Clothiers, and even the Mompessons, would stop at nothing to destroy or to regain it respectively?"

"Precisely. And if the Clothiers killed your grandfather and your mother in the process and took custody of your father as well, then so much the better from their point of view. And so your grandfather's chief preoccupation was how to ensure the safety of your mother and father and protect the will once it was delivered to him. And this was what was discussed between the three of them, your father, your grandfather, and Mr Escreet, that night that your parents agreed to marry. And it was then that they hatched the conspiracy that was to have such fatal and unforeseen consequences."

"A conspiracy!" I exclaimed. "Against whom?"

"Against your mother, for one. For your father and grandfather were determined to keep as much of all of this as possible from her in order not to worry her."

"But did they not think of what anguish that would cause her!"

"But they could not have known then that their scheme would go terribly wrong. And, moreover, to take part in the plan required the ability to act a part which they did not believe that your mother possessed. In order to understand what happened you must consider the situation as it presented itself to them that night. They needed to encompass the following ends: your mother had to be kept from the knowledge of any of this, at least until all was safe; your father had to be spirited away to a place where he would be secure from his father and Dr Alabaster who, remember, were at this time armed with a writ from the Commission of Lunacy which permitted them to take him into custody as soon as he left the protection of your grandfather's house; the Mompessons and Clothiers were to be deceived into believing that your parents had not received the will and the codicil from your grandfather; and, finally, in case the attempt to convince them of this failed, both documents — the codicil and the will — were to be conveyed out of the reach of either the Mompessons or the Clothiers and their numerous agents and intelligencers."

"How could they hope to achieve all these ends?"

"Well, Mr Escreet devised a very ingenious way of going about it. He suggested that your father and grandfather should stage a mock quarrel in the presence of Mr and Mrs Fortisquince and your mother, at the climax of which your father should storm from the house with your mother."

"The charade of which he spoke at the inn in Hertford!" I exclaimed.

"A charade, yes. Exactly that. And so you see why your mother could not have been forewarned? She would not have been able to deceive the keen eye of Mrs Fortisquince. Your grandfather entered into the spirit of the thing wonderfully, and Mr Escreet was also very convincing, but your father often told me how poorly he himself acted the part."

"Yes, my mother recorded that she thought his manner was strange, but she was completely taken in by my grandfather and Mr Escreet."

"It was an unfortunate necessity that your mother had to be deceived, seeing that things turned out so unexpectedly and terribly. But all was done with the best of intentions. I assume that you understand that the purpose of the charade was to lead Mr and Mrs Fortisquince to believe that there had been a complete rupture between Peter and his new father-in-law? And it was crucial that Mr Fortisquince, in reporting this — with no malign intentions — to the Mompesson family, would mention that he had only passed the gift to your grandfather after Peter had left the house. For by then Sir Perceval would have learned that the will had been removed from his house and put into your grandfather's hands by Mr Fortisquince's unwitting agency. Mr Fortisquince would be believed as one whose reputation was that of a gentleman incapable of the smallest act of deceit. His assertion that the newly-married couple had left the house after such a scene and gone no-one knew whither, would forestall any attempt to find them, and the Mompessons would have no reason to anyway if they assumed that your grandfather still had the will."

"And Mrs Fortisquince would report the same to the Clothiers!"

"Exactly so. And they too would therefore reject the idea that your grandfather had entrusted the will — and also the codicil — to his son-in-law, would abandon the attempt to take custody of him under the writ of lunacy, and would instead concentrate their efforts to obtain the codicil and the will — the one to lay before the court and the other to destroy — on your grandfather himself."

"Then do you suspect that what happened to him ... "

"I must leave you now," he broke in. "Yallop has not done his rounds yet and is certain to come very soon."

"A little longer, I beg you!" I urged.

"A few minutes. No more. To return to my story, then. It was a considerable attraction of the ruse proposed by Mr Escreet that even if it failed to convince your family's enemies that a breach had taken place between your father and your grandfather, at worst your parents would be safely out of London, and in possession of the two documents, in a place whose whereabouts only your grandfather and Mr Escreet knew. And so in the week preceding the one appointed for the wedding of your parents, all the necessary preparations were secretly made. Your grandfather entrusted to your father both the codicil and the letter he had written to explain the significance of the purloined will. (He wrote this because he knew that, as you have just implied, he was putting himself in grave danger.) Now it was crucial that when Mr and Mrs Fortisquince arrived it should be demonstrated to her that her husband did not give the package he had with him to your grandfather until your parents had left the house. She would not bestow much attention on this at the time but would realize its significance later when the loss of the will by the Mompessons became known. And so it was agreed that your grandfather would decline to accept the package until your parents had departed after the argument. They chose the subject of money as the one that the Mompessons and the Clothiers would find most plausible as the cause of a rift between son-in-law and father on the former's wedding-day. Only after your parents had driven away would your grandfather ask Mr Fortisquince for the package. He would then slip it surreptitiously to Mr Escreet and then your father ... "

"Would secretly return to the house to take it from him!" I cried in delight.

"Precisely," said Mr Nolloth. "Mr Escreet would leave the back-door unlocked and since the servants would be out of the way celebrating the marriage below stairs, he would be seen by no-one."

"But Mr Fortisquince saw him," I said. "Though he did not recognise him at the time."

"Yes, many things went wrong."

"Then please tell me what happened!" I almost cried out.

"No, I must not stay any longer. It is getting light. I will be found and then I will lose all power to assist you."

"I don't care. I must know what happened."

"Tomorrow, if I can," Mr Nolloth whispered and slipped quietly away.

I lay down on the hard straw-bedding but I knew that sleep would not come for many hours, for what the old gentleman had said had started a train of thought that I needed time to pursue. So my grandfather had had an irrefutable claim to the estate. Then surely I had inherited it? My great wish might yet be fulfilled! But I must not allow myself to think of this for it all depended on the will, if it had ever even existed. Could I be sure that it had? If it had, then what had become of it? Presumably it had been destroyed. How strange that I understood now more than my poor mother had ever done of the events of that fateful night, and in particular, the benign purpose of the charade. In the light of what I now knew, could I say that her fear that her husband had killed her father was unfounded? For one thing, it seemed to me certain that acquiring the purloined will was the motive for the murder, and I could not see what Peter Clothier had to gain from this.

A little later the night-porter came along the passage and held his lanthorn to the grille for a moment before he passed on.

CHAPTER 79

The day that arrived — insofar as it was distinguishable to me from the night in my dark, underground cell — was exactly the same as the previous one. In the morning Hinxman brought food which I left untouched. About an hour afterwards, Mr Nolloth managed to push a large piece of bread through the bars and this time he accompanied it with a small stone jug of water which I was quick enough to take from him, and which I concealed beneath the straw. This was enough to keep me alive a little longer, but I knew that my strength was ebbing.

Mr Nolloth failed to keep his promise to come again that night. I was more disappointed by this than by the fact that the next day he did not bring me meat and drink either, so that all I had was the food brought by Hinxman which, hungry as I was, I left untouched.

I could not help blaming Mr Nolloth for having let me down, irrational though I knew this was. Or was it so irrational? For during the long blank hours of day and night alike, I could not keep from my thoughts the question whether I could trust him. To distrust him was to imagine that there was a complicated conspiracy directed against me in which he was a participant, and to suspect this seemed to me to be an indication of insanity. And yet there did seem to be a design against me for Barney and Joey Digweed had risen from my past and shewn themselves to be implicated in some kind of secret combination against me, unless I could ascribe their reappearance in my life to the effect of mere coincidence. But I could not do so, for had not Joey led me to the Clothier (or "Porteous") family who had most certainly conspired to deceive me?

So a plot against my life and sanity certainly existed, and if the very family whose name I bore could organise it, then how could I trust a stranger? And yet there had to be some fulcrum of certainty on which to rest or I would doubt everything and surely that was the quickest road to madness? Mr Nolloth's look of pity when he saw me dragged by Hinxman and Rookyard through the night-ward, and his expressions of affection for Peter Clothier, seemed to me to be the signs of genuine sympathy which it would be madness *not* to trust. Finally, I concluded that, circumstanced as I was, I had nothing to lose by believing in him.

Late in the afternoon — as I assume it was — of the second day following Mr Nolloth's last visit, the door was suddenly unlocked and Hinxman came in with Rookyard following him.

He smiled strangely and said: "Your dad has been askin' arter you most tenderly. So, since the doctor is always anxious to accommodate those under his care, he has arst me to take you to visit him."

When they had led me back along those dark passages to the cell in which I had been placed on my first night in that house, I found that the wretched creature was no longer there and that the place had been transformed: fresh straw had been laid and there were now two chairs facing each other across a small table. Seated in one of them was a stranger who looked at me intently as I entered. He was a little under forty, clean-shaven, and neatly dressed in a blue coat with a white stock, a white waistcoat and dark trowsers. Hinxman pushed me into the chair opposite him and pressed me into it by leaning heavily on my shoulder. The stranger still stared at me fixedly and at last I recognised him.

Instead of the wavering light of madness in his eyes there was a deep melancholy. He looked much younger now that he had lost his tangled beard and his ragged mop of hair; and since he was free of the strait-waistcoat, I could see how thin and frail he was. Beneath the edge of the stock I noticed a raw wound on his neck. Altogether I found the appearance of this man towards whom I stood in such a strange relation, even more disturbing in this new manifestation than what I had been braced to encounter.

We faced each other for a few moments while Rookyard and Hinxman looked on. I had some idea of giving him my hand but the gesture seemed too formal.

"They have just told me that my wife had a child," he said gravely. "They say you are he. And yet I cannot believe it. Is it so?"

He spoke hesitatingly as if unused to speech, but his voice was soft and gentle. I was unable to speak or even to nod my head.

He went on: "But I see that you are Mary's child. You feature your dear mother's fa... " His voice broke and he stopped.

"In course the boy's your son and heir, Peter," said Hinxman. "Why, it's plain to see he's inherited his father's wits."

"For he wouldn't be a scholard in Dr Alabaster's 'cademy if that wasn't so," added Rookyard.

"Yes. These gentlemen are right. I am mad, you know." Then he said eagerly: "But tell me, how is your dear mother?"

Unable to speak, I shook my head.

"I broke her heart. Do you know what I did?"

I shook my head to try to stop him.

"I murdered her father," he said almost in a whisper. "Your grandfather."

"No, no, that's not true."

"Oh but it is. Though I don't recall how or why but, you see, that's because of my madness."

"Why, you took a haxe," said Hinxman, "and you chopped the old genel'man in three eq'al pieces. And an uncommon scaly way to show respect for your miss'is' dad it was. Pertickerly on your wedding-night."

"Not an axe, Mr Hinxman. It was a sword."

"Which only makes it worse, Peter," put in Rookyard, "as you'll see yourself if you think about it. Or you would do if your wits wasn't addled."

"Some things I remember clearly. Others not at all. After your mother and I left the house, I went back secretly. I remember that very well."

"Yes," I said. "But it was by arrangement with Mr Escreet."

He frowned: "No. You've been misinformed. Nobody knew. At least, I don't believe so. I remember passing the door of the dining-room which was open and averting my head so that anyone in there should not see me. So you see, I must have meant to do harm, mustn't I? I went to the library and there I found Mr Escreet. I remember that very clearly. Then it seems that I attacked him and Mr Huffam. I used a sword. We were in the plate-room. Sometimes I can almost remember doing so, but this part of it seems like a dream. Apparently I stole some money. But I certainly remember that I could not leave the house for the back-door was locked. And I recall cutting my hand as I broke the glass of the vestibule-door. So you see, I must be a murderer. But Mr Escreet survived, thank God."

My belief in what Mr Nolloth had said dissolved and I believed I was staring into the mild brown eyes of the murderer of my grandfather.

"You feature your grandfather very nearly," he said. "The same eyes. The very mouth that your sweet mother has. What is your name?"

"John," I managed to say. Seeing no sign that he recognised the name I added: "John Clothier."

"I remember that name," he said with a shudder. "It is mine. Or it was. Once I was proud to bear it. I loved my father, and I admired him as sons do their fathers. Though I saw how unhappy he made my mother — a gentle creature who could do nothing right in his eyes. For long I knew nothing of the business that my father and brother drove, for I was a shy, dreaming schoolboy who wanted nothing more than to be left alone with my books. I wished to become a book-seller. But when the time came for me to leave school, I found that I was expected to enter and to bear my full part in the family's trade. And now I discovered what it was." He paused and sighed. "In brief, they had a hand in every low, snivelling trick that is perpetrated in London against the poor or the unworldly or the defenceless: They ran illegal pawn-shops that charged too high a rate of interest and were used as a cover to receive stolen goods. They lent money to young gentlemen with expectations and then blackmailed them or their friends for extortionate repayments. And they owned some of the worst properties in the metropolis: the stinking dens of the most poverty-stricken from which they wrung blood-rents, as well as the haunts of every imaginable and unimaginable vice from which they reaped a dividend."

"Now, now," said Rookyard. "You mustn't slander one of the finest old genel'men in London."

"Imagine what such a discovery meant to me," he continued, apparently not having heard this remark. "The father and brother whom I so revered, revealed to be no more than crimping cheats and blackmailers! When I refused to have anything to do with all of this they tried every means to make me give way from bribes to threats and eventually to violence. Is it any wonder that I became as I did? After my mother died I had no allies. I believed that everybody was against me, and that all the people in the world were either weak and therefore victims, or strong and so behaved as my father and brother. Your mother and her father were the first decent people I had ever known. Because I came to love your mother I found the strength to resist." He broke off and gazed at me as if he had newly awakened from a dream: "That wasn't what I meant to say. I wanted to ask you how your mother is." His voice trembled. "I don't know what to believe. The people here tell me such stories."

"You've been told often and often enough," said Hinxman. "Turned w---- and died mad."

I looked at the man's jeering face and could not tell if he had spoken merely at hazard.

"She is alive and well, is she not?"

"Yes," I stammered. "She is alive and well."

My voice only trembled slightly but the tears welled from my eyes and ran down my cheeks.

The gentle, melancholy face studied mine: "You are lying to me as they all do. I see that she is dead, isn't she?"

I could not speak but I nodded.

"I feared it. I only want to know that she did not die in misery and want, as Mr Hinxman and the other gentlemen tell me."

I tried to finds words to reassure him, but he read my mother's history in my countenance and covered his face with his hands.

I rose and moved towards him but a heavy hand gripped my shoulder and Hinxman's voice said coarsely: "I don't have all day to listen to you two chat about old times, pleasant though it is to hear you."

As he raised me from the chair and began to push me towards the door I managed to turn and say: "I will talk with you again."

He gave no sign of having heard me, and in a moment I was out in the passage and Rookyard had swung the door shut behind us.

On the way back along one of the passages Hinxman met a turn-key I had not see before and shouted to him: "Hey, Stillingfleet. Take this young wronghead back to No. 12. I've got to get ready for the night-coach to Gainsborough. I'm going north this evening on business for one of the doctor's customers."

He thrust me at the other man and went off. Remembering that this was the turn-key whom Mr Nolloth had mentioned as the only one there possessed of any humanity, I said to him: "Mr Stillingfleet, supposing I were to offer you a sovereign to help me get away? Would you do it?"

"No," he answered without hesitation; "for that would be bilking my master."

I had expected a refusal and, strangely, his answer cheered me for it was at least honourable. And, after all, he might have cheated me by taking it and doing nothing. But if I could do nothing for myself, I could at least help another and so, remembering the hideous wound I had seen beneath the stock, I said: "You know Peter Clothier?"

"Aye, poor devil. What of him?"

"If I offered you the money to help him as you can, what would you say?"

"I'd say I wanted to see your blunt fust."

I decided to trust him and he let me halt while I retrieved the sovereign that Daniel Porteous had given me from its hiding place in the hem of my night-shirt.

As I handed it to him I said: "Try to stop the chain biting into his neck so tightly."

"I'll do my best," he said as he took it.

Once I was alone in my cell again I laid myself down on the straw and wept. In the hours that followed I could not efface the memory of that delicate, suffering face nor disguise from myself that I had been made the unwitting means of inflicting further pain.

Moreover, I now had no reason to doubt that he had indeed committed that terrible crime — not that Mr Nolloth had been lying to me, I assumed, for he had himself been deceived. I believed that at least life had no further horror to threaten me with for my death now seemed inevitable and to be welcomed.

CHAPTER 80

Despite this resolve, as the evening wore on I listened anxiously for the faint sounds from elsewhere in the building to die away in the hope that Mr Nolloth would soon come. If I could not share my fears with a sympathetic hearer I believed I would truly forfeit my sanity. During all the long hours of darkness that dragged by, the only people who passed were the turn-keys whose heavy tread I recognised. But at last, at what must have been after midnight, I heard faint footsteps in the passage and went to the grille where I found Mr Nolloth. He apologised for having failed to come before, and then passed through the bars some more food and drink which, eagerly as I received them, were less valuable than the chance to tell him of my encounter that day and to find my own anxieties shared. First I told him how the interview had ended.

"Do not believe for a moment that I am blaming you," the old gentleman said kindly when I had finished my account; "but I hardly like to think of the consequences."

"If only I could have disguised my feelings," I cried.

"Don't reproach yourself. You did what was expected of you."

When I told Mr Nolloth how Peter Clothier had described murdering my grandfather, he sighed: "He believes it now, but I assure you it is not the truth. It is not even plausible. The account he gave me of that night when he first entered this place is self-evidently the truth."

I bid him continue with it from the point at which we had been interrupted the other night, and when he did so I forced myself to play devil's advocate because I wanted to be convinced that the confession I had heard was false.

"As you know from your mother's account, the charade of the quarrel took place as planned and your parents left the house and went to the coach-office at Snow-hill. There your father changed his coat to make recognition more unlikely in case he were seen, and he returned to the house."

"He now denies that this was by prior arrangement."

"I know," said Mr Nolloth. "But if the back-door was not left unlocked by Mr Escreet, then how did he get in?"

"He did not explain that," I happily admitted.

"He went to the library which he found empty. A minute later Mr Escreet entered from the plate-room and told him that your grandfather was engaged with Mr and Mrs Fortisquince, but that he had given him the package which Mr Fortisquince had brought. Your father took it and then made to leave. How does that square with what he told you?"

"He said that he met both my grandfather and Mr Escreet in the plate-room and attacked them and left them for dead."

"That is impossible. For one, the sword that was used to kill your grandfather hung upon the wall of the passage between the plate-room and the street-door — in other words, on the opposite side of the house. No, the truth is that he simply took the package from Mr Escreet and made for the back-door without even meeting your grandfather."

"Mr Fortisquince saw him as he passed the dining-room," I said. "But because he was wearing a different coat he did not recognise him."

"And that was as well since it meant that he continued to believe in his innocence for longer than he might have done otherwise. But when Peter reached the back-door he found that it was locked and the key gone."

"That is strange," I said.

"Very strange. (You see, his original account is much more puzzling and therefore more credible than the simple version he now believes.) He assumed that one of the servants had come upstairs in the interval and, needing to go into the back-yard, had locked the door on entering the house again. Realizing that he would have to leave by the street-door, he went to the front hall."

"And Mr Fortisquince saw him again as he passed the door and now began to wonder who he was."

"Indeed? So you see how this version tallies with the evidence given by others! Now here is the strangest part of the story. Your father found that the glazed door between the hall and the vestibule was also locked and the key gone. Now that, he assured me, was quite contrary to the usual custom of the house, for the key remained always in the lock and the door was only secured at night as an additional precaution. He was about to break the panes of the door into the vestibule when he saw through the glass that the key to the street-door itself was similarly missing."

"How strange!"

"Wait. There is something even odder to come. For he then noticed that the great key of the street-door was lying at his feet by the vestibule-door."

"That is wonderful indeed! What explanation did he offer for this?"

"None that satisfied him. But at least he now saw his way out. He broke a pane of glass in the vestibule door as quietly as he could and in doing so cut himself slightly and tore his coat."

"Thus accounting for the blood on his hand and the tear in his jacket that so alarmed my mother!" I exclaimed in delight.

"Yes, exactly. But your father could not account for the blood inside the package that he found when he and your mother opened it early the next morning at the inn in Hertford. Nor for the fact that the will was not there. That remains a mystery."

"Yes, my mother described how there was nothing in it except the bank-notes covered in blood, although he apparently expected to find something." After a silence I went on: "And what about the question of who did, then, murder my grandfather?"

"Your father and I believed we had resolved that question."

He paused and I realized that he was listening to some faint and distant noises. We almost dared not breathe until, after a few moments, absolute silence returned.

"There appears to be a disturbance in the house. Perhaps one of the poor wretches has become violent. I must not stay." Mr Nolloth paused and then said gravely: "As far as the murder of Mr John Huffam is concerned, I fear that your father was, in a sense, responsible."

"What?" I exclaimed. "After what you have told me?"

"Oh, not in the way that you fear. When he left the house he was unable to secure the street-door behind him since it had no spring-lock. Someone must have seen him leave, entered the house immediately, taken down the sword as he passed through the side-lobby and gone into the plate-room. He must have found the two gentlemen standing over the strong-box, struck Mr Escreet from behind, killed your grandfather, ransacked the box, and then left by the way he had come. This must have happened so soon after Mr Escreet had spoken to your father that it is not to be wondered at that in his confused state, after recovering his wits, he should have incriminated him."

"Yes," I said. "That is entirely possible. Yet it still leaves some of those other questions unanswered. And I believe that regaining the will was the motive for the murder, and therefore that the explanation cannot lie simply in a chance intruder."

"But my dear young man, I did not mean to imply that your father believed for a minute that the murderer was a mere speculative housebreaker. On the contrary, he suspected ... "

He suddenly broke off as we realized that there were people approaching along the passage from the left, for we had been too engrossed in our conversation to hear them until they were almost upon us.

Mr Nolloth moved swiftly away along the passage in the other direction out of my sight. But to my horror, just as lights appeared from the left, I heard Rookyard's voice from my right say:

"So that's your game, is it? I guessed there was something of this kind afoot. You've been a-bringing him wittles, ain't you?"

He had crept up upon us while we had been distracted by those arriving from the other direction. As they rounded the corner their lanthorns illuminated him as he pressed himself and Mr Nolloth up against the grille of my door to let them pass. The newcomers — who were the turn-key, Stillingfleet, and a man

I had not seen before — were carrying a heavy burden between them which was hidden from my view by the door.

As they passed us Rookyard, with a nod of the head towards me, said to the stranger: "This is his boy."

The man looked at me curiously. "Looks like he's aimin' the same way," he commented.

Rookyard laughed shortly and began to push Mr Nolloth in the other direction. As they went the old gentleman turned back to me an agonised face on which there seemed to be written a feeling much stronger even than regret at his having been discovered. A moment later the passage was deserted and veiled in impenetrable darkness again, and I was left to speculate on how I would survive now, to worry about how my friend would be punished, and to brood on the words that had passed between Rookyard and the stranger.

What had the old gentleman been about to say? That Peter Clothier had suspected that the murderer was someone who had been watching the house on his father's orders? That made sense for Silas Clothier wanted both to capture his son and regain the codicil — and the will, too, if he knew of its presence in the house. I thought again of Barney! He had hinted that he had killed a gentleman at exactly this date. Perhaps his connexion with the Clothiers went back as far as that. Could he be the murderer of my grandfather?

There continued to be unusual sounds from somewhere far away in the house for an hour or two — gates clanging, feet running, shouts — then the night returned to its earlier silence and I managed to fall into an uneasy sleep.

BOOK II

The Release

CHAPTER 81

Let me return you to that mournful place by the riverside, that area of tumble-down wharves and abandoned warehouses and delapidated landing-stairs — in short, that district which my colleague's eloquent and fashionable pen could describe so much more vividly than mine.

What a comfortable, not to say absolutely charming scene! The boy is sitting with his feet on the fender and roasting chestnuts on a toasting-fork held at the fire while Mr Vulliamy is slumbering at his desk with his head resting upon his papers.

Then the street-door slowly opens and their employer enters softly and steals on tip-toe across the room. When he is upon the boy he cuffs him suddenly about the side of the head.

At his cries of alarm Mr Vulliamy wakes up and looks around in confusion.

"Damn you, Vulliamy, you were asleep again!" the old gentleman cries. "I don't pay you to sleep in my time!"

The clerk mumbles blearily and rubs his eyes: "Bless me, sir. I was dreaming about toads and then I wake up and see your face. It's most upsetting."

"What in the name of the devil has got into you, Vulliamy?" the old gentleman asks. "You're constantly falling asleep these days." Lowering his face to within a few inches of his clerk's he sniffs: "Yet you seem not to be fuddling as much as before."

"I'm sure you'll find that I'm as wide-awake as you could wish me, Mr Clothier," the clerk answers. Then he mutters under his breath: "Maybe a deal more so."

"Eh, what?" the old man asks sharply. "What are you whispering to yourself about?"

But the clerk merely smiles and begins to mend his pen.

"Wide awake!" the old gentleman sneers. "You weren't wide awake when you stopped Ashburner raising those rents in Hatton-garden."

"It's too much, sir."

"Too much? What gammon is this? It's my property, isn't it, to let as I choose? If they don't want to pay they can go elsewhere. That's fair, ain't it? All I want is justice."

He breaks off and, lowering his voice with a glance at the boy, asks: "Has it come yet? Has he sent a message?"

"Who do you mean?"

The old gentleman scowls and whispers: "Him. My son."

"Why, you know he don't write to you," the clerk exclaims.

His employer flinches and seems about to retort, but at that moment a ticket-porter enters the outer office bearing a letter.

Seeing this, the old gentleman grins at his clerk, seizes it and, while Mr Vulliamy settles with the porter, looks at the direction: "It's from him!" he cries. He glances slyly at his clerk: "You see? He hasn't forgotten me."

He beckons him into the inner office where he tears the letter open. As he scans it his face lights up: "The boy is safe! He is safe!"

And yet strangely enough, Mr Vulliamy does not look very pleased at the spectacle of his employer's exultation.

CHAPTER 82

I awoke early and lay for hours hardly aware of the faint traces of the dawn that crept sluggishly in through the grating. Late in the morning another turn-key, a thick-set man with a pugnacious expression whose name was Skilliter, brought me food. Though I decided that I would hold out a few hours longer, I knew that before the end of the day I would have to eat, let the consequences be what they might.

Just as I was reflecting that it seemed to be my fate to bring misfortune upon any who tried to help me — first Sukey, then Miss Quilliam, and now old Mr Nolloth — I became aware of distant noises. Or were they inside my head? I could not determine this, and then they seemed to recede. The passage in which my cell was located remained silent and deserted until, a little after midday, I heard footsteps approaching and hurried to the grille. Rookyard and Skilliter passed towards my door and I strained to hear their words:

"So the doctor didn't git the roastin' what he was a-feared on?" Rookyard asked.

"No, the crowner wasn't too hard on us. I suppose he reckons he'd miss his Christmas box."

"Even so, an inkwich don't do the house no good," Rookyard commented as they moved out of my hearing.

I could make little of these words. However, my hunger-pangs had by now become so fierce as to drive all other considerations from my mind. I reasoned with myself over and over again: I had no certain proof that an attempt was being made to poison me, while what was certain was that I was facing death by starvation. I was doing my enemies' work for them!

By late afternoon I had resolved to eat some of the porage and was just on the point of doing so when I heard steps approaching, and in a moment Skilliter had unlocked my door and swung it open for Dr Alabaster to enter.

He looked at the untouched platter and said: "You still persist in your obstinacy? Then so be it."

He smiled unpleasantly and nodded to the turn-key who seized me and pushed me before him. Followed by Dr Alabaster, we went along the passage in the direction of the main block of the house, climbed some stairs, and then passed quickly through a day-ward. A number of inmates were assembled there, some writing letters, playing cards, or reading, but others sitting alone and staring blankly before them. One old man was rubbing his hand up and down his face so savagely that the skin was quite red and raw with the friction. Several were wearing strait-waistcoats and one gentleman was chained to the wall and peaceably reading a newspaper as if at his own club.

Just as I was shoved out through the door, I caught sight of Mr Nolloth, who was sitting in a corner alone. He looked up and I saw from his red and swollen eyes that he had been weeping. Worse than this, he directed towards me a gaze of such sadness that I shuddered as if at an ill premonition.

I had turned my head and dragged my feet to watch him for as long as I could, but Skilliter, with an oath, hit me on the side of the head and I had to turn away from the last sight I ever had of the brave old gentleman.

We passed along a draughty passage into a cold, damp outbuilding that might long ago have been a dairy, and came to a locked door. While Skilliter fumbled to find the right key from those on his chain, I stood on the cracked flag-stones shivering in my night-shirt that the Porteouses had given me and trying to blot out the memory of a valiant soul reduced to tears, which both chilled me and disappointed me.

Skilliter swore and muttered: "My fingers are so damn' froze I can hardly hold the keys."

Dr Alabaster laughed drily and said: "There's no call to hurry, Skilliter. He won't go away."

Skilliter snorted in a toadyish manner to indicate his appreciation of this piece of drollery, and as he finally managed to unlock the door Dr Alabaster said to me with a sneer: "We thought you would probably care to see your dear papa again."

My emotion at the prospect of another interview with the pitiable being was tinged with surprise at the venue for our meeting. When the door swung open and I was pushed in, my bewilderment increased for since it was a small, well-lit chamber I could see immediately that it had only one occupant. This was a large woman dressed as a laundress who had her back to us at the far end of the room. She was bent over something on a table or sideboard at about the height of her waist, but straightened up and turned her head as we came in.

"Thank you, my good woman," Dr Alabaster said. "You may stand aside now."

"It's 'Mrs Silverleaf', if it's all one to you, Doctor," she answered.

As she moved aside I was able to see what the object on the table was, and before I saw the face I knew who it had been. I halted where I was, not wanting to see more, but Skilliter gripped me from behind and shoved me forward until I was standing over the dreadful thing, and at the moment that I saw the features — looking even more than before like the youthful countenance I bore in my memory — I saw that the throat was jaggedly slashed. The wound had been washed and crudely stitched, but that only made the ugly red tear in the pale skin the more horribly apparent.

I heard the voice of Skilliter from the other side of the room: "He don't seem too keen to pay his respecks."

At that moment a dark mist clouded my vision and my legs ceased to bear my weight. However, my slide to the ground was halted by a strong hand beneath my shoulder and I felt myself being assisted into a chair that stood against the wall. As the dark circles of black mist cleared away I found the face of the woman looking at me with an extraordinarily intense expression of interest and concern.

"Respects, Skilliter!" came the doctor's jeering response. "To such a father?"

"What!" exclaimed Mrs Silverleaf. "You mean this boy is the poor creatur's son? That's beyond everything."

She muttered something to herself but I could not catch it.

Dr Alabaster said: "Did you say something, my good woman?"

"You didn't ought to have broke it to him so sudden," she said.

"Finish the work for which you have been paid and be on your way," he replied.

She sniffed and went back to the table. I saw that she was holding a linen cloth and that a bason of water stood on the table with a folded length of cotton whose shape and purpose I recognised from my memory of Mrs Lillystone.

Then turning to me, Dr Alabaster said: "I regret to have to inform you that your esteemed parent destroyed himself last night. I assume it was in grief at the news you conveyed to him of the death of your mother."

"You really didn't ought to have let him know," said Skilliter sarcastically.

"Indeed, I fear that you are to blame for your father's death," Dr Alabaster said. "It seems to be a family tradition. Be that as it may, the coroner sat on the body this morning and his jury returned a verdict of self-murder."

"I never heerd on sich a cruel thing as the way you're treating this boy," said Mrs Silverleaf.

I, however, had no strength to be angry at their taunts. All my thoughts were for the lonely, wasted life that had just come to so premature an end.

"That's enough from you," Skilliter said to her.

"Why," she went on, "to break it like that! I never did!"

I looked at Mrs Silverleaf's broad red face and it came to me that I knew her from somewhere.

"That's almost as cruel," she continued as if unstoppably impelled by the force of her indignation, "as to lock him in here alone with the poor thing all night."

"Why, listen to the good soul," said Dr Alabaster with a kind of malign delight. "I believe she may have hit upon something you and I have neglected to think of, Skilliter. For do you not consider that it would be only right and proper for the young gentleman to keep vigil by his father's body?"

Skilliter laughed sycophantically but the layer-out appeared not to have heard this remark, for she was now engaged upon unfolding the shroud and shaking it out.

"Lock him in here for the night," said Dr Alabaster to his deputy. "After all, he has known his father so briefly that it would be a pity not to spend with him what little time remains. Be sure to tell Yallop before you go off."

Skilliter nodded and Dr Alabaster left the room directing towards me a last gleeful smile.

"Will you help me with this, Mr Skilliter," said Mrs Silverleaf, who appeared to have heard none of this for she had made no comment upon it. While

I tried not to watch, she and Skilliter worked together to pull the shroud over the body and when they had succeeded, she tied it securely at the top.

At that moment the door was suddenly kicked open and Rookyard and the strange man I had seen the previous night outside my cell staggered into the room carrying a coffin, panting and swearing at the effort. They placed it on the table beside the body.

"The boy stays in here tonight, Yallop," Skilliter said to the stranger. "The doctor's instructions."

The three men grinned at each other and when the newcomers had regained their breath they set to work again and with Skilliter's assistance the body was lifted over the sides and dropped into the coffin. Meanwhile Mrs Silverleaf was collecting her possessions and packing them away into a large bundle ready to depart.

Then Rookyard, who was carrying a hammer, picked up one end of the lid and told the others to help him lift it onto the base.

"Shouldn't that wait for the undertaker's men?" asked Mrs Silverleaf looking up at that moment. "They usually like to do it theirselves."

"Why, what do you know about it?" Rookyard sneered.

"A great deal," she replied spiritedly. "I've laid out many a better-looking gentleman than any what I see before me now."

Rookyard reddened with anger but Yallop laughed and said: "Yes, she's right. Leave it for 'em."

"No, that ain't right," Rookyard persisted, and an argument broke out between the three men.

The layer-out reached across me to pick up a piece of sponge and as her face came close to mine she whispered: "Hide in the coffing."

I was stunned by these words and thought I had misheard them. I stared at her in amazement, but she was now packing her bundle with an expression as unconcerned as if she had not spoken.

Meanwhile the argument ended with the decision that the coffin should be left unsecured and, with ironical good wishes to myself for a pleasant night, the two turn-keys departed, leaving the night-porter behind.

As Mrs Silverleaf was securing her bundle she enquired conversationally of Yallop who was waiting with unconcealed impatience for her departure: "Who's doing the burying?"

"If it's any of your consarn, Winterflood and Cronk buries for us."

"Is that so?" she said. "I wondered if it might be Digweed and Son."

The room seemed to heave as if I were on board a ship in a squall and I leant back against the chair for support. That Christmas of long ago rose before me and I knew the woman now.

"Never heerd on 'em," said Yallop disparagingly. He picked up the blanket on which the body had been lying and folded it over his arm.

"When will they come?" she asked.

"Before first light tomorrer. We like our bodies to be out of here at night. It looks bad by day."

"It'll be a bitter cold night for this lad if he's to stay here until dawn," she said. "Spare him that blanket at least."

"I wasn't told nothing about no blanket," Yallop said doubtfully.

Mrs Digweed turned towards me and stared at me hard as she uttered the next words: "I think you'd best, Mr Yallop, or Winterflood and Cronk's men won't hardly know which on 'em is to be took when they come tomorrer."

I understood her and to my relief Yallop reluctantly relinquished the blanket into my hands. With a last glance of deep meaning towards me Mrs Digweed passed out of the room.

"Shall I leave him this light?" Yallop mused aloud, picking up his lanthorn and looking at the stub of candle left by the coffin. "Or would it be worse to be altogether in the dark?" He reflected for a moment: "I reckon it would be worse to have the bit o' candle left and see the shadders moving on the walls and know that in an hour or two it was going to burn out."

He left it where it was and went out, locking the door behind him.

I understood what I had to do, though my conscience and my stomach alike revolted against it. Perhaps it was fortunate that I had little time to reflect — beyond the conviction that if I failed to seize this chance, I would die — because I needed to act while the candle still burned. And so I began with excessive haste to try to raise the body and lift it over the side of the coffin. After some minutes of struggling I realized that my panic-stricken actions were achieving nothing except further to exhaust me. I forced myself to pause until my thumping heart had quietened and I had considered my next step rationally. It became clear to me that, weakened as I was by hunger, it would be a long and laborious task even if I could find the right way of going about it. But my approach was clearly the wrong one.

Suddenly I remembered the hideous song that I had heard from Isbister's company, and now I connected it with what I had seen them doing that night in Southwark. I realized that what I should do — despite my horror — was to kneel straddling the legs and embrace the shoulders in order to pull it so that it sat up.

This proved effective though I made only slow progress, and all the time as I struggled my hearing was alert to detect the approach of the night-porter. Eventually I managed to manoeuvre it out onto the table and from there to roll it to the edge. In order to lower it gently to the floor — for I could not bring myself to push it over the rim and let it fall — I had to position myself beneath it and pull it down onto me, going down on my knees as my legs buckled under the weight. I managed this successfully and once it was on the ground untied the shroud and after a long struggle pulled it off.

Now I rolled the body into the furthest corner of the room and arranged it to look like a sleeping figure, laying over it the blanket which I was sure Mrs Digweed had intended that I should use for this purpose. As I was doing this the guttering candle burned out, but I did not need its light for my last action which was to climb back onto the table, pull the shroud over myself, and then clamber into the coffin concealing the untied end beneath my head. I found that I could breathe through the cheap cloth, though with some difficulty.

CHAPTER 83

There was so much that I wanted to avoid thinking about as the long cold hours dragged by. I seized gratefully on the extraordinary nature of my encounter with Mrs Digweed. How was it that she had reappeared in my life in this of all places? Was it by means of a series of meaningless coincidences or by a chain of carefully-linked connexions? Either possibility seemed implausible. Whichever it was, how strange a part she and her family seemed to have played in my life — assuming, of course, that Barney and Sally were members of her family. And there was Joey, too. And now that I thought of him it occurred to me that I was blindly trusting the mother, when it was the son who had led me into this very trap.

I found myself, despite the extreme cold, breaking into a perspiration at these reflections. Was I delivering myself voluntarily to some kind of horrible death? If so, then never had victim more laboriously prepared himself for it. But if my worst fears were well-founded, then what could I do? If I passed up this chance now, then surely only a longer-delayed death awaited me? Was I, then, trusting Mrs Digweed only because I had no alternative? Surely not. There had been true kindness in her manner, and I could not bear to believe that she had acted a part in order to lure me to a cruel death. And yet Emma had taken me in! And even if I had done right in trusting Mrs Digweed, what was to be gained by my concealing myself in this way? Surely I would be discovered by the undertaker's men?

I grew colder and colder under the thin shroud as the night deepened, and many strange thoughts came to me: that I was at least appropriately attired and positioned should the cold overcome me, and that after all it was not so terrible a thing to die. I wondered who would be affected by my passing from the world. Perhaps Mr Nolloth would be the sole mourner, and now that I thought of him it came to me that it had not been for himself that he was grieving but for his friend, and, I supposed, for me. Miss Quilliam would be sorry for me if she ever heard of my death — and Henry Bellringer, too. Then I wondered if Henrietta would ever learn of it and, if by some chance she did, whether she would grieve for me. The one thing I tried not to think of was the silent presence in the corner of the room whose place I had sacrilegiously usurped.

At last I heard the door being unlocked and the sound of footsteps as if several people were entering. I began to breathe as infrequently and as shallowly as I could. Through the thin cotton I could even see the faint illumination of lanthorns.

Then Yallop's voice, disconcertingly close, said angrily: "I'm damned if I know why you've come so early. It's a good three hours to first light."

A man's voice that was strange to me said: "Them was the orders what I had of Mr Winterflood."

"You nivver had 'em of Winterflood," said Yallop. "He's been dead these twenty year."

"Then it must have been the other genel'man, for I ain't but jist started and don't know the names yet."

"Well, Cronk ain't nivver sent no-one so early a-fore. And it's most irregular not to have brung a proper growed man. I nivver heerd on sich a thing. Especially as, beggin' your parding, you're sitiwated as you are. I suppose you'll expeck me to help carry the box?"

"Why, the guv'nor give me a shillin' for that wery purpose."

"Oh did he?" said the night-porter's voice, slightly mollified. "Well, there it is. But where's that damned boy? They told me to watch out for him in case he tried to hook it. Why there he is fast asleep in the corner over yonder! And sleeping like the dead hisself."

To my dismay I heard him move towards the far corner saying brutally: "See how much respeck he shows for his own dad! I'll soon give him somethin' to dream about."

Quickly the other voice said: "Help me with this lid will you, Mr Yallop?"

"You're arstin' a lot for that shillin'," said Yallop irritably, but I heard his footsteps moving back towards me.

There was a brief silence which was broken by the grunts of the two men, then the lid was banged down only an inch or two from my face so that I had to force myself not to flinch.

"Hold that there nail steady, will you, Mr Yallop," said the stranger's voice.

"Can't your boy do it?" protested Yallop.

"He can't reach while it's on the table," said the strange voice.

A moment later I was nearly deafened by the crash of the hammer. And then as I listened to one nail after another being driven in my heart began to pound as I wondered how long I would be able to breathe in that confined space and tried not to imagine a horrible possibility.

"Why bless me," said Yallop, "if that boy ain't still asleep, though this noise would wake the wery dead. I'll try what a kick from my boot kin do."

Almost with relief, I resigned myself to the inevitable.

However, I instantly felt myself being tipped up and the strange man cried: "Bear a hand there, will you, Mr Yallop. I can't hold both ends by meself."

"What the divil did you do that for?" said Yallop indignantly. "You should have waited until I was ready."

As he spoke I felt the coffin being raised to the accompaniment of alarming groans and then lowered slightly, I presumed onto the shoulders of the two men. We advanced a few unsteady steps and I judged that we were out in the passage.

Suddenly Yallop said angrily: "Put it down, for Gawd's sake."

I was in a state of terror, fearing that he had realized the deception being practised for now I desperately wanted the attempt to succeed.

"I have to lock the door agin that blessed boy."

The door clanged shut and the key rasped in the lock.

At that moment I heard a boy's voice very close to me — he must have had his mouth pressed up against the coffin: "Hold on just a minute longer, Master Johnnie!"

I knew the voice: it was indeed that of the boy who had led me to the house in Islington!

The coffin was raised again and after a while I could tell that we were descending stairs. At last I was deposited on the ground with a jolting thud, and heard the elaborate unlocking of what I guessed to be the main street-door. There was the sound of footsteps on gravel and a moment later I was jarred by the crash of the coffin hitting, as I guessed, the tail-gate of a cart.

"There's your shillin'," said the stranger's voice panting with exertion.

"Why, here's a start!" said Yallop, also gasping. "That ain't the reg'lar dead-cart what Winterflood and Cronk allus sends."

I heard the stranger clucking his tongue: "Hurry up, Gunpowder!"

I was beginning to grow dizzy and though I knew I recognised that name, I could not remember where I had heard it.

At that moment Yallop cried: "Why's this hiding the name?"

"Leave that be!" cried the boy and at that instant I felt that the cart was in motion.

"Why ain't it Winterflood and Cronk?" Yallop shouted. "Who the devil is Isbister?"

Isbister! Of course! This was his horse and cart! Then I had after all entered some kind of hideous trap! I tried to cry out and to beat on the sides of the box, but the air I gasped was hot and choking and no sound emerged from my throat. The effort was too much: there came the sound of rushing water in my ears and a flood seemed to be closing over my head as I began to lose consciousness.

We drove for some distance though I had no idea of how long we had been in movement before the cart drew up. I heard the clatter of tools against the lid, and then, to my inexpressible relief it was raised and I took draughts of fresh cold air through the cotton. A hand helped me to sit up and drew the ghastly covering from my head and face.

As my face came free of the cloth my eyes, accustomed to the darkness, were dazzled by a bright light very near. After a moment I realized that it came from a lanthorn which was being held aloft by someone on the seat of the cart, and that its glare was preventing me from seeing the figure of the person who had helped me to get free of the shroud.

"Shut that down, Joey, and watch out for Yallop," came the stranger's voice.

As the shutter of the lanthorn was lowered I found myself staring straight into the most horribly disfigured face I had ever seen. The skin was everywhere pitted and deeply scarred, the features had been brutally squashed leaving the nose a swollen lump and the lips twisted so that the few teeth that remained were exposed, and, worst of all, one eye was no more than a leering, red socket. I saw, too, that this terrible figure had only one hand: the other was an ugly hook that protruded from the sleeve of his coat. I flinched, wondering what I had delivered myself up to. It came to me that I had indeed died and that this was what lay beyond death.

My horror must have been only too obvious for the man said, in a strangely gentle tone: "Don't be alarmed, young master. Though I know I ain't a picter o' roses."

"Are you all right, Master Johnnie?" the boy asked.

I nodded and looked round, putting one hand over my forehead to try to shield my eyes from the light of the lanthorn which was still making it impossible to see him.

"Shut it right down," my rescuer said. "We don't want the watch to see us. I have a notion what game they'd suspect was afoot if they was to see us now, eh, Joey? Especially with this cart and hoss."

The light was suddenly reduced to a narrow beam as a plate was slid across the eye-hole. Now I saw that the boy holding it was indeed the youth who had come to me outside my grandfather's house.

"Joey Digweed!" I exclaimed.

He looked at me rather shame-facedly and squirmed into place on the driver's seat holding the reins.

"That's right," said the man. "And I'm his father, George."

While I was struggling to understand the significance of these revelations, Mr Digweed helped me to clamber out of the coffin and then free myself from the shroud. Then, to my surprise — but I was beyond being surprised — he deftly rolled the cloth up, put it back into the box and then lightly nailed the lid down again.

While he was doing this I had leisure to notice my surroundings, and saw that the horse and cart were drawn in at the side of a wide and deserted road which was unpaved and unlit. The houses around us were in darkness except for the flickering light of an occasional early riser's candle.

"We've only come a few hundred yards," Mr Digweed explained. "Yallop roused the house by ringing the bell when he thought he knowed what we was doing, so I reckon they'll be upon us in a minute."

"Then why are we delaying?" I cried.

Mr Digweed laughed: "They'll take a fair bit of time to put a hoss to the shafts at this time o' night. And if they come a-foot, we'll leave 'em behind soon enough." He nodded at the coffin which, working skilfully despite his handicap, he had nearly secured by now: "But I ain't taking this. I never stole nothing in my life and I shan't start now."

"Here they come!" Joey cried excitedly.

I looked back the way we had come and saw lights approaching.

Unperturbed, Mr Digweed dismounted from the cart and gently lowered the coffin to the ground.

"Give me that lanthorn," he said and Joey passed it to me to hand to him. To my surprise he put it on top of the coffin.

"All right, Joey," he cried and, as he jumped back on board, Joey shook the reins.

"The lanthorn will show 'em where it is," he explained, "and slow 'em down in the bargain."

Gunpowder — a horse, as I well remembered, with a mind of his own — failed to respond. Joey shook the reins again and shouted at him. I looked behind us and saw that the approaching figures were now only a hundred yards away. I could make out Yallop and two night-shirted figures whom I took to be Rookyard and Skilliter.

Mr Digweed clambered past me onto the seat to take the reins from his son, then shook them and clucked with his tongue — but still to no effect. Our pursuers, now only a few yards away, began to bellow in triumph as they saw our plight. At this, however, Gunpowder put his ears back in fright and instantly set off at a fast trot. I sat as close behind the other two as I could and described to them what was happening behind us. Rookyard and Skilliter continued to chase us, though Yallop, who was more portly, stopped by the coffin. Mercifully, our pursuers fell steadily behind us and after a few hundred yards they gave up.

Mr Digweed turned back and smiled gleefully: "How I'd like to see Yallop's face now. It *will* puzzle 'em to find the coffing there."

For the first time the grave expression on Joey's face lightened as he looked from his father to me.

"I reckon I know what they think we've got on this cart," Mr Digweed went on. "But if the watch stops us they won't find what Yallop and the others thinks. It won't be till later that they figure out what's happened when they find you've gone and ... " Suddenly he broke off and said gravely: "I beg your pardon, young genel'man. I meant no disrespeck."

I clasped his arm and tried to speak of my gratitude.

My face must have been more eloquent than any words, for my deliverer shook his head and said: "Whatever we done is all the old lady's doing, not mine, sir."

"I don't know what I can say," I managed to utter.

"Say nothin', sir. That's allus best I find."

"But why have you ... ?"

"I'll let her explain, sir."

"Here's a coat she said I was to give you," said Joey, picking up and passing to me a man's great-coat — shabby but serviceable — that lay on the box beside him.

I wrapped it around myself gratefully for the night was exceedingly cold. As I did so I brushed against something hanging over the side of the cart and I recognised it as the piece of tarred sacking which I remembered so well, and which Yallop had pulled aside just now.

"But Mr Digweed," I said, "please tell me how it is that this cart belongs to a man called Isbister of Parliament-street, Bethnal-green, a man whose trade I know to be ... ?" I broke off.

"Why, you know him, do you?" said Mr Digweed turning to look at me in surprise. "That's a strange thing. But the old lady will explain that, too. If I tried I'd on'y get muddled up and you'd be more posed nor ever."

The little cart rattled at a spanking pace down the dark road. In contrast to the surrounding gloom, faint glimmers of light were beginning to appear ahead of us, for we were heading south towards the metropolis. As the darkness slowly lifted, the sky grudgingly disclosed itself as grey and overcast, but I had never witnessed a more joyous dawn.

I found myself taking pleasure in the most trivial and unremarkable sights. Increasingly now there were lights visible in the houses that we passed and I wondered about the people in them who were getting up and washing and dressing and preparing breakfast and making ready to go to work or to school or to scavenge for food.

We were at the hour when the market traffic is at its heaviest and the cart was over-hauling one rumbling waggon after another headed for Covent-garden or Spitalfields, each heavily laden with market produce and drawn by a team of great dray-horses with jangling bells and blinkers, recalling to my mind my earlier escape from the Quiggs and the waggon which had aided me. And market women balancing their huge baskets of eggs and fowls and garden-produce on their heads and bound for the same destination were striding along at the edge of the road with the long swinging gait of country-people, which is so different from the quick, nervous walk of the city-dweller.

We passed several droves of cattle on their way to Smithfield and herded by men with dogs and long whips, and once we were held up when some of the beasts spilled across the carriageway in a kind of doomed bovine uprising, and I remembered the clumsy lumbering beasts which had crowded down the farm-lane past our garden-gate when I was a little child.

Once a mail-coach came up behind us, its guard signalling to us to pull out of the way with a long arrogant blast of his horn. And I, on a foolish impulse — intoxicated, perhaps, by exhaustion and excitement — stood up on the swaying floor of the cart, while Mr Digweed and Joey clutched my legs, and halooed and cheered. As the coach swept magnificently past, I saw the tired faces of the outside passengers — some asleep with their heads leaning against each other's shoulders and others waking up and staring at me with sullen listlessness —

and I laughed aloud that anyone should look so miserable at the start of a new day.

Everything was a source of interest and delight to me. Why then did I suddenly become aware that I was weeping and have to hide my face in the sleeve of my new coat? At first I thought my tears were shed in joy at my unforeseen deliverance, but then I realized that I was also sobbing for one whose death I had hardly had time to think of, and sobbing the more because it meant so little to me.

Despite my attempt to conceal my tears, Mr Digweed noticed my grief. "Oh dear, oh dear," he said in deep embarrassment. Then he struck his forehead: "What am I thinking on!"

He reached into his coat and brought out from a capacious pocket a flask of hot coffee and a packet of sandwiches, both of which he insisted I take. Faced with food and drink, I now found myself to be extremely hungry and consumed far more than my fair share of both.

So I ate and drank as we rolled along, and Mr Digweed turned his head at intervals and smiled and nodded at me to signify that I should eat as much as I wanted, and shook his head to indicate that, no, he did not want any of the food. And as this nourishment took effect, my spirits revived again, and I began to speculate on where we were going and what I should find there. The only blot upon my peace of mind was the solemn face of Joey Digweed who, the few times he looked round to take a sandwich or a pull at the flask, stared at me with an expression that I could not interpret as anything but resentful hostility.

We had been passing down Brick-lane but now turned right into Flower-and-Dean-street. A little way along it, Mr Digweed pulled up the cart at a corner where there was the shell of a burned-out house. He dismounted and led the horse down a narrow way into a little back-court of four or five low, mean dwellings like cottages (though of two stories) constructed in the rear-gardens of the big houses in the street.

As we approached, the door of one of them opened and Mrs Digweed came hurrying out smiling broadly.

I got down from the cart.

"How can I thank you?" I said, taking her hand and shaking it vigorously.

She looked at me for a moment and then suddenly moved forward and embraced me, holding me to her for an instant.

"Bless you," she said, and then stepped back apologising for her familiarity. But immediately she seized me and hugged me all over again. She sniffed several times, then I heard her mutter something I didn't quite catch about "Your poor blessed mother" and I saw that there were tears in her eyes. She pulled an enormous red handkerchief from somewhere about her person and held it to her face dabbing at her eyes and rubbing her nose savagely as if it had done her a wrong.

"My mother ... " I began, but she interrupted me gently.

"I know. You don't have to say nothing."

Mr Digweed, who had been looking on benignly, now said: "I'll have to take the hoss and cart back now, old lady. I said I'd return 'em before half arter seven o'clock and it must be past seven by now."

"Very well, George," Mrs Digweed answered in a voice that was trembling slightly.

So while he and Joey turned the cart and went back the way we had come, Mrs Digweed led me inside the house.

It consisted of a single chamber on the ground floor a couple of feet below the level of the yard, and another one above. Once across the threshold, therefore, I found myself immediately in a room which, though small, served as kitchen, living-room and bed-chamber. It was clean and neatly — if sparsely — furnished and altogether very superior to what I had seen of the habitations of the poor. At one side there was a wooden ladder to the room above and at the back a door which led to a tiny wash-house in a small yard.

Mrs Digweed sat me at a small deal table before the hearth and then stepped back to look at me, saying gleefully: "I jist knowed they'd work it."

"Why have you done this? And how in heaven's name, Mrs Digweed, did you find me?"

"All that can wait," she said, smiling as if at a secret source of satisfaction. "It's a long story and it needs Joey here to say his piece, too. I can see you're fair done up, so fust things fust."

She had some broth already prepared for me and now keeping warm over the fire and, despite the sandwiches, I realized that I was still hungry. I consumed it with thick slices of bread, and meanwhile she continued to parry my questions with a laugh and a shake of the head.

As I finished, she busied herself making ready a place for me to sleep on a settle in a corner.

Feeling suddenly tired I laid myself down and Mrs Digweed pulled some blankets over me. Suddenly it occurred to me that I was in Spitalfields — the part of London which seemed to have some mysterious connexion with my mother's past, though her account had not made it clear. I was quickly asleep and enjoyed a deeper repose than I had experienced since the eve of the occasion, not much more than a week before, when I had been taken before the Court of Chancery.

I became aware of the murmur of voices and opened my eyes to find that Mr and Mrs Digweed, together with Joey, were sitting at the little table before the hearth at the opposite end of the low chamber, and talking quietly together. Now that the excitement of my escape had worn off I felt growing suspicion. I watched them for some time through half-closed eyes wondering if I could really believe that they had rescued me solely from altruistic motives, and that they were not part of a complex conspiracy against me. Finding that I could not catch their words I could not suppress the suspicion that they were speaking softly in order that they should not be overheard. I would bide my time and try to discover their real motives while I regained my strength. Meanwhile I would tell them very little and see how much they told me. At that moment Mrs Digweed glanced towards me and I saw in her face such an expression of good-natured concern that I forgot to maintain my small deception and opened my eyes fully.

She smiled and said: "Come and eat with us. We were waiting for you."

Dressed in some clothes borrowed from Joey, I joined them and, finding myself again hungry, shared their meal of bread and herring.

Though I tried to restrain my curiosity, at last I said: "There are so many things I don't understand."

"In course," Mrs Digweed said. "Well, it's Joey's story. Leastways, to begin with, for it was he that fust found you."

"How was it," I said to him, "that you met me at that house at Charing-cross?"

"Why, I dodged you there from Barney's crib."

"I thought somebody was behind me! So you were the 'Joey' I heard Barney mention." The boy who had been needed for some secret purpose that night, I recollected, wondering if he would tell me about this. "But why?" I asked.

"When I come to the crib out by the Neat-houses that night," Joey answered, "Barney told me to watch you the whole time in case you tried to cut and run. 'Stick to him like bricks,' he said. He told me there weren't no harm in it. Well, I didn't expeck that you'd try nothing that night, but as it happened I was woke up a few hours later by the bolt clattering when you let yourself out."

"And you stuck by me for two or three days?"

"Aye," he said shame-facedly.

So Barney was being paid by someone to watch me, as I had suspected. Presumably it was Sancious working for the Clothiers. And Joey's answer merely put back the need for an explanation to an earlier stage: "But how was it," I asked, "that you and I should both come to be there in Barney's company?"

There was a silence and no-one looked at me.

"It was just chance," Joey said.

Now I knew he was lying — and presumably his parents, too. Did they know that Barney was the housebreaker who had burgled my mother and me at Melthorpe? Surely they did. But they did not realize that I had discovered this and that therefore I knew that it was stretching coincidence too far not to assume a connexion between him and them. I was almost sure that he was Joey's uncle, and that made him the brother of one or other of his parents. And I was pretty sure that Sally was their daughter. I would give them the chance to confess.

"What is your connexion with Barney?" I asked, looking from face to face.

All avoided my eye and the parents looked at their son.

"I got mixed up with him," he said. "That's the long and the short of it."

They all studied their wooden platters which they had by now turned over to receive the pudding.

I was sure I was right. Someone — though I could not conceive who it might be — must have paid them to rescue me and gain my confidence. But why, if Barney was working with Sancious to have me trapped by my enemies — the Porteouses and their collaborator, Alabaster — why had Joey and his parents rescued me? Was the rescue a mere charade? If not, then in whose interest was it to make me safe from the Porteouses? Surely it must be the work of the Mompessons!

"How did you come to be in that place, Master Johnnie?" Mrs Digweed asked, after a silence.

I described how, two years ago, my mother and I had gone to Cox's-square to search for Mrs Digweed and had been told by the old man, Sam'el, the addresses of Isbister and Pulvertaft, and how, although we had gone to the former on that occasion, I had remembered the latter's address and gone there more recently and been directed by him to Barney.

"Why, that accounts for the whole business!" exclaimed Mrs Digweed. "Old Sam'el told you wrong. He always was a muddle-headed old cove. My George never worked the sack-'em-up line."

"Then what is your connexion with Isbister?" I asked.

"We was neighbours a good few years back," Mr Digweed said. "And I hire — I mean borrer — his hoss and cart now and then."

I considered this. It occurred to me that Sam'el might have confused George with Barney, in which case it was possible that there might be no connexion between the Digweeds and him — for he had, after all, never admitted to the name — so that the only coincidence would lie in the fact that they and he had once been friends or neighbours of old Sam'el. The old man's mistake, then, had led me to Barney. However, since I knew that Barney had burgled my mother's house before Joey and his mother had come there, I knew that this explanation was inadequate. Moreover, the Digweeds' manner was guilty and suspicious.

There was another question I could put to Joey to see if he was lying:

"Why did you lead me to that particular house in Islington?"

"Why, it wasn't no pertickler crib," he said sullenly, and did not meet my eye. "I chose it at a ventur'."

This, of course, was a lie and made it clear that the whole story was a fabrication or at the very least involved huge omissions. But I thought of something else:

"Joey, Barney stole some things from me that night just before I left. Do you know what became of them? They were very precious to me, though of no value to anyone else."

"You mean that pocket-book and them other papers that he give to ... to one of the gals?"

"Yes, it was Sally. Don't you know her name?"

He reddened and avoided my eye. His parents looked equally conscious.

"Yes, that's right," he said. "Sally. Well, she told me arterwards they was prigged of her right arter that."

It was as if my last link with my mother had been snapped.

"But I haven't said yet what I done arterwards," Joey went on. "I felt ashamed at what I'd done. You rec'lleck, Master Johnnie, what I said when you was being carried into the crib and you thanked me so nice?"

"You asked," I said, "if you could come and see me."

"I did, for I wanted to know that no harm would befall you. And it was because of what you said to me then. You rec'lleck, you said to 'em, 'be good to this boy'? Well, arterwards I worrited and worrited about what I'd done. Barney give me five shillin' and that made it worse. It didn't seem right to put a down on someone who hadn't no more tin than what I did. I mean to say, taking it off of them as has got plenty of it and is too green to know how to keep it don't seem wrong to me."

He was addressing these words with an air of defiance to his parents who looked at each other gravely.

"I went back to Barney but he was in a sad way arter what happened that night, and we was moving from crib to crib like hunted rats. I begun to think about things and to reckon that mebbe he wasn't so great as I'd believed. For I'd always thought he was a fine fellow with his adventures and his free-spending ways and his disrespeck for the law. Well, anyways, the long and the short of it is that I decided to cut away from Barney and so one night right arter that I lit out and come back here."

"Heaven be thanked," said his mother.

"And I told me mam and dad everything what I'd done."

"And that's when we vowed that we would help you," Mrs Digweed said, "in order to make up for what Joey done, and because of the kindness of your sweet mother that Christmas-time."

"But if you chose that house you led me to at random," I asked, "why did you later come to think I was in danger?"

Joey blushed and they all avoided my eye.

At last Joey said: "It was 'cause when I told Barney what I'd done he was very pleased. So I guessed you was in danger."

This was a feeble evasion of the truth. However, I pretended to believe it and encouraged him to go on.

"So," Joey began, "me and me dad kept watch on the crib day and night, turn and turn about. Arter around a week or so we heerd you banging and shouting at the back, and the sarvints told us there was this poor mad boy kept there and nobody wasn't to take no notice of the noise he made. We were very worrited about that but we couldn't think of no way to get you out. Then one night three or four days back, I was watching in the street when I seen a coach draw up and some men went into the crib and then come out again holding you, and they put you into the coach. So I run behind it all the way to Clapton. Then I come back here and told Ma and me dad where they'd took you."

"And we guessed what kind of a place it was," Mrs Digweed continued, "and so we wanted to get you out of there as quick as we could. So I spent a couple of days in the boosing-ken nearest to it in hopes of befriending the sarvints when they come in for their wet."

"The old lady is precious good at making friends," her husband put in.

"Well, I had the notion of trying to get laundress-work there for that's mostly how I've kept meself these last few years. But the sarvints told me there weren't none, 'cause they sent it all out. Well, then" — here she looked grave and lowered her voice — "jist two days ago one of the maids as I'd got to know come into the public and said there'd been a death in the house and could I lay out? In course I said I could, which were nothing less than the truth, for it's somethin' I've done often and often."

Her voice quavered slightly and she paused for a moment.

"The gal went back to speak to someone and then come agin and told me that was all right. Only fust there was to be a crowner's inkwich later that day. It was to be held in an upstairs room of that wery same tap. So I went up and sat at the back. In course, I didn't know it was your poor dad, but jist thought it was a way of gettin' inside."

"How did he die?" I asked.

"He managed to get free during the night," she said softly, "and break a bottle and ... " She hesitated. "One of the keepers was got to tell the crowner that he hadn't fastened his chain as tight as he should. The crowner said the keepers shouldn't be so soft with the inmates from now on. He even said he suspicioned that the keeper had been bribed."

That fatal sovereign! The coin that had been given me by Daniel! That I had passed to Stillingfleet with the best of intentions, hoping that it should bring relief to the wretched sufferer. Well, in the event it had.

Mrs Digweed had paused but now went on: "And then when you come in last night I recognised you and larned as how the poor genel'man was your dad. I seen the way they was trying to drive you out of your wits by affrighting you. So I put the notion into that doctor's head to make you stay there all night."

Mr Digweed laughed and nodded at me as if to draw my attention to his wife's resourcefulness, and then took up the story: "She come back here arter that (nigh on midnight!) and told me to find a hoss and cart that very minute and get up there with Joey a-fore dawn. She told me what to do and that I was to tell the night-porter that I was from Winterflood and Cronk. So me and Joey went round to Jerry Isbister's and luckily he didn't have no need of them that night. But he was mighty curious and I think he must have wondered if I was going into the resurrection line myself."

"Which you was, in a manner of speaking," his wife put in.

"Aye, I reckon I was," Mr Digweed said reflectively. Then he concluded: "And you knows the rest, Master Johnnie."

"I believe you have saved my life," I said, for whatever their motives might be, I was sure of this.

But what were their motives? Money, presumably. It was obvious from the appearance of the room and the nature of our meal that they were very poor, so someone had paid for the hire of Isbister's horse and cart.

"Well, and if it comes to that, Master Johnnie, I don't reckon as you are altogether safe even now," said Mrs Digweed. "Them people at the madhouse, they'll want to ketch you agin, won't they? And they seen George, and there ain't many in Lunnon as looks like him."

The same thought had already occurred to me, but I was struck by how sincere her concern appeared to be.

"And, besides, he seen the name on the cart," said Joey.

"But Jerry will jist say it was borrered without his leave," said Mr Digweed.

They were right. I was still hardly out of danger. Although it was only late afternoon I found myself to be extremely tired again, and seeing this Mrs Digweed suggested that I retire for the night with a hot posset of rum. I was making myself comfortable on the settle again when I learned that Mr Digweed and Joey were making preparations to go to work. It struck me as a very late hour to be doing so, but I did not long concern myself with this for I was soon fast asleep.

CHAPTER 84

Although I had fallen so rapidly into a slumber, I slept badly and awoke tired and feverish at a very early hour. I felt too weak to get up, and seeing my pale face Mrs Digweed, who was alone in the house and making ready to go out to her laundress-work, insisted that I remain there. Despite my protests she sent a neighbour to make her excuses at the house to which she had been engaged, and remained at home to nurse me. She must have realized then — for she had had experience enough of sickness — that I was very ill, and my last clear memory is of her bustling about the room preparing hot cloths and basons.

After that I remember nothing except being very hot and yet, strangely, at the same time icily cold; being haunted by fevered dreams and parched by a raging thirst. And I recall the presence always when I awoke of Mrs Digweed who nursed me with great kindness and skill. It was as if, without my realizing it, my strength had been at the limit of its endurance during the privations I had endured over the previous weeks, and now that I was safe it took the opportunity to collapse. (As I learned only later, they sent for a surgeon from the London Dispensary nearby, who prescribed medicines which I was sure they could not afford, and my conviction that they were receiving money from someone was strengthened.) For the first few days I remained in the lower room because it was the warmer, but when on the third day the fever broke and the crisis was past, Mr Digweed carried me upstairs and laid me on a straw mattress in the other chamber; and from now on this was where I slept while Joey made his bed on another mattress on the floor nearby. During the weeks that followed I stayed in bed and slept most of the day while my strength returned.

When I was better I was carried downstairs during the day and sat in a chair by the kitchen fire. Now that I was able to take notice of what was going on around me, I was struck by the amount of noise coming from the houses nearby: dogs barking and drunken shouts and fierce arguments all day and all night. It seemed to me that the neighbourhood was worse even than Orchard-street — and later I came to know that, indeed, it was perhaps the worst part of London and jocularly called Jack Ketch's Kitchen. Flower-and-Dean-street was its most notorious thoroughfare, consisting of big old houses, now decaying, which had been "made-down" and were dens of thieves — and worse than thieves. Because the Digweeds' cottage was up a "slumber" at Deal's-court, which had been thrown up in the back-gardens of the big houses, it was somewhat secluded from the goings-on in the street. And I soon noticed that the Digweeds seemed deliberately to keep themselves apart from their neighbourhood, although of course Mrs Digweed's gossips came in to borrow cups of sugar and pass the time of day, and boys came looking for Joey. (My hosts' visiters stared at me curiously but were given no explanation of my identity.) Also, Mr Digweed went to the pub every day and Mrs Digweed often accompanied him, and I'm afraid I could not help noticing that they frequently came home the worse for drink.

Most of all, I remarked that Mr Digweed and Joey were out for much of the time but at hours that varied strangely. Sometimes they set off during the morning, sometimes in the afternoon or evening, and occasionally Joey woke me when he rose in the middle of the night and went downstairs. Once or twice I watched from the little window that over-looked the yard in front and saw him and his father leave the house, each wearing worsted stockings up to the waist, greased knee-boots, a loose blue shirt, long oil-skins which were not like the loose-hanging garments that sailors wear but fitted closely around them, and a fan-tailed leather hat. Between them they bore a bag worn on a strap over the shoulder, a large sieve, and a long-handled implement like a kind of hoe or rake. And each had a short knife, a stick, and a trowel worn at the belt, and carried a closed lanthorn even when they went out and returned during day-light hours.

I could make little of this or their hours: they were never away longer than about six hours, the only times they never ventured out were when it was wet (for they went out on Saturdays and Sundays), and they always came home exhausted and filthy. Now I recalled that when Mrs Digweed had come to our house in Melthorpe she had mentioned that her husband was "working the shores", and my mother and I had guessed that this meant scavenging along the river. This would explain the hours since they could only do so during a low tide, though it did not account entirely for their dress and the equipment they carried.

Since the little house was kept scrupulously clean by virtue of a great deal of hard work by Mrs Digweed — with a little assistance from her husband and son — it was some time before I realized how extremely malodorous the male Digweeds' work was. Once I was well enough to spend most of my time downstairs I perceived that at whatever hour Mr Digweed and Joey returned they always entered the house by the back way, and eventually I grasped that the point of this was that they removed their oil-skins and boots in the little back-yard and washed their hands and faces under the common cistern-pump. Their things were then cleaned — usually by Mrs Digweed — before being brought into the house, and it was for this reason that I took so long to realize how foul their original state was and to wonder how this could have come about. After performing their ablutions and in a state of absolute exhaustion, Mr Digweed and Joey made a light breakfast and then lay down and slept soundly for several hours.

When they volunteered no explanation and my hesitant questions were turned aside in evident embarrassment, I began to become suspicious, and the more so when I noticed that they quite often came back with injuries — particularly Joey. These were usually nothing more than slight cuts or bruises, but once every couple of weeks or so one of them — usually Joey — had a wound that incapacitated him for a day or two. (Was this the way Mr Digweed had received his injuries?) There were other things: they purchased newspapers and Joey — since Mr Digweed could not read — pored over them. I could not help remembering how Sally and Jack had done the same.

Whatever it was, they appeared to be making very little money for the signs of poverty were everywhere. Their clothes were patched and threadbare, they mashed tea two or three times from the used leaves which were boiled with milk, and they ate little but herring, the rough bread of the poor, and occasional faggots or blood-puddings. Yet the rent was paid every week when the deputy came round for it, and they were able to keep themselves in coals, clothes and candles. I was certain that they were being paid by whoever it was who was taking an interest in me, and that this was why they were providing my keep without any prospect of recompense from myself.

Mrs Digweed, moreover, was working as a laundress, which necessitated rising and going out very early in the morning to help some establishment — often an hour's walk away — with their weekly wash. Despite this, I could see that their situation was precarious for they had no savings to rely on and, which was much more to be looked for, no valuables to pawn in the case of illness or accident.

One night at the beginning of April when I had been there the best part of two months, I awoke in the early hours and, hearing voices, I crept down the ladder. Mr Digweed and Joey were sitting at the little table before the fire at the other end of the room while their wife and mother slept on the settle. They were counting coins into piles and I believed I saw the glint of silver and perhaps even of gold. I watched for perhaps a minute and then, fearful of being seen, crept back to my bed. What were they up to? Was that the money that they were being paid by someone to take care of me? I determined that I would ask some direct questions the next day.

So the following evening as we were gathered at the table for our meal, I said: "You've been very kind to me, but now that I'm recovered I must leave you."

Though I thought Joey looked pleased, his parents were as alarmed as I had expected if they were receiving payment for keeping me.

"Why you ain't well enough yet!" Mrs Digweed exclaimed. "And wherever would you go?"

"I can't stay here costing you money," I objected.

They looked embarrassed at these words, as I had anticipated.

"Wait until you're stronger," she said.

"Well, just a little longer since you're so kind," I said sarcastically, and I thought she blushed.

"We're on'y paying you back," she said. "You and your mam for your kindness that Christmas-time."

"Yes," I began. "I meant to ask you, how was it that you and Joey happened to be in Melthorpe then?"

I wanted to draw them out for I was sure I would find gaps and inconsistencies in their story.

They all three looked at each other in some perplexity.

Then Mr Digweed began: "It all goes back to when I couldn't find no work in my own trade so I had to take a job with the Gas, Light and Coke Company in their new works in the Horseferry-road."

"I remember you mentioning it that Christmas-time, Mrs Digweed!" I cried. I turned to her husband: "And you were injured in an explosion there."

They looked at each other in surprise.

"No, it wasn't that," Mr Digweed said.

He seemed unwilling to say more, but, recalling my suspicions, I prompted him to go on.

"In them days the other companies was trying to lay their pipes in our district. They would break up ours and we'd do the same to theirs if we got the chance — especially when we found they'd laid their pipes overnight." He chuckled but then looked grave and said. "But there was worse. Some of our foremen would let on they was trying to win their men over with gin, and then when they was disguised in liquor, they'd go at 'em with pikes and bludgeons. There was men killed in the gas wars. But I never took no part in that. Not until one day when I got 'tacked by the lads from the Eq'itable, and they throwed me into one of our braziers for heating the tarmacadam, and put out my eye and smashed my arm bad."

"They took George to the cutting-ward of St. George's and had his arm off," Mrs Digweed put in with a shudder. "And they couldn't save the eye."

"So when I come out I had to be nussed by the old lady. In course, I didn't have no work to go back to like this." He indicated the hook.

"Did you not get any compensation? I mean, set-off?" I asked, feeling rather ashamed of my suspicions.

"Aye," Mrs Digweed said. "I must do 'em the justice to say they gived George a hundred pound hurt-money."

"That was a great deal!" I cried.

"Aye," she said quickly; "but we lost it all soon arterwards."

"Lost it? How?" I demanded, suspicious once again.

They looked embarrassed and then Mr Digweed began:

"Well, it was somebody ... somebody as I knowed. He'd got hisself mixed up in this building spec over by the Neat-houses and he arst me to j'in him in it. Well, I thought it was a good thing and so I went in with him on one o' the houses. And so did others that he knowed. And we sub-contracted to do the plaistering and j'inery work on a few on 'em. Well, I worked for nearly a year while we lived on our hurt-money and Maggie here went out washing."

I was sure he was referring to Barney. Why did he not admit it? It could only be because he was trying to conceal this criminal connexion from me.

"How did this friend of yours become involved?" I asked.

Would they tell me what was surely the truth? That Barney had become involved in it through Sancious?

"I don't rightly know," Mr Digweed replied. "But I believe it was through someone he used to do things for. A genel'man. Howsomever, me and him nivver got nothing for the work we done."

"The work *you* done," his wife interrupted indignantly. "Precious little he done!"

"Aye," Mr Digweed acknowledged ruefully. "The spec failed and so me and the old lady was worse off than a-fore, with the hurt money gone and everything hocked, and debts we'd run up besides."

"Aye," she put in. "That was a bad time. Yes, pretty bad, I should say, taken all round."

"And that was when you went north?" I prompted.

"That's right," Mrs Digweed answered, "for that same ... friend of George's told us about work near your village. So we went down — me and George and Joey. We left ... we left ... "

She broke off and her husband said: "We left the other children here."

The other children! Now, would they mention Sally whom I recalled Mrs Digweed referring to when she was at my mother's house, and who I was sure was the young woman I had encountered in Barney's gang.

"But when we got there," Mrs Digweed went on, "we found there wasn't no work for me and Joey, so we went on to Stoniton. Then I got word that the children was ill and started back. That was the time me and Joey come to your mother's house."

"By chance?" I prompted.

She looked at me in such innocent surprise that I shuddered inwardly at the thought that she might be dissimulating: "Yes. I knowed nothing of you before that. And when I got back here ... "

Her voice trembled and she stopped speaking.

Her husband gently took her hand and said: "When she got back here she found them desperate bad. And they died a week arter."

They were implying that Joey was their only surviving child. So they were suppressing all mention of Sally! I was sure of it. Again, this must be because they did not want me to know that she was in Barney's company. What else were they concealing? I would give them the chance to admit the connexion with Barney.

I watched them carefully and then remarked conversationally: "When you and Joey came to my mother's house, do you know, you weren't the only visiters from London we had? For the house was broken into and burgled not many years before that?"

The effect of this was dramatic: they all stopped eating and lowered their eyes.

"Yes," I went on; "and I saw the burglar."

Nobody looked at me or spoke.

"Don't you want me to tell you what he looked like?"

There was a silence.

Then Mrs Digweed asked: "Why, what did he look like, Master Johnnie?"

So I described Barney in as much detail as I could. They said nothing and none of them met my gaze. I was certain that they knew that the burglar was Barney. Why did they not tell me? Presumably because they did not realize that I had recognised him and discovered their relation with him.

Mr Digweed and Joey did not go to bed that night but prepared themselves for one of their mysterious nocturnal departures, and left the house a couple of hours after midnight. I heard them leave, for I had retired to rest for the night with much to reflect upon many hours before that and had been lying awake wondering what I should do. If they were in the pay of the Mompessons, then I was surely safe, though I was made uneasy by their connexion with Barney — and even more so by their failure to admit it. I would stay with them and wait for the hidden hand that had been guiding my destiny to reveal itself.

CHAPTER 85

I slept late the next morning and awoke to find that Mr Digweed and Joey had not yet returned. Already they had been out for much longer than usual and Mrs Digweed was growing anxious. I shared her anxiety — though without having any precise idea of what I should be worried about — and by ten o'clock we were both in a state of considerable alarm.

Suddenly the street-door opened and Mr Digweed's hook appeared around its edge, and when after a moment he himself entered sideways we realized to our horror that this strange mode of entry was because he was supporting his son who now staggered in behind him hardly able to stand. He was pale and trembling and blood was running down the leg of his boots. As I took this in my senses were assailed by the appalling stench that came from them now that they were inside the little chamber.

With some help from me, Joey was eased into a chair. His mother carefully removed his boots and stockings and cut back his trowsers so that we could see that there was a deep gash several inches long just above the knee on his right leg.

Mr Digweed threw off his oil-skins in the back-yard and hurried off to the Dispensary while I assisted his wife in removing Joey's filthy outer garments, washing the wound, and carrying him upstairs.

A medical student came, applied a pledget to the wound and bound it up, bled his patient, approved of the treatment he was receiving, came downstairs again and, as he pocketed his fee, announced:

"He'll be all right so long as it doesn't become infected. If it does, send again for me. Keep him in bed for a few days and then at home for a couple of weeks."

When he had gone Mrs Digweed busied herself in making a sleeping draught for her son who was now in considerable pain, while Mr Digweed went into the back-yard and occupied himself in cleaning the oil-skins.

I went out and helped him. He was less talkative even than usual and we worked in silence for a few minutes.

"Mr Digweed," I said, "for the next couple of weeks you'll need help, won't you? Please let me take Joey's place."

He shook his head vehemently: "No, that wouldn't be right."

"But why not?" I persisted.

"Well, the work don't suit everyone."

"But," I added at a venture, "you can't work easily without assistance, can you?"

He stared at me and exclaimed: "Easily? Why, you can't work at all on your own!"

"Then how will you manage?"

He shook his head gravely.

There was a long silence while we rinsed the boots under the pump and then he said: "Well, we'll see what the old lady says. But let it lie till tomorrer."

Joey slept well that night, and the next morning there was no sign of the wound turning bad. Mr and Mrs Digweed's spirits having lifted, I raised the subject as we breakfasted:

"Mrs Digweed, I want to work the shores until Joey is recovered."

"Why," said Mrs Digweed, "then you knowed all along what they was doing!"

I explained that I had recalled her words back in Melthorpe.

"Then you know how dirty it is, and dangerous. No, it wouldn't be right for a genel'man's son, Master Johnnie."

They were concerned about the danger, I imagined, because they were being paid to keep me safe. I persevered and Mrs Digweed resisted hard and long until at last, seeing that I was determined, she gave her grudging consent.

Mr Digweed nodded and said: "Very well. And you're small enough to suit." (It was true that I was of a size with Joey, but I was puzzled by this remark.) "There's a low tide at midnight, so we'll go tonight."

I was restless all day until at last the time came for us to make ready for our departure. Mr Digweed helped me to put on Joey's boots and oil-skins and showed me how to trim the bull's-eye lanthorns and work the shutters.

By the time we left the house it was almost dark. To my surprise we headed away from the river and walked towards Bishopsgate. In this district there were many little work-shops, most of them connected with the slops trade, so that when I peered through windows as we passed I often saw tailors sitting cross-legged on the floor sewing in the light of a candle. No wonder so many of them became blind, I thought, and remembered my childish fancy many years before of the blind mole stitching a coat for Mr Pimlott.

We turned into Dorset-street, walked some way along it and then stopped. I looked around in bewilderment and, in the near-darkness that surrounded us in this unlit district, saw merely a quiet back-street with nothing remarkable about it, except perhaps an old brick culvert beside us of the kind so much more common at that date when many open sewers and drainage ditches could still be seen even in the fashionable parts of the metropolis.

While Mr Digweed lighted our lanthorns I leaned over the low and crumbling parapet of the shaft and saw that there was a trickle of water running along the brick-work of the culvert's bottom. A little further along there was an arch-way leading into a tunnel, protected by an iron grille.

Mr Digweed now warned me to be ready to follow him and always to do exactly what he told me. He glanced cautiously around and seeing that the dark street was empty, he suddenly sprang over the parapet and seized with his hook the topmost of the series of iron rings driven into the brick-work, then lowered himself down the wall by their means and dropped into the shallow water below us. In surprise I followed him and we splashed our way towards the arch-way.

Now I discovered by the light of our lanthorns that the iron grille which had looked impenetrable from above, was so rusted and broken that it presented no obstacle. My companion pulled it towards him and squeezed round its side and I followed him without difficulty. As we advanced into the tunnel the smell assailed me and I gasped for air through my mouth as well as my nostrils.

For a few terrifying seconds I was overcome by dizziness and heard a loud rushing in my ears and thought my legs would give way and that I would lose consciousness, but then I recovered, the fear and nausea left me, and I found I was able to keep moving. By the glow from his lanthorn I could see Mr Digweed a few yards ahead of me, picking his way quickly along the bed of the foul stream, glancing back occasionally to make sure I was following him.

Once he let me catch up and then raised an eyebrow interrogatively. I nodded back with a forced smile and he placed his mouth next to my ear and shouted: "This is a very pretty shore. But you has to keep moving or you starts to notice the smell."

I nodded and we moved on. Suddenly he turned up a side-tunnel. Since it was lower and narrower we had to stoop so that progress became more difficult, and the level of the water rose which meant that as it was rushing more quickly it made more noise and speech was now impossible.

After a few yards this tunnel branched and Mr Digweed chose one fork as unhesitatingly as if he were sauntering through the streets of his own neighbourhood. Now we were going discernibly downhill and the surface was so slimy that it was difficult to avoid slipping. In addition to this the stench was almost over-powering.

We walked for some time — I cannot say how long for I found distance difficult to judge and time impossible when every moment was crowded with new fears and sensations. Indeed, here where it was absolutely black and there was only the rushing of waters in my ears that might have been the rush of blood, I could not tell what was I and what was not I. When I stretched out my hands to touch the rough sides I could not tell whether I felt my own frozen fingers or the cold stone. Involuntarily, I thought of the great weight of earth and buildings and paved streets that was above us, and felt such a blind terror that I had to force myself to think of something else.

Although I now understood much, I was still puzzled by the purpose of this activity until suddenly Mr Digweed stopped and waited for me to catch him up. Then he bent down — I should say, bent even further down for we were both hunched over — and lowered the lanthorn, indicating that I should look at what he was studying.

I did so and noticed that there was something standing upright in the space left by the erosion of the mortar from between two of the stones. The object gleamed in the light and I saw that it was a coin. My companion lifted it out and held it in the beam so that I could perceive that it was a shilling, then slipped it into the leathern pouch that hung from his shoulder.

There was money lying down here for anyone to find who took the trouble to look for it! I could not understand why — apart from the noxious smell — more people did not venture down here.

We now passed along tunnels of many different sizes and characters which must have owed their variety to their having been constructed at widely-separated periods. Some were medieval, though most had been built during the re-construction of the City after the Fire and its extension into the suburbs that made up the modern metropolis, and were therefore between a hundred and a hundred and fifty years old. Since, therefore, they had been constructed by means of quite different methods, through varying soil conditions, and at different angles and gradients, conditions in them were quite distinctive.

I walked behind my companion and both of us — though we were of small stature and I was not fully-grown at that date — had to stoop, which I found extremely painful to the neck and shoulders. All the time Mr Digweed was scrutinizing the surface, and once or twice he reached down to lift a coin.

Most of the tunnels were shaped like an egg, curving around us above and below; others — and these were the biggest which dated from the medieval period — were much wider and flatter and had a deep ditch, with a narrow and crumbling path-way along the side. Here the sound of the rushing water was almost deafening, though in other tunnels it glided or trickled silently, and in yet others there was no water at all but only a layer of wet or dried mud.

"Is it so easy?" I asked my patron when next we were passing through a dry tunnel and could hear each other's voices.

"Bless you no," he exclaimed. "Why, I've on'y found that shillin' and a few coppers so far."

"But we haven't been looking for long."

"Why, how long do you reckon?"

"I don't know. Do you not have your watch?"

He laughed: "A watch wouldn't last long down here."

"About a half-hour?" I suggested.

He shook his head. "Nearer two. You see, we won't find much up here. We've got to get down to where the mud builds up for that's where everything gets washed down to. But we can on'y stay down there for about an hour at the most."

I was about to ask him to explain this when I noticed a dark shape scurrying quickly out of the light of the lanthorn. Then there was another. And another. I realized with horror what they must be, though they seemed too large.

Seeing me shudder my companion said: "Aye, rats."

"But so big!" I gasped.

"Brown rats. They ain't the same as the house-rats."

"Aren't they dangerous?" I exclaimed.

He laughed: "You don't want to get bit by 'em. They're p'isonous. But they don't as a rule go for a man unless he's bleeding a'ready. Seems the smell of blood drives 'em to it."

I swallowed hard to fight down the panic I felt rising within me at the thought of those knife-like, envenomed teeth. But if Joey had been able to endure these horrors, then I was determined to show myself no less courageous.

We went on and now I could tell that we were making our way consistently downhill. I discovered that the deepest tunnels were generally the most ancient and the most foul smelling and treacherous, for the brick-work of the narrow ledges along the sides was often crumbling so that it would suddenly give way beneath your weight, and the surface was pitted with deep ruts on which one could easily trip. And to miss your footing here, where the water was deep and the current swift, was to face a certain and very horrible death.

Gradually I began to sense another odour distinguishable from the acrid, sulphurous stench that I had already grown somewhat inured to, and eventually I realized that it was that of the river: a deep, ancient smell like the stagnant ponds that I had found so fascinating as a small boy. Now the different sewers broadened out into wide, flatter basons rather as a river widens at its mouth, so that the water ran down the middle leaving banks of deep mud exposed at the sides. Instead of being cast back at us from the dank wall, the lume of the lanthorn was lost in the gloom that opened around us.

"You can only stay down here when the tide is at low-water," Mr Digweed explained. "And that's not long."

So that explained the hours he worked!

"As the tide rises the low-lying tunnels back up," he explained. "Very sudden sometimes. There's many as has been caught that way, by not keeping a reckoning of the time. And the spring and neap tides can be devilish tricky, too."

Now we set to work and I understood why two of us were needed, for the shore-hunters' technique was quite different, in these vast stinking sumps where Thames and sewer came together, from that used higher up. Instead of coins being trapped in the crevices where the angle of descent was steep enough so that the mud and filth were washed away by the running fluid, here the effluvium was left behind by the retreating tide whose action, as it went out, formed a kind of vast sieve, leaving the mud and its contents to sink to the floor. And it was upon this expanse of crumbling brickwork covered in layers of thick mud or worse — on which it was easy to lose one's footing — that we had to work in the absolute darkness and as quickly as possible.

Now Mr Digweed showed me my duties which involved holding the lanthorn for him while he raked through the mud and filth that accumulated in smooth heaps like the sand left along the foreshore of a beach. He now brought the trowel and sieve into play, sifting through the mud and occasionally finding a coin. Or he would start prodding with the rake at a particular shoal of foetor while I had to direct the lanthorn as he indicated. Sometimes he would detect something — a lump of rusted metal, an iron baccy box, a spoon — and hook it back with the rake. I was amazed by the way in which he saw coins and other objects that were invisible to me in the mud, and I realized that although it looked easy enough, he had a knack of spotting them when I would not have noticed them — even though I had the advantage of two eyes.

It was very hard and unpleasant work. We had water swirling about our feet while we laboured on the mud-banks at the edges, and when we crossed from one side to another the water in the centre of the ditch frequently came up to our knees and often dead cats, dogs, and rats as well as all manner of beastliness, were swept up against us. The tunnels were very cold and damp and the cramped position that was required was uncomfortable and even painful. Above all, of course, the stench was appalling.

Because I began to realize that Mr Digweed was much sharper at spotting coins and other things buried in the mud than I, I was pleased with myself when I noticed a metal object that he appeared to have missed several feet away protruding from the mud. I pointed it out to him and he nodded and smiled as if to indicate that he had seen it, but when I suggested retrieving it he shook his head.

"Mud's too deep," he said.

I expressed surprise for it looked to be no deeper than elsewhere. I made to go forward but he held out his hook to stop me.

"That wasn't like that a-fore," he said. He leaned forward and probed with the rake. To my surprise it sank several feet.

He smiled at me: "The brick-work's given way there. See, it's as rotten as gingerbread. There's shallow vaults beneath here. Then the mud goes through and fills it up so as it looks solid."

I shuddered to think how easily I might have ventured across it.

"Aye," Mr Digweed added reflectively. "It's allus different down here every time."

He went on to explain that even on the very lowest levels, the ground was cracking and giving way, for the whole network of sewers was sinking slowly into the soft London clay. So even here when I thought I had reached the very bottom, I found that there was nothing firm beneath my feet.

After some time I became aware that as well as being cold and exhausted, I was also extremely hungry. I had no idea whether we had been down there for a few hours or for the whole night, but we had taken nothing to eat and I understood why, for the very idea of consuming food in those conditions made my gorge rise.

Mr Digweed must have guessed what was in my mind for he said: "The tide ain't turned yet but I see you're tired so we'll come up now."

I was delighted to hear him say this and so we retraced our steps, making our way towards the upper tunnels. But suddenly, just when we had turned into the mouth of a new one, the flames of our lanthorns sank down and spluttered as if gasping for air.

Mr Digweed who was in front of me turned and said calmly: "Gas. We'll have to go back."

I looked at him in dismay, for everything that I had heard or read about coal-mines came flooding into my mind: "Can it explode?"

"No, this is choke-damp. But it can drown a man if he don't know it's there."

I felt a blind terror. To die in that darkness! To be stifled! To lose your very body to the malignant tides!

"It can come down a tunnel on you very sudden. Breathe it and you're finished."

"How can you avoid it?"

"Why, you jist has to watch for it."

We continued along the main tunnel we had been in before, but after a few yards the lanthorns began spluttering again and the flames guttered low.

My companion stopped and said: "We'll have to turn back. You have to watch that it don't put the lanthorn out for it's hard to strike a light in this damp."

As we turned back, it came to me how terrifying it would be to lose one's light down there. I knew how impossible it would be to grope my way back to the surface, and wondered if it could be done even if one knew the labyrinthine system as well as my companion. I shuddered as I imagined trying to pick my way along the slippery edge of a deep water-filled ditch.

The lanthorns guttered several times as we made our way, to my surprise, back to the lowest level again, but we reached there without further danger. Now we proceeded down a broad ditch which sloped very gradually, and I grew increasingly alarmed at the idea that we were going deeper and deeper into the system. However, as smaller tunnels fed into it, the bore of our tunnel grew larger until it was more than twice the height of a man. After some time I discerned a slight mitigation of the absolute darkness ahead of us, and at last I saw a great circle of faint light.

When we reached it I realized that we had arrived at the mouth of one of the great sewers where it disgorged into the river. At that time many of the grids intended to prevent people from getting into the tunnels were so far rusted away as to present no obstacle. And since there were no tide-gates as there are now, it was very easy to lower ourselves down the brickwork to the muddy foreshore where the tide was encroaching, then walk along until we reached the water-stairs at the end of Northumberland-street — oddly enough, I reflected, very near my grandfather's house.

It was strange to come to the surface and find that we were in quite another part of the metropolis and that the dawn was streaking the sky with pale light. As we made our way home and then conducted the ritual of stripping off the oil-skins and pumping ourselves down in the yard, I was too tired to ask the many questions that I wanted to.

When we entered the house Mrs Digweed smiled at me anxiously and said: "Well, how did you find it?"

I was so exhausted that I could not respond and merely nodded and tried to muster a smile.

"He done prime," Mr Digweed said.

Feeling proud at this accolade, I went upstairs and lay down beside the sleeping Joey. Within seconds I too was profoundly asleep.

The next day I succeeded in making Mr Digweed talk about the work and as we sat over a late breakfast, I found him more eloquent than I had ever known him.

"Folks don't know as there's nigh on two hundred miles of main shores," he enthused, "with near the same number of outlets into the river. But then there's another fifteen hundred miles of district and private tunnels as you can get into. Though some on 'em — the two-footers — is tighteners."

"What about the smell?" I asked.

"Why, you hardly notice it. There's even some as reckon it's healthy, for they say the toshers live to a great age. But there's some things that ain't too nice, like the blood-tunnels beneath Newport-market and Smiffle. Though they ain't so bad as the b'iling-shores where there's sugar-manyfact'rers, for the sugar is drove into the shores by steam." He grimaced. "And then you've to watch out for the soap and tallow manyfact'ries, too. And you don't go near the lead-works at all if you can help it."

He told me about the other hazards: the falling of rooves (which is how Joey had been injured), the collapse of floors where one sewer was constructed over another, and the sudden rise in the water-level because of a heavy downpour.

"And then there's the tide," he added; "for it can back up in the most surprising ways. And it has a reach of more nor twenty foot."

I was determined not to be deterred. And so we went down again the next day — or, rather, the next night. And while Joey convalesced during the following three weeks, I accompanied his father regularly on his underground expeditions.

As I acquired more and more experience of the "shores" I began to wonder how I had ever imagined that it was an easy way to make a living. It was my second week when I first encountered direct evidence of the dangers. In a sloping side-tunnel somewhere under Blackfriars we saw a large shape rising up from a thick deposit of mud.

My companion grimaced: "Reckon that's a used 'un, like they used to say in the army."

When we got close enough he employed his rake to pull it a little towards us and we saw that it was indeed the body of a man.

"Poor devil," my companion said. "I have to see if I know his face. If he has one."

He managed to pull the body over and held the lanthorn down to the pale face: "No," he said. "He ain't one of us."

"Do we leave him here?" I asked.

"We have to. It's a long job to get one up. We only do it for one of the S'iety. There's some as takes what they find and even strips the togs off 'em, but I don't."

"What will happen to it?"

"This tunnel leads into one where there ain't no grid across the mouth, so it'll be washed into the river. That's to say, what the rats leave."

I felt my stomach heave at these words, but Mr Digweed continued without noticing: "Then, most likely, one of the river-scavengers will find it. Anything he finds on it will be his reward, which is another reason for leaving what's on it, or it's robbing another of his trade."

"How do you think it got here?"

"He might have come down without someone that knowed his way around. Or he could have fell in, or he might have been bellowsed and throwed into a culvert, in course. There's many and many a way."

Isbister's warning about dropping me in the Fleet-ditch came back to me and I asked: "Do you find them often?"

"Now and then," he answered. "Not so much full-growed, but a mort o' babbies."

As we were returning to the surface we came to a place where there was a grating above our heads every few yards through which I saw dim lights. I thought I heard the noise of horses and carts, but dismissed it as a trick of the running water until I realized that the gratings were those at the side of the street and that I could indeed hear and even see the traffic and foot-passengers. How strange it was that, just a few feet beneath the everyday world, here we were in the darkness and stench of a dangerous underground realm.

At that moment I heard a strange noise — a hollow but rhythmical banging.

"A storm!" my companion explained. "Lucky we're near the top."

We hastily made our way to the surface and once out of the system, he explained to me that when there was a downpour, the gong-fermors — as the men who were employed by the parishes to clean the sewers are known — warn their fellows who might be below ground by raising and dropping the metal covers of the manholes.

Mr Digweed had told me that there was ill-feeling between the toshers and the gong-fermors who regarded us as interlopers who were poaching on their domain — although we went into shores that they shunned as too dangerous — in order to take the rewards of their own work. And he had warned me that they would sometimes attack us if they encountered us below. But there was a great deal of fellowship amongst the toshers — the most experienced of whom jealously controlled entry to their Society.

I had proof of this a few days later for suddenly, as we were proceeding along a tunnel where there was a long straight stretch ahead of us, we saw lights approaching. As we drew near Mr Digweed reassured me that it was another party of shore-hunters. We halted and exchanged greetings.

"There's bad gas beneath Fetter-lane at the Fleet-street end," one of them reported.

"How's the roof under Chancery-lane?" Mr Digweed asked.

"Dunno. I ain't been up that way for a few weeks. After what happened to Jem I've kept clear of there."

We continued on our way.

During these weeks I realized that the secret of successful shore-hunting was to cover as much distance as possible in the most promising of the upper tunnels, to venture into the lower sewers as soon as the tide rendered it safe, and to stay down there as long as caution allowed. For the whole art lay in knowing when it was safe to enter different parts of the system and how long it was prudent to remain, and in guessing which parts would be most profitable in view of a range of factors: the tide, the recent weather, and the time of the year. There was a competitive element involved for it was desirable to beat other hunters to the best grounds, though at the same time (as I have said) there was a generous spirit of mutuality among the shore-hunters. Interlopers, however, would receive no assistance, and the fact that it was so dangerous unless one had expert knowledge, meant that the craft had descended from father to son in some cases for many generations. Mr Digweed explained to me that he had been taught it by an old man, Bart, to whom he had done a favour once many years before. From him he had learned how to scrutinize the ground as quickly and thoroughly as possible, and had acquired his knowledge of the tunnel-system and the ability to "read" changes in it upon which not merely profit but life itself depended, for as I had already seen the system could be as unpredictable and as dangerous as the sea.

Proud though he was of his knowledge, he lamented often — particularly when he had just returned from the public-house — that to work the shores was a waste of his skills for a craftsman who had served his time.

When, after three weeks, it became clear that Joey was almost fully recovered, I wondered whether his father would still want me to accompany him underground. Although the thought of doing this work indefinitely repelled me, I could see no other way of earning my living for I had very little education and without capital or friends had no chance of establishing myself in a gentlemanly profession. Yet soon, I reflected, whoever it was who had been paying the Digweeds to rescue and foster me would surely reveal themselves — for good or ill — and until then I could accept this work as a temporary expedient. And it had its attractions, for while I shrank from the filth and degradation of the shores, I was strangely drawn by the idea of working beneath the surface, setting my hours by the mysterious movements of the tides, often labouring at night and sleeping by day, and dwelling here in the haunts of the most wretched and impoverished. Although it was partly because I felt I was safe from my enemies in a secret underworld and, moreover, fending for myself and surviving, there was some further appeal that was stronger even than these and that I was only vaguely aware of at the time.

One evening in the middle of May, Joey announced that he was determined to go under again the next day and, despite Mrs Digweed's protests, his father agreed.

"Does that mean you don't need me?" I asked.

"Why, don't you want to?" Mr Digweed asked.

I hesitated for a moment and Joey saw this.

"I suppose it ain't good enough for you?" he said.

"Now hold your tongue," his mother ordered.

"For the time being at least," I said, "I'd like to."

Mr Digweed nodded approvingly: "Three's much safer than two."

"On'y," said Mrs Digweed cautiously, "it don't hardly seem right for someone like you to earn his living that way."

Joey glanced at me with a half-smile that I interpreted as a sneer.

"What shall we say about the money?" I asked.

Mr Digweed glanced at his wife. "This is what we reckoned," he said. "Let's say we'll split what we earn into five shares. You and Joey take one each and I'll take the rest. Then you pay us eight shilling for board and lodging with washing found."

These terms seemed suspiciously generous. It was virtually an admission that they were receiving money from someone. I looked at Joey's face and thought I saw there resentment that I was being treated on all fours with him.

So it was agreed. And now my life settled into this strange routine. And yet, however often I went down the shores, I never lost entirely the sense of terror I felt that first time. It was all the stranger, then, that in the face of all the hazards, I felt a kind of safety in this way of life. At least I was no longer the play-thing of accident or the unknowing victim of a conspiracy, for I had reached the very nadir of human existence and yet had found that I could survive, and do so not by something as humiliating as begging for charity in the streets but by a means that demanded courage, skill, and endurance. Down here the frivolity of chance could do little against me and I no longer laboured under the delusion of freedom (as I conceived it) for I knew that someone was manipulating my life — even if I did not know yet who it was. Though the shores were in one sense degrading, they represented a merely physical danger and my pride and independence were uncompromised, for apart from injury, death, or disease I had nothing to fear from them. All I feared — and yet longed for — was the unveiling of the hidden hand that had guided the Digweeds towards me.

Mr Digweed was so skilful with the rake and trowel and, with the assistance of myself and the more experienced Joey to help him, was able to cover so much ground, that we made a reasonably good living, and my share of our takings after paying my eight shillings was usually between two and three shillings a week. I tried to save the seventeen shillings I had borrowed from Sukey, but I never managed to reach that figure and, unwilling to send her less than that, I put off writing to her.

As time passed I began to understand why Mr Digweed went so frequently to the nearby public-house.

"You need it to clean you out," he explained. "For it's dry work down there, very dry."

I found it remarkably damp, but I could appreciate how, after the darkness and confinement of the shores, he needed the bright lights and sociability of the Pig and Whistle. But Mrs Digweed similarly found her laundry-work "wery drying" and also needed to visit the public-house frequently, so that most of what little spare money they had went on beer and gin, and it seemed to me to be largely for this reason that both of them had to work so hard. They always invited me to accompany them there but I rarely went at first.

When I did, I discovered that Mr Digweed had professional reasons for his frequent attendance there, for the Pig and Whistle in Petticoat-lane was the house of call for the Society of shore-hunters. Here they exchanged intelligence about conditions below ground and administered a benefit-club to which they all contributed in case of accident or illness.

Joey often visited the public-house with his parents, but spent much of his time with a gang of boys searching for scrap wood and metal which they sold to rag-and-bone dealers. He was often getting into one sort of mischief or another, and his parents were worried that he would get involved again in something criminal. He wasted much of his money on fine clothes and tobacco, for he now cultivated a pipe. His manner towards me hardly improved at all as time passed, and he remained reserved and even hostile, though we worked well together underground. Once he invited me to join him and the other boys "for a lark" but I declined for I thought it necessary to keep a difference between us.

It would be very easy to succumb to these temptations and so gradually slip into the way of life of these kind, sociable people who lived for the moment and took little thought for the future. My destiny, however, was to be very different from theirs as my origins were different. I reflected often that if what Mr Nolloth had said about the will of Jeoffrey Huffam was true, then great wealth was mine by every criterion of morality, and yet here I was grovelling for coppers in the filth when I should be master of one of the greatest estates in England. Having worked myself into a state of rapture at this thought, it gave me a strange kind of pleasure to raise objections to it, and argue to myself that I had no proof that the will had even existed and no chance of regaining my rights unless it could be found, for these obstacles made my day-dreams seem the more plausible. But then I would go too far, for when I realized the impossibility of the will's ever being located — even if it still existed, or had ever existed — I became quite downcast and my bright phantasies faded.

Moreover, to make any such attempt would be once again to expose myself to danger from the Clothiers and, tempted as I was to obey the motto of my Huffam ancestors and seek safety through confronting danger, I felt even more strongly the appeal of the anonymity and oblivion that I had now found.

My phantasies were not entirely selfish dreams of wealth, I assured myself, for having forgotten nothing of what the Clothiers and the Mompessons had done to their opponents, I was possessed by the desire to wreak justice against them. Justice would humble them and make them regret — if not repent — what they had done to me and mine.

Driven by a grim pleasure in watching the Mompessons enjoy their stolen wealth, I went sometimes at night to Brook-street and walked backwards and forwards before their house. Was I watching in secret those who were secretly providing for me? I wondered. Several times I saw Sir Perceval and Lady Mompesson arriving or leaving in their carriage, and once I glimpsed a young lady who might have been Henrietta.

The sight of the usurpers sent me back to my books. If I was to gain the estate I had to know a great deal about Law and Equity. And so, although I returned from our subterranean expeditions exhausted, I spent much of my time reading. I was glad that the others were out so much and that I had the little cottage to myself, for I missed my privacy. (The life of the poor, I discovered, is wholly social and the Digweeds could not understand my desire to be alone.) Many and many a time as I sat alone by the fire with a book open upon my knee, I thought of my mother and remembered our happy times in the village.

There was a second-hand book-shop in Maiden-lane, Covent-garden, where I befriended the bookseller who was an interesting and thoughtful man. He permitted me, on payment of a small fee and a deposit on each book borrowed, to take home anything from his stock. I read mainly legal works but also odd volumes of *The Spectator*, *The Tatler*, *The Rambler*, as well as the English classics: Shakespeare, Milton, Hobbes, *Rasselas, The Vicar of Wakefield*, and Goldsmith's *History of Greece and Rome*; and lighter works like *The Castle of Otranto, The Monk*, and *Peregrine Pickle*. But these were mere diversions from my study of the Law and Equity, and I felt that I was acquiring the knowledge that would both win for me my rights and permit me to enjoy them.

Though I was with the Digweeds as little as possible, I watched and listened all the time for a clew to who was giving them their instructions about me. I learned nothing, however. Their reticences were eloquent, though, for I was struck by the fact that Sally and the other children were never mentioned.

As the months lengthened into a year, I gradually began to see the absurdity of my hopes of regaining the estate. More than likely, the will had never existed, for the evidence was indirect and tenuous: probably Mr Nolloth had misrepresented or misunderstood what Peter Clothier had said, or the latter had done the same with what my grandfather had allegedly told him. And so as a second year passed by, my law-books gathered dust in the chamber upstairs that I still shared with Joey. I still hungered for justice and occasionally allowed myself to dream of great wealth, but I now came to see the suit as a delusive will o' the wisp that was in danger of leading my thoughts into dangerous phantasy as it had my grandfather's.

I tried to convince myself that it was better to accept the inevitability of my situation and of my bleak future than sustain myself on empty dreams. But I could not bear to think that I would spend my life like this; that I had sunk to the bottom and there I would stay. And yet, of what worth was I? As Mr Pentecost had said, a man's value was his price on the market and mine was nugatory. So increasingly I became frustrated and restless as I saw my life stretching emptily and oppressively before me. Anger and hatred burned inside me and the little house seemed a prison. Now I went with the Digweeds almost every night to the Pig and Whistle, finding the bright lights and noise a welcome contrast to the solitude and darkness of the tunnels. Gradually I discovered the release and escape that drink offered and am ashamed to admit that I frequently found myself staggering home with the others. I wasn't sure whether I was trying to blot out the thought of the past or of the future. Either way, what I sought was oblivion, a kind of death which was the counterpart of my life in the shores.

BOOK III

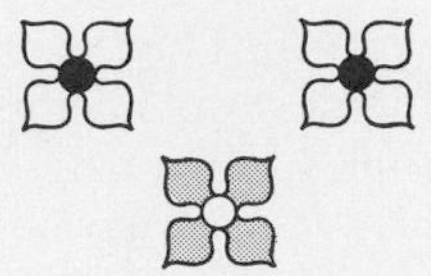

Grandfathers

CHAPTER 86

One evening in the middle of May almost exactly two years after the Digweeds had effected my escape from Dr Alabaster's refuge, I was reading in thc downstairs room. No sign had ever come from the party who, I assumed, was paying them for their attentions to me, and consequently I had begun to have serious doubts about the validity of the assumption I had made about this. This evening I had the house to myself for Joey was out and Mr and Mrs Digweed were, of course, at the public-house whither I had for once declined to accompany them.

The street-door opened suddenly and I heard Joey speaking to someone who was entering the room behind him, and then a woman's voice answering him. Joey came in looking rather mysterious.

Behind him was a young lady — at least, that is what I took her for. She was very finely dressed in a beautiful scarlet silk gown and a hat with a peacock feather. She was tall and handsome with bold blue eyes and a high nose. Her golden hair was worn in ringleted tresses and her cheeks were faintly rouged. She carried an elegant parasol and seemed strangely out of place in that mean little chamber that was now filled with exotic perfume.

To my surprise she looked at me as if she knew who I was.

"My," she said, "haven't you jist growed!"

Joey watched my face curiously.

Then I recognised her: "Why, it's Sally!"

"I wondered if you'd know me," she said. "I wouldn't hardly have knowed you agin if I'd passed you in the street."

I looked at Joey: "She's your sister, isn't she?"

He nodded in surprise.

"And what relation is Barney to you?" I asked them.

Sally was about to speak but Joey said quickly: "That's for the old folks to say if they choose to. But they mustn't know nothing about Sal coming here."

"They think I'm bad for Joey," she said with an unconvincing laugh.

"They're at the tavern," I said.

"Joey knowed that. I wanted to speak to you."

"To me!"

"It's about that night you left the crib, you recall, when Barney needed a boy and you wouldn't make one of us? So I went and found Joey?"

I nodded. "What was it they wanted you for?" I asked her brother. "What were they doing?"

"I don't rightly know," Joey said. "They had something on but I on'y seed a small part of it for I jist had to stay outside with the carriage. (They wanted a tiger to make it look like a swell's.) But Sally knows the whole story."

"Well, I'll tell you," she said. "It can't do no harm now and will show you I mean to deal plainly with you. This is how it was. Barney and the rest of us gals, Nan and Maggie and some of the others, was going up West together for months a-fore that and they was letting on that they was rich publicans and we was their friends. Well, we'd got acq'ainted with some genel'men what had lots of tin. And we'd been going to this hell with 'em."

"Hell?" I asked.

"My, you are a downy! It's a gaming-club. This one's in Henrietta-street. Very respectable. Well, that's to say, in course it's agin the law, see, to run one of them places, which you have to know to understand what I'm telling you. They have people at the door what won't let you in unless they know you in case you're one of them traps — you know — that don't wear the uniform. And they search you for weapons, too."

"Hurry up, Sal," Joey protested.

"Well, Barney and the other culls have knowed the coves as runs it for a long time. In fact, they've worked for 'em as buttoners — bringing in gulls and letting on that they're winning a lot of money and all that kind of thing. So Barney had got Sam work there as one of the files what guards the door. But the coves what run the place didn't know that, in course. Now these flatts what I'm telling you about have lost so much blunt there that Barney and the rest of us are completely trusted by the coves there. Now that night we'd told the gulls that they should bring lots of blunt with 'em because Barney had tipped the croupier a bit to rig the game in their favour. (Which was a wrinkle, in course.) Naterally everyone was searched at the door that night same as usual. But Sam let Jack in and Jack was letting on that he was a gamester, but he was carrying a pair of pistols. Suddenly he and Sam brings out their pistols and holds everyone up. Barney and the rest on us let on that we were as frightened as everyone else, and we encouraged all the others to part with all the money they had with them. It *was* funny to see Barney playing his part. He was stunnin'. So when they'd got every piece of money and joolery in the house, Sam and Jack took off."

Sally and Joey were grinning at the memory. But I remembered how upset she had looked that evening when Jack described how he had shot Sam, and so I said:

"And all the time Sam was intending to cheat the rest of you and shoot Jack stone dead."

Sally flinched and said: "You know about that, then?"

"I was looking down through the ceiling when Jack got back." Then I added carefully: "But it wasn't true what he said, was it?"

She flushed. "What do you mean?" she stammered.

Joey looked from one of us to the other in bewilderment.

"It was really Jack who cheated the rest of you, wasn't it?"

She bit her lip and said nothing.

"You see," I said, "I know something about Jack already. About him and the Cat's-meat-man."

She looked startled at this and exclaimed: "He told you?"

"So you do know," I said.

"I don't know nothing!" she cried.

"Then I'll tell you," I said. "It goes back a long way but I think I've puzzled it out."

I reminded her of the account of the past that I heard Barney giving to the others the night after the raid when he had explained how Pulvertaft's spy was Sam all the time, and had described how he and Jack had pretended to believe it was Nan in order to lull Sam's fears that he had been detected. Everything that Barney had said, I now suggested, had been correct with one crucial exception:

"For you see, it wasn't Sam who put the mark on Barney that summer in '17 when he had to cut from Town and go north. It was Jack, wasn't it?"

"I dunno," she said nervously.

"And when Barney got back to London later that summer someone put a down on him and had him taken up. That was Jack again, wasn't it?"

"How do you know?" she demanded.

"Then Jack and Blueskin, whom you knew as Peg, worked with Pulvertaft — unbeknownst to Barney — to destroy Isbister," I went on relentlessly as she stared at me in amazement. "It was exactly four years ago that Blueskin lured him into a trap at a graveyard in Southwark and Jem was killed. I know Jack was involved in that."

"How can you say that?" she cried.

I answered calmly: "Because I saw him there."

She gasped and turned pale.

"Blueskin joined Pulvertaft," I went on, "and after that they had the market pretty much to themselves and could fix their own price for ... for what they were selling. I assume Jack took his share of that. And I'll wager that he played a big part in the combination against Blueskin when Pulvertaft 'peached on him and got him knocked down."

Joey had been staring at us open-mouthed: "Tell him it ain't true, Sal!" he cried. "Jack ain't no scrub."

"And the worst thing of all," I went on, "was how he killed Sam to put the blame on him."

She was very frightened: "Jack and Barney are still working mates (in Thrawl-street now) and if Barney knowed what you jist said, he'd bellows him. I sometimes wish he would. On'y Jack would bellows me fust. He told me once (when he was scratched or he wouldn't have) that he set up the whole fakement with Pulvertaft. Arter that I seen him looking at me in a way I didn't like. He's been looking at me like that more and more often. That's why I've left him. I don't want to have to go back. See, I knowed he was lying about Sam from the fust, for he made me promise to tell Barney as I'd seen Sam talking to a bald cove with a wooden leg. I nivver thought no harm to it at the time. But Jack used that to make Barney b'lieve as how Sam had blowed on us to Blueskin and Pulvertaft. I on'y knowed what he was up to when Jack come back that night and said he'd bellowsed Sam."

"I believe you," I said. "For I was watching you through the ceiling and I saw how upset you were."

She looked at me curiously for a moment, then cleared her throat and said: "That reminds me: I've brung something for you."

"For me?" I said in surprise. What in my references to that night could have reminded her of anything to do with me?

At that moment we heard the sound of footsteps approaching.

"I said you should've gone," said Joey reproachfully.

Sally looked bold but not alarmed, I thought, and I wondered if she had always intended to be found by her parents.

When they came in they froze in surprise at the sight of the strange lady. The four members of the family stared at each other for several moments.

Then Mr Digweed stepped forward, lifting his hand to his forehead: "Why, miss, we didn't ... "

"Dad, it's me, Sally."

Mr Digweed stopped in amazement. Then he seemed about to move forward.

"George!" his wife cried, and he halted.

The parents looked at each other for a few moments, and then Mrs Digweed said eagerly: "Have you gave it up?" Then she stepped back: "But I only need to look at you. And to smell you. Faugh! You stink like an alley-cat."

"How can I give it up?" Sally broke in impatiently. "What could I do?"

"I could find you work, decent honourable work."

"Doing what?"

"Why, as a laundress, working with me."

Sally grimaced in distaste. "What, up before dawn, working all the hours of daylight, ruining my hands, and working alongside servant-girls and dolly-mops. Ketch me at that!"

"Then go now, Sally," her mother said. "And don't come here again. Not nivver."

"Why are you like this, mam? Why can't you forgive me?"

"Forgive!" she exclaimed. Then she said more calmly: "And that's twice you got Joey mixed up in all that."

"What else could I do?" Sally cried. "You was starving and you wouldn't take money from me. Would you rather he'd died?"

"No, in course not!" Mrs Digweed said with a troubled expression. "Oh Sally, I don't understand it. I only know that what you're doing is wrong and shameful." Her voice broke as she went on: "Why have you come? And how did you find us?"

Joey said: "I brung her. We've been meeting now and agin."

Mrs Digweed looked at him reproachfully: "That was wrong of you." Then a new thought struck her and she cried: "So Barney knows where we are!"

So I was right! She knew all about Barney! Surely my suspicions of her were justified!

"Steady on, old gal," her husband murmured with a glance at me.

But his wife turned to me and said: "No, it's time we should tell you everything, Master Johnnie. Most likely it was wrong of us not to say it a-fore, on'y we thought it was for the best. You see, Barney is George's brother."

"He is, I'm mightily sorry to say," said Mr Digweed. "He is a regular right-down bad 'un and allus was from a boy."

"But there's more than that," Mrs Digweed went on. "It was him what broke into your mam's house."

At last she had told me! And she and her husband seemed so ashamed and guilty that I didn't know what to think now. Had I been mistaken in my suspicions of them?

"There ain't no danger of Barney finding us," Joey said. "Whenever I met Sal I was allus very careful not to let nobody dodge me back here."

"Well," said his mother, "but this time you've brung her."

"I won't tell him," Sally said.

"But he might have follered you here."

"Why should he do that?" Sally asked with a smile.

Involuntarily Mrs Digweed glanced towards me.

"Oh," Sally said, "I know Barney wants to find Master Johnnie. And I know why, too."

The rest of us looked at each other at a nonplus.

"That reminds me what I come for," Sally went on. "I've brung something for him. Look what I've risked for your sake, mam, because I knowed you'd want him to have these back."

She reached into her handsome reticule and then, to my delight, held up my mother's pocket-book. I almost snatched it from her and tore it open. To my relief, it was intact and I found the copy of the codicil I had made and the letter — or whatever it was — written by my grandfather which I had been about to read just before Barney had stolen it. Even the pages of the map which I had long ago given to my mother were still there. The letter, I reflected, would be a great deal more significant to me now after what I had heard from Mr Nolloth.

"Barney gived them to me to read for him," she explained to me, "that night when he took them of you. But I didn't want to give 'em back, so I told him I'd had 'em prigged. He hit me for it." She laughed and looked at her mother: "He wanted me to read 'em so that he could know how much to ask for 'em when he come to sell 'em. And I know who he meant to sell 'em to. It's that split-cause, that lawyer, what he got onto years back when I read him that fust letter what he'd stole. I brung these to show you I don't go along with everything Barney tells me to do. I want to make peace with you. I've left Barney."

So I had been right! It was Sancious who was the link between the Digweeds, on the one hand, and my mother and myself, on the other. And the link with Sancious was through Barney.

"You could have brung them papers back two years ago," her mother said; "and saved Master Johnnie a mort o' grief." Then she scrutinised her daughter's face: "What's really happened? What are you keeping from us?"

"Nothing! I've told you the truth."

"You've fell out with your fancy-man, haven't you?"

Sally flushed.

"I want to come back," she said. "That's all."

"Why?"

She glanced at Joey and me. "I'm ill," she said very softly.

Her mother stared at her. "No I won't help you, Sally," she said sadly. "Not if you won't promise never to go back to Barney but to work honest."

"Don't arst it, mam," Sally said. "I won't."

"What will become of you? You know what happens to gals like you when they gets too old."

"Oh that's a long way off. Time to think of that when it happens — if I live that long. Until then I've got plenty of tin."

She removed a purse from her reticule and showed that it was full of gold.

"And I can be useful, too, and warn you what Barney's got it in mind to do about Master Johnnie." She held the purse towards her parents: "Here, take some."

Before I could ask her what she meant in reference to myself, Mrs Digweed said angrily: "How dare you! Git out of this house a-fore your dad throws you out."

Mr Digweed muttered something that might or might not have been confirmation of his wife's threat, but at this outburst Sally herself turned red, rose and stamped her foot.

"Very well, I'll go. And maybe I won't nivver see any on you agin. And you'll be sorry if Barney has his way with your precious Master Johnnie. Why, Barney was right about you. You really are a pair o' gudgeons! No wonder he took you in over that building spec!"

"What do you mean?" her mother asked.

She laughed: "That split-cause arst him to find flatts."

"You mean Barney knowed from the start that it was a take-in?" Mr Digweed asked.

"In course," she jeered. "You see, that big builder was in it with the split-cause and the coves what owned the land, and they only put up a few carcases as call-birds to draw flatts like you into doing the work on the rest. It was planned from the start that they would screw you all up to selling out for far below the value of the work what you'd put in. And, like I say, that lawyer is up to other things. I was going to tell you but I shan't now."

She flounced out banging the door behind her.

There was a silence. Mr Digweed shook his head and said: "My own brother. I can't hardly credit it."

So much was becoming plain to me. The Digweeds had been victims of the same fraud that my mother had been ruined by. And the common factor was again Sancious and behind him, I suspected, Silas Clothier. More and more — and especially now that Mr and Mrs Digweed had been so frank with me — I was wondering if I had been correct in assuming that they were being paid by an agent of the Mompessons.

Mrs Digweed said: "You didn't ought to have met her, Joey."

"She's my sister, ain't she? Why are you down on her so hard? Dad, *you*'d let her come and see us now and then, wouldn't you?"

Mr Digweed looked extremely discomfited at this.

"Well," he said at last, "if it's 'no' what your mam says, then I reckon she's right."

"You don't really think that," Joey cried. "Why can't you forgive her?"

"Forgive her!" his mother exclaimed. "Have you forgotten what she done? How she left Polly and the little boy in Cox's-square when they had the fever, and went to Barney and ... ?"

Near to tears she broke off. Sally had left her brother and sister that time when the rest of the family were up North! Left them, in the event, to die! So that was the explanation of the family's reticence about that period. I blushed with shame at the memory of the motives I had attributed to them. Now that I saw them unguardedly in conflict with one another, I realized that I had grievously misjudged them.

"Another thing," said Mrs Digweed. "Master Johnnie ain't safe here from

Barney no more now. Even if nobody didn't foller Sally here, I don't trust her not to tell him where we are jist out of spite."

"She wouldn't do that," said Joey.

"Oh no?" Mrs Digweed said darkly. "I think I know my gal better than you do, young man. So it's right away from here we'll have to go. And that means I'll have to build up a new connexion in the launderin' line and your dad will have to give over the S'iety. You see what you've cost us, Joey?"

"It's your fault, not mine," he cried. "You should make up with her."

He made towards the door.

"Where are you goin'?" cried his mother. "You're nivver goin' arter her, are you? You ain't going back to Barney?"

But Joey ran out without answering.

As I watched and listened, I was thinking how wrong I had been in my suspicions of these good people. And when I remembered how, thinking they were profiting from me, I had bargained so hard for the largest share of the toshers' spoils I could win, I burned with shame. And now it seemed to me that I was the cause of the trouble that had come upon this family.

"You mustn't move simply on my account," I said. "You stay here and I'll go away."

"No," Mrs Digweed said. "It ain't entirely on your account, Master John. I don't want Joey meeting her and mebbe Barney again. So it'll have to be another part of Town altogether."

"From what Sally has just said, I begin to understand more of the connexions between us," I began. "But I still don't really understand why you went to such lengths to rescue me?"

"Well," said Mrs Digweed glancing nervously, as it seemed to me, towards her husband, "for one thing, it was shame at what Barney had done to you and your mam."

"You mean that time he burgled our house?"

She nodded and said: "And more than that. And we was grateful for how your mam sarved us that time she give me and Joey our coach-fare back to Town."

How wrong I had been about them! Far from their being rewarded for guarding me, I had been costing them all that money — for medicine, for my food, for my clothes, and for lost working-time! Well, they had certainly paid back my mother's kindness in full and with interest. And yet I still didn't understand how it was that first Barney and then Mrs Digweed had come to our house in Melthorpe.

"Please tell me about that time Barney burgled us," I asked. "I know he had to leave Town just then, but why did he go to that particular village?"

"Well," said Mr Digweed, "it's like this. Our dad — that's his and mine — come from your part of the country. You might have noticed as I don't speak quite like a Lunnon man. He come up to Town from a village not far from Melthorpe when he was a boy."

"I see. And you have connexions still down there?"

"Aye, a few, but they're mainly cousings as I don't know no more. Now my dad's heart was allus set from a tiny boy on being a j'iner and comin' up here. His old feller was a day-labourer so it wasn't easy, but his uncle Feverfew was a stone-mason — and a mighty 'cute 'un — and respected by the fambly he was in sarvice with at the big house nearby. So he got my dad a place there, and fust he worked for the estate carpenter and he was so keen and willing that he got gave inside work — cabinet-making and that — for the fambly. They had a land-agent that took notice of what a steady worker he was and give him the chance to better hisself. So at last he come to Town one year when the whole household come up for the Season — for they only lived down in the country for part o' the year. Well, arter a few years he left the sarvice of the fambly and with the help of the genel'man what I mentioned, he got hisself 'prenticed and when his time was sarved he set up in trade for hisself. And at fust he done well for the agent give him work at the fambly's house in Mayfair and that give him his West-end connexion. But then the drink became too much for my old feller for he had always liked his glass. And by the time me and Barney had served our time, he didn't have much of his connexion left, though we still done a little work for that fambly ourselves now and again. But we had to fall back on jobbing work and Barney quickly tired of that. The hours was too long and the money too short."

"And then he took to breaking into houses?" I prompted.

"Aye, he did, I fear. That and many other things. But it was a long time a-fore I guessed it."

"So he had relatives in Melthorpe he could visit?" I asked.

"He was up there doing some work for the fambly what my dad fust worked for."

"And it was while he was coming back from there on his way to Lunnon," Mrs Digweed went on, "when he broke into your mam's house. It was jist chance that he chose that one, as he told Joey, for he was angry because he had been turned away with ill words when he asked for money."

"That was my nurse's doing," I said. "And mine, too, as I remember."

"Well, all he stole was a silver letter-case," Mrs Digweed said. "There was a letter inside it and he thought it might do him some good. But not being able to read hisself and not trusting nobody that wasn't fambly (not to say that he trusts us, neither) he had to wait to get it read and that wasn't until Sal j'ined him quite a long time later. Something she read there led him to a lawyer called Mr Sancious who, it seemed from the letter, was desperated to larn where your mam was living."

"I see!" I cried. "That is how he discovered our whereabouts. I had never understood that!"

So another piece of the pattern fell into place.

"And that led to all the harm that befell you, didn't it?" Mrs Digweed asked, fixing her troubled gaze upon me.

"I fear that it did," I replied. "For Mr Sancious found his way by that means to our enemies and it was at their prompting that he cheated my mother of her little fortune."

I was beginning to understand at last. But there was much that was still puzzling. "Then if Barney came to my mother's house by chance, surely you and Joey did not come by coincidence all that time later?" I said to Mrs Digweed.

"I told you when George fust brung you to this house," she said, meeting my gaze without flinching; "that it was not by design that I come to you and your mam that time, and that's the solemn truth. But Joey must tell you about that."

I blushed at the implied reproach. I could not doubt her, though I was very puzzled as to how such an apparent coincidence could not have been premeditated. Then something else became clear and I cried: "And it wasn't simply because of old Sam'el making a mistake that I was directed to Barney!"

"No, you arst about a Digweed and he sent you to one," Mrs Digweed admitted. "But we weren't lying when we told you that, for it was true that we knowed Isbister. What we didn't tell you was that we knowed him on account of how Barney worked mates with him and Pulvertaft. That was when he got Joey mixed up in their lay."

She shuddered.

So that was why he was so knowledgeable about burial-grounds that time we had argued in Melthorpe!

"We was very green, Master Johnnie," Mr Digweed said. "We thought they were running an ornery carrier's consarn. It was a long time a-fore we larned what they was up to."

Though I now believed that Mr and Mrs Digweed had done me nothing but good, I was still puzzled by the fact that she and Joey had come to my mother's house. And, moreover, how was it that Joey had led me to the house of Daniel Porteous? And what of my suspicion that Barney had been involved in the murder of my grandfather?

Seeing that Mr and Mrs Digweed were preoccupied in discussing their children, I took a candle upstairs and, making myself comfortable on my straw bed in the corner, examined the letter. The design of the quatre-foil rose on the seal was very familiar to me, and I knew now what the dark stains were. But this time I saw ambiguities in the superscription that I had not perceived before: "My beloved son — and my heir: John Huffam". Not merely could it be addressed to Peter Clothier as my grandfather's son-in-law and heir, or to my mother as his heir-at-law, but also to anyone who became his heir-at-law as I myself now was. Feeling that it was therefore in a sense addressed to myself, I unfolded the sheet and began for the second time to read my grandfather's words:

"Charing-cross,
"The 5th. of May, 1811.

"Claim to Title of Hougham Estate:

"Title in fee absolute held by Jeoffrey Huffam. Allegedly conveyed by James and possession now Sir P. Mompesson. Subject of suit in Chancery.

"Codicil to Jeoffrey's will of '68 criminally removed by unknown party after his death. Recently restored through honesty and perseverance of Mr Jeo. Escreet. Creates entail vested in my father and heirs male and female. Legality of sale of H. estate? P. M. not dispossessed but now only dependant right of base fee, while fee absolute to self and heirs?"

This was the point at which I had stopped reading on the earlier occasion. Now I read on:

"Very recently informed by unimpeachable informant: Jeoffrey H. made second hitherto unknown will also criminally suppressed after death. Disinherited James in favour of self. So sale invalid, no title to convey. Assuming will regained and rights restored, self and heirs owner of fee simple. Informant avers: will concealed for thirty years by Sir A., now by Sir P. Promises to obtain.

"John Huffam.

"Lay before Chancery. Heir to take name of Huffam."

The last words — "Lay before Chancery. Heir to take name of Huffam." — appeared to have been added in a different hand from the one that had written and signed the rest. And this was the crucial clew for now as I puzzled over it, the solution seemed to come to me. Surely this was a kind of aide-memoire — the summary of a conversation between my grandfather and his new son-in-law about the claim to the estate. It must have taken place after they had resolved on the charade and the flight from the house of the newly-wedded pair. My grandfather was telling Peter Clothier about the legal implications of the codicil and also of the purloined will. (He knew he was in danger and this suggested that he feared he might be killed.) He was telling him what action to take and I assumed that it was Peter Clothier who had added the last words undertaking, in case my grandfather was unable to do so, to pursue the claim and to adopt, either on his own behalf or that of any son who might be born, the name of his wife's family. Now I saw another meaning in the superscription: the letter was addressed in a sense to the son of Mary and Peter Clothier who was to take the name of "Huffam". But the important thing was that the aide-memoire was further proof of the existence of the will that Mr Nolloth had told me of and which was to have been given by Martin Fortisquince to my grandfather on the evening of the marriage and smuggled into the possession of Peter Clothier later that night. Or at least, it proved that my grandfather had believed that it existed. Yet I was still puzzled, for if he had been right, then what had happened to it? Why was it not found when the bridal pair opened the package in the chamber of the inn at Hertford?

As I lay on the straw mattress in that dark shabby room, it now became apparent to me that if it existed and could be found again then I would have an unassailable claim to the Hougham estate. I recalled the wish I had made that Christmas many years ago when I had heard from Mrs Belflower the story of how the Huffam family lost their land to the Mompessons. Was it to come true?

Darkness fell without my noticing. Mr and Mrs Digweed called up that they were going to the tavern and did I wish to accompany them? I answered in the negative and heard the door close behind them.

The crucial question therefore was, Had the will existed? And assuming it had, then who had stolen it from my great-great-grandfather as he lay dead or dying? And was it the same individual who had misappropriated the codicil? Where had both documents disappeared to for all those many years? Who was my grandfather's "unimpeachable informant" and what had happened to the will on that fateful night when he had died? Had this individual failed to secure it and pass it to Mr Fortisquince? Or had he secured it but failed to pass it on? I realized that the only person who might have the power to answer these questions was Mr Escreet, and so I resolved to go back and make another attempt to speak to him.

I heard the elder Digweeds returning from the Pig and Whistle and found that it was very late and that Joey had still not come back. Now I wondered how much of the situation I should explain to them. They had risked so much on my behalf that it seemed a kind of meanness not to confide in them. Yet it was a poor return for their generosity to impose upon them the burden of worry about my affairs. And though I believed I trusted the parents, yet I hesitated to put anything into the hands of Joey that he might convey to

Barney. And that made me reflect that it would be wrong to bother them with these matters while they were worried about whether their son would return.

Towards dawn I resolved on one other thing: as a token of my determination to succeed in the task begun by my grandfather, I would henceforth call myself "John Huffam" whenever it was appropriate to do so. (One's "real" name was surely the name one chose for oneself.) Never, I vowed, would I use again the name that was so hateful to me.

So early the next morning, as we made our breakfast, I explained to the Digweeds that as a consequence of things I had learned from the papers that Sally had brought, I intended to go to my grandfather's house; but I said nothing of my purpose. Protesting that now that Barney might know where I was, I could be in danger if I left the house unaccompanied, they insisted that Mr Digweed should go with me.

I agreed and so when, after the morning's work, we had returned above ground, washed, and dined, we set off together towards midday.

It was a bright but chilly mid-May afternoon when I arrived back in the gloomy, malodorous court. I asked my companion to wait nearby but out of sight of the house in order not to alarm the old man. Then I knocked, remembering how I had beaten my fists against that door on that earlier occasion. And now I reflected that it was no wonder that Mr Escreet had refused to open it since I had announced myself under the name in the world he most hated and feared: Clothier.

So this time, when once again it seemed to me that the judas-hole slid slowly back, I said: "I am John Huffam. Please let me in."

I heard bolts being slowly withdrawn and the sound of a great rusty key being turned, then the door swung open. A huge old man with rounded, stooping shoulders stood looking down at me. He had a long, drooping face whose flesh hung in flabby folds beneath the cheeks and that ended in a jutting jaw; and he had a bulbous reddish nose between ancient, bleary eyes with heavy lids. He appeared not to have shaved for several days and the skin of his face, where it was visible through the white stubble, was mottled. He was dressed in the costume of the last century which was threadbare and ragged in places: ancient drab breeches with stockings below the knee, a faded green coat of old-fashioned cut with an embroidered waistcoat yellowed with age, and buckled shoes. There was a strong smell of spirits.

He stood for a moment blinking at me as if he had just awakened from a profound sleep and then, to my astonishment, he said: "I was expecting you, Master John."

Standing aside he gestured to me to enter. I stepped from the sunlight into the gloom of the vestibule and then through the glass door and thence into the hall where I looked around in the dim light. There was a smell of damp and decay like a cold steady breeze blowing up from the cellars, and many of the black and white marble squares were cracked and there were weeds growing between them. Before me was the wide staircase, and on a wall at one side of it and to my left I could just make out a crossed halberd and curving sword. I shuddered.

Mr Escreet was watching me with an expression I could not interpret. I turned to look at him feeling that this ancient man held the secrets of so many of the mysteries of my family, and wondering how I could induce him to divulge them. It had looked to me at first as if he was in the last stages of senile decay but now, apparently having awakened from his dream, his eyes were focused on me with keen penetration. Yet his wits must have gone. How could he possibly be expecting me? Unless he had recognised and remembered me from my earlier attempt to gain admittance? But surely that was not possible!

"Come this way," he said, and, turning, led me through the hall, past the staircase, and into a small and dark room at the side of the house.

He sat down in an old elbow-chair and gestured towards a similar one opposite him: "Seat yourself, pray. Treat this house as your own, for it was your grandfather's once, though it is mine now for he willed it to me."

I was puzzled by this, for I remembered my mother having written that Mr Escreet had inherited it from her great-grandfather.

"This was his cabinet," Mr Escreet continued. "God rest his soul. I served him faithfully for many years and was with him when he died."

I was amazed by what I took to be such a calm allusion to my grandfather's murder.

"It was in this very chamber," he added.

Feeling a cold chill run up my spine I said: "Will you tell me about that, Mr Escreet? My grandfather's death and ... " I hesitated and then said: "My parents."

"About your parents' death I know little," he answered, misunderstanding me.

I was astonished that he had heard of these events. He had given my mother to understand that he had heard nothing of her for many years on the occasion when she came to this house, so who had informed him of her death? And how did he know anything of Peter Clothier's circumstances?

"In truth, I hardly knew your mother," he went on. "I knew your father much better."

But surely this was the precise opposite of what I knew to be the case? Was the old man quite wandering in his wits? Yet it seemed not for as if my words had accidentally touched some hidden spring, he began to speak with great readiness and fluency, recalling details, names, and dates without effort. As I listened, however, it became apparent that though his recollection of the events of long ago was vivid and clear, he was confused by their relation to the present — or, perhaps it would be truer to say, by his own relation to the past.

CHAPTER 87

I hardly knew your mother. I knew your father much better, for I was little more than a boy when I first came to this house to work for old Mr Jeoffrey Huffam — indeed, I was about the age that you are now, begging your pardon, Master John, and no disrespect intended.

I don't suppose it would interest you if I were to tell you much about myself, so I won't burden you with my own life's-story, beyond saying that I was the child of poor folks, or so I always believed. However, as I grew older I discovered that they weren't my natural parents, though I could never persuade them to tell me who those might be. It's very well for you, Master John, coming of an old family with a deal of family pride, so you cannot fancy what it's like to have no knowledge of who your father is, nor yet your mother.

Though even in your case, there is a difficulty in proving your legitimacy, as I shall tell you.

I was taken from school at fifteen years of age and put to be bred attorney in the office of Mr Paternoster, who did a great deal of law-work for Mr Huffam. Now it happened at the time I am speaking of that the old gentleman wanted a kind of secretary — a factotum or scrivener, you might say — to help him with his correspondence and legal affairs, for he was always going to law over one thing or another. So he asked Mr Paternoster to find a promising youngster, and he brought me here and the old gentleman — and very old I thought him for he was then over sixty, though that doesn't seem so old now — appeared to take a liking to me. I remember it to this day, though it was a long time ago. It meant giving up the chance of articles and a good chance, too, for though I knew that with no fortune of my own and no friends it would take me a great many years, Mr Paternoster had been good to me and I believed I had reason to hope for assistance from him. However, he urged me in the strongest terms to accept Mr Huffam's offer, so I reckoned I would have a fairer chance of bettering myself if I did so.

As it turned out I believe I chose wrong. But for the first years of my time here everything went well. Of course at that time the Huffams were still a powerful, wealthy family and Mr Jeoffrey had a large amount of business to transact, so it was very exciting for a young man. What kind of work was it? Humble enough to start with. I was a kind of under-steward to him. Of course, he had his land-steward then, Mr Fortisquince, to manage his property in the country and receive his rents, and Mr Paternoster was his town-agent. All he wanted was someone to write his letters and make copies of his papers and deal with all his business here, for this house was always full of people coming and going. Ah, it's sad to see it so deserted and delapidated now.

Because Mr Jeoffrey wasn't in good enough health to travel down to Hougham very often, I used to have to go down there now and then to do business with his steward and the tenants. The big new house was not finished, of course, and work had come to a stop a few years before when Mr Jeoffrey had got into severe money-difficulties. I hear, Master John, that the new proprietors have gone on building there, though I don't know if they've followed the design that your grandfather had set his heart upon, for he was bent upon having the finest and biggest house in the county and he intended that it should take the form of an "H" — though one squashed flat, as it were — to celebrate his own name: a central block to represent the cross-bar of the "H", with wings at either end. (He loved such designs and the first thing he did when he came into his estate as a youth was to plant a quincunx of trees before the Old Hall with a statue before each one.) Alas, the house was not completed in his own lifetime, though the main block had been up for some years by the time I knew the place, and that is where the rest of his family lived when they were down in the country. When I last saw the estate the village that stood near the Old Hall had not been taken down nor the park landscaped as I believe has been done since. It must be beautiful now, though I don't suppose I shall ever see it.

It was there that I first met your father for he was often down for the game. He was at the 'Varsity then and used to come with friends of his. He was of an age with myself, though with his horses and dogs and fine friends he took very little notice of me. But how strangely things turn out! For there he lies now in his grave and has lain for — what is it? — a good fifteen year. And all the wealth and the lands that he expected to inherit — what has become of it all? For here you are, his son, almost as poor as I was when I first came to this house about the age you are now. And now this house is mine and you have almost nothing. It's almost enough to make a body believe there is a pattern to events.

Well, I didn't stay in the Great House on my visits, of course, for I was only a paid retainer and not a member of the family, and so at first I put up with Mr Fortisquince who at that date lived in part of the Old Hall with his wife. She was a beautiful young woman, and her husband was many years her senior. How she hated that dark, gloomy old place. But you know what it's like, for that's where you've been living yourself until now, isn't it? It must be even more of a ruin by this date, for this is many years ago that I am speaking of and it had been closed up twenty years before that when your grandfather and his wife and daughters moved into the main block of the new erection.

Mr and Mrs Fortisquince didn't have all of it for there was one wing that was kept shut off. And there was someone kept there. Someone they didn't want known about, but whom I met without their knowledge. Well, on account of that — and other things, too — it came about after a time that Mr Fortisquince wouldn't let me stay there any more. Well, these things happen and I wasn't such a bad-looking young fellow as you might suppose from seeing me now.

Well, so things jogged along for a few years and your grandfather and I agreed very well. He was not an easy gentleman for he had his crotchets, and he possessed a fierce temper and lost it very readily, so he had to be humoured. He kept me on a low salary and very short commons here in the house for he was not generous, not in many ways. But he used to say to me that if I worked hard and served him honestly he would do well by me. I would take the opportunity to remind him now and then of what I had given up by accepting the post with him, and I used to hope that he would make me land-agent in succession to Mr Fortisquince when he grew too old for it.

I trusted him when he said he would see me right for I believed he had taken a fancy to me. And I needed money for I was betrothed about this time, and I could hardly think of marriage and an establishment on the salary that your grandfather was paying me. He used to say sometimes that he wished I was his son instead of the son he had. Oh, I mean no disrespect, but you must know that he and your father did not agree well together.

To speak frankly, Master John, your father was a sore trial to my employer. When he came down from the 'Varsity he lived in this house and I soon came to understand how things lay between them. Mr Jeoffrey had become somewhat near, but Master James was what his father had been at his age. He belonged to a Lodge — a drinking club, and a wild set of young fellows they were who called themselves Mohawks. He lost heavily playing Hazard at Almacks in Pall-Mall where the lowest rouleau was for fifty pounds. Fifty pounds! (Why I've never staked more than twenty-five!) Sheer madness! He and his father quarrelled often and had come to hate each other. The arguments were about money for his father kept him on very short allowance and Master James chafed under this. And so he started borrowing money against his expectations. The worst of it was that he got into debt to a parcel of rogues that your family have long had reason to fear. That's the Clothiers and that old devil Nicholas — may God have mercy on his soul, though what God he might worship I hardly know. A turtle-eating Cit from the wrong side of Temple-Bar, Mr Jeoffrey called him. And much worse.

Once your father was of age he began signing post obits in favour of old Clothier and your grandfather feared what would happen when he died, for he knew that Clothier's heart was set upon acquiring the Hougham property and that that was why he had got his claws into your father. He feared this for he knew Clothier of old and saw events repeating themselves in his son's recklessness and indebtedness to the old man. Of course, you won't understand that unless I explain, as I shall do if you'll bear with me so far.

Well, the year after your father came of age your grandfather was so alarmed by this state of affairs that he decided to make a new will. (For truth to tell, Mr Jeoffrey went in for will-shaking, and had done this before.) I remember the occasion well, Master John, and I shall describe it, for it was to have important consequences for you. But first, I should say something of the connexions between your family and the Mompessons, and make clear who the Clothiers were — and are, for there is one of them still left to plague us — and how they came to be involved with your grandfather. And in order to do all that, I have to go back a long way and explain some things that you might not know, for I doubt that Mr Fortisquince would speak to you of such matters, and yet I believe it is right that you should understand them, and I have a particular reason, as I shall make clear to you.

CHAPTER 88

The Huffams — or Houghams as they originally spelled the name — are a family of auncient and honourable lineage. The original founder of the family was given a grant of the manor of Hougham by the Conqueror himself, and in later centuries some of their wives came of royal stock. The blood of the Plantagenets flows through your veins, Master John. They held the estate quietly for the next few hundred years, gradually extending and improving it. They built the Old Hall while Henry IV was on the throne and very cannily managed to avoid the consequences of the civil wars between the factions of the white and red roses that did so much harm during the rest of that century. At the Dissolution they acquired considerable new lands from the old Carthusian monastery that had owned much of the property around there, and thus they became one of the greatest families in the county. But they adhered to the Church party — some say they were secret Papists — and so it was that during the Civil Wars in the following century they backed the King and thereby forfeited part of their estates when the Royalist cause was lost and many estates were sequestrated. Much of their land went to a family who had been small squires in the neighbourhood for many years and who had been shrewd enough to have backed Cromwell — I speak of the Mompessons. They claimed equal antiquity with the Huffams, insisting that they had given the name to the nearby village of Mompesson St. Lucy. But your own family always looked down upon them as upstarts and said that they had been yeomen-tenants of theirs and that they had taken their name from the village and not the other way round.

Then the Huffams tried to win back what they had lost by making friends with the Parliamentarians and they came down fiercely against the Papists. Well, who can blame them? We've heard plenty about families trimming in their faith in order to better themselves. Yes, and converting from more than Papistry. However, they had misjudged the temper of the times, while on the other hand the Mompessons were long-headed enough to foresee the Restoration. So the Huffams regained nothing at that happy event and the Mompessons retained what they had acquired, and by the beginning of the old Queen's reign they were fine gentlefolks — though nothing like as rich as us for we were still among the largest land-owners in that country. For it was a very fine property that your grandfather inherited and without any burdens since he was the only son, though he had two sisters, Laetitia and Louisa. I fear that as a young man he was wild and reckless, almost as much as your father, and racketed around the Town with other young bloods and they got into all manner of scrapes. He gambled and drank and spent his time and money in the way of wealthy young gentlemen at the time — indeed, at all times, I suppose. And he borrowed money, a great deal of it, for he needed it to set up his carriage and his horses and his ... Well, everything that a young gentleman on the Town needs. He had already begun to borrow against his expectations even before he attained his majority, although the security he could give was in law worthless unless he chose to honour it. When he came into the estate at his father's death he honoured these debts (despite the advice of Mr Paternoster that he should repudiate them) and in order to do so he borrowed heavily against the security of the land he had inherited.

Now the individual to whom he became most deeply indebted was Nicholas Clothier who was a merchant and money-lender and projector and all manner of bad things. Your grandfather called him a mushroom man for he had risen quickly and in the dark. He referred to him as Old Nick and said he was rightly named. Clothier was already very rich and what he sought was to ally himself with a respectable old family and buy his way into landed society. So he fastened upon your grandfather and within a few years the estate was so deeply mortgaged to him that Mr Jeoffrey was very near to failing to keep up the interest payments and thereby giving him the chance to foreclose. But then, at the very last moment, he saved the estate. You see, your grandfather had a great deal of pride in his family and could not abide the thought of our ancestral lands falling into the clutches of a low bill-broker. So he shut down this house and went back to Hougham and lived there, taking the management of the estate entirely into his own hands. And by this means he retrieved his position and within a few years was safe from Clothier, who was furious at being cheated — as he conceived it — at the last moment of what he had expected to fall into his grasp.

Well, all went well for some years and would have continued so had your grandfather not taken the fever for building that was all the rage amongst the gentry then. For instead of redeeming the securities still held by Clothier when they fell due, as would have been prudent, he renewed them so that he could spend his money on bricks and mortar. The Old Hall seemed to him not to be fit for a gentleman, and so he resolved to build himself a fine new house nearby. It was strange that he never cared much about where he lived in Town and was content to go on living in this house, though it was no longer in a *tonish* quarter once they built those new streets beyond St. James and even out as far as Tyburn. (For this district has declined sadly. The gentry have been moving away from here for the last fifty or sixty years, so this house is worth much less than when your grandfather promised it to me. You'll maybe have noticed the Bagnio next door at No. 16 with the line of carriages and chairs outside it? And the soldiers' tuppenny drabs along the wall of the Privy-gardens? This was why your grandfather turned the house around and stuck on a vestibule so that the back is now the front.) Of course, now that he had thrown up his old ways, he only came to Town on business about the building and furnishing of his new house. But it was while he was here that he made the acquaintance of Mr David Mompesson, the eldest son of that family, who was of an age with him. He was ambitious to establish himself in Society and, claiming the privileges of a fellow-countryman, succeeded in making the acquaintance of Mr Jeoffrey. He was determined to ally himself with your family and, knowing of your grandfather's pecuniary embarrassments, paid his addresses to his younger sister, Louisa, and after a time was so bold as to request of Mr Jeoffrey her hand in marriage.

But your grandfather, remembering how the Mompessons had gained what wealth they had and considering them to be beggarly upstarts, was furious at his impertinence and refused him in somewhat insulting terms. Mr Mompesson took this very ill and, as you will hear, resolved upon gaining satisfaction for the slight. Determined to elevate his family's fortunes, he found himself as rich a bride as his rank could bring him, the daughter of a Bristol merchant. He went into partnership with his father-in-law and, shortly after the birth of his son, Hugo, he sailed for the West-indies, where he remained for upwards of ten years. His wife also bore him a daughter, Anna, who was born some months after his departure.

Your grandfather, too, spending more and more money on his building mania, began to look about for a rich bride and also found himself an heiress. And her money was all he ever cared for, I fear, because there was no love between them — and this led to trouble. And shortly afterwards his first child, a daughter whom he named Alice, was born.

Then Mr David Mompesson returned to England, having made a great fortune in the West-indian trade and acquired sugar-plantations and ships and I don't know what not. He bought himself that new house in Brook-street which his family still occupies. Then he went into Parliament and purchased a baronetcy, (and your grandfather used to say that though the king might have made him a baronet, the Devil himself couldn't make him a gentleman). And he took out a grant of arms incorporating the Huffam quincunx into his blazon, claiming that it had aunciently been the device of the Mompessons — though your grandfather was mighty angry at the impertinence. But he did not buy himself a landed seat for he had set his heart by one means or another on acquiring the Hougham property, partly because of the villages nearby named "Mompesson" which he believed would vindicate his family's claim to auncientness, but also in order to get revenge for your grandfather's out-of-hand rejection of his suit. But because his health was broken down by the tropics, he died soon after his return to England. His son, the present Sir Hugo, inherited his father's West-indian plantations along with his ambition to own your grandfather's estate.

And he believed he had a good chance, for at that time, of course, your grandfather had no son, for your father was not born until some years after Mr Jeoffrey's second child, Miss Sophia. Knowing of your grandfather's pressing need for money, Sir Hugo calculated that, wealthy and titled as he was, he might succeed in forming an alliance where his father had failed, for your grandfather's elder daughter, Miss Alice, was then almost of marriageable age.

So Sir Hugo set out to renew the acquaintance with your grandfather which the two families had distantly maintained. But when he offered for her hand, Mr Jeoffrey insisted that she was too young to think of marriage and Sir Hugo feared that he was putting him off with excuses and that he would be rejected as an upstart, just as his own father had been. However, one way or another Mr Jeoffrey was brought to agree to the marriage. And the terms he accepted in the articles of marriage were very favourable to Sir Hugo, for your grandfather bound himself to settle the estate on the eldest son of the marriage if he himself died without a son. (His wife was then well advanced in years and was believed to be past the age of child-bearing.)

There was a grand wedding, by all accounts. Sir Hugo loved pomp and splendour and heraldry and all that kind of thing and he had the house in Brook-street ablaze with lights and filled with heraldic emblems. But how briefly the truce between the two families lasted! The trouble came when Sir Hugo and his lady's first child turned out to be a girl — christened Lydia — and was followed by no other child, and your grandfather refused to make a will in the infant's favour. He argued that he had promised to favour the eldest son only. And perhaps the reason why she grew up such a strange creature, by all accounts, is that she was resented by her parents — for if she had been a boy everything would have been quite otherwise.

Well, the next thing that happened was that, after all, it became known that your grandmother was expecting another child. And when your father was born the rift between your grandfather and the Mompessons became very wide. As you must know, your grandmother died in childbed and the infant was a weakling, and I suppose that it was because of this and being his father's late-born son and having a doating elder sister, Miss Sophia, that your father grew up spoiled and indulged.

All these years your grandfather had been building at Hougham instead of putting money into improvements on the estate, and therefore he had been getting deeper and deeper into debt to Clothier. (It cost a deal of money for he had to clear the village that stood near the Old Hall, in order to lay out the park.) At last, about ten years after the birth of your father and about six years before I entered Mr Jeoffrey's service, Clothier was once again ready to foreclose. Your grandfather, however, proposed a bargain whereby his younger daughter, Miss Sophia, who was then a beautiful and sweet young lady of eighteen, should marry the old man. In return for Clothier's agreement to extend the mortgages, Mr Jeoffrey consented to a marriage settlement which stipulated that the eldest son of the marriage be made heir to the Hougham property next after your father. Clothier reckoned that your father, then a sickly child of ten, would not survive to his inheritance. Your grandfather bound himself by covenant to make such a will, hoping, of course, that his son would survive to father an heir so that the clause would be worthless.

Well, a son was born to Clothier and Miss Sophia the following year, and that was young Mr Silas of whom you may have heard something — none of it good, I'll wager. When, however, Mr Jeoffrey did nothing about making a new will as he had undertaken to do, old Clothier began to threaten once again to foreclose. Your grandfather resisted making any new will at all since he was determined not to risk making young Mr Silas his heir in remainder until your father had married and fathered a child. But since, as he approached the age of majority, he showed no sign of doing so, eventually Mr Jeoffrey decided to make a new will but to do it without mentioning Master Silas.

CHAPTER 89

So this was how the land lay at the time I was speaking of just now, almost exactly twenty years ago. Mr Jeoffrey's attorney, Mr Paternoster, drew up the will with my assistance and I was very gratified when your grandfather said that he intended to bequeath me this house as a mark of his gratitude and good-will towards me. (He had also increased my salary and all of this meant that I could marry at last.) Apart from that bequest, the new will simply confirmed the terms of his previous will making your father his outright heir, though your grandfather was sorely afraid that he intended to sell the estate when he should come into it. Mr Jeoffrey did not even mention his grandson, Silas, in the will — contrary to what he had covenanted to do.

Well, Clothier insisted that your grandfather should show him the will in order to satisfy him that he had done what he had bound himself to, and when Mr Jeoffrey refused he went to law and got nearly all that he sought, for when the court ordered your grandfather to discover the will and it was found that he had ignored his undertaking, he was ordered to add a codicil to it naming Master Silas as heir in remainder and to have it witnessed by Mr Clothier himself.

Well, now, your grandfather and Mr Paternoster and I had many a long discussion about what should be done both to prevent your father from selling the estate if he should inherit it, and to reduce Silas Clothier's chance of inheriting in default of him. Mr Paternoster came up with a way of atchieving both ends: the codicil should entail the estate on your father (though since he had no heir, the entail was only upon him and it would not be difficult for him to break or bar it), and should name Master Silas as the heir in remainder if the entailed line should fail. This meant that he could only inherit if he were still alive when all the descendants of your father were dead. And if young Mr Silas were no longer alive at such time, then the entail passed to the only member of his family with whom Mr Jeoffrey had not quarrelled at that date — his elder sister, Miss Laetitia, who had married a gentleman called Maliphant. Finally, to allay your grandfather's fears altogether, Mr Paternoster pointed out that there was nothing to stop him either revoking the codicil or making a new will if he chose, except that the Clothiers would contest this in Chancery — as, indeed, they have done. And so the codicil was drawn up in these terms and witnessed by Clothier himself.

Naturally, your grandfather was very anxious that your father should marry as soon as possible in order to preserve the line, but when, shortly afterwards, Master James told him he had chosen a bride, Mr Jeoffrey very strongly opposed his choice. He believed that her family was not rich or well-born enough. And there were other reasons why he was against the match. For one thing, the whole family had been set at odds by a scandal over the fact that the daughter of Sir Hugo and Lady Mompesson — the queer young creature I told you of

— had fallen in love with the lady's brother, John Umphraville. Her parents opposed the match and your grandfather supported them over this. His nevy, George Maliphant, on the other hand, took the young people's part and as a consequence Mr Jeoffrey quarrelled with him and determined to strike out his remaindership. Conversely, your grandfather's sister, Louisa Palphramond, supported Mr Jeoffrey and so came back into favour with him. In the event the marriage between the girl and young Umphraville did not take place because of your grandfather's opposition.

Your father, however, succeeded in defying your grandfather for he and your mother made it up to run away together and be married. Because he had to do it secretly he acquired a special licence and arranged for the ceremony to be performed somewhere where his father would neither know of it nor be able to prevent it. Because of this there has always been a mystery about the marriage. And though it grieves me to say it, Master John, you must know that the accursed Clothiers have doubted the marriage — that is to say, they are claiming that it never took place and that therefore you are illegitimate. And since your parents are dead and no witnesses to the ceremony are known, nor any record of it in any of the parish registers that have been examined, I am afraid that they have a very strong case. So your grandfather's opposition may have brought about what he most feared: the disinheriting of his own descendants.

CHAPTER 90

Well, early in the Spring of the following year your grandfather became very ill and when he realized that he was dying, he was haunted by the fear that your father would dock the entail and sell the property to Nicholas Clothier or, which was hardly less agreeable a thought, to Sir Hugo. He besought Mr Paternoster to think of a way to prevent this, but in vain. Then everything changed suddenly and you were the cause of it, Master John. For as soon as news came of your birth Mr Paternoster perceived a means to thwart your father's intentions and outwit both Clothier and the Mompessons. However, I knew nothing of this at the time for I was down at Hougham, and everything I am now about to tell you I discovered only long afterwards.

Following Mr Paternoster's design Mr Jeoffrey made another will cutting out your father entirely by entailing the estate upon you. Yes, Master John, you are in Equity the entailed heir to the property and should be in possession of it at this minute. But be patient and I will tell you what happened. (I might also mention that your grandfather chose to take the risk of leaving out all mention of Master Silas and defying the Clothiers to contest it. And because he had quarrelled with his nevy George and made up with his niece, Amelia, he wanted to punish him and reward her. And so the entail, instead of going to him and his heirs in default of your issue, now passed to his niece Amelia and her heirs.)

Now I have to tell you a terrible thing. Immediately after making this will, your grandfather died and so no-one knew that it existed except Mr Paternoster and the other witness to it who was one of his own clerks. And Mr Paternoster removed and suppressed it; and not only that but he also removed the codicil from the original will. (I will explain his motives in a moment.) So he produced the original will and said that your grandfather had revoked the codicil shortly before he died, and his clerk confirmed this for Mr Paternoster had paid him to hold his tongue and say what he was bid. Consequently, that earlier will was sent to probate. Of course Nicholas Clothier challenged it in the Court of Consistory, alleging that the codicil had been illegally suppressed, but since he had no evidence the case was dismissed after only a few months.

So your father inherited the estate. And Clothier, furious at having been cheated, set about foreclosing on the mortgages and the post obits and resorted to Chancery in the attempt to prove that the codicil was illegally suppressed and that, since the marriage of your parents never took place, his son, Silas, was the rightful heir. He offered to abandon this suit if your father would sell the estate, but your father outwitted him for he did not wish to sell his ancestral lands to a counter-jumping Cit any more than his father did. So, less than a year after his father's death, he conveyed the estate to his brother-in-law, Sir Hugo Mompesson, who, now that he had a son — the present Sir Augustus — was keen to obtain it. Since Sir Hugo could not put down the whole of the purchase-money, it was settled that an annuity was to be paid as a charge on the estate to your father and his heirs in perpetuity.

Your father died soon afterwards and so did old Clothier, but the Chancery suit continued, for it was taken over by Mr Silas. Now, Master John, this is the important intelligence that I have for you. Just before Mr Paternoster died a few years ago he confessed to me what he had done and why. He told me he had gone to your father and told him that Mr Jeoffrey had just made a will disinheriting him. And so your father bribed him to suppress it and, for good measure, to conceal the codicil to the earlier will so that he would not have to go to the expense of breaking the entail before he could sell the estate.

However, what Mr Paternoster told me on his deathbed was that he did not destroy those two documents, as he led your father to believe. He kept them for a number of years and not long before, he had approached the Mompessons and told them about the will and that it was still in existence. They were naturally horrified for it would have the effect of disinheriting your father retrospectively and thereby invalidating their purchase of the estate. And so they purchased it of him for a large sum of money. I fear they will have destroyed it, Master John, and so there is no evidence now that it ever even existed.

The codicil, however, offers more hope. Mr Paternoster dared not offer it, of course, to the Clothiers but he sought out the heir of Mr George Maliphant — upon whom, you may remember, the entail devolved in default of your father's issue provided that the death of young Mr Silas had taken place — and he offered it to this gentleman, a certain Mr Richard Maliphant. However, Mr Maliphant declined to purchase it. Mr Paternoster told me he had then sold it to another member of that family, but he refused to tell me who this individual was.

Now, if you could regain the codicil and lay it before the court you might have a chance of being declared owner of the Hougham estate, for it would retrospectively create a base-fee instead of the fee-simple the Mompessons believed they had purchased and the court might find that the sale was therefore invalid.

I dare say all of this will require a great deal of money, Master John. So you must begin now to save what you can from your annuity, and start to acquire the knowledge of the law of real property that will permit you to prosecute the suit most effectively. Why don't you come and live here? (You may pay me something for your board and lodging.) And bring that other young fellow, Martin, the son of poor Elizabeth Fortisquince. I will teach you what I know of the Common Law and of Equity. So you must ... you must ... What the devil is that row, Master John? I say, what the ... Master John? By God! Who are you?

BOOK IV

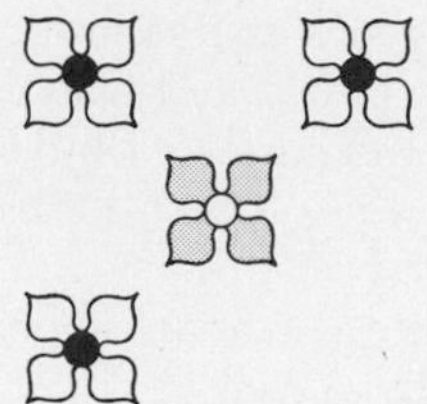

A Friend on the Inside

CHAPTER 91

It is late in the evening and Mr Clothier and Mr Sancious are alone in the counting-house or, rather, almost alone for Mr Vulliamy is still at work in the outer office where he can surely hear the sound of raised voices.

"Those bills of Quintard and Mimpriss that you advised me to buy for my client — they were worthless!" Mr Sancious is shouting.

"I didn't know the house was in danger," the old gentleman exclaims indignantly. "Why, I got burnt myself holding their paper. And so did my informant."

"Your informant," the attorney sneers. He looks as if he is about to say something else, but then he goes on: "I'll wager it was your informant that got us into this pickle! See where your bill-dealing has got us! Every penny the Pimlico and Westminster Land Company made out of that spec — lost! And the company itself going to smash with the prospect of gaol for someone!"

"Why should you care?" cries the old gentleman. Then, jerking his head towards the door and hushing his guest with a gesture of his hands, he goes on in a hoarse whisper: "It ain't you that will suffer for it."

"Nor you either!" the attorney retorts. "And I wonder if you've bubbled me all along. Why, I'll wager you've been selling your own slang bills to the company and making me pay for your losses!"

"That's a lie!" the old gentleman screams. "And if it comes to that, *you* haven't been square with *me*. It was you who arranged the Huffam boy's escape!"

"What are you talking about?" Mr Sancious exclaims in amazement — or a fine imitation of it. "Why would I have done that?"

"Don't play with me. Do you take me for a fool? I know you were behind it. And I'll stake my life you know where he is now."

"That's absurd. What motive could I possibly have for doing such a thing?"

The old gentleman looks very cunning at this: "Don't think I don't know exactly what your game is, Sancious," he says. "I know how you've been trying to trump me. But you won't succeed. I've been one too many for you. I know all the cards you hold. You see, I ... "

The old gentleman falters and starts gasping for breath. Then he sinks to the floor moaning: "Loosen my collar. Help me."

The attorney stands looking down at him while his host splutters and clutches his chest.

In a low strangled voice the old gentleman gasps: "Call Vulliamy, for heaven's sake!"

Mr Sancious remains motionless.

After a few minutes the old gentleman falls silent and lies quite still. Instantly the attorney crosses to the strong-box and tries to raise the lid. It is locked. He goes to the desk and begins opening drawers and looking through piles of papers.

At that moment, however, the old gentleman suddenly jumps to his feet: "Not so quickly, my dear friend."

As Mr Sancious looks at him in horror, he smirks at him and sneers: "You thought you were in luck, didn't you?"

He advances towards him and Mr Sancious backs out of the door into the outer office where he cries out: "Your governor has gone mad!"

Then he turns and hurries out of the street-door.

In amazement Mr Vulliamy looks up from his desk at his employer who is standing in the door-way to his inner closet and hugging himself in glee.

CHAPTER 92

The reason why the old man broke off his narrative so suddenly was that there had come a violent hammering at the street-door. It was a strange and distinctive knock: the blows fell in a quick succession of three, followed by a pause, and then a single knock followed by another pause before the pattern was repeated. Mr Escreet had started at the noise as if he had been suddenly awakened, and he was looking at me now as if he was seeing me for the first time: "By God! Who are you? You're not Master John! Who the devil are you?"

"As I told you, Mr Escreet, I am John Huffam."

As I spoke, my mind was in a tumult as I tried to think about the implications of what he had told me.

"No you're not. John Huffam is dead." He stood up: "Whoever you are, you must go. *He* must not find you here."

"Whom do you mean?" I asked. "And how do you know who is there?"

He looked frightened: "Nobody else knocks like that. Hurry, he has his own key."

He seized me and almost pushed me out of the room. As we were passing through the hall, he raised his finger to his lips and while we crept on tip-toe across the broken tiles, the sound of the street-door opening came to us. We were by now hidden from the vestibule by the staircase and paused here while we heard the door close and realized that the newcomer had entered the house. Then the vestibule-door opened and shut and we heard footsteps almost passing us as the stranger went into the side-lobby. We set off again down the long passage and reached the back-door safely. Mr Escreet almost pushed me through it and then locked the door behind me.

I made my way along the dark little alley-way into bustling Charing-cross, and then going up the street, returned along the public way into the first yard of the court. There I found Mr Digweed waiting for me where he could see anyone coming or going but could not be seen from the house. To my surprise,

Joey was with him and was panting as if he had been running. I was pleased to see him, though only because I knew how worried his parents were.

"Who was it who arrived just now?" I asked them.

They both shook their heads.

"What did he look like?"

"He was quite young," Joey answered; "dressed like a genel'man, but out of blunt, I should say. I can't say no more than that."

"I'll wait and see him when he comes out."

"You can't," Joey said. "*He's* jist come to the house."

"Who?"

"Barney. Sally must have told him where we was."

"You ain't safe there now, Master John," his father put in. "You must be got away."

I saw the force of this, though I was reluctant to give up my chance of observing Mr Escreet's visiter.

"But where to?" I wondered.

Mr Digweed and Joey looked at each other.

"Meg's," Joey said.

"That's what I was thinking."

I looked at Joey. Was he telling the truth or was this another trap that he was going to lead me into? How had he learned of Barney's return to the house? Was it not probable that he had gone back to him with Sally and that they had concocted another design against me?

"I'll take him there, dad," Joey said, "for if one of Barney's men dodged me here I can lose him better than you can."

Mr Digweed nodded.

"So you came back, Joey?" I asked.

He reddened but his father, who I could see was torn between his pleasure that his son had returned and his alarm on my behalf, said: "Aye, thank Gawd. He says he didn't never go back to Barney but jist walked about and slept out."

Joey's manner was less sullen than I had ever seen. It seemed to me as if he was truly pleased to be able to do something for me and with this reflection, I decided to trust him.

So we left his father, and Joey led me on a headlong chase across the metropolis, weaving our way between the foot-passengers on the crowded pavements, dodging up alley-ways, and diving across busy roads so suddenly that horses reared their heads and drivers shouted and cracked their whips at us. With many digressions and doublings back, we were heading steadily East along the riverside.

We passed the Tower and cut through a district all of whose streets were either cleared away or in process of being demolished. This was St. Katharine's parish where a medieval college and hospital together with more than a thousand houses were being taken down (and their inhabitants evicted) to make way for the new dock. The rubble and soil extracted from here were being shipped up-river to fill the Grosvenor-bason in Pimlico — an undertaking which I had seen while crossing the Neat-houses in search of Barney.

Beyond that we suddenly entered a district where men with wind-burnt faces in stiff clothes walked the streets, brazen-faced women flaunted their finery, and all about us were ships'-chandlers, biscuit-makers, rope-makers, and, in short, the manufacturers and suppliers of everything to do with ships. Sea-gulls cried above us and London was suddenly a sea-port.

At last we reached a shabby, run-down district near the river and here, in a dirty, narrow way called Brewhouse-lane, Joey stopped and knocked on a low door set deep in the wall. (We were, in fact, in Wapping and almost beside Execution-dock where pirates and mutineers were formerly executed by the incoming tide.) We were both gasping for breath and I had had neither time nor wind to ask any questions.

Meg's turned out to be a clean and respectable lodging-house — a most unlikely occurrence in that part of London where the crimping-houses lay in wait to prey upon discharged sailors. Meg herself was a friendly, honest woman of about Mrs Digweed's age. Although she was an old companion of hers, their friendship was, Joey assured me, quite unknown to his uncle. She showed Joey and me to a small but spotless room, and when she had withdrawn, I expected Joey to say he would leave me and was about to ask him to convey my thanks to his parents, when he made it clear that he wanted to say something. I was impatient for him to go for I had much to think about.

He seemed to be having difficulty in beginning, but at last he blurted out: "It was all down to me. Ma didn't know nothing about it."

"What are you talking about?"

"Jist a-fore we went down to the North that time, Barney got Sal to bring me to him and he gived me four shillin' and promised me more if I'd do what he wanted. I was to get inside this crib in Melthorpe, and he told me exackerly where it was and what it looked like. I was proud that he trusted me. And that was why I led Ma back through Melthorpe and straight to you and your mam."

"I see. And what did he want you to do?"

"I was to prig a door-key if I got the chance. But most of all I was to look out for any screeves — papers — that might be lying around, and to see where anything vallyable might be kept hid." Then he cried: "But I didn't do none of them things."

"Because I caught you!"

"No!" he exclaimed indignantly. "I didn't want to do nothing arter your mam was so good to us. I reckoned I'd jist take a good look round so I could tell Barney what I seen, but not tell him nothing that'd help him to prig nothing of you."

Was this the truth at last? Presumably his parents had known this but wanted Joey himself to tell me. And now he had done so at a time when, having rescued me from his uncle, he felt in a morally stronger position. I was almost certain that I now knew the reason for his sullenness towards me: there is nobody we resent as much as someone to whom we feel we have done wrong.

"I believe you," I assured him.

"That ain't all," he said. "That time I dodged you from the carcase, there was more to it. When you found your shake-down at the Common-garding that night, I spoke to the boy what you'd gived a ring to."

"Luke!" I cried.

"That's the ticket. I got him to watch you and dodge you if you went anywheres, and then come back and tell me where you were. I gived him my last four-pence and promised him another six-pence. Then I went back to Barney and found they was getting ready to clear out of there. Barney told me he'd got his orders about you from whoever it was that was paying him."

"Who was that?"

"I dunno. But he told me how I was to make a pall of you and lead you as if by chance to this crib out towards Islington. He even drawed me a map so as I should find it. Which as you know I done."

I said nothing but suddenly he broke out: "Well, I nivver knowed what they meant to do, did I?"

I nodded distractedly. What he had said confirmed my assumption that Sancious was the connexion between Barney and the Clothiers.

"So I left Barney and went back to the Common-garding," Joey went on; "and Luke took me to your grand-dad's house."

Almost everything that had still puzzled me about the role of Mr and Mrs Digweed was now explained and my fears about them were all but laid to rest. And though Joey had done my mother and me wrong, he had been too young to be held responsible and the very fact that he had for so long resented me was proof of how guilty he felt. Even so, I could not be entirely sure that he would not return to his former allegiance to his uncle, and therefore I felt I could not trust him too far.

As Joey was leaving, Meg asked me to come and eat in the kitchen, so it was only after I had returned to my chamber later that evening that I had leisure to reflect on the things Mr Escreet had told me — and told me, as it were, by mistake. His confusion about time and my identity had given me a window straight into the past so that I believed I now possessed knowledge that no-one else alive had apart from us two. I now knew that the purloined will of Jeoffrey Huffam had indeed existed and that it was the attorney Paternoster who had misappropriated it and sold it to the Mompessons. I also knew that instead of destroying it (as Mr Escreet had assumed they would), the Mompessons had kept it, for shortly before my grandfather's murder he had received that mysterious promise from someone in their household that he would return it to him through the agency of Martin Fortisquince. I was puzzled by why the Mompessons had held onto the will since its effect was to disinherit them. (Presumably it had been by an oversight and surely they must have destroyed it by now?) And I was intrigued by the identity and motives of the person who had undertaken to steal it back from them.

I settled down to try to sleep. In the middle of the night there was a noise at the front of the house and when I looked out of window I saw the three Digweeds standing in the street with all their possessions loaded onto a hand-cart. As I came down, Meg rose and let them in. We went into the kitchen and they explained that they had decided to flee from their house under cover of night and in the utmost secrecy, in case Barney or any of his gang were keeping watch. They intended to find somewhere to live in this part of the metropolis so that I could dwell with them again. I was very surprised by this and it confirmed my assumption about their real motives.

In the morning they succeeded in finding a little cottage nearby in Peartree-alley off Cinnamon-street, and we all moved into it. Having become strangers here, they had no credit at the chandler's, could score nothing on the slate at the tap, and had no relationship with the pawn-broker. And so, moved by this evidence of their loyalty to myself and feeling guilty for having misjudged them, I decided that I owed it to them to tell them at least a little of my story. Yet since I was still not sure if I could trust their son so far, I resolved to wait until Joey was out of the house.

It happened that the next time he went out his mother, as if aware that I might not want to speak frankly before him, asked me: "Did your grand-dad tell you anything useful, Master John?"

I started. *My grand-dad?* What did she know? How could she know it? Then I understood how we had misunderstood one another for she had been misled by my reference to my grandfather's house.

"You mean, Mr Escreet?" I said. "The old gentleman at the house by Charing-cross?"

She nodded and so, fortunately, I had no need to deny that Mr Escreet was my grandfather. It was, after all, my grandfather's house. I explained that the old gentleman I had visited was the confidential servant of my mother's father and I began to recount some of what he had told me.

However, as soon as I mentioned the Mompessons Mr Digweed broke in: "The Mumpseys! Why, that's the fambly what my dad worked for down in the country before he come up to Lunnon. What I told you of a-fore."

"That's a strange coincidence," I said. He looked puzzled. "I mean, the odds are very long against it."

"Oh I don't know so much," he replied. "Arter all, they was the big fambly in them parts, so seeing as how that's where my old feller come from it ain't no wonder that he should have gone into sarvice with 'em."

"Where exactly did he come from?"

"Why, a village called Stoke near 'Ougham, what got took down about fifty year back. So my dad's fambly had to leave."

"I know it. They rebuilt it and called it Stoke Mompesson."

"Aye, but then 'twas for freeholders on'y so they wouldn't be a burden on the paritch."

It was an extraordinary coincidence that there should be this further link between myself and the Digweeds. Had I been premature after all in allowing my suspicions of them to be laid to rest? But if they were concealing something from me, then they would hardly have admitted to this.

Mr Digweed went on: "My fambly — the Digweeds and Feverfews — has been masons and j'iners for the Mumpseys since time out of mind."

Then a thought occurred to me and, trying to hide a note of suspicion, I asked: "Then is Barney connected with them?"

"He was for a time but hasn't been for many a year," his brother answered, "for he fell out with the steward over payment for some work he done and held a grudge agin 'em ever arter."

I knew something of Barney's grudges. Relieved that all was beginning to fall into place, I said:

"I remember you told me that you and Barney went on doing work for the family your father served. So was that why Barney was up there that time he broke into our house?"

"Aye, that's right," said Mrs Digweed. "Do you mind as how the Mumpseys opened up their big house in 'Ougham not long arter that? Well, Barney got took on beforehand to help make it ready which is why he was passing through Melthorpe that day."

So there was no coincidence! Now I saw that I had misread this connexion and got it the wrong way round: it was that original link between the Digweeds and my own district from which all the other apparent coincidences had followed! Then I had been completely wrong to suspect Mr and Mrs Digweed of being involved in some vast conspiracy! (Indeed, I remembered now that when Mrs Digweed and Joey had come to us in Melthorpe, she had mentioned her husband's connexion with Mompesson-park. How strange that I had forgotten that.)

I felt now that I trusted them enough to tell them more. So I explained briefly how an ancestor's last will — together with a codicil attached to an earlier will — had long ago been stolen, and how all the ill suffered by my family followed from that: my grandfather had been murdered, my mother ruined, and I myself persecuted in the way that they knew about. Now that the codicil had been obtained by the Clothiers and laid before Chancery, my life was in grave danger for Silas Clothier would come into the Hougham estate upon my death. What I had learned from Mr Escreet was that the Mompessons had bought the purloined will from its thief, and I guessed that it was in the attempt to regain it from them that my grandfather had been murdered — and in such a way that suspicion had fallen upon his new son-in-law.

They shook their heads at this story, and then Mrs Digweed asked: "Ain't there no way you could make yourself safe?"

"Only if that purloined will still existed and could be laid before the court, for it would overturn the codicil and there would be no advantage to anyone in my death. But it must have been destroyed long ago."

"Are you sure?" Mrs Digweed asked. "Don't you think that if the Mumpseys kept it for forty year, then if they did get it back that time arter the poor genel'man was killed, they'll still be keeping it?"

"Yes," I said, my heart racing at this confirmation of my hopes, for I had earlier pushed that very thought from my mind. "But if they did have a reason for keeping it — which I can't believe for it does them nothing but harm — then it's probably in a bank-vault or some other secure hiding-place."

"Hiding-place!" Mrs Digweed exclaimed and turned to me, her face flushed with excitement: "What year was it that your grand-dad was done to death?"

"Why, it was in May the year before I was born."

"And you was born about six months a-fore Joey, ain't that so?" She turned to her husband: "Why, then that was the May of the year of the Great Comet. Do you not rec'lleck it? 'Twas as big as a cheeseplate." He nodded and she continued: "That was the time I was nussing Polly and it was jist then that you done some work for the Mumpseys!"

Mr Digweed stared blankly at her.

"A cove come from their steward," she went on, "to say they needed some j'inery work done."

"Mr Assinder?" I asked.

"No, the one a-fore him," she said to me, and then turned back to her husband: "And you wondered why they didn't use one of their reg'lar men, for you'd done no work for 'em for many a year?"

"Aye," he said. "I recall it now."

Mrs Digweed cried: "So don't you see, the job you done was that very time they must have got Master John's dockyment back!"

"I see," I said.

"George, tell Master John what they wanted."

"Well," he reflected. "There's a big chimbley-piece in one of the grandest rooms. The Great Parlour, so they call it. Made of the finest marble and dowelled something beautiful. They'd had a mason cut a slab in it jist below the mantel and holler out a space behind and below it. I was to make a kind of wooden box to fit behind it and to swing upwards and for'ard by means of a pulley when the slab was lowered."

"A hiding-place!" I exclaimed.

"That's right," Mrs Digweed said. "That's why they didn't want to use none o' their reg'lar workmen."

I could not speak for I was possessed by the thought that if this was correct and if I could obtain the will, then I would immediately become the owner of the estate. What a complete restoration of justice in recompense for the wrongs done to my family by both the Mompessons and the Clothiers! And Sir Perceval had shewn himself by his actions towards the local people to be wholly undeserving of the property. I had more than a right — I had a duty — to possess the estate! But how could I hope to regain the will? Not wishing to let the Digweeds suspect my thoughts I made an excuse, left the house and walked briskly around the neighbouring streets until my mind was calmer.

Even if I had the means, I could not subpoena the will for the Mompessons would simply deny that it existed. It was clear to me that the only way to acquire it was by some means to break into the hiding-place. But how could I hope to do that?

Mr Digweed, Joey and I went back to work the next day, and now that we were living in a different part of the metropolis, we had to enter the system through another outlet and this meant that we had to travel some distance to get to the most fruitful tunnels which slowed us down and lowered our earnings.

One evening when Joey was once again from the house, I brought the subject of conversation back to the hiding-place.

"Did Barney help you to make it?" I asked Mr Digweed, mindful of my earlier suspicion of his involvement in my family's story.

"No," he answered in surprise; "for he wasn't in Town then."

"Do you know where he was?"

He shook his head: "He went missing for a few months about that time."

Though not conclusive, this was further evidence that he might have been the murderer of my grandfather.

After a moment I said: "I'm afraid that the only way to get the will back is to remove it."

There was a pause.

"You mean, steal it?" Mrs Digweed said.

"It's not stealing," I protested. "It was stolen originally and it rightfully belongs to the courts. All wills do."

"Then it is for the courts to get it back," Mrs Digweed said.

"But they neither will nor can. If justice is to be done, then I must take it upon myself."

There was an outcry at this:

"If you're caught you could be hanged," Mrs Digweed said. "At the least you'd be transported."

"My life is already in danger," I said. "Am I to spend the next years hiding from Barney until Silas Clothier is dead?"

They looked taken aback at this and I saw that my reference to the role in my life performed by a member of their family had scored a hit.

"Only when I have laid the will before the Court will I be safe. So all I ask, Mr Digweed, is that you tell me how I might open the hiding-place?"

His wife nodded slightly and he began:

"Why there's a difficulty. You see, there was a space left to insert a lock, but that was to be done by a locksmith."

"Do you know who this was?"

"I do not."

"But the lock may be easy enough to pick or to force," I suggested.

"Aye," he said uncertainly. "That may be so."

"Now that I know of the secret hiding-place, all I have to do," I said, "is to work out how to get into the house."

The Digweeds shuddered at my words and seeing this, I turned the conversation.

During the next few days as the difficulty of what I had embarked upon dawned upon me, I gradually realized that I had no chance of attaining my goal without help, and I therefore decided to take Mr and Mrs Digweed more fully into my confidence and ask for their assistance. I would emphasize that only by regaining the will could I make myself safe and say nothing about the virtual certainty that this would confer great wealth upon me.

And so I argued with them about the rights and wrongs of what I was proposing over a period of several days, always keeping our conversations secret from Joey. All I wanted, I told them, was what was right, for, as I had learned from Mr Escreet, the purloined will represented my great-great-grandfather's final intentions for the disposition of his estate and should therefore be put into force.

Eventually my efforts paid off and one day Mrs Digweed said: "Very well, Master Johnnie, we will help you. If you think it's right to take back that dockyment, then that's good enough for us. For we still owe you amends for what Barney and Joey brung upon you and your poor mam."

"Don't talk of amends," I protested. "I only wish I might have the power to reward you."

"We don't want no reward," Mr Digweed interrupted. "It's enough to us to see justice done."

I felt slightly embarrassed, but I had achieved what I sought and was satisfied.

Although the three of us attempted to keep our intentions secret from Joey, it was difficult to conceal anything in that tiny cottage, and so it came about that he overheard me one day when I did not realize he was upstairs, and thereby discovered our design.

Of course he insisted on being involved, and although I supported him — for it seemed to me to be a way of preventing his 'peaching on us to Barney — his parents resolutely set themselves against this and there was a bitter argument.

"You don't know nothin' about crackin' a crib," he said. "But I do from my time with Barney."

"All the more reason to keep you out of it now," his mother said.

Joey scowled.

"At least you may give us some advice," I said.

"Aye," he said, "for there'll be the watch, and the police patroles, as well as a nightwatchman inside the house. Which parish is it?"

"St. George's, Hanover-square," I answered.

"The best patroled of all! You'll never do it without a plant."

Seeing our bewilderment, he explained: "A friend on the inside what can let you in or at least tell you what to look out for and when's the best time to crack it."

"But I have some of that information," I cried.

I had told them a little about Miss Quilliam and now I recounted that part of her story which concerned her entry into the house late at night after her escape from the night-house in Panton-street.

"To the best of my recollection," I went on, "she could not rouse the nightwatchman because he was so soundly asleep, and therefore she had to go round to the mews. So he may not be a very dangerous obstacle."

"When was that?" Joey asked.

"Almost five years ago," I confessed.

He snorted: "That ain't worth nothin'. You need better than that a-fore you try to break in. They might have dogs now."

Mr Digweed shuddered at these words, but his wife gamely said: "I'll try to make friends of the sarvints and larn what I can. Where is the house, Master Johnnie?"

"Brook-street. Number 48."

Suddenly Joey said: "If you let me come in on it, I'll help you to a better way."

"Joey, this ain't no game," Mrs Digweed said. "Anyone as breaks into a house at night can be charged with burglary and can be hung — as many poor wretches are every year."

"I don't need to go in," he said. He turned to his father: "You'll need a bo-peep."

"A what?" Mr Digweed exclaimed.

"See how green you are! A bo-peep's the cove what stays outside and gives the look-out so them inside can cut away. Let me do that!"

"Not while I breathe," Mrs Digweed said.

Seeing that she was adamant, he got up and flung out of the house.

Despite my attempts to persuade her, Mrs Digweed continued to insist that Joey should not be involved, even though I argued that we could learn a great deal from him. So, during the weeks that followed, while Mrs Digweed hung around in various of the taverns near Brook-street, her husband and I spent whole evenings in the "flash-houses" of our own district winning the confidence of suspicious strangers who had been recommended to us as experienced cracksmen.

As a consequence of what we learned from them, Mr Digweed and I spent a considerable amount of time learning to master the bull's-eye lanthorn, which could be made to give a very narrow beam, and the "spider", a device for picking locks.

When I had leisure to take notice of Joey, he seemed very quiet and to have become even more distant towards me as if it were my fault that he was being excluded. He went about looking bitter and noble, answering only when spoken to and then very curtly.

One afternoon a few weeks later, Joey, his father and I were finishing a spell underground and returning to the surface by way of a tunnel beneath Soho.

Suddenly Joey, who was carrying one of our two lanthorns, said: "I'm going another way fust. I'll see you back at home."

This was a breach of the most fundamental rule — that you never ventured into the system alone — and we were so taken aback that he was almost out of sight round a curve before we acted.

We started after him but he had chosen his site well for when we rounded the corner no glimmer of his light was discernible. He had vanished into one of the many branch-tunnels which joined the main tunnel just here, and since it was impossible to guess which, we reluctantly gave up the search and made our way home.

Mr Digweed was as silent as usual, but his silence now was of a different kind. We had reached the surface and were making our way home along the Strand when he asked me to wait for him and went into a shop. He came out carrying a long cane stick.

When we got home and had washed and changed our clothes, there began an anxious period of waiting. After a couple of hours we heard a step at the street-door, but it turned out to be Mrs Digweed.

She came into the house in great excitement: "I've made friends of one of the laundry-maids!" she cried, but broke off when she saw our long faces: "Why, whatever's amiss?"

We told her and she sat down heavily on the battered settle.

"What are the dangers?" she asked.

"The tide will have backed up by now," said Mr Digweed. "If he loses his light or misses his step and hurts hisself ... "

All thought of Mrs Digweed's news was forgotten as we continued our anxious vigil. I wondered if Joey had gone back to Barney and speculated on the consequences for myself if he had. If only his parents had let him in on our design!

To our relief, however, he appeared a short time afterwards wearing a defiant and yet triumphant expression. Mrs Digweed threw herself at him and hugged him, though he was still in his filthy work-dress. Looking over her shoulder, Joey kept his eyes on his father.

Mr Digweed raised his cane: "I ain't going to arst you what you thought you was doing because there ain't no reason can make what you done right. You can tell me arterwards if you've a mind to."

"I have a reason and a good 'un," Joey said defiantly. "But I shan't tell you. Not until I choose to."

"When have I ever beaten you a-fore now, Joey?" Mr Digweed asked.

"The two times when I come back from Barney," he said sullenly.

"Change them togs and wash," his father said.

Joey hesitated and then went to obey. When he returned Mrs Digweed went upstairs saying she would change her own clothes. Since I had nowhere to go now, unless I went out, I stayed.

Joey stood in his shirt with his back to his father. Mr Digweed raised the cane and then brought it down upon his son's shoulders and back. The blow was a hard one for Mr Digweed was gasping and Joey's face was red and his lower lip trembling. Four times the stick rose and fell with a terrible crack across the youth's back.

No word was spoken. Joey went and sat in a corner of the room. A few moments later, Mrs Digweed came down and shot a compassionate glance first at her son and then her husband.

"Now tell us what you've found out, old lady," Mr Digweed said, still panting slightly.

"I've got to know one of the young maids that works in the laundry there," she began. "Nellie she's called. She sleeps over the laundry-house in the mews. She says that when she starts work in the morning she has to hammer and hammer at the back-door to wake the nightwatchman. He sleeps in the back-scullery which is the warmest place, and she says he's always screwed by the time he arrives and then he falls fast asleep."

Mr Digweed and I looked at each other with delight.

Mrs Digweed continued: "Once the butler has locked the house up for the night he gives the keys to the nightwatchman so that he can let in any of the fambly as comes in late. But when he thinks they're all in, Nellie says he hides the keys for safety and goes to the scullery and shakes down. So if anyone wants to get in arter that they can't unless they knocks up the coachman and grooms to get through the mews-door, and he leaves the door into the kitchen unlocked so they can get into the house from the yard."

"Yes," I said. "Miss Quilliam did that! So nothing has changed and the nightwatchman will pose no problem. The danger will be from the other servants. And of course being seen in the street."

"But how shall you get in?" Mrs Digweed asked.

"I don't know yet," I answered.

At this there was a strange noise from Joey, as if coming from deep in his throat.

Ignoring it, I said: "We will somehow have to enter by a window either at the front or the back of the house. But I wish there were a better way."

The same sound came again from Joey's throat and he exclaimed: "Hah, wouldn't you jist like to know!"

"Yes, we would," I said to him.

"I ain't going to tell you unless I'm 'lowed to make one with you."

"That you nivver will," his mother said firmly.

"Do you have an idea, Joey?" I asked.

"More nor a hidea. I knows exackerly how you can get in and out without no chance at all of being seen from the street. But I ain't going to say."

I tried surreptitiously several times to make him say more during the next few weeks — but always without success — as the difficulty of the undertaking was increasingly borne in upon me. For when Mr Digweed and I visited Brook-street a few days later we discovered that all the basement and ground-floor windows were stoutly barred with iron, and that the area railings were topped by fierce spikes — including a fan-tail palisade where the railing met the house which made it almost impossible to climb up to a window above the ground-floor. We went round to the mews at the back and, negotiating our way between the piles of horse-dung, discovered that, as we had feared, the back-wall of the house-yard comprised the stables and coach-house and since the story above them obviously held the living-quarters of the coachman and grooms, there was no possibility of entry by that means. We noticed, however, through the open stable-door, that the wall into the back-yard of the neighbouring house, No. 49, was badly broken-down. This house, which was on the corner with Avery-row and much smaller, was shut up and appeared to be empty, though unfortunately it was just as well defended as No. 48.

When Mr Digweed reported back on what he had learned from an acquaintance he had cultivated in the public-house, we were even more downcast: "It would be a divil of a job to get in through a winder. You need the best part of twenty minutes with an auger and centre-bit to take out each of them bars. That's if you're lucky."

"We'd need to remove two before even I could squeeze through," I said. "Isn't it possible to do it any faster?"

"You have to go slow to keep the noise down."

"Forty minutes!" I exclaimed. "Even on a moonless night that would be a risk. What then?"

"Lift out the panes and cut the glazing-bars. That's j'iner's work and I could do that in five minutes."

"So it could be done in under an hour?"

"No, for I'd need to keep stopping for the watch and the police-patroles. We'd need someone else so as you and him could keep look-out both ways up the street and warn me when to lay off."

"We dare not trust anyone else," I said. I hesitated for I had had it in mind to put a proposal to them for some time. At length I asked: "Would you consider letting Joey act as look-out?"

Though at first they were resolutely opposed to this, at length I managed to persuade them that it would involve little risk to Joey and would considerably increase his father's safety.

Joey was informed of this concession when he returned later that day.

"Oh, prime!" he cried, clapping his hands. "Now tell us what you've fixed to do."

We summarised the plan and when we had finished he laughed and said: "I ain't never heerd nothin' so green. You wouldn't hardly have time to get your bit agin the bar a-fore you was nabbed. I knows a much better way."

"Then tell us!" I cried.

"Well, it was the name of the street that fust set me to thinking."

"Brook-street?" I asked.

He nodded: "I wondered if that meant the street follered the course of an old river."

Baffled by this I glanced at Mr Digweed but he was leaning forward intently with his mouth slightly open in the position that indicated a readiness to be enlightened.

"There's a number of them as has been bricked over — oh, years and years ago. There's the Fleet, in course, and the Wallbrook."

"And is Brook-street one of these?" I asked.

But I could see Mr Digweed shaking his head.

"No, it ain't," he said.

"No," said Joey, that's right, it ain't." He paused and looked slyly triumphant: "But I found out that it crosses one such and that's how it got its name, I s'pose."

I began to perceive what point he was aiming at and saw that his father was following his exposition with growing excitement.

"You see, years and years ago," Joey went on, "the Tyburn-brook (not the one by the park but the old King's-Scholars'-pond) run down that way from across the New-Road, and there was a bridge where Brook-street crossed it."

"Avery-row!" exclaimed Mr Digweed.

"That's the ticket," said Joey.

"So one of them big old brick shores runs across the street and ... "

"And the house next door — No. 49 — is on the corner!" I exclaimed.

"That's right!" Joey said.

"So why does that matter?" asked Mrs Digweed.

Joey looked embarrassed and said: "Well, you mind that day I went off alone ... "

His father nodded grimly.

"Well, I went there. You know how the old houses that are built beside a main shore sometimes drains straight into it?"

Mr Digweed nodded again.

"Well, No. 49 is one of 'em!"

"What do you mean?" I asked.

"You're sure?" asked Mr Digweed.

"I counted the streets going that way twice over."

"Then that's our way in!" Mr Digweed said.

Joey nodded and went on excitedly: "There's just a rusted grate that you could lever off with a jemmy. Then you'd have to climb up into the petty-house."

"Then where would you find yourself?" I asked.

"In the back-yard."

"And the wall from there into the yard of No. 48 is easy to climb and the door into the house is left unlocked!" I cried.

We looked at each other in excitement, all speaking at once. When we had quietened down we discussed the details: In order to be able to get to the house and back by underground ways we needed a night on which low-tide would occur at about three o'clock in the morning, for this would permit us to have an hour and a half in the house and still leave time to get away. Far from the river as Avery-row was, there was little danger of being caught by the tide but, in case we had to make our escape by the streets, we also needed a moonless night.

CHAPTER 93

We learned from the almanac that we did not have long to wait for a date that met all the necessary conditions. The night of the 23rd. of June — only ten days away! — would be moonless and there would be a low tide at exactly the right hour. We made our preparations for the enterprise and when the evening of the 23rd. arrived — a fine summer night — all was ready. Since our best advice was that we should carry the incriminating tools with us for as little time as was necessary, it had been decided that Mrs Digweed should bear them — hidden beneath a bundle of laundry in a basket — as far as the entrance to the shores at Chancery-lane where Mr Digweed and I would rendezvous with her. He and I would make our way underground to Avery-row and enter the house by the means that Joey had discovered. Meanwhile Joey would get to Brook-street by the surface and take up his position opposite the house, from where he would make a sound like a tawny-owl if we were in danger of being detected from inside, and imitate a night-jar if the danger came from the street. (This trick he had learned from his experiences with his uncle.)

"If we fail to get the will," I said, "we must not let it be known that we possess the secret of its hiding-place, for then they will move it and there will be no second chance. So we must make the attempt appear to be an ordinary crack."

Mr Digweed shook his head: "I won't steal nothin' else to put them off the scent."

I made no answer. I felt a sudden stab of excitement at the thought that the will and all that it carried with it might be in my hands within a few hours.

The hour came at last. We concealed in Mrs Digweed's basket a crow, a spider pick-lock, a rope with a grapple (to be used only if we had to escape through the window), and a drill and bit for the back-door if it should prove to be locked, and she took leave of us. A few minutes later Mr Digweed and I set off by another route carrying our usual equipment — a lanthorn (though of the bull's-eye design), a small trowel and a shore-hunter's rake — leaving Joey to make his more leisurely way to Mayfair.

All went well and at about three in the morning we were beside the culvert of No. 49. When my companion had dislodged with the crow some of the bricks holding the grate and moved it out of the way, he held me up and, putting down the rake, I clambered up the funnel. Then I helped him to ascend after me and a moment later we found ourselves in the little yard behind the house. From there we clambered over the derelict wall and made our way to the back-door which we discovered, to our relief, to be indeed unlocked. As we passed into the house I masked the lanthorn and only the smell of oil and hot iron betrayed its presence.

Now the darkness around us seemed absolute and we waited until our eyes were adjusted to take advantage of the faint starlight that came through the single dirty window. My hearing seemed — as always in the dark — unnaturally sharpened and, as we crept across the stone-flagged floor and passed the scullery-door, we could hear snores which indicated the whereabouts of the nightwatchman. Once we had gained the hall I released a narrow shaft of light and by its aid we made our way up the stairs until we found ourselves outside the high double-doors to the Great Parlour.

Mr Digweed tried the handle and gently pushed: the door was locked. Instantly he set to work with the spider while I held the lanthorn, and within a few minutes he had opened it. We passed through and, as we had been advised, took the precaution of locking the door after us and placing a wedge beneath it to obstruct any attempt to force it.

I opened the eye of the lanthorn a little more, conscious of the danger of accidentally directing the beam towards the window for, despite the thickness of the drapes, the light might be perceived from the street if the shutters were not closed. By now Joey would be out there.

I turned the lanthorn and the shaft of light circled the room picking out furniture and objects at random. The shadows almost made it seem that there were figures seated on the sophas and chairs or lounging by the beaufet at the side of the room, as there probably had been a few hours before. I felt a surge of excitement as the beam fell on the great marble chimney-piece at the end of the room opposite the door, higher than a man's head and gleaming palely.

I longed to start to tackle it but first we had to attend to other matters. The professional advice we had received was that as soon as you got into a house you made sure of your means of egress. (I vividly recollected how Barney, having entered my mother's house, had found himself trapped inside it.) So we crossed to the window and, as we had previously agreed, carefully drew back the curtains to reveal the shutters: they were closed and their bars drawn. We very gently and quietly released the bars and the window catches, watching out for the spring-alarms — common on ground-floor windows but occasionally found on the first-floor — about which we had been warned, but to our relief there were none.

Now we brought out the rope and under my companion's direction, I attached the hook of the grapple to a heavy sopha which stood with its back to the window, and left the rope coiled on the floor. Our efforts meant that we could now open the window within seconds and lower ourselves (though Mr Digweed only with considerable difficulty) down the side of the wall, and yet there was nothing that looked suspicious from the street. However, the window over-looked the area and would be difficult to escape from on account of the long, sharp spikes on the railings and the fan-tailed cluster at the juncture with the wall of the house, and I earnestly hoped that we would not have to make use of this means of escape.

Now at last we could turn our attention to the point of our efforts. We crossed the room and I shone the beam onto the entablature of the over-mantel behind which lay the hiding-place. I perceived a large heraldic device embossed upon it which, to my surprise, was already familiar to me — at least to a degree.

My companion was as surprised as I, though for a different reason.

"That were never there a-fore," he whispered. "The safe-place must be behind it."

The device was an elaboration of the design I had known all my life both from the crests on my mother's plates and from the Mompesson and Huffam tombs in the church at Melthorpe. There the arrangement was of the kind known as a quincunx: five objects, in this case quatre-foil flowers, were so disposed that four occupied each of the corners of an imaginary square and the fifth was placed in the centre. Here, however, the quincunx was multiplied five times for the quincunx device itself was the element that made up the larger arrangement. In short, it was a kind of quincunx raised to the power of two, a quincunx of quincunxes, apparently carved from a single and enormous slab of white marble.

The over-mantel was so high up that we had to carry a couple of foot-stools over from near the windows and stand on them in order to examine it properly. Now Mr Digweed scrutinized the entablature closely, running his hand over its cold, smooth surface. After a few moments he pointed out to me that what I had taken for a single expanse of marble was in fact a number of dowelled segments fitted together.

"What's more," he whispered, pointing to a portion of the marble immediately above the design, "I'll wager this piece drops away, for there's a j'in here that's wider than the others."

I followed his hand and saw the crevice in the marble which my less skilled eye would probably not have noticed.

"But how is it made to move?" I asked. "And by what means is it secured and released?"

He frowned and continued his study for what seemed an age. First he ran his hand over the marble, paying particular notice to the joints and to the flowers, and then to my surprise he pressed his face to these last, touching them with his lips like a superstitious worshipper at a shrine.

Suddenly he turned to me and, hoarse with excitement, whispered: "The buds of them flowers ain't stone. They ain't so cold. Try it."

I leaned forward and touched with my lips first the marble and then the central part of a quatre-foil. He was right: both were cold but the marble became warm after a second or two whereas the bud of the quatre-foil did not.

I looked at him in surprise: "What does it mean?"

"The middle bits of them flowers ain't marble. They're of iron." As he spoke he looked at me as if expecting to see on my face that I knew what he meant.

I stared back in bafflement.

"Look," he said and rested a finger on the central portion of one of the quatre-foils: "I'll wager this is the head of an iron bolt."

He gently inserted the blade of a knife behind the bud and levered it upwards very cautiously. He was right in his surmise for the bud instantly began to move towards us and revealed itself to be a long iron bolt whose head was painted white to match the marble. It came out about four inches and then stopped, held firmly by some obstruction.

Now I understood what Mr Digweed meant: the heraldic device concealed a number of bolts which, like the wards of a lock, formed a mechanism for holding in position the section of marble behind which should lie the hiding-place.

"Do you imagine that all we have to do," I whispered, "is to pull out all the bolts and then the slab will drop?"

I could see that he was puzzled.

"I reckon so. And yet it seems too simple."

"Try the next one," I suggested.

He did so with exactly the same result, and so proceeded to the next. In a minute we had withdrawn all of the five bolts along the top line of quatre-foils. As I removed the last very slowly and gently, Mr Digweed pressed his hand against the slab above it in order to hold it back and restrain its drop for we expected it to fall a few inches and reveal a space. However, it did not move.

"It must be that they all need to be pulled out," Mr Digweed said, clearly as puzzled as I was.

In a few minutes we had withdrawn all the remaining twenty bolts except for the last one on the bottom row of quatre-foils. But when we cautiously repeated our earlier manoeuvre as we withdrew this one, once again the slab failed to move.

I looked towards my companion in despair. He reflected for a long time, holding his chin thoughtfully as he stared at the design.

"I believe I understand," he said at last. "It's a form of lock, and we ain't got the key."

"Key?" I repeated. "But where's the key-hole?"

"Shsh," he whispered suddenly.

We froze.

"I thought I heerd a sound at the door," he went on. "No, there ain't a real key. The key's in your head, for this is fashioned on what they call the 'combination principle'. That's to say, you can't jist pull all them bolts out and expeck the slab to fall, for the bolts make up like it were the wards of a lock, and so you have to know which pertickler bolts you have to withdraw — jist the way a key has to fit a lock."

"I see," I said. "Then should we not try out different combinations?"

"No, there ain't no purpose to that. We wouldn't open it that way, not if we was here all night and for days and weeks to come. There's hundreds and hundreds of combinations. We won't hit on the right one by hazard, we have to know the design."

I saw that he was right, and it was a bitter blow. There was obviously no possibility of using force to open the hiding-place, for the heavy slab of marble was locked into position and we would have to make far too much noise and work for far too long to have any hope of evading discovery.

Standing precariously on the foot-stool, I leant forward and thumped the marble with my fist in my rage. I struck against one of the infernal quatre-foils and bruised my knuckles. As I did so I remembered how I had beaten my fists against the door of the old house at Charing-cross that first time when Mr Escreet had refused to open it. The quatre-foil design on the knocker had grinned down at me then, and I remembered the same mocking indifference from the cold marble quatre-foils on the tombs and memorial tablets and the old stained glass in the church at Melthorpe that had so fascinated me as a child. I felt tears prickling my eyes as I reflected that even though I had penetrated to the *sanctum sanctorum* in the very house of the Mompessons, yet I was met by the same cruel unconcern that I had experienced in seeing the design on the pannel of the carriage belonging to Sir Perceval that had so alarmed my mother all those many years ago.

That recollection, however, recalled to me that there was a difference, for in the designs I had always been familiar with the quatre-foils were in different colours varying between the Huffam and the Mompesson versions. As I remembered this, the faded red of the ancient glass in the East window of Melthorpe church came to mind, and the black and white of the design on the side of the yellow chariot. Yet in this case the whole design of twenty-five quatre-foils was entirely white.

I was about to explain this to my companion and ask him if he thought there could be any significance to it, but at that precise moment there came the whirring sound of a tawny-owl: there was danger within the house!

Instantly Mr Digweed began to move towards the door.

"The bolts!" I hissed. "We must put them back!"

With a look of terror he turned back to help me and hastily we pushed the bolts home. Then we both hurried — though still moving as light-footedly as we could — towards the door. Just before we reached it the handle slowly turned. We looked at each other in horror.

"The window," I whispered.

Less cautiously now we gained the window and Mr Digweed thrust back the curtains, pulled the shutters away and raised the sash. Dawn was just beginning and there was only faint light in the street. I picked up and handed the rope to him and he leant out of the window and lowered it. At any moment the street-door below us might be opened from within the house and our escape cut off.

Just then we heard heavy feet running up the stairs and someone tried the door-handle again. There were shouts and then the sound of men hurling themselves against the door. By now Mr Digweed had clambered out of the window clutching the rope as best he could with one hand, and with his feet resting on the top of the entablature of the ground-floor window immediately below, he was trying to reach across to a conductor-pipe. At this moment I heard a window open above my head. I looked up and against the dark grey sky saw a cylindrical object protruding from the window directly above my head. To my horror, I realized it was the barrel of a gun. I glanced down and it was clear that Mr Digweed, intent upon his escape, had not seen it. As

I looked up again the barrel suddenly disappeared as if it had been snatched away.

In trepidation I clambered out onto the sill clutching the rope in my turn. At that moment Mr Digweed pushed off from the entablature with the intention of seizing the conductor-pipe. I glanced up and saw the barrel appear again. Suddenly it was violently jerked upwards and sideways, and at the same instant it went off with a loud report. Mr Digweed staggered as if hit — though I was sure the gun had not been pointed towards him when it had fired — and so missed the pipe he was reaching towards with his hook. The rope slid from his grasp and he lost his balance and fell.

As if in a nightmare I watched as his body descended, his hand scrabbling desperately and unavailingly at the bricks of the wall, towards the long spikes of the fan-tail waiting below. I closed my eyes and a moment later opened them to see him slumped awkwardly across the cruel device. I noticed a figure run across the street towards him.

I had to think of my own situation now, and realized that I had no alternative but to follow Mr Digweed in the hope that I could get away while the gun was being loaded. I gripped the rope as hard as I could and swung across towards the pipe.

I missed it but, still clutching the rope, managed to get back for another attempt. This time I succeeded in seizing the pipe and instantly let go of the rope. With the aid of the pipe I lowered myself down the rusticated stone-work of the bottom story. I was haunted by the idea that the gun was being pointed at me and so, against my better judgement, I glanced up and saw a head appear at the window from which it had been fired. In the dim light I could see enough of the face to recognise it as that of a man of about thirty-five and to see the expression of keen eagerness on his face. He appeared to be arguing with someone whom I could not see, but when I looked up now he gazed full into my face. Even at the time it occurred to me that if I could see his face so clearly, he could see mine.

I reached the ground and joined Joey who was tending to his father. He had fallen between the fan-tail and the wall in such a way that one of the spikes had penetrated his side and he was wedged against the wall.

"Help me lift him!" Joey cried.

"Shouldn't we leave him? It might kill him to move him," I shouted, all sense of caution lost in the horror of the situation.

"He's a dead man for sure if we leave him. He'll dance at Newgate if they don't let him die!"

I saw the force of this and felt that it was Joey's decision to make. And so we began as gently as we could to lift his father off the spike which had pierced his side.

He was still sensible and his face was contorted with pain, but he uttered not a sound except to breathe once: "Good boys."

We were standing on the front steps and the strangeness of our situation struck me even then. I expected that at any moment the street-door before us would burst open and we would be apprehended. As we lifted him it became clear that the spike had not penetrated very far into his body, yet somehow he had been severely injured for the amount of blood that gushed forth was most alarming. I assumed that he had been hit by the bullet despite my own impressions.

We eased him off the fan-tail and still no-one came from the house. It occurred to me that the servants might not be able to open the street-door because they did not have the key. If this were so it could only be a few moments before whoever had it was found or before they got out through the back-door into the mews, and came round the corner of the street. I was also alarmed that the watch would be roused by the noise, or even that people in the surrounding houses would intervene against us. Our only advantage lay in the comparative darkness and that was passing from us with each succeeding minute.

We began to carry Mr Digweed down the steps, Joey in front holding him under the shoulders and I clutching his feet, and then broke into a kind of run when we reached the street. As I glanced back to see if we were pursued I saw that we were leaving a tell-tale spoor of blood behind us.

Just as we were about to round the corner I looked back and saw a number of men come running into our street from the direction of the mews. Since they were carrying torches and we, of course, had no lights, they might not have seen us in the near-darkness, dazzled by their own flambeaux. This must have been the case for when we dived up the next street and then turned again and then again in the hope of baffling our pursuers, we found that we had indeed shaken them off.

By now, however, it was getting so light that I feared that even if we continued to elude those chasing us, we might encounter the watch or a patrole and, incriminating as our appearance was, be taken up merely on suspicion of having committed a crime.

Joey had obviously been fearing the same thing for he suddenly whispered hoarsely: "Mount-street!"

It was a moment before I understood his meaning, but then it came to me. We bore his father to the culvert there (just opposite the Workhouse) from which we had often reached the surface in the past. There was nobody about and so we lowered him into it, and then carried him a little way under the arch so that we could not be seen from the street. Here we tried to staunch the flow of blood and found that as well as piercing his side the spike had ripped his thigh in a deep gash that had almost exposed the bone. This was the source of the blood and I had been right in believing that he had not been hit by the bullet.

While Joey hastened home, I stayed to tend Mr Digweed as best I could. It was not easy even to keep him dry in that damp place. The time dragged past. He was in great pain and I had difficulty in stifling his cries. To my relief, Joey returned a couple of hours later accompanied by his mother. When we had helped her into the culvert as discreetly as we could, she quietly and calmly did what she could for her husband.

"He should go to the Dispensary," I said.

"No!" Joey insisted.

His mother shook her head: "We dare not risk it, if that man got a good look at him ... "

She was right. Her husband was only too easy to identify.

"And they'll be looking for toshers," I said. "We left the rake beneath the privy-drain." We were silent for a minute. "But if he ... if he needs to go to the hospital," I began.

Mrs Digweed shook her head again: "We don't have no ticket anyway. And I don't know no-one what would give us one."

"We must get him home," Joey cried.

And so, after a brief discussion, he hurried off again to Bethnal-green.

For the rest of the morning Mr Digweed alternated between periods of terrible pain and blessed — though worrying — lapses into insensibility. Towards noon Joey returned with Isbister's horse and cart, and we now took the considerable risk of manoeuvring him from the concealment of the culvert into the cart in broad daylight. Our audacity was rewarded for though several foot-passengers noticed us, no-one apprehended us or sent for the watch, and by this means we succeeded in conveying the wounded man home. There Mrs Digweed stripped and cleaned the wound and then made up a composing-draught of brandy and laudanum while Joey and I carried him upstairs. When he had drunk it he fell into a deep sleep.

In the course of the evening the patient grew fevered and delirious and Joey and I — now sleeping in the lower chamber — were kept awake by his cries for much of the night. He was quieter in the morning and slept most of the day with a grey, drawn expression that struck a chill into my heart.

He was a little better the following day, but worse the day after that. And so he continued, varying between one day and the next, sometimes fevered and at other times weak but collected in his wits. The wound did not become poisoned, but neither did it heal.

Everything had gone wrong and it was my fault — though I was the least affected by it. Mrs Digweed offered no reproaches, but I saw Joey gazing at me more balefully (it seemed to me) than ever before.

Our anxiety over Mr Digweed's condition could not prevent us from facing the fact that we had to earn money, for our failed burglary attempt had exhausted what little we had, and the situation was the more critical now that Mrs Digweed was often unable to go out on her laundress-work for having to watch her husband. And so, two days later, Joey and I ventured into the shores alone.

Now it was that I realized the full extent of Mr Digweed's skill and knowledge, for the amount that Joey and I were able to glean dropped dramatically without his father's guidance, and this was because we covered less distance and made poorer judgements of which tunnels to explore under the prevailing conditions.

More worryingly, our inexperience led us to make serious errors of judgement. On one occasion, the tunnel we were in, which was built over another and more ancient one, began to collapse as we walked along it and we were lucky to escape. And several times we came perilously close to being trapped by gas. We kept these incidents from Mr and Mrs Digweed, but it was quickly becoming apparent to me at least that we had to find a means of earning our living that was at once safer and more profitable.

After a little over a month Mr Digweed's condition seemed to settle at a steady level. He would have feverish periods which lasted several days and were then followed by a slight recovery. He remained too weak to leave his bed, but at least while Joey and I were at home Mrs Digweed was able to go out and look for work. And we badly needed the money, for Joey and I were only able to make about twelve shillings a week between us.

So things continued for the following three months. As the autumn drew near it became clear to me — and, I am sure to the others, though we did not speak of it — that Mr Digweed's strength was slowly ebbing. He now slept most of the time and could speak only with considerable difficulty.

Then one day towards the end of October, when Joey and I were in a shore near the river with which we were unfamiliar, we had our most serious misadventure. It began when Joey was venturing cautiously into an area of deep mud, probing ahead with a rake, while I held the lanthorn. Suddenly he found himself sinking rapidly where a mass of compacted material had deceptively borne his weight for a few seconds and so lured him further before giving way so that he sank to his waist. Placing the lanthorn on the ground, I waded into the mud up to my knees and held out my hand to Joey who was now immersed in thick mud up to his shoulders. After a struggle, I pulled him free but as he returned to safe ground he kicked over the lanthorn and the light was extinguished.

The darkness was absolute. Luckily the tinder, which had been in my pocket, was dry but in that damp atmosphere it would be difficult to get a match. We worked in growing desperation, well aware that without light our chances of finding our way out were slender. At last, we succeeded in nursing a spark into flame and hurriedly set off for the surface.

When we reached the larger shore into which ours debouched we found that it was several feet deep in water.

"The tide!" Joey cried.

We had lost more time than we had realized.

"But it shouldn't be so high," I exclaimed. "There must have been a shower."

This was the combination that was most feared by under-goers. And our plight was now grim for the way we had come was already blocked and all other ways led down towards the river.

"I know a way out, if I can remember it," Joey said. "My old feller took me once. We have to find the Fleet and follow it."

"But that's towards the tide! It'll be higher the further we go!"

"I know, but it's the only way out from here when the tide is so high for there's ladders from the tops of the vaults."

I didn't understand what he meant but there was no alternative but to follow him. And so we waded down the shore until we reached the Fleet — the oldest and most ill-reputed of London's hidden rivers — now a subterranean ditch that runs beside the ancient prison in which my mother and Mr Pentecost had been immured.

There was a path on our side and we followed it downwards, though even now the tide was backing up over its banking so that water was swirling about our ancles. As we descended, its level rose higher and higher. Suddenly we came to a flight of steps and as we stood at the top and peered down, saw water several feet below us. I raised the lanthorn and we made out that the river and its banks widened out and the roof soared above us twenty or thirty feet in a series of high vaults whose limits were lost in the gloom. Now we had reached the Fleet-market where the river was actually a canal built by Sir Christopher Wren more than a hundred years before; and in front of us, beneath the water, were broken wharves lining a row of vaulted warehouses. They had never been used because they flooded at high water since the water-gates — the first of which we had arrived at — had from the very beginning failed to hold back the tide. In token of this, all the stonework we could see was blackly encrusted with nitre and as I gazed, I thought of the fortunes quite literally sunk here by speculators all those years ago.

"Too late!" Joey cried out. "There's a ladder in the top of each vault that goes up to a trap. But we can't reach it now, the water's too high."

The tops of the vaults were still just visible, but their entrances were now below the water-line.

"Yes we can," I said, remembering those summer afternoons when Job had persevered (and Harry had succeeded) in teaching me to overcome my fear of the water and to swim beneath the water-gate of the mill-pond at Twycott. "We might be able to dive and swim through the top of the arch."

"I can't swim!" he cried.

We stared at each other in horror.

"We can try it," I said. "We must. I'll try it now myself."

I removed my boots and great-coat while Joey watched me. It would be hard in the dark to know where to come to the surface and then to find the ladder. And perhaps the trap-door would be locked? However, there was no alternative. And the lanthorn would give me light enough at least to know where to dive. I plunged in and was shocked by the cold. Even to stay in it for more than a few minutes would be dangerous. This water was not a living creature like the river at Twycott, but a dead thing that was yet claiming an intimate familiarity with me. I swam towards the first arch. Then I dived, felt my way down the wall until it gave way, swam through the space and then came up. I had hoped that there would be cracks of light coming from around the sides of the trap-door which should be far above me, but I found myself still in utter darkness. I groped about above my head and to my relief hit my hands against the cold iron of a ladder. Thinking that I had better verify that the trap-door was open — for otherwise I would need to try another vault — I climbed it until I banged my head (fortunately, not too hard) against something. I pushed, and the heavy wooden object lifted a few inches. It suddenly occurred to me that I could escape now rather than risk trying to save Joey at the peril of my own life, but the reflection came to me as an intellectual fact and not something that had any emotional appeal. I could not imagine facing Mrs Digweed or living with myself if I did not at least attempt to rescue him. Though whether he could be saved depended on how far he would trust me.

I descended the ladder, dived again and rejoined Joey without difficulty. I could see how pleased — and surprised? — he was to see me. I must have seemed a long time away. Now he began to remove his boots and coat.

Pulling myself onto the slimy steps, I told him what I had found and he managed a grim smile. Then while I slapped my limbs to restore warmth, I gave him directions (just as Job Greenslade had done to me) on how to let himself be drawn under the surface:

"Whatever you do," I stressed, "don't panic and try to cling onto me or you'll drown us both. Just let yourself go and I'll hold you."

Whitefaced, he nodded and lowered himself into the cold water. Then I held him from behind by the shoulders and kicked with my legs, slowly moving us towards the arch. Now came the hardest part.

"Keep your eyes shut and trust me completely," I urged.

Joey turned his head and nodded.

I could see his eyes glittering in the lume of the distant lanthorn. Then he closed them. I dived, pushing him down so that our heads went under together and, though I knew that all his instincts were urging him to rise again, he stayed beneath the surface. So down we went, I holding his hand and with my other feeling down the wall until I found the top of the arch. I pulled him under it, swam a few strokes, and then we rose to the surface. Joey was spluttering and sobbing with fright and relief. I pushed him onto the ladder and climbed after him. When we reached the top we had more difficulty than I had anticipated in raising the door, but at last we found ourselves sprawled in the dark on the floor of a cellar amidst the reassuring smell of musty straw and rotting wood.

I waited for him to say something.

After a silence he spoke: "I nivver thought you'd come back for me."

That was as close as he came to expressing his gratitude. And this episode led to no improvement in my relations with him. In fact, it sometimes seemed to me that it had given him a further cause for resentment.

We lay for some minutes, too exhausted to move — although in our soaking garments we were both shivering violently.

"We should get out of here. Some of these cellars get flooded, too," Joey warned, though this one seemed dry enough.

Groping in the blackness it took us some time even to find the door, leave alone to open it. But at last we were out in a passage that led to a small door which was merely bolted on the inside, so that in a moment we found ourselves out in the street. And there before us were the wooden market-stalls, the bustling crowds, and the shouting barkers of Fleet-market!

Fortunately, when we got home we found that Mrs Digweed had set off for her work without waiting for us, so that no explanations of our bedraggled appearance were required. We changed our dress and then sat watching over Mr Digweed who was sleeping restlessly.

For a long time neither of us spoke. Then at last:

"Well, that's the toshing finished," Joey said.

Apart from any other consideration, we had lost everything: rakes, lanthorns, boots, and great-coats.

"Yes," I agreed. "But what can we do instead?"

"There's lots of other things," he said.

I looked at him suspiciously.

However, before I had a chance to ask what he meant, Mrs Digweed came in and I could she that she was excited about something. As she removed her bonnet she went across to her husband, took his hand, and studied his sleeping face for a few moments.

Then she turned back to us: "You'll never guess where I've been!"

"Tell us quick, Ma," Joey said shortly.

"Why, what would you say to Brook-street?"

Joey stared at her. By an unspoken agreement we had never mentioned the events of that ill-fated night.

"I reckoned it was safe by now, so a week or two back when I started doing some work up that end of Town, I went to the tavern nearest the house a few times, hoping to meet that gal I got to know before, Nellie. Well, she come in today so that's why I'm late now."

"Did you ask her about the crack?" Joey asked.

"In course not. I ain't sich a downey. Jist like a-fore, I was careful never to ask no questions but on'y to listen and hold my peace."

I managed to stifle a smile at the thought of Mrs Digweed holding her peace.

"And sure enough, arter a bit, why, naterally, she told me everything I wanted to know. She said when they gived the alarm the men-sarvints couldn't wake the watchman for he was boosed so deep. Nor they couldn't find where he had hid the key of the street-door. So they had to get out through the back of the house and go round by the mews."

"That's what saved us," I exclaimed.

"She said it was the tutor, Mr Vamplew, what fired the gun."

I recalled the sallow, sinister face I had seen.

"He got a good look at the man and the boy with him, so she said. And she told me the cracksmen didn't manage to take nothing."

"Well, so what have we larned that we didn't know already?" Joey jeered. "You didn't ought to have done it, Ma."

"I disagree," I said. "We might have learned something important."

"Oh, but I did," Mrs Digweed said mysteriously. "I wanted to pick up something useful and I did."

"Useful?" I asked in bewilderment.

"For getting the will back, in course!" she exclaimed.

I was stunned by this and seeing my surprise she said: "You didn't think I'd gived up, did you?" she asked. "Why, I'm more bent upon it than ever."

Though I had not consciously thought about it, I now realized that I had never abandoned the idea. But that *she* should have gone on thinking about it!

"Then what did you learn?" I asked.

"A deal of things. That girl is a fee-rocious rattle. She told me about one of the footmen, Bob. (For it seems he's sweet on her.) Well, he has a boy to work to him — Dick — but she said Dick was a-goin' back to his dad in Lime'us to be put to the caulking-trade, and so Bob is looking for another hall-boy."

"A plant!" I cried. "But can you be sure of getting him the place?"

Her face expressed bafflement.

"Don't you mean Joey?" I asked.

She looked conscious and said after a moment's hesitation: "Why, Master Johnnie, to tell the truth, I thought you'd take it."

I was stunned and a thousand ideas rushed into my head. To become the humblest of menials! To exchange the independence of the gulley-hunter for the servitude of a domestic! In that house! I saw Joey watching me curiously and wondered how much he suspected of what I was thinking. Then I saw the appeal of the idea of entering that arrogant house in such a disguise in order to work its destruction.

However, an obstacle presented itself to me: "What about the tutor, Mr Vamplew? He might recognise me."

"Nellie said he's gone abroad with his young gentleman and they're goin' to be there until Christmas."

"Well," I said, "I'm ready to take it on. But would Bob give me it?"

"There's a good chance," she said. "I told the gal my husband had a sort of nevy, begging your pardon and may God forgive me for the lie. I said you'd jist come up from the country — I'd told her last time that my George's dad come from down in the North, so that was as well — for she said Bob wanted a country-boy as bein' healthier and not so artful as a Town-bred younker. So she took me straightaway to Bob in the Tap. 'Send the lad along,' Bob said to me. 'Send the lad along and I'll take a look at him and see if he'll sarve.' So you're to go along fust thing tomorrer morning. And if he wants you, you'll start straightaway."

"And what wages would he pay me?"

She made a face: "You won't make your fortun'. You'll get your board, a set of clothes and two aprings a year, and washing found. As for wages, I didn't think to ask. Maybe ten shillin' a quarter, I suppose. Out of that you've only to find yourself in tay and sugar and soap."

"That's not much."

"Hardly worse than we've been doing," said Joey with a grim smile. "And as for me, why I'll find something."

"What?" I asked suspiciously.

"Come, Master Johnnie," said Mrs Digweed. "We've work to do. You must larn your name and history, for you'll have to take each word out of your mouth and look at it a-fore you use it."

We chose for my place of origin a district near the Scottish borders, and Mrs Digweed took great pleasure in inventing a complex set of circumstances to explain how her husband's aunt down in the North country had met and married a grazier from even further north.

"May the Lord forgive me," she broke off once. "I suppose we ain't doin' nothin' wrong?"

"Surely," I said, "it's no more wrong than making up a story in a book?"

She frowned over this and seemed unconvinced.

"What is my name?" I asked.

"I said you were called Johnnie," she said. "I doubt if he'll ask you for any other."

"But if he does, I'll say it's Winterflood," I said laughing.

Mrs Digweed looked surprised for a moment but when she remembered where the name came from, she laughed with me.

Later that night I lay awake beside Joey wondering what lay ahead of me. To enter my enemies' house in this manner was indeed to grasp at the rose in disregard of the thorns. But the shame worried me more than the danger, and I felt a bitter-sweet excitement at the prospect of coming so close to Henrietta in such a role. Close? Surely it was unlikely that I would even glimpse her! But however that might be, the will was the main thing.

CHAPTER 94

In accordance with Mrs Digweed's instructions, I reached the mews at the back of Brook-street at about half-past seven o'clock the next morning. Since No. 48 was next on from the one on the corner, it was easy enough to find the right set of buildings in the mews behind it. The main gate of the coach-house stood open and two men were cleaning a carriage which I recognised as the one in which Mr Steplight had come to Mrs Fortisquince's house those many years before.

"Who are you?" the elder of the men said to me when I made to enter.

"I've come to see about the hall-boy's place," I replied.

"Very well, look alive then," he said, jerking his head to indicate that I should pass through the coach-house.

I did so and found myself in the back-yard where I saw three laundry-maids at work carrying baskets of linen from the laundry-house to a big rinsing-trough. One of them glanced at me in a friendly way and I crossed to her.

"Are you Johnnie?" she asked, with a smile.

When I confirmed this she said: "I'm Nellie. I'll take you to him." She turned to a stout woman nearby: "Can I take the boy inside, Mrs Babister? He's come to see Mr Bob about a place."

"Very well, but be quick about it," the woman answered ungraciously. "And none of your nonsense."

The girl led me into the house by the door which I remembered from that ill-fated night. Then we went down the stairs, along a gloomy passage and into a dark little room without windows and lit only by a tallow-dip, where we found a tall man a little over thirty, wearing a shirt and breeches with a long green baize apron reaching almost to the ground.

As we came in he was polishing a pair of boots, but when he saw us he dropped them, removed the apron and playfully made to seize the girl who dived away from him, but not so quickly or so far that he could not catch her briefly and plant a kiss on her lips.

She pulled herself away and said: "Why, Mr Bob! I nivver did! I've only come to bring the boy what his aunt spoke to you yesterday."

"Come here, you fascinating creatur'," Bob said, and made to catch her again.

However, she ran out with a giggle and the man turned to me, muttering something I didn't catch. He was above middle height and quite handsome, though his features bore a somewhat spoiled and petulant cast and he had an air about him of feeling rather hard done by and owing the world a grudge in consequence. He now stared at me hard with cold blue eyes, and yet it seemed to me he was looking at me in an oddly evasive manner as if gazing at a point a yard in front of me.

"What have you done a-fore now?" he said, looking me up and down sceptically.

"I'm used to hard work, Mr Bob," I replied. "I started by tenting crows when I was five and went on to helping my father with the cattle and the feed, singling turnips and swedes, winnowing corn, stone-picking, and all that manner of thing. I was nearly doing a man's work when he died and my mother gave up the lease."

Clearly this battery of rural terms conveyed nothing to him, but he grasped the main point: "Farm-work, eh? Well, you should be strong and hardy, though you don't look too strong to me, for all you're bigger than the last boy. He was a tiger, but you're too tall and wouldn't fit the livery. You won't be found in livery, so don't go whining arter one. I'll give you new togs twice a year. Not new, you know, but good enough. And if you don't take proper care on 'em, you'll feel the weight of my hand."

I noticed with mingled feelings that these threats were couched in the future, rather than the conditional, tense.

"Now you works to me, is that clear? If 'Arry or Roger or anyone else tells you to do somethin', you tells 'em it ain't their business to give you orders. Is that understood."

I nodded, and he went on: "But if Mr Thackaberry or Mr Assinder tells you to do anything, you do it jist the same as if I told you."

I nodded again.

Then I asked: "What will my wages be?"

He looked at me in surprise and then laughed without humour: "I say, you are a flatt. You don't get no wages for skinking. If you settle to the collar and work hard I'll give you somethin' now and then. Arter a bit, maybe I'll start to give you a share of my vails. Anyways, we'll see. That's all."

He suddenly flung a piece of rag at me that was foully black.

"Make a start on them and we'll see how you do."

He indicated a pile of boots and shoes and a pot of blacking and so I stood at the sideboard and began to polish as hard as I could.

Bob hung the apron on a nail on the back of the door, donned a jacket, seated himself on a low chair beside me, and put his feet up comfortably on the board by my elbow.

"Now listen careful," he began. "The fust time you do somethin' wrong or don't do somethin' what I tells you to do, you get a thump on the ear. The next time you get a thrashing. If you do it again, you're out, and I promise you'll leave here singing the Black Psalm on account of a few bruises to remember your uncle Bob by."

He pulled a short pipe and a tobacco-pouch out of a capacious pocket in the jacket and began to stuff the bowl meditatively.

"Now I'm 'Mr Bob'. Not 'Bob'. And when you're talking to the other sarvints I'm still 'Mr Bob'.

One of his feet suddenly moved sideways and hit me hard in the ribs.

"Is that understood?"

"Yes, Mr Bob," I gasped.

"Jist so's we knows where we stands from the start. Now you haven't been in sarvice a-fore, but that don't matter because you won't need to do nothin' but what I tells you. Now this here's below stairs and you don't nivver go above without I say so. The only times you ever goes above stairs is with me when I cleans the rooms and when I does my lamps and candles last thing at night. If you're ketched above stairs on your own when you haven't no business to be there — and I wery much doubt if you ever will have the right to be there when I ain't — then you're goin' to be in Chancery. That's all."

"What are the other rules?"

He started up from his chair: "What did you say"?

"What are the other rules, Mr Bob?" I hastily repeated.

He relaxed again: "That's better. You'll find 'em out. There's jist one rule what you needs to know for now," he said. "And that's 'Do what Mr Bob ... '"

At that moment he broke off suddenly as a fattish, middle-aged man came in. He was wearing a green coat and white trowsers with a yellow and black checked waistcoat and a fine white stock. He had a lowering face which was covered with brandy-blossoms.

Bob jumped to his feet and shoved the pipe into his pocket still cradled in his hand.

"Are you doing those boots, Edward?" the man demanded.

"Yes, Mr Thackaberry. That's to say, the new boy's jist a-doin' of 'em now."

"Keep at your work," Mr Thackaberry snapped at me, for I had turned to look at him while I continued to polish as hard as I could. "There was a good half pint of sherry left in the blue glass decanter last night, which I want to know what happened to it?"

"Oh no, Mr Thackaberry, with respeck, sir. There weren't no more nor a couple of fingers."

"I'm not going to argue about it, Edward. I'm just going to say, for the last time ... "

"Excuse me, please, Mr Thackaberry," Bob broke in deferentially. "Let me send the boy away."

The man nodded and Bob turned to me: "Dick, go into the scullery and help Bessie clean the pans."

Taken aback, I did not move for a moment.

"Is the boy half-witted?"

"Excuse me, Mr Thackaberry," Bob said apologetically and then a blow landed on my head from the flat of his palm.

"Are you deaf?" he shouted.

I staggered dizzily into the passage and making my way further along it, found myself in a gloomy, foul-smelling cellar that I took to be the scullery. Amidst the smell of damp and the reek of tallow-candles there was something sharper that pricked my nostrils. In a corner I now saw that there was a little hunched creature bent over a sink and scouring a huge copper.

"Are you Bessie?" I asked. "I'm Mr Bob's new boy."

Without glancing at me she nodded towards a number of vast pans stacked up beside the sink. I now saw that she was a girl of about my age but her body was twisted askew and her face was so thin that she looked like a very old woman. She said in a high-pitched voice: "Second table. Quick."

"I'm Johnnie," I said, as I picked up a pan. "That's my real name, though they call me Dick here."

She made no acknowledgement. I watched how she was rubbing a mixture of fine sand and caustic soda — that was the smell I had noticed! — onto the inside of each pan and then scouring with a stiff brush. I saw that her hands were red with numerous tiny splits in the skin that were bleeding in places and that their backs were covered in blisters.

So I began to work and found that the soda burned my hands painfully. I was much slower and less adroit than the girl but although she worked furiously and without stopping it took us nearly three hours without a break to clean the coppers and boilers, scraping the burnt food off the pans and then scouring them with lemon and sand and using soda for the dirtiest until they shone like looking-glasses.

Occasionally Bob wandered in and stood watching me for a few minutes, and two or three times a fierce-looking red-faced woman whom I took to be the cook came in from the other direction and encouraged us to work harder with a rain of curses and a shower of light blows about the head and shoulders.

By eleven o'clock I was exhausted and my hands seemed to be on fire with the pain, but we had finished the coppers. I noticed that my shirt and trowsers were now filthy.

Just then Bob came in and tossed something to me: "Put this on. Look at the mess you're in. You should have arst me for your apring."

What he had given me was a long white apron. I noticed that he had taken off the dark green one he had been wearing.

"Wait," he said as I began to don the apron, and to my surprise he reached into one of the pockets of my trowsers and pulled out the contents: a six-pence, three pennies, and some ha'pence and farthings. He investigated all my pockets in the same manner, though no more contents were disclosed.

He counted the money: "One shillin' and four-pence three-fardens," he said, then put the coins in his pocket. "This blunt goes in your box. And I have the key to it. So if you're ever found with blunt or anythin' what I didn't give you, I'll know how you come by it. Understand?"

I nodded. Now he placed his hand in my pockets again and ripped out the linings of each of them in turn.

"Now put that on," he ordered, and I tied the apron around myself. "The green 'un is for working and the white 'un is for above stairs and waiting in hall and the housekeeper's room, so don't you get them the wrong way round, because if that white 'un gets s'iled I shan't be too pleased." He pointed to the pocket of the apron. "Now there's your pocket. And if I ketches you with them pockets of your own sewed up agin or with anythin' hidden on you, may God A-mighty presarve you."

He turned and walked away. At the door he looked round angrily: "What the deuce are you waiting for? It's ha'-past eleven."

Interpreting this as an instruction to follow him, I caught up with him at a run. Other servants were making in the same direction down the dark passage. After a few yards we entered a large, low-ceilinged room with a sanded floor where a number of people were taking their places at a long deal table in the centre. Those at the top and the bottom of the table sat on high-backed oaken settles but in the middle there were only forms. The room was windowless and lit by tallow dips that stank terribly. I saw that the men-servants sat at one end and the women at the other, but what I did not grasp until later was that they were seated in strict order of precedence with the head-coachman at the top and beside him the under-coachman, the first, second, third and fourth footmen, then the grooms in the same order of precedence. The women were headed by the head-kitchen-maid, then the head-laundress, the house-maids, the kitchen-maids and the laundry-maids so that the most inferior men and women met at the centre — though they were forbidden to talk to each other.

Bessie and I had to carry in the food and serve it to the women's and the men's end of the table respectively, when everyone helped themselves in the old-fashioned style. It was very hard work and Bob kept shouting at me and drawing the attention of the rest of the company to my deficiencies for comical purposes. I was myself faint with hunger and wondered when I would be permitted to eat. I whispered this question to Bessie as we collected the great serving-dishes.

"Arterwards," she replied.

When the meal was nearing its end we had to start carrying the empty and used dishes back to the scullery. On one occasion as I arrived there, I noticed Bessie quickly seize a piece of bread and run it round the bottom of the boiler she had just put down. I followed her example, but there was very little left by our fellow-servants. I slipped a piece of bread in my apron-pocket to eat later.

Bessie saw me and shook her head, for, as I learned, we were only permitted to eat what we could scavenge at the time, and to save anything for more leisured consumption was a serious offence.

When I had carried the last of the dishes to the scullery I hurried back to the servants'-hall. Bob now stood up and looked at me commandingly: "Come along. Second table."

As he delivered these mysterious words he looked at my white apron and saw small smears of grease from the heavy pans I had been carrying pressed against my chest.

He cuffed my head: "That apring's on'y changed once a week. Keep it clean or you'll answer to the palm of my hand for it."

He led the way back to the scullery and this time we passed into the kitchen — a large, high-vaulted room with an enormous fireplace hung with spits and roasting-grids. Here we picked up more containers of food, though this time the dishes were more elegant. We carried them back along the dark passage but on this occasion we went beyond the servants'-hall and into a large room with a barred window through which a little light entered. It was deserted, but in the middle of it there was a handsome old table which was set for eight.

When we had placed the dishes on the sideboard Bob said: "Now don't forget to bow when the ladies and genel'men come in."

Then he went out closing the door behind him, but only a few moments later he flung it open and stood, bowing respectfully, holding the door back.

A number of people now processed into the room from a chamber opposite. They were led by the butler, Mr Thackaberry, arm in arm with a tall, crow-like woman wearing pince-nez and whom, to my dismay, I recognised. It was Mrs Peppercorn, the housekeeper whom I had briefly met at Hougham all those years ago the day I first encountered Henrietta. I quickly bowed to hide my face, but as I did so it occurred to me that though she was unaltered, the same was hardly true of myself.

The company seated themselves, Mr Thackaberry at the head of the table and Mrs Peppercorn at the opposite end. On Mr Thackaberry's left was the cook and on his right a gentleman with a very shiny bald head and a prominent red nose. Then there were three young ladies whom I took to be lady's-maids and at the bottom of the table a young gentleman and the head-house-maid on either side of Mrs Peppercorn.

"Do what I do," Bob hissed at me and began to hand round the plates in the new style.

The food was exquisite and each course was accompanied by a different wine.

"What do you reckon, Mr Thackaberry," the gentleman sitting next to the butler remarked, "to the fact that the family is not to go down into the country for the festive season?"

Pointing to the gentleman, Bob held out a dish and whispered to me: "Give this to Sir Parsivvle's valick."

Mr Thackaberry looked at Bob's back and waited until he had gone to the sideboard. Then, forgetting or discounting my presence, he first wiped his mouth with his napkin and then opened it, but before he could speak Mrs Peppercorn cut in: "The intention is to economise, of course."

"There is," Mr Thackaberry said solemnly, "another reason. The Chancery suit is at a delicate stage, I understand."

"Fiddlesticks!" Mrs Peppercorn said. She added dismissively: "That suit has always been at a 'delicate stage'."

"Ain't it rum," the cook began pacifically, for the Tartar of the kitchen seemed to be resolutely emollient amongst her superiors; "that Sir Perceval is so keen for Mr David to marry Miss Henny rather than the young lady he has in mind. They say she's fearfully rich."

"But she's a nobody, ain't she?" boldly put in one of the young ladies who had the most charming curls and the prettiest dress. "They say her father was just a nabob who was bred apothecary and made his fortune nobody knows quite how."

Mr Thackaberry looked at her severely: "Sir Perceval would never give his consent to such a match."

"Why, Sir Perceval don't know anything about it," she exclaimed. "It's Sir Thomas who is trying to bring it about."

With considerable dignity, Mr Thackaberry said: "If Sir Perceval did know of it, then I'm certain he would oppose the marriage. His sense of family pride would assuredly lead him to value rank above merely mercenary considerations."

Speaking as if to one of feeble understanding, Mrs Peppercorn said: "The truth is, Mr Thackaberry, that Sir Perceval does not realize that Mr David is so deeply in debt that he must make a good marriage or go under."

The butler flushed.

"They say that Sir Perceval is furious with Mr David over his losses at Hazard," the bald gentleman — whom I now knew to be the valet — commented.

"And yet he does not know the half of them," the same young lady cried. "Goodness knows what will happen when he finds out!"

Mr Thackaberry glared at her but to no effect.

"Ned told me he had a fearful row with his mamma last week," she exclaimed in delight.

"Joseph had no business to tell you," Mrs Peppercorn said severely. "Mr Thackaberry, I trust you will warn your men-servants against spreading gossip."

"And likewise you, ma'am, your women-servants against listening to it," the butler said.

"I can't believe this story about Mr David marrying Miss Henrietta," the cook said quickly; "for she has no expectations at all."

"Very true, ma'am," said Mr Thackaberry. "She would be a penniless orphan if it were not for the goodness of heart of Sir Perceval and Lady Mompesson in bringing her up as their own child. And how in character it is that they should now want to make her one of the family by marrying her to Mr David."

"You've got it all wrong," Miss Pickavance cried. "Mr David is to marry the heiress. It's not he who is to marry Miss Henny."

Mr Thackaberry flushed again and Mrs Peppercorn, smiling at his discomfiture, said: "Yet you are at least right in praising their generosity towards their ward. After recalling her from school in Brussels they are now paying for a governess."

"Governesses!" exclaimed Miss Pickavance with deep significance.

Mrs Peppercorn glanced at her: "You are right. In reality, a governess is an upper house-maid with leave to wear no cap."

"And just because she is occasionally invited to dine with the family when they have no company," Miss Pickavance commented, "that Miss Fillery thinks she lives on a footing of equality with them!"

"In my experience, Miss Pickavance," Mrs Peppercorn put in magnificently, "governesses always do. Consider the last one."

"Designing creature!" the young lady exclaimed. "Only recall the odious way she tried to ensnare Mr David! She even persuaded him to take her to Vauxhall-gardens once!"

But now she had gone too far. With a glance towards Bob and myself at the sideboard, the housekeeper frowned her into silence.

When we had served and cleared the first course, Bob whispered to me: "Help me take them dirty dishes and plates out to the scullery and mind you don't touch nothin' or I'll skin you."

We did this and in the scullery I noticed that he was helping himself to a couple of small fowls and some slices of beef left in two of the dishes.

When we returned to the housekeeper's-room, Miss Pickavance was saying: "Of course, a body-servant who attends upon his or her employers must necessarily be more in their confidence than those who, however exalted, merely oversee the arrangements of their establishment. Would you not agree, Mr Sumpsion?"

The bald valet looked at her in astonished terror and was fortunately saved the need to reply by a fit of coughing.

We were serving the coffee a few moments later when suddenly Miss Pickavance looked at me and screamed: "What is this boy thinking of!" Everyone stared at me and she continued: "To come in here like that! That apron is absolutely filthy!"

I had been taking pains not to dirty it any further, but Bob cuffed me on the head again: "He done it jist now, miss," he apologised, "and I give him a row for it. It's his fust day."

"Don't come near me, you horrible creature!" Miss Pickavance exclaimed.

"You stand back there and hand the cups to me from the sideboard," Bob admonished me in a fierce whisper.

"This is adding insult to injury," Miss Pickavance announced. "I'm not used to being waited upon by servants in undress. At Lord Decies' such a thing would never have been thought of."

"Indeed?" said Mrs Peppercorn very drily. "I was under the impression that in Lord Decies' establishment the lady's-maids did not dine at the second table."

The rest of the company sniggered and Miss Pickavance flushed.

When we had served the coffee the butler said: "That will be all, Edward."

As we bowed and went out Bob seized my arm and twisted it behind my back to emphasize his words: "If you get me into a scrape agin, I'll see you out of here with something to remember me by for the rest of your life. Is that plain enough?"

I cried out in pain and he released me. "Now when they ring the bell you go back and clear. Is that understood?"

I gasped: "Yes, Mr Bob."

"Until then you go and help that gal." He went off down the dark passage towards the servants'-hall and I returned to the scullery where I found Bessie cleaning the crockery that we had just brought in, and scouring the boilers. For the next hour I worked with her as before.

After a short time I caught glimpses of magnificent figures passing the door into the passage clad in scarlet and chocolate livery with gold-braided froggings and shoulder-knots, ruffles at the sleeves, plush knee-breeches with white silk stockings and padded calves and shiny black pumps with bright buckles. They were all tall but seemed even more so now because of their heightened shoulders and powdered wigs. I had difficulty in recognising in them the mortals I had served at dinner. A new dignity and sense of their importance now hung upon them so that the fastidiousness with which they avoided anything that might soil their clothes partook almost of a moral quality that separated them from those of us not in livery. Bob appeared eventually, more magnificent even than the others, and too grand even to notice me as he passed through the scullery towards the kitchen.

Now I heard bells ringing above stairs and suddenly there was a tremendous bustle and a procession of footmen came from the kitchen carrying smoking hot dishes. The family's luncheon was being served and the commotion attendant upon it lasted for about an hour and a half.

In the middle of it one of the bells above us rang and Bessie glanced up: "Pan'ry."

Not realizing she meant me I did not pay any attention until she screeched: "Pan'ry!"

I returned to the room where we had served dinner. It was empty. I tried knocking at the door opposite and there I found Mr Thackaberry and Mr Sumpsion, Sir Perceval's valet, slumped in their chairs before the fire.

"Take 'em away," muttered Mr Thackaberry, indicating the array of articles on the table.

I did so and then worked all afternoon assisting Bessie. At intervals Bob came back into the kitchen to make sure I was not idling, but most of the afternoon he spent playing cards and drinking in the footmen's room.

The work was unremitting and by late afternoon I was in a state of staggering exhaustion. By now the kitchen was preparing tea for the servants'-hall, supervised by the under-cook, and dinner for the upper servants and the family under the exigent eye of the cook.

At six the livery-servants reassembled in the hall for their tea and Bessie and I brought in loaves of bread and cheese and small-beer for the men. The women drank tea, and this was a complicated operation since each of them had their own locked tea-caddy and sugar, and had to have a separate pot each. This time I managed to seize several pieces of bread and a small lump of cheese — mainly the rind — while removing the dishes.

By the time Bessie and I had cleared and washed up after this, the bustle over preparations for the first and second tables was increasing.

"Parlour-dinner for five," I heard the under-cook say to the first footman. "And three trays."

Towards seven o'clock Bob came in, staggering slightly and looking extremely ill-tempered, searching for me so that he and I could wait on the upper servants at dinner in the housekeeper's dining-room as before. This time she had company so there were two more to be served. Just as at luncheon Bob ensured that I had no opportunity to take anything from the food that was left uneaten.

At the end of the meal the ladies withdrew to the housekeeper's private sitting-room. Bob told me to serve their tea there while he waited on the gentlemen for their dessert.

When I had done as I had been ordered, I tried to sit on a bench in the scullery and rest for a few minutes but Bob came in and just as he was cuffing me to my feet the bell rang in the housekeeper's room.

"You heerd it," he said. "Go and clear up."

I went back and found Mr Thackaberry and the valet, just as before, dozing in front of the fire. I cleared up here and in the sitting-room and then helped Bessie to wash up.

By now the family's dinner was being served and the soiled dishes and pans from each course were beginning to arrive for our attention. Our task now, however, was merely to fill them with water, mix in caustic soda and leave them to soak overnight to be scoured and polished by us the next morning.

It was after half-past nine before Bessie announced that we had done all we had to do for the moment. I sank onto a bench, wondering as I did so where I would sleep now that at last this interminable day seemed to be finished. Almost immediately I dozed off, but in that last assumption I was mistaken, for after a few minutes Bessie shook me awake to tell me that it was time for us to serve supper in the servants'-hall.

We did so and then had to clear it and deal with the dishes. As I was engaged upon this a sour-faced man of about sixty dressed in a long greasy gaberdine top-coat and carrying a battered hat, came along the passage. As we passed he stared at me intently, swinging his head to follow me with his watery, somewhat protuberant eyes. I noticed that he went into Mr Thackaberry's pantry without knocking.

By now I was so exhausted that I had no thought of eating. Shortly after this Bob and I carried tea to the housekeeper's room and cleared it away afterwards. At half-past ten the man whom I had seen arriving appeared from the pantry with Mr Thackaberry, the latter flushed and slightly unsteady. They made for the stairs.

"Come on," said Bob, seizing me by the shoulder and pushing me towards the stairs after them.

As we passed his little closet he reached in and picked up two wooden boxes, one small and the other large. He thrust the large one at me and I seized it and followed him and the other two men up the stairs. I realized that we were to accompany the others and, tired as I was, I felt a stirring of excitement at the reflection that this would bring me closer to the purpose of my being here.

First Mr Thackaberry, taking the key from the impressive bunch that he carried threaded on a chain, locked the back-door into the yard — the door that had always been left unlocked! This was a serious blow to my hopes. Then we went above stairs and into the hall where Bob turned off the gas-jets which were installed only on this floor.

We went to the door of the Blue Drawing-room and as the nightwatchman — for so I now guessed him to be — and the butler went in I made to follow them, but Mr Thackaberry turned and said angrily: "Where the deuce do you suppose you're going? You never go into any of the rooms above stairs except to clean them in the mornings. Is that clear enough for you?"

He spoke as if I were an ideot and this idea seemed to have taken currency. (As it turned out it was quite useful for me that this was believed.)

I nodded: "Yes, Mr Thackaberry."

"Mr Jakeman, if this boy gives you any trouble, deal with him as you think best."

The nightwatchman nodded, eyeing me speculatively.

So I stood outside each door and held the lighted candle that Bob handed to me before he went in. The others passed in and, under the supervision of Mr Thackaberry, closed the shutters and locked them. Bob went round the room extinguishing any candles that were still burning, and collecting the candle-ends which he placed in the smaller box. As the little party came out of each room the butler locked the door.

When this operation had been performed on each of the ground-floor rooms, the butler and the nightwatchman secured and locked the street-door.

"Who's yet to come?" asked Jakeman.

"All the fambly's back," said Ned, one of the other footmen who was on hall-duty, "save Mr David."

"Damn his eyes," snarled Jakeman. "I suppose it'll be another of his late nights to keep me from my sleep agin."

I noticed Ned and Bob snigger at each other at these words.

"Good-night, Joseph," Mr Thackaberry said, and returning the greeting the footman went below stairs, off duty now that the street-door was locked.

Now we all passed upstairs and went through the same procedure for each of the rooms on this floor, including, of course, the Great Parlour in which I was so interested. When we had completed the circuit of the rooms, Mr Thackaberry handed the keys to Jakeman and, to my surprise, took the box of candle-ends from Bob. (I later learned that it was one of the butler's prerogatives to sell them to the chandler.) He and the watchman then went down the stairs again while Bob and I ascended to the next floor.

Here we — or, rather, I — collected the boots and shoes from outside each door and placed them in the large box. Thus I learned that Sir Perceval and Lady Mompesson's chambers were on this floor, as were those of "Mr David" and "Mr Tom" and any guests of the family who might be staying in the house.

After this we went up to the next floor where less important members of the family and superior members of the staff — the steward, the governess, and Mr Tom's tutor — had their apartments. We went no higher for above this was merely the attic-story in which the house-maids and kitchen-maids slept. Later I learned that most of the men-servants, as well as the housekeeper and the cook, slept in the basement. The remaining servants slept outside — the coach-men and grooms above the stables and the laundry-maids above the laundry-house.

My box was full and very heavy by the time we returned below stairs to deposit it in Bob's closet ready for me the next morning.

"Bright and early tomorrer," Bob said. Then he turned and began to walk down the passage.

"Please, Mr Bob," I said, "where am I to sleep?"

He turned, shrugged his shoulders and yawned, but answered with what, for him, was a remarkable degree of amiability: "The last boy found hisself a shake-down on the bench in the scullery, I b'lieve."

"Have you any blankets?"

"Blankets?" he exclaimed, his good humour instantly dissipated. "No I ain't. What do you take me for, a maid-sarvint?"

He strode out and feeling that I was so tired I could sleep anywhere — even on the hard and narrow bench he had mentioned — I went into the scullery where I found only a small fire still weakly smouldering. I moved the bench as near as possible to this faint source of warmth and stretched myself out. Even here it was cold now and without any covering I feared that I would be too chilled to sleep. But I was wrong for, worn out as I was, I fell quickly and deeply asleep.

It seemed only a few minutes later that I felt myself being physically dragged up from my slumbers. I realized that I was being held and shaken, and opened my eyes to find myself blinded by a lanthorn.

Then it was dimmed and I saw the nightwatchman's face close to mine and glaring at me: "Git out o' here. This ain't where you shakes down."

"Can't I sleep over there, please Mr Jakeman?" I asked pointing towards a more distant part of the room, for I was reluctant to be banished from the comparative warmth of the fire.

"Not in here," Jakeman insisted.

"But I'll freeze anywhere else," I protested. "Where can I go?"

"To the devil, for all I care. You'll find it hot enough for you there, I dare say. Now move yourself."

He seized my shoulders and pushed me towards the door. So, without even a candle I blundered down the passage and felt my way into the servants'-hall. As I did so I noticed a faint but acrid smell and in the pale moonlight from the subterranean window, I glimpsed a movement below and around me. As my eyes grew accustomed to the near-darkness, I realized that the floor was thickly covered with black-beetles so tightly packed together as to form a shiny living carpet. I shuddered, but I had little choice and so I stretched out on one of the narrow forms. It occurred to me that I had earlier wondered what form of life in this house was lower and more despised than myself, and now I had learned the answer.

This time the cold was so intense that I could not sleep even though I was exhausted. The edge of my tiredness had been blunted by my brief repose, and I was distracted by the ceaseless, loathsome movement beneath me.

The document I sought was now only a few yards from me — assuming that it was in the hiding-place — but I still had to deal with the nightwatchman, the locked door of the Great Parlour, and above all the combination-lock that guarded the hiding-place. I also had to consider the question of how I would make good my escape. There was no point in securing the will only to find myself unable to get out of the house, like the servants pursuing Mr Digweed and myself! And now that I had learned that the back-door was locked at night, I saw that this would prove to be a major obstacle for though I believed I could get through the small lock on the door into the Great Parlour, I could see that the locks on both the street-door and the back-door were not of the kind that could easily be picked by someone as inexpert as myself. The alternative to escaping immediately after securing the will, would be to conceal it somewhere in the house and hope to be able to get clear with it before its absence was discovered. But what a risk that would be! At the very thought I became so alarmed that sleep eluded my grasp even further.

Eventually I must have fallen into a restless, dream-haunted sleep for the next thing I recall is a soft noise — strangely insidious and insistent — which gradually awakened me. When I opened my eyes I found it was still absolute night. The noise came again: Tap-tap-tap.

I went into the passage and it seemed to be coming from the scullery, so I cautiously opened the door and went in. To my surprise it was empty. The meagre fire had gone out. Where was the nightwatchman? There was a faint yellow gleam at the window and now that I went closer I saw a face on the other side of the grimy pane. It was the laundry-maid, Nellie, who was holding a candle and tapping on the glass. I put my face against it and she smiled and nodded at me to indicate that she wanted to come in. I shrugged to show her that I could not comply for the door was locked and the watchman had the key.

Nellie frowned, pointed to my right, and then, putting her face as close to the dirty window-pane as the iron bars on the outside permitted, called: "Wake him, will you."

Cautiously I went into the kitchen and there I found Jakeman fast asleep, sprawled on a bench before the banked-up fire with a stone-bottle of gin, uncorked and empty, lying beside him. It was much warmer in here, but why had he driven me from the scullery if he did not intend to sleep there himself? I went across and addressed him. He did not stir. I spoke louder, then touched his arm, then seized him by the shoulders and vigorously shook him. He muttered irritably and when he opened his mouth I inhaled the perfume of gin, but his eyes remained firmly closed. I began to search for the keys, reflecting that if I could find them, then here lay the answer to how I could escape from the house. They were, however, not hanging from his belt nor in any of the pockets that I could reach. I continued to shake him and slapped his cheeks until at last I managed to wake him.

He glared at me with deep though drunken suspicion.

"Where are the keys?" I asked. "Nellie wants to be let in."

"Nivver you mind that," he said. "I'll let the damned b---- in meself."

He shook his head muttering to himself and ran his hands through his hair. I waited but he looked at me ferociously: "What are you standing there for?"

"If you give me them, I can let her in."

"I'll git 'em. You cut away!" he snarled.

As I left the kitchen he followed me into the scullery and as I went out closed the door behind me. Of course! He had hidden the keys somewhere in there so that he could drink and sleep without any danger of their being taken from him. So that was why the other servants had been unable to unlock the street-door that night! And it was that that had saved Mr Digweed and me! Then could I find out where he hid them?

I waited in the dark passage for a few moments. Then Nellie opened the door and gave me a conspiratorial smile. Jakeman was not there.

"I've had a divil of a job to wake him since Dick's been gone," Nellie said to me. "I've had to stand out there in the cold and wait on Bessie to finish her work in the housekeeper's rooms and come and let me in."

"Couldn't the back-door be left unlocked for you?" I asked.

"They used to do that, on'y there was a burglary that way a few months back and since then Mr Thackaberry has made him lock it. But never mind that now. What are you standing there for? You've work to do or you'll ketch it hot from Bob."

"What's the time?"

"I dunno. Between five and six."

So, though tired and unbreakfasted, I had to carry baskets of coals up from the cellar, help Nellie to lay and light the fires in the scullery and the servants'-hall and get the kitchen copper boiling, and then, having completed these indoor tasks, go out into the cold yard coatless as I was. The acrid smell of burnt coal that hangs over London in the winter and lies like a thick blanket on foggy mornings pinched my nose, filling me with a sense of the earth as something ancient and inimical to men. Now I had to pump water into the cistern (later in the winter often having to unfreeze the pump by pouring hot water over it) and then carry it upstairs in buckets to pour into the boilers.

After an hour or so other servants appeared and began to start work. Bessie was the first and I learned that she had been at work even longer than I, making ready everything for the female upper-servants' morning toilet and breakfast.

Towards seven o'clock Bob came into the scullery, yawning and stretching. "You'll do a full day's work today," he said reflectively. "No half-holiday like yesterday, my lad."

Bessie and I had to serve breakfast in the servants'-hall a little after seven, clear it away and wash it up. Then I had to carry breakfast to the butler's pantry on a tray for the male upper-servants while Bessie served the same repast in the housekeeper's room for the women. I had to clear that away and wash up the utensils. After that, under Bob's guidance, I had to go upstairs and carry down the chamber-pots that the maids had left outside the doors, and empty them into the privy. As I did so I noticed without surprise that the dust-hole had been freshly bricked up and an iron grille clamped across it. I cleaned and polished them and when they had passed Bob's inspection, took them back to leave outside the bed-chamber doors for the house-maids to restore. Then, just as on the day before, I had to clean the boots and after that set to work on the pots and pans from yesterday's dinner. The rest of the day unrolled on the pattern of its predecessor.

During the first week I learned that this was the almost unvarying daily routine except for Sundays and holidays, and I came to understand how the day was divided up. But most important of all, I grasped the way the different areas of responsibility were shared amongst the various upper servants. The butler presided over the men-servants in livery and had charge of the serving of meals in the dining-room and of everything to do with wine (and other drinkables) and the wine-cellar. He also controlled the state-apartments on the ground-floor and the first-floor. The housekeeper was responsible for all the female livery-servants (except those within the cook's domain) and the rooms on the floors above the ground and first floors. The cook — slightly but crucially lower in the hierarchy — was responsible for everything to do with the kitchen, scullery, still-room, larders, and so on, and had charge of the four kitchen-maids, the two stillroom maids, and the scullery-maid, Bessie. These were the three great areas of indoor responsibility, and like great neighbouring empires jealous of each other's power, they fiercely contested their rights and areas of prerogative amongst themselves, forming alliances that shifted as rapidly and shamelessly as those of the European Powers. Below these three members of the staff — but only in the sense that they had no underlings for in other respects they were, or regarded themselves as, at least the equals of the three just mentioned — were the lady's-maids and the valet. At the next level were the servants responsible for out-of-doors functions: the head-coachman and the head-laundress (and, I understood, when the family was at Hougham this included the head-gardener) who, since they were liveried servants and yet had underlings, occupied a niche that was in uneasy relation to that of the body-servants. This was the cause of a great deal of friction — though I may say that the head-coachman, Mr Phumphred, was never the originator of it — and Lady Mompesson's lady's-maid and the head-laundress particularly detested each other.

Above the upper servants in a dizzy region I knew nothing of directly was the steward, Mr Assinder, to whom the butler, the housekeeper, and the cook were responsible for the smooth and economical running of the household. He ate in his own apartments — this was the "steward's table" I had heard reference to —

or sometimes with the family. On certain gala days, however, he was the guest of the upper-servants and I heard these mentioned as occasions of considerable delicacy when his hosts had to steer a narrow course avoiding either miserly parsimoniousness or extravagant indulgence. On the same level as the steward but of negligible importance within the economy of the household, there were also the governesses and tutors who existed in a hideous limbo and, as an outward token of their insignificance, usually took their meals alone on trays in their rooms.

Apart from Sir Perceval and Lady Mompesson, Mr David, and Miss Henrietta, the only other member of the family in residence was an old lady usually referred to by my fellow-servants (without rancour) as the "old cat" but more formally as Miss Liddy. The first three had apartments on the second floor, as did Mr Tom who, as I knew, was out of the house, and the two latter on the floor above that, on which were also the rooms of the steward, Mr Tom's tutor and Miss Henrietta's governess.

I felt increasingly, as the time dragged by, that though I was tantalisingly close to my goal, yet I might never reach it for the profundity of the gulph that still divided it from me. For example, one of the duties that Bob and I discharged was to spend two mornings a week cleaning in strict rotation various of the ground-floor and first-floor rooms. On Tuesdays we cleaned the Great Parlour, and since this was the only occasion on which I was permitted to enter the room, I hoped to be able to make use of the opportunity. When Bob had set me to polishing everything that was visible — rubbing the brass fittings with lemon-juice, cleaning the fireplace and grate by scouring the bars with brick-dust and black-lead and then brushing this off — he took charge of the more skilful work of sweeping the dirt and dust out of sight beneath the floor coverings. I learned some useful things for when we opened the shutters I saw that there were now bells on spring-handles secured to them against burglars, which would make that mode of exit very difficult. If nothing else, I was able to record in my memory the precise appearance of the entablature and its mocking design for it fell to me to clean it. This involved smearing it with a compound of verdigris, finely-powdered pumice-stone and newly slacked lime mixed with soap-lees, and then washing all this off with soap.

Knowing how essential it was to comprehend the workings of the household if I was to achieve my design, I worked out as quickly as I could the principles that regulated the structure of the day — or, at least, the normal week-day, for Sundays and holidays were different. The first division of the day — the forenoon — lasted from dawn until the moment when the dressing-bell for luncheon rang as the signal for the footmen to don their livery and make ready to serve that meal. During the forenoon they were in "undress" livery and I could be above stairs so long as I was under the control of Bob. Now all the work above stairs was completed: cleaning the rooms, making the beds, changing the linen, lighting the fires, and so on. The family either breakfasted late in their rooms and remained there, or kept out of the way of the servants in the breakfast-room, the morning-room, or the library. No visiters were admitted except those on business to Sir Perceval who received them in the library, where he was often closeted at this time with Mr Assinder or his legal advisers.

Once the dressing-bell for luncheon rang shortly before one o'clock, the "afternoon" had begun. This meant that no unliveried servants — kitchen-maids, laundry-maids, and so on — or livery-servants in "undress livery" could be seen above stairs. The evening began when the dressing-bell for dinner rang at half-past seven o'clock. The rules forbidding access above stairs were even stricter now, for liveried servants had to be in evening livery. One of the effects of these rules was that Bob and the other footmen spent a great deal of time dressing and undressing.

Tea was served to the family and guests at half-past nine. This period ended — unless there was a late dinner or supper — at half-past ten when the house was locked up in the ritual I have described. During this brief in-between period we lower servants were allowed once again to venture above stairs to perform our duties: carrying up lamps, candles, warming-pans and heated bricks. But after about eleven o'clock it was, in principle, part of the nightwatchman's responsibility to ensure that no servants were moving about the house. In fact, since he fell rapidly into a drunken slumber he was not able to enforce this, and I soon became aware that quite a lot of movement between the different sleeping-quarters of the servants took place up and down the back-stairs.

All of this made it difficult to imagine how I could get access to the hiding-place for long enough to find how to open it — and I still had no idea of how that might be done. Night was obviously the only opportunity. Since I was fairly confident that I could pick the lock of the door to the Great Parlour, I would get Joey to bring me his father's "spider" — though how or where I could conceal it I could not imagine. (I had arranged to meet him in the back-lane of the mews on Sunday evening, since Nellie had told Mrs Digweed that that was the only time the most menial servants had any chance to be free.) However, I still had the problem of how to get out of the house after my attempt.

During that first week I discovered how very hard the work was. Bob often slept late — and sometimes made me bring him his breakfast — so that the burden of his duties often fell very heavily on me. If I slacked then my share fell to Bessie, and if she got behind she received a worse drubbing from Mrs Gustard, the cook, than I did from Bob, so I tried not to let that happen. However, at least I became more adept at seizing food during the brief moment when I had the opportunity — the time when I was clearing the table after servants'-hall dinner and supper. But occasionally it happened that there was no food left and if I found any I dared not keep it for often Bob or Mr Thackaberry or even the housekeeper would, on meeting me in the scullery or the passage, stop me and almost absent-mindedly slip their hands into my apron-pocket. Once Bob found a piece of cheese that I must have put there quite without knowing it, and struck me fiercely on the side of the head.

So with the hard work and the near-starvation and the growing conviction of the impossibility of my task, I became increasingly dejected. How could I have been foolish enough to think I had any chance of securing the will? I was at the very lowest level of the household with the under-maids, the stable-lads, and the knife-boy, so that the life of the Mompesson family — their visiters, their dinner-guests, Mr David's comings and goings down to Hougham for the game, and so on — impinged on me hardly at all. I felt myself to be like some low crustacean clinging to a rock on the sea-bed unreached by the ripples of the vessels passing high above me on the surface. All the difference I felt from the family's comings and goings was that I had more or fewer boots to clean, coal-scuttles to carry, chamber-pots to empty, and knives to scour. Though frustrating in some ways, my remoteness from them was fortunate in other respects, for I feared — perhaps quite irrationally after all these years — that I might be recognised. Once, collecting the boots early one morning, I saw a lady come out of the door to the apartments which I had gathered belonged to the master and mistress, and recognised Lady Mompesson. Late one night Mr Thackaberry's locking-up party found Sir Perceval still in the library and backed off respectfully after opening the door a little way. He came out, affably remarking to the butler that he had not realized how late it was, and passed without even glancing at me.

And always it seemed there was more rather than less work, for my initial exhaustion did not decrease as I became accustomed to it but grew greater as I became worn down by it. I had not started from a basis of robust health and it was an abiding fear of mine that I would fall ill.

That first Sunday when I was due to meet Joey in the evening, I found that the Sabbath-day's routine as it affected me was slightly but significantly different. Although I had to rise at the same early hour, almost everything happened later for nearly everybody else in the household. So, for example, Nellie did not wake me at about five for she had the forenoon as a holiday. I performed the same early morning tasks with Bessie while Bob lay in bed late, secure in the knowledge that Mr Thackaberry would not be seen before noon. The rest of the upper servants breakfasted at eight o'clock instead of shortly after seven, while the family — those of them who breakfasted at all on Sunday, for this rarely included Mr David — had trays brought to their apartments at half-past nine. Then at eleven the carriage was sent round to take the family to their devotions at St. George's nearby, and most of the upper servants and some of the others accompanied them thither on foot.

However, if Sunday was a day of rest for some, it meant even harder work for the others — at least in the forenoon. For instead of the family and the upper servants taking a small luncheon at midday and then dinner in the evening, one large dinner was eaten in the afternoon both above and below stairs. The family dined at two and the servants — both upper and liveried — had dinner together in the servants'-hall at about half-past three. This meant that while many of the household were at church, the kitchen-servants had to work particularly hard to prepare not merely parlour-dinner for the family who often had company, but also "hall-dinner" for the servants, as well as the cold suppers that would be required in the evening.

At one o'clock the family returned and the carriage and horses were put away for their one day of rest. No drive in the Park or to pay visits took place in the afternoon and if any of the family went out, a hackney-chariot was ordered from the nearby stand.

Towards half-past three when the family had had their dinner and tea had been served, there came the week's great event below stairs: "hall-dinner". This was the single occasion — other than feast-days, when all of the servants (except for Bessie and me and our fellow crustaceans) dined together, and they all dressed up for it. The household's coxcombs, the footmen, appeared resplendent in their full dress livery, Mr Thackaberry and Sir Perceval's gentleman were no less smart in their best coats and waistcoats, while even Mr Phumphred and his grooms presented themselves in carefully waxed top-boots and freshly-laundered neck-cloths. The female upper-servants, of course, vied with each other to appear in fine gowns, and even the maids in their muslin dresses competed with each other in the area of bows and ribands.

A great deal of ceremony was observed. First of all the lower servants assembled in the hall, standing beside their places. When all were present Bob went to summon the upper-servants, reappearing a few moments later with a haughty and remote expression on his face as he flung open the door and they marched in. Mr Thackaberry said grace and then the upper-servants seated themselves in places assigned to them — and the subject of much bickering — strictly in accordance with their rank. The butler occupied the head of the table with the housekeeper on his right. The rest of the servants sat in descending order of importance as the august presence of the butler grew remoter: first the upper servants with both sexes inter-mingled, then the livery-servants with the women first and then the men, ranked according to seniority. Finally, the head-coachman, Mr Phumphred, having ceded his week-day position to Mr Thackaberry, fortified himself at the opposite end of the long table with one of his grooms on either side, resplendently clad in plush knee-breeches and gold-laced coat.

On this occasion Bob took his place at the table and it fell to Bessie and myself to serve everybody. During the first course the upper-servants made conversation amongst themselves, and their inferiors had to remain silent unless addressed.

While we brought in the second course, Bob served wine to the upper servants and Ned handed round porter for those in livery. As Bob poured a first glass for Mr Thackaberry that gentleman said affably:

"Come, fill the glass, Edward." He turned smiling to Mr Sumpsion: "To stint the wine is to insult our employer with the implication of close-fistedness, don't you think."

He agreed. And now Mr Thackaberry began an animated discussion with the housekeeper concerning the scandalous price of oranges. (For in front of their inferiors, they treated each other with courteous geniality.) When everyone at the upper end of the table had had the chance to air his or her views upon this topic, and the right of the upper servants to ignore the rest of the diners had been demonstrated, the butler, with great condescension, then bellowed down the length of the table:

"Very fine weather we've been having, don't you think, Mr Phumphred?"

"So it is indeed, sir, you're very kind to say so," Mr Phumphred answered, clearly embarrassed by the public part he was called upon to play. "I thought my lady looked remarkably well at church, Mr Thackaberry."

"She did, she did," the butler replied, turning to Mrs Peppercorn for confirmation.

"Indeed she did, bless her," that lady sighed. "Especially when you consider how much she has to vex her."

The top end of the table exchanged sighs. The collective curiosity of the lower end expressed itself in Mr Phumphred's cautious query: "They say Mr David is causing her a great deal of consarn?"

Mr Thackaberry and Mrs Peppercorn smiled at each other and shook their heads.

"And that that's why the family ain't going down to Hougham this Christmas," Mr Phumphred persisted.

Mr Thackaberry placed his finger beside his nose: "Ah well, verb sap, you know, Mr Phumphred. There are various matters at issue here that I ... in short, my lips are sealed."

"Is there any news of the Chancery suit, Mr Thackaberry?" the head-coachman asked after a suitable pause. "They say it's going against us."

"Much more complicated than that, you know, Mr Phumphred," Mr Thackaberry said briskly. "As you know, the Huffam heir has disappeared and it's said that the judge is about to declare him dead."

"And what would that mean for our people?" Mr Phumphred asked.

"It would be grave," the butler answered, shaking his head and reaching for his wine-glass. "Very grave."

"Why would that be, Mr Thackaberry?" Miss Pickavance asked innocently.

"Why, because ... That's to say ... It's a complicated matter of law, young lady, that I don't believe you'd understand if I were to explain it."

"Did you not meet the Huffam heir once, Mrs Peppercorn?" the head-housemaid asked sycophantically.

The housekeeper beamed at her: "Indeed I did. More than ten years ago when I was keeping house down at Hougham. In fact, I may justly say it was I that found the Huffam heir. He was a mere child at the time, of course, and living under an assumed name. But you know, I saw something in him that made me feel that he belonged to an ancient and honourable family. One can tell, I think, if one has spent one's life among the gentry. I mean the real gentry." (Here she glared magnificently at Miss Pickavance.) "And I was correct for he — or, rather his mother — was the last representative of the Huffam family from which Sir Perceval is himself descended. (For as you must know, Sir Perceval's grandfather, Sir Hugo, married the daughter of Mr Jeoffrey Huffam.) But as for that little boy, he made such a great impression upon me that I told Sir Perceval about him and he guessed the truth, and this was how he and his mother were traced. Sir Perceval was most grateful. Most grateful." She paused to let the implications of this sink in and then went on: "Though the heir has been lost sight of more recently, I am certain I would know him again for his nobility of bearing. But alas! he must have perished, poor child."

"And the worse for the family if that is so," Mr Thackaberry said, shaking his head.

When the third course had been removed Mr Thackaberry, after exchanging a glance with the housekeeper, rose — slightly unsteadily — to his feet, and this was the signal for Bob to jump up and hurry to open the door and for everyone else to stand. With an elaborate exchange of bows and curtseys on both sides, the upper servants now filed out of the room. The atmosphere instantly relaxed. Mr Phumphred moved to the top of the table, everyone made more room for themselves, and the conversation quickly became animated and unconstrained.

"Go on," Bob said to me, seeing me still in the room after a few moments. "Dissart's in the pantry. Git on and sarve it."

I did as instructed and a few minutes later left the upper servants drinking and eating nuts and comfits as they gossiped and quarrelled all the more unrestrainedly after the united front they had just had to present. When I went back an hour later the ladies had withdrawn to the housekeeper's room for their tea, but the gentlemen were still there and discharging devotedly their duty to demonstrate their employers' open-handedness.

Their inferiors in the hall were just as jealous of the family's reputation, and by the end of the afternoon it was clear that very little work was going to be done during the rest of that day, except that Bob had one or two trays to carry upstairs. Bessie and I, however, still had to clear up and perform our normal duties. Under the conditions that now prevailed it was at least easier to obtain food, and Bob even pressed me, with uncharacteristic good humour, to eat some slices of boiled beef and the remains of a preserved damson-pie.

Meanwhile, the family consumed a cold supper which had been set out for them in the dining-room immediately after their luncheon, and so required no further work. I realized in course of time that on Sundays they either ate such a collation or dined out, for there was no parlour dinner and certainly no "company dinner" on that day. The effect of this was that on the Sabbath the majority of the servants had no further duties from shortly after midday, and they made use of this freedom in the way I have described. When I had cleared the hall and Bessie and I had washed the dishes, it was about seven o'clock and for the first time during the whole of that week I felt relatively free and unobserved. Consequently I was able, watching for my opportunity, to slip out into the lane at about half-past seven.

There I found Joey waiting and hugging himself with cold.

"What took you so long?" he demanded.

"How could I help it?" I protested. "I couldn't get away any sooner."

I told him that although I had made little progress, I was reasonably optimistic about my chances of acquiring the will; and I asked him for the spider. Before parting we agreed that I would try to meet him at about the same time on Sunday a fortnight hence.

"My dad's about the same," he said just as I was leaving him, for in my haste I had not thought to ask. I turned back but he hurried away.

In the week that followed I made no further progress, except that I came to understand more clearly how the household functioned. The following Sunday Bob had been more devoted than usual to the family's reputation. When I went into the servants'-hall to remind him (on the instructions of Bessie) that it was time for him to take up the cold trays to Miss Liddy, Miss Henrietta, and her governess, Miss Fillery, he stood up and staggered a few steps. The other footmen and maids who were in the room laughed.

"Dammit, give me a moment or two and I'll be right as five-pence," he protested, but at that moment he stumbled backwards and sat down heavily on the form. "One of you will have to do it," he said, looking at his confrères.

"Well, *I* shan't," declared Will.

The others murmured agreement with this sentiment.

"It's the boy's place to take 'em up if you can't," Ned pointed out.

"Hear that?" Bob said to me. "Put on your pantry-apring and take them trays up. But don't let no-one see you."

"You'll ketch it if she noses on you to Assinder," Will said warningly to Bob.

"Who?" enquired Bob.

"Why, that b----," he answered somewhat enigmatically, and the others muttered in agreement.

"Assinder!" Bob exclaimed. "Why, I ain't a-feared o' him. It's he should be a-feared o' me."

The others laughed but not very affably for I don't think that Bob was much liked.

However, the upshot was that a few minutes later, laden with the three trays, some rather incoherent instructions from Bob and much advice from the footmen — most of it facetiously designed to set me disastrously astray — I ascended the back-stairs and passed through the baize-door onto the landing of the second floor. I felt a thrill of excitement at being for the first time alone on that side.

However, as I made my way along the passage I was alarmed to see the housekeeper coming towards me. She stopped and stared at me in amazement.

"What in heaven's name are you doing here?" she demanded.

"Please, Mrs Peppercorn," I said; "it's Mr Bob ... I mean, Edward. He's not well, so I am carrying the trays up for him."

"Very well," she said, "but I will speak to Mr Thackaberry about this, you may be sure. And do not forget to tell Edward so."

She strode on, and a moment later I knocked on the door of the governess's apartments.

"Come in," said a commanding female voice.

I entered and found myself in the presence of a lady of middle years who was seated on a chair before the fire in a somewhat austere parlour. Sitting opposite her and therefore with her back to me was a young lady whom I dared not even glance at.

"Who are you?" Miss Fillery said sharply.

"Please, miss," I said, "I'm the new hall-boy, Dick."

I noticed that the young lady turned her head to look at me when I spoke but I resolutely kept my eyes on the countenance before me.

"And why are you here?"

"Bob is not well, miss."

"Bob? Whom do you mean?" she said with a shudder.

"Edward, miss."

"How dare you come up here out of livery!"

"I'm sorry, miss, but I'm not a livery servant."

"Indeed? Then tell Mr Thackaberry that a servant out of livery must never be sent to attend upon me again."

This revealed so mistaken a notion of the kind of relations I had with the butler that I felt I had to point this out: "Please, miss, I think you'd better tell him yourself."

Her face whitened and her eyes seemed to become little points of darkness: "How dare you be impertinent!"

"I didn't mean to be, miss. I just meant that Mr Thackaberry wouldn't pay much heed to ... "

"I have no interest in hearing what you meant to say," she interrupted. "And neither do I intend to bandy words with you any longer. Finish your work and go. I shall report this to Mr Assinder himself."

Now I knew whom the footmen had been referring to in such unflattering terms! I placed the two trays on the sideboard and took the covered dishes and the cutlery from the topmost one. As I began to place the articles on the table in accordance with Bob's directions, the young lady rose and came across as if to seat herself at the table.

As she did so we exchanged glances and I recognised my solemn-faced little companion whom I had thrice encountered at Hougham and had glimpsed a few times entering and leaving the house when I had been watching in the street.

She was almost my height and very slender. Her countenance — all the paler for the contrast with her black hair — had grown longer and thinner, though it still wore the same melancholy expression, and was a little too pinched to be called conventionally beautiful. She appeared to have looked at me with no more than idle curiosity and I felt a sharp sense of disappointment, but as she seated herself she put her left hand on the table and then looked directly at me and then down at her hand. To my amazement I saw that she had slightly raised one finger and was drawing to my attention the ring I had given her in the park at Hougham all those years ago. I glanced at her, keeping my face as impassive as I could and the look I received in return impressed itself deeply upon me. It was curious and speculative as if I offered some possibility of something. I wished I could acknowledge it but with the governess's sharp eyes upon me, I dared not. I glanced at Miss Fillery now and even though Henrietta had her back to her, she seemed to have noticed that her charge and I had exchanged looks.

"Miss Henrietta," she said, "leave the servant to do his work."

It was almost in a daze that I finished setting out the table, picked up the remaining tray from the sideboard and, not forgetting the bow at the door whose importance Bob had impressed upon me, left the room.

Outside in the passage I paused to try to recover my composure before going on, for seeing Henrietta again under these circumstances had brought back the past and in particular that last summer down in the country.

However, I dared not be caught idling here so I went down the passage until I reached Miss Lydia's room. When I knocked and opened the door I found myself faced by a tiny old lady with a deeply wrinkled face, but the brightest blue eyes I had ever seen. The chamber was small but cozy and she was seated in an old elbow-chair on the other side of the hearth, wearing an old-fashioned muslin gown, horn-spectacles, and black finger-mittens. In a reverie though I was, I became aware that her glittering eyes were scrutinizing me closely:

"Where is Bob?" she said suddenly. "Oh I know Edward's real name," she said, seeing my surprise.

"He is unwell, ma'am," I said.

She smiled: "He is always unwell on Sunday afternoons, but he comes anyway."

"He is more unwell than usual, ma'am," I said, as I laid the tray on the little table she indicated and began to remove the dishes.

Though she was still smiling, her gaze did not falter: "Your manner of speech surprises me. Where are you from, young man?"

Though I had narrated my account of my origins several times to fellow-servants, I now found myself strangely reluctant.

I stammered and said: "Far from here, ma'am. The Border Country."

"I see," she said thoughtfully. Then suddenly she asked: "What is your name?"

"Dick, ma'am."

"That is what Bob's boy is always called. What is your given name?"

"John, ma'am."

"John," she repeated softly, and I believed I heard her murmur: "Yes, of course." Then she said aloud: "But you have another, I assume?"

"Yes, ma'am," I said.

"Will you tell me what it is?" she asked.

I hesitated for a moment: "John Winterflood, ma'am."

She looked at me as if she were disappointed, yet whether it was the name I had told her or the fact that she had guessed that I was lying, I did not know. I felt myself reddening.

"Very well, John Winterflood," she said gravely; "I hope I shall have occasion to see you again."

I bowed and left the room. I had much to think about as I made my way below stairs. How had Henrietta felt at seeing me in the guise in which I had appeared to her? She had not appeared upset or even surprised. Was there any chance of being able to speak to her? If so, how much should I tell her? And why had Miss Lydia taken so much interest in me? I had heard the other servants say that she was "queer", and part of her queerness presumably lay in her way of talking to the servants.

Throughout the week that followed my thoughts turned, whenever I had leisure, to what had happened during those few minutes in the governess's sitting-room. I longed for the following Sunday to come, bringing the possibility of another encounter with Henrietta. And yet I could not imagine how this could be, since Miss Fillery had so expressly prohibited my coming to wait upon her.

When Sunday came I watched Bob anxiously all afternoon whenever I had the chance, and he did not fail me. I was polishing the coppers in the scullery with Bessie when at about four o'clock the governess's bell rang.

When I went to tell him he exclaimed furiously: "What the divil do she want! Let her ring for all I care. Git back to your work."

I did so and a few minutes later the bell rang again, this time continuing angrily for so long that when I reached the servants'-hall the noise was still coming from the scullery and I did not have to announce my message. The other footmen and the maids laughed but Bob staggered to his feet with a terrible curse and made off.

He returned a minute or two later.

"The young lady wants to go a walk in the Park," he announced indignantly. "But Miss Fillery don't, so she wants a footman to go with Miss Henny."

I held my breath at this. Surely Henrietta was trying to arrange to meet me!

"What did you say?" asked Will.

"I told her I was keeping the door and couldn't on no account be spared."

The others laughed.

"I ain't putting myself out on a Sunday for no governess," Bob declared.

"Could I not go in your place?" I asked.

They all turned to me in amazement.

"What?" Bob said, "a sarvint out of livery accompany one of the fambly (for all it's on'y Miss Henny)?"

"I nivver heard on sich a thing!" Ned exclaimed.

"So I may not?" I asked.

"Sartinly not, for the honour of the house," Bob said.

At that moment the bell began again to ring insistently.

"That's that b---- agin," said Will. "She don't care what Miss Henny wants to do, but now she thinks you're defying her, she won't let it go."

"Be damned to her," Bob said.

"You'll ketch it from Thackaberry," Ned warned.

"You'd best go," said Will.

Uttering a fearful oath, Bob rose unsteadily to his feet and began to button his heavy coat and smooth his powdered head. The others helped to sober him a little and he went out unsteadily still muttering imprecations.

"Git on with your work," said Will suddenly and I realized that he had been watching me.

Hoping that he had not noticed how eager I had been to take Bob's place, I quickly hurried back into the scullery where I found Bessie still hard at work over the pans.

CHAPTER 95

For several weeks Henrietta insisted — to the indignation of the servants — on going for a walk on Sunday afternoon and though I guessed her intention, I could find no way to play the part required of me.

By now Christmas was approaching and since it was spoken of by my fellows as a kind of heightened Sunday when the everyday pattern of events was even more disrupted, I looked forward to it in the hope that I might find some way of taking advantage of the general relaxation of rules.

It was an understood thing that the family celebrated the festival on Christmas-eve and so made only the most modest demands on the servants' time on the day itself. So when the 25th. came, my fellow livery-servants rose late and, when they had donned dress-livery, began keeping the day in the hall which was now hung with branches of holly and where the Christmas candle, wreathed in greens, burned on the sideboard. A bunch of mistletoe was hung above the table and there was much flirting and kissing beneath it, and at each kiss one of the white berries was plucked until all were gone and there were supposed to be no more kisses — though this rule was quickly set aside.

Hall-dinner was to be a long and elaborate meal with a great deal of toasting. It began at two when the upper servants entered in greater state than usual, and at first conversation was somewhat stilted because of their attempt to maintain their dignity amidst the informality of the occasion. I noticed that Mr Thackaberry kept a seat empty on his right and this was explained when, after the first course, the door opened and a strange gentleman entered and took the place of honour beside him.

The newcomer was small, in his early forties with a handsome, high-coloured face which wore a somewhat petulant expression. This, I understood, was Mr Assinder who was graciously partaking of a single course, and his arrival was the signal for Mrs Gustard to enter the room followed by two of her staff carrying on a vast charger between them a boar's head decorated with rosemary, stuffed with sausage-meat, and with a lemon in its mouth, and preceded by the rest of the kitchen-servants bearing mountains of good food.

Conversation was still restricted to the upper servants though there was some giggling and whispering at the inferior end of the table, until, as usual, the moment came when Mr Thackaberry addressed the head-coachman:

"You have less work this Christmas than usual, I fancy, Mr Phumphred, with the family staying in Town?"

"That's true, sir. Though it's a shame not to get down to Hougham. But I suppose Sir Parsivvle needs to spare hisself the expense now."

"How dare you," Mr Assinder exclaimed, his features suddenly flushed, "speak of your employer in that manner. It's not for you, Phumphred, to speculate on Sir Perceval's financial circumstances."

Everyone was astonished at this breach of good manners which was also a rebuff to the hospitality of the servants'-hall. There were some suppressed laughs and many were divided between their annoyance at the steward and their pleasure in seeing one of their superiors so publicly put down. Mr Phumphred looked taken aback and Mr Thackaberry hastily poured his guest a glass of wine. When Mr Assinder withdrew shortly afterwards the mood was immediately lightened, and conversation became general and increasingly unrestrained.

When the upper servants had themselves withdrawn, the footmen — Bob, Dan, Will, and Jem — and Nellie and three or four of the other maids took over the whole table. The Wassail Bowl was filled with lambs'-wool and circulated rapidly. The outburst over dinner was the first topic to come *sur le tapis*.

"Why did he drop down on old Phumphred so sharp?" asked Nellie, whose waist was encircled by Bob's arm.

"Why, do you not know that?" he exclaimed. "It goes back a few years now. He once lent the carriage to someone. And Phumphred made trouble — I reckon Assinder didn't square him — and so the old flatt went to Sir Parsivvle hisself."

So that was how Mr Steplight (in fact, Mr Sancious) had obtained it that day he came to my mother at Mrs Fortisquince's! Then the Mompessons had had no knowledge of the deception practised upon her.

"What did Assinder get?" Nellie asked.

"No more than a good telling off for Sir Parsivvle is wery partial to him on account of his uncle, the steward that was. But he wouldn't be if he knew that Assinder does more than jobbing with what don't belong to him. I could tell you things about him," Bob said, winking one eye knowingly.

"Why, if it comes to that," Will said to Bob with a scowl, "you was gived a bit to bubble that last governess."

Bob merely laughed: "Aye, we done her brown, me and Mr David. I let on as I was bringing her a letter from Sir Parsivvle and my lady but it was a flatt-trap, for Mr David got a friend of his to write it."

"That was the night she come in through the mews?" asked one of the house-maids, giggling.

"That's right, for she went out on the town with Mr David on account of the letter, and that's why she was sent out of the house."

There was laughter at this.

At that moment the bell rang to summon me to wait on the uppers in the pantry. As I entered I heard Mr Thackaberry say to Sir Perceval's gentleman:

"Phumphred touched him on a sore point. The truth is that our people are in deep, very deep. Mr Assinder has told me some grave news. The rent-roll down at Hougham has been falling for years and has recently dropped further because of the bad weather. He is being told to squeeze more and more money out of the land and my lady doesn't take enough account, he says, of the stupidity and dishonesty of country-people. He has been trying to demolish and evict to keep down the poor-rates, but he's had no end of trouble with the vestry-men and the tenants. He's trying to make the best of the place, but it's a poor country. The house is in no condition to receive the family in the winter."

I went back to the hall just as one of the chamber-maids came in:

"Bob," she said, "it's that governess. She sent me to say that Miss Henny wants to go a walk in the Park."

"On Christmas-day!" Bob cried. "Well, she shan't, that's all."

"Then there'll be trouble, for Miss Fillery's mighty high today," the maid warned.

"What do I care?" Bob cried drunkenly, and the other footmen cheered him on, perhaps with no very benign intentions towards him.

A few minutes later Ned, who was keeping the door, hurried in to say: "Bob, Miss Henny's waiting now in the front hall, for the governess told her to come down. So git yourself ready and come on out to her."

"I ain't a-goin' to," Bob announced.

"Why then," Ned returned, "there'll be the divil to pay if nobody don't go out to her, that's all."

"Well it shan't be me and that's flat."

"Be careful, Bob," Ned warned him. "That governess is out to make trouble for you. Didn't she complain to Assinder about you the other week?"

"Assinder be damned! He daren't touch me!"

"What do you mean?" Will asked, while Ned hurried away.

Bob grinned at him with drunken triumph and, laying his finger along one side of his nose, shook his head.

"Let me go, Mr Bob," I said.

There was an outburst of disapproval from the other footmen at this, but Bob eyed me with an unsteady gaze and said: "Why, that's jist the ticket. Let her high and mighty la'ship see how she likes that."

"Come on, Bob," Dan protested. "He can't go in them togs."

"Yes he can," Bob insisted. "That's jist the beauty of it. If anyone makes trouble, why I'm in the clear aren't I? I've sent the boy. Ain't that good enough for a governess on Christmas-day?"

"All right," said Dan, "be it upon your own stupid head." Then he turned to me: "But don't let none of the fambly or the upper sarvints see you."

"He'll need a coat," Jem said. I was grateful for this for it was a very cold day and, of course, I had no top-coat. Then Jem added: "For that will sarve to hide that he ain't in livery."

So, with much drunken joviality, they found me an old carriage-coat kept in a cupboard in the footmen's room in case of emergencies which, since it was several sizes too large for me, served to conceal the outrage represented by my costume, though it made me look rather absurd. They found me a nosegay but none of them would entrust to me his gold stick.

Thus attired, I went up the stairs and passed into the front-hall where, to my delight, I found Henrietta patiently waiting. We played our part to perfection, under the watching gaze of Ned who was sitting in his box by the door.

"Please Miss Henrietta," I said, "Edward has sent me to escort you to the Park."

I heard Ned's sharp intake of breath at these words.

"Why could he not come himself?" she answered, speaking so coldly that for a moment I believed I was mistaken in thinking she had recognised me.

"I'm afraid he is indisposed," I replied.

"Very well," she said and without even glancing at me she walked towards the door with an imperious glance at Ned who sprang up to open it.

I followed her out, taking the umbrella that Ned put into my hand as I passed him, and we went down the steps. I had seen footmen in the streets escorting their employers often enough to know that it was my duty to stay three paces behind her.

We walked a few yards along the pavement and then, without turning her head, she said: "We must not attempt to speak until we are in the Park."

So I had not imagined her recognition of me! It was agony to have to walk so near to her in silence when there were so many things I wanted to say.

When we had passed inside the gate she chose the emptiest avenue. Luckily, since it was Christmas-day and the weather was cold and threatening rain, the Park was deserted and Rotten-row empty of the fashionable parade of horses and carriages that was usually to be seen at this hour. A light but icy wind rustled the leafless branches that waved lazily against the grey sky.

Henrietta began to walk slower and I moved up until I was a little closer to her. Now she turned her head for a moment allowing me to glimpse her pale face with its dark, intense eyes, and directed towards me a melancholy gaze before turning her head away again.

"You have become very handsome," she announced.

"How did you know me?" I asked.

"I knew you would come one day. After all, we pledged our troth, didn't we?"

We walked on for some yards in silence for I could not think how to begin.

"I have always remembered you," she said. "You were the only stranger, apart from Miss Quilliam, who was kind to me." She turned back to me again: "Amn't I beautiful? You're supposed to say I am."

"You are beautiful," I had to say. "Though I don't believe I should say that to a young lady — I, the humblest and wretchedest creature below stairs."

"You may say it to me — the humblest and wretchedest creature above stairs. But tell me your story. How do you come to be in that hateful house?"

We were in the middle of the Park by now and there was nobody in sight, so I came abreast of her.

"First tell me what has been happening to you," I insisted.

"Oh that is soon told. I was sent to Brussels where I was most unhappy. Since I returned I have had Miss Fillery as my governess. I hate her. And yet she is no worse nor better than any of the others. The only one I ever cared for was Miss Quilliam. I sometimes wonder if that is why she was dismissed, for I could never learn the reason."

Then she urged me to give an account of myself, saying: "It may surprise you to learn that I know something of your story already, for you have been much discussed by Sir Perceval and Lady Mompesson. Do you know that they are desperately looking for you?"

I nodded and began my tale. I had decided I would tell her nothing of the burglary or my intention to regain the will for after my experience with Emma, I could not be sure that she would not betray me. More important, I felt that she might not understand how my actions were justified unless I explained everything. And even then, she might make objections.

So as we walked together along the deserted, gravelled avenue of elms, I went over the events of the five or six years since we had last met. I described how my mother and I had been cheated of everything by Mr Barbellion and Mr Sancious and betrayed by Bissett; how we had fled to London, lost everything to bailiffs set on by Mr Barbellion, and had fallen into deepest poverty. I said nothing of either the Isbisters or Miss Quilliam, and softened the details of much of my narrative. I explained that my mother had possessed a document which certain enemies of ours were anxious to obtain. Somehow we had been traced by agents of these people and had been attacked in an attempt to seize it. Though we had escaped on that occasion, we had then been led, by a complicated series of misunderstandings and betrayals, into surrendering it into the hands of our enemies. I told her very briefly how I had been sent to Quigg's farm and something of what I had suffered there, and described how I had escaped and returned to London.

"I found my mother in even more wretched circumstances than I had feared," I went on. "She was also weakened by consumption and ... In short, she died a few hours after I found her."

Henrietta seemed to be deeply moved by these last passages in my narrative and turned her head away as if to prevent me from seeing her tears.

We were now by the bank of the Serpentine-river which at that time was a stinking cess-pool. It was a bleak spot, and especially so now that the mist was gathering and obscuring the trees around the perimeter and the sky was merging with the thickening fog to form an oppressive canopy overhanging us.

"I like it here," she said. "Miss Fillery hates it."

"It's not a proper river, you know. It's a sewer that follows the course of the old Westbourne-river."

"How do you know so much about it?"

I blushed: "I will tell you, but we should turn back now."

Amid the gathering darkness lights were appearing through the bare branches of the furthest trees, reminding me that we had to return to the house soon or risk drawing attention to ourselves. Henrietta consented and as we made our way back, I told her briefly the later part of my story: my encounter with Barney Digweed and his gang in the half-built house, the reading of my mother's account of her life and my realization of the nature of the crime that had always over-shadowed my life, and the way I had been lured into the custody of my Clothier relatives and taken before the Court of Chancery by them, and then consigned to the madhouse. I told her whom I had met there and how I had learned more about the night on which my grandfather had been murdered. Then I recounted how I had been rescued by the Digweeds and explained that I had lived with them since then and earned my living below ground.

"Have you come to my guardians' house to rescue me?" Henrietta asked.

I was wondering how to answer when I saw her bite her lip as she stared ahead with an expression of alarm. I looked in the direction of her gaze and saw to my dismay that a gentlemanly figure was approaching us from a few yards ahead. The mist had allowed him to approach so closely without being noticed. Already he was raising his hat to greet her, and as he did so he was looking curiously at both of us. I instantly fell a few paces behind her, but it seemed impossible to me that he should not have noticed that she had been engaged in earnest conversation with her page.

"Why, Miss Henrietta!" he exclaimed as he came up. "Fancy meeting you out walking on Christmas-day. Alone and in weather like this!"

He stood smiling quizzically, a handsome figure in his early forties, wearing a magnificent merino great-coat and Hessian top-boots. His gaze passed briefly over my face as I touched my forehead.

"Good day, Sir Thomas," Henrietta replied with a blush. "I wanted some air."

"On such an afternoon? It is spitting rain and the fog is thickening!"

"Indeed, and therefore I was just turning back."

"So I should hope, for your governess will be becoming alarmed, even though she is not as solicitous — nor in any way so charming — as the admirable Miss Quilliam. Let me accompany you back to Brook-street. Your servant can go on ahead." He added: "If that would be agreeable to you."

Henrietta consented and I gave him the umbrella and, with a couple of quick bows, hurried off towards the house.

I had much to occupy me and when I reached Park-lane, decided to take a long way back to give myself time to reflect. Could I trust her? Did I dare tell her that I was planning an action that would destroy her guardians' wealth and position? For the first time it came to me that my design might appear a shameful thing to one who did not know what I knew. And with a part of my attention I wondered who the gentleman was who had accosted us and whether he had overheard us.

I made my way into the house through the mews and the back-yard and returned to the scullery. As I came in Bessie turned from one of the pans she was scraping and jerked her head: "Mr Will."

Assuming he wanted the coat back, I went to the servants'-hall. As I entered I saw that Bob was lying fast asleep on one of the forms, and I also noticed that my fellow-servants were looking at me curiously.

Will scrutinised me and said: "Well, Dick, I don't know what you've been up to, but the old tabby wants you. You're to go to her right now."

My first thought was that Sir Thomas had told her that he had seen Henrietta talking to me, but then I decided that in that case it would surely be the governess who would have been concerned rather than Miss Lydia. I made my way up the back-stairs and along the second-floor landing and knocked at the door.

When I entered I found the old lady sitting in her elbow-chair facing me and staring at me with a strange expression: a kind of suppressed excitement mingled with fear.

We looked at each other while I might have counted to ten and then she said: "John Huffam."

Before I could stop myself I uttered the fatal words: "How did you know?" Instantly I could have bitten my tongue. "I have told you my name," I said.

At my words she looked surprised herself: "So you are another John Huffam?"

I could make no sense of this remark but I felt that having revealed so much I had to trust her.

"My name is not John Huffam," I said. "Though it is one that has associations for me."

"Yet you answered to that name as if to your own," she said sharply. "Though I only said it to you at a venture to see if you knew it."

"Why should you think I might know it?"

"Because I knew your face as soon as I saw you. At first you put me in mind of Martin Fortisquince and I believed you must be his son."

I waited in astonishment for her to say more. The resemblance between myself and my progenitors had been referred to more than once before, and I recalled how Mrs Fortisquince had commented upon it.

"But then I remembered," the old lady continued, "how much he and your father resembled each other when they were boys."

I was so amazed that I blurted out: "My father? Do you not mean my grandfather?"

"Of course," she said and smiled. "How could John have been your father? What a foolish old creature I am. He was a generation too old. And besides, I know he had no son. And yet, only think, I last saw him when he was about the age that you are now. And I was already past my youth then. You see how very ancient I am? I expect you think I'm out of my mind. Perhaps I am."

As she looked at me with her glittering blue eyes I felt that I had never seen a face that expressed more acutely sharpness of intelligence.

"I set eyes on your grandfather only once," she went on. "It was just after he came to London, when he paid a call for the first and last time on his Mompesson cousins. The resemblance between you is striking."

"So I have been given to understand," I said, remembering how Mr Escreet had received me.

"He came to ask about things he had been told by an old retainer of his grandfather. He had requested him to tell him about his parents and old Jeoffrey Huffam."

So I had asked Mr Escreet exactly the question that my grandfather had put to him more than forty years ago! No wonder the old man had been confused.

"So you see," the old lady went on, "I have guessed who you must be: you are the Huffam heir that everyone is in such a pother about."

I nodded for it seemed pointless to try to hide the truth from such sharp eyes.

Suddenly she cried: "Then your mother was that poor child that I tried to save!"

I was about to ask her to explain this remark when she went on: "But I knew you even before you came to my room. I recognised you the night the house was broken into."

I must have looked alarmed for she smiled and, patting a chair beside her, said: "Pray be seated. I mean you no harm."

I obeyed.

"Now tell me, what did you mean to steal?" Seeing me hesitate she said: "I believe I know it already."

I was beyond being surprised.

We gazed at each other, our eyes undeviating, unblinking and hardly daring to breathe:

"An old piece of parchment," I said.

"A legal instrument?" she suggested.

I nodded: "A will."

"Of one," she continued, "who died many years ago leaving a will he had drawn up earlier and that was substituted for this one?"

"While the real one was concealed in this house for many years," I said.

"The will of Jeoffrey Huffam," she murmured.

"Dated the eighteenth day of June, 1770," I added.

I saw that there were tears in her eyes.

"Perhaps there is Equity after all," she mused. "And yet, how strangely events seem to conspire to thwart Justice. I have longed for many years to see that will restored to the heir of Jeoffrey Huffam, and yet it was I who raised the alarm that night."

"You?" I asked in bewilderment as other questions prompted by her words crowded into my mind.

"Yes," she said. "And when I reflect that as a consequence you might have been shot, or hanged or at the very least transported ... " She broke off with a shudder. "But mercifully, no harm seems to have befallen you."

"No, I was lucky," I said.

"I must tell you what happened. I sleep very little now. At my age one needs less, and, besides, so little time is left. I see you smile, but I am very old, you know. No, not old. I am ancient. I am a relic of another age. Anyway, on that night I was reading in here when I heard a noise. Oh, not from downstairs. You were very quiet and I did not hear a thing. The sound that caught my attention came from up here. Now the family were not here but at Hougham at that time, with the single exception of Tom. He sleeps downstairs, that is, when he sleeps in the house at all. So I believed I knew what the mysterious sound was, for I had heard it once or twice before in the preceding weeks and on those occasions I had quietly opened my door and seen Mr Vamplew, whose rooms are also on this floor, going downstairs. That seemed to me to be rather strange, and I had resolved that the next time I would follow him if I could. So on this particular night I was still in my day-clothes and it seemed a good opportunity. I crept out into the passage without a candle and saw a figure descending the stairs. It was indeed Mr Vamplew. But perhaps you do not know who he is?"

"Yes. He is Tom's tutor."

"Well," she replied, "that is the word used, though another might be more appropriate. Tom is well over nineteen now and hardly needs a tutor, though he does need someone to keep him in order. So Mr Vamplew is his keeper, shall we say? He is a sly creature and I suspect him of being up to no good, and so that is why I determined to follow him, though I suspected that all I would discover would be some sordid intrigue with a servant-woman. He made his way down the stairs without seeing me and once on the ground floor, he began to behave very strangely, raising the carpets, looking in cupboards, feeling beneath the side-tables in the hall, and, in brief, clearly looking for something. I watched him at this work for ten or twenty minutes and then at last he appeared to abandon his search and went back up the stairs as if to go towards his own apartments. I followed him after a cautious interval and it was then, while I was on the first landing, that I heard a faint noise from the Great Parlour. I crept over and listened at the door. I heard voices faintly whispering."

"Yes," I cried. "We thought there was someone at the door just before the alarm was raised!"

"I tried the door and found it was locked. If only I could have known who it was," she sighed. "Naturally I imagined it was an ordinary burglary. I crept downstairs to find the watchman, that odious, sottish lout Jakeman. Of course he was asleep and so drunk that I could not rouse him. I searched his pockets for his keys but could not discover them. And so I decided to find Mr Vamplew since I knew he was awake and dressed. I went up-stairs and knocked on his door and told him of my belief that there were housebreakers in the Great Parlour. He said he would summon the men-servants and told me to return to the watchman and get his blunderbuss. He was most particular about the blunderbuss. He went below stairs to waken the men, and before he could warn them, one of them struck one of those new lucifers."

"And our watcher saw it from the street! And that's what made him warn us."

"Thank heavens for that!" said Miss Lydia. "Meanwhile I went back to Jakeman but still I could not find the keys. I had no intention of fetching his gun. By now I could hear the men running upstairs from the basement and trying to break down the door. I went up to tell Mr Vamplew that I could not get the keys and pointed out that if the housebreakers escaped through the window, our men could not get out through the street-door to pursue them without the keys to unlock it. He swore terribly and said: 'But that damned rascal of a watchman has them hidden somewhere.' That was strange, was it not?"

"Yes," I said. "And presumably it was the keys that he was looking for when you observed him."

"That is what I assumed. Then he asked me to give him the gun and when I said I had not brought it he was very angry that I had been wasting my time, as he put it, in looking for the keys. I said I believed we had no right to take the life of our fellow-men when they were not threatening to do us any harm. He rudely suggested that I should see how Sir Perceval appreciated that sentiment. By now it was clear that the men would take a great deal of time to break down the door. So Mr Vamplew ordered two of them to stay and the rest to go through the back-door into the yard, rouse the coachman and go through the coach-house and run round the mews to cut off the burglars' escape. He ran down with them and I followed, but met him a moment later in the hall coming back carrying the gun. At this moment Mr Thackaberry appeared from below stairs clad in his night-gown and cap and looking very frightened." The old lady laughed. "I besought Mr Vamplew not to fire but the butler urged him on with the reflection that Sir Perceval would reward him. The ground-floor windows are all barred as you know, so that he could not fire through them, so we went back up the stairs. We must have looked very ridiculous, I trying to hold his arm and Mr Thackaberry trying to pull me away. Mr Vamplew opened a window and pushed the gun out. I managed to snatch it away once but then he did the same again despite my efforts to pull him back, for the butler held me. However, just as he fired I succeeded in jogging his elbow and spoiling his aim. He swore dreadfully."

"Thank heavens you did! For that saved my companion from being shot dead, I am certain. At that distance Mr Vamplew could not have missed. Yet though the shot went wide, the poor man fell onto the spikes."

"I am grieved to learn it! Was he badly injured?"

I told her what had happened and she said: "Blood was found by the railings afterwards, but we did not see what occurred for there was the most comical struggle between the three of us when I tried to prevent Mr Vamplew from re-charging the piece. However, before he fired he looked out of the window and I am afraid that he got a clear view of you. He described you very accurately to the constable of the watch."

"I feared so."

"You must be sure to keep out of his sight. He is away with Tom at present, but they are to return in a few weeks. Sir Perceval gave Mr Vamplew ten guineas for his night's work." She smiled mischievously: "He was very angry with me."

"But he had no suspicion that this was anything more than an ordinary house-breaking?" I asked anxiously.

"To the best of my knowledge, none at all."

"But why was Jakeman not dismissed?" I asked.

"Because Mr Thackaberry spoke up for him and, I suspect, paid Mr Vamplew to do the same, so that his disgraceful conduct was not known to the steward. You see, he pays a share of his wages to the butler. Many of the servants do so because they are indebted to him for their places. I protested, but you see, no-one takes any notice of me. The only precaution that was taken was the blocking up of the privy-drains and the rule that the door into the back-yard was henceforth to be locked at night — though there is no way into the back-yard save through the coach-house and stables."

"I dare not stay longer," I said and stood up. But I could not go away unsatisfied on one matter at least: "Will you tell me why, as you said, you wanted the will to be restored to Jeoffrey Huffam's heir when such an event would ruin your family?"

She cast her eyes down and I wondered if I had been tactless. Then she looked up and said: "You refer to 'my family' as if you did not know that you and I are close kin. The Huffams and the Mompessons were united by the marriage of Jeoffrey Huffam's elder daughter, Alice. For she married Sir Hugo Mompesson and they were my parents. So half of me is a Huffam."

I started at this: "You are so close to me as that!"

She nodded: "I am your first cousin twice removed, if that is close."

Then I remembered Mr Escreet mentioning the daughter of Sir Hugo and what a "queer" young woman she had been. He had referred to some scandal or something involving her, but I could not call it to mind.

"And may I ask what relation you are to Sir Perceval?" I enquired.

"I am his aunt. He is the son of my younger brother, Augustus." She paused. "For certain reasons, I had a particular affection for your grandfather, John. And a few years ago I had the opportunity to do something for him. And it was an action that gave me particular pleasure for it meant undoing some of the evil that my family had done him. And it also meant preventing a young woman from being forced into a hideous marriage against her will for the sake of her family's pecuniary interests."

I was confused by her words until I realized that "a few years ago" referred to a time before I was born.

"Nobody in this family has ever trusted me enough to tell me anything. But over the years I've kept my ears open and I came to know how my brother and then his nevy acted to protect their interests, even though that involved the suppression of legal documents and other criminal acts. Well, at the time I am speaking of, Mr Martin Fortisquince happened to make one of his visits to the house to pay his respects to my family. And it came about that he mentioned something in my presence that made a great impression upon me."

She broke off and I noticed her hands restlessly moving on her lap, the fingers of one intertwining with those of the other.

"I know something about the way young women can be forced into marriage. Well, Mr Fortisquince told us, merely in the way of conversation, how your mother was at loggerheads with her father because he was determined that she should marry someone whom she detested. I was very concerned. And surprised, too, for your grandfather had seemed such a nice boy that time I met him. But then Mr Fortisquince mentioned that the intended groom was the elder son of Mr Silas Clothier. (He was the son of Abraham Clothier — or Nicholas as he later called himself — who was a money-lender who had battened upon my grandfather and forced him into marrying one of his daughters to him.) My nevy and his wife were very put about at this, for the idea of a marriage between two of their enemies appalled them, though nothing was said before me or Mr Fortisquince. I took him aside as he was leaving and asked him about it and he confirmed what I had suspected: that it was all to do with that wretched suit. I gathered that your grandfather and Mr Silas Clothier were forming some kind of combination which was being ratified by the sacrifice, as it were, of your mother. Well, I knew a very sure way of upsetting any such alliance between the Huffam heir and the Clothier remainderman. And I saw my way clear since I knew which was the drawer of his bureau where my nevy kept his title-deeds and other important documents. So I wrote to your grandfather."

I stared at her. "Do you mean to say that ... ?"

She smiled. "Yes. I decided that very instant that I would regain that document that you and I spoke of just now, from the possession of my nevy."

At last I knew the identity of my grandfather's mysterious friend inside the Mompesson household who had written the letter that had so excited him, and in learning this I had discovered something that not even my mother or Martin Fortisquince had ever known.

The old lady continued: "I knew that Perceval and his wife would be abroad the following Monday, so I decided that on that day I would go into his closet and force the drawer."

"And," I interrupted, "you told Mr Fortisquince to come that day and receive a gift to give to my grandfather!"

"Yes!" She smiled delightedly. "But however did you know?"

I explained how Mr Nolloth had recounted to me Peter Clothier's story of the events of that fatal day.

"I had to be so devious," she said, "for dear Martin would have been dreadfully shocked if he had known how I planned to involve him in what I believe he, with his scrupulousness, would have regarded as a crime."

"Then what happened?" I asked in excitement.

"I obtained the will exactly according to my plan," the old lady replied.

"But then did not your nephew suspect that you were ... ?" I asked and broke off in embarrassment.

"The person who removed the will?" she said quickly. "He did indeed, and accused me of it in the most dreadful scene. But I denied it and he had no proof. And only think what a perplexing position he found himself in. He could not reveal the nature of the document he was missing since he had neither a moral nor a legal right to possession of it. But he and Isabella themselves searched my rooms and my person."

"And they did not find it?" I asked.

She stared. "But you must know that they did not. For all went exactly as I had arranged with your grandfather. Right here in my nevy's house, I passed it to Martin."

"And so what went amiss?" I asked.

"Amiss?" she said in surprise. "Why nothing went amiss."

"Then why did Mr Fortisquince not give it to my grandfather?"

She looked at me thoughtfully. "Now I understand the misconception you are under. Why do you believe that he did not?"

I looked at her in amazement: "Because Peter Clothier's account of that night's events makes it clear that Mr Fortisquince did not pass the will to my grandfather for it was not in the package he received from him when he opened it at an inn in Hertford later that night."

"But only reflect," she said, "on whose word your father had for believing that Martin had not given your grandfather the will. Only that of Mr Escreet. Now I know that Martin did in fact pass the will to your grandfather, for I questioned him about this without letting him guess why I was so interested. He suspected nothing of what he had been involved in. He never knew that Sir Perceval had lost the will — indeed, he never believed that it ever existed except in John Huffam's imagination."

Suddenly I realized something: "So that means Sir Perceval does not have it!" I cried. "Then everything has been in vain: Mr Digweed's injury and my working here. All gone for nothing!"

A bitter rage welled up inside me. The will had vanished and I had no chance of ever regaining my rights!

Miss Lydia seemed about to speak but at that moment there came a knock at the door.

"That must be my great-niece," she said.

I rose in alarm for I had no idea who she could be referring to and it occurred to me that it might be Lady Mompesson.

The old lady put her finger to her lips and then raised her voice: "Come in, my dear."

The door slowly opened and to my intense relief and delight, disclosed none other than Henrietta.

"You here!" she exclaimed.

The three of us were equally astonished.

"How is it that you know each other?" asked the old lady.

"Dearest Great-aunt," Henrietta said, smiling, "I was just about to tell you the most extraordinary thing. Do you remember how I have spoken of a little boy I met at Hougham many years ago who stayed in my thoughts?"

The old lady nodded and looked at me, her eyes bright with excitement: "Who claimed the name of Huffam!"

"You remember!" Henrietta cried.

I blushed, for I remembered only too well that it was my divulging of that connexion before Mrs Peppercorn that had led to the Mompessons' discovery of my mother's hiding-place with all its evil consequences.

"Well a few weeks ago I believed I recognised that little boy, now grown up, of course, in the hall-boy who brought up the trays to Miss Fillery and myself. I decided not to mention it to you until I was sure. And I have come to your room now to tell you that he and I managed to converse this afternoon and that he confirmed that it was indeed he. And he has a very extraordinary tale to tell. But how is it that I find you friends already?"

"Well, I declare!" Miss Liddy exclaimed. And she described how she had recognised me from my resemblance to my grandfather (rather than to my father), omitting all reference, of course, to having seen me during the burglary.

"John," said Henrietta, "will you not be missed from your work?"

"Not for a little longer," I said. "The other servants are less punctilious about their work than usual on high days and holidays."

The old lady smiled drily: "Then make yourself comfortable and let me tell you some more."

So I seated myself on the chair by the door and our hostess poured us each a glass of madeira.

"Now first, my dear," the old lady said to Henrietta, with a conspiratorial glance at myself, "we must put this young gentleman on an equal footing with us by explaining how we are connected."

"That is very simply done," Henrietta said. "This is my Great-aunt Liddy, who is my only friend in the world."

She went over to the old lady's sopha and kissed the faded cheek. "Many and many a time when I was a frightened, lonely little child did I creep up to this room to find comfort."

"And comfits, my dear," the old lady said, laughing.

Henrietta seated herself beside the old lady: "Dearest Great-aunt, I believe you alone prevented me from becoming a morose, embittered creature."

"If only I could have done more for you," Miss Liddy sighed. "And if only I could do anything to avert the fate that awaits you and you, John, because you are both members of this family."

Henrietta looked as puzzled at these words as I did.

A thought struck me: "Miss Liddy, are Henrietta and I are related?"

"Yes, but very distantly. You share a great-great-great-grandfather, Henry, who was the father of Jeoffrey Huffam, and that makes you fourth cousins. And so you are both related to me, though neither of you has any Mompesson blood. For you see, I am half Huffam and half Mompesson. I am much more closely related to you, John, than to Henrietta for she and I are only second cousins twice removed. So I think that if it is right for her, then you, too, ought to call me Great-aunt."

"But not before anyone else," I said, smiling.

The old lady had not heard.

"Two young people," she said looking at us keenly but distantly. Henrietta turned towards me and I avoided her eyes. "I was your age once, you know. I remember your grandparents, John. What a handsome bridal couple they were, Eliza and James." (Of course, she meant my great-grandparents. But hadn't Mr Escreet said something about this wedding?) "Eliza was the sister ... was the sister of someone I meant to marry." She turned to me and I saw tears glistening in her eyes: "Another John, for your father was named for him. The wedding was to have been on the same day."

She broke off and after a silence Henrietta asked: "What happened, Great-aunt?"

"He died," she said softly. "Ah, how many young lives have been blighted by that wicked business! And will be. Now I find the heir to the Huffam inheritance working as a hall-boy."

"But why in this house?" Henrietta demanded of me.

Miss Lydia looked at me as if to imply that I should not answer. I felt strangely guilty at the idea of confessing to what I had come here for, and even angrier when I reflected that if I had understood Miss Lydia correctly, then the will had vanished and so was no longer in the hiding-place anyway. I found myself almost resenting Henrietta for making me feel these things.

"My dear Henrietta," Miss Lydia said, "Joseph will be bringing our supper at any moment. He must not find John here."

"No, of course not," she said.

And so, relieved at not having to answer, I quickly rose to take my leave.

"Try to come at this time next Sunday," Miss Lydia said.

"I will do my best," I replied. "But I may not be able to. If we need to communicate quickly, we can leave each other a note. Put it in your boots when you leave them outside the door and I will find it and return it, for cleaning boots is one of my duties."

They laughed and I added: "Only be sure to make your note unclear in case someone else finds it."

Then I cautiously opened the door and slipped into the passage and down the back-stairs. My long absence had been over-looked in the general hilarity that was still in progress in the servants'-hall. But when I saw how late it was I realized that the nightwatchman would arrive at any moment and the back-door would be locked. It was therefore too late to meet Joey, and I thought somewhat guiltily of the long cold Christmas vigil he must have had in the mews.

I laid myself down on my narrow form that night with mixed feelings. Could it be that the will really no longer existed after all? In that case my undertaking was pointless. Why should I stay on in this demeaning position? On the other hand, suddenly I had found two friends where I had thought I was surrounded by enemies. But could I trust them? Surely I could. But perhaps even they, like so many others I had encountered, had motives that were far other than they appeared. Everything I had gone through had taught me to trust no-one. I resolved to keep an open mind.

BOOK V

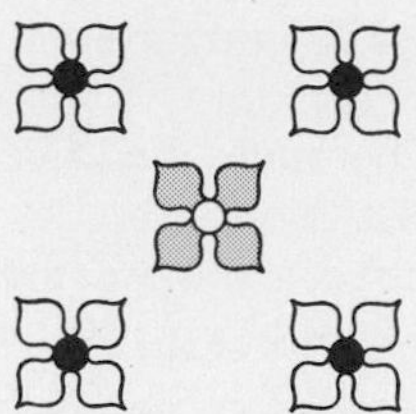

Marriage Designs

CHAPTER 96

We have done our best to reconstruct events as they must have occurred beyond your own experience, and to do so (in my case, under protest) without speculating. I must, however, now be permitted to mention that I have the darkest suspicions about the motives of Mr Mompesson and his mother. For though you may say what you like about Sir Perceval — and he, beyond contest, embodied the vices of Old Corruption — yet for all that he was a gentleman of the fine old English school. His son, however, is a product of a more grasping and less honourable age.

Imagine the scene in the Great Parlour. The baronet is seated on an ottoman with his right leg on a stool. His wife sits opposite and his elder son stands before him with a bold expression — and yet, for all that, looking somewhat shame-faced.

"You have no objection, however, to the girl?" Sir Perceval says.

"None at all," Mr Mompesson answers. "She's a decent enough little chit, and fond of me, I believe. Confoundedly so. Though she's a trifle too long-faced for my taste. Let Tom marry her. That would animate her if nothing else."

"Certainly not," the baronet says angrily. "And apart from any other objections, such a course of action would not save the estate anyway. Not with the codicil accepted and now a Receiver appointed."

His wife and son look at each other and she shakes her head very slightly.

"There are ways of achieving that end by this means, Sir Perceval," she says.

He glares at her: "I understand your meaning very well, but I will countenance nothing that would be dishonourable."

"Dishonourable!" she repeats scornfully. "Is it honourable to be publicly bankrupted, to be sold up and see one's house and possessions fall beneath the hammer for the amusement of one's friends?"

"There's no question of that. I insist that both the honour and the security of our family demand that David do as I require."

"And I insist that he need not."

"Then, madam, how dare you defy me!"

"Pray calm yourself, Sir Perceval."

"I am calm!" he shouts.

"I don't believe you appreciate the gravity of the situation," his wife says coldly.

She glances at her son and nods slightly.

"I need rhino, Father," Mr Mompesson says. "Soon. And a great deal of it. And that is why I must marry Miss Sugarman. She has a clear ten thousand a year."

"I forbid such a thing!" the baronet cries, his face quite purple. "Our family ... one of the oldest ... the most honourable ... English!"

He falters and breaks off, gasping for breath.

The other two watch him in silence until he regains his normal rate of breathing.

Then his son says coolly: "You don't understand. I'm in over my eyebrows, pa."

"Your creditors will have to wait," the baronet says bitterly. "Wait patiently until I die. That won't be far away. This thing has almost eaten my vitals away. *You*'ll have to be patient, too."

"That won't help me much," Mr Mompesson says. He and his mother exchange a glance and he says: "To tell you the truth, I've compromised my expectations."

His father stares at him and then asks: "Do you mean post obits?"

"Yes. Everything's mortgaged."

"Everything?" Sir Perceval demands. "You told me it was two thousand."

"That wasn't quite the whole truth. To be absolutely frank, Father, it's twenty thousand."

"So much!" the elderly baronet gasps. He pauses and then continues slowly and indistinctly: "You signed away your inheritance to the Jews while I've been struggling to hold it together?"

"I had to have tin, Father. How do you expect a fellow to live without it?"

"Who holds your bills?" his father asks, speaking thickly.

Before answering Mr Mompesson glances at his mother. After a moment she nods. (And if I may be permitted for the first and last time to venture such a remark, I believe that nod amounted almost to murder.)

"Old Clothier has been buying them up. Deuce take him!"

"What?" The baronet's visage goes a purplish-blue and he begins to gasp for breath. Then he turns onto his side, clutching his left arm.

His wife and son exchange a look. Then she rises and moves towards her husband while young Mompesson slowly crosses to the chimney-piece and pulls the bell-rope.

CHAPTER 97

During the next few days I thought constantly about my new friends and longed for the moment when I could meet them again. The opportunity came the following Sunday when I managed to get to Miss Lydia's room as before. I found her alone and immediately blurted out the question I had been brooding on all that time:

"So the will no longer exists?"

"Why do you say that?"

"You said it was passed to my grandfather by Martin Fortisquince and so I assume that it was lost."

Miss Lydia stared at me and said: "You are wrong. Far from being lost, it was restored to my nevy only a few days later. He had a hiding-place in the Great Parlour constructed to keep it safe. It is there now."

Relief flooded through me. So the hypothesis about the chimney-piece that the Digweeds and I had elaborated was correct. This augured well.

I told Miss Lydia how we had stumbled upon the existence of the hiding-place and how Mr Digweed and I had failed to unlock it.

Then a puzzle occurred to me: "But how was the will restored to Sir Perceval?"

"That has always been a complete mystery to me," Miss Lydia answered. "Have you any idea?"

"No," I said, "for this revelation upsets the most probable explanation of that night's events."

I explained to her the hypothesis that Mr Nolloth and I had accepted as the most likely: that my grandfather had been murdered and Mr Escreet assaulted by an unknown person who had entered by the street-door which was left unlocked by Peter Clothier as he left the house.

I went on: "Mr Nolloth and I assumed that the murderer was either a chance robber or an agent of the Clothiers who had been watching the house. But neither of these explanations accounts for the will being returned to Sir Perceval: a chance robber would not have taken it or known what to do with it if he had, and an agent of the Clothiers would have taken it to them and it would never have been seen again."

We reflected in silence for a few moments.

"You don't think it could have been Mr Fortisquince?" I asked, for I had long had certain suspicions concerning him. There was a kind of appropriateness, it occurred to me, in finding him responsible for this, too. "That in fact," I went on, "he did know that it was the will that you had given him to pass on? And that he removed it from the package and then gave it back to your nephew?"

"Having murdered your grandfather in the bargain?" Miss Lydia scoffed.

"Well, somebody did," I said.

Perhaps her jesting words were the truth: Mr Fortisquince gave the package to my grandfather without realizing what it contained. When he saw it opened and realized its significance, he killed him and restored the will to the Mompessons. It would be very neat if he turned out to be the individual who was responsible for all the mysteries that haunted me.

"My dear boy," she said, "you could not possibly suggest such a thing if you had known Martin. He was gentleness and honesty itself, and quite incapable even of the tiniest act of deceit, let alone anything else. That is why he was so well-suited to my purposes."

"It is true," I said, "that he was very kind to my mother afterwards, though ... "

I broke off, for the old lady was staring at me hard and now said:

"Go no further or you and I may have to quarrel. But for the matter of the will, whoever returned it, I will help you to regain it. But listen, John. Henrietta will be here in a moment, and I want to say something to you. Do not mention any of this to her for she might be upset if she knew what we were planning. She is a strange girl and I fear she would oppose our design against her guardians."

"Surely she feels no affection for them."

"That is true. She is very unhappy and has had a miserable life. She was left an orphan at an early age and abused by her first guardians. Though my nevy and his wife have treated her generously, they have never shewn her any kindness." The old lady paused and seemed perplexed. Then she went on hesitantly: "I don't know if you'll comprehend me if I say that I think she almost takes pleasure in her own misery. I know how she feels. I was like that once myself."

"I don't understand."

"Well, for instance, when she was a child she used to inflict injuries upon herself. Quite severe ones."

At these words I remembered the welts I had seen on her arms that time we had met in the great house at Hougham and which she had told me had been inflicted by her cousin, Tom.

"The only person who has ever gained her affection — apart from myself — was a young governess, a Miss Quilliam."

"I knew her," I said.

"She did not stay long. I'm afraid she let Henrietta down by trying to take advantage of her position here."

I raised my eyebrows and Miss Lydia began: "It's an unattractive story. She tried to ensnare first David and then that near-ideot, Tom, and had to be dismissed the house. I believe she became David's mistress before they quarrelled."

I was going to answer, but at that moment there was a tap at the door and Henrietta came in.

When we had re-arranged ourselves on the chairs she asked me bluntly: "I beg you to tell me, John, what are you doing in this house?"

I glanced at Miss Lydia. "I'm hiding."

"Hiding? From whom?"

"From my enemies, for my life is in danger."

"In danger!" she cried. "Why, this *is* just like a novel! Why?"

"Because of that document I mentioned to you in the park."

"Please explain to me," asked Henrietta, "what it was."

"'Is', I am afraid," Miss Lydia corrected her.

I glanced at her. Perhaps she knew something of its history after leaving my mother's possession?

"It's a codicil," I explained. "It all centres around the Hougham estate which my great-grandfather, James Huffam, inherited under the will of his father, Jeoffrey, almost exactly sixty years ago. Now there were rumours that there had existed a codicil to that will affecting the inheritance, but it was not found at Jeoffrey's death."

"And so not long afterwards," Miss Lydia continued, "my father, Sir Hugo Mompesson, bought the estate from James in the honest belief that he had a clear title to it."

"But in fact," I said, "Jeoffrey's attorney, a man called Paternoster, had misappropriated the codicil."

"Is that who it was!" Miss Lydia exclaimed.

"He confessed on his deathbed to Mr Escreet," I explained. "He had been bribed by James to do this in order to prevent the entailing of the estate on himself, for that would have interfered with his intention to sell it to your father, Miss Lydia. The Clothiers suspected this and tried to prevent probate. But Paternoster, with a suborned witness, testified that Jeoffrey had revoked the codicil."

"But what is the significance of the codicil now?" Henrietta demanded.

"If it were laid before the court and put in force," I said, "it would retrospectively entail the property on James even these many years later, substituting a base fee in the estate for the fee simple which Miss Lydia's father believed he had purchased. The base fee would terminate when the succession from James failed: that is to say, if I died without an heir for I am the sole surviving heir of James. In that event Sir Perceval and his heirs would lose all interest in the estate. In plain terms, they would be ousted without compensation."

"Then who would inherit it?" Henrietta asked.

"That's the point: it would go to the next remainderman under the entail who is Silas Clothier," I answered. "He has to be living at that time for if he were dead it could not go to his heir."

"And what became of the codicil after Mr Paternoster stole it?" Henrietta asked me.

"It disappeared for many years and I assume that he sold it to someone in the Maliphant family, for it was they who stood to gain the estate if Silas Clothier were dead when the Huffam succession failed. Perhaps their line failed. Do you know, Miss Lydia?"

"No, I haven't the slightest conception."

"Strangely enough," I said, "there was a boy at the school I was sent to whose name was Stephen Maliphant. Though that must have been merely a coincidence. But whatever had happened to the codicil for all those years, someone offered it for sale to my grandfather (in fact, to Mr Escreet) a few months before his death. He purchased it, and it was in order to do so that he formed an alliance with Silas Clothier as part of which my mother was to be forced into marriage with his elder son. However, then things changed," I said, glancing at Miss Lydia who had sighed at my reference to my mother. I went on, trying to suppress all reference to the part she had played at this juncture: "For one thing, my grandfather realized that once it was before the court it put him and my mother in danger from the Clothiers."

"And was your mother forced into that marriage?" Henrietta asked.

"No. In fact, she married the younger brother."

She looked at me with her eyes widening: "So this horrible old man, Silas Clothier, who is endangering your life, is your grandfather?"

"Let me go on with my story," I answered, after a moment's hesitation. "Well, my grandfather — I mean, John Huffam — died shortly after that and the codicil passed into the possession of my mother. She wrote to Sir Perceval a few years later to say that she had it and sent him a copy. And he, realizing that it threatened his possession of the estate, tried to purchase it. However, my mother refused to part with it because she had promised her father to pass it on to her heir. But eventually it fell into the hands of the Clothiers, as I explained in the park. What I don't know is what has happened to it since then."

"I can tell you," said Miss Lydia. "Silas Clothier laid it before the Court of Chancery."

Just what I had guessed!

"I leave it to you," the old lady went on, "to imagine how horrified my nevy and his wife were by that. Since then they have been closeted with Mr Barbellion for hours every week."

"What was the judgement of the Court?" I asked.

"It upheld the validity of the codicil and retrospectively entailed the estate on James Huffam, ruling that the heir in succession to James is the nominal holder of title to the estate."

I needed to take a deep breath for it was a shock. Title to those vast and rich lands which had been owned for centuries by my ancestors was now vested in me. Even though I knew it meant nothing in actuality, it was profoundly exciting and gave me a foretaste of what real ownership would be like.

"That confirms what I had assumed," I said, and explained how Daniel Porteous and Emma had lured me into their trap and then led me before the Court.

"I believe," I explained, "that their intention was to establish my identity so that my death would be accepted beyond question."

The other two shuddered and Miss Lydia said:

"You are quite correct. By bringing you before the Court the Clothiers prepared the way for your death to be accepted. It was clear from your appearance that you were very weak, and their counsel stressed this and implied that you had inherited your father's mental alienation. That is why Mr Barbellion tried to prevent the Clothiers gaining custody of you, but since they are your nearest kin, he was only able to obtain a stay of execution. During that period they had you committed to Dr Alabaster's madhouse which you were never intended to leave. However, you foiled their intentions by escaping and they therefore had to come before the Court and confess that you had disappeared. They moved a motion to have you declared dead, and brought on witnesses — a justice of the peace and Dr Alabaster himself — to testify to your poor state of health and to your insanity. The burden of their testimony was that, having absconded from the skilled care of the asylum, you could not hope to live very long."

I smiled at this.

"But the situation is grave, John," she said. "Perceval's counsel naturally opposed this since it would dispossess him immediately, and the Master of the Rolls compromised by ruling that if you could not be found within a certain period you would be declared dead. Upon the expiry of this period, the property will pass immediately to Silas. The court has appointed a Receiver of Rents and is making an inventory of the estate."

As I reflected on this many implications occurred to me.

"What is the period?" Henrietta asked.

"It was four years from that date."

"A little over two years from now," I said. "Well, if the Clothiers and their agents could find me, I wonder what my life would be worth, for Silas Clothier is already a very old man."

Miss Lydia smiled and said: "More than ten years younger than I."

I blushed and faltered.

"You were going to say," she said, "that he cannot hope to live very long. And since under the codicil he must be alive at the moment of your death, the Clothiers will try to kill you even before the time-limit expires."

I nodded.

"They may not need you to be dead," Miss Lydia said, "if they can prove you illegitimate."

I stared at her in horror, wondering what she meant and how much she knew.

"You see, John, the Clothiers have always tried to have your grandfather's service as heir set aside on the grounds that he could not prove filiation for there is no proof that his parents, James and Eliza, were legally married."

I understood what she was driving at now: "Yes," I said, "I remember that Mr Escreet mentioned this."

"No record was ever produced, nor any witness. The Clothiers have been able to produce evidence that James and Eliza lived together for some time before the alleged marriage took place, and that supports their case."

"This explains what Barbellion was looking for the first time I ever saw him!" I exclaimed.

I repeated what Mr Advowson had told me about Barbellion's interest in the records of the Huffam family.

"But the marriage did take place," the old lady said. "I know that for certain, though I cannot prove it."

I stared at her in amazement. Before I could speak I was interrupted.

"Can it really be true that your own family are trying to kill you?" Henrietta asked.

"Why, yes!" I cried, and told them about the way Emma had tried to poison me and about my treatment in the madhouse. Miss Lydia was very upset by this but I thought Henrietta looked a little sceptical.

"If your own family are trying to kill you, I don't understand why you are safe in this house," she said.

I looked at Miss Lydia and she nodded and said: "There is something we have kept from you. John, tell her."

So I explained how Jeoffrey Huffam had made a new will on his deathbed when he heard of the birth of my grandfather and realized that he now had the means to disinherit his profligate son by entailing his property on the infant.

"However," I continued, "after his death Paternoster substituted the earlier will for the later one, first removing the codicil from it as I've explained. And he acted for the same reasons, for if the entail had stood, James would have been a mere pensioner of his own son."

"And presumably this Paternoster was the villain," put in Miss Lydia, "who sold the will to my father?"

"That is so," I confirmed.

"Your father bought it?" Henrietta exclaimed.

"Indeed he did, and for a very large sum. For he realized that since James had had no title to sell, this meant that his own title would be void if it ever came to light. I only learned of it long after my father's death, and it seemed to me to be a shameful act."

"Yes," Henrietta cried. "A mean, unjust deed! But what has this to do with us? It all happened many years ago. What has this to do with your being in this house, John?"

I wondered if I dared to tell her that only by regaining the will could I make myself safe from the Clothiers.

Before I could speak, however, Miss Lydia, holding her with her glittering eyes, said: "Do you conceive how I thought it right to try to restore justice?"

"Yes I see that, but what could you do?" Henrietta asked. "Your father must have destroyed the will?"

"Indeed he did not and it passed into the possession of your guardian."

Henrietta started.

"Oh yes," the old lady went on. "Perceval has continued to profit from this act of injustice. And though I suppose it seems ancient to you, yet it all happened when I was already nearly ten years older than you are now. And as John knows, it blighted and even shortened the lives of his grandfather and his parents. But as you will hear, it has continued to exercise its baleful effect and has profound consequences for both of you."

She spoke so gravely that I asked: "What can you mean?"

"You wonder that my father and after him my brother and now my nevy did not destroy the will?"

"Yes," I said. "That has long puzzled me. It could only destroy their right to the estate, surely?"

"Let me try to explain," the old lady said. "I have told you that the probate of the original will was unsuccessfully disputed, and this was done by the Clothiers — Mr Nicholas Clothier and his son, Silas. Well, after the failure of that case, they instituted a Chancery suit which has continued down to this very day. They were now disputing the validity of my father's purchase of the Hougham estate from James, and he feared — and after him Augustus and then Perceval continued to fear — that one day they would be successful. And in that event the only way to save the Mompessons' title to the property would be to produce the will."

"Why should he and my guardian have feared that they would lose the suit?" Henrietta asked.

"And how would producing the will save them?" I added.

"Oh dear," said Miss Lydia, "I am explaining it badly. The reason is that when Mr Paternoster sold my father the will, he quarrelled with him over the price, and as an act of spite he warned him afterwards that the disputed codicil was also still in existence."

I nodded at this since I had long known about the wretched codicil, but Henrietta looked puzzled again.

"However, my family were never sure that it really did exist and that this was not just a cruel joke. Indeed, I believe it was first known for certain that the codicil existed only when your poor mother, John, sent a copy of it to my nevy in support of her claim to the annuity."

"But I still don't understand how the will could protect them!" I protested.

"Well," the old lady went on, "to explain that I have to tell you a great deal of ancient history."

It was not to be, however, for Henrietta glanced up at the clock on the mantelpiece and exclaimed: "Gracious heavens! Look at the time! John, you must go this minute."

There was no gain-saying this and so, with agreement from both sides that we would try to meet at the same time the following Sunday, I left the room and returned to my quarters.

CHAPTER 98

I thought about Henrietta over and over again during the days that followed. Why did I care so much that she might disapprove of my having carried out the burglary and of what I was planning now? I hated not having told her the whole truth and resolved to tell her as much of it as I dared. Why was her opinion of me so important? Why was I so hurt and angry that she appeared not to believe me when I told her that the Clothiers and their agents had tried to kill me? I must be in love with her. Was this what was meant by "love"?

The next Sunday when I came to Miss Lydia's room I found only Henrietta there. We were embarrassed at finding ourselves alone.

"My great-aunt will be along soon," she said. "Aunt Isabella has asked to see her."

I seated myself. I had the chance to plead my cause and I wanted to confess to my part in the burglary:

"Henrietta, you wanted to know why I am in this house. You have heard how the will was misappropriated and my grandfather cheated. I am his heir. Don't you think I have the right to the estate?"

"Are you not confusing legality with justice?" she asked. "Are you not making the mistake of believing that you can found a moral claim upon the quirks and accidents of the law? By doing that you are doing what you say the Mompessons and the Clothiers have done, though I grant you that your legal and moral claim may be better than theirs."

"There is no comparison! Jeoffrey Huffam wished to entail the property upon his grandson's heirs and that wish was illegally and immorally frustrated!"

I now told her much of what Mr Escreet had told me, but the consequence was not what I had hoped.

"I perceive," Henrietta persisted, "that in making that final will Jeoffrey Huffam was breaking his undertaking to Silas Clothier's father, disinheriting his own son, and getting his revenge against members of his family with whom he had quarrelled. Do you really believe that such a man's last will should carry any moral weight?"

I said nothing and she went on: "And, after all, Sir Hugo bought the estate in good faith, so do you have a moral right to dispossess his heirs even if you have the legal right?"

"But when he found out about the purloined will he did nothing. And Sir Perceval has continued to suppress it, thereby cheating my family."

"But what could you expect? To have admitted the truth would have meant ruin: the loss of the property and the purchase-money."

"Of course you defend Sir Perceval and Lady Mompesson," I exclaimed.

Could it be that her motives were simply self-interested? That she could not forget that the prosperity of her guardians was to her own advantage? Did she even have designs on David?

She flushed: "I care nothing for them. They have never been kind to me. I have never understood why they adopted me."

"Don't you at least feel gratitude?"

"Gratitude? For charity offered out of mere duty and concern with appearance? For I can only assume that those were their motives."

"Then why do you defend them?"

"They have their rights."

Her attitude was perverse.

"But what of mine?" I protested. "Here I am penniless, barely educated, and friendless. What hope have I of being able to live not merely as a gentleman but in any tolerable way at all? Not only that, but now that the codicil is in force my life will be in danger for as long as Silas Clothier lives. Only by regaining the will and overturning the codicil can I become safe. Do you really deny that I have the right to do that?"

"I understand!" she cried. "That is why you are in this house! You intend to steal the will!"

So the secret was out now. Nothing was to be gained by denying it.

"To regain it!" I cried. "To restore it to the Court to which it belongs."

"Then use the law to do it!"

"That would require money," I objected. "And anyway, Sir Perceval would destroy it rather than surrender it for, as your aunt and I have explained, if it came to light he would forfeit the estate."

"Are you certain? For in that case I don't understand why he has kept it?"

"Neither do I. Your aunt was going to explain that last time."

There was a pause while she scrutinised me.

"Why are you so set upon this?" she demanded suddenly.

"I have told you!"

"No, I mean what are your real motives? You talk of rights but I believe you want revenge."

"Revenge?" I repeated in astonishment. "No. I simply want Justice. I want to make order and meaning out of the randomness and injustice I have seen all my life. If I cannot do this then nothing has any meaning. If the Mompessons can lie and cheat to obtain and keep their wealth, then why should any other criminal be condemned? All that my family has endured — murder, the madhouse, what was done to my mother — all these things will have counted for nothing if I cannot regain the will."

"This is the language of revenge," she said passionately. "I understand, for I too have reason to hate my guardians. Oh, not so potent as yours, nothing like."

"What do you mean?" I demanded.

"Oh, it's of no matter now. And yet you saw how Tom tormented me that summer at Hougham. Though in some ways Tom is the least unkind of them. But to desire revenge is to repay one injustice with another."

"But in my case it is not the wrongs that I, but that others whom I loved, have suffered that inspire me."

"Then if it is not revenge," Henrietta said sadly, "it is vengeance, and that is much more insidious. For you can so easily disguise your motives as the desire for justice."

"That is not true!" I exclaimed, and without reflecting I blurted out: "Your great-aunt had no desire for revenge."

"What can you mean?"

There was nothing for it now but to tell her the truth: "Do you remember how I said last week that when my grandfather had bought the codicil, he intended to lay it before the Court but then suddenly changed his plans? The reason was that someone in this household wrote telling him about the will and promising to obtain it. That was Miss Liddy and she was as good as her word, though somehow the will was returned to your guardian."

Henrietta was clearly dumbfoundered.

She shook her head: "Great-aunt Liddy could do such a thing?"

At that moment Miss Lydia entered the room: "I am glad you are still here, John," she said gaily, smiling at both of us. "My niece sent word that she wished to see me which is most unusual, so I went to her room but she did not come. It is most puzzling. Perhaps Perceval's surgeon is with her. I know he was weaker today. He has been steadily worsening since his seizure last week."

She broke off when she saw the way Henrietta was looking at her. She glanced at me as if for an explanation.

"Miss Liddy," I said, "I'm afraid I told her how you helped my grandfather."

"And you are shocked," she said to Henrietta. "My dear, I did it because I thought it a shameful thing that my father had done. I had long contemplated it but I only acted at last because by doing so I could save a young woman from a terrible fate."

Henrietta looked at her in surprise.

"Did you not explain, John?" the old lady asked. "You remember, Henrietta, that John's grandfather was trying to force his daughter into marriage with the odious elder son of Silas Clothier? That is something that I could not permit. By offering him the will, I rendered the match of no advantage to him."

"If ever it could be right to steal," Henrietta said slowly, "then I suppose it was so then."

"'Steal'! Don't use that word!" Miss Lydia cried.

"No, 'regain' is the right word," I said. "It was right then and it is right now. For by laying the will before the Court I become the outright owner of the estate, and that is the only way I can be safe from the Clothiers." Watching Henrietta closely I said: "Therefore I shall go ahead with an attempt to regain the will."

"Yes," cried Miss Lydia. "Of course that is what you must do!"

"Why," Henrietta asked, "can you not declare yourself to the Court as the Huffam heir before the time-limit expires and put yourself under its protection?"

"As I did before when I was handed over to Daniel Porteous and then Dr Alabaster?" I objected. "You don't seem to believe me when I say that I am in peril until old Clothier is dead."

"If your safety is your main concern," Henrietta said, "then why do you not simply allow yourself to be declared dead by the Court?"

I was taken aback.

"Then your guardians would lose the estate," I pointed out, "for it would pass immediately to Silas Clothier."

She nodded. Then her motives were not simply mercenary as I had feared, for if the Mompessons were bankrupted she would be destitute. And by accepting this suggestion I would prove to her that mine were not mercenary either. Miss Lydia was watching me closely and gravely with her piercing blue eyes.

"I believe that is the right course," I said. "I will give up this degrading work and try to find a place worthier of me, though with no money and scant education I have little hope."

Henrietta smiled and, leaning forward, pressed my hand: "I am sure that is the honourable solution."

"My dear children," said Miss Lydia, "I have something important to tell you in the light of which I am certain you will change your minds."

Henrietta and I looked at each other in alarm.

"What can you mean, Great-aunt?" Henrietta asked.

"It is the question of the purloined will that I was about to explain to you last week when we had to break off. Since it establishes that the Mompessons have no title to the estate, then why has my nevy — like his father before him — kept it instead of destroying it?"

"This is the very point that has puzzled me ever since I learned of its existence," I said. "For they ran the risk of its being used to dispossess them. What possible benefit could it confer that made that risk worth taking?"

"It's all so complicated that I don't know if I can ever make it clear," the old lady began with a droll smile. "My poor head begins to ache when I start to think about it. I believe I understand it until I start to ponder on it and then the explanation goes flying off in a thousand different directions in a shower of words: codicils and judgements and instruments and orders and all those other ugly terms associated with the law and Chancery that have cursed our families for more than half a century. But first I have to explain a lot of family history so that you will understand why it is that as soon as the Huffam line is declared extinct, my nevy will produce the purloined will."

"And so it will supersede the codicil!" I cried. Then as the further implications struck me, I shouted: "So Silas Clothier will have no claim!"

"That is so," the old lady replied. "But what do you imagine will become of the estate?"

"I don't know," I said, "since I do not know what the will specified beyond the fact that it entailed the property on my grandfather. But surely the estate will no longer belong to your nephew?"

"You are right," Miss Lydia agreed smiling with pleasure at the game. "This is better than 'Speculation'. And I hold the highest trump."

"But dear Great-aunt," Henrietta protested, "if that is so, then why have they kept the will?"

"Because of the identity of the next entailed heir to whom, under its terms, the estate passes once the Huffam line has been declared extinct."

Henrietta and I looked at each other blankly and then at the old lady.

"Who is that?" I asked. "Isn't it the Maliphant heir as in the codicil?"

"No," the old lady said. "The terms of the entail in the will are quite different from the entail created by the codicil." She paused. "You see, by then Jeoffrey Huffam had quarrelled with his nevy, George Maliphant, and so the will created an entirely new situation in which, if the entail upon his grandson, John Huffam, and his heirs failed, then it went to another branch of our family. The surviving heir of that branch would become the absolute owner under the will."

"Who is that?" Henrietta and I both asked.

"Wait," she said, glancing down for a moment. "I will tell you everything. It all goes back many many years to when I was about the age of you children. And that is nearly seventy years ago." Seeing my surprise she said: "Yes, I am as old as that. (Why, I am almost as old as this house, which was built for my father.) I have never told you this story, Henrietta, for it is too painful. But you should know it. You are old enough now." She paused for a moment with her head lowered again, then raised it and went on: "When my grandfather, Jeoffrey Huffam, added the codicil to his earlier will in 1768 he was on bad terms with almost all of his kin. He was not on any sort of terms then with my parents nor with his niece, my Aunt Amelia. George Maliphant was the only member of his family he was still speaking to. But then he quarrelled with him over this business that I have never had the courage to admit to you, Henrietta." She hesitated. "I fear I was the unwitting cause of the quarrel between my grandfather and my parents, for he had agreed to name their heir as his own since at that date he had no son. But because I was not a boy and therefore would not inherit my father's title, he refused to do this."

As she went on, Mr Escreet's account of these same events came back to me.

"Then a little later his own son, James, was born," she continued. "The rift was not healed and he never became fond of me as I grew older. I was believed to be 'queer'. And that reminded him of ... There was madness in our family, you see. It angered him that I befriended my aunt."

"You mean your great-aunt Louisa?" Henrietta asked.

"No," the old lady said with distaste. "I never loved *her*. But when I was about fifteen I grew to be very fond of my aunt Anna who was my father's younger sister. She was considered somewhat odd. She had had an unhappy life and at that time lived at Hougham where I used to spend the summers. The Fortisquinces were living in another part of the Old Hall."

"I remember," I said. "Martin Fortisquince and my grandfather were brought up there."

"My dear child, this was long before either of them was even born. I am speaking of his parents, his wicked mother and his poor father."

She seemed to be looking into the distance at something that Henrietta and I could not see. Then she began to speak in a soft rapid undertone:

"There was a young man whom I wanted to marry called John Umphraville. He was in holy orders. His sister, Eliza, was your great-grandmother, John, and your grandfather was named for his uncle. (That is why I took a particular interest in the poor boy.) So you, too, are really named for John Umphraville. The Umphravilles were an ancient land-owning family who had held property in Yorkshire for almost as long as the Huffams, and certainly much longer than the Mompessons, for we are quite upstarts compared with you, John. But they had lost most of their lands and all of their money, for the father of John and Eliza was a drunkard and a spendthrift who, having driven their mother to an early death, himself died while they were still children. I met John in Town — in fact, in this very house. But my grandfather, Jeoffrey Huffam, and therefore my parents, opposed the match. There was a great to-do about it and it was involved with the business of your great-grandparents' marriage, too, John. So you see, both John and Eliza were rejected by my parents and grandfather. But John was strongly in favour of James marrying his sister, and since Jeoffrey was opposed to this match he was even more furious with John."

"I know about this," I said. "Mr Escreet explained to me that Jeoffrey Huffam believed that Eliza was not rich or well-born enough to be allied with his family."

She hesitated and then said: "Yes, that is part of the truth. But there were other obstacles." Her hands were moving restlessly across her lap. "Although he was the only son and the family very old and respectable, he had the most meagre expectations. And there were ... other difficulties."

Here she glanced at me timidly.

"His sister ... that is to say. My father. In short ... "

She faltered and for several moments tried to speak but failed.

"In short, my parents prevented our marriage."

She broke off and, remembering that she had mentioned on an earlier occasion that the man she had wanted to marry had died, I did not dare to ask her more.

"On the other hand," she went on, "the marriage of James and Eliza went ahead."

"Can you be so sure?" I asked. "For that marriage has been disputed by the Clothiers."

"I am quite sure. One day you must hear the full story, but the long and the short of it was that my great-aunt Louisa turned against me in order to make favour with Jeoffrey on behalf of her daughter, Amelia. The only person who supported John and me was my uncle George, and this was because he had a particular affection for me and also for John who was a *protégé* of his. And that cost him his place in Jeoffrey's last will, for whereas in the codicil the entail passed to him and his heirs, in the new will it passed to Amelia and hers."

She ended as if her point was made but Henrietta and I looked at each other in bewilderment.

The old lady resumed: "I see you do not know your own ancestry, Henrietta. Do you not know that your great-grandmother's name was Amelia? She was Jeoffrey's niece and she married a gentleman called Mr Roger Palphramond."

Henrietta grew pale.

"Yes," said Miss Lydia. "You, my dear, are the Palphramond heir and will become the owner of the Hougham property on the failure of the Huffam succession." She continued gently: "I am afraid that it was for that reason and no other that my nevy and his wife adopted you and became your legal guardians."

"I don't understand," Henrietta muttered.

"I do," I cried. "They wanted to be able to produce the purloined will, and the heir that it created as well!"

"Precisely," the old lady said and then, addressing herself to Henrietta, she continued: "Have you never wondered why they left you in poverty and neglect with your uncle's widow for the first few years after your parents' death?"

"Yes, often and often."

"You see, it was only after John's mother had confirmed that the codicil really existed by sending them a copy, that they sought you out and took you into their family."

How strange that my mother's action should have had such profound consequences for a child of whose existence she surely knew nothing!

"But why?" Henrietta asked. "What could they gain by it?"

The old lady shook her head gravely: "If it ever became necessary, they would marry you to one of their sons."

"Marry my cousin!" Henrietta cried.

I scrutinised her face. She had flushed. Was she dismayed at the prospect?

The old lady reached across to Henrietta's chair and gently took her hand: "My dear, I'm afraid that they have begun to execute this design."

"But he wishes to marry that ugly heiress!" Henrietta gasped. "He does not care for me."

"But my dear," Miss Lydia said, still holding Henrietta's hand; "you have leapt to the wrong conclusion. The bridegroom intended for you is not David but his brother."

Henrietta drew back with a cry of horror and covered her face.

Now this was real horror!

"That is, I believe," Miss Lydia went on, "why he has been ordered back here in the last few days. That, and his father's recent attack."

"But surely," I said as I gazed from one to the other, "if Henrietta were to inherit the estate while still unmarried, she would be rich and independent. How could they force her to marry?"

Henrietta looked expectantly towards Miss Lydia who smiled sadly, still watching her great-niece: "They will not produce the will until you have been forced into this marriage. And since Chancery some years ago appointed them as your guardians (together with Mr Barbellion), you will be completely under their control until you attain your majority; and remember that in the case of real property, the age of majority for a woman is twenty-five. You will find them very persuasive. And they will make it clear that it will be a marriage only in name. That will be as much in their interests as in yours, Henrietta."

Henrietta looked down blushing.

"There is division amongst them about how to proceed," Miss Lydia went on. "It is Lady Mompesson and Mr Barbellion who, together with David, are anxious to implement this design, but Sir Perceval has been holding out against it. Oh, only because he believes marriage to David would be a surer means of safeguarding the family's interests, and he objects to the young woman David has chosen for his bride. (He says he could not abide another such marriage in the family after his great-aunt Sophia marrying Nicholas Clothier!) He has not been permitted to know how deeply in debt David is, and therefore how desperately he needs money, for David and his mother have kept this from him. But this is why they are determined that he will marry the heiress, and now that my nevy is so ill I believe they will have their way."

"But what advantage would such a hideous marriage afford them?" I asked, and Henrietta removed her hands from her face to listen.

"Nothing less than continued possession of the estate," Miss Lydia replied. "For as you know, when a woman marries, her property becomes vested in her husband."

"But then," I objected, "Tom would have the title to the property!"

"Tom will be declared *non compos mentis* immediately after the marriage and his property will be vested in a trust controlled by his parents and his brother. Mr Barbellion is a past-master in the design of such arrangements whose sole purpose is to deprive one member of a family of his property in favour of the others on the pretext of lunacy. It is a flourishing branch of Chancery business. In effect, they will continue to own and enjoy the estate as before. Tom will either be sent abroad or, more likely, be confined to a madhouse — and there will be no heirs. Consequently the entail will cease at your death, Henrietta, and the property will pass by the terms of the trust to David or his heir."

"Then that explains," I exclaimed, "why my mother's request for help when she came to this house was refused by Sir Perceval: knowing by then that the codicil had been laid before Chancery, he had already decided to implement this hideous project and therefore had no need for my mother to remain alive."

"No," Miss Lydia said. "That is wrong. He did not turn her away. It was always in my family's interests that your mother and yourself should remain alive to block the effect of the codicil."

Remembering my mother's account, I knew she was wrong but did not pursue the point. I reflected that if they had decided to produce the will, then they actually needed my mother and myself to be dead since under its terms our claim took priority over Henrietta's.

"I will never consent to such a marriage!" Henrietta exclaimed.

"And this project assumes that I have been declared dead!" I cried. "But if I come forward now and declare myself to the Court after all, then there is no danger of the estate passing to Silas Clothier."

Miss Lydia said nothing but Henrietta shook her head and said: "No, for you have already said that this would put you in danger. I will not buy my own safety at that price."

So she did accept that my enemies had tried to kill me! Or was she mocking me? I was in a quandary for if I played down the danger now she would think I had been melodramatising earlier.

As I tried to find an answer Miss Lydia said: "You will never be safe, Henrietta. Now that the codicil is in force, Isabella and David will not stake everything on John's surviving since they know how determined his enemies are to kill him. They will persevere with their plan to force you into this marriage so that they can produce the will if it becomes necessary." She turned to me: "So by coming forward you would merely put yourself in danger without helping Henrietta."

"There is only one way for you to be completely safe," Henrietta said to me. "You must die."

I started and she flushed and said: "I mean, of course, that you must let yourself be declared dead."

"But then you'll be forced into this marriage!" I exclaimed. She shook her head and I said angrily: "In that event the Clothiers will inherit! I can't let that happen." Another implication occurred to me: "Your guardians will be ruined and you will be left penniless!"

"Is poverty so terrible?" Henrietta asked.

"Yes," I answered. "And you are at least young. Can you ask your great-aunt to be evicted from the house in which she has spent all her life?"

"I have a little annuity left me by my father, and it is yours to dispose of, my dear," the old lady said to her. "Unfortunately, it is only fifty pounds a year and it dies with me, but I might be able to sell it."

"I forbid it!" Henrietta cried.

"You see how powerless we are without money!" I exclaimed, and the bitterness of my outburst took me by surprise. "All my life the lack of money has robbed me of my freedom. Think what we could do if only we had money."

Both of them were watching me intently, Miss Lydia nodding her head vigorously and Henrietta gazing at me thoughtfully.

As far as I was concerned, the decision was clear: "Then if I can neither come forward nor let myself be declared dead," I said, "I must get the will back myself."

Henrietta flushed but the old lady cried out with delight: "Yes! Heaven be thanked! There's the Huffam spirit! I hoped you would say that."

"If I succeed, Henrietta, then your guardians lose everything to me and there would be no advantage in forcing you into this marriage. You would be free to marry whom you chose."

We gazed at each other for a long moment.

"So it comes back to that, does it?" she said slowly. "Well, I wonder what your motive really is or if you understand it yourself. If your purpose is to help me, then I am all the more opposed to your stealing the will. It is not necessary, for I can resist being forced into marriage."

"So you say now," Miss Lydia cried, "but my dear child, I have heard that before. I know only too well what can be done."

She spoke with such force that we both looked at her curiously.

"What can they do to me?" Henrietta asked. "They cannot beat me or starve me. Or if they do I can run away."

"My child," Miss Lydia cried, "I know what they can do. They can do terrible things. Don't believe you can withstand them. I believed that once and I was not as young as you are now."

"Dear Great-aunt, pray don't distress yourself."

"You must let John get the will back. That is the only way you will be safe."

"Yes, for I will be rich," I said. "And so we will all be safe."

Henrietta looked at me mournfully: "When you say that you make me worried," she said. "I can accept poverty for myself but by advising you to give up the idea of stealing the will and to pretend to be dead, I am suggesting that you renounce the chance of great wealth. Am I asking too much of you?"

I could not answer for I was in a dilemma. If I said I cared nothing for the inheritance I would earn her good opinion but leave her to her fate, whereas if I said I wanted the estate for itself she would despise me but allow me to steal the will and thereby save her. In this torment of indecision I wondered what truly I did feel about my claim to the property? Was it greed and nothing better that motivated me? Surely not. I had such plans for it. And yet I now began to feel unsure of what I should do.

At this moment Miss Lydia, looking suddenly much older, rose from the sopha, crossed to Henrietta's chair and knelt at her side. Looking earnestly up into her face she said:

"You must go away from this house. Immediately. This very night."

"My dear Great-aunt, you are alarming me. There is no necessity for that."

"You will need money," she cried. "It always comes back to money, doesn't it? Just as the boy says."

Henrietta glanced reproachfully towards me.

Miss Lydia took the girl's hands in both her own and began playing restlessly with them: "I only wish I could give you some, but you know I have never had any."

"Dear Great-aunt, I am not going away. Please rise."

"All I've ever had is the annuity on the estate, but I have some good things that I can sell or — what is the right word? — pawn. Things people have given me." She began looking distractedly around the room. "Look, that piece of china was left me by my poor aunt, Anna. It might be worth a few guineas. And there is that clock on the mantelpiece. And I have some jewels. Oh, only paste, I'm afraid. I was so plain and so queer when I was a girl that nobody gave me anything much. Only dear John."

"Don't distress yourself, Great-aunt," Henrietta begged, trying to stand up and pull the old lady to her feet.

"It's all to do with money!" Miss Lydia cried, gripping Henrietta's gown and gazing passionately up at her. "That was why they wouldn't let John marry me. My darling girl, I can't bear to see your life blighted too."

At that moment there came a knock at the door. It was instantly thrown open and a strange man stood on the threshold. I quickly stood up, but the new arrival must have seen that I had been seated on the sopha. However, his gaze was drawn to the even stranger sight of Miss Lydia still on her knees before Henrietta's chair.

"I beg your pardon," he said softly.

The old lady started at this and slowly began to get to her feet with Henrietta's assistance. Meanwhile I had realized that the newcomer was not an entire stranger to me.

He withdrew his gaze from the other two and, while Miss Lydia smoothed down the rumpled folds of her gown and rearranged herself on the sopha, kept his eyes on me with a thin smile that was not intended for my benefit.

At last Miss Lydia spoke, panting slightly but with admirable dignity: "This is a very unceremonious introduction, Mr Vamplew. I think you should have waited for my permission before you entered. I was hardly even aware that you were in Town."

He now withdrew his gaze from me and directed it towards her: "I beg your pardon for surprising you, Miss Mompesson. Mr Tom has returned because of the illness of his father."

"Oh well, no matter," she stammered. "We were just getting this boy to move the table so that we could play a hand of whist."

Mr Vamplew smiled slyly: "It was because I was so preoccupied with the gravity of my news that I entered so abruptly. The tidings have clearly not yet been brought to you." He paused as if calculating his effect: "I regret to inform you that Sir Perceval was gathered to his ancestors about an hour ago."

Henrietta gripped her great-aunt's arm and, involuntarily, looked at me.

Mr Vamplew followed her gaze with interest.

"This is grave news indeed," Miss Lydia said and I saw her patting Henrietta's arm reassuringly. "I had feared this event."

"He was carried away by an apoplexy," Mr Vamplew added.

As if suddenly remembering my presence Miss Lydia said distantly: "That is all, John. I mean to say, Dick. You may go now."

I bowed slightly and made to leave the room. Mr Vamplew stood aside for me, watching me closely as he did so.

Just before I reached the door I heard Miss Lydia say: "I would have asked you, Mr Vamplew, to do me the honour of taking tea with me, but under these sad circumstances ... "

"Oh quite, Miss Mompesson," Mr Vamplew said smoothly. "I perfectly understand and you are very kind to have thought of saying so."

By now I was out in the passage and could not resist glancing back. Mr Vamplew was closing Miss Lydia's door behind him but he turned his head and stared directly at me. I should not have looked back, but probably the harm had already been done for it seemed to me to be almost certain that, his attention having been drawn by the sight of a hall-boy seated like a guest on the sopha, he had recognised me from the night of the burglary. As I descended the back-stairs I speculated, in an anguish of uncertainty, as to whether he had or not. I was almost certain that he had, and so, almost with a kind of impatience, I waited for the consequences. I expected him to alert Mr Thackaberry and for both of them to appear in the scullery, armed and accompanied by two or three of the footmen. Should I therefore flee from the house while I had the chance?

It was, as it happened, the usual time to meet Joey so I went out into the dark mews-lane. As I waited, walking up and down to try to keep warm, I heard the sound of hammering from our house: the hatchments were being erected to mark Sir Perceval's death.

Dared I go back and risk arrest and trial? If I did not, then what had I to live for? At the end of half an hour, Joey had not come and now I had to make my choice. I decided to risk staying and returned to the house. As I resumed my duties in the hall and scullery, I found my fellow-servants excited and hushed by the news of the death of the master. They went about their work in a state of shock, preoccupied with the uncertainty about their future.

However, as the minutes and then the hours passed and nothing happened to me, I began to wonder if I had been wrong and Mr Vamplew had not, after all, recognised me. And now I had time to think of the implications of Sir Perceval's death. Above all, what would it mean for Henrietta? That she would be forced into this hideous marriage? And how would it affect my chance of getting the will? Indeed, how would it affect my position in the household? And would the will continue to lie in its hiding-place in the Great Parlour — assuming that it was indeed there? For the succession of David — Sir David as I supposed he must now be referred to — might well bring about so complete an upheaval in the domestic arrangements within the house as to throw all my plans into jeopardy. It became clear to me, therefore, that if I were going to do it, I should undertake my assault on the hiding-place as soon as possible. Yet I still had no idea of how to defeat the lock on the chimney-piece which had baffled Mr Digweed and myself on our earlier attempt. And, of course, I had to think first about Henrietta's opposition to the undertaking.

The evening unfolded as usual: the watchman arrived for his chat with Mr Thackaberry — which lasted longer than usual as if the open-handedness of the family had to be upheld on such an occasion with particular scrupulousness — and the ritual of locking-up began.

As I accompanied the little party around the house, still half-expecting to be denounced at any moment, it occurred to me that Mr Vamplew might be delaying his exposure of me for some reason connected with the confusion now reigning in the mansion. Although it seemed so important to me, in the midst of these great events it might have struck him as of little significance. Yet I still felt that this explanation did not fit with the peculiarly piercing gaze that he had directed towards me.

I learned something of interest, however, for just as we were about to ascend the stairs after securing the street-door, someone hammered at it. Grumbling, Jakeman took the bunch of keys from Mr Thackaberry, went back to the door and inserted one of them in the lock. There was a pause, then he bellowed instructions through the door, and after a few moments it was opened and Sir (formerly Mr) David staggered in cursing him volubly. (He had obviously been marking the death of his father.) So it was a double-lock and could only be opened if the corresponding key was used on both the inner and the outer wards! That meant that even if I could obtain the keys, I could still not get out of the street-door.

That night when I went to my shake-down in the servants'-hall I found it so cold that I ventured into the scullery (for Jakeman had already taken up residence in the kitchen) and sat before the dying fire. As I stared at the flames that flickered languidly around the smouldering coals, I found myself seeing pictures just as I used to when I was a child in Melthorpe. Henrietta's disapproving face came to me and I thought of her hostility towards my intention to regain the will. Had she no sense of Justice? Miss Lydia had, and had striven nobly in pursuit of it when she had tried to return the will to my grandfather. Was she right, however, to defend Mr Fortisquince from my suspicions? Or had it indeed been he who betrayed my grandfather over the will? Perhaps even murdered him? Presumably Miss Lydia defended him because she believed that Peter Clothier was the murderer, and yet I was determined not to believe this if I could help it. Probably, however, I would never establish the truth of what had happened on the night of my grandfather's death.

What a dilemma Henrietta had placed me in! The only way I could rescue her was at the cost of earning her contempt. How dared she accuse me of being motivated by nothing more than revenge! And imply that I coveted the estate! It was not vengeance I sought but Justice, and since that entailed the completion of a pattern in such a way that everyone got what they deserved, then if that meant that some suffered so that others could benefit, this was an incidental effect.

As for coveting the estate, why, I had never thought of anything but the weighty responsibilities that the ownership of such a vast property would impose upon me — and the opportunities to do good. I remembered what Sukey and Mr Advowson had told me about the management — the mismanagement — of the Hougham demesne and the injustices and wastefulness that it involved: the demolitions and evictions, the murderous spring-guns in the preserves, the crumbling walls, and the flooded, ill-drained meadows. And yet it could all be so different: I thought of the charming park with its huge house, the villages of Hougham, Mompesson St. Lucy, Stoke Mompesson and much of Melthorpe, the thousands of acres of rich farm-land, and all the woodlands and streams and commons that encompassed the estate. The Mompessons cared nothing for the land or the people beyond what they could extort from them in the short term. How differently I would manage it! I would dismiss Assinder, the rapacious steward, along with the brutal gamekeepers, and take the management of the estate into my own hands.

As I sat in the cold and darkness in the bowels of the house with the beetles rustling on the floor and the drunken snores of the watchman audible from the kitchen, I drew up schemes for the rebuilding of the cottages, the draining of land, the construction of walls, the fairer management of tenancies, the foundation of schools for the education of the poor, the relief of the aged, and so on. Then the fire finally died and I returned to my hard form in the servants'-hall.

Before I fell asleep I reflected that it was not solely my right to decide what to do. If Henrietta chose to take the risk of being forced into a travesty of a marriage rather than seize the chance to be free to marry whom she chose, then I had to give some weight to that.

CHAPTER 99

All that week the house was in an uproar and it was like a continuous Sunday. The servants were drunk most of the time as if, fearing dismissal, they wanted to enjoy what they could while it lasted. Yet since the mansion was under siege from tradesmen with unpaid bills, only meagre provisions were coming in and the larders and cellar were being emptied. Sir Perceval's funeral took place that Thursday — though of course I saw nothing of it — and this was another occasion for a Bacchanalia.

I longed for the chance to win over Henrietta to my view for I wondered — as I carried coals, brushed boots in that dark and airless hole, and scoured pots in the scullery — what I was doing these things for if not to oust the Mompessons and, as far as was possible, redeem the sacrifice of my grandfather's, my mother's, and Peter Clothier's lives. Because of the changes in the household's routine, however, I found it impossible to meet Henrietta and Miss Lydia the following Sunday. I had another disappointment that evening for though I waited in the mews for Joey for two hours, he once again failed to appear. This meant I had not seen him for several weeks and I was somewhat indignant at his remissness now. Or had he even abandoned me?

It was not until the third week after the occasion last described — the first Sunday in February — that I managed to come to Miss Lydia's room again. (Joey had not come on either of the intervening Sundays.) I found the old lady alone and she explained that Henrietta had been summoned to an interview with her aunt earlier in the afternoon and would come to us afterwards.

"But I am glad that we have this opportunity to talk by ourselves," she said. "Tell me, what have you decided about the will?"

"I want to go ahead, but I don't believe I can in the teeth of Henrietta's opposition."

"You must!" she exclaimed with so much force that I was quite disconcerted. "I know what they will do to her! She is not strong enough to resist."

I studied her face and believed I understood her meaning: "Very well," I said. "As long as she does not positively forbid me."

I could see that the old lady was disappointed by this condition.

"But you don't know her!" she cried. "She *will* forbid you. There is something in her that almost craves to be hurt. Remember what I told you of how she used to wound herself. You must go ahead whatever she says and whatever she makes you promise."

I nodded and was about to speak but at that moment the door opened and Henrietta entered. Miss Lydia and I started guiltily.

"I will secure the lock," said the old lady, "so that none of the servants — nor that odious tutor — can interrupt us."

"You were right, Great-aunt," Henrietta began as she sat down. "Aunt Isabella and David wanted to see me in order to tell me they desire that I should marry Tom."

"And poor Perceval is hardly cold in his grave!" his aunt cried.

"What did you say?" I asked.

"What do you imagine?" she replied. "They told me that it would not be a real marriage, but I still refused to consider it."

"Then," I asked, "do you withdraw your objection to my taking back the will?"

"Certainly not," she replied. "I can resist anything they can do to me."

I looked at Miss Lydia and said: "Then I cannot go ahead."

The old lady cried in anguish: "Oh but you must. All this is my fault. I have not told you enough, Henrietta. I have been selfish. And so you don't understand what will happen. What has happened in the past."

Henrietta and I looked at her in surprise.

She went on: "I told you that my grandfather, Jeoffrey Huffam, quarrelled with most of his family, but I did not tell you why." She paused and seemed to be collecting her strength: "It goes back to the time when my father asked Jeoffrey Huffam for the hand of his elder daughter, Alice, and he refused on the grounds that she was too young. This was many, many years ago. Almost a century. My father believed that he was being repulsed because he was not well-born enough, just as his father had been rejected when he had offered for the hand of Jeoffrey's sister. And he deeply resented this second rebuff to his family who now had wealth and a title and were, he believed, at least the equals of the Huffams who, for all their ancientness and the extent of their lands, had no title and were deeply in debt."

"I know this story," I said. "Mr Escreet told it to me. And I wondered then why Jeoffrey Huffam suddenly changed his mind. It seemed quite out of character that immediately after opposing it he should give his blessing to the match and promise to make the child of the marriage his heir."

"You're right!" Miss Lydia cried. "There was a reason for it, though I fear the story reflects deep shame on some of my nearest relatives. Mr Escreet could not have told you the full story for he could not know it. Well, my father had a younger sister, Anna, a beautiful young woman, but wild and wayward. He knew of Jeoffrey Huffam's reputation for gallantry, even though he was now a reformed man after the excesses of his youth. Your grandfather was now a little past forty and it was widely known that there was scant affection between himself and his wife, for it was a marriage of convenience. So my father threw Anna in his way. Well, I need not dwell upon it. Poor Aunt Anna often told me that she had had no idea of her brother's designs. At first she hated Jeoffrey but he had considerable charm and I fear that it was not long before she became his mistress. This was precisely what my father had hoped, and he now took advantage of his knowledge."

"You mean, he blackmailed him?" I asked, glancing at Henrietta who, in obvious embarrassment, averted her gaze.

The old lady cast her eyes down for a moment and then looked directly at me and said: "I fear so. That is why Jeoffrey consented to the match and agreed to a treaty of marriage upon such generous terms. But it wasn't long until Jeoffrey tired of Anna and cast her off. She became quite wild with grief and despair, it seems, especially when the threat of exposure and ruin loomed." She looked at Henrietta who blushed and glanced down. "For the following year," she went on, "she secretly bore a child. My father and Jeoffrey Huffam took the baby from her against her wishes. Imagine her anguish. Her pain and grief. And then later ... later, they told her it had died."

The old lady broke off and it was some moments before she could continue. As I watched her I reflected that this had happened before even she was born. The grief that was nearly a century old was living again in her and through her in Henrietta and myself.

At last she was able to go on: "Then my father tried to force her into marrying a rich acquaintance of his, but she held out against this. Oh, Henrietta, they did such terrible things to her! At last she was brought to a state of complete mental alienation. All of this had profound consequences. For one thing, this is why my father was on such bad terms with my grandfather. And that is why he used the excuse of my not being a boy to avoid making me his heir. But there were other consequences that affected events many years later when Jeoffrey Huffam opposed the marriage of his son, James, to Eliza Umphraville. I did not tell you the whole truth about that, either."

She turned to me.

"I am afraid, John, that your great-grandfather, James, was a drunken and dissolute spendthrift, although he had great charm. The real reason for my grandfather's opposition to his marriage to Eliza Umphraville was that she had been openly kept by him for some years. He had seduced her when she was hardly more than a child, but she was a very fast young woman who had little regard for modesty. Later on, the fact that she had been his acknowledged concubine was exploited as proof against their ever having married."

"Mr Escreet explained none of this," I said. "But considering that he believed he was addressing the son of James and Eliza, that is hardly to be wondered at."

"Of course. Anyhow, John Umphraville quarrelled with James about his treatment of Eliza and forced him to marry her. Meanwhile Jeoffrey was trying to prevent the alliance, and this is why Jeoffrey hated John: he blamed him for the match. And then something else happened and made Jeoffrey even angrier with him: John and I met at about this time because of this business between James and his sister, and we fell in love. It was because of his sister's disgrace — and also his poverty — that John Umphraville was so unacceptable to my family as a suitor for my hand." She paused for a moment and then went on: "John and I decided to elope and marry. And since John had forced James to agree to marry Eliza, we were to have a double elopement and wedding. John arranged for a clergyman who was a friend of his to come with us and perform the ceremonies."

She stopped and seeing that she was in distress, Henrietta said: "Dear Great-aunt, pray do not continue if it gives you pain."

The old lady smiled and squeezed her hand: "No, my dear. I must tell my story or I will take it with me to the grave."

"And are you sure that they were married?" I asked.

"Quite sure."

"Then where did it take place? No record has ever been found."

"Where should we flee to but Hougham?"

"But there is no church there," I objected. "The church at Melthorpe serves the whole parish which includes Hougham."

Miss Lydia smiled: "That is only partly true. I assure you that James and Eliza indeed married. Let me tell you the story. We obtained two special licences and set off. We guessed that we were being pursued for we knew before we left Town that Jeoffrey had found out our plans and we feared that he had sent some agent of his to prevent both marriages. However, we reached the chapel safely late at night. We entered it very quietly in order not to disturb the Fortisquinces, for they were living at this date in another wing of the Old Hall. James suggested that the two young gentlemen should spin a coin to see which ceremony should be performed first. John protested at this levity but he agreed to do it. He and I were unlucky. My life was determined by the spinning of that coin." She stopped for a moment and then smiled at me: "So you see, I know for certain that James succeeded in marrying Eliza. I was present throughout the ceremony. Indeed, I was a witness."

At these words a thought occurred to me: the record might be in that ancient chest that Mr Advowson showed me which he said had come from the old chapel! Would I ever have the chance to look for it?

Miss Lydia dabbed at her eyes and then went on in an unsteady voice: "As the ceremony was ending we heard a horseman riding up. John ... John went out to see who it was. It must have been the man sent by Jeoffrey."

"Was there a sword-fight?" I asked, remembering Mrs Belflower's story which was being so strangely confirmed.

"I will tell you. I looked out of one of the old windows in the chapel and saw John come into sight below me and then stand amidst a group of trees that stood between the Old Hall and the high ground."

"I know!" I cried. "There are four elm-trees just there planted in a square."

"No, there are five," Miss Lydia said. "They were planted by Jeoffrey to form a quincunx many years before. There is a statue before each of them. And they are oaks."

"It must be the same place," I insisted. "Just beneath the Pantheon!"

"The Pantheon? Do you mean that Greek building just above the Old Hall?" she asked, and I nodded.

"Where you and I met that day, John," Henrietta said.

"I know where you mean," the old lady said, but her next words plunged me back into confusion about whether we meant the same place. "But that is the Mausoleum. It was built by Jeoffrey in order to improve the view from the Old Hall before he decided to abandon it altogether and build the new house. He is buried there."

"Then that is why his name does not appear in the graveyard at Melthorpe!" I exclaimed.

"Go on with your tale, Great-aunt," Henrietta urged.

"As I looked out I could not at first perceive what John was doing. He appeared to be looking at the statue that stood before the tree in the middle. (I should say that the statues were very famous, for though they had been sculpted by a local workman — a man called Feverfew — he was a very gifted mason, and they were considered as good as all but the best Italian work.) Then I noticed that there seemed to be a new figure behind it. It was as if there were not five statues, but six which was quite contrary to the pattern. Then to my amazement it moved and I realized that it was a man. I saw his face full in the moonlight. I did not recognise him. I am sure I would have known him if I had ever seen him. It was such a strange countenance: a big bulbous nose and deep eyes. But most of all I was struck by the expression. I have never forgotten it: such a terrible picture of suffering on such a young face."

She paused and I said: "I believe that very statue now lies in the garden of my mother's cottage in Melthorpe, for she told me how Martin Fortisquince's mother brought it with her when she came to live in that house when she was widowed."

"She was not widowed," Miss Lydia said. "She and her husband were estranged a few months after the events I am speaking of and that is when she went to Melthorpe. It was suspected that she knew something of the stranger. In short, that ... And she believed the statue saved his life. But never mind. She died in childbirth a few months later and her infant, Martin, returned to his father — such a kind, generous man — to be brought up by him at the Old Hall."

There was a silence. How complicated things were! New possibilities occurred to me as a result of these words, and I wondered if I would ever know the truth. Each time I seemed about to grasp it, it receded further.

Then I said: "But I interrupted your story. What happened when the stranger came forward?"

"He drew his sword," the old lady continued in quavering tones. "John did the same and they began to fight. Suddenly a woman came running out from another door of the Hall. She was in a long white dress. I still recall how pale it seemed in the moonlight. Then I realized that it was my aunt, poor mad Anna. I had not seen her for many years and they had not told me that she was living here under the charge of Mr and Mrs Fortisquince. She came up behind the other man and they both turned to look at her for she called something out. Something extraordinary. Then she cried: 'Watch out behind you!' Because of this John must have thought she was warning him that there was another assailant, for he turned his back on his opponent. I saw the man ... he stepped forward and .... He stabbed him."

She broke off and fought against her tears. What had the madwoman cried out? I felt there was something crucial here. Something I needed to know that was being kept from me.

"What was she calling?" I asked, but Henrietta put her hand on my arm and shook her head at me.

The old lady looked up, however, and said with terrible sadness: "She was calling out, 'My son, my son!' She must have taken John for her lost child."

"Of course," I prompted, "it was because she was mad that she forgot that the child had died?"

At this, Miss Lydia suddenly looked very old and terribly frightened.

"What happened then?" Henrietta asked quickly, with a reproachful glance at me.

The old lady wiped her eyes on her handkerchief and said softly: "My parents tried to force me into marriage with a man I loathed. I managed at last to resist."

Henrietta and I stared at each other. What a hideous tale! What struck me most forcefully was the brutality of Jeoffrey Huffam. He had seduced and discarded a young woman, possibly ordered the murder of his granddaughter's lover, and then tried to force her into marriage with a man she hated. This was the man whose last will I had believed I had a duty to uphold! He had written his first will, his codicil, and that final testament in order to frighten, reward, and bribe his heirs. If I no longer had the duty to do it, did I still feel I had any moral right to steal a will that had been made by such a man and with such motives?

At that moment Henrietta said: "Take comfort, dear Great-aunt. I will not try to dissuade John from regaining the will any longer."

Miss Lydia clapped her hands and cried through her tears: "Thank goodness! Oh, Henrietta, I have been so afraid for you!"

So now I had to do it for Henrietta's sake! I felt a profound relief that the responsibility for making the decision was being lifted from me.

"But before I can try," I pointed out, "we have to work out how to open the hiding-place."

"Will you help us, Henrietta?" Miss Lydia asked. "For three heads are better than two, and your young one will be of more use than my poor old one?"

"Don't ask me, Great-aunt. I have withdrawn my prohibition but I have not said that I approve."

"Very well, then you and I, John, will do our best alone. First of all, please explain exactly what happened when you and your poor friend tried to open the hiding-place."

Henrietta looked at me sharply and I blushed. Miss Lydia realized what she had revealed and glanced timidly at her great-niece. There was nothing for it and Henrietta had to hear the whole story. When we had done, she said nothing but looked thoughtful.

So now I began to describe the design of the "quincunx of quincunxes" on the entablature of the chimney-piece which Mr Digweed and I had discovered was a lock, while all the time Henrietta sat with a book in her lap, glancing towards us occasionally. As I went over our actions that night, Miss Lydia found a large sheet of paper and a pen and, sitting at the little round-table, I drew the design of twenty-five quatre-foils.

"There appear to be twenty-five bolts," I explained, "each representing the bud of one of the quatre-foils of the design. We found that each bolt may be drawn out several inches, for we did this to all of them. But nothing happened, and it seems that only certain of the bolts must be withdrawn. I suspect that if any superfluous ones are moved, they serve actually to lock the slab of marble more firmly in place."

"Or do worse than that!" Miss Lydia said and I nodded, not understanding what she meant but anxious to continue.

"So I believe," I went on, "that the solution lies in establishing precisely which combination of bolts should be drawn out."

"The quincunx of roses," said Miss Lydia, "is the device of both the Huffams and the Mompessons, but I am not sure that I have ever seen such an arrangement as this quincunx of quincunxes, as you aptly called it. Though it seems familiar."

"I know the quincunx, too," Henrietta said, looking up from her book; "for it appears on some worthless pieces of china that I inherited from my parents. (Everything of any value was sold before I knew anything of it.) So I suppose it must have been on the Palphramond coat-of-arms, too."

"I believe," Miss Lydia said, "that all the families descended from Sir Henry Huffam — the Palphramond and even the Maliphant families — adopted variants of the quincunx. I have even heard, John, that the Clothiers took it for their blazon when Nicholas changed his name from Abraham and applied for a grant of arms."

"Then this design," I said, indicating my drawing, "appears to me to be a kind of monstrous assertion of the triumph of the Mompesson branch of the family over the rest of it."

Miss Lydia seemed about to speak but Henrietta said, laying down her book: "There is a difference, however. For although it seems that the design of the different quincunxes in each of the family's devices is identical, the colours are not the same, are they?"

"Colours?" Miss Lydia exclaimed. "The correct term is 'tinctures'."

Seeing that Henrietta's point was important, I said: "In the Huffam version of the device — which is surely the original and which I have seen on the family vault in Melthorpe church-yard — the four quatre-foils at the corners have white petals and a black bud, while the arrangement of tinctures of the central quatre-foil is precisely reversed: black petals and a white bud."

As I spoke I took the quill and inked in the appropriate parts of the first figure of the design.

"And," Miss Lydia said, "the Mompesson design is precisely the same except that the central quatre-foil has red petals — 'gules' in the language of heraldry. (Black is 'sable', you know, and white is 'argent'.)"

She likewise inked in the next figure, blacking the buds of the four quatre-foils at the corners as I had done, and then covering with dots the petals of the central one to represent red.

"I remember my father telling me," she went on, "that the original device of the Mompessons was the *crab gules*. He made up a new device by combining the Huffam blazon with it. So our shield has a crab and the quincunx of quatre-foils like the Huffam design, except that the central one is in gules to distinguish — or 'difference' — it. But you know, John, the quincunx of quincunxes represents not the triumph of the Mompessons over the other branches, but the union of the two founding families."

Before I could answer this, Henrietta said: "The tinctures of the Palphramond design are the same as those of the Mompesson one."

"And I believe the Maliphant design is identical to the Huffam," Miss Lydia said.

Henrietta came across to the table and looked over my shoulder: "Then I believe that we are beginning to solve the puzzle."

"Why do you say that?" I asked.

"Because I suspect that the answer to the question of which of the bolts should be withdrawn lies in the different tinctures."

"Yes," I exclaimed. "I believe you may be right."

"I'm only a very foolish old woman," said Miss Lydia smiling, "so I do not understand unless you explain it to me very slowly."

"Well," Henrietta began, "it seems that the petals of every quatre-foil may be black or white or red. But notice that in both designs the bud is always black or white, never red. What I'm suggesting is that this choice may correspond to the possible positions of each bolt: if black it should be withdrawn, if white left in position."

"Or, of course, vice versa," I said.

"Yes, that is true, I'm afraid," Henrietta said. "It must be quite arbitrary."

"I begin to see," Miss Lydia said. "And this is exactly the kind of puzzle that my father used to love, for he had a passion for designs and conundrums and heraldry, and I believe it must have been he who devised this pattern in order to celebrate the alliance of the two families. (Indeed, I'm certain I once saw a memento of the wedding that looked like this.) So if I have understood you, the choice of which part of the design should be which tincture depends on how the three tinctures of the Huffam and Mompesson quincunxes have been incorporated to form this larger design?"

"That is so," I said. "But is there any way we can work that out or is it entirely arbitrary and at hazard?"

"From what I recall of what my father told me, it is a principle of heraldry," Miss Lydia said, "that nothing should be arbitrary. For one thing, the design should be ... What's the word? Like the reflection in a looking-glass?"

"Symmetrical!" Henrietta exclaimed.

"Yes!" I cried. "That is a great help. For the other two designs are merely replicas of the first two. So let me draw them in and let us see what results."

I began to do so but Miss Lydia cried: "Don't make those directly opposite mirror each other. Make the diagonals do so. That is much more like true heraldry."

Seeing that she was right, I added to the design before us so that the first and fifth quincunxes and the second and third reflected each other.

"The difficulty with that," Henrietta pointed out, "is that we have quite arbitrarily assumed that the first quincunx is the Huffam crest and the second is the Mompesson version of it. It might easily be the other way around."

"Surely not," I protested, "for the Huffam crest is the original motif and that family is the more ancient, so that it might fairly be assumed to be the point of departure."

"On the other hand, since it was a Mompesson who devised it," Miss Lydia suggested rather tartly, "one might expect that my family's version of the quincunx would be not the first but the central one."

"Or the Huffams'!" I objected.

"I had no intention of provoking another round in the feud," Henrietta said, smiling, and Miss Lydia and I laughed uneasily. "But if we are right that the other four designs reflect each other, then the central one must surely be different from them in order to maintain the logic of the pattern. And in that case, whether the Huffam or the Mompesson is the first makes no odds, for the tinctures of the buds are white in each case and it is only the petals that differ."

"Yes," I said in excitement. "And that suggests that it is those four central bolts that should be withdrawn."

"Or," Henrietta said teazingly, "that it is they which should not be withdrawn."

I had to admit that she was right.

"In that case," I said, "I could pull out all the 'white' bolts except the central one and then pull that one out. And if that didn't work, try it the other way around."

"No!" the old lady cried, looking at me in alarm. "For there is a rumour that the lock incorporates a device of the kind which the French call a *machine-infernale*. A booby-trap. It was added after your attempt."

"Do you mean it would be triggered if someone tried to force it?" I asked.

"Or," she answered, "if the wrong bolts were withdrawn."

"I see," I said. "And what would be the consequence?"

"I have heard that there is a spring-gun inside which has been adapted from a game-keeper's man-trap."

I recalled what Harry had told me of the fate of his and Sukey's father, and shuddered.

"But I have also been told," Miss Lydia went on, "that it is only an alarm-bell that is released."

"Then we must decide if the central bolt is white like the others or black, so that I know at least whether the bolt should be in the same position as them or not."

"I think it must be black," Henrietta said. "For if it were white then the design of the central figure would be the same as the Mompesson and Palphramond designs which would surely not be right. It will only be different if it is black."

"Yes," I agreed. "But in order to be sure, we need to know how the two original designs are merged in that one."

"I should be able to work that out," Miss Lydia said, laughing, "for I am myself the sole living result of the alliance between the Huffams and the Mompessons. My father had many books and papers concerned with genealogy and heraldry which must still be in the Library. I will hunt through them and try to find a clew."

"But even if we could work it out," Henrietta asked, apparently having quite forgotten her original disclaimer of interest; "how will you manage to get into the Great Parlour?"

"If necessary, I could pick the lock of the door (provided that my friend, Joey, brings me the tool I need), but that might take a long time so it would be better to get the keys. But there is a difficulty in stealing them from the nightwatchman ... "

"Because he hides them!" Miss Lydia exclaimed.

"Precisely," I said. "However, I believe I may be able to secure them, for I have a suspicion about them. But the real difficulty lies in getting out of the house afterwards. I cannot pick the locks of either the back-door or the street-door, and the first-floor windows are now barred."

"But surely if you have the keys you can escape through either door!" Henrietta exclaimed.

"No, for the street-door has a second lock, the key to which is not held by the nightwatchman but only by members of the family."

"That, too, was added after the burglary," Miss Lydia put in.

"And unlocking the back-door would only get me as far as the yard," I continued. "To get into the mews I would have to go through the coach-house and stables which are themselves securely locked at night and, moreover, the coachman and grooms sleep there."

"Then there is no way out?" Henrietta asked.

"By night, no. Therefore if I can find them, I will use the keys to get into the Great Parlour, return them, and wait until the nightwatchman unlocks the back-door to let the laundry-maid in. About two hours after that the coachman unlocks the coach-house and then I can escape."

Henrietta shivered: "You mean you will be waiting inside the house with the will in your possession and the knowledge that at any moment the opening of the hiding-place might be discovered?"

"Yes, it will not be pleasant. But there is little likelihood of its happening at that early hour."

"Why do you believe you will succeed in finding the keys?" Miss Lydia asked.

"Well, when I tried to sleep in the scullery on my first night, Jakeman moved me away from there and yet that is not where he sleeps himself. So I believe that is where he hides them."

"What will you do afterwards?" Miss Lydia asked.

"I will go back to my friends, the Digweeds, and then take steps to lay the will before the Court."

"Be very careful, for my nevy's solicitor, Mr Barbellion, has an intelligencer close to the Court. I have heard them speaking of it."

"Do not fear," I said. "I will not let the will out of my sight until I place it in the hands of the Lord Chancellor himself."

They laughed and Miss Lydia said: "It should be someone almost as elevated. But dressed as you are, you will not get beyond the door-keeper."

"I have a friend I mean to go to who will help me."

"But you must allow me to give you some money," she insisted.

"I cannot accept it," I said, surprised that she had any and guessing that it would be very little.

"Yes, you can. For Henrietta's sake if not your own. And for mine and John Umphraville's."

She opened a small wash-leather-bag which was lying on the table and turned out its contents so that a clinking shower of bright sovereigns scattered across the sheets of paper on which we had attempted to solve the problem of the quincunx.

"Great-aunt!" Henrietta cried. "Wherever did you get this?"

The old lady smiled. "That is fifty-one pounds," she said with modest triumph, putting the coins back.

"But what did you sell?" Henrietta asked and we both looked round the room. I could see none of the usual objects missing, but I knew that not one of them, nor all of them together, could amount to a sum a quarter this one.

"Let that be my secret," said Miss Lydia.

Henrietta looked penetratingly at the old lady who, to my surprise, began to blush.

"I believe I understand," Henrietta said. "Will you not get into terrible trouble? And what will you live on from now on?"

"My dear child, I am a very old woman. I cannot be held responsible for my actions. And as for living, it's a bad habit that people of my age often get into, and I intend to break myself of it before it becomes irremediable."

I thought I began to comprehend and was about to speak when there was a loud knock at the door. We looked at each other in alarm. We had been so engrossed in our conversation that we had heard no approaching tread.

"You must not be found here again, John," Henrietta whispered.

At this moment the door-handle was turned several times.

"Quickly," said Miss Lydia taking my arm and pushing me towards the door into her bed-chamber. "In there. And take the money."

I grasped the bag that she thrust into my hand and hurried into the dark little closet as she closed the door behind me.

After a moment or two I heard a voice I had not heard for many years and that had grown no sweeter with the passage of time:

"Why was the door locked? I suppose you've been encouraging this wretched girl to hold out in her resolve. I think the time may have come to forbid this intercourse between you."

There was a murmur and then the voice came again:

"Leave us, child. Your great-aunt and I have something to discuss in private."

"Very well, Aunt Isabella."

I heard the door into the passage open and close and when Lady Mompesson spoke again her voice was cold with barely suppressed fury: "Well, Miss Mompesson, your most recent outrage exceeds all the others. Are you so foolish as to believe that it could fail to come to my notice? At such a critical juncture with a great deal of wild speculation about the solvency of my husband's estate and my son's indebtedness, it was the worst step that a member of this family could have taken. But then, I suppose that is why you did it. All your life you have sought to damage the interests of your nearest. You, who were born into it, have passed up no opportunity to harm this family, while I who only married a Mompesson, have devoted my whole being to furthering their interests. I presume you never forgave your parents for that scandal which was entirely the consequence of your infamous conduct and which brought shame and humiliation upon them. I know you are obsessed with the desire for revenge. I don't know quite what you imagine your parents did, but the truth is that it died. You were told so at the time and it was the truth."

She paused and I heard a barely audible mumble.

"But to part with it for so little!" Lady Mompesson continued. "Did you not see how that would damage our credit? Instantly all the promissory bills that my son has been so ill-advised as to accept during the last few years, were presented for payment. My husband's own debts and David's post-obits will require new mortgages to be taken out, but already the existing mortgagees are threatening to foreclose. What have you to say for yourself?"

I heard only an indistinct mutter.

"I do not understand you," the harsh voice resumed. "You become more incoherent every day. I can only suppose that this was an act of foolish senility. What could you want with so much money all at once? You have all an old woman could need, haven't you? Well, you have made your bed and now you must lie upon it. Henceforth you may expect no charity from anyone in this house."

There was another pause and then Lady Mompesson resumed: "Either this is a device, or you have really lost your wits. But in either case, you have shewn yourself to be incapable of managing your own affairs and must take the consequences."

I heard rapid steps and then the door slammed.

I lingered for a moment, speculating on something that Lady Mompesson had said. An idea came to me. Was this the answer to why the old lady had been so moved by Anna's story and so evasive about her aunt's connexion with her own? I felt as if the final piece of the puzzle were now in my hands, but because I could not make out the pattern I did not know where it belonged. And I dared not challenge her.

Cautiously I opened the door into the sitting-room, not knowing quite what I would find.

To my relief, however, the old lady's bright eyes were sparkling at me from her flushed face: "Wasn't she angry! I could almost have done it just for that alone!"

"Miss Lydia, what have you done!"

"Brought the whole family upon the parish, I am to believe," she cried in delight. "What stuff and nonsense!"

"I cannot take this money," I insisted, holding it out to her.

"Fiddlesticks!" she cried. "I will be all right. And it is the dearest wish of my heart to see Justice done." She lowered her voice and came forward a few steps to grip my arm: "And to see Henrietta made safe. You will make her safe?"

"Yes, to the best of my ability."

She gazed at me earnestly: "I believe you care for her."

What did she mean? If she meant what I thought, was it true? Under this scrutiny I blushed.

"I thought as much," she said in glee. "And I know she cares for you. (I have suspected for some time that she is in love with someone, and now I know who it is.) Once that will is before the Court, I believe all will be well. Now take that and go before anyone else comes."

"I cannot. I have no pockets and the bag is too big to hide. Let me take just a few coins now."

"No," she said fiercely. "You must take all of it. I don't know how much time is left."

Before I could ask what she meant she had seized my jacket and turned it inside out.

"Look, the lining will serve," she said, tearing it open.

She poured the coins into this makeshift: "Can you take them straight to a hiding-place?"

"Yes," I answered, thinking of the coal cellar.

Very cautiously I opened the door and established that the passage was deserted. I bade farewell to the old lady, but to my surprise and before I knew what she was about, she stretched up and kissed my cheek.

"God speed you," she said, her eyes sparkling.

I went out, squeezing the door shut behind me. As I was making my way along the landing towards the back-stairs, I noticed a door that was half-open. As I passed, it suddenly swung back and I felt myself being seized from behind.

I tried to struggle but my assailant was too strong.

Mr Vamplew's voice hissed close to my ear: "What were you doing with the old tabby?"

"Moving furniture for her."

"For two hours? I saw you go in. And the girl and her ladyship were there, too. What have you to do with them?"

"Nothing."

"Tell me what's afoot or it'll go the worse for you."

As an encouragement to me to speak he tightened his grip and at the same time shook me. To my horror two of the sovereigns were dislodged from the lining and fell. He looked down at them and, still holding me fast, bent and picked them up.

"Did you prig 'em or what?" he asked in surprise.

Calculating my best answer I replied: "She gave them to me."

He put them in his pocket and said: "I know who you are. I remember you from the crack. Are you in league with the old crone to rob the family? Is that why she wouldn't let me fire?"

I said nothing and he whispered: "Cut me in on the fakement or I'll 'peach. Why else do you think I didn't before?"

When I still didn't answer he shook me again and I said: "Yes, Mr Vamplew."

He whispered: "Have you any more?"

To my dismay he began to search the lining with his free hand. But at that moment we both heard someone approaching. He pushed open the door of his apartments behind him and tried to pull me into the chamber, but I struggled and he, realizing that the third party was almost upon us, hissed:

"I'll be watching you. Don't try to gammon me."

He relinquished his hold and I was able to escape. As I hurried through the door to the back-stairs I glanced back and saw Will, carrying a salver towards Miss Lydia's door, looking at me in surprise.

I made my way back to the nether regions and found Bob still in a drunken slumber in the servants'-hall. He would not miss me for a little longer. So, taking a stub of candle from his greasy little closet and lighting it in the scullery, I picked up a scuttle and went down to the coal-cellar. Here, in the only place in the house where I could be fairly sure of being left undisturbed, I removed the coins and counted them over: there were just two missing. I tore out a large piece of the lining of my coat and wrapped them in it. Then I lifted the biggest of the great lumps of coal which it was one of my tasks to break up before carrying upstairs, and in the space left beneath it I placed the package.

As I returned to my duties I wondered if Mr Vamplew would dare to reveal what he knew of me now and guessed not, since he hoped to profit from his secret. It seemed that I was right for after a few hours no-one had come for me. Mr Vamplew's interest in me, however, would make it more difficult to visit Miss Lydia and to carry out my great undertaking.

When Bessie and I had finished the pots and pans I went back to the dark little closet and spent the next twenty minutes working on an old piece of wash-leather I used for cleaning. I clumsily stitched it into a long pouch which I then threaded onto a piece of string. This would carry the sovereigns, and once I had the will I would put it in this and wear it around my neck for safety.

At nine o'clock I saw my chance to sneak into the mews. I collected the money in the cellar, putting it into the pouch round my neck. The chill assailed me once I left the house in my thin garments. To my relief, Joey was waiting for me at the corner of the mews, stamping his feet and hugging himself for it was extremely cold. He thrust into my hand the "spider" — for picking locks — that I had asked him for so long ago.

"I've missed some of the last few Sundays," I said, "because I couldn't get away. But I came last week and the time before that and you weren't here!"

"Been busy," he said sullenly. "And I seen Barney near our crib last week, so I didn't come."

This was worrying, though I had no time to consider it then. Quickly I told him what had happened and, first making sure that in the dark no-one was near enough to see what I was doing, pulled open one of his pockets and emptied the bag of coins into it.

"Do you trust me with all this?" he asked with a sly smile.

"Don't waste time," I said angrily. "First, take what you need for yourself and your mother and father."

"Dad don't need nothing," he said bluntly.

"Don't be proud now that at last I can do something for you," I said. "Then take decent lodgings for me for a month in a good district. Say you're taking them on behalf of a young gentleman who is about to return to London from abroad."

"What name shall I say?"

I reflected for a moment and, remembering from the distant past what I had interpreted as a friendly gesture, I said: "Parminter. And say I will arrive there very early next Monday morning. For if I can work out how to open the hiding-place, I will make the attempt a week today. Now this is very important: buy me some good clothes. You're about the same figure as I, so buy them as if for yourself. And can you meet me here a few hours before dawn that morning?"

He nodded.

"I must go now. How's your father?" I asked as I turned away.

"Died two days arter Christmas," he said flatly. "That first Sunday that you never come."

I turned back but he was already round the corner. As I returned to the house I wondered how long Joey had hung about in the cold out there that day while his mother grieved alone. His family had more than paid their debt to me. Well, once I had come into my rights I would make it up to him and his mother, but there was no time to think of the Digweeds now.

If I was to succeed, however, I still had one crucial task to perform. And so, when I laid myself down for the night, I forced myself to stay awake. A long weary wait of it I had, for Jakeman had to stay up to let Sir David in. At last the young gentleman hammered at the door and I cautiously followed the old nightwatchman as, grumbling to himself, he put down his jug and went to admit him. Both were so intoxicated that it took some time to engage the two keys, during which they cursed each other from opposite sides of the door, the young gentleman more audibly and with a wider vocabulary: "Damn your imper ... imper ... your insolence!" he shouted as the muffled oaths of the nightwatchman reached him in the street.

When Sir David had ascended the stairs, Jakeman went into the scullery and, as I had anticipated, stooped near where I had lain down on my first night there, removed a loose brick from the hearth, and slipped the keys behind it. Then he stumbled off to his usual sleeping-quarters.

Now all was ready for me to make the attempt, if only the solution to the quincunx could be found.

CHAPTER 100

All day I had thought about, and now that night I dreamed about, the quincunx. It came at me mockingly out of the darkness, at one time like a flower whose bud was unfolding in coruscating geometrical designs too dazzling for me to catch; and then like a heart whose centre, as I tried to peer into it, was burning so fiercely that it seemed black, and my aching eyes could not penetrate it.

The next morning — an even colder one than the day before — I overheard Bob telling Will that Mr Thackaberry had given instructions that henceforth Miss Liddy's bell was not to be answered. Then a little later it became known that all the servants were to be addressed by the butler at noon in the servants'-hall. Bessie and I, of course, were not included in this summons and continued with our work while the rest of the staff crowded into the hall.

When the assembly dispersed it was some time before I could even learn what had happened, for the rest of the servants were too busy in lamenting their fate or expressing their relief at being spared to waste time answering my enquiries. Piece by piece, however, I was able to put it together from brief explanations and overheard fragments. The house was to be shut up immediately and the family was to remove to Hougham until at least the beginning of the Season. Certain servants were to accompany them there, others would remain in London on board-wages unless they chose to leave, and yet others were warned that they would be paid off at the end of the week. Mr Thackaberry had read out the three lists, and Bob's name was among those to be dismissed. I ventured into the servants'-hall and found him seated on a form drinking gin and hot water, swearing viciously and complaining loudly to Will and Nellie and some of the others that footmen junior to him were to be kept on.

"I can't understand why Assinder let me be sent out," he kept saying. "It must be a mistake. I could make things difficult for him, and he knows it."

"Oh everybody knows about that," Will said. "You mean that old story of Assinder hiring out the carriage?"

"No I don't mean that," Bob said angrily. "I've got something much better agin him."

"Don't you know," said Ned who had just come in, "Assinder's been dismissed too. He's to be sent away fust thing tomorrer."

"What?" Bob cried.

"Seems her la'ship and Mr David and their man of business reckoned as how he was stealing from 'em," Ned continued; "but old Sir Parsivvle trusted him and wouldn't let 'em do nothing agin him."

"So your pull on him don't count for nothing, Bob," Will sneered.

Bob had turned white with rage and bafflement.

"What was it, Bob?" Nellie asked curiously.

"You might as well know for all the harm it'll do him," he said. "It was three or four year back, one summer. This ooman — lady, I s'pose on'y she was in caggy togs — come to the street-door while I was on hall-duty. The thing was, she was in custody of a sheriff for she was being held on a warrant. In course I told her to go round the back but she said she was fambly or something. I couldn't make much of it for I believe she had the sun in her eyes, or something worse. Well, I went and told Assinder for none of the fambly was at home. And he come and seen her in the library while the sheriff stood out in the hall. And arter a few minutes she come out and went off agin singing the Black Psalm. Then Assinder told me never to say nothing about it to nobody and give me five sovereigns."

"Five!" the others exclaimed. "Why, it must have been something important."

I knew what it was. I hurried out of the room into the dark passage for I needed to be alone to think over what I had heard. So it seemed that Assinder had taken it upon himself to turn my mother from the house in tears without telling his employers. But why? This only made sense if he was working on behalf of the Clothiers! Then he was the agent they were believed to have in the Mompessons' trust! What were the implications of that? And if it were true that the Mompessons had not turned my mother away, then had I the right to act against them in the way that I was intending?

At that moment Will came out of the servants'-hall and I asked him (for he was one of those being kept on board wages), what would happen to me.

"To you?" he jeered. "You're out, too, in course, along with Bob. Bad cess to him for a mean scrub."

Now that the household was breaking up, no-one felt constrained to conceal their real feelings.

"When is the house to be shut up?" I asked.

"He's paid up until Saturday, but you might both be sent out of the house before then."

He looked at me curiously and remembering that he had seen me being accosted by Vamplew, I asked no more questions but turned and hurried into the scullery.

Clearly I had to bring forward the attempt to regain the will if I was going ahead with it! My fear was that I would be dismissed that very day, for I foresaw that Bob might have high words with the butler and be sent out of the house instantly. And there was another danger: would the Mompessons take the will with them to Hougham? Clearly the quincunx had to be solved without delay.

By the time the hour came for Bob and myself to accompany the locking-up party, he was in a suppressed drunken rage and was so insolent to Mr Thackaberry that had the butler himself not been too inebriated to notice, I believe he would have been dismissed on the spot. When the two of us reached the floor on which Miss Lydia's rooms were, I saw a pair of boots outside her door and bent to pick them up.

"Leave 'em," said Bob. "She's in disgrace. She's been sent out of the house same as me."

As I lowered them I noticed a small piece of paper in the right-hand boot.

Bob was ahead of me, so I quickly slipped the note out and into my apron pocket.

Once I was safely alone in the hall, I read the paper by the light of the dying fire: "Solution found. Come after midnight."

I thrust it into the flames and as I watched it blacken and curl up felt a gathering sense of excitement. I waited until I heard Jakeman's snores, crept up the back-stairs and in pitch darkness felt my way along the passage to Miss Lydia's door, counting them to ensure that it was the right one. To my surprise there was no light under the one which ought to be hers. With Mr Vamplew only across the passage, I dared not risk knocking so I gently turned the handle and slipped in.

The only illumination came from a faint glowing amongst the embers of the dying fire and there was no light under the door of the bed-chamber, either. The sitting-room reeked of a candle that had burnt itself out. Knowing that there were usually candles on the mantelpiece, I took the fire-tongs and picked up a glowing coal. By its light I found one, held the ember to it and, while I waited for it to catch, listened to the absolute silence around me.

Then the candle-flame flickered into life and with a stab of ice in my innards, I saw that there was someone sitting in the chair by the fire. In the next moment I recognised the figure as that of the old lady, though the rapid thudding of my heart hardly grew less at this realization. She must be very deeply asleep not to have been awakened by my entrance.

"Miss Lydia," I said softly, but still startling myself with the sound of my own voice. When there was no response I spoke a little louder: "Great-aunt Lydia?"

I moved closer and touched her arm. Instantly, her head lolled forward and I started back. In horror I realized that I was after all alone in the room.

I moved forward again as my first moment of terror passed. There was no reason why I should be frightened. I touched her hand and found that it was quite cold. She had sat here waiting for me to arrive, as the fire died down and the candle guttered and drowned in its own wax, so that she could supply the final element needed in order to bring about the consummation she had desired for so long; and at the last she had been cheated by a few hours. Perhaps even she had died of excitement at the prospect of succeeding at last. I studied her face. The expression seemed peaceful. I tried to imagine what she had been like as a young woman and I could not think that she had ever been a beauty.

I looked round the little room in which she had passed her wretched, narrow life. After more than eighty years of living, how much would her absence be noticed in the upheaval now taking place in the household? Henrietta alone would be saddened by the death of her only friend and ally, the only person she loved. And the old woman had loved her — I was sure of that — had loved her like her lost child; though her love for her must have seemed a mere tail-piece at the end of so long a life. Surely what had mattered to her had been the acts of injustice against herself and those she had loved — Anna Mompesson and John Umphraville — that had blighted and embittered her youth. Was it her desire for revenge or her love for Henrietta — for the child she should have had — that had made her so determined that I should regain the will? I was sure she had sold her life-interest, which was a charge on the estate, at Doctors' Commons. Well, since she could not give me the solution to the quincunx, I now had no chance of doing what she had hoped.

I was about to leave the room when I noticed that there was a battered old hat-box, whose lid had been removed, on the floor at her feet. Glancing inside it I saw a heap of bric-à-brac: a bouquet of flowers that had been dried to preserve it, some paste-board tickets granting admission to ancient balls, and underneath them a christening-robe trimmed with lace that was now yellowed and which had been made, I suspected, for a child which did not live to be baptised. (Perhaps if the old lady had lived I might have asked her about the words she had attributed to her Aunt Anna, but probably not. For I understood now that I could continue for ever to hear new and more complicated versions of the past without ever attaining to a final truth.) Clearly she had been going through her most cherished possessions. And now I noticed that there was something on the old lady's lap which she must have been holding when she died, and which had slipped from her fingers. I picked it up and held it close to the candle.

My heart began to beat faster as I examined it: a faded piece of printed silk stretched over a rectangle of paste-board and adorned with a silken tassle which declared itself to be an invitation to a ball given by Sir Hugo Mompesson to celebrate his marriage to Miss Alice Huffam. Embossed on the front was a sentence in Latin: "*Quid Quincunce speciosius, qui, in quamcunque partem spectaveris, rectus est?*" I smiled for the words were a boast that the pattern of quincunxes represented rectitude, rightness, and justice. Well, I thought, I would do my best. I opened the invitation and there was the very design which we had laboured over a few days before, except that here the three tinctures — white, black, and red — were indicated! As we had anticipated, the arrangement was symmetrical with the first and the fifth, like the second and the fourth, elements exactly reflecting each other, and the Huffam motif was indeed the first as I had suggested it should be. The crucial central quincunx was identical to the second and the fourth, except that the bud of the middle quatre-foil appeared — as predicted — not to be white. But what was it? I held the candle closer and peered at it, wishing I had a lanthorn. The tincture gules was represented, as on the design that Miss Lydia had drawn, by dots and it was very difficult to make out whether the central bud was filled with dots or was entirely black — or was even white after all but marked with slight discolourations of the paper. After staring at it for a few moments in the flickering lume of the candle I was sure it was black. It had to be so for the sake of the pattern of the whole.

I had the solution after all! All that remained unclear was whether the black or the white bolts should be withdrawn, and it would not take long to try it both ways, though I was concerned at the warning Miss Lydia had given me. The decision had been made for me: I would make my attempt that very night! It might be my last opportunity, for the next day anything might happen. I only wished I had some way of getting a message to Joey to tell him to meet me early tomorrow instead of next Monday.

Thrusting the paste-board into the lining of my jacket, I left the room, crept downstairs and, listening to the deep snores of the nightwatchman, stole along the passage and retrieved my bit of candle and the tinder-box from Bob's little pantry.

Very cautiously I made my way to the hearth of the scullery, dislodged the brick I had seen Jakeman remove, and found the keys. I took a knife from the drawer where I had hidden it earlier that day and then, feeling my way step by step through the absolute darkness, I climbed the stairs and unlocked the door of the Great Parlour. (So I did not need the "spider" after all.) As I turned the handle and pushed one half of the lofty door open, it gave way and I stepped inside the room.

I felt a profound impulse to light the candle and begin work immediately, but I resisted it. I must keep my head and think carefully or everything might still be lost since there was no way out of the house until daylight and Mr Vamplew — or anyone else — might be prowling about. So I should lock this door again in case anyone tried it while I was inside. As I made to thrust the stolen key into the lock I found that there was a key already there. Of course! I had forgotten that there was one permanently here to enable the door to be locked from the inside. An idea came to me. I could appropriate this key to lock the door behind me when I left, and this meant that I could return Jakeman's keys to their hiding-place now.

I removed the key from inside the door, locked it behind me and made my way back towards the scullery. As I passed the back-door I recalled the advice given by the housebreakers whom Mr Digweed and I had consulted, concerning the importance of securing one's escape as soon as one entered a house. I hated the thought of being trapped inside for the next few hours and so, although my reason told me it was pointless since I could not get out of the yard until the coach-house was opened, I unlocked the back-door before replacing the keys.

Then I returned to the Great Parlour, and only when I had locked the door on the inside did I light my bit of candle. Now I was sure the central bolt was black. I knew it could not be white. And red seemed highly unlikely. So it was surely black. The only problem now was whether "white" indicated that the bolts be withdrawn or "black" meant that. I decided to withdraw the four "white" bolts first, since that would be quicker than trying the twenty-one "black" ones. Using the blade of the knife, I slid the two top ones out and then, not daring to breathe as I watched for signs of movement, pulled out the two lower ones wondering if I had indeed found the "Open, sesame" of Al Adeen that would give me possession of what I sought.

It worked! To my delight the central slab of marble dropped smoothly down and a space was revealed behind it. I brought the candle closer and peered in. Inside were a small bundle of bank-notes, some gold coins wrapped up in tissue-paper, some jewel-cases, a number of letters and documents, and two tin deed-boxes stamped with the Mompesson arms. Foolishly, I had not anticipated that I would have to search through so many items and I wondered where to begin.

Then I saw a small packet of soft leather beneath the bank-notes. I lifted it out, unwrapped it and in the dim light of the candle-stub which I stood on the edge of the mantelpiece, I read: "I, Jeoffrey Huffam, being of sound mind … " It seems strange to me, now that I look back, that I felt so little at this moment. But perhaps it was because I knew I had so much to do if I was to secure my acquisition. I merely pushed it into the lining of my jacket from which it stuck out, intending to conceal it more effectively in a moment when I had restored the hiding-place so that the fact that it had been opened could not be detected.

I gripped the slab and raised it so that I could slide the two lower bolts back in place, and had just pushed the second of them home so that the recess had moved out of sight, when I heard a noise at the door of the room.

I felt the hair stiffen on the nape of my neck. The door was being unlocked! For some reason Jakeman must have awoken and had his suspicions aroused, perhaps because I had unlocked the back-door. How foolish to have done that! I still had the top two bolts to push back but my first thought was to try to hide and to conceal the will in the hope that the bolts would not be noticed. So I left them as they were, blew out my candle, and crept away from that part of the room. As quickly as I could, I concealed the will in the pouch around my neck which I had prepared for it. A moment later, in the dim light that came through the drawn curtains, I saw a shape by the door. At that instant a beam of light shot out at the raising of the shutter of a dark lanthorn the newcomer was carrying. To my dismay, the beam instantly found the chimney-piece and dwelt there on the incriminating bolts. Then it slowly swung round the room, blinding me for a moment where I was crouching behind a high sopha.

It must be Mr Vamplew! He must have found at last where the nightwatchman hid his keys! If only I had not put them back! I knew that there was no possibility of escape as long as he stood by the door, and my only hope lay in making some kind of bargain with him.

A voice suddenly said in a carrying undertone: "I know you're there, Dick or John, or whatever your name really is."

It was not Mr Vamplew but Mr Assinder!

"What do you want?" I asked and the beam instantly swung onto me.

"You know what I want. The same as you."

I felt despair and bewilderment. How could he have learned about it?

"I don't know what you mean," I said.

"Come, do not prevaricate or I will give the alarm and bring the house about us. I will be well rewarded for my pains. So you will do better to obey me. You see, I know all about you from Vamplew. You and the old woman."

Mr Vamplew was not acting on his own behalf but was being paid by him! So that was why he was so anxious to find where Jakeman hid the keys!

He directed the beam back onto the chimney-piece: "I see you've been clever enough to penetrate that damned trick-lock."

"No," I lied. "I haven't opened it yet."

"But it's half-open," he said, his voice trembling. "So you must know the secret. The old pussy must have told you. Tell it to me. Come over here so that we need only whisper or we'll be heard."

Reluctantly I went over and as soon as I came within reach he seized my arm and, while he gripped me tight, searched my pockets and the lining which Mr Vamplew must have warned him about. He found the piece of paste-board — though luckily he did not notice the pouch round my neck.

He looked at his find in bewilderment, then exclaimed: "Why, it's the same design as the chimney-piece! So I was right. I thought when Vamplew told me he had recognised you that I would keep my counsel and see what came of it. When he told me you were so thick with the old woman I guessed you were plotting something like this." He held up the paste-board: "Did she give you this?"

"I had it from her, yes."

He laughed softly: "The damned old b----! She'd rob her own kin, would she."

All the time I was listening to him I was trying to think of a means to make him move away from the door for this was the only chance I had of escaping. The sole advantages I had were that I already had the will and that unknown to him I had unlocked the back-door. I reckoned that, holding Jakeman's keys, he would assume that I had no way of getting out of the house. And yet, what would it profit me to find myself trapped in the back-yard rather than in the house?

"It's the solution, isn't it? How does it work?"

I shook my head.

"Give me half of what we find in there," he said, "or I'll go for the reward."

I had misunderstood him! He knew nothing of the will and all he was interested in was money! In that case I had a chance, and yet I shrank from conniving at simple robbery even against this family. However, it seemed that I had no choice, for if I was to get out of that room I had to distract his attention and the hiding-place was the only thing that would do that.

He drew me over to the chimney-piece, twisting my arm painfully behind my back.

"I had only half-opened it," I said, "when you came in."

"So I see," he said, releasing me a little. "What is the secret?"

"The centre of each of the flowers is a bolt but you withdraw certain of them only," I explained. "This block of marble is balanced on a pulley in such a way that when you pull out the correct combination it will sink and another will rise behind it containing the safe-place."

"And which are the ones to pull out?"

"Those which are white on that design in your hand," I answered.

"Devilish clever. Now do it."

He smiled at me in a way that aroused my suspicions. Did he then know of the possibility that there was a booby-trap?

I was in a dilemma: I could see no way to avoid opening the hiding-place again, but if I did so then there was nothing to prevent him from harming me once he had what he sought.

"I can't make out the pattern," I said, clutching at a desperate hope.

He brought out the paste-board and studied it under the lanthorn.

"The top two are white, sure enough," he exclaimed. "And the bottom two." Then squinting at it more closely he said: "But I'm damned if I can tell what the middle one is. It could be white or dotted like other parts of the design or even black!"

If he thought the central bolt was white and tried to remove it, then he might trigger the trap. And yet if I were to warn him, then I was surely lost. And why should I risk my life to warn him? The man who had fraudulently used the name of his employer to turn away my mother? Who had been embezzling money from that employer? And who had been paid, I assumed, by my enemies to spy on their behalf?

"White should be safe enough," he said to himself.

Safe! Then it seemed he did know of the rumour! And yet he had been prepared to force me to brave the lock. He was now engrossed and, seizing my chance, I crept away into the darkness of the room.

"Where are you going?" he said, glancing round as I was almost at the door. "Well, be damned to you if you don't want your share."

I knew he believed I had no way to get out of the house, and I suspected that my share would be to be beaten into insensibility — or even worse — and left by the ransacked hiding-place while he secured his escape.

In an instant I was out on the landing, had hastened as silently as I could in the darkness down the stairs and across the hall and was sliding back the bolts of the back-door. Thank heavens, after all, that I had thought to unlock it! Yet

I still had no idea of how I would escape from the back-yard as I opened the door and slipped out.

The cold air with its acrid taste of soot and burnt coal rasped in my throat and lungs, and I remembered my first shock at a winter dawn in London. It was bitter now and I had no coat. In a moment I had scrambled over the low and derelict wall between the two back-courts in the hope of finding a way of escaping from the abandoned timber-yard. Once inside, however, I found that the wall surrounding it was about fifteen feet high and topped by tall spikes. Moreover, as I discovered when I ran my hands over it, the brick-work was so smooth that there was nothing to get a hand or a foot-hold on. There was no escape this way. I crossed over the wall back into the yard of the Mompessons' house.

At that moment I heard a sound like a roll of thunder. Then the silence became absolute. I looked at the rear of the house and saw that candles were being lit on the upper floors. So the hiding-place had indeed had a booby-trap! I had no time to speculate on Mr Assinder's fate for as a consequence of his having roused the house I was myself in danger of being discovered. At any moment someone might run out to alert Mr Phumphred and the grooms above the coach-house and stables.

Of course! I suddenly knew precisely what I had to do.

I ran across the yard to the door of the coach-house and hammered on the iron-bound oak. When I glanced back I could see that a number of lights were now ablaze in the house and I heard shouts and the ringing of bells. Everything betokened uproar as manifestly as I could wish.

After an agonizing wait, the door opened and Mr Phumphred stood in his night-shirt holding a candle and sleepily gazing at me as he must have gazed at Miss Quilliam all those years ago.

"There's an alarm in the house," I cried. "They sent me to wake you."

"An alarm?" he said and looked up at its windows above us.

"They want all the men inside at once! I'll go for the grooms," I cried and made to push past his large figure.

To my relief he moved aside and I ran up the steps to the loft above the coach-house. I found it was partitioned with one half reserved for the hay, and two mattresses on the floor of the other half. Here I could see the two grooms lying fast asleep.

I shook them awake shouting: "Hurry! You're called for to go to the house quickly. It's burglars!"

They took some time to wake up, grumbling and cursing all the while. I kept up a constant shout of "Thieves! Robbery! Quick!" and pointed out of window towards the lights in the house.

My pantomime of alarm and the evident disorder within doors convinced them. They pulled on their clothes over their night-shirts and stumbled down the steps still in the dark.

When they had gone I wasted not a moment in sliding open the window that looked into the mews. Then I clambered over the sill and lowered myself from it until I dared to drop the last few feet. My luck held for the watch, drawn by the noise, might have been running thither, but at the moment the mews-lane was deserted.

I made my way cautiously towards the street. At last I was free. I had nearly fifty pounds! I had Jeoffrey Huffam's final will in my possession! And then it came to me suddenly that it was a few hours into my birthday.

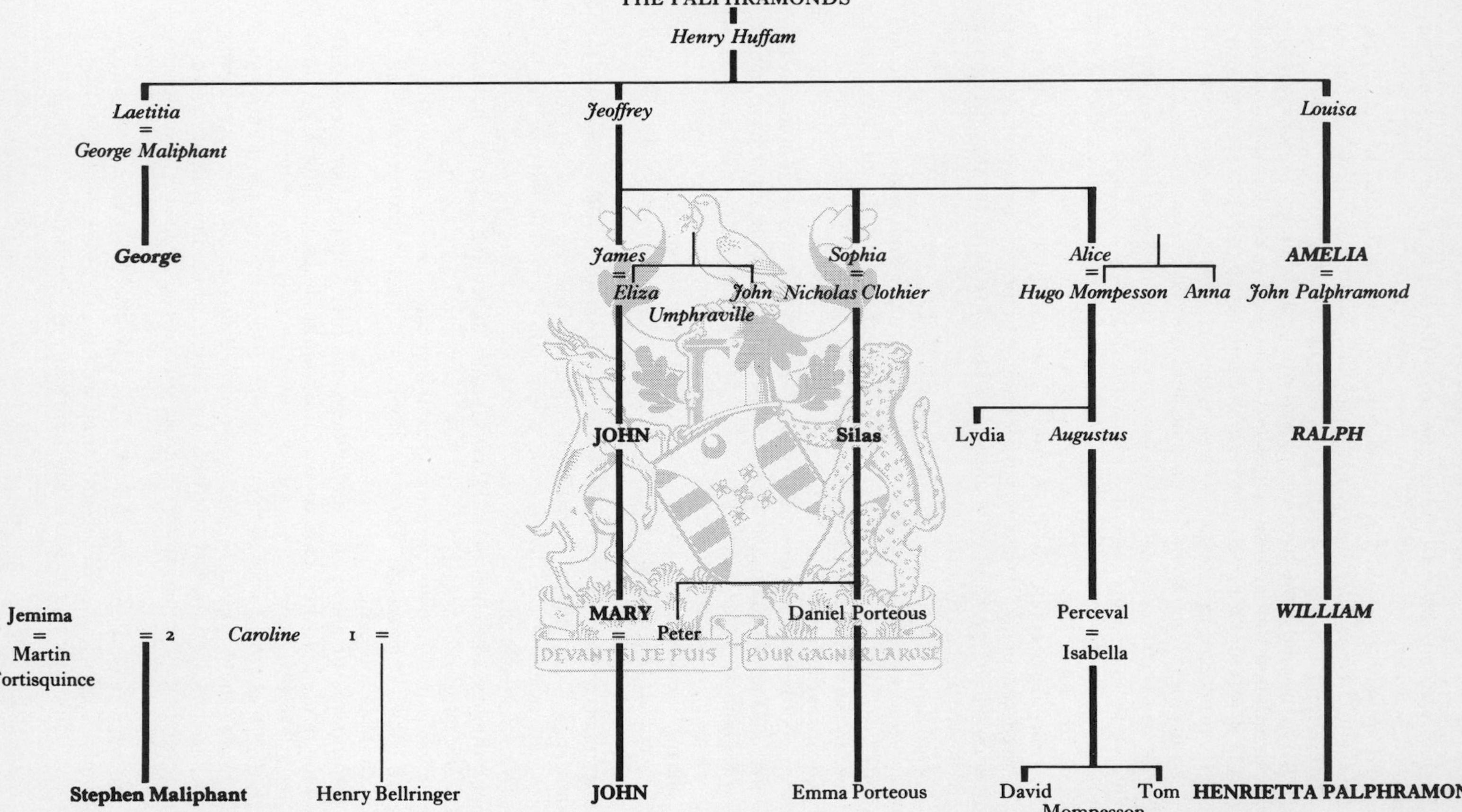

Characters who never appear directly in the narrative are in *italics*. Those who might possess the estate if Jeoffrey Huffam's suppressed codicil were in force appear in **bold** typeface. Those who might possess it if his purloined will were laid before the court are in **BOLD CAPITALS**.

PART FIVE
THE MALIPHANTS

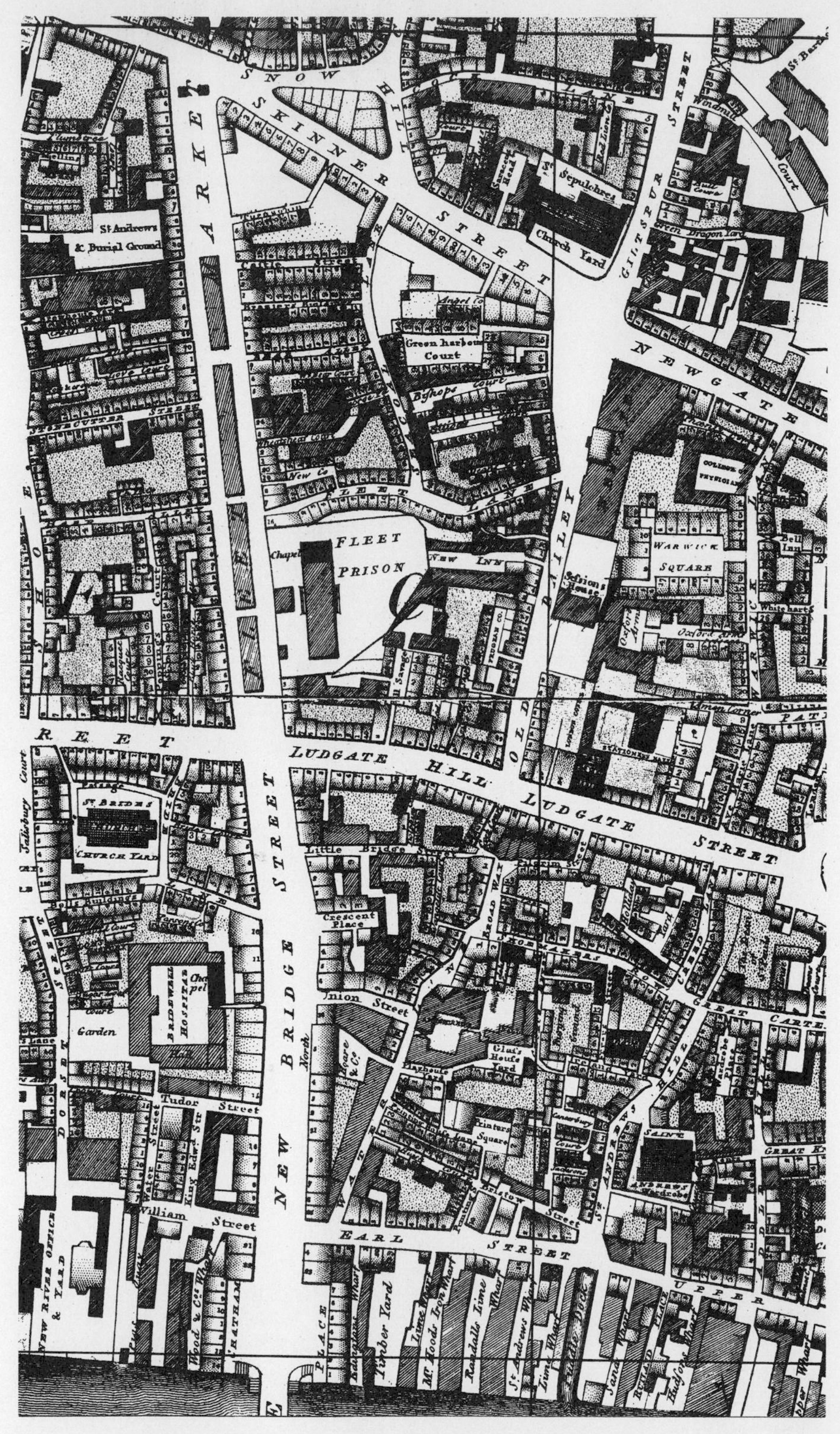

SMITHFIELD, NEWGATE AND BLACKFRIARS (Scale: 1″=105 yards)

The top of the page is North

BOOK I

The Wrong Hands

CHAPTER 101

How much pleasure it gives me to imagine the discomfiture of Old Corruption! Here are Lady Mompesson and Sir David hastening in their night-attire to the Great Parlour with their servants running around them calling out and bumping into each other. As they enter, the footman, Joseph, is lighting the gas, and then he and the other lower servants are shooed from the room by their employers with orders to run for a surgeon and the watch. At the opposite end of the chamber Mr Thackaberry is bent over something lying on the ground. In the dim light of the single mantle it can be seen that the beautiful Turkey-carpet is being disfigured by a dark, spreading stain.

"See if anything has been taken," Lady Mompesson says.

Sir David steps over the object on the ground and searches the hiding-place. Then he hurries back to his mother and whispers: "It's not there!" He adds in horror: "Nothing else seems to be missing!"

"What is not there?" she demands, but reading the dismay on his countenance she looks down at the body. "Search him!" she commands imperiously.

He kneels beside Mr Thackaberry who is pulling open the injured man's coat and who says: "Oh, leave him to me, sir. Don't dirty your good linen. The wretched betrayer! First the Hougham rents and now this! He isn't worth your concern."

"Get out of my light, you old fool!" Sir David exclaims.

With as much dignity as he can muster in his night-shirt and night-cap, the butler stands up and moves away as his employer goes through the pockets of the injured man.

"It must be here," he cries after a moment, and starts to search them over again. Again, he finds nothing. Then he leans over the face and says: "What have you done with it?"

Mr Thackaberry looks down at him and then glances at Lady Mompesson: "I beg pardon, your ladyship, sir, but I believe Mr Assinder is ... "

"It must be here!" Sir David cries. "He was shot as soon as he opened the hiding-place!"

"Then he must have had an accomplice," his mother says.

Sir David stands up and says to the butler: "Assemble all the servants immediately. They must all be searched. Their persons and their boxes."

"Very good, sir. But if there's something been taken, I fear it's too late now. Some of them have left the house to go for assistance."

"Nevertheless, do as I say. A valuable paper has been removed."

When the old servant has hurried out, Lady Mompesson says: "Remember, we dare not reveal the nature of the document for no-one must know that it even existed!"

"If it fell into the wrong hands ... " her son begins and breaks off with a shudder.

"It won't. It must have been taken by mistake by one of the servants working in colleague with Assinder. I suspect Vamplew for I have seen them whispering together. When he finds what it is he will destroy it. How should he know its significance?"

"But, Mamma, it appears that that is all that was taken! As if they were looking for it!"

"That is an alarming possibility," Lady Mompesson concedes. "And it suggests that I was right to suspect Assinder of being in the employ of our opponents. If only the Huffam boy were still alive! For as soon as he is declared to be dead, Silas Clothier inherits."

"He is old. What will happen if he dies before that happens?"

"Unless we can find the will, then the Maliphant heir will inherit under the codicil."

A few minutes later the servants are all mustered and not one of them is found to be missing (for no-one recalls the knife-boy). Mr Vamplew is roused indignantly from his bed and subjected to the indignity of being made to assemble with the servants. Then they and their possessions are thoroughly searched by Mr Thackaberry and the watch. (One of the footmen — Edward, I believe — is very drunk and angrily refuses to be searched until the watch restrain him by force.) Although, to the embarrassment of many, numerous small articles — bottles of wine, items of table-silver, clothes — are discovered on the servants and in their boxes, no document is found.

It is long after dawn when one of the scullery-maids suddenly asks where the knife-boy, Dick, is.

CHAPTER 102

While I made my way out of the silent mews I was thinking of nothing but the danger of being pursued. As I went a little further I found that everything was enveloped in the darkly yellow gauze of the freezing fog. I had no idea of the time since the sun was not visible but only present as a faint lightening of the fog whose cold hands seemed to reach under my thin clothes and run clammy fingers down my body. Once clear of the neighbourhood I found myself heading eastwards without reflecting. Then a sudden upsurge of exultation seized me and I rejoiced to think that I had escaped and triumphed. But as soon as I had leisure to consider my situation I realized how disadvantageous it was. Although I at last had the will — and I pressed the package to my side reassuringly, longing to open and read it but not daring to — my possession of it now put me in considerable danger from both the Mompessons and, above all, from Silas Clothier. The latter would do anything to destroy it — and myself along with it.

The obvious course, which was to go to the Digweeds, was barred to me by Joey's warning that Barney might have someone posted to watch the house. If only I had had time for Joey to do what I had instructed, I could have gone straight to my new lodgings and been assured of my safety. As it was I was literally homeless and penniless. There must be still some hours to go before dawn and in my thin clothes and without a great-coat I was feeling the cold severely.

I had been walking briskly to try to keep warm and by now I had reached Regent-street. There was little traffic at this early hour and not many foot-passengers. I walked down to the Quadrant where there was a baked-potato-seller's stand on the corner, and I loitered within a few yards of it, deriving some feeble heat from its glowing brazier.

There were two women in bedraggled finery standing near it. One of them shivered and the other laughed mechanically and said:

"I amn't cold, Sal. My vartue keeps me warm."

Desperate for the warmth, I hovered nearby as close as I dared. The number of waggons and market-carts trundling towards Covent-garden increased, and herds of sheep and cattle came past on their way to Smithfield. After a time I saw one of the horse-patroles returning from duty in the suburbs around the metropolis. Some working people were passing now, though it was still too early for the clerks walking into the City, as I knew from my memories of my street-trading career.

Only by laying the will before the Court of Chancery could I gain any security, for then there would be less point and more risk in killing me. For at present, unknown, and even believed to be dead, I was very vulnerable. Yet, given my present appearance, I had no chance, as Miss Lydia had pointed out, of getting past the door-keepers of Chancery and I was determined not to give up the document except into the hands of a high official and before witnesses, for I remembered Miss Lydia's warning that the Mompessons had an agent in the Chancery-office.

However, there was Henry Bellringer, Stephen Maliphant's half-brother. I had seen him in the Court and I knew he had some kind of connexion with Chancery. He had been kind to me — as kind as his circumstances permitted — and was the friend I had mentioned to Miss Lydia, and so I resolved to go to him.

It was still some hours too early to think of that and so I walked about to keep warm, stepping carefully for the paving-stones were slippery with frozen dew, and watching the metropolis struggling into wakefulness on a raw, foggy winter's dawn.

Shop-boys awoke from their frozen slumbers beneath the counters and lit the gas-lights which struggled feebly against the growing fog. Then they began to take down the shutters, blowing on their freezing hands which must have been painful against the wood and iron. Now the lamp-lighters set about extinguishing the lamps which were casting tiny amounts of light in the thick fog. People were hurrying to their place of work not from enthusiasm but to keep warm and get in out of the cold. Around Leicester-square I encountered groups of finely-dressed young gentlemen roistering their way home.

CHAPTER 103

I reached Barnards-inn and, wiser now than on my previous visit, I did not declare myself to the porter but waited until his attention was distracted by a gentleman who was giving him some instructions, and then hurried past.

I made my way through the two courtyards and up the stairs to the garret where, finding that the outer door stood open, I knocked on the inner one. After a moment Henry opened it and gazed at me in surprise. He looked exactly as before except that he was wearing a flowered chintz dressing-gown, a velvet night-cap with a gold tassel, and Turkish slippers.

"Do you remember me?" I asked, recalling that it was about two years since he had seen me.

To my relief he looked at me with delight and exclaimed: "Indeed I do, John! You brought me the news of poor Stephen! My dear fellow, I'm very pleased to see you again."

He ushered me in and closed the door. The room was much more cheerful, for there was a new sopha and a second table, and a bright Turkey-carpet and some pictures. I had interrupted him in the preparation of his breakfast for a frying-pan stood on the hob containing three rashers of bacon and a couple of kidneys. At the sight and — more particularly — the smell of this food, a sharp pain seemed to attack me in the stomach.

Henry must have seen this for he insisted that I sit at the little table from which he cleared a jumble of books, papers, pens, pen-holders and other paraphernalia, and, despite my protests, he served me with his own breakfast.

For some minutes I ate in a greedy, unashamed silence while Henry watched me with a quizzical expression.

"Upon my soul," he said, "you look as if you haven't eaten for a week."

Seeing the ill-concealed expression of regret with which I finished the last of my food, he cut two slices of bread and toasted and buttered them for me, and then made coffee for both of us.

"Am I keeping you from your business?" I asked as I embarked upon them. "It is still early, isn't it?"

"It wants five and twenty minutes of eight," he said, taking from his pocket a rather handsome silver watch.

"I thought it was earlier. I was afraid of waking you if I came too soon."

"Too soon! By Jove, have you been up all night?"

I nodded, still intent on chewing.

"Indeed? Then I hope I am to learn the reason."

"I will tell you," I answered.

Seeing that I had consumed all of his breakfast and was still unsatisfied, he gave me a large piece of pound-cake to eat with my coffee.

"Did you recognise me that time?" I asked. "When I saw you in the Court of Chancery at Westminster?"

"When was that?"

"It was two years ago. Shortly after I last came here, in fact."

"And what were you doing there?"

"Well that's a long story. But I want to tell it to you. I need to be able to trust someone."

"You know you can trust me, old fellow. For poor Stephen's sake. I only hope I can do more to help you than I could last time. I have often remembered how I let you go off like that without doing anything for you, but I was deuced short of the ready then."

"I believe you may be able to help me. Do you know anything about Chancery?"

"Indeed I do. I'm articled there."

This was better than I'd hoped!

"I'm a Sixty-clerk. That means," he went on, "that I work to one of the Six-clerks. (Of course there ain't six and sixty.) One day I shall become one, I hope. I don't suppose any of that means much to you. But look here, what the devil is all this about, old chap? You're being confoundedly mysterious."

"I need to sleep," I said.

I was exhausted and yet my mind felt strangely sharp and almost painfully clear.

"Then by all means sleep first and then tell me your story."

"No, I must tell you first."

And so during the rest of that morning I told him enough of my story to let him know that I was the Huffam heir and that I had in my possession a long-lost will that would resolve the issue. He professed himself amazed to learn this and revealed that he knew quite a lot about the suit since it was, he explained, absolutely the most infamous. When I described how I had obtained the will he applauded my actions as bold and high-spirited. Finally, I impressed upon him the grave danger I was now in.

"And so," I concluded, "I need help in laying it before the Court. I can pay you, for the old lady I spoke of gave me some money which some friends of mine are keeping for me."

"The money be hanged," he exclaimed. "I would be honoured to act for you without a fee. Though that shows you how bad a lawyer I must be! But am I to understand that you have the document with you at this very minute?"

I opened the lappels of my coat and showed him the package that was hanging round my neck.

"And so you have not looked at it yet! Then the first thing is to read it."

While he cleared a space on the table I removed the document and unfolded it. Seating himself beside me he looked through it rapidly and then exclaimed:

"By heavens, this is the real thing all right. My word, this brings to an end one of the longest suits in the long cobwebby, spidery history of Chancery. Won't the lawyers just stare when this comes before the Master!"

He laughed and, because I was unfamiliar with the Chancery engrossing hand in which it was written, he read aloud the part that concerned the entail: the estate was settled upon "the infant, John Huffam, and upon the heirs male and female of his body". He scanned it and said: "And it's witnessed in proper form."

He lowered the document and said gravely: "Well, that's simple enough. Even muddle-headed old Chancery can't do much to obfuscate and complicate this, old fellow."

At his words a great tiredness fell upon me. It was as if at this moment all that I had striven for was achieved and the strength that had borne me up for so long failed now.

"I must sleep," I said.

"Then you shall," he said. "And while you're doing so, I'll con over this a few more times and decide on the best course of action."

He said it with such a bright-eyed, trustful expression that I felt ashamed of the powerful reluctance I felt welling up inside me to relinquish my hold on the document.

Unwilling though I was, I was about to insist that he return it to me, but he had perceived my hesitation for he went on: "No, you're quite right, old chap. Don't let it out of your sight. We'll look at it together when you awake."

He handed it back to me and I took it with a deep sense of shame. Had I become so suspicious that I could trust no-one?

"I've an idea," he said with a smile. "My bed-chamber will be infernally cold. So why don't you sleep on the sopha in here? You won't disturb me."

I thanked him and he began to re-arrange the furniture: "You'll be too close to the fire there. I'll move the sopha back."

He did so and I protested: "But now it's jammed against the door."

"No matter for that," he answered cheerfully. "I'm going nowhere."

I was still smarting from embarrassment at letting him see my suspicion, and now it occurred to me that I could make some amends since I could sleep secure in the knowledge that no-one could leave the chambers without waking me.

"Would you like to look at it while I sleep?"

"Yes, that's a good idea," he replied.

So I handed it to him and made ready to sleep on the sopha. It was the middle of the morning now, though on account of the thickening fog, only a feeble yellowish light crept in through the small grimy windows. My last memory before sleep engulphed me was of Henry sitting at the table and busily writing.

CHAPTER 104

I slept without dreams. Once I awoke, or half-awoke, and saw Henry sitting at his desk with his back to me just as I had last seen him. I drifted into sleep again and when I woke up was still wondering where I was when I felt something by my head. I reached for it and found that it was the package. Instantly, remembrance flooded back. Glancing up and satisfying myself that Henry was sitting with his head averted from me, I quickly looked inside it. No miser ever greeted his gold with as much delight as I recognised the will. I raised my head and, seeing that Henry had turned round and was smiling at me, blushed to think that he had seen and understood my act.

"Well, what do you think?" I said standing up.

"Your case is iron-cast for the terms of the entail are perfectly clear," he said and I saw that there was a reddish spot in each of his cheeks. "If the will is genuine — as I am satisfied that it is — then it will be set up in place of the other one. Equity recognises no statute of limitations in such a matter."

"I believe you're as excited as I am," I said.

"The prospect of resolving this ancient suit quite takes my breath away," he said. Indeed, he was breathing rapidly as he smiled at me. "My dear John, all you have to do is to issue a writ of right to the land and you'll soon be the owner of the Hougham estate. May I be the first to congratulate you?"

He reached out his hand and shook mine so warmly and generously that I was deeply moved.

"There is at least one obstacle," I said.

I explained that there was doubt about the marriage of my grandfather's parents and therefore the legitimacy of my grandfather, and Henry acknowledged that this might be an impediment. I told him, however, that I believed I now had the solution to that, though I did not bother to tell him that it was based upon what Miss Lydia had said about the wedding in the chapel at the Old Hall.

My repose had lasted so long that already the wintry dark was returning, all the darker for the fog that was even thickening. Now, once we had moved the sopha back to its position and seated ourselves before the fire, we made our dinner of some potatoes and two small beef-steaks he had purchased the day before. Then Henry, apologising for the meanness of the hospitality he had to offer me, brought out a bottle of claret which he insisted upon opening in my honour, though neither of us drank more than a glass.

When we had eaten he said: "What I propose is this: I will go this very evening to the private house of a very high official of the Court of Chancery. Insisting that I am speaking to him in the utmost confidence, I will tell him merely that an extremely important document has come to light and that the party in whose possession it now is wishes to place it directly in his hands in the presence of a witness, namely myself. I will impress upon him the need for absolute secrecy. And I will suggest that we come to him at his own residence tomorrow for this purpose. What do you say to that?"

I nodded, and, unable to speak for a moment for my gratitude, took his hand and pressed it.

"Thank God," I managed to say at last. "I will not feel safe until this is done. Beg him to let us come tonight. I don't wish to pass another day with this burden upon me."

"My dear fellow, for a Chancery lawyer next year would seem precipitate. But I promise you I will do my best. You are safe here, and I think I need hardly tell you to open the door to no-one while I am gone."

I shuddered at the thought and he put on his hat and coat, remarking: "While I am away, you may read the precedents I have found. I have left papers in the books to mark the places."

He took his leave and only when I had barred the outer door behind him and locked the inner one, did I feel safe enough to sit before the fire with the will before me and read it. One clause I noticed stipulated that "Mr Jeoffrey Escreet" be left merely fifty pounds, and I was sure that I recalled my mother mentioning that he had inherited the house at Charing-cross under the original will. Could that be of any significance? When I had read it over several times I began to study the tomes Henry had indicated. As far as I understood them, the relevant judgements appeared to be very encouraging.

CHAPTER 105

No-one came to the door. There were footsteps on the stair but they all stopped at the landing below ours and no-one ventured up the last narrow flight to the single door of Henry's garret-chamber.

So it was virtually all over and I had nothing to do but wait until the time came for me to enter into my inheritance!

When, however, a couple of hours had passed I began to grow worried. Surely it could not be taking Henry so long? Was I right to trust him? If not, should I flee from there now? Might he return with Barney? Yet how could that be? There was no connexion between him and anyone else involved in my story, was there?

At last, very late that evening, I started at hearing someone on the stair outside. Whoever it was had a key and unlocked the oak. Then to my relief Henry's voice called out to me to release the bolts on the inner door.

When he came hurrying in I saw that he was in high spirits. He was carrying several parcels which he flung down on the sopha as he removed his coat.

"All is arranged," he cried. "We are to see my principal later tonight at his own residence."

"That is excellent news!" I answered. Yet I could not help wondering why he had been so long.

"There is more," he gasped. "Only let me get my breath back. The fog is in my lungs and it's getting so thick that you have to walk like a blind man and that is slow going, I can assure you."

He hung up his hat and coat and turned to me with a bright smile: "And I stopped at Oxford-market to buy these: two bottles of wine, a couple of hot meat-pies, and a plum-pudding."

He began to arrange these articles, putting the meat pies and the pudding on the hob and starting to open the bottles.

"My principal was intrigued by my story and I had a capital time teazing him. It can't be often that one of his junior clerks has known so much more than he. His eyes grew quite round when I told him the matter concerned the ownership of a vast estate and the fortunes of one of the most respected families in the land." He poured out two glasses of wine: "He lives in Harley-street and is expecting us there between eleven o'clock and midnight."

"So late!"

"My dear John, what time do you imagine it is now? It's already past eight o'clock. We must leave within the hour. But the reason why I was so long is that I called on a friend of mine in Great-Titchfield-street on the way back."

"You have been busy," I commented, my suspicions lulled.

"He is on his way here now. We will eat now so that we may depart as soon as he arrives."

"Do you mean that he will be accompanying us?" I asked.

"Precisely. For it occurred to me as highly desirable that another individual should be present at our interview."

I looked doubtful at this.

"My dear John, consider it for a moment from my principal's point of view. Here is a junior clerk of his, a young rapscallion of whom he knows little good — though equally little harm — who turns up late at night claiming to have with him the heir to a large fortune and the long-lost will which proves his claim. And who does this fortunate individual turn out to be? Now don't take offence if I say that he is a very young gentleman indeed and hardly presents an appearance calculated to inspire confidence in the breast of one who has worked all his days in the legal dust-mill."

He said it so charmingly that I smiled to show that I was not offended.

"But now consider his feelings if these two are accompanied by a gentleman of the most unimpeachable respectability — an ordained clergyman, no less! Now the case presents itself in a very different light, does it not?"

"A clergyman?"

"The Reverend Mr Charles Pamplin. An excellent fellow who holds a fine living down in the North."

I could not imagine any way in which this addition to our party could be a cause of concern, and yet I felt a slight unease.

"And from your point of view," Henry continued as he laid out knives and forks, "he will be a witness of the handing over of the will — not that there is really any need to worry about that."

We addressed ourselves to the good things that my host had brought and made a pleasant, lively meal of it. We had "done justice" to the meat-pies, as Henry expressed it, and were close to a "judgement" on the pudding when there came a knock at the oak.

Henry jumped up to let the newcomer in and he entered glancing round the room with an air of slightly condescending amusement. I stood up and he held out to me a pale, scented hand studded with rings. He had a fleshy face which, though he was still a little under thirty, was already heavy-jowled. His eyes were black and very bright and had a lazy, spoiled way of resting on one as if he were bored by what he saw but it were too much of an effort to shift to a more interesting prospect. His gaze fell to my feet and then languidly elevated itself back to my face. He was wearing a clerical shovel-hat and a magnificent great-coat which he removed (handing it, with his hat and fine kid gloves, to Henry rather as if he were a footman) to reveal a beautiful coat with a great deal of fine linen showing, an embroidered waist-coat and white trowsers.

"So you," he began, holding my hand in his own pale and rather damp one, "are the young man who ... " Here he broke off and turned to Henry, relinquishing my hand: "But then I have not been told enough to say quite what, except that it is something very important. It's all very mysterious, Bellringer. Am I to be permitted to know nothing more?"

"Nothing, Pamplin. But I don't see that you have any grounds for complaining. You're a clergyman so mystery is your province. You'll have to take it from me that I can say no more. But you must have taken more implausible things on trust before now or you wouldn't be in orders."

"You're a damned infidel, Bellringer, and I promise you'll go to Hell for it," the clergyman replied affably.

"Mind your tongue, Pamplin, or you'll spoil your role in this evening's proceedings which is to vouch for our respectability. Though that's like one beggar offering to stand surety for another."

"Your respectability! Well, if you're expecting me to perjure myself you'll have to bring out that '09 you promised me."

He seated himself at the table and Henry poured each of us some of the port.

"We must leave soon," he warned.

"It's a damnable night to go out in and you shan't get me down those confounded narrow stairs of yours until I've prepared myself with some of this."

The wine was too thick and soup-like for me, but the two gentlemen — particularly Mr Pamplin — drank a considerable amount, though it seemed to have no effect upon them.

"Before I forget," the clergyman said. "Sir Thomas is up. I saw him at Crockfords last night and he gave me a message for you."

"None of that now," Henry said and looked frowningly at me.

"By Jove! I wasn't going to say any harm."

"Where that gentleman is concerned, to mention his name is to do harm."

"Now Bellringer," Mr Pamplin said affably, "you can't expect me to listen to my patron being scandalized."

The conversation turned to other topics and as the other two spoke Mr Pamplin occasionally turned his heavy-lidded gaze upon me with a speculative air.

BOOK II

Caught in the Web

CHAPTER 106

I have to bring you once more back to the old counting-house beside the tumbledown wharf. Mr Clothier is in his private closet with his managing-clerk and is obviously in high spirits. He rubs his hands and suddenly chuckles, then dances a few steps off the ground. Mr Vulliamy keeps glancing at him curiously, as if wondering what the old gentleman has to be so pleased about.

"Who was that who came here while I was at supper, Mr Clothier? I saw him leaving as I was returning just now?"

"Never you mind!" the old gentleman cries gleefully.

"I thought it might be on business, you see, or I shouldn't have asked."

"Private business," his employer returns, less affably. "And nothing important."

"Indeed? And yet it's such a nasty foggy night to be out in."

"You're blessed inquisitive all of a sudden!" the old gentleman cries. Suddenly he changes his tone: "Pray be seated. There's something I have to tell you. Old friend." He stops and then after a pause goes on: "How long have you worked for me?"

"Man and boy, Mr Clothier, upwards of thirty years."

"And have you ever been in doubt about my good intentions towards you?"

Mr Vulliamy eyes him closely and says: "Not for the last few years, no. No doubt at all, sir."

"Very good," the old gentleman says, looking at his clerk rather uncertainly. "Now you remember the Pimlico and Westminster Land Company?"

Mr Vulliamy nods.

"Of which I made you nominal owner. (See how much I've always trusted you!) Well, the truth is ... The fact of the matter ... The company's unfortunate speculation ... That is to say ... "

"You mean, Mr Clothier, that I may be taken up on a warrant for debt to answer for your losses on the money-market?"

"Why do you have to make it sound so bad?" the old gentleman exclaims indignantly. "The truth is, if it comes to the very worst, the very worst, mark you, why, you may be in the Fleet for a month or two."

"And if I refuse to take the penalties on your behalf?"

"Refuse?" the old gentleman cries, his affability forgotten. "Why, then I have those bonds of yours and can send you there on my own account for much longer!" Then he recollects himself and says sweetly: "But I know you won't refuse. For if you agree to do this for me, then I will look after your family most generously while you are detained."

"I am sure I can rely on you for that," his managing-clerk replies so meaningfully that the old gentleman is quite taken aback.

At that moment there is a hammering at the street-door.

A minute later the boy, pale-faced, opens the door into the inner closet without knocking and says: "Sheriff's officers, Mr Clothier, sir."

Leaving his employer sitting in surprise, Mr Vulliamy briskly gets up and walks into the outer office where he says: "Good evening, gentlemen. I believe it is I whom you are seeking."

"Why, that's wery pleasant of you, sir." the sheriff says. "I wish all our customers was eq'ally obleeging."

While Mr Clothier stands at the door to his inner sanctum, Mr Vulliamy places himself in the custody of the officers and is led away so very calmly and looking at his benefactor so very strangely as he goes, that he leaves the old gentleman quite pale with astonishment and unease.

CHAPTER 107

Shortly before ten o'clock Henry rose and said: "We should go now or we'll be late."

He went to one of the windows and pulled back the shutters: "I can't see a blessed thing," he announced. "The fog has closed down."

"Can we not put it off until tomorrow?" asked Mr Pamplin.

"By no means," Henry replied firmly.

"But the hackney-coach will take hours, if we can even succeed in engaging a driver who will venture out."

"Precisely," Henry said. "So it will be much quicker and more certain to go on foot."

"What!" Mr Pamplin cried. "You're out of your senses. I would not dream of walking so far on such a night."

"Nevertheless, that is what must be. I know the way and could find the street if I were blind-folded."

"Oh very well," said the clergyman ungraciously, and he poured himself another glass from the decanter, draining it as he got to his feet.

Henry took up and lighted a lanthorn. Then he passed a great-coat to me and when we were all wrapped up against the weather we set off.

The bitter choking air that we encountered as we went from the bottom of the staircase into the courtyard made me gasp. It tasted so powerfully of smoking coal fires that it was like being in a room in which the smoke is blowing back down the chimney. We could see only a few paces ahead and as we left the inn the noise of what little traffic there was seemed muffled. Because of the density of the fog the lanthorn cast only a dim light.

"I'll go ahead," Henry said as we reached the street. "We shall march like

Roman legionaries, *haeret pede pes*, each one's foot sticking to the other's. You keep behind me, John, for as Ovid says '*medio tutissimus ibis*' — it is safest in the middle."

"I say, it's too beastly cold for Latin, Bellringer."

"And as for you, Charles, I think you'd be happiest keeping up the rear."

Mr Pamplin snorted and we set off. Though I quickly lost all sense of direction, Henry clearly knew exactly where we were and kept striding purposefully ahead.

We had been walking for some time through almost deserted streets when, as we were descending a long narrow lane I fancied I heard another party ahead of us.

I asked Henry to stop and we paused to listen.

"Deuce take it, Bellringer," Mr Pamplin said, "we could be murdered. It was a damnably foolish idea to come on foot."

"Hold your tongue," his friend ordered.

We strained our ears but heard nothing.

"It's your fancy, John," Henry said, and we walked on.

However, just before we reached the mouth of the lane several figures suddenly emerged from the fog behind us and in an instant a strong hand was placed across my mouth and my arms were gripped so that it was painful for me to move. In the darkness and fog I could make out little of what was happening, but I heard sounds indicating that Henry was fighting back and saw the lanthorn fall as someone grappled with him. Then I thought I saw him knocked to the ground. Mr Pamplin had disappeared into the fog at the moment that Henry and I were attacked. I tried to struggle but was punched hard in the ribs and rendered breathless.

A voice from nearby that I thought I had heard before said: "Search him. Quickly."

A hand rifled my pockets and found nothing. In the midst of all this, I congratulated myself for my forethought in concealing the precious document around my neck.

The man holding me cried in a voice that was also horribly familiar: "I can't find nothing!"

Then I was bodily dragged down the lane to the entrance towards which we had been making our way so that it occurred to me even at that moment that we had walked into an elaborate ambuscade. Here I was suddenly lifted up and caught a glimpse of a coach-door before I was thrown onto the straw of the floor. I found myself sprawling at the feet of a man who was already in the coach who spoke from the darkness:

"Excellent work!"

My assailant knelt upon my back still holding a hand over my mouth while the third man boarded the coach, slamming the door and calling out to the driver as the vehicle moved off. I was in despair for by now I had recognised both my assailants and the man who had been waiting in the coach: they were Dr Alabaster and his assistants, Hinxman and Rookyard.

CHAPTER 108

As I lay on the floor of the rocking coach with Hinxman's weight still upon me, I wept with vexation, not for the danger to myself so much as the fact that after all that I had endured in order to obtain the will it was going to be taken from me, and whatever happened I would lose my chance of regaining my rights and obtaining justice against those who had wronged my mother. But how had it happened that I found myself once again in the power of my enemies? How had they known where to find me?

As for my fate, I expected to be taken back to the madhouse and there to be imprisoned for the remainder of my life — however long or short that might be, for I could not expect another opportunity to escape. There was no point in struggling or trying to scream. And so, as the coach moved at barely walking-pace through the dense fog, I gave way to tears of rage and misery.

However, it seemed that my surmise about our destination was wrong for after only some ten or twenty minutes, the vehicle came almost to a halt in order to make a sharp turn and then it very slowly descended a steep slope. I knew that must mean we were approaching the river and indeed I could smell its salt-stale fragrance mingled with the fog. Now the coach came to a complete stop. I was carried out, still gripped in such a way that I could not struggle or cry out, taken through a door and then flung onto the ground. For a few moments I was dazzled by the bright gas-lights above me.

Then I looked up and found myself gazing into the face of a little old man who was smiling down at me with the most curiously intense expression. I had seen him before. But where? And when was it? He was pale and skinny and, with his legs encased in tight pantaloons which emphasized this, his bulging paunch was all the more obvious. All of his costume — the fly-blown and powdered perruque like a black cauliflower perched on his balding scull, his torn and dirty frock-coat, his neckerchief of yellowing cambric, his black finger-gloves, his green horn-rimmed spectacles, and his salt-and-pepper breeches — seemed appropriate to an earlier age.

"Good work," he said to Alabaster with a smile — if it can be called that, for his mouth merely opened slightly while his tongue licked his upper lip. "You'll be well paid. Tie him up and take him down."

Hinxman secured my hands and he and Rookyard carried me down two flights of steps into a dank cellar lined with ancient hogsheads and empty casks. The smell was more than mere dampness; it was a sharp rivery smell.

They threw me on the ground near an open trap-door that was like the top of a well, and then went away leaving me in darkness. After a few minutes the old man came down carrying a lanthorn and approached me, walking with a curious crab-like sideways motion. As if I were nothing more than a parcel, he reached down, tore open my coat and felt for the cord around my neck. As his hands groped for it I wondered how he could have known to look there. He removed it and tore it open. Holding it near to the lanthorn, he read it avidly while the light cast a huge flickering shadow on the damp wall behind him. Then he folded it, opened the lanthorn, stuck the document into the flame and held it as it burned.

After all I had gone through! After all that Great-aunt Lydia had endured and died for! To lose all hope of restoring my family's fortunes, of achieving Justice to redress the balance for their sufferings!

He held it the other way around until it was completely burnt and then broke it up and scattered the ashes down the trap-door.

Now that he turned and looked down at me thoughtfully, his face illuminated from below by the lanthorn so that it threw shadows across his face, I found the solution to what had been troubling my memory: "I saw you that time I was ill at Daniel Porteous's house!" I cried.

He was the old man I had seen during my fever and not known when I awoke if I had seen him in my dreams or in reality.

He looked at me as if surprised that I could speak.

"You're Daniel Porteous's father!" I exclaimed. Then the further implications of this struck me: "You're Peter Clothier's father! In that case, you're my ... "

His countenance darkened as I broke off. So this was my mother's and my Enemy and the prime mover of all my and my family's woes!

He stared at me piercingly.

"Your nothing," he said. "I'm the father of the unfortunate husband of your mother." He said something further about her and then reached into his pocket and pulled a small object out and thrust it at me, holding the lanthorn for me to see it by. "This woman," he said.

What he was holding was the locket that my mother had prized so highly and whose loss had saddened her so much. It still had the circlet made of two intertwined locks of hair.

"It was this that led me to your precious mother," he said. "For one of my pledge-takers recognised my son."

As he spoke he held it for a moment over the trap-door and then dropped it. There was a brief silence and then I thought I heard a faint splash. Was the river beneath us? I recalled the occasion when Joey and I had escaped from the rising tide through the vaults of a warehouse and wondered if I were once again near the Fleet-market.

"Why did you hound her to her death?" I demanded. "Why do you hate her?"

"What a lot of questions!" he said with that sinister smile that was no smile.

"Tell me! Tell me the truth!"

"Why, I'll tell you whatever you want to know," he said, still smiling. "It can't hurt now and we've a little time, for the tide is low."

What did he mean? Was he planning to ship me abroad? The sight of the locket had awakened painful memories and made me reckless of my own safety. I had to complete the pattern, whatever my fate was to be.

"Was it you who had my grandfather murdered?" I asked.

"No," he said.

"It *was* you," I insisted. "You paid a man called Barney Digweed."

"Never heard of him," he answered.

Could that be the truth? That my surmise that Barney had been involved was quite wide of the mark? It was true that I had only inferential evidence.

Then as if suddenly angry the old man shouted: "I'll tell you the truth, but you won't want to hear it. Your mother drove Peter to it. The fact is, he thought himself too fine a gentleman to have an honest money-lender for his dad. He was happy enough to take my money though he professed to be horrified to find out what kind of hard work had paid for his fine manners and his book-learning. I had such hopes for him. But he didn't love me enough to justify the money I spent on him."

While he was speaking he attached a stout rope to an iron ring in the wall:

"Then he met your mother and she and her father turned him against me. Poor lad, they pulled him in so many directions there's no wonder that his wits addled. Mind you, he had good cause to make an end of Huffam for he stood to gain by his death. Just as she did."

"That's not true! She wasn't like you say!"

"She trapped Peter with her woman's wiles and drove him to it as surely as if she'd plotted it herself. (This rope is devilish long! No matter.) I had nothing to gain from Huffam's death. On the contrary, for it turned Daniel against me. Against his old dad who has worked all his life to make him what he is and leave him a wealthy man! He changed his name shortly after that when he married a rich widow, saying he was afraid of the scandal of the murder and the trial. Oh, he told me it would mean that he and I could do business together without anyone knowing that we were kin. And it's true that he contrived to bring his banking-house, Quintard and Mimpriss, to underwrite some of my little undertakings. But I know it wasn't just that. What started as the pretence that we were strangers has now become the truth."

Quintard and Mimpriss! Of course! That was the bank which was implicated in the speculation that Sancious had involved my mother in. I recalled the name from one of his letters to her about it. And then I had heard the name mentioned in Court as that of Porteous's employer.

"Yes, Daniel is ashamed of me now just as Peter was," the old man went on. "It isn't fair! He'll have everything when I die. All my properties in Town and now he'll get the Hougham lands, too. But he can't hide his contempt from me. And that girl of his, does she care for her old grand-dad? She wrinkles up her elegant nose when I come into the room. But she won't refuse her share of my money, I'll be bound."

Now he was securing the other end of the rope tightly around my waist: "I never sought revenge against your mother. All I ever wanted was my rights. They were taken from me when I was barely out of my teens. Those proud Huffams and Mompessons despised my father and me, but they needed us. Oh yes, they came running to us when they wanted money for their grand ways, their houses and carriages. When did I ever enjoy such things? And yet I could have done so a thousand times over."

"It was for your rights that you killed my mother!" I cried. "You put Assinder up to turning her away from Sir Perceval's house!"

"So you know about that!" he exclaimed. "Well, what harm can it do now? Yes, I pay him to watch out for my interests. For one thing, he makes sure those damned Mompessons aren't trying to convert the assets of the estate before it falls into my grasp. Though I know he helps himself to their rents, so it won't be long before they catch him."

"You drove her to her death!" I cried.

"She took the codicil that I had a good claim to and held onto it and tried to keep me from my rights," he shouted and began to push and pull me along the floor towards the trap-door.

"But it wasn't just that! You needed her to be dead before you could inherit. Just as you need me to … "

Of course! He intended to push me into the trap and let me be drowned as the tide rose! But why the rope? Presumably he wanted to be able to pull my body out again for some reason. Then it came to me: He needed my body to prove that I was dead!

"What about Henry Bellringer?" I cried in despair. "Is he an agent of yours like Sancious and Assinder?"

"Enough questions," he answered, panting with his exertions.

I began to struggle as far as I was able to, given that I was securely bound, but though I kicked out at him with my feet he managed at last to push me over the edge. I hit the water only five or six feet below the level of the cellar floor, fortunately descending feet first. It was freezing. The old man held the lanthorn above me and I saw him looking down with a strangely solicitous expression. Then he dropped the trap-door and I was in utter darkness.

I kicked with my feet to stay upright. And I struggled to get my hands free, but they were fastened beyond any possibility of release. In less than an hour the rising tide would be pressing me against the trap-door. He would have locked it or would be standing on it. Judging by the stench I had noticed, the tide probably covered the floor of the cellar. I would drown. I would drown sooner if I became too numbed to keep my head above the water. So this was death. And nobody but he would ever know the truth of it. What would Joey and his mother think of me? How would they remember me? As the one who had brought about the death of their father and husband? What other claim upon their remembrance did I have? I had killed him, and even if I had rescued Joey once from certain death that could not efface my responsibility. Even though I had saved him at risk of my own life.

Then it came to me! Saved him from death by drowning! Saved him from a vault that was under water! And we had come up into a cellar that was like this one! Then perhaps where I was now was the top of such a vault for I remembered that they were separated by pillars which were submerged as the tide rose. It occurred to me that if this was where I was then I might be able to get into the next vault and the cellar above it by going under the surface and coming up again, as I had on that occasion. The difficulty of doing this when tied to a rope and with my hands secured terrified me, but I had no choice. And if I did not do it soon I would be too numbed by cold to have any chance. It meant rushing upon danger rather than merely waiting for it to come upon me.

The rope was long, perhaps long enough to let me get so far. But what if it was not? Trying not to think of that, I dived beneath the surface and felt for the hollow beneath the arch. I could not find it. Was this vault, then, different from the one from which I had rescued Joey? I rose to the surface for breath and dived again. This time I found space and went under it. I kicked my legs and moved some yards. Then I came up in absolute blackness. But there seemed to be space above me. I shouted and from the nature of the echo I deduced that there was indeed a void above me. I was surely in the next vault! Terrified that the rope would hold me back at any moment so that I would merely drown in that vault rather than the first one, I felt for the ladder and began to climb it. In a few moments I was at the top! The trap-door was the next obstacle. I pushed and it rose a few inches. I heaved again and at last managed to raise it. I scrambled into the cellar unable to see a thing, and as I rose to my feet I reached the full extent of the rope's length! Was I yet above the reach of the tide? Well, I would find out. So I stood like that as the tide rose to the lip of the trap, bubbled through it, and began to rise about my ancles, then my knees, until it reached my waist. Was I going to drown after all like a rat in a trap? I waited, my eyes wide open in the dark, my forehead feverish in the icy cold, recalling what I had read of the poor wretches waiting for the rising tide at Execution-dock.

Hours passed that seemed like days, like weeks. Scenes from my life paraded in review before my eyes. Those early years in Melthorpe. My mother, Sukey, Bissett, and Mrs Belflower. I had never repaid Sukey for the money she had lent me! Henrietta and the Mompessons. And what of Henrietta? Did I love her? Had she loved me?

Suddenly I felt shame at so much that I had done — and, worst of all, not done. I had been so quick to judge. I had condemned my mother a hundred times. I had refused to forgive poor crippled Richard for betraying Big Thom at Quigg's. Now I did not feel I had to forgive him. I felt I had no right to. And if only I had thought more of Joey and his mother and less of gaining my rights. Rights. Justice. What did these words really mean? I had deceived myself. My motives were much baser than I had allowed myself to believe. If only I could live, I would behave so differently in the future. What had I ever done for anyone else? I thought of all the times I had brought my mother to tears and now I wept myself, and the more when I thought of the suspicions of her that I had nursed. Mother, father. Grandfather. What did any of that matter? Suddenly I saw in this horrible, pitiable old man my real affiliation. I knew the story he had told me — his quest for justice, his brooding sense of ill use, his attempt to measure love. It was hideously familiar to me. So now I made a thousand promises and resolutions with no certainty that I would have the chance to break them.

I dared not believe it, but the water seemed to be rising no higher. It was surely falling! It *was* falling! But I was not saved yet. I had to go back for there was no other escape from the rope that bound me fast. Go back! (Always it seemed that I had to go back! Would I never be really free?) How long should I wait? The only chance I had was to hope that Clothier had left the cellar and had not secured the trap-door. If I delayed too long he would return and start to haul me in. I would wait until the tide had gone down to a foot beneath the trap-door. That would give me just enough space to breathe while I tried to open the trap-door.

I knelt as the level fell and reached down to feel at intervals until the moment came. Then I lowered myself into the water and swam back, following the rope. I rose to the surface and as I felt the trap-door with my hands found that it was not secured. Of course! He had not been able to bolt it because of the thickness of the rope holding it ajar! No light was coming in round the corners so I assumed that he was not waiting in the cellar or I would have detected the lanthorn. As I was trying to raise the trap-door I was bracing myself against the ladder when it suddenly began to give way. It was rusted through and my weight had broken it free of its mountings. I was terrified until I realized that it did not matter for the water supported me, of course, and by hauling myself against the rope instead I was able to push back the trap-door and enter the cellar in the darkness. I closed the trap-door again, but what worried me was that Clothier would surely notice when he returned that there were now two lines of rope coming from beneath it when there should only be one. I would have to jump out upon him before he got close enough to notice this. So I found a place to hide near the bottom of the steps.

Soaking wet, I was numb with cold, and a long time passed before I heard the cellar-door opening and saw the light of the lanthorn. He stood by the door presumably listening to the slopping of the tide beneath the trap-door and waiting for it to fall further. Then he came down the steps a little way and I saw him more clearly. He was carrying a knife to cut the rope! Here was a new danger but also an unexpected chance, if I was lucky. Fearing that at any moment he would notice the two ropes, I wondered whether to seize the initiative by throwing myself at him even before he came past me. I would try to get the knife from him and cut myself free, for though my hands were tied together, I still had the use of them. Then I could use the knife to force him to let me out of the building.

I believe I was about to throw myself at him when suddenly I heard a noise from above. He obviously heard it too for he put down the knife to open the door, and went through it. As soon as it closed I crossed to where he had been and fumbled for the knife which I then used to cut myself free. Even that took some time and to free my hands would be much harder. Groping my way back, I threw the end of the rope down the trap so that there was once again only one line coming from it. Cautiously I passed through the door, went up the next flight of stairs, and peered into the main room of the counting-house. I had the knife and I would use it if need be!

The old man was shouting at someone I could not see: "What are you doing back here? And at this hour?"

"What am I doing?" the man answered. "Why, I'll tell you with great pleasure. More pleasure than I've ever had in obeying you, sir — I mean, Clothier."

I moved into a position from which I could see the speaker. He was in late middle age and round of figure as of countenance, almost completely bald and very red-faced — though whether this was constitutional or caused by the stress of the occasion I could not know then. He was shabbily clad in an old brownish coat with lustreless brass buttons, a canary waistcoat, and pale blue pantaloons.

"What is this madness?" Clothier cried.

"Madness? No, the madness has been to go on doing the things for you that I have done. Wringing the poor for their last pence, fastening on young heirs and sucking them dry, crowding people into rooms that a fair man wouldn't keep a pig in. Above all, persecuting that poor young creature — your own daughter-in-law, sir — I mean, Clothier. Cheating her of her little money with the aid of that leech, Sancious, and then hounding her into shame and an early grave."

Listening, I had to resist the impulse to come forth and embrace the good little man.

"Get to the point, Vulliamy," Clothier snarled. "How did you get out of the Fleet?"

"I've never been in it," he returned. "And now I'll tell you something. I had a key to the street-door copied some time ago. Ever since then I've been coming back of nights to transcribe papers. (That's why I haven't always been wide-awake during the day, sir — I mean, Clothier.) When I was arrested, I took them with me to the sheriff's and showed them to an attorney — a precious fly 'un, too. He advanced me the monies for the caption and a sham bail bond and told me to come back and get more evidence."

"What papers?" the old man asked, his voice trembling slightly.

"Why, pretty much everything. Most particularly on the Consolidated Metropolitan Building Company and its dealings over that piece of land. Especially with Mimpriss and Quintard. But many other things, too."

"Why, you don't think I'll let you leave here alive, do you?"

"I think you'd better, sir — I mean, Clothier. For I've left 'em with the attorney who has instructions on what to do with them if he does not hear from me."

There was a brief silence.

"Come," said Clothier in a very reasonable tone. "State your terms. You've got the better of me this time, but business is business and I'm sure we can come to an arrangement."

"Why, I couldn't reconcile it with my conscience to let you go on doing what you have been doing."

"What, not for anything at all?"

There was a pause, and then the little man answered: "Not for less than fifty thousand pounds."

So he was no better! Though perhaps he was, for at least he set a high price on the value of his conscience!

"You're mad!" Clothier shouted. Then more calmly he said: "You must know I don't possess anything like that amount!"

"You do now."

"What do you mean?"

"I heard what passed in the cellar not an hour ago. Now that the boy is dead and the will destroyed, you're the owner of the Hougham property and that's worth a tidy sum."

There was a brief silence, and then the old man said in a silky tone: "Why, you *are* up to the game! But if I'm to claim the estate, you must help me in the cellar."

"Very well. But none of your tricks."

They came towards where I was and because there was no other way to go, I quickly retreated back down into the cellar and hid behind a cask.

"Let's have a look at him," Clothier said and seized the rope. "What the devil!" I heard him cry a moment later on finding it attached to nothing. "He must have drowned whatever happened," he said. "For I stood on the trap-door until the tide reached my ancles. The rope must have frayed on a sharp edge. I must have the body to prove to the Court that the Huffam line is extinct. But I don't want it found with the hands tied. Nor in the vaults, for that's too close to home, but out in the river. You're five and twenty years younger than I, Vulliamy. Go down and see if you can find it."

"Not for the world."

"Come, don't be a coward. We need that body. Climb down while I hold the lanthorn."

"I know a trick worth two of that," Vulliamy said.

"I'm not trying to kill you, you fool," Clothier growled. "I'll do it myself if you won't, but remember that your receiving the money depends on my remaining alive to inherit! Hold the lanthorn."

He began to climb down. I knew the ladder was unsafe and the old man had no rope to save him as I had. Yet if I tried to warn him I would be killed. I recalled the choice I had had to make when Assinder opened the hiding-place. I felt even less compunction now.

Suddenly there was a cry: "It's giving way! Help me."

I heard a desperate scrabbling of hands and nails on stone, and then a long scream and the thud of the body landing. Then there was silence. Since the tide was right out now he must have hit the wharf twenty feet below. I looked round the edge of the cask and saw Vulliamy peer down into the trap as he stood at its edge holding the lanthorn. After a moment he hurried to the steps and ran up them and out of the cellar.

After leaving time for him to get well clear of the building, I felt my way in the dark out of the counting-house. Towards the top of the lane I heard footsteps and pressed myself back into the shadows. A moment later Vulliamy passed me with the watch behind him. I ran up one street and then another until I found a quiet place. Then, my teeth chattering and my fingers numbed with cold, I managed to use the knife to free my hands.

CHAPTER 109

As I hurried away from the river-front I reflected that for the second time within twenty-four hours I had no idea where I should go. The first time, I had gone to Henry believing that I could trust him. Had he betrayed me? Someone must have, for how had my assailants known where to find me in the dark lane? And how had Clothier known that I had the will hidden around my neck? I could not avoid the suspicion that Henry had blown me up. But how could he have come to form a combination with my enemy? And he had put up a fierce struggle against our attackers. Had Barney then somehow traced me? That seemed much more probable. In that case I still dared not go to Joey and his mother. Then I would return to Henry, but I would be very suspicious of him. I crossed Fleet-street and hurried up Fetter-lane.

It was still very early when I reached the entrance to Barnards-inn but the gate was unlocked for, as I could see from the dim glow from his window, the porter was awake. I glanced in and saw that he was preoccupied in making his breakfast, so that with the aid of the fog it was not difficult for me to steal past.

I ascended the stair and as I reached the top I noticed that the oaken outer door of Henry's chambers stood open and I heard voices. After all that I had been through I hope it may be understood — if not excused — that I tip-toed up to the inner door and pressed my ear against its pannel.

Henry was speaking: "I very much fear, Pamplin, that we won't see our young friend again."

"What the devil do you mean by that?"

"Well, from what he told me I know he had enemies who wished his death."

"His death! What have you got me involved in, Bellringer? Do you mean to say that you believe those villains who attacked me intend to murder him?"

"I very much fear so."

I heard a long, low, and most unclerical whistle and then Mr Pamplin said, in a voice shaking with fright: "What the deuce do we do now?"

"We go to the police-office and lay an information before the beak."

"But only think of the scandal if our part in this gets abroad."

"But we have to, Pamplin. It's the only chance we have of saving the boy."

"Do you know who those men were and where they've taken him?"

"No, I have no idea."

"Then what purpose is served by going to the authorities? It'll only get me into the most infernal scrape. My bishop won't like it. You know how much trouble I've already had with him."

"I'm sorry, Pamplin, I'm afraid you'll have to take the consequences."

"Really, Bellringer. It's your fault for getting me into this. I agreed to do you a favour because you've helped me in the past. If you do have to go to the beak can't you keep me out of it?"

"I don't see how. I need someone to vouch for my innocence in all of this."

"Your innocence! What about me? We're both innocent, but how is our story going to sound when it's reported in the papers? There's always some damned journalist hanging about the police-courts waiting for stories of this kind. And why should the justice believe us, anyway? It all sounds improbable enough to me: a missing heir, a mysterious document of some kind. And a young fellow in the middle of it! You seem to forget my circumstances. This could be the end of my hopes of advancement."

"Why should you care for that? You have a rich enough living already, haven't you? But it's barely dawn and I'm confoundedly hungry. Before we do anything, let's have some breakfast."

"Excellent idea. The Cocoa-tree should be opening about now."

"Then you go on ahead and I'll follow when I've washed and changed my dress."

As I heard footsteps approaching I moved away from the door. I had heard enough to have my suspicions allayed.

The door opened and Mr Pamplin stood gazing at me in amazement. I believe that for an instant he thought I had returned from the grave and in the face of a miracle every one of his profoundest beliefs was shaken. He stepped backwards into the room, his mouth drooping speechlessly, and I followed him.

Henry turned and presented to my gaze almost as ghastly a spectacle as I: his face was bruised and since he was in his shirt and trowsers I could see how badly torn his clothes were, and that the shirt was covered in blood.

He looked at me for some moments with the strangest expression: "My dear John!" he exclaimed at length. "It really is you! Thank Heavens you're safe!"

He moved forward and, dirty and wet as I was, embraced me. In my weakened state I felt tears rising at his obvious pleasure in seeing me again.

"Awfully glad to see you safe, old man," said Mr Pamplin, having recovered his composure. "Spares me some uneasiness, I can assure you."

Henry led me tenderly towards a chair before the fire. "What happened?" he asked. Then he glanced warningly towards his friend who was watching us intently and added in an undertone: "Tell me when he's gone."

I saw the danger and though I had much to say and many questions to ask, I kept silent.

"You got away, evidently," Henry went on in a more natural voice. "Well, don't tire yourself by telling us now."

"What happened to you?" I asked.

Henry laughed: "Your friends knocked me to the ground and kicked me. When they had gone, Charles and I spent a comical half-hour blundering about in the fog trying to catch each other."

"Comical!" the clergyman protested.

"Very comical in retrospect, though hardly so at the time. You see, John, I unwittingly frightened him half to death so that he would run off whenever I came near, taking me for one of our assailants. But in the end we found each other. Then we looked for the watch, but of course it was not abroad. The Charlies are always safe and snug in the watch-house on a night like this. We decided to come back here and clean up before going before the beak." Then with a warning smile at me, Henry said to his friend: "Be a good fellow, Pamplin, and order us over breakfast, will you?"

"Very well," he answered rather irritably and departed.

As the door closed behind him Henry smiled at me conspiratorially and said: "Tell me quickly what happened before he gets back. And change into some dry things."

He gave me a dressing-gown and while we talked, I removed my soaking garments and he hung them before the fire.

"The men who abducted me were agents of Silas Clothier, who is the claimant under the codicil if I die. He tried to kill me but I escaped and he died instead."

"Died?" Henry repeated.

"Yes. But not before he had destroyed the will."

"You are sure he is dead?" Henry asked.

"Certain," I answered, rather surprised that he was so much interested in the old man's fate and so little in that of the will. I told him briefly what had happened. "What do you think I should do now?" I asked. "Should I go to the magistrates?"

"What purpose would that serve?" Henry asked rather distractedly.

"I believe none," I agreed, "for I am safe at last from that family, for the Clothiers — or, rather, the Porteouses — have no claim on the estate now that I have outlived the old man."

"Yes," Henry muttered. "They have no claim."

There was a silence, and then he said: "If you reveal yourself to be alive, that has far-reaching implications."

I looked at him in surprise.

"For the suit!" he exclaimed, seeing my puzzlement.

We were both silent for a moment.

"You keep the Mompessons in possession!" Henry exclaimed.

"That is true," I said. "But I also expose myself to danger."

"What danger?" he asked quickly.

"Well, with the destruction of the will the codicil remains in force and if I remain concealed until the time-limit expires, it is the heir of George Maliphant who would inherit. So there is still someone in whose interest it is that I should die."

"You are making an unwarranted assumption there," Henry said.

"Oh?" I asked.

"Are you sure that there is such an heir in existence? I have never heard of a claimant from that side of the family."

I was a little nonplussed that he seemed to know so much about the suit and the genealogy of the parties involved.

"You are right," I said. "The line may have failed and in that case I am safe. But then what would happen to the estate? Would it remain in the possession of the Mompessons?"

"By no means. Only while you are alive do they have any title. Once you were declared dead, if no heir descended from George Maliphant could be found, then the estate would escheat to the Crown."

So by remaining in hiding or coming forward I could determine the fate of the Mompessons. It was a deeply gratifying reflection and I meditated on it in silence for some time. Henry also seemed to be lost in his own thoughts, so we sat without speaking. I would need time to think about this and to consider how my decision would affect Henrietta. Certainly, now that the will was destroyed, there was no advantage to anyone in forcing her into marriage. Indeed, her guardians would lose all interest in her. She could surely marry whom she chose.

We were still sitting in this silent state when Mr Pamplin came back, followed by a waiter bearing our breakfast in a tower of silver dishes.

When the servant had set down his burden and departed, Henry said cheerfully: "You'll be relieved to learn, Charles, that we've decided that nothing is to be gained by going before the magistrates."

Mr Pamplin brightened visibly, applauded our judgement, and made a good breakfast of the devilled mutton-chops, crumpets, and coffee. He departed shortly afterwards, declaring himself exhausted after the night's alarms. Henry and I were also so tired that we decided to sleep, although the day was by now far advanced on its foggy, freezing course. He insisted that I take the bed while he made himself comfortable on the sopha. It hardly mattered to me for within a minute of falling into bed I was fast asleep.

CHAPTER 110

I awoke towards noon and lay thinking about the events of the last two days. I had seen a man risk death — and perhaps die — for the sake of gold. And I had made no attempt to dissuade him from taking a gamble that I knew was more dangerous than he had believed. Yet I felt no responsibility for what had happened to Assinder. And I had seen another man die and had let him go to his death because to save him was to destroy myself. Though hardly guilty, I was at the very least involved. Whatever this madness was, I could not tell myself that I was outside it. Not any longer. And what had old Clothier's motives been in trying to kill me and in risking his own life? The love of gold again? Or was it something more insidious — the desire for justice? If I could acquit myself of the former, as I believed I could, I had to plead guilty to the latter. And the list of those whose death had come about because of this quest for justice did not end with Assinder and old Clothier. I had led George Digweed to his fate, even though he had gone willingly. And even Miss Lydia might still be alive if I had not come into her life. Perhaps Henrietta had been right to imply that her great-aunt had confused justice with the desire for revenge, and perhaps I had done so myself.

I dressed and went into the sitting-room, where I found Henry, clad as he had been the night before, sitting at his desk. I gained the impression — I do not know how — that he had not slept.

He greeted me warmly but seemed preoccupied.

"Are you not going to your work today?" I asked.

"Yes, in due course," he said off-handedly.

"Will not the gentleman whom you appointed to meet us last night wonder why we did not arrive?"

"Oh, I'll see him and explain."

"What will you say? Surely not the truth?"

"Heavens, no," he exclaimed with a mirthless laugh. Then he added confidently: "I'll gammon him with something. Leave that to me."

Lying open before him was the evening-paper, *The Globe*. I looked over his shoulder and read it. At the foot of the second page was an item headed "Unfortunate Accident to City Merchant and His Grandson: Heroic Death of Mr Silas Clothier, of Edington's-wharf, Blackfriars, and Bell-lane, Spitalfields". From the story that followed it was clear that Mr Vulliamy had reported to the authorities that the old gentleman had died in attempting to save the life of his grandson who had fallen through a trap-door into the river and presumably drowned, though his body had not yet been found.

The allusion to Bell-lane gave me the explanation of why my mother had been so horrified when Mrs Sackbutt had mentioned the name when we were in Cox's-square: it had revealed to her how near she was to the house of her enemy.

"He'll cut up pretty warm," Henry said meditatively. "Daniel Porteous will be the heir and will be pleased at his old feller's death since Quintard and Mimpriss have got into trouble and he's in a pickle over it. But you'd have a very strong claim to a half-share of Clothier's estate, I believe."

"Never!" I cried.

I began to explain to him why I wanted nothing to do with the matter, but he listened to me with increasing irritation and before I had finished interrupted me:

"And what are you going to do about the Hougham claim? Don't tell me you're not interested in that either. The time-limit when you will be presumed to be deceased runs out in two years, though now that you've been reported to be dead (though they won't find a body, of course) I suppose that might be brought forward. When are you going to declare yourself?"

"I haven't decided that I will," I said lightly.

"But don't you see how much hangs upon it?" he exclaimed brusquely.

I looked at him in surprise that he should seem to be so concerned on the Mompessons' behalf: "Then you think I should come forward?"

"Of course not!" he cried. Then he smiled awkwardly and said: "Don't you see, old fellow, that you have a great deal of pull on 'em, but only by not coming forward?"

I stared at him in bewilderment for I could not follow his reasoning.

"Once you declare yourself they have no further need of you for your life keeps them in possession," he explained. "So stay out of sight and negotiate with them through a third party."

So that was it. A kind of blackmail. I saw it all now and I did not need to be told who the third party was to be.

I stood up: "I must go now. Thank you for your assistance."

He flushed: "Don't be a muff. After all, you stole the will from them. What I'm suggesting is no worse than that."

It was quite different. I had regained the will in order to see justice done. What he was suggesting was mere self-interested exploitation of the situation.

I hurried to the door and he called out: "Where will you go?"

"To my friends."

"How are they called? Where do they live?"

"I know the house but not the name of the street," I said, reckless of how I might offend him.

"Send word of your address, will you?" he cried as I opened the door.

I looked at him as I stood in the door-way: "Goodbye, Henry."

I hoped never to see him again for his suggestion had re-awakened the darkest suspicions in my mind. He faced me, flushed with annoyance but trying to smile his old smile that reminded me of Stephen but that took me in no longer. I slammed the door and hurried down the stairs.

As I made my way out of the inn I glanced back several times to see if he were following me. And then as I hurried East I began to regret my conduct towards him and to ask myself, what kind of suspicious, ungenerous being had I become constantly to suspect that others had designs upon me? What proof had I that Henry's interest in me was anything but benign? He wanted me to benefit from the position I was in and was prepared to help me. So why should he not be rewarded for that? And yet as I went I took precautions to ensure that no-one could follow me by several times crossing a busy street suddenly in front of oncoming vehicles — cursed and whipped at by the drivers for my pains — and darting up a side-lane on the other side.

When I reached the lane in Wapping in which the Digweeds lived I approached their house with the same circumspection. As far as I could establish, nobody was lurking nearby.

As I entered I found Mrs Digweed and Joey seated before the fire. They greeted me with surprise since Joey was expecting to see me next in the mews at the back of Brook-street at dawn nearly a week hence. They had, of course, not read the reports of my death in the public prints. Examining their faces, I saw nothing but pleasure at the sight of me on Mrs Digweed's and something of the same but still alloyed with resentment, on her son's. I wished I could overcome that gnawing suspiciousness that had tainted me.

First I expressed my condolences for the death of the father. Then I answered their questions and when I told them what had happened, they rejoiced at my escape but grieved at the destruction of the will after all that we — they and I — had been through.

Joey told me that he had done what I had asked about engaging lodgings by paying a month's rent in advance, and he returned to me the balance of Miss Lydia's monies, insisting on rendering me a full account of what he had spent on my clothes and linen — a sum which amounted to four pounds. He and his mother adamantly refused to take a shilling for themselves.

Later that day I went with Joey to the lodgings he had taken in Chandos-street with the intention of getting the money back since my intentions had changed now that the will no longer existed. However, the landlady, Mrs Quaintance, absolutely refused to return more than a derisory amount of the rent (two pounds, for it was ten shillings a week) or to countenance my under-letting the rooms. It occurred to me that there would be advantages in living there and so I arranged to move in after all.

When I was alone I sat on the edge of my bed and thought with relief that I was now free of the Clothier connexion. They had no further interest in me nor I in any of them. My relation to the Mompessons, however, was less clear-cut.

During the days that followed I tried to decide what to do. The idea that Henry had hinted at — of blackmailing the Mompessons — filled me with repugnance. Either I would come forward and save them with no advantage to myself, or I would let them be dispossessed. But how would that affect Henrietta? And what of my own situation? I had the forty-seven pounds left from the gold that Miss Lydia had given me and that was a great deal of money, but I was by no means certain that I had a moral right to it since it had been given me to pay for laying the will before the Court in order to rescue Henrietta. (That was why I felt I could not use it to repay Sukey.) But if not to me, then to whom did it belong? In a sense, I held it in trust for Henrietta and I could best serve her interests by using it to establish myself so that I could help her in the future. As for whether to declare myself, I decided not to make a decision yet since I still had nearly two years before the time-limit expired.

I realized after some time that the destruction of the will was actually a blessing, and I felt as if a great weight had been lifted from me. Now I could decide what to do with my life with no regard for factors wholly beyond my control, for it came to me now that the whole of my life had been dominated by the past — the early experiences of my mother, the murder of my grandfather, and even the deeds of my great-grandfather and his father before him. Now the future, whatever it might be, was at least my own.

How would I live? What would I do with the rest of my life? The best I could hope for — barely educated and without friends to advance me — was a lowly clerkship at a salary of twenty pounds a year. And I would be fortunate even to gain such a position for I did not write a good hand or cypher well or know how to reckon up accounts. The idea of entering one of the professions that I had long cherished, was out of the question for I would need not only a premium but the means to keep myself for the period of my articles — at least two hundred pounds. So I concluded that my wisest plan was to search for a post as clerk while continuing to educate myself in the hope of improving my prospects.

BOOK III

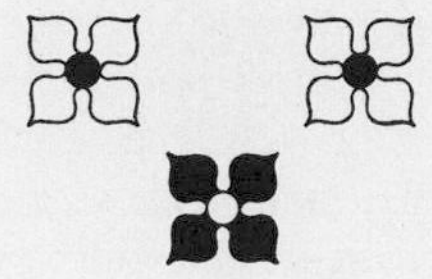

Old Friends in a New Light

CHAPTER III

The months that followed were a period of relentless, grinding disappointment. I began by studying the newspapers and writing in response to every advertisement for a post for which I felt myself to be at all qualified. In no case was I even invited to present myself for examination. Meanwhile I laboured at my books and penmanship, trying to acquire those skills that I lacked.

Once the month that I had paid for was up, I moved from my set of rooms into a small garret-chamber under the roof for four shillings a week, frightened of the way my money was running out. After a couple of months more I realized that I had been too optimistic in believing I could rely upon advertisements in the press, and so from now on I spent a part of each day trudging from one establishment to another asking if there were any vacancies. The great disadvantage I had — beyond my lack of experience — was that I could offer no written character, nor provide a respectable person to be referred to, nor even describe my life in full and accurate detail up to that moment. So I was constantly rebuffed — usually off-handedly, often coldly, and occasionally in a friendly enough manner.

In those cases when it was admitted that there was a vacancy it always happened that it had been set aside for the nephew of the managing-clerk's wife or a lad known to the family of the senior cashier. Gradually it came to me that English mercantile life was a vast system of uncles, nephews, friends and neighbours from which I was excluded.

Even when on one occasion I was offered the position of office-boy with the prospect — but a distant and dubious one — of working up to a junior clerkship, I decided I could not afford to take it. The salary of about five shillings a week, intended for a boy younger than I and living at home, would barely cover my lodgings. I could not consider a salary of less than twelve shillings.

By the time that six months had expired since my escape from the river, however, I realized that I should have taken that post and eked out the salary with my little capital in hopes of being promoted before it ran out. For the prospect of being reduced once again to pennilessness faced me now. My money had not lasted as well as I had expected, principally because the expenditure involved in searching for work was so high. I had to have serviceable boots and I found that I could not avoid the occasional expense of a hot meal from the cook-shop. Over and above my rent, I was living at the rate of about nine shillings a week.

Living some distance now from the Digweeds, I saw them infrequently though the mother, at least, fairly regularly for she was working again as a laundress and insisted on doing my linen. There was little enough of it, but every three weeks she collected it and Joey usually delivered it back to my lodgings a few days later. He had found occasional work as a barrow-boy at Covent-garden and I knew she was anxious that he should not be tempted to return to the criminal pursuits of his early boyhood, especially when he saw his friends who had remained in that course possessing money to spend and plenty of time to enjoy it. I was reassured that they had seen nothing of either Barney or Sally since the occasion when Joey had spotted his uncle shortly before I managed to regain the will. I assumed that I was safe since now that Silas Clothier was dead nobody, as far as I knew, had any interest in my death. Yet I could not altogether put from my mind the clause in the codicil which stipulated that at the failure of the Huffam line the estate passed immediately to the heir of George Maliphant.

After some reflection, I decided to allow Henrietta to believe with everyone else that I was dead, for I saw no advantage to either of us in my taking the risk of disabusing her of this notion — and it even gave me a certain pleasure to know that she believed me to be no more. Yet several times I hung about in the street outside the house in Brook-street (muffled up around the face) and was occasionally rewarded with a glimpse of her coming or going.

One day in the middle of October in the same year, I had a chance encounter that was to have important consequences. As I was hurrying along Fleet-street one afternoon I caught sight of someone I thought I knew. Just before I averted my head and began to move away in instinctive recoil from anyone from my past (since I wished it to be believed that I was dead), I saw that she was a peak-faced young girl in a cheap cotton gown.

I was too late, and she hurried up to me and called: "Sir! Please wait!"

I turned and recognised Mrs Purviance's little servant, Nancy. I had nothing to fear from her and stopped to talk. She told me that Miss Quilliam had returned to London about a year ago and had quarrelled with Mrs Purviance, and she added that she had seen her fairly recently coming out of a night-house in King-street, St. James-square. I thanked her and gave her a penny.

I felt that Miss Quilliam was one of the few people I had known in the past whom I might not have tried to avoid now. Yet I remembered how she had been in one respect a baneful influence upon my mother, even though acting for the best motives, and I also recalled what Miss Lydia had said about her and the gossip of the servants at Brook-street. I did not know what to believe, but I knew that she had been kind to my mother and myself with no selfish motive. No, I would not avoid her in the event of my meeting her.

That was improbable, however, since I was rarely abroad at night. Yet it now happened that I found myself occasionally in or near that notorious part of the Town late in the evening, for one of my few consolations and almost my sole luxury at this period of my life was the theatre, for which I now developed a passion. I formed the habit of going late and therefore gaining admission to the gallery at half-price, losing myself for a couple of hours in the near-darkness and the glamour of the stage-lights in the only moments of happiness I then experienced.

One evening, as I was walking down Haymarket, I was struck by the face of a young woman turned in my direction and registering utter horror at the sight of me. I could not look away, so compelling were her pale countenance and staring eyes. It was Sally! And she had clearly recognised me and believed that I was dead. Now I turned my head and hurried up a side-street, cursing my ill luck for of all those whom I least wished to know that I was alive, Barney was the chief.

One night a few weeks after this, I had been to the theatre at Covent-garden and having stayed for the after-piece was making my way home along Maiden-lane very late when a woman came past me whom I thought familiar. I followed her as she progressed along the street stopping occasional foot-passengers, and at last went into the Court-end of Town. She seemed to become aware of me for she glanced backwards once or twice and appeared to slow down, and shortly afterwards she turned into a house in King-street. I followed her in, pushing past a porter who stepped towards me in the dimly-lit hall, and entered a large salon hung with chandeliers whose bright lighting showed up its faded elegance.

People in the costume of ladies and gentlemen were standing or sitting in groups around the room and somewhat down-at-heel waiters were serving refreshments, so that it might — waiving a certain unsteadiness of gait or shabbiness of dress — have been an At Home in any of the drawing-rooms a few streets to the north.

Miss Quilliam was already seated upon a chaise-longue and turned to me as I came in. As I crossed to her I saw that her face was much older, despite the rouged cheeks. Though she smiled, her blank eyes were gazing at me unsteadily and because her speech was indistinct, her first words were difficult to understand, though their import was clear.

"You have misunderstood," I said. "I am an old friend of yours."

It took some time to make her understand who I was. When she remembered me she was manifestly moved. Now she became more collected and her first question was about my mother. At my intelligence she cast her eyes down and bit her lip.

"I have thought of her often," she said. "And of you too. That time we spent in Orchard-street, it was the last ... I cannot say 'the last period of happiness' but at least ... "

She broke off and I laid my hand on hers and told her that I understood her meaning.

After a few moments' silence, she ordered a waiter to bring coffee for both of us. At her prompting I told her briefly some details of my mother's death and a little of what had happened to me since then: my persecution by the enemies who had pursued my mother, my consignment to and escape from the madhouse, and finally my period of service in the Mompessons' household for a purpose which I left unspecified and about which she did not enquire.

"Tell me," she asked eagerly, "do you have any tidings of Henrietta? I have never ceased to worry about the fate of that strange child."

I replied that I had spoken to Henrietta a number of times and that when I had last seen her some six months ago she was in good health. Then I told her I had a particular reason for wanting to know about the Mompessons and begged her to tell me everything she could about her time in that household.

"I once told your mother my story but I suppressed much of it," she said. "If only I had told the whole truth then it might have saved her, but I was ashamed. And I wanted to protect her innocence."

She laughed without amusement.

I did not tell her that I had overheard her account on that occasion, and she now related it to me again in exactly the same terms except that this time she said much more about the circumstances in which she had come to Town:

"When my grandmother died in my fifteenth year I was sent to the workhouse. It was after my request for assistance from my grandfather had failed that I appealed for help to Sir Thomas."

"Is that the gentleman who is a friend of David Mompesson?"

"Yes, Sir Thomas Delamater. It was he who gave the living to Mr Charles Pamplin that his uncle had promised to my father."

"Pamplin!" I cried.

I described to her Henry Bellringer's friend and she confirmed that it must be the same gentleman.

"He played a part in my story," she said with a bleak smile, "for he wrote to me at the prompting of Sir Thomas and encouraged me to feel safe in trusting that gentleman. In his letter Mr Pamplin told me he regretted having — entirely unwittingly — been the instrument that precipitated the misfortunes that had fallen upon my family. We maintained a correspondence and a few years later, when my apprenticeship at the sisters' school was out, he suggested I come to Town in order that he and Sir Thomas might aid me to find a post as governess. In all innocence, I accepted the invitation. Need I say more? He found me lodgings with Mrs Malatratt who appeared to be an entirely respectable woman. What could be more natural, I thought, than that my benefactor, Sir Thomas, should visit me?" She sighed. "I was scarcely seventeen, ignorant of the ways of the world, and utterly penniless. However, I insisted on regaining my independence after a year, and it was then that Sir Thomas found for me the governess's post with the Mompessons, who had long been friends of his. He believed that in this way he would retain power over me. I had to leave my trunks containing gifts from him at Mrs Malatratt's when I went to Hougham, which turned out fortunately for it was thus that I met you and your mother again. My troubles were not ended by my new independence, however, for the reason that Sir Thomas told Mr — I should say, Sir David — Mompesson of my relationship with him, and that is why he was so importunate in his pursuit of me. However, I was happy at Hougham for those months with Henrietta, truly happy for the first and last time in my life."

So it was from Sir Thomas that she had received the silk dresses that Mrs Purviance's servant had told me were in the trunks. I believed she was telling the truth now.

She went on with the story she had told my mother. While she described the events of the fateful night on which she had been taken to Vauxhall-gardens by David Mompesson, Mrs Purviance, and "Harry", something — some dim echo of something in her account — began to stir in my mind, but I could not drag it into the light of day.

"When I left the house in Brook-street and returned to Mrs Malatratt," she continued, "she refused to let me remove the trunks whose contents were my only fortune. The reason was that Sir Thomas owed her rent for another wretched young creature whom he had installed there before me. Finally she was paid by Mr Pamplin when he brought to her house yet another victim, for he is, to speak plainly, Sir Thomas's procurer. And so Mrs Malatratt released them to me shortly before you found me at Orchard-street."

I asked her about my mother's telling her, or showing her, the account of her life she had been writing at that time, and whether she therefore knew the full story of my grandfather's death and my own conception.

"I can't remember," she answered.

"Do you mean you can't remember whether you knew, or you knew the story but have forgotten it?"

She shook her head and I saw I would not receive an answer, but I believed I knew anyway what it would have been.

She told me briefly what had happened to her since my last meeting with her after which Mrs Purviance had sent her to Paris. On her return she had broken with her protectress and, as a consequence, spent some months in the Fleet-prison. Now it was that she told me — with what fortunate results you know — of a meeting there with our friends from Orchard-street, whom she had found happily (or unhappily!) reunited and reconciled. After this there was no more to be said, and with a sad heart I took leave of her and hurried home.

As for what became of her, my friends, (to address you directly for a moment) then if you are curious to know about a former acquaintance, you will be interested to learn that I heard a little a couple of years after that last encounter — though since then I have heard nothing. It appears that about a twelvemonth after the meeting just described, her situation improved considerably when she was re-united for a few months with a younger woman who was an acquaintance from earlier and happier days and who had herself fallen into unfortunate circumstances and was consequently encumbered. They shared lodgings in Holborn and I understand that for a while they maintained themselves by their needles. Then the little household suffered the sad loss of one (the youngest) of its number and sank under this blow. Helen was lost from sight and her companion as well — though I have been informed that the latter went to France and was last heard of in Calais.

So matters stood with me late on a cold wet afternoon at the end of the November following the events narrated in the previous chapter. I had spent the morning at my books and the afternoon in a fruitless search for work, and was now expecting Joey who was due to make his regular visit to return my clean linen.

The rain was falling steadily and lowering clouds were massing in the western sky. As I waited I sat at a little table at the window and occupied myself by grimly reckoning up my accounts as a way of practising that skill and finding out where I stood. After nine months I now had left a little over twenty pounds and reckoned that at my present rate of living I could survive for another six, at which point I would be wholly destitute.

As I reached this gloomy conclusion there was a loud and peremptory knock at the street-door. Since I was now the only lodger and my landlady had few visiters, I assumed that it was Joey. And yet it was much more exigent than the way in which he habitually knocked and reminded me of something — some earlier occasion — that I could not call to mind.

Since my little chamber under the roof was at the back of the house I could not look out into the street, but a moment later I heard feet upon the stair as if several people were coming up. There was a gentle knock on my door and then Mrs Quaintance opened it beaming broadly:

"A gentleman to see you, Mr Parminter," she said, and was obviously very gratified to be able to make such an announcement for the first time to her lodger in the garret.

She withdrew and the gentleman entered. It was Henry! And very gentlemanly indeed he now appeared in a white beaver hat and a magnificent great-coat beneath which he was wearing a bottle-green frock-coat of excellent cut and adorned with silver buttons.

"My dear fellow," he cried, "how very good it is to see you again!"

Although he spoke with his wonted vivacity it seemed to me that he was ill at ease.

"How did you find me?" I asked.

He wagged a gloved finger at me and as he removed his white kid gloves said: "You didn't send word of your address. I only found you by the most extraordinarily fortunate coincidence. I saw you coming in here one day as I was going past. I was in too much of a hurry to stop then but I noted the number and here I am."

It was indeed an extraordinary coincidence and I had learned to be suspicious of them.

"What is your business?" I asked.

He seated himself with considerable assurance and said: "The Mompesson suit."

"Then I will detain you no longer, for I am not interested in it now."

I thought he flushed.

"You most certainly are interested in it," he exclaimed, "at least in the legal sense."

"Hardly. Now that the will no longer exists I can hope for no advantage from any outcome."

He turned his head away and bit his lip: "Can you dismiss it so lightly?"

"Although I was very upset," I answered, "when the will was destroyed, I am now relieved not to be concerned in the business any longer. No strangers seek to encompass my death and that, I assure you, is an honour that I am very happy to forego."

Henry looked at me with a strange kind of triumph: "You believe you are no longer in danger?"

I nodded in surprise.

"Then you do not know what has happened? You see, you should take an interest in the suit. The Maliphant claimant has come forward."

"Has he!" I exclaimed. "And who is he?"

"His identity has not been revealed. A solicitor acting on his behalf has given formal notice to the Court that such an individual exists, and that since the codicil is now in force, the death of Mr Silas Clothier means that he is now next in succession to the estate and will claim it when the Court declares you dead."

I felt a cold chill as if I were being clutched and dragged down once again by something that I had thought to have escaped from.

"Then I will let that happen," I said. "I will let the Court declare me dead and the estate pass to this individual rather than to the Crown. Why should I care?"

"But you see, it isn't as simple as that. You are alive and therefore your existence is — or, rather, would be — of considerable interest to both the Mompessons and the Maliphant claimant."

"You obviously take a very close interest in the suit. You say that this individual's identity has not been revealed, but may I assume that it is known to you?"

He smiled at me so coldly that I began to wonder how I had ever thought him kind and good-hearted. And now, as I looked at him, the strangest idea crossed my mind.

"Forgive me for not answering that question," he replied. "But you do see, don't you, that you cannot remain safe simply by allowing yourself to be declared dead? Too much is at stake."

"You mean, to this individual my life is an insignificant obstacle?"

He merely flicked at his polished boots with the edge of his pocket handkerchief.

"But you forget," I said, "that to the world I am already dead."

He smiled and said softly: "But you see, I know the truth."

As I looked at his face I felt that I was reading his very soul. How could I have imagined that anything but greed and self-interest motivated him? The blood rushed to my head with shame as I remembered how trusting I had been. I had gone to him with my hideous story of the death of Stephen and he had brushed it aside. The death of Stephen! I recalled that Stephen had told me how it was Henry who had persuaded him to trust his aunt. Surely he had been implicated in his death! What a fool I had been! How dared I blame my mother for her fatal trustfulness!

"Then I assume," I said in as steady a voice as I could muster; "that you have come to put to me once again your infamous proposal that I should blackmail Sir David and Lady Mompesson?"

As I spoke I moved towards the door to make it clear that I wanted him gone. However, he remained reclining in his chair, idly swinging one leg. His self-confidence had grown in proportion as my peace of mind diminished.

"You are quite out," he answered.

I was so surprised that I sat down.

"Imagine," he began, looking up at the ceiling reflectively, "how very different the situation would be if that will which you and some of your friends went to so much trouble to retrieve, should still exist?"

"But it doesn't," I replied. "I saw it destroyed in my very presence."

"Yes, but supposing it had not been destroyed?" he persevered.

"Then if it could be laid before the Court I should be in danger no longer."

He gave a sharp, angry laugh: "Is that all that strikes you? Don't you care that it would make you the owner of the property?"

"That too," I agreed.

"That too," he echoed, leaning forward and gripping the arms of the chair.

I shrugged my shoulders.

"Are you really so unconcerned?" he muttered to himself. He stared at me for a moment and then suddenly said: "What if I should tell you that the will does exist?"

I started: "Then I should tell you again that I saw it burnt to ashes before my eyes."

He hesitated a moment and then said: "What you saw old Clothier destroy was a careful copy of the will made on parchment of an identical type and written in an accurate legal hand."

"Nonsense," I said. "The document I took from the hiding-place was the original. You said so yourself."

He nodded: "I did. And so it was."

"And it never left my possession until it was taken from me and destroyed."

"Except once," Henry said softly with a smile. "When you slept on my sopha for a few hours the morning you came to me."

I gasped and immediately anticipated what he was going to say.

"And while you slumbered I sat at my desk," he went on, "and made as accurate a copy of it as lay within my power. And given my experience as a law-copier and the fact that I had all the materials I needed at hand — including an old and blank sheet of parchment — I was able to make a very good copy indeed. Certainly good enough to deceive you and old Clothier."

I did not doubt that what he was saying was the truth.

"Why did you do this?"

"As a precaution in case anything happened to it."

"And where is it now?"

"Safe where it belongs."

I could make nothing of this.

"And you see how far-sighted I was to take such a precaution," he went on; "and how grateful to me you ought to be?"

I tried to collect my scattered wits. This did not make sense: "But why should you fear that?" I cried. "We were about to take the document to your principal. It would not have deceived him."

I faltered and broke off for even as I spoke, it all became clear to me.

"There was no such appointment, was there? It was Silas Clothier whom you went to see and not your principal. It was you who arranged to lure me into that trap."

"Stuff!" he said. "You saw how badly injured I was."

"False! False! You were not badly hurt. Or if you were, that was the price you were ready to pay. It was all a charade!"

"This is absurd. You don't surely imagine that a man in Pamplin's position would involve himself ... "

"I don't know. I think I could suspect him of anything, for all he is a clergyman. (I know more about him than you think.) And yet I believe you duped him as much as me. Yes, I see it now, you wanted him there precisely because he would be an unimpeachable witness to my abduction and your resistance to it in case it ever came to light."

As if he had for once no answer to this, he turned his head away.

"I think I understand it now. You sold me and the will to Silas Clothier, though I don't know how you knew how to find him. But you also intended to cheat him as much as you betrayed me and so you made that forgery. And once I was dead and he expected to claim the estate under the codicil, then I imagine that you intended to go to the Mompessons and tell them you had the will. Or rather, that you represented someone who had it. And in that situation they would have given you almost anything to have it back."

"You're very clever," he said and I took his remark as sarcastic.

"No, what you mean is that I've been a complete fool. But I believe I understand now. There is more. You betray anyone who trusts you if there's an advantage to be got from it. Poor Stephen trusted you and I'd stake my life that you betrayed him, though I don't understand how or why. But when you urged him to deliver himself into the power of his aunt who sent him to that wicked place to be done away with, I'll wager you did so for a reward. And by doing that you helped to murder him. Why, that's why you were so poor the first time I came to you and so much more prosperous the next time!"

He stared at me without smiling but did not make any effort to answer my charge.

"But when it was Silas Clothier who died that night instead of I, you were taken by surprise," I continued. "How dumbfoundered you were to see me again! Your scheme was in ruins, for since I was still alive the Mompessons were not in the grave danger you had hoped for. That is why you wanted me to remain hidden so that I could join you in blackmailing them."

"Hardly that," he protested gently. "Let us say, 'arriving at a composition advantageous to both parties'. But it was clumsy of me to have suggested it. I hadn't realized what high principles you have. And yet since they apparently permit you to burgle a house and steal the property of another, perhaps it was pardonable in me not to appreciate this."

I flushed: "I believe there is a difference. I thought I had a moral right to the inheritance even if I had to steal the will back. But I don't see any need to justify my actions to you."

"Just don't be so ready to accuse me. Now, on that basis, let us be perfectly frank with one another. Will you hear what I have to say?"

"I will at least hear it. Be quick."

"I am no longer interested in the Mompessons. I have a much better proposal. I was delighted to hear you say just now that you have a moral right to the will, for I am offering it to you."

"To me? I have nothing to pay you with, and I don't imagine you are offering it as a gift."

"You would not make a good man of business. Only consider for a moment. Who else derives any advantage from the will? Not the Mompessons for while you are alive, they can make no use of it. If they laid it before the Court you could come forward and claim the estate. In order for it to be of any value to them, they would have to know that you were dead and then marry that mad girl to the half-wit."

I shuddered for I had not considered the implications of the re-discovery of the will as they affected Henrietta. Perhaps she was no longer safe from a forced marriage, as I had believed. But how did Henry know so much about the Mompessons?

"You are the one who stands to gain the most," he went on. "For you would go from beggary to opulence."

"Then what do you want from me?" I asked.

"I want you to agree to convey to me a third share in the property."

"A third share!" I exclaimed. Then I added: "Have you not forgotten one thing? I am not yet of age and therefore have no power either to alienate any real property I may possess or to bind myself to do so in the future."

"My dear fellow, you seem to forget that I am a Chancery lawyer. Of course I have considered that. All I want from you at this stage is your consent. I will retain possession of the will but I will file a bill on your behalf — acting through a third-party, of course, in order to conceal my role — serving notice to the Court that the succession of the Maliphant claimant under the codicil is objected to. There will be no difficulty in drawing out this process until you are of age and can then execute a bond by which you will bind yourself to the conveyance of the property in my favour."

"I merely asked from curiosity," I said. "For the bargain itself, I can give you your answer now. You inferred from what I said a moment ago that I believe I have a right to the will and therefore to the estate, but if you had attended to my words more carefully you would have heard that what I said was that I once believed that. I believe so no longer, and I assure you that I will never consent to what you propose."

He was clearly surprised and, from the way his face darkened, very angry.

"You're mad," he exclaimed. "If you agree to this you will inherit vast wealth. But if you refuse ... "

"As I will, I assure you," I broke in.

"Then you leave me with only two choices. Either I can sell the will back to Sir David."

Then Henrietta would once again be forced into marriage with Tom!

"Or, on the other hand," he continued, "I can offer it to the Maliphant heir who will, of course, destroy it and with it your chance of ever inheriting the estate."

"I tell you, I do not care."

"No? But you forget that in both cases the other party needs your death, the Mompessons so that that girl inherits and the Maliphant claimant in order to inherit under the codicil."

From the way he looked at me I knew precisely what he was threatening.

"So there is your choice: on the one hand, wealth and safety; on the other, poverty and ... at the least, danger."

His words strangely recalled the choice offered me by my mother many years before, but now the terms were much more starkly opposed for it was not wealth and danger against poverty and safety, but a choice that presented itself quite unequivocally to self-interest. And, though Henry did not know it, the choice was all the starker because of Henrietta. In rejecting wealth and safety I was also condemning her to marriage with Tom. And yet I did not hesitate.

"I have given you my answer," I said. "And I assure you that I will never change my mind. Once I was prepared to go to almost any lengths to gain that estate for I believed that I had Justice on my side. But I did wrong and brought harm and unhappiness to myself and, what is more important, to others."

I believe that until I spoke these words he had thought that my refusal was merely a bargaining ploy, but now he realized that I meant what I said.

"You believe that merely because harm to other people came of your actions, that proves that you did not have Justice on your side?" he said mockingly. "What a naive view of the world. You think there are rewards for Justice and punishments for doing wrong?"

"You have misunderstood me again. I still believe I had Justice on my side, but what I have learned is that I have no right to Justice. Society itself is unjust."

"You talk so easily of Justice and Injustice," he suddenly cried with extraordinary venom. "What do you know of those things? What right have you, a Huffam and a Clothier, to talk of Justice when your two families — and the damned Mompessons — have done so much wrong to mine?"

"What are you talking about?" I asked in amazement.

"I have as much right to a share of the estate as you. If my great-grandfather had received his due ... "

He broke off as if suddenly realizing that he had said too much and sat for some moments making an effort to compose himself again.

A right to a share of the estate? Did he then have some kind of connexion with my family?

He stood up and said: "If you change your mind, you know where to find me. We have a short while, since the time-limit does not expire for a little longer."

"I have given you my reply," I said.

"In that case, you must abide by the consequences," he said and left the room.

I sat down to consider the implications of what I had learned. First I tried to work out who the Maliphant claimant could be and how it was that Henry knew his identity. My own connexion with him came through Stephen Maliphant. Had Stephen been sent to the school to die because he was the heir? In that case was the claimant Stephen's aunt or someone closely connected with her? If that assumption were correct, then was Henry himself related to the claimant? Was he himself, even, the Maliphant claimant? His proposal was hardly consistent with that, for in that case he would surely have destroyed the will. (Unless he was playing his hand even more deviously than I understood.) Yet his reference to his own family's rights suggested that he had some blood-connexion with me. Was he related to one of the five families descended from Henry Huffam: the Huffams, the Mompessons, the Clothiers, the Palphramonds, and the Maliphants? Where then did he fit in the pattern?

The evening advanced without my noticing until I found myself in absolute darkness and had to find a lucifer. Only then did I realize that Joey had not arrived as had been agreed, and in my present state of mind this was further reason for disquiet. My visiter had made me so restless that I could not think of staying idly indoors and so, putting on my great-coat and hat, I stepped out with the intention of walking to Mrs Digweed's cottage to see what had become of Joey.

I had only gone half the length of Church-lane towards the Strand when I heard a rapid step behind me. Before I had time even to be afraid, I was flung head foremost against the wall and pinned by a powerful grip. The blow to my head stunned me and a wave of nausea rose within me. Then a face was thrust close to mine and a harsh voice came out of the darkness:

"Well, ain't this a pleasant surprise! And there was I a-thinking as you was dead and gorn. Wasn't I glad to hear as how it wasn't true! I thought I'd come and see for meself. And I *am* pleased. On'y it quite shakes a cove's respeck for the public prints, don't it?" He pulled something from his belt. "I reckon I should prove 'em right, arter all. And the beauty of it is I can't be lagged for it for you're dead already."

I knew there was no point in struggling nor in crying out in that lonely place. My only chance lay in an appeal to self-interest. But on what grounds? On whose behalf was Barney doing this? Surely not Daniel Porteous' for now that old Clothier was dead my death was of no benefit to his heirs. Was he getting revenge against me on his own behalf? In that event I was lost. But there was another possibility.

"Sancious put you up to this, didn't he?" I cried.

Even as I said it, I had no idea what the attorney's motives could be. But whatever they were, they must be based on a mistaken assumption. And so I played the one card I had:

"But he doesn't know that the will still exists! It wasn't destroyed any more than I was! Tell him that!"

Barney wrenched me round to face him and stared at me thoughtfully, breathing heavily and stroking the blade of his knife with his thumb.

"This is a bubble," he said at last.

"If you kill me now Sancious won't profit. Only the Mompessons. Do you want that?"

This was inspired, for I recalled his brother telling me that he had a grudge against them over payment for some work.

He stared at me for the longest moment of my life, then he suddenly pushed me from him and rapidly made off.

I hurried on towards the Strand and only felt safe once I was among the crowds and the street-lamps.

Why should Sancious want my death? Who could he be working for? That remained a puzzle, but suddenly I both understood how Barney had known where to find me and knew why Joey had not come that afternoon! He had sold me to his uncle. I found my eyes watering and realized that I was close to tears. I had come to have faith in him after a long period of suspicion, and just when I had in effect entrusted my life to him he had betrayed me. Something was running down my face. I realized that it was not tears but blood, for now that I was more collected I found that I had a cut on my forehead that was bleeding profusely. My head throbbed and I felt weak and dizzy. Where could I go now? I had nowhere. Only my dismal lodgings and they were now dangerous. Yet I had no choice. With a heavy heart I hastened home, sneaked up the stairs avoiding my landlady, and locked my door. I bathed my wound and stemmed the bleeding, then lay on my bed as the room spun around me.

CHAPTER 112

How magnificent the house must have looked that night! I might have passed it just then for I have often walked about the West-end of Town at a late hour gazing at Old Corruption's display of wealth and ostentation (and deploring it, of course). I can imagine how the crush of carriages arriving formed a lock in the street that quite blocked the way — another gesture of contempt for the convenience of one's fellows.

I may lead you inside the mansion as it was that night. We pass a door-footman at the entrance and our names are announced by a hired groom of the chambers and called from one landing-place to the next as we ascend. Fine sophas and elegant beaufets are disposed around the walls and Collinet's quadrille band are already playing waltzes and gallopades, though it is only ten and unfashionably early (but we are not of the *bon ton*!) to have arrived.

Lady Mompesson and Sir David are preparing to receive their guests at the door to the great Salon at the top of the main stair. They appear so at ease that surely their guests almost doubt the rumours of their impending smash. From the lavish expenditure one would not believe these stories. Surely they are the usual spiteful gossip that the fashionable world is only too prey to from idleness and viciousness?

Now Sir David advances smiling and bowing towards two of the guests: a lady of about fifty and a younger lady. The latter is not very beautiful but she seems pleased to see the baronet and smiles at him in a way surely calculated to inspire the strongest emotions in the male breast.

Now here comes Sir Thomas in the company of the Countess of H------ and her son, the Honourable Percy Decies. Is that a wink that Sir Thomas bestows upon Sir David as he sees him addressing Miss Sugarman?

And there is a rather burly young gentleman in regimentals. Why, it is Tom Mompesson! Yet surely he has been sacked from his regiment? However that may be, he is looking rather fine in his scarlet coat with gold froggings, his canary-yellow waistcoat, and his shiny Hessians. Who is that smartly-dressed gentleman with him? His bottle-green coat, though handsome, seems not quite to fit him. Why, it is Mr Vamplew! What is the tutor doing at the ball? Has a sudden access of the democratic instinct led his employers to invite him? Is the butler, too, a guest rather than the master of ceremonies here? No, for Mr Vamplew seems not to be enjoying himself but is watching the young gentleman very closely — and, in particular, the number of glasses of champagne he is consuming. For on one occasion he slightly shakes his head at the footman, Joseph, as he advances towards them and the servant instantly moves away.

CHAPTER 113

About an hour or less before midnight, just as the ball is getting under way, a young gentleman approaches the front-door of the house. He is stopped by the door-footman who, after a brief exchange, calls for Mr Thackaberry who comes, magnificently dressed and strapped almost to the point of insensibility. After some conversation the young man is admitted. He mounts the stairs and shakes hands with Sir David at the entrance to the Salon.

"What the deuce are you doing here?" his host exclaims in an undertone.

The guest flushes and says in an urgent whisper: "I must speak to you and your mother immediately."

"Not now, for Heaven's sake! You'll look like a damned bailiff!"

The young gentleman twists his mouth into a smile and says softly: "The Huffam heir is alive!"

Sir David stares at him for a moment, then points towards a door at the end of the landing: "Go into the Chinese Room. I'll fetch my mother."

A few minutes later Sir David and Lady Mompesson enter the darkened chamber. Sir David carries a candle-stick which provides the only light. As he places it on a side-table he says: "Mamma, you have often heard me speak of my friend, Harry."

"How do you know the Huffam boy is alive?" Lady Mompesson demands without ceremony.

Harry flinches briefly and then says: "On the best evidence, Lady Mompesson: that of my own ears and eyes. I met and spoke with him today — yesterday, in fact."

"But how can you be sure it was he?" Lady Mompesson objects. "Nobody has positively identified him since he absconded from the madhouse to which his uncle sent him. And that was nearly four years ago."

"By the most remarkable coincidence," Harry replies, "I met him just a few months before he escaped and disappeared. But I did not realize that it was he. He was known to me then merely as a school-friend of my half-brother. It was only very recently that I connected him with the Huffam heir."

"That is indeed an extraordinary coincidence," Lady Mompesson says coldly.

I believe she meant to imply that she did not believe him.

Harry seems to take her remark in this sense for he addresses his next words to her son: "He came to me immediately after escaping from his grandfather, and that was when he told me who he was."

"But that was last February!" Sir David exclaims. "Why did you not tell me this before, Harry? You know very well that we have been in fear of being dispossessed as soon as the Court declares him dead."

"He swore me to secrecy because he knows his life is in danger," Harry lies. "And then he disappeared and I had no idea where to lay hold of him again. But now I have found him. But to the main matter: the fact that he is alive after all is wonderful news for you."

"It certainly is," Sir David agrees. "With old Clothier dead and reports in the papers that the boy was murdered by him, and then the Maliphant claimant having come forward, things were looking deuced bad."

"So I take it that if the boy can be persuaded to come before the Court, the situation will be as before," Lady Mompesson says. "We will be safe as long as he remains alive."

"It is not quite as simple as that, Lady Mompesson," Harry says. "There is the complication of the will."

She looks horrified and turns to her son who stammers: "You see, Mamma, I asked Harry's advice about the trust we were going to create when we wanted Henrietta to marry Tom. After all, he's an Equity man."

She scrutinises her son's friend who stares confidently back at her: "Perhaps he shouldn't have told me, but I'm bound by confidentiality in the matter, I can assure you, Lady Mompesson."

"Then since you know so much," Lady Mompesson says, "you probably know that we assume that the will was destroyed, for we believe that Assinder's accomplice — improbable though it seems — was a knife-boy employed in this house. He was by all accounts almost an ideot. However, he must have conveyed the document out of here after Assinder's misadventure, though he could have had no idea of its value. We assume that he subsequently lost or destroyed it."

"You are right in thinking that the knife-boy made away with the will. But he was no ideot and I promise you that he had a very precise sense of its value. He had entered your house for the sole purpose of stealing it. In short, he was the Huffam heir."

"This is absurd!" Sir David cries, but his mother puts her hand on his arm.

"Continue with your story," she commands.

"He told me that he managed to become a servant in this house and spent several months here before he succeeded in making away with the will. (Assinder was not in colleague with him but was working on his own account.) When he left here he was somehow caught by his grandfather's agents and delivered to his death though, contrary to what was reported in the newspapers, he managed to escape."

"And what happened to the will?" Lady Mompesson asks impatiently.

"It passed from his possession into the hands of someone whom I cannot name. In short, it still exists."

"Who has it?" Sir David cries.

"I said I cannot name the party and that is the literal truth. I have been contacted by this person and instructed to negotiate with you for the sale of the will on his behalf."

Sir David and his mother look at each other.

Harry watches them narrowly and says: "You have nothing to lose and everything to gain by obtaining it. Once you have it back you need not worry about the Huffam heir dying. Marry Miss Palphramond to Tom and if the boy dies without an heir, produce the will and you are safe."

"How can we know that this extraordinary tale is the truth?" Lady Mompesson asks.

"You may have the document certified before you buy it," Harry replies stiffly. "If it is false then you have lost nothing."

Lady Mompesson and her son confer in whispers and then she announces: "We can offer you a thousand pounds, but not a penny more."

"I fear that is not enough," Harry says sadly. "Not nearly enough."

"But we are close to a smash," the young baronet protests. "The Court's Receiver is collecting our rents. My credit is exhausted and I have to sign the marriage-treaty before it's known how close to I am to going entirely to pieces, or Miss Sugarman's friends will break it off."

"I will beg my principal to hold back for a few days," Harry says. "But my fear is that if you do not purchase it, he will sell it to the Maliphant heir."

"Then the boy must be induced to put himself under the protection of the Court," Lady Mompesson says.

"He is too frightened," Harry answers. "And I fear he has good reason to be."

"What do you mean?" Lady Mompesson asks.

Harry shrugs his shoulders: "He is an obstacle to the Maliphant claimant. That is all I meant."

The other two look at each other in dismay. Then Sir David reaches for the bell-pull and tugs it impatiently.

CHAPTER 114

The guests are now collecting in groups to discuss the strange behaviour of their hosts and there are subdued whispers of "Bailiffs" and well-bred giggles hidden behind hands. Miss Sugarman is seated beside her mother in the supper-room. Sir Thomas Delamater comes up to her and engages her in conversation. She continues to frown however and at last he moves away.

Meanwhile in the street outside the house a tall figure in black steps hastily out of a hackney-cabriolet, enters the house, and quickly mounts the stairs behind a footman who leads him to the door of the Chinese Room.

Another hour passes. The guests are in confusion now. The carriages have not been ordered to take up until about four o'clock. Tom crosses to Miss Sugarman rather unsteadily, followed by Mr Vamplew who appears to be remonstrating with him. Tom pushes him away and says something to his brother's intended bride. A moment later, Sir Thomas hurries over and pulls him away. Mr Vamplew takes charge of him and leads him out of the room. Miss Sugarman, however, says something angrily to her mother who signals to one of the footmen. Sir Thomas seems to be pleading with her. I haven't been able to establish what passed between them, but I assume he was begging her to stay and she was pointing out that Sir David had ignored her for three hours.

Miss Sugarman and her party leave. Shortly afterwards a footman assists Mr Vamplew to escort his charge to the Chinese Room where his mother and brother, together with Mr Barbellion, are waiting for him. The tutor waits outside with the servant, and ten minutes later, they are summoned to help the young gentleman to his bed.

Now that the exodus has begun, other of the guests begin to send for their carriages and by three o'clock most of them have gone. By four, the ices have melted, the bees'-wax candles burnt out, and the hired servants are clearing up the food and beverages that are left over.

Then at five in the morning a footman is sent to the coach-house with orders that Mr Phumphred be woken up and told to get the horses ready to travel a considerable distance.

By six o'clock the house is hushed and in darkness.

Now as I approach the end of my task, I unloose the jesses from my Imagination so that it takes flight, haughty and daring, and soars at last in search of prey.

In the glittering state-rooms that only hours ago were thronged with the pampered denizens of the *beau monde*, the vast looking-glasses between the lofty windows, which so recently reflected all the staring vacancy of Fashion, now reflect only each other. On the marbled beaufets lie heaps of sweet-meats and delicacies rejected by fastidious Appetite, whose cost would feed whole streets of the poor — nay, entire villages in Erin, our sad sister-island. In the cramped attic-rooms and damp cellars the exhausted servants sprawl on their mean beds in all the prostration of honest Toil; while amidst soft linen sheets slumber newly-inheriting Wealth and greedy Arrogance. May honest dreams delight the former and ill nightmares haunt the latter!

CHAPTER 115

Oh Happiness! I have done at last with the cankered parasites of Old Corruption for whom the day of judgement will surely come. And now that my contribution is drawing to a close, let me cast aside the constraints that have hemmed me in and boldly assert the obligation upon us all to judge — and more than judge: to *condemn* — a society in which honest Merit is held back, Talent is passed over, and Insolence and Rank arrogantly usurp the prerogatives of all. Let the Cynic ask by what right we condemn it: we condemn it at the bar of the Court of Conscience that is seated within the breast of each of us! And which is the model of Justice upon which our (sometimes fallible) Courts of Equity are based.

Only from Judgement comes Pattern and therefore Understanding. I am proud to have played my part in the process by which you have come to see unfold in your own life — and thereby to understand — the great Design of Reason and Justice.

Neither must one spare oneself from judgement, and that requires an act of confession. Your part in our undertaking has been such a confession, for you have not concealed your motives even when they might have exposed you to reproach. I reverence you for that. I too have known the release that confession brings; in my case to a friend who might have believed I had betrayed him from mere self-interest. For (as you have so often heard me say) we have to understand motives or otherwise we will condemn too rashly. Even what appears to be a dishonourable action, if properly understood, may be revealed to be wholly just. For example, a lawyer may be suspected of an act of betrayal of his client, a woman of her husband's honour, or a political Radical of his fellow-conspirators. But in each case the accused and vilified individual might have been motivated by the Higher Duty we all owe to Justice.

So judge, my friend, but only when all motives are known. And judge your own motives as only you are able. Then if you are sure your motives are pure, you may entrust yourself with Wealth and Power. Think of the good you could do! the Injustices you could right! the Talent and Merit you could bring forward! As you know, I despise Wealth and Power, and so when I urge you to seek them you know how to interpret my motives.

I therefore urge upon you, in conclusion, the Universal Duty to seek Justice and so gain the means to exercise Philanthropy.

BOOK IV

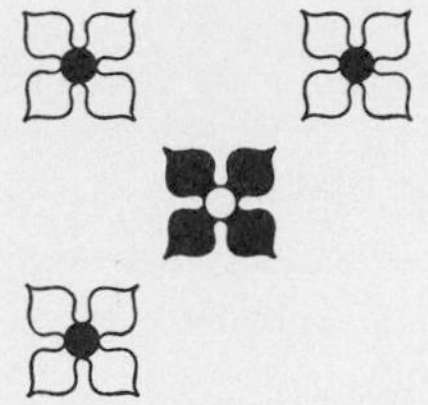

Weddings and Widows

CHAPTER 116

Philanthropy? Fiddlesticks!

However, I must restrain myself for my contribution to our common task is not yet completed.

I believe it happened more or less like this:

As the wind is rising a figure strides up Aylesbury-street in Clerkenwell. He stops at a small house and rings the door-bell. The maid-servant who opens the door stares at him in surprise, listens to what he says, then puts the door on the chain and leaves it ajar while she disappears into the house.

A minute later Mr Sancious himself opens the door, pale and trembling, and hisses: "I told you never to come here!"

"This couldn't wait."

"You'd better come in," the attorney says, looking anxiously up and down the street.

The man enters and is shewn into the parlour where he finds a lady: "Good evening, mum," he says. Then he grins at the attorney.

Mr Sancious ignores this and demands: "Well, what have you to tell me?"

"Sally wasn't wrong. He didn't die that time like it said in the papers. She seen him all right."

The other two stare at each other in dismay and then the little attorney whispers: "Go on. Have you found him?"

"Yes. Jist like I reckoned, Joey led me right to him."

"And?" enquires Mr Sancious.

"I was jist doing what I'd 'greed when he told me something that brung me up short. It was something I thought you'd want to know. So I gived over and come straight to you."

"You mean you let him go?" the lady demands.

Mr Sancious waves her down with one hand without looking at her: "What did he tell you?"

"He said as how the will still exists."

His auditors are thrown into consternation by this intelligence.

"Still exists? How can that be?" the attorney cries, turning to his companion.

"The old man destroyed it. Vulliamy himself told me so."

"The boy was lying to save himself," the lady rejoins. "It would be just like his audacity."

"No, I believe he was telling the truth," Mr Sancious says. He suddenly turns to Barney and cries: "Then did he have it?"

"No. I searched him."

"Then where can it be?" Mr Sancious exclaims. "Who has it?"

"You did right not to ... That is to say, you were right to let him go," the lady says to Barney. "But find him again. He must lead us to the will. And when he has done that, then do what you have been paid for."

Mr Sancious opens the door as a hint to his guest. With a little bow, Barney leaves the room and the attorney follows him towards the street-door and lets him out.

When he comes back a moment later, he and the lady stare at each other for a minute. Then he says: "What if the boy doesn't lead him to the will?"

The lady answers coolly: "Set your mind at rest. I believe I have an idea about that."

CHAPTER 117

I had little sleep that night for the pain of my wound, and all the next day I stayed in my room thinking over the previous day's events. I had been betrayed by two of the few people I had come to trust. Though Henry's treachery had hurt me, Joey's had wounded me much more grievously for it had re-awakened my own feelings of guilt towards him and his mother over what had happened to Mr Digweed. I had imagined that Joey bore me no grudge for that, and I had clearly been very wrong. Did his mother, then, also nurse a desire for vengeance? I hated even to speculate upon so uncomfortable an idea.

Towards five in the afternoon I was sitting and gloomily revolving these thoughts when there came a knock at the street-door. I heard the voice of Mrs Quaintance and footsteps on the stair and then someone tapped at the door.

"Who is it?" I asked.

To my amazement Joey's voice said: "It's me."

"Is he alone, Mrs Quaintance?" I called out.

"He is, sir," she answered in surprise.

I unlocked the door, Joey entered and I quickly locked it again. He was smiling broadly though with a quizzical expression as if at my odd conduct, but as soon as he saw my bandaged forehead and pale face in the light of the candle he cried out: "Why, whatever has happened to you?"

His surprise and his concern were so manifestly sincere that I am not ashamed to say that I seized him and began to weep. Why I wept I did not know then and hardly know now, but I believe it was not merely relief at having found him a true friend after all but remorse for having ever doubted him. (And, remember, I was weakened by my injuries.) Joey patted my shoulder and muttered something as unintelligible as my own words.

"Forgive me, Joey," I said. "I doubted you. I thought you had deserted me when you didn't come, and then that you had 'peached on me to Barney."

He was moved too. I had never seen him look as he did now: all the suspiciousness and the reserve had gone for once.

He led me to the sopha and sat me down. "And why shouldn't you think that," he said, "when I've done it twice a-fore?"

"No, no, I had no right. You've taken such risks on my behalf and given up so much." I paused and tried to say: "Your father, Joey. I want to tell you how I ... how ... "

"Never mind saying it," he said gently. "I know what you mean, Master John."

When we were both more collected I told him about the attack by his uncle. He must have learned (I now understood and explained to Joey) that I was still alive from Sally, who had seen me one night in the West-end a few weeks ago.

Then Joey said: "I'll tell you where I've been since yesternight and why I nivver come. I was on my way here when I noticed someone dodging me. Well, I went roundabout and roundabout and thought I'd been one too many for 'em, though now I reckon it was Barney and he must have stuck close to me arter all. So that's how he found you, I'm 'shamed to say."

When I had protested that I blamed him not at all, he went on: "So about six o'clock I was just outside here when I seen someone leave. Do you know who it was?"

"Yes, I had a visiter and he left about then. I must tell you about it. It was Henry Bellringer, whom I have told you of. Have you never seen him?"

"I didn't think so, but when I seen him last night I knowed him all right."

"What can you mean?"

"Why, do you rec'lleck that time I come to your grand-dad's crib at Charing-cross? You was inside and my old feller was waiting outside?"

I nodded. Someone knocking at the door had interrupted old Mr Escreet's story and I had left the house by the rear and found Joey waiting with his father.

"Well," Joey went on, "that was the cove I seen coming to the door then."

"By Heavens!" I cried. "Of course! That was what his knock reminded me of!"

This was astonishing news for I could not begin to understand what business he could have with Mr Escreet. Here was another extraordinary connexion that I could make nothing of.

Now, casting reserve aside, I told Joey what Bellringer had come to tell me: the will — the document for which his father had lost his life — had not been destroyed after all.

"But that's not what I meant to tell you," Joey said when we had briefly discussed the implications of this. "I remembered that you had wanted to know who this cove was, so I decided to dodge him. And can you guess where he went? To the Mumpseys' crib in Brook-street!"

This was stranger and stranger!

"It was all lit up for they was having a big party. And in he went, straight past the door-keepers as if he was knowed there."

"What!" I exclaimed. "That's extraordinary!"

Not merely was Henry connected with Mr Escreet but with the Mompessons too!

Now I told Joey about the conversation I had heard between Henry and Mr Pamplin in which they had referred to "Sir Thomas" and how I had discovered from Miss Quilliam (because of the connexion through Mr Pamplin) that this was Sir Thomas Delamater who was a friend of David Mompesson. I had taken these links for random coincidences, but suddenly they began to come clear to me. David Mompesson's friendship with Sir Thomas linked him with Mr Pamplin (who held a living in the gift of Sir Thomas) and with Miss Quilliam (whose father should have been given that very living). Sir Thomas had found Miss Quilliam her post with the Mompesson family, so all of that was straightforward enough. But how did Henry come to know David? Through Mr Pamplin? Suddenly it came to me that it was the other way around: Henry was a friend of David Mompesson's and through him had become acquainted with the clergyman and Sir Thomas, for Henry was none other than the "Harry" mentioned by Miss Quilliam in her story of the evening that led to her dismissal! I had half-known this for a long time, but now it all fell into place. The way she had described him in age, appearance, and manner of speech all matched the man I knew. Then how did Henry come to know David and how was he connected with the Mompessons? I could make no headway with that, but at that moment another realization came to me: He was the spy of the Mompessons in Chancery whom Lydia warned me about! So I had taken the will straight to the worst person in the world!

Then it struck me that Henry had betrayed me not to the Mompessons but to Silas Clothier! How had *that* link come about? And, most perplexing of all, how was he connected with Mr Escreet? And then I recalled that I had come to know Henry through Stephen Maliphant whose name suggested yet another mysterious link with my own kin. Beyond that point, however, I could not go.

Having followed this through to a dead-end, I returned to Joey's account and asked him to go on:

"The Mumpseys was having a great ball and I thought he must be a guest," he continued; "on'y he weren't togged up like the other swells getting out of their carriages. Well, I waited outside all night and at last the carriages started to collect their masters and mistresses and drive away and the lights in the ball-room went out. But my mark didn't come out. Then very late — oh, about two or three — I seen a genel'man arrive in a hackney-coach who didn't look like no guest but more like a parson or a lawyer for he was in a great hurry and wasn't finely dressed but wearing black. I was a-feared my mark had gone out through the mews, but at last, towards seven o'clock this morning, he come down the steps."

"So late!" I exclaimed. "What business could he have there that would keep him overnight! And in the middle of a ball!"

Joey shrugged and went on: "Then I followed him to a house in Great-Titchfield-street."

"Mr Pamplin!" I cried, remembering the address that Henry had once mentioned.

"He come out with a cove in a slabbering bib."

"A clergyman! Yes, that's he!"

"He was there an hour or two — most like having breakfast," Joey said wistfully.

Taking the hint I laid before him what alimentary resources I could muster and he went on:

"Then they went to Fozard's livery-stable in Piccadilly and I got close enough to hear him order a post-chaise."

"Did he say where he was going?"

"No, but that stable on'y posts along roads to the North. Then they took a hackney-coach and I had to run after them as best as I could. Luckily the traffic was heavy. They went to a crib near St. Paul's, something like a church with arches and pointed winders. I arst the gate-keeper what it was and he said something that sounded like 'doctor's coming'."

"Doctors' Commons!" I cried.

"Aye, that's the ticket. So I give the gate-keeper a shillin' and arst him to larn the business of the two genel'men as had jist arrived. And he come back and said they'd sweared out an alligator for a special licence."

"An allegation, Joey."

"Alligation," he repeated.

"For whom was it?"

"Why, for himself, Henry Bellringer. But I couldn't catch the lady's name."

I was puzzled and explained why: "Whom is he marrying? And why at this moment? Surely now that he has the will, it is in his interests to sell it to either Sir David or the Maliphant claimant?"

"But supposing he knowed that Barney had been paid to kill you? How would that change things?"

Why, at my death the will makes Miss Henrietta the heir."

I broke off and stared at Joey in horror. He understood my meaning and we both rose to our feet.

"But," I said, "she would never consent. She ... "

I fell silent for I had recalled that of course she believed that I was dead! Oh Heavens! What had I done by my decision not to enlighten her? But then another thought came to me and I cried:

"But why are the Mompessons allowing him to? What do they gain by it?"

There was no time to be lost in such speculations.

I began to dress, crying out: "Run for a coach, Joey." As he made for the door I shouted: "Stop. What time did Bellringer order the post-chaise for?"

"I couldn't hear the hour. But it was for today."

"Then we have no time to lose."

While Joey ran down to the street I opened my bureau and carefully pocketed all the capital — twenty pounds and a few shillings — that remained from Miss Lydia's gift. Now at least I was using it in a cause that would have been close to her heart. Then I boarded the coach Joey had hailed, and we set off for Brook-street.

CHAPTER 118

Reaching the house at half-past six, we agreed that Joey would go round to the mews and see what he could glean from the stablemen. Meanwhile I went up the steps and boldly rang the bell. The footman who opened it was Joseph (Ned) and he did not recognise me.

"I wish to see Sir David and Lady Mompesson on a matter of urgent business," I said impressively.

He eyed me sceptically and I became acutely conscious of the bloody kerchief around my head and my shabby and now blood-stained clothes.

"May I have your card, sir," he said; "and I will send to enquire if they are at home?"

My printed card bore my assumed name so I said: "Tell them that I am Mr John Huffam."

As I had anticipated, the name which had had so powerful an effect upon old Mr Escreet served to unlock yet another door, for when Joseph returned he asked me to follow him. We ascended the stairs and, somewhat to my embarrassment, I was ushered into the Great Parlour.

Lady Mompesson sat on a sopha and Sir David stood behind it. As I came through the door which was held open by Joseph, their eyes were fastened on my face. They seemed to start when they saw me, though whether it was because they recognised me or because of the somewhat gruesome sight I presented, I did not know.

We stared at each other in silence and then, after a few moments, David glanced at his mother's face.

I spoke aloud the question that I was sure he was putting to her silently: "Well, Lady Mompesson, do you recognise me?"

"I saw the Huffam heir once only and briefly more than six years ago when he was a small boy. It would be otiose to speculate on whether you are he."

"I remember the occasion," I said. "Considering that my resurrection from the dead now safeguards the title to your estate, you seem surprisingly unwilling to recognise me."

"You are mistaken," Lady Mompesson said. "You appear to be unaware that the legitimacy of the Huffam heir — setting aside the question of whether you are he — is about to be declared invalid by the Court of Chancery."

"On what grounds?" I demanded.

"The heirship of John Huffam is being rejected because no proof of his parents' marriage has ever been found," she said. "Nor, indeed, is there any evidence of the birth of a legitimate heir to his daughter, Mary Clothier."

I flushed at the reference to my mother's marriage and, as I took it though I was not clear precisely what she meant, to my own origins. Insolent, cruel woman! But at least now I understood their lack of interest in me. If there were no longer a Huffam heir, their only means of preventing the Maliphant claimant from inheriting would be to produce the will.

"We have nothing to say to you," Lady Mompesson went on. "It was you who sought this interview. Kindly state your business."

"I have come," I said, "to appeal to you on behalf of Miss Henrietta Palphramond."

"What impudence!" Sir David cried.

"Will you be good enough to make your meaning clear?" his mother asked.

"I refer to her marriage," I said. The way they glanced at each other confirmed for me the correctness of my surmise that the licence was for her. "I cannot believe that you approve it."

Lady Mompesson said haughtily: "Your impertinence is astonishing."

"You cannot approve," I continued, waxing indignant as I spoke, "a hasty, half-clandestine marriage by special licence performed by a clergyman of vicious personal habits. You are surprised that I know so much about it? A trusted servant of mine — a friend, I should say — saw Henry Bellringer at Doctors' Commons earlier today. I know enough of her proposed husband to believe that you would be condemning her to a life of wretchedness."

"You have over-stepped the limits," Lady Mompesson said with icy fury. "We need detain you no longer."

Her son reached towards the bell-rope.

"Wait," I said. "If I cannot appeal to your honour and generosity, I appeal to your self-interest."

Sir David paused and turned towards me.

"I do not understand your motives," I went on. "How are your interests being served by this marriage?" He seized the bell-rope and I cried: "Bellringer has the will! Don't you see what that means?"

They stared at each other in amazement and then directed their gaze at me.

"What can you mean?" Lady Mompesson exclaimed. "Mr Bellringer is only an intermediary in this affair."

"Is that what he has told you?" I cried. "That he is merely acting for someone who has it? Then I understand it all now." Seeing that I had guessed aright, I went on: "But I know he has it for he stole it from me. Yes, it was I who took it from that hiding-place."

I walked across to the chimney-piece and, using my pen-knife, pulled out the appropriate bolts so that the inner recess slid open. I turned back with a smile that I could not repress:

"I worked in this house as a lowly domestic and one night I stole in here and removed it. Did Assinder not tell you?"

"He died without regaining the power of speech," Lady Mompesson said.

I shuddered at this news for until now I had not known what his fate had been.

"Mr Bellringer, however, told us of your dishonourable and criminal conduct in stealing the will," she went on.

"But he did not tell you the truth about what happened to it after that," I said triumphantly.

I briefly described how Bellringer had copied and substituted the will while I slept and had then betrayed me to Silas Clothier.

When I had finished they looked at each other in unconcealed dismay. This was one of the sweetest moments of my life.

Then Sir David turned to me: "That's enough," he said. "Leave this house now."

"One last thing," Lady Mompesson interrupted, holding up her hand. "What were you saying about Miss Palphramond's marriage a moment ago? I do not think I understood you perfectly."

"That it is because he has the will that Bellringer is marrying her. As her husband he will, in all but name, possess the estate that she inherits under the will."

"Bellringer marrying her!" Sir David cried.

"Yes," I answered in surprise. "Of whom else but he were we speaking?"

"You are certain that the special licence was in his name?" Lady Mompesson asked.

I studied their faces: "In whose name do you suppose it was?"

Her face grew suddenly pale. "You must leave instantly," she commanded. "David, ring the bell."

"Be calm, Mamma," her son said as he obeyed her. "Phumphred will do what he is told."

"Yes," she said in exasperation. "But told by whom?"

"Damn him!" Sir David suddenly exploded, his features turning an ancestral hue. "I suppose this is his revenge on behalf of his great-grandfather!"

"I think I see!" I cried in the darkening face of Sir David. "He was to have arranged it all, except that he was to have been the groomsman, not the groom!"

He advanced towards me looking so dangerous that I hastily withdrew from the room and ran down the stairs. Leaving the house I hurried round to the mews where I met Joey. I sat on a low wall to listen to him for my haste had made my sore head throb.

He had learned that at about five or six in the afternoon a party made up of Miss Henrietta, Lady Mompesson's lady's-maid (Miss Pickavance), and Mr Pamplin had set off in the great family coach driven by Mr Phumphred, with Mr Tom and Mr Bellringer accompanying it in a hired chaise. The coach held only four so that presumably explained why they had needed the chaise. But most important, Joey had learned that their destination was Hougham!

I told Joey what had passed between the Mompessons and myself while we hurried to a nearby livery-stable. There they told us we had no chance of finding a post-chaise that day for there had been a run on the road because of the bad weather. This seemed to be the case, for we hurried from one stable to another without success. At last, however, and very late we found what we were seeking — for a carriage had been unexpectedly returned — and so we set off at nearly midnight. At fifty shillings for each stage and with the tolls to pay as well, my little store of money would be exhausted by the time I reached Hougham. They had six or seven hours' start on us, but they were travelling in the much slower carriage. And presumably they would break their journey overnight. If they were indeed going to Hougham, then we had a good chance of overtaking them.

At only the second stage on the Great-North-road we passed a slower phaeton — though going at full spank — that I recognised by the arms on the pannels. I had no doubt that Sir David was inside.

A thaw had just started so the roads were very bad. As we journeyed north, the wind was rising steadily, and, as it swept inland across the flat landscape to our right, it buffeted the carriage so that it rocked alarmingly. We were delayed by having to enquire of the ostlers at every inn to know if our quarry had halted for the night. They were easy to identify and we soon found that we were indeed upon the right track. As time passed, we learned that we were gaining on them. By the early hours of next morning, however, it began to seem that they must be travelling overnight; though even in that case we reckoned that we should still overtake the lumbering family coach by an hour or two after breakfast-time.

However, when we stopped at an inn in Hertford at about five or six o'clock, one of the ostlers told us that the party we sought had arrived a few hours before. And indeed, there the coach was still in the coach-house though, worryingly, the chaise was not to be seen.

Joey and I entered the inn and I sent a startled maid-servant for the landlord who appeared in his nightgown and nightcap with an expression of alarm on his face. At first he would say nothing, but when I had frightened him with talk of an action for aiding and abetting the abduction of a minor, he agreed to tell us what we wanted to know. The party we were pursuing had arrived very late last night at an hour or two after midnight, and had engaged rooms as if intending to stay. However, after only a few hours all but two of them had risen and, leaving those two behind, had set off again in the lighter and faster vehicle. Their own coachman had taken the reins and they had been accompanied by two mounted postilions — one riding ahead at the gallop to pay the tolls and order fresh horses. They had gone barely an hour ago!

Those left behind were a young gentleman and a young lady. The latter was, from her description, Miss Pickavance, who was still asleep and whom he refused to let us awaken. As for the young gentleman, the landlord said, well, he was still pretty much in the condition he was in when he was helped from the coach. I asked to be taken to him and very grudgingly he led us upstairs.

As we were crossing the landing I looked out through the window over-looking the stable-yard on my right and saw the arch into the street. It had begun to grow a little lighter than it had been when we arrived and I could just catch part of a shop signboard in the street across the way: *amphy*.

"Landlord," I asked. "What is the name of this inn?"

"The Blue Dragon, sir," he answered, panting from the stairs.

I stopped and looked up and down the passage.

"Did any of the party use this room?" I asked, indicating a door on my right on which was painted a faded crescent on its back with its cusps rising like the horns of a bull.

"The Half-Moon? Why, the young lady slept there," the landlord said.

I opened the door and saw a large sitting-room looking into the yard and with a view through the arch. The furniture was battered and the walls were hung with shabby papers. There was a door into a small bed-chamber which I looked into. It contained a chair and a big old hanger-bed. The room was damp and oppressive. I gazed into it for a few minutes, my heart filled with forebodings for the past and the future. I was there for so long that Joey came to find me and jogged my arm, looking at me curiously. Then I closed the door and went back to the landing.

We continued up another flight and along a passage to a private sitting-room. There we found (as I expected) Tom Mompesson sprawled on the sopha, reeking of brandy, and profoundly insensible.

Taking some refreshment with us, we hastily resumed our journey. It was clear that since those we were pursuing were now travelling in a vehicle that was at least as rapid as our own, we could not hope to overtake them, but we should be able to remain no more than two or three hours behind.

At intervals I slept but my injured head was throbbing painfully, the more so as it bounced against the seat as the vehicle lurched and swayed in the eddying gusts.

CHAPTER 119

Lashed by the rising winds, we travelled all that day and the next night, calculating that we would arrive towards noon. We would go straight to Mompesson-park, for we assumed that that would be the destination of the party ahead of us. The wedding would presumably take place as soon as possible — perhaps within an hour or two of their arrival, in which case we would come too late. Most probably it would be celebrated in Thorpe Woolston church which was the nearest, or perhaps Melthorpe which was hardly any further, but it was unfortunate that Joey had not been able to learn which of these the special licence specified. Assuming we were not too late, how would we go about rescuing Henrietta? We decided that Joey — since he was unknown to anyone there — would boldly enter the house pretending to be an express courier with a letter to put into her hands. He would tell her that I was still alive and give her a note from me. The next time we stopped to change horses I wrote a few lines pledging myself to rescue her from Bellringer and telling her to trust the bearer.

I speculated on the likely effect on her of discovering that I was still alive. Was it only because she believed I was dead that she had consented to this marriage? Presumably Bellringer had put it to her that marriage to him was the only alternative to marriage to Tom. And he might have deceived her into believing that he admired her for her own sake, for she obviously had no conception that he had the will. My letter explained all of this and when she had read it, Joey would lead her from the house and I would be waiting with the chaise to drive her to safety.

The wind had dropped slightly but the dark clouds were lowering threateningly when, at about noon, we reached the village of Hougham. A few minutes later we reached Mompesson-park and, having passed through the high gates where I had first met Henrietta, drove round to the front and halted at the foot of the pincer-like flight of steps up to the portico.

I waited out of sight inside the vehicle while Joey ran up and hammered at the door.

I heard it opened and then Joey said:

"I must see Miss Henrietta right away. I've rode express from Town with a urgent message from Lady Mumpsey."

"Why, don't you know no better than to come to the front door, old feller?" the footman (whom I recognised as Dan) answered. "Anyways, she ain't here. The fambly's all up in Town, as you oughter know."

The voice of a woman whom I took to be the housekeeper down here said: "Is there anything amiss, Robert?"

I descended from the carriage and mounted the steps, saying as commandingly as I could: "Come, I know that Miss Palphramond is here."

Both servants stared at me in surprise. Did Dan recognise me?

"I am privy to the secret," I said to the housekeeper. "I am charged by Lady Mompesson with a letter for Miss Palphramond which I am to put into no other hands than her own."

She stared at me as if I had taken leave of my senses: "I have not the slightest conception of your meaning, young gentleman."

Her demeanour was so convincing that I was at a non-plus.

"Then we have over-ridden them on the road and they have not yet arrived," I said. I turned to Joey: "We will retrace our steps and meet them on the way." Then I said to the housekeeper: "But if they arrive without having met us, be sure to tell Miss Palphramond that Mr John Umphraville has business with her and that she must do nothing before seeing him."

I had hit upon that name as a way of conveying to Henrietta the gravity of my message — and perhaps even my identity, though (as far as I knew) she believed me dead — without being understood by her companions. The housekeeper consented to deliver this communication and while I returned to the post-chaise and ordered the driver to halt just out of sight of the house, Joey went round to the stables.

He rejoined me a few minutes later: "The groom's-boy said there ain't been no carriage come and I believe he's telling the truth. There ain't no cattle in the byres nor no ruts in the mud."

"*Can* we have over-ridden them?"

His face indicated how unlikely he thought this and I agreed.

"Then," I said in despair, "Bellringer must have changed their destination from Hougham."

"But you told me as how Sir David said the old coachee had his orders from Lady Mumpsey! And I larned from the stable-men as how the orders was for Hougham."

"That's so! Then they must have come here. But perhaps they have gone straight to the church!" I stared at him in horror: "But to which one? Melthorpe or Thorpe Woolston?"

"We must try 'em both. Which is nearer?"

"Thorpe Woolston."

"Then I'll run there and you take the chaise to Melthorpe." He looked at me anxiously: "Are you well enough?"

"You don't know the way!" I objected.

"Set me on the road and I'll enquire it out."

Joey's suggestion was a good one, so we took the chaise back to the lodge-gates and then parted: he set off in the direction I showed him while I told the driver the way to Melthorpe along the turnpike.

It was already dusk when we drove up the High-street where nothing appeared to have changed. Yet how different were my circumstances from when I had last seen these familiar sights! When we reached the church I could see no lights inside. I got down, crossed the road and hammered at Mr Advowson's door.

After what seemed a long wait he opened it a few inches and peered out.

"Do you know anything of a wedding here?" I cried.

"A wedding, sir?" he answered, clearly not recognising me. "There's no wedding due, for there's no banns been called."

"This is by special licence."

He shook his head: "Even so, sir, I've heard of nothing of that nature."

Then unless Joey had more success, I had lost all chance of thwarting the marriage!

I was about to turn away when the old parish-clerk said: "Ain't it Master Mellamphy? 'Mr', I suppose I should say."

I nodded.

"Why, I'm very glad to see you, sir. Will you have the goodness to step across to the vestry with me, for there's something I wish to show you?"

In some surprise, I agreed for there was no reason for haste now. He fetched and lighted a lanthorn, and then we crossed the road and went up the path between the graves. All the while he maintained an unbroken flow of gossip about the changes that had been taking place in the village, but my attention was elsewhere. He unlocked the great door and ushered me through the dark and empty church into the vestry.

And now he explained: "About three or four years ago — not long after you were last here yourself, Mr Mellamphy — a stranger came to my house and asked to see the baptism-books for the last twenty years. Well, it appeared that he needed to copy a number of entries, so I left him alone here for an hour or so. He thanked me and departed, but as I was putting the books away I recalled that business about the record of your baptism and noticed that the last of the registers he had been looking at was the very one that it was in. Well, something made me look at it again." He turned to me and said impressively: "Why, it had been torn clean out."

So that was what Lady Mompesson had meant when she said that even my existence had not been proven! She and her advisers must have learned that someone had removed this record — for it was in their interest that my claim should be upheld. It must have been the Clothiers who had done it when they laid the codicil before the court. I hoped that the copy Mr Advowson had made that time I had passed through the village on my way from Quigg's farm was still safely concealed in Sukey's thatch.

Now Mr Advowson was groping in the darkness amongst a pile of huge old registers.

"But here's the strangest thing," he went on, panting as he lifted one of them onto the table. "The stranger who must have done it, I knew him. I didn't recollect then, but it came to me afterwards. I could not be mistaken, for he was the tallest man I have ever seen." A cold chill ran down my back as he turned to me and said: "That man that came all those years ago with the young lady, sir."

"Hinxman," I muttered. The man who had helped Emma when she had tried to abduct me! Alabaster's agent! It made sense, for I was sure he had been employed by Silas Clothier to destroy the evidence on which my claim to be the Huffam heir rested in order that the provisions of the codicil could be put into effect. And then I remembered that I had overheard him saying to another of the turn-keys that he was going to the North while I was a prisoner of Alabaster's at exactly that time.

"Is this the register?" I asked, looking at the book he had retrieved.

"This? Oh no, sir. This is something quite unconnected with that, though I believe it has a connexion with yourself. I hope you won't think it impertinent of me, but after you had gone that last time, I fell to thinking about how Mr Barbellion had examined the marriage-records going back fifty years but had not found what he sought. And then I remembered how you had asked me about the Huffam family as if you had an interest in them. And then I recalled the quatre-foil that Pimlott noticed on one of the chests. (I sent him about his business after what you said, sir, by the way.) Do you recall, Mr Mellamphy, he said he had seen the same figure on one of your mother's possessions? Well, I put all this together afterwards and looked through the chest. And I found this." He indicated the mouldering volume. "It's from the time when the chapel in the Old Hall was used by the family for christenings and suchlike. (According to what they say round these parts it was de-consecrated after a murder there, but that's an old wives' tale.) So I wondered if it was what Mr Barbellion was looking for."

"Of course it was!" I cried, remembering Miss Lydia's story of the elopement of my great-grandparents and the wedding at the chapel.

I leafed through it and found the right date, 1769. And there at last was the piece of evidence that had been sought by so many for so many years: the record of the marriage of James Huffam and Eliza Umphraville. Miss Lydia was indeed recorded as a witness just below the signature of John Umphraville.

Mr Advowson confirmed that the entry was formally correct and duly witnessed. Thanking him for his efforts, I begged him to keep the book safely and then left him and climbed back into the chaise.

"Where to, sir?" asked the postilion.

"Back to Hougham," I said. Then a thought came to me: "No, go down the High-street and bear sharp right at the Green."

Remembering the copy of my baptism-record that I had left with my old nurse-maid and reflecting that it was now crucial, I had decided to call on Sukey. The postilion was disgusted when he saw Silver-street for after the thaw and several days of rain, it was like the bed of a muddy stream.

To my astonishment, however, there were no cottages here and no sign among the flourishing grass that there had ever been any. My first thought was that the copy had been destroyed and my claim to the property therefore fell. Then it occurred to me to wonder where my old friend and her family might have removed to. I ordered the postilion to circle the Green and then return to the High-street in the hope of finding informants. Nobody was abroad in the heavy rain so at last I stopped and knocked at a cottage door. I was directed by an old woman there to another part of the village and hastened thither.

By the time I reached the cottage to which I had been referred it was the middle of the afternoon. At the place I had been directed to I found a sad little group of wattle-and-daub cottages scattered higgledy-piggledy on a bare patch of waste land, as randomly as if they had fallen off a waggon.

I chose one of them at hazard and, since there was no door to hammer on but only a leathery curtain to keep the rain out, I called into its dark interior: "Hello there! Sukey?"

Immediately Sukey — older, more careworn, thinner — came forth blinking in the weak light. She took a moment to recognise me but then with an exclamation moved forward and flung her arms around me.

Then she drew back red-faced: "I didn't ought to have took the liberty. You're a growed man now a'most, Master Johnnie, and quite the genel'man agin."

For answer I seized her and hugged her.

"Dear, good Sukey!" I cried.

"Why, this *has* been a day for seeing old faces," she said, standing back to survey me. "But yours is the fust that I cared to set eye upon." Before I could ask her what she meant, she cried: "What's wrong with your head?"

"A slight accident," I said. "It's of no importance."

She looked at me disbelievingly. Then, noticing the chaise a few yards away, she exclaimed: "You've come into your inheritance!"

I shook my head: "I fear I'm no richer now than when I last saw you."

"But the grand carriage and sarvint?"

"Hired with the last of my money." Then I blushed and said: "Sukey, I never sent you the money I borrowed the last time I was here."

She nodded gravely and I wished that I had done so with Miss Lydia's money as soon as I had escaped from old Clothier and moved into lodgings with Mrs Quaintance.

"So much has happened," I went on. Falteringly I began: "My mother ... "

"Come in and seat yourself," she said. "You look pale."

I followed her and found myself inside a small windowless hovel with a low roof of furze branches and a floor of bare mud. There was no fire and it was illuminated only by a tallow rush. There were two battered chairs and I sat on one of them.

In a few words I told her of my mother's death, by which she was deeply moved, and a little of what had happened to me since I had last seen her. But I quickly turned the conversation:

"Why have you moved house?" I asked.

"Why, they've destroyed them cotts in Silver-street and elsewhere. It was done to bring down the poor-rates, for this is outside the paritch now, and so we get nothing from the Guardians."

"That's terrible," I said, my indignation against the Mompessons rising.

"Oh, there's many and many in the same case now. Like poor old Mr Pimlott. That puts me in mind of something, Master Johnnie. That time that man broke into your mam's house, 'twas Mr Pimlott as helped him."

"So I believe, but how can you be so sure?"

"He died a few months back. While he was on his deathbed my aunt tended him. (Bless her soul, for she passed on herself not a week arterwards.) He told her there was something he wanted to say to me a-fore he died. I went to him and he told me he was sorry that what he had done that time had injured me and Job. He on'y done it to wound your mam on account of she was gentry, for he was dreadful bitter agin 'em. See, he had worked for the Mumpseys all his life, but then he got to be bad with the rheumatiz from labouring in the wet fields, and so the steward — not the old steward who was a decent man, but his nevy — turned him off. And he 'victed him and his good-wife from their cottage on the estate, and all they could find was that damp little cott nigh to your mam's house. He reckoned the old woman died on account of it being so cold and wet."

"Well, but his part in the burglary?" I prompted.

"That day when the tramping man was turned away from your garden-gate, Mr Pimlott seen it and called out to him and offered him meat and a night's shelter. Then they got to talking and the long and the short of it was they planned it together and Mr Pimlott helped him to carry it out. He told me how arterwards he seen some drawing or something on a letter-case that the man took and he knowed as how that meant that your mam was connected with the Mumpseys, so he reckoned he'd had his revenge. But when he seen you agin that time you come here from up north it begun to prey on his mind for you looked so ill and miserable, he said. And when Mr Advowson suddenly told him the next day that he hadn't no more work for him, he believed it was a judgement upon him for what he done to you and your mam. And then his own cott was pulled down not long arterwards, like I was saying, and he tried to make himself one like this that Harry built for us, but it blowed down in a high wind and he fell ill and lay for days with no shelter over his head, a'most, and all the time it was gnawing upon his mind what he'd done."

I was silent for some time thinking back over the past and how things had turned out.

Then I asked: "How is Harry? And the other children?"

She looked down: "It would be better if they didn't see you."

Mention of Harry reminded me of the agreement he had extorted from me in connexion with the copy of my baptismal entry.

"Sukey," I asked, "have you still got that piece of parchment?" Before she could answer, however, I remembered something she had just said and a sudden and terrifying thought occurred to me: Mr Advowson had said that it was Hinxman who had removed the entry from the vestry and I tried now to recall if Sukey had seen him on that distant day when he and Emma tried to abduct me. Could it be that he had somehow followed me and was here now?

Hastily I demanded: "Sukey, what did you mean by saying I wasn't the first face from the past that you had seen today?"

"Why, I was walking back from Nether-Leigh when I noticed lights in amongst the trees. You mind as how the wall along the park is broke down there? Well, I went a little way up the old carriage-drive and seen as how the lights was in the Old Hall. So I went closer and who do you think ... ?"

"Lights in the Old Hall!" I exclaimed. "But it's a ruin. It's deserted."

Suddenly I thought of the old chapel there in which James and Eliza's marriage had taken place. Surely any building that had been once consecrated could be the venue for a marriage by special licence!

I jumped up: "I must go there!" I cried.

"Where?"

"To the Old Hall."

"Not in this clashy weather," she cried for the wind was now roaring above us; "and you looking so wan!"

She made a feeble effort to seize me, but I dodged her exactly as I had when I was a mischievous child trying to postpone my bed-time, and ran out and boarded the chaise, shouting to the driver: "Back the way we came. And then turn off where I tell you."

As the chaise set off Sukey ran alongside for a few yards in the pouring rain shouting something I couldn't hear above the clattering hooves and driving wind, but we soon left her behind.

CHAPTER 120

The postilion urged the horses into a fast trot, and as I retraced in the swaying chaise the course of walks I had so often made as a child, the long-threatened storm broke. As we breasted Gallow-tree-hill, it grew quite dark and rain came slashing against the windows with impassioned vindictiveness. Then I remembered: there was something I had wanted Sukey to tell me! Of course! The record of my baptism! What had become of it? I cursed my forgetfulness in neglecting to ask her.

It was early evening as we passed between the stone pillars that marked the rear-entrance to the old Huffam estate and followed the over-grown carriageway as it wound through the decaying timber down towards the lake, taking the route that my mother and I had walked all those years ago when she made her fruitless appeal to the honour and generosity of Sir Perceval and his lady. So strong was the wind now that the elms were waving like willow-trees, and black towers of cloud were piling up against the face of the pale moon. As I peered forth I thought of what Sukey had told me of the actions of the Mompessons' steward, Assinder. They had no right to this land: they had obtained and held it by fraud and had failed in their obligations towards it. If Bellringer could be made to give up the will the estate would be mine.

As we crossed the bridge at the head of the lake, I leaned my head out to search for the old house to the left. We were still a quarter of a mile short of it, but the drive swept past it towards the new house leaving nothing but the water-logged meadow-land that lay between the lake and the hill where Jeoffrey Huffam's mausoleum was, at the foot of which the Old Hall stood. There was no alternative, and so I ordered the reluctant driver to venture cautiously across the ill-drained ground.

The old house was visible now about a mile away as a blacker shape against the gloom, and whatever Sukey had seen, it appeared to be in complete darkness. Or was it? Was that a gleam from within or merely the dim light of the sky reflected off one of the window-panes? Now it was lit up by a flash of lightning and, with the gaping roof of the wing that was directly ahead of us suddenly exposed, it looked a complete ruin. I peered around in the hope of spying the chaise Bellringer had hired, but unless it was that dark shape beneath the trees in the distance, I could not see it. As we advanced, our progress grew slower and slower as our vehicle's wheels sank in the soft grass.

At last I called out to the driver to stop and, ordering him to wait, jumped down and hastened towards the crouched hump of the old house. Exhausted by long hours of travel and with my head still painful, I soon out-ran my strength and, gasping for breath and my ears ringing, was forced to pause to recover. I went on more cautiously, finding myself crossing what must once have been a terrace of gravelled walks between balustraded walls, where there were still ancient fish-ponds dark and thick with weed. Now I saw the mullioned windows gleaming faintly where the leaded glass panes still remained. I headed for the arched entrance at the side where I discovered that the great wooden door was unbarred, and I passed in.

There was a warm, earthy smell I could not identify and my feet seemed to be standing on broken tiles. At first I was in pitch darkness and cursed myself for not having brought a light, but as I grew accustomed to the gloom, I found that the roof was high above me and realized that I was in a great hall. I had never forgotten Mrs Belflower's story of the elopement and duel which had been so surprisingly confirmed by Miss Lydia. So it was here that it had happened sixty years ago!

As I gazed upwards there was a flash of lightning and my eyes, though dazzled by the brightness, glimpsed the great timbers of the vaulted roof bearing illuminated armorial insignia on the corbeilles, the ogival hoods above the lofty windows, and ancient portraits hanging below them still with shreds of the yellowed muslin clinging to them with which they must once have been wrapped for protection. Beneath my feet I noticed the pattern of tiles making black and white lozenges like endlessly proliferating and ramifying quincunxes, it occurred to me, whose centre changed as I advanced.

Though there was no sign that the house was anything but deserted as it had been for so many years, above the occasional roll of the thunder and the continuous moaning of the wind and pattering of the rain I thought I heard voices. Yet they might merely have been the sounds of the eddying gusts and for anything I knew to the contrary I was alone in the great building.

Suddenly a huge shape loomed up before me and I heard a harsh breathing. Then it was followed by a deep trumpeting note and I realized it was a cow. So that was the smell! The ancient hall of my ancestors was now a cow-byre!

I ventured further, recalling that the chapel figured in the stories of both Miss Lydia and Mrs Belflower and trying to remember if either of them had suggested where it might be. As I groped my way towards the back of the hall, there was another flash of lightning and I started as I saw a shape ahead of me and to the left. At the realization that it was my own shadow I laughed aloud, and the noise sounded so hollowly that I was frightened again. I passed through an ancient screen hung with painted leather which was now cracked and hanging in strips, and found that I was in a smaller chamber where there was a strong smell of damp. At the next flash I saw that the walls were still hung with glazed linen and tapestries that were billowing in the draught, except where they had come down and lay in a rotting pile leaving the bare frames exposed. I passed a lofty old tester-bed — perhaps that in which Jeoffrey Huffam had been born, it occurred to me — still with its damasked wall-hangings in faded scarlet and gold.

In a corner there was the entrance to a spiral staircase and I began to ascend, finding the old stone treads badly worn but still in place. As I groped my way upwards in the dark, I suddenly thought I heard voices. Remembering Miss Lydia's account of how her aunt, Anna, had dwelt there in her madness, I felt a profound unease.

Suddenly someone spoke from the darkness very clearly and very close to me. But what made me start and caused the hairs to rise on the nape of my neck, was that I knew the voice before I understood the words:

"Master Will-Not must perforce give way to his better, Mr Thou-Shalt."

My wits must have turned! I had imagined it. This was Bissett's voice. Yet how could that be? I must be mad or dreaming. I rounded the last twist of the spiral and found myself at the back of the old chapel behind an ancient wooden screen. The roof was derelict and rain-water was running down the walls and across the floor and splashing through the broken windows where only remnants of coloured glass remained. What light there was came from two coach-lamps and a pair of lanthorns which were hanging from poles at the altar end. Standing side by side with their backs to me were Bellringer and Henrietta, with Mr Pamplin facing them. Mr Phumphred was standing beside Bellringer. On the other side of Henrietta stood — yes, it was indeed Bissett!

"I ain't your sarvint to command, Mrs Bissett," Mr Phumphred was saying. "It's my dooty as giver-away to make sure that the young lady truly does wish it."

"Thank you, Mr Phumphred," Henrietta said in a low voice that I could hardly catch. "I know you mean well, but I assure you that I am not being forced into this in any way."

"Very well," said Mr Pamplin irritably. "We have established that there is no just cause or impediment ... "

At that moment I stepped forward from behind the screen and cried: "Hold!"

They turned and I saw horror and dismay — though of different kinds — written upon every countenance. Henrietta screamed and backed away, holding up her hands but staring at me through her fingers that were splayed across her face. Bellringer uttered an oath. Mr Pamplin looked dismayed, while Bissett and Mr Phumphred were pale with shock.

"I am not a ghost," I cried. "I did not die in Fleet-ditch."

I advanced up the shattered aisle and all but Bellringer and the clergyman moved away. I held out my hand towards the old coachman and he cautiously shook it. Henrietta was hunched against the altar-table watching us with fearful intensity.

I went up to her and, as if still believing me to be an apparition, she backed away.

"Forgive me," I said to her in an undertone. "I believed it was for the best that you should think me dead. For your sake as well as mine."

She shook her head in bewilderment: "You should have let me know!"

"I'm sorry," I said.

Surely I could see in her face that she had loved me and had suffered! This was why she had listened to Bellringer.

"I did not mean to surprise you this way, but I had to prevent this marriage." She was still staring at me in horror. Continuing to speak softly so that the others would not hear, I went on: "He is deceiving you. He means simply to enrich himself through you."

As I was speaking Bellringer came up to us and stood beside her with an expression of solicitousness that I remembered well.

"That is not true," Henrietta muttered, looking from one of us to the other. "He knows I am penniless."

"No," I said. "The will has appeared again. It was not destroyed as we all believed. That means that if I really had been dead, then you would have inherited the estate."

"Don't listen to anything he says, Henrietta," Bellringer said. "He hates me. He wants to injure me in your eyes."

"But I know the will was not destroyed," she protested to me. "That was why they wanted to marry me to Tom: so that I would make the estate safe for them. But I'm not marrying him. Harry has rescued me from that."

I was baffled by her words. Was she, then, collaborating with Bellringer in outwitting her guardians? But at her next speech all became clear to me:

"And so, you see, when Aunt Isabella hears what I have done, she will destroy it and that will be the end of my prospects."

"He has lied to you," I said. "Lady Mompesson does not have the will. Bellringer himself has it."

"That's not true!" Henrietta cried, turning to him as she spoke.

"Dearest, he is lying," Bellringer said and gently took her hand. To my dismay she allowed him to do so.

I was in a turmoil. This wasn't how it should have turned out. What was happening? Did Henrietta feel nothing for me? Did she love Bellringer? Did she even know that he had the will and was that why she was so dismayed to see me: my existence disqualified her as heir? Surely that could not be!

"How could it be the truth?" Bellringer went on. "For even though I see that he is alive, yet I still wish to make you mine. But you know that the Huffam heir stands between you and the estate, so if I only cared for your inheritance, would I marry you now?"

"Yes," I cried, "because you know that my life hangs by a thread. Look at me, Henrietta," I said to her, indicating my bandaged head. "His friends have tried to kill me once and he knows that they will try again."

"I don't believe you," she said. "You have a crotchet about people trying to kill you." She turned to the clergyman and said in a firm voice: "Mr Pamplin, pray continue."

"No!" I exclaimed, raising my voice so that the others would hear and trying one last desperate means. "He has tricked you, all of you! The marriage of Miss Henrietta that Sir David ordered you to bring about was to his brother, Tom."

"That is what he has saved me from!" Henrietta cried, flushing. She turned to me with an expression I had never seen on her face: "What are you trying to do to me?"

"Is that true?" demanded Mr Pamplin. Seeing Henrietta's discomfiture he believed me and said: "In that case, you've made a damned fool of me, Bellringer."

"But you showed me that letter from Mr Barbellion," said Bissett, in alarm; "saying that it was Sir David's wish as how I should accompany Miss Palphramond to her wedding with you."

I knew that Bellringer was an accomplished forger: he had devised the note that Miss Quilliam had said had been the undoing of her and he had forged the copy of the will that had taken me in. But there was no point in trying to persuade them of this.

"You're quite right, Mrs Bissett," Bellringer said. "Don't believe him."

She shot me a malevolent look and nodded her head as if remembering all the times I had shewn myself to her to be unreliable.

"Do your work, Pamplin," Bellringer said. "The bride is willing and the licence is in form."

The clergyman nodded and those present took up again the positions in which I had interrupted them. I had played all my cards and had none left. So the ceremony was resumed and I discovered I had never desired her so much as now when I was forced to stand by and see her wed to another. I hated him as I had hated no-one before. In my powerlessness to oppose my fate, I was reminded of how I had crouched in the darkness beneath the Thames wharves and waited for the tide to rise and kill me.

"Listen!" Mr Phumphred exclaimed a few moments later.

Against the roaring of the wind I heard the hooves of a galloping horse.

I looked out of one of the western windows and saw the moon peep from behind some scurrying clouds whose paleness threw into silhouette the mausoleum on the hill that rose beside us. In the foreground were the four great elm-trees of Miss Lydia's story bowing in the gusts of wind. And in a flash of lightning I saw a horse and rider approaching the house at a gallop.

I called out to describe what I had seen and Bellringer hurried to the window beside me. At that moment the rider threw himself to the ground and ran towards the building. He was carrying something heavy that I could not make out. I did not recognise him, but I saw Bellringer blench as he looked out.

Then he ran to seize Henrietta and cried: "Quickly! He is coming in the back way."

Though none of us — except Bellringer — were sure who the rider was, we were immediately united in a kind of guilty fear and followed the newly-wed couple towards the stair at the back of the chapel.

"Leave the lanthorns, you ideot!" Bellringer cried as Mr Phumphred made to pick one of them up.

When we reached the bottom of the stair, we listened but could hear nothing. Bellringer led us towards the great hall and we had picked our way in the darkness halfway down its length when suddenly a voice that was so harsh with anger that I did not know it, shouted from behind us: "Stand where you are!"

We all froze. The man strode forward until he was within a few paces of us, peering to make out who was who in the gloom. I saw that he was carrying a duelling-pistol in each hand and I heard the locks click.

"Is that you, Bellringer, you snivelling cheat?"

I recognised the voice now: it was David Mompesson.

"It is I, John Huffam," I said.

"Then stand clear, meddler," he said. "Justice must be done." He stepped forward until he was level with me.

"Don't be a fool, Mompesson," I warned him.

He was staring intently at something over my shoulder and I turned in that direction. There was a flash of lightning and I saw a figure caught in silhouette slipping silently towards the great door behind us. Seeing this Mompesson raised his right arm. I moved so that I was between him and his quarry.

"You can't shoot him now," I cried.

I saw Mompesson's face like a white mask and knew that he was going to fire, but I found I was powerless to move. Suddenly I was violently pushed from behind. There was a vivid flash in front of my eyes and what seemed like a blow to the head. My lungs were filled with acrid smoke. I could not breathe. Then I found myself on the floor, gasping and blinded, my eyes seeing fireworks. Someone was lying beside me. Instantly there was another explosion, this time from a safe distance.

There was a high, terrible scream.

Then Joey's voice beside me said hoarsely: "Are you all right, John?"

He had saved me. He had entered the Hall just as we came in and had pushed me out of the way of the first shot. (Later he explained how he came to arrive just then: he had seen my chaise as he was returning from Thorpe Woolston and had followed it to the Old Hall.)

He helped me to my feet and with his aid I staggered towards the rest of the party. Mr Phumphred had brought two of the lanthorns from the chapel and by its light I could see that the others were standing around Bellringer who lay on his back, except for Bissett who was kneeling beside him and had loosened his coat and shirt which were covered in something that looked black in the pale moonlight. Henrietta was cowering nearby, staring at Mompesson.

As we drew near Bellringer gasped: "I've done for you now, Mompesson. "You'll hang for this, and nothing can save you."

His face wore an expression of triumphant malice.

"He was trying to escape," Mompesson protested to the rest of us. "I had no choice."

Looking down at the injured man I could see that the ball had entered his chest from behind and left the body just below his heart.

"I'm finished," he said suddenly. Then with something between a laugh and a gasp he added: "So Umphraville is avenged."

Astonished by this allusion, I was about to ask him what he meant and how he knew of that ancient crime, but at that moment two figures appeared at the door — a lady and a gentleman carrying a lanthorn. As they drew near I recognised them as Lady Mompesson and Mr Barbellion. (Sir David, I learned later, had parted from the coach some miles away and had taken one of the carriage-horses and ridden into the park from the rear, which explained why he had reached us ahead of them.)

"What has occurred?" asked the solicitor, looking at the pistols that his client was holding.

Mompesson seemed about to speak but Mr Barbellion raised a hand to stop him: "If you please, Sir David. I advise you to say nothing."

"He shot him in the back," said Mr Pamplin laconically.

"Did anyone of you witness this alleged incident?" Mr Barbellion asked, glancing keenly from one face to another.

Bissett looked at him expressionlessly and Mr Phumphred fearfully, glancing also at Lady Mompesson who was gazing fixedly at him. Mr Pamplin looked away.

"Are you going to try to cheat me of my revenge?" gasped Bellringer. "Charles, damn you, you saw it."

"It was too deuced dark to see anything," the clergyman muttered.

"Henrietta?"

She said nothing. Was she too shocked to speak?

"I saw it," said Mr Phumphred looking straight into Lady Mompesson's face.

"You ideot!" Lady Mompesson screamed at her son and swiftly struck his face.

"Then I can do nothing for you, Sir David," said Mr Barbellion. "You have very little time. I advise you to make the best use of it."

To my amazement Lady Mompesson knelt over the dying man and began searching his pockets. Seeing this her son knelt down and did the same, laying his weapons on the ground.

"You'll find nothing," Bellringer gasped.

They pulled everything out onto the broken tiles of the floor. Lady Mompesson found his pocket-book and looked through it.

I stepped forward: "I protest at this. The man is seriously injured. Someone must be sent for a surgeon."

The two ignored me. They reminded me of a pair of thieves I had once seen rifling the pockets of a corpse on a piece of waste ground near Bethnal-green.

Then a more sinister consideration struck me. The will would only be of value to them if two eventualities occurred: my death and the marriage of Henrietta to either Mompesson himself or Tom. It must be that their keenness to find the will was because they knew very well that someone was determined to procure my death.

Mr Barbellion was watching me and now smiled thinly in greeting. I must have presented a strange and unimpressive appearance for, in addition to the injuries received in the attack by Barney, my eyebrows were now singed and my face blackened and scorched by the blast of Mompesson's pistol.

"Ah, the Huffam heir welcoming us to the mansion of his fathers," the lawyer said.

I heard a chinking sound and saw Mompesson drop several keys from Bellringer's pockets onto the worn squares of the floor. One of them was enormous.

"I do not have it," said Bellringer. "I am not such a fool." He paused and fought for breath, raising his head a little so that he could watch Lady Mompesson and her son who had given up the search and were now looking at him eagerly. "It's safe," he said. The words were coming faintly and at longer and longer intervals. "It's back. Back where ... where it came from."

His head fell onto the broken tiles.

"Back where it came from!" I repeated to myself, staring at the huge key. And he had said to me at my lodgings that it was "safe where it belongs". Those words had reminded me of something that someone else had said, but I could not recall who.

"You fool," Lady Mompesson hissed at her son. "You've destroyed us all."

"What shall I do?" he muttered.

"I cannot advise you," said Mr Barbellion. "To do so would be to become an accessary after the fact."

I saw Mompesson clench his fist and move forward, but his mother took his arm and held him back.

"I can only describe to you," the solicitor went on, "a desperate course of action that a man who has committed a serious felony might take. He might go abroad as swiftly as possible. Therefore he would need to get to the nearest port — which I believe must be Boston — and take the packet-boat to one of the Dutch ports. I fear he would have to reside overseas for the remainder of his life."

"Wait," I said. "This man has committed murder. It is our duty to apprehend him."

"Damn you!" cried Mompesson.

"Is this your way of seeking revenge?" Lady Mompesson cried.

"Well spoken, young gentleman," Mr Barbellion said ironically. "But unfortunately Sir David is a desperate man and armed." He paused. "You are armed, Sir David?"

Mompesson hastily picked up the pistols.

"What can we do?" Mr Barbellion went on. "If the men amongst us were to rush upon him now, one of us might be fatally injured. The law does not require us to endanger our persons."

"Indeed not!" Mr Pamplin breathed.

"Both pieces have been discharged," I said.

"You want revenge, don't you, you low, sneaking fellow!" cried Lady Mompesson.

The words stung me but I could not think how to reply without conceding her charge.

"Let him go," said Joey, glancing down at Bellringer. "That one wasn't worth risking our own skins for."

"I've re-loaded this one," said Mompesson, dropping one of the pistols onto the tiled floor where it clattered and echoed, and pointing the other at me.

"You're lying," I said.

I glanced towards Henrietta who was watching the proceedings with a strange intensity.

"Very well," I said. "Go."

I stood aside and he passed with a kind of stupid leer of triumph.

"Come, Phumphred," Lady Mompesson said, turning to the old coachman; "Take Sir David to Boston."

The old coachman hesitated.

"You don't have to," I said. "And if you do you may regret it."

"Is this loyalty?" exclaimed his mistress, seeing his indecision.

"Was it loyal in you to have me take this young lady to a marriage agin her will?" he replied. "But very well, ma'am, I'll do as you bid."

Lady Mompesson turned to her solicitor: "Will you not come with us?"

"No, Lady Mompesson, I will not compromise myself any further. My duty is to find the nearest justice and lay an information against your son." She opened her eyes wide at this, but he went on: "However, if I have to walk in quest of one in this weather and ignorant of my way, I doubt if I shall even reach him before Sir David is at the next post-town between here and the coast."

Lady Mompesson smiled briefly and then turned to Henrietta: "Go to the house hard by and wait for me to return."

Henrietta did not look at her. "David!" she cried. "Take me with you!"

Mompesson shrugged his shoulders in embarrassment. She was clearly hysterical and confused.

"*She* won't marry you now!" Henrietta cried. "*She* won't follow you abroad."

Mompesson moved towards the door with a foolish smile.

"Calm yourself, Henrietta!" Lady Mompesson said sharply.

I moved towards Henrietta to take her arm but she ducked away from me and ran further back into the shadows.

Mompesson and his mother had almost reached the door when Mr Pamplin said: "Lady Mompesson, let me explain my part in these proceedings lest I lose your good opinion. I was the unwitting dupe of Bellringer. He said he wanted me for a divinity-job and ... "

With no more than a glance of irritation in his direction, Lady Mompesson walked out followed by her son with Mr Phumphred behind him. The clergyman turned to us and finished his sentence: "And, in short, I had no conception of his real design."

"That may be so," Mr Barbellion said. Then he turned to Bissett: "As for you, woman, what the devil were you playing at?"

"I obeyed your instructions," she protested.

"What can you mean?"

"Why, Mr Bellringer came to me last night in Huntingdon with a letter from you telling me to do what he bid and promising that I would be amply rewarded. But he tricked me. I didn't realize it was Mr Tom that Miss Palphramond was intended to marry."

"A letter from me?" the lawyer repeated.

She fumbled in her pocket and pulled something out. Mr Barbellion seized it.

"You'd do anything for a reward, wouldn't you?" I said. "It was because Mr Barbellion bought you those many years ago that all the ill consequences followed for my mother and myself."

"That's a wicked thing to say!" she retorted. "I only done what I thought best for your mother, for Mr Barbellion meant well."

"This letter is most convincing," the lawyer said admiringly. "The young man had much ability."

Indeed he had, I thought. And not merely as a forger of documents.

"But you must not reproach either your old nurse or myself, young gentleman," Mr Barbellion went on. "I meant no harm to your mother but merely wanted to purchase the codicil from her. And how much misery might have been avoided if I had succeeded, you are better placed to know than I."

I reflected that it was not his fault that my mother had mistaken him for an agent of the Clothiers. And if we had not fled that time that Miss Quilliam brought him to Orchard-street, all might have turned out well, so perhaps I had been unfair to him. And he could help me now.

As he moved towards the door I said: "I believe I might be able to find the will!"

He stopped immediately, swung round, and looked at me with interest. "Go on," he said.

"Suppose I could? Would the property be escheated or would it be mine?"

"You know some law!" he exclaimed. "Indeed, the property of a fugitive felon escheats to the Crown, so that if Sir David is convicted then he loses everything. However, if the will were found, a claimant under it could argue that it retrospectively altered the devolution of the estate: in brief, that Sir David has no title to lose and that title passed down to the claimant. But I have to inform you that the will is of no use to you. It would benefit only Miss Palphramond, for you have no claim since it cannot be proved that you are the Huffam heir."

"You are referring to the absence of a record of the marriage of James and Eliza Huffam?" I asked and he nodded.

At that moment Sukey entered, soaking wet: "There's the chaise out there and the postilion grumbling that he has been waiting a good two hours," she said to me, looking round in the half-gloom. She started: "So you found Mrs Bissett, Master Johnnie," she said, staring at her with hostility. "I was going to tell you, that was who I seen here today when I come up to the Hall to look at the lights."

Bissett nodded curtly at her.

Sukey brought something from under her shawl: "I brung that package you left with me last time."

In delight I seized it from her and unwrapped it. Mr Advowson's copy of the entry was in perfect condition, though I noticed that the home-made ink of the contract that Harry had required me to sign had faded away.

Suddenly Sukey gave a cry. She was staring at Mr Barbellion: "Why, that's the genel'man as frighted us in the burying-ground all them years ago!"

"That's right," I said to her. Then I turned back to the lawyer: "I know what you were doing then. You were examining the Huffam vault."

"That is so," he said in surprise. "I hoped to find a clew to the venue of that marriage we were speaking of."

"You were very close," I said. "If you had been franker and told the clerk, Mr Advowson, that you were interested in the Huffams he might have told you about the chest from the old chapel where we were just now. That is where the wedding of my great-grandparents was solemnized. Though I know you were so discreet because you did not want to give away what you were looking for."

"So you have found proof of it?" he asked in excitement.

I nodded. "Mr Advowson has it safe."

"Then if only you could prove your own parentage ... " he began but broke off. "However, as you might know, the record of your baptism has been stolen from the church."

"But not before I had it copied," I said, and handed the piece of parchment to him.

At that moment I heard a cry of horror from Sukey as she caught sight of the body. Then I saw her cross to Henrietta who was still sitting against the wall. She put her arm around her and although Henrietta at first shook it off, she then allowed herself to be held.

"Then this changes everything," Mr Barbellion exclaimed after perusing the piece of parchment. "For if the will could only be laid before the court, you would have an unassailable claim. Where do you believe it is?"

He spoke as if casually but I thought I heard a tremor in his voice.

I shook my head with a smile. I could be as circumspect as any Chancery lawyer.

He reached into his pocket and held out his card: "Come and see me if I can be of any assistance."

Seeing my hesitation he placed it in my hand with the copy of the entry, and asked me where my lodgings were. Not knowing quite why I did so, I gave him this information and told him the name I had assumed, and he wrote the details down in his pocket-book.

"Now, Miss Palphramond," Mr Barbellion said; "if you will permit me, I will escort you to the house."

As if she had not heard him, she made no move.

"Let her be for now," I said, "and we will take her there later."

Mr Barbellion shrugged his shoulders and went out, Bissett and Mr Pamplin following him without either of them even glancing in my direction.

I explained to Henrietta who Joey and Sukey were, but she stared dully back at me without looking at them, though Sukey was sitting beside her still holding her. What would become of her? Now that I could prove my claim, there was no advantage to the Mompessons in marrying her to Tom so long as I lived. But until the will was safely before the court, my life was in danger from the Maliphant claimant, and so Henrietta was in peril of another forced marriage.

I walked over to her and Sukey tactfully withdrew to the door where the rain was still lashing down and the lightning flickering at intervals. So Henrietta and I sat alone in the great dark hall with the harsh breathing of the cows around us and the silent third not twenty feet from us.

I took her hand in mine and she did not resist. It was very cold.

"You must try to put the past behind you," I said.

"I once believed he loved me."

"You must not reproach yourself, Henrietta."

"He seduced me," she said simply.

"He seduced me, too," I said, and now she looked at me in surprise. "He can be very charming."

"I don't think you understand," she said, shaking her head.

"Then tell me," I urged.

"I don't want to."

"Then if it distresses you to speak, I will tell you," I said. "For I believe I have been able to deduce all that has happened. Just nod if I'm right."

She glanced up for a moment, but lowered her head as I began to speak: "There was a ball that night," I said and she nodded. "Bellringer came to tell your guardians that I was still alive and the will was for sale after all. So Tom was made to sign his consent to the trust that was to strip him of his legal rights. In the early hours you must have been told by Lady Mompesson that you were to go down to Hougham under the protection of Pamplin and accompanied by your aunt's woman, Pickavance. I imagine that you were not told that Tom and Bellringer would be accompanying the carriage in a post-chaise. It was only that night when you reached the inn at Hertford that you realized that they were travelling with you. Tom was, of course, hopelessly drunk, for Bellringer had been plying him with brandy on the way. Rooms were engaged for the whole party, though in the event you only stayed a few hours. Am I right so far?"

She looked up and nodded, her eyes wide in amazement.

"And am I right to suspect that later that night Bellringer came to you?" I asked. Henrietta flushed and cast her eyes down. "I know how convincing he can be," I went on. "He told you that the Mompessons had regained the will and so had instituted the plan to force you to marry Tom. Perhaps you would be kept here in the Old Hall until you gave in. He said that he had pretended to go along with it, but now he said he could save you. The only sure way was by marrying you himself. Am I right in saying that he swore that he had loved you since he first met you?" She nodded without looking at me. "Of course, not realizing that he had the will, you did not know what he stood to gain. Indeed, you probably told him that you were penniless and he assured you that he cared nothing for that."

"He said that David's engagement showed how little he cared!" Henrietta exclaimed, still keeping her gaze lowered.

"For anything but money, you mean?" I asked, after a moment's puzzled reflection. "So he said that David was marrying for money but he was marrying for love? I understand and, Henrietta, nobody could blame you for succumbing as you did. And, of course, you believed that I was dead. Forgive me, dear girl. That was wrong of me, but I meant it for the best. So I imagine that Bellringer explained that he could frustrate your aunt's design by discarding Tom at the inn and leaving Pickavance behind (since she had her orders from Lady Mompesson). Presumably he reassured you by saying he would furnish you with a respectable woman in Huntingdon who would accompany you. He would do this by making her think she had been hired by Mr Barbellion to help him as she had in the past. He knew this because I had told him how Bissett had betrayed my mother and myself to Mr Barbellion long ago. You see, he took me in, too, so you need not be ashamed. I have guessed it all aright, haven't I?"

She made no acknowledgement and did not raise her head, but I could see in her face that my words had awakened painful memories and so I did not press her.

"So when you set off very early the next morning Tom was abandoned in a drunken stupor and Pickavance was left behind still fast asleep, and later that day Bissett was picked up in Huntingdon to fill her place. Then you travelled overnight and reached Hougham this morning."

She nodded and now looked at me.

At that moment Sukey came over from where she had been standing with Joey: "Shouldn't we take Mrs Bellringer to her people?" she asked me gently.

For a moment I had no idea whom she meant. Then I understood and saw that she was right. I left her with Henrietta, went over to the body and raised the lanthorn to look down upon it.

There were coins scattered about and I put them back in Bellringer's pockets. This reminded me that I had very little money left — just enough, once I had paid the postilion, for my coach-fare back to the metropolis and a few shillings for Joey to make his way home on foot. I picked up the huge key and, feeling that I had every right to, I pocketed it. It was this that had led me to tell Mr Barbellion that I believed I had a chance of regaining the will. For I had recognised it while Lady Mompesson and her son were picking the dead man's pockets. Remembering that, as Joey had told me, Bellringer was Mr Escreet's mysterious visiter, I had realized that it was the key to the old house at Charing-cross. Perhaps, I reflected now, it was the very one that Peter Clothier had said he had found lying on the floor before the vestibule-door. But what could the link be between Bellringer and Mr Escreet? His remark about the killing of John Umphraville had confirmed that he had some secret connexion with my family, but what could he have meant by saying that that murder had been avenged by his own death? And was I any nearer to resolving the mystery of who had murdered my grandfather? Finally, what about the will? As long as someone had it then I was in danger of being killed and Henrietta of being forced into marriage, if not with Tom then with some other unscrupulous adventurer. I believed I had a chance of regaining it, for I had remembered what Bellringer's phrase about the will being "back where it belonged" had stirred in my memory.

I went back to Henrietta and Sukey, and called Joey over. "Henrietta," I said, "we'll take you back to the house now. I must return to London today so you and I, Joey, will go back to Sutton Valancy in the chaise and I'll take the night-mail from there. I have just enough money left to travel as an outside. But I'm afraid you'll have to make your way home as best you can from there."

Joey and Sukey protested that I was not well enough to travel, and Joey warned me that I was still in grave danger from Barney and should not venture onto the streets of the capital alone.

"I must go back," I said. "Something Bellringer said has given me an idea."

"About that accursed will?" Henrietta said suddenly.

"About the mystery of my grandfather's murder," I returned indignantly.

"No, it's the will you want really," she insisted. "That's why you tried to prevent my marriage. It wasn't me you were pursuing but the will! That's why you're going back to London now."

"Take care of her, Sukey," I said. "She's not well."

Sukey gently took her arm and so we went out to the chaise — picking our way across the old terraces and the muddy parkland with increased difficulty now that it was completely dark — where we found the driver indignant on his own behalf and that of his horses.

There was only room for two and so I took leave of Sukey and then, while Joey ran behind, the chaise returned to the big house. Henrietta and I said nothing as it jolted through the darkness. When it stopped she got out and stood with her back to me at the foot of the steps but with her head turned towards the way we had come. Joey boarded the vehicle and as we rolled away I looked back and saw her standing motionless where we had left her.

BOOK V

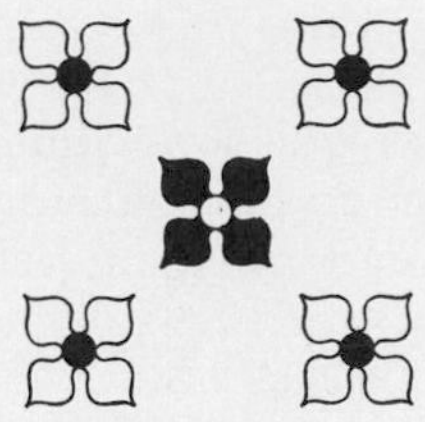

The Key

CHAPTER 121

Though it is true that we can understand nothing without finding a pattern, I must warn you against the course of action that our misguided friend (with whom I am now chumming again, as when we first met) advocates, for it risks imposing rather than discovering a design. (How I hope that my poor understanding has not led you into that error in helping you to comprehend your past experiences!) Now that I take my leave of you, I urge you not to impose such a pattern on the future.

Let me illustrate what I mean by taking the case of Barney Digweed in his pursuit of yourself. For Digweed, as a criminal, is the exemplary member of such a society as ours in that he seizes his opportunities where he finds them and is blinded by no prejudices as to how matters ought or ought not to be. Living in and for the moment merely, he can adapt easily to the situation as it changes.

From what you found out from him a little later that day, this is what must have happened:

He had pursued you the previous day, but you eluded him (without knowing it) by travelling down to Hougham. Learning from the servants at Brook-street that that was where you had gone, he deployed members of his company to watch out for your return and so had them hurrying from one livery-stable to another and visiting each of the inns that deal with the Great-north-road all that day and the next. This responsiveness to events was rewarded for it came about that you stumbled unwittingly into his net. But with what result, you know better than I, and so I shall leave it to you to recount.

Let me conclude by advising you to learn at least this lesson from Digweed: the concatenation of events is always more complicated and inexplicable than we like to imagine. We must remember that a pattern — whether of the past or the future — is always arbitrary or partial in that there could always be a different one or a further elaboration of the same one. In the end we have to make a guess or hazard all upon the throw of the dice, just as you did when you chose to withdraw that particular combination of bolts in Chapter 100.

And therefore, as I fondly take my leave, I beg you, my dear young friend, not to trust too much to Justice and Equity in your designs for the future.

CHAPTER 122

We reached the inn at Sutton Valancy within a couple of hours. Learning that the night-mail was due in an hour, I purchased my ticket and gave my remaining money to Joey — except for my last shilling with which I bought us some food and drink in the travellers'-room. The coach arrived on time to the minute and we took leave of each other.

My outer garments were inadequate to keep off the driving rain as I sat on the roof during the long journey South. Exhausted, I fell asleep against the broad shoulder of a fellow-traveller and awoke to a grey, cold dawn as if the storm were wearily recuperating before another onslaught. All that endless day and the next I revolved in my mind the mysteries that surrounded me and the question of what I should do when I reached my destination. I recalled the last time I had traversed this road in the same direction, walking the weary miles or riding a cart at the invitation of a friendly carrier. And I remembered the occasion before that when I had been safely inside the coach with my mother. This memory returned to me with particular force as we approached Hertford that evening and I recalled what I had learned since then about my mother's experiences there. All day I had felt weaker and weaker and now, when I left the coach during the change of horses at the Blue Dragon, I fainted in the yard. I was picked up and borne inside by one of the ostlers and ordered to bed by the landlady, despite my protests. Even my insistence that I had not a penny upon me had no effect except to produce the accusation that I was half-starved, which was followed by a bowl of broth. So I stayed there overnight, regretting that I had lost the initiative and might not now reach Town ahead of the news of Bellringer's death and Mompesson's flight.

The storm overtook me that night and roared above my head. The landlady would not permit me to go on the next morning and, besides, I did not feel strong enough. I slept most of the time but awoke in the evening feeling refreshed and well again. Now I insisted on continuing my journey and late in the evening boarded the very night-mail which I had been on the previous day. The storm was still blustering, but by the time we clattered under the arch of the Golden-Cross-inn a couple of hours past midnight, it had almost blown over. I was so preoccupied that it did not occur to me to look out for anyone who might be watching for me, and I could not have evaded detection even if I had — though perhaps if I had guessed, I would have requested to be put down on the outskirts of the metropolis and have made my way from there on foot.

So it was about half past two o'clock when I reached the old house at Charing-cross that I thought of — rightly or wrongly — as my grandfather's. It was in darkness and, reflecting that in both law and justice it had belonged to my mother's father and that since I was the heir-at-law of his heir, the house was mine, I took out the great key and gently turned it in the lock of the street-door. The wards clicked and I passed in. The vestibule-door was unlocked so, first locking the street-door again, I found myself a moment later in the front hall.

Suddenly, to my horror, I heard a loud banging noise. For a moment I believed it came from my own heart, but then I realized that someone was hammering at the street-door. I froze. Had I been pursued? The knocking was repeated and then I heard an answering noise from upstairs. I moved swiftly round to the lobby at the side of the staircase where I would be hidden from the street-door. The moonlight coming through the windows cast enough light for me to see with a shudder that the sword and halberd were still hanging on the wall — *back where they've always belonged* — as Mr Escreet had said to my mother. Pressing myself back into the shadows, I was just able to see Mr Escreet, carrying a candle and clad in a dressing-gown worn over his night-shirt, reaching the bottom of the stairs. On his face was an expression of terrible, harrowing sorrow and his bulbous features seemed to me to resemble nothing so much as a weathered piece of sculpture. As he descended I moved round in the shadows towards the door of the plate-room to keep out of his line of vision.

I heard him speaking through the judas-hole and then the door opened. There were voices, one of them surely a woman's, and then the sound of several people. They passed through the vestibule and then stood in the hall at the foot of the stairs, just out of my sight.

"Come, we know you have it."

To my astonishment I recognised the voice as that of Sancious — the attorney who had cheated my mother and whom we had later encountered at Mrs Fortisquince's in his disguise as Steplight, and whom I had believed I saw while ill at the house of Daniel Porteous.

"How can you say that?" Mr Escreet protested. "You know that it was destroyed when the boy was drowned."

"We believed that at first just as we believed that wretched boy had died," Sancious sneered.

So, as I had guessed, Sally had told Barney about seeing me that night when I had noticed her staring at me in the Haymarket, and he had gone to Sancious and been instructed to kill me. Presumably they were here because Barney had told them that I had said the will still existed when he had attacked me outside my lodgings a few days ago. But why had Sancious come here to get the will? And why was he so anxious for my death now that Silas Clothier was dead and so his heirs could not profit by it?

There was a long sigh from the old man. "If only he had."

Then Mr Escreet knew that I had not drowned! How could he have learned that? From Bellringer, presumably! The more I learned, the more puzzled I became.

"Leave us alone for that," Sancious said brutally, and I slunk further into the shadows. "But for that, we need the will."

"Why do you think I should have it?"

"We know that Bellringer got it from the boy by a trick. And one of our people followed him to this house not long ago. We assume he gave it to you for safe-keeping."

Bewilderment and enlightenment flooded in upon me. How did they know so much? Why had they had Bellringer followed?

"To me?" the old man exclaimed. "Why should he have given it to me?"

This was what puzzled me: what was the connexion between him and Bellringer?

"Don't play with us," said a woman's voice.

I stifled a cry of amazement. I was truly going mad. My wits had turned.

Then she spoke again:

"We know everything. You had the will originally. You were involved in its theft."

It was indeed she! It was Mrs Fortisquince! Why was she there? What was her connexion with Sancious? What interest could she have in the will? And what did she mean by accusing the old man of having stolen it? He had told me the thief was Paternoster. Was he lying about that?

"What do you know about it?" exclaimed the old man. "You weren't even born when it happened."

"Mrs Sancious knows a great deal about it," said the attorney.

Mrs Sancious! I was astounded. Why should the proud, wealthy widow ally herself with a pettifogging attorney?

Mrs Fortisquince — or Mrs Sancious as I now had to think of her — spoke again: "I do. Above all, I know of the child that was born in secret to Anna Mompesson more than ninety years ago."

I heard the old man gasp.

"Born as the consequence of a shameful and illicit intrigue," Mrs Fortisquince went on. "And I know that the child was taken from her by its father, Jeoffrey Huffam, and given to his attorney, Paternoster, to be put out to adoption. I know how Paternoster conceived the design of blackmailing Huffam, and to that end had the child adopted by one of his own clerks. I know that he instructed that it be baptised in the name of its natural father: Jeoffrey."

She paused and suddenly the name I had seen mentioned in the purloined will when I had read it at Bellringer's lodgings flashed before me: Jeoffrey Escreet!

This affair between Jeoffrey Huffam and Anna Mompesson was the story Miss Lydia had recounted. Yet even she had not known the fate of the child — or had perhaps confused it with the fate of another such inconvenient infant.

And then, confirming my surmise, Mrs Sancious went on, speaking very deliberately: "And I know that that clerk's name was Escreet."

Of course! Escreet was the founder of an illegitimate line combining the two families of Huffam and Mompesson!

"Aye!" cried the old man bitterly. "Escreet! Neither 'Huffam' nor 'Mompesson' though I am half of one and half of the other — and the only being upon this earth who can say that, now that old Lydia Mompesson is no more. My curse upon both those families. And curse Paternoster for what he did! Better to have left me in ignorance, but he used me like a piece in a game of chess. He contrived to have Jeoffrey Huffam take me into his service as his confidential agent without either of us knowing of the connexion between us. Then he persuaded me to marry his own daughter — an ugly squinting creature that nobody would take for the pitiful dowry that was all he could offer — with the promise to reveal something to my advantage. And what was it? Why, the secret of who my natural parents were. A bitter secret that was. I used to go down to Hougham on business for Jeoffrey at that time and once I knew my parentage and would see my half-brother James wasting his money on horses and women and gambling, and that great new house a-building, and that poor madwoman that they had driven insane ... Well, it all preyed upon my mind, the injustice of it."

"So that is why you blackmailed Jeoffrey," Mrs Sancious said.

"No, it wasn't like that. When I told him I was his son he was delighted. By that time he was disappointed in his legitimate son and was pleased to have one whom he could trust."

"That's not true," she returned. "You frightened him with the threat of a scandal for he had begun to be received at Court and had hopes of a title."

"You're lying!" the old man almost shrieked. "Why, as soon as I told him, he made a new will leaving me this house and a thousand pounds."

"You forced him to," she insisted. "He asked Paternoster for advice, not realizing that he was the very man who stood to gain because his daughter was secretly affianced to you. And a couple of years later Jeoffrey tried to annul his bequest of the money by adding the codicil to his will without your knowledge."

"Another lie!" he cried. "He did that because he was worried that James would sell the property to Nicholas Clothier after his death. That is why he added the codicil entailing the estate on James."

"Have you deceived yourself after all these years?" Mrs Sancious jeered. "Why was it that he concealed from you what he was doing if it was not that he was trying to disinherit you? But Paternoster told you and promised that he would make it all come right. And he said the same, didn't he, even when your natural father was dying in the Spring of '70 and made another will in which he cut you out altogether?"

"He did that in order to disinherit James in favour of his new-born grandson!"

"Yes, that too," she conceded, but went on: "But he rescinded the bequest to you of this house, did he not? So when he died Paternoster and you removed the codicil from the first will and hid the second one, and got a reward from James for doing so for that meant that he inherited the estate outright and was able to sell it to the Mompessons. And, of course, it also meant that you got this house and a thousand pounds."

I recalled that the purloined will made no mention of the bequest of this house to Escreet. So that was part of the reason why it had been stolen!

"No, it was Paternoster who did it all!" the old man insisted. "I knew nothing of it."

"You knew all about it," she sneered, "for Paternoster and you had to bribe his clerk to keep quiet about what you had done and to say he witnessed Jeoffrey's revocation of the codicil. And as part of the bargain made between you to keep his silence you affianced your young daughter to the clerk's son. His name was Bellringer and Henry is the grandchild of that marriage and therefore your great-grandson."

So that was Henry's connexion with the old man! The final pieces of the puzzle were falling into place.

"Yes," Escreet said. "Henry is my great-grandson, but you are wrong about the rest of it."

"And that," said Sancious, "is why he was as determined as you to get revenge on the two families and a share of the estate."

"A share!" cried the old man. "By this time he has secured the whole estate!"

"What do you mean?" Mrs Sancious asked quite calmly. "How can that be?"

"He has married the Palphramond claimant," the old man cried.

"Indeed?" she responded coolly.

"So do you think I'll give up the will now that what I have hoped for all my life is about to happen: my own family — my descendants! — are about to take possession of the Huffam lands? Be damned to you. What do you want with the will anyway?"

"Nothing at all," Mrs Sancious said. "It must be destroyed."

"Destroyed?" the old man gasped. "The only party who could want it destroyed must be ... "

He broke off.

"Yes," she said. "I am the Maliphant claimant."

So that was the explanation! That was why she was here! That was why Sancious had paid Barney to kill me! With Silas Clothier dead, the Maliphant claimant inherited the estate — so long as the Huffam line had failed! And, of course, that was why she and Sancious were married: she had the claim and he had the means to implement it.

"Henry warned me about you!" Escreet cried. "He told me how he had helped you to take care of your nevy because he stood in the way of an inheritance."

Then I was right in suspecting that Stephen's aunt had sent him to Quigg's farm to die! And yet I had not guessed who that aunt was and that it was because of her that Stephen and I had been sent to the same place!

"You are rambling, old man," she said coldly.

"Give us the will," Sancious ordered.

"I won't!"

"Give it to us," Sancious repeated. "It is of no use to you, for your great-grandson has failed."

"You're lying!"

I heard the rustle of paper as Sancious said: "This will be on the streets at dawn."

Then the old man's quavering voice came faintly to me: "'Baronet Flees After Death of Cousin in Duel. *Sutton Valancy, Tuesday 2nd. December.* Sir David Mompesson, Bart., is believed to have fled the country after the death of Mr Henry Bellringer ... '"

He faltered and broke off. After a few moments there was another rustling and then Mrs Sancious continued: "'... the death of Mr Henry Bellringer, understood to be a remote connexion of Sir David, in a duel between the two gentlemen. Mr Bellringer is reported to have eloped with Miss Henrietta Palphramond, and Sir David, who was opposed to the love-match because of his own attachment to the young lady, to have followed the lovers and to have interrupted the ceremony. Our correspondent states that the two gentlemen then fought a duel in which Mr Bellringer fell mortally wounded.'"

"Killed," the old man said. "Killed by a Mompesson!"

"And now the Huffam heir will inherit if he gets hold of the will," Sancious said. "Do you understand what I'm saying? It's of no use to you now. Give us the will and we have a man waiting for a word from us to make the boy quiet."

The old man said in a dazed voice: "So Umphraville is avenged."

That was what Bellringer had said as he lay mortally wounded! What had he meant? What did the old man mean now?

"What are you talking about?" Sancious asked irritably.

"He sent me after them," the old man began in a dazed tone. "The two couples. He was bent upon preventing their marriages. He promised ... promised to increase my inheritance. I rode day and night."

"He is wandering in his wits," Mrs Sancious remarked.

I, however, was hanging on his every word, trying to fit this story to what Miss Lydia had told me.

"When I reached the Hall," the old man continued, "it was in darkness. Then Umphraville came out and challenged me. I drew my sword and fought him. He was the better swordsman, but then she came running from the Hall behind me. She saw that I was in danger. She cried: 'My son! My son! Watch out behind you!' He believed she was speaking to him and turned his back on me, and I drove my sword home."

There was a brief silence.

So that was the "extraordinary" cry — as Miss Lydia had called it — that the madwoman had uttered! She had recognised her child and seen that he was in danger. It was not John Umphraville but Escreet whom she was trying to protect!

Then the old man went on: "I did this for him. For the Huffam family. My family. The Umphravilles weren't good enough to be allied to us. That's what he said to me. But afterwards he was angry that I had failed to prevent James' wedding to his harlot. And that I had killed Umphraville. And then Paternoster told me how he had tried to cheat me, to disinherit me of the house and money. I didn't believe him until he showed me the codicil and the will he made while he was dying. And then I saw that while I was away from here on his business, he was trying to cheat me of my rights!"

Bellringer had referred to his great-grandfather being denied his rights! So that was the explanation of his words that had so puzzled me!

"After all I had risked! I had the right to be considered one of the family. That's why I consented to help Paternoster when he made his suggestion. But we didn't *steal* the codicil and the will. They were lies and I had the right to suppress them. And what pleasure it gave me to extort so much money from James for the codicil and later to sell the will back to the Mompessons! If I could not belong to them, then I wanted to exploit and destroy both families by setting them against one another as far as lay in my power. So when I sold the will to them, I warned the Mompessons of the existence of the codicil so that they would know that they would never be safe. And many years later I tricked John Huffam into buying it from me, believing he was buying it from some third party."

So all the time that my grandfather, John Huffam, had been saving money from his annuity and had then plunged into debt to old Clothier in order to buy the codicil, Escreet had it in his possession! The purchase of it through a third party that my mother had described had been another of his charades!

"So you murdered a man all those years ago, did you?" Mrs Sancious said. "But Umphraville is not the only one, is he?"

I felt my mouth go dry with excitement. What could she mean?

"Yes, the only one," he protested. "Isn't one enough for you? God knows, it is for me!"

"Give us the will," Sancious hissed. "You don't want the Huffam boy to inherit, do you?"

"No, but nothing would make me give it to you!"

"Nothing?" Mrs Sancious repeated. "Not even if I was to reveal what really happened on the last occasion you and I met?"

The last occasion! Now it occurred to me that of the people present in that house on the night of my grandfather's murder — my mother, Peter Clothier,

Martin Fortisquince, Mr Escreet, and Mrs Sancious — the only two survivors were present once again. Except, of course, for the murderer himself. Perhaps I would learn something about what had happened that night. My heart began to pound at the thought.

"I don't know what you are talking about," the old man said.

"Then I will tell you," she said. "I was suspicious from the first about that evening. Why should Huffam have invited my husband and me after such a bitter division? And when I discovered that he had married his milksop daughter to the addle-pated young Clothier, I was more and more curious. Particularly when my husband told him he had brought something for him, and Huffam instantly turned the conversation as if he was anxious not to receive the gift so soon. What was in that package, I wondered? And when that quarrel broke out between Huffam and his son-in-law, why, I saw that it was a charade, though it deceived my gullible husband. So I resolved to watch very carefully. When Clothier and his bride left the house I was puzzled, for I had so far seen nothing untoward. Then I had to withdraw upstairs while the gentlemen sat over their wine. And that was when my husband gave Huffam the package, as he told me later. Then you and he left my husband and went into the plate-room, Huffam saying that he was going to unlock the strong-box in order to put the package away. Now we all know what he was in fact doing: he was bringing out the codicil to give to you to pass on to his son in-law. Is that not so?"

"Yes," said the old man.

"But now we come to something that nobody knows except you and I. When Huffam said he was going to unlock the box, you had to leave the room since not even you were allowed to know where he kept the key hidden. And so you passed into the hall."

"No!"

"Yes you did. You cannot deny it. Where do you imagine I was at this moment? Safely out of the way in the drawing-room upstairs? No such thing. I had come quietly down the stairs as far as the landing."

"You are lying! You couldn't have seen anything from there."

"You can see a great deal. Do you doubt me? Then I will show you. Stand just here and I will go up to the landing."

I heard footsteps and realized that Mr Escreet and Sancious were coming towards me. I retreated, my heart pounding and possessed by a terrible fear of being caught like a thief in that house. The plate-room, whose door was behind me, was my only refuge. Was it locked? To my relief, the door opened and I retreated into it, finding myself in near-darkness for the shutters were fastened. I left the door slightly ajar and, though I could see nothing, I could hear clearly.

Then I heard Mrs Sancious calling down from the landing: "I see you. Now do what you did then."

There was a pause then she spoke again: "Come, do not be shy. Take it down." After a pause she said: "Give it to him, Mr Sancious." There was another silence and then she spoke: "You have it in your hand now. At this moment you are lowering it to the ground. Do you believe me now? Well, no matter. Then you went back into the plate-room and a minute later — no, less than a minute, you came out again without the sword. I watched you go round to the front hall treading very quietly. I was intrigued, as you may imagine. But I was even more puzzled by what you did now. You unlocked the vestibule-door with your own key and removed the great key from the street-door. Then you locked the vestibule-door again and hid the street-door key on top of that grandfather clock. Yes, I can see it from here. Then you waited for a few minutes, at intervals taking out your watch as if expecting someone. But you never thought to look up and peer into the shadows of the landing and see me, did you? After a minute or two I heard someone come in through the back-door and make softly towards the library. It was Clothier. Now I guessed that the whole point of the charade was to smuggle that package to him, but I was still perplexed by your conduct. Won't you tell me now?"

There was a silence.

Then she went on: "You waited until he had passed into the library and then crept towards the back of the house. I know now that you went to lock the back-door in order to trap him inside the house, though I did not guess that then. You spoke to my husband and left the door to the dining-room open so that he would see Clothier as he tried to get out through the back-door. Then you came back here and passed into the plate-room. And as I later knew, you went from there into the library through the door which you had left locked to prevent Clothier from going into the plate-room. And you had a very good reason for not wanting him to do that, hadn't you? Meanwhile I came down the stairs."

I could hear her voice coming nearer again.

"I retrieved the key from the top of the clock and laid it by the vestibule-door. Why did I do that? From sheer deviltry, wishing simply to interfere with whatever design you were attempting to carry out. After a few minutes I saw Clothier come to the door. He had discovered that the back-door was locked and therefore that he could not leave the house. But now he found the key where I had put it and so he broke a pane of the vestibule-door — cutting himself in the process — and let himself out. Then I went back upstairs to the drawing-room and waited. After a few minutes you raised the alarm. How surprised and angry you were when, after naming Clothier as the murderer, you discovered that he had escaped from the house when you intended him to be caught on the premises with Huffam's money — and his blood — upon him! Then you changed your story and spoke of an intruder, didn't you? But there was no intruder."

I understood what she was suggesting. And surely she was right! Peter Clothier was innocent and had been the unwitting dupe of a plot to incriminate him which had gone wrong because of her own interference. Everything she said provided a satisfactory explanation of the hitherto puzzling facts of the crime. But was it true or was she saying all of this merely in order to intimidate the old man? Suddenly I realized that her voice was getting much closer to me. I moved round the staircase but she kept on coming.

"No intruder," she repeated. "And Huffam was dead before young Clothier even entered the house."

The footsteps were approaching. I hurried back into the plate-room. Then my heart nearly stopped. The others were coming in here! I crossed the room and pulled at the door into the library but found that it was locked. I was trapped! Suddenly I knew what to do. I went to the plate-cupboard which stood open and concealed myself inside it, pulling the door to so that only a crack was left through which I could see a little.

I was just in time for they entered the room at that moment. I could not see them but their candles lit up the part of the chamber that I was able to observe.

"There *was* an intruder, there *was*," the old man was insisting.

Clearly, he had convinced himself that this was the truth.

"No," Mrs Sancious said gently. "For even before Clothier re-entered the house, you came in here with the sword, didn't you? Huffam had unlocked the strong-box, hadn't he?" In a caressing whisper she urged: "Show me now."

The old man, moving as if he was sleep-walking, came into my line of sight still carrying the cruelly curved sword and with a candle in his other hand. He placed both of them on top of a large chest on the floor below the window and then knelt down, pulled up a section of the floorboard and removed something. A key! Still kneeling he opened the chest. Then he looked towards another part of the room as if dizzy and confused.

"He took something out," came the gentle voice.

"Yes," the old man muttered, and reached into the chest.

"After thirty years you saw it again," the voice went on cajolingly. "Unless you could get it back to the Mompessons, Huffam would regain the estate after all. Your revenge against his family would be undone. And, moreover, you might lose this house since the will disinherited you. From the moment he had told you that someone — in fact, it was that mad old creature, Lydia Mompesson — had undertaken to restore it to him, you had begun to plot. You knew Sir Perceval would pay almost anything to have it back. You had planned it all so that Clothier would be blamed: the son of your old enemy. What sweet revenge! Just as you came in Huffam pulled out the package that my husband had given him, didn't he? And perhaps he opened it and when he saw that it was indeed what he had hoped to find, he said something that goaded you past enduring, something like: 'Last throw wins all. The estate is mine'."

The old man turned towards the voice, muttering: "No, no, it wasn't like that at all."

"It took no more than a few seconds to do what had to be done. Now all you had to do to get your revenge and put it out of the power of the Huffam family ever to enjoy the estate, was to take the will from the package and hide it somewhere in this room. Then spread blood on the codicil and the letter that Huffam had written that evening and on some of the bank-notes from the chest, and put them all into the package. Then lock the door to the library so that young Clothier could not get in from there when he arrived. Then go out into the hall as I have already described and take steps to ensure that he could not escape. So he never knew that when you gave him the package in the library, Huffam was already lying dead a few feet from him in here. And when he had left the library all you had to do was come back in here, smear some of Huffam's blood on your forehead, and raise the alarm."

The old man got to his feet and stood dumbfoundered. "No," he muttered. "You've invented all that."

Sancious now came into my line of sight and bent over the strong-box as Mr Escreet had before. He began to search through it. As I watched him I thought about what I had just heard. Was it true then that Peter Clothier did not kill my grandfather? How could I be sure since the old man was denying it? Was certainty to elude me even now?

At that moment Sancious raised something in one hand and exclaimed: "I have it. The estate is mine!"

Instantly I knew what was going to happen. I stepped from my place of concealment, calling out: "Watch out behind you!"

Unfortunately, Sancious was so surprised by my sudden appearance that he turned towards me rather than to face the source of danger behind him, and at that instant Escreet drove into his back the sword which I believe he had used to kill John Umphraville nearly sixty years before. I saw a look of astonishment on the attorney's face, but whether at the blow or at my sudden manifestation I could never know. He looked as if he was trying to speak to me, but his face became twisted so that his eyes seemed to be starting from their sockets. Then he fell to his knees, his head sank against the chest, and without a word he collapsed to the ground and lay still.

Mrs Sancious and I stared at each other. The old man, as if he did not see us, crossed to the door of the library and locked it. Then he took the will from the lifeless hand of his victim, reached into the strong-box to take out a bundle of bank-notes, went to a bureau by the window and placed them inside a drawer.

All the while I looked at Mrs Sancious. She was now staring fearfully at the corpse of her husband. This was the woman who had allowed Peter Clothier to suffer for a crime of which she knew him to be guiltless, who had betrayed my mother to her death, who had sent her young nephew to die, and who had tried to encompass my end, too. I believed now that Peter Clothier was innocent and my doubts about the truth of what she had said had gone, for by his action Escreet had surely confessed to the murder in a manner more impossible to retract than any words.

The old man left the room, presumably in order to wait for the arrival of Peter Clothier by the back-door from Charing-cross.

As I came forward Mrs Sancious looked at me fearfully: "I did not mean it," she stammered. "I only intended to goad him into giving us the will."

What was she saying? Simply that she had not meant this to happen? Or that she had made her story up? Or had merely guessed at what she had not seen? There was no time to ponder these things now.

"He might be dangerous," I said in a low voice and, because she seemed frozen, I seized her forearm with the intention of hurrying her away before we found ourselves trapped inside the house.

"The will," she muttered, and, wrenching herself free, she crossed the room, stepping around the body, and removed it from the bureau.

Her self-possession was remarkable.

Taking care to avoid the old man, I hurried her into the lobby and out through the vestibule. In a moment we found ourselves in the mean little yard in absolute darkness for though the storm had quite abated, the blanket of cloud hung dark and heavy.

"We must go to the authorities," I said. "The old man must be taken up before he harms anyone else."

Then I almost said: "It must all be told. How you suppressed the evidence that would have freed Peter Clothier. What you and Bellringer did to Stephen." But I saw that she was shivering and could not find it in me.

"Come," I said, and we began to cross the unlit court.

Suddenly, as we reached the jutting angle of the next house, a shadow moved in the corner of my eye and instantly I felt a hand across my mouth and I was seized from behind. My first thought was that the old man had somehow pursued us but then a voice that I knew too well rasped in my ear:

"Has he got it, mum?"

Barney! I knew that the moment of my death had come. Mrs Sancious now had the will and she only needed me — the sole person who knew of her nefarious acts down the years — to die, and she came into the estate. She had known all the time that Barney was here! So she was only pretending to surrender so meekly for she knew he was waiting for us to come out! He must have come to the house with her and Sancious.

"What are you doing here?" she exclaimed.

So that surmise at the least was wrong!

Barney held me from behind so that I could see her but not him.

"Why, mum," he began pleasantly, "I had my company out watching for him like the genel'man arst, and Jack seen him come in at the Golden-Cross not two hours back. He dodged him here and then come and found me. Does he have the dockyment?"

"No," she said. "I have it."

"All the better. Where's the genel'man?"

"He's still inside the house," she said flatly.

"Well now, mum, you'd best leave me and I'll do the job. It ain't fit for a lady to watch. There ain't no-one about now. This place will do as well as any other."

What could I do or say to save myself? Then I thought of something. His mention of Jack had given me my clew for I had assumed they had parted company long ago. Sally must have kept her secret! I struggled to speak but could say nothing with his hand clamped across my mouth.

Mrs Sancious stayed where she was and seemed about to speak, but just then Barney removed his hand from my mouth in order to be able to reach into his jacket for something.

I had an instant and was able to cry out: "Jack's your traitor!"

He covered my mouth again with his hand which was now holding a knife. "Sing low," he enjoined.

Then he removed his hand just enough to let me speak with difficulty.

"It was Jack that plotted with Pulvertaft, not Sam," I gasped. "I know because I saw him there that night at Southwark when Jem was killed."

It crossed my mind that in revealing this I was condemning Jack to death, but I recalled what he had done to Sam and felt no remorse.

"You're lying," he snarled.

He listened, however, as I told him how past events known to him in one form should be re-interpreted by substituting Jack for Sam as the traitor. He must have seen that this version better explained what had occurred for he began to look perplexed and asked me several questions which I was able to answer without hesitation. And all the time Mrs Sancious stood a few feet away watching us curiously.

"Sally told you that she'd seen Sam talking to a bald man with a wooden leg, didn't she?" I asked him.

He nodded.

"But Jack got her to say that," I explained.

"Why would she do that?" he asked, looking at me thoughtfully. "She was soft on Sam."

"Don't blame her," I cried. "She didn't understand that it meant his death. She didn't know it was a description of Blueskin!"

He saw how the trick had been worked and gave a cry of rage and thrust me back against the wall. He believed me now, but what a fool I was to think that this would save my life. He was so angry he would take out his rage on me.

He raised his knife and I closed my eyes.

Suddenly Mrs Sancious said: "Don't!"

I opened my eyes and saw that she had stepped forward and put her hand upon his arm.

"What do you mean?" he said, almost indignantly. "It's what you and the guv'nor paid me for, ain't it?"

"He's dead," she muttered.

"Is he?" Barney looked alarmed for a moment. Then he said: "But I must be paid same as if I'd done it. I've spent a lot of time watching out for him. Me and the others."

"You will be paid." She opened her reticule and flung a handful of sovereigns on the ground. "Now be off."

Barney released me to stoop and pick the money up, watching us both warily as if he suspected a trick. He had to run his hands over the dark cobbles for there was little light there.

While he was doing this I stared at Mrs Sancious in amazement: "Why did you do that?"

She merely shook her head.

Was she in a state of shock? Had the killing of Sancious so upset her that she had acted in a way she would later regret? I found that I wanted to think so for otherwise I would have to try to feel gratitude towards her. And then I would be cheated of my right to hate her.

Barney straightened now, counting the coins. "It's been a pleasure to do business with you," he said. "I'll be very happy to obleege you agin. For I like to keep up a connexion that's been established to mutual advantage."

"Wait!" I said. "I want to ask you something. You told me once you killed a gentleman."

He looked at me in astonishment.

"I have a good reason for asking. You said it happened not long before I was born. Tell me the truth now. Where was it?"

He merely smiled as if at a private source of amusement.

I wanted to believe that Mrs Sancious had been telling the truth, but there was also this other possibility.

"Tell me," I pleaded. "No harm will come of it. Was it in this house?" I gestured with my hand to the dark mass behind us.

With a half-smile that was directed at both of us he slunk away into the darkness.

Mrs Sancious and I began to walk slowly across the empty yard. After a moment I could not prevent myself from beginning: "Your account just now of what you saw the night my grandfather was murdered ... " I paused and went on: "You implied just now that you only said it because you wanted to goad the old man into giving you the will. What did you mean?"

"What does it matter?" she said dully.

"It matters to me. Did you mean that you invented those things?"

She shrugged her shoulders: "I saw Clothier."

"Then if you saw all that, why didn't you come forward when he was indicted?"

"You assume too much. And why should I? I hated your mother. She was a spoilt child. She had everything — a loving father, fine dresses, music, so much — when I was poor and despised, though I was cleverer and more beautiful than she. I was happy to see her suffer."

I shook my head for I wanted to protest that my mother's life had not been as she imagined.

"I was envious of her then," she went on. "And later, I was jealous."

I looked at her sharply: "Did you have any reason?"

Suddenly she stopped and turned to me: "I'll tell you bluntly, then: I never believed that the murderer was your father. Though of course I have no conclusive evidence of what happened or didn't happen that night."

"Tell me what you mean!" I begged, for in the light of things I had been told or had come to suspect, her words were capable of more than one interpretation.

She would say nothing more, however, and we walked on in silence.

Then she said: "I have something that belongs by right to you."

She reached into her reticule and handed me the package she had taken from the bureau. We had by now reached the corner of Charing-cross and the Strand, and I approached a street-lamp and slid the contents out. I read the opening and recognised it as the purloined will which I had last had, briefly, in my hands some ten months ago. Now that I was to be let to live it was of no use to her, but her motive for restraining Barney puzzled me.

"I do not understand," I said. "You have devoted so much to the pursuit of the inheritance." (I bit back the impulse to say that she had helped to bring about the death of people who stood in the way.) "Why did you throw away your chance just now?"

"There's been too much death," she said softly.

"Come," I said. "We must lay the events of this night before a magistrate's office."

She would not move and I saw that she was shivering. I took her arm and so, grotesquely arm in arm with one who had done so much harm to me and those I loved, I slowly walked through the streets as dawn began to paint the eastern sky.

CHAPTER 123

We went to the police-court at Bow-street where I told the authorities what had happened. A constable was sent with the watch to the house and Mr Escreet was taken up and found to be so wandering in his mind that he was confined to a madhouse to await trial.

Before I took leave of Mrs Sancious later that morning, I asked her to explain to me some things that I did not understand. She would say nothing more, however, of what she had or had not witnessed the night my grandfather was murdered. But there was something else I was puzzled by: exactly how she and Henry Bellringer were related. I knew now that she was a descendant of Jeoffrey Huffam's sister, Laetitia, who had married George Maliphant. What I did not understand was how her nephew Stephen, should come to be the half-brother of the great-grandson of Mr Escreet. She explained that the wife of her brother, Timothy, who was called Caroline and was Stephen's mother, had been married and widowed previously. Her first husband was Michael Bellringer, the father of Henry and grandson of Mr Escreet. (It was not merely coincidental that this connexion should have come about for both the Maliphants and the Bellringers lived in Canterbury where Henry Huffam had once owned property which Paternoster, Michael Bellringer's great-grandfather, had managed on his behalf.)

I went back to my lodgings and, exhausted as I was and with my bruises aching, looked for a safe place to hide the will. One of the bricks around the hearth-stone was loose so I removed it, folded the document, and replaced the brick on top of it. Then I threw myself on the bed and slept for the rest of that day and all the night.

In the weeks that followed I had no desire to see Henrietta for I was upset and hurt by her behaviour at the Old Hall. I had much to preoccupy me for Mr Barbellion wrote to me repeating the offer of his services which he had made on the last occasion when we met. He told me that if I had succeeded in obtaining the will I should be made aware of the following facts: Sir David Mompesson had been indicted and convicted in his absence for the murder of Bellringer and this meant that as a felon his property would be escheated — that is, pass to the Crown rather than to his heirs. This would happen despite the existence of the codicil, for the Maliphant claimant — now revealed to be Mrs Sancious — had lost her rights under it since I was now known to be alive. He therefore urged that if I had the will I should lay it before the Court and obtain a judgement that the estate had never belonged to Sir Hugo Mompesson in the first place, but to my grandfather. He believed that this would be relatively easy to achieve and that consequently the estate would be mine. If I did not have the will, he went on, I could at least claim the annuity which the Mompessons had for so long refused to pay, and he said that a judgement in my favour to this effect would soon be achieved. I wrote to him and, without revealing whether or not I had the will, told him merely that I had no interest in pursuing my claim either to the annuity or to the estate itself.

Why did I answer in this way? You know that I had come to see what kind of deeds the desire for the estate had led others into. Moreover, I did not want to continue to be a play-thing of Chancery. I wanted to be free to plan my own life. Besides, I knew that the pursuit of a claim to have the annuity restored to me would require a great deal of money. Money was my dominating preoccupation, for a month after the events at Hougham I was three weeks in arrears of rent to Mrs Quaintance and was now penniless. I had seen Joey and his mother a few times and knew that if necessary I could go to them for help, but I shrank from the thought of doing so. I often wondered what had become of Lady Mompesson — or, more precisely, of Henrietta — and walked past the house in Brook-street a number of times. It appeared shut up and empty. I bought a newspaper occasionally and scanned the fashionable columns but saw nothing about either of them.

I might mention here that Escreet died raving in the madhouse a couple of weeks after the death of Sancious, without ever being brought before a grand jury.

CHAPTER 124

Then one day at about this time, a stranger came to me at my lodgings. He revealed that his name was Mr Ashburner and that he was a money-lender. He told me he had come to make an offer to me: he was prepared to lend me money against my expectations. When I expressed my surprise that he should know anything of my affairs he pointed out that such intelligence was the basis of his profession, but he would not tell me how he had come by it. I dismissed him as politely as I could (not very politely, I fear!).

This incident made me reflect, for it raised the possibility that it was known that I had the will. It was more probable, however, that it was the annuity that was known about, and in that case the implication was that it was widely believed that I had a good chance of obtaining it — though I assumed that it would not be worth much now. I thought of the good I could do to others if I had even a little money. I could help the boys at Quigg's, try to free old Mr Nolloth, and look for Mr Pentecost who might still be in the Fleet, and perhaps even Mr Silverlight. And to obtain the annuity when my mother had failed would be a kind of justice, I reflected.

So I wrote to Mr Barbellion and, at his invitation, went to see him at his office at No. 35 Cursitor-street. He explained to me that now that the estate was in process of being escheated, its administration was entirely in the hands of a Receiver appointed by Chancery; and he warned me that the mismanagement and corruption this would involve would destroy it within a very few years. He made it clear that he was no longer acting on behalf of the Mompessons, and he even warned me that Lady Mompesson was trying to rescue what she could of the family's property from the escheatment and that therefore she and I would be on opposite sides if I were to press any kind of claim at all. I was impressed by his frankness.

He informed me that he was prepared to act on my behalf if I chose to pursue my claim either to the annuity or, if I possessed the will, to the estate itself, and he tried to learn from me whether I had it. Without actually lying, I prevaricated and insisted that I was only interested in the annuity. I reminded him that in his letter to me he had said that he believed this undertaking could be successfully concluded soon, and asked him how long he considered it would take and how much it would cost. He answered that no more than five years should suffice, and I was startled to learn that this could be considered "soon". I said that I would like to retain him but had no money at all. He said he was delighted to accept my instructions and as for the cost, well, he had one or two ideas about that. Had I considered whether I had a claim upon my grandfather's estate? It was some time before I understood what he was referring to, and when I did I insisted that I had no interest in that at all. He seemed surprised and said he had some ideas that he would prefer not to disclose at this stage and that, with my permission, he would pursue them but take no action without prior reference to me. To my amazement, he then offered to advance me monies against my expectations, saying that it would give him considerable pleasure to see me come into some of my rights at least.

I was utterly confounded by this. Had I always misjudged him? Was he really a generous man who believed in justice? I stared at him as he smiled at me, and wondered. On the other hand, could it be that he was after a share of the Hougham wealth for himself and was trying to lure me into his toils?

Obviously guessing something of what was passing in my mind, he explained that he had been associated with the estate for most of his professional life for he had first worked as a very young man for the father of Sir Perceval, Sir Augustus, who had begun a series of improvements to the property that his son had abandoned. Because of this, it grieved him very much to see it fall into decay. He had worked hard for the various improvements he had carried out — many of them, in the twenty years since the death of Sir Augustus, against the wishes of Sir Perceval, who was profoundly traditional and hated change of any kind. His only ally had been Lady Mompesson and she had not always taken the long view, either. What had caused him most pain, however, was his discovery some dozen or more years ago that Assinder had been assiduously embezzling rents and falsifying his accounts. Although he had at length and with difficulty persuaded Lady Mompesson of the truth of this, he could never convince Sir Perceval that the nephew of his faithful old steward could be cheating him; and he had been deeply hurt by this lack of faith in his own judgement.

When I told him of my concern at some aspects of the policy that the proprietors had been following, he said that he owed it to himself to make it clear that it was only Assinder's greed that meant that the policy of enclosing the common land and closing the villages had borne so heavily upon the poor. He concluded by saying that since the accession of Sir David, who begrudged putting a penny back into the land, he, Barbellion, had made no advance at all with his designs for the improvement of the property; and that he wanted nothing more than to see justice done after all this time and the property restored not merely to its rightful owner, but also to the condition in which it had been at the death of his first employer.

When he had finished I sat silent for some time, and then said that I was deeply affected by his offer but that he must understand that I was interested in the annuity only. I had no desire to claim the estate itself for I had come to believe that great wealth represented a commensurate moral danger to its possessor. Now he looked at me in a rather droll fashion and asked me how much I thought the estate was worth if it were to come on the market at this very moment. I said I had no experience of such matters, but he encouraged me to make a round guess. I chose a large figure of so many tens of thousands of pounds and he laughed drily and said I was quite out. The property was worth precisely nothing. Quite literally, nothing. And even that might be an over-valuation. I asked what the meaning of this riddle was and he explained that the estate was so heavily burdened by a number of charges — post-obituaries and mortgages and annuities, of which mine was only one, though it was the first — that its net worth was either nothing, or even much less than nothing. But now that it was in Chancery and the process of escheatment had been begun, he doubted if it would ever absolve its own debts and be able to be sold. Its fate was to be mismanaged and further run down for decades to come.

This was astonishing news and it set me thinking. I could see that Mr Barbellion expected that this would prompt me into confessing that I had the will, but I adhered to my resolution to say nothing about it. I accepted, however, his offer of a loan of forty pounds per annum at a compounded rate of interest of six per cent and to be repaid out of the annuity. I received my first quarterly advance from his managing-clerk that very day, and Mr Barbellion undertook to set my claim in motion.

I am pleased to be able to say that the first thing I did was to send to Mr Advowson the money that I owed Sukey — with an addition to represent notional interest. I also went to see Joey and his mother and insisted — in the teeth of their opposition — on paying them five pounds to make up for all that they had spent on and done for me. It was now that Joey told me that a few days after my last encounter with Barney outside the house at Charing-cross, a body that he suspected was Jack's was found on some waste-ground near Flower-and-Dean-street, the district to which Barney and his company had removed after leaving the Neat-houses. I might mention here that that was the last I ever heard or saw of any of them.

Now I had just enough to pay my rent and keep body and soul together until the next quarter's remittance. As the weeks passed I spent a great deal of time thinking about what I should do. I would often take the will from its hiding-place and sit by the hour studying it and trying to decide. Mr Barbellion's revelation about the estate placed my relation to it in a new light, for there was no question now of its being a temptation. No question of my being corrupted by great wealth. On the contrary, its possession would be an onerous and perhaps crippling responsibility. I thought over and over again about what Sukey had told me of the depredations of the Mompessons against the poor. What would happen to them if the estate remained in Chancery? And now it began to seem to me that to reject the estate was to act selfishly and to shirk my responsibilities. Moreover, I had never given up the idea that Justice required that my great-great-grandfather's will be executed.

Then in early June of the following year, Mr Barbellion wrote asking me to meet him down at Hougham a few days hence, for he said he had much to explain to me that could best be clarified there. He enclosed a bank-note for ten pounds to cover the expenses of the journey. Though I was somewhat puzzled, I welcomed the opportunity to look at the property — not with the clear intention of pursuing my claim but merely in order to assess the difficulties that would lie ahead if I were to come into possession. Down there I might be able to judge the issues more clearly.

Since I am close to bringing to a conclusion my share in these pages, I will anticipate now events that have taken place in the period since that visit by addressing you directly a second time, my dear friends, in order to tell you of the fate of those of my former companions whom I have been unable to find again. Keeping the promise I had made to myself at the time, I sought to have Mr Nolloth released and Alabaster's madhouse closed down. I found, however, that the good old man had died less than a year after my escape. The serjeant whom I consulted about bringing a suit against the mad-doctor assured me that it would be almost impossible to prove anything against Dr Alabaster. The same lawyer dissuaded me from trying to pursue a charge against Mrs Sancious that she had brought about Stephen's death, and remembering that she had saved me from Barney, I decided not to go ahead. After all, the death of her husband under such circumstances was a kind of punishment.

Since I had not forgotten my undertaking to myself to do what I could for the boys at Quigg's academy, I wrote to an attorney in the nearest town to that institution to ask him to visit it as my representative on the pretext that I was searching for a school for a nephew of mine. The lawyer reported back that he had gone to the farm and found that the Quiggs had given up the scholastic profession and gone back to agriculture. He was emphatic that he had not seen a living boy on the premises.

Since his flight, Sir David has been living in penurious exile in Calais on remittances from his mother who has a small property secured to her independently. She lives in a very diminutive house in Mayfair and some of her income has to go to keeping Tom in the private retreat (not, unfortunately, Dr Alabaster's!) to which the consequences of his intemperance (of various kinds) have condemned him. Daniel Porteous set up in trade in Lisbon — a place with which his bank had connexions that were close enough to allow him an *entrée* and not so close as to make it necessary for his conduct in England to be bruited abroad. His wife and son went with him, and so did Emma.

As for Henrietta, I must go back to that visit to Hougham in June.

CHAPTER 125

I took the coach to Sutton Valancy as an outside and then with the money I had saved thus, I hired a horse and hacked to Melthorpe — for I had a fancy to see the little place again and the old house where my mother and I had lived.

The village seemed unchanged. The yellow-red brick of its better houses was mellow in the sun of an early summer afternoon, and the trees and grass were still clad in the bright green hues that would fade as the summer advanced. No-one recognised me, though I saw Mr Advowson crossing the High-street from his house to the church, and reflected that he was returning to the vestry after his dinner. Why should he pay any attention to a strange young gentleman riding a horse through the village?

Our old house looked shut up and abandoned and when I asked a passer-by about it I learned that it had stood empty for six or seven years. So far from needing to raise our rent, Mrs Sancious had not bothered to find another tenant! She had seized on the excuse as a cover for her malice. I went up the farm-lane that ran along the side and, lifting the latch of the well-remembered gate, ventured into the garden. It looked very small now, and the smaller for being over-grown to such a degree that it was impossible to see where the grass-plat ended and the Wilderness started.

This was where my story began! Began on that other summer day when Bissett's cry had summoned me from here to an encounter with a stranger at the gate — that encounter from which so much had followed. How much more I knew and understood now than when I had last looked upon this place before our flight to London! And yet there was still so much that was mysterious. I had been told and had overheard so many stories since then — Mrs Belflower's, Miss Quilliam's, my mother's, Mr Escreet's, Miss Lydia's — and had heard so many lies and inconsistencies and distortions and omissions.

I remembered the sculpture that Martin Fortisquince's mother had brought to this garden from Mompesson-park or, rather, Hougham-park as it should, and might once again, be called. I advanced the length of the grass-plat and pushed through the brambles of the Wilderness until I saw it. Moss had grown again over the inscription and now when I had scraped it all off, I found that although I had been certain of my earlier reading, the words in fact were:

Et Ego in Arcadia. An enigmatic phrase. And what was the meaning of that ravaged, time-worn countenance? And of the arms seizing the figure from behind? Whom were these struggling figures intended to represent? Was it the story of a chase — Pan and Syrinx or Tereus and Philomel or Apollo and Daphne — or of an amorous encounter? I could never know. And, anyway, did it matter what the sculptor (the great-uncle, I believed, of a man whose death I had brought about) or his patron (my own great-great-grandfather) had intended? Looking into the empty eyes I saw that I could read from that palimpsest of a face anything that I chose. As I tried to grasp it, the pattern receded endlessly, like the tiles of the broken floor of the Old Hall.

And then there was the mystery of why the banished wife had brought this sculpture here. Yet I believed I understood that as I thought of the concealed sixth that always breaks the pattern of fives. The disgraced woman had brought the sculpture with her because it had saved the life of her secret lover and, perhaps, father of her child. And perhaps had died of a broken heart because he — and I was sure I knew who he was — had never visited her. And this brought my thoughts, as so often, to Martin Fortisquince. So much was still unresolved. He had written in the register of my baptism "godfather and father" and that whole entry and what Mr Advowson had described of its composition could bear a particular explanation.

So many omissions. So much that my mother had kept from me or on which she had been mistaken. (I knew that she had been wrong about Miss Quilliam's treachery, for example, and about Mr Pentecost.) I thought of the words from her account of her life that had echoed so often in my memory: "I could not bear to think that the father of my child had killed my Papa!" How much she had had to bear. I remembered how while we had sought shelter in the yard of St. Sepulchre after fleeing from Mr Barbellion, she had talked wildly of the "crescent moon" and the curved sword and the blood. And hence, surely, the name she had once chosen: "Halfmoon". If she could not forget the truth, had she succeeded in making it more bearable? And then what Mrs Sancious had said so recently came into my mind: "I never believed that the murderer was your father." What had she intended to convey? What should I believe now?

At last I left the house and rode towards Hougham. As I passed Sukey's tumbledown cottage I wondered whether to call upon her, but by the time I had decided it might be a friendly thing to do I had gone past it and felt that I could not spare the time to turn back. Afraid of keeping Mr Barbellion waiting, I urged my nag into a canter, although I knew I had more than an hour to get to Hougham. A few minutes later I passed a country-woman who, wearing a scarlet cloak and carrying a basket, was going the same way as myself, and, perhaps because I was thinking of Sukey, I was struck by her resemblance to my old nurse.

A quarter of an hour afterwards I rode up the carriage-drive to the big house and gave my horse to a boy who issued from the stable-block at the sound of my arrival. Mr Barbellion had explained to me that the Chancery Receiver had retained just enough of the servants to maintain the house and that, as an officer of the Court of Chancery himself, he had been able to obtain permission to visit it on this occasion.

I entered the hall and a figure came forward to greet me with a curtsey. To my astonishment it was Mrs Peppercorn:

"How very good it is to see you again, sir," she said. "I met you hard by here once many years ago when you were very young. You will have forgotten my existence, I am sure."

"On the contrary," I replied. "I recall our last meeting very clearly."

"You are very kind to say so, Mr Huffam," she said with a smile. (For I had taken my grandfather's name in accordance with the wish expressed in the paper written by him on the evening of his death.) "Mr Barbellion is expecting you in the justice-room," Mrs Peppercorn went on. "I will conduct you there."

Though I believed I could find the way unassisted — for it was the very chamber in which Sir Perceval and Lady Mompesson had received my mother and myself on my first visit to the house — I allowed her to lead me there. All the while, as we passed through state-rooms whose furniture and pictures were muffled up in great swathes of brown Holland like so many crouched monks, she kept up a stream of talk. She told me of the tragic vicissitudes that had recently overtaken the Mompesson family and explained that as one of their most long-serving and, if she might be permitted, most loyal retainers, she had been allowed by Chancery to end her period of service at the house where she had begun it in the happy days of Sir Augustus. And it was now that I learned most of what I have repeated above of the recent circumstances of the family. She made no mention, however, of Henrietta.

As I entered the justice-room Mr Barbellion, who was sitting at the far end reading some papers, rose to shake my hand. We exchanged pleasantries and seated ourselves, once Mrs Peppercorn had withdrawn, on one of the sophas (I) and an elbow-chair (he) from which the coverings had been removed.

"I have asked you to meet me here today, Mr Huffam," he began, "because I wish to put before you in the most vivid terms the certain fate of this great responsibility" (here he waved his hand to take in the house, the park, and the tenanted lands and houses beyond it) "which is now drifting rudderless in the dangerous waters of receivership. I suppose it will eventually be auctioned, but what will be left of it I shudder to imagine. I therefore beg you to tell me whether you have the purloined last testament of Jeoffrey Huffam. If so, the estate may be saved."

When he ended I hesitated, looking over his shoulder through one of the windows whose curtains had been drawn. I could see the branches of the great elms of the park waving gently in the wind against the pale blue sky and at that moment a great longing welled up in me to feel this place my own.

"I have it," I said.

A reddish flush appeared in his cheeks and he stood up quickly and took several turns around the room.

Then he said: "Though the estate is encumbered in the ways I have told you, the situation may be very different once the will is accepted — as it surely will be. In that event all charges secured upon it since its inheritance — its improper inheritance — by James Huffam would arguably be invalid."

I stared at him in amazement.

"I don't understand," I protested.

"It's very simple. Once it has been proved that James had no right to sell it and that therefore the Mompessons never had legal title to it, then none of the obligations that they have entered into are valid."

"Is that certain?"

"Nothing is certain in Equity, but no-one has a better chance of gaining such an outcome than myself."

He had told me at our last interview that the estate was worthless because of all the encumbrances upon it. Now he was saying that the purloined will could be used to repudiate them. But had I the moral right to do so? To render valueless the various mortgages and post obits and other charges that had been imposed upon it? Surely I had, since they had been undertaken by those who had no right to the estate? And, besides, I would be doing so in order to ensure its future well-being and that of its dependants.

"It would cost a great deal," I said.

"You could find a way," he answered with a mysterious smile.

"You mean borrow it?" I asked. "A man came to me several months ago to offer to lend against my expectations."

"I know," he said. "His name was Ashburner."

I started. How did he know this?

"There is much that I have to tell you, my young friend," he went on, seeing my astonishment. "You say that Ashburner offered to lend against your expectations, but he was not referring to the annuity — much less to any claim on the Hougham estate itself. The man was sent by an individual of the name of Vulliamy."

This was becoming stranger and stranger.

"I see you recognise the name," Mr Barbellion said. "You may know, in that case, that he was your late grandfather's managing-clerk."

I had recognised more than Vulliamy's name, for I now recalled that I had heard the name "Ashburner" before: the woman who had been kind to my mother and me when we had left Mrs Malatratt's, Mrs Sackbutt, had mentioned him as the landlord's deputy. Did that mean that those wretched dwellings she had inhabited were owned by the Clothiers? And then it came to me that the rent-taker at Mitre-court had uttered his name as well.

Mr Barbellion went on: "I have spoken to Vulliamy in the course of my enquiries into your claim upon your grandfather's estate."

"I did not give you leave to do so!" I cried.

"With the greatest respect, Mr Huffam, at our last interview that is precisely what you did. Don't you remember that I undertook to take no action in the matter without instructions from yourself?"

He was correct and I had to apologise, while still insisting that I wanted nothing to do with the Clothier estate.

"At least hear me out," he went on, "while I tell you what has been happening since the death of your grandfather nearly eighteen months ago. As you presumably know, his heir was Daniel Porteous, your uncle. Now it appears that Vulliamy possessed evidence of various wrong-doings on the part of your grandfather." Here Mr Barbellion looked down and shuffled his papers in embarrassment. "It seems that the resourceful old gentleman, doubtless in his eagerness to oblige his borrowers despite the poor security offered, lent money at rates above the legal limit of twenty per cent. And some of the pawn-shops he owned were — surely without his knowledge — acting as 'fences' for the receipt of stolen goods."

None of this was new to me for I had heard it from the lips of Peter Clothier.

"There were other matters, too," the lawyer went on. "But the main point is that Vulliamy had evidence of Porteous' involvement in these undertakings. And most seriously, he possessed copies of papers — goodness knows how your grandfather allowed him to obtain them! — showing that Porteous perpetrated a fraud in colleague with your grandfather in which he improperly used the name of his employer, the banking house of Quintard and Mimpriss, and thereby incurred considerable losses on its behalf. (It seems that it was a building-speculation and that your uncle exposed his bank very gravely by advising it to take up a mortgage on a lease where the freeholder was a nominee concealing his father and himself. The lease became worthless when the mortgagor defaulted and the freeholder re-possessed. Combined with the banking crisis of a few years ago, this embarrassed the house to a degree that at one point threatened its solvency.)"

Again, I knew about this for I had overheard Vulliamy blackmailing Clothier about it the night the old man died.

Mr Barbellion went on: "Vulliamy bargained with your uncle for a share of your grandfather's estate as the price of his silence — conduct which is inexcusable, I need hardly say — but he became frightened when an attempt was made by a pair of ruffians to kill him one night."

I thought I could venture to put a name to at least one of the pair, but I listened in silence.

"In order to obviate the danger to himself, therefore, Vulliamy had to lay his evidence before the board of Quintard and Mimpriss. As a consequence Porteous fled abroad with his family to escape prosecution by his employer, and so his attempt to intimidate Vulliamy — for I assume it was he who was responsible — precipitated the very result he was trying to avert."

I felt I knew where his words were tending.

"Your uncle having fled and been indicted for a felony by a grand jury, you are consequently the sole heir to your grandfather's estate," he continued. "It was because he knew of this turn of events that Vulliamy sent Ashburner to you."

Here was an astonishing reversal of expectations! Instead of coming into the Hougham estate, I found that the Clothier inheritance was mine virtually for the asking. But what kind of inheritance was it? And in what sense was it mine? *I could not bear to think that the father of my child had killed my Papa!*

Mr Barbellion had been watching me closely and now said: "I understand that in addition to a large sum of money in securities and government bills, the estate is principally comprised of extensive properties in the metropolis, most of them in the poorer districts — though I believe them to be fairly remunerative. (There is also, incidentally, a large mortgage on the security of this very property which your grandfather had bought up through a nominee. You may know that he was very anxious that his descendants should possess this estate, for I understand that his mother was a Huffam by birth. And so — I hope — you will achieve his ambition.) Vulliamy is ready and willing to continue to manage the properties and other interests in Town on your behalf. If you accept the suggestion I have just made, then you will be a wealthy man, and on that assumption I will proceed with your suit to set up the purloined will."

His words had stunned me. My ears rang and I felt dizzy at these successive revelations. My one idea was that I must do nothing in haste.

"I must think about what you have told me, Mr Barbellion," I said.

He nodded, keeping his gaze closely upon me.

Wondering if my legs would support me, I rose and left the room. Without paying attention to where I was going I descended a flight of back-stairs and then, in search of the way out, traversed a series of long, gloomy passages with never a sight or a sound of another human being, constantly finding myself brought up by a dead-end or a locked door or a flight of stairs leading only upwards. One of the passages, wider than the others and hung with many chandeliers, was a picture-gallery and as I laboured down its length I wondered which of the portraits on the wall (all of them muffled in yellow muslin as if in mourning) represented Jeoffrey. When I came to this gallery a second time and realized I had been right round the great square of the central block, I admitted to myself at last that I was hopelessly lost in the huge house. And huge it was, even though it had not been completed according to the original design that Mrs Belflower had told me of so long ago. This, I mused, was the house whose building had cost Jeoffrey Huffam so much that he had fallen into debt to Nicholas Clothier and married his daughter to him, thereby inciting him and his son to the ambition to own the property that had brought such harm upon his (Jeoffrey's) descendants.

It came to me now that a kind of justice was being offered to me. Could I not claim my Clothier inheritance — whether or not I felt entitled to it and despite my revulsion from it — and use it to restore the Hougham property? But could I convince myself that Vulliamy's management of the loans and properties could be conducted in accordance with the principles of justice and fair dealing?

Then by good luck I ran across a service-door and at last left the house, finding myself in the stable-yard at its rear.

Someone suddenly spoke to me from behind:

"Master Johnnie!"

I looked round and found Sukey standing before me clad in a scarlet cloak and carrying a basket.

"Why, I couldn't hardly credit my eyes!" she exclaimed.

I greeted her and she asked eagerly: "Are you here for Miss Henny?"

Preoccupied with what I had just learned I shook my head. I did not want to discuss Henrietta with her.

"I thank you for the money you sent by Clerk Advowson," she said. "It was more nor I lent you."

"Sukey," I asked, "do you recall that piece of parchment that Harry made me sign when I borrowed that money from you?"

She nodded.

I began walking and Sukey accompanied me. I didn't know where I was going so I allowed her to guide our steps.

"You know, when you brought it to me at the Old Hall the last time I was here, the parchment was so faded that it was almost illegible. And Harry forced me to sign it, really. So it would have no standing in a law-court."

She nodded again, looking at me curiously. We were walking across the park now towards the head of the lake and the old house beyond it.

"Anyway, the property is worthless," I concluded. "It's weighted down by debts."

She looked at me blankly.

"Do you understand what I'm saying to you? All of this," and I waved my arm at the great house behind us and the park stretching before us, "is worth nothing."

"Harry wouldn't hold you to it, sir," she said.

"Wouldn't he?" I said. Then I added: "I don't believe he could."

"Besides, he's at Chatham now," she said sadly.

"The Hulks?"

She nodded and almost whispered: "Poaching. He's to be transported, most like."

"I'll see you all right, Sukey," I said. "You and your brothers and sisters."

She thanked me and we walked on in silence. We reached the square of four ancient oaks at the foot of the hill on which the mausoleum stood, and she halted and looked around. I remembered how Miss Lydia had described this place and recalled that she had insisted that there were five trees when I had known that there were only four. Ahead of me now, however, I saw in the exact centre of the quincunx planted by Jeoffrey Huffam the decaying stump of a fifth. So we had both, in a sense, been right.

At that moment a figure glided from the direction of the ancient building to our right and came towards us. Then, too far away for me to make it out, it paused.

"She's shy of you, sir," Sukey whispered.

I turned to her in amazement and seeing this she said in surprise:

"Didn't you know, sir? I believed you were come a purpose to see her."

I shook my head.

"She has been living in the Old Hall ever since ... since that time I last seen you." She indicated the basket. "I've brung her food and so has some of the sarvints from the big house — at least, until they shut it up and turned 'most all on 'em away. The housekeeper will have nothing to do with her."

"She spent the winter in that draughty old ruin?"

Sukey nodded. "She couldn't be made to leave it."

Was she so devoted, then, to the memory of Bellringer that she would not desert the place of his death? In that case, how would she regard me? Did she blame me for playing a part in bringing it about?

The distant figure slowly came on again and then halted about thirty feet away. Now that I saw her more clearly a new shock struck me. I looked at Sukey who met my gaze briefly and then lowered her eyes.

"Dear God!" I whispered.

"I don't know that she'll come no nearer with you here, sir," Sukey said. "I'll go to her. Shall I say you wish to speak to her?"

"She can't stay there alone!" I protested. "Not like that."

"Do you wish to have a word of her?" Sukey asked again.

Unable to answer, I shook my head in bewilderment.

Sukey moved forward and handed her the basket. They exchanged a few words and then Sukey came back to me.

"She knows who you are. I b'lieve she'll speak to you if you wish, sir."

I reached into my pocket and took out all the money I had. Reserving a few shillings for necessities on the journey back, I pressed into her hand the remainder — nearly twenty shillings — saying: "Do what you can for her."

Taking it without protest, she nodded and then set off in the direction from which we had come.

I walked slowly forward. As I had seen from a distance, her hair was down so that it hung upon her shoulders, she wore no bonnet, and her dress (the one she had been wearing the last time I had seen her) was patched where it had been let out. Her face was even paler and thinner than on that occasion so that it occurred to me that she looked once again — in respect of the countenance at least — like the little girl I had first met a few hundred yards from here more than ten years ago.

As I approached she was staring at me unsmilingly. I halted and for a moment did not know how to start.

Then I said: "No reproaches, Henrietta?"

"You have nothing to reproach me for," she answered sullenly.

"That's not what I meant," I said, distressed that she should have interpreted my words amiss. I said gently: "You can't stay here."

"Have you come to take me away?" she asked calmly.

Where could I take her? She must have read my expression for she said: "I believe you wanted to marry me once."

"Go to the big house," I said. "Let the housekeeper there write to your guardian." Then I added, though I doubted what I was saying even as I spoke: "I am sure Lady Mompesson would take you to live with her."

She looked down.

How could I marry her, almost penniless as I was and with my prospects so uncertain? And my origins. The circumstances of my mother's end. My paternity. For (to express myself with brutal clarity), if I was not the son of a man who had committed murder and then lived in a hell of near-madness until a hideous death for which I myself was to some extent responsible, then I was at least the grandson of such a one. Besides, I felt pity not love. Although she had hurt me, I would do for her what little lay in my power. I had so many difficulties facing me on my own behalf that I could not think of taking on responsibility for others. I would help her with what money I had, but by one means or another I had my own way to make in the world. As for marrying ... It came to me that, all other considerations aside, I could not face the possibility that if I were to regain the Huffam estate, it should be inherited by anyone tainted with Mompesson blood.

"I must stay here," she said dispassionately. "I am expecting a summons. He will send for me. He will expect me to be here."

I felt a chill at these words for I took them as confirmation of what I had feared when I first saw her. It had been over six months since her elopement with Henry, since her journey north with him, since the night at the Blue Dragon inn, and since his death before her eyes. Had she been waiting all that time for her lost lover to communicate with her?

And yet as I looked at her now she seemed quite composed and sane. I felt a dizzying sense that there was something here that I did not understand and I suddenly wanted to leave that place.

"I have given Sukey some money for you," I said. "I will try to send her a little more. I am still very poor now but I may be richer one day."

She looked at me impassively and, deciding that it would not be wise to offer her my hand, I turned and walked away.

As for what became of her, she disappeared shortly after this and you have heard as much as I know of her later life when I described Helen Quilliam's fate and that of her companion.

When I reached the first of the trees that surround the great house, I turned and looked back once and once only, just as on that summer's day when as children we had exchanged love-tokens. At my last sight of her, she was still standing motionless holding her hands crossed in front of her in the centre of the square of trees beside the dead stump where Miss Lydia's lover had died by my grandfather's sword.

The End.

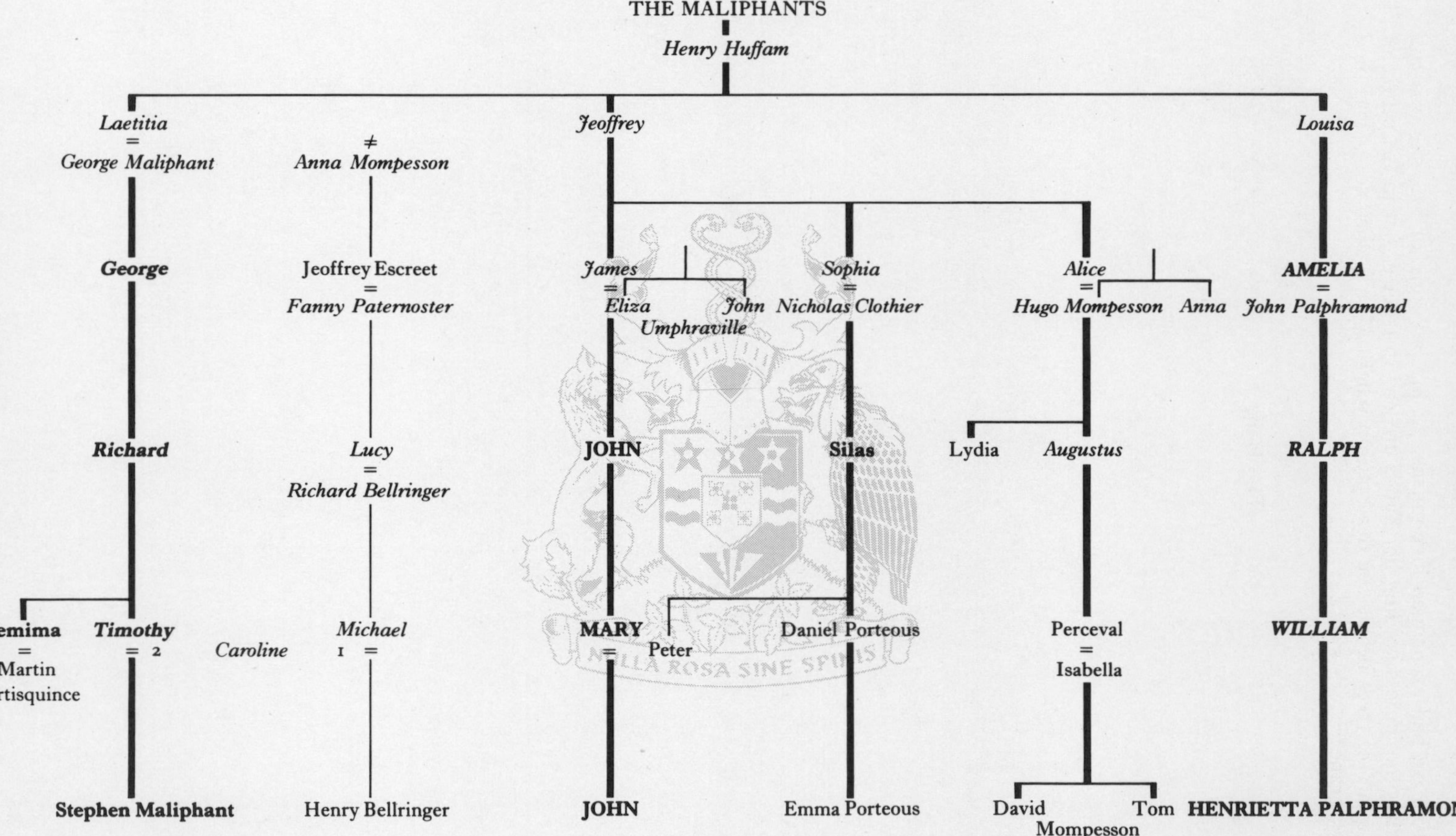

Characters who never appear directly in the narrative are in *italics*. Those who might possess the estate if Jeoffrey Huffam's suppressed codicil were in force appear in **bold** typeface. Those who might possess it if his purloined will were laid before the court are in **BOLD CAPITALS**.

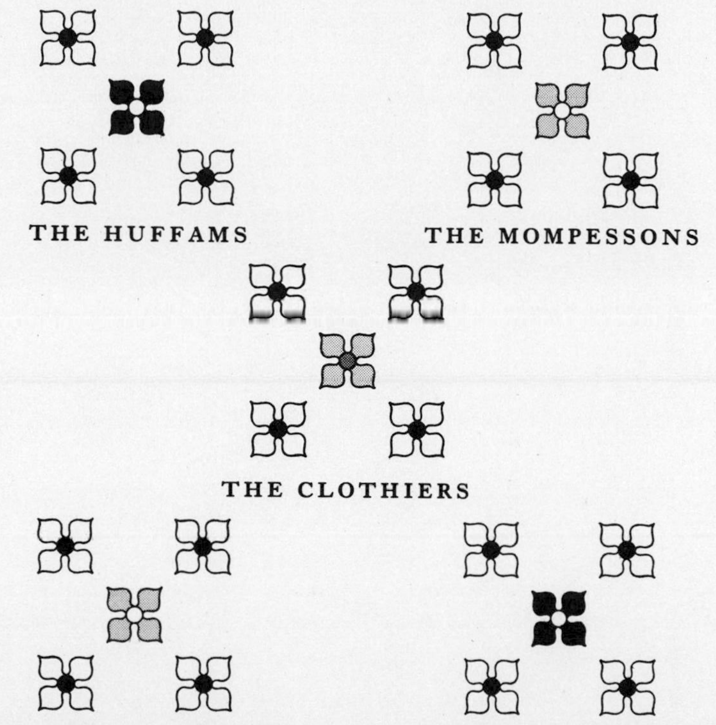
THE HUFFAMS
THE MOMPESSONS
THE CLOTHIERS
THE PALPHRAMONDS
THE MALIPHANTS

ALPHABETICAL LIST OF NAMES

Characters are listed under both first name and surname, with the full entry coming under the surname where one is mentioned. Some place-names and company-names are included.

Advowson: The vestry-clerk at Melthorpe.
Alabaster: A madhouse doctor.
Anna Mompesson: See under Mompesson.
Ashburner: Mrs Sackbutt's rent-collector whom John meets in Chapter 124.
Assinder: The Mompessons' steward.
Barbellion: The Mompessons' solicitor and town-agent.
Barnards-inn: Henry's lodgings.
Barney Digweed: See under Digweed.
Belflower, Mrs: The cook at Melthorpe.
Bellringer, Henry: The half-brother of Stephen Maliphant.
Bissett: John's nurse at Melthorpe.
Blackfriars: Silas Clothier's counting-house is at Edington's-wharf.
Blue Dragon, The: An inn in Hertford.
Blueskin: A member of Isbister's gang.
Bob: The Mompessons' footman "Edward".
Bob: A member of Barney's gang.
Brook-street: The Mompessons' house is at No. 48.
Cat's-meat-man, the: See under Pulvertaft.
Charles Pamplin: See under Pamplin.
Clothier, Daniel: See under Porteous.
Clothier, Emma: See under Porteous.
Clothier, Mary: John's mother.
Clothier, Nicholas: Silas' father.
Clothier, Peter: Mary's husband.
Clothier, Silas: Peter's father.
Coleman-street: Mrs Malatratt's house is No. 26.
Consolidated Metropolitan Building Company: The company organising the building-speculation.
Cox's-square: Mrs Sackbutt lives at No. 6.
Cursitor-street: Mr Barbellion's office is at No. 35.
Dan'el Pulvertaft: See under Pulvertaft.
David Mompesson: See under Mompesson.
Delamater, Sir Thomas: A friend of David Mompesson.
Delamater, Sir William: The patron of Miss Quilliam's father and the uncle of Sir Thomas.
Digweed, Barney: The man whom John meets in the half-built house in Pimlico.
Digweed, George: The husband of Mrs Digweed and father of Joey.
Digweed, Joey: The son of George.
Digweed, Mrs: The woman who comes begging in Chapter 18.
Digweed, Sally: The elder sister of Joey.
East-Harding-street: Mrs Purviance has a house at No. 12.
Edward: The Mompessons' footman "Bob".

Eliza Huffam née *Umphraville*: See under Huffam.
Emeris: The constable at Melthorpe.
Escreet, Jeoffrey: The old servant of the Huffam family who lives on in the house at Charing-cross.
Espenshade: The man whom John sees in Melthorpe talking to Bissett in Chapter 22.
Fortisquince, Elizabeth: The mother of Martin.
Fortisquince, Jemima: Mary's cousin who has married "Uncle Martin".
Fortisquince, Martin: An old friend of Mary's father and the son of the Huffams' land-agent.
George Digweed: See under Digweed.
Golden-square: Mrs Fortisquince lives at No. 27.
Gough-square: Mrs Purviance lives at No. 5.
Greenslade, Job: The young man whom Sukey walks out with.
Halfmoon: Mary's false name when she pawns the locket.
Harry: The young man whom Miss Quilliam meets at the pleasure-gardens in Chapter 39. See also under Henry.
Harry Podger: See under Podger.
Henrietta Palphramond: See under Palphramond.
Henry Bellringer: See under Bellringer.
Hinxman, Jack: The extremely tall man who is Alabaster's assistant.
Huffam, Eliza: The wife of James Huffam, *née* Umphraville.
Huffam, James: The father of John Huffam.
Huffam, Jeoffrey: The father of James Huffam.
Huffam, John: The father of Mary.
Isabella Mompesson: See under Mompesson.
Isbister, Jerry: The man John and his mother find in Bethnal-green who is a former associate of Barney.
Jack: A member of Barney's gang and Sally Digweed's fancy-man.
Jack Hinxman: See under Hinxman.
Jakeman: The Mompessons' nightwatchman.
Jem: A member of Isbister's gang.
Jemima Fortisquince: See under Fortisquince.
Jeoffrey Escreet: See under Escreet.
Jeoffrey Huffam: See under Huffam.
Jerry Isbister: See under Isbister.
Job Greenslade: See under Greenslade.
Joey Digweed: See under Digweed.
John Umphraville: See under Umphraville.
Liddy, Miss: See under Mompesson, Lydia.
Lillystone, Mrs: The parish layer-out whom John first encounters in Chapter 52.
Limpenny, Mr: The parish clerk whom John first encounters in Chapter 52.
Lizzie: The old woman who befriends John and Mary in Chapter 49.
Luke: The boy whom John meets at Covent-garden-market.
Lydia ("Aunt Liddy") Mompesson: See under Mompesson.
Maggie Digweed: See under Digweed.
Malatratt, Mrs: Miss Quilliam's former landlady.
Maliphant, Stephen: The boy whom John meets at Quigg's school.
Marrables, Mrs: John and Mary's first landlady.
Mary Clothier: See under Clothier.

Martin Fortisquince: See under Fortisquince.
Meg: A member of Barney's gang.
Meg: A friend of the Digweeds who runs a lodging-house.
Mellamphy: A false name used by John's mother.
Melthorpe: The village of John's childhood.
Mint-street: Pulvertaft lives "down the Mint" in Blue-Ball-court in Southwark.
Mitre-court: The Rookery to which John and Mary go in Chapter 49.
Mompesson, Anna: The sister of Sir Hugo Mompesson and so Lydia's aunt.
Mompesson, Sir Augustus: The father of Sir Perceval.
Mompesson, David: Sir Perceval's elder son.
Mompesson, Sir Hugo: The father of Lydia and Augustus.
Mompesson, Lady (Isabella): The wife of Sir Perceval.
Mompesson, Lydia: The daughter of Sir Hugo.
Mompesson, Sir Perceval: The son of Sir Augustus.
Mompesson, Tom: Sir Perceval's younger son.
Nan: A member of Barney's gang.
Neat-houses: Barney's half-built house is in Pimlico beyond the Neat-houses.
Ned: A member of Isbister's gang.
Ned: The leader of the boys at Quigg's school.
Ned: The Mompessons' footman "Joseph".
Nellie: The Mompessons' laundry-maid.
Nicholas Clothier: See under Clothier.
Nolloth, Francis: An elderly inmate of Alabaster's mad-house.
Offland: A false name used by John's mother.
Orchard-street, Westminster: Miss Quilliam lives at No. 47.
Palphramond, Henrietta: The little girl whom John first meets at Hougham in Chapter 5.
Pamplin, Charles: A clergyman and friend of Henry Bellringer.
Parminter, Mr: The gentleman who gives directions to John and his mother in Chapter 29.
Paternoster: Jeoffrey Huffam's attorney.
Peachment: The family at Orchard-street who befriend Miss Quilliam.
Peg: See under Blueskin.
Pentecost: One of the Punch and Joan men whom John meets while living with Miss Quilliam.
Peppercorn, Mrs: The Mompessons' house-keeper.
Peter Clothier: See under Clothier.
Philliber, Mrs: Mary and John's second landlady.
Phumphred: The Mompessons' head coachman.
Pickavance, Miss: Lady Mompesson's lady's-maid.
Pimlico and Westminster Land Company: The company which owns the freehold of the land involved in the building-speculation.
Pimlott, Mr: The old gardener and under-sexton at Melthorpe.
Podger, Harry: Sukey's brother.
Podger, Sukey: Mary's servant at Melthorpe.
Porteous, Daniel: The elder brother of Peter Clothier.
Porteous, Emma: Daniel's daughter.
Pulvertaft, Dan'el: A former associate of Barney and Isbister. Also called the Cat's-meat-man.

Purviance, Mrs: The woman who appears in Miss Quilliam's story and who offers shelter to Mary in Chapter 42.

Quaintance: John's landlady at the lodgings found for him by Joey.

Quigg: The headmaster of the school to which John is taken by Mr Steplight.

Quilliam, Helen: Henrietta's governess whom John meets again in London.

Quintard and Mimpriss: The banking-house which is involved in the building-speculation and is the employer of Daniel Porteous.

Richard: The crippled boy at Quigg's school.

Rookyard: Alabaster's turn-key.

Sackbutt, Mrs: The friendly woman at the Digweeds' former lodgings in Cox's-square.

Sally Digweed: See under Digweed.

Sam: A member of Barney's gang.

Sam'el: The old man at Cox's-square who directs John to Isbister.

Sancious: The attorney retained by Mary.

Saracen's-head: An inn at Snow-hill, near Newgate-prison.

Silas Clothier: See under Clothier.

Silverlight: One of the Punch and Joan men whom John meets while living with Miss Quilliam.

Snow-hill: St. Sepulchre's church and the Saracen's-head coaching-inn are both here.

Stephen Maliphant: See under Maliphant.

Steplight: The man who comes to Mary and John as Sir Perceval's representative while they are staying with Mrs Fortisquince.

Sugarman, Miss: The heiress whom David Mompesson wishes to marry.

Sukey Podger: See under Podger.

Thackaberry: The Mompessons' butler.

Thomas, (Sir) Delamater: See under Delamater.

Tom Mompesson: See under Mompesson.

Twelvetrees, Mrs: Sukey Podger's aunt.

Umphraville, Eliza: See under Huffam.

Umphraville, John: The brother of Eliza.

Vamplew: Tom Mompesson's tutor.

Vulliamy: Silas Clothier's managing clerk.

West London Building Company: The company which is the main-contractor in the building-speculation.

Will: A member of Barney's gang.

Will: The Mompessons' footman "Roger".

William, (Sir) Delamater: See under Delamater.

Yallop: Alabaster's nightwatchman.

About the Author

Charles Palliser, a graduate of Oxford, is now lecturing in nineteenth- and twentieth-century fiction at Strathclyde University, Glasgow. His radio play The Journal of Simon Owen was broadcast on BBC Radio 4. He has spent the last twelve years scrupulously researching period detail and writing this, his first novel.

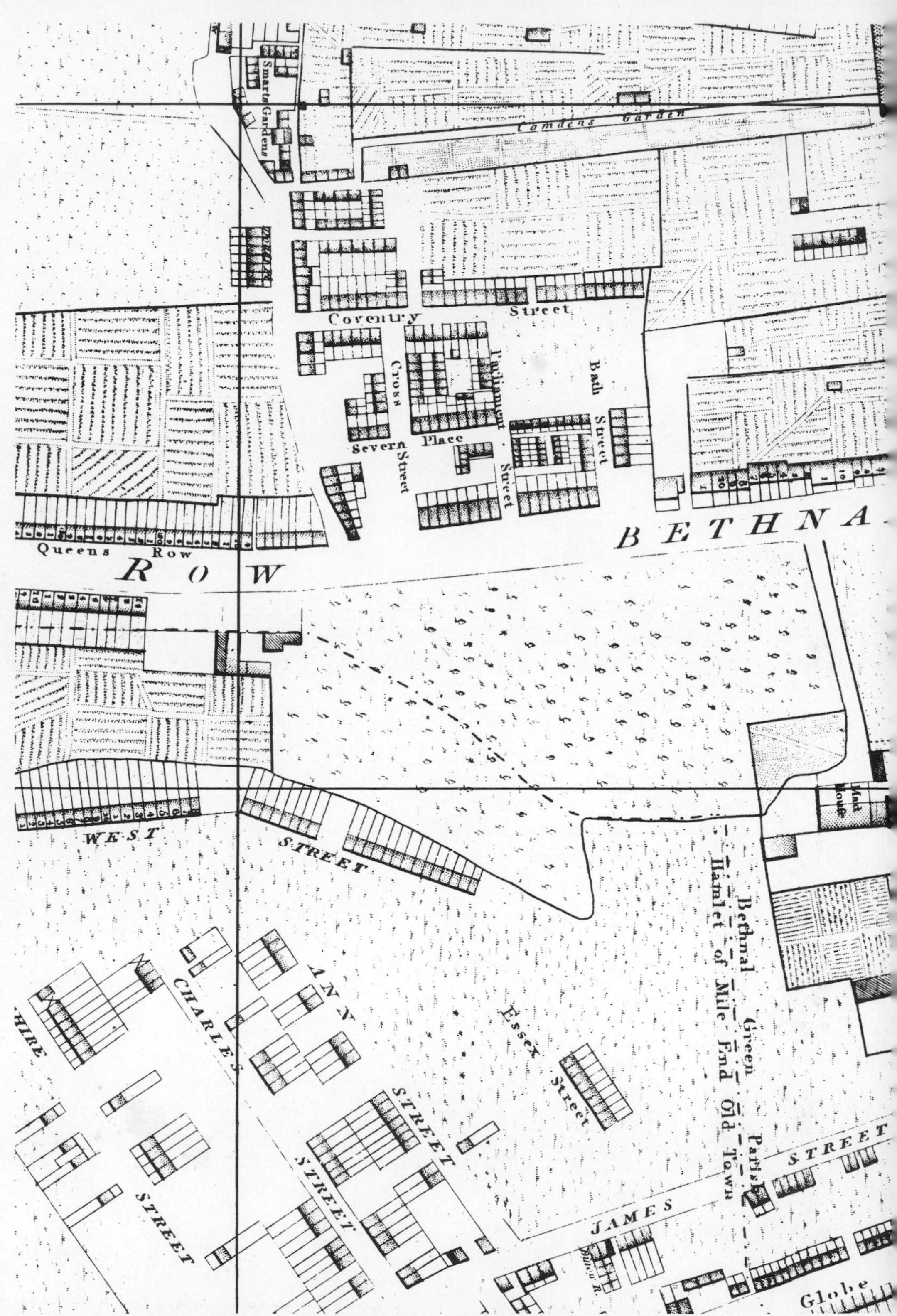

The top of the page is West